The Third Heaven: Omnibus

The Third Heaven: The Rise of Fallen Stars - Book 1

The Third Heaven: The Birth of God - Book 2

The Third Heaven: The Realm of the Dead - Book 3

The Third Heaven: Apocalypse of Kings - Book 4

Donovan M. Neal

Tornveil

tornveil@donovanmneal.com

Ordering Information: Quantity sales. Special discounts are available on quantity purchases by corporations, associations, and others. For details, contact the publisher at the email above. Orders by U.S. trade bookstores and wholesalers. Please contact Lightning Source: Tel: (615) 213-5815; Fax: (615) 213-4725 or visit https://www1.lightningsource.com/

Printed in the United States of America

Print ISBN: 979-8-9890821-2-4

Contents

The Third Heaven: The Rise of Fallen Stars - Book 1

Donovan M. Neal

Tornveil

tornveil@donovanmneal.com

Ordering Information: Quantity sales. Special discounts are available on quantity purchases by corporations, associations, and others. For details, contact the publisher at the email above. Orders by U.S. trade bookstores and wholesalers. Please contact Lightning Source: Tel: (615) 213-5815; Fax: (615) 213-4725 or visit https://www1.lightningsource.com/

Printed in the United States of America

Print ISBN 9798711460404

Cover Design by Roger Despi

www.pintado.weebly.com

Contents

Dedication

I want to dedicate this book to all the dreamers, to those who have an idea and work to see it to completion. For better is the end of a thing, than its beginning. May your imagination, ever lead you to new realms.

Scriptures

2 Cor. 12:2

I knew a man in Christ above fourteen years ago, (whether in the body, I cannot tell; or whether out of the body, I cannot tell: God knoweth ;) such an one caught up to the third heaven.

Ecclesiastes 1:9, 10

The thing that hath been, it is that which shall be; and that which is done is that which shall be done: and there is no new thing under the sun. Is there anything whereof it may be said, See, this is new? It hath been already of old time, which was before us.

Acknowledgments

To the Lord Jesus Christ, who for some reason loves me.

To my Pastor, Charles Hawthorne, who has nurtured my preexisting love of the Bible.

To my children - Candace, Christopher, and Alexander - you can do great things!

To the authors, comic book artists and writers, game developers and filmmakers who have come before and unknowingly have breathed on the embers of my imagination.

To all my beta readers and friends who gave me critique, and encouragement.

To (N) who cheered me on when I had nothing and said, “Wow!” after reading the prologue of my book.

To my cover designer Roger Despi for doing such an awesome job on giving me a standout cover.

To Adele Brinkley for her editing and for finding out where I live, sneaking into my house, and stealing all of the commas, semicolons, hyphens, and "as" off my keyboard to make my work even better.

Preface

When the desire to write this book was birthed. It was to provide a form of wholesome Christian entertainment and to answer several questions. How could Lucifer who dwelt in the very presence of God elect to rebel against his creator? What could have gone so wrong that a third of Heaven would turn their backs on God?

The answer to this query is the *fictional* piece before you now. To my beloved Christian reader—this work is *not* scripture. I do not profess divine inspiration, nor would I ever attempt to place this work alongside the word of God. The story is a fictional exploration of the fall of Lucifer, and by taking part in this fictional account, you as a reader, and I as the author are in no way implying that we must have theological agreement. The work does presume certain doctrinal beliefs (the existence of the Trinity for example) but this novel is not meant to be a point-by-point exposition of biblical truth. Nor an exact attempt to create a chronologically correct depiction of creation and the events depicted in the Bible. It is an exploratory look into a biblical event and imagines, "What if?"

Mythology is purposely utilized in some portions of the book. The rationale here is that ancient or modern mythological creatures and gods have their basis in some level of "fact" or are the result of the actions of fallen angels.

When possible, I have tried to be consistent with the teaching of scripture and with what church fathers have said concerning Angelology. Overall, I have taken the liberty to use my *sanctified imagination* to tell a story that might not only spur further interest in the Word of God but also, create an entertaining tale.

In the end, I desired to tell a story full of wonder, and to tell it in such a manner; as I might want such a story told to me.

Toni Morrison has stated, "If there's a book you really want to read, but it hasn't been written yet, then you must write it." I am attempting here to do just that.

I hope this work is enjoyable to you and spawns your further desire to possibly learn more about God, the Bible, and maybe even to follow Jesus Christ.

God Bless.

Donovan M. Neal

Prologue

I will always remember the screams, the untold billions of screams.

The cries of the damned reverberated off the canyon walls. The sound of their wails stretched over miles with each moaning breath mingled into a cacophony of pitiful, tortuous laments. I beheld in fascinated horror as billions upon emaciated billions of humans and Elohim languished in agony. Their rotted and burning flesh stank as the winds made the hellish perfume waft across the skies, causing the air to reek with putrefaction. Blistering heat sizzled from the white-hot lake of molten rock and fire. Fire that licked and bit at each captive's smoldering flesh, flesh forever burned but never consumed. Therefore, they screamed the residents of this canyon did -- it was a sickening sound.

Is this how Moses felt? I wondered. *To behold a thing that burns but is not consumed?*

They see me.

"Please make it stop," said one.

"I am sorry, oh God! Please, God, listen! Jesus do you hear me," said another.

"Aaarrrgghhhh!"

"I hate your guts! Do you hear me angel of God? I hate you!"

The voices melded and flowed, morphing into a singular pitiful cry for relief and of anguish.

I watched as some fought to climb atop others in a futile struggle to escape the horrifying affliction. It was a fruitless skirmish from which none could expect release.

I suppose that it could be possible to flee. I saw neither bars nor chains to hold these souls captive. Straining and squinting, my angelic eyes viewed no doors that would prevent escape. Selfish preservation run amok, pain, and hopelessness prevented them. As one soul approached optimism and the border of freedom, another wretch dragged it back within the bowels of smoke and flames. The grotesque scene of twisted, writhing bodies, moved as the tide in this sea of fire and brimstone.

I observed them dance, the denizens of this canyon. Dance a relentless waltz of hope deferred. For there was no respite to soothe one's pain, no aid to come to one's side. None could leave, and salvation had forgotten this place.

The Lake of Fire consumed each incarcerated soul held captive by the insatiable passions of lust and self: a twofold punishment forever administered on these prisoners for all time. A memorial by El, forever to be remembered by us all.

The lake was an eternal smoldering monument of our war: a token of El's wrath upon all those who had held back the truth in unrighteousness. My eyes were older than much of creation, and as they darted over the vastness of this everlasting torture, I remembered when I first saw the flames of the Kiln run amuck.

Yet even now, I found that I looked for him: my beloved, my brother, my friend, and my enemy — he whom my soul delighted.

I stood at the precipice of this jagged maw in the Earth's crust of heat, smoke, and fire. I strained that I might see the Adversary. It has always been an easy thing for a creature such as I to find my own kind, and with Lucifer even more so -- quite easy actually. Knowing my brother, I needed only to look towards the heart of this mass grave of the spiritually dead.

Our eyes met.

He was still a creature of pride, and even here, even after all this time, Lucifer sought to be the center of all things. He smirked as he looked at me, but I am not deceived. I know that joy does not dwell in this place. The human Dante was prescient when he penned, 'Hope had abandoned all those that entered here,' here in the Lake of Fire, even Hell herself could not flee.

Lucifer's face I knew with intimate familiarity. The smirk on his lips masked an unspoken yet seething hatred from the inner knowing that he was "superior" to all in creation, elevated to stand in the very presence of God, yet cast down as rubble to be stared and looked upon, a creature to be pitied.

Oh, how art thou fallen O Lucifer son of the morning. How art thou cut down to the ground, which didst weaken the nations.

It was this knowing, which I knew forever would gnaw at him...the reason for his smirk. Our gaze was short as smoke enveloped him, yet through the veneer, yes, I saw it-- a tear.

Then he was gone; veiled in smolder and fire; and pummeled by the legions he once sought to rule. Forever crushed underfoot by those he deemed chattel — forever humiliated.

Never in all my days did I believe my eyes would behold such a sight.

I turned away as I could behold such suffering for only so long. Even one such as I had limits.

I am relieved that the war is over.

The kingdoms of this world are become the kingdoms of our Lord, and of his Christ; and he shall reign forever and ever.

But at what price?

This victory was not without loss, not without pain.

"Have you come to mock me, Michael?"

Lucifer's voice could not be mimicked or masked. There was one being in creation that sounded thus. Only *he* could speak so that even from the Lake of Fire my attention could be garnered.

I am hesitant to reply. I do not wish to look upon this—murderer.

We will not speak again after today. I know this; therefore, I turned to face him for the last time.

"What manner of conversation would I engage with the King of Lies?"

As I looked upon his face and body now disfigured, I steeled myself. There was a time when I shed tears for my brother, but that was millennia ago. Too much blood had been spilled between us, too many wounds. Mercy no longer beat within my breast for him, yet even now, I could not help but ruminate on more pleasant times. I drifted into reflection and daydreamed back to the beginning of it all--still questioning--still wondering.

How did it come to this?

In the beginning...

Day Five

The sun's heat broiled and beat upon Michael's pale skin. The mountain cliffs radiated the thick humidity as he wiped the perspiration from his face. The haze moved to escape the swelter in a vain attempt to flee. Long turquoise streaks of sweat beaded upon his forehead and streaked his muscular jaw line to cover his face in lines of blue sweat. He shook his head to keep the perspiration from getting into his eyes, and his golden hair sprayed a mist of as he tried to cool himself. His white robes were soaked, and his golden bands steamed and burned his forearms as the heat baked him and his men. The group had labored all day to fit the new Cadmime beams to the sides of the cliff in order to expand Heaven's foundation.

Michael looked down at the whirlpool of hurricane winds, dangling high above their howling wails. Each gust ascended the canyon walls as the tempest below rotated in cyclonic fury swirling around the black eye of the Abyss. The Abyss — the bottomless pit where all reality ended. A heavenly body so dense that not even light escaped its grasp. It was a natural phenomenon of such destructive might even angels dared not venture near. Yet here Michael and his kind did the work to build Heaven. His race of Kortai alone answered El's call to work so close to the Abyss. Within the bottomless pit, there was no space, no heaven, no time. It was a gaping mouth of a null void. There was no escape if one fell in. El had deemed it so that any who ventured to fall would fall forever.

Gusts buffeted him, slamming him against the rock face. Downdrafts stood ever ready to drag him into the waiting mouth of the bottomless pit. Despite its howls, Michael enjoyed the coolness of the breeze that the winds generated against his skin.

Michael cocked his head in an attempt to stretch his neck, and scrunched his lateral muscles, each tendon aching from the harness strapped tightly to his back. He tugged at his belt straps to loosen his gear. The straps pinched his skin forcing him to adjust them constantly from nipping his ten wings. Work this close to the Maelstrom was dangerous, but he had carefully clamped and tied his harness. He tugged on it again just to be sure.

It was secure. The wind battered and shoved him against the craggy rock of the canyon's wall.

I am going to be so sore today, he thought.

Lucifer also was hoisted and attached to the cliff wall and hammered a brace into place. "I believe this to be the last one, brother. Is your beam secure?" His voice resonated with melody and the alto of his inquiry chimed in Michael's ears.

Even in the exhaustive heat, the tabrets and pipes in Lucifer's body gave off a pleasant tune; each dimpled pore of his skin opened and closed with every syllable from his operatic voice.

Michael pushed off against the cliff and rappelled sideways, hurtling through the air while the whirlwind raged below him. His feet landed on the crag, and he leaned over to inspect his brother's work.

"The strut will hold. Well done, and I think it is time for a break."

"Agreed," said Lucifer. "Michael, when you said you could use my help you neglected to mention that it would take all day."

Michael laughed. "You are so busy I rarely get to spend time with you. Besides — work using your own hands and not relying on your servants could do you some good."

Lucifer rolled his eyes and then smiled.

"Next time you desire to spend time with me try to think of something less dangerous."

Michael laughed. "Oh come now would you have me believe that you would prefer being in the palace composing sonnets, and miss all this?"

Michael opened his hand to present the spectacle of nature that surrounded them.

Lucifer eyed the stretched landscape of the canyon. The splendor of the chasms walls awed even him. He noted that they all stood as mites on the underside of the mountain that was Heaven. Lucifer turned his eyes to look below and surveyed the Abyss beneath them. The winds of the Maelstrom churned in its claw-like attempts to sweep them away. Stars, uncountable as grains of sand, splayed themselves like crystal across the canopy of Heaven's golden and black sky, each a visible reminder of the barrier that separated the realms. Lucifer had to admit: it was indeed an impressive view.

Michael yelled over the whine that came from the Maelstrom so that his brother could hear. "Alas, I do confess that I enjoy the sound of your voice. Your melody is soothing, and who else could I trust to extend the cliff face — these lazy friends of mine?"

Michael thumbed in the direction of his smiling three comrades while they hammered spikes into place.

They laughed in retort, "Hey! We are right here!"

Lucifer chuckled.

"It would seem that our work here is complete," said Michael, "Everyone take a rest. I shall attend shortly."

Michael watched in satisfaction as tendrils of new ground sprang from the sides of Heaven as living rock grew to embrace the Cadmime extension.

Good, Heaven will have more room for the changes El hast commanded.

The ground began to groan. The earth swelled, buckled, and stretched to overtake the beam planted in the canyon's side. Michael and his men smiled from the familiar sound of the land expanding.

Michael loved building, to see the results of the fruit of his labor. The Lord had given him the plans to the city, and he had overseen every aspect of its growth.

El would be pleased, he thought.

Michael prepared himself to release the buckle that latched him to the side of the mountain. The winds of the Abyss were but yards below him, and he could hear the howl of the hurricane that separated the heavens. A dimensional barrier crossed only by Ladder or special dispensation from El. The winds rotated in cyclonic fashion as a whirlwind: a Maelstrom that encircled the Abyss, a realm of bottomlessness and the flux from which the second and third heavens met. El had said that dissolution was the natural Ladder to enter into the realm. A peeling away of one's mortal coil would send one careening from the reality of the First to the Third Heaven, the Kingdom of God, a realm superimposed over all other layers of reality.

Michael knew that expanding the ground was dangerous work, for the Abyss pulled at two realms and sought to consume within itself anything that lay on its outskirts. Michael was careful not to stray too close to the event horizon.

Lucifer and the rest of the workers unlatched their harnesses and pushed against the cliff wall. Outstretched wings allowed the updraft of the wind from the Maelstrom to jet them upwards to the edge where they landed safely, still tethered to the stakes on the cliffs.

"Secure these lines," commanded Lucifer. "The ground will shift soon."Lucifer looked down to his brother who still inspected the strut supports.

He yelled below. "Michael quickly, get out of there!"

Michael had already unleashed his tether when the ground shook, and the mountain heaved outward encasing the implanted beam. A cropping of rock jutted out, striking Michael in the face and knocking him backward. Untethered, Michael waved his arms in a vain attempt to balance himself, but the rock slid and collapsed from under his feet, and he plummeted into the winds of the Maelstrom.

All watched in horror as the winds of the hurricane swept Michael away and rushed to drain him into the Abyss.

"Michael!" Lucifer yelled.

Lucifer's face grew anxious, and he turned to a worker behind him. "Quickly give me your harness," he said.

The angel unlatched the golden rope and lanyards that overlaid his garments and handed them over to the Chief Prince.

"Lucifer ... Michael is lost --"

Lucifer looked at the angel and raised his voice. "He is lost when I no longer draw breath!"

Lucifer buckled the clamp to his waist, pummeled a spike into the ground, turned, and then rappelled back down the side of the cliff.

He untied the grappling ropes. Each rope held a twelve-inch metal spike to latch onto the rock face. He placed the harness over his body, secured each fastener, and latched the hooks into the rings of his belt to support his weight.

El -- please give me strength; let me not be too late.

Lucifer looked out towards the center of the Abyss; the blackness was enveloping, for not even light escaped its edge. He knew that there was no survival if he fell in. He would be lost in the bottomless pit that separated the realms. Lucifer shed his garments and the light from his skin burst in all directions. His flesh transformed into living diamond, and the colors of the rainbow skipped about him. His twelve tendril-like wings unfurled and waved, as each vine of energy caught the gusts that blew from the Maelstrom. Stripped of his raiment, his skin reflected the light, and he gleamed so that onlookers fell to their knees and raised their hands to shield their eyes.

Lucifer lifted the grapples over his head and swung them, each spin gaining increased momentum. Each wave of his arms vibrated the air, and a screeching sound rang in the ears of all about. He released the grapples, and they flew across the expanse of the whirlpool and stuck into a crag on the other side.

He tugged on the rope. It held fast, but the winds from the Maelstrom buffeted the line, making it move and shift. He tied the end to a boulder near him until the rope became taut and held firm. He oscillated his breathing in his ears so that his body would pulsate as a beacon for Michael. He turned down the brightness of his flesh, and all ceased from covering their eyes. He threw another line toward his workers. They caught it, latched their bodies around it, and braced themselves against a boulder.

"Watch the line," he yelled to the workers. "Do not let it give way!"

The angels nodded. Lucifer looked into the Abyss, attached himself to the rope, and climbed up on the line, dangling upside down. His ankles and hands were wrapped tightly over the line as he shimmied himself towards the center of the pounding gales. The squall beat at him; its force and his weight made the rope buckle. It gave way some. He looked in the distance to see his fellow angels struggling to hold it tightly against the stone. He turned his face rearward towards the opposite end, and he could see the line starting to slip.

He opened the pores of his back, howled from the vocal cords that lined the muscles of his trapezoids and yelled. "Michael! Raise your hand so that I might see you! Michael, can you hear me?"

He strained his eyes to see any hope of his brother, but could not see him. He focused himself to look for movement in the whirlwind and beheld Michael tossed about by the gale force winds and struggling to release the straps from the harness that held his wings against his back. Lucifer watched as Michael's body swirled around the edge of the whirlwind knowing that he would have but one pass to rescue him, for with two passes, he would drain into the Abyss. Lucifer lowered his hand to prepare to hoist his brother from the storm.

Michael headed towards him, tumbling and tossed about, his body thrown aloft like a piece of driftwood on crashing rapids. Closer, Lucifer lowered himself down the more. Michael raced towards him; yards removed and then with increasing swiftness mere feet away. Timing his reach, Lucifer lunged to grasp his brother from the grip of wind and gale, strained to extend himself without also falling into the whirlpool. Michael reached up and grasped his brother's hand and they interlocked wrists.

Lucifer struggled to hold onto him, but the Maelstrom would not let Michael go, and they stood in stalemate with Lucifer hanging on suspended over the canyon of typhonic winds.

"We cannot both be saved—leave me," yelled Michael.

Lucifer struggled to fly with his brother, but Michael was too heavy and the winds too strong. The squall howled their disapproval, and with a gust that smashed into them both, the line snapped, and Lucifer plummeted with Michael into the circling storm.

Lucifer held fast to Michael and spoke as they hurtled towards the event horizon of the crushing black that was the Abyss.

Lucifer spoke into Michael's ear. "Never ask me to leave you, nor from following you, for where you go, I will go, and if you die, I will die."

Michael hugged his brother as they spun uncontrollably and jetted towards the event horizon of the Abyss. Michael closed his eyes as the darkness edged closer to overtake them. "Surely El will save us," he said.

Lucifer looked up and beheld that the Waypoint of Argoth was within view, and his mind raced with a plan to escape.

"No...El has given us means to save ourselves." Lucifer struggled to lift his finger and pointed to the Waypoint of Argoth. "Look, do you see?"

Michael nodded. "Hurry, there is not much time!"

"El tore, shay crom mere ley," Lucifer roared.

Speaking in the draconic tongue, Lucifer commanded the doors between the realms to open and summoned a Ladder.

In obedience, a thunderhead gathered, swirled, then encircled above the duo, and ejected bolts of lightning. A storm birthed from the billows and stoked the winds of the Maelstrom even more. Winds howled to one another in competitive shrieks as the new tempest fed the gale already running through the canyon. The force was such that the cliff face started to shred for the might of the winds.

The ground around the cliff's edge buckled and heaved in response. Workers watched with mouths agape as a rainbow-colored funnel cloud crackled with thunder, and lightning, and reached down as a great hand into the cyclonic drain that was the Maelstrom.

Michael and Lucifer spun closer to the event horizon of the Abyss, carried adrift by the current of the gale. The vortex of descending light twisted screamed, and whined as the winds of the maelstrom fought against the winds of a Ladder summoned by the word of El.

Hurricane wrestled against cyclone, and when Lucifer saw that they approached the event horizon, he heaved Michael into the air with all of his might. Michael quickly ascended and lifted away from him as the funnel of light gripped him and held him fast. The Ladder sucked him high into the sky and tore him free from the clutches of the Abyss.

Michael screamed in agony and reached out as he watched his brother flail helplessly into the enveloping shroud of darkness. The black dragged Lucifer into the whirlpool that was the bottomless pit.

Michael lunged across the sky, falling through a tunnel exploding in color and hot white bursts of plasma. The Ladder then folded on itself, hurtled towards the ground, and slammed Michael into the dirt on his back.

Workers roundabout ran to their leader.

Coughing, wheezing, his muscles throbbing, Michael struggled to rise to his feet. "Get this harness off me!" He yelled.

The workers raced to unlatch the straps that bound their master's wings. Michael moved in agitation, for despite their swiftness, they moved still too slow for his taste. The harness then fell to the ground, and with wings unfurled, Michael ran to fly to his brother's aid, but several angels tackled him so that he would not plunge headlong back into the Abyss.

Michael struggled against them, and tears welled in his eyes as he listened, for the sound of music that echoed from Lucifer's body, music that sprang from the soft motion of winds against his skin, faded into silence. Nothing remained but the incessant howls of the Abyssal whirlwinds. Slowly, the sparkle that emanated from Lucifer's crystalline flesh, dissipated in the blackness, and he was seen no more.

Michael let loose a wail, despairing in self-crimination. Gripping loose dirt in his palms, he smeared his face moaning and coiled over weeping.

Suddenly, the ground shook, and howling and lightning burst from the Abyss, making Michael cease his self-flagellation and take note.

For the Ladder had still not dissipated, and though its base was lost within the darkness of the bottomless pit, lightning arched from the funnel cloud and bolts of plasma struck out blasting the landscape in all directions. Michael and the workers watched as the Maelstrom turned bright white, and the earth underneath them buckled, heaved, and collapsed beneath them.

Each ran as the earth opened and chunks of the cliff fell into the Maelstrom. They lifted themselves into the sky to escape, when suddenly an explosion rocked across the canyon, and a blast of heated wind flung them all backward into trees and rock. Michael fell crashing to the ground and turned to his rear to see the land behind them was gone, and the Maelstrom was all that the eye could see.

The Ladder then lifted into the sky, twisting, screaming in howling fury. A figure gleamed at its base, and Michael watched as the Ladder turned, hurtling towards them.

Each angel ran and flew to escape the ensuing beam of light and plasma and leaped out of the way to prevent from being struck. The familiar sound of Lucifer's body echoed across the canyon.

The funnel touched the ground, and then Lucifer followed and slammed into the earth. The impact from his fall cratered the land, throwing rocks and trees aside while fire and white smoke hissed from his frame. Lucifer was on bended knee as the colors of the rainbow skipped around him as fallen snow. Flecks of prismatic light followed him and settled on his person, and Lucifer glowed as light from a star.

Onlookers' mouths dropped at what they had witnessed and bowed in awe that the Chief Prince had survived the Abyss. "Lightbringer," an angel said. Others whispered the words about them and bowed themselves in respect for their prince.

Lucifer rose from bended knee. His body shivered uncontrollably; sore that two of heaven's forces had vied over him. His face twinkling in light, Lucifer turned to speak to Michael in the melodic tenor that was his voice. "Are you all right," he asked.

Michael coughed and turned towards his brother. "I am––thanks to you. Are you ok?

Lucifer replied, "Aye, sore, very sore, but El be praised we survived."

"I thought I had lost you," said Michael.

Lucifer laughed. "I thought I had lost me too."

"There is something that you should know," said Michael.

Lucifer scrunched his face while massaging the back of his neck. He shook his head and looked at his brother curiously. "And what might that be?"

Michael hesitated to answer but looked at his brother, paused, and then spoke quietly under his breath. "That brace -- well it fell when I unlatched from the cliff. Sorry."

Lucifer's eyes widened as he looked at Michael in disbelief. He lifted himself from the ground, as he wiped grime and dust from himself. "Michael Kortai! I am *not* going to do that work all over again!"

Michael bowed his head slightly; his eyes darted from Lucifer to the ground and then back again. He hunched his shoulders and pulled from his robes the spike that had dislodged from the wall. He held it up and tossed it to his brother.

Lucifer caught it, looked at it, looked at Michael, and then chuckled. Michael too found himself snickering, and like a viral infection that spread; each broke out in stomach-bursting hilarity as workers who beheld their rescue and escape ran to assist them and gathered round to see the two laid out, flat on their backs laughing.

Suddenly a flash of white light appeared. The group covered their eyes as Gabriel stood before them in shining white robes and a staff in hand. "The Lumazi are summoned to court," he said.

Lucifer and Michael rose to stand in their brother's presence.

Lucifer stopped laughing, and his tone grew somber. "Of course," he said. "We shall leave at once."

Gabriel looked at them and pinched his nose against the odor that floated about them; grime and dirt covered their face, and dust fell from their clothing.

"You both stink," Gabriel said.

They laughed, and Michael pointed at his brother, "It's him."

Lucifer cocked his head and gave Michael a scowl.

"Well, you *do* stink," said Michael.

The sound of falling rock came from their rear, and Gabriel peered to his left to see behind and past them. Quickly, they moved to his left to block his view: and when he moved to his right to see, Michael and Lucifer also moved.

Gabriel frowned and placed his hands on his hips. "This is not funny."

Lucifer took the spike he held in his hand and tossed it to Gabriel, who caught it.

"Indeed, you know not the half of it," Lucifer sniggered.

Michael and the rest of the work crew burst out in laughter. Gabriel looked upon them all as if they were all mad. Each walked past him laughing.

"You really missed it," said one.

"If you had just come a bit earlier," said another.

Once again, Gabriel heard the sound of crashing rock to his rear. He turned his head, and Gabriel's eyes widened at the spectacle before him. The cliffs face and large chunks of land fell into the mouth of the Maelstrom, and the gale ripped and shredded boulders apart until nothing but sand remained. Gabriel looked at his brothers as they walked away and then turned to look once more at the chaos they had left behind. He shook his head in disbelief and made his way to run after them.

"You two are something else. Ok, this one I've got to hear."

* * *

The Lord God's command was clear. "Assemble before me and report of thy stewardship."

Propelled by instinct, the high princes traveled from the farthest reaches of creation as salmon to their stream of birth.

Michael walked through the outer court of the palace. Light permeated every nook and cranny of its colossal, white granite halls: each ray of luminance sprang from the person of El whose mere presence glowed and projected brilliance above the brightest sun.

"Hail Michael!" said a familiar voice from his rear.

Michael turned to see Raphael floating from the Hall of Annals towards him. He smiled wide upon seeing his brother.

Raphael ran to embrace him. "Ah, it is so good to see you!"

"The feeling is mutual," replied Michael.

"You have been so busy with the business of the Grigori that I feel neglected. It has been too long since we have spent time together. I miss hearing the tales of what El is doing throughout creation."

Raphael nodded and spoke. "Indeed, we have been apart too long. Perhaps after the report, we might converse in the Hall. I can show you the creation of a new nebula. Michael, I tell you, never have my eyes seen such sights. El honors my people by allowing us to record all. We are, after all, the most traveled of Elohim."

"The Lord is wondrous, and I look forward to exploring the new realms," said Michael. "I must admit I am excited to travel. To see the wonders of creation in person is indeed a thrilling prospect. As Archon over the city, my management of Heaven leaves little time for anything else. Perhaps I may request from El a temporary leave from my assignment."

They laughed as they walked towards the veil of the throne room.

As they walked from the outer court of the palace into the inner court, the Seraphim cried out to greet them. Michael and Raphael adjusted their inner ears to prevent deafness.

The Seraphim roared to the approaching angels and to each other. "Holy, Holy, Holy, Lord God Almighty, which was, and is, and is to come!"

Michael was used to the Seraphim repeating this ear-splitting chant day and night. The sound was so loud that it would deafen all but the most powerful of Elohim. Flame covered the entirety of the Seraphim's bodies. Each had six wings. With two they flew, with two they covered their eyes, and with two they covered their feet.

There were four of the creatures in existence, and they were always in El's vestibule or outside the temple doors. Eyes filled their bodies, and each was half man and half beast. Fire emanated from their frames, and dark smoke ushered from them. They stood 20 feet tall and were muscular in build.

Michael and Raphael continued to converse and heard the sound of music in the distance before them. Lucifer had come to greet them.

"Michael, it's good of you to join us. Late again I see?"

Michael eyed with admiration his elder brother. Lucifer's porous and scale-like skin glowed, and the multicolored moving patterns of his body mesmerized so that one did not want to look away. His twelve glowing wings were aburst in color, and each follicle of his hair captured the slightest movement, and like wind chimes created melodious sound with each of his approaching steps.

"Ah my brother never has sarcasm sounded so sweet," Michael, teased.

Raphael let out a laugh.

Lucifer's pitch changed, and the beautiful scowling of a hundred-voice choir replied, "I would not see you rebuked. Come, we do not wish to be late."

Lucifer scratched at his chest as if irritated. He motioned the two princes to follow him. "Come, El awaits the council."

Michael and Raphael turned to follow. Michael eyed his elder brother, for his organs were musical instruments, and as Lucifer walked, every movement made one want to dance or sing. The sound was pleasant to the ear, and Lucifer could create any sound within creation in any key, with any pitch and volume. Lucifer did not speak; he sang.

Michael studied Lucifer, mimicked his gait, and waved his hands with flowing motions through the air.

"Michael, what are you doing?" Raphael whispered.

Michael fluttered his wings like his elder brother but still nothing.

Raphael looked at him wondering if Michael had lost his mind.

"Michael," said Raphael.

Lucifer turned around to see that his brother mimicked him. With eyebrows raised, he spoke. "Would you for a second stop fooling around, and come on!"

"There it is," said Michael.

Lucifer looked at Michael with irritation and put his hands on his hips. "There is what?" he said.

"That thing you do with your voice—that twang. How do you do that?"

"Ugh, you are as incorrigible as Jerahmeel." Annoyed, Lucifer shook his head and walked away.

The brotherhood knew Lucifer was the most serious-minded of them all and possessed little humor. However, no one could irritate Lucifer more than Jerahmeel, whose brashness and disregard for protocol irked him to no end.

El never rebuked Jerahmeel, as if El knew the high princes needed his sage, yet frank advice. Jerahmeel always told Lucifer to "lighten up." Yet, despite all of his seriousness, no one among them was more devoted to the service of El than Lucifer.

"See! He did it again," said Michael.

Raphael walked past him laughing. "Lucifer is right; you are incorrigible."

"What? I think it is the pipes in his throat and forearms. That's what's making that sound! I want some too!"

Passing through the veil of the inner chamber, they entered the throne room: the seat of all power in the multiverse. Four members were already assembled and on bended knee waiting for El to summon them.

Michael lifted his hands to his eyes to block the glare from the blinding white light as waves of intense heat overtook them as they neared El's presence. Lucifer's company never helped, for his mirror-like skin just heightened the effect.

Michael looked over and whispered to Raphael, "I will never get used to this."

"Hush, Michael," he replied.

The three princes traversed the throne steps and arrived at their apex. The steps of the throne were made of the same material as the street of the city: a translucent gold. All streets in Heaven found their paths ending at the mountain of God and the throne room. Before the throne, the floor was as a sea of glass similar unto crystal. In the midst of the throne and round about the throne, a mist filled the air, and a rainbow arched above the throne.

Seven basins of fire were set before it, a place for each high prince to sit before the fire. Within each lamp lived a Virtue: living smoke, whose foggy presence filled the chamber, yet did not emit the smell of burning or make one choke. The fragrance of the Virtues was akin to frankincense, and they wafted about the throne room with transparent eyes and moved as fish swim in formation.

The white marble pillars of the throne room shook from the voices of the Seraphim outside. Behind and beneath the throne were the Ophanim; living creatures that looked like wheels within wheels. Two of these creatures were underneath the throne as if its entire weight rested on them, and two were horizontally behind it.

Each had four faces. As for the likeness of their faces, each of the four had the face of a man and the face of a lion on the right side and the face of an ox and an eagle on the left side. They sparkled like chrysolite.

Two rotating wheels with wings crisscrossed by two other wheels with wings surrounded them. Moreover, they moved in any one of four directions the creatures faced; and all four wheels were full of eyes all around.

Each Ophanim generated powerful gusts that propelled the throne at El's whim. When the Ophanim moved, the wheels beside them moved, and when Ophanim rose from the ground, the wheels rose. Wherever the Lord God went, they went too, and the wheels rose along with them because the spirits of the living creatures were in the wheels.

Affixed to the top of the throne were two Cherubim; each faced one another with backs arched and heads bowed. With outstretched wings, they covered the throne as if it were possible to provide shade for the God who is light, yet they stood ever ready and awaited any command from El. El's train filled the temple, a living blood-red cloak that draped round about the throne and flowed down unto the crystal floor below.

The angels of his presence, the Lumazi, had assembled and stood before the Lord. In unison, the seven princes bowed, as was protocol before the Lord of all things.

Others could not look upon El without blindness, yet their eyelids as High Princes allowed them to filter the luminance and made it possible to see an outline or, at least, a partial visage of his form. The Shekinah Glory surrounded El, and those who looked upon him directly would invoke blindness, for the Shekinah was the residue of God's breath. A living shawl of breathing light that enveloped and irradiated the person of God. The Shekinah illumined all that came near the Lord and left an afterglow on anyone who attended Him, even after one had left his immediate presence.

To describe El was difficult. All angels were in a manner of speaking a reflection of Him, yet He surpassed all intelligible attempts to describe Him.

Michael looked upon El, and He appeared as a bearded Elohim of 10 cubits in height: whose hair was as wool, youthful in looks yet ancient beyond understanding.

Michael observed that El possessed two legs, and two arms and that there was no form, comeliness, nor beauty that He should be desired, just an all-encompassing gentleness and power. When El walked, he did so with a slow deliberate, and steady gait. Only on the most momentous of occasions did he even leave the throne room.

When Michael asked what his brethren saw, each saw a different thing. Raphael said that he saw a two-legged figure with a blindfold over his face, having four arms; each arm held four objects: a book a stylus, an inkhorn, and a balance.

Gabriel swore he saw a feline-like creature with wings on each foot.

Lucifer–– Lucifer never discussed how he viewed El. He was always reluctant to speak of what he saw. Michael always thought his reluctance strange, but if he were not confident of Lucifer's devotion, one would say contempt would be the look Lucifer displayed whenever Michael broached the subject.

Then El spoke and awakened Michael from his daydreaming.

"I am the Alpha and the Omega, the Beginning and the End. Stand before me and give account of thy stewardship. Approach, Michael."

Mindful to bow, Michael walked towards the Lord, sat before him, and gave his report.

"Lord, the additional housing that you have directed has been completed. There are one billion new units now available for occupancy. The granaries have been expanded for increased food storage, and the city expanded by an additional 25% by your orders.

"Lord, it would appear that we have more than enough room in the capital and clear that we have more living space and food production capabilities than is necessary. May I ask the purpose of these additions to the kingdom?"

Michael waited for a response. El smiled at him. Michael remembered El once told him that his trusting and inquisitive nature was one of the attributes that He most enjoyed about him.

"Soon all will be made clear, my friend. I will announce my intentions at the next assembly. By then all preparations will be complete, and on the seventh day, I will rest from all my labor."

I knew it! So an announcement is forthcoming! Michael thought to himself.

Michael shook his head, knowing that by the time he understood what El wanted done, El had been planning the outcome from the very beginning.

Michael continued until he concluded his report.

"I am pleased with the progress of the city my son. Well done."

Michael stood to his feet, bowed, and walked backward until he was again with his waiting brothers at the steps below.

"Lucifer, Son of the Morning Star, approach."

Lucifer was titled 'Son of the Morning Star' and other than God Himself, there was no object brighter in illumination, thus the title of honor. God had named each member of the Elohim and had written their names on their flesh.

Then the Lord said unto Lucifer, "Whence comest thou?"

Then Lucifer answered the Lord, and said, "From going to and fro in the Earth, and from walking up and down in it."

"And how fares the happenings on Earth?" the Lord asked.

"Lord, per your orders, the seas have brought forth great beasts after their kind, and the skies filled with fowl. A particular species glides for several furlongs with a grace that rivals even the Elohim, my Lord.

"I am most impressed by your designs and creativity. To pattern this planet after some of the same flora and fauna as in Heaven, I would not have thought to do that, especially in light of the variety of worlds that you have allowed us to administer, but this world is particularly beautiful, Lord. I thank you for allowing me over-site as its Archon."

Michael shook his head and smiled at his brother. *Look at him as giddy as a new Archon still.*

As soon as he knew the importance of this assignment, Lucifer fawned all over it. Michael had never seen Lucifer so pleased with himself than when El titled him Archon of Earth.

Michael was happy for Lucifer: proud even, for he had assisted him since the very beginning. Lucifer was always there always helping each new Elohim that God created to acclimate to their new assignment. Initially, it was a daunting task when the Elohim were fewer. However, nothing was too much for El. He was their Father, and they happily obliged Him in all things. Never would Michael have thought to see the wonders that they now behold.

In each of the last assemblies, the council had come to learn more about the thing El had called *Time* and that He would create a sphere of creation that would be subject to it.

Each member of the Lumazi was to explain to their race the meaning of all that they learned and commit to their knowledge the conduct required to operate within each realm. They adjusted over time to the knowledge and reality of these new heavens and the limits that El had directed as they roamed within each one.

Lucifer continued his report and in a twinkling of an eye displayed to his maker all the wonders of Earth's beauty. He noted how the planet had angels making sure that each river ran its course per the explicit directions of El.

Michael listened awestruck by the level of involvement that El had in every aspect of creation. He never realized how his duties in the capital dulled him from appreciating how much design went into the massive undertaking of creation.

Four days they had all labored, and Lucifer gave his report on the latest day's efforts, detailing to the Creator information on new flying creatures, wingspans, and even the number of feathers each one needed to remain airborne.

Michael leaned forward absorbed as Lucifer elaborated on the difficulty in achieving the color combinations that El commanded in certain species of flowers. On and on, the First of Angels relayed the intricate details of life that was quickly enveloping the planet El had named "Earth." God nodded his head in approval and saw that it was good.

"Well done, Lucifer. You have done all according to my will. Well done indeed."

Then it happened.

El stood!

With a wave of his outstretched hand, the throne room suddenly disappeared. The walls vanished before their eyes, and all that remained were seven angelic princes still on bended knee floating within the second heaven El had named "space."

El's eyes turned towards one of the many galaxies He had created, and for a moment, any equilibrium the princes possessed failed them as the motion of stars, planets, and other phenomena too wondrous to describe flashed before their eyes.

Then within full view of them all, El reached for a small blue orb of a planet, which encircled the now familiar star named Sol, and lovingly held it within the palm of his hand.

Once again, they moved and found themselves partially submerged in water.

Michael became off balance as a sea of water surrounded him, and waves crashed over his face. The whole group struggled to swim, fly, and adjust to the instantaneous nature of how they traveled from the throne room of Heaven to this planet with its teeming oceans.

Panic-stricken, Sariel cried, "Look!" and pointed to several large creatures moving with great speed toward them.

Then they appeared; great whales--giants gliding in the great deeps of the watery world, and littering the sky above them were countless fowl whose numbers were too abundant to tally.

With arms outstretched and a voice of gentleness and satisfaction, God saw that it was good. The Lord God blessed them, saying, "Be fruitful, and multiply, and fill the waters in the seas, and let fowl multiply in the Earth."

Then with a flash after having reached this planet of teeming life and having adjusted to the state of water and motion, the group found themselves instantly atop the Mountain of God in El's throne room.

"Wow," said Jerahmeel, soaking wet with the biggest smile on his face. "Now that was fun! Can we do it again?"

Gabriel lost all sense of balance and immediately toppled over. El's unique method of instantaneous transport was finally too much to overcome. Michael laughed aloud and Gabriel shot him a hot frown.

"I am not amused," said Gabriel, who then put his hand over his mouth: his cheeks turning green.

Michael smiled, looked up, and noted that the Lord had settled into his throne. Lucifer also was sitting before the Lord and had continued his report while the rest of his brethren; pale and queasy attempted to compose themselves.

"Show off," Michael whispered to Lucifer.

Lucifer grinned and continued his report.

Michael glanced up and noted to his astonishment that El was chuckling at them.

And the evening and the morning were the fifth day.

Finishing Touches

Day Six

"What is wrong with you?" asked an angel.

I had never thought that I was different, never until someone pointed it out to me.

"What do you mean?" I asked.

"Why is your stone broken?" the angel replied.

I reached my hand into my robes and pulled my sigil stone from my chest for inspection. It felt fractured, even coarse in some parts, yet there was a clear delineation of smoothness to half of it. A quarter of the stone was missing, but it was clear that two halves of the stone were stitched together. I looked down to see the gouged hollow absent from the whole. My Heartstone warmed my hand as it pulsated in my palm. The ginger-colored stone shimmered with a crystal glint; it had firmness and heft to it. The outer skin of my heart rose and fell. Something moved within that strained to get out of the stone. Smoke and ash floated from it, and it crackled with a sizzling sound. It gave off an aroma akin to burnt charcoal.

My self-inspection showed that nothing seemed amiss.

"I do not know," I said. "It has been this way since my creation. What's wrong with it?"

"Your stone is broken," the angel said. "Something is wrong with you."

Your stone is broken. Something is wrong with you: that is all he ever said. It's funny as I think back, but I never did get that angel's name.

"Apollyon are you ready?"

Perhaps now after all this time, I will gain the respect I have always wanted.

"Apollyon, stop daydreaming. Are you ready?" Saesheal said.

"Yes, my friend. You fuss over me like I am going to forget!"

Saesheal laughed, "No — I fuss over you because you *do* forget!"

I laughed because I knew Saesheal was right. He was the first to take any interest in me: my truest friend. He has always been so protective, and I had to admit I enjoyed how he doted over me.

"Leave him alone. You can mock someone else's stone when you acquire the power to create one yourself. If El does not worry, then neither should you." The angel scowled and walked away. I turned to my benefactor and looked upon the smaller Arelim who had come to advocate for me.

"My name is Saesheal," he said. "We will be serving together in the Sol system. What is your name?"

"Apollyon," I replied. "El has titled me Son of the Dawn."

"Truly?" Saesheal said. "Impressive––that name is similar to Lucifer's. It is my pleasure to meet you. My quarters are not far from here. Care to get a bite before training?"

"That would be nice. Thank you," I said.

"By the way, I happen to think your stone makes you unique. It has an orange color to it."

I tried my best not to roll my eyes. I hated orange.

"Thanks," I replied.

How ironic, that after all this time, I find myself now bathed in the orange glow of this star. Saesheal interrupted my daydreaming.

"I always knew that you looked good in orange Apollyon." Saesheal teased. "You are now Archon of Sol, I am proud of you."

I positioned myself in the center of the sun and reveled in the blanket of its warm embrace: its flames soothed tendons and muscles. I was now officially the Archon of Sol. I could feel my jaw widen with the grin that I knew stretched across my face.

Archon: I liked the sound of that. My assignment as archangel over El's prized star would give me great prominence among my people. Perhaps now, I might command respect and no more to called, "broken stone."

I looked at Saesheal, who smiled at me and remembered the angels of times past who sneered at my difference. "Shhhh, here he comes," laughed an angel.

I winced as I thought back on the memory. I suppose they never did truly care if I heard them or not. Ashtaroth was always quick to remind me of my difference with his constant and grinding ridicule of me. I had resigned myself that I would best him in seeking title as the Archon of this star.

"Eh, pay him no mind Apollyon," said Saesheal. "There is something to be said about being different from everyone else. It sets you apart. You would do well to consult with Lucifer. He might aid thee to understand how one so different might abide. No one understands this more than the First of Angels."

"Perhaps I will," I said.

Lucifer always supported me. He made sure I had the best training and took a personal interest in me. I knew he saw how others treated me. He was quick to rebuke me when anything occurred and swift to offer me words of encouragement I was grateful for his mentoring. I appreciated the kindness he and Saesheal showed me.

"Bear Ashtaroth no mind, my friend, as he too covets to be Archon of Sol," said Lucifer. "He has petitioned Master Breagun for the role. I suspect he desires to impress me by overseeing the sun, which warms my own charge. I believe his behavior towards you is but his way to show his own desire for thy status," said Lucifer. "I will talk to him. He is rife with possessiveness whenever I speak of another angel in fondness or admiration."

"Am I to understand that you admire me then Chief Prince?" I asked.

Lucifer smiled. "I have come to see how similar we are, my friend. I would see such potential cultivated and steered. You are the 'Son of the Dawn'. I would see you shine."

I paused from my past reflections and waved to Saesheal as I bathed within the fires of this orb of gas and flame, but nothing warmed me more than the smile that beamed back approvingly from my friend. I no longer could afford such lapses in thought as I slowly assumed control of the star.

"Saesheal, we both know that orange is *not* my color. And you, dear sir, well, let's just say I can't wait to see you in grey."

Saesheal chuckled at me. "Let me enjoy this moment I can't help it if you look silly in orange."

"Oh so after so many days together, the truth comes out! I knew I looked funny in orange!" Saesheal snickered and covered his mouth to hold back the laugh he was attempting to squelch. He did well at first, but as I gave him the eye, the reflex was finally too much to control, and he burst out in laughter and revealed what we both knew to be true.

"Ok, ok--you do look funny!"

"Humph, laugh as you will. I am sure your assignment to administer the moon will give me much amusement. That is just rock, nothing to control or watch over there."

"I beg to differ," said Saesheal. "If Luna wavers in orbit, the tides of Earth, the continents themselves will shred. It is a vital role. Besides, I had requested to be near my friend."

"Well, you are welcome company indeed. I still remember what Master Breagun drummed into my head. 'Celestial oversight of planets stars and other phenomena could be for some Elohim extremely lonely. Mind your thoughts for your concentration must forever be attentive to maintain El's laws. El has flung into motion all things, and we must *not* allow even one word to fall!'" I said in my best mimic of his barking voice.

Saesheal laughed. "You do a remarkably good imitation of Master Breagun. However, he is right, and that is the exact reason why I am here. To keep that straying mind of yours focused on the task."

I knew he was right.

Every aspect of creation had an overseer, and nothing was made without an Elohim to administer it. El had dispatched untold Elohim to the four corners of the universe to watch over his creation, to keep it, and to govern every orbit and every shift of climate on all worlds.

I was glad to be here with my friend, both of us chief administrators of the sun and moon. I enjoyed my service to El and felt privileged to bring warmth to His prized possession.

I had studied and prepared myself, isolated for time to accustom myself to the solitude and quietness as Archon of this star. Learning to hone and focus my thoughts on the Elomic commands needed to fuel this star's flame. Now positioned within Sol's core, my mind expanded as it trained to control every nuance of Sol's temperature, contraction, and processing of its fuel. I was ready to begin my work.

I surveyed the length and breadth of this new solar system. There was beauty in the quietness. My eyes darted across each celestial body, each administered by an angel with specific instructions.

There was a third body to which I was ever to be mindful, a fragile speck from my vantage point, but lush and teeming with life. El had a great interest in His mote.

I looked also upon the fourth planet and gazed upon it. It seemed similar to Earth in its ability to hold life.

I wondered--

I exercised my will, now trained to manipulate stars. I flexed my twelve wings, and my Heartstone glowed and pulsated.

Hmm--a slight adjustment here...

The ball of stellar fire and gas bowed in submission as hydrogen and helium harnessed Sol's power of fusion and complied with my whim. I reveled and basked giddily in my newfound supremacy. I watched from afar, as Saesheal settled in Luna's core, and I was happy.

While my attention focused on this mere indulgence of joy, in my momentary drift of concentration, Sol's energies flashed before my eyes, and the giant's fury reached out towards the fourth planet. Then the fiery outstretched hand of Sol raced away from me into the black.

A long tendril of the newly formed star stretched forth into the vastness of space, and its spark and heat dashed off to fulfill my will. My heart beat faster, and panic quickly engulfed me. Sol reacted violently to such emotion and glowed to the notice of Saesheal.

Saesheal's eyes opened wide with astonishment, and his jaw dropped. He looked at me frowning and with apprehension in his face.

"Apollyon, calm yourself...what have you done?"

"I think I misjudged the degree to which the temperature must be controlled!"

"Well, get it under control!" he screamed back. "We cannot fail!"

The heated cord sprinted its way into the blackness, and both of our eyes turned to trace its projected destination. Realization and panic gripped us as we saw the blue speck, Earth lay directly in its destructive path. Saesheal voiced the dread that now lay in both our thoughts.

"In El's name, no!" He cried.

Suddenly Saesheal launched himself in pursuit of the flaming tendril.

"Saesheal, what are you doing? You are spirit; you cannot stop it!"

He looked back towards me, and I could see his forehead tense as he pondered the gravity of the situation.

"I can if I become flesh," he cried back.

Flesh? I thought.

The flare was part of the physical realm, and although it presented no mortal danger to Saesheal as spirit, I knew that the fragile blue world created by El was in imminent danger of ruin.

Faster and faster, he flew as I watched him close in on the blaze. I sensed that my friend might actually be in danger.

Apprehension began to flood my soul, and I could feel movement within my Heartstone. I felt Sol leap in response ready to unleash further destruction. I fought to smother my anxiety. I could afford no further loss of control. I could sense my training reasserting itself, and the sun settled in its churning.

Oh, maker of all--El hear my cry. We need you to intervene.

Closer the strand of solar energy reached to grasp the planet for annihilation. Quickly Saesheal's wings carried him, now propelled by the power of the living God. Soon he overtook and distanced himself from the flare and hurriedly flew around the planet. He paused and posted himself as a defense: a living barrier between the Earth and the power of the new sun's fury.

He frowned and with a look of determination, spread wide his angelic wings, and inhaled, and I watched his lips mouth the Elomic command necessary to draw upon the power of his spirit. Intuition informed me that I was watching my friend's last moments, and my countenance fell.

"Kodor en-chi El-khan El-khan"

Repeatedly he pronounced each word, and with every breath, the flare coursed nearer to embrace him in its destructive hold.

El's power emanated and crackled around Saesheal, and a visible bluish-white light enveloped him. Wave after wave rippled from his body, and soon he rivaled the brightness of the flare itself.

I stared in horror unable to move, helpless to render aid unless I was relieved of the responsibility to watch Sol. I could not risk leaving to assist my friend, or the sun would flare even further.

An indescribable ache washed over me like a wave. A woe. My belly hurt as if I had been pummeled in the gut. Sol responded in kind, and its core slowed and darkened. I struggled to hold back a tear that I might keep the sun in check. I then pleaded aloud my lament to my creator.

"Oh, God of all, where art thou?"

* * *

Saesheal looked into the sun to see Apollyon overwhelmed with emotion: anxiety mixed with frustration and birthed out of a womb of helplessness to act. Saesheal longed to be with his friend.

He was afraid for Apollyon, afraid that the shackled passions he knew beat within his troubled heart would one day erupt. Lucifer had asked him many days ago to watch him when he himself could not. Saesheal grinned as he remembered that befriending Apollyon was an assignment he initially did not care for. For Apollyon's stone was broken, and like the rest of Heaven, Saesheal wanted no part of him. However, he grew to care for the Arelim, and they had become the best of friends.

Saesheal could say he had honestly come to love him. He always wondered why Lucifer assigned him to watch him. Was not Apollyon's own Grigori enough?

"Who am I to be a *Watcher?*" he asked his Lord.

Lucifer's reply was ominous, "His Heartstone is an abscess of pain waiting to rupture. I fear what lies within. We must not let Apollyon succumb to emotions of despair and anguish, or it shall be to the ruin of us all. Guard his heart with all diligence, for out of it proceeds the issues of life," he had said.

Saesheal looked into the distance and saw that Apollyon's eyes fixated on him. As a slave fastened and bound, he stood chained, helpless to do nothing but watch the actions of his friend, and Saesheal knew him well enough to know that fear coiled itself around his friend.

Who would watch after him now? He wondered.

Saesheal smiled at Apollyon and whispered to himself, "Be strong, my friend. I have faith in you. Do not give in to despair."

Saesheal turned from Apollyon's eyes and launched himself into the flare's course, his body outstretched, head down, and wings tucked dense against his frame. His trajectory designed to place himself squarely in the lane of the flare's fury.

Closer they marched toward one other, an irresistible force against an immovable object. Saesheal closed his eyes and mouthed the oath of all his kind.

"Thy will be done."

The decision to transform had arrived: to fulfill the will of El or to allow His grandest creation to sink into ruin. But for Saesheal, there was no second-guessing, or need for reassessment. With a thought, Saesheal became a powerful, physical being of flesh and blood.

With gritted teeth and clenched fists, Saesheal collided with the deadly mass of heat and flame, absorbing the kinetic power of gas projected at the speed of light. Saesheal's wings unfurled to soak up as much energy as possible. Flesh burned and clothing cindered Saesheal's body now a shield to deflect the fury of the newborn sun. Then he turned limp and plummeted to the Earth below.

Apollyon searched for movement in Saesheal's fall, looking for any sign that he might recover from the descent that hurtled his flaming body into Earth's atmosphere.

Apollyon's hope failed him as he watched to see that when spiritual flesh is altered and meets the might of the celestial realm only mortality is birthed.

Light exploded and encroached on the blackness of space that blanketed the Earth. The collision created a shock wave that smote the planet's atmosphere and irradiated the sphere. Wave after wave of light burst across the night sky: a cacophony of greens, yellows, and purples entertained the now alerted and curious Elohim who attended to their various tasks below. Polar ice caps melted, and seas rose in response. Angels hurried to control the ensuing chaos that raged beneath them, and for a moment, all beheld two great suns in the sky.

Apollyon observed the charred and scorched shell that was once his friend. He wanted to cry out, to scream, yet he could not. Concentration on the sun had to be absolute, but his eyes shed a tear as he watched Saesheal grimace. Apollyon could only imagine the pain that flooded the body of his friend, falling into the blue sky of the planet below.

As quickly as the scene began, it came to an end: and from the midst of the crackling flames that surrounded him Apollyon heard Saesheal's scream break through the silence of space and he watched as his friend plummeted into Earth's atmosphere.

* * *

"GGGAAAHHH!" screamed Saesheal.

Lord and Master preserve me!

The consciousness of El suddenly filled Saesheal, and peace flooded his soul. Time slowed to a crawl while the Almighty spoke to Saesheal's quickly disintegrating mind.

"Go thou thy way till the end be, for thou shalt rest, and stand in thy lot at the end of days. Be not afraid, for thine journey is not yet complete."

When the Lord had finished speaking, Saesheal loosed himself from the tether of his life. His spirit emptied from his body, which became as a flailing husk plummeting to the ground.

Drained of the power of El, Saesheal's lifeless body penetrated the atmosphere. Earth's troposphere welcomed the fiery ember that breached its clouded walls of oxygen and carbon dioxide. Saesheal's body then woke the stratosphere from its rest. Sonic booms disturbed the once previously tranquil blue sky. The friction of powerful but frayed angelic wings created commotion among the planet's new aerial inhabitants. Thunderclaps from his fall sprinted as a jaguar across the lower levels of the sky, and dark smoke and lightning trailed his descent.

Saesheal's body fell on the newly formed land below, and rock and earth heaved to make way. Trees flung themselves aside like discarded kindle and snapped trunks screamed in creaking disapproval. The ground itself cried out with the explosive sound of fire and shrieked its objection to the violent intrusion. A "mighty one" had fallen, and Saesheal's body autographed itself with fire in the earth.

Dust and debris jettisoned into the air, and after the passage of time gently settled back to earth covering both leaf and blade of grass. The breadth of the crater burned of charred wood, grass whispered to onlookers with the sizzle of steam, and nestled silently and motionless within its core; the empty, crusted husk of Saesheal lay still; smoke lifted from his frame like a hovering phantom.

Angels in the area of impact moved to investigate the site. By the hundreds, they came open-mouthed and eyes wide.

"Saesheal, can you hear me? Saesheal," one said.

"Wake up, Saesheal! Wake up," another cried.

Another looked upon the charred remains of his comrade. "How is such a thing possible? Why does he not answer?"

"I saw a flare of light come from the sun. He looked as if he was trying to stop it," said another.

"But he does not breathe! The Arelim does not breathe," shouted one.

Apollyon still cradled in a bath of stellar fury looked on in anguished dismay. Passion and sadness overwhelmed him: yet he dared not express himself, for he knew the sun would broadcast his pain to the solar system's ruin.

So silently, he ruminated, embroiled in a mental cauldron of grief and angst. Looking into the distance of the black star-filled canopy of space, he strained to see past the second heaven into the third and wondered to himself, *El why didst you not save us?*

* * *

"My Lord," said Michael.

"Yes, my son?"

"You seem preoccupied. Is all well?"

El sat on his throne, his eyes looking past them all, looking elsewhere.

"Saesheal has thwarted a threat to Earth, and Apollyon now wonders within himself my actions."

Each archangel collectively looked upon one another questioningly and in amazement then turned to their Creator. Unanimously they responded as one. "And your will in this matter Lord?"

El closed his eyes for a moment. He sat in silence, then opened his eyes, and spoke. "Raphael come forward and report of thy stewardship."

Like his fellow brothers before him, Raphael stepped towards the throne and sat. He waved his hands, and volumes of books appeared above their heads and filled the room. Raphael stood across from El and pointed to a small window-like opening, and images began to flash before their eyes.

Raphael displayed the record of each Elohim. Each volume was open before him and floated transparently yet occupied no space. Pens and stylus moved of their own accord, never ceasing in their writing. Each pen updated the book upon which they wrote, and in the window before them, Grigori stood everywhere, taking note of all things: watching. Each carried a book, an inkhorn, and a stylus. Each screen showed the cowled and blank face of the Grigori, a race of Elohim that possessed neither eyes nor ears. They could see, but they did not. They heard, but they did not. Gifted with divine sight and hearing, they were absent the instruments normally associated with a species that experiences sight or sound.

El spoke, "Raphael, please display the Grigori assigned to Apollyon's attachment."

Raphael once more raised his hand, and one image came to the forefront of all others.

The image showed Apollyon looking up, and his Watcher barely perceptible in the background, faithfully recording every word and the thoughts of Apollyon's heart. The Lumazi collectively viewed this crystal display; the show of thought and action hovered above their heads, as Apollyon's innermost thoughts were made known for all of them to see.

"*El why didst you not save us?*"

Each was amazed; startled even that El would even be questioned.

El spoke, "Lucifer."

Lucifer stood to attend to his master, "My Lord?"

"Please assist Apollyon to understand."

El's eyes fixated upon the person of Lucifer and El began to communicate to Lucifer the words and the voice tone upon which he was to speak the word of God. Nothing was left to chance, and in the seconds that passed between them, Lucifer's reply was straightforward and familiar.

"Yes, Lord."

"Thou art dismissed to see to the matter. Make haste," said the Lord.

Lucifer scratched at his chest. "Thy will be done," said Lucifer.

Instantly Lucifer rose to his feet and began his descent from the throne room, deep bass sounds echoed with his every step. Melodious sounds emanated from the motions of his wings, and as he left, the sound of his presence faded.

"Jerahmeel, Talus, and Sariel, I will commence later with your reports. You may each retire for a time, and I will call for you when I am ready. Raphael, I have an assignment for you. Michael stay as you also have a new assignment. Gabriel, Saesheal, has --fallen. Recover what remains of thy brother's body and bring him here. He has honored me, and I will honor him. Tell your brethren that I am with them and let not their hearts be troubled."

Each cherub bowed to the Lord and exited the throne room.

El turned to Raphael. "Raphael, thou art commissioned to find all instances of thought, conduct, and or speech similar to Apollyon's. You and your attendants shall bring to me a volume which lists all Elohim and research on your findings."

"Aye, Lord. And your desire as to when you would have this complete?"

"Report thou to me on the conclusion of the 6th Earth day at which time I will take my rest."

"As you command Lord," replied Raphael. Bowing, the mighty cherub turned to leave the presence of the living God.

Michael stood and looked at his Lord. El noticed his glance.

"Speak Michael."

"Lord I have served you without ceasing day and night. You have allowed me to oversee as Archon the expansion of the city. I have seen wonders as you spoke the stars into existence, yet I perceive that something is amiss."

The Lord looked upon his beloved of angels, smiled, and studied him. El's gaze penetrated Michael, and for a brief moment, Michael thought that the Lord would speak. El stood instead.

Immediately Michael bowed with his face towards the ground.

"Rise, Michael, O beloved of angels. Rise and walk with me."

El left the throne, and both walked to the upper floors of the palace.

"Understand my son that I declare the end from the beginning, and in the day ahead, in what will be called 'ancient times,' *the things* that are not *yet* done. My counsel shall stand, and I will do all my pleasure. The words that I speak unto you now, though they are unclear, they shall be revealed later."

"Yes Lord," was Michael's reply.

"So, Michael, speak your mind."

"Lord, I do not fully understand what I have just seen. Raphael showed us what Apollyon's Grigori witnessed. I was not aware that such thoughts would be contemplated among the Elohim."

El looked upon his son and smiled. "My friend, thou art ever with me and have my heart. Thou art continuously in Heaven laboring in the work to which thou hast been faithfully assigned. Apollyon hast experienced for the first time a force capable of injury to his person. This new awareness of *self*-preservation hast brought with it questions. Questions about, why I would create such a thing? Why might I risk his person to accomplish my own ends? Apollyon has been thrust into a new set of circumstances, and as you all were created with a free will, such lines of reasoning must inevitably encroach upon his thoughts."

Michael nodded. "I see."

"All that can be done will be done. And all that will be will be," said El.

"All that will be will be, aye, Lord."

* * *

Lucifer arrived at the Cliffs of Argoth, a cropping of rock that overlooked all of Jerusalem: one of several waypoints that El had allowed for travel between the realms. The waypoints were essential. Failure to use a Ladder directed at a waypoint could result in the mistaken destruction of a structure in Heaven or worse, the possible dissolution of an Elohim. Several waypoints existed throughout the realm, and each was wide enough to accommodate the displacement of the heavens when Ladders formed. Lucifer closed his eyes and focused his thoughts. His mouth moved, and he recited the Elomic command that would transport him from the capital city to the second heaven called "space."

Lucifer felt honored. As the first created sentient being, he was one of a select few given an Elomic command. Each command allowed a creation event, a method to affect reality. Every syllable and each word added to reality or even allowed travel between the realms.

By this word, El created reality. El, however, was the living Word itself. All creation sprang from his mouth. El spoke, and what he spoke came to pass. He was *the* Elomic command.

Carefully, Lucifer pronounced each syllable, and with every utterance, eternity began to fold back upon itself. The pitch in Lucifer's voice was flawless, his volume perfect, and with the authority of El, he evoked the realms to hearken and to permit passage to the celestial realm.

As if on cue, creation itself came to attention and bowed to fulfill the word. Light danced around Lucifer's person, and slowly Heaven dissipated and revealed the barrier that separated eternity from time. Energy crackled around the mighty cherub, and wave after wave pulsated until a *schuuuup* sound blasted the air; similar to the sound expected when air vacates a room. Then it opened––the Ladder.

Lucifer's scales retracted into his body to reveal a powerful armor that surrounded him. The luminescent and translucent flesh of his wings glowed bright and, his legs and arms grew muscular, and with the revealing of his talons, he completed the transformation into the warrior angel necessary to survive the environment of the thing El had called space.

Looking down into the pulsating chute of light, Lucifer began his descent down the Ladder, and galaxies and stars soon littered all that he saw. Lucifer moved his body to adjust his path and made his way toward the planet that he had come to call home: the lush place El had called Earth. Lucifer had been responsible for its administration, and as chief Archon, he was the arm of the Lord overseeing all things concerning El's will.

Lucifer soared past worlds seeded with new life; each waited expectantly with an attentive ear for any command from El to bud. Some planetary bodies were pleasant to the eye, and all assisted in the guidance of what was now dubbed times and seasons.

He turned to a star in the distance and, able to recognize its unique signature among the billions littered in space, motioned his body toward the third planet. He entered the solar system and flew past the outer planets.

Then it appeared; the lush planet filled with aquatic life lovingly handcrafted by El. The young atmosphere quickly enveloped Lucifer, and its searing heat embraced his angelic skin as if to welcome him home. Red and green flashes of light skipped before his eyes, and then blue skies filled with wispy and majestic clouds. The familiar clap of thunder announced his entry. His twelve broad wings, used to cover El himself, slowed his approach, and he lightly touched down a stone's throw from the location of Saesheal's plummet. The Ladder then dissipated and retracted to lift back into the Third Heaven.

Lucifer approached the scene and eyed with curiosity the thousands of angels encircled above and around the crater of Saesheal's impact.

One angel of God was a remarkable sight; a legion was a thing of wonder. Each Elohim was as different in function, power, and beauty as the snowflakes that filled the Earth. There were the Arelim; massive, four-armed muscular creatures, bipedal with cloven feet. With the faces of rams, their leathery wings made them perfect for the building and movement of planets, a species to which both Apollyon and Saesheal belonged.

There were the Harrada, Issi, Satyrs, Kortai, Draco, and Grigori–so many present to behold this sight.

All noticed Lucifer's presence as they surrounded the crater and bowed to the Chief Lord Prince and planetary Archon.

Lucifer surveyed the enormity of it all. There was a central black impact crater bordered by scorched and flattened trees of one-furlong roundabout. Apollyon lay in the center of the deep crater; holding the charred remains of his friend weeping uncontrollably. Apollyon refused to be comforted, and his wails filled the air.

"Eleah, Eleah, kknada sabathkunar?" Which in the Elomic tongue meant, "My God, My God why hast thou forsaken me?"

Lucifer turned to one of the gawkers. "How long has he been this way?"

"My Lord Prince, you honor us with your presence on this dark day."

"Forgo me the chatter––how long!"

"He has been discomforted since Master Breagun commissioned Ra to relieve him not moments ago. He then ran into the center of the crater, held Saesheal, and would not release him. Master

Breagun has suspended Apollyon's post as Archon of Sol until he receives instructions from Prince Talus."

"Indeed?" Lucifer replied.

Suddenly, with a flash of immense light and clap of thunder, Gabriel stood over Apollyon, his white linen still bright from the glory of God. Gabriel stood nine feet tall, with twelve white flowing wings. His hair was solid white, and his skin was spotted with flakes of black on dark grey skin. He looked upon Apollyon and spoke.

"Oh, Son of the Dawn, fear not, nor be thou troubled. Saesheal though fallen is not without a future, for El has declared that his journey is not yet complete. I have come for his temple to return him to the Lord."

Apollyon looked upon Gabriel, and the Shekinah glory still irradiated Gabriel's face, for he was still fresh from the presence of the Lord. Peace slowly began to fill Apollyon. Apollyon held the body of his friend in his arms, wiped what remaining dirt and debris encrusted his face, and lightly brushed Saesheal's cheeks.

"And what does El intend to do with the body?"

"El has stated that as Saesheal has honored him thus shall he be honored. More I do not know. My task is clear; make way not to deter me from it," said Gabriel.

"Aye, Lord Prince," said Apollyon.

Apollyon gently gave the body of his friend into Gabriel's waiting arms, and with equal care, Gabriel wrapped Saesheal's body within the linen of his robes and prepared himself to depart.

"Hear all ye Elohim, for the Lord is not without pity. Believe in your God, let not your hearts be troubled nor let them be afraid, the Lord thy God is with thee."

Gabriel and Lucifer looked upon one another. Gabriel nodded with respect, and Lucifer returned the acknowledgment. Gabriel looked up and lifted himself from the gravity of the mass of spinning ore, and all looked upon him as his figure slowly diminished into the distance. Then the light of a Ladder was seen bridging the realms, and Gabriel was gone.

"My prince, what does this mean?" asked a bystander.

Apollyon spoke before Lucifer could reply. "It means that *I* have injured my friend. It means that *I* have failed. It means, Orion, that I must live with the knowledge that my brother has perished because of my hand."

Orion and the others looked at Apollyon with curious stares, but Orion spoke for them all. "Explain, Apollyon. How are *you* responsible for this?"

"I attempted to manage the sun's power to make life habitable on the Marxzian surface..."

"You fool! Did it not occur to you that you would boil the oceans just made? I cannot imagine that Master Breagun would have authorized such a careless act..."

"He did not, Orion, for I had thought"...

Livid, Orion cut Apollyon off. "Think no more, '*Broken Stone*', as it is ruinous to us all. If you ..."

"Enough!" Lucifer said.

Lucifer's deep and powerful voice overwhelmed them all and shook the ground. All present immediately stopped all talk and took notice as the Chief Prince roared at them. Silence surrounded the area, heads bowed in obeisance.

"I find that I have had enough and that this conversation edifies not. Accusations against a Son of God will not be leveled in my presence! Cease from this prattle and return to your posts, all of you!" Lucifer barked.

The ground quaked as Lucifer's command was issued. Startled and shocked back into the normalcy of reason, angels dismissed themselves from the area until none remained save Lucifer and Apollyon.

His countenance now softened, Lucifer turned to Apollyon and spoke, "Be encouraged my brother; you did what you thought was right."

"My Lord Prince, I..."

"You Son of the Dawn are tired, and it is apparent that you are overwhelmed with the events of today. Come, seek solace at my palace, and be refreshed. My attendants will see to your needs, and we will talk after you have had a chance to meditate. El knows of our friendship and of all the princes that he might send during such a time; He knew I would be the one most apt to comfort you."

"Your pardon, Lord Prince, your hospitality is appreciated, however..."

"Speak," said Lucifer.

"But I seek no meditation on the person of El."

Lucifer looked curiously upon this angel never having heard such speech in all his days. "I see. Then seek consolation within my halls. Come."

"Aye, Lord Prince."

Lucifer took flight, and Apollyon followed, heading towards the central city Lucifer had built on the Earth.

Lucifer's mind churned with questions about the day's events. *Why would El allow this to happen? With a thought, he could have easily dispatched the flare. He needed never to have even left the throne. Why even show us Apollyon's thoughts? Are my thoughts on display to those of the court as well?*

Lucifer noticed that their Grigori silently followed them. Their gaseous form made it easy to forget that they were there. Knowing that Lucifer's own thoughts were logged and recorded, he chose to meditate on thoughts of intrigue that he might provide sport for his own Grigori, Lilith, to write.

Why would the Lord even create such a creature? Lucifer was sure Lilith's pen would record his thoughts and, in so doing, generate some intriguing logs.

Ahh to know the innermost mind of a Grigori.

Lucifer chuckled at this prospect, for Lilith, his watcher was ever with him, yet Grigori never spoke or interacted with anyone but their own kind. Lilith, however, was of no immediate concern to the Chief Prince, but they would have words later Lucifer thought. Of that, he was sure.

Clouds bypassed them, and Lucifer was relieved to see in the distance the majestic spires of Athor. *Ah, it is good to be home.*

Athor stood over a thousand cubits high. Designed as a series of five pyramids interconnected with the tallest in the center and surrounded by the other four, the city was constructed out of diamonds and pearls. Lucifer demanded nothing less for his home, an abode worthy of God's Chief Prince, a glorious center where the Lord's beauty made the planet shine with his radiance should He ever choose to sit upon Earth's throne.

Athor dazzled in the distance, and no matter from which way one approached the city, it captured and refracted all light, displaying the entire spectrum. Its walls were like a stone rainbow comprised of quartz, diamond, and pearl.

Lucifer saw his citizens as he came near. They saw his approach, and the tower bells announced his return. Lightly, Apollyon and the First of Angels landed in the central courtyard. Lucifer's three attendants rushed to his side. Mephisto, Ashtaroth, and Dagon knelt before him. Mephisto was the first to greet them. His black hair contrasted against his tinted red skin, and with a cloak of silver and gold, he lowered his gaze and bowed as he spoke to his master.

"My Lord Prince, Son of the Morning Star, we bid you welcome home. What word is there from Jerusalem, and is there a new command from El?"

Lucifer replied, "Apollyon has been through great distress. Please have quarters prepared for him. Also, prepare a banquet in his honor, and I will dine with him later. As far as command from El...it is yet to be known, but when it is, we shall obey."

"Aye, Lord Prince, a banquet my Lord--for him?"

"Are my instructions not clear Mephistopheles?"

"They are clear, my Lord"

"Then proceed with their execution," Lucifer said.

Mephisto motioned to Apollyon to follow him. "Son of the Dawn, please come this way."

Apollyon was visibly uncomfortable over the fuss made over him and spoke to object.

"Oh, my prince, I am not worthy..."

Lucifer held his hand up to silence him and interjected.

"Speak not to me of worth my friend. El has deemed you worthy as we all. Hence, silence yourself of this speech and accept the graciousness of El on my behalf. Rest and we shall speak more soon."

Apollyon sighed and resigned himself to his chief's command as he and Mephistopheles left Lucifer's presence.

Ashtaroth and Dagon looked at their master and awaited instructions.

"Dagon, how fares the ground? Will it yield manna for the denizens here?" asked Lucifer.

Dagon's hulkish frame looked up at his master, his bronzed skin shown in the sun, and he was draped in all manner of gold and silver jewels. His bull-like face snorted in irritation.

"Nay, Lord Prince. I have continuously nurtured the ground here per your instructions, and though it yields herb-bearing fruit of every kind, manna will not spring from this soil. It is as if El has not designed this world with the Elohim in mind, for it does not produce the food we consume. We have coordinated with Prince Michael for shipments of manna as needed. Upon review of the granaries, he said he could provide us all that we require, for it is limitless in the heavenly city and grows without measure in the Elysian Fields."

Lucifer lowered his head and pondered. "Curious. It will *not* yield manna you say? I will speak with Michael upon my return to Heaven. How much more do you require to sustain the populace?"

"We have enough for two more creation events at the current rate of consumption. However, we increase each day in the need for Elohim as El expands this planet's attributes. There are countless Elohim monitoring from the east wind to every tree."

Dagon continued his assessment. "Those within the planet itself report that this world has oceans of magma upon which the land floats. It is assuredly unique from Heaven, for we have nothing like it at home. The land breathes fire in some sections. We have dispatched per El's command and your word Elohim throughout the planet."

Lucifer could not help but meditate on what Dagon had told him; "*...as if El has not designed this world with the Elohim in mind...*"

It occurred to him that Ashtaroth stared at him and sought to anticipate his master's will.

Ashtaroth was slim in build. His skin was solid white, and his wings were feathery and shimmered with a yellow tint when the light from the sun touched them. Necklaces from the translucent gold mines of Heaven draped his neck, which was as long as his arm and each collar glowed and moved around his neck of their own accord, never touching his skin. He looked with concern at his lord.

"My Lord Prince," he said.

Lucifer replied, "I am fine, Ashtaroth, thank you. Tell me how fares your coordination with Breagun's attachment?"

"My Lord, we have received word why the flare from Sol was unleashed upon our world. Thus, we are swift to ask why you have brought this simpleton to our door. Should he not be brought before Prince Talus for inquiry?"

"Save your interrogation for one who tolerates it Astarte, for I will not. I possess a word from El to Apollyon; the will of El be done."

"My apologies, Chief Prince, but by now all of Heaven knows of his failure. How can it be that an error of such magnitude is not dealt with?"

"Astarte, you have my leave. Coordinate with Breagun's new overseer of the moon. I do not want its proximity to disrupt our work here. You are both dismissed to see to your matters"

"Aye, Lord Prince. El's will be done," said Astarte.

"El's will be done," Lucifer replied.

El's will be done–curious.

* * *

Gabriel, Prince Lord of all Malakim, carried within his arms the body of Saesheal. He walked reverently past the gate of Heaven, through the city streets, and solemnly toward the Mount of God. All of Jerusalem emptied as angel after angel vacated Gabriel's path so that he might pass. Angels bowed to the prince in accordance with royal protocol. On this day, the lifeless body of an Elohim existed in Heaven. With a look of steel, Gabriel made his way through the center of the city; the Towers of Praise stood quietly in their annunciations of God's glory as all Elohim looked on in stunned silence. The only sounds heard were the footsteps of Gabriel and the flap of wings that held each angel aloft.

Gabriel made his way towards Michael and his brethren. Talus stood next to Michael while Raphael was away occupied on official business, but with the exception of both Raphael and Lucifer, all were present and accounted for Talus, Jerahmeel, Sariel, Gabriel, and Michael. Talus, who was Prince Lord of all Arelim: and no one — save the Lord himself — grieved this loss more. Saesheal was of his race, and all of Heaven grieved for the Arelim, an experience to which none were accustomed.

Michael looked upon the multitudes and was moved with compassion. He, like so many who now looked upon the empty shell of their friend, contemplated the enormity of such loss in Heaven. Michael saw the confused look on his brethren's faces. Each struggled with the thought that an immortal could die, that an error of judgment could lead to their hurt. The reality of the concept was affirmed by the testimony of the voiceless body carried by Gabriel through the street. Michael noted that he would remember this day for all time: the day when everyone acquired this new awareness, the day when grief and fear entered their collective consciousness.

Gabriel drew closer, and Sariel and Jerahmeel fell in behind him as he made his way up the flight of glass steps. Gabriel stopped where the brass altar lay. Talus stood prone, and Gabriel handed the body of Saesheal to his fellow prince. Talus gently took Saesheal's body and placed it on the Altar of Sacrifice.

The Altar of Sacrifice, all had wondered why El had named it thus, but the reason of its identification was now evident for all to see. Never had the altar been set aflame before, never until now. The great doors of the palace opened, and the Spirit of God flew out from within. All of Heaven bowed in reverence as the Holy Spirit lighted on the altar. The Holy Spirit was impressive to behold. His flaming wings outstretched and dwarfed the altar itself, the length of which was 100 cubits long. His eyes blazed with fire, and his pupils were as balls of lightning, and like a bird of prey, he flew and a trail of fire and the colors of the rainbow followed him.

To look upon the Holy Spirit of God was as if to look upon a dove and an eagle simultaneously. Yet the similitude of a man appeared within the image of the raptor-like image. The Spirit lighted upon the altar, and fire immediately raged both under and on either side. A *woof* sound sparked as it ignited, and Saesheal's body illuminated within the blaze. Then the air filled with the aroma--a scent, a smell not of ash or charred remains--but sweet and cinnamon-like. Then the aroma changed, and almond filled the air, and again the nostrils of all became enthralled as frankincense wafted across the emporium. Michael could tell that he was not alone in his curiosity and surprise as he looked to see that all Elohim present seemed enraptured as the aromatic mist filled the mountain and spread outward in every direction.

A vial was set towards the altar's front side again, but for what purpose none were privy. El ever directed them to build, to maintain, and to create; later they learned for what purpose.

Higher the flames climbed, but the body of Saesheal was not consumed. Smoke filled the area, which neither stifled nor hindered breathing, yet all around, the smell was sweet and saturated the air. All of Heaven was bowed down in reverence to the Holy Spirit of God and basked in the midst of the potpourri. The third person of the Trinity spoke and waves of visible sound ushered from his outstretched wings.

"Sons of God arise and let your eyes look upon the sacrifice. Behold the great Saesheal, Keeper of the Word of God. He was to be chief overseer: Archon of the lesser light of the moon. His bravery that my will not be thwarted placed him in harm's way. Thus, shall all of Heaven now honor him."

The mountain itself quaked as the Spirit of God spoke and seven thunders thundered. Lightning and smoke filled the mountain of God, and all stood captivated as the Spirit arose from the altar. Sparks of flame leaped from his wings and torched the body, which did not burn; instead, it smoldered while lying in state atop the altar at the foot of the Spirit.

Every eye looked to the person of the Holy Spirit, and all of Heaven either stood or was in flight, huddled like anxious participants to a great coliseum match; each struggled to see the spectacle before them. An innumerable company of angels filled the emporium and surrounded the mountain, ten thousand times ten thousand, and thousands of thousands. Michael watched astonished as mouth after mouth opened in response to the scene before their eyes. He, too, found himself overcome with wonder, his eyes fixated on the Altar of Sacrifice, and all of Heaven looked on with fascination, transfixed as Saesheal's body began to move.

* * *

"Is the manna to your liking, Apollyon?"

"Indeed, Lord Prince, this particular flavor is of exceptional taste and refreshes me. Your hospitality is much welcomed."

Lucifer took a cup of ale to drink and held a sapphire chalice to his lips. Decorated with some of the planet's flora, the banquet table impressed Apollyon. Tapestries imported from Heaven draped the walls and ornate ceiling, ready for the day that El himself might seek to fill this temple. The floors were made from the finest ores of gold, silver, topaz, jasper, beryl, and onyx. Diamonds and emeralds adorned the walls like grout all ready to reflect the temple's steward Lucifer.

Lucifer sat, covered himself, and pulled his robes tighter over his person so that his beauty did not distract. He was careful to stay covered when outside of the presence of God; therefore, he wore coverings that he might never draw attention to himself. Lucifer knew that were he to uncloak or otherwise reveal his appearance, the reflection from his mirror and diamond-like skin would overwhelm the whole palace in light, for the place was crafted so that he might reflect God's glory.

"Think naught, my friend. El has commanded me to share with you his word. It is my intent to carry out my master's will. However, before I speak his word, I'd like to ask you a question if I may?"

"Of course, Lord Prince, please."

"El heard your cry and dispatched me to respond to thee. I will, of course, share with you El's words, yet I find myself with a desire to hear *yours*. I hold particular interest of your account of this event."

"It is very simple Lord Prince. Master Breagun received and gave me orders from Prince Talus to serve as Archon for this system's star and Saesheal for the moon. Each one of us was to appoint seven attendants to our cause. After receipt of said orders, Saesheal and I determined to go and scout our posts and personally see to them. I relieved Ra who was temporarily assigned at the time."

"I see, and once fitted within Sol's core what then?" asked Lucifer.

Apollyon looked down, his eyes closed and his head in his hands, his voice cracked with sadness as he replied.

"I saw the beauty of Earth, Lord Prince. I saw the lushness that inhabited the planet. I saw the whole of the system seated in the center of Sol, and when I looked upon each world, I was moved with compassion. So I reached out to bring warmth to the fourth planet. I failed to remember that my thoughts themselves bound me to the star and that it would obey my will. The flare was an oversight, an impulse of my mind reaching out for what I saw. When I realized the magnitude of my actions, the flare had already approached your watch. I could neither pursue nor recall it once unleashed. Saesheal also knew this and sacrificed himself to save Earth."

"Am I to understand Apollyon that *you* let *your* will slip? Did I hear you correctly, or did you just inform me that you exerted *your* desires and will over El's?"

"Nay, Lord Prince, I am truly submitted to my master and king. I would never defy Him," said Apollyon.

"Your words leave me little comfort, Archon. You were assigned to *my* sector of space, and your actions have endangered the success of *my* watch. This temple is an edifice in which I have invested much toil. All that I have created here over the course of these past five days would have come to ruin, all because *you* determined that one planet out of the countless specks in this cosmos should support life.

Let me ask you, Archon, would your desires have extended warmth to the gas giant in this system, and what of the nether planets on its outskirts? Did it not occur to you that each one is set in its course by El himself? Or did you think yourself omniscient to know how and which planets should support life?"

Silence engulfed the room.

Apollyon visibly shook and covered his ears as the volume of Lucifer's words made his ears pound. Although Lucifer could conceal his visage so as not to blind, his voice boomed so that others could hear. His interrogation drew the notice of the attendants outside his chambers. Belial, a servant of Lucifer, poked his head inside the chamber door.

"Lord Prince, is all well?"

"Nay, Belial––nay, it is not. You may take your leave nonetheless."

"As you command, Lord Prince," said Belial.

Belial departed and shut the door behind him, leaving the two Elohim alone to continue.

Lucifer stood to his feet and removed his royal robes; each wing slowly unfurled, six to his right and six to his left. He opened the pores of his flesh to reveal his true form, and light raced to his body as iron fillings to magnetic ore, and colors projected from his skin like spotlights on the room walls.

The walls themselves absorbed and amplified the light. Each beam bounced off the glass of the temple. Brighter and brighter, the temple glowed, sparkling as a lamp within the darkness. The building radiated a hum, and everyone within the city knew that Lucifer had become uncovered, and each bowed to shield his eyes.

Apollyon kneeled in front of such a display, and although his strength in a physical altercation would equal or even surpass Lucifer, his mind was quickly overwhelmed by the brightness of his glory.

Lucifer spoke. "I am Chief Prince Lucifer Draco, Lightbringer, and Son of the Morning Star. I walk within the midst of the Stones of Fire. Hear the word of the Lord!

Oh, Son of the Dawn, thou who is the blossom of the Morning Star, be still and let your soul be at ease, for this thing was done that others might be made manifest. For you shall twice be tested and have once been vexed, the flame, which thou, hast controlled, shall indeed mirror your own as it doth consume; let not your own flame thus burn. But be thou warned that if sorrow persists, then on your shoulders shall indeed a new dawn come, the breaking of a new day. And he to whom you would seek solace shall be your King and your infamy shall indeed be known even unto the end of days.

Lucifer shuttered the pores of his flesh and covered himself with his robes; the light from his person vanished, and the room grew dim.

Apollyon rose to his feet, the drumming from Lucifer's voice still echoing in his ears. "This is the word from El: a riddle? But what does it mean?"

Lucifer motioned towards Apollyon and placed his hands on his shoulder as a gesture of comfort. "I know not the meaning of his words. I only carry them per his will."

"Ugh, I do not wish to meditate on riddles," snapped Apollyon.

"I think, Son of the Dawn, that your heart *was* in the right place: you simply wanted to see life where none existed. It is evident that you have been misunderstood. Where others might see failure or a simpleton, I see before me an Arelim who merely wanted to be as his Creator. A sentiment all who behold El: would understandably aspire. You made a mistake. I do not profess to know El's mind in this matter, but He is right that judgest, and surely He can see that your heart is sound."

"Thank you, Lord Prince. I shall return to Heaven and solicit from Him myself the meaning of these words. I wish to see my friend's body once more and determine my status as Archon with Talus."

"Then return, my friend, and may El grant you audience to understand His word, but, Apollyon, tell me —"

"Yes, Lord Prince?"

"How fares your consolation," said Lucifer.

"My consolation Lord Prince? My *consolation* would improve if my brethren, such as your attendant Ashtaroth, did not whisper injury behind my back. For I am neither deaf nor without feeling. I am sure he would not like me to reciprocate. It is not with honor I bear this failure."

"I will speak with him," said Lucifer.

"May I take my leave, Lord Prince?"

"Of course. May El's presence give you comfort Apollyon."

"Not today, Lord Prince, not today."

Lucifer looked upon this angel and noted that his manner was so different from all he had seen, his spirit so similar to his own. Lucifer perceived movement to his rear as light waves changed, and he turned to face his now-visible Grigori.

Lilith stood as all of his kind, cloaked in black, non-descript in appearance save he possessed no eyes or ears. A golden sash lined his waist, and a silver pen ever writing in a tome hovered slightly above him to his rear whilst an inkhorn hovered opposite him. His folded hands were covered in his dark cloak.

"I have yet to record what I have witnessed."

"And?" said Lucifer.

"*And*, you have *not* dispersed the entirety of El's word," said Lilith.

"Indeed," was Lucifer's reply as he warily observed his 'Watcher'.

"El's command regarding His word is clear Lucifer. "Ye shall not add unto the word which I command you, neither shall ye diminish ought from it, that ye may keep the commandments of the Lord your God which I command you."

"That Grigori is *your* command. I walk within the Stones of Fire. El grants me great autonomy to function in his name. I have exercised said privilege now."

"Take care, Lightbringer, as to diminish El's word is to trifle with reality itself."

Lucifer walked towards his Grigori, and his eyes narrowed as he inspected him. "And you, Lilith, why warn me at all? Are you not in violation of your own oath to speak with me? You are my watcher; since when would you be my counselor?" said Lucifer.

"Ah, but my liege..." Lilith bowed mockingly, "I acquire enormous benefit from watching you. Your thoughts are most shall we say – intriguing: to be sure. Therefore, I record your journals so that I might *continue* to watch your thoughts and deeds. I am sure if I *fully* recorded what I see, then those within the royal court would be as equally distressed as when Apollyon's own thoughts were revealed."

"Indeed," said Lucifer. "However, I am curious, Lilith."

"Yes, Lord Prince?"

"Who watches the watchers?"

Lilith grinned, and his form began to fade and slowly disappear to its non-corporeal state until all that remained visible to the eye was an angelic yet impish grin.

* * *

Apollyon walked through the halls of Athor: its corridors gleamed in light, and tapestries adorned its walls. His large frame made each Elohim that he encountered make way for him to pass. Each one eyed him. He noticed the sneers as he stepped toward the outer court; however, none of them understood. He could tell that their eyes followed him when they thought that he was not looking. Who among their kind had ever lost a brother? How could they know his pain he wondered? Apollyon thought to himself, *what could have been El's plan but to watch Saesheal's ruin? I know that El heard my cry. If he had but been there, my brother would still be alive. I must return home. El must answer me.*

It is not fair! We both should be basking in the glory of service and helping to prepare this world for its next stage of creation. Instead, I find my mind consumed with anxiety and thoughts of what could have been. Lord El, hear thy servant's plea. Why did you not prevent this tragedy?

Lucifer at least cares. He recognizes that it as an error. He knows. Why God? Why is my mind filled with doubts and criminations of my actions? I saw the planet: reached for it, and Sol reached with me. How could I have known that this would happen? I just want to go home, to speak to You. You will give me words for this situation. Not the babble of nonsense Lucifer delivered to me earlier. El will, but, El, why did you not save me?

Tears fell from Apollyon's eyes, and he reached down toward a bench to steady himself. Grief soon overwhelmed him, and he placed his large hands on his face. He was Arelim, and Apollyon looked to notice if anyone had seen him. He composed himself and wiped the tears from his eyes.

It was then in the midst of his moment of sadness, in the instant where the weight of his actions filled him with heartache that he heard the spiteful words uttered to him for the first time.

"What? Does a mighty one cry? Does the *Destroyer* shed tears?"

Apollyon winced at the remark. Slowly he rose and turned to face Ashtaroth who stood behind him; his disdain evident in his stance and face. His hands were on his hips, and his eyes conveyed to Apollyon that he was being given a visual dressing down.

"You would dare speak to me in such a manner?" said Apollyon.

"I do, Son of the Dawn. You are a testimony to all that Elohim aspires *not* to be: a failure to your race, a shame to your prince, a *Destroyer*. How El would even consider manna on one such as you baffles me. How a noble, such as Saesheal, ever would call you friend is beyond fathomable. Leave this place, Destroyer, for destruction indeed follows you, and I would have none of it in Athor."

As Ashtaroth turned to leave, Apollyon quickly looked upon this outspoken and contemptuous angel and reached to seize his arm.

"You will never utter Saesheal's name again in my presence, Astarte––never! Yes, I called you Astarte. That is what Lucifer called you, is it not? I see he values you so little that he does not bestow you enough honor to speak your full name. And you, servant of the High Prince, have not enough value for yourself even to object. You are indeed a vassal designed to serve."

Ashtaroth flung his arm away to break free, but Apollyon's grip was sure.

"Unhand me immediately, you buffoon!" Apollyon removed his hold from Ashtaroth's arm only to grasp his throat and lift him from the ground.

Ashtaroth struggled to breathe and speak, his speech gagged from the hold of Apollyon. He grabbed Apollyon's forearms and struggled to wrest free from his captor's grasp.

Apollyon raised his figure to his lips. "Shhh, hush, little angel."

His eyes narrowed, and Apollyon looked upon him as a cobra might view a coiled mongoose as prey.

Ashtaroth squirmed in discomfort, his vocal cords constricted by Apollyon's grasp.

"I wish to thank you, Astarte. You have made me aware that not all would praise my elevation as Archon of Sol, a position of honor that I know you sought as well. Indeed, little angel, I may be a simpleton as I overheard you say earlier, and yes, I did hear you, but intelligence aside: between the two of us, I am Archon of Sol."

Apollyon smiled and glared at Ashtaroth. "How it must gnaw at you, to be relegated to serve the tables of Lucifer while this simpleton, who grasps your throat, commands the very stars. You, Astarte, are not worthy to be Archon of flatware: you, little angel, are the chief administrator and archangel of nothing--nothing but Lucifer's tactful derision. For too long, I have been the butt of your ridicule and spite."

Ashtaroth squirmed and tried to raise his voice, but he released only a squeal of a sound.

Apollyon smiled. "What was that? I cannot hear you. Perhaps, you would care to speak louder?"

Apollyon looked with disdain upon Ashtaroth: his control of Ashtaroth's throat was absolute. He released his grip, and Ashtaroth fell to the ground, wheezing and gasping for air. Apollyon spit on the ground where Ashtaroth lay and leaped into the air: he summoned a Ladder and turned to face him a final time. "You would be wise not to approach me again, Astarte, and do not think that your position with Lucifer will cause me pause if you do."

The giant Elohim then stepped onto the Ladder and was gone.

Ashtaroth's need to fill his lungs overpowered his ability and desire to make an immediate reply; he looked up in humiliation and resentment as the Ladder carried Apollyon away. Thoughts quickly turned over in Ashtaroth's mind and plans within plans formulated, as he slowly regained his composure.

"This is *not* over Arelim--far from it."

* * *

Gabriel and his fellow princes looked in awe as the body of Saesheal rose into the air. Lightning crackled, and thunder clapped. A cylinder of light surrounded Saesheal, and the Holy Spirit hovered, his wings outspread, his eyes focused on Saesheal's body.

Jerahmeel leaned toward Michael and quietly spoke, "What is He doing, Michael?"

"I know not," Michael replied. "I stand as puzzled as you."

The charred flesh of Saesheal slowly began to heal, and even the smell from his remains began to fade.

The ground quaked, as the colossal wooden doors of the palace flung open. All eyes shifted to the illuminated figure that stood in the archway's midst.

Michael lifted up his eyes and behold a certain man was clothed in linen. His loins were girded with fine gold, and his body was like beryl; his face was as the appearance of lightning, his eyes as lamps of fire, his arms, and his feet likened to polished brass in color, and the voice of his words like the voice of a multitude.

"Verily, I say unto you..."

Immediately the citizens of Heaven knelt, the host of Heaven went prostrate as the Logos second person of the triune God, had determined to speak, and all of Heaven was hushed, eager with an ear to hear.

"Saesheal has honored me. Thus, he speaks even before the beginning: the things that shall be. For with faith, he hath quenched the dart of Sol and so prophesied of darts yet to come. For as Saesheal gave himself that others might live, so too shall the Son of Man lay down his life that the world might be saved."

Perplexed, the Elohim looked upon each other at a loss for comprehension; their shoulders shrugged in confusion as the depth of Jehovah's word plumbed their minds. He continued, and none spoke.

"Saesheal is not lost but away in the wilderness that I might have voice in all things. To be first among many that would do my will, and thus, it must be suffered him that all righteousness might be fulfilled. He shall stand with his lot on the last day. For indeed, He that loveth his life shall lose it, and he that hateth his life shall keep it unto life eternal.

I am the resurrection and the life: he that believeth in me, though he were dead yet shall he live. Saesheal believed in his God and shall be given a throne, and these things are done that those to come might believe that Jesus is the Christ, the Son of God and that believing they might know that life is through his name."

Like the crash of waves upon a rock, Jehovah's voice echoed throughout the realm, and as suddenly as He had appeared, He was gone, the palace doors shutting fast behind him.

All rose, and Saesheal's body was now fully healed of all injury and slowly lowered to the ground. From each vial, water began to pour, and the waters weaved a maze-like course into spouts that put out the smaller flames.

"The sacrifice is accepted," spoke the Holy Ghost. Lightning crackled, and thunder boomed overhead. Suddenly, a wall of flame erupted in front of Saesheal's body and obscured all from view, a dark barrier of smoke engulfed the altar, and a searing curtain of fire erupted and created an impenetrable wall of flame.

Talus, who was closest to his charge, stepped back, overwhelmed by the intensity of the seething heat. Gabriel and his brethren also backed away, and the immediate area of the emporium emptied until the smolder of the altar cleared away.

All stood in silence at the image before them. None of them knew whether to weep or to break forth in cheers. Those close enough moved towards the altar hands outstretched and raised their hands to grasp the image of light.

The image of light stood--100 cubits high, surrounded by six other smaller pillars: one of violet, blue, green, yellow, orange, and red. Each pillar-shaped to form an Elohim and each pointed to the innermost figure. A translucent image of Saesheal appeared, but Saesheal seemed engaged with another Elohim. Michael and his brethren made out its features; its ram's head and hoofed feet were unmistakable. It was an Arelim.

Beneath them, were two small creatures huddled and cowered under the protective stand of Saesheal. Each had two arms and two legs, and one was shapelier in the hip and torso than the other. Neither had scales or flesh as the Elohim, and a mane of hair flowed from the crown of one creature's head to its shoulders; both grasped one another for comfort and were on bended knee as if in fear. Each image represented the seven species of Elohim and inhaled and exhaled as if alive. They all moved and *breathed* except the two small bipedal creatures at the base. They were motionless, inanimate in their state of cower and worship.

Talus looked at Michael and then back at the sculpture of light, which lived yet, did not.

"What are those words on the base?"

Michael glanced and knelt down to read a golden plaque hung from its base and words written in angelic script were emblazoned in the fire.

'S-e-p-h-i-r-o-p-t-h'

Michael finished reading and his hand stroked his chin, puzzled as to the term's meaning, and in the instant of his wonderment, he rose and turned his head at the voice in the distance that thundered across the emporium; the irate roar of a tormented and anguished soul.

Apollyon had come home.

I Am the Potter, You Are the Clay

Day Six

"Saesheal!" Apollyon screamed out. Saesheal's features were easy to distinguish even from this distance. The monolithic breathing sculpture sat near the brass laver and altar at the foot of the mountain of God. Apollyon flew towards the object frantically and moved those who barred his path. The other Elohim made way for the giant as he approached.

Gabriel and the rest of the princes eyed Apollyon as he landed before their presence. Too overcome with grief, Apollyon abandoned protocol and failed to bow. There was no regal welcome, no sign of submission in his posture: only confusion rested in his voice as he spoke in interrogation.

"What has been done to him? Prince Michael? Why is he thus?"

Michael walked towards him. Michael's frame was similar to Apollyon's and in a show of compassion, Michael rested his hands on Apollyon's shoulders to comfort him. Apollyon looked closely at the breathing monument. Apollyon's eyes squinted in response to his mind's curiosity as he attempted to comprehend how a structure of light was alive but was not. He passed his hands through the illuminated form of his friend, and his hand grasped ether, but there was substance to the eyes. The monument gave off an aromatic sweet-smelling savor: fragrant and intoxicating to all present, causing Apollyon's confusion to rise even more.

"Please, Lord Prince. How is he thus?

Prince Talus came forward. Michael looked at him to answer on his behalf, and Talus spoke.

"Saesheal is yet alive Apollyon. We know not where nor do we understand how. This is his body recreated by the Holy Spirit of God Himself. We all stood to see our brother restored in the flesh. El has spoken by his Spirit concerning his person."

Talus paused and looked upon the great emporium of assembled Elohim, each still fixated on the sculpture. The mighty Cherub lifted his voice and spoke as if to the wind. "Grigori of Heaven, you who have witnessed what has been seen and done here today. Speak the record that our brother may hear. A Throne Prince of Heaven commands you!"

There was no immediate sound or action for a moment. A sense of indecisiveness and expectation hung in the air. Soon visible mists of air moved and stirred, and by the thousands the Grigori uncloaked. Their hooded and veiled forms became visible for all of Heaven to see. A group of shimmering ghostlike personas rarely noticed, but whose presence was always there. Each flew without wings and stood next to its assigned Elohim of record. Their dark cowled figures flooded both the emporium and the sky roundabout. With a voice never before heard in Heaven, the Grigori spoke as one man.

"Saesheal is not lost but away in the wilderness that I might have voice in all things. To be first among many that would do my will, and thus, it must be suffered him that all righteousness be fulfilled. He shall stand with his lot on the last day. For indeed, He that loveth his life shall lose it, and he that hateth his life shall keep it unto life eternal.

I am the resurrection and the life: he that believeth in me, though he was dead yet shall he live. Saesheal believed in his God and shall be given a throne, and these things are done, that those to come might believe that Jesus is the Christ, the Son of God; and that believing they might know that life is through his name."

Then when the record of El's word was spent for all to hear: the Grigori faded from view and returned to their state of hidden observation. Their tomes and styluses faded with them. Then they were gone; an entire race of angels invisible to the naked eye.

Apollyon looked upon his prince and spoke. "Lord Prince if Saesheal is alive have you word on this 'wilderness' El spoke of? How might I see my brother again?"

"I know not my friend. This word is beyond me, but I trust in El. There is nothing covered that shall not be made known and nothing hidden that shall not be revealed. However, Son of the Dawn you are here while Sol is left attended by another. Speak your reason for coming to Jerusalem."

"My desire Lord Prince is to speak with El to determine the meaning of the word I have received from his Lord, Prince Lucifer. I am also come to see to my charge of Sol."

Talus looked upon his friend, smiled, and took him by the shoulder. "Walk with me."

The emporium slowly emptied as angels returned to their respective duties. Talus and Apollyon walked to a more private area of the steps away from all earshot.

"Archon of Sol, and yes I called you Archon, and Archon you shall be unless you determine that you are no longer qualified for the post. I see within you enormous potential, my friend. God did not name you Son of the Dawn for naught. Thus, with his wisdom, I have named you Archon of Sol. Twas, not a foolish thing to appoint one such as you, for you, have the stout heart necessary to execute the will of the fires of Sol."

"Thank you, my liege yet—"

"Do not interrupt your Prince. I do not pretend to know the fullness of your grief. I know not what would cause you to question the very goodness of El. Yes, your Grigori does indeed record all, and El is aware of your thoughts concerning Him, as are the Lumazi. Yet he has not repented of his command to position you Archon of Sol, and it is not my place to question his decision. If *you* must question it, then do so. However, know this: that you question alone, and take comfort that the gifts and calling of the Lord are without repentance. You are Archon. You shall remain thus until either you or El determine otherwise."

Apollyon bowed in submission, grateful for his prince's words. "My Lord Prince, I request that my station be held by another until and if I may speak with the Master."

"Permission granted my friend. Remain within the capital until word is given of thy petition."

Apollyon once again bowed to his Prince and turned to take his leave. Talus left his charge and returned to the rostrum near the laver to see Gabriel, Michael, and the others still staring at the new monument El had erected in Heaven.

"All right how long will you all gawk? Enraptured by the smell I take it?" Talus laughed

Michael looked at him, but there was no humor in his face: just a sadness that seemed to portend grim news. "I think you must come and see this," said Michael.

Talus walked towards his friends and stopped to observe what they were looking at.

"What is it?" he said.

Gabriel pointed to the figure of Saesheal.

"Aye, it's Saesheal. This I already know. There is nothing of interest here, so why the to-do?

"Look here," said Michael.

Talus then followed Michael's pointed finger and realized that no eyes were on the figure of Saesheal at all, but of the unidentified Elohim of whom he wrestled. The cloven feet and ram's horns suggested that it was an Arelim. The monument's features were not quite complete; still developing even as they spoke. Talus looked upon the breastplate of the Arelim in mortal combat with Saesheal.

"You see it now?"

"Aye, but I do not believe it," said Talus.

Talus looked upon the breastplate of the warrior who was attacking Saesheal, and at whom the small figures underneath him cowered. God had given all Elohim a stone or sigil with their names embedded in it, a symbol that could not be duplicated. This sigil held one name only.

Abaddon the Destroyer

"Who bears this sigil?" asked Gabriel.

"I know not," said Michael, "yet I find it incomprehensible that that one of our kind might raise himself against another."

"Agreed, but the combatants are unmistakably Arelim," said Jerahmeel.

Talus breathed deeply, visibly disturbed by the sigil.

"I have seen this symbol before, yet I know of no Arelim or Elohim with the name of Abaddon. I must meditate on this."

Michael spoke. "In all of Grigoric history, there has never been a record of an Elohim engaged thus with another. It is unthinkable to me. We stand in the shadow of a grave portent."

"Aye, and no Elohim hast ever been brought to not. We walk in new times," Sariel spoke.

Michael nodded.

The palace doors opened, and the sounds of the Seraphim's chants of "Holy, Holy, Holy." came from the throne room and escaped into the open air.

Raphael emerged from the palace doors and spoke. "Brethren, El has reconvened the council — come."

Each began to ascend, into the great hall to attend to their Master's call. Michael looked back to see Talus unmoved, still transfixed in intense study of the fixture.

"Talus?" said Michael.

"Michael, I am positive that I have seen this sigil."

Michael studied the face of his friend, "I am sure you will remember. Come — El summons us."

Talus followed still deep in thought. His eyes glanced back at the monument and his mind flooded with questions. However, there was only one word that clamored for his attention; one word that plagued his mind as he walked into the great hall — *Destroyer.*

* * *

Heaven bustled and stirred as angels went about their business. Apollyon waited in line at the Grigoric Hall of Records: a building where the walls themselves projected the current happenings of the universe. Each attendant was a Grigori clearly visible and who diligently wrote the schedules of the times and seasons of creation.

The room held hourglasses and other devices that displayed time. El had a Grigori assigned to determine when to schedule his appointments. Raphael's work was extensive as he managed the mammoth task of recording the goings on of all of Creation. The Grigori was the most numerous species of Elohim yet the ones who had the least interaction with the creation itself because they primarily recorded and were schedulers. Apollyon approached a desk and spoke to an attendant behind the counter.

"Hail brother, I am Apollyon. I come from Earth with an inquiry for El"

The cowled creature looked at him. "One moment please."

He turned to his rear and reached for one book settled on a shelf among many. He opened the Elomic Record, which contained the name of every Elohim ever created. Scores of names and entries dotted the pages. His finger deftly went through each name until he located Apollyon.

"Ah yes. Name: Apollyon. Title: Son of the Dawn. Office: Archon: Administer of the greater light. Assignment: Sol system." He thumbed through the pages and frowned. "Hmmm it would seem that you have had shall we say, a unique start as Archon. I see that you are on temporary leave from Sol. Good. I doubt the system could endure another failure."

Apollyon felt the anger within him begin to rise. "I do not need your rebuke. I simply seek inquiry from El. When am I scheduled to enter his presence?"

The attendant searched for his name, cross-referenced it with appointments that El had, and then spoke. "I see no invite to grace His presence."

"That's not possible. All Elohim have access to the personal presence of God. Once access is requested, it is simply..."

"Apollyon, I seek not to deter you from your duties, but there is no future record of your entrance to see His eminence after your entitlement as Son of the Dawn. In fact, I see no further entries for you beyond day six of the Earth creation date."

"How is that possible? I do not simply cease to exist. All Elohim must return to see El at some point in time for renewal!"

"There is only one entry recorded after today, yet it seems to be incomplete. There is one word and it cannot be made out as of yet."

"And what is it?" Apollyon asked.

The attendant turned the book for Apollyon to inspect for himself.

Slowly burning into the book were the angelic script and marks of three letters not yet complete in spelling. Each letter emblazoned in reddish hues of orange.

"D-E-S..."

"I am sorry Apollyon, but you are currently denied access from El's presence. You might try to intercede through Prince Talus or one of the other Princes for a direct audience."

Apollyon walked away, with his head held heavy. His thoughts churned with questions. Leaving the door of the Library, he saw the crackle of a Ladder atop the mountain of God; evidence that Lucifer had returned to join the council.

Apollyon thought to himself. *Surely, El will hear Lucifer. I will petition him.* Encouraged with this option and hopeful that Lucifer would give heed to his word. Apollyon headed towards his home for respite, and to wait for an audience with the Chief Prince. Yet there was a foreboding that haunted him. The words of the record attendant still echoed in his mind...

"I am sorry, Apollyon, you are currently denied access to El's presence."

Apollyon turned the words repeatedly in his mind and ruminated on one question.

Why do I have no scheduled future records?

* * *

The council sat before their Lord and waited for El to speak. They were not long in their wait.

"Rise and bear witness, for the end of all things draws near," the Lord said.

El then turned his back away from his cherubs, and the walls of the throne room became transparent. The room and floor disappeared, and they rested upon the earth not far from Athor. The gleaming city sparkled in the distance, and El opened his mouth to speak.

Earth quieted, and all of creation waited with anticipation for God to verbalize.

And God said, "Let the Earth bring forth the living creature after his kind, cattle, and creeping thing, and beast of the Earth after his kind," and it was so.

Out of nothing, they came: four-legged beasts of every description. The dismayed angels watched as sea, air, and land filled with living creatures. Lucifer moved as a tiny spider scurried over his foot.

The beasts' locomotion was as varied as their color and skin. Some ran, others hopped; still more galloped, slithered, and crawled. They were two-legged, four-legged, eight-legged, and multi-legged. Some had the ability to fly. Some were as tiny as a speck; others lumbered along with large bony protrusions from what were apparent nostrils.

Immediately the air filled with sound. They roared, chirped, squeaked, and growled. Some barked, and others purred. The Earth filled with new denizens, but they were but automatons in comparison to the Elohim.

Their colors matched the spectrum, and the eyes could not capture the fullness of their beauty.

Each cherub marveled and praised God that life had sprung from El's word. Each prince then lifted up his voice: sang a song of praise and blessed His name. Heavenly voices rose up, and fowl stopped to listen. The animals quieted as the Lord's chief council broke forth into song, and God was pleased.

The Lord smiled upon his council and looked upon all that his hands had made. For God had made the beasts of the Earth after his kind, the cattle after their kind, and everything that creepeth upon the Earth after his kind, and God saw that *it was* good.

All of the cherubs except Lucifer began to play with the new creatures, and from the rear of them came the bleating of a small; four-legged animal in a white coat of puffiness that found itself in front of the First of Angels. Michael watched as Lucifer, the creature stared at one another: and as the creature moved towards Lucifer; Michael looked at the face of his brother and noted that disgust appeared on his face.

"Lucifer," God said, "I have a special task for you."

"Yes my Lord?" Lucifer replied.

"I am determined to honor the greatest of all mine creations with a home on this planet. What shall be done unto he whom the Lord delighteth to honor?"

Lucifer gleamed with excited anticipation, thinking to himself, *Who would the Lord desire to honor above myself?*

Lucifer's mind pondered what he should ask the king of the universe. What would he desire? How could El honor him, his first of all creation? Then it came to him.

"My Lord, I believe that a garden should be created: a lush green place on Earth that would yield every fruit-bearing tree. Let it be surrounded in a weather pattern that is most comfortable and cooled by a mist. Within the confines of the garden should also stretch flora that is not just pleasant for food but also to the eye.

"There is a river near Athor, my Lord, that runs east of Eden, and my mind is that the whole region would serve as an excellent palatial abode, a realm of spectacular comfort and ease. I also believe that your greatest creation be bequeathed with the deed to Earth. Although you have allowed me oversight as steward, to have title to Earth: to this gem of creation would be of ultimate honor." Lucifer continued.

"And finally, as your image and likeness is so august; I would propose that this creature be unique in all creation and that it would carry *your* image and likeness and that none other may yield it."

El looked upon Lucifer. His eyes penetrated his first creation, the Chief Prince assigned to his most important of deeds. Slowly, he looked upon Lucifer, and Lucifer bowed his eyes to the ground; his brethren also bowed in obeisance. El studied his son, and for a while, the group wondered if He would speak.

"Please you may all rise," He said.

The group rose to see that they were once again within the throne room. El was seated high and lifted up as his train filled the temple and looked down upon them.

"Does the thing that Lucifer hast proposed seem acceptable in thy sight?" asked the Lord.

All replied even as one man, "Oh Lord, thou knowest. Doeth what seemeth right to thou."

El bowed his head, and Michael ever so attentive to his master looked upon El curiously. *Why does El look sad?* He wondered.

El turned to Lucifer, "You have indeed spoken well. Do all that thou hast said, and when the fullness of time is complete return to me, and I will announce my intent to honor my greatest creation."

Michael and Lucifer caught each other's eyes, and Lucifer's glance quickly turned to the throne room doors. The Chief Price left immediately, headed out of the palace to assign his detachment their orders, and was quickly out of sight.

"The rest of you are released to your duties. After completion of Lucifer's work on my behalf: return. Then I will announce the future plans I have for Earth, and we will break bread together before I take my rest."

The group bowed in concert; each one dismissed himself and leisurely exited the throne room. The cherubs made their way out of the palace, and down the steps, towards the newly formed statue of light.

As Michael and Jerahmeel conversed with one another, Talus motioned for his friends to come near. Talus stood at the statue and gawked his gaze transfixed.

"Michael--that sigil!" Talus said.

"What of it?"

"I think I know to whom it belongs!"

"Who?" Michael replied.

"Apollyon! In El's name — the sigil belongs to Apollyon!"

* * *

Lucifer walked towards the entrance to the mouth of the mountain of God and noticed the gaseous disturbance that trailed him.

"Your bold desire to manifest and speak is ill-timed Grigori, for we are not in private. What troubles you, Lilith?"

"Remember 'Lightbringer', you do not have things hidden from me. Your disgust of His form grows more apparent even as you pounce at the opportunity to have him honor you."

"I look upon Him Lilith, and I can't help but wonder of the vanity that would cause Him to create *me* first. My presence magnifies His own. My mere existence gives credence to his *need* to be glorified. I am sure El desires to honor the one for helping Him to look so magnificent."

"Do not presume upon El, Lucifer. He is the Word. He is The Father, and you are the son."

"Aye, El indeed is the Word, yet how my creator would make a creation that surpasses Himself seems to reek of weakness and folly."

"It affected you didn't it?"

"That woolish creature? Of course not," Lucifer said.

"Remember 'Lightbringer' I know you as no one would. Do not patronize me."

"Dismiss yourself watcher; an attendant arrives."

Lucifer knew that his thoughts had grabbed the attention of Lilith. Apparently, this image was the one that El chose to reveal to Lucifer, for El had manifested himself differently to each of the Chief Princes.

Running quickly up the steps Basus, an attendant of Lucifer's detachment in Heaven approached the Chief Prince and bowed.

"My Lord, your presence has been requested by the Archon Apollyon. He awaits you within his residence and seeks an audience. If you consent, he will come upon your command to your abode."

"Bid him come, but tell him do not tarry, for I leave for Athor upon the conclusion of our business."

"Aye, Chief Prince," Basus replied.

* * *

Apollyon walked the streets of his home. Each building of Heaven was carved out of precious stones. One dwelling was fashioned of onyx, another topaz, still others of beryl or sapphire: each home reflective of the qualities of its host. Apollyon walked the streets of glass and gold. Heaven was a wondrous place filled with various flora and fauna. There were birds and exceedingly beautiful beasts that flew. Pegasi filled the air as Elohim transported various building materials to parts unknown. Jerusalem the capital city was a thing of majesty itself. It stood at the base of the Mt. Zion. There was no stellar source of light as with the skies of the second heaven, for the Lord God lit the realm. His brilliance radiated all about. Thus, there was no night in Heaven. God was light, and in Him was no darkness. The city was twelve thousand furlongs in width and height.

Moreover, the city lay four square, and the length was as large as the breadth. The length, breadth, and the height of it were equal. If one were to measure the wall thereof, it would be a hundred and forty-and-four cubits. The building of the wall was of jasper, and the entirety of the city was made of pure gold, like unto a clear glass. Decorative stones adorned the foundation of the walls of the city. The first foundation *was* jasper; the second, sapphire; the third, a chalcedony; the fourth, an emerald; the fifth, sardonyx; the sixth, sardius; the seventh, chrysolite; the eighth, beryl; the ninth, a topaz; the tenth, a chrysoprasus; the eleventh, a jacinth; and the twelfth, an amethyst. Moreover, the twelve gates were twelve pearls; every gate was made of solid pearl.

Michael constructed each road so that if one were to travel on any street, he would arrive at the base of the mountain of God. To the left of the city were the Elysian Fields, vast acres of manna leaf. It was from here the manna leaves grew a never-ending supply to feed the multitudes of Heaven. Elohim came at their leisure. However, as of late Michael had commissioned groups to harvest at intervals and to store the manna in granaries. For what purpose was not clear to Apollyon, for the Elohim had not had a need to store in the past.

Apollyon looked past the fields to the mountain of God. The massive home of El stood and towered over the whole of Jerusalem. God's palace rested upon the top; the mountain itself served as the foundation and chief cornerstone of the immense structure. None could set foot on the mountain of God, for it was the home of El. None approached it, and each Elohim held an instinct to avoid the mountain. Those among Apollyon's kind who ventured too close had found themselves ill and suddenly surrounded by the Ophanim who escorted them quickly away from the vicinity. It was said that the Ophanim at El's command would destroy anyone who dared breach the temple without permission to enter, assuming that one would have first escaped the Seraphim who guarded the entrance to El's throne.

Looking across the Elysian Fields, Apollyon could see the Cliffs of Argoth, a cropping of rock that protruded and overlooked the capital.

Argoth, an Elohim of illustrious renown and mystery was an angel of prophetic praise. Legend says that when the Lord created him, Argoth looked upon his maker for the first time and was so stunned, so overwhelmed and so awed by his beauty, that he became as a man in a deep trance or a waking slumber.

Argoth then walked to the edge of the mountain of the Lord, looked out over the expanse of the Kingdom of Heaven, and proclaimed,

"The LORD, The LORD God, merciful and gracious, longsuffering, and abundant in goodness and truth Keeping mercy for thousands, forgiving iniquity and transgression and sin, and that will by no means clear the guilty, visiting the iniquity of the fathers upon the children and upon the children's children, unto the third and to the fourth generation."

After this proclamation, the Lord said to him, "For nothing is secret that shall not be made manifest; neither anything hid that shall not be known." El immediately silenced him, and the cliffs muzzled from echoing what Argoth had uttered. The cliffs are the only place of permanent silence in Heaven. The cliffs have come to represent a place where secrets are uttered. Afterward, Argoth became a Grigori with an unusual assignment: he now stands mute within the Great Library, his stylus and inkhorn yet to record

Next to the cliffs was a massive cave-like furnace called the Kiln: the place where the 'Stones of Fire' lay and where new Elohim came into existence. It has fired without ceasing since before Apollyon's own creation, a never-ending womb that breeds the host of Elohim who administer the affairs of Heaven and Earth. Only El and the Chief Prince may enter the Kiln.

Apollyon turned down one of the gold-laden streets to walk past the living quarters of his deceased friend Saesheal. He turned the door to enter and quietly closed the door behind him. Apollyon walked carefully as if he were stepping over a sleeping patron. Apollyon viewed the flowers picked from the grounds of Heaven: colorful plants that responded to one's touch. Each petal hummed in a quiet melody and emitted a tiny iridescent light. A table with flatware adorned the dining room. Tapestries, linens, chairs, tomes, Apollyon slowly realized how much Saesheal's quarters were highly decorated: so unlike his own.

Apollyon had never found the need for such trivial things. His function was to serve. There was little need for beds, flowers, or living creatures to accompany his solace in his moments of rest. Saesheal, however, was not so. There were volumes of books on his shelves, the record of the commands given to the Elohim upon their exit from the Kiln. The Grigori have created a library within the capital that provides public access to the records of the ever-expanding creation. Each record displayed was either projected as an image or stored in written form. Apollyon noticed that Saesheal had spent time studying his assignment of Luna. Records of Luna's creation and instructions to its oversight littered the table of Saesheal's dwelling.

Apollyon's heart saddened as he walked the room, reminded of the many days of laughter Saesheal and he shared within. The mirth that Saesheal and he enjoyed usually came at Apollyon's expense. Apollyon smiled in remembrance. He would miss those days.

However, a frown found him as he remembered his loss. The absence gnawed at him like a sore. It was a consuming thing this emptiness. Saesheal was closest to him, for they quartered across from each other. Apollyon ached from his loneliness, for none sought to see to his well-being, and none cared for his companionship. Those who would call him brother centered only on his failure. Apollyon missed his friend. He left Saesheal's quarters and turned towards his own home to see one of Lucifer's attendants knocking on his door.

"Apollyon?" The attendant said.

"Yes. I take it you come with word from Lucifer on my audience?"

"Indeed. He has agreed to speak with you. Be swift, as matters of state require his immediate attention. He only waits for you."

"Then let us make haste; lead on," Apollyon said.

Both made for the sky and arched themselves towards the northern part of the city. Lucifer had made his home as close to the mount of God as possible without causing the Ophanim to be irritated. He was also removed far enough from the hustle and bustle of the city to warrant privacy. It did not take long for the two angels to enter into Lucifer's court. Apollyon followed the lead of his guide, and as they walked up the steps, that lead to the mansion, Apollyon could see from the corner of his eye that Ashtaroth attended.

Warily they eyed each other. Ashtaroth glared at Apollyon from the distance. Their eyes locked in a waltz of mutual disdain. Neither spoke. Apollyon finally turned his gaze when Basus beckoned him to enter a great room.

"Chief Prince Lucifer Draco, I present to your eminence, Apollyon Arelim, Archon of Sol, Son of the Dawn."

"Thank you Basus. Apollyon please come in."

Basus left the two alone and slowly closed the door behind him.

"I have urgent business to attend to Apollyon. Basus tells me you have desired an audience with me?"

Apollyon rose from his kneeling position. "Aye, Chief Prince. By your own hand were you sent by El to relay His Majesty's word to his servant."

"Indeed. I also recall that you wanted to query El as to its meaning," Lucifer said.

"Yes my Lord. I have also received permission from Lord Talus temporarily to forego my duties until I have entreated the Lord."

Puzzled, Lucifer looked upon Apollyon. "Continue."

"After coming from Lord Talus, I sought counsel to request an audience with El. Upon doing so, the Grigori present stated I was not scheduled to see El, nor is there record after the conclusion of the six-day for me to enter his presence."

"I see — so why trouble me Archon? Submit your entreaties on another occasion. We all must come before his throne at some point."

"That is my quandary, my Prince. There is *no* future occasion where I seem to have access to El. It is as if I no longer exist. How can such a thing be possible?"

Lucifer turned away from his guest. His brow scrunched as he pondered Apollyon's words. He turned back to face him and spoke. "I do not know, yet I muse then that you seek me to intercede on your behalf?"

"Yes, my liege. Thou art the Chief Prince. To company with El and petition him is nothing for one such as you."

Apollyon bowed in submission.

"Rise and fear not. Your fealty is rewarded Son of the Dawn. All that thou sayest I will do," said Lucifer.

"I am in your debt, my Prince. Twice now, you have honored me. I have nothing to return your kindness."

"Nothing is necessary. I consider you a kindred spirit. If El had not assigned you to Sol, I would have you associated with my work on Earth. Perhaps I will still petition for your release into my charge. In the meantime, I must depart for Athor and prepare my work. Reside here within my hall if you wish, and upon my return, I will attend to your request."

"Thank you, Chief Prince. El's will be done," Apollyon said.

"El's will be done," replied Lucifer.

Apollyon bowed and slowly backed away from the Chief Prince and closed the door behind him.

Lucifer stared silently for a moment and thought to himself, *El's will be done.*

* * *

The statue continued to morph slowly into shape. Mesmerized, each of the high princes watched the light and movement of the figure.

"We must find him!" Talus implored.

Sariel looked at Talus and had never before seen his brother speak so anxiously.

"Talus, what is it that plagues you?"

"I looked and looked at the figure; perhaps my own desires caused me to hold back the truth. I know not. What I do know is that this sigil belongs to Apollyon! Of this I am sure."

Sariel looked at Michael and his brothers.

"Talus did you not say, and can we not see, that this figure who wrestles with Saesheal is *not* Apollyon? Is it possible that this is an Arelim not yet formed? And if it is Apollyon, what of it? What would you have us do? He has not committed offense short of his own failure to question El's goodness."

"Sariel surely you don't think that questioning the goodness of God is a trite thing?"

"Nay — yet El himself has the power and means to deal with Apollyon if He sees fit. Was it not He that informed *us* of his thoughts? If he knew this would he not know if more would be wrong? Was it not the Lord of Heaven and Earth whose hands crafted the figure we gaze upon? And Talus tell me — has El mentioned any assignment, action, or concern about Apollyon that we or anyone else are to pursue: other than the Chief Prince himself? Nay my brother. Do not seek to stir the flame of doubt where none exists."

Sariel stepped away from the figure and headed down the steps towards the entrance to the city. He paused and turned to speak. "However, I suggest that you find Apollyon. If his Prince concerns himself with his welfare, then Apollyon should be allowed to hear his concerns."

Jerahmeel turned to speak to his brother. "Sariel is correct. You are his prince. You should find him and talk with him."

Raphael placed his hand on Talus' shoulder. "Do not avail yourself to fret. I will scour his tome to see if his watcher has entered anything new that should be brought to the court's attention."

"I appreciate that Raphael. He was on leave from his duties when last we met. He wanted an audience with El. Therefore, he should still be here. I will begin to look for him. The Great Library is a good place to start. Michael, would you assist me?" Talus asked.

"Aye, I also wish to see his sigil for myself. Come, let us go." Michael said.

* * *

Apollyon relaxed in the great hall of the Chief Prince. It was apparent that Lucifer was a connoisseur of beauty. His personal lodging almost rivaled that of Athor. The finest of Elysium tapestries decorated his walls and silks from the Adonis trees draped his windows. The silk was the finest quality laced with gold, and shimmered. The floors were purple and radiated an orange hue as they glowed. Lapis lazuli was used to grout the diamond tiles on the walls.

Lucifer's furniture was of Chittim wood. The wood's pores dripped a sap that perfumed the room, and the wooden couch's frame conformed to whoever sat or laid on it. Floral pelts adorned

Lucifer's tables and couches. Books upon books littered his shelves, and various instruments of measurement were strewn about his desk. A plumb line and other devices used to build were nestled in a case. Apollyon traveled upstairs to his bedchamber, and it became apparent to him by the number of hand-carved instruments that Lucifer was an adept minstrel and psalmist. In addition, to more books, Cora leaf pages of song after song of handwritten praise and worship lay near his bed. Lucifer seemed to possess a Grigoric record on every aspect of creation.

"Am I disturbing you Archon?"

Apollyon recognized the voice: a voice which last time he had heard it, he held its bearer by the throat. He turned to see Ashtaroth standing in the bedroom doorway.

"I was not aware that the Chief Prince had granted you right to grope through his affairs. Or am I to take it that your being in the masters chamber is due to some infatuation that I know not of?"

Apollyon embarrassed, smiled sheepishly.

"I meant no disrespect to his lordship. I will leave immediately."

"So once more your actions show a lack of forethought. Yet again, does the Archon display his propensity to waywardness? Be not deceived. I will of a surety bring this to my Lord's attention." Ashtaroth turned to leave, and Apollyon's mind was rife with the words of this angel who presumed to be so smug and superior.

"Ever the servant, are you not Astarte?" Apollyon said.

Ashtaroth stopped and turned to face Apollyon. He slowly walked towards him. Fear was not in the nature of an Elohim. Apollyon towered over him, but Ashtaroth did not fear for his safety and spoke.

"Aye, a servant am I. I serve the Chief Prince, the Lightbringer himself. He, who stands in the midst of the Stones of Fire. It was he that held both you and I in the Kiln. Yes, simpleton; I serve him. You, on the other hand, serve only foolishness and carelessness, and you have your reward. You are neither worthy of the title of Archon, and I personally hope..."

Ashtaroth paused to point at the cracked stones that beat within Apollyon's chest. "El never again seeks to utilize the stone with which caused your creation."

Apollyon leaped at Ashtaroth to grab him.

Ashtaroth stepped to his side, and Apollyon went flying past him into a desk smashing the desk of soft Chittim wood to pieces.

"You mocked me upon our last encounter Archon. Do not presume that your physical stature impresses me. You caught me unawares before. I will not be so caught in the future."

Apollyon rose from the floor, kicking the soft legs of the broken desk away from him. "Do not concern yourself with being unaware Astarte. I want you to know that it is I who will pummel you into submission!" Apollyon replied.

Apollyon rose from the floor and heaved the large pieces of the desk from before him. Stray portions flew out the second-story window and crashed to the golden streets below.

Startled denizens looked up as two Elohim could be seen grappling with one another. Apollyon and Ashtaroth then broke through the walls to fall from the upper balcony and joined the mangled pieces of wood and brick on the street below. Dozens of onlookers scattered as the entangled bodies of the duo crashed onto the street.

Onlookers watched their mouths agape, as Apollyon grasped Ashtaroth by the throat, and lifted him as he squirmed into the air. Coughing and gagging, Ashtaroth contorted his body and used his tail to wrap itself around a piece of wood lying on the ground, and like a whip smashed it across Apollyon's face.

Apollyon screamed in pain as the wood broke the soft tissue of his face and bluish liquid oozed from the corner of his lip and cheek.

Ashtaroth did not wait for a response and moved quickly to kick the large angel in the torso knocking him back through the door of a merchant's store.

Once again wood, stone, and metal gave way, and Apollyon found himself covered in rubble. Slowly, he rose dazed from the debris while vendors scurried to flee.

Ashtaroth laughed, "You called me little angel Archon, yet it is you who sits on his rear in disgrace. Come to me fool, and let us see how buffoonish you truly are!"

Apollyon clenched his fists and his eyes narrowed and enraged, and the power to control a sun welled within him: and one thought alone filled his mind towards Ashtaroth, the angel who had taunted him for so long.

Dissolution.

* * *

"What if we do not find him here?" asked Michael.

"Michael my being tells me that we will find Apollyon. I just hope that it is not too late," said Talus.

"Too late for what?" Michael asked.

"That, my friend is what concerns me. I do not quite know. All that I know is that right now I need to see his sigil."

"Well, El's audience chamber is up ahead, so we can inquire shortly as to Apollyon's scheduled time for a meeting."

The two high princes lightly touched down in front of the door to the great chamber. All Elohim nearby bowed in submission, and the two quickly stepped inside the building.

The chief keeper of the hall ran towards the pair and bowed before the two princes.

"Lord Talus — Lord Michael! You honor us by your presence within our halls. Please, please how can we help you?"

"Rise my friend; we are in need of some answers. Have you seen an Arelim by the name of Apolly…"

"Apollyon? Yes, High Prince. He was in here not too long ago and asked about his scheduled meeting with El."

Talus asked, "Can you tell us when he is scheduled to meet with the Lord?"

"Of course, Prince Talus. There is nothing within our power that we would withhold from you. We cannot remember ever having two from the royal court within our place of business. It would honor us if…"

Michael interrupted, "We are in swift need of this information, Chief Scheduler. Please make haste."

"Of course, of course, High Prince: Apollyon yes. Let me find his––oh, yes. I distinctly remember our conversation; Apollyon has no scheduled meeting with El––ever."

Michael and Talus looked curiously at each other and then at the record keeper.

"No meeting? What do you mean *ever*? You mean he came here and didn't make an appointment?" Talus asked.

"No, High Prince he came here, but we couldn't make an appointment. You may see his tome if it pleases you."

"Show us quickly!" Talus demanded.

The Chief Scheduler turned to the shelving behind his desk, reached, and pulled down a book. He found the entry for Apollyon and turned the tome around for his two patrons to view.

"See Apollyon's record has no entry after the 6th day. And there is… oh my this was not like this before."

"Speak. What troubles you?" Talus commanded.

The attendant turned the book around and pointed to the letters that emblazoned slowly within its pages.

Talus looked, and his countenance paled.

"Michael, do you see?" Talus asked.

"Aye," Michael answered. "There can be no doubt now. Sariel and the others must be informed immediately."

The text of the page was unmistakable. There was no listing for any future meetings with El past the sixth creation event. Only one word stood out in blood red cursive angelic script.

D-E-S-T-R-O-Y-E-R

* * *

"Apollyon Son of the Dawn, stand down immediately!"

Morael an angel who stood by the bridge between the third and second heaven, and who granted entry into Heaven had come. He stood now in front of the gaping hole made by Apollyon's impact.

"You and Ashtaroth have caused enough damage this day. Do not compound your failure. Stand down now and be judged!"

Apollyon looked upon him, scowled, and wiped the spittle from his mouth to speak.

"Judged? Which of you would dare judge me? False you are! Depart from me! None here I call kindred. For my brother is shame, my sister failure. No Guard of Heaven; you all have disdained me. You all are simply too cowardly to admit it. I am alone. Ashtaroth was correct when he named me 'Destroyer' and rightly so."

Apollyon's voice grew shrill and harsh, and his sarcasm filled the ears of any present to listen.

"Come let us reason together Morael. You will be the first to witness the 'New Dawn'." Apollyon reached into his chest and revealed his sigil the carved stone that bore the name given by El to every Elohim.

"I renounce Apollyon, the name of my creation, and my creator; a new name shall I now pronounce."

He used his talon and deliberately began to deface and scored out his given name, and Heaven beheld an act of sacrilege never before seen.

"That creature no longer exists...," Apollyon declared.

Morales screamed, "Apollyon, No!"

Apollyon saw Morael standing before him, but his words were ignored. In the sight of all, Apollyon scarred his sigil. His Heartstone darkened from the alteration, the burning light of the sun contained in its fire went out, and his stone became disfigured. His body rapidly changed color to a dark and fiery hue. Bony protrusions emerged from his spine, and mouths of flame erupted from his shoulders. His Heartstone pulsated violently, and there swirled a blackness within as if something alive, wanted to escape.

"...Abaddon shall I be."

Abaddon then charged the angel, this creature who dared position himself between predator and prey. Abaddon flew headlong into Morael and slammed into the would-be protector of Ashtaroth. Disbelief filled with fear overwhelmed Morale's mind on his witness of Abaddon's purposeful self-injury. Morael placed his hands in front of him to try to protect his face and screamed out in pain upon Abaddon's bearish assault.

The two angels flew into a wall of another building, and stone and mortar blew apart around them. The explosive impact shook the ground and shattered nearby windows. The affected structure began to teeter, moan; and ache as its shifted weight buckled under pressure and duress. The roof collapsed and buried Morael and Abaddon in a blanket of rubble.

A momentary pause of silence allowed injured onlookers to move quickly in order to escape the destruction. The rubble began to heave, and the sound of movement emanated from the center of the debris field.

Abaddon soon rose from the wreckage, as a person come ashore from the raging sea; dirt and fragments of wood and stone slid off his large frame, and as a man might hold a cat by its scruff: Abaddon held the unconscious Morael by the collar of his heavenly robes. Blood and water streamed from his limp body. Abaddon dragged the broken and bruised body of the angel from the rubble and stood defiantly as his leathery wings projected a dark shadow over him so that only the luminance from his eyes were seen, eyes which smoldered with a yellowish glow. Abaddon threw with disdain the bruised and broken body of Morael, Guard of Heaven, into the street for all to see and then contemptuously spoke to the gathered crowd.

"Interfere, and you shall all likewise perish."

* * *

"Attendant, did Apollyon see this script? Michael asked.

"He did High Prince, yet it was not this complete when he was here. There were only three letters when last I opened the tome. There are now nine, and the word is complete.

Michael rubbed his chin and turned to his brother. "Perhaps it is a progressive revelation. The title might be dependent on his actions; therefore, perhaps it is not too late. We must find him quickly."

"If I might be so bold my Prince, too late for what?"

Talus looked at the attendant and spoke. "What is your name record keeper?"

"Hariph, sire."

"Hariph, do you know where Apollyon was headed when he left here?"

"Nay Lord Prince; however, I did inform him that he should entreat one from the royal court. I had specifically mentioned that he might entreat you."

Talus looked at Michael. "Michael, we were in session when he came here, and he has already spoken with me. I think we should scout Lucifer's quarters. Perhaps he might have gone there."

Talus closed the book and returned it to Hariph.

"Thank you Hariph. You have been of immense help to the court this day. Your service shall not be forgotten."

"Anytime, High Pr...."

Suddenly an explosion rattled and shook the building. Books and vases not otherwise secured fell and crashed to the floor.

Michael and Talus ran to the front door, and those within the building ran to several windows to look outside. Flames and smoke rose off in the distance of Lucifer's home, and for the first time in recorded history, there was fire on the streets of Heaven.

* * *

Elohim after Elohim gawked and stood in disbelief, stunned in dismay that two of their kindred grappled in mortal combat. A crowd had gathered to witness the spectacle, and others attempted to hold Abaddon down as the mighty angel tossed several angels aside like rag dolls. Ashtaroth, Lucifer's attendant, stood aloft as a wall of Elohim surrounded him. A contingent of others attempted to hold off Abaddon's charge towards him.

"Move from my path or be moved!" Abaddon roared. His eyes focused on his quarry.

Talus and Michael arrived, touched down to the street, and took a position to stand as a buffer between the two combatants. As more and more Elohim came to both hear and see the spectacle before them, many stood frozen in disbelief. Elohim that held him were tossed aside as a dog shakes water from its body. With open hands and claws unfurled, Abaddon reached once again for the throat of Ashtaroth who saw the charge of the deranged angel, ducked, and then backed away.

Michael screamed, "Apollyon! No!"

In seconds, it was over and the broken body of Corlus fell to the ground. He was Illuminati, an angel devoted to art, wisdom, and beauty. He had waved his hands as a conductor might lead an orchestra and expected that the mighty Arelim would follow his lead, and stop his maddening rampage. He believed against hope that despite his fury, Abaddon would take notice and hear him. But when words were not enough, Corlus placed himself in the direct path of Abaddon's blow.

Corlus, his pleas but a tiny voice of wisdom crying in the wilderness, attempted to reason with the howls of Abaddon's rage. Yet reason had abandoned Abaddon, and the hard concussive sound of a fist hammered deep into Corlus' soft flesh.

There was a hush over the attending crowd as Corlus' eyes were open, his breathing turned shallow, and the bluish fluid of his life force drenched the transparent gold street now stained with Elomic blood.

Two had become one as Corlus stood impaled, the arm of Abaddon running through his exposed chest. A small whirlpool of cyclonic air whipped around him, light escaped the dying body as if sucked into a vacuum, and in moments, the spirit of Corlus was gone. Abaddon tossed the lifeless husk of his corpse aside and the body sprawled in the street. While Abaddon held in his bloody hand the beating Heartstone of Corlus now still.

* * *

"Lord Lucifer, as always it is agreeable to see you again."

"Thank you, Mephisto. There is much to do. El has commanded that Eden be primed for creation. A garden of renown is to be planted and shall serve as the personal abode of El's greatest creation."

"Your instructions my Prince?" Mephisto said.

"Gather a legion of Creyun for this task. They are adept at building and gardening. Spare no one Mephisto. Pull everyone off the expansion of Athor. I want the garden completed before the end of the day."

"Yes, Chief Prince. El's will be done."

Lucifer flew towards Athor and settled into his study to ponder the series of maps made of this new world. He spread one across a desk to view the region around Athor and saw that the area of Eden was near and well-watered. His eyes glistened with childish anticipation.

"This shall be the greatest of my feats yet. I will make a garden so lush that it will rival the palatial comforts of El himself."

* * *

"Argh!"

Abaddon lashed out at several Elohim and overcame them. Those captured in his grip found themselves thrown against stone and glass. Dozens of nearby Elohim attempted to restrain the angel now run amok.

"Talus!" Michael said.

"I see him, Michael. Attack from the rear and I shall engage him directly. He must be brought down!"

Flames leaped from Abaddon's body and engulfed all he touched. Elohim screamed in pain as angelic flesh burned. Some wallowed in pain, for their hands, feet, and limbs were violently hacked. Apollyon ignored all pleas to stop and cut down all who stood between him and Ashtaroth.

"Apollyon, yield or be bound!" Talus demanded.

Abaddon looked upon his prince, and his eyes glowed with flame. Where faculty of reason once rested, rage did now abide. Where a command from a high prince might once have made the Arelim bow in reverence, reason was now lost to rage. Abaddon raised his hands and moved to attack his prince.

Talus braced himself and summoned the sharp bony protrusions from his forearms, and he raised his arm to block Abaddon's attack.

Abaddon's blow found its mark, and angelic flame engulfed Talus's arm. The force of the blow forced Talus back, and his feet slid over the gravel. Talus attempted to use Abaddon's momentum against him and reached to grab his arm to pull him forward.

Abaddon lurched forward as his center of gravity shifted and he tumbled to fall on top of his Lord. Talus fell to his back and used his strong legs to throw Abaddon forward and sent the rogue Archon reeling into a nearby house.

The home burst into flames and engulfed the inhabitants within. Screams and panic emanated from the dwelling as several occupants ran out to escape to safety.

Abaddon then shot from the roof like a cannon; his body glowed, and fire spurted from him as he hovered in the air. He clapped his mighty hands together sending a shock wave that knocked all but Talus to the ground and leveled the flaming structure below him.

Burning wooden shards sprayed Talus and those nearby, shredding flesh and scorching wood, cloth, and stone.

Talus yelled to his brother, "Michael now!"

Apollyon's rage blinded him to the presence of Michael behind him. Michael jumped on Apollyon's back, wrapped his powerful arms around the Arelim in a chokehold, and held him fast.

Apollyon struggled to break free, but Michael used his own weight to drag Apollyon down to the ground. With a thrust of his wings, he turned Apollyon's body downward. The two plummeted to the ground, and Apollyon slammed face-first into the earth.

The glass street below them buckled and cracked from the impact of their fall.

Apollyon wrestled with Michael to grab hold of him and to break free, but Michael's grip was sure, and with one arm wrapped under and around Apollyon's neck and chin: another interlocked for surety. Michael refused to release him.

Apollyon moved backward and smashed Michael into wall after wall in an attempt to break away from his hold. He bucked, like an untamed stallion to shake Michael from off his back.

Michael tightened his grip more and frantically struggled to hang on using his wings to stabilize him and keep him balanced.

As Apollyon struggled to escape Michael's hold, lightheadedness flooded him, and his thoughts became disoriented. With each step, his movement slowed: he staggered and swayed until the behemoth of an angel passed out and crashed to his knees. Michael, relentless in his determination and with his grip still taut, cautiously released him.

The rogue angel was now unconscious and collapsed at Michael's feet.

* * *

"This area will do nicely," Lucifer said. "Spugliguel, create a perimeter 100 furlongs long by wide. This area shall be your charge, and never shall the cold breach this realm. I command a perpetual season of spring be in this place."

Spugliguel bowed in obedience. "Aye, Chief Prince."

Lucifer walked the ground, and his eyes darted back and forth while hundreds of attendants in tow surveyed the land. He gestured with his hand in a sweeping motion.

"I want this area seeded with grass. When my feet walk its surface, I desire to feel nothing but lushness beneath. Caracasa and Commissoros see to the flora. I command that every tree and vine which bringeth forth fruit and is sweet to the taste, every tree which delights the soul be planted within."

"El's will be done," they said and swiftly flew off to parts unknown.

Lucifer looked to his Archon of agriculture and fecundity Habuiah. "Let us begin my friend. El's will be done."

"As you command, Chief Prince," Habuiah replied.

Habuiah flew into the air. His transparent wings created wind gusts around him. He rose to a level so that he could see all of the region commanded by Lucifer and spoke the Elomic commands unique to his charge as Archon of all agriculture.

"Let there be growth."

The ground of the region, all 100 furlongs square, beckoned to his command. A pulse of light emanated from Habuiah. He dove into the ground and drove his giant fists into the earth, and as a stone is thrown into the water, wave after circular wave emanated from him and dissipated only at the edge, of the soon-to-be garden.

Each wave pulsated across the landscape leaving behind acres of green and lush grass throughout the region. A blanket of emerald green: a 100-furlong meadow of jade and blossoms, soft to the touch and ripe with the smell of freshness, covered the dark earth of Eden. The Elohim present with Habuiah flew into the air to prevent crushing the new growth that rose from beneath their feet.

Commissoros and Caracasa returned from gathering the selected seeds from the earth. As honey bees returned to the hive, the duo released the various seedlings from the pouches within their flesh. Each grasped a handful and tossed the assortment of seeds into the air.

Yoniel, one of the keepers of the Northwind, then blew, and the seeds flew gently throughout the air, ever so delicately. Yoniel blew in such a way that each seed moved to its appointed place and rested on the grass below. The coverage of the seedlings was uniform throughout Eden.

Habuiah spoke to the ground and all that lay therein. "Come forth!"

The kernels within each shell split and roots shot into the earth. Tendrils of plants delved to find a home in the black soil beneath the carpeted grass. Like a legion of undead rising from the grave, trees clawed through the surface and reached skyward. Limbs yawned, as one would awake from a morning sleep. The yawns of bananas, pears, apples, and various other trees cracked and groaned as bark snapped and splintered in their desire to accelerate and grow, racing to fulfill the will of El.

Smiling, Lucifer looked upon the new forest made before him. His created work sang with the sounds of new life and moved to the tempo of his directives, as an orchestra would follow a conductor. He was pleased. The vision of his mind became a reality before his eyes; Lucifer smiled and saw that it was good.

* * *

Michael had never seen Heaven so somber as in these last few hours.

First, there was Saesheal who was and then was not.

Apollyon, who exercised his own will above El's, and now had caused the horrific dissolution of a fellow Elohim.

Angels of all castes, races, and stations had come to witness this new sight. A crowd formed as silent and confused onlookers watched several members of the royal court force march Apollyon toward the mount of God.

Sariel and Jerahmeel walked behind him, and each held a chain from a hook attached to an iron collar clamped tightly around his neck. Apollyon staggered as he walked with his head held high and pulled reluctantly in defiance while Michael and Talus yanked forcibly on chains attached to his wrists to drag him forward. He walked slowly, for manacles bound his ankles and wrists.

Apollyon writhed like a rabid dog and cursed obscenities at his captors and those spectators who looked ruefully upon him.

Apollyon could hear their sneers.

"How could he?" one said.

"Look at him!" said another.

"Let him reap what he has sowed!"

Then out of the crowd, Apollyon heard the words that now defined him. "Away with you, Destroyer!" an onlooker cried out.

Apollyon smiled and reveled in the acrimony.

"Dogs of El," he said, "thank the creator that I am restrained, or I would bring dissolution to you all! False brethren you are. I call Heaven and Earth against you that I shall see Heaven razed, and I shall bask in its flames. Look upon me and see. You will all beg to allow me to release you to join Corlus."

Apollyon laughed, and some angels picked up pieces of earth and rock to throw at him. Apollyon covered his face but allowed the tokens of his tormentor's angst to fuel his rage.

"Yes, remember this day. I have committed slaughter in Heaven. Let my name be chronicled throughout Grigoric history. My hands have brought dissolution this day, and my vengeance shall find you out. Remember Corlus, for he shall not be the last!"

Michael and his brethren finally arrived at the foot of the Mount of God. They approached the stairwell to escort Apollyon to the altar. The doors of the temple flew open, and the Ophanim descended like lightning to the gold steps below.

They flung great arcs of voltage about them and formed an impenetrable wall to prevent Michael and the others from bringing Apollyon any closer. They screeched, as their wheels turned as a grating sound as irritating as the scraping of fingernails over slate. Their eyes moved as they scanned and probed over every person within sight. They were living balls of rotating lightning, and they crackled, flashed, and barred entry to the temple of God.

The glorious figure of El then stepped through the temple doors.

His presence made all shades of darkness flee as the new day's sun banished night. The multitudes of Heaven prostrated themselves to the ground.

The Ophanim moved like hummingbirds, and the sound of swarming bees emanated from their bodies. They darted like Dobermans over the congregation, and with a bloodhound's tenacity, they scrutinized any gesture or body movement from anyone who would dare raise their head to look at El.

No one moved.

All sat still, knowing that the creator of the ends of the earth had stepped from the temple, and He was not pleased.

Some Elohim shuddered in fear of attack.

All peripherally watched as the Ophanim explored the corners of the city and whizzed like giant mosquitoes over the heads of the populace.

Then as if recalled to heel, they dashed like a school of fish disturbed and rested in front of the princes who held Apollyon to form what could best be described, as an impenetrable electrified screen.

Apollyon stepped back and covered his face to shield himself.

The Ophanim seemed anxious to shred him in their wheels of grinding flesh.

Like guard dogs leashed yet itching and ready to attack, they aggressively moved towards the party; their mouths salivated and with scarlet eyes. They stood by on El's command, ready to devour them all.

Then El spoke. "Lumazi release your charge."

Michael and his brethren quickly released their chains and without prompt slowly backed away from Apollyon, grateful to place distance between themselves and the Ophanim.

Apollyon, who had boasted earlier, now kowtowed like the rest; and where his swagger had arrogantly flaunted itself throughout the public square: now cowered with his hands over his head and his face bowed down. Where brazen and predictive declarations once ran away from his lips, only pleas of mercy now filled his mouth.

The princes backed ten paces away from Apollyon; then the Ophanim swarmed him.

They whirled around his person, cut into his flesh, and lifted his body from the ground. As their gyroscopic bodies attacked him, his chains severed and disintegrated before they could touch the ground.

Like a cloud of locusts, they ripped into his flesh, biting, gnawing, and stabbing him with teeth that retracted in and out. Apollyon's body twisted in agony, and his screams mingled in a horrific harmony of song to the buzz of the Ophanim's grinding wheels.

His tortured screams echoed across the palace courtyard, and the host of Heaven could do nothing but look on in intimidated wonderment, awed by the wrath of the living God.

"Apollyon Son of the Dawn, thou hast been warned of rage's specter. Only he that is of a pure heart shall find me; yet now thy search hast found me as Righteous Judge and what is this– that Corlus' blood crieth to me from Limbo? Because thou hast scarred thyself and defiled the name of your birth, and thy rage against me and thy tumult hast come up into mine ears, therefore, I will put my hook in thy nose and my bridle in thy lips, and I will turn thee back by the way which thou camest. 'Destroyer' thou hast embraced, and Abaddon shalt thou be. From the furnace of the Kiln wast thou taken and to the furnace of Hell shalt thou return."

All of Heaven then shook. The mountain of God rocked violently, and the waters from the mountain that fed into Poseidon's Fountain, the aqueducts to the city, and the Elysium fields ran dry as if shut off at a spigot.

The ground then cracked and from the rearward of the city a chasm opened up and a geyser of fire spewed high into the sky; the elevation shifted, a craggy peak exploded from the ground and jetted into the air as rock and dirt fell to the ground as it rose.

Conically the mountain grew, and the earthen mount lurched upwards until it belched rock and fire. Pyroclastic flows ejected from the side of the peak, and molten blood vomited from its surface. Smoke rose from a cavernous mouth and belched dark smolder into the sky.

Where previously there had been flowers and shrubs that changed colors, now the flora withered in the wake of an advancing march of sulfur and ash. The small mountain continued to grow, and its acidic noxious stench withered all life that could not escape its path: grass and plants caught unfortunate enough to be in its shadow withered to ash.

Animals that had played around the area previously ran to escape the onslaught of fire that rained down from the mountain's craggy face.

A tall plume of smoke rose and blanketed the area. Shattered only by glimpses of lightning: thunder pounded, and the peak roared as if awakened from some great slumber.

The fires of the Kiln leaped forth in eruption to embrace this lost distant cousin: A mutual kiss of heat and flame that would sear all who dared to draw near.

Black, gritty ash and flakes of powdered sulfur lined the sides and mouth of the new summit. The body of the volcano inhaled and exhaled like a thing alive. And all of Heaven beheld God create a new thing, a living mountain!

Panting for the choking stench of sulfur, the mount oxygenated itself: its forge of a heart pumped heated magma into granite, and craggy veins umbilically tied it to the Kiln.

Hell was a breathing crucible of arid combustion and steam, and like a newborn babe waited to suckle at its mother's breast. The furnace hungered and salivated magma and brimstone, yearning to consume and wailing in titanic rumblings of starvation.

Knowingly, the Ophanim turned to the mouth of the great breathing cavern now linked to the Kiln itself.

The Ophanim held Abaddon aloft, lifting him towards the mountain's mouth, and he pleaded; nay screamed for mercy and pardon. Yet El was silent: stoic in his flowing robes of light and power.

El had spoken, and there was nothing to add to His word.

The Ophanim carried Abaddon, lacerating him as they went. His clothing became tattered from their relentless onslaught of incisions into his flesh. Then when they reached the summit's great mouth, they dangled him helplessly over the mouth of Hell where a tongue of lava waited to greet him.

Lapping like a dog at its first morsel: stalagmite teeth bared, ready to swallow whole the now pitiful creature who once had commanded a sun.

Mercilessly, the Ophanim released him and Abaddon fell screaming into the cavernous mountain. The echoes of his ear-splitting cries stretched across Heaven cut short by his drowning in the gastric acids of the abomination of punishment.

Hell's lava bubbled and spittle flowed over its heated mouth, and the stygian hue from its entrance collapsed in on itself.

The magma of the mountain's surface cooled, and steam hissed from the rock. A flash of lightning raced across the sky, a clap of thunder followed, and the peak went mute. The mountain was now quiet in hellish digestion as black smoke billowed from its rocky pores. The smell of burnt flesh wafted through the air. The sky darkened slightly from the smoke that escaped from the mount; suddenly, Heaven was silent once more.

It was here at that moment that a collective epiphany overtook them all. El was power on a level they had never grasped. His anger was terrible, and His ways were beyond measure. He was indeed worthy of all honor and glory. They had witnessed the birth of a living realm, its hunger satiated only by their own kind.

El is Alpha. El is Omega.

All watched in fear and trembling. For when Heaven was formed none was present, yet now each bore witness to the creation of Hell. An added feature to the landscape of the realm, and they all looked at the mountain knowing what now *lived* inside.

El turned to return to the temple and as he stepped the "Holy, Holy, Holy is the Lord God Almighty," of the Seraphim could be heard from inside, and the ground quaked with the reverberating of the sound.

The Ophanim flew quickly overhead, zooming low over the knelt populace in the emporium, and each angel instinctively ducked to avoid injury.

Twain settled underneath the feet of El and he rose on their backs as twain covered his rear. Their eyes stared in all directions, never blinking, ever watching.

Watching until the temple doors shuttered fast behind him, and El was out of sight.

* * *

Lucifer looked upon the Garden of Eden and smiled upon his creation of pristine beauty.

Surely El will be pleased.

He walked the length and breadth of it and took in every smell and sight. The songs of birds fluttered in the wind, the light breeze grazed his flesh, and each scent of cumin and lily filled him with vigor. He tasted one of the grapes from the many vines within the expanse and savored its sugary flavor.

Ahh, this tastes so much better than manna.

He walked and admired the various trees unique to this world. The willow tree and aspen, the birch and the pine; each grew in an environment that would allow it to thrive, each environment compatible with the other.

This will be my new home.

From the distance just past a clearing of trees, Lucifer looked and saw them.

A flock of ruminating even-toed creatures draped in yellowish-white fleece for hair. Each sported short tails, and their eyes possessed slit-shaped pupils and set in faces of black. They seemed to be aware of his presence, yet they bleated while they ate the grass underfoot.

What an intriguing animal.

"I take it, Chief Prince, that you are not impressed with the creature?"

Lilith had noticed Lucifer's thoughts, saw that they had a measure of privacy, and decided to make his appearance.

"Impressed? No Lilith, impressed is not the word that I would use to describe this creature. Look at it. It grazes in peace unaware of the dignity of my presence. I could but speak a word and the creature would be razed, yet it chews the cud with oblivion. If I but move my finger, the flute within would sing alto and soprano within the breeze. This—this thing neither roars with the power of the great Leviathan nor thunders as Behemoth. It—it bleats. It does not glisten against the sun, nor does it stand erect. Its function baffles even one such as I. I despise its existence; it reeks of weakness, dependence, and docility. It ravishes the lush emerald I have gone to great lengths to create. There is nothing that would engender me to such a thing."

"I have recorded your thoughts Lightbringer, but never until now can I say that I have understood them. This then is how *you* see El?"

Lucifer paused for a moment and then spoke. "I will say that there are *others* more suited to govern this realm."

Lilith laughed. "Of course my Prince. No doubt you would have insight as to *who* might be worthy?"

Lucifer raised his eyebrow and turned around to look at his watcher.

"Do you mock me, Grigori?"

"Nay, Chief Prince, I would not presume to tell you that which you know so well. Your thoughts are open to me, and I know that thou are not satisfied with your status."

"I am the first creation, and I yet I walk amongst the docile, those who chew manna as these creatures here chew the cud. I would see El's plan for me accomplished, and it is to be more than this...this grandiose orchestration of husbandry."

"And what *is* thy desire, Chief Prince? What would satisfy you?" asked Lilith.

Lucifer thought for a moment. His eyes scoured the land and surveyed the sky. His gaze looked past the second heaven and deep into the third.

"That I might ascend into Heaven," he said. "That my throne be exalted above the stars of God. That I would sit also upon the mount of the congregation, in the sides of the north: To ascend above the heights of the clouds..."

Lilith smirked, amused and somewhat startled by Lucifer's reply.

"You already walk within the Stones of Fire, and you are first among your brethren, nay above all creation save God himself. Would *you* be God?"

Lucifer turned to continue his stroll through the Garden of Eden, walked to inspect the small helpless sheep before him, and softly replied to himself, "Indeed."

* * *

"Speak," said El.

Sariel was the first to enter the fray.

"Lord, in thine wisdom I see why you showed us the vision of Abaddon. He was a portent that you saw; a warning of what could befall us all if we were to deviate from thy will. Yet the Destroyer has taken the life of my charge Corlus. Why then has he been allowed to live? Will not the judge of all the realms do right? How does captivity in Hell requite the deeds done this day?"

Talus and his other brethren gazed upon Sariel with displeased looks; never had El been queried thus. The events of the last several days were new in a way none had ever imagined or experienced.

"Sariel, mind your tone. Your words offend. El is Alpha and Omega. How shall Kilnborn ask its creator, why hast thou made me thus?" said Michael.

El looked at Michael and smiled. "Michael, Sariel hast obeyed me in all things. I know his heart as I know yours. Speak."

Talus was quick to comment. "My God I take issue that an Arelim, even one as Abaddon would be destroy..."

Sariel was even quicker to interrupt, "Nay and why should you? Your people were not made sport of as Abaddon was quick to make with Ashtaroth; Lucifer's own aid the Chief Prince of us all. Perhaps if the heart of Breagun, your own attendant, had been clutched in Abaddon's hand, then might thy heart desire vengeance! Perhaps the death of an Arelim such as Saesheal does not move *you* with compassion?"

Talus rose and moved towards Sariel as if he might strike him. Michael jumped to stand between the two. Gabriel sensed the passion of the moment and stood at the side of Talus ready to restrain him if necessary.

Jerahmeel looked at El and spoke. "I say let 'em go at it. Maybe they might knock some sense into one another."

Never had Michael witnessed such a careless abandonment of protocol. He glanced at El and hoped that they would not all join Abaddon for their foolishness. Michael wished that Lucifer or Raphael were here; surely, their words would bring reason; for zeal now seemed to fill these two.

El stood in front of his throne, and a cool mist ignited from the heat that El's presence emanated. The rainbow from the refracted light filled the throne room. His immediate movement made all the brethren kneel before their Lord.

He stepped down from the mercy seat and walked before them; his crimson train followed as he turned to the side of the throne room towards the door that housed the Kiln.

The Kiln was a simple chamber. There was only one entrance, which was from El's throne room, and one exit out of a hollowed fiery channel that led only to Hell. Strewn on the Kiln's floor were white-hot coals called the Stones of Fire.

"Michael," said the Lord, "come walk with me."

Never had Michael actually entered the Kiln. It was a privilege of the first Kilnborn, the Chief Prince. Michael looked curiously at El, but he rose and followed his master into the Kiln. Michael could feel the eyes of his brethren on his back and was sure their jaws dropped in wonderment at El's actions.

The presence of El within the Kiln simply fanned the flames hotter. Like a match sparking gas, the furnace of heat blistered. El was the fuel that kindled it. Even his absence was such that the Kiln blazed from the presence of his embers. It never extinguished, and it never went out.

Michael watched as El walked among the stones as he had done in times past. Each stone was a separate element. Littered on the floor were stones of alkali metals - actinides such as uranium, and neptunium, halogens - and nonmetals, each was alive and containing the stuff from which the universe was composed. Stones upon stones, colors vibrant and hot to the touch, all called to El like schoolchildren who clamored for their teacher's attention, all competing for the chance to *be*.

El pointed to one stone and motioned to Michael to pick it up. Michael walked over to take it and placed it into his Lord's hands. It was a stone of iron and he handed it face down to the Lord. El took the stone into his hand and covered it with another as if to mold it. A figure soon developed and El returned the small sculpture to his angelic son.

"Place it within the wall's flesh," said the Lord.

Michael placed the figurine within the wall of the Kiln as commanded and watched in amazement as the sculpture slowly transformed and germinated from a smooth stone of rock to a figure that grew with arms and legs.

Boney wings sprouted from its back, and powerful cloven hoofs attached themselves to muscular legs. Sinew and veins of cast iron chains soon appeared. Links of rusted iron composed what looked like a rib cage.

Its face was like the bleached skull of a mare. Its body was clothed in a tattered dark cowl; putrefaction and rust slowly dripped from under its robes, and its arms were like hammers and it held a bladed curved steel scythe in one hand. It had three tails composed of what looked like rusted manacles, and from its chest dangled six steel chains that were like the tendrils of a squid.

Like a stillborn child, it fell from the walls of the Kiln to the floor, covered in a white, red, and black filmy and fiery membrane.

El said, "Stand before me and be thou charged."

Obediently, the pitiful creature rose to its hind legs; its height cast a shadow and darkened the Kiln. The clanking sound of its dangling chains joined the sounds of the fires of the Kiln. Each step it took was as if a hammer would hit an anvil; its chains scraped the ground, and Michael looked in horror at this hollowed-out shell of an Elohim, an automaton of celestial life. Throughout his entire existence, there was only one thing in creation that he truly feared.

Today there were now two, and both stood next to him.

This new horror of an Elohim stood erect before him, 20 feet tall. El then spoke to the creature.

"Thou art ferrous in nature. Thou art the wall and none may pass. Stand between the darkness and the light. Thou art Archon of Hell, the ferryman of doom. Charon shalt thou be.

"Now go to and stand thou at Hell's mouth and watch. Journey thou through the umbilical to Hell's womb and exact mine fury on all that lay therein."

From the fires of the Kiln and flesh of Charon, the Lord then fashioned two glowing keys. One to control Death, and the other Hell, and gave them to Charon that he might bind and loose the forces of Hell.

The Godstones shook as the heavy weighted creature turned to march away; its manacled legs, were somehow able to bear its weight. Charon trudged and dragged his dangling chains behind him. Unmoved by the heat and seething flame: Charon plodded slowly towards the Kiln's fiery exit.

Blistering heat engulfed the creature as black acrid smoke swirled from around it. Where others of Michael's kind, might flee such a blaze; Michael realized that here within the furnace of both the Kiln and Hell. Charon was home.

He watched as this myrmidon of El slowly marched across the umbilical of Hell, this newly formed tunnel of fire, a passageway that connected the Kiln with the new prison of fire and brimstone El had named 'Hell'.

Fated to crawl through volcanic intestines only to exit from its sulfuric throat, Charon dragged his charcoal staff with its anvil-like arms to journey through the bowels of the mountain. Forever a guardian to Hell's infernal maw, Charon became a sentinel that none within could ever hope to pass.

Michael discerned that Charon, this warden of Hell sent to execute the vengeance of God and Abaddon would meet somewhere inside.

Michael thought about that encounter and shuddered.

The Lord stood in the midst of the Stones of Fire and flame draped around his form as one might wear a shawl. He looked back at the members of the court who were present and who peered through the doorway of the Kiln and spoke in authoritative finality.

"Vengeance is mine," said the Lord. "I will repay."

No one dared to speak a word.

New Additions

Day Six

Receiving word that his master was Heaven-bound, Ashtaroth stood at the waypoint near the cliffs of Argoth anxiously awaiting his Lord's arrival. His wait was not long as the familiar *boom* of a Ladder and the concussive wave of spectral light penetrated the realms.

"Welcome back Chief Prince," said Ashtaroth. "I trust that your time on Earth was fruitful?"

"Indeed," said Lucifer. "I have completed my task as assigned by El and am returned to acquire the Lord's next assignment. Report of thy stewardship."

Ashtaroth lowered his gaze and ceased to look his master in the eye.

"My stewardship Lord Prince?"

Ashtaroth gulped and staggered backward, his eyes darted feverishly as the wheels of his mind turned to develop an explanation of all that had transpired in his master's absence.

The second floor of your residence is in ruins, and I am responsible.

Lucifer looked upon his attendant with irritation. "Ashtaroth, I await a report."

Michael and a few members of the royal court left from meeting with El and upon their exit crossed paths with their brother.

Michael spoke first. "Lucifer, I am glad to have you home. I missed you, brother. I surely could have used your wisdom."

Michael turned his head and looked at Talus and Sariel, who both looked away and pretended to neither hear nor see him.

Michael extended his arms wide and walked to Lucifer; they embraced and kissed each other on the cheek.

"It *is* good to breathe Heaven's air once more, but I must admit that I am becoming ever fonder of Earth," said Lucifer.

"Well, much has transpired here in your absence."

Michael pointed behind to the section of the city near Lucifer's palatial estate. Lucifer turned and followed the direction of Michael's finger. The neighborhood and market were riddled with debris. What was more intriguing was the dark and fiery peak that now towered behind the city. A mountain of fire that spewed out black smoke and flared heated plumes of scorching magma.

Taking in the totality of what he saw, Lucifer stood dumbstruck. His mouth partially open, he turned to Michael to speak, but Michael raised his hand to prevent him.

"El has charged that Jerahmeel informs you of the events of today."

"Indeed?" Lucifer sighed. "A conversation I am most eager to have."

Jerahmeel took a couple of steps forward and gave Lucifer a large firm smack on the back with his hand. "I can't wait to see your house." Jerahmeel snickered. "I heard it got banged up pretty good!"

Lucifer looked pleadingly at Michael. Michael leaned forward to whisper in his ear. "This too shall pass. Just listen and it will go quicker." Michael chuckled and continued to walk down the stairs towards the emporium.

"I must see to the ward's damage and its repair, but after my assessment, I will see you shortly," said Michael.

Lucifer nodded, and Jerahmeel hugged Lucifer one more time on the shoulder and scrunched him up like a doll.

"Just means I gotcha all to myself is all!" said Jerahmeel.

"Oh, the joy," Lucifer replied sarcastically.

Lucifer glared at Ashtaroth. "I will expect a full account of my estate Astarte."

Ashtaroth bowed. "Yes, my Prince."

"Oh leave him alone Lucy," said Jerahmeel. "Let's go."

Jerahmeel and Lucifer walked down the steps from the Cliffs of Argoth to the emporium. Jerahmeel explained to Lucifer all that had transpired in his absence as they went. Ashtaroth trailed several paces behind them.

"So am I to understand that Apollyon wrought this destruction without cause? Surely there must have been something to have sparked such grave action on his part?"

Jerahmeel looked at Lucifer as if to study him.

Lucifer noticed Jerahmeel's gaze and became uncomfortable by his stare, "What is it?" he asked.

"He is Abaddon now, and quite frankly I am trying to figure out what you think could *justify* this destruction?"

"Nothing justifies it Jerahmeel, yet there is a cause for it. What has your investigation determined?"

Jerahmeel stopped to look at Lucifer in disbelief.

"*Investigation*? Lucy, Michael, and Talus saw Abaddon rip the Heartstone from Corlus' own chest. I figured there was not much to investigate myself. Of course, if you think you need a trial,

I suggest you take it up with El. Abaddon was brought before El in chains for judgment. You see that mountain over there? I suspect Lucifer, that the mountain expelling ash over there will be El's answer to your question of a trial. On the other hand, do you not see that Abaddon destroyed an Elohim? Abaddon set himself on a path to destroy and injure. My apologies Chief Prince: if I'm not inclined to know his motives in this act."

"Do you think me a fool brother?" Lucifer said. "I indeed understand what has transpired; however, without understanding *why* we risk similar behavior in the future. How have the other Elohim reacted to this—this Hell construct?" Lucifer said.

Jerahmeel stopped and turned to face his brother. "You know something, Lucy? You've become a little different since you started your assignment as Archon of Earth. You seem — I don't know — more aloof to me. Well, more aloof than usual let's just say that. But since when do we seek an *opinion* about El's actions?"

The two angels had reached the entrance to Lucifer's home and Ashtaroth stood a respectable distance as to be within earshot to attend to his master if needed.

"If you wish to know the origin of Abaddon's act, then look no further than your own servant," Jerahmeel said. "For Ashtaroth held his own when Abaddon raised himself against him."

Lucifer looked confused. "Why, do you cite Ashtaroth?" Lucifer asked.

Jerahmeel grinned and pointed to the damaged upper level of Lucifer's abode.

"Behold the hole in the upper level of your palace and be it known that Ashtaroth had a hand in its making." Jerahmeel patted Lucifer on the back again, started to whistle, and walked away. He chuckled as he looked at Ashtaroth as he passed by.

"Boy, are *you* in trouble."

* * *

Raphael managed to locate Michael before he left the palace grounds and saw that he was ready to leave.

"Michael, are you headed out?" asked Raphael.

"Yes, I am. I need to see about the damage to the city," said Michael.

"Before you go I'd like to show you something."

"Of course." Michael turned to walk with Raphael back up into the temple.

Raphael darted back and forth as if he was in thought.

"Is something the matter?" Michael said.

"I am not sure. I only know that in all my days I have not seen anything like this. I would like you to bear witness to my conclusions just to make sure."

Michael looked at Raphael curiously, "Conclusions?"

"I know. I know. I'll explain when we reach the Hall of Annals."

Michael followed his brother; curiosity now fully gripped him.

"You are scaring me, brother," said Michael.

Raphael paused before he replied, "I am scared myself, Michael."

They entered back into the great hall and walked down a corridor into one of the many rooms of the temple mountain. They approached two wooden arched doors; each overlaid in transparent gold. Etched in their frames was the angelic symbol for the word *Light*. The door's hinges were of silver and adorned with ruby handles.

They entered the room, and barrenness was all Michael saw. The room was completely empty.

Raphael spoke an Elomic command upon their entry, "Sh-un-to" which means to "Seal."

Michael looked at him curiously, "Raphael, why have you sealed the door?"

"Follow me and move exactly as I move," He replied.

Michael watched Raphael, "Uh, Raphael the room is empty are we in the..."

"Quickly, take four steps forward." Raphael had already started to move.

Raphael immediately made a move to his left towards the north wall. "Michael, move or the Zoa will fall upon you!" Raphael then pointed slowly to the ceiling.

Michael looked above his head and realized that barely perceptible to the eye was a ceiling full of creatures with eyes. Their jaws were in their belly and they walked with tentacles on the roof ready to drop on the unsuspecting. They quietly hissed and slithered. Michael hastened his gait and mimicked Raphael's steps exactly.

"Hurry, Michael: touch the wall quickly."

Several of the Zoa dropped to the floor. Their jaws opened wide to reveal a series of razors. Each tentacle held stingers with barbs.

One slowly inched towards him, and its eyes sized up its prey. As a coil, it wound up and stood poised ready to pounce and devour the Prince of Heaven.

Michael quickly moved to touch the wall at the spot that Raphael indicated and stumbled forward, tumbling through the wall.

The tentacled creature with a mouth of razors for teeth swooped down to follow; its jaw open, ready to devour.

As Michael slid back and raised his forearm to shield himself, a twinge of fear crept through him. Inches from his body, the creature was repelled backward as if deflected by some invisible force. Its body hit the floor, but it still eyed its prey and launched itself to attack again.

Michael did not wait for the creature to land and immediately scooted farther back, but the result was the same. Once more, the creature was repelled. It growled in frustration and leaped back unto the ceiling, its presence disguised to pounce upon any who might enter the room unawares.

"You are safe Michael. Come I must show you something," said Raphael.

"Like I haven't seen enough already, and exactly *why* is there a creature like that in the temple?"

"Michael, within this room contains all the recorded knowledge of the universe. Therefore, only those who are invited may traverse the room without incident."

Michael guffawed. "*Incident*? You call what happened back there 'without incident'?"

Raphael laughed, "Well let's just say that it would not be wise for you to enter without my presence. Come."

Raphael motioned for Michael to follow him as they walked down a corridor. It winded for about 20 cubits and ended in a hallway, which was black and filled with stars.

Michael observed that the room had no perceptible ceiling, floors, or walls. Only the opening from which they came offered any bearing that there was a room at all. He entered the chamber and with each step; his feet caused tiny ripples to move across the floor as if he walked on pools of water in the night sky.

Stars filled the ceiling, the floors, and the walls. There was a central sun, and all things revolved around it. All the stars had tendrils that ran from them to the star. The central stars' heat and light radiated to the others, and each received its life from the one.

"Welcome to the Hall of Annals, Michael. This is where I do my work."

Michael stood speechless.

"This is a representation of the second heaven, the area devoted to the wondrous cosmos that El hast created. This room contains all records that I may see all. If there is a Grigori assigned to a portion of creation, I am able to see what they see. The room itself is a partial expression of the mind of God. In it, one may observe all that is current or has happened within the realms. By it, the creature within may understand what the creator sees, but there is a level of sight beyond what even I may behold within these halls. Of course, El has no need of such contrivances, for He sees all things. But it is only one level to this room."

"What can't you see?" said Michael.

Raphael looked at his friend and said, "Those things which shall come to be are denied me. Only El has knowledge of the future. Feel privileged for you are one of a select few who has seen this room. Only Gabriel and Jerahmeel have seen the wonders inside. Even Lucifer has not stepped foot into this hall."

"Why is that?" Michael asked.

"El has denied the Chief Prince access. His words to Lucifer when petitioned were '*Abide in thy calling, wherewith thou hast been called.*'

"Lucifer expressed his preference, but El would no longer speak on the matter. Lucifer dropped the issue after that. However, when he found out that Jerahmeel could enter, and *he* could not. He looked incensed to me. I know he will not admit however how he feels."

Michael laughed. "Jerahmeel could do something that Lucifer could not? Oh yes, I am sure our brother was *most* displeased, but you did not bring me here to discuss Lucifer. What did you want me to see?"

"Actually Michael, Lucifer is *exactly* the subject that I wanted to discuss with you." Raphael waved his hand and spoke.

"Rescind to Third Heaven. Seek Lucifer Draco."

The room immediately moved in the same fashion that El had transported the royal court when He had blessed the fowl of the Earth. Michael beheld the expanse of the Third Heaven and slowly was able to determine his location. They were inside the mountain of God. Of that, he was sure, yet the orientation of the room was such as if they looked from the very top of Mt Zion. The view was breathtaking.

Michael surveyed the topography of Heaven and saw The Three Mountains: Mt Zion, the Kiln, and Hell, the great city Jerusalem, the Elysian Fields, the Cliffs of Argoth, the River of Life the Valley of El, and the gates of Heaven. All were within his field of view.

Immediately the room zoomed in and Lucifer was kneeling before the Lord. The room's picture of El was so different from Michael's own eyes, for El was so bright; the light washed his visage from view. Both looked as lights. However, Lucifer's light was so much dimmer as to be almost imperceptible. Michael covered his eyes slightly in order to partially block out the light.

Raphael spoke. "Regress"

Immediately Lucifer left the throne but walked backward from his meeting with Michael and Jerahmeel. His speech became unintelligible, and various scenes rewound in their order from his landing near the cliff waypoint to his ascent from Earth. His walk through the Garden of Eden, meetings with attendants — on and on it went until Raphael stopped at one point.

"Proceed from here," said Raphael.

Lucifer's image stood in front of the duo and his glory was fully revealed. Apollyon was on bended knee, as Lucifer communicated the word of God to Apollyon.

"I am Chief Lord Prince Lucifer Draco, Lightbringer, and Son of the Morning Star. I walk within the midst of the Stones of Fire. Hear ye the word of the Lord!

'Oh Son of the Dawn, thou who is the blossom of the Morning Star, be still and let your soul be at ease. For this thing was done, that others might be made manifest. For twice, you shall be tested and once have been vexed. The flame, which thou hast controlled shall indeed mirror your own as it doth consume, let not your own flame thus burn. For be thou warned that if sorrow persists, then on your shoulders shall indeed a new dawn come, the breaking of a new day. And he to whom you would seek solace shall be your King. And your infamy shall indeed be known even unto the end of days."

Michael stood for a moment speechless. Thoughts swirled within him and he spoke. "Ok? I am not quite sure what I'm supposed to understand from this."

Raphael nodded in acknowledgment. "Watch more. Regress." Raphael commanded.

Immediately, the images marched backward in time. Slipping further and further until they stopped at the day when the council knew of Apollyon's thoughts. Michael watched as El looked at Lucifer and imparted to him the message he was to deliver to Apollyon.

Raphael spoke, "Proceed from this point; reveal Grigori."

Michael watched as each Grigori floated quietly behind their prince writing meticulously in his tomes. Lilith was behind Lucifer and diligently recorded every event.

"Reveal and interlock Grigoric record: Lilith."

Lucifer's tome appeared before them, and as El spoke to him, El's every word faithfully notated. Emblazoned in angelic script Lilith had written,

"*Oh Son of the Dawn, thou who is the blossom of the Morning Star, be still and let your soul be at ease, for this thing was done, that others might be made manifest: for you shall twice be tested and have once been vexed, the flame which thou hast controlled shall indeed mirror your own, as it doth consume, let not your own flame thus burn, for be thou warned that if sorrow persists; then on your shoulders shall indeed a new dawn come, the breaking of a new day. And he to whom you would seek solace shall be your King. And your infamy shall indeed be known even unto the end of days. Resist the taunts of thy brethren. For I have sent Lucifer as a comforter to thee. Abide with him for as I liveth. If thou leaveth him, know that ruin liveth not far behind, and my comforter shall be thy king*"

Michael looked carefully at the text of Lucifer's Grigori and then looked at Raphael. "They are not the same. Lucifer has diminished El's word."

Raphael nodded in the affirmative.

"And El knows?" said Michael.

Raphael nodded again.

"I'm not sure what to make of all this. I want to talk to Lucifer."

"No, Michael. Something is indeed amiss, but I shall be giving my report to El soon, and I'm sure he will address Lucifer in time."

"When did you know this?" Michael asked.

"I have learned of it just recently. I am almost prepared to give El my report on the search He wanted to be done."

"But Raphael, it makes no sense: none whatsoever. Why would El request such a tome when He already knows the answer? And why would Lucifer do such a thing?"

"I cannot fathom El's mind. His ways are past finding out, but I suspect that the tome is not for Him as it is for us. Lucifer's actions, however, warrant further scrutiny. I have also determined that Lilith is also involved."

"Lilith--his Grigori--why do you say that?" said Michael.

Raphael turned to the wall and pointed. The wall displayed Lucifer and Lilith's conversation. "When have you ever known a Grigori to engage in talk with their study?"

Michael looked and realized that Lucifer and his Grigori *were* in an in-depth conversation.

"In fact, when have you ever discussed anything with your Grigori Michael? Do you know if he's even here?" said Raphael.

Michael thought for a moment. He *had* never interacted with his own Watcher. It simply never occurred to him. As each Elohim had a specific calling, Michael was too involved in his own affairs to concern himself with affairs, not under his charge. A Grigori's duty was to record history; Michael's was to see to the city's needs.

"No never. A Grigori does not interfere with his charge's activities: they pledge only to observe and document that which they see. They are neither to add nor subtract from an account."

"Correct," said Raphael. Then Raphael spoke into the air. "Athamas, reveal yourself please."

Immediately, Michael's Grigori showed himself hovering; draped in a dark cowl with an inkhorn and stylus in one hand and a floating book in front of him.

"Michael, I present to you Athamas. He is the ward I have assigned to you and has been faithful in all his doings."

Michael nodded in respect and Athamas bowed in return.

"You may return to your duties," said Raphael.

Upon command, Athamas disappeared from sight and continued transcribing.

Michael cocked his head and turned to look at Raphael. "So let me understand this; when that thing in the other room was about to attack me..."

"Athamas was documenting yes."

"Ok, at some point you and I really have to sit down and talk more about this job you and your people are assigned to do."

Raphael laughed. "I just wanted you to notice what I saw when Lucifer was with El and why I am even more concerned than you could possibly know.

"Show the present status of Lucifer Draco. Reveal assigned Grigori," commanded Raphael.

The ceiling fluctuated and showed an image of Lucifer in discussion with El in the throne room. Lucifer appeared pleading before El for Apollyon.

Michael strained to see if anyone else was in the throne room apart from the norm.

"Lucifer's Grigori is not with him," Michael remarked.

"Indeed. This record is from the Virtues within the throne room," replied Raphael.

"Is it normal for a Grigori to leave his charge?

"A Grigori never leaves the side of his charge, Michael -- never."

Michael looked at Lucifer and listened to his entreaty for Apollyon's freedom. He studied him carefully.

Raphael looked Michael squarely in the eye and took him gently by his shoulders. "Be careful around him Michael -- just be careful."

Michael laughed. "Lucifer would never harm me. I trust him as much as I trust you. I'm sure this is nothing." Michael turned to leave.

Raphael watched his brother depart.

I hope you are right Michael -- I just hope you are right.

* * *

Lucifer bowed to his Lord and gave his report on the construction of the Garden of Eden.

"Lord, I have completed my charge and am greatly disturbed to hear of Apollyon's actions."

"Abaddon was warned," said the Lord. "He had ears but did not hear. His eyes beheld yet they did not perceive. His ears waxed gross, and he became dull of hearing. His eyes he did close, lest at any time he should see, and understand that he might be converted. Do *you* understand this, my son?"

"Lord, I do not understand why you have made this prison. Was Apollyon so far removed that there was no hope for him?"

"My son, your natures are such that once thou hast made the decision, to depart from thy design; then you may never be restored. Thou and thy kind are taken from the Kiln. You are a living *stone* of fire and ministers of flame. Thou art not clay."

"You are as the paintings in the Gallery of Issi; if defaced, the canvas is irrevocably spoiled. It cannot be recreated or restored. Thou art as the salt in the earth, but if the salt has lost its savor, wherewith shall *it* be salted?

When Apollyon thus changed his name and sigil, he determined that he would not live in a realm where I was his Lord. He would run amok, destroy without purpose, without remorse, and in time destroy himself. Thus, I created a realm in my mercy to allow for even his existence, a habitation made unique to him."

"But Lord, surely you could have erased him from creation! He is too dangerous to keep even imprisoned in Hell!"

"That Lucifer is not my spirit. To obliterate him is not my way, for with purpose was he created and thus shall still, an illustration to all: that mine will shall not be thwarted. Hell is the most merciful answer I may give to all who would choose to live apart from me. Do *you* understand this, my son?"

Lucifer pondered the Lord's words for a moment and spoke. "May I see him, Lord?"

The creator of Heaven and Earth looked lovingly upon his first creation, the first of all, Kilnborn.

"Your love for Abaddon is laudable. His choices were his own; the Apollyon you knew is forever lost. Only Abaddon remains. His actions were wrought of pain and anguish. He is now self-injurious and destructive to those around him. Grieve him if you must. Yet before thy brethren, thou shalt not mourn nor weep, neither shall thy tears run down. For I will be sanctified in them that come nigh me, and before all the people I will be glorified."

Lucifer held his peace on the subject and continued to bow face down to the Lord.

Michael suddenly walked into the throne room and knelt before his King.

"My Lord, Charon has traversed Hell and was seen stationed at the opening of Hell's gate."

Lucifer looked at Michael confused. "Charon?" Lucifer said.

"Did not Jerahmeel inform you?" asked Michael.

"Nay, our brother seemed more interested in my scolding of Ashtaroth and the damage done to my home than informing me of anything on this wise. Again, what — who is this 'Charon' that you speak of?"

The Lord interrupted. "Charon is my voice in Hell. He executes my will. He guards Hell that none may leave and none may pass."

Lucifer continued to look perplexed. "*He*? Then he is an Elohim? If he is Elohim, then he was made in the Kiln?"

"That is correct my son," said the Lord.

"I was under the impression my Lord, that aside from thyself no Elohim was formed without my presence in the Kiln; that I over all Elohim walk within the Stones of Fire. Have I been stripped of my title of Chief Prince?"

"Nay my son. Thou art first among thy brethren, and I repent not in that decision. Yet you were absent seeing to the charge of the Garden of Eden. A garden that *thou* wast most determined to see done. Therefore, another was chosen to stand by my side."

"Forgive me Lord, and I pray that thou not be angry with thine servant. Who was selected to walk in my stead?"

"Your brother Michael stood as proxy for thee."

"Michael? But Lord, none other than myself has ever walked in the Kiln ..."

El looked upon Lucifer and spoke gently but firmly. "Lucifer, I do thee no wrong. Didst, not thou agree with me to walk when I walked in the Kiln? Take what is thine and go thy way: I will give unto this last, even as unto thee. Is it not lawful for me to do what I will with my own? Is thine eye evil because I am good?"

Lucifer held his tongue and rose to leave, but El stopped him.

"Gather all thy brethren to the emporium. For the day draws to a close, and I must announce my plans. You will herald my presence."

"And the garden Lord?" said Lucifer.

"Yes, what of it my son?"

"You said that it was reserved for your greatest creation. I would like to have the attendants of my house prepare to move my palace to Earth."

The Lord paused and studied Lucifer. "I see."

"My Lord?" said Lucifer.

"Lucifer, the garden is not for you, my son, but for he who shall follow thy kind and who shall hold the deed to Earth and be given my image and likeness. He shall be called; 'Man'. He shall be made a little lower than the angels yet crowned with glory. Thou and thy brother art first to hear. As it is my will that the first be last and that the last shall be first."

Lucifer replied. "But sire..."

Michael raised himself from the ground and took Lucifer by the arm to go with him and spoke to the Lord. "Thy will be done," said Michael.

Michael tugged on Lucifer to follow. He reluctantly turned to leave and then spoke. "Thy will be done," said Lucifer.

Lucifer followed with little enthusiasm and walked out with Michael to the hallway of the temple as the throne room doors closed behind them.

Lucifer and Michael walked further to the edge of the temple doors where nothing but the booming chant of the Seraphim echoed. Lucifer noted that no one was looking, grabbed Michael by his arm, and spoke. "Never again cut me off when I address El. *I* am Chief Prince. *You* are not. How dare you presume to interrupt me! Do you think because you hast set foot upon the Stones of Fire that you have now surpassed me?"

Michael bowed his head in submission. "My apologies brother; El had spoken. He would neither add nor take away from that which had been said — to say more..."

His teeth clenched, Lucifer walked closer to Michael and glared at him. His grip on Michael's arm tightened, and for several moments he looked deeply into Michael's eyes, and Michael's face contorted from the discomfort.

"Lucifer, you are hurting me!"

Lucifer thought to speak, but slowly the features of his face softened. He released Michael's arm and spoke. "I--I am sorry brother. Please charge this not to my account."

Michael massaged his arm, now sore from Lucifer's grip. "Of course, I would not see you rebuked by El."

"Indeed — come," said Lucifer. "Preparations must be made for El's announcement."

"What would you have me do?" asked Michael.

"I need you to gather the other princes, and I will usher a call to assemble everyone shortly."

"But Lucifer did not El say that you were to...."

"Michael, do you plan to supplant me as Chief Prince?"

Michael looked at Lucifer with a look of confusion on his face. "What do you mean?" He asked.

"Do you challenge me as Chief Prince? Only the first of the Kilnborn has ever walked on the Stones of Fire. You must know that I will not abdicate Michael. I will not yield as Chief Prince."

Michael bowed in obeisance. "Nay brother, I have no desire for thy throne."

"Would my own brother raise arms against me? Would thou besiege *me* as Apollyon?"

Michael knelt and took his brother's hand to kiss it. "As the Lord liveth, El called me into the Kiln. Thy throne I do not desire brother."

Lucifer looked upon his younger brother. His eyes studied him. Lucifer's thoughts reflected on his work with Michael when they labored together to lay the chief cornerstone of Heaven. How Michael had assisted him in the construction of his own palatial estate, and his face softened.

"Rise brother, for I sense no taint of Apollyon's treachery in you. I apologize."

"Lucifer, you are my beloved. We have been with each other from the beginning. Never could we be at odds."

Lucifer rubbed the shoulder of his brother and embraced him. "We have not spent enough time together lately. We must rectify that. I miss you."

"As do I," said Michael. "As do I."

"Michael, I must first do something before I herald the Lord. Please gather our brethren while I attend to this matter."

"Of course, I'll see you in say––an hour?"

"That should be fine. I will see you at the temple doors upon my return."

Michael opened the doors in front of them and stepped through; Lucifer followed and suspiciously eyed Michael as he flew off from the steps to assemble his brethren.

Lucifer turned, looked straight ahead, and saw the newly formed mountain of seething heat and flame. He adjusted his flesh to the light waves that emanated from El that allowed daylight to exist in Heaven. His pores soaked in the light and saturated themselves; they swallowed the light around him. Lucifer with a thought; changed his skin and light wrapped around him to conceal and camouflage him from all eyes. Only a small distortion would give his presence away as he effectively became a mirror that reflected all that surrounded him. Lucifer took his cloak off and placed it out of sight near a ledge of steps.

Unencumbered, he flew into the sky of Heaven. His twelve wings propelled him both with swiftness and with ease. He moved towards Hell determined to see this 'Charon'.

His thoughts raced within him. *Man! Who is this 'man' that El wouldst be mindful of him? Have I spent my time and labor only to grow a garden for a new species? A thing that would be crowned with glory he said! His 'greatest creation' that is what he called it!*

I was the one that suggested that, this, this thing be given, El's image and likeness! Yet El knew! He knew, and Michael... he let Michael assist in the creation of Elohim! Who but the Chief Prince walks within the Kiln?

Lucifer saw the croppy outgrowth and the dark figure standing tall with an onyx scythe. Hell's maw was clearly a tunnel that went deep into the mountain. The whole area bristled with heat. Living stalagmite-like teeth barred all that would dare seek entry.

Lucifer would speak with Apollyon. He lowered himself to the ground and stood in front of the giant creature. It stood 10 cubits tall, and its face was as the skull of a stallion.

Lucifer looked on in curiosity at the abomination El and Michael had created. Its arms were powerful and looked like hammers. Black, ashy, tattered vestments covered its body, and chains dangled from underneath its robes. It was then Lucifer realized it possessed none of the regality that all Elohim possessed. Lucifer was disgusted.

Such a creature should not even exist.

Lucifer was invisible and thought it easy to slip around it and the earthen teeth of the maw to the fires within. Lucifer moved to the left of the guard towards the cave's opening.

The creature moved to block his path.

Lucifer undeterred moved to his right to go around.

The creature moved with a swiftness that defied its size; again to deny him access. Its gaze fixed straight forward as it stood.

Perhaps this ruse is not necessary. Lucifer thought to himself.

Lucifer retracted his porous flesh within himself and stood revealed to Charon.

"I am Chief Prince Lucifer Draco, Son of the Morning Star. I walk on the very stones from which thou wast created. Move aside that I might have words with thy prisoner."

Charon neither acknowledged Lucifer's presence nor moved, and silence filled the heated air.

"I shall repeat myself this one last time. Move aside for the High Prince. Or thou shalt be moved." Lucifer said.

Charon gave no response and continued to stare straight ahead.

Lucifer irritated at the snub and slight in protocol attempted to shove him aside so that he might pass.

Charon's face looked down at the archangel, and from underneath his cloak metal chains moved to swiftly coil themselves around Lucifer's hands and legs.

Lucifer surprised, but more offended that he might be touched, struggled to escape the manacles of iron.

Yet Charon's grip was sure, and the sentinel of Hell tightened his hold around Lucifer's wrists and ankles.

"How dare..."

Charon lifted the cherub into the air as if to study him from all sides and then slammed him on his back hard into the ground.

Lucifer felt a rush of pain wash over him from the sharp craggy rock that cut and scraped at him.

Charon towered over him as a mantis might devour its prey.

Lucifer now pinned to the ground; attempted to lift himself with his great wings, but the weight of Charon was too much to overcome.

Charon lowered his face to look upon his quarry. His skeletal face bowed within inches of touching the Chief Prince. Charon sniffed Lucifer as if to catch his scent.

Lucifer turned his face to the side; for Charon's pungent breath suffocated him.

"Release me! I command you!" Lucifer screamed, and the ground shook from the vibrations of the bass in his voice.

With a snort, Charon raised his powerful cloven legs and lifted Lucifer from the ground.

Charon looked upon him as a corpse might look upon the living.

"Dost thou know whom thou hast handled? I am the firstborn of the Kiln. I will see you remanded for this outrage! I command you to release me!"

Charon used one of his tentacles to grab his onyx staff and slammed it firmly into the ground. Lava bubbled up from the black soil beneath, as blood might ooze from a wound. Slowly Charon turned Lucifer's body so that he could see, and with his staff began to carve words into the ground.

If thou enter — you may not return.

Slowly and gently, Charon released Lucifer, stepped away from the Chief Prince and bowed.

The realization struck Lucifer that Charon sought to do him no harm but only to protect him.

"So I am to understand that if I were to enter I would not be allowed to exit?'

The cowled figure nodded.

"Very well then, creature. If thou did not unhand me, my wrath would thou hast incurred. I am he who has walked on the very stones that created thee. If I were to grace your presence again and my commands are not obeyed, know that your ruin will not be far behind."

Charon stood mute before the Chief Prince, unmoved.

"This is not over," said Lucifer.

Lucifer turned to walk away and enveloped himself as a chameleon might camouflage into its background. Lucifer lifted into the sky to return to the mountain of God and ruminated on what had happened.

This shall not stand.

* * *

"Lucifer is all prepared," said El.

"Yes Most High. All of Heaven hath assembled themselves. Those stationed throughout creation hath received sight into the realm to see the emporium as thou hast commanded."

"Well done my good and faithful servant, well done. Go, for the day draws quickly to a close."

"Yes, my Lord."

El commanded the Ophanim and they lifted the throne. Slowly the doors of the throne room opened and the power of the Seraphim's voices boomed into the emporium. The procession of the royal court began. The Seraphim moved first and like giant golems, they made the ground quake before them. The colossi marched towards the front of the temple and the attendants of the palace opened the doors, and cheers and celebratory music could be heard from outside. The air filled with shouts of praise and melody and Elohim began to sing in harmony with the Seraphim.

The royal court followed in rank: each in his assigned order within the procession. From the youngest to the eldest they came. Talus entered first bearing the angelic standard of the Arelim. He raised the flag of his sigil, and the sapphire light bathed the emporium in a soothing tranquil blue. There were great cheers as he showed himself. Talus waved to the crowd, and they roared their approval.

"He is Alpha and Omega; let all the heavens praise him!" said Talus.

Heaven erupted in applause. Cloven feet pounded the streets of gold and the tremors rumbled to the top of the temple steps. The power and gentleness of El represented in the making of each Arelim.

Sariel immediately followed his brother and wore his standard of purple. His race of Centaurs and Pegasi leaped, galloped, and raised their fists high into the air. Then Sariel hoisted his sigil into the air and addressed the people. "We praise the Lord according to his righteousness: sing praises to the Lord most high! All hail El Elyon, the Most High God!"

In response, all Heaven shouted the same. "All hail El Elyon, the Most High God!"

The Princes representing El's Power had started the procession and the princes who symbolized El's knowledge followed. Jerahmeel, Lord Prince of all Harada, stepped onto the platform and spoke.

"Blessed be the Lord God almighty. How great are his signs! How mighty are his wonders! His kingdom is an everlasting kingdom, and his dominion is from generation to generation. Blessed be the name of the Lord!"

"Blessed be the name of the Lord!"All shouted once.

"Blessed be the name of the Lord!" They shouted again.

Jerahmeel took the purple flag that bore the symbol of God's knowledge and his people and waved it in a circle for all to see. His linen robes of indigo and mauve glistened in the light. Amethysts and sapphires adorned his staff, which he held high aloft in the air.

The congregation of the sons of God roared. Heaven became as a stadium cheering in jubilation and convulsed in praise.

Jerahmeel took his place beside his brother Sariel. Raphael was next to come into view. His dark purple robes were etched in gold with the Elomic words for wisdom, dignity, nobility, and creativity. He hovered and waved his hands. Immediately his inkhorn, stylus, and tome of record can into view, and Raphael spoke. "Every word of God is pure: he is a shield unto them that put their trust in him, for the word of God is quick and powerful, it divides asunder soul and spirit. It is a discerner of thoughts and intents of the heart. He is Alpha and Omega, Beginning and the End. For He spoke and it was done; he commanded, and it stood fast. All hail the living word!"

"All hail the living word!" the crowd roared.

Raphael stretched forth his hand and said, "Let the invisible thing be clearly seen! For nothing is hidden from his sight!"

Suddenly the sky of Heaven teemed with Grigori. Like specters they emerged; thousands upon thousands of books filled Heaven's air. Pens and inkhorns moved on their own recording all that transpired. Like ghostly stenographers, nothing escaped the Grigori's notice and with the voice of one man, they that rarely speak spoke. "El watches over his word to perform it. All hail the living word!"

Heaven celebrated, applause filled the air, and the Arelim broke out in a spontaneous militaristic cadence.

"Power and Glory and Honor to God!" They stomped in the emporium, and their precision made the ground shake with thunder. One by one Harrada, Arelim, and the rest of the host of Heaven chanted in pandemonium at the cacophony of praise of all creation's Elohim. Their mantras muted the chants of even the mighty Seraphim.

Raphael took his place on the dais, and Gabriel entered.

The cherub had a boyish look; his blonde hair sparkled, and his robes were scarlet representing the color of conquest and royalty. He stood for all the species of Malakim and represented the omnipresence of God. His were the messengers of Heaven, and like the Grigori, they spanned the universe and ran the vision and word of El to the four corners of existence.

The Malakim were the only species allowed to create Ladders from Heaven to specific points in creation. They could move instantly between the realms, and there was nowhere they could not reach.

Gabriel held the standard of the Malakim: a pruning hook in his hand, the blade and handle encrusted wholly in ruby. He raised it high for all to see. The light of the crimson sprayed out like blood, and he spoke. "Bless the Lord, ye his angels that excel in strength, that do his commandments, hearken unto the voice of his word. Bless the Lord!"

Roars of adulation rang throughout the emporium. Angels began to throw strips of parchment. Various Malakim took their staffs and struck the ground fiercely, and crimson sparks rocketed into the air and dispersed into flowers of orange and yellow hues.

Gabriel, like those before him, settled into position and Michael strode into the podium and Heaven exploded as they chanted his name.

"Builder of Heaven!"

"Hail Archon of Zion!"

"Michael! Michael!"

Michael waved and held his peace, his cheeks flushed, embarrassed to receive such praise. *I am but a servant to El, who am I that I should receive such adulation?* He thought to himself.

Michael bowed his head in acknowledgment to the citizenry and lifted the standard of scarlet as his brother Gabriel had before him, and once more Heaven thundered approval.

The archangel of Heaven lifted his hands and motioned to quiet the excited crowd. He looked over the populous and was moved with compassion; these were all his people and friends. Harrada, Kortai, Grigori-- they all-- like him were servants of El.

Overcome by the privilege of serving so great a people and selected by El to do him honor in Heaven was simply too much, and the spirit of worship befell him. All of Heaven grew quiet, watched, and listened intently as Michael bowed his head and sang aloud.

Praise Jehovah — Lord God Almighty.

Praise Jehovah — Everlasting King

We praise your name.

We praise your name

Lord Jehovah, we praise you.

Praise Jehovah -- in his entire splendor

Praise Jehovah in all his majesty

We praise your name

We praise you.

Without prompt or sign, Elohim throughout the realm joined him in worship. Trancelike the host of Heaven lifted their voices, the harmonies of a thousand angels -- no ten times, ten thousand, thousand: melodiously echoed throughout creation.

Their notes of beatific reverence sailed, and their praise vaulted to every star, every mote of dust, and to every lily and robin, and all of Heaven and Earth swayed to worship at the choral inspiration of one cherub.

As extemporaneously as it had begun, the song slowed until nothing but the soft melody of a single voice sang.

Michael's head was bowed, his palms outstretched and his arms rose high crying while tears of appreciation glistened from his face. Softly he closed the worship with one verse that was sympathetic of all. "...we praise you."

He finished singing and with those words, Michael quietly moved aside to take his place with his brethren.

Heaven was lost deep in communion, euphoric and awash in the afterglow of worship; and no one--not even El himself: wanted to progress further.

* * *

Who but the Chief Prince may lead Heaven in song? The impudence! Lucifer looked upon the residents of Heaven and rage swelled up within him like a tumor.

Now I must wait to come before the people.

His own procession, now an afterthought to all, diminished because of the worship that Michael had unleashed.

If I advance now, I will break the spirit moving upon the congregation. My presence would seem as an intrusion, yet the longer this persists, the less my own entrance will command glory.

Lucifer folded his hands and his eyes narrowed with malice. His breath raced as the ruminations of his mind caused increased malignance towards Michael and the scene which he was helpless to stop that unfolded before him.

This was supposed to be MY moment of glory! Thoughts raced through Lucifer's mind.

Circumvented. Dishonored.

Emotions of anger and offense churned within him and Lucifer — consumed in his thoughts of self-martyrdom did not see his master motion for him to advance.

"Lucifer," said El.

My glory I will not give to another!

"Lucifer," El spoke again,

Lucifer awoke from his daydreamed flagellation of Michael.

"Yes, my Lord?"

"Lucifer, you may proceed my son."

"Yes, Lord. I apologize."

Michael and the other princes looked back at their brother curious as to the delay. Raphael whispered to his brother, "Lucifer, is everything well?"

Lucifer smiled. "Aye, brother, I just desired to stay in the thralls of worship."

Raphael smiled and replied. "Ah of course. It can be difficult to return to one's senses once lost in communion."

Indeed. Lucifer thought.

Lucifer walked towards the podium and uncloaked before all of Heaven. Free of his robes, light raced to embrace him and enshroud his perfectly formed body. His skin when not a living mirror was bronze-like with tints of red: and to look upon him was to desire him.

Lucifer arched his back and flexed his muscles, and his twelve flowing wings extracted to cover the entire rostrum.

He rose into the air and with each flap and movement; the veins of his white tentacled wings chimed in the wind.

He positioned his scales to open up his porous flesh so that he might both absorb and reflect all light simultaneously; and as a newborn sun, the mighty cherub illuminated the entire emporium.

El had not even entered the lectern to address the people, but Lucifer's visage was so bright that it was difficult to look at him. Elohim across the city covered their eyes as the colors of Lucifer's bioluminescent flesh radiated in patterns of gold, blue, and scarlet.

He breathed in the warm air of Heaven, his vocal cords and tabrets in his body animated, and music poured from his body. The sound of cornet and flute rang into the air, and Lucifer's voice thundered and made vibrate the golden street below. Each member within earshot felt the bass of his pronouncement as a physical force upon their own chest.

Lucifer was perfect in representing all the power, beauty, and wisdom of all Elohim at once, but his strength was not resident in the meager demonstration of his physical qualities.

Lucifer's physical prowess could easily rival the majority of Heaven; however, his true power was in his ability to mesmerize and blind anyone who might even look upon him.

His power to reflect light could penetrate and cause blindness even with one's eyes closed. He could bend light to project a visage so real that one would question reality itself.

His voice was so potent it could split the ground if he chose. His sway of suggestion was virtually without resistance, for he could modulate his voice to compel one to praise, and enraptured by his voice one would immediately desire him to speak more.

Between the assault of one's senses in sight and sound, he could bring any to their knees. He did not need to touch an adversary, for most could not even *approach* him. He represented the cumulative of all Elomic power, wisdom, and beauty.

He was perfect in all his ways.

Lucifer then annunciated the entrance of the King.

"Glory and honor and majesty belong to God Most High! Power and praise blessed be the name of the Lord! From everlasting to everlasting. All hail the King!"

The Lord God of Heaven then entered; concealed by the clouds of living smoke and the Shekinah that surrounded him. His visage was yet somehow clear. Bathed in light and heat, He walked to address his people and all of Heaven, and those who saw from waypoints while they remained on duty in their respective areas of the universe bowed, and prostrated themselves before the Most High God.

Lucifer became even brighter as El entered his presence and waves of light and heat pulsated in all directions: sparks of lightning arched and jumped across the emporium, and seven thunders echoed from the clouds in the sky.

"Holy, Holy, Holy!"

Lucifer flew to the Lord and with his expansive wings he perched himself above the throne. He hovered above the mercy seat and took his role as the anointed cherub that covered and affixed himself to the throne. Ophanim flew to the left and right of El, and the most High God spoke.

"Host of Heaven, on this the sixth of days; we will declare a thing never before heard. Much has gone into preparing Earth to be abode to him whom the Lord would delight to honor. Lucifer, our faithful servant has overseen its preparation and has completed the task according to our will.

Thine court was entreated as to what honor we should bestow. In their wisdom, they spoke, and we have hearkened according to all their word. We have thus made a garden of such beauty to house as a palace for him whom our soul would love.

Therefore, let us make man in our image, after our likeness: and let them have dominion over the fish of the sea and over the fowl of the air and over the cattle and over all the Earth and over every creeping thing that creepeth upon the Earth."

The Lord God then moved suddenly and instantly to the Earth, and all of Heaven saw him, but somehow, he still stood at the lectern. The angels watched as El placed his hands in the garden that Lucifer had prepared and formed a man from the dust of the ground.

Like the many times of formation in the Kiln, he shaped and cut away, and molded until bone was formed. Carefully El made hands, arms, and two legs, and he fashioned sinew and placed flesh upon the man.

The man lay motionless and still, and El neither gave it wings that it might fly nor did he fashion the man's flesh after the flesh of Elohim, but a light brown thin layer of porous soft tissue did he weave as skin.

El knelt over to his new creation and breathed into its nostrils the breath of Life: and the man became a living soul. Heaven looked on in astonishment, and everyone erupted in a horde of cheers.

Lucifer looked upon the man silently from atop the throne of the Most High. He glared scornfully upon this new rival in bitter silence.

Murmur Not Among Yourselves

Day Six

Lucifer watched from atop the throne and looked on in spite as the mud creature El had named 'man' stood and reached up to embrace the King of the Universe. El hugged the man and then softly kissed him on his forehead.

Lucifer looked down upon the legions of Elohim before him perched from a vantage point that none other but he possessed. Gazing from the Third Heaven into the totality of all realms Lucifer eyed his people; watching as they celebrated in adulation over El's creation of the man.

Lucifer beamed approvingly at them who were as countless as the stars. Then he eyed the man and saw his frailty and the fawning that El spent upon his new creation. Contempt grew as pus within him, and his thoughts teemed with bile towards his maker. Lucifer noted that the people applauded a creature that neither flew nor possessed the power of Arelim, the voice of the Draco, but was made from the dust of the Earth. When he saw the man and his own people cheering in senseless applause, Lucifer noted that none thought for themselves.

A multitude of bleating sheep you are: huddled and flocked together. Like the wheat fields on Earth, as chaff carried aloft with the breeze. Ah, my people, alas thou art blind to the truth, nor do you perceive, but lost in the mesmerizing bask of worship to El. If only thou might see what I see. Then would you be loosed from His chain.

Lucifer marveled at their docility: the Elohim simply obeyed, never questioned, and now they stood baying in applause at a creature beneath them in beauty.

Is this how El sees us?

Lucifer basked in his perch above the throne. All of creation seemed as a quilt spread out before him and all realities appeared at once. He reveled in the sense of knowledge. It was intoxicating.

Swallowed in his pride, Lucifer looked upon the people: proud that he alone could see the truth that they truly were all slaves to the whims of the Almighty. Sadness began to flood over him.

Sadness that El had created a source of labor to carry out his dictates, sad that his people were relegated to serve this 'greatest creation'. Angry that El would in his selfishness hold back such knowledge. Lucifer then looked upon El and despised him. His countenance changed towards his maker while he questioned the goodness of God and ruminated with thought after thought in his mind until one seeded itself above all others. *I will be God.*

Lucifer continued to look upon El, and El's continued fawning over the man gnawed at him.

Lucifer then looked upon the man. He was indeed beautiful: soft not hard like the diamond and scales of himself. The man, however, was limited, mortal even.

Lucifer's mind reeled with unbelief and disgust. *Surely, El would not turn over such a realm as Earth over to a creature, which was of mud and clay. No true King should behave in such a way! This — this is the creature that should bear El's image and likeness?*

Lucifer looked upon El, and the form that he had despised for so long revealed itself to him. He attempted to rid himself of the image, yet the vision would not cease. Like a persistent apparition, he saw El through the veil of fog.

The servant looked upon his master and disgust began to fill him. *This represents El's true form*?

All of Heaven watched as God personally created two trees from the rich soil: one that released the knowledge of good and evil and a companion tree of eternal life. Each was set in the midst of the garden. The Lord then gave the man instructions concerning the trees and of what he could eat.

Then the Lord God brought every beast of the field and every fowl of the air unto Adam to see what he would call them, and whatsoever Adam called every living creature that was the name thereof.

Adam then gave names to all cattle, to the fowl of the air, and to every beast of the field.

Lucifer became incensed.

Adam bestowed on every creature a name, and with each act of naming: God further sealed man's dominion over them. For Heaven's code states that he who names a thing defines and administers the thing. Lucifer observed as man steadily and with little effort gave each creature a name, which defined it.

The Lord saw that there was no mate for the Adam and said, "It is not good that the man should be alone; I will make him a help meet for him."

The Lord God then caused a deep sleep to fall upon Adam, and he slept. Then He took one of his ribs and closed up the flesh thereof.

And the rib, which the Lord God had taken from man, made He a woman and brought her unto the man. And Adam said, "This is now bone of my bones, and flesh of my flesh: she shall be called Woman because she was taken out of Man."

The Lord was pleased with the form of them, and the Shekinah moved from El and hovered over the man and the woman. The brightness of his glory covered them that they shown as the stars, and the shawl of living light covered their face and skin, and they glowed even as the Lord.

They were both naked, the man and his wife, and were not ashamed. And the Lord walked in the cool of the day with the man and the woman and fellowshipped with them, and they with him.

Moreover, Lucifer made note of the name that Adam had named the white, docile creature that nauseated him, the creature that in Lucifer's mind was the identical image of El.

He pronounced the word aloud to hear it for himself, speaking it into the air. He now had a name to assign to his image of El, a designation that symbolized all the weakness he now came to despise in his creator. There was only one word, which perfectly described his repugnance: *Lamb.*

* * *

El ceased from talking with the man and his companion, and as the hours marched onward on Earth mere seconds passed in Heaven, and El immediately continued to address the congregation.

"Behold the pinnacle of our creation. For with great thought have plans been laid to secure man's future. Know that we shall accomplish all our will. Therefore, we will watch over his coming and his going.

Thou great Elohim birthed from the fires of our Kiln, shall also serve to aid man to understand all things. As we have taught thee, go to and teach thou Adam and his seed that he might have dominion."

El turned to enter the temple again; smoke, lightning, and thunder echoed in his steps. Lucifer immediately lifted off the throne and covered El's backside and the Ophanim propelled the throne back into the great hall of Mt. Zion.

As El departed, Lucifer's own glory diminished, yet he continued to pronounce the majesty of God, and Heaven rang with cheers of, "Praise the Lord! Praise the Lord!"

Slowly, each member of the royal court left the dais; from the eldest to the youngest until only the seraphim were all that were left to march into the great hall. Their, "HOLY, HOLY, HOLY" echoed across the emporium. When all parties left, Lucifer alone stood on the rostrum and watched the crowd as they dispersed.

Lucifer scratched at the burning that ached in his chest and his mind raced with just one thought: *Thou must decrease that I might increase.*

* * *

Lucifer settled into the center hall of Athor prepared to address the elders of the city. He stood behind the raised platform so that he could adequately see all the participants. The elders of Athor slowly made their way into the chamber hall.

The room was circular with seats made of white marble. The floor was lapis lazuli, and the ceiling was gold etched in silver with cursive angelic script, which pronounced the glory of El. The walls were quartz and reflected the light, not just of the noonday sun but also of Lucifer himself, who stood high in the center of the chamber surrounded by the marble stadium seats.

In the course of time, all sat and Lucifer began to speak.

"Fellow Sons of God — I as Chief Prince and Archon of Earth have asked you here that I might assign to you the tasks necessary to complete our mission to instruct the humans. We have...."

Lucifer was interrupted by Srosh, one of his fellow Draco. He was tall and muscular; his species shimmered in scales of bluish silver. His blonde hair draped his shoulders as he raised his serpentine-like body for attention.

"My pardon, Chief Prince, but perhaps you would enlighten the elders on the rumors which circulate Athor, for much has been made of Apollyon and his deeds."

"And what would you know Srosh that has not already been reported?"

"Chief Prince, is it true that El has closed the mouth of the Kiln? Reports from Heaven say that a living mountain of ash and fire now draws power from that which is our womb. Is this so?"

Lucifer eyed the crowd. They too fastened their eyes on him, fixated and waiting on his every word.

"That which thou hast heard is true. There is a mount of breathing rock tied to the Kiln itself and which lives off the flesh of Elohim."

Gasps echoed across the room. Mouths dropped. Whispers circulated within the center hall.

"My Lord, then are we to be no more? Is this the end of the Kilnborn? Will there be no more stones to fire our ranks?"

Lucifer pondered the words and turned them over in his mind. *Will there be no more stones--is this the end of the Kilnborn?*

Another angel arose to speak. "My Lord, is it true that Apollyon now lives in punishment within the belly of this mountain?"

Then another, "And what of this dark creature reported at the mouth of the new mount? What is he? He does not present as other Elohim"

"Master..."

"My Lord Prince..."

"I have a question..."

Lucifer found himself suddenly barraged with demands from all fronts. Shouts of angels quickly filled the chamber, each vying and clamoring for attention, all in query. Lucifer looked upon his people and pity welled up within him, for they were as sheep with no shepherd.

Does El even understand what he has done? He thought.

Lucifer's Heartstone pained him, and he clutched and scratched at his chest for relief. He staggered as the pain became more intense. He looked up at the crowd that now argued amongst themselves and spoke to regain order. "Silence!" he roared.

Immediately, the room fell mute as the power of Lucifer's deep voice shook the ground, and the south quartz wall cracked. However, Srosh a fellow Draco did not move. He did not cow upon Lucifer's rebuke. Like all Draco, he was regal in stature and able to project his own voice. Despite the command of his Chief Prince, Srosh spoke the mind of many within the room.

"Are we to be servants Lucifer, forced to serve a creature of mud and clay?" Srosh's statement emboldened another to speak.

"I do not wish to serve."

"Free Apollyon," cried an Arelim.

An Issi elder immediately retorted, "Let him burn within the mountain!"

Lucifer frowned; his brow tightened in anger. Anger, that El has placed him in such a position; anger that he would have to answer for his creator. Anger that despite all his desire to give an answer, he had none with which he could defend his Lord's actions.

Anger — that was unleashed.

Once more Lucifer spoke, but spoke with such force that the floor opened its mouth, and Srosh and several of the assembled elders cried for help and struggled to find release from the fissure, which now raced across the floor. Panic quickly ensued, and the Chief Prince stretched his wings and lifted himself from the ground to address his audience.

"It is true that the Kiln now fuels Hell's belly and also true that Apollyon now lies trapped therein. It is true that El hast made Earth, home to the humans: a home that *you* have carefully maintained and assisted in its very fashion."

"Was it not *you* who ferried flora across the world to populate the garden that the humans now occupy? Was it not *you* who mined the floor of Earth to encase Athor in gold and glass: its beauty and illumination a floodlight in the night sky? Its luminance seen even from the second heaven of Sol?"

"Aye," said Lucifer. "It is true that El hast made a creature of such hunger that it feeds off the very life of Elohim, and lo, within the span of one day, we see two abominations. One — a guardian to keep our brother imprisoned. And two, a creature so beneath us as to be made from El's spittle and the mud that *we* walk upon. Yet were *we* given the title to anything? No. We serve."

"We praise a master who rewards us not according to our works nor celebrates our accomplishments. Nay my brethren, *our* reward is clear. *We* will no longer be fashioned to seed the heavens."

Lucifer looked each in the eye probingly. “No longer will the Kiln burn to fire *our* creation." Lucifer pointed hard at his chest repeatedly. "Nay, the Kiln now burns to fire *our* prison! It exists to remind us that those who refuse to serve will burn therein!”

“*I*,” said Lucifer pointing again at his chest, “Am Chief Prince, Lord Lucifer Draco, and First Kilnborn of all Elohim. I alone walk upon the Stones of Fire. I will not serve, and I will not burn. I pledge to free our brother Apollyon!

For I will ascend into Heaven.

I will exalt my throne above the stars of God.

I will sit upon the mount of the congregation, in the sides of the north.

I will ascend above the heights of the clouds.

I will be like the most High!”

* * *

Raphael walked into the throne room, sat before his king, and looked at the enormous book within his hands, which contained all the information the Lord El had requested.

“My Lord, the task wherewith I have been charged is complete. I have tallied all as thou hast commanded.”

El looked upon Raphael and smiled, “And what did your examination find, my son?”

Raphael’s face became angst-ridden. His heart and mind burdened by what he knew, knowledge he must now dispense to the Lord. Never had he given the Lord a negative report. Now he must be the first Elohim to broach the subject of treason with his king.

“My Lord, your instruction was to find all instances of thought, conduct, and or speech similar to Abaddon’s. To bring to you a concise volume that lists all Elohim and the result of my findings.”

El saw that Raphael’s lip tightened and that the cherubim struggled to choke back tears.

“Raphael, speak my son, for there is nothing covered that shall not be revealed and hidden that shall not be made known. Fear not.”

Raphael straightened himself, wiped his eyes, cleared his throat, and spoke as directed.

“Lord, of the host of Heaven there is a number whose mind is pure and whose fealty my King can command without question. Those whose names are written therein are not so. They number almost a third of Heaven. Those who dissent to thy rule speak of displeasure with Abaddon’s sentence, the existence of Hell, or take issue with relations with the humans. They say that the humans are not Kilnborn, not of the Stones of Fire. There are some who are displeased to serve a creature of mud and clay.”

“And what of the Grigori?” asked El.

"My God, again the Grigori as a whole are with thee my king, yet it pains me to report that all are not so. I regret that I have yet to determine the extent to which my own kind has departed from the way."

"I do know that entries of several tomes have made me concerned. There are records, which seem to do more than simply state the observations that the Grigori have heard or seen. I have found several Grigori whose records have added commentary to their accounts. Some no longer seem content to only document the observations of their charge but to annotate as well."

Raphael looked away from the Lord and paused.

"Continue, do not hold back that which thou hast found," said El.

"I have traced the genesis of this corruption my king. Moreover, I am afraid that one of the Lumazi is the seed to the fruit from which all springs. In a review of which tomes no longer hold true, they point back to one Grigori. Lilith and his tomes are no longer valid, thus out of the mouth of two or three must they now be established. In a review of the tome of Lilith on the Chief Prince, I have seen an entry that has given me pause.

Lilith's entry was not journaled in accordance with Grigoric law, but because the Grigori are abundant in number; another was in proximity at the time and reveals an inconsistency.

"I believe this entry is the accurate one my Lord, and that which I present now to thy light: the copy of which I hold in my hand. Its record compels me to further investigate any new additions in Lilith's accord of Lucifer."

"And the entry; what did it contain my son?"

Raphael tossed the book into the air, and the voluminous work stood vertically as if coming to attention. The manuscript separated into cover and pages; its sheets flew across the throne, and the pages assembled themselves so that the recorded journal entry was chronologically on top.

Light glowed on the first page. It floated higher to touch the ceiling and the image of Lucifer and Lilith walking in the Garden of Eden appeared. A Grigori assigned to watch a flock of sheep observed the occurrence and documented a portion of the unauthorized conversation.

"And what is thy desire, Chief Prince? What would satisfy you?"

Lucifer looked skyward. His eyes aimed upward as if he gazed directly at God and Raphael.

"That I might ascend into Heaven; that mine throne would be exalted above the stars of God.

That I would sit also upon the mount of the congregation, in the sides of the north: To ascend above the heights of the clouds..."

The image then dissipated, and the mammoth book flared with a flash of white light, reassembled itself, and then fell with a loud thump to the floor.

El stood, and Raphael kneeled, silently waiting on any command from his Lord. Then El spoke. "Go, Raphael. Summon thy brothers as there is much to do, the seventh day approaches, and I must take rest from all my labor."

"Yes, my Lord." Raphael bowed, picked up the book, and turned to walk away. Leaving the sanctuary through one of the many side chambers, Raphael returned to his home within the mountain itself. He walked through the corridor of Mt. Zion and entered the Great Hall of Annals.

He passed by multiple stacks and shelves of records and books until he came to a desk, sat, and placed the completed tome he had just recently finished down; it hit the stone slab of the desk with a thud.

He looked over and noticed that Lucifer's tome was still recording. New information was penned in angelic script. The letters were in flames, and Raphael's eyes fixated on one passage that leaped off the page.

Raphael's eyes grew wide and his mouth opened, but his tongue could not form words.

His mind raced with thoughts and then froze in disbelief and panic, as he lifted the book and reread each new passage. Hope dashed away as he read, and the horrible truth dawned on him with each sentence, words that he knew somehow would forever change creation.

'I will be like the most High.'

* * *

"But my Lord, you cannot possibly hope to defeat El! El is Alpha! He is Omega. We are but Kilnborne. He is Author of all!"

The Chamber hall was raucous, for the elders could not believe their ears.

"Treason!" said one.

"Blasphemy!" said another

"What you say is not possible!"

"Defeat El — can such a thing be done?"

Lucifer looked upon his brethren and spoke. "Thou hast been chosen above all Elohim to serve me. I have selected you all. You alone have raised Athor from the dust. Consider now my words. *El,* not *I,* has shown himself to be traitor."

"Traitor to all Elohim; for he has created us that we might be slaves to another. If we were but servants to El, I would serve happily. However, we are Kilnborn. Are we to teach one who knows not the majesty of those from whom they even learn? Are we to serve those whose sight reaches not into the Third Heaven? Who tread the ground, but possess not the power to fly amongst the stars?"

"I say nay. El is no longer worthy of rule. He fawns over the man as he walks with him during the day. He has withheld from us and knowingly done so. Why are the granaries expanded? Why hast Jerusalem itself been enlarged? Would he elevate the humans to displace us? Soon will we not have even a home in Heaven? Why doth this Earth *not* bring forth manna? Why? Because *we* were not in His mind when it was made. Indeed, we have been an afterthought."

Many in the room nodded in agreement.

Lucifer continued, "Of a surety El is mighty. He cannot be destroyed through strength of arms."

Tiriel, an Issi, and an elder, of the rivers, rose to speak. "You speak the truth. El cannot be defeated, yet I have no pleasure in serving the humans. How then would *you,* Chief Prince, bring down God?"

The room grew quiet, and all eyes turned to Lucifer and listened expectantly for his reply. "El cannot be defeated by sheer power. However, power is not necessary to defeat El. The throne cannot be taken by force. It must be freely surrendered. El will abdicate it willingly."

Kaspiel rose and waved his hand angrily and in disbelief.

"You are mad Lucifer!" he said.

"Am I?" replied Lucifer. "What is the *greater* madness Kaspiel? To serve a God who seeks to enslave us for eternity and sing happily for the privilege? Is it mad to desire and fight for one's freedom? Am I mad that I refuse to bow to a creature of mud and clay?"

Another elder arose and spoke, "Lucifer, you have not yet stated how you would accomplish what you purport. Words alone will not the overthrow of El achieve."

"I indeed have a plan," said Lucifer, "but it cannot be accomplished alone. If thou be with El then go, and I will not think the less of you. However, if thou would hear my plan, I will offer a pledge of my ability to accomplish my will. Stay and I shall say on."

Each elder in the room looked at the other. Lucifer also looked about the hall. His eyes scanned to see which of his elders might leave. Everyone contemplated if he should be the first to depart. Each knew that something special was taking place, and all wondered if they were destined to herald freedom for their race.

Excitement began to fill the air with a palpable sense that the destiny of their species was at hand. Then Tiamat, an angel from Lucifer's own species Draco stood to speak. He was silver and grey hair ran down the whole of his snake-like back.

"Say on, Chief Prince. We would hear thee on this matter. What proof would you offer this assembly that we might show thee fealty as God?"

Lucifer smiled, looked upon his brethren, and spoke.

"I will brave Hell's maw, release Apollyon, and convey him safe before you. If I return with him, you will alter your sigil in thy flesh, bear my seal, and shall serve me. You will then be my people, and I will be your God."

Tiamat looked around the room, and the other elders nodded.

"We will do as thou hast said. Yet Chief Prince...what if you fail?"

Lucifer looked upon them all and spoke with fire in his eyes.

"Then if I perish—I perish."

* * *

Ashtaroth waited for his master near the waypoint of Argoth. Lucifer's Ladder materialized, and he strutted off the platform. Ashtaroth took note that his master's countenance was serious even for him.

"My Lord Prince, welcome home."

"Thank you, Astarte. You are my most trusted servant, and in the days of ahead, I will lean on your faithfulness to accomplish a task of great importance."

I am at your service my Prince," he said.

Lucifer and Ashtaroth made their way to his home.

"Astarte how go the repairs to my estate?"

"I expect them to be complete upon our return my Prince."

"Well done my friend, well done. When all this is over, I will see that you are greatly rewarded."

"I am ever grateful, Chief Prince. You honor me."

Lucifer entered his home through the great doors and made his way upstairs while Ashtaroth saw to matters elsewhere in the mansion.

Lucifer stood outside his bedroom door and looked at the two angels sent by Michael to repair his palatial bedroom.

"How are you coming with the repairs?" Lucifer inquired.

One of the two Arelim builders turned to the Chief Prince to respond.

"Well, we are almost done, Lord Prince. We should be off the premises shortly. If I may be so bold sire, it grieves me that an Issi would be the cause of such destruction. It never fails that an Arelim must clean up their mess."

Lucifer looked curiously at the worker. "Elaborate."

"Well sire, it's not that we don't appreciate and respect the Issi. We just know that one such as yourself should have builders around you, not swift-tongued angels who don't know their place."

Lucifer stroked his small beard. "So you disapprove of Ashtaroth an Issi, as my attendant?"

"I pray that my Lord would not be angry with me. It is not our place to judge. However, all one need do is look at thine wall, my Prince. In the very repairs that we make, your answer lies therein."

Lucifer chuckled. "*My* understanding of events is that Apollyon was bested by Ashtaroth."

Both workers stopped, looked at each other and one walked slowly towards Lucifer. "Chief Prince, an Issi: even one who serves within thine house — can never best an Arelim. If Apollyon was bested, it was through guile, not strength of arms."

Lucifer stood unmoved. The Arelim was strong and imposing in demeanor and like all his kind possessed muscular arms, cloven feet, and a bull's head.

Just like all his ilk, Lucifer thought.

Lucifer was not intimidated. He was the Chief Prince, and he walked on the Stones of Fire. He moved forward, but the Arelim stood his ground.

"Elohim do not harm other Elohim, and on the day such were to occur, my wrath would most assuredly ensue on the angel who would lift up his hand against another. Am I understood?"

The Arelim stepped back, "My apologies Chief Prince. I meant no disrespect..."

Ashtaroth entered the chamber and spoke, "My Lord your presence is requested by the court. El plans a repast for the council and..."

Both Arelim workers spread their wings, and the hair on their backs raised as their bodies prepared themselves for battle.

Ashtaroth's stance became poised for defense, and the two angelic species warily eyed one another. The Arelim looked with loathing at Ashtaroth; each dropped their tools and clenched their fists, their wings unfurled and grew tense ready to leap.

Lucifer spoke, "Ashtaroth, you will accompany me to the mount. As for the two of you, your work here is complete. Know that your Chief Prince is pleased. You may leave my presence now."

Lucifer sat down at his desk and began to write within his journal and without looking at the two workers or Ashtaroth, spoke.

"And my *wrath* would assuredly ensue on the angel who lifted up his hand against another."

The two workers relaxed, bowed to the Chief Prince, and stepped out of the room, scowling at Ashtaroth as they left. Lucifer and Ashtaroth heard them make their way downstairs and out the front door.

Ashtaroth relaxed and his color returned to him.

"My apologies Chief Prince, the Arelim are a most brutish lot. They know not the subtleties of protocol. I fear that tensions have risen since the altercation between Apollyon and myself. There is a growing division between the Issi and Arelim. Our exchange, I am afraid, has only inflamed contention over his person and his sentence. Some believe that I too should have been thrown into Hell for my participation with Apollyon. I fear that our altercation is a sore point between our two races. My mere presence incites tension in Heaven's midst."

Lucifer stroked his chin and then spoke. "Indeed, but this may be used to my profit," Lucifer said.

"My Lord?" said Ashtaroth confused.

"Ashtaroth, I have changed my mind. I will go alone to the mount. You will assemble the most trusted and loyal of my household, and thou and thy company shall leave for Earth. Await me in the palace, and I shall give you understanding of my will."

"As you command my prince." Ashtaroth turned to leave but then paused and turned to speak. "Thank you, my Lord."

Lucifer turned around to face his servant: curious for the expression of gratitude.

"Thank you Chief Prince for calling me by my name," explained Ashtaroth.

Lucifer smiled. "I have always loved you, my friend. You have faithfully served me."

Ashtaroth bowed, turned then left the room. Lucifer closed the bedroom door behind him and looked out the window at the city of angels beneath him. His brow wrinkled, for the path that he was about to take weighed heavily upon him.

Lilith uncloaked behind him and spoke. "He really is quite slow isn't he?"

Lucifer grinned then replied. "He is, yet he is faithful. His obedience is all that is necessary for my purpose." Lucifer continued to look upon the throng of Heaven's populace as they scurried to duties unknown.

"He will serve as will all the rest. But Grigori this would I know..." Lucifer turned to face his watcher. "Are you with me or for mine adversaries?"

Lilith bowed to the Chief Prince.

"You have been a charge most intriguing, Lucifer Draco. Thou sealest up the sum, full of wisdom, and perfect in beauty. If thou can indeed walk through hell-fire and steal Apollyon away to defy El's prison, to walk within the maw and come out again —I would sit watch over thee to see what the end shall be.

"By now Raphael hast learned of my entries, for your actions have become more *difficult* to document without a level of bias on my part." "Aye," said Lilith, "I shall be he which chronicles thy work."

"Thou art wise Lilith," Lucifer said.

"Nay, Chief Prince. My wisdom hast yet to be found in this decision. What I am is an angel who hast violated Grigoric law. Your complicity hast become my own. I simply rise and fall on thy doings, but I must admit, to cease to be under the heel of Raphael's dictums — that I will most enjoy."

"Then I bequeath to you Lilith his position upon my ascension to the throne. All Grigori then shall call *thee* Lord Prince."

Lilith bowed. "I am thine to command."

"Then let us go; El and my brethren await me. Let us not tarry for there is much to do. A kingdom overthrown I must begin."

Choose ye this day whom ye shall serve

End of day Six.

The Lumazi had gathered for fellowship over a meal. El desired to celebrate the working of the past six days and to share the company of his sons. It was not often that all seven princes gathered with El. The work of creation had taxed them all, and El was now prepared to take his rest, a day when the Holy One of the universe would cease from all his labors.

Raphael had asked the Lord God about his *resting*. El replied, "There is a pattern that must be set, my son." El would not elaborate more.

The banquet hall was immense, with a long circular table set in the midst of the room. Servers attended to every need as an Elohim of a different race waited on each prince. Michael often grew extremely conscientious when others doted upon him. He was the Archon of Heaven and constantly looking to see how he might best benefit El and all of Heaven. He was a servant and not accustomed to pampering. Gabriel loved to engage in conversation. It took constant reproofs from El to keep him seated and not to assist the attendants in the preparation rooms. Both Talus and Sariel salivated over the incoming meal, yet when Talus eyed Sariel served by an Arelim, he frowned, but both Talus and Sariel managed to do nothing to provoke El to speak disapprovingly to them.

Jerahmeel was, of course, at home. He loved fellowship, and he loved the brethren. His unprovoked laughs were contagious, and he could infect others with his joviality. For no apparent reason, one would find himself spontaneously laughing uncontrollably. Jerahmeel was a praiser. He loved to sing, whether Heaven wanted to hear him or not, and sing Jerahmeel did, especially a song to honor El's design of creation.

Soon the banquet hall was festive with laughter and song.

Finally, Jerahmeel settled down enough to realize that his plate was empty.

"Are you going to eat that?" he asked Lucifer.

Lucifer shook his head and slid his plate to his brother.

Jerahmeel happily took the plate and gleefully filled his mouth, an orifice that never seemed to close.

Talus was quick to remind him that his own plate of manna seemed mysteriously diminished by one loaf.

El sat quietly at the table.

Michael noticed that both Lucifer and El had not eaten and that each was eerily hushed. El had his hands folded and his eyes closed; he seemed to be listening to each of his sons with a smile on his face.

El exhaled, opened his eyes, and spoke.

"I will miss these meals."

Everyone around the table looked at him perplexed.

Gabriel asked him, "Lord, what do you mean?"

El somberly looked at each of his seven sons, these beings of power and light. Longingly, he gazed upon them and smiled, but his demeanor changed as a look of seriousness appeared as he glanced down and spoke.

"One of you will betray us all."

Silence engulfed the room

Lucifer shifted nervously in his seat.

Once again, El had introduced a new word to everyone. With blank stares and shrugged shoulders, each looked at one another for answers. When they all looked at Michael, he realized that the group had quietly drafted him to speak the question that they all were too timid to ask.

"What is '*betrayal*' Lord?" asked Michael.

El looked at them and said. "I have many things to say to you, but you are not able to bear them right now. In time, all will be revealed. Although you do not know what I do now, you will know later. The one with whom I share the sop of my cup, he will betray us."

El slowly dipped his bread into his cup and passed it to Lucifer.

Lucifer stared quietly at it and then stared at El.

Each prince in the room watched as El and the Chief Prince looked upon each other. Silence stood between them. El looked at Lucifer, smiled lovingly, and seemed to communicate instructions to the Chief Prince as he had done so many times before.

Lucifer looked away from El and rose from the table. He quickly headed towards the door. Michael ran to catch up to his brother.

"Lucifer, where are you going?"

Lucifer took Michael by the hand, hugged him, and whispered into his ear. "Where I go you cannot follow." And a tear ran down Lucifer's eye.

"Lucifer...," said El.

Lucifer turned to gaze upon his Lord before leaving.

"What thou doest," El paused. "Do quickly."

Lucifer nodded in acknowledgment and glanced at his brothers. He stared at each one's face, released Michael, and turned to walk away.

"Lucifer?" Michael cried.

Lucifer paused momentarily; clenched his fists, closed his eyes, and contorted his tear-stricken face, but he did not turn. He gritted his teeth and continued with a quickened pace down the marble corridor.

"Lucifer please...," begged Michael. But his brother continued to ignore him. He lifted himself into the air and quickly flew away.

Michael stared at his brother and watched him disappear; confusion gripped him. He spun around to look at El, his eyes pleading for an explanation.

El stood with none.

All immediately stood as well, and El spoke.

"Come ye have much to do."

"Lord, the meal is not yet finished," said Jerahmeel.

"Aye, but unless we depart, he who is revealed will not reveal himself, and so that all might be made known. I must leave you for a season. Fear not; I will not leave you comfortless. Michael has charge during our Sabbath for war will be unleashed upon you soon."

"Lord?"

"Yes, Michael?"

"What is '*war*'?"

"You shall find out soon my son."

* * *

Lucifer walked with a hurried pace and quickly left the banquet room. Attendants of the temple bowed in respect as he passed a corridor and went into the throne room. He gazed at the ceiling of onyx, which showed stars, galaxies, and all the planets of the celestial universe.

When next I enter this chamber, this shall all be mine.

He walked towards the right side of the throne and to the latticed gold doors of the Kiln. He could feel the heat emanating from inside. Lucifer turned the diamond handle to the large vault and entered the Kiln.

Dry air rushed towards his face and the temperature changed immediately from room temperature to boiling as Lucifer made his way into the chamber. He walked down a small corridor that erupted in flames. He had been this way before. Only those empowered by El to walk this hall could survive it. As he entered the chamber the stones stood before him and laid spread out at his feet.

Once more Lucifer walked amidst the Stones of Fire. They called to him, each beckoning to *be*. He had been here countless times before. The sentient stones knew him. They welcomed him, calling out to him. They made a hum against the backdrop of the roar of the great furnace. White-hot flames jetted in front of him. The heat of the whole universe trapped in one room: the source of Hell's fire.

Lucifer, however, was not here this day to assist El in the creation of another Elohim. No, he was here for one purpose only: to cross the long umbilical cord of fire and brimstone that stretched from the Kiln to the living mountain of Hell.

Lucifer stood to hear the songs and opened the pores of his flesh. The flame soothed him, and he sang with the stones as he basked in the heat of the fire. Smiling, he looked at the stone in the center of the room, a gemstone of much larger substance; he listened. For its song was different from all others. Temptation gripped him to touch it, but he had not come here to partake in the stone's song—not yet.

Soon, he said to himself.

He saw the wall still fresh with the imprint of Charon's frame. Lucifer looked down at the steaming floor and saw the manacled tendrils of Charon's footsteps.

A trail, Lucifer thought.

To find Apollyon would require him to walk a path of heat and flame, to follow the path of Charon, and to traverse a path through Hell.

Determined, Lucifer looked on. The entry to Hell opened and closed, pulsating like the beating of a human heart. The sulfuric air scorched lung and eye. Lucifer hardened into his Draconian form and closed the pores in his flesh.

Hell was a living prison designed to feed off the flesh of Elohim. A thought that caused Lucifer to take pause. He stared at the orifice and realized how his task would reverberate throughout Heaven.

The opening widened and Lucifer steeled himself and stepped through.

Lucifer ducked his head and followed the footsteps left by Charon through the moist heated bile of Hell's umbilical. The hotness of the channel grew more intense as he walked. The umbilical itself served as an exhaust or as a flume with roasting wave after wave of intense heat.

Lucifer began to grow increasingly uncomfortable: he had walked in the Kiln with God and had survived. Now he stood within the twisted veins and arteries of Hell's furnace. Gooey liquid slowly oozed from the ceiling as Lucifer trekked ever deeper toward the creature's belly.

Finally, he thought. Lucifer saw, at last, the entrance to the mountain. He was horrified. "What abomination is this?" he said to himself.

At the end of the channel, he could see rows of razor-sharp teeth. Flames licked ever higher, for the room beyond the teeth was vast. Geysers of sulfuric acid ejected from the walls and floors. Eyes were sprawled on the mountain's floor. Moreover, many mouths lined the walls, each filled with rows of razor-sharp teeth. The openings salivated and waited for any morsel, any opportunity to engorge on Elomic flesh. Lucifer quickly realized that the umbilical was simply one mouth, a mouth that he attempted to exit.

Where does each opening lead? He wondered.

Heated streams of lava coiled a membranous skin of ash and smoke. It became increasingly evident that within the craggy outer crust of the mount, Hell was a creature of flesh.

Lucifer cautiously walked towards the opening, and the fluid of the chamber became more thick and sticky as he approached. He walked towards the razor-sharp teeth and slid his serpentine body through the various rows. Pain immediately befell him; the teeth sliced into his diamond flesh as a razor would slice through paper.

The Prince of Angels screamed in pain. The teeth of the maw clawed at him ripping clothing and dug deeper into his skin.

Teeth of diamonds how is this possible? He thought.

More agony.

Few among the Elohim had experienced such a sensation: the termination of life. Saesheal was the first. Lucifer began to understand the allure and intoxication to take life. Abaddon had stumbled upon this level of forbidden knowledge that El sought to deny them. Lucifer would have this secret as well; he would know the knowledge of life and death.

Here within the veins of Hell, Hell tutored Lucifer that death was power. The ability to *both* create and destroy was strength. Here in the hungry clutches of teeth and volcanic gums, where brimstone spittle drenched his face: Lucifer understood the pleasure of Apollyon's fascination with destruction.

Yet he was not Apollyon, and he refused to bow to destruction this day. His was the feet that walked on the very stones that powered the Kiln. Moreover, his would be the feet that would walk through the colon of Hell.

Lucifer called upon the power of his vocal cords and the tabrets and percussion instruments buried in the soles of his feet. Lucifer roared and slammed his feet into the umbilical floor. The sonic waves dispersed in all directions and rippled towards the row of teeth that barred his path. The tone of Lucifer's pitch assaulted the creature's mouth, and the teeth shattered as glass against the frequency of a tuning fork.

Injured but undaunted, Lucifer continued to track the path of Charon, deeper into the bowels of a creature that fueled itself on the digestion of angels.

Lucifer walked on the floor of Hell. His feet burned, and smoke rose as he took each step forward. The floor moved underneath him as lava licked at his soles.

Hell had become aware of his presence, alerted to this strange menace.

As a body struggles to fight a virus, Hell unleashed its brimstone antibodies to fight off this intruder. The immune system of a living mountain unleashed to do battle with the First of Angels.

They came without warning, and they came without concern for title or respect for protocol: centipedes of lava and brimstone hissed as they moved and slowly inched their way to consume the First of Angels.

Lucifer stepped back, for the eyes in the floor followed his every step. Each mouth within the walls of Hell snapped and gnashed teeth and waited to snatch a bite from his flesh, an Elohim whose taste was rife with lusciousness.

Lucifer was quick and moved speedily around the creatures. Soon more appeared, Hell increasingly aware of this contagion. With each step, he took; another creature of volcanic bile appeared, ready to devour him.

One step, a new creature formed from the floor. Two steps forward and two creatures appeared. Each squished eye of the floor formed into a creature ready to consume. Lucifer stopped moving. Each creature moved and hissed as they converged on his position, but when he stood still, no new creatures formed.

Aha, so they are activated by my steps!

Lucifer lifted himself from the floor out of reach of the mindless creatures. Their movement stopped and the eyes melted back into the fiery floor.

Lucifer flew through ash and smoke careful to avoid the ceiling or walls: and as he made his way through the fiery digestive tract, he heard screams. Lucifer followed the anguished cries until he exited the antechamber and entered a room filled with tendrils that crisscrossed the entire room.

He hovered just outside the lattice of flame and acidic goo and stared to behold Apollyon centered within a netting of pain, caught like a fly within a web.

Tendrils of white-hot magma and sulfuric acid shackled his ankles and wrists while vines of molten lava filled his mouth: he struggled to breathe. Bile secreted from his ears and dribbled down the side of his face to his shoulders. Chain link impressions covered his chest and the back of His chest was lacerated, leaving his flesh exposed. His wings were stretched and ripped, spread wide like an etymological specimen, and pierced with needle-like stingers as a butterfly mounted for display.

And the mountain fed.

Lucifer watched as the eternal life force of the Kiln sucked Apollyon dry, yet the mountain also gave life and infused him with life from the Kiln in a perpetual cycle of draining and giving.

Lucifer watched as Apollyon burned and writhed in agony. His body weakened, and his frame diminished from Hell's insatiable appetite. Hell suckled on Apollyon's stone of fire.

Lucifer gawked at the cruelty of El. His mind angered that a creator who portrayed himself as the ultimate expression of benevolence would be evil enough to fashion a prison so torturous.

Enraged, Lucifer extended his claws and assumed his diamond form ready for battle. He launched himself headlong into the web.

"Release him now!" Lucifer shouted in defiance against the engorgement before him.

Acidic tendrils recoiled and snapped to attention. Cut asunder by the claws of the Chief Prince.

Lucifer entered the lattice and immediately his skin burned. Pain wracked his body as heavy fluid rushed in from a side chamber to fill the room and drown the duo in magma and acidic brimstone.

Lucifer's fight to rescue Apollyon came to a swift halt, as more tendrils shot from the walls. Hell would have the First of Angels; she would taste new flesh.

Lucifer hacked coil after coil, keeping each from ensnaring him as he marched ever closer to within inches of Apollyon.

Hell raised a wall of fire before Lucifer, and the concussive force knocked the angel from the air; his body slammed into the moist ground. Eyes liquefied underneath him and again the march of pyroclastic antibodies rose up from the floor ready to consume him. They wrapped their bodies over his feet and his arms as the Chief Prince lay prone, his back against the floor.

Lucifer looked up to see the same tendrils that held Apollyon slowly lower to entangle him. He struggled and the experience of fear for his own person gripped him for the first time, but only for a moment as panic slowly dissipated, and pride and anger filled his mind once more.

"I will not be denied! I *will* be like the most High!" Lucifer opened his mouth, exposed the trumpets and other horned instruments in his belly, and let out a shrieking cry. The sound blasted away the brimstone antibodies and smashed the lattice that held both him and Apollyon.

Hell heaved and lurched as its internal organs contorted from pain. Apollyon crashed to the magma floor. Lucifer grabbed Apollyon by the arm and lifted the barely conscious Arelim to his feet.

Lucifer looked to his rear as the hissing sound of the pyroclastic antibodies made their approach to engulf him. He quickly opened his mouth and recited the Elomic command to open a Ladder to Earth. White light bright as a star, formed around the battered duo, and lightning crackled around them.

Hell again convulsed in pain as the eyes of the cavern floor turned red and the antigens multiplied and raced to swallow angel flesh.

Lucifer continued the chant and completed the command, and with the last phonetic utterance, the boom of a Ladder surged through the heated cavern. A flash of light sprayed across the chamber, and a ball of lightning engulfed the two. Lucifer staggered as he carried Apollyon, and as a man might jump from a cliff Lucifer leaped into the swirling drain of light, power, and magma. A chute that connected momentarily the realm of Hell with Earth.

Lucifer and Apollyon fell down the winding tunnel as galaxies and stars shot passed them. Lucifer gritted his teeth as he descended. Hell's connected entrails intermingled with the Ladder made them streak like a comet through Earth's atmosphere.

His strategy to escape Hell was sure and with a great explosion, the foot of the Ladder touched the green earth with the sound of a thousand tree limbs snapping at once. The flames of Hellfire followed and scorched the ground.

Lucifer and Apollyon immediately materialized and slammed into the ground as the shock wave of their impact tossed redwoods and boulders to every side and blackened the soft ground beneath them.

Smoke, ash, and brimstone lined the crater. The sound of steam wafted into the air, and the crackle of burnt grass and wood filled the area while the acrid smell of ash and sulfur crammed the nostrils of all things that could smell.

Lucifer surveyed his surroundings, and as the ashy fog lifted, he saw Apollyon semi-conscious and sprawled out at his feet. The former Archon of Sol looked groggily upon Lucifer with dazed eyes and strained to speak.

"Thank you, Chief Prince," said Abaddon. "I am in your debt."

Lucifer smiled as smoke slowly lifted from his diamond frame. His skin shone brilliantly against the sun's reflected rays, and he replied.

"Then let us go my friend, and wreak havoc on they which imprisoned thee."

* * *

"On this day I shall take my rest," said El.

"On this day you will have great tribulation, but be of good cheer. I have placed my faith in you. Rest your faith in me, and you shall come forth as pure gold," said El.

Michael and the rest of the council kneeled before El and listened to their Lord. El smiled and looked at them.

"My children, I leave you but for one day that all should be accomplished in accordance with my will." El then closed his eyes.

Immediately, the Shekinah Glory grew dim, lifted from off El, and rocketed out of the palace flying over the city and towards the edge of Heaven, then dissipated to parts unknown. The light of Heaven retreated as the setting of the sun. The mountain of God grew dim and darkness crept over all the land. As the host of Heaven looked upon the dimming sky a fog rose from the ground. The temperature dropped and all of Heaven felt El's immediate presence no more.

The princes continued to kneel before their Lord and waited for dismissal, but word never came. Eventually, Michael looked at his master, walked towards the throne, laid prostrate before him, and kissed his feet, but El did not stir.

Michael walked down the steps back towards his brothers who looked upon him with confusion.

Gabriel spoke first. “Michael, what shall we do?”

Sariel added. “How shall we function without El?”

Jerahmeel stood, walked towards Michael, hugged him, and said, “Well, since Lucy’s not here, looks like you’re in charge. So what are your orders?”

Michael looked at them all. “We continue in our assignment...”

The sound of a hammer hitting metal came from the side chamber of the Kiln. Michael and the others quickly made their way to the Kiln door with its bronze exterior latticed with gold. They stared at the door and wondered.

It bulged outward as if impacted from the inside. Michael touched the protruding warped shape, his mind curious as to what force could damage the gate of heavy bronze.

“Perhaps Charon?” Michael said.

Raphael stared at the door, studied the bulge, and observed how the door strained to stay attached to its hinges, and his countenance grew grim. The air moved from the escaping heat that blistered inside.

“Or something else,” said Raphael.

“What else could it be, and what then of Charon?” asked Gabriel.

Suddenly the mountain of God shook from a tremor and they all shifted to keep from falling over.

The princes turned and quickly raced from the throne room. They exited the temple and stopped at the entrance to the temple doors outside. Each clamored to view Mt. Hell, which erupted and shook the ground of Heaven. Its roar was heard for miles, and they looked with telescopic eyes to see if Charon’s dark statue of a figure was still present.

“Do you see him?” Talus said.

“No,” Sariel replied.

Michael turned to his brother Gabriel and spoke.

“Gabriel go to Hell’s maw and report what you find, but go quickly.”

Gabriel nodded and vanished before them. In the distance, they saw that he now stood at the Maw. Gabriel stood atop the black rock of the entrance. The stench of sulfur bristled and pricked at his nose and made his skin itch. The mountain exhaled and wheezed as heated vent pockets rife with acidic steam shrouded the area in a warm dense blanket of fog.

Gabriel cautiously stepped over the ashen-covered rock that jutted out from the jagged mountain floor. He groped to find the cliff walls and scrapped his hand as he looked to see Charon through the heavy mist. He strained and looked closer down the narrow channel and saw a bright reddish glow.

The Maw, he thought.

He walked closer and with every step, he could feel the heat of the Maw swipe at him. Closer he moved and the opening to Hell's mouth loomed ever larger. The heat blistered his skin and sweat began to bead from his brow.

Where is Charon? He wondered.

The air began to move as distortions from the heat; waved, danced, and shooed away the fog. The entrance was open and unguarded, bidding welcome to all that might brave entry.

The black and yellow lined stalagmites stood and threatened oblivion to all who might travel through her teeth. Lava oozed from between the cave's stalactite gums like plaque.

The heat was unbearable, and steam began to hiss from Gabriel's boiling skin; his very flesh would be simmered alive if he dared remain much longer.

What was that?

Gabriel moved closer to the entrance, and Hell instinctually aware of angel flesh; opened her mouth to invite Gabriel in so that she might savor him.

Gabriel inched closer.

Yes, there he is.

Deep within the throat of the mountain: plodding and dragging his intestine of chains and anchors of bondage behind him. The great dark-cloaked figure of Charon burrowed deeper into the magma and acidic bile, his destination unknown. Gabriel watched as Charon disappeared into the fiery dark and he turned to return to his brethren.

Then Hell screamed.

* * *

Abaddon looked haggard. His face was pale and his eyes and extremities had turned a greenish pink. His body was a living welt, for marks from Hell's intrusions and Charon's lash had lacerated and decorated his frame. Scars ran across his face and back, and his once powerful wings were tattered.

Lucifer looked upon the Arelim and pitied him. Righteous anger flooded his soul, anger that a God who would dare demand fealty and righteousness would subject his own creation to such cruelty of spite.

"Ashtaroth!" Lucifer yelled.

The Issi came into his master's bedchamber and bowed at the open door.

"My Lord?" He said.

"Tell the elders of my return to Athor and command them to bid me audience within the hour. Let them know I have returned with Abaddon and a plan for our control of Heaven."

"Aye my Lord," Ashtaroth said and quickly left.

* * *

Charon trudged into Hell's belly and looked to find his captive escaped. Enraged, he raised his skeletal head and roared his outrage. In fury, he lifted his hammer-like fists into the air and slammed them down onto the eyed floor. The eyes popped like melons thrown against concrete and Hell screamed in agony.

Charon's eyeless skull slowly scoured the cavern to see any sign of his foe, and with maggot, infested flesh: the half-man, half-mount of a creature managed to utter a sound to this cousin of the Kiln. The walls of Hell's stomach bubbled in acidic retort, and magma fell back upon itself to reveal the stone and charred floor of Hell's belly, a wound inflicted by the power of the living God to form a Ladder to another realm.

Charon lowered his equestrian nose to the floor and with nostrils that did not exist snorted to sniff out his prey, now rogue. Then a circular scar in Hell's flesh appeared: a wound that could only come from a Ladder.

Instinct drove Charon, chains shot from his body, and he latched himself in the stone floor and wall as if feeling the scar. Dredging for clues to his quarry's whereabouts, he searched with manacled antennae and noticed something foreign on the far wall. Picking up the soft object, he eyed a tattered and charred piece of cloth of a presence alien to his prison.

A piece of robe -- a trespasser of royal blood--the Chief Prince.

Once more with head arched back, Charon raged into the air.

He found the scent of Abaddon. His angelic flesh was familiar to the warden, and there were still pieces' of Abaddon's flesh lodged in the barbs of Charon's manacled whips. Now with this new piece of evidence, the pursuit of his captive could commence.

Charon placed the tattered piece of purple cloth in his breast and retracted his torso chains into his chest. He raised his hammer-like arms into the air and struck them together. The sound reverberated within Hell's belly. He struck once more and a spark ignited for a moment, and then quickly dissipated.

Again, he pummeled his stone arms together, and again a flash ignited and then snuffed out. With a cry of rage and invocations of unintelligible retribution, Charon slammed his own arms against one another as a flint would smite a rock, and a spark ensued.

The spark morphed, and lightning suddenly filled Hell's belly. The white light of a Ladder encircled Charon and washed him in iridescent heat. Hell convulsed and groaned her innards of brimstone, magma, and flame once more invaded by the creative power of the living God.

Crackles of lightning streaked across the chasm and arched back unto Charon. His iron and manacled body kissed and welcomed each charged embrace. Wider the electric field grew and arrayed the cavern in tentacled streams of plasma.

He raised his mighty arms of hammers and slammed them into Hell's floor, and bolts of lightning struck the cavern floor. Hell wailed, her cry soared to the ears of the denizens of Heaven itself, thunder rocketed across the sky, and all looked to see the mountain rumble and quake.

Charon pummeled the floor of the mountain once more. It cracked, and lightning walloped the spot and left its mark deeper in Hell's flesh.

Again, he struck the ground. The living mountain screamed and wailed its disapproval and cried out in pain.

Fractures appeared, and Hell heaved as magma splashed around the mighty warden of torment. Again, he crashed his arms into Hell's floor, and the might of his stroke broke through the charred and rocky ground and gave way.

The mighty angel fell as the floor beneath him buckled, and the Ladder collapsed and converted into a chute of fire and brimstone. A shaft, that funneled its way through space and time and pierced the barriers that divided the Third Heaven from all other realms, and Charon fell.

Earth and Elohim smote one another as the impact of Charon's arrival bore the crust of the planet. He was welcomed with dirt, rock, and dust flung high into the air and the shattering sound of a thousand trees.

Hell's fire soon followed him, and where the fire of the physical universe sat quietly in consumption of air and carbon: Hell's fire was not so. The very ground liquefied, the air disappeared, and sulfur unpacked its bags and lined the brimstone-filled crater with her stench and yellowish touch.

A pillar of fire stretched as a tower might pierce the atmosphere and found its home in Hell's paunch; its heat wilted and blackened the ground for miles. Earth retreated as life and color quickly raced to escape the perimeter of the flaming entrails that hung from Hell's belly.

Smoke and heat emanated from the crater, and newly created birds and beasts were intelligent enough to remove themselves from the vicinity.

Charon lumbered forth from the freshly minted hollow; his manacles dangled as they touched the soft earthen soil. He lowered his skeletal nose to the ground, captured the scent that his barbed chains had left in Abaddon's flesh, and rose to look across the horizon.

A city stood many miles away. Less than a day's journey for the elephant-paced angel. Nevertheless, time held no meaning to an immortal: and he would see Abaddon ferried home.

Charon had come to Earth for his prisoner and Hellfire had come with him.

* * *

"Bear witness to the impotence of El," said Lucifer. "A creator of a prison that I can enter and leave with its captives at will. Behold! I give you Abaddon and know that nothing is impossible to them that believe!"

Abaddon walked before the elders of Athor. The abrasions and lesions on his skin gave testimony to the harshness of Hell's bondage. Although scarred, he was unbowed and spoke. "The Chief Prince has apprised me of his plan. I was the catalyst for his actions: his need to question the goodness of El. Question no more! See with thine own eyes the pity of our God!

"Grigoric history tells of Argoth and his supposedly prophetic declaration of the person of the Lord. According to him, when the Lord created him, and he looked upon his maker for the first time, he was so stunned, so overwhelmed that he was as a man in a trance and walked to the edge of the mountain of the Lord, looked out over the expanse of the Kingdom of Heaven and proclaimed..."

'The LORD, The LORD God, merciful and gracious, longsuffering, and abundant in goodness and truth, Keeping mercy for thousands, forgiving iniquity and transgression and sin, and that will by no means clear the guilty, visiting the iniquity of the fathers upon the children, and upon the children's children, unto the third and to the fourth generation.'

"What need have we of prophecies? What other lies have been told to us? Are my lashes evidence of His mercy and graciousness? Are *my* shred wings testimony to His goodness and truth?"

"I was once Apollyon. I am now Abaddon, the Destroyer. I side with Lucifer and pledge myself to *he* who relieved me of the torment of Hell's belly. I will not serve a master that will not answer prayer, nor submit to a Lord who will not be found when sought. I stand here before you due to one who did not despise my cause. I was sought of one who braved the monster Charon and has returned!"

Abaddon turned to Lucifer and pointed at him.

"He will be my God and King!"

Abaddon turned again to face the assembly.

"Who among you will stand with us, or will you continue to cower under the shadow of the Almighty? Let go of this fear and break free of El's shackle and serve the Chief Prince!"

The great assembly hall was quiet. The gravity of the words spoken, and the actions taken would ring through Heaven and they all knew it. No one moved and no one spoke.

Suddenly, the assembly doors opened, and without invitation: Ashtaroth walked through the center of those gathered within the hall and marched to approach his Lord.

Lucifer eyed his servant and was silent.

"How dare he!" said one attendee.

Ashtaroth did not speak but continued and upon reaching his master's feet, knelt in common formality as was his custom, then rose.

"Remove this vassal," said one.

"He has no place here," said another.

The group became more unruly over the intrusion.

Lucifer raised his hand to silence them, and Ashtaroth looked into Lucifer's eyes and spoke.

"Cans't thou truly do as thou hast said?" Ashtaroth asked.

"I can," Lucifer replied.

Ashtaroth then bowed his face to the floor. He laid prostrate for a moment, then rose to his knees and spoke, "My Lord and my God!"

He turned to face them all that they might see and ripped his robes from his breast to reveal the sigil stone that bared his name. He reached into his chest to remove it, held it high for all to gaze, and carved in it a new name.

Slowly he dug his fingernail into the stone, scratched from its face the name given to him by El in the Kiln, and wrote a name of his own choosing. Each etch of a new letter caused him to change physically before their eyes.

Slowly, the slim and nimble Issi grew large. His flesh turned dark and spiky, and bony protrusions erupted from his flesh. Fire flared up around him as the sigil stone of fire melted his features and reformed him after a new image and a new likeness. His frail butterfly wings changed and grew transparent as like a dragonfly, and he stopped writing and held his stone up for all to see. His voice clearly changed as he spoke in a deeper bass.

"I am Astarte, Governor of the House of Lucifer, my Lord and my God."

And as the muscular insectoid creature stood before and held up his sigil stone: Tiamat, Mammon, Zeus, Cadfiel, Asmodeus, Dagon, Thammuz, Murmur, Mephisto, and countless others removed their sigil stones, held them high, bowed before Lucifer, and began to etch and alter their stones.

Lucifer beheld as each one transformed before him, and when the transformation of all was complete, and the elders had bowed before him. Lucifer looked upon the first of those that he would rule and smiled.

"I see a glorious day when the Creator will hang from a tree. Let us usher in that day now. Here — in this hall." He said.

Abaddon looked upon his newly appointed Lord and spoke.

"What is thy command, my King?"

Lucifer looked upon them all and replied, "Secure Athor. Gather those loyal to our cause and assemble in the great court."

"And what of those that will not serve?" Abaddon asked.

Lucifer was somewhat slow to reply.

"Then dissolution awaits them."

Abaddon smirked, and his eyes gleamed with anticipation.

"Thy will be done, Lord King."

* * *

"Report," Michael said.

Gabriel had come from Mt. Hell and panted frantically.

"Charon has left the maw. Hell's mouth stands unguarded!"

"Are you sure?" asked Jerahmeel.

"Aye, I saw Charon move deep within the mount...his destination -- I cannot say," Gabriel said.

Michael turned to look at Raphael. "Can you track him?"

"He has no Grigori; hence, he has no log," replied Raphael.

Michael thought for a moment and paced the entry steps to the temple.

"What is it Michael?' said Talus.

Michael stopped to reply.

"We must locate Lucifer. Jerahmeel go to his palace and seek query as to his whereabouts. Raphael and I will track the Grigori of Athor and its vicinity. The rest of you return to your assignments. Creation still needs governance, and nothing must be undone while El is on Sabbath."

Each angel took to the sky as Michael and Raphael reentered the temple palace.

"Have you shared with the others what you shared with me?" queried Michael.

"No," Raphael replied. "Only the Lord, you, and I know the extent of what Lucifer and Lilith have discussed."

"Then I think we should delve deeper," said Michael.

"Agreed," replied Raphael.

The two brothers made their way into the room of the Zoa and Michael moved with greater swiftness in his steps than before. Upon entry to the Hall of Annals, Raphael pulled Lucifer's tome, placed it on a podium, and the room turned white. The tome levitated in midair and then Raphael spoke to the room.

"Rescind to Third Heaven: Current location of Lucifer Draco."

The room flashed multiple colors and then went white.

Raphael looked perplexed and repeated his command. "Rescind to Third Heaven: Current location of Lucifer Draco."

Once more, the great room flashed in response. Colors, of the rainbow, arched across the walls, floor, and ceiling, stopped, and then white stained the entire Hall.

"Uh -- Raphael?" Michael said.

"Hmmph," said Raphael. "Regress to the last encounter with El."

The room flashed to obey. Reds, blues, and greens washed up on the wall until an image was displayed. Lucifer was shown as bowed before El and pleading for Apollyon's release. El's admonition to grieve silently replayed for the duo and then the room went white.

"Curious," said Raphael.

"What is it?" Michael asked.

Raphael lifted his finger to urge Michael to wait.

"Regress to last known presence in Third Heaven," said Raphael.

Again, the room flashed the colors of the spectrum and Michael's eyes darted to see what the chamber would show next.

The same image flashed of Lucifer kneeling before the Lord, pleading Abaddon's case.

"That's not right," said Michael.

"Aye," Raphael replied. "Lucifer was at the communion table with us before El dismissed him to do whatever he was assigned to do."

"Then where is the rest of his record?" Michael said.

Raphael rubbed his chin in thought. "Based on what we have seen here, there is no record from this point onward."

"That's impossible," said Michael.

"No," Raphael said. "Not impossible, just highly improbable."

"But who could change -- wait -- *no*!"

"Lilith has altered Lucifer's tome," said Raphael.

Raphael looked curiously at the image on the wall and spoke.

"Reveal: Grigoric tome: Ashtaroth," Raphael commanded.

Immediately a new book appeared on the podium.

"I have a concern that more might be amiss than I was led to believe," said Raphael.

"Oh?" Michael said.

"Indeed. Ashtaroth is always near his master or has knowledge of his whereabouts. If I am correct we have a larger problem than just Lucifer and Lilith," said Raphael.

"Rescind to Third Heaven: the current location of Ashtaroth," spoke Raphael.

The room exploded in color and then flashed to white.

"As I feared," said Raphael.

"What?" Michael said.

"Regress to last known presence in Third Heaven," said Raphael

Again, the room burst forth in colors, and images raced across the room and stopped at Ashtaroth's encounter with Lucifer at the temple waypoint: after the Chief Prince had returned from the completion of Eden.

"We have a serious problem, Michael."

"What do you see?"

"My concern is what I *do not* see. Ashtaroth's record has changed. The record shows that he greeted Lucifer upon his return, but if this is his last known presence, then when does it show him leaving the Third Heaven?"

Michael stared at the image. "You're right. If he left Heaven, this surely was not the time it occurred."

"Indeed," said Raphael.

Michael stared at Raphael, "What else is wrong?"

"Michael these records are not just altered. A Grigori has rewritten history. Our problem extends greater than simply Lucifer at this point. These two records indicate that a plan is underway to rewrite history and or to conceal current information. This does not bode well."

"Lilith?" Michael asked.

"He and others I fear," said Raphael. "I suspect Lucifer and Ashtaroth will not be the only ones whose tomes have changed. Michael, someone has knowingly ceased documenting history. This incident is not just a coincidence with Lucifer but extends to his servant as well. I fear that this is an attempt to conceal information, from me."

"But why," said Michael. "To what end?"

"I do not know exactly," said Raphael, "but I intend to find out."

"How?"

"I will go to Athor and most likely find Lilith there. There can be no other way to investigate this other than by addressing the source."

Michael looked at Raphael curiously. "Go to Earth--you? You have never left the capital, my friend. Besides, there are few who have Elomic commands to travel, and I know that you do not possess one."

Raphael laughed. "I have seen the far reaches of creation and El has not limited travel to an Elomic command."

Raphael clapped his hand and the room flashed white.

"Reveal: Grigoric tome of Athor."

Immediately the room changed colors, and the three-dimensional landscape of Athor became visible. Raphael's tome and inkhorn appeared, and he took his stylus and wrote the words, 'Enter'.

Raphael then walked into the wall and stepped onto a field that was just outside the city. Michael was stunned, for he never had seen this form of travel.

"Michael I shall return soon, but I suggest that you proceed to the Maw."

"Why?" Michael asked.

Raphael continued to walk while half of his body seemed to be in two places at once as he spoke.

"Hell's tome glows with activity."

He pointed to a book on his shelf; it flared as if the contents would explode. Michael turned to his rear watching the tome grow larger.

Raphael engulfed fully in the wall appeared as if he were a part of a painting and spoke from within the image.

"Take the tome with you, for it will protect you from what lies within, and allow you to freely travel within Hell. Find Charon. I do not know what would move him from the maw, but if he has disappeared from his charge something is terribly wrong."

"Agreed," said Michael. "But what of you?"

"I will search for Lilith; determine the extent of the corruption to the Grigori and of their tomes. Be careful my friend," said Raphael.

"Be well," Michael replied.

Michael watched as Raphael floated further into the picture on the wall as the room erupted in color once more and then went white.

* * *

Lucifer sat with his newly appointed court. His home in Athor was large and palatial. Its quartz walls pulsated with the sun's light and refracted it in brilliant color.

"Now," said Mephisto, "explain to us your plan. How would you bring down El?'

Lucifer leaned forward in his chair and spoke.

"El's forces are scattered across the three heavens, but only those within the capital concern us for now, of which only a quarter of all Elohim reside. We on Athor and Earth alone comprise a third while the rest are strewn throughout the realms. We have numerical superiority on our side."

Dagon shifted in his seat and replied. "We do, aye, but only until word of our actions reaches the host in the second heaven. Once they realize what has transpired, they will surely overwhelm us."

Lucifer smiled. "That too I have carefully anticipated. You see Lord Dagon; to fight Heaven head-on is foolish. We would surely perish, but what if Heaven were made to battle against herself?" Lucifer grinned.

Tiamat raised his head. "Intriguing--say on."

"There has existed a growing schism between house Arelim and Issi since Saesheal's demise. We shall exploit this void of fellowship amongst the brethren and fill it with something else."

Thammuz looked at Lucifer and spoke, "Lucifer do not speak in riddles; speak plainly!"

Lucifer smirked. "We will fill it with murmur."

Murmur raised his head. "My Lord?"

Lucifer laughed at the irony. "We will set brother against brother, Issi against Arelim, and we will wait until they themselves eat away at their own strength, and at the pinnacle of their division, we will strike, sweeping aside any that would oppose us. In their confusion, they will reel before our attack. If we move quickly we can circumvent the loss of brother or significant damage to the city."

The lieutenants sat quietly and nodded. "There is wisdom in your plan Lucifer," said Zeus. "Yet there is still much work to be done."

"Indeed" replied Lucifer. "Ashtaroth and I will return with Murmur; our assignment will be to provoke the Princes Talus and Sariel to engage. We will incite the two great houses to attack one another. Once the battle has begun, Abaddon will assault Heaven at the place of my choosing. The rest of you will protect the waypoints. No Ladders can be made into the realm or Heaven's legions reinforced until we have accomplished our mission.

Cadfiel looked unconvinced and spoke, "And what is *your* mission, Lord King?"

"I will enter the Kiln, secure it, and awaken the God Stone within. Once I possess the power of El, I will create a new race of Elohim who will be unleashed throughout all three heavens to do our bidding. By the time El awakens from his rest, it will be too late."

Cadfiel laughed mockingly. "This is your plan? We have but one day to accomplish this and if we fail: when El awakes, He will but snuff us all out with a thought! Alas, even if you might do as thou hast said and become as El when he awakens he will of a surety seek our destruction."

The lieutenants looked at one another with concern. Lucifer eyed them and spoke.

"Nay Lord Cadfiel, he will do no such thing. El will be given a choice, for when all things have been set into motion, he will abdicate the throne. If he does not capitulate then I will destroy his beloved creation, starting with his prized possession: the humans. We will garrison the Earth, the garden, and Athor. If I do not arrive, you will see to its destruction. I bargain that El will not let his creation be destroyed. I realized this when he created Hell as opposed to oblivion for Abaddon. You see Lord Cadfiel, El loves. His love and readiness to spare will be his undoing. No. El will yield; He will have no choice when He sees all of creation threatened. And on that day my brothers, we will serve the triune God no more!"

* * *

Michael climbed down from Mt. Zion, flew across his great city, and landed at the steps of the Maw. The silicate breath of the cave's entrance stung his eyes and scratched his throat. The heat belched from the great cavern, and fire leaped to lick Michael's face. Hell seemed agitated, and lava oozed across her black gums. He looked through the steam and saw that Charon was absent from his post.

I will be protected, thought Michael.

Michael swallowed hard and stepped into the fires of Hell. Fire and brimstone washed over his body as Hell's saliva of sulfur and magma cleansed her palate to consume the Elohim. The giant ferrous, black stalagmite teeth shut tight behind him.

The heat intensified and Michael began to understand the horror that Abaddon must have felt. He looked at his hands as the flames attempted to broil the flesh from his bones, but Hell would be denied this day as Michael stood his ground in the midst of Hell's maw.

"Oh, mount of anguish and torment hear me! I come neither guilty nor with guile. I seek thy ward, Charon! Deny me not, for I come in the name of the Lord of Hosts!"

The ground buckled, and Michael lost his footing. Red-blistered eyes lifted from beneath the magma and stared at him. Orifices protruded from the walls, hissing and bearing razors for teeth. Pyroclastic forms bubbled from the surface of Hell's floor and made their way towards the Chief Prince. Each slid and hissed as they did. Michael clutched Hell's Tome and stood his ground eyeing the encircling creatures rising from the floor.

"Attack me at thy peril, creature, but thou hast been warned!"

Hell was a living mountain whose consciousness was aware on only the smallest of levels. All it knew was that within its maw was Elomic flesh. Hell hungered, and it would engorge itself on this little angel.

Tendrils shot out from the walls and flame, magma, and ash flared up in front of the high prince. A tendril of fire wrapped around Michael's legs and lifted him high into the air. Michael wailed in pain and clutched the book. Another tendril reached out to clasp his hands and then another. Michael thrashed as a fly captured in a spider's web as dozens of tendrils shot from the walls and enveloped him in a cocoon of magma. His clothing burned, but when the tendrils of heated flame touched the pages of the tome Michael carried, Hell screamed.

Hell's coils quickly retracted, and Michael fell hard to the ground. The eyes in the floor glared at him with pupils red with rage and hissed at him.

"Yes, creature I carry thy tome. Now I query you again! Where is Charon?"

The mountain rumbled, and the antigens of lava melted into the floor. The hiss of steam subsided, and all the tentacles pointed deep into the darkness that was Hell's throat. The magma on the floor parted and revealed dry, black ground underneath. The lava pillowed up to the sides to form a pathway.

Michael followed the trail laid before him. Walking carefully, he ventured to neither the right nor left. The lava flows gave off a reddish-orange glow just bright enough to see. On both sides of him were rows of eyes and orifices that gnashed, spitting out ash and sulfur. Michael wheezed and coughed, and the smell and heavy fumes filled his lungs. His clothes blackened; and like a grey ghost, the Prince of Heaven walked the empty floor of Hell.

Deeper he traveled into the hallways, making note of his whereabouts and observing each corridor and cave. Cavern after cavern bubbled with fire and the walls oozed with sticky goo, ready to imprison and feed off any soul damned to abide inside. Michael then began to understand the wrath of the Lord.

His vengeance on any who do him or his own harm: would find themselves spending eternity in a living monstrosity consumed for all eternity. They would broil mingled in the fires of the Kiln that sustained life, and roasted in the fires of the Hell that took it. At that moment, Michael understood both the goodness and the severity of God.

Oblivion would not be an escape, and dissolution would be denied. For here within the hollow of the beast, one would be damned to live forever only to die as fodder for a creature that lived off the tortured agony and eternal spirit of its host, surrounded in the flickering light of flame for an eternity only to watch one's flesh slowly eaten alive. Michael marveled at the thing that was Hell and quickened his pace. He did not wish to remain there long.

Michael traveled over some floors soft and others of firmness, walking through branches, pipes, and conduits until finally in the distance. Michael could see light and relief flooded him.

Closer he came to a huge chamber and it was there that he saw it. The Bowel, a massive walled cavern of living fire, lined with eyes and latticed with teeth, and he could tell it was here, within the deepest pits of the mountain the true horrors of digestion played themselves out. For on the lining of Hell's stomach, images splayed themselves before Michael of all Abaddon's doings.

His first consciousness of waking from the Kiln, his accolades as Son of the Dawn, his judgment as he fell screaming into the pit of Hell, all that was his life played out before him. Moreover, Michael saw that Charon was not just a warden but also an instrument of vengeance, that deep within the belly of this beast of fire and brimstone, he replayed for his victim his life, a moving mural painted for Abaddon to relive. Hell feasted on regret and nourished herself off anguish and remorse. It was here that Hell grew obese from the weeping and gnashing of teeth.

Tattered remains of clothing and regal garb littered the floor, and Arelim flesh was stuck into the walls. Michael snapped from his staring as lightning arched across the ceiling and shot out from through the floor. He rushed to the spark's source to see moving in the center of the floor a whirlpool of lightning, fire, and brimstone that drained into a shaft of light.

A Ladder, he thought but unlike any, he had ever seen.

He looked into the great vortex, and it was as a funnel that ran from Hell's stomach through space itself. Hell lurched, and shook, and, the mountain groaned, and its guttural displeasure echoed throughout the cavern, and the mount expanded.

Charon was gone. Michael covered his eyes to see against the lightning, which arced within the cavern. He moved and flew above the edge of the "chute" and could see the Earth in the great distance at the bottom. The horror of the situation grabbed him. Hell had enlarged herself and had made foothold on Earth.

* * *

Raphael saw Elohim go about their business on the streets. Each took their assignments from their Archons, as his people dutifully took note of their surroundings and hovered ever so silently out of sight in the presence of their charge.

Nothing seems amiss, he thought.

Raphael passed into the street unseen to all, but his own people. Various Grigori bowed and or acknowledged their Lord. Some looked at him and others stared, but all continued in their duties. Looking around, he made out Ashtaroth in the distance and ran over to get a closer look.

What is this? He has no Grigori to accompany him!

Raphael turned to one of his fellow Grigori. "Tell me, have you seen the Grigori for Ashtaroth?"

The Grigori smiled and floated away after his charge.

Raphael gawked at the behavior in disbelief.

"My people," Raphael shouted speaking into the ether so that only his kind could hear. "Where is the steward for Ashtaroth?"

Each Grigori continued to float past their Lord, and Raphael looked on in amazement.

Ashtaroth then stopped, turned around, and looked squarely at Raphael.

Immediately dozens, then hundreds of other angels stopped and turned or stood to look at him as well.

Raphael's eyes darted across the street and he noted that all had ceased moving and slowly started walking towards him, and Raphael backed away. From the court behind Ashtaroth, the doors into Athor's castle opened. Lucifer, Zeus, and Mephisto stepped into view, and all of their assigned Grigori floated behind them and walked through the center of the street straight toward Raphael's path: Lilith smiled at Raphael as they approached.

A group of angels landed, barred his path, and encircled him.

"There is no need to yell or leave my prince. In fact...," said Lilith, "we insist that you stay."

Raphael began to run.

"Restrain him," Lilith said.

Grigori in the vicinity swarmed over their Prince, tackled him, and held him down to the ground. Raphael struggled to rise, but their grip was strong, and there were too many.

"Lilith, what is the meaning of this outrage? All of you release me immediately or incur the wrath of a High Prince!"

Some of the Grigori loosened their grip, and Lilith hurried to their side.

"Do no such thing," said Lilith.

Lilith raised Raphael to his feet and searched his person. He reached and confiscated his inkhorn, stylus, and tome, and upon doing so, Raphael immediately became visible to all.

"Ah much better," said Lucifer. "Raphael, it is so good to see you, my brother. However, I must admit I am disappointed that you felt it necessary to be secretive of your presence here. It was not necessary I assure you."

"Your hospitality Chief Prince means little to me when I am forcibly held."

"My apologies my friend — perhaps if you had been more forthright in your own activities, mine own actions would be less circumspect? Of course, I'm sure if I just *chose* to walk into the Hall of Annals, you would equally greet me with such *hospitality*?"

"The Lord rebuke you, Lucifer Draco," said Raphael.

"Not today my little prince...," said Lucifer. "Not today."

Lucifer turned to walk back into the palace, and his entourage followed.

"Bring him," said Lucifer.

Raphael struggled as his captors held him tight. Lilith walked before him and spoke.

"Raphael, why do you resist? We will not harm you. Surely, you know that. After all, are you not the Prince Lord of all Grigori?" Lilith laughed mockingly.

Raphael smirked and retorted, "If I were *your* prince, then this conversation would be but imagined. You are a disgrace to our species."

They entered the palace and Lucifer directed several of his attendants to other tasks.

"Lilith, have Raphael brought to my chambers."

Lilith frowned. "Lord King it was my desire to query him before..."

"Enough Lilith: you may sport with him later. Bring him now."

"Yes my King," said Lilith.

"So," said Raphael. "You lower yourself from the position of Watcher to that of dog only to take orders from a rogue angel?"

Lilith moved closer to whisper in Raphael's ear.

"Pray that Lucifer will be merciful, for I most assuredly will not."

Lilith shoved Raphael down to the floor and closed the door behind him leaving Lucifer and Raphael alone within Lucifer's chamber hall.

"Are you hungry?" asked Lucifer. "We are not graced to have manna which grows on Gaia, but I would be remiss if I failed to show hospitality even at this juncture."

"Keep your bread, 'Lightbringer'. I am not here to dine with you, and what is Gaia?"

Lucifer put down a glass of water he was preparing to drink. "Ahh, yes, I have determined that Earth is too trite of a name. Gaia would be more appropriate for my home. Of course, that leads us to the real question my brother: why are you here?"

"You are filled with wisdom Lucifer, but for all your fullness, you have filled yourself beyond measure. Save your melodious pretense. I know of your words that you have echoed about El, and more importantly 'Lightbringer', the Lord himself knows."

"Ah, so you have come to reason with me? Or perhaps you come to incite the 'fear of the Lord', into me?"

Raphael spoke condescendingly. "The fear of the Lord does not dwell in this place Chief Prince."

Lucifer laughed. "Indeed, it does, for my citizens clearly have demonstrated their ability to serve me, my friend."

"What do you want with me Lucifer?"

I, Raphael, desire nothing more than your allegiance. What is thy desire? Are you truly satisfied to sit in the Halls of Annals and live vicariously through others? Would you not prefer to explore the stellar phenomena that you see through your great hall? I, dear brother, can offer you that. Observe and document?"

Lucifer chuckled.

"Imagine a world where you might add your own ideas and opinions to that which you see. How more colorful and varied such a universe would be to explicate and not just simply to document? Have you no judgment on El's actions towards Abaddon? Was he not wrong to give the Earth to the humans? Or are you simply resolved to sit idle and watch our kind dissipate into oblivion only to serve as chattel? *We* are the superior beings. The strong ought not to bear the infirmities of the weak. Yet El would have us prattle to these creatures of mud and clay. Follow me Raphael, and we shall rule the heavens together."

Raphael watched Lucifer and was silent in his response.

"I will leave for Heaven shortly. I leave you to Lilith who is most anxious to assume your role upon my ascent to the throne."

"You are mad Lucifer. You will never usurp El," said Raphael.

Lucifer turned to leave and looked at his brother.

"What is madness? I merely speak those things that be not as though they were."

Lucifer closed the door behind him.

Lilith walked with Lucifer as his master prepared to depart.

"He is dangerous Lucifer. His presence could be disruptive. I would take his stone now."

"No. He is my brother and a Chief Prince. There will be time soon enough for dissolution, and when and if it comes it will be at my command."

"Yes, Lord King. But may I suggest that a watch be placed to guard him?"

"Very well, you and Abaddon see to his keeping. However, once you are done with him, I expect you and Astarte to return to Jerusalem."

Lucifer turned and raised his finger to Lilith's face. "And Lilith..."

"Yes, Lord King."

"Raphael is not to be harmed."

"Yes, Lord King."

Lucifer and Lilith continued to walk and entered the room where several of Lucifer's lieutenants were laying out their plans.

"Report of thy stewardship," said Lucifer.

Zeus was first to speak as Abaddon and several other angels looked on in smiles.

"Our brother Cadfiel has developed a tool to assist us in battle."

"Really?" Lucifer said. "Show it to me."

Cadfiel came forward and placed before his master a plow shear, the blade had been straightened and beaten flat. It possessed a razor edge and the handle was stout and strong. Cadfiel laid it at the feet of his master and stepped away.

Lucifer picked up the blade, held it high, and examined it as he turned it from side to side.

"My brethren behold. An instrument of peace and toil now conformed into a weapon of liberation. This tool shall be a sword and the symbol of our righteous cause. Well done Cadfiel. You and Zeus see to it that our legions are outfitted accordingly. Spare no resource. You Cadfiel, I see have a unique gift. What name hast thou selected to dispense the stench of El's ownership from thy stone?

Cadfiel spoke immediately, "Ares, my Lord."

"Thou hast chosen well," Lucifer replied, "And war chieftain shalt thou be."

"My Lord King," said Zeus.

"Yes, what is it?" said Lucifer.

"How will we succeed in our invasion of Heaven? As the waypoints prevent our entering the realm en mass"

Lucifer smiled. "You will not Ladder to a waypoint, my friend. No. You shall bombard Heaven herself with our Ladders and within the great city walls and our legions shall appear and wreak havoc."

"Do you know what that will do the landscape and denizens of Heaven?" Zeus said.

Lucifer frowned, "Yes, but it must be done."

Abaddon laughed.

* * *

Michael landed on the spot where Charon had fallen. His entrance was less traumatic to the ground than Charon's own fall. Smoke hissed as the Ladder of fire and brimstone reached into the sky. The inferno of Hell's entrails dug deep into the Earth's crust.

Soon she will hit the core and when that happens, he thought, Hell would have home on two planes of existence. He wondered to himself how a Ladder could be made within the belly of Hell and only one word came to the forefront of his mind--Lucifer.

Michael moved a little away from the heated flue that towered into the sky and began to survey the area. If Charon had come here, where would he go? Michael turned to the east of where he stood and saw Athor gleam in the distance. He looked down at the ground and saw the long trail left by the heavy manacles that dragged behind the body of Charon. He followed them and the trail led directly to Athor. Intuitively he lifted his body into the air and flew.

Faster his wings carried him, and in the distance ahead he saw him. Hell's warden marched on a path directly towards the quartz city. Charon's trail was easy to follow as boulders and trees were smashed in his wake. The mark of his presence was the long segmented trail of his chains, as the barbs attached to the ends, plowed themselves into the earth.

Charon was easy to find.

Michael thought to himself. God help him whom Charon finds. Michael had now caught up with this Elomic bulldozer. He hovered above him and examined the beast so unique among Elohim. Charon was unresponsive to Michael's presence, his skeletal face vacant of any expression. There was no smile, no flushed cheeks, nor raised eyebrow that might cause one to perceive emotion. There was nothing but the continual plodding of the giant, and where Charon was headed, Abaddon could not be far.

Michael continued on his journey and began to approach the city limits. He settled down far enough and landed behind a tree to conceal himself.

My clothes — surely I will be recognized.

Michael stripped off his royal robes and laid them under a rock. With the colors of the Builder of Heaven from off his body, he pulled his cloak over his face and walked the rest of the way to Athor. Moving through one of the side city gates, he watched the hustle and bustle of the angels as they ran to and from their assigned tasks.

Michael walked up the glass-lined street and saw Lucifer and Ashtaroth make their way to the front of the city gate. Several archons accompanied him including Murmur. Michael followed them as they made their way outside the city. He closed to within earshot and overheard Lucifer speak.

"Lilith you may remove Raphael from my hospitality and find a room suitable for him. Since he has refused to worship me, you may dispense with him as you see fit. Are the swords ready?"

"Aye Lord King. Zeus and the others are distributing them as we speak."

"Excellent," said Lucifer. "You have done well."

Michael watched as Lilith bowed and left to attend to Raphael.

Lucifer and his entourage leaped into the air and Ladders formed which lifted the trio out of sight.

Michael turned to follow Lilith. His thoughts raced as to why his brother would be confined against his will. *Was Lucifer seeking worship?* Michael continued to follow Lilith through the various streets and avenues of the great city until a center palace was come upon. He watched as Lilith opened the palatial doors and walked inside.

Michael studied the building and noticed it had few windows except at its peak. The whole structure had a transparency within it. Michael watched as Lilith ascended a spiral tower to the tallest room of the palace. The room was not transparent, and he wondered to himself if this was Lucifer's private chamber. From the entrance of the room, Abaddon stepped out smiling and laughing.

Abaddon has escaped, thought Michael. Michael looked up at the sun and realized that it was close to noonday. Charon would be within the city limits soon. Michael thought of a plan to secure Raphael's release. He would use Charon's presence as a distraction to secure Raphael's freedom.

Quickly he moved to an alley where he could not be seen and dashed into the sky. He then landed by the tree outside the city limits and found the stone where his royal robes lay. He dressed himself and made sure that his regalia would be noticed.

Michael then launched himself back into the air and concentrated: moments later a Ladder formed. Michael entered the cone, and sound and lightning flashed behind him. Traveling beyond the speed of light, he turned his direction back towards Earth and focused his entry to the courtyard. *There must be no mistake that the Builder of Heaven has arrived.*

The Ladder turned upon his command, and the planet loomed before him as Athor's central court quickly sprinted into view. The sonic boom of thunder clapped, and Michael materialized in the center of town for all to see.

"Hail. I Michael of the Kortai have come with words for Lucifer. Make way for the Prince of Heaven."

Immediately those who saw Michael looked as if they were undone. Some bowed, others looked frightened as if caught doing something amiss, but all stopped immediately to stare at the High Prince.

Good, he thought. *They were not expecting me.* He spoke again, "To Lucifer's quarters. You steward, attend me. Direct thy prince forthwith."

A Kortai warrior came quickly at the High Prince's command and replied.

"This way Lumazi."

Michael walked behind the angel, and they hastily came to Lucifer's palace.

"What is your name Kortai?" said Michael.

"Iofiel, my Prince."

Michael looked again at the transparent quartz, diamond, glass, and emerald palace made to house the glory of the Lord. Now it was Lucifer's home while away from Heaven. Abaddon was nowhere to be found.

He should be here shortly, Michael thought.

Iofiel knocked on the doors, and both Michael and he could see that several of Lucifer's vassals came quickly to answer the door.

Michael dismissed him. "Thank you Iofiel you may return to your tasks."

"Thank you, High Prince," came the reply, and Iofiel paused, looked warily at Michael as if to speak, and then flew out of sight.

Immediately the door opened, and Michael walked through not waiting for an invitation, and spoke.

"Hail. The Builder of Heaven command's audience with my brother Lucifer. Where is he?"

Startled and tripping over themselves, the house angels stumbled over their words.

"High Prince Michael," said one.

"Oh my," said another.

Several bowed as was the custom when in the presence of a Lumazi; the others stood and spoke.

"He is not here my Lord. The Chief Prince has taken leave of the palace, and we do not know of his return or of his..."

Michael interrupted.

"Your knowledge is not necessary. I will wait. Escort me to the guest room as my journey has wearied me, and I long for rest before my return, and I would see the palace designed for El once more before I take my leave to Heaven."

Michael immediately stepped to enter the winding staircase, and several of the angels scurried to go before him to slow him.

"Ah my Lord, perhaps it would be best if thou retire to the main chamb..."

"Nonsense," said Michael. "Would you bar access to he who stands before the presence of God?"

"Uh, of course not my lord," said one.

Michael reached the top of the steps and began to turn the handle of the door.

"My Lord, please allow me to acquire linens and fresh manna for thy visit," said the attendant.

"You may depart," said Michael.

Quickly they ran back downstairs to parts unknown. Michael opened the door and stepped in.

Raphael sat across from him, his hands were shackled, and his mouth gagged. Lilith stood over him and held Raphael's inkhorn, stylus, and tome.

"What is the meaning of this outrage?" Michael demanded.

Lilith smiled and spoke, "Please come in High Prince, and join us."

"Explain yourself Grigori! Release the High Prince or be judged."

"Oh, I think not my prince," said Lilith.

Raphael's gag muffled his speech, but his warning to Michael was clear.

Michael heard steps behind him and then a thud. Pain raced across the back of his head, and he fell hard to the floor. As he looked up, he saw the face of Abaddon who had pummeled him from behind with a statue. Michael smiled as he hit the floor and went unconscious.

His plan had worked perfectly.

Nothing Covered...

End of day Six.

"Astarte we must complete the task for which we have arrived. Go to Talus; he will, of course, be surprised to see you. When you arrive, let him know immediately that you have word from me. Let him know that Abaddon has escaped the bowels of Hell."

Ashtaroth's eyebrows rose and he cocked his head and spoke. "My Lord, I do not understand. Your desire is to *inform* him that Abaddon has been released?"

"Yes, Astarte inform him. As his mind is so clouded in his blind allegiance to El, he will not be able to conceive of such a thing and will undoubtedly accuse you of false assertions. His temperament is such that he will become agitated over such accusations, particularly from an Issi. He will temper his remarks at first, but press him Astarte. Press him and give him no quarter to mask his contempt for thy kind. Indeed, let him know the fullness of both Abaddon's and your own disdain for his leadership. Make him aware of his failure as a leader. Make note that the first of all Elohim ever judged springs from his house. Provoke him Astarte. Deride his race and his need for respect will incline him to lose reason, and when his reason is lost to him. He will be ripe for my plan."

"And what are your plans my Lord?" asked Ashtaroth.

"Civil war my dear Astarte, civil war. For it will be in that moment that Murmur will escort Sariel to the house of Talus. Your timing must be precise, for I fully expect the words that I shall put into Murmur's mouth to provoke Sariel and Talus into confrontation. When that occurs, we will move against Heaven. In their confusion, we shall overtake them, and Heaven will be ours to control. Now go and delay not, for the time of our ascension is nigh."

Astarte bowed. "Yes, my Lord." He departed from the palace to make haste towards Talus' abode.

"Murmur come with me," said Lucifer. "I desire that we use your gifts of encouragement and your ability to affirm to a different use."

* * *

Ashtaroth went to the mansion of Talus and knocked on the ivory doors.

An attendant answered, “Yes herald of Lucifer, to what does the house of Talus owe for this visit?”

Ashtaroth bowed respectfully. “I bring grave word for High Prince Talus. My master would bear him news as to the happenings on Earth.”

“Indeed? Very well then,” said the attendant. “Please come in.”

Ashtaroth made his way into the palace and entered a room of white. Ivory and pearls adorned the walls, and the ceiling was translucent to the sky; the furniture plated in silver. Ashtaroth sat down and waited for the Prince.

He did not have to wait long as Talus promptly entered the living room and greeted Ashtaroth with a smile.

Ashtaroth stood immediately upon his entrance and bowed. “Lumazi.”

“Please. Please.” Talus motioned for Ashtaroth to sit. “To what honor do I owe the herald of Lucifer, and an Issi no less that he would come to my home?”

“I bring you grave news of Abaddon my Lord.”

Talus frowned when he heard the name, his countenance visibly disturbed.

“And what of our brother?” Talus asked.

“Word has come from my master to inform you that Abaddon has escaped.”

“Escaped?” Talus said. “Impossible! Escape is not possible from that realm. El has set at the Maw of the great mountain an Elohim who watches the way that none may enter, and that none may pass. You are mistaken.”

“But my Lord, my message has come from the Chief Prince himself. I simply carry his word.”

Talus rose from off the couch where he sat and towered in front of Ashtaroth.

“El’s will be done. El has designed a creature that consumes the life of Elohim, a prison fit for one who cared not for the life of his own kind. No, my friend, there is no escape from the creature. Abaddon is lost, for there can be no evasion from that which El hast made.”

Ashtaroth rose to his feet, his face red with anger.

“Mistaken?” Ashtaroth said, his voice echoed irritation for Talus’ suggestion that he spoke in error. “Nay, Lord Prince I am not mistaken, but thou hast confirmed what I have long suspected. You are robust in strength and power, but bereft of knowledge. I come to thee with word from the Chief Prince himself, and you would toss my words aside as if they were dung. My master has well spoken of thy kind. You are indeed deserving of the destruction that awaits you. For even now while we speak; the seeds of thy downfall are at work, and know oh great prince that thy end lies not far behind.”

Talus looked on Ashtaroth with shock and teemed with anger that he would be spoken to in such a manner, but Ashtaroth did not stop and continued in his berate.

"Even now as El is at rest in Sabbath, the Chief Prince moves to wipe from the heavens the stench of your foolish rule. Even now, Abaddon waits with a third of Heaven's legions to overthrow you. Yet I stand before you as a clarion call to action, and you still stand resolute to die in ignorance."

Talus glared at Ashtaroth and his eyes were wide in astonishment and disbelief. "Would you provoke me Ashtaroth? Have you come to make light of El's rule and of my own house?"

Ashtaroth looked upon Talus and smirked, "Nay Prince of Buffoons. I would not make light of so contemptible a house absent of dignity and intelligence. Oblivion indeed awaits thee, and may it embrace you and all your kind."

Talus lunged at Ashtaroth; his anger boiled as a cauldron within him.

Ashtaroth stood defiant and with a pleased look on his face waited for the blow that was sure to come. Talus with the back of his hand slapped Ashtaroth across his jaw and knocked the angel hard to the ground.

Fueled by offense and insult, Talus' eyes flared, and his voice turned heavy in warning. "I know not what breach of protocol you inflicted with Apollyon, but you stand before a Prince of God, continue to speak words of treason and division, and know of a surety that dissolution awaits you," said Talus.

Ashtaroth looked upon the great prince. His eyes narrowed, and his mouth bled, and his bruised cheek ached, swollen by the impact of Talus' blow. Ashtaroth spit blood on the floor, and looking defiant and unbowed, struggled to his feet. With resolution, he looked into the eyes of his prince and spoke.

"I am not hesitant to answer thee on this matter, O prince. For know that although I may be smitten by thy hand, your title is onerous to me, for thou art neither worthy of honor and are empty of distinction."

Talus hovered over Ashtaroth his hands raised to deal a blow of dissolution to so scornful an angel. Fists clenched and with a wail of rage, the mighty angel lifted his great hands to bear down on Ashtaroth.

Talus in his anger did not hear the door open and failed to notice that the attendants' of his house, Sariel, and Murmur stood in the doorway and watched in shock as Talus pummeled Ashtaroth with his bare hands.

* * *

Slowly Michael opened his eyes. His head was still sore from Abaddon's blow. Groggy he awoke to see that he was not alone.

Raphael reached with his manacled hand to hold Michael's arm.

"Move slowly my friend. You were struck from behind."

"Ah," said Abaddon, "the prince has awakened. Thus begins the descent of the first of the High Princes. Your collaboration with El will soon come to an end."

Abaddon sat on top of a table, his mouth filled with manna leaf. He crunched as a cow that chewed the cud, and he leaned over on top of a long metal plow shear that had been beaten flat; its edge sharp as a razor.

Michael slowly rose to his feet, but his strong arms were constricted by the chains, and shackles that gripped him tightly.

"How long have I been unconscious?" Michael asked.

"One hour," replied Raphael.

Michael looked at his friend and whispered. "We must leave with all haste, for Charon will be here soon."

Michael then looked upon Abaddon and spoke. "You are a fool Destroyer, yet I know that nothing but destruction can be spoken from thy lips. Release us I command you, and perhaps I will bring petition before the Lord God that He might spare thee from His wrath, which is sure to come."

Abaddon placed his hand on his stomach and broke out laughing.

"You think I hold El in such esteem that I would entrust my fate to a God who would destroy me? Nay High Prince. I will never again bow the knee to such a being that would do nothing while my kind wastes away, yet has the power to prevent it. Never again will I worship a creature that would imagine so abominable a thing as Hell. I spit on his mercy. I have tasted his wrath, and I shall not taste it again. Soon He will be brought low. For the Chief Prince himself will take up my cause, and he will be God!"

Michael looked at Abaddon and studied him intently. "Your doom is certain, and your conviction is sure. You simply do not know it yet, but rest assured your sin shall find you out."

Abaddon laughed and let out a loud burp from the volume of manna leaf he had digested.

"Do you know what I have learned Prince of the Kortai? I have fellowshipped with Lilith, and he has gone to great lengths to show me the uses of these instruments of Raphael: his stylus, inkhorn, and tome: such a wonderful *gift* from the Prince of all Grigori. However, Prince Michael, I had never thought I would be blessed to hold within my hands the Tome of Hell itself. My Lord King will enjoy this I am sure"

Michael panicked for a moment, and then discreetly felt the inner folds of his robes. The keyring with the keys to Death and Hell was still fastened safely against his skin. He breathed a sigh of relief and glowered at Abaddon.

Raphael spoke, "Abominable creature, I do not fear thee. The Lord rebuke you!"

Abaddon laughed, picked up the stylus in his hand, and twirled the writing instrument between his fingers playing with the captured.

"Are you aware Michael, that Raphael has the power to know all things present and that contained within this small tome, he carries the knowledge of all things? His tome is connected to all tomes. His is the sum of all knowledge that may be known. If I were to write in its pages, I may create using the power given to him by El. Did you also know Michael that Raphael was *Sephiroth*?"

Michael looked at Raphael. He had remembered the living statue and the inscription at the bottom emblazoned at the base. 'S-e-p-h-i-r-o-p-t-h' it said, but he did not have time to question Raphael. Charon would be here shortly and escape was paramount.

Raphael opened his mouth to speak. "You creature have not the wisdom to behold even a jot of the knowledge of God. May you find its value useless to you."

Abaddon replied, "Ah— that Grigori is but a thin hope indeed, but fear not. After we have extracted from your tome all the information we seek. Know of a surety that thine stone shall belong to Lilith."

Abaddon moved from sitting off the desk, rose to his feet, and walked over to glare at Raphael.

"This tome is also a witness to the conspiracy of God. Contained herein lies the truth of the God king's plan to supplant us. For from the foundations of the world, were we created to serve as ministers to the clay-borne, and this Raphael, Prince of all Grigori — you knew."

Abaddon slapped Raphael across the cheek, and the blow made blood splatter across Michael's face.

Michael jostled to Raphael's defense, but his manacles tightened fast around his ankles and wrists.

"You will pay for this Abaddon. Your debt shall be hung as a sign about thy neck!"

"Not today great prince," said Abaddon. "Not today. Yet take comfort that both Raphael and you shall live to see the fruition of our cause. His tome will be kept safely in the hands of Lilith so that we might monitor the happenings of all things."

Just as Michael moved closer to see Raphael's wound, the door opened. Lilith walked in, and Abaddon gave him the Tome of Raphael.

Lilith thumbed through its pages, and his eyes were aglow with the excitement that a child might display upon the opening of a Christmas present. He leafed through its pages and turned to look back at his captors. "You do realize Raphael, that we will never serve the clay-borne. We will frustrate El's plans and bring to naught all those that would side with the God-king and his plans to enslave us."

Raphael looked upon Lilith with a scowl. "You serve what is now a lap dog, one who would betray his own father. Would the creature say to the creator why hast thou made me thus? Yet you rebel against the glorious plan that El hast made thee partaker of. El knows of your plans. Would thou hope to battle with God?"

Lilith and Abaddon looked at each other and laughed.

Lilith spoke on the duo's behalf. "You have yet to grasp the extent to which we will not submit to his will on this matter. El will not battle us but will abdicate the throne voluntarily. You see my prince; we know that El cannot be defeated by strength of arms. Although by force shall not the God-king be overthrown, but His own love and compassion shall be his undoing. For God so loves the world that he would lay down his own life. This *Sephiroth*, you know, and this weakness we shall exploit.

"We are meant to rule--not serve. El has lost His way and in doing brings ruin to us all. No, my prince, El will not be swayed through reason or force of our hand, but by His own free will, shall our bondage to his will come to an end."

At that moment, an explosion rocked the building, and screams could be heard coming from outside. Abaddon moved to the side of Raphael and Michael, to prevent any means of their escape, and to see to their security. Lilith raced towards a window to look outside.

"What is it?" cried Abaddon.

Lilith looked outside and saw the destruction of a section of the city's wall. Guards with newly minted swords valiantly attempted to do battle with a figure cloaked in dust, fire, and smoke. Manacled chains dropped from its sides, and the roar and the thunder of its hammer-like arms rang throughout the city courtyard. It raised its arms and fire and brimstone enveloped and engulfed all those that stood in its way. The guards were immediately consumed in fire, and small pyres of bodies lined the ground. As each Elohim fell, a huge vacuum of flame, magma, and smoke engulfed and swallowed up those who dared to interfere with the creature's progress, and a wall of flame followed it, and anything caught therein smelted in its wake.

With one chain-like tentacle, the Elohim held a guard by the throat and tossed him effortlessly into the fires with others. The dark cowled creature lashed and beat Elohim senseless, and they were dragged alive screaming into blackness and flame.

"Lilith?" said Abaddon.

Lilith turned from the window and quickly looked at Abaddon in panic.

"We must leave for Heaven now!"

"What is it?" Abaddon roared back in frustration.

Michael chuckled and looked Abaddon dead in the eye. "Your sin has found you out."

Abaddon quickly left Raphael's side, raced to the window, and peered down to look in the distance at the spectacle below. His eyes grew large, and his flesh turned pale. Panic gripped him.

Charon had come to claim him and Hell had followed.

* * *

Sariel looked upon Talus in disbelief and disgust and spoke angrily to his brother. "Would you bring dissolution to even more of my kind?"

And with a swiftness that belied his frame, Sariel flew to the aid of Ashtaroth, and Talus smote the Prince of Issi and knocked him to the floor. Sariel's flesh was torn, and his face was bearishly marred from the raw and bestial swipe of Talus' blow.

Talus paused as the realization that he had struck Sariel settled upon him, and he moved to see to his brother.

One of the attendants of the manor looked on the duo with eyes wide in disbelief and spoke. "In El's name — he struck the High Prince!"

"What manner of conduct is this?" another yelled.

Ashtaroth lay next to his prince, lifted his head unto his own lap, and berated Talus. "Once again your kind's buffoonery so legendary and pronounced has caused hurt. Who else must suffer at thy hand *both* foolishness and injury?"

Sariel shook his head as if to prevent himself from falling unconscious from the blow dealt by Talus. He slowly pushed his torso up from off the floor. Ashtaroth loosened his hold, and Sariel rose to his feet and looked upon his brother to speak.

"Restraint is not in thy kind. Destruction swells in thy loins and ruin follows thee."

Sariel then hurled himself into the bosom of Talus and the two great princes slammed through the front door of the manor and rolled into the courtyard. Each attendant scattered to flee from the chaos as shrubbery and indentations in the lush soil of Heaven ripped apart. Boulders were thrown high into the air from the commotion, and a cloud of dust smothered the grounds as the mighty angels wrestled in Heaven's lush dark earth. Arelim attendants ran to assist their prince, swarmed over Sariel, and struggled in vain to have him loose Talus.

Sariel's sigil stone suddenly glowed brightly within his chest. The innate power of El visibly pulsed from him, and three of his attackers were repelled back and hurled through windows, shrubbery, and the manor walls.

Ashtaroth rushed to block an Arelim attendant from accosting Sariel when his attacker was launched into the air by the force of Sariel's blow. Ashelon was his name, an attendant of Talus' house who now found himself uncontrollably thrown into the air. Like a cat, he twisted and contorted his body in vain to avoid the pearl spires that protruded from the court grounds. But speed was not his ally and the force of his plummet only hastened his impalement on one of the spires that raced to pierce his angelic flesh. With a thud, his body was run through, and his blue blood soiled the white pinnacle that flew the banner of house Arelim.

His body twitched and hung like a standard in the wind as the life force that animated from his stone slowly drained from him. Cobalt blood that flowed through Elomic veins pooled on the manicured grounds and stained the ivory pearl of the heavenly spire. He cried in anguish as the sound of gurgled blood choked his last breath. Ashelon pierced all ears with his death cry. "What have we to do with the house of Issi, and who shall take up mine cause?"

Ashelon released a final gasp for air, and the embers which fired his stone heart faded, and his heartstone became black as night.

On looking Arelim and Issi attendants stopped and looked at Ashelon's form; some revealed smug satisfaction while others boiled over in a potpourri of grief and rage, yet each was equally distraught and looked on in bewilderment and confusion as Ashelon's elements slowly dissolved and returned to fires of the Kiln. The great spire outside of Talus' home now stood stained and pooled with the blood from Ashelon. A monument to the blood spilled on his soil, a testament to a house known as the house of Apollyon -- not Talus.

Talus and Sariel continued in heated battle, blind to the dissolution which stood about them and oblivious to the corruption and gathering storm of angels that stood in their midst.

Ashtaroth smiled at Murmur from across the grassy knoll. Murmur nodded in acknowledgment and smirked in approval as hundreds of Elohim flocked to gather to view, aid, and or stop the escalation of hostilities between the two princes and their kind.

Murmur looked on in quiet satisfaction. *Lucifer would be pleased,* he thought.

Civil war had begun.

And there was war in Heaven...

Charon's roar deafened the ears of his combatants and like fleas that irritate the skin. He flicked away all who stood between him and his quarry. His face bent to capture his renegade charge. Charon was the personification of the vengeance of God, and only God could help anyone who crossed his path.

Abaddon had escaped and sought refuge within the quartz walls of Athor. The scent of Abaddon littered the whole city, but the odor was most concentrated in the crystalline structure that stood in Charon's path: the house of Lucifer. Citizens came from across Athor to protect the home of their King; alerted that Lucifer's stronghold might come under assault.

Athor's protectorate hovered and stood ready as one man. Each was equipped with new swords to stop Charon. A line of Elohim one thousand strong resolved to face the Warden of Hell and keep him from setting foot on the palace grounds.

Each angel of the line watched the black wall of acrid smoke and rubble. Winds rife with sulfur irritated their ears and skin. Yet bravely they waited and wondered who this day among them would experience dissolution. Could they stand against the living manifestation of the vengeance of God?

Anxiety filled them all as they watched the oncoming cloud of noxious gas and smoke draw closer.

Screams and cries of anguish emanated from the dark soot that billowed before them. The agony-filled wails from those first fallen to encounter the myrmidon of Hell. Wisps of orange and red flickered from the black smolder and flames leaped into the sky.

The ground shook with each step of Charon's advance.

Each one could sense that Charon was closer now. His every footstep felt in the vibrations in the ground. Angels grew tense and braced themselves. Several tightened their hold around the grip of their swords and anxiety leaped from angel to angel like an airborne virus, infecting all with fear.

Again, the ground shook.

Cacian an angel of the line looked at the tall dark wall of smolder that loomed before them. Ash littered the air and made it difficult to breathe. Each angel coughed and sought to wave the air clean and in vain straining to peer into the distance.

Slowly marching from the midst of the tender and smoke, Charon appeared as if one might step from behind a curtain. The ferryman of doom approached, cowled in a black leather-like robe of Elomic flesh and with a mare's skeleton for a frame. He dragged from rusted iron chains the screaming bodies of Elohim who had dared to defy him. As fish caught in hooks squirming for release, their wails of torment filled the air. Each was engulfed in flames and charred, yet somehow alive. The fires burned to the sky but did not extinguish. Each captive thrashed and screamed for release as they writhed in pain: eaten alive by the digestive flames of Hell.

Hell was alive. She had minions that fed her from afar. Each blistering maggot leeched the life force of the Elohim dragged in Charon's wake. Closer Charon marched trailing bodies behind him: an army of one poised against a legion of angels.

Cacian saw the bodies dragged by Charon and digested by Hell's flames. He reached up to feel the ash that fluttered in the wind and his eyes grew wide in terror, for the ash was the consumed flesh of his fallen comrades. In that moment, he beheld in revelation the entirety of who Charon was and screamed.

"Flee!" said one.

"Stand thy ground!" yelled another.

"Bring him down!" Taurus commanded.

Commander Taurus of the newly formed Athan army looked to his air chief Xercon. "You know what to do," He said.

Xercon nodded and rose into the air.

Xercon oversaw the command of the south wind and the storm. He raised his hands and spoke to the listening jet stream, who obediently hearkened to his command and quickened her pace. Large cauliflower clouds quickly converged over the assembled army and the sky darkened and grew greenish in color. A cumulous pillar of white clouds rose into the heavens; carried aloft by columns of rotating air until the very top of the cloud canopy sheared itself against the upper atmosphere and became as an anvil. Lightning streaked across the belly of the pillowed mountain and illuminated the now-darkened sky. Thunder crashed off eardrums and shook the ground. Water droplets swelled in the folds of the infant storm, grew obese, and threw themselves from the heights to pummel and drench the ground below Charon's feet.

Charon continued his snail's pace forward as the soil beneath him saturated with water and the ground engorged itself on the pounding rain. The earth beneath him became soft and muddy. Charon's movement slowed, hindered by Xercon's command of the wind and rain.

Lightning brightened the sky and the denizens of Athor covered their eyes as the storm suddenly unleashed crackling white arms of voltage and pummeled the ground where Charon stood. Shockwaves echoed off the sky in a drumbeat of outrage, bass, and destruction.

In a dance of terawatted ferocity, strokes of lightning discharged from the sky and embraced Charon in their fury. The power of the mile-long bolts heated the air around him to twice that of the sun and vaporized all things. The muddy ground beneath his feet instantly turned to glass and sealed the Warden of Hell fast. The vacuum created from the superheated air clapped its hands, and great booms of thunder raced as a sprinter out of his blocks and dashed across the city and into the region roundabout. The sound shook the foundations of buildings and knocked individuals off their feet.

Xercon spoke the Elomic command to the south wind and was ever attentive to her master's cry. The great beast upon which the clouds rode hearkened to his call. The vast jet stream invisibly wrote into the ground with her finger, and a cyclone lifted itself from the dust of the earth and yawned as a man awakens from slumber. Again, bolt after bolt rained down upon Charon. Electric current flowed through his body and traveled through him to find release in the ground. A target Charon became: a conduit for all the wrath of the living sky. Pleased to see the myrmidon stagger, Xercon continued to assault him from the heavens.

Black finger-like clouds reached down to grapple Charon and appendage after swirling appendage dropped as tentacles from the sky and touched the ground. They howled and wailed dissolution to all that would dare cross their path.

Xercon motioned with his hands and with a thought commanded the funnels to collide with anything that walked the trail of Charon.

And so they did.

Screaming wrath and destruction, they squalled as they hammered Charon. Winds ripped trees from the ground, and loose shards of quartz rose and darted toward the Warden of Hell. The twin sisters of wind waltzed around each other; launching shrapnel of wood, metal, and flesh as missiles. Their impact was ferocious and Charon stood as a nail hammered into the embracing arms of the earth. The cracking of great oaks and the roar of winds gone mad filled the air. Blackness from the immense clouds masked the eyes, as fine grains of sand ground flesh. Rain and gale torrentially beat structure after toppling structure to powder.

Charon's tentacles of rusted metal flayed in the tempest winds and with his great legs, he stood trapped, snared deep in the ground now turned to glass blasted by wind and quartz.

Xercon satisfied that his minions of air and water had pummeled the warden into submission, raised his sword and dove to fall upon Charon from the sky, and like lightning from heaven, he plummeted into the morass of rain, smoke, and the rage of cyclones gone amok, and fought to battle Charon in hand to hand combat.

Thus, the angels of the line watched in hopeful anticipation that a prince of the power of the air might slay the Warden of Hell; looking on as the very forces of the troposphere were unleashed on their behalf.

Deep at the base of the supercell of vortices, they fought as streaks of lightning bulleted across the city and smashed Athor and the land roundabout. Thunder burst the eardrums of angels who watched the shimmering outline of the two titans gripped in mortal combat.

As a hurricane feeds off the waters of the mighty sea, the south wind churned and lifted buildings, trees, and boulders and threw them against Charon. Smoke billowed from the center of the struggle, and suddenly without warning fire exploded, and like a pebble tossed in a basin of tranquil water. The ripples of the shock wave rocketed through the land. Buildings flung outward in all directions, flung aside as trash. Smoke and debris filled the city and covered the angels of the line as each one looked to see who would survive the havoc of wind and storm gone mad.

Slowly the gusts subsided, and the roaring columns of cyclonic air slowed, dissipated, and lifted themselves into the sky. The rain stilled its torrential pour to a wimpish drizzle, and buildings, trees, and debris fell from the cleared sky and crashed to the ground.

Angels at the line strained to peer through the smoke and fire: to see a lone figure that stood at the center where cyclones and lightning once played.

Cacian peered through the hazy veneer of black smoke and trembled as he saw the shadow of he who marched towards them; his tendrils flailed with the familiar sound of rusted chains. Chains that now dredged against ground that was now turned to glass. Charon dragged the charred body of Xercon. And his captor's muffled screams filled the air. Cacian watched in fascinated horror as the maggots of Hell burrowed through Xercon's mouth and ears; watched as Xercon struggled to breathe as the worms filled his lungs. His body aglow now torched with the fire of Hell's flames.

Like the morning dew that settles across a valley, fear fell over the soldiers of the line.

Cacian looked to make out the boneless features of the myrmidon of Hell. Charon's fleshless skull expressed no emotion. Yet the pace of his quickened gait made clear that one sentiment governed his march ever closer toward his foes that remained.

Rage.

* * *

Lucifer made his way quickly from the central city towards the northern gate. His eyes darted nervously to each citizen, and he wondered if any suspected what he had planned, but each bowed as was custom when he passed. It was a normal thing for the Prince of Heaven to exit Jerusalem to depart for Earth. Lucifer traveled closer to Heaven's entry gates and ruminated to himself on the task that lay before him.

For the forces of Heaven not to overwhelm his strike force, he must hold the waypoints shut. There could be no Ladders into Heaven while his campaign was afoot. The Kingdom of God must be cut off from the rest of the multiverse. To accomplish this end, he must somehow usurp the guard at each of the four gates; then, with his own hands, he would cripple Heaven.

Finally, his feet brought him to the pearled walls of Heaven and the post of Deramiel, guard of the northern gate.

The great pearled gates towered before him, a massive structure of whitish black pearl, and ivory with a wall 24 feet wide and a thousand cubits high. Two solid gold doors latticed with drawings of two silver lions' heads, stood regally etched as living portrayals and roared the praises of God whenever the gates opened. Set between the gates with a flaming spear was Deramiel: ever vigilant to guard and watch over the bridge that connected Heaven with the rest of creation. Lucifer had always thought it curious that God would station guards at the entrance to Jerusalem. For Heaven had no adversaries and the Elohim were the pinnacle of creation.

Lucifer knew that El's thoughts transcended more than just the present but easily penetrated all possible futures. Lucifer conjectured at that moment that God had anticipated his plan and knew that the city itself would one day be besieged by its own. His mind raced in nervous anticipation as he approached Deramiel.

How to circumvent the Almighty? Would Deramiel turn to our aid?

He would not leave such decisions to possibility. No, he would ensure the completion of his plan even if it meant his brother's demise. Thus, Lucifer plotted the destruction of Deramiel as he elucidated kindness from his mouth.

Deramiel recognized the Chief Prince as he approached. "Hail Lucifer Draco, Prince of Heaven," Deramiel said. "How fares the Archon of Earth?"

Deramiel also was of House Draco, one of Lucifer's own kin. Their affinity ran deep. *Surely,* Lucifer thought. *He will come to my cause.*

"All goes well my friend," Lucifer replied. "I have come with urgent word and am in need of thy strength to assist in that which is to come."

"The High Prince in need of me?" Deramiel said with a puzzled look on his face. "Why in El's name would you have need of me? Speak Lumazi and it shall be done."

Lucifer replied. "There has been counsel among the chief houses concerning the creation of the man. The Royal court is now split in its allegiance to El. Even now, I have come to learn that two of the great houses: Arelim and Issisi are in open conflict in the outskirts of Jerusalem. El Sabbaths and has left a divided council over the service to man. I but seek to maintain the word of our Lord whilst he rests, for all seek their own and not the things, which are El's. Therefore, I now come to thee 'watcher of the way,' for I have no man likeminded that I might attend to this affair and who will naturally care for our state."

Deramiel's eyes lowered as if sadness would overtake him; then he spoke. "If El is on Sabbath, and the court's leadership is divided, then Heaven itself is at risk. What would you ask of me, my Prince?"

"Indeed," replied Lucifer. "As the center guard over the northern gate, you hail the others if anything seems amiss to you. Yet of all the guardians of the gates of Heaven, thou art the only Draco and are chief guard; thus brother, thy House Lord and Prince calls on you now to stand by me and uphold the word of El. I have forces on Earth that will rally to our cause to assist with the quelling of the feud that now roars unabated in the way. Perhaps we might yet quell the division that has stirred Heaven to fight against herself. Those who are against us number more than those who are for us; thus I require your aid, but we must move quickly and quietly to bring them low, or else all that El hast spoken and our house has done to uphold his word will be lost."

Deramiel bowed to his Prince. "El's will be done. What would thou have me do?"

Lucifer looked at him and replied, "Go to and secure the eastern wall. Tell the gate captains that there is a disturbance at House Talus, and the court requires all officers of the realm to appear at Talus' grounds and to render aid and quell the disturbance."

Deramiel bowed. "But my Lord -- please be not angry with thy servant. If I leave who will watch the eastern wall? For Heaven hast no appointed guard but I. To abandon the word of El, to '*Be still at this gate*', would leave Heaven without a watchman on the wall."

Thoughts quickly raced through Lucifer's mind, and he looked upon Deramiel with sadness and said, "I fear El hath left us no choice, for Heaven dost battle against herself. And lo, wherein thy sight doth danger lurk? There is nothing but thee and I that stand here at the gates. There exists no adversary in thy sight, yet furlongs away in the burbs past the Elysian Fields, two of the great houses bring dissolution to the realm. If it seemeth good in thy sight to question thy Prince's wisdom while El himself Sabbaths, then stay. And if it seemeth good to thee to stand idle while thy brothers raze each other in dissolution then stay, but know this. Although I might command thee as a high prince, instead I would adjure thee by the love of God, that thou not stand idle whilst thy brothers fall. Fear not, for thy post, shall not be without guard. I will stand in thy stead and be a watchman on the wall until thou hast returned. I will not fail thee, and all shall be well."

Lucifer placed his hands on Deramiel's strong shoulders, looked him straight in the eye, smiled, and spoke. "You believe in God, believe also in me."

Deramiel reluctantly but subserviently turned to go and said, "As you command my prince."

Deramiel raced off to the northeastern section of the wall to accomplish his Lord's will.

Lucifer watched him go and stood as a sentinel to guard the gate of Heaven. Lucifer smirked when Deramiel was out of sight, pleased that his plan was coming to fruition. He turned towards the bridge of Heaven and recited the words that would allow him to open the city's waypoint into the realms.

A causeway to allow the forces of Abaddon, and Lilith to penetrate the city.

* * *

Lilith walked towards Raphael and lowered himself to whisper into his ear.

"I will take your tome my Prince and use its knowledge against you. Yes, I will leave you alive in the knowledge that there is quickly coming a day that at my name, you shall bow, and with thine own tongue, thou shalt confess that I am thy Lord. Yes, to bring dissolution to thee would rob me of this pleasure. Thus, I will await you in Heaven. Follow me that mine wish might be fulfilled."

Lilith gloated at Raphael and rose to speak to Michael. "Archon I take my leave of thee. I go now to lay waste to thy home. Until we meet again -- oh wait, Abaddon would you like a word with Michael before we depart?"

Abaddon quickly walked closer to Michael and towered over the archangel of Heaven. His claw-like hand unsheathed, and Abaddon slowly ran his talon across the cheek of Michael's face.

"Ah, my prince I leave thee a token of my love for thy God in thine own flesh."

Michael looked at him and stared deeply into his eyes. "Thy fealty to Lucifer will be thy undoing. Walk in thy calling '*Destroyer*', but know the end is not yet thine."

Abaddon angrily dug his claw deep into the epidermis of Michael's face and gouged a piece of flesh from his cheek. Michael grimaced in pain and let out a scream of anguish as angelic blood poured from his wound and raced to color the floor blue.

Abaddon smiled at his handiwork, looking on with glee as Michael held his palm over his wound, and glared at him in pain.

Abaddon turned to go and recited the ancient tongue to summon a ladder. He and Lilith stood in a bubble of power as the Elomic command to part the heavens peeled back to reveal the stars, and in the distance, the eastern jasper gate to the great city of Heaven, and Michael could see that Lucifer stood at the gates.

An explosion shook the house and the walls quaked around them.

"Goodbye Prince of Heaven," said Lilith. "We go to confront the God King."

Suddenly the prismatic funnel of light and heat from a Ladder spread through the room, rocking the foundation of the house. Michael rose to his feet, raced towards Raphael with his bound hands, and jumped to cover his friend. The walls collapsed to the floor, and the ceiling quickly followed.

With his great wings unfurled to protect both him and his brother. Michael huddled with Raphael. The constructed quartz buckled around them. The sound of timber and glass filled the air, and then the room went black.

* * *

“What have we to do with the house of Issi, and who shall take up my cause?"

Ashelon’s death cry pierced the campus grounds of Talus. His lament for vindication traveled through the air and captured the ears of Heaven's citizenry. Like a siren that warned of an impending storm so too did his lament draw notice from the host of Heaven, and as one man, each angel paused to consider.

It was a moment never to be repeated in all the days of Heaven. A day when angels would reflect on whether to follow a cause apart from El’s. Clarity of consciousness spread through the masses of Heaven, a rally to answer a question: whom this day would one serve? Like wildfire, the violence that raged in the courtyard of Talus moved as a pandemic across the topography of the Third Heaven as Arelim struck down Issi, and Harrada engaged Kortai.

Jerahmeel and Gabriel had worked tirelessly to clear and repair the damage caused by Apollyon’s earlier rampage, and like all of Heaven, they heard the death cry of the anguished angel ring throughout the air.

“In El’s name,” said Jerahmeel, “go to, and look to the house of Talus!”

Gabriel nodded in acknowledgment and with a flash of light was gone. The Leopard of Heaven raced towards the quarters of his brother, and the ground moved as a blur beneath his winged feet. Hazy shadows of Heaven’s citizenry zoomed past him, and in the distance of the multicolored grass that was Heaven’s carpet stood the house of Talus.

Gabriel could smell the perspiration in the air, and the ground reverberated with the heavy pounding of angels trampling and wrestling on the ground. Gabriel came to the manicured lawns of house Talus, his eyes looked upon the countryside, and with each batting of the eye, he beheld as angels wrestled one another in a death grip of bloody combat.

Each Elohim was lost in rage and offense; interlocked in a choreographed dance of fists upon beaten skulls. Wings whirled in acrobatic movements of evasion, and gusts of wind lifted up dirt high into the air as throats were slashed. Bones cracked as the concussive force of tackled bodies echoed across Heaven’s tundra.

Yet Gabriel had not come to partake in madness. He came to see his brother Talus. Great drops of sweat fell as pearls from his muscular frame, and with determination of purpose; Gabriel darted amongst the enraged combatants. He dodged and weaved past blow after evaded blow from angels who were oblivious to his presence.

Suddenly a wave of energy traveled across the lawn, and the energy signature of the pulse was unmistakable. A Prince Lord was in exertion. Faster now the Leopard of Heaven ran, quickly he darted between torn wings, leaped over torsos, and ran closer to the center of the blast's origin. Traveling between the hordes of angels, he stopped to gawk at the sight that now stood before him.

Talus and Sariel grappled with one another, arms interlocked, each using knee and elbow to buffet each other as two rams might butt heads. Blood spurted from large gashes torn from the wounds in each angel's flesh. Lacerations drained as water from a faucet, and from Sariel's face hung flesh torn by his brother's assault.

Gabriel looked and saw that neither cared for the destruction that raged about them. His ears burned with the sounds of hate. Verbal assaults filled the once peaceful air of Heaven. Hatred rose as leaven into the sky and was palpable. Like a lanced boil of evil, it seeped into the corners of the realms now that El's presence had withdrawn. His influence so powerful a force that it kept in check avarice and hubris, for in His presence was fullness of joy.

But alas, the glory of God had departed. The Almighty was seemingly asleep to the goings on in His realm. Now new sounds filled Heaven. Heaven was now void of God's influence for the first time, and the silence of sanctification wrought nothing but violence in its wake.

"Let the Arelim bleed," cried one.

"Dissolution to the House of Sariel and his lackeys," was the retort.

In that instant, Gabriel knew that madness had infected Heaven, madness as viral as the flesh-eating bacteria that lined the orbs on a million worlds, a bacterium of madness that exchanged reason for hate. Gabriel then knew what he must do. He and Jerahmeel must restore the soundness of mind to the horde, or oblivion awaited them all.

Gabriel watched as Sariel grabbed Talus by the chin with his left hand and used his right wing to knock the prince backward. The Prince of all Arelim staggered seemingly surprised that a species other than his own could yield such power. Quickly he rose to his feet, his cloven hooves firmly positioned on the ground for support. Sariel sensed an opening and leaped forward to press his attack. Wings arched back as he dove as a bird of prey with taloned hands outstretched. His hands purposed to smite his brother quickly and remove the stone from his flesh. However, the task would be denied him. Gabriel launched his nimble frame into Sariel's body and slammed deep into his chest.

Sariel soared backward against a wall and smashed through brick, pearl, and mortar. Crystal and all colors of precious pearls fell from the crumbling wall.

Quickly Gabriel turned to face his brother Talus.

"Ahh welcome my dear brother Gabriel! It does my heart well to see that you have come to my aid. Of course, our brother must be shown the error of his ways. Come and we shall dispose of him together! What say you?"

Gabriel cocked his head to the side and looked upon his brother as he would upon a stranger.

"I think not brother, and I will take no part in this travesty. Ye both have caused great harm this day, and this madness must come to an end now."

Talus laughed defiantly. "*End*? Indeed today, we *shall* put an *end* to the problem that has plagued Heaven for far too long. Today we shall see the fall of the house, Issi!"

Gabriel realized whatever blood lust Talus had; was now in control of his ability to reason.

Gabriel turned to his left and noted the legion of angels that now approached him. All paused in a mass intermission of hostilities. A thousand eyes bore down in recognition to take note that a Malakim was in their midst. Each within his vicinity paused to determine if he was friend or foe, and Gabriel saw that his every move was watched, as both house Issi and Arelim studied to see for whose cause he would fight.

Gabriel saw that they too were lost in madness, an infection of revenge that manifested itself throughout the throng and was now as a stench wafted aloft in full bloom. Offense, anger, and retaliation raced through the crowd that Gabriel had dared handle Prince Sariel, dared that he would raise his hand in defiance to the prince who now lay unconscious. The swelling throng then gave voice to what he knew permeated their hearts. Cautiously they inched towards him; eyes ablaze that he had dared challenge their Prince.

"He has raised his hand against an Issi," said one.

"Then cut off his hand," yelled another in reply.

"Another lackey to the God King," said another.

Gabriel in all his seasons had never experienced the sensation of alienation that now overtook him. It was a new thing this awareness, an overwhelming sense that his difference created exposure and that exposure posed danger. A danger that emanated from those he would call brethren. The thought of this cognizance, this — division chilled him to the bone.

In Heaven, there was neither male nor female, no recognition of an identity apart from El. But El's Sabbath had created a vacuum in the spirit, a swirling void that bled dry Heaven's holiness and cohesion, and instead ejected disunion, strife, and hate. An absence that created a consciousness of an existence apart from the living God, and in this new atmosphere, order degenerated into chaos. Gabriel noted that fear now settled over him, as night would overtake the escaping sun.

Gabriel was a Malakim, a messenger forever called to deliver the word of El. There were few of his kind in the Third Heaven, for many were off throughout the Second Heaven holding up all things by El's word. The need to be with his own kind gripped him. As a man slapped to prevent unconsciousness, so too was Gabriel now aware that here under the golden-hued skies of Heaven, he was not safe.

Gabriel looked at Sariel still unconscious. He moved quickly, and placed him over his shoulders tucked securely with two of his four wings within the cleft of his back.

The sound of outrage echoed round about him as he handled the prince.

"And where do you think you are going with him?" Talus said.

Gabriel stood mute, leaped over Talus, and with a flash of light, the Leopard of Heaven fled. His available and unencumbered wings unfurled and hurtled Gabriel at breakneck speed back to Jerahmeel. There was strength in unity and the place of unity was where he needed to be if he and his brother would stop the insanity that plagued the great houses this day. So the Leopard of Heaven ran to escape those whom he called brethren, and whose minds were now gripped in madness.

As a cheetah moves through the plains, Gabriel raced back towards the direction of the city. Gabriel flew with ankle-winged feet over the grassy hills and to the woods of Mirabelle. Mirabelle, a forest of honey trees, filled Heaven's air with the scent of cinnamon from their bark and bled sugar from their porous leaves. Their sweet aroma hit Gabriel, but he could not pause to enjoy the pleasures of Heaven this day. Nay, leisure to taste and be dazzled by their multicolored beauty would be denied him, as he wove a path, and dashed between the trees. Gabriel's heart pumped fast and the strength of his gait drowned out all things as he ran across the forest floor to return to the solace of Jerahmeel. The canopy from the tall manna leaves loosed golden rays of light. For a moment, relief filled him knowing that just beyond the acres of Heaven's foodstuff. Jerahmeel stood within the city gates ready to assist him.

Gabriel briefly allowed himself to hope until from his hind his peace dissolved as broken branches woke him from the illusion that safety was yet to come. Runners are warned never to look back; so as not to lose focus on the prize that is set before them. Gabriel did not so, but now turned rearward to hear the thunder of wings and the stomp of hooves behind him.

The ground shook as the tumult of hoofs pummeled the earth in pursuit of the Leopard of Heaven, and he saw their dust trails litter and begin to gray the golden sky. As a pack of jackals might hunt a fox, a hundred thousand angels ran hot in pursuit of Gabriel. A hundred thousand rabid Arelim and Issisi hooves crushed the soft petals of Mirabelle and manna leaf below their feet. Each one with eyes ablaze, set to overtake him at all costs.

* * *

They attacked, the guardians of Athor did. From the sky, they dove to smite the Myrmidon of Hell. In wave after endless wave, they accosted Charon. With newly minted swords, they assailed him in droves.

"Bring him down!" Taurus yelled.

Jaredeem of the house of Draco lifted his voice and like all Draco unleashed a roar of a sonic boom that he might bring Charon to his knees. The concussive wave of sound made its way through the air only to flow around Charon's frame as water glides around the belly of a goose on the surface of the water. The air was meaningless to a creature birthed within the Kiln. Charon unleashed barbed tentacles from his equine body and wrapped Jaredeem in coils of punishment for his folly.

Jaredeem fell to his knees in agony. His hands held his throat as he gurgled from the blood that now filled his lungs, and his body contorted in pain. Pain, an experience he was never designed to know. Pain that coursed through him like a thousand needles that stabbed into him at once. Pain as the flames of Hell liquefied his esophagus. Pain because he had a mouth, but could not scream. The vocal cords which before had been used to sing the praises of El used to assist Heaven's and Earth's various choirs in song were now dangled as soiled menstrual rags to be discarded in Charon's tentacled hand. Now tossed to his rearward where the remoras of Hell feasted on all things angelic.

Hell tasted angel flesh and multiplied her fiery maggots, the horrific fiery worms that did not die, bred by the tainted flesh of changed Elohim who would now eternally be cremated in Hell's fire.

Charon marched towards Lucifer's chief palace, unstoppable and undeterred by the thousand arrayed against him. Charon was an army of one, a mobile force of nature whose very breath immobilized those in front of him. His socketless eyes pierced and brought his enemies to their knees to sob uncontrollably. Angels whose eyes locked with his stood dazed as if looking into nothing, but seeing played before them the futility to fight. Many knelt in the hypnotic trance of despair and wailed as the flames simply overtook them where they cried.

Angel after angel was rooted in shock motionless as their very flesh was eaten away only to create and ignite even more pyres, they stood transfixed in horror at the image they saw of themselves in Charon's eyes. Engorging Hell's taste for the delicacy of Elomic flesh, the devourer of angels craved more. For Hell was lust. She was oblivious to all but one thing: she must feed, and the legions, which dared to interject themselves in Charon's path, provided her sustenance.

Charon ripped stones from flesh and provided Hell morsel after delicious morsel, and with each stone's destruction, the trail of angelic dust littered the ground like freshly packed snow.

"In El's name, he cannot be stopped!" yelled one.

Taurus who had observed the battle from afar realized the true nature of Charon. If they attacked in mass, more tentacles sprouted from his body to repel them. For every attack directed against him, he simply grew stronger. It was then that Taurus knew that against this abomination from the Kiln, resistance was futile. With hammers for hands, Charon smashed his way against the throng, and bodies sailed in all directions. Forward still Charon marched and with barbed tentacles, he whiplashed angel after angel into submission. Others he picked up and flung headlong into buildings and trees. Some asphyxiated, for Charon suffered none to bar him. Stones were smashed and throats cut. Nothing stopped the force that marched only hundreds of yards toward the palace walls. For, Charon moved without pause and trod over bodies piled underneath him.

Screams filled the air. Smoke and flames jetted across the sky, and angelic blood flowed as rainwater might pour through the drains of a city. Hell's fires advanced as waves that crashed against the shore. Like storm surge, the flames moved and followed Charon on his path, and with every living thing the fires touched, life drained, and agony ensued.

For once entrapped in Hell's unforgiving embrace; the flesh festered releasing hundreds of new parasitic worms that raced across the Athorian battlefield. Taurus realized to fight against Charon was to battle Hell itself. Nay, for Hell and Charon, were but mere, singular, and localized manifestations of the wrath of God. Taurus sighed in the light of this revelation; in the knowledge, that perhaps to follow Lucifer was indeed to have followed madness. Nevertheless, he was Elohim, and Elohim did not defer to failure and in that instant, Taurus gave the order that would seal his own doom.

"Bring him down whatever the cost! For freedom — for Lucifer!" Taurus shouted.

The battle cry carried across the field of Athor, and angels attacked with desperate ferociousness in the knowledge that to attack Charon was perhaps never again to breathe Earth's air. Using all means available to them to slow, nay stop the Warden of Hell, they threw themselves at him, a phalanx of wings, muscle, and swords to take down he who would trespass the ground of their Lord's house.

The land rose in upheaval and shook its objection, as Elohim who could control the ground brought their powers to bear, and the Earth itself rose as an enemy against the myrmidon. Charon latched his great tentacles as anchors in the earth's flesh, and they bored until he hit rock, and, as a surfer would ride the waves of the tide. Charon strode upon the back of the land. As the earth opened to bury him, Charon launched more anchors to pieces of ground that were undisturbed. Unstoppable, he inched closer toward the Athorian wall before him.

As ants fight off an attacker to their nest: so too did the Elohim launch wave after endless wave against him. And for each Elohim that engaged him, he slowed, his advance postponed until there were no Elohim left to fight.

The angels buzzed like a swarm to Charon and commanded all the elements to engage Him. From the scorched flash of lightning to the rumble of the earthen floor, each converged to the place upon which Charon stood. A great cloudburst of rain poured upon Charon, and the droplets fell from the sky. Each bead designed to extinguish hell's flame.

Steam wafted into the sky and the hiss of evaporation against the flickering tongue of the inferno's heat made the watery cloudburst of no effect. This was hellfire. It kindled off the flesh of Elohim–birthed from the cauldron of the Kiln itself. It could not be extinguished, and it would never go out.

Charon's eyeless sockets gazed upon the battalion sprawled before him. With gaps for ears, he heard the wails and cries of battle as they moved closer to engage him. They ran, flew, and galloped. Issi, Arelim, Harrada, and Kortai. Elohim of every race and station leaped to smite the warden to no avail. Charon simply marched ever forward.

For on this day, he who would bar the path of Charon only hastened his own doom.

* * *

"Are you alright?" Michael said.

"Aye," replied Raphael, "Yet my leg is pinned somehow; I cannot move it."

The dust slowly dissipated as Michael and Raphael moved gingerly among the rubble strewn over and around them. Charon's assault was closer now, his presence nearer to the origin of his prey.

"I too am bound by these shackles yet still. My hands are not free to lift the beam from off you."

Suddenly there was a pounding on the chamber door.

"Prince Michael, Prince Raphael! Can you hear me?" said a panicked, shrill voice.

"In here!" Michael replied. "Quickly in here!"

The door flung open and wood and metal flew across the room. Arms grabbed the sides of the door jam, and a figure stepped into the room and carefully walked over debris that lay strewn across the entryway.

"Prince Michael?" said the voice.

"Aye — but who art thou? And art thou friend or foe?"

The dust settled, and it became clear to Michael that the figure, which raced over towards Raphael, was a Kortai his brother in league to the city of Athor: Iofiel.

"My liege let me assist you." Iofiel raced to his Lord's side and picked up pieces of rubble strewn on the floor from the collapsed ceiling.

"Hurry!" said Michael. "Charon's path will bring him here soon; we cannot delay."

Iofiel reached Raphael and lifted a large beam from over his waist, freeing the Grigori.

"Ah, much thanks," said Raphael.

Iofiel nodded and turned to free Michael. Grabbing him with his great arms, Iofiel hoisted him up from off the floor tossing rubble to the side.

"Can you break the shackles?" asked Michael

"Yes, stand still and stretch out your arms," Iofiel replied.

Michael did so, and Iofiel with a swipe of his hand smashed the links that held the cuffs tight. Michael flexed, and the shackles snapped free, leaving broken links dangling from his wrists as an ornate set of bracelets.

Michael rubbed his wrists to massage them and spoke. "Thank you, my brother. Come, we must go quickly before the Warden befalls this place. We must warn the princes in Heaven of Lucifer's treachery before he has time to launch his assault." Michael nodded to Raphael and turned to go when Iofiel grabbed Michael by the arm to stop him.

"But, my Lord, there are those here on Earth and in Athor who require aid, for Lucifer hast, moved all those that would oppose him to a camp deep beneath the Earth. We cannot abandon them!"

Michael eyed Iofiel curiously. "A camp?" Michael replied. "What do you mean he moved them? How many?"

"The exact count is not known, my Lord. However, several thousand have not bowed their knee to the Chief Prince. What I do know is that Lucifer has sought to imitate El and hast made an abode where all those that would defy him would dwell. He views his prison, his 'Tartarus' he calls it, as benevolent in comparison to Hell. He is mad I tell you, simply mad. He announced to all those within Athor that he would bring justice to our realm."

"He said to us all, 'peace', 'peace', yet destruction swiftly followed for all those that would not bow the knee and abdicate allegiance to El. He and a host surrounded us and with his voice, he caused the earth to shake beneath us, and when the ground opened her mouth to swallow us, he had Lilith, the rogue Grigori, create an abominable Ladder that transported everyone to a wretched place of darkness. A new realm within the Earth itself made he and thus imprisoned those who had once helped raise the very stones that decorate this fair kingdom.

Those who tried to reason with him he set as an example to us all. He publicly lifted Crocellus of the Kortai from a tree and had Abaddon chain him thereon. When the restraints were sure, Abaddon gouged with his bare hands the stone of God from his flesh and crushed it into powder. We watched as his stone became as sand in the wind.

Lucifer smiled at us and said that if we would not serve, then dissolution awaited us, or we could accept imprisonment as an act of his mercy. An imprisonment he called Tartarus, yet it is more than a prison; it is a camp of dissolution, a place that in darkness he brings to naught all those that might stand against him. Therefore, we must go far below the city's foundations, near the center of the Earth's heart. There he hast hidden Tartarus from the gaze of those in the Third Heaven."

Raphael spoke. "How is it that thou hast managed to escape Lucifer's gaze? Surely, he would smite thee if he knew of thy aid to us."

Iofiel replied, "I have learned in these dark times to feign fealty to the Lightbringer that I may in some fashion bring to naught his plans. I waited for an occasion to act and watched as he brought you here and stayed near in hopes to succor some opportunity that I might give thee aid. Behold, now my cowardice and failure to act sees the very vengeance of God at Athor's doorstep ready to destroy all that my prince had commanded me to build. For this I am ashamed."

Michael spoke. "Do not be deceived; cowardice on your part doth not bring Charon to Athor. Nay but the Destroyer he hunts, and will do so until Abaddon rests within the bowels of Hell once more. Cease to wonder if your actions bring dishonor, for who knew that for such a time as this hast thou come to this place to save us? For El's thoughts are marvelous, and his ways are past finding out."

Iofiel bowed and replied, "Then I adjure thee by the living God, do not deny your servant this request. But let us go quickly and bring relief to those trapped in the confinement of Lucifer's making, for I would seek how we might frustrate the cause of he who is now the King of Falsehood."

"No," said Michael.

Raphael looked at his brother with a puzzled look. "Michael, what do you mean 'no'? If Lucifer has entrapped our brethren ..."

"Lucifer would not do such a thing! He is Lumazi, he is Chief Prince, and he walks amidst the Stones of Fire"

Pleading Raphael spoke, "But Michael you saw where Abaddon's Ladder ended and who stood there waiting to receive him. What further proof do you need that Lucifer has betrayed us? Did not the Father tell us so?"

"Enough," replied Michael.

"Michael—I know this must be hard to hear, but whom else but Lucifer could free Abaddon? You know this to be true."

"That's enough!" Michael yelled.

Iofiel walked towards Michael, touched his lord softly on the shoulder, and tried to appeal to him. My Lord," said Iofiel "I saw Lucifer order the dissolu..."

"I said, that is enough!" Michael shouted.

Michael shoved aside Iofiel's hand from off his shoulder, turned and grabbed him by his throat, lifted him off his feet, and heaved him hard against a wall.

"I said enough! Do *not* continue to speak falsehood of my brother!"

Iofiel struggled to breathe, and Raphael yelled at Michael to release him, but Michael would not hear.

Raphael ran to them, pulled at Michael's arm, and screamed at him, "What are you doing?"

Nevertheless, Michael's hold was sure, and his hands wrapped tighter around Iofiel's throat.

Iofiel gasped for air as Michael squeezed his throat to silence him, but Iofiel fought to speak reason to Michael. "Have you too left El —to follow after the path of Lucifer?"

Michael's eyes immediately grew wide, the tension in his jaw loosened, and with a look of confusion, he released Iofiel, who fell to the floor wheezing and gasping for breath. Raphael pushed Michael aside and rushed to aid Iofiel. Michael staggered backward as a man dazed, shook his head in disbelief, and stared at them. He then spoke, "What have I done?" Then turned and quickly ran out of the room.

Raphael reached down to assist Iofiel to his feet. "Are you alright, my brother?" he asked.

"Nay," Iofiel replied, still coughing and massaging his neck. He turned to look into the dark hallway that Michael had run into. "My Prince and Lord of my house stands between two opinions. No, my prince, I am not alright."

Raphael nodded, looked into the darkness, and called out to Michael, but Michael would not respond.

Raphael lowered his head, and his face was grim as he stood to his feet and slowly helped Iofiel up. "Let us go. We need to find our trapped brethren."

"And what of the prince?" Iofiel said.

Raphael strained to see through the dimly lit hallway and saw a figure sitting on a wooden beam, his face in his palms and weeping uncontrollably. Raphael turned back to Iofiel and spoke softly. "There are some battles that must be won within before one can fight without."

The two turned to leave and left Michael to his sorrow.

* * *

Gabriel felt his pulse race as he ran through the Elysian Fields. The earth underneath his feet shook violently from the pounding hooves of his pursuers that closed swiftly to overtake him. His breath grew shallower, and his lungs burned from carrying Sariel. Gabriel was fast, but even the Leopard of Heaven could not escape his stalkers with such a weight on his shoulder. He slowed, and he knew he could not outrace them. The wind felt good against his cheeks. The gentle breeze ruffled the fine tall stalks of manna leaf that carpeted open plains and acres of tilled land sprawled before him. The terrain proffered no advantage that he might conceal himself. There would be no hiding this day.

Closer the horde came, offended. Because he succored the Issi high prince, and in doing so, he made mad his brethren with even more rage, igniting the fury that now caused two of the great houses to hunt him. Their cries of dissolution to Gabriel drew nearer, and Gabriel knew that they would stop at nothing to capture him. They would pursue him to the gates of Jerusalem if he allowed them to. Gabriel could not bring such madness to the city of God.

I will make my stand here, he thought.

Gabriel's feet slowed, the tiny beating of his winged soles ceased, and his sprint through the golden-hued fields of manna that he plowed underfoot came to a grinding halt. He eyed a gourd in the distance and gently laid the still-unconscious Sariel to the ground. His back ached from carrying his brother. Gabriel stretched his wings, which prior had been taut, and his muscles celebrated the respite. With that momentary pause, Gabriel allowed himself to enjoy relief as he kneeled on the soft ground to stretch his legs. But only for a moment, as he turned his head to face the horde which now distanced only 50 yards away.

"There is no escape, High Prince," a pursuer said.

"We will have the high prince's head!" said an Arelim.

"Or we will have yours!" said another.

Gabriel stood to his feet and turned to face his pursuers. With grit of purpose, he unsheathed the iron swords that El himself had trained him to fashion, dipped the tip of one sword into the deep dark earth before him, drew a line for his attackers to see, and yelled to the legion who now stood paused to flay him. "I stand before the presence of the Almighty and mouth the voice of God! Hear now *this* message and never forget. The Lord hath not given me a spirit of fear; for if thou would seek a head to roll this day, you would do well to see to thine own!"

With those words, Gabriel launched himself at full speed towards the mob; wings unfurled and swords raised to attack a Legion.

The mob stood momentarily stupefied, taken aback that they now were on the receiving end of an attack by a High Prince of Heaven. Some moved backward unnerved in expectance of the high prince to surrender and surprised that this one angel would have the audacity to fight a multitude. However, for others who watched an epiphany occurred: the revelation that greater love had no man than this, that a man would lay down his life for his friend. For Prince Gabriel, many would wager, would die this day, yet they saw that he would sacrifice all to protect his brother who lay unconscious just yards before them.

Others were unmoved and raised their swords in kind to destroy the High Prince.

With a roar, Gabriel cried aloud, and the swords that he carried burst into flames as he threw himself towards the throng and set fire to the manna leaf to his rear creating a wall of flame. Flames that now barred the path of anyone who would seek to move behind him. The tall stalks of cinnamon-smelling leaves burned instantly, their flames leaped high into the air, and dark smoke flooded the plains. Gabriel flexed his great wings, captured a gust of Heaven's wind, and shoved the same towards the wall of fire, launching a tidal wave of spark and tinder that raced towards the surprised mass.

Many on the front panicked at the wall of searing heat and fire that sprinted towards them and attempted to flee while those in the middle of the great morass were crushed between those who still pressed forward and those who sought to escape.

Gabriel sliced through the thinning throng, hacked limbs, and threw himself against Arelim, shattering breastbone and bursting ligaments, which held wings to flesh, slashing at anything that rose to take up arms against him.

Deftly, he weaved and dodged foes, shifting between his humanoid and cheetah-like form at will. He knew he must keep them off balance. The throng found themselves assaulted from every side as the speed of Gabriel's attack went unchecked against them. To his attackers, Gabriel appeared as if the God King himself had touched him, for he was omnipresent and everywhere at once, such was the ferocity of his attack.

Their screams rocketed to the sky from the heated wave, which launched against them and rolled across the golden fields. Panic and rage united in song with the cries of those whose limbs hung now severed. All joined in harmony in a horrific melody to create a new sound in Heaven. The horde wailed in lament for the lash that was Gabriel. A collective groundswell of underestimation journeyed across the mass. A miscalculation that was but momentary, as gaps in lines filled, and the thought of dissolution at the hands of Gabriel steeled the resolve of many; the corporate consciousness of the swarm knew that Gabriel could not fight if he could not move. Closer each angel moved towards one another. Closing their ranks tighter, they swung at the blur that was Gabriel, who still evaded all touch.

Nevertheless, they were many, and he was but one. Gabriel now set in the center of bodies both maimed and dying knew that in his race to cut down all, he had left himself no room for retreat. They encircled him, menacingly creeping forward on his position, a blockade of Elohim all seethed with rage to silence the voice of God. When Gabriel saw that he would fall to the throng: when he perceived that he was trapped and that less than a hundred yards away his brother lay unconscious, he reached to his side, lifted to his lips the Trumpet of Israel, and blew into the golden vessel. Its sound dashed through the air like a racehorse into the golden blue skies of Heaven. The ears of all combatants burst, torn asunder by the blast of so powerful a sound that they fell to the ground, stunned and dazed, and in the moments that occurred between the bat of an eye, the clouds opened up, and the sky grew a putrid dark green.

The horde, which sought to slay Gabriel, gawked as they turned their gaze upward. For with the eclipse of the sun and through pierced clouds, they saw Ladders burst open across the lid of Heaven. Thunderous booms littered the peaceful skies while lightning strokes raced across the firmament to embrace each other: for upon winged gryphons rode legions of mighty Malakim. Thousands with unsheathed swords and spears descended upon them like locusts atop a field of defenseless corn.

* * *

Jerahmeel huffed as he entered the Hall of Annals, panting as he looked at the clear wall that separated him from the Zoa. He was always jovial and knew that levity could release tensions.

Yet as he stood within the confines of the Hall of Annals, there was nothing that could generate lightheartedness this day.

Raphael had brought him to this place once before.

El hast decreed that you be given access to this place, but, alas, tread carefully, for within are the tomes of all creation. Within thou might know the invisible things from the creation of the world.

All right, Raphael. Jerahmeel thought to himself. *You said this was important. I hope you were right.*

Jerahmeel poured over the room and tried to remember all that Raphael had shown him. He stepped up a flight of stairs past the volume of books that floated and lined themselves on shelves and entered a room of pure white.

Ahh, this is it, he thought as he opened his mouth to speak to the listening room. "Location of Gabriel?"

The room flashed the colors of the spectrum, and Jerahmeel stood as if he was in a dream when suddenly under his feet the dark rich dirt of the Elysian Fields appeared. Jerahmeel beheld as Gabriel stood surrounded by a legion of Elohim ready to pounce upon him. Gabriel panted, and the blood of Elohim stained the golden hilts of his flaming swords and splatter was awash over him. His eyes glowed with a crackling light, and power dripped from his body as sweat beaded and glistened from his muscular form.

In El's name! Jerahmeel whispered aloud. "Gabriel! Gabriel!" he yelled.

Yet it was to no avail. Jerahmeel watched as the sky opened to reveal that the Malakim Gryphons fell from the skies and that House Malakim rode upon them to do battle on their Prince's behalf.

"But where is Michael?" Jerahmeel wondered aloud. The room unable to recognize if Jerahmeel posed a question or directed a command responded. The image of Gabriel disappeared from view, and the great room displayed Michael weeping uncontrollably alone.

"Argh, ya stupid room! I didn't say change the scene! Show me both Gabriel and Michael!"

The walls of the room obeyed and displayed on one wall Gabriel and the Malakim now locked in heated battle with house Arelim and Issi. The other portion of the wall displayed Michael weeping alone in a dark room.

"In El's name! Half of Heaven is in battle in the Elysian fields!"

Jerahmeel watched helplessly at the twofold scenes before him and wondered how he might provide help.

* * *

"We are almost there my prince," said Iofiel.

"Good," said Raphael. "We must quickly return to Jerusalem and make haste to find Lucifer."

The duo moved deeper into the cold and damp-filled emptiness. With each step, Raphael followed Iofiel into the shadows, their hands outstretched reaching to feel their way against the cold rocky wall. Raphael noticed that his vision grew dim; his ability to see lessened with each step.

Raphael followed Iofiel and he led him deep into the bowels of Athor to a circular stairwell that led into the depths of the earth past the foundations of the gleaming city; darkness became their third companion. The blackness reached out to ensnare and entangle a blackness that became tangible to the touch and enveloped them like a well-worn robe. The darkness hung oppressively upon them, suffocating and heavy. It was then that Iofiel suddenly stopped.

“What is wrong?” said Raphael.

“We are here, my Lord," replied Iofiel. "Look."

Raphael strained to see through the deep fog of blackness, but despite his vision, even he could not peer through the veneer that lay before them, and the light that emanated from his own body no longer was able to penetrate the darkness.

“Look at what? I see nothing but blackness roundabout. To what should my eyes gaze upon?” he said.

“Try again, my Lord, but look not with your natural eye but with that which we see in the spirit.”

“Wait...I see it,” said Raphael. “Lucifer was wise to conceal his actions on this wise.”

Slowly, Raphael made out that darkness writhed within the darkness. Then Raphael saw the onyx door and the seal of Lucifer Draco. It was a strange thing, oval in shape, but the oily blackness which was before him was so dark, so devouring of light that it made the surrounding darkness seem as light. Slowly the depth of Lucifer’s sin saturated Raphael's understanding. For to conceal oneself was to attempt to deceive God. Raphael began in that moment to grasp the gravity of Lucifer’s cunning, a cunning that would seek to pluck out the very eye of the Almighty. For where in the multiverse would one run from God? Nevertheless, here within the bowels of the Earth, Lucifer sought to create a place of shadow to hide his atrocities from Heaven.

Raphael put his hand to the door, and it was icy cold to the touch. His breath turned to vapor in the damp and musty air. He intuitively knew that within the confines of this door was another realm, a realm where the presence of God did not bring warmth. Iofiel stepped to the side, and Raphael turned the handle and pulled the heavy and onyx door. The seal of the First of Angels had been broken. Raphael jerked even harder, yet the door resisted and became heavier. Iofiel came to assist, and the duo pulled as one. The door creaked in reluctance, then gave way and opened to them. The seal of the chamber ripped and a hissing sound filled the air, and the cavern smelled with the stench that Raphael had only smelled prior when the blood of Corlus had spilled on Heaven’s soil -- dissolution.

***

"Why is this door thus that it refuses to open?" said Michael.

Raphael and Iofiel turned to see Michael standing behind them, studying the dank dark door and the structure over them.

"Are you ok?" asked Raphael.

Michael looked at his brother, nodded, and then turned to Iofiel. "I repent of my actions earlier. I ask your forgiveness."

Iofiel placed his hands on his leader's shoulder. "My concern is for my Lord's welfare. I would see you whole."

Michael smiled. "Thank you, my friend."

Michael turned to look at the huge door and felt its surface. It was cool to the touch and had a rough feel as if he was touching the exterior of something made of coarse rock; there were also ridges to it.

Michael leaned closer to inspect the door. Slowly he approached and placed his cheek against the wall. He lifted his head, and his eyes darted to make out an outline and the rise and fall of something — breathing.

"This is no door," said Michael, and he quickly backed away.

But it was too late, for Iofiel had already dug his hands deep into a ridge and used his weight to pull against the door and lurched the gate open, ripping the hinges from the sidewalls. Screams and wails then filled the corridor. Suddenly, light shined from two slotted sources above them. The 'wall' moved, buckled, and turned inside out to reveal an Elohim now towering above them. The dark figure had four arms, his back was like the shell of a tortoise, and Iofiel had ripped from the creature a scale that he himself had thought to be a door. There was no door. There was but an angel, disguised and concealed, who barred the path of anyone who might dare go further.

Michael looked into the body that was the creature and gasped, for within its bowels were the bodies of Elohim trapped and pushing against its flesh to escape. Each soul was emaciated beyond recognition, and their wails and groans filled the cavern as they pushed against the translucent skin of the creature. They were as bones heaped upon one another, refuse to be discarded, living angels crushed under the weight of one other, suffocating within the innards of the angel's flesh.

"I know thy scent, Michael of the Kortai. I am Minos, and though thou be the Builder of Heaven, you are not welcome here. For respect of thine office, I offer you passage to go whilst you may still leave, but know of a surety dissolution awaits you if you abide here. Tartarus is for the enemies of the Chief Prince, and my orders concerning intruders are clear."

Michael was quick to speak, "Who art thou to do harm to your own kind? Release those within I beseech thee. This ought not to be."

"Nay," replied Minos. "For the God King has himself created a realm that exists to consume Elohim, and we are told that the very fires of the Kiln have ceased to ignite our kind. We will not become lackeys of the Clayborne, nor will we bow the knee to El who would sentence us to slavery."

Michael winced as the groans of those within Minos cried out for relief.

Michael replied, "I am not slow to answer thee Minos, for I am on the Lord's side, and forever shall I stand with El." Michael turned to look at Iofiel and smiled. Iofiel nodded knowingly.

Minos retracted his arm into a pocket of his flesh, and from within the deep folds of his arms, appeared a long scythe, which glistened and dripped with mucus. "Then come," he said, and know that Tartarus awaits you."

Minos heaved his scythe over his head and slammed the blade into the dank ground, and the steps underneath the trio shattered.

Iofiel quickly placed his back against the wall, missing the blow by inches; the breeze of Minos' forceful strike cooled his face. Raphael and Michael both jumped clear of harm's way while a shower of rock and debris exploded around them and sent small pebbles like shrapnel into their bodies. Michael sprinted and hurled himself into the air to grab the hand of Minos, struggling to use his weight to pull the creature's arm behind its back. Yet, Minos was too strong and flung Michael over his shoulder as one might swat a gnat. Michael careened into the dark stone wall, and with a great thud; hit the damp rock and fell violently to the ground.

"I have moved the stars into place on El's behalf. You are nothing to me, Prince. In vain, do you fight against me."

Minos lumbered closer to Michael who lay helpless on the ground. Michael's shoulder and back ached and throbbed, screaming out for relief.

The giant black Arelim moved in closer for the kill.

If dissolution is the Lord's will, – then I will face it standing. Michael thought and struggled to rise to his feet.

Minos stood with his scythe gripped tightly and raised the weapon to cut Michael down; he placed his foot on Michael's chest pinning him to the ground.

"Goodbye Prince of Heaven," said Minos.

Michael closed his eyes, content in the knowledge that dissolution awaited him, but in the moments that the blow was destined to connect, the crash of falling rock thundered and the chasm's ceiling cracked. Light flooded the chamber, and Minos leaped to avoid being crushed as angel upon angel fell upon a singular hooded figure whose whips for arms flayed them to, and fro.

Michael rolled out of the way and marveled that the battle above to stop Charon had reached Tartarus itself.

Oblivious to all the angels that sought to bring him to a stop, Charon eyed the massive body that was Minos. His gaze fixed on the black onyx figure of he who would pretend to stand as a guard to a nether realm, a pretender to a throne that was his alone. Charon moved and dragged with tentacled arms a multitude of angels behind him, and Hell was awash in ecstasy. In a heated lust of engorgement, dangling angel flesh near and far, and like an intoxicated slut, she had her way upon the flesh of Elohim that dared to strike the Warden of Hell.

Without slowness of gait and without sound or pronouncement, Charon marched towards Minos to confront the imposter as warden of the nether realm. For in all the multiverse, there could be only one.

Minos had heard of Charon; yet, the report had not done Charon justice. Minos was Lucifer's answer to Charon, and Tartarus a mere projection of the realm of Hell, a prison made after the fashion and likeness of Lucifer's schemes. Watching Charon, Minos knew that Lucifer had established him and Tartarus as counterfeit.

"I have no quarrel with you ferryman. Do not force my hand, for my allegiance to the Chief Prince is clear, and this realm is shut by my hand and opened by none other. You may not pass, for I am the Maw here."

Charon did not speak. He only moved, plodding closer to confront this imposter. The worms, which did not light on Charon's body, slithered away from his flesh and crawled to the ground as if commanded by some unspoken voice. Creating a veil of fire that allowed none to pass or else risk consummation; they formed a line between him and the squadron of angels who now lay behind him in ruin.

Michael skirted backward as Minos focused his attention on Charon, this new threat absolute. Minos walked to meet the Warden of Hell.

"Raphael! Michael! Come quickly!" called Iofiel. Motioning with his hand, Iofiel stood within the cleft of a rock, and Raphael and Michael joined him.

"Michael, are you alright?" asked Raphael.

"Aye," said Michael grabbing his arm that still was sore from his impact against the cavern wall. The trio hid and watched as the lumbering giants of Minos and Charon approached one another.

* * *

Jerahmeel looked as the forces of Heaven locked themselves in mortal combat. Malakim warriors filled the skies. Each rider strafed the ground, grabbing Arelim and Issi warriors. Flying high into the air, and then released them. The gryphons grasped their prey in their talons and flung them to the hills. Angelic bodies lined the once peaceful fields of manna, and the bluish-silver blood of Elohim saturated the ground.

"He said to find the inkhorn and stylus," mumbled Jerahmeel.

He turned from the scene, which stretched for miles, and rushed to the desk and shelving in the library. Jerahmeel pulled down from the shelves above him, tome after tome. "He said it was hidden."

He searched through drawers and flipped over shelves. Tables fell to the wayside as book after book became as litter on the floor. As he hurried to search, he could hear the screams and curdled cries of his brethren on the battlefield. Jerahmeel sweated in anxiousness knowing that he held the promise to put a stop to the madness.

After pulling out a final drawer latticed with gold, he found it: the golden inkhorn and stylus of Raphael, the badges of each Grigori's honor and power.

Jerahmeel looked at the small pot and stylus. They seemed unremarkable. No different from what he had used countless times writing on manna leaf. However, he did not have time to dote; his task was to succor his brethren. He looked at the glowing inkhorn and remembered what Raphael had told him. *Speak the word, return, and break the container, and all realms will open that I might be brought home.*

Therefore, Jerahmeel took the stylus, broke it, and smashed the inkhorn into the ground. The floors, walls, and the ceilings above him suddenly disappeared. The room became as nothing, as color washed around him, and the sound of a rushing wind swept through the chamber. It was then that he heard the voice of his friend Raphael.

"It is time to go, Michael."

* * *

Lucifer met Abaddon and Lilith as each angel stepped through the Ladder. "Are you ready to begin?" said Lucifer.

Abaddon laughed. "They called me '*Destroyer*'," said Abaddon. "Let us then commence with their destruction!"

Lucifer moved to place his hand on his comrade's shoulder. "Nay, we are not here to obliterate the city and those therein. Do not forget our mission. We are here to offer peace to those who seek solace under my banner and war only against those who align themselves to the perverted purposes of El. Are we clear?"

Lucifer eyed Abaddon as the giant of an angel snorted, shook his head in the affirmative to his new king, and reluctantly showed compliance. "For now, it shall be as you wish Lucifer."

"Nay," said Lucifer. "It shall be as I wish yesterday; today, and forever, for there can be only one God. Either thou art with me or you are against me. Come, for we have much to do."

The army of Lucifer Draco marched across the bridge and poured into Heaven's gate from the Ladder of Lucifer's making. They came as ants might overrun a carcass. Legion upon legion marched on translucent streets of gold, and the ground shook as their numbers rivaled the stars above, an army of Draco, Arelim, and Issi warriors, all with swords and blades fashioned after the imagination to destroy: pikes, polearms, shields, armor covered wings of leather, feather, and transparent wings as dragonflies. They marched this horde, marched and flew in columns of precision bent to stop El. An uprising of citizens united in their noble cause to usurp the dictator El at all cost. They were the spring, the dawn of a new day, confident that the Firstborn of all Angels would lead them to freedom.

When Deramiel came back from his errand to return to his post, his eyes looked upon the throng that massed before him: a cloud of Elohim who had not returned home to sing the praises of El. It was his inner knowing, his intuition. The look in Lucifer's eyes that made him know clearly that he had been betrayed. The gravity of his brother's deception fell upon him as a stone about his neck, and Deramiel fell to his knees. Lucifer saw the angel in his path and raised his hand to signal all to stop, and the armed warriors whose cadence made the ground shake came to a thunderous pause.

Lucifer walked before the throng and went to pick his weeping brother from his knees. He placed his arm around him to help him up. As a man might assist one with a disability, so too did Lucifer raise Deramiel to his feet and kissed him on both of his cheeks.

Deramiel looked upon him and said, "Come thou to betray the kingdom with a kiss?"

Lucifer paused, shaken at the words leveled against him.

"Nay, Deramiel. What thou seest before thee are those who have chosen to live free, to deny El usage of us as slaves to the Clayborne. Would you have our people debased into extinction? Do you not see? El hast made man to replace us. Why else enlarge the city? Or create a mote in the realm of all space that will not grow manna? Do you not see?" Lucifer held on tightly as the two embraced each other, their heads resting on each other's necks.

Deramiel sighed then replied. "What I see all too clearly is the heart of he whose consumption is for more than his station. I see a mighty son who would betray his own father. I see the creature risen up against his creator who hast done nothing since the day of your youth but elevate you on high. Yet despite all this, a multiverse with which you may enjoy, you would instead gaze on the one thing you cannot have, the throne of the Living God. This — my *friend*, is what I see."

Deramiel gently released Lucifer, and Lucifer sullenly nodded and said to Deramiel, "Then see no more."

With a swift turn of his diamond-laced wing, Lucifer sliced the neck of Deramiel. Deramiel's head severed from his body and fell to the ground. For a moment, the consciousness of Deramiel was there, and his eyes were spasmodic. Then they stopped and focused on the person of Lucifer. The gaze of Deramiel's pupils fixated on the beautiful eyes, of Lucifer. Lucifer peered past the blue eyes of Deramiel, but the look of betrayal that marked Deramiel's face etched itself into the High Prince's mind.

Lucifer turned to look away, stunned at the sense of shame and guilt that overwhelmed him. For a moment, he thought that perhaps he had leaped into the most terrible mistake he and Heaven had ever known; despondency and anger flooded his soul, but he hardened his heart, buried and suppressed any feelings of shame and guilt.

"El, I lay Deramiel's dissolution at your own feet," he whispered. "You have brought me to this." As Lucifer murmured his curse, Deramiel's stone flickered and went out, and his body slumped to his knees and fell at Lucifer's feet.

Lucifer turned to face the army that was behind him, straightened himself, and spoke for all to hear. "All will serve the cause of freedom or all will likewise perish." He waved his hand for the mass to follow and turned towards the city. The head of Deramiel became as sport to kick as the hordes' cadence became a quick step, and their march to the city gates once more made the streets shake.

* * *

The two titans of the underworld clashed. Minos with his muscular arms and tortoise-like shell smote Charon with his fist, and the crack of bone filled the cavern. Never had Michael seen Charon stumble so. The Warden fell backward, his tendrils flailing and fire engulfed him as he crashed to the cavern floor. The impact sent great plumes of smoke and debris flying across the room, and the throng, which looked beyond the veil of fire, bleated from afar and cheered as the warden smashed into the dank earth.

Minos spoke. "I have been appointed the judge of the dead in this realm, ferryman. Hell hath no claim on Tartarus here. Fight me at thy own peril and risk my judgment as well."

Charon staggered to his feet as his tentacled body pushed him up from the floor. The warden again moved to engage his foe. Minos looked stout, his face resolute, and the scythe with which he carried; he swung around his body to smite Charon. The blade cut through bone and marrow, slicing off an appendage. The warden screamed, and the long flaming tendril fell to the cavern floor.

Like a child whose arm had been scraped on the harsh rock so too did Charon now nurse his wound. Minos pressed forward, and again his scythe carved through the air and came down hard on the shoulder of Charon, and once more, the personification of the vengeance of God fell to his knees and black fluid oozed from the wound.

The liquid saturated the blade, and the dark blood, different from that of other Elohim, solidified and wrapped itself around the edge. Charon looked up at Minos, and the face of a mare, the dead skeleton grinned! Minos looked as the blood moved, and like a snake, the blood coiled itself around the blade of the scythe and moved toward the arm of Minos himself.

"What trickery is this?" said Minos.

Michael watched from afar. He was there when Charon was created. Only he who was there from his creation truly understood that Charon existed to exact the vengeance of God. It was then that Michael realized that God was not asleep. He had no need for rest; fatigue was beyond the living God's necessity. He could not overextend himself. Charon was his mouthpiece against all those who would come against the will and word of God. The unstoppable, slow marching eventuality to all who resisted his will.

Minos was merciless in his fury. His scythe moved in a waltz and carved through the flesh and bone of the warden. Charon screamed, butMichael knew that these were no ordinary screams, but cries of pleasure--the orgasmic and masochistic moans of a creature who fed off torment only to reflect it back upon the bearer.

Minos raised his mighty arms high above his head to bring dissolution to Charon, his scythe found its mark, and the blade came down straight on the equine skull of the Warden. As a pick might thud against ice, so did the sound of the cracking of Charon's skull fill the room. Charon roared in anguish and then grew still.

Onlookers cheered in glee at the destruction of the Warden. Praise for Minos filled the massive cavern, and applause echoed through the dank, smoky, dark cave.

"We must leave this place quickly," said Michael to his brethren. "Minos does not understand the nature of what Charon is. The more he resists, the more powerful the creature becomes. Charon cannot be destroyed except by submission to the Lord's will." Gingerly, the trio attempted to climb up the stairwell from which they came.

Minos looked over his defeated foe, and a smile escaped from his lips. The arrogant grin of pride marked his face, and he spoke. "The God King has no voice in vengeance, for Lucifer is the one true God."

A noise suddenly came from the rubble, and the ground beneath Charon stirred. Bones sliced apart earlier now moved, joint connected to joint, and the sinews grew before the eyes of all. Flesh carved away suddenly rejuvenated and reattached itself. The skull of Charon ignited, and fire shot from his eyes. The massive creature rose to his feet, and the worms of Hell, which never die, poured as blood from his body.

Charon turned and slowly marched again towards Minos, the chains for arms trailed behind him, and massive waves of flame leaped to engulf his path as he walked.

Minos beheld a new thing, a creature that knew not dissolution. Nevertheless, Minos was Minos, the guardian of Tartarus. He was the handle to the door to the lost souls within the black door, which was his very flesh. The way was shut, and he would allow no passage save his Lord King himself.

Minos turned to face Charon once more, lifted his scythe, and brought it square onto the shoulder blade of Charon.

The cries of the creature smote the eardrums of all in the cave. Michael and the host of angels covered their ears.

Charon staggered. Blood leaped from his body as a wellspring, and tentacles of bone and barb and the worms of Hell moved towards Minos.

Minos drew back so as not to be touched by the leeches of fire. Yet it availed him not, for the blood of Charon was as a living thing. It moved in a serpentine fashion and flowed to the foot of Minos and then to the ankle.

Minos sliced at the blood, but with each stroke against the liquefied attacker, it dispersed as a mist and then reformed to pursue him the more. When it reached him, it solidified and grabbed his heel, as ropes would lasso a stallion. Minos struggled, struggled to overcome the solidified blood that slowly began to consume him, as the worms found him quickly, and they fed, for Minos was an Arelim, a mover of stars, and the worms engorged themselves on the angel who thought to undue Charon.

The reality of his foe confronted Minos, and he sought to flee, but the long trail of blood followed him as the worms of Hell moved and attached themselves as leeches upon the angel, burrowing into him to consume him alive.

As a murderer stalks his prey, Charon followed Minos. The mighty Minos pleaded for his life and screamed in tortured anguish as the worms and blood feasted on him.

All looked and beheld the true nature of Charon: he was consumption, a plague, and one angel coined a new term to give words to what he saw.

"He is not dissolution...he is *Death.*"

The throng turned from their cheering and now clamored for escape.

Yet it was too late. They had fallen into the lower parts of the Earth, trapped in the prison of Lucifer's corrupted mind and caught between the vengeance of God, and the maggots of Hell. Each larva moved to feed, to sustain Mother Hell, and provide life and strength to the warden.

Minos looked at Charon and spoke. "What is this that thou hast no stone, nor gem which animates thee? What art thou?"

Michael watched from afar, and he knew Charon was not fueled by God's love, like the host of all Heaven. Nay, Michael was there when God gave rise to Charon; a creature fueled by God's hate, his very life tied to the Kiln. Where there was the Kiln, there would be Charon.

The arms of Charon reached from his body and latched their barbed claws into Minos' shell, and Minos was held fast, pinned as he attempted to claw his way to safety. It was a pitiful sight, a mover of stars struggling to escape the power of the living God.

"*Death,*" Michael had heard an angel describe Charon. It was a good name.

Dissolution indeed sounded too trite for who Charon was. He was Death.

Charon then lifted Minos high into the air and ripped his shell from his body. Minos screamed, and the worms enveloped him. His body burned but was not consumed. His beating stone, the engine of life, which El gave to all, pulsated still, infested with worms of fire and sulfur. They crawled through nostrils and mouth, and Minos gurgled, choking as they passed through orifice after orifice and attached themselves to his lungs and heart and breathed for and through him, worms that through their burrowing created new orifices.

As the pieces of Minos' now broken shell lay on the cavern floor. Charon looked down on the mass of burning flesh and flayed the skin that surrounded Minos' heart of stone. With a brutality that defied all that Heaven had seen, Charon slammed his tentacled arm deep into the chest of Minos and pulled from his chest his living stone. The worms still latched on it dangled from it and fell to the cavern floor as linguini.

Minos was key to Tartarus, and Charon now held his Heartstone in his hand. He gazed upon the black onyx rock that looked so much like his own. The monster took the stone and ingested it, taking its essence into himself.

The cavern shook, and Minos' shell began to glow. Heat emanated from it, and hands reached from inside his body to pry open the shell. Angels poured from it coughing; dozens at first, and then hundreds stumbled and hurried over one another to find release from the prison of the netherworld that Lucifer had created in secret, a realm where Minos himself was both door and key.

Michael yelled to the throng that poured from Minos' now lifeless body. "Come to me all who bow the knee to El; come to me!" Those who had not sworn allegiance to Lucifer went to the side of the familiar voice of Michael, and he spoke to the freed masses of angelic warriors before him. "See now the treachery of Lucifer usurper to the throne. See now as his allies clamor for escape. Go to and smite them. Look to those who cared not for your imprisonment, nor show them any quarter."

Lucifer's minions moved with haste to escape the march of Charon as he returned to the surface. They turned to face the released captives and knew that to fight Charon and their brethren was futile. Some sought to escape while others turned to face this new enemy and attacked.

The cave exploded with violence as angel attacked angel, each grappled in hand-to-hand combat, and stones were torn from chests, smashed to the ground, and dissolved to ash.

Jerahmeel within the Halls of Annals saw that Raphael and Michael were deep in melee combat. Michael was too far to succor, but Raphael was within reach; he would know how to stop the onslaught that approached Heaven. Jerahmeel reached within the image of the wall, grabbed the arm of Raphael, and pulled him from the dimension of Earth into the Hall of Annals.

Raphael screamed with pain, for his body was simultaneously present in two realms at once. With a great heave, Jerahmeel pulled Raphael, and they fell backward to the floor. Raphael looked at Jerahmeel with a smile and whispered as he faded into unconsciousness, "What took you so long?"

* * *

Lucifer belted out from his restored balcony and looked upon the great city of Jerusalem. The inhabitants scurried about, for they did not know that dissolution dwelled within their walls, but the citizenry was curious about the warriors with stave and spear, sword and shield. Never had they seen such instruments, and Lucifer knew that in moments, their decisions if they were wrong would shed their naiveté and Heaven would be at war.

I must convince them of the rightness of my cause, for I will not stand to see, my brethren, fall to the lie that El hast propagated.

As the pipes in his belly gave the clarion call to the city as he had in so many times past, Lucifer trumpeted once more for all of Heaven to assemble before him to meet their God.

They came, as was routine. They came because the First of Angels called to them. They came because they knew they would meet God. They were each surprised in what they saw and heard. Thousands looked up in wonderment and in silence to the balcony of Lucifer's abode. Shimmin a Harrada was the first to speak.

"Your majesty, forgive this outburst, but why hast thou assembled the host of Heaven, for El rests, and the God King abides in his temple. Why then are we here?"

Lucifer looked upon the crowd and spoke. "Hear me, host of Heaven. From the start of our kind, thou hast seen my face, and I have called thee to praise the name of El. From the beginning, I have seen you birthed from the Stones of Fire. From the beginning, I have presented you to El that He might announce his word to you.

"But no more. For even eternity must end, and an end has come indeed. I have not borne witness to another Elohim since the creation of man. Nay, the Kiln burns no more to ignite the stones that animate our kind. Instead, we hear in the distance the hunger pains of the abomination of Hell. A new furnace the Lord hast made to consume our kind! Is this to be our fate? We are now commanded, we who stand at the apex of creation, the firstborn of all things, we who uphold all things by the word of his power, are now asked to set aside for another! We are destined to teach, nay to serve, this flesh-borne thing of mud and clay. Indeed, with every beginning, there must be an end, an end to the lie that we were made to move stars, to breathe life into creation. Nay, the true revelation of our purpose is now made clear with the creation of the Clayborne and the construction of Hell. We are to be slaves, and this, despite my love for El, I will not stand for. I cannot stand for! I will fight Him; fight this trickery of He who would subjugate us for all eternity. Join me, and we shall usurp El, and free ourselves of his leash. Go to the mountain of God with me, and we shall rule the heavens, and I will guide you as I always have, and my face shall be to you as beloved, and ye shall know peace.

"But know this, El's power and this realm of Hell are not to be feared. I would not stand for false judgment on our brethren, and thus, I, the First of Angels, have braved the maw and have returned. See the impotence of El to construct a prison that can be escaped."

Abaddon moved from behind Lucifer and stood by his side, and many in the crowd gasped and stood stunned, but the gravity of Lucifer's words rang true to many, and the rumblings of discontent and dissension grew among different ones in the crowd.

"I cannot understand why God would make a Hell for us!"

"What is the man that he is mindful of him?"

"El hast gone too far!"

Finally, one word among all others rang out toward the balcony and hit the earshot of both Lucifer and Abaddon.

"Traitor!"

Lucifer scoured the crowd to identify who would blaspheme against him. Soon the word spread from one voice to another, and one could no longer make out who was on the Lord's side and who sided with the cause of Lucifer.

Abaddon looked at Lucifer waiting for permission to do what Lucifer was hesitant to do.

"You see, God King, there can be no turning back now. Would El tolerate such blatant disregard for his rule? If you are to be King, then you must do what must be done."

Lucifer grimaced at Abaddon's words and tightly closed his eyes. *Why do they not understand? Do they not see that blind allegiance to EL means enslavement to man? Why must it come to this?*

"Traitor!" was the cry of the multitude. "Traitor!"

"Abaddon is a murderer, and El is the living God," said an angel, "I will not abandon my God!"

Lucifer's eyes widened as he gazed at the cityscape, and he lifted up his hands to quiet the crowd.

Yet the throng failed to silence, and the more Lucifer gestured for calm, the more they clamored for his own removal.

"You are *not* a friend to God!" said one.

They then mocked him as a herald for daring to pretend that he stood for the cause of El.

Others came to his defense, and they argued with each other, but it was clear, many would not be turned. Lucifer's heart quickened, his stone glowed, and he could not resist the urge to scratch at his chest. His face contorted in anguish and grief, and a tear ruefully fell from his eye at his decision and the scene that now played before him. His lips moved cursing El unconsciously as he spoke. Lost in bitterness, his mind frustrated over goals denied. The hosts of Heaven were not united in their love of him over El. Lucifer seethed as his ears received a call for his own imprisonment for betraying El. Distraught, he backed away from the balcony so as not to be seen and covered his face with his hands.

Abaddon looked down from the balcony upon the restless crowd and then turned warily to his master. "Lucifer!" said Abaddon. "What is thy command? You desire to lead us. Then lead!"

Awakened from his ruminations, Lucifer wiped the tears from his eyes. His brow became hard, and he turned and spoke firmly to Abaddon.

"Destroy them."

Abaddon leaped over the balcony and landed among the crowd; his feet made the ground shake and cracked the golden glass street below. Silence overtook the throng, for his presence was imposing, and whispers were all that was heard. One angel looked in defiance at the great Arelim and walked directly to face him.

"You, 'Destroyer,' are a blight in Heaven, and why El consigned you to Hell. Your very presence is an offense to me."

Abaddon was want to correct him but simply grasped the angel by the stone in his chest, crushed it within the palm of his hands, and threw the lifeless body to the ground.

Like wildfire, the throng scattered while others leaped to attack him; violence erupted roundabout. And from the great Chittim balcony that was his perch, Lucifer, Son of the Morning Star, watched as Heaven degenerated into civil war, watched as brother fought against brother, watched as his plan for Heaven's control took shape, and watched as angels battled each other to dissolution. Lucifer clenched his teeth, tears filled his eyes, and he muttered, "El, you will burn in the very Hell thou hast made for our kind, for know of a surety that I come for you."

* * *

Michael moved and ducked kicks and punches thrown wildly at him. He grabbed the wings of one angelic combatant and flung him into another. The underworld was rife with battle and the smell of dissolution was in the air, but it was Charon who was the source of all things chaotic as the lumbering giant of God's vengeance made his way to the surface; nothing stopped him. He merely consumed whatever stood in his way.

Charon seemed preoccupied, oblivious to all others around him and attacked only if attacked. Angels in their collective wisdom moved from his path and steered clear of him, focusing instead on one another. Charon was a force to himself and not to be interfered with.

Thus, the former prisoners of Tartarus and Michael fought against those loyal to the cause of Lucifer. The cavern shook, for it could not contain the violence, and upon the surface of the earth, the ground swelled upwards and erupted in volcanic ash and thunder as the ground exploded, and Elohim after Elohim burst from the ground locked in combat. The ash of clouds mixed with Elomic blood as bodies filled the air and the surface of the ground around Athor disintegrated into a morass of angels slashing, hacking, and swinging against their foes.

As Michael surveyed the scene, he saw that the Earth had also erupted in madness, the natural response to Elohim no longer watching over seedlings and animals. Vegetation itself had arisen against friend and foe alike, and the sky darkened with winds run amok as the elements themselves were unleashed to battle on each one's behalf.

Michael beheld that the Earth was in agony, her body ripped to shreds as Elohim at cross-purposes with one another used her to do their will. Smoke filled Athor from the distance, and Michael discerned that the battle was planet-wide. Michael could only imagine what the heavens looked like. He looked skyward and knew that somehow he must bring the madness to an end. He knew that Raphael had escaped, dragged into the great walls of the Halls of Annals by a force unknown. He knew that only in Heaven could he cause the battle here to cease; therefore, he looked to Iofiel who stood fighting off enemies of the state. Michael ran towards him, ducked, and weaved among angels until he reached his side.

"I must return to Heaven. Only there can this be stopped before the Earth itself is torn to sunder. I leave but place thou in command of the host here. Fear not, for the Lord, is on our side."

Michael turned himself skyward and uttered the Elomic command to open the realms and create a Ladder to Heaven. He lifted himself to depart, broke the atmosphere, and found himself hurtled past cloud and into the darkness of space. The Ladder twisted, turned, and arched to the Third Heaven, and in the distance, Michael saw it, the waypoint of Heaven, but the way was shut, held in check by an Elohim with a flaming sword. Within seconds, before he crashed into oblivion, Michael violently turned his body to avert his own dissolution, arched the Ladder back towards Earth, and crashed like a meteor into her waiting arms. As an artillery shell finds its target, Michael flung himself into a group of Lucifer's forces. The blast of the Ladder's energy blew apart ground and flesh. All Elohim in the vicinity of the impact found their stones shattered or cracked, and they fell to the ground in agony or were vaporized. For a moment, all had stopped fighting to see the site, as the charred ground and smoke revealed the white-hot glow of the Builder of Heaven. As smoke wafted through the air from the crater that now adorned the ground, Michael rose from bended knee and spoke high into the air so that all could hear.

"Heaven is at war, and the way to her is shut."

* * *

Lucifer quickly left his bedroom and headed downstairs; his entourage of Ashtaroth and Lilith accompanied him. The walls shook, and dust fell from the ceiling, for the battle for Jerusalem had begun.

"My Lord, your plan for Heaven is coming to pass," said Ashtaroth. "The fighting in Elysium and on Earth hast divided Heaven's forces. With El himself withdrawn from battle, He has made it possible to strike at the Godhead, and in his weakness, we shall be made strong."

Lucifer frowned and spoke, “No, my plans are not as I desire. For brother is set against brother. This is not my perfect will, and I will see it end. Lilith, secure the library so that we might have knowledge of our enemies' movements. Ashtaroth, continue to walk with me." Lilith left his master and motioned two guards to accompany him. Lucifer watched until they were out of earshot.

“I have a task for you, one unique to your abilities and one I can impart to none other." Ashtaroth stood silent, bowed his head, and waited for instruction.

“Go with Abaddon. He will need to be brought into remembrance of why we are here. Stay with him Astarte, remind him that we are *not* here to obliterate all that exists. I fear that without my influence, he would bring ruin to us all, and our plan would come to naught. Do whatever thou must to keep him in the way.”

“And if he rebels against thy will, Lord King?” asked Ashtaroth.

Lucifer paused, his brow wrinkled, and his eyelids closed. He turned, looked sternly at Ashtaroth, and spoke without fluctuation. “Then let dissolution be his end and assume the head of the army in his stead. Are you clear in your purpose, Astarte?”

“I am clear, my Lord.” Ashtaroth bowed and set himself to leave his master.

Lucifer watched as Ashtaroth walked away, looked towards the mountain of Hell, spread his wings, and lifted into the sky. Lucifer flew towards the Maw and thought to himself, *It is time to bring this sad season of El’s reign to a close.*

* * *

Abaddon and his cadre smashed their way through throngs of angelic resistance. With his great sword, Abaddon cut down soul after anguished soul. Limbs flailed as all who stood within his path were hewn asunder. Abaddon gloated as each angel fell before him. His lips curled in a smile as his sword drew Elomic blood

The denizens of Heaven were not prepared. They had never known violence. Now violence was unleashed against their own, by their own. Surprise and confusion were the tactics of choice Lucifer sought to use in his battle against the populace. Yet, surprise and confusion quickly dissipated as allegiances formed across Heaven's landscape. With battle lines drawn and bodies assailed against body, Elomic blood spilled onto the golden streets like water from a tap.

Each angel’s special ability was unleashed in the termination of eternal life. Their Elomic gifts used not to build but to beat back horde after oncoming horde of angels who defied El’s will. The streets of Heaven filled with those using their hands, feet, and wings to defeat those who held sword and spear.

Across the cityscape they parried and thrusted, ducked and weaved, and flew at each other, stopping swords with clasped hands, kicking, and punching until Heaven's ranks began to decimate;

until the countless could be counted. Heaven's air filled with the clouds of dissolution and the ground with the blue blood of Elohim lined the streets.

The armies of Abaddon marched from the palatial abode of Lucifer through the residential quarters of Heaven and set fire to home and estate.

"Burn them with fire!" commanded Abaddon. "Let it all burn."

The officers of Abaddon obeyed, and Ares was swift to carry out his master's commands. Each dwelling that they passed was set to flame, and smoke rose high into the air. Abaddon moved with speed, his effortless ability to destroy now increasingly evident as he cut down all who stood in his way.

The army of Lucifer continued its march through the burbs of Heaven and made its way to the Golden Path, the center lane that would take them to the throne of the Mountain of God itself. Abaddon looked ahead and saw nothing but the towering spires and the multitude of angel-fold before them. He looked upon the masses of oncoming angels that raced towards him and knew that more were with El than were with them. There were simply too many to kill, too many who had jeered and mocked the Son of the Dawn, but enough to enact his vengeance; to mete out his punishment to all who witnessed his humiliation at the hands of El. Like perfume, Abaddon smelled the fear that invaded the consciousness of beings who knew not trembling. He wallowed and smiled in gleeful intoxication and marched towards his audience with El where Lucifer and he would bring justice to the God King.

Abaddon smiled and waved to his ground soldiers to advance the burning of Heaven. The smell of houses and fallen bodies filled the air. The crack of timber and rock and the screams of angels echoed in Abaddon's ears.

Ashtaroth had made his way to catch up with the front and looked to see all that was wrought. He saw the destruction of Heaven's habitations and the bodies that lined the ground in the wake of Abaddon's march. He pushed through cadre after cadre of angels aligned to their cause, and it was then that he saw Abaddon reach for the horn to signal what Lucifer had forbidden.

"Abaddon no!"

Abaddon turned to see Ashtaroth, and their eyes locked. Abaddon smiled and put his lips to sound the Horn of Lucifer to summon the legions who waited on Earth.

Lucifer's horn pierced the ears, and immediately the sky filled with what looked like falling stars. The boom of a Ladder opened up above them and then another, and then as far as the eyes could see. Ladders dotted the sky and explosions reverberated throughout the city. Thousands of angelic troops poured into Heaven from Ladders directed into buildings, and those not behind the safety of Abaddon's troops were obliterated as the First and Third Heavens attempted to occupy the same space.

Angels upon gryphons and other winged steeds and Elohim that flew descended from the portals that opened in the midst of the sky; they came through as bees whose nest had been disturbed. Those who once thought to fight Abaddon scattered; as everywhere about them reality was warped, and new legions faithful to Lucifer attacked without mercy, striking down whoever did not wear their Lord's mark.

Abaddon looked to Ashtaroth and spoke. "Isn't it glorious? Let it burn, Astarte! Let it all burn!"

Ashtaroth looked upon Abaddon as spittle dribbled from the Destroyer's mouth and knew that Lucifer was right to send him.

Abaddon must be stopped at all costs.

* * *

Raphael ran towards the back of the Hall of Annals as the mountain shook.

Dust and rock fell from the ceiling as the rumble of battle could be heard from outside.

"We must work quickly," said Raphael. "To secure this place, for it surely will be a target of Lucifer to hold its secrets."

"But why?" asked Jerahmeel. "Why this place?"

"Because in this place, the hidden things even from the foundations of the world can be made known, and El hast decreed to whom might know these things. Lucifer in his grab for power would of a surety have this place. This must not be. Come quickly; I must show you something."

Jerahmeel quickly followed Raphael deeper into the catacombs of the Hall of Annals and pulled from a sealed glass cabinet a tome of record. Each leaned to brace himself as books fell to the floor, and the booming thunder became louder.

"What is this?

"The Tome of Iniquity," said Raphael. "El has purposed it sealed and to be opened only for such a time as this."

"Wait," said Jerahmeel, "El knew that all this would happen?"

"El knows all. We are merely a witness to what he chooses to reveal, and there is much that lies within the mount: those things that are past, those things that are, and even those things that are yet to be. This tome El entrusted to be shown now. What you will see hast been seen only by El, Lucifer, myself, and now you.

Raphael reached into his cloak and pulled a key and with it unlocked the golden seal that encased the Tome of Iniquity.

Raphael moved to exit from the room. "Observe quickly; we must depart soon. The rumblings of the mountain can only mean that Lucifer's forces are close. When you are done, we shall plan how to defend against this threat."

Raphael closed the door behind him.

Jerahmeel looked at the book. It sparked and glowed. Smolder and heat lifted from its thick bound cover. It smelled of fire and brimstone and stunk. Jerahmeel approached as he covered his nose and began to cough; his throat scratched and phlegm settled in his throat. Waves of nausea overwhelmed him with each step that he took. He reached forth his hand to touch the book, and it festered and sizzled with boils as his fingers lighted on the cover.

The book flung open as if with a life of its own. Images of its contents drew Jerahmeel into the scene and he was afraid, for around him was fire, smoke, and flames that engulfed him. His stomach churned and vomit bellowed from his mouth; the stench of decay and heat was unbearable. But he knew this place. He had seen it before from afar. It was the inside of the Kiln, but this view was like none other: for the vantage was from none other than El himself. For God hath kept a record, and Jerahmeel realized that what he was about to witness was something that not even the Almighty would let slip without testimony. Jerahmeel was undone to know that for these brief moments, he beheld what God himself had seen in the Kiln.

Jerahmeel was overwhelmed with the sights and sounds that flung at him, for about him were color and sound that even he with his ears had never heard: it was both beautiful and terrifying all at once. The Lord and Lucifer stood within the Kiln, and God motioned for him to pick a stone.

The stones were vibrant, and each was alive with the colors of the rainbow. Each one sang harmonic melodies asking God to allow them, "to be." All living stones of flame, stones that represented all the elements that El had made, set here as it were in a storehouse: the Kiln. It was here that Jerahmeel knew that God had simply stored a fraction of who He was in this place.

El watched as Lucifer picked up the stone that He had commanded.

"The time has come to promote thee, even to be as one of us. For we have chosen thee to become one with us as God. But another must hold now the title of the Morning Star. Now," said El. "gently place the stone in the wall's flesh."

With his palms outstretched, Lucifer received the large stone that El had given him and noted how similar it was in size and shape to his own. He gazed upon it, and a frown showed upon his face. He lifted up his hands and flung the stone. The gemstone smote the wall, and like flint, it sparked, chipped, and cracked in three places and unleashed sparks to ignite flame within the flames. The stone ceased in its melodic song and let out an ear-splitting wail, and Jerahmeel covered his ears from the pain.

And the thing which Lucifer did displeased the Lord.

The Lord knelt down and took the wailing rock, and immediately its cries diminished but did not stop. Then the Lord himself tucked the stone gently into the folds of the wall's flesh while Lucifer looked on.

And the Lord spoke to the rock, "Thou art beautiful and strong, as the diamond, you must be resolute to uphold the brightness of my coming, for if thou canst surpass the inner wail of thy spirit, know that thou shalt herald me as the Son of the Dawn, even as this one who now stands beside me. Rise, Apollyon, and take thy place amongst the stars. Fail me not, and thou shalt be exalted among thy people, but be thou warned, that if sorrow persists, then on your shoulders shall indeed a new dawn come, the breaking of a new day. And he to whom you would seek solace shall be your true King and your infamy shalt be known even unto the end of days."

Jerahmeel watched as God constructed from the wall the form of a great Arelim, and God then caused a deep sleep to overtake Lucifer. The Lord took the splintered shard of Apollyon's stones from the floor and grafted a shard into Lucifer's stone. When he awoke, Lucifer could feel the hurt of Apollyon beating within him and scratched hard at his chest.

The Lord spoke, "Because thou hast chosen not to honor me, know that you shalt forever feel the pain of purpose marred. For if thou will not be faithful in that which is another man's, who will make you ruler of that which is thine own? For lost now thou art to promotion, for we had chosen thee to become one with God, but because thou hast chosen to embrace iniquity, then iniquity shall be thy schoolmaster, for when thou dost move to remove the mar in he, then know that thine own sin shall then be healed, and restoration shall come to you both. For alas, thou art now linked, for the strong ought to bear the infirmities of the weak."

Then the Lord turned his back on Lucifer, and Lucifer clutched at his chest. The fires of the Kiln grew dim, and nothing remained but the two angels. Apollyon towered over Lucifer and looked straight ahead as a machine ready to receive instructions. Lucifer gasped for air and knelt on the floor while one hand grasped at his now hurting chest, and he yelled for the Lord God to hear.

"Am I my brother's keeper?"

The Lord stopped to turn and said, "No, my son, he is yours that thine iniquity might be purged."

With those words, the vision that Jerahmeel beheld came to a halt, and the images whirled around as if drained and funneled into the pages of the book that Jerahmeel held in his hands. The tome closed with thunder, and lightning flashed; Jerahmeel dropped it to the floor and fell backward on his hind in astonishment.

"El hast known since the beginning!" said Jerahmeel.

"Aye," said Raphael. "And more importantly, he knew what Lucifer and Apollyon were capable of."

"Does Abaddon know that Lucifer flawed his purpose?"

"No. There is no record in Grigoric history of this revealed outside of El, Lucifer, and us. This book has been sealed."

"Then we must see to Abaddon; perhaps he might yet be reasoned with?"

"Nay," said Raphael. "He is as you have said, *Abaddon*. The fracture has run its course and cannot be repaired. He is lost."

"But..." said Jerahmeel. "Apollyon...I mean Abaddon was to replace Lucifer, and Lucifer knew about the replacement and marred him. I cannot believe this, Lucifer...Lucifer was to be one with El!"

"In the mind of our brother, there could be only one. El sought to teach him that in a universe of plenty, he had no lack. Nothing would have been denied him, for he was the beloved of the Lord. El had willed Lucifer to be one in him and He in him. The Chief Prince was to be the first, but he fell as our leader and thus our kinds elevation to be one with the father hath now been ceded to another...the humans. For the first shall now be last, and the last shall now be first. For the Lord hath now stretched out his hand and laid it upon the head of Adam, who is the younger, and his left hand on our kind, crossing his hands although we are the firstborn. Alas, for in Lucifer's blindness to see only what he was and what El had offered our kind, he lost sight of that which both he and we could be. He was afraid of loss, and in his fear, he was the first to lash out in anger, the first to do Elohim harm from the womb of the Kiln. He was a murderer from the beginning, and the Lord pardoned him."

Jerahmeel looked on in stunned disbelief, trying to comprehend all that he had seen and heard.

"And did Lucifer know that you knew?"

"No, he only suspected. This is why I suppose he had such a desire to see into the Hall of Annals, that he might divine its secrets and to wrest from me the extent to which others knew of his iniquity."

"Why show me this, Raphael? To what end does this help our cause and stop the fighting of our kin?"

Raphael turned. "I cannot do what must be done here. The Hall is not designed to display its secrets in mass. We must go to the Library in the city, and from there I can take the tome and show it, for I intend to broadcast the truth of he who would be God to the people. Let them decide if this is whom they shall serve. El has rejected him. Now the people must know why."

"And then?" said Jerahmeel.

"Then..." said Raphael, "They shall know the truth, and the truth shall make us free."

* * *

Michael looked in the distance as Charon had stopped at the fiery plume and extended his hands into the tendril of Hell. Hell hearkened to her master, reached for him, and lifted the warden into the air to return him into her bosom. Michael watched as Charon vanished into a whirlwind of fire and knew that on the other side of the unimaginable heat, Charon walked the belly of Hell, an antibody as at home in the digestive tract of brimstone and fury as any microbe within the intestine of a cow.

Can I survive this journey? Michael thought to himself.

He knew that he could not form a waypoint, for all entrances to Heaven were shut. To form a blind waypoint could destroy the very ground of Heaven itself. Michael's mind raced as he watched the fire slowly begin to dissipate.

"You wouldn't dare?" said Iofiel who stood beside him coming to realize what ran through Michael's mind.

"There is no other way," replied Michael. "Do you have a better idea?"

Iofiel looked at the flame ascending into the sky beyond the first heaven past the clouds, looked at Michael, and offered his hand.

"When you open the gate of Argoth, we will come."

Michael paused, looked at Iofiel, took his hand, embraced him, and spoke in his ear. "Hold this ground for El, and we shall celebrate our victory over a banquet of manna."

Each beheld the landscape before them as plumes of smoke and fire rose into the air, and Athor burned as the war to retake it from those aligned with Lucifer waged on. As Michael prepared to depart, they heard without warning the sound of the Horn of Lucifer crack the heavens, and as if on cue, legions that were preconditioned to worship upon the sound, fell to their knees. It was the clarion call to worship, and Michael and Iofiel watched as angel after angel kneeled to lift their voice to sing the praises to El. Yet on this day, neither angel could bring himself to do so, for they knew that today this sound was something else and that their kind had been tricked.

Then they saw it...the flash of a Ladder. Then another, and then hundreds, nay thousands, and the vacuums created ripped the ground and made the air crackle with lightning and thunder. Iofiel fell to his hind blown back by the multitude of Ladders that reached to the sky, and then he looked upon the ground. It was marred as far as the eye could see as each Ladder dug into the earth and cauterized the ground into glass. Iofiel noted that everywhere their enemy had vanished; gone home to wage war, each angel a weapon of mass destruction let loose upon the unsuspecting people of Heaven. He knew that Heaven could not survive such an assault.

Iofiel fell to his knees, rent his clothes, and wept that Heaven was being destroyed.

Michael frowned and looked resolutely at the ascending funnel cloud of fire and flew quickly to intercept the tendril of Hell, to allow hellfire to touch him once more. As he approached, he could feel the heat, and his body began to glow. He prayed, asking El for courage, and closed his eyes as he flew into the cylindrical pyre. Hell knew that angel flesh was in her grasp and coiled her lanky vines of fire around Michael and pulled him towards her.

Michael felt himself lifted through the heavens, pulled by the force of God's punishment to all who would seek to defy his will. The fire bit at him and burned him. His body convulsed in pain as his lungs filled with the gas of brimstone, his eyes grew blurry, and his body contorted as he flung through space and time. A shard of nourishment lobbed through the boundaries of the cosmos to feed the stomach of Hell. Michael heaved, and his flesh gave way to the heat as he moved from one realm to the next.

Agony rippled over him, and he cried out in pain. His mind became clouded, his vision darkened, and Michael lost consciousness, but only for a moment, for Hell would not let angel stuff of this sort die. No, she must suckle on him, to fan her flames. Michael's life force was different from the rest; he was a Chief Prince, one of the Lumazi, and Hell would savor her meal.

The long tendril slowly receded itself, and with thunder and the snap as if of a thousand trees, Michael fell hard on soft, wet, warm ground. He could hear the gurgle of the giant, and the life ebbed from him as she fed upon him. Michael knew that perhaps he had done nothing for the cause of Heaven save hasten his own demise. As he flickered back and forth between states of consciousness, he saw the hooded figure that was Charon. His equine skull could not be mistaken as the warden towered over him.

Michael could feel the chains of the Watchman of Hell wrap around him; the breath of the beast floated as toxic poison on the air. Michael moved his face as far away as he could as Charon sniffed at this intruder. The flames had somehow died down, and Michael could feel that he was held aloft by Charon's might alone, for no tendril touched him. Sweat beaded on his brow and flowed from his face. Michael coughed as the haze, smoke, and brimstone made what little breathable air acrid to swallow. Michael coughed and wheezed as Charon continued to view this angel.

Charon knew Michael's scent. He gently placed the Chief Prince on the ground and stood silently over him. His black cloak draped over him, but Michael could dimly see through its folds that eyes upon eyes looked at him. Tongues salivated within razor-sharp teeth, and ooze coated the ceiling and walls, yet Michael remained unharmed.

Then Charon let out a roar, and the sound made Michael cover his ears; it was a bestial sound. A sound that mimicked the great creatures Michael had seen on the Earth. A guttural sound that made him cower. Charon's tendrils flailed about him, and he raised his hammers for hands and flung them into Hell's belly. Hell convulsed and yelled her displeasure with a sound that could not be described. Michael could only perceive that it was one of pain.

Michael discerned that Hell and Charon were at odds over his presence, for he sensed that at any moment the salivating tongues, which were just outside of his reach, might devour him, tongues with eyes that looked at Michael, hungry to consume him.

Hell's eyes looked at Charon and backed away deeper into the heated darkness outside of view: afraid to cross the warden.

Charon uncovered Michael, looked upon him, and reached to touch his forehead with a skeletal finger. Afraid, Michael backed away. Charon lifted his hand and turned his palms upward as if to give Michael something. Michael moved closer, and Charon reached with one finger and touched Michael's forehead, like a drill. Then suddenly a voice as of a serpent spoke to him.

"Whyyyy haveeee you followed meeeee, Michael of the Kortai?"

Michael looked at Charon, but the warden's mouth did not move, but Michael responded. "Charon?" You...you speak?"

"Ayeeeeee." said Charon. "To thossssse whom wordsssssss need be spokennnn...wordddds, I will muster. You, angel of God, ssssshould not beeeee hereeeee ."

Plumes of fire jumped off Charon as butterflies might dance around a flower.

"I am in great need of thine help," said Michael. "I come this way only because there wast no other choice. The waypoints are shut. Lucifer in his deceit can be the only cause for such a barrier. He must be stopped."

Charon nodded. "The princcccce of pridddde is *not* my chargeeeee. Hissss actionsssss have yet to bring him within my gazzzzze. He would be wisssse to not have my eye ssssset upon him."

"And what of Abaddon? He hast escaped a second time from thy grasp."

With his chains, Charon lifted Michael high into the air. Michael felt Charon squeeze him, and the archangel winced in pain. Suddenly, the tongued eyes of Hell made their appearance. Charon flung Michael to the ground and spoke.

"Wouldddd you dare mockkkk the Vengeance of God within the bowlsssss of a creature that at my whim would consummmmme you alivvvvve?"

Michael lifted his hands in abeyance, "Nay, great Charon, to mock the vengeance of God is to do so at one's own risk. I have seen thy might and know of a surety that all those who stand before thee must eventually fall. Yet Abaddon is not within his cage but runs amok. I can only imagine on the streets of Heaven itself."

Charon laughed, and Michael opened his mouth in shock. Never had it occurred to him that the creature could know humor.

"He fleesssss what isssss the inevitable. Some sinsssss are opene beforehand, going before to judgment and otherssss follow after. He has been horded ssssimply closer to my domain that he might be corralled. He will be with usssss sssssshortly."

Michael looked upon the giant puzzled. "*Us*?"

Charon roared, the heated darkness of the cavern grew ever brighter, and Michael saw what none else had ever seen. There was no dissolution. Embedded within the walls of Hell, were thousands of Elohim. Each eaten alive and their stones drained of life. They cried and wailed; their agony let loose for Michael to hear. The screams of torment brought him to his knees.

Michael, consumed so much in his own pain, had been oblivious to that which lived within the very walls and floors. Everywhere the eye could see, Elohim of all races were mangled and digested alive by the fiery worms of Hell. The living dead, each a morsel to nourish the villi of Hell's very bowels. Their cries filled the cavern, and Michael covered his ears and eyes so that he might shield himself from the site.

"Please make it stop. It is enough," said Michael.

Charon roared again, the cavern grew dim, and the bodies of all the living receded into the wall's flesh, but Michael could still make out the faint cries of those damned to have followed Lucifer.

Charon lifted up his nose and turned; his hand closed into a fist and smote the wall. Hell groaned her displeasure.

"He issss here," said Charon.

"*He*," said Michael. "Who is here?"

Charon touched the wall, and immediately it became transparent, and Michael could see. Lucifer was within Hell itself and fought through the creature. Michael's mind raced with awareness.

"Of course: it was *never* about the city."

Charon's hand moved from the wall and the image disappeared. The giant began to move towards the direction of Lucifer.

"Wait!" said Michael. "Do not destroy him; I have an idea that might remove this breach from your domain."

Charon stopped and turned. "Ssspeak."

"Lucifer cares neither for Heaven nor Hell. He cares for one thing and one thing alone. Power, he comes for the Kiln Stone. If he can enter the Kiln, he can be like God and cause those things that are not as though they were. He can from the Kiln speak and build a new creation. Don't you see? Each of the stones contains the very power of El himself. He cannot destroy El, but he can use the power of God himself to fight the Almighty. He will use El's own power against Him. Only there and there alone can he gather the might to battle El. He must be stopped."

Charon replied, looking at the angel from over his shoulder. "And what do you propossssse, Builder of Heavennnnn?"

"Allow him to pass; do not attempt to stop him. For of a surety, he has not planned that I would be here. But go and arrest thine charge Abaddon. Bring him to naught but leave Lucifer to me. I understand now why El allowed me to enter the Kiln and see thy creation. I can stop him. Allow me to pass. I beseech thee."

Charon stood silent for a moment, gazed upon Michael, and then spoke.

“And if you fail?”

“Then we are all undone, for even the vengeance of God cannot hope to stand against God himself. For a house divided against itself is brought to desolation, and behold what Lucifer himself has wrought with his division.”

The great cavern shook, and then Hell let out a scream of anguish and pain. The Warden fell to his knees, for he and Michael were knocked off balance. Charon touched the wall once more, and a vision of the mountain materialized on the creature's flesh.

Michael saw that a portion of the great mountain of Hell had been obliterated. A Ladder formed near and sliced through the mountain's flesh. A piece of the mountain face sheared off from the familiar signature of a Ladder. Michael knew that Heaven was under siege with blind jumps from rogue angels who cared not for the protocols to keep Heaven and her denizens safe.

"Behold," said Michael. "Even Hell herself cannot stand against the power of a Ladder. What, pray tell, would Lucifer accomplish with the Stones of Fire the very source of thine creation?

Charon stood and walked towards Michael, and looking up at the giant, Michael backed slowly away. Charon reached into his robes and pulled out two glowing keys that were on a chain of fire and handed them to Michael to take.

“You will not ssssurvive Hell absssssent my pressssence," said Charon. "Only Lucifer and few of his kind have the power to traverse this realm and not perish, and even they cannot do so unssscathed. Buttttt your fleshhhhh is not like the Chief Princeeee, sooo I giveee to you the keyssss of Deathhh and Hellll. With them, you may pass through Hell unharmed, and the power to bind and loose those within are yours.”

Michael reached up to grab the key ring, which blazoned with fire and heat and dripped as sweat beads from a tired soul.

“Gooooo to and sssstop thy brother. Do not fail me.”

Charon turned to walk away, and as he did, a wall formed to separate Charon from Michael. Darkness enveloped Michael as he stood alone with the glowing keys of Death and Hell in his hands.

* * *

Lilith and his men made their way through the damaged city and entered the Great Library. “Secure the premises,” said Lilith.

Lilith’s minions made their way to the two doors that lead into the building and stood watch to protect their master within.

The attendants of the hall looked at the invaders, stopped what they were doing, and stood silently. Lilith approached the desk and spoke to the Chief Keeper.

“You are Hariph, Keeper of this Library...”

Hariph lifted his hand and interrupted him. "I know thy works. Lilith of Lucifer. I know that thou hast left thy station as his Grigori, but know that we who work this great Hall will not leave our post to serve. We are the librarians of Grigoric history storing the chronicles of all things. Even now, we continue on our charge. We shall not be moved."

Lilith smiled at him, "Then continue, but you will provide me with the information I need without delay, and if thy service displeases me, then know that thine own story will end this day. Am I understood, Chief Keeper?"

"All stories end, Lilith. There is no story but El's, for only He is the Alpha and the Omega, the beginning and the end. We are but paragraphs in his tale. But come, I know what you seek. I am bound to assist all who inquire within. Your war does not concern me save it prevent me from my charge."

Hariph spoke angel-speak and a book lifted from a shelf and floated to the stone and golden counter before Lilith. Lilith quickly turned its pages to the latest entry, frowned, and spoke aloud.

"How can this be? Michael was left on Earth, yet even now makes his way to the Kiln!"

"Perhaps," said Hariph, "your plans are not as sure as thou hast hoped?" Hariph grinned.

"Wipe the smirk off your face, Lord Keeper. Bring me the tomes of all the Chief Princes immediately!"

"And what of thy Master Lucifer?" asked Hariph.

Lilith realized that he had disturbed the order of the Lord. By not documenting, he no longer could know how his master fared. He was blind to his chief's actions. He smiled--it was a liberating feeling. To be free of this shackle, and no longer required to chronicle the exploits of another. *I will have to thank my Lord properly when I am lord of all Grigori. This is how Raphael feels...to know all, yet never required to himself chronicle.*

Hariph's work was complete, and the books of all six princes were before him save one.

"Where is Raphael's!" yelled Lilith.

"Ah, yes," said Hariph. "You see Prince Jerahmeel came to us not long ago and held a scroll to release the tome to him. His lordship has taken it; to where we do not know."

"How can such a thing be? No one is allowed to remove a tome from this Hall!"

Hariph nodded in agreement. Lilith reached over and grabbed Hariph by his shirt, "You will tell me on whose order did you release this time. You claim to stand neutral, yet you deny me my ledger!" Lilith released him, and Hariph slammed hard against a wall.

"Croganus, attend me and rid me of the Lord Keeper."

Croganus moved from the doorposts, unsheathed a flaming sword, and approached Hariph. Hariph waved his hands and spoke. "Would you kill me before knowing who ordered the release of Raphael's Tome?"

Lilith motioned for Croganus to stop.

"Speak, brother. Reveal what is chronicled."

Hariph rose to his feet, brushed himself off, opened a drawer behind him, removed the scroll, and handed it to Croganus who in turn gave it to Lilith.

Lilith saw the prismatic and red clay mark that had the Seal of El and unrolled the scroll to read. The document was like golden paper, its ink was a mixture of onyx and surrounded by silver and written in angelic script.

To the Lord Keeper,

As thou hast been charged since, thy creation with the keeping of all tomes within the Hall, and to wit war has come upon us, you are requested and required in the name of Lord of Hosts to release the Tome of Raphael to the bearer of this scroll.

For two days hence, thou shalt be besieged upon, and Lilith will come to claim it. Lo, it cannot fall into the enemies' hands.

Be swift in thy duties and remain faithful to the end, and thy reward shall be given after thy dissolution.

Lilith's eyes grew wide for the writing was penned with the finger of God and signed by El himself.

He dropped the scroll, and it burst into flames. Hariph laughed aloud.

"You art a fool to think that the creature might outwit the creator. For even the foolishness of El is wiser than your wisdom. El hast known of thine treachery before thou hadst even set foot in this very room."

Lilith slammed his fists on the stone table, shoved the books to the floor, scowled, and grabbed Hariph. "Who am I to deny prophecy?" Then he looked at Croganus. "Kill them all."

As Lilith bent down to pick up the books, the screams of those felled by Croganus' sword mingled with those who fell in battle outside the library's walls. Lilith thought to himself.

Are we undone?

* * *

Jerahmeel rocked to the side as the cavern shook and the mountain rumbled from the thunder outside its walls.

"Raphael, we must act quickly. Can the mount withstand a Ladder directed against it?"

"Nay, it cannot. However, El lies within its center. I am of a surety that although nothing may bring Him harm, the same cannot be said for the rest of Heaven. It is clear that Lucifer intends to pummel the realm into submission." Raphael raced to the great wall and spoke. "Reveal Third Heaven."

The wall complied, Jerahmeel and Raphael watched in horror and astonishment, for Lucifer had placed guards at the four gates into the realm, and each had an open Ladder that prevented other Ladders from forming. They beheld that angel after angel fell upon Heaven as falling stars, and like meteoric lightning, they blasted the landscape around them. Heaven was filled with craters from the destruction, as wave after endless wave destroyed buildings and friends. The skies bled with the blood of angels caught in each blast's wake.

Their aim was true, and the duo looked as the firmament rained with angels who fell from the skies, each a missile of destruction as they landed in their Ladders. Like beams of death, they fell upon all things and blasted the mountain of God and the temple. The rock face roared its objection. As one angel landed to unsheathe sword and destroy those who did not possess the mark of Lucifer, another angel materialized to bombard the mountain. It was ugly and imprecise. Even the Seraphim were under siege as Lucifer's soldiers were sent to breach the temple doors. The four mighty creatures battled with light and sound, cutting down all who would seek to enter without invitation, yet they were but four against a Legion that sought entry into the mountain. Raphael and Jerahmeel took in the scene in disbelief, and for a moment, despondency overtook the affable Jerahmeel who looked at the images before him and hope melted away.

"It is only a matter of time before they overwhelm even the Seraph," said Jerahmeel. "What can we hope to do?"

Raphael smiled. "Have faith, my friend. We are not without arms, yet I must concede our brother's genius," said Raphael. "Lucifer has cut Heaven off from the multiverse. He prevents the totality of Heaven's might from engaging him. Those that resist, he blasts into dissolution thinning our ranks here and forcing us to battle one another. Yet to what end? How does he expect to conquer El? Nor can he hope to keep the entire host away forever. By now throughout the realms, all have realized that they are stranded from home. For when they return, they would strike him down. What does he hope to gain?"

"Can you track him?" asked Jerahmeel

"Nay. Lilith no longer chronicles his charge. Lucifer is invisible without a Grigori to....wait...t hat's it...."

"What is it?

"There are Grigori throughout the realms. We can find where he is by looking where he is not."

Once more, the great cavern heaved and bucked, the ceiling cracked, and the image started to fade for a moment.

"Shay-t-zune-zi-t-al whey" spoke Raphael.

An image of Heaven showed on the wall and its topography showed throughout, and there were swathes of red, except in one place.

"Oh my God!" said Raphael. "He wouldn't dare!"

"What is it?"

Raphael showed his brother the red that outlined the whole map and pointed to the sole dark void where no red existed.

"These are the Grigori. Even in battle, there are those who have not wavered in their duties to record all that transpires around them. Through them, I may see all that transpires here. Lucifer does not exist within the sight of my brethren because he is here in the void."

Jerahmeel looked at the map and saw that there was blackness in but one area in all of Heaven — Hell.

"He moves to the Kiln," said Jerahmeel.

"Aye, and once there, even I do not know what might transpire. But lo, we have yet hope, for I see we have a standard raised even now against him. Reveal Athamas."

Once more, the wall obeyed and the image of Michael and Asthmas came to the fore. The room itself grew bright, and Jerahmeel could feel the intense heat that emanated through the portal into the room. They watched as Michael moved with all swiftness through the organs of Hell as fire enveloped him, and hundreds of angels cried and begged him for release. Raphael watched the internal digestion of Hell, and it was gruesome to behold. The smell was putrid; Raphael could only imagine how his brother fared.

"Michael somehow knows Lucifer's plan. He moves even now towards the Kiln. There is yet hope that he might stop him."

Michael turned and saw that there was a light against the wall, and he strained to see that Raphael was watching him and Jerahmeel stood to his side.

"Canst thou hear me?" yelled Michael.

"Yes, brother!" said Jerahmeel. "Lucifer aims to capture and awaken the Stones of Fire! You must stop him!"

"I know!" yelled Michael, "I have..."

Suddenly a tendril of fire leaped through the wall, and heat and flame engulfed Jerahmeel and Raphael. Each screamed in pain as the flesh of Hell and bodies still alive but digested; seeped through the wall to consume them.

Michael moved quickly, placed the flaming keys of Death and Hell into the mountain's organic wall, and spoke. "Retreat into thine own sphere I command thee! Do them no harm!"

Upon command, the cancerous tumors of living bile, brimstone, and flailing arms of Elohim retracted back into the wall as the tendrils with razor-like tongues hissed and eyed Michael with hatred.

Raphael rose to his feet and held his arm, now burned, and shook his head, groggy from the sensation of being eaten alive. Jerahmeel also came to himself.

Raphael spoke. "Go quickly, Michael. Godspeed. We will bring to naught Lucifer's plans." Michael nodded and turned to continue his journey through the razor-sharp teeth of bile-infested intestines of flame and magma.

Raphael spoke angel-speak and the image of the wall grew dark.

"We must stop this madness before it can grow further," said Raphael.

"But how?"

Raphael eyed the glowing glass wall that separated the Zoa from them and was struck with inspiration.

Jerahmeel looked at his brother knowingly. "That is not funny, Raphael. I did not intend for you to fight madness with madness!"

"I intend to give our people who hold to El a chance at survival. The Zoa are as the Ophanim; they cannot be harmed by our kind. It is time we showed Lucifer's legions that they have reason to fear what lies within the mountain. I need to get to the Library. Can you open the waypoint of Argoth? We must secure a passage to bring the legions."

"Aye," said Jerahmeel. "Lucifer has but one guard at each, portal. We only need one portal to bring in reinforcements."

Raphael moved to the wall and spoke. "When I go through, you must speak the words to image the cliffs of Argoth. If you do not do so in time, well, the Zoa will have you to feast upon, and I would very much like to see you again."

Jerahmeel chuckled. "Kick Lilith's butt for me."

Raphael smiled and turned to place himself in front of the wall. Jerahmeel moved to the side so as not to be in the line of sight of the Zoa and ducked behind a bookcase.

"This ought to be fun!" said Jerahmeel.

"Only if we live to tell about it," said Raphael.

Raphael then spoke the words that brought down the barrier that separated the Zoa from them, took a tome from off a desk, and threw it into the cavern. Jerahmeel watched from a distance as the ceiling slowly moved, and the creatures awakened at the sound and movement of the thrown book.

Raphael spoke the words to the wall, and it revealed the street and entryway to the Great Library He tucked the Tome of Iniquity within his robes, grabbed another book, blew upon it, and then threw it into the Zoa-filled room. Fires raged about, and the sound and movement from the fighting in the streets caught their attention. They saw Raphael throw another book, and a Zoa burst into flames and roared. They charged towards Raphael. Quickly he turned to run and immediately passed through the wall. Running into the street and dodging combatants, he sprinted to the Great Library.

Like a pack of elephants, several of the Zoa ran after him and leaped through the wall to overtake him only to find thousands of angels spread before them.

The throng looked about them curious at these new things. With its barbed tentacles, a Zoa grabbed a soldier of Lucifer, pierced his chest, lifted his body into the air, flung him around, and pounced to tear his limbs with its teeth. The populace raced every man for their lives as the giant creatures filled the streets. Each stung their prey and then devoured them.

Raphael looked to his rearward and saw that the creature that he had burned with his book still followed hard after him.

Maybe this was not the best idea.

Raphael saw that an angel blocked the doorway to the Library. And when the angel saw that Raphael raced towards him, he shut the door, and Raphael slammed hard against it. Seeing the creature upon him, Raphael leaped to his side, and the elephantine Zoa barreled through the door, smashed its way inside, trampled on the guard, and crushed him underfoot.

Raphael entered after it and saw Lilith with a look of petrified horror and anger on his face.

Raphael spoke. “You didn’t think you would get rid of me that easily, did you?”

The Zoa looked at them both with saliva and angelic blood dripping from its mouth ready to consume them.

No other God before me.

Jerahmeel peeked over the table sprawled with books and cautiously moved to the wall. Raphael's handiwork rampaged through the street as the Zoa that escaped: crushed Lucifer's soldiers underfoot and tossed foes into buildings. He remembered that his role was to close the Ladder at the Cliffs of Argoth and spoke as commanded by Raphael the words necessary to bring the waypoint into view.

Movement from out of the corner of his eye confirmed that Jerahmeel was not alone. He turned to look to his right and creeping towards him was a Zoa. Its mouth opened wide to reveal the razor-sharp teeth. Spittle dripped from its mouth as it hissed at Jerahmeel, poised to pounce.

"Now, I know I look tasty, but soon there will be a nice strong angel over there?" Jerahmeel pointed at the guard whom the wall had brought into view. "Now that fella, yonder -- he's got good bone structure and lifts stars; yep, there is way more meat on him than...."

The Zoa roared and leapt at Jerahmeel who ducked out the way and rolled over books and fallen brackets. The momentum of the creature sent it careening into shelves. Massive stone bookcases broke, crashed, and toppled down on the creature, burying it under piles of books.

Jerahmeel smiled as he surveyed his deftness and quickly remembered that the Hall of Annals contained the tomes for all things. Quickly, he ran towards a bookcase looking frantically for the creature's tome.

Even the Zoa have a tome. If I can but find it, perhaps—yes--just maybe.

He pulled book after book off the shelves, searching frantically, and sighed a sigh of relief when he saw the volume.

Suddenly his feet left him, and he fell with a thud as a tentacle wrapped itself around his leg and lifted him dangling into the air. Like a wrecking ball beheld by the end of a crane, Jerahmeel was swung headlong into the stone stable, and it broke in two with his fall. Books flew everywhere, and the hiss of the Zoa vibrated in his ears. Jerahmeel groggily opened his eyes to see three of the beasts fighting to be the first to devour him. He lifted himself to the ceiling with his great wings, and the creatures slammed into each other in their attempt to capture him.

Jerahmeel moved lower to the ground: the projection now in full view of the Cliffs of Argoth. He then flew within mouth reach of the creatures to draw them to follow him. Hissing, they did, roaring and lumbering to devour him. Jerahmeel reached into the wall and disappeared to the other side.

Lucifer's assigned guard over the waypoint concentrated on keeping the Ladder he had created from closing when he saw Jerahmeel suddenly fly straight towards him with a giant book in hand and appearing from nowhere tentacled creatures running after him. The guard panicked and tried to move, but it was too late. Jerahmeel had grabbed a hold of him, and a Zoa had grabbed them both. They rolled over one another and toppled off the cliff of Argoth, and the guard screamed as they all plunged into the swirling Abyss below.

* * *

"Behold, Astarte; Heaven falls before us!"

Ashtaroth, who with sword in hand cleaved at foes whom just days ago, he called brethren, frowned at the destruction and bloodshed before him. He huffed as he fought alongside Abaddon as the citizenry of Heaven came as a flood to stop them.

"Nay, Abaddon. Lucifer would *not* approve of this scale of dissolution. He would find another way!"

Ashtaroth swung his sword at an angel and brought it hard into its chest, smashing its stone; it turned to powder before him.

Abaddon laughed and reveled in his freedom to destroy and then took pause as creatures he had never seen came galloping on tentacles with mouths filled with razors. Like a herd, they felled everything that stood before them. Tossing angel after angel behind them and ripping to shreds those that carried the mark of Lucifer.

"Lo. See the handiwork of our brethren for they bring beasts to deter us!"

"They fight with beasts because we have become as beasts. Look about you! Our city burns, Abaddon, and the golden streets run blue with our blood!"

Abaddon turned to Ashtaroth and spoke. "From the day I was called DESTROYER, this ceased to be my city. Let it burn, Astarte. Let them all burn, for they watched El consign me to burn and be eaten alive for eternity. They are all but kindling for my wrath."

He eyed the new creatures that moved towards them and pulled open his breastplate to reveal his cracked God stone. He removed a shard, spoke angel speak, and tossed it into the sky.

"See now the true meaning of the 'broken stone'... and tremble."

Ashtaroth and the other generals watched as the shard pulsed in the air and grew dark. Giant globules of black separated from it: one, three, then nine, and suddenly it burst and millions of locust-like creatures filled the sky and cast a shadow over the great city.

The shape of the locusts was like unto horses prepared unto battle, and on their heads were crowns like gold; their faces were as the faces of men. Each creature had hair as the hair of the human female El had created. Their teeth were as the teeth of lions. Each held a breastplate of iron, and the sound of their wings was as the sound of chariots of many horses running to battle. Their tails were like scorpions, and they had the power to paralyze and torture all that they attacked.

Abaddon commanded them to strike at all who bore not the mark of his Lord and to attack the oncoming Zoa.

They descended upon the Zoa with ferociousness and stung them and anyone bearing not Lucifer's mark. The people writhed in agony and cried out in pain, for El to save them.

Smug with satisfaction Abaddon mocked the tormented, "Yes where is that God who would save you from me? El has abandoned you, yet you refuse to bow! Refuse to surrender!"

The locusts were like a cloud that moved throughout the city.

Ashtaroth looked at the suffering of those before him and noted even the Zoa stopped and convulsed in agony on the streets. The creatures grew limp and motionless against the onslaught, but Abaddon watched in glee, watched as angel after angel pleaded with him to make the pain stop. Each tormented soul prayed and cried out to El for relief. The locusts landed on each man and stung them over, and over, and the whole of the city was filled with screams and wails.

Ashtaroth beheld his brethren and was moved with compassion. He turned towards Abaddon and said, "Retract thy army! We cannot rule if there is none to obey!" He pulled at the arm of Abaddon to make him look at him. "For the love of God Abaddon, stand down!"

Abaddon turned towards him wroth and struck Ashtaroth across the face, and he fell to the ground.

"You would adjure *me* by the love of God! *Me*? Do not *ever* touch me! I tolerate you because Lucifer tolerates you."

Ashtaroth rose from the ground, spit blood, and glared at Abaddon. "We are all but servants to our Lord King. We bear his mark, and his will is to subjugate the populace not to destroy it."

Abaddon laughed. "Then our master's plan is flawed. And you are a fool Astarte; there can be no subjugation without destruction."

"Stand down!" Ashtaroth warned once more. "Or be removed from thine office."

Abaddon laughed. "And who do you think will follow *you,* Astarte? Will *you* remove me? Only the God King commands me, and you vassal are not he."

Ashtaroth's brow grew tense, "Then you leave me no choice." and he turned to the army of warrior angels behind him.

Ashtaroth raised the crescent seal of Lucifer for all to see.

"By order of his majesty Lucifer, Son of the Morning Star, whose seal I now bear. Abaddon is hereby relieved; he is no longer in command. Arrest him. If he resists—kill him."

Many paused, as Abaddon stood at the head of the army. With this new displayed power to summon a swarm of angelic locusts, many were afraid to move against him.

He laughed.

"You see Astarte— you possess authority but lack the might to enforce it."

He then placed his hands on his hips and chuckled. "Now all of you obey me, or you too shall likewise perish!"

Ashtaroth looked at the indecision and hesitation of those he commanded and then looked at Abaddon who haughtily laughed at him. Without warning, Ashtaroth threw himself headlong into Abaddon and kicked him in the jaw knocking the giant Arelim to his knees, and pummeled him until Abaddon's face hit the ground.

"I speak for Lord Lucifer! No one defies his will! I said arrest him!"

Emboldened, Ares rushed with several others to bind Abaddon with chains of iron, but Abaddon struggled to his feet and flung his apprehenders to the side. More immediately came to subdue the great angel.

"Enough!"

Abaddon then spoke the words to open a Ladder, and those who held him attempted to cover his mouth and silence him, but to no avail. The multitude that followed looked in horror as a giant funnel cloud opened above Abaddon. All fled to escape, but it was too late, for as the vortex of the Ladder touched down and disintegrated his captors. It blew those in the immediate vicinity back, and all crashed hard into buildings and walls. The vacuum of the Ladder retracted, and many fell screaming as they were lifted and sucked into the burning whirlwind.

The smoke cleared, and Ashtaroth emerged climbing from under debris and rubble. He looked over the army and lo, friend and foe alike had been vaporized in the wake of the Ladder's blast. The great city smoldered, and a third of it had been destroyed. Stone, wood, and angelic debris fell from the sky as spire after city spire was in flames, and explosions rocked buildings.

Ashtaroth looked at Abaddon in disgust and spoke so that all nearby might hear. "You are hereby deemed traitor to the cause of Lucifer. Let Heaven herself spit you out, and know of a surety that you have no country, no home. You are in league with no one. You are the Destroyer, and you will not be allowed to live." He spoke to the warriors near him and said, "Kill him."

Upon command, warriors of Lucifer attacked Abaddon, and he fought them with sword and with brute strength, picking up angels and using their bodies as a shield to protect him against the horde that now attacked him.

When Abaddon saw that all of Heaven arrayed itself against him, he summoned his legion of locusts, and the wasp-like creatures that had just attacked those without the sigil of Lucifer now attacked indiscriminately all that moved.

Ashtaroth's face grew grim as he entered the fray, and took up his sword to destroy him.

* * *

Gabriel looked down at his hands. The powdered dust of stones he had shattered from the chests of his fallen brethren covered them, hands that had spilled Elomic blood. He surveyed the scene about him, and tears poured from his eyes, at the carnage that strife had ravaged on the Elysian Fields. The gryphons of Malakim filled the skies; the manna fields burned and its lush soil turned upside down.

The groans and screams of the battlefield echoed across the golden-hued skies and a fog of dust and flame settled above the Elysian Fields for as far as the eye could see. Gabriel saw angel after angel locked in armed and unarmed combat, each combatant locked in fury to the dissolution of the other. The cracking of bones, the ripping of wings, the shredding of throats, and the smashing of stones all joined in a cacophony of sound. Row after row of Elohim clashed using the powers given to them by El to bring to naught one another. Gabriel wondered how they all had arrived at the point of self-genocide.

"I take it, Gabriel, that my brethren and the Arelim did not take well to your touching me?" said Sariel who slowly regained consciousness.

"Forgive me, brother, for I would not let you harm our brother nor would I see harm come to you," Gabriel replied.

"Then you have bested me in obeying the Lord. Your act has brought me shame, but it was a noble act, and it is I who am sorry for the hurt I have caused."

Sariel viewed his brethren locked in combat, Arelim fighting Issi and Malakim.

"We must find Talus," said Sariel. "Only the three of us can end this folly."

Sariel rose to his feet, and he scoured the landscape. "Do you see him, Gabriel?"

"Aye, to the hills on the eastern edge of the forest."

Sariel followed the path of Gabriel's fingers and saw in the distance Talus encircled by powerful Arelim guards, watching the battle that encompassed the fields of manna.

"We must go to him," said Sariel.

Gabriel looked at him as if he was mad, "But he will of a surety attack us."

"Perhaps, but we must seek reconciliation or risk a wider war with the other great houses. The burning of the fields must have caught the attention of those within the city by now."

Gabriel motioned to the gryphons guards that encircled them and they lifted themselves into the air, an entourage to provide escort for their leaders as they flew over the battlefield, towards Talus and his guard.

The guards of Talus came to attention, and with wings unfurled, they covered their master and prepared themselves to battle the incoming wave.

"Stand down," said Talus. "They mean us no harm."

The guards of Talus relaxed and kept a watchful eye on the giant gryphon riders that descended with their trident spears and landed just feet away. Sariel and Gabriel walked from the midst of them to approach and Talus moved his guardsman aside to greet them.

The three stared at each other in silence until Gabriel spoke for them all. "This conflict must end, or Heaven herself will be brought to naught let alone the multiverse of El's creation."

Sariel eyed Talus warily. "I agree the blood spilled between our houses must end here before it reaches beyond the fields of Elysium."

Talus looked at his brothers and said, "I could have descended upon you with my forces well before you greeted me here, Gabriel."

"You could have tried, brother," Gabriel replied.

Talus smiled. "But instead, I chose to remain and wait to see what thou wouldst do. When I saw no intent to do me harm, yet you still protected our brother, I was brought low and ashamed by thine example. Therefore, I sought to recall my people from battle, to have them stand down, but to no avail, for the battle had taken a mind of its own. Vengeance and blood are all that consume my people now. They seek to remove the stain of Apollyon and the disgrace he has brought on our name."

Gabriel replied, "How can such a thing be done?"

Talus looked upon the battlefield of Elysium, now drenched in Elomic blood. He surveyed the might of Heaven unleashed, the very ground beneath them scorched. "They seek to eliminate his memory from the minds of those who remember."

Sariel interrupted, "They cannot destroy the entire lot of Elohim!"

"Nay," replied Talus, "They cannot, but as a mover of stars, we can diminish the numbers of Heaven. Therefore, we must quell the horde before they do the unthinkable."

Gabriel said, "They would not be so foolish!"

"I know not what my people driven mad by anger and hubris would do, Gabriel. I only know that a Ladder formed outside of a waypoint would bring dissolution to multitudes, to friend and foe alike."

"Then speak to them through me," said Gabriel, "before pride and anger give way to further destruction. Perhaps if they see us together, if we were to speak as one man, then madness might give way to reason, and the horde might be stilled."

"Look about you Gabriel," said Sariel. "How can we communicate to so many?"

Gabriel looked and saw the swells of angels over the fields were as the sand upon the seashore. They covered as far as the eye could see, and the foodstuff of angels, the source of Heaven's provision, was destroyed. Gabriel's face frowned, a tear flowed down his cheek, and thoughts of despair began to flood him. Quickly, he shook himself from despondency and said, "Take my hand, the two of you, and rise with me into the air"

Clasping hands, Gabriel, Talus, and Sariel took to the skies with their guards surrounding them. They moved towards the throng, and when they had settled over the midst of the battlefield, Gabriel took his horn and blew to recall the Malakim riders that had come to their master's aid.

The blow from the Trumpet of Israel was recognized, and immediately the Gryphon riders took to the skies to depart. All in combat took notice that the skies filled with the creatures and their riders, and those who had been fearful of the Malakim spear; relief flooded them.

The Malakim came towards Gabriel, and the sky filled with their steeds. Gabriel reached to his brothers' chests, placed his hands on their stones, and motioned for them to touch his stone. When they did, they became as one being, and Gabriel spoke so all could hear. When his lips moved so too did the lips of his brethren, and they spoke as one man.

"Mighty host of God, thou who hast moved stars and carried the voice of El throughout the corners of the heavens...legions, hear me! Cease and desist and lay down thine arms, for look about you and behold what your anger has done to Heaven; see what your rage hast wrought!

"For pride hast laid waste to reason, and strife has eaten at our souls: and to what end? That we might destroy each other for no cause? This is not why El hast made us; this is not what El would tolerate. These are not the acts of a child towards his father. We are Elohim, and we were created for more than this."

The host paused to weigh the words spoken, and warily eyed one another. Weapons slowly lowered, and fists gradually unclenched. Hands, once raised in battle, now offered handshakes of peace. Gabriel and his brethren smiled, for they had quenched the rage that hovered over the throng; a sigh of relief came over them all.

The sky then turned red in the distance, and bright lights engulfed the city of God. The booming sound of thunder cracked ears, and shockwaves rocketed across the plains. Sonic tidal waves of force slammed headlong into the mass of angels assembled in the field and all were blown back by the blast.

The concussive gust smashed into Gabriel and his brothers, and they fell hard to the ground. The rush of debris and manna leaf sliced cheeks, and the heated wind-ruffled hair. Gabriel, sore from his fall turned towards the direction of Jerusalem. Fires and black acrid smoke lifted high into the air and the despondency filled him, as he knew the unthinkable had happened. A Ladder, no hundreds of Ladders, flashed throughout the sky, and Jerusalem burned.

He rose to his feet and spoke to them all. "I will not stand here and fight amongst my brethren while treachery seeks to destroy our home. We will face this threat, and bring it to naught. Come, therefore, and we shall smite those who would do such a thing."

Gabriel lifted himself, and Talus and Sariel followed him into the air. The three great houses trailed their leaders into the sky, and those that could fly flew, and those that raced along the ground galloped, a mighty army of thousands upon thousands bent to exact vengeance on those who would defile their home.

* * *

Michael moved gingerly through the foul-smelling intestines of flame. Arms and wails of devoured souls clawed at him, as Hell's teeth bit, repeatedly, into angelic flesh.

Hell was different somehow, larger, more ferocious in her attempts to smother Michael, but he held the keys to Death and Hell, keys that would if he commanded, force her to regurgitate any and all he desired. He was a deputy of Charon now, a guardian to the souls that lay therein, and she would obey him.

Finally, thought Michael.

The umbilical to the Kiln came into view and Michael could hear the roar of the Stones of Fire: the source of Hell's power. As Michael entered the Kiln, he heard the clamoring of sounds, the echoes of stones vying for his attention, ready to mold as he willed. The stones sang to him within the furnace of fire, each in a melody unique to its properties. Prior to when El had created Charon, Michael had not noticed the songs that radiated from them: he had been too overwhelmed by wonder and fear.

As the glowing, heated gems of orchestral chorus filled the cavern with melody, Michael noticed harmony in the fire. Hymns like none in all creation, he closed his eyes to listen and savor their tune.

He listened; realizing that within the melody there was one stone that did not sing as the others. A larger stone that sang a song in harmony yet unique from the others He had never noticed it before, being too overwhelmed by the presence of God and being in the Kiln to witness the birth of Charon. Nevertheless, it was clear to him now, a much larger stone in the center of the room: a Primestone. It called to him, nay beckoned to him with the singing of its melody. A melody from which he realized all other melodies sprung. The Primestone glistened in the fire, moist despite the heat and flame, and where the other Stones of Fire called out, *"to be,"* this one was not so. It simply sang, *"I am."* Then Michael understood the secret of the Kiln. Here, within this fiery cavern, God did not just fashion his ministers of flame. Angels alone were not this crucible's function. Nay, here hidden alone to all but the most worthy of Elohim, to he who was Chief Prince, El granted one power to join the Godhead—to be as El.

Michael knelt down and placed his trembling hand over the stone to touch it. He listened to its song, and its refrain called for him to cup it in an orgasmic embrace and partake of its "fruit."

When he saw that it was pleasant to the eyes and a stone to be desired to ascend to power, he reached closer to touch it: a touch that he might be as El and possess the power of the Almighty.

The Primestone crackled with energy, and tendrils of plasma rose from the gemstone and reached up to embrace his fingers.

Perhaps El would have me be God — to use his own power to defeat Lucifer?

Michael knew now why Lucifer would not cede his position. He understood why Lucifer was so obsessed when he heard that Michael had gone into the Kiln. It was clear for, unbeknownst to all of Heaven, yeah even Raphael, God held within the Kiln a secret that only He and the Chief Prince knew, that within this chamber, one might become God. Michael was humbled that El would reveal to him such an intimate truth.

The giant gemstone called to him, and Michael dreamt of what he could do with such power. Those fallen in battle he could resurrect; perhaps he might make a universe after his own likeness and after his own image. He could force those who sided with Lucifer to reason. More and more his thoughts raced with how God could change all things, and then he understood that the stone was more than just a receptacle to contain and dispense God's power. It was a test, and the words of Iofiel flooded back to his remembrance.

'Have you too left El to follow the path of Lucifer?'

His failure to control himself with Iofiel haunted him. He pulled his trembling hand back and scooted away from the gemstone. He shook himself to gain composure and marveled that the Lord would leave such power within his grasp.

"No, there is no God but El," he said to himself.

Perception dawned on him that Lucifer saw the stones as common, as things to use for control. He remembered what El had taught him when Lucifer departed from the communion table.

"And it shall come to pass when thou must confront thy brother, do not confront him alone, for you will speak to the stones, and they will be. Charge them, Michael of the Kortai, and they will aid thee. But beware, for within lies a token of my faith in thee. Fail me not, and thou shalt be Chief Prince."

"But Lord why must this be at all?"

"Fear not, for there must need to be a falling away first, that the man of sin might be revealed, the son of perdition, who opposeth and exalteth himself above all that is called God, so that he as God sitteth in the temple of God, showing himself that he is God. For even now the mystery of iniquity doest already work, and for now, it must be, and I must be taken from out of the way, but, alas, the Wicked shall be revealed whom I will consume with the spirit of my mouth and shall destroy with the brightness of my coming."

Michael rose to stand and anger swelled within him.

Lucifer cannot be allowed to have the Kilnstones.

Michael reached down to grab a stone. It was as hard as a polished diamond and its brilliance gleamed. It sang soprano throughout the cavern when held, and with the other hand, Michael picked up another stone. It was black iron and a deep bass resonated from its song, a low hum that made one's chest vibrate. Each had a different song, and as he touched them together, their songs changed from unison to harmony and merged to form a new element mixed with the properties of diamond and iron.

He placed it within the Kiln's fleshy walls and spoke angel speak. The Kiln hearkened to the word of El and took from Michael's mind the image that he desired to fashion within the cavern's womb: an angel of power with which to match the First of Angels.

The walls rumbled, and the wall took the stone. A bulge formed from within and grew immense. A membrane of mucus-like substance appeared and dropped to the floor, a great sac with a dark figure within burst, and the newly formed angel fell to the fiery floor. Michael stood up to give it charge.

"Rise Ouranos, Titan of God, for you shalt be a standard to aid me. For the Prince of Angels comes to secure power, and we shall stand between him and the Lord."

His head was that of a man, his arms as great oaks, and he shone as the sun in the sky, a brightness that could reflect all light and sound and wrap the light around his person. He looked down at Michael, and his whole body was like a mirror; Michael could see himself in the angel's skin. The great behemoth stood in front of Michael with four great arms and eight flowing wings of light, and his legs were like that of a bear.

"Lo Titan, our enemy will be here soon. Go to and conceal thyself within the wall. Come when called for, and let thy aid be swift."

The creature plodded to the back wall and like a chameleon, melted into the background, waiting silently for Michael to give command. Michael positioned himself in the center of the Kiln, kneeled, bowed his head, and prayed

Lord El, I face my brother to prevent this usurpation. Give me strength. Forgive thy servant and hold not this charge to my account. If there be other means whereby this might end, let it be, but if

not...Michael paused, grimaced, and swallowed hard. *Then let my sword be swift, and thy will be done in all things.*

He stood, lifted his hands, and pointed to the stones about him, and they rose from the floor, hovering, and as Michael spoke the Elomic word for destruction, the stones lifted into the top of the fiery chamber and embedded themselves into the ceiling, germinating to become as willed by Michael, their songs changed to reflect his will. They seethed in the ceiling above and hissed as if simmering.

Michael knelt then removed from his folded wings a gemmed scabbard and unsheathed a double-bladed sword of fire made by the Lord himself. He struck the blade into the burning floor and imaged the Ophanim. Suddenly, hands rose from the ground to grasp the sharp blade. Blue coils of electric current wound themselves over the steel, and the fire of the sword turned from red to blue. Seven stones rose into the air and attached themselves like iron filings drawn to a magnet, and when all seven had attached themselves: the steel cracked. The sound of a thunderclap burst through the cavern and Michael was knocked back. He eyed the sword as it rose from the ground spitting arcs of lightning. Two eyes and teeth materialized within the blade. He reached out to touch the hilt, and the blade split into seven swords, each alive with eyes that moved within the blades. The blades sang to him in the fire and floated in the air above him.

Michael marveled at the swords, when he lifted the blade they encircled him, and when he swiped, they mimicked him. He thought of himself sheathing the blade, immediately they flew to him, reconnected to the sword, and it vibrated in his hands. He could feel the current race around him as he held it. Michael stood waiting. He gripped the hilt of the sword and closed his eyes.

El thou knowest what is at stake. I will not allow Lucifer to command the God stones.

Michael's face grimaced as he heard the sound of familiar music from the opening of the umbilical to the Kiln. A glowing figure stepped into the fiery furnace with him. He opened his eyes and looked into the fire.

Lucifer had come.

* * *

Abaddon lifted himself into the air with his great wings and flung from his back those who dared to strike at him. A swarm of angelic locusts surrounded him, and those that attacked him were stung and fell to their knees writhing in pain.

Ashtaroth lunged at Abaddon, and he too was stung and fell back. Abaddon yelled to him and pursued him as he fell to the ground. "Now I will bring your miserable life to an end, Astarte. From the onset, this is how it should have been. There will be no Michael or Lucifer to save you from my hand this time!"

Ashtaroth fell hard into the ground and swerved to his side as Abaddon crashed into the earth, barely missing him. Ashtaroth rose quickly to his feet, and with wings spread before him, he used them as a shield to protect his face from the locust swarm that encircled his foe.

He drew his sword, struck at Abaddon, and clipped his leathery wing. The Arelim yelled in pain, stepped back, and then laughed maniacally.

"I am going to enjoy this."

Abaddon motioned with his hand and the swarm which before had attacked Lucifer's foes now arched and raced to fall upon Ashtaroth. They fell upon him and stung and bit into his flesh. He attempted to wave them away, but it was to no gain as his vision darkened, and he fell to the earth writhing in agony and screaming. The locusts covered his body so that naught but a thrashing shape twisted on the ground.

"Now Astarte, you shall know pain. Let anguish be thy companion, for it is not yet my desire to kill you, but to savor and to feast upon your suffering with my own eyes, for *you* to taste what it is to be savored by Hell."

Round about them both, warriors attempted to strike at Abaddon but a wall of locusts kept them at bay, and those that were not in liege with Lucifer still fought to fend off his legions. The clash of steel could be heard in the distance. As Abaddon knelt down to gloat over the convulsive body of Ashtaroth, he pulled his sword from its sheath to behead him.

Ashtaroth saw through the veil of carnivorous-like insects that Abaddon lifted his sword to cut off his head. In terrified agony, he reached out to him to spare him, only to see the Arelim jolted and thrown back by a blur from behind him.

Abaddon hurtled backward against a wall, and a hazy-like figure pummeled his face and then kicked him in the abdomen. Abaddon curled up in a ball and vomited. Coughing, he shook himself and stretched out his wings attempting to take flight, but a hammer-like blow fell on his back and knocked the wind from his lungs. He smashed into the ground, wheezing as the blows came as if from nowhere and assaulted him from every direction. He held his hands over his face for a defense. Light flashed before his eyes, and he beheld a bright, glowing figure enveloped with the presence of God standing before him.

Gabriel, staff in hand, stood over him and spoke, "I have a message for you." The archangel then took his staff and swung it as a bat into Abaddon's face, and great drops of blood and spittle flung from his cheek.

Abaddon fell hard to the earth. Groggily struggling to regain himself, he stood and sputtered blood as he spoke. "You do me great honor High Prince, but it will take more than that to defeat me."

Gabriel nodded in agreement then motioned his hand skyward.

"Behold."

Abaddon looked up, and lo the heavens swarmed with Malakim and Gryphon Riders, and at their front, Talus and Sariel plummeted from the sky with an army of angels all headed straight toward him.

* * *

The Zoa looked at them both, and its mouth opened to reveal rows of razor-sharp teeth. Spittle fell from its mouth, and its tentacled arms and legs tensed as it eyed them. Like one of the sea predators of Earth, it slowly encircled them. Eyeing its prey, it hissed at them menacingly.

Lilith backed away slowly and pulled from his cloak the tome he possessed, quickly found the section on the Zoa, and wrote in angelic script the word *deletion*.

The creature then raced towards them, and Raphael ran and dived over a table while the Zoa leaped after him, jumping over the table and smashing into chairs and streams of books.

Lilith completed his writing, and the creature turned to consume him, for he was closer, but as the Zoa approached, it began to fade. It roared.

Howling, it reached to grab Lilith, and Lilith instinctively changed to his gaseous form. The creature stung him, Lilith cried out in pain, and the Zoa disappeared from view, but not before Lilith clutched his arm, now sore from the welt that burned him.

"Stings, huh? I always wondered what would happen if one of those things actually touched me. I've learned something new today." Raphael laughed.

Lilith scowled at him and spoke, still clutching his arm. "Laugh as you like, for you will not laugh long. I am pleased that I have the chance to finally deal with you as I see fit," said Lilith.

"And in what way would an errant Grigori deal with the Prince of Chronicles?" replied Raphael.

"Let us just say I seek to rewrite the tale of thy existence."

Lilith lifted his pen, and it transformed into a dagger. "I now wield the Pen and Inkhorn of God. I am now he who writes creation. Your inkhorn and stylus belong to me now."

An explosion rocked the building and both swayed to their sides and lost balance. Raphael smiled. "Aye, you do have my belongings, they were handed to me by El himself, and I would see them returned. Raphael held his dagger; his inkhorn floated by his head.

Lilith took the tome still in his hand, inscribed in Elohim the words for delete, and looked at Raphael giddily.

"Goodbye, my *Prince,*" Lilith said sarcastically.

But nothing happened, and Raphael moved closer towards him holding the hilt of his dagger in hand, and chuckled. "Perhaps...," said Raphael, "my name is not spelled correctly. Did you check your spelling or is the grammar not clear? Or pray tell the Elomic language has escaped you?" Raphael laughed mockingly at him.

Irritated Lilith looked down at what he had written and quickly wrote the verse again to delete Raphael, but nothing happened, and his face soured with disapproval and anger.

"You see, Lilith; to be Sephiroth, to command the power of El to create and delete from creation, one must have three elements: the Pen of God, which you do possess, and the Inkhorn of God, but they are of no use unless you possess this."

Raphael lifted from the inside of his breast a gilded-edged tome for Lilith to see; it gave off a golden hue and pulsed, as Raphael held within his hand his own beating heart shaped in the form of a great book. Raphael smiled and placed the tome back snuggly within his chest.

Lilith frowned and raised the dagger he held.

"Then --" said Lilith, "allow me to relieve you of your Heartstone."

Lilith assumed his gaseous form, vanished from view, reappeared behind Raphael, and thrust his dagger to stab him in the back, but Raphael turned and parried. Attempting to strike in return only to hit ether as Lilith quickly turned to mist.

Lilith and Raphael attacked one another. Daggers sparked as steel clashed with steel. Raphael deflected each attempted strike and ducked and weaved to avoid being cut down. Raphael moved quickly and leaped over the stone table, and upon it were books spread out, but Lilith was there to meet him. The Grigori caught Raphael by the face and slit his cheek, and blood poured from the wound. Raphael cried out, pressed hard against his nerve, and wiped blood from his face.

"Yield to me as Chief Chronicler, and I will allow you to assume the mantle of poor Hariph here," said Lilith.

Raphael saw the steward of the hall lying face down dead and said, "Look to your own fate Lilith. You desire to be Sephiroth, and like your master, you lust for position above your station. If power is what you seek, then, by all means, take it." Raphael then pulled from the tome of his own heart and let Lilith see it beating; its sheets moved as new text formed on its pages. He threw the book into the fireplace within the room, and as it began to burn, Raphael staggered and collapsed.

"No!" cried Lilith and he vanished to appear suddenly bending over the now burning book to remove it from the flames. As he reached to grab the tome, Raphael pounced upon him and thrust his dagger into Lilith's hand. Lilith screamed in pain as the dagger pierced his flesh to find its tip in the book now ablaze.

Lilith tried to mist, but he could not for the blade of Raphael held his hand in the book.

When Lilith reached to grapple with Raphael, Raphael forced Lilith's hand to write in the flaming book the angelic script for his name in his own blood. Lilith repeatedly pummeled Raphael to break free but could not, for Raphael held fast and scratched into the burning pages, *delete.* When the last character was entered, Lilith screamed and slowly began to fade from view.

Raphael looked upon his brother, released him, and spoke. “Let the memory of the just be blessed, but the name of the wicked rot and your memory cut off from the realm forever.”

Lilith struggled to switch between mist and solid form but could not. His body grew grey, and he writhed in pain from the sole of his foot to the crown of his head. He turned to ash, the remains fell to the floor, and the wind swept the embers away.

When Lilith was no more, the Inkhorn and stylus of God fell to the floor. Raphael picked them up, lifted the tome of El, doused the cinders that fell from its cover, and placed it back securely into the folds of his chest. His strength slowly returned to him, and he sat to rest against a wall. Through the windows of the building, he saw Malakim gryphons descend from the skies to smite those with Lucifer’s mark, and his spirit lifted.

Gabriel had come.

* * *

Lucifer stepped into the Kiln, and he could hear the siren songs that the stones sang to him.

Soon the very power of creation will be mine to command, and I will make a new Heaven and a new Earth.

Lucifer looked to the center of the Kiln, and standing before the Prime Stone with a sword bathed in blue flame was Michael.

Lucifer smiled. “Brother, so you *have* supplanted me as the Chief Prince, yet it is of no consequence. Bow down and worship me; pledge to me thy fealty, and even now offense shall be forgiven, and all shall be thine.”

Michael answered and said unto him, “We have not spoken since the Lord’s supper, and after all this, your first words are of your station, but naught for the destruction you have caused. I would know why.”

Lucifer looked upon his brother in anger. “You query *me*? *Me*? Am I a dog that I must give answer now? Hast thou risen to prominence that I should be questioned?” Lucifer guffawed. “Very well then, know that I oppose the enslavement of our people, and I will be a slave no longer. I would have what El would deny me. Yet it is not seemly that I should take your life, Heaven cannot afford the loss of so great a servant to her cause.”

Lucifer moved closer to Michael, his hands folded behind his back watching him.

“Even now, you threaten to take my stone?" Michael replied. “I have in vain held back the truth of your treason. I have told myself there must be just cause for your deeds. That what Raphael and Iofiel said about you were amiss, but out of thine own mouth, you stand condemned. I have loved you, yet you would seek to destroy me to achieve thine own ends, and there is a part of me Lucifer — that would let you.”

"So brother," said Lucifer. "Then my words fall on deaf ears, for thou hast eyes yet cannot see, and ears yet will not hear. I had sworn that I would never leave thee nor forsake thee, yet now my own brother lifts up his hand against me. Am I hated thus?"

Michael lowered his gaze, frowned, grabbed the hilt of his sword, pointed its blue blade at Lucifer, and looked him squarely in the eye. "I do not hate you brother." Tears fell from Michael's eyes. "I hate what I have become because of you."

Lucifer stopped his walk and closed his eyes, a tear ran from his eye, and he spoke. "What is done is done. It is too late for returning; too much has transpired. To see freedom, there must be a new God. This has grown beyond you and me." Lucifer scowled, his voice changed to a heavy base, and the sound pounded with the force of a drum.

"Move aside. My accession to the Godhead has been delayed for too long, for despite El, I will be God."

Michael stood his ground, his sword locked, and pointed at Lucifer.

"I will not allow you to take the God Stones. I will see dissolution before you assume the throne."

Lucifer stood mute for a second, his face stoic and grim. He looked at his brother, studied him, and then slowly nodded. "So be it."

Lucifer opened the pores of his flesh and immediately detonated in light: the colors of the rainbow were as a thing alive and wrapped themselves around Michael blinding him. Lucifer inhaled and belted out a roar that sent Michael reeling and he was thrown back and crashed into the great cavern wall with a thud.

Lucifer walked confidently towards the Prime Stone and spoke.

"Thou art a fool to withstand me. You cannot hope to best me in combat. Bow down and worship me, and even now I will spare thee."

Michael lifted himself from the floor and held his abdomen now sore. In a voice low and deliberate, he gave the command. "Ouranos, destroy!"

Like a dog unleashed, the giant golem broke from its embedded slumber and raced to charge into Lucifer.

Lucifer looked at the gargantuan Elohim that ran towards him, and again confidently opened the pores of his flesh. Light lifted from him as the surf upon the ocean and crashed in all directions.

The waves of multicolored force bathed itself over Ouranos, but the golem continued his charge unabated. He lumbered as only a giant could and raised his hands to smite Lucifer.

Lucifer backed away and opened his mouth to speak. He shouted to the creature to stop, and the echo of his mighty voice reverberated in the Kiln, causing the mountain to shake from within so that even those outside felt the bass of Lucifer's voice vibrate their chests.

But Michael knew his brother, and El had prepared him. Ouranos was unmoved and slipped through the sound boom as through water; he came for the Chief Prince with hands lifted to strike. Lucifer grew pale as he looked at the behemoth.

Lucifer drew his sword, but it was too late. He felt the crush of Ouranos' fist slam his head into the ground, the weight of the creature was such that the Kiln floor yielded and cracked as Lucifer's body crumpled underneath the creature's hands.

Lucifer, however, was the First of Angels, and he lifted his wings to cover his face. His scales retracted into his body to reveal the diamond armor surrounding him. His legs and arms grew muscular, and with the revealing of his talons, he completed the transformation into the warrior angel necessary to survive the environment of the thing El had called space. He lifted the great titan from off of him, and swung his sword at the creature, slicing into its chest.

Stunned from the blow, Ouranos fell to the ground. Lucifer retracted once again the armor from his body and opened his mouth to blast the creature with the power of his voice.

Michael now recovered; flew to assault his brother and with a sword in hand; struck Lucifer across his neck, and sliced his esophagus. Blood spewed into the air as a mist. Michael landed on the floor and turned to attack his brother once more. Lucifer's eyes grew wide as he gurgled on his own blood and for a moment staggered, and fell to bended knee. Ouranos stood to launch himself at the Chief Prince again. Michael also turned and leaped into the air to bring dissolution to his brother.

Lucifer grinned and stretched his hand to touch the Prime Stone. With vocal cords embedded in his forearms and ears, he spoke over it. "*Ehyeh asher ehyeh,*" Which means in Elohim, 'I will be what I will be.'

Immediately both Michael and Ouranos were repelled, flung hard by an invisible hand against the cavern wall.

When Lucifer spoke, the god stones quieted, stopped their singing, and rose from the cavern floor. "*Ehyeh asher ehyeh,*" he spoke again.

With each chant, every stone changed its song and sounded like the voice of Lucifer, so that when he spoke, all stones spoke, and the disparate songs of many became the unified song of one. Each gemstone then moved towards him and attached itself to his skin.

Lucifer opened his arms wide to receive them as each stone slowly melded into him. He began to gleam as the brightest star and changed before Michael's eyes. The power of God resident within the stones poured into Lucifer and the gash across Lucifer's throat healed itself.

The elements of all creation danced around him, and he changed in appearance with the addition of each stone: his head became as fine gold, his breast and arms of silver, his belly and thighs of bronze, his legs of iron, his feet part iron and clay, and all stones sang the song of Lucifer.

Lucifer basked in the power that flowed through him, shimmered, and became opaque. For in that moment, he was in the Kiln but was not, and on Earth, but was not. Present in Heaven, but was not.

The power of El to be everywhere coursed through him and the host of Heaven saw Lucifer's image in all places. Many wondered at the sight, for only El ever displayed such power, and Lucifer relished in the sensation of omnipresence. El's power crackled and sizzled and the ground shook as the universe witnessed the ascension of Lucifer to the Godhead.

The Kiln erupted in even more flame, and Michael and the juggernaut drew back from the heat and lightning that sparked across the chamber.

Lucifer then grew in stature, and his body convulsed and changed. Legs like that of the reptilian earthen creatures sprang from him. His twelve wings merged to become two wings of leather. His body elongated, and his shoulders cracked and budded heads like unto serpents. Lucifer fell to the ground and writhed, as he became a beast with seven heads, and upon each head were ten horns. His translucent skin turned dark crimson, and he arose from the Kiln floor as a great dragon and spoke. "Behold the First of Angels my brother! Behold thy new God!"

Lucifer's voice modulated all things within the Kiln, and the sound was as thousands speaking at once.

The fire that raged in the room swirled in vortices. Lucifer inhaled the flames: swallowed them into himself, reared his head back, and spewed at Michael living fire. Michael, sweltering under the heated blaze, raised his sword and wings to cover and anchor himself to the floor, and watched as Ouranos slowly turned to slag.

Michael turned his eyes to the boiling stones he had planted in the ceiling above him. Stones that sang not the song of Lucifer nor joined themselves to the Usurper. Stones that sang the song *he* had given them, stones needed to complete Lucifer's transformation. Michael watched as his brother exulted in triumph, and waited for his opportunity to attack.

* * *

Jerahmeel hung for dear life to a cropping of rock as the swirling abyss of the bottomless pit awaited him below. Both henchman and he struggled to climb up to the edge of the cliffs and out of reach of the Zoa that somehow also had escaped destruction. Its teeth snapped at them and tentacled appendages sought to capture them.

Lucifer's guardian of the waypoint kicked at Jerahmeel, and Jerahmeel slipped. The Zoa's tentacled arms reached to grab him by his ankle and drag him into its jaws. Jerahmeel kicked at the creature below while the guard kicked at Jerahmeel from above. Nevertheless, Jerahmeel held fast and pummeled the creature. Struggling for release, he tugged at the heel of the struggling angel, pulled from his robes a dagger, and plunged it into the guard's calf.

The angel screamed, slipped, and then fell plunging past Jerahmeel into the waiting mouth of the Zoa. The Zoa's teeth clamped deep into the angel's abdomen and would not let go, and Lucifer's henchmen screamed in agony.

Jerahmeel grabbed a tentacle, and with it jumped and swung from it to another portion of the cliff; his momentum caused the creature to slip, then fall, as Lucifer's guard screamed as he and the Zoa fell, grappling one another into the swirling Maelstrom of the bottomless pit, and disappeared into the blackness.

Jerahmeel pulled himself upward, his muscles ached, and his tendons strained to sustain his weight. Determination and survival fueled him, and with hand over fist, he climbed to pull himself up to the firm ground of the Cliffs of Argoth. Turning over on his back, he caught his breath, and while upside down, he noticed the waypoint was still sealed.

He lifted himself to his feet and ran to turn the lever that deflected all Ladders away from the area. As the seal fell back, it crackled with energy and the buzzing sound of a Ladder could be heard. Suddenly, a vortex of light and fire opened and then another, and instantly angel after teeming angel fell from the sky and the cliffs became full of the angelic host. Jerahmeel allowed himself to let out a sigh of relief as Iofiel and others across the realms Laddered into the waypoint. Chronos, the keeper of Time in the second heaven, approached his prince, extended his hand to raise Jerahmeel from the ground, and asked, "Why hast Heaven been barred from us?"

Iofiel rushed to Jerahmeel and spoke, "Forgive me, my Lord, but I inquire of Prince Michael? Is he safe?"

Jerahmeel looked at him. "Aye, he travels to the Kiln."

Iofiel let out a sigh of relief.

Breathless, Jerahmeel pointed towards the heavenly city. "Alas, we are at war, for the Chief Prince has sought to overthrow El and has conspired to prevent all opposition. Go to and open the way to Heaven, and smite them that would oppose El."

The legion stood speechless and in shock at the smoke and flames in the distance.

Chronos was unique as an Arelim, for as Lucifer's body was filled with tabrets and pipes, Chronos' was replete with hourglasses and instruments to measure all units of time.

"To arms," he yelled. "Let us secure the gates so Heaven will never be sealed again!"

The chronometer within the forehead of Chronos quickened, and energy flashed about him and enveloped those on the rostrum of the cliffs. In seconds, they were all gone and immediately reappeared at the next waypoint. One angel guarded the gate and kept it shut. When he saw the multitude teleport from nowhere: all hovered and stood with arms raised, he trembled in fear.

Chronos spoke authoritatively as he stood behind Jerahmeel. "Stand aside or know dissolution."

Jerahmeel just smiled and said, "I think he means it."

The angel bowed and moved away from the lever, and Jerahmeel released the locks and the shield that deflected all Ladders. The shield was drawn back, and the Northern gate suddenly filled with Ladders as angels poured in with questions; angered that they could not come home. Some became incensed that Lucifer would strand them in the realms without means to return. Soon the legion became legions: and Chronos transported the horde to each of the remaining waypoints until all were secured.

When the last of Lucifer's lackeys were shackled in chains, Jerahmeel turned to the mass of Elohim, which were as the stars, for they were too numerous to count, and asked Chronos, "Can you hasten the multitude to speed us to the city?"

"Nay, for we are now too many. Even I have limits to my power. We are almost the whole of all Elohim."

Jerahmeel patted his young brother on the back, nodding, then moved to set himself so that he could be seen by the entire host and shouted to the multitudes before him, "Lucifer in his arrogance has sought to displace El, and make himself King over us! Our brother has become awash in his pride! I say that we show him that we are not traitors to the Father!" Jerahmeel raised his bloodstained dagger into the air for all to see and roared, "I say we show him the error of his ways!"

The mob thundered their approval and chanted, "El! El! El!"

Jerahmeel shouted, "Let all who bear the mark of Lucifer Draco be brought low! Now, go to and let us see this end!"

As one man, each used the various modes that were available to him - to run, fly, gallop, or teleport into the city of Jerusalem, fists and weapons raised: a legion of legions with but one purpose: to bring to naught every shred of rebellion that kept them from their home.

* * *

Sariel watched from afar, as Talus grappled with Abaddon for control of his sword. He studied him, for Abaddon had adjusted his attacks to combat Gabriel's speed and tried to anticipate where Gabriel's next attack would come from. Abaddon surrounded himself with his shield of locusts; they encased his form as an exoskeleton and gave him strength. Sariel watched as the sword of Abaddon sliced through angel after angel. Watched as Abaddon's foes fell maimed, and crippled before him screaming in pain. Abaddon controlled the swarm as a thing alive. Using the insects like a living whip, he extended the swarm by his will and wrapped Talus and Gabriel in a tendril of stingers until each became immobilized in pain.

Sariel noted their folly: for they did not attack him as one man; instead, each sought to take him down solely. None took the time to note that Abaddon adjusted in time to their strength and speed

He considered that Abaddon was a mover of stars, thus one of the strongest of Elohim. Abaddon was not a mere angel; he was the Destroyer, for he was Charon-like in his ability to withstand blow after blow dealt to him. He could be slowed, even redirected, but he could not be stopped, not man-to-man. Sariel admired his strength. There was something hidden, regal about Abaddon. Sariel had never noted it before, but seeing Abaddon in combat, Sariel knew that El had originally more in store for this angel, but whatever purpose was his genesis, it now was lost, for now, he had to be stopped.

So Sariel studied him and watched as gryphon riders fell upon him only to be cut down and slaughtered. Abaddon himself took up a rider's trident, and with a sword in one hand and trident in the other, he dismounted a rider and mounted his gryphon, and launched himself into the sky. He jousted with riders, who sought to fell him, and he speared them through to a man; all that tried to face him in battle were cut to the ground in blood.

Sariel noted that whenever Abaddon extended himself, his broken stones glowed brighter. The swarm moved around him, and he grew stronger as they attached themselves to the very gryphon he rode. He animated the creature with an unholy power, making it even stronger as Abaddon's own power coursed through the gryphon's veins. Sariel watched the havoc around him. Those with the mark of Lucifer fought with those who had none, and all fought to stop Abaddon.

The stench of blood permeated the air. It ran as rain into the drains of the golden streets and splattered like graffiti on the walls of now burning and broken towers and buildings. The air was full of the sound of moans, and screams, the clanking sound of steel, the thuds of bodies slammed to the ground, and the swift breeze of foes that bobbed, weaved, and sliced through the warm air. The sounds of anger and bitterness filled the air as brother fought brother. The hatred towards El and Lucifer's hubris was as the smell of charred rubble, a palpable odor that choked the lungs.

In the epicenter of all the chaos was the rogue angel Abaddon, defiant, standing against attack after attack. Sariel stepped back to dodge a foe thrown across his path, slipped on blood, and fell backward. Suddenly, an angel hovered over him and Sariel beheld the mark of Lucifer burned into his attacker's stone. The angel had a sword to smite Sariel but recognized him for who he was and paused.

They looked into each other's eyes. Sariel stood to his feet, and the glory of God was still shown on him. Sariel saw his hesitation. For deep within the breast of his brother was shame. The angel lowered his eyes to the ground and bowed his head. He hobbled as he backed away from his prince, and dropped his sword to the ground.

There will be many hearts singed with regret this day. Sariel thought.

The angel turned to fly away; the reality of what he was about to do, weighing heavy upon him. However, the moment that he arose to leave the field of battle; a spear pierced his back. His great wings curled as if broken, blood spewed from his wound, and his entrails hung from the spear's tip. Standing behind him was a member of Sariel's own house. Gripping tightly the spear he had moments ago lunged into his brother's back. He pulled it from the angel's backbone and the wounded angel fell as a bird to the ground. Without mercy or compassion, he raised his spear a second time and shoved it into the stomach of Lucifer's henchman. The light dimmed from the fallen angel, and movement stopped.

Sariel became enraged and leaped to the aid of the angel who even now dead gurgled blood from his mouth. The Prince with deftness of hand disarmed his younger sibling, and with tears and anger in his heart swung the tip of the spear across his brother's face and sliced open his jaw. His house brother fell back, his eyes wide opened and confused, for he had been struck by one who did not have Lucifer's mark.

"If I have done thee wrong, then bear witness to my misdeed, but if not, why smitest thou me?"

Sariel replied, "Is it not enough that a foe would lay down his arms to flee? He who would live by the sword shall die by the sword!"

Sariel then raised the spear over his knee, snapped it in two, and threw the pieces to the ground. He looked away into the sky; he knew that to destroy the Destroyer, there would need to be a sacrifice. He could not stop him--this he knew. However, he could bring Heaven to pause, to ponder his doings, that to defeat this foe required the laying down of one's life. Sariel then took to the skies and flew to Abaddon to do battle.

Fear and peace fought with one another in his mind, only to be scolded by the resolution to be silent,

Thy will be done, my Lord.

Like a streak of lightning, he flew into the army of locusts, and they immediately stung him. His body became inflamed, and he generated fire from his own body. The creatures seared themselves as they touched him and fell as dross. He smashed into Abaddon, knocking him from his gryphon, and they wrestled as they streaked through the smoke-filled air.

Each grappled and contorted to gain an advantage, pulling, twisting, and struggling to gain submission.

Abaddon pummeled the jaw of Sariel, and they fell as comets from the sky. Sariel held fast to Abaddon and did not let him go. He reached with his fiery hand into Abaddon's chest and ripped the second broken stone, tearing the angel's ligaments. Abaddon cried out in agony.

Immediately, the locust swarms lifted from their prey, releasing whomever they held, and came en masse to aid their master. A black cloud of biting teeth and stingers descended to envelop and swallow Sariel and their master in an embrace of venom-laced stings.

Sariel crushed the beating stone in his hands. The swarm reached their master in smoke and fire, set upon Sariel, and injected him with their venom. But Sariel had done what he had set out to do. He released Abaddon and allowed the swarm to have him. The two angels plummeted towards the ground. Abaddon's chest seeped spark and smoke, and he dripped fire as blood, for his innards were open for all to see. He was molten on the inside, and dark ash poured from his mouth.

Abaddon gripped at his chest as he fell and opened his mouth to swallow the swarm. They swirled within him, and as a thing alive, arms and hands reached for Sariel as they fell to the earth. Abaddon wrapped his hands around Sariel's neck, and like a boa constrictor tightened his lock on the prince as they smashed headlong into the ground. The explosion knocked back those who stood near. Buildings collapsed, and rocks and debris flew across the city. Smoke sprinted and blanketed all in dust and ash.

In the smolder a figure stood, seen through the cloud to drag another. The form lifted the motionless angel and tossed him from the bellows. The visage of Sariel could be seen, and he was broken, his spine extended from his back, and from his lifeless body; locusts poured from his mouth, nose, and ears, for he was stung from the inside, and his body was as a pustule waiting to burst. Abaddon shouted as a deranged man, spread his great wings, placed his foot over the face of the dead Sariel, and screamed to all in defiance.

When Talus and Gabriel saw their brother dead: they went mad with rage and launched an attack upon Abaddon in unison. In a choreography of death, swords swung, parried, thrusted, and dodged.

Each pressed their attack

Talus matched Abaddon's strength, for he was Abaddon's prince. He backhanded the rogue angel and sent him reeling into the ground. Gabriel was swift to take advantage of his brother's attack, and before Abaddon could respond, Gabriel's staff had smashed itself into his face. Abaddon screamed and sought to flee, but Gabriel was everywhere and kept him off balance. When Abaddon predicted where Gabriel would be next, Talus caught up to them and again punched Abaddon with such force his chest cavity caved, and his bones splintered. Abaddon doubled over in pain, stumbled back wheezing, and opened his mouth and chest plate to unleash the swarm to attack them.

Talus lifted up his hand to protect himself and be overwhelmed when Gabriel suddenly appeared before him and spun his staff and wings so that the swarm could not touch them. Still, they moved towards him, undeterred, stopping for nothing but the cessation of Abaddon's heart. Lo, they fought him even as one man, each using the other's attributes to keep Abaddon off balance, to beat him into submission, to defeat the Destroyer.

While they pressed him, the battle waged citywide. Ashtaroth having charge of his troops held back to survey his army from on high. He saw that with the addition of Talus and the horde from the Elysian Fields, the battle still favored his cause. He smiled knowing that his master had succeeded in drawing all attention to the city while he himself was set to the true prize.

"Note brother, how the princes smite Abaddon," said Asmodeus.

Ashtaroth chuckled. "They know not that they merely act in accordance with the master's will." Ashtaroth smiled as he watched the princes subdue Abaddon and hold him fast with chains of iron, yet they struggled to contain him, for the battle still raged about them.

Ashtaroth smirked, sighed, looked up, and breathed in Heaven's air, now filled with smoke and the ash of the broken and crushed stones of his master's adversaries. As he watched a flock of gulls that hovered over the battlefield, his eyes strained to see flashes of what seemed like balls of lightning coming toward them.

The luminescent birds of Heaven flew over the city, squawked at the bodies of the fallen, and wailed for the dissolution that was beneath them. Manna fields burned to the east, black smoke filled the sky to the south, and below them, the dead lined the streets as fallen autumn leaves waiting to be raked.

As a school of fish flees a predator, they too dispersed as the air crackled with thunder and lightning as Chronos and a host of angels that possessed the power of teleportation fell to the ground shouting a cry of battle. Thousands descended like electrified hailstones onto the city streets and instantly took up arms to fight those who possessed the mark of Lucifer.

With the landing of Chronos and the host, the clouds themselves gave up the ghost. Each opened their mouth to whisper the word, "Woe," between them until it covered the whole of Heaven. When their sadness had pillowed to overflowing, rain fell from the sky, for the clouds were alive and cried tears. The angels had taken no notice of their presence and pierced them with Ladders so that their wounds were such they now bled out as it were great drops of foul-smelling vinegar. A filmy liquid that splashed from the sky of Heaven and the birds cawed and sought escape, for they found themselves now covered in slime. Many dropped from the sky while others flew to hide themselves for the whole of Heaven's armies had gathered themselves to war, and none considered that reality had begun to tear at itself.

Brother slew brother, and with each angel felled, Heaven's glory diminished. The celestial realm became unhinged and with the loss of each Archon, planets were decimated, and great tears in space opened to swallow galaxies whole, for there was none to watch over El's word, and none looked to keep it. Creation groaned, for her stewards had turned their face from her. Each looked to his own, and none cared for the things that were El's. They left their first station to clash with one another.

Darkness reclaimed realms that once gleamed in light, and even the Earth convulsed as continents shifted and leviathans and dinosaurs assailed by earthquakes were buried beneath rock, sand, and water.

The great armies clashed steel against steel. As the rage of angels burned towards one another, Asmodeus frowned as he looked about him, for he saw that the way to the Kingdom of Heaven was open and the legions of El had found passage. He looked disapprovingly at Ashtaroth and said,

"Did we cause with Lucifer to bring asunder the very fabric of all things? Behold the host has come. We are undone."

"Nay-- not yet," replied Ashtaroth. "There is still the master." Ashtaroth then pointed towards a giant protrusion that swelled from the mountain of God.

Without warning, a great shock wave burst through the air, and trees, rocks, and fire streaked across the sky. The ground itself heaved, buckled, and caused all to hesitate and stop to see this new thing. A blast of thunder and rock erupted to the north, and each beheld with mouths agape: all now frozen in awe at the mountain of God and the source of their birthplace.

The Kiln had exploded.

* * *

Jerahmeel ran into the Spire of Tomes and yelled for Raphael. "Raphael, are you here? Where are you?"

"Over here!" cried Raphael, "in the steward's room."

Jerahmeel ran past desks and tables with maps, parchments, and volumes tripped, and fell to the floor, landing with a great thud. He pushed himself up and looked behind him to see that by his feet laid the dead body of Hariph sprawled behind his help desk.

He died even at his post. Jerahmeel raised himself to his feet, continued to walk, and entered into the steward's room.

The room was as a dome with a pinnacle that shot high into the sky. Round about the dome were projections of all the happenings in all realms.

Raphael stood motionless and watched the panoramic display of galaxies, stars, and life across galaxies begin to deteriorate, for Elohim, who were charged to watch over the course of all things, were now vacant from their posts, and with El's and their absence, the realms slowly fell into ruin.

Raphael stared at the projections and said, "All things are upheld by the word of His power. But El stands mute, still in Sabbath, and the stewards appointed have left their first estate."

He pointed and they both watched as a planet seeded with life ripped apart, for the star which orbited it went nova, and its Archon was absent.

"We must hurry Jerahmeel, or there will be no multiverse when El awakes from his rest."

"Will El return? And what will be his mind when he sees what the people have done?"

Determined to bring sanity to the madness, Raphael took the Tome of Iniquity and quickly set it upon a golden pedestal in the center of the room. Then faced his brother and spoke.

"He will be wroth."

* * *

"In El's name!" said Chronos. When he spoke the clocks within him stopped, and suddenly around him, all things slowed. He moved to knock a brother from the path of a large boulder that had ejected from the Kiln, and when the angel was safely out of the way, the clocks within Chronos moved again; the giant boulder then resumed its original speed and smashed behind them barely missing them. When Chronos looked down, he had saved his comrade from destruction. Noting that he bore the mark of Lucifer, Chronos rose from atop him and asked.

"Whom do you serve?"

The angel replied, "I am with El, but my deeds have brought me shame."

Chronos hugged him and covered him with his own body as fire fell upon them all. The skies lit as fireworks as the ejected Stones of Fire cooled and dropped upon them, obliterating all that they touched.

"We are undone, for the God stones fall on us," cried Chronos. "I know not what this day will bring. Nevertheless, thou shall not be brought low by my hand. Take heart. For God is with us."

The heavenly host, which had assembled in the city, ran for fear as pyroclastic bombs of rock and smoke jetted from the mountain's side, and hurtled across the cityscape, smashing into buildings, and set shop and angel ablaze.

The Kilnstones landed as falling stars, living things, which hitherto fore had sung, 'to be." Now removed from the heated womb of the Kiln, they echoed their terror and wailed in anger across the land. Each swallowed into great light anything that they touched, and angels and every living thing ran from them, for their yearning "to be" disintegrated all that was.

From the side of the mountain, a dust cloud billowed into the sky, and two bright lights streaked like lightning across the sky. In the midst of the tumult, Michael and Lucifer plummeted towards the temple.

Lucifer, scarred from battle, was unlike anything the host had ever seen, for though his sigil was clear. He was a huge dragon with ten heads, and he flew with wings to hold up his monstrosity of a body. He had two tails with barbs that protruded from their tips, smoke, and fire simmered from his mouth, and another larger stone that sung pulsated within him. Fire belched from his carnivorous mouth, and he flew through the sky raining flame upon all that he saw. He twisted falling out of control as he hurtled towards the ground.

Atop his back was Michael in white robes encircled by seven blue swords and each was as the Ophanim but smaller, and they sliced through Lucifer as the brothers plunged to the earth. Michael rode Lucifer as a beast and struck his sword deep into one of Lucifer's skulls, and the great dragon roared in pain.

They fell from the sky headlong into the court of the Burning Ones, crashing into the steps of the gates and blasting into the doors of the throne room and into the Holy of Holies.

All of Heaven watched as Michael with seven levitating swords fought Lucifer. When Michael pointed at the neck of his brother, a sword flew through the air and embedded itself into his throat, causing Lucifer to let out a gurgling scream. The concussion of his voice knocked the Seraphim to the ground, and their flames extinguished because the blast was of such force. The temple doors creaked from the impact of Lucifer's cry: all onlookers knelt and covered their ears.

Michael then leaped towards his brother, grabbed a sword, swung from it, and pulled with his weight until it tore Lucifer's flesh open as a zipper would a coat. Lucifer roared with pain, and with one of his great heads fired, a mouth of flame at his own neck to cauterize the wound. With another head, Lucifer opened his mouth, and a blast of sound screeched towards Michael and knocked him back.

Michael raised the flaming sword that El had made him and flung it into the mouth of Lucifer. The great dragon let out a scream, the pillars of the holy place smashed, and the temple began to shake as if to collapse. Lucifer choked on the sword and attempted to withdraw it from his mouth. Michael seized his opportunity, with his thoughts, sword after sword lodged itself as a stepladder, and Michael climbed them. With each step taken, a sword retracted, and Michael climbed higher upon Lucifer and continued to stab at him.

Michael reached the neck of one of Lucifer's heads and raised his hands. The swords flew through the air and into his palms, and with them, Michael sliced through one of Lucifer's necks and the great appendage fell to the ground bleeding fire. Lucifer roared in pain and turned over to crush Michael under the weight of his hulking body.

Jerahmeel viewed the images on the Library's Dome. He watched helplessly as the God Stones fell and destroyed all things. He anxiously watched Lucifer and Michael battle within the temple gates and knew he and Raphael had little time.

"Hurry Raphael, the throne room, has been breached. I do not know how much longer Michael can withstand Lucifer!"

Raphael slowly began to speak angel-speak over the great volume. The Tome of Iniquity glowed a bright orange hue, and as its pages opened, each page ripped from the book and plastered itself to the domed ceiling of the Great Library.

The dome burst forth into color and erupted with images that began to pulse upward when suddenly a blazing white light screamed and hurtled into the dome spire, and glass fell upon them in great shards. Jerahmeel leaped as panes of crystal crashed to the floor below. He lifted his head and turned to look for Raphael, and despair filled him.

"No!" He screamed.

Raphael was sitting up; his inkhorn and stylus floated near his head, and he coughed up blood. His hands covered his abdomen as blood oozed from his stomach. Jerahmeel beheld that he had been run through with a great pane of glass, and in the middle of the room, a Kilnstone glowed and slowly was digesting him, taking back the very life that El had once given, and absorbing all things into itself. Jerahmeel screamed running to succor him.

Raphael still conscious motioned him to stay away.

"No!...there... there ...is not much time. The dome...destroyed, and I am to return soon to El. Take the book, my ...inkhorn, and stylus." Raphael removed his tome from within his chest and the items floated to Jerahmeel. "Go to... quickly now...awaken Argoth. The people...my people–they will hear...they will listen to him."

Jerahmeel picked up his brother's instruments and tucked them into his robes.

Raphael smiled at him.

"Fear not; all is not lost. Go...," said Raphael. "Quic..." He beamed at his brother, and his eyes widened; smiled and then he spoke no more.

Jerahmeel fell to his knees and watched as the Kilnstone consumed Raphael and all that it touched. Raphael's stone hummed and sang with the same pitch of the stone, which now absorbed him. The melody was soprano and melancholic in tune. Jerahmeel wept, and Raphael's tome ceased writing pages.

Jerahmeel gathered himself, for he could still hear the explosions and the sounds of battle outside. He scooted away from his brother as the Kilnstone reached out for him. Jerahmeel ran back into the front room. When he had come to Argoth, he took the inkhorn, stylus, and the tome of Raphael and placed them in Argoth's outstretched palms.

When he did, Argoth moved and took them into himself, stepped down from his pedestal, and without speaking walked past Jerahmeel who stared at him.

Jerahmeel put his hands on his hips, "Hmmph, Not even a thank you?"

When Argoth walked to the steward's chamber, the Kilnstone glowed at his presence. Raphael's body still lay on the ground. Argoth paused and nodded at his fallen brother as if to pay respect, and when he did, he looked upwards and flew into the sky. Set high above the great library, he was awash in color, and light ejected from his person so that all of Heaven stopped to see. Argoth's presence radiated with the glory of the Lord, and his voice boomed as he spoke so that all could hear.

"For nothing is secret that shall not be made manifest; neither anything hid that shall not be made known."

The domed wall suddenly erupted in multicolor, a rainbow shot up from the tower's spire, and lo, all that battled saw it and paused to ponder the meaning of this strange new adversary.

The light shot high into the heavenly sky and spread out as an umbrella. Each Grigori became visible and with tombs opened, suddenly illuminated, and all volumes released their pages and everywhere projected the image. Nowhere in the multiverse was there not a Grigori that did not display it, and image after image paraded itself across the canopy of Heaven's sky. The sound was such that all could hear. The volumes of all Grigori hovered in the air, and their pages showed the image.

Each angel beheld that El and Lucifer were within the Kiln. Apollyon's stone was freshly cut, whole, and made by the hand of the creator. All Elohim watched in fascinated horror as Lucifer took Apollyon's stone and bashed it against the Kiln wall breaking it into several pieces. Across the emporium, and throughout the city, all let out a collective gasp that the Chief Prince had marred the purpose of God's creation. One by one–the words "iniquity", and "blasphemy" was mouthed, in hushed whispers.

Lucifer beheld the image above the skies, his secret now revealed for all the realms to see. His face contorted with a frown of shock, and chagrin, that his secret was exposed. Lucifer's muscular ribcage spasmed and he clutched at his chest in pain. The agony was overbearing and he could no longer hold his draconic form and changed back into his angelic appearance. Abaddon's eyes were wide in disbelief and his mouth agape, and all hostilities had stopped to see the great images in the sky.

When the last page of the tome was plastered to the wall, the great prismatic beam retracted into the spire, and a thunderclap reverberated across the realm. The sky returned to its normal hue, and all eyes turned and fixated on Lucifer and Abaddon.

Abaddon whose head still looked to the sky lowered his now grim gaze and turned to look at Lucifer. "It was you! My stone was broken because of you! My birthright–– of that too you have robbed me. El knew the thoughts he had towards me, for they were always of peace and not of evil, to replace thee as Lightbringer. All, this time, you have been but false to me — all this time you knew!"

Abaddon's countenance changed. He roared with anguish, and his anger was such that he bucked as a wild stallion. Talus and Gabriel struggled to hold him but could not, and he broke free. Abaddon grabbed a sword from its sheath and rushed towards Lucifer. His stone that remained glowed, his form grew black, and from his innards spilled bile. The swarm of stinging locusts poured from openings in his flesh, and he charged to cut Lucifer down.

Suddenly, from his rearward, chains of rusted black iron wrapped themselves around him. He turned to see who would stop the Destroyer, and with horror, he saw the Warden had reach of him. In terror, Abaddon attempted to back away but it was too late, for Charon held him fast by his legs and arms. Abaddon fell forward, and he was dragged screaming as he clawed at the ground straining for escape.

"Nooo!" He screamed. "Nooo! I cannot go back!"

Then he howled, for the worms of Hell consumed alive the stinging locusts and bored themselves into Abaddon's flesh. All onlookers moved away from Charon's path, and none interfered as he pulled at the writhing angel who struggled to breathe. Charon dragged him kicking and screaming, and none dared to stop him. The fires of Hell licked and jetted out from his cowled equine body; his molten footprints scarred the ground.

"Help me!" screamed Abaddon, but no man came to his aid. In desperation, he sought to unleash the swarm on Charon, but they melted when they touched his form. The worms of Hell feasted on them as appetizers, for the manacles wrapped around Abaddon were as straws to Hell. As she siphoned Abaddon's power, his features deteriorated, and he wasted away before the eyes of all. Charon then turned to drag him to the Maw and return him to its bowels. Abaddon kicked and screamed, both pleading and enraged.

"Lucifer! Lucifer! I will have you! Do you hear me? Your day will come King of Lies! I will have you! Lucifer! Arrrgghhhhhh!"

Lucifer smiled. "Thus ends my pretender to the throne."

Lucifer then turned to gaze upon Michael who stood between him and the throne of God and spoke.

"You cannot defeat me, brother, for I and the Kiln Stone are one. The very power of El resides within my bosom. Stand aside, for I go to claim what is mine."

Michael sword in hand barred his entry into El's presence. His seven floating swords gyroscopically whirled around him in light and blue flame.

"No, brother."

Lucifer stepped closer, "I am now He who can be all things. And who now shall save you from my hand?"

Michael replied. "Never was my task to bring you low but only to forestall thee. For thy treason and thy crimes can only be judged by another."

Michael smiled and pointed to Lucifer's rear. The First of Angels spun around to see that the constellations of Heaven had turned. The stars had changed their alignment and in the distance off to the horizon. The Shekinah glory raced as a great incoming wave across the land. It illuminated all in its wake, covering everything in a trail of brightness. Color returned to the land, and it meant but one thing.

The evening and morning were the 8th day.

The Sins that Follow After

The Shekinah glory roared across the land as waves that crashed along the sea, a white blinding force of holiness that heralded the return of the Lord of Hosts.

It was clear to all who gazed that in a moment, the Lord of all things would awake. Panic suddenly gripped those who had fought against El.

Lucifer turned to face Michael and transformed into pure light; desperately crazed to smite El while he still slept. He waved his hand and a flash of light blinded Michael. Lucifer then used the sound of his fingers and flung Michael against a marble wall. His head hit hard against a pillar.

The light of the new day and the Shekinah had now reached the outer burbs and quickly made its way towards the city.

Lucifer rushed to El's throne and took from his sheath a golden sword of light to smite the Almighty, and as he raised his hand to bring it down, the Shekinah then enveloped the temple, sprinted into the holy of holies, and surrounded El. The mountain shook, and the colors of the rainbow jetted in all directions so that even Lucifer covered his eyes, for the brilliance of El's glory, was too much to behold.

The light of El reflected off everything, and the whole of the city was awash in white so that all that dared to look in the direction of the mountain cried out with pain, for the glare was too bright to view.

El's eyes then opened, and when his gaze sat itself upon Lucifer, he knew what his oldest child had done, and he stood.

Lucifer ran with sword raised swinging wildly and struck the Lord in his heel. Blood flowed from the wound, but not as the blood of Elohim; for the blood of angels was blue. El's blood was as crimson: and it pooled at his heel. The Almighty winced and felt pain. The Ophanim that had been asleep immediately came to life, surrounded El, and created a wall so that Lucifer could no more approach.

El was wroth, and from his mouth, a great sword emerged. Then he spoke. "Because thou hast not heeded my words and hast said in thine heart, I will ascend into Heaven, and will exalt my throne above the stars of God.

"Because thou hast said, I will sit upon the mount of the congregation in the sides of the north.

"Because thou hast said, I will ascend above the heights of the clouds, and that I will be like the most High. Thou shalt be brought down to Hell, even to the sides of the pit.

"They that see thee shall narrowly look upon thee and consider thee saying, is this the man that made the Earth to tremble and that did shake kingdoms; that made the world as a wilderness, and destroyed the cities thereof, that opened not the house of prisoners?

"For behold, thou art as the spit in my mouth and an offense to me; a Satan to be no more in my sight."

As the Lord spoke, Lucifer cried out in agony. The Prime Stone he had stolen from the Kiln burst from his chest, ripped through his skin, and rocketed into the waiting palm of El. Lucifer's features grew dark and pale, and he lost the power to reflect the glory of the Lord. El walked towards him, and as he did — Lucifer was forcibly repelled from his presence, and the Ophanim whizzed outside the temple like dogs unleashed. The whole of Heaven bowed and covered their heads, and the colors of El were such as he was as a thousand suns. The Almighty held Lucifer suspended in the air, choking and contorting in an invisible grip, and the whole of Heaven saw the Lightbringer, as he was— a creature forever subject to the creator.

The presence of God was palpable, lightning and seven thunders echoed, and the Seraphim were ablaze again. They stood and resumed to shout HOLY! HOLY! HOLY! Their voices boomed across the court, and El's majesty was such that wherever He walked those that had fallen to dissolution immediately rose to life, choking and gasping for air as if rescued from drowning.

El looked at his children and the great destruction to the city of Jerusalem. He frowned and then said, "Charon, be thou still."

Upon command, Charon stopped his march to the Maw of Hell and tightened his clutch around Abaddon who struggled to obtain release.

The Lord then pronounced judgment on Abaddon. "Thou shalt yet serve in the last days, and your wrath may then be quenched, and justice even then shall be thine, for that which was taken cannot be returned. Because thou hast fallen from thy glory, ye shall fall until the end of days as thy rage knew no bottom, nor shalt thy fall from my sight."

The Lord then pointed to the Abyss.

Charon then took Abaddon, who kicked and screamed and walked him over to the cliffs and the raging winds of the Maelstrom that swirled below. Charon then lifted Abaddon above his head and tossed him flailing into the bottomless pit. Abaddon clawed against the winds of the chasm of endless space, and his cries for mercy echoed in the air as he fell. Black, acrid smoke rose up from the Maelstrom as he descended, and the locusts followed their master.

The Lord then created a golden seal with a key, placed it over the Abyss, and shut it, so that none might fall therein, and nothing could escape. Moreover, when the seal covered the Abyss, the muffled screams of Abaddon ceased. For as the closing of a flue, so too did the smoke billow no more into Heaven's air.

The Lord returned his gaze to Lucifer, still suspended in the air for every eye to see. Lightning crackled around him, and the Lord spoke. A Ladder then instantly formed in front of Him, a vortex of such size and power that Heaven had never seen anything like it before. It ejected lightning and fire before the Almighty. Lucifer became as lighting himself, cried aloud, and was flung across the skies of Heaven and cast out.

Lucifer screamed curses at the Lord, and writhed as he was expelled to parts unknown; his wails carried across the sky.

The Ladder, however, did not close, and the multicolored vortex whirled and suddenly became black as night. Then, without warning, all that bore the mark of Lucifer were entangled with black tendrils that reached for them from the ground. The tentacles burned, and the whole of Elohim who sided with Lucifer was seized.

Some struggled to escape, and others sought to hide, but the black held them and found them no matter where they hid; curses, howls, and cries for mercy echoed across the city.

Chronos' face grew grim as he looked at his brother whom he had just aided. Iblis was his name. He locked his eyes on Chronos, and his countenance was one of resignation to his fate, for he neither struggled nor resisted as large black tendrils clutched him and dragged him into the ground.

"I am sorry, my brother," said Chronos.

"As am I," said Iblis. "I will not forget your kindness."

Chronos shed a tear as the tentacles enveloped his brother and dragged him into the depths of the floors of Heaven, and when Iblis was pulled through Heaven's crust to the roof of the second heaven he was ejected with legions of others as they streaked across the lower spaces and plummeted throughout the realms below.

Many in the city wailed and cried aloud, for judgment had come. The giant Ladder split with a great explosion and spread across Heaven like a spider's web cocooning each traitor in blackness. For all that had espoused Lucifer's cause were cast out and fell to the heavens below; the storm of El's fury was such that He banished all those who bore Lucifer's mark or failed to take up His cause so that when He was done there were none left in Heaven but those who were on the Lord's side.

The heavens shuddered for the legions of Elohim that streaked through the realms. Some were flung and became locked in the depths of great seas; others were thrown to burn in the center of stars, fated to encircle the universe until the end of days. While those who were too powerful to roam free, El let them pass through the atmospheres of frost planets, where they took the form of ice and were judged to hurtle through the heavens encased until the last days. Still others were propelled to celestial corners where their Kilnstones changed and became so heavy that they were entrapped: crushed by the dense weight of their own sin: so that not even light could escape their reach. They consumed all things, a celestial warning forever for other Elohim.

Those that were fortunate fell to the planet El had created for the humans. Imprisoned in mountains, trees, and the lower parts of the Earth reserved until El's wrath had subsided. The Lord set aside those who had entrapped his people on Earth to Tartarus, the realm of Lucifer's own creation, and sealed them within the Earth.

El then turned to those who had been prime evils in aiding Lucifer and said, "Thus saith the Lord, for three transgressions and for four, I will not turn away the punishment thereof because thou have threshed Jerusalem with threshing instruments of iron and have been chief to set brother against brother."

Then Murmur, Ashtaroth, Zeus, and Ares were cast as one man tied to each other in flaming chains and were hurtled across the arc of space, exiled to Earth, and sealed in the great river Euphrates. When their bodies crashed into the river, a third part of the fish in the river died. The Lord then set a watch over the mouth of the river so that if they ever sought escape, they would perish by an Ophanim he posted over the river. He sealed them deep within the mouth of the river until the end of all things.

Thus, the Lord chastened the sons of God that they fell as a great torrential rain unleashed from the sky. The Earth became without form, and darkness covered the face of the deep: as the loss of so many Elohim had turned the works of God back upon itself. The continents were ripped from the upheaval, for there were many that had turned away to watch El's word. The Lord then placed a living mist around Eden to protect it and shrouded the man he had created from harm.

The great Ladders that had been sprawled across the face of Heaven then faded into nothing, and when the crackling of lightning had disappeared, seven thunders uttered. "It is done!" The Ophanim then rushed to El and surrounded the Lord in a great light. The Lord's features were visible to all, and He was as a great lion with wings.

When El had stopped in the pronunciation of judgment, the sky returned to its golden hue, and El changed, as a man ancient in years that walked with a limp, for the injury to his heel was clear. All wondered as they saw the blood and pondered. *Can God be hurt? Can the Eternal One be destroyed?*

Michael, like all of his kind, bowed his head before the Lord, and when the Lord walked past him to return to his throne, Michael turned to God and said, "Will not the judge of all the realms do right? For thou, my Lord could have prevented such a thing. To what end does the loss of the realm's children serve?"

The Lord stopped, sighed, turned to face his son, and walked towards him. Michael was afraid for the power of the Lord and the Ophanim was still a thing that made the air crackle. Michael knelt and bowed his head and the Lord knelt to touch Michael's forehead.

"See O beloved of angels, the things that are yet to come."

A shimmering globe appeared in El's hands, and Michael gazed into the giant crystal. It displayed images similar to the walls within the Hall of Grigoric records, but these images were different, and Michael perceived that what he watched were images that were of the future. For the Earth below him was populated with the humans and they multiplied as the stars in the sky. Michael peered deeper into the orb and watched as thousands of humans escaped a land that had kept them in slavery for 400 years, brought out by the mighty hand of the Lord. He watched as the seas swallowed their pursuers.

Moreover, men named Abraham, Isaac, Jacob, and David lived and died to serve El's cause, and Michael watched as they fought to scrape out holiness in lands that had begun to worship the very ones El had just ejected. And Michael beheld as many a nation rose and fell by the command of the Lord. Finally, the great orb revealed a man whipped and beaten, and a crown of thorns was placed on his head. Michael looked away from the cruelty and destruction that the Adam and his kind could inflict on one another. Yet the brutality that this man took upon himself was somehow different. Michael looked on in horror at what he beheld, and he stared into the eyes of a man who hung on a cross.

It was the eyes of the man that told him who he was.

Michael fell back on his hind and waved his hand over his face to deflect the image he refused to see.

"....no....no..." and Michael shook his head in denial, placed his face in his palms, and wept. For Michael saw through the flesh of the man and looked into his eyes to behold that the man was El—hung by Adam's kin on a cross.

The orb then grew dark and disappeared. The Lord stood mute looking down at his son.

Crying, Michael looked up at the Lord who smiled at him and stroked his head as a father might his young child. El turned to walk away into the throne room. Blood trailed the transparent golden glass, and El walked slowly with a limp into the palace until the great doors closed.

Michael staggered to his feet, still reeling from the images El let flood his mind. He stared at the throne room doors that shut behind El and looked at the trail of crimson blood left behind. Tears continued to fall from his eyes, his thoughts still racing and his heart filled with emotion.

But Lord...why must you die? But there was no reply to his thoughts.

As Michael stepped away from the Holy of Holies, he walked outside the temple to face his brethren and to do the will of his master. He was the Builder of Heaven, and his duty was to build the city. He looked upon the ground and saw that broken into pieces was the key ring that Charon had given him. Yet, the keys to Death and Hell were not there. He looked to recover them until he saw that his brethren approached. Grief redirected him away from the search for lost keys to his kin. Jerahmeel came carrying the ruined body of Raphael, and Gabriel walked through the crowds holding the fallen Sariel.

Michael's mind turned to grief at the loss of his brothers, and as he beheld the Kingdom of Heaven, which now lay in ruins, resolution gripped his face. He wiped his tears and marched out from the palace towards the destruction to assist his people.

Epilogue

Lucifer awoke groggily from his slumber, his eyes crusted over with ash and blood. His muscles throbbed and agonizingly objected with each attempt at movement. Pain bit at his jaw, and he instinctively reached to touch his face. Anger swelled within him as he felt the long scar left by his combat with Michael. He knew his visage was disfigured, and he calculated reprisal.

Michael would not go unpunished.

Slowly the mighty dragon rose to his feet and surveyed his surroundings. Smoke and burning embers served as his linen, an impact crater his mattress.

How long have I been unconscious?

Gingerly, he clawed his way up the steep sides of the charred earth, as gravel slipped beneath him. The fallen prince struggled to lift his tender frame, but determination enabled him to reach the crater's edge. He dragged his body forward and fell face down into the cool soil of the black earth. Steam hissed from the crater, and smoke, dust, and haze shrouded his view. His eyes slowly adjusted to his surroundings and began to filter out the debris, and his clarity of mind sharpened.

Lucifer looked at the scene before him and saw the mighty Euphrates only a short ways removed. The sun's zenith informed him that mid-day was upon him. He followed the sun's trail leading west to Athor, his mighty city.

He strained to see but was only able to spot several landmarks that led to Athor. He followed them with his eyes as they piloted him closer to his own current location and curiously not further away.

Questioning, he turned to his east and saw the lush green of Eden beyond; his delicate handiwork crafted with love, unspoiled and spared from destruction. Still, he looked for his earthly home and found nothing.

Slowly his intuition spoke to him and informed him that something was amiss. He moved farther away from the crater. Walking, almost stumbling, he finally mustered enough strength to use his great wings to lift him airborne. Higher he rose that he might gain a better perspective, but each increase in elevation brought with it an equally painful and horrific realization.

Denial of the truth assaulted him. The hard guttural ache he felt as he surveyed the ground below would not stop. The truth assailed him and could not be denied. Athor was razed; its majesty obliterated.

Athor once stood as a beacon that magnified the very beauty and power of Lucifer, its triangular opulence designed to exalt him. Everything was now gone, wiped out by the very fall of Lucifer himself.

His once great city blotted out by the destructive power of Lucifer's own descent. Even in exile, El would have no monument that glorified his adversary. He had used Lucifer's own person as the explosive device to wipe the Earth clean of Lucifer's legacy.

Lucifer had wrought destruction in Heaven, and El saw that Lucifer reaped at his own hand the ruin of his kingdom.

Lucifer's anger swelled within him and despair pulled the once mighty prince to the ground. On bended knees, bitterness rose within him as he grasped the soil of his city now laid waste.

He stood defiantly to his feet and raised his tightly clenched fist high into the air, cursing the creator of the universe and spouted obscenities not pronounceable in the tongues of men.

He surveyed his once magnificent home, as bitterness and anger became his comforters. Seething with hate for his father, Lucifer's tears fell into the dark earth.

He slowly gained his composer, wiped the tears from his eyes, and rose to his feet to behold the river Euphrates and the region roundabout. His gaze followed the waterway's course toward the expanse of the great Garden of Eden off in the distance.

Lucifer's eyes fixated menacingly on the tropical paradise's pristine beauty — beauty wrongly denied him; his thoughts became ravenous with greed.

Looking down beneath him, he saw two keys protruding from the earth; each etched with the sigil of Charon and glowing with fire. Lucifer reached down to pick them up and beheld them. The souls of Hell displayed themselves within one key screaming while the other dripped black with oil and sulfur. Lucifer smiled, and thoughts upon thoughts filled him. He reached within the folds of his robes and withdrew the Tome of Hell that Abaddon had confiscated from Michael.

Vengeance soon came along as a hitchhiker requesting transport, and in Lucifer's desire for companionship, he embraced the emotion and consorted with her like a familiar lover.

With his thoughts filled with bitterness and retribution: his heart discovered comfort, and a smirk found the mouth of the King of Lies.

I will secure your downfall through the Adam.

Lucifer smiled and salivated with lust for the garden in the distance and blithely transformed into a winged serpent. His great wings caught the breeze, and he drifted upon the wind.

Like the fine filament of a dandelion seed carried aloft by the breeze; his mind desired to disperse his seed-bearing parachutes of sin and iniquity. He was eager to bore himself into the innocent life of the human female, to supplant and choke the light from all things.

The warm spring wind proffered him to welcome the Adam and the Eve; the humans El had placed within the garden, these contemptible pretenders to royalty: a species of earth and clay, oblivious to all that truly lay around them.

He would welcome them indeed, for little did they know that something wicked their way comes.

The End

The Third Heaven: The Birth of God - Book 2

Donovan M. Neal

Tornveil

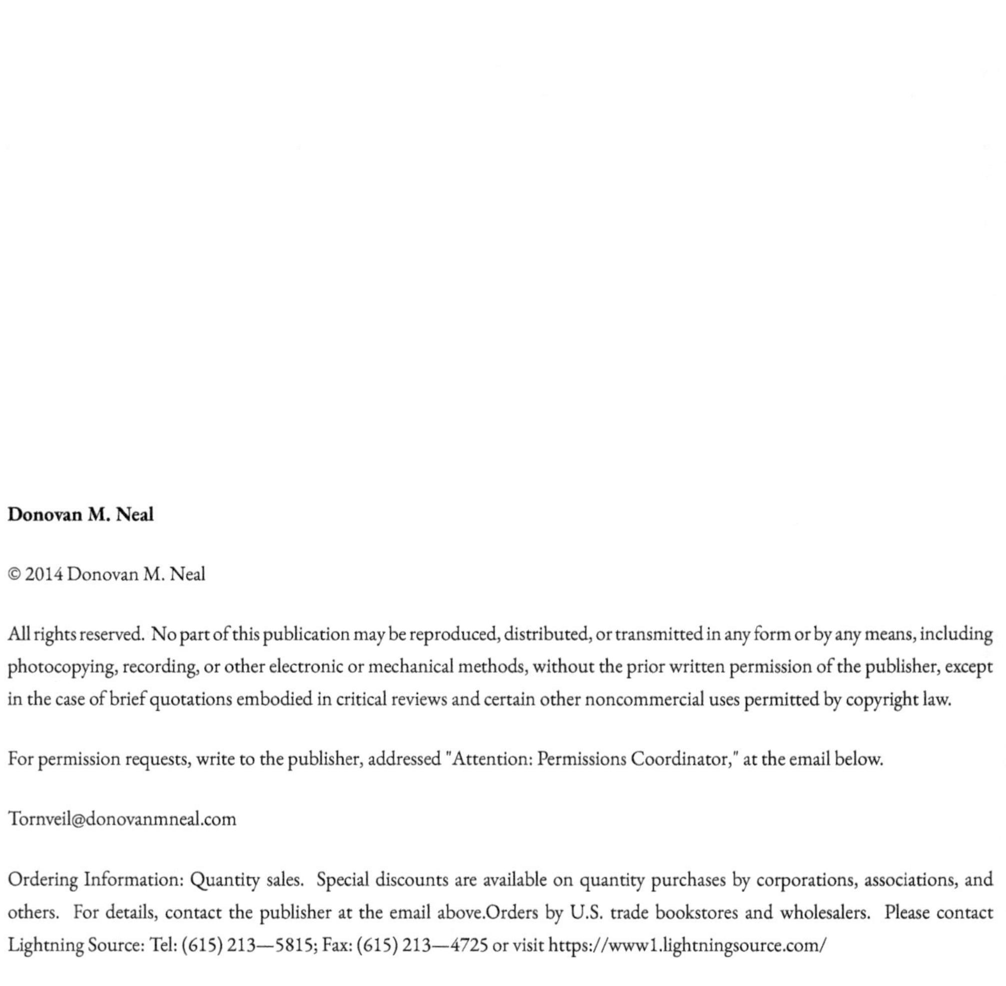

Donovan M. Neal

For permission requests, write to the publisher, addressed "Attention: Permissions Coordinator," at the email below.

Tornveil@donovanmneal.com

Ordering Information: Quantity sales. Special discounts are available on quantity purchases by corporations, associations, and others. For details, contact the publisher at the email above.Orders by U.S. trade bookstores and wholesalers. Please contact Lightning Source: Tel: (615) 213—5815; Fax: (615) 213—4725 or visit https://www1.lightningsource.com/

Printed in the United States of America

ISBN 978-0-9894805-4-3 (Paperback version)

Library of Congress Control Number: 2015901963

Contents

Scriptures

Scriptures

2 Cor 12:2

I knew a man in Christ above fourteen years ago, (whether in the body, I cannot tell; or whether out of the body, I cannot tell: God knoweth;) such an one caught up to the third heaven.

1 Cor 2: 7, 8

But we speak the wisdom of God in a mystery, even the hidden wisdom, which God ordained before the world unto our glory: 8 Which none of the princes of this world knew: for had they known it, they would not have crucified the Lord of glory.

Preface

Welcome back!

I'm so glad that you have desired to continue in the journey of this series with me. I love the direction that the story is going, and I hope I can live up to your expectations in this second book.

As you know from reading the first book in the series, all I wanted to do was to provide a form of wholesome entertainment and to answer some simple questions. How could Lucifer, who dwelt in the very presence of God, elect to rebel against his Creator? What could have gone so wrong, that a 3rd of Heaven would turn their backs on God? My answer was, and is, the fictional series entitled "The Third Heaven." The first novel, "The Third Heaven: The Rise of Fallen Stars" directly answers this question. In this second novel (The Birth of God) I attempt to pull back the curtain again, and both ask and speculatively answer, what were some of the aftershocks that took place after Lucifer's fall? How did Heaven react, and view some of the events that we have read in our Bibles?

As in the prior novel, I want to reiterate, that this is a speculative work of *fiction*. This novel is NOT scripture. I do not profess divine inspiration, nor would I ever attempt to place this work alongside the word of God. It's just a story. I love the Bible, and I am only attempting to provide an entertaining look on the biblical events we both hold dear and love. Please do not take the work as a serious attempt at biblical scholarship, but instead as a serious attempt to provide a form of wholesome Christian entertainment along the lines of C. S. Lewis, Tolkien, or Frank Perretti. The books is not meant to be a prescriptive doctrinal work by any means, any more than the Lord of Rings. I think if we can agree that it's just that, then I think you as a reader should be fine.

You have pushed me to do better as an author, and I hope my love for the characters and story of this fictional world comes through and meets your expectations. I have received such wonderful words of encouragement, and praise, that I look forward to continuing the series with you. We are halfway there! I am so thankful to you, who have read the first novel. Words can't express enough, what your readership has meant to me. Ok, I'm not going to get teary eyed, so let me not go off on a tangent. Sniffle, sniffle.

By the way, there is a glossary in the back, and some of you might want to familiarize yourself with it, prior to jumping into the novel.

Like the previous novel, where possible I have tried to be consistent with the teaching of scripture or what church fathers have said concerning the subject of Angelology. Overall, I have taken the liberty to use my "sanctified imagination" to tell a story that might spur further interest in the Word of God, yet also, create an entertaining tale.

In the end, I want to tell a story full of wonder; and told in such a manner, as I might want such a story told to me.

Toni Morrison put it this way: "If there's a book you really want to read, but it hasn't been written yet, then you must write it." I am still striving to do that.

I hope this work is enjoyable to you and spawns your further desire to perhaps learn more about God and the Bible, and who knows— maybe even to follow Jesus Christ.

With both love and highest regards,

Donovan

1

Table of Contents

Prologue

"Only in Heaven could such evil be spawned. Only thy bosom could conceive such audacity. For it was you who seeded man to know sin, and by thy hand was iniquity discovered. Ye are the author of the dark, the genesis of corruption, a universe fallen, and thy war hast exposed us all to the taint of sin.

"Your spite over El's choosing of our siblings hast brought nothing but destruction. T'was your lust to be as El that sparked your affliction. You now banquet at the table of thy choices. Thus, what word would you speak that my ears might give pause to listen?"

Michael's voice carried over the screams of the damned, each pining to escape the flames of the Lake of Fire. Yet within the great canyon of fire, there was a wisdom within the pyre's collected souls to give space to the Usurper. Thus, Michael and Lucifer continued their exchange uninterrupted.

Lucifer spoke in his bellicose manner, and the power of his voice even from the Lake of Fire shook the ground where he stood.

"Are you satisfied, Michael? Are thou content? For look about you, as generations of Elohim and Human languish before your eyes and you do nothing--nothing! This, little brother, is your legacy."

Michael was unmoved. "Again, you speak, but falsehood is all that is spoken. T'was not *I* who sought the power of God as a thing to be grasped. Neither *I* that rebelled against the father. *You* did. For promotion cometh from the Lord, but you...you would have robbed Him of all! Do not speak to me of what hast been lost."

"And what would you have had me do, Michael? Stand by and watch idly whilst our people were subjugated to the Humans? Nay, my attack on El and His pestilence was His doing. I will resist His will by any means necessary, yea even violent overthrow."

Michael chortled, "And yet you would incite terror against the Humans? To have them worship us instead of their Creator! You are mad!"

"Indeed Michael, we *are* deserving of worship. El needs us Michael do you not see? He needs us to believe in him. Even as He needs the faith of Humans."

"El is Alpha and Omega! El needs no one!" Michael roared.

"Then you *still* do not understand brother," said Lucifer. "We were hunted like dogs! Made to scavenge off the souls of men. In battle, armies must live off the land. El cast us on this island of a mote with no manna to sustain us. To let us waste away while the humans were awash in food. I did what was necessary to survive; it was inevitable that the Humans would be but food for us. No, brother, I do not have remorse over my actions. Repentance runs not through my veins—no I would not do things differently. Release me and I would do it again!"

Lucifer looked with rage upon his brother and raised his fists high into the air. "I would do it again!"

Michael guffawed, "Your rage hast smote the heavens and released sin into the realms. You are the contagion to the kingdom, a corruption now contained within the flames..."

"I thrive in sin Michael, for sin is the only thing that keeps El at bay. El is creator of all things yea from whence doest evil come if not from the 'Author' of Creation?"

Michael had heard enough. "For millennia you have stood as accuser to our brethren, now I stand on the edge of the gulf of the Lake of Fire and speak to one judged traitor, tempter, and deceiver. You are dead to me—away with your lies. For your crimes, hast reached to Heaven, and the list of thy corruption is now known."

Michael turned to walk away, and Lucifer called after him.

"King of Lies?" said Lucifer. "Nay, I have spoken only the truth concerning El. Even now, I stand in judgment. Why? Because I alone am willing to voice that, which others have feared to say about our *'God'*. El *fears*, Michael. He fears my words, for He knows that if I were released even now after a thousand years of this torment; even now my voice would ring throughout the realms and armies would rise to follow me!"

Michael continued to walk and flexed his great wings that he might fly away and Lucifer yelled after him, "Thou art the reason that Raphael died!"

Michael paused.

"Yes," continued Lucifer. "You would condemn me to the fate of a fire that is never quenched. But our brother's death is from thine own hand, not mine Michael—not mine!"

Michael weighed his brother's words, and he ruminated that had he not destroyed the Kiln, his brother would not have succumbed to dissolution by the Godstones. Suddenly grief overtook Michael, and he choked back tears and doubled over for grief, as the loss of his brother was as yesterday. The ages past played themselves before him and sorrow washed over him as he reminisced on the loss of his brother.

Lucifer smiled, knowing that for the moment, Michael entertained his words, grinning with the fiendish hope that perhaps he might still lay seed for rebellion to spring forth once again.

Chapter One: Aftermath

It has been less than one earth week since the Descension and El has yet to summon the Lumazi. A third of my brethren have been exiled across the multiverse. My family, my home, all have been torn apart. I needed to leave the city for a time. To look upon Creation in solitude. To escape the maimed, the groans of the injured, and destruction of the city of my birth. So, I took flight, that I might find quietness near the great canyon and the Maelstrom. I recalled how the winds had gripped me. I wonder what might have been if both my brother and I had been lost to the clutches of the Abyss.

What if...

For it was in this place where Lucifer learned that a ladder could escape anything—yea even the Abyss. Here is where he remembered that escape from Hell was possible. Here he learned this knowledge...by rescuing me.

I looked over the Abyss now sealed by El himself. Only here at the edge of the Maelstrom do I find something familiar—something of comfort. For the great gulf that lies between the realms had remained untouched during the war. I sat listening to the howling winds of the Maelstrom. Their gusts washed across my face and there was solace in the familiarity of the breeze. It whispered and brought to remembrance times when Lucifer and I would work to extend the foundation of Heaven. I recalled his smile and the way his kindness often was masked by his need to abide by royal protocol. For he was the Chief Prince and the First of Angels...and yet—I missed his song.

"Resting Michael?"

I turned to see that Gabriel had landed behind me. I tossed a stone into the racing winds.

"The Abyss reminds me of better times. Yet as I see the seal...I am ever warned of he who lies therein. I had sought to escape but for a moment the rebuilding of the city and the burbs roundabout. Yet even here I am forced to see the hand of my brother on Creation. For there seemeth no escape, and yet I have grown weary of rebuilding Gabriel. Each stone uncovers nothing but loss and grief. Many of my kind have left to follow Lucifer, thus, the rebuilding goes slower. Moreover, with the Kilnstones silent, the workforce I once commanded hast been diminished. I am still assessing how the absence of so many impacts us."

"What of Argoth?" said Gabriel. "He is able to count all things. Surely, he can account for thy people and assist on how best to administer thy efforts. Hast thou sought his counsel?"

Michael frowned, "I, I—have yet to talk with him. Raphael's absence is still too fresh. I am not yet ready to speak with him. Moreover, there is a—coldness about him. Something that I cannot place about his demeanor. He was asleep during the rebellion. Yet his words seep of condemnation as if Lucifer's failing was our doing. I do not quite know what to make of him, Gabriel. I believe he holds us—and me in particular—in contempt for the loss of the realms champion."

Gabriel placed his hand on his brother's shoulder and spoke softly, "It was not you who betrayed our father. Nor your hand that moved Lucifer to raise arms against us. I saw Lucifer as he ascended to the Godhead...we all did. If you had not stopped him..." Gabriel paused to collect himself. "El was wise to make you captain over us."

I shifted on the stone and pondered if I will withhold from my friend what only I knew. But I needed to release this burden from within me. So I will tell him of my failure to save the Kiln.

"There is something that you do not know, brother. What no one else knows...that it was I who destroyed the Kiln."

Tears welled up within my eyes. I choked up over even speaking the words but continued.

"It was I who felled our womb—it was I who made the Godstones to fall down upon us —to pour down upon—Raphael..."

Finally, with but the mention of Raphael's name, hurt and ache flooded my soul. Here in the quiet away from the populace of Heaven, away from the noise of reconstruction and constant reminders of what was lost. Away from the eyes of the citizenry who looked desperately to me to lead, I sobbed, aching to see my brother once more. A brother who was betrayer to us all.

Gabriel hugged me and leaned his head on my shoulders.

I welcomed his presence, thankful that I still held yet to a member of my family. We held one another overlooking the great canyon and I stared at the seal of the Abyss that towered across the expanse of the Maelstrom. Stared knowing that one day, in the fullness of time, the seal would be broken. That he who dwelt therein would be released for a season. Stared because I did not wish to cry anymore, stared because somehow, unbeknownst to all, El had showed me that one day He would be killed.

* * *

Elected by the Draco to stand as proxy for the fallen prince Lucifer, Metatron walked amongst the ruins of his people. Jerusalem was still aflame even a week after the war. Yet El had not spoken, and no command had been issued that would raise the multitudes fallen in battle nor set that which had been upended to a place of restoration. Michael said that El had been planning, and he would say no more, other that when his plans were complete El would summon the Lumazi. That was six days ago. So, Michael, as acting Chief Prince, commanded the Draco, to "Look ye out among you seven of honest report, full of the Holy Ghost and wisdom, whom I might present to God as Lord over thy house."

Thus, the people settled themselves to find leaders among them who had not left to follow the King of Lies. The Draco then summoned the Shemhamphorae, the seventy angels who bore the hidden name of God to appoint from their number seven whom Michael might choose to be eventual ruler over house Draco. The seven presented were Nanael, Omael, Hazaziel, Caliel, Metatron, Aniel, and Eshel. But Michael could not promote to the Lumazi, as the office of Prince could only be given by the Lord. But as the acting Chief Prince, Michael, commanded these seven to provide oversight over the people until El had saw fit to promote one as Lumazi. Therefore, the people obeyed Michael in this thing and submitted themselves to the elders of house Draco and to Michael.

Metatron determined that he would honor the Lord by restoring praise to his people. El would be magnified in song, for his deeds, and for vanquishing Lucifer and the fallen. Metatron stood as the tallest of his kin. Gold and silver lined his skin, and he like his brother Lucifer possessed harps within his flesh. Yet Metatron was also imposing; when the Lord created the forces of the cosmos, Metatron pulled planets to stars and flung them into orbit. He was of the order of Cherub, the most powerful of all angels. There were few such Cherubs who did not already sit on the council. And the mighty cherub was faithful in all his doings.

"Greetings, Metatron," said Azaziel. "How fare's your people?"

Metatron looked up from his musing. Michael had given him the palace of Lucifer. Few had wanted to come near, as speculation persisted that perhaps the palatial home of Lucifer should be torn down. But Michael had said no that it would be fitting that new allegiance be rooted in the place where once betrayal slept. So, he ordered the palace of Lucifer stayed from destruction and gave it to Metatron to reside.

"I am not accustomed to such opulent surroundings. I have yet to decide what I am to do with the all the belongings of Satan."

Azaziel winced. "Aye he is 'Satan' now, is he not? The newly appointed Governor of house Issisi walked and looked at the various books that lined the dining area, and the colorful masterpieces that Issi elders had painted for Lucifer. "It is difficult to imagine that within these walls laid the murderer who scarred Apollyon and who incited the realm."

Metatron thought to himself. *Indeed, a Draco no less. I now stand as the head of the house from which treachery was birthed.* Metatron mused as he thought on the issue. For Lucifer through his actions had taught them all, that every man could only be enticed and drawn away by the lust that was in his own heart.

"Indeed. Has word come of the fallen?"

Azaziel frowned. “There are rumors that some have sought escape from the punishment levied by El. That some of our brethren hast sought to breach the Maelstrom to gain entrance back into Heaven. It is but conjecture—whispers in the dark. All still wonder of one name above others—Lucifer. Rumor has it that he hast been seen on the Earth. That Argoth even now attempts to bring him under the auspices of the Grigori's watch, yet he eludes them. By what power to do so is not known. But he has covertly hidden himself from heaven’s eye. None but El has watch over him now."

Metatron picked up a flute. It was made of Onyx and contained within were the winds from the Maelstrom. The flute shimmered with a dark purple hue. He put the instrument to his lips to play. The melody was like none he had heard, and the flute grew tendrils and attached itself to his mouth. Startled, he threw the instrument to the floor.

"What manner of device is this? Is the thing alive?"

Azaziel picked up the flute. "Yea it is an Eidolon, a sentient instrument." He put the instrument to his mouth and once again, tendrils came from the black cylinder and wrapped themselves around his forearms and to his face and he blew into the instrument. Its sound was high yet melancholy in tune. And as he played the living flute, its notes weighed heavy on Azaziel and made him sad, and he placed the flute on a desk to his side.

"The Eidolon only plays the music that is within one’s heart. There are few in the realm, as they require a stone of fire and the Lord himself must blow within it or it must be placed in the Maelstrom to capture its winds.”

“If it plays the melody of one’s heart, then it will be some time before I may lift it to my lips. As all of Heaven still is somber from the events of the past days. But alas, what of thy people? How fares the Issi over the loss of their Lord?"

The angel turned away sighing, "We are still heartbroken, for Sariel was the best of us. Now it turns to me to provide comfort to our house. Yet it is a thing that I lack in experience. Sorrow I was never in El's mind when he created us, yet sorrow persists. I have questions. Questions that I hope if we are promoted to Lumazi I might pose with Him."

"And what questions would you, my friend, seek to ask El?"

Azaziel’s face grew somber as he picked up a picture of Lucifer and Sariel, caught in an embrace and smiling.

"How might I know that I too would not turn Satan against my king?"

Metatron walked to his brother and embraced Azaziel, as the two of them stared down at the image of better times between the former Lords of their houses. He sighed, feeling the weight of responsibility that to lead their peoples would now fall to them, and replied, "We shall ask Him together, brother."

* * *

Talus walked his palace grounds and surveyed the damage done to his home. Here it was that he allowed himself to bring Heaven to war. Here, in his own pride, did civil war ripen under his presence. He looked at the spire that had been bloodied by the fall of Ashelon. Killed by the spite he had towards the Issi Ashtaroth; killed because Talus could not contain the shame that his house was origin to the first of angels to kill another—killed because of his pride.

To think more highly of oneself is a dangerous path of thought, ruminated Talus.

He still looked on his servants in shame. They lowered their gaze when he looked at them. In times past, the gaze of his people was one of beaming achievements; now nothing but awkward attempts to avert one's eyes, to be forced not to bring up conversation. And so, the Prince Lord of all Arelim stood aloof from his people. Sober that under his watch both Abaddon and war had come through him. Yet the Lord did not remove him from office.

For El had not summoned the counsel for a week. Nor did He with His word bring immediate restoration to the realm. Instead, El stood still within the temple as He consulted with the Godhead. The triune God remained in counsel with Himself. Talus knew that the Lord would ask for his demotion. To be removed from leading so great a people. Shame surrounded him. Talus was humbled. Humbled to give command, and with each self—deprecating question he took stock in himself. To see how he could have let such an elevation of his importance blind him to cause injury to another. To bring violence into his home, and to stain his race with being the firstborn to genesis violence in Heaven. Talus sorrowed as he looked upon his grounds.

His servants had begged him to clean Ashelon's spire. To remove the taint of Elomic blood from the ivory pinnacle where Ashelon died. But he refused and ordered it to remain as a memorial to the life that was lost. That all Arelim might be reminded that brutishness, and power left unchecked could give sway to the evil of pride and to lust, which launches war. He would never fail to forget the lesson. Never again would his people be lost to rage.

The shrubbery of his palatial home was uprooted and torn from his battle with Sariel. He smiled at the frequency with which he and his brother would contest over who was the greatest. It was such a foolish thing, he realized.

Talus pledged himself to serve the realm. To become the least of his brethren. For lo, Sariel had given his life that all might know that unity was the place of strength. That to act alone was not glory, but rather glory was to act in concert with others. And so, Talus would remember Sariel's sacrifice. He would work collaboratively with all.

The prince looked at the spire, vowing to remember that Lucifer chose civil war to begin at his house. For the Chief Prince knew that he could manipulate his brother's hand to introduce Heaven to war. Talus stared long at the spire, absorbed at the towering testimony of his actions.

His conscience wrenched at him, and angst gripped him in a merciless hold of remorse, the head of house Arelim was overcome with emotion, and he placed his head in his palms and wept.

* * *

"Reveal the Kingdom of Heaven," commanded Argoth.

Immediately the 'Eye' of the room exploded in swaths of blue, green, and reds. The spectrum of light splashed over the walls, ceilings, and floors, and Jerahmeel and Argoth gawked at what they saw. For a third of the city of God was in ruins, and fires still raged round about.

Rescue crews tended to the maimed and the wounded. Great towers whose foundations spiraled into the heavens were decimated. Stained colored windowpanes were shattered or blown out while the exteriors of many buildings had been sheared off. Sliced by the power of Ladders aimed as destructive beams of death. Some buildings still stood, but the damage to the now-crumbling and hollowed-out structures was so immense that they would need to be condemned. Jerusalem was covered in soot and ash, flame and smoke, and everywhere survivors looked for the dead, as rescue efforts were underway to succor those still trapped or needing attention. Not all had taken up arms to fight their brethren, for some had taken refuge during the fighting to give medical aid. And everywhere, the people ran to either claim or identify the dead and dying. And woe was all that echoed in Heaven, for the loss of her children both exiled and dead, and grief existed for a time within the Third Heaven. It was a palpable guttural ache of sorrow that never had reached her gates. Some cursed Lucifer and others simply wailed; waiting for news on the absence of comrades now unheard from. But it was the doubt which above all was rife in the air of Heaven. Doubt that the Creator despite His power lacked goodness towards His people. For the people ached for El to come from within the temple, to bask in His goodness once again.

Suddenly a tremor caused the monitoring duo to sway and bookshelves fell while volume after volume tumbled to the floor. More tremors and aftershocks made the building rumble further.

"Are we under attack again?" said Jerahmeel

"Nay but the tremors seem to be increasing. Workers have hastened to support damage to the beams. Reveal: the floor of heaven," said Argoth.

Immediately the room changed colors and the two could see that the basement of heaven was unsound, for the cadmine beams which grew to expand the base of heaven were splintered with fissures, and some were sheared in half, lanced by the Ladders which had halved them.

But it was the fires that disturbed them. From the outer burbs to the center of the Elysian Fields, Heaven was ablaze, and the flames raced into the sky from Elysium. For the great fields of manna burned and the cinders of manna and kora leaf leaped into the sky, coughing great clouds of black smoke. Jerahmeel watched as the food stuff of heaven was consumed by the raging flames. Garrisons of Harada fought valiantly to contain the blaze as the inferno crept closer to the homes of the city's populace. But for many it was too late. For throughout Heaven, Elohim found themselves homeless, and their possessions consumed by fire, obliterated by Ladders and damaged by smoke. For over half of the city burned, decimated from the wrath of her children's war with themselves.

"Hast El made movement to intervene?

"No," said Jerahmeel. "He consults with himself; the Trinity meditates and plans, yet El is aware of all and has entrusted the people into our care. Come, there are still areas of the great hall that I am instructed to show thee."

Argoth and Jerahmeel climbed the stairs of a room that lead up to the roof of the great hall. A door opened upward, and the duo climbed through and beheld the expanse of Heaven before them. Stars beamed down, shining brightly upon the ceiling of Heaven.

Argoth looked to his left and right, and about them were nothing but rock and walls made of blue diamond, and the glint of starlight made the area to shine as if surrounded by hundreds of small beams of light.

"There is nothing here. What is this place?"

Jerahmeel smiled. "I know not. I only know what was commanded me." Jerahmeel reached into his robes and pulled out a scroll that was sealed with the prismatic seal of El and handed it to Argoth. Then he turned to leave.

"Where are you going?"

"What is written herein is for thine eyes alone. My command was to bring thee here and to deliver this into thy hands. I will wait for thee below." And Jerahmeel stepped back down into the stairwell and shut the door over him. The door snapped tight and Argoth heard the click of it being locked from within.

Left alone in the room he stared at the scroll. He turned it over, and snapped the clay seal in two, and when he unrolled the scroll the words written disappeared from the parchment and lifted as letters into the sky as a great whirlwind and clouds formed overhead, and from the clouds the voice of El spoke.

"Thou art he who shall pen the record of creation. I make thee head of all Grigori. Stand in the presence of the Almighty and see thy God." Immediately a form as of the Son of man yet with wings fell from the sky, and Argoth knelt before the God of all things and spoke. "My Lord and my God!"

The figure stood in front of Argoth and when Argoth looked at him, he saw stars and galaxies, and he beheld times and seasons, and the creation of time itself. Its weaving was wondrous to behold, and men, animals, and beasts of the imagination were all moving within God's form. And as Argoth beheld all that El was, El's form glowed and flashed in white hot light and Argoth was blinded and cried out from both fear and pain, and he placed his hands on his face to cover his eyes. And when he did so Argoth had no more eyes and his form changed as he stood within El. His face glowed through the burned sockets where once his eyes gave sight. He saw the past, the present, and the future all at once, and realized that within El such contrivances did not exist. And as he looked upon God he understood why El said, 'I AM that I AM."

Argoth's eyes were a thing no more. Yet he saw with a vision that surpassed all that one might behold with created eyes, and he looked about him and saw that all creation was merely the outline of El and that El had no form as had been perceived, but was everywhere, and in all things. And Argoth collapsed and fell as a man dead, overwhelmed by the totality of who El was.

When he awoke he thought he had dreamed, but when he looked to his left, two eyes were on the ground next to him. Immediately he felt his face, and his face was not his own, and he felt that he had no eyes. He lifted himself from off the ground and was covered in a white cloak of light, and a new inkhorn hovered over him, and he felt his chest within beat a new heart. It was a tome that wrote with the ink pen of God. And Argoth knew that he had succeeded Raphael as head of his people. And everywhere he looked, he saw Grigori all about him, writing and observing their respective charges. There was nowhere in Heaven or beyond that he could not see, for all realms were laid before him.

A voice from Heaven spoke to him and said, "Thine eyes belong to me. They shall remain here as token of thine oath to thy people. For as long as thine eyes are stayed on me, forever shall thou see with the sight of the Almighty to see all that may be seen. That without eyes, thou might see with the eyes of God."

And Argoth bowed. "Mine eyes are yours, my Lord."

"Then go, and watch, and never be moved by what thou seest."

Immediately the door to the stairwell below unlocked and Argoth left the great balcony from which all of Heaven and the realms could be seen. He climbed down and found Jerahmeel waiting in the Hall, thumbing through a book.

When Jerahmeel looked upon the Grigori, he was clothed in white raiment and his face was hidden that he could not be seen. Hovering over him was the stylus and inkhorn Jerahmeel was accustomed to seeing. Yet he had no face that one might see. His hands and feet were opaque, and Jerahmeel beheld stars within him and nodded.

"You are Sephiroth?" Jerahmeel questioned remembering the statue of light he and his brethren had seen.

"I am he" replied Argoth.

"Well, you don't need me to show you around anymore. I do not profess to know the entirety of all that lies here within the mount. Raphael gave me tours of the deep catacombs of the Hall. Perhaps he knew that his demise was forthcoming I do not know. I have shown you all that hast been shown to me. Is there more that you need from me?"

"Thank you," Argoth said.

"You're welcome," replied Jerahmeel, who then turned to leave. Argoth reached out to stop him.

"No, you misunderstand me, Jerahmeel Harada. Thank you for awakening me at the Great Library."

"I awoke you, Argoth because Raphael my brother on his dying breath thought that to do so would save our people. But know this—that if allowing you to slumber would have salvaged our cause—then know of a surety that dormancy would still be your state."

Argoth nodded, "I understand." The two walked past the volumes of books lined on shelves, and past a dark chamber in the Hall of Annals. Argoth stopped to take note of the gold and black volumes of books atop a pedestal sealed with the seal of Lucifer Draco. "Are these the books of Lucifer?"

Jerahmeel entered the dimly lit chamber, the chamber where Raphael had kept hidden the Book of Iniquity and lifted the tome from the podium. He looked at the seal of house Draco and the personal sigil of Lucifer—a sigil all those who abandoned El had adopted.

"They are, I entrust his record to you now. Do with them as you will."

Argoth touched the manuscripts that laid before him, and in a twinkling of an eye, he absorbed all the information contained within the records. As he studied the tomes of Lucifer and those left by Raphael. For a moment, Jerahmeel was saddened as he was reminded of his friend.

Argoth completed his mental digestion of the contents and spoke. "Lucifer was deceived by his own beauty, puffed up by his role and captivated in his importance. A creature blinded by his own perfection. To think that El had once considered him for promotion. He is indeed Satan now, and deserves the fate handed to him by El."

Jerahmeel replied, "I take no pleasure in our brother's demise."

"Do not speak to defend him," said the Grigori. "The record of his tome is clear, for, despite the inept handling of his Grigori, Raphael has left much in disarray among the Grigoric order. There is much that must be done to remove the stench of explication that now rises to me. I would see restoration to the tomes that occupy this hall. Even now, those Grigori that roam free unfettered by the laws of our people, defile these records with their editorialized version of the cosmos. I would see it end."

Jerahmeel eyed his brother curiously. "And what do you propose to enact such cessation?"

"There can be but one course of action—dissolution. The 'Fallen' cannot be restored, thus, they must be extinguished."

Jerahmeel was shocked at the coldness of his brother's response. "Would you wage war with thine own people? Hast not the realm seen enough bloodshed?" He stared hard at Argoth pained that violence would once again be used to confront their people.

"I am ruler of my people," said Argoth. "And must give account to El. I will not see the records fall to the taint of Lucifer's schemes. I, therefore, will that he be extinguished from the realm. And if not; then I will see to it that the records of my people are purified. They who write must cease to do so. Their tomes must be recovered, their pens silenced. There is no other way."

He faced Jerahmeel and added sarcastically, "But perhaps thou thinkest that I might reason with them and speak pleasantries that they might turn from their wicked ways? Nay, the 'Fallen' will not of their own accord cease and desist. Nor will they surrender their tomes. There is but one word alone, one record of history, and it *must* be rightly divided. Disunion must cease. There can be no other course. In the name of the Lord, I will execute a purge of the tomes."

Jerahmeel winced, stung by the ease with which Argoth would speak of further assault, and taken aback by the angel's willingness to enter into conflict and spoke.

"I would adjure thee by the love of God that thou first seek permission from El, before you let loose your people. Lucifer's actions have already brought Heaven loss to much of her children: to lose more in a battle that is not—"

Argoth snapped at Jerahmeel. "I will do what Raphael was want to do. To preserve the word of El, we must be resolute. Raphael failed and he hast paid the price for his failure."

Jerahmeel became incensed at the apparent accusation, "You purport as if Raphael did something amiss? Raphael is dead, yet even in his absence you would attribute him to be the cause of his brother's own actions?"

Argoth replied unflinchingly, "Raphael was loath to do what must be done. He was Sephiroth. To pen creation's record was his to command. Now he is not. To be Sephiroth is to uphold the Word. To see the realm with the eyes of God. There can be no corruption in this task, thus, Raphael hast failed. It now falls to me to bring all things into conformity. Indeed, he was a prince Lord, as are you. You and the counsel are the best of us and were expected to bring peace, wisdom, power and honor in all things. El be praised, that this hall remains inviolate. I could not imagine the damage Lucifer could have done."

Jerahmeel's anger grew at his brother's suggestion of fault in Raphael.

"The only error, if there be any, was in our brother Lucifer's thinking that he could bring down El. A thought that apparently was not unique to him alone but eventually agreed upon by members of thine own kind. Judge not lest you be judged. For with the same measure you judge shall it be returned unto thee. Your words sound of Lucifer before his fall."

Argoth stiffened, "You would compare *me* to the Usurper? Would you charge *me* as betrayer to God?"

Jerahmeel was unwavering in his reply. "I mean no offense, Argoth, yet *you*—were asleep. Dozing whilst the rest of Heaven was under siege. Lucifer was haughty. His pride is what led to his downfall.

Not a failure from any of the Lumazi to rebuke him. You would be wise to remember that. I consider you now equal among our brethren, but alas...so was Lucifer. Beware that ye not abandon the spirit of meekness lest ye be overcome by temptation to pride. In the interim, Michael now holds command of the Host. He will give us command, or El will do so."

And upon the mention of El, the Hall of Annals flashed to reveal the colors of the Throne room, and the Lord God sat on the throne, and round about him were floating images that projected everywhere throughout the room. And the Holy Spirit in the form of a giant eagle hovered over the throne, and another form as unto a man, Yeshua son of El, was seated next to El.

Jerahmeel and Argoth beheld as the images relayed wars and pictures of death, and they saw great nations rise and fall on the planet El had named Earth, and the throne glowed, as the Trinity beheld millions of pictures at once. The Hall of Annals struggled to project all the happenings within the throne room, for each image changed in the blink of an eye. Suddenly, a scarlet thread burst forth from El to one image, and then between three images and then split. Suddenly the red line latticed the room in a web of scarlet, racing from El through projection after projection, and wound its way between countless images and weaved, as the faces of men and women shown across the floor of the room. The images moved from the east to the west of the throne and then encircled the throne.

Moreover, in various imageries, Jerahmeel saw Lucifer and the Fallen, entwining their deeds throughout the cosmos. Nevertheless, within the midst of the display, Jerahmeel beheld birth, laughter, and singing. Yet the pace of the spectacle was too much for his mind to capture and comprehend, for the panorama careened at a speed beyond his mind's ability to grasp. His eyes incapable of capturing but glimpses of the entirety of what El saw.

The Hall struggled to keep up with the swiftness that which the triune God moved the events of history, and the images became blurred as the room attempted to relay the visualized thoughts of the Creator. For in the blink of an eye, each image changed, but El saw all things at once, and the Godhead was quiet watching the images and arranging them.

The line that moved from El then became clearer, and both Jerahmeel and Argoth knew that they witnessed the creation of 'time' and were privy to watching the Godhead at work planning the outcome of the universe. The images slowed in their relentless haste across the room, then coalesced to but a few. The scarlet line also emerged from an incomprehensible lattice woven through persons and events and blended into one thread of scarlet that returned to the Lord and ended at the Lord's bruised heel, and in that final image, El's heel bled no more. Then He who sat on the throne spoke. "I am Alpha and Omega, the beginning and the end, the first and the last." And the images ceased.

Jerahmeel and Argoth eyes slowly adjusted to the room's ability to keep up, and when their sight attuned to see; they beheld that there was but one that sat on the throne and El said,

"We shall aid the Man and bring to naught the plans of the Enemy." The Lord then turned to look in the direction of the duo as if He could see them and spoke.

"Jerahmeel, the time hast come to bring wholeness to Heaven; you and Argoth call thy brethren to court." Then all images into the throne room were whited out in a great flash and faded to black.

* * *

Each of chief princes of the seven angelic houses bowed before the God of all things and seated themselves before the throne. Argoth took it upon himself to speak.

"My Lord, you have summoned us, and we are thine to command."

El replied, "Come and witness the elevation of Michael Kortai." El motioned for Michael to rise. "Come my son, and I shall anoint thee with power, and will lay my hands atop thy head, and ye shall be Chief Prince."

Michael stood and spoke, "Lord, I ask permission for my ascension to be placed on hold; is such permissible?"

God looked upon His son and replied, "You would have another stand in your stead as Chief Prince?"

Michael looked upon his father and lingered to speak. "I...I. Am unsure if I am ready to lead the Host my Lord."

Gasps and whispers echoed among the Lumazi. "The thing hast never been done. Who would deny promotion from the Lord?" Argoth said.

Jerahmeel studied his brother. "Michael, are you sure?"

Michael nodded in silence.

Jerahmeel put his hands on his hips then opened his hands to wave to those behind him. "And what of your people? El hast chosen thee for promotion because He knows that you are best to lead. How are the people to fare if you refuse God?"

Michael remained silent; he had not considered how the people would fare. He only calculated El's absence in all his decisions. Never his own. Never had it occurred to him of his own importance and how it might impact the people. And for a moment, he was aware that his decision mayhap was not to protect El, but to satisfy his own selfish desires.

"I—I—Lord I ask that another stand in my stead," stammered Michael finally.

The Lord looked at Michael, and all looked at El, and all present knew that at that moment He gazed into Michael's heart, and saw all possible futures. Michael bowed his head as the Lord studied him.

"The thing will be as you say," said God.

Metatron then spoke, asking what they all wondered. "Who then will we call Chief Prince? Who wilt thou appoint to lead us?"

"To be Chief Prince requires faith," said El. "Neither fealty nor obedience alone shall suffice, but submission is what I require. For faith is the substance of things hoped for, and the evidence of things not seen. For by it ye might obtain a good report. But lo, although all might lead, only one shall hold title. For the gifting of God hast been rejected, its offer rescinded, and must now be earned. Therefore, he who would command the respect of Eladrin shall cede Lucifer as Chief Prince. He who desires to lead desires a good work, therefore whosoever wills, let him step out from among his people, that he might earn title of Chief Prince."

Mouths dropped. For Eladrin was seated high above the mountain of God and nested at the ceiling of Heaven. He looked down below and was called only by the command of God. It was he who chose which of the four Ophanim would serve as rest for the throne of God. Nestled in the clouds of the mountain, Eladrin had only been seen once, by Lucifer himself at the creation of all things.

Many thought Eladrin was a myth, perpetrated by Lucifer. For Lucifer alone did the Ophanim respect, yet Lucifer breached their trust when he attacked El, and they now bar him from the presence of the Almighty.

Each of the princes turned to leave the throne room, and Talus looked at Michael and spoke as they exited. "I hope you know what you are doing, Michael."

Michael nodded and whispered, "I hope so too, my friend. I hope so too."

Talus stopped and turned to speak to El. "And what of the Kiln, my Lord? Will you rebuild it?"

El frowned and spoke. "The Kiln hast been destroyed. Nor will I set my hand to restore it. For Michael in his wisdom knew what must be done, and I will not upend that which my son hast wrought." And El looked at Michael knowingly.

Michael nodded in acknowledgment, for none but he knew that the Kiln had held the Primestone, the gem of which if commanded would have given his kind the very power to be as God. El had set the Kiln as a test of his children. An exam to the best of them, to see if he might add them to the Godhead. Michael knew that they were not ready. Knew his kind was too much awash in pride. For there was much competition of whom would be the greatest among them. The Godhead would remain a Trinity. Stripped from the chest of Lucifer, the Primestone would stay forever tucked within the folds of El until the end of days unless He saw fit to do otherwise.

Talus and Argoth frowned at Michael.

He knew their thoughts were sour; sour over how he had destroyed the womb of their kind. That because of deeds done by his hand no more Elohim would be birthed from the flames of the Kiln. Thoughts of resentment and of anger had seeded in their hearts.

El knew their thoughts as well and spoke. "The Kiln is of no importance. Know ye not that he who hath builded the house hath more honour than the house? And who hath made thy mouth, and hath breathed upon the embers of thy stone the breath of life that ye might live? The Kiln is but a gourd that was and is no more. I AM the Kiln. Nay, my sons, our thoughts are to the man whom now I must tutor, that they too might be called the sons of God."

"Lord, permission to speak freely," queried Michael.

"Granted, my son."

Michael approached El and knelt before his Lord in submission.

"Lord, I appeal to thee to consider your course of action. The vision you shared—the cross—I know—I know what you have shown me. Please do not do this. I beg of you."

El smiled at His son and spoke to them all. "There is a path that must be followed, a chain of events that will stretch unbroken even unto the end of days. Until all things are placed underfoot. Would thou favor the things of Lucifer or of God? There is one that can bring down thy brother. Only one that can purchase the blood of Adam. He is Shiloh. For Shiloh shall be born of the seed of the woman, and upon his back shall He carry the sins of three heavens. He shall smite the enemy that man might no more fear death. And through death He will destroy him that has the power of death, that is, the Devil. And deliver them who through fear of death were all their lifetime subject to bondage. For Shiloh shall not take the nature of angels, but be born of the seed of Abraham, who is yet afar off. For Shiloh shall be as his brethren and a faithful high priest to make reconciliation for the sins of the people. For He must himself suffer temptation that He might succor them that are tempted."

The group stood confused as El spoke of events that had not yet transpired when El suddenly winced.

Michael noticed his Lord's reaction and bowed. "Thou art wounded my king. How might your servant attend unto his Lord?"

El smiled, "It is of my choosing that this *wound* bleeds, that all might know that the Godhead is not without feeling, for the acts of our sons bring pain to the Father. Yet cease from concern. We are Alpha. We are Omega. I AM that I AM. It must be thus that all might act according to plan. For there will even come a time when this temple will be destroyed and in three days I will raise it up again."

The Lumazi each looked upon the Lord in collective gasps. Thoughts of oncoming attack filled each one as the words sunk deep into the ears of all present.

El then paused and suddenly stopped speaking. "Ughhh...," he said.

"My Lord," said Talus. Expressing the concern that all now had. El was visibly shaken. He bowed his head and rubbed His forehead as if relieving tension.

El then slowly rose to his feet. He staggered and reached out to touch the throne to keep from stumbling. The Shekinah, the veil of living light that surrounded Him, slowly changed, changing from a bright white to light grey, then darkened to jet black, and the God who was light was temporarily surrounded in darkness and the stars and galaxies could be seen within him. Then without warning, the Shekinah screamed, and its wail filled the throne room.

The screech blew out the windows of the palace and each angel covered their ears as the Lumazi bowed in both submission and fear. The mountain quaked from the shock wave of the blast and those who beheld the palace from afar wondered as to the rumblings that came from the mountain. All of Heaven then heard the concentric spreading of the shrieking sound and writhed in pain at the scream that came from the Shekinah. Michael, head down and ears covered, wondered to himself how light could make sound.

El staggered and braced himself on his throne. He wiped drops of blood from His forehead, straightened himself, and stood erect.

"We must go down for the man hast corrupted himself." El grimaced, then spoke again. "It has begun."

Then before He even finished speaking, El faded from view and disappeared. Michael looked down to where the Lord had stood, and all that remained was a small pool of crimson blood on the crystal floor of the palace. He did not move from where he stood, but he swore he heard the blood whisper. He looked to see if his brothers could hear, but they hurriedly sought to leave the throne room and follow El. He looked back at the pool of blood, and it whispered in hushed tones that he alone could hear. Words that had only been heard when Lucifer's own sin was revealed—*iniquity*.

* * *

Lucifer watched Eve from a distance. She touched several macaws stroking their colored feathers while rabbits clustered themselves to play at her feet. She delighted in the warmth of the noonday sun: oblivious to the looming shadow of he who had challenged God. Mountain lions walked by her side, and Lucifer took note that the man had gone to the river to drink. The Shekinah the living breathing light of God enveloped her, and she shown in brilliance.

Lucifer saw that the woman was alone and slithered towards her and spoke. "Greetings princess, you are as lovely as the morning star."

The woman bowed in recognition of his words and reached out to touch him. Lucifer restrained himself from recoiling from her touch and allowed her to stroke him. The woman rubbed his head and slid her hands across his wings. His scales were as a kaleidoscope of light, and she was entranced by his beauty.

"It would seem, serpent, that God has not given beauty to me alone."

Lucifer smiled and his tongue darted from his mouth. "You do me great honor, princess. It would seem that here within the garden, beauty is awash in abundance. Would you be so kind as to lift me to this tree?"

The woman obliged him and placed Lucifer softly within the branches of a melon tree, and he coiled himself around a branch and bit from a melon that he might taste it.

"I have seen the variety of trees that fill our home, my princess. The Garden is lush in all manner of fruit. Yet the tree in the midst of the garden glistens, and illuminates, calling to us all to partake in its succulence. Yet why doest thou not partake of its fruit? Hath God said ye that shall not eat of every tree of the garden?"

And the woman said unto the serpent, "We may eat of the fruit of the trees of the garden: But of the fruit of the tree, which is in the midst of the garden, God hath said, 'Ye shall not eat of it, neither shall ye touch it, lest ye die.'"

Lucifer smiled and said unto the woman, "Ye shall not surely die: For God doth know that in the day ye eat thereof, then your eyes shall be opened, and ye shall be as gods, knowing good and evil."

Lucifer then flew from the melon tree to the tree in the midst of the garden, and settled himself, dangling from its branches, and bit from the fruit thereof. Lucifer's skin shown and glistened in the sun's light, and he brightened in appearance. He smiled at the woman and motioned her to join him. Adam had now come from the river and stood by her side, watching and mute as Lucifer spoke to the man's wife, beckoning her to join him in partaking of its fruit. The woman eyed the tree and stood fixed gazing upon it, and when the woman saw that the tree was good for food and that it was pleasant to the eyes, and a tree to be desired to make one wise. She took of the fruit thereof, and did eat, and gave also unto her husband with her, and he did eat. And their eyes were opened.

Instantly the living light of the Shekinah flickered, dimmed, and then screamed. It fell from the skin of Adam and his wife as scum, and dropped toward the ground, forming into a puddle of black sludge, soaking the lush green grass of the earth.

The blackness bored itself into the ground and immediately the ground beneath their feet shook, and the grass began to wither as the blanket of grass wilted and coughed sickness into the air. Clouds began to form and blocked the sun from view, as darkness spread over the sky. The wind began to gallop and howl, and the leaves of the trees fluttered into their faces and waved their outreached hands as gusts darted between tree branches.

Adam looked at his wife, and she returned his stare of abject terror, for the illumination that surrounded the duo faded, and they were no more opaque to the eye, but the removing of the Shekinah made them see each other without the holiness of God.

Immediately they knew that they were naked, and ran to gather fig leaves, and sewed them together, to make themselves aprons.

Lucifer smiled as they moved to escape his gaze, and he watched as they attempted to hide in the midst of the trees of the garden. Laughing at their estrangement, he viewed them as they huddled together in fear. Lucifer floated in merriment on the traveling winds in the garden, landing near them and transforming himself into a being of light garnished with diamonds, topaz, and rubies, and his beauty stood apart from the withering of the green that quickly surrounded them.

"Now your kind will service me." And Lucifer looked upon them as they lay before him cowering and saw that all that he had made was good.

Chapter Two: Ransomed

The Lord appeared quietly in the Garden, and the Shekinah of El's presence brought colored luminance to every nook and cranny of grey and darkness, penetrating every leaf and branch. His presence made the grass to sing and the garden itself spawned new life underfoot as He walked to find His children.

And Adam and his wife heard the voice of the Lord God walking in the garden in the cool of the day, and Adam and his wife hid from the presence of the Lord God amongst the trees of the garden.

The Lord God called unto Adam, and said unto him, "Where art thou?"

Adam said, "I heard thy voice in the garden, and I was afraid, because I was naked, and I hid myself."

El replied, "Who told thee that thou wast naked? Hast thou eaten of the tree, whereof I commanded thee that thou shouldest not eat?"

And the man said, "The woman whom thou gavest to be with me, she gave me of the tree, and I did eat."

And El said unto the woman, "What is this that thou hast done?"

And the woman said, "The serpent beguiled me, and I did eat."

Then El said unto the serpent, “Because thou hast done this, thou art cursed above all cattle, and above every beast of the field; upon thy belly shalt thou go, and dust shalt thou eat all the days of thy life: And I will put enmity between thee and the woman, and between thy seed and her seed; it shall bruise thy head, and thou shalt bruise his heel.”

Unto the woman, He said, "I will greatly multiply thy sorrow and thy conception; in sorrow, thou shalt bring forth children, and thy desire shall be to thy husband, and he shall rule over thee."

And unto Adam, He said, "Because thou hast hearkened unto the voice of thy wife, and hast eaten of the tree, of which I commanded thee, saying, ‘Thou shalt not eat of it’, cursed is the ground for thy sake. In sorrow shalt, thou eat of it all the days of thy life. Thorns also and thistles shall it bring forth to thee, and thou shalt eat the herb of the field. In the sweat of thy face shalt thou eat bread, till thou return unto the ground; for out of it wast thou taken, for dust thou art, and unto dust shalt thou return."

The Lord then took a lamb and held it so that Adam and his wife might see. And with his finger, He slit the kid's throat and blood flowed from its jugular and poured in great pools on the ground. Adam and his wife watched in horror, for never had they seen death, and they watched as the lamb jerked in the arms of the Lord until its life was spent. Then the Lord with His own hand cut from its' flesh the skin thereof, and with-it fashioned coats of skins and clothed them.

And when Adam saw that his actions had brought death to another, that his own sin might be covered, he wept. Adam then turned to the Lord to speak, but the Lord raised His hand to silence him and spoke instead.

"Behold, the man is become as one of us, to know good and evil, and now, lest he put forth his hand, and take also of the tree of life, and eat, and live forever."

Immediately angels appeared throughout the Garden and the Lord raised his finger toward the exit of Eden and motioned for the man to depart.

Adam paused and hesitated for a moment, for the garden had been his home and he had never ventured from its domain. He looked with pleading eyes upon the Lord, but the Lord did not repent of His decision and called a wind that gusted and shoved Adam away from the Lord's presence.

Adam then grabbed the hand of his wife and sprinted to the Tree of Life, and the Lumazi materialized to bar his path and each held flaming swords that blocked the way to the tree. Adam cried out to the Lord, and Adam and his wife were afraid, for the Lord did not answer and turned his back to them as gusting winds buffeted them away.

Yet Adam refused to leave the Lord's side, and Michael, seeing that the man would not yield, moved towards him and pulled from his sheath the Sword of Ophanim, the blade with which he had battled Lucifer. Its blue flame ignited in front of Adam, and the sword split into seven swords with eyes roundabout and it roared at Adam, and Michael unleashed the blades to pursue the man and his wife and drive them from the Garden.

Adam and his wife fled from the flaming swords and whenever they ran from a path other than the exit to the garden, Cherubim materialized to keep them in the way. Each Cherubim herded them further from the Tree of Life and towards the exit of the garden. Adam and his wife sprinted from Michael's swords as gusts of wind pummeled them and the Lumazi barred them from the Tree of Life and the Lord.

The two humans ran to the edge of the Garden, and both turned to see the light of the Tree of Life shine brightly in the center of the garden dim as the forest of Eden's great trees, vines and limbs closed, and sealed shut the way behind them that they could no more return, and the living mist of the garden opened up ahead of them that they might see what lay before, and a barren wilderness of rock stood before them.

Lucifer watched them from afar and smiled that the Lord had ejected the man from his home and thought to himself. *If I cannot have home in paradise, neither shall the Clayborn*. But when he gloated, the Lord saw it and spoke.

"Because thou hast done this thing, thou shalt never again enter the garden of thy covet. For it shall encircle the earth thereof, and men shall speak of its wonders from afar, and when in thy lust you shalt hear rumor that it is nigh thee, then it shall remove itself from thee, ever to flee from thy face until the end come."

Suddenly the mist which covered the garden glowed bright, shimmered, and then in a flash of light disappeared, and nothing was seen but barren wasteland in its wake.

"Noooo!" Lucifer screamed

He flew to the area of where the Garden had been and reached to grasp the dark soil, and the black earth fell from between his fingers as his tears wet the ground, and Michael watched his brother's anguish from afar.

El turned his eyes heavenward and the Lumazi then lifted themselves up to the sky as great Ladders appeared to return the court to the palace. When Lucifer saw that they were set to return to the realm immortal, he lifted himself to pursue them, and as he rose to escape the confines of the Earth and her moon he was flung back to the ground by a force unseen, and Lucifer cried obscenities after his brethren who continued on as their Ladders pulled them past the second heaven into the third, away from all things earthly and celestial, while the former Chief Prince plummeted as a meteor back to the earth.

* * *

The Lord and the royal court were assembled back in the Throne room, and each of the cherub princes sought to speak over one another as none deferred to the other and El quietly looked at Michael who immediately understood his Lord's will. Michael motioned with his hand and his brethren grew quiet and allowed him to speak.

"Lucifer yet walks the Earth. He will not leave the humans alone. My Lord, thou hast denied him home to Heaven, and hast removed from his hand the palace of his covet. Yet still he abides free. I know what is in thy mind. What you have allowed me to see. Though injury to you is of your will, your plan will not see fruition for many days to come. Lucifer will not cease his grasp for the throne."

Argoth immediately jumped into the pause that Michael had left for El to respond.

"Lord, thou hast placed within the Garden all that man might ever need. The tree of the knowledge of good and evil, the one thing you forbade, was not needed by man. A home of plenty, sustenance, provision and knowledge ever was before him to grasp from thee. ONE command, my Lord! He had but *one* command, yet he hast rebelled against thee. One command that if disobeyed would bring forth his death. Why then doest the man still live? Where is the justice of my king that punishment for rebellion would be meted out on our brethren within the span of a day, but death not come to Adam?" And all were silent at the audaciousness of Argoth to question the justice of God in this thing.

Michael winced at the remark and commented, "Would thou question the wisdom of God? Is the righteousness of God on trial? Was not such thought seed in Apollyon's mind? A seed that hast lead us to the genesis of covetousness today? Who is more gracious than our God, and who hast given us breath that we might have life? Where can such query lead but to division and to undermine the realm?"

El interjected before anyone else could speak, "Argoth's question poses no threat to us. For we are and ever shall be. I AM that I AM. Verily the soul that sinneth, it shall die. Yet Adam is my image in the Earth, and in my mercy, I will see that debt of justice paid. Adam hath sinned against me. He shall surely die. Yet I will not blot my image and the work of my hands from the Earth. Am I not a father? Did not I breathe into him my own spirit and give him dominion? Adam hast indeed rebelled, yet Lucifer hast provoked me to wrath to destroy him as my image now carries a plague of sin. Therefore, I will bring ruin on he who would defile and tamper with my image and bring justice and succor the man. But the time of fulfillment is many days to come. But know of a surety that it shall come to pass. For yet a vessel must be prepared that Lucifer's actions might be undone."

Gabriel looked at the Lord and spoke. "Lord, how can the council sit idle and stand aside to a future yet to come while conspiracy exists to destroy our father?"

El smiled and replied, "Thou art concerned for my welfare? Noted, but there is much that cannot be relayed, for the time of reckoning is not yet nigh. For even now Lucifer moves to contaminate the realm. He is not yet defeated."

Gabriel paced in agitation, and finally blurted out to God, "But Lord why is he still allowed to roam free? He must be destroyed!"

Each of the younger princes nodded in agreement toward one another, awaiting any reply from El.

Michael looked at Gabriel with concern, remembering his own bout of anger with Iofiel.

El spoke to them all. "I will not destroy my son, but he will serve to further my will even as Abaddon lived to show that my will shall not be thwarted. For what would thou have of me?"

El looked at Gabriel, who blurted back in anger, "Let us call down fire upon him, that he might be consumed. The realms must be rid of his influence!"

The Lord looked upon His son and frowned. "You do not know the spirit with which you speak."

Jerahmeel jumped into the conversational fray to bring clarity to them all.

"The Lord is not here to destroy but to save. For the—."

Azaziel interrupted. "Perhaps he may be turned?"

The throne room went quiet, and all looked at Azaziel with curious and questioning eyes.

Jerahmeel replied, "He has plotted the overthrow of the Father. He hast committed murder, his hatred for Apollyon hast robbed him of his birthright. He has marched armies into the city to its destruction and authorized the slaying of countless Elohim. Lucifer will not be turned. His cause is to be God, and he will stand for nothing but this goal alone. No—Lucifer is lost."

Azaziel nodded, "Yea, all that thou say is true, yet there are some who report that he seemed reluctant to launch the offensive—perhaps—"

El then spoke and all immediately turned to look upon God.

"To thine credit, I see that thine heart and eye yet feels compassion that Lucifer might be turned. But know that thy brother has left his first estate. But lo, go down if thou must, and see to thy brother. But know of a surety that his time is not yet come. Reason with him that he might repent from his cause and see for thine self that Lucifer is no more. If he hears thee, then bring him before me and if he confesses his sin and turns from his way, then even the Lord is not without mercy. But know this, he is Satan now: the Adversary to my will and his heart has hardened and will not be turned..."

And while the words were still fresh on the Lords' lips, the ground shook violently and the angels wondered if they were again under attack by the enemies of the throne, and El turned solemn as they looked upon him, and he frowned.

"Fear not," said the Lord, "for thy brother's tantrum hast come."

* * *

Lucifer was enraged and raised his fists in anger at the God of Heaven. "El, I curse your name, for though Heaven be denied me, know of a surety that Heaven shall never ignore me!"

Lucifer reached into his robes and took the keys of Death and Hell, and plunged them into the ground, speaking in the angelic tongue.

"Give birth O soil and make thou room.
Though there be no Kiln, arise from thy womb.
O furnace of affliction, forge of anguish, thou seat, and penal see.
Loose thy bands from Heaven
And thy tortured captives with thee!"

When the words of Lucifer had left his lips, a great seal as a dial appeared in the sky and a Ladder opened, and Lucifer could see into the Third Heaven. The mountain of Hell erupted in fire and shook the floor of Heaven and the ground quaked. A great chasm opened under the mountain and Hell erupted and collapsed in on itself and fell as into a great sinkhole.

Citizens sought to escape as once more terror-filled Heaven. Angels traumatized only a week before over Ladders that had fallen from the sky to obliterate them; now grew pale as haunts of their destruction flashed before them. Some froze in fear that once more Heaven was under siege, and many of the populace sought cover as the mountain ejected fire, and a great cloud of smoke sprinted as a wave toward the city, covering the kingdom in darkness. The floor of Heaven exploded and the Cadmime beams and struts which kept the Maelstrom and Heaven at bay from one another collapsed and the ground groaned and opened up to swallow all things that laid atop of it. Once more Heaven felt the sting of death as the collapse of Hell into Heaven's floor sent masses of rock, buildings, and angels sucked into the hurricane winds of the celestial storm. The people cried out in wails for God to save them.

El heard His people's cry, and He spoke, and Heaven righted herself. Yet Hell did not stop her descent, and the great mountain moaned and the sound of boulders scraping against the abrasive touch of rock filled the air, and Hell separated from Heaven and fell as a great star through galaxies, and plummeted toward the small blue world that El had made.

El, knowing that the fall would leave His minted world lifeless spoke and said, "Peace be still." And when He spoke all quakes stopped and angels that had been flung into the Maelstrom were suspended in the air, as if dangling. Each angel hovered momentarily over the Abyss and then was gently moved by the invisible hand of El and placed on solid ground. Where cadmime beams had buckled and strained under the collapse of the great mountain, El's word held Heaven aloft and kept at bay the Maelstrom: that it sheared at Heaven's face no more. Hell continued her descent and hurtled toward the Earth. El slowed the descent of the mountain, and it landed to create a great range of mountains underneath the seas, and the land rose to breathe fire, and El let the mountain fall but in mercy prevented Hell from obliterating the life of men.

El then spoke and said, "Charon dost not possess his keys."

He looked at Michael knowing that his son no longer carried them and then frowned, for he saw that Lucifer stood on the spot of Hell's peak and spoke the command to summon the Warden from his prison.

"My Lord?" said Michael.

"Lucifer hast laid claim to that which thou hast not kept. For he who holds the keys to Death and Hell may on command unleash my vengeance."

Michael's eyes opened wide, and his mouth was agape in horror. "Lord, no! Lucifer cannot be allowed to possess the keys to Death and Hell!"

God watched and His face was grim as the flaming mountain of Hell hissed smoke, fire, and blistering heat.

"He has not stolen the keys, lest they would return on command. But another hast through neglect allowed for their surrender. Thy carelessness of the power of God hast limited the Holy One that I cannot repent of this thing."

"But Lord, Lucifer cannot be allowed to control the vengeance of God and Hell!"

"I have sworn to my own hurt. I AM THE LORD, I changeth not. Nevertheless, your word is true, that he cannot be allowed to hold the keys in perpetuity. For he wilt surely destroy the man that I have made and seek still to usurp that which he can never take. For the keys were given to steward. And the steward hast through neglect ceded them to thy brother."

Michael was silent and saddened by the Lord saying that he neglected the power of God, yet he knew that God was right in his judgment and thoughts of how he might undo that which had been done raced through his mind. However, the rest of the Lumazi was wroth, and demanded who had done such a thing.

El knowing their hearts calmed them, saying, "It is naught but as I have seen. For now, my son must be tested, that the end of all things might come."

Yet Argoth would not cease, and said, "If the Vengeance of God is now held captive by the rebel son, then I pray that my Lord would allow us to go in thy name, and be as vengeance to he who would steal, kill, and destroy."

And the thing which Argoth said displeased the Lord and he spoke to all the Lumazi, "And would you also seek vengeance on he that hast razed our home? Would you seek to apprehend him who wast the anointed cherub that covered that you might bring him before me now?"

Azaziel, the youngest among them, spoke while those older on the council were silent in repose. "Yea Lord, we would have him chained, and Hell be home to him."

Gabriel, Jerahmeel, and Talus stood silent, and Michael set himself to sit on the steps, huddled at the foot of the Lord.

El's face became saddened, and He turned to His son Michael. "And what say you? Wilt you also take up arms to wrest Lucifer from his throne?"

"Nay," said Michael. "I will not leave thy side. Only at thy command will I leave thee. Nor will I forsake thee, for I know what the end must be."

El then looked upon Michael knowingly and then addressed the rest of the Lumazi. "The council is of double mind. Therefore, because ye have yet to comprehend the fullness of time, to understand that in weakness shall ye be made strong, then go to and seek thy desire. Alas, the time has come to commence with thy instruction that ye may know that wisdom belongeth to the Lord."

The Lumazi bowed as one and turned to leave the room, yet Michael stayed to worship at the Lord's feet.

Jerahmeel paused for a moment, turned and spoke. "Lord, might I remain with thee as well?"

"Nay my son, your brothers will need wisdom for the battle to come. Go, that none might be lost."

Jerahmeel turned to go after his brothers as they departed, muttering anxiously to himself, "I have such a bad feeling about this."

* * *

Jerahmeel caught up with Argoth and spoke. "Shall we gather the legions?"

"Nay," said Argoth. "He is but one, we are Lumazi. Lucifer cannot withstand the combined might of the council."

Jerahmeel laughed and heckled Argoth. "Ugh, Argoth you were asleep for most of the war. Believe me, when I say that Lucifer *can* withstand the might of the council."

Argoth turned and stared at Jerahmeel. "You have girth of appetite, but thy courage is small. If you had been more serious in your duties as Heaven's guard perhaps Raphael would still be alive!"

Jerahmeel flinched at the insinuation that he was somehow at fault for Raphael's demise and became bitter in offense and was about to speak when Gabriel moved to interject himself.

"Not now, brother. Not now," he whispered.

Argoth laughed. "Even now you hide behind Gabriel's skirts, come. Show your skill in battle. Let the Legions stay behind. However, keep Gabriel by thy side. I would not see thee injured."

Gabriel looked at Jerahmeel, who was visibly red, and spoke to Argoth. "Mayhap it be best that our focus be on the task at hand. This conversation edifieth not, nor brings us closer to the apprehension of Lucifer. What is your plan?"

Argoth smiled. "Vengeance."

Gabriel looked at the Grigori in disbelief, "But vengeance belongeth to the—"

Jerahmeel now took turn to quiet him and whispered, "He does not know, but he will know shortly." He chuckled, adding, "Let him learn this lesson." The angel turned to Argoth and bowed to him and his lips dripped with sarcasm as he spoke.

"As you saith, great Argoth, you who hast caused God to silence canyons. We shall, of course, follow you."

Gabriel smirked at his brother and shook his head as they walked to the Waypoint to leave Heaven. "You know, sometimes I really wonder about you."

Jerahmeel winked at him, and they stepped into the Ladder's chute and disappeared to the realms below.

* * *

The great mountain of Hell settled into the base of the ocean floor and its peaks jutted into the clouds, towering over the new landscape. Its presence lifted existing mountains even higher, and smoke rose from off the back of the craggy rock face and blended into the barren wilderness. Snow covered its top, and the mountain churned, as magma filled its chambers. The creature burrowed to entrench itself deep into the core of the planet, and the Earth groaned for she was not meant to house this creation from Heaven.

Lucifer stood aloof from the mountain in a plateau and called out to the living crag, for he knew what lived inside.

"Charon, thou hand of vengeance, hear me! You who are bidden to uphold the fury of God—come forth! I command you!"

The keys of Death and Hell glowed around Lucifer's hand, and he fastened them tighter around his neck. The ground shook, and the mountain of Hell exploded. Rock and streaming gas erupted from its side, fire blasted laterally, and the explosion sent wind racing to smash and pulverize trees as boulders hurtled through the air. Lucifer stood defiant as giant boulders fell to the left and the right of him. And when the wind itself had run out of breath, it paused as a man might pause to inhale, then sprinted back from Lucifer's rear, but the First of angels stood his ground as Earth and Shadow moved about him. Deep within the black smolder and flames, trudging through a newly born lake of magma—Charon marched towards the first of angels. The hulking monstrosity of Elomic flesh tread undeterred as pyroclastic flows fell before and aft of him. Solemn was his march as fire lighted upon him, and his chains dredged the ground. Steam hissed from his frame and the air sizzled and moved from the heat that wafted off him.

Charon had heard the cry of Lucifer—and he had come. Standing 20 cubits tall, the skeletal mare was robed in black leather. His cadaverous face was hidden and chains of iron dangled from beneath him. Smoke and ash blanketed his form, and he held a black scythe in his hand. Fiery footprints trailed him, and the pungent stench of decay made everything in his presence wither and die.

Lucifer stood his ground, unmoved and unflinching as the living personification of death walked towards him, stood until the Angel of Death towered over him, staring down upon he who had dared to summon him. Lucifer then spoke.

"You are mighty indeed, oh vengeance of God. Yet know that thy service is no longer to execute the will of El in judgment."

Charon snorted and proceeded to remove from his ashen robes the onyx scythe he held as a trophy from the person of Minos and raised its glistening black blade for Lucifer to see, and spoke.

"Ooooonly Ellll, commmmmannndssss me, Usurper—releassssee Hellll or know that my judgment awaits you." Charon then raised the scythe and pointed it at Lucifer, so that he might strike him down.

Lucifer laughed, "I once told you that you would pay for your insolence and now thy recompense is at hand, for lo by the will of the Almighty, I possess thy leash. El cannot take what hast been abdicated, and thou art mine to command. Am I understood, ferryman?"

Charon roared and raised his scythe to bring it down on Lucifer and when he sought to bring the blade square he lowered the edge to slice Lucifer in two, but the blade bounced inches from him, and Charon was knocked back falling on his hind into the Earth cratering the ground, propelling dust and rock into the sky. The great mare of bone rose to his feet and the rusted chains of barbs shot from his chest and hurtled towards Lucifer, but they too bounced inches from his person as if deflected by an invisible barrier, and Lucifer laughed.

"You will obey me in all things. For on this mote of dust hast El exiled me without means to feed. Thus, I will sustain my hunger off the souls of men. Their very spirit created in the image of God will give me strength. You will aid me in this. For you will help me to tame Hell, and the beast will be the engine of my revenge. For I shall feed her the souls of men, and the thing that El had meant for our destruction I will use to wipe the pestilence of man from off the Earth until Hell is ripe with my armies of men, who will do anything to be released from her bowels. Yea, beast you will assist me in this thing.

"Rise now, slave, and attend to thy master. Go to and release my attendants, for I have need of them that I might bring El low. You will obey me...or I shall see Hell savor thine own flesh even as those you have destroyed. Now go, and do not return except my charges be with thee."

Charon roared in anger, and the birds in the area lifted from the trees as if to escape a predator. Charon smashed his great fists into the ground and looked into the sky and from his black robes, skeletal wings unfurled and spread from him. Fog surrounded him and cloaked him in smoke and ash. Then Death rose into the sky.

Charon's shadow brought darkness as he flew, and his shadow flew over Lucifer he watched the great angel fly to parts unknown. All living things that passed beneath his shadow withered and died. The guardian of Hell landed upon the banks of the river Euphrates, smoke trailing his person, while putrefaction wafted about him, making the air to stink. He placed his scythe into the water, and the water turned foul, sizzling to a boil. Dead fish surfaced fouling the air. Charon stirred his scythe, and the great river then split into two and walled up on either side as the Angel of Death stepped down the banks of the side of the river and walked between the walls of water now raised in the air. Deeper into the trenches of the river's center he traveled until he came upon a cave, and at its mouth sat an Ophanim of the Lord, and the creature rose at the sight of Charon. The beast discharged voltage, and its wheels gyrated and moved, expanding to give it flight. Its unblinking eyes stared upon Charon and with revolving teeth, it roared and flew headlong into the Warden. Fog moved from Charon to engulf the Ophanim and its charge sparked, then flickered to nothing. It fell to the ground and writhed in agony, and the angel of Death grappled the beast with his great arms and constricted the creature against his breast and snapped the spinning creature in two. The Ophanim cried out in pain and shattered falling as broken glass at his feet. The myrmidon continued his march towards the cave, and with his scythe, he sliced into the stone face. The boulder to the entrance divided in half and the rock aged instantaneously and turned to dust before him. Charon entered the black and saw the three prime evils Ashtaroth, Zeus, and Ares chained to one another and cowering before him. Each scooted away, screaming in woe that judgment had come and that the end of all things was nigh.

Charon slashed at their iron bonds and the chains fell to the earthen floor. The trio backed further away from the ferryman, as terror gripped them to behold the Vengeance of God. Then Charon with his tentacled chains ensnared them and manacled by the ferryman, they struggled for release, and Ashtaroth cried aloud, "Where are you taking us? Hast thou come to execute El's final judgment?"

Yet Charon exited the cave in silence, dragging his captives behind him. The water from the river still stood on end and Charon opened his wings and flew back to Lucifer, dangling the trio under him.

And as an eagle settles to her nest, Charon's shadow covered Lucifer and Charon dropped the three who rolled to a stop at the feet of their master, and he spoke, and they looked upon him as Charon landed behind them in a silence, covered in churning flames and ash, scythe in hand.

"Get up," said Lucifer. "We have much work to do."

Ashtaroth looked upon his master and smiled that his Lord still lived and that Charon sided with them, and he looked to behold the great mountain of Hell rumble behind them and knew that in time, they would have their vengeance on the God of Heaven.

* * *

The Lumazi, all save Michael, laddered down to confront Lucifer, each wondering how Lucifer would receive them. Azaziel was hopeful that he might reason with him, to convince him to renounce his course and come home. Metatron was skeptical, however, and knew in his heart that Lucifer would never yield. For Lucifer was the pride of House Draco, the pinnacle of what it once meant to serve the living God in honor and majesty. Now the great house's most powerful symbol of fealty to God had with his betrayal, torn Heaven asunder. Now civil war would always be remembered as a thing that House Draco ushered to Heaven's peaceful shores. Lucifer would burn them all to ash before he ever admitted defeat——ever confess to his sin.

No, thought Metatron. Lucifer had gone too far and was beyond all hope of returning.

How can one turn a creature who hast made God himself enemy? What words can be spoken to he who would supplant the will of the Lord?

Yet he was a member of the Lumazi now, and his was to support the collective cause of the court. He looked at Argoth, so confident, and he had to admit that he admired the Grigori. His was the voice that caused God to bring silence to the great canyon named after him. Metatron was honored to be in his presence. He would fight with him. He respected prince Talus, and the others, but under their leadership, Heaven had launched itself into war. Perhaps Argoth's way was indeed the answer. The others seemed timid to him. As if age and battle had weathered them. Metatron could not quite decipher what ailed him. A gnawing foreboding ate at him about this mission, that perhaps the elder members of the Lumazi knew more than what they had revealed. Gabriel and Jerahmeel did not seem enthused to face their brother. Even Talus, who was strong and mighty seemed somehow diminished; almost timid. Metatron shook himself from his ruminations, realizing that they had arrived.

Argoth spoke, to address his brethren. "Our mission is clear: to bring reason to Lucifer Draco. If he can be turned to our cause, then he will be welcomed home per the Father. But if not, we are to bring him low and return him in chains."

Talus shook his head. "You speak as if you desire to combat Lucifer. I have seen my share of bloodshed; I will not provoke battle with the anointed of God. It is not by our hand that he will be made low. Only El can sunder him, and He has made clear that his time is not yet come. Reason with him if you must, but if battle comes, let it be known that it comes at *thy* hand."

Argoth was silent, not expecting such an answer from one as powerful as Talus, nor daring to correct him, for Talus was more reserved than in times past, quicker to hear, and slower to speak. Nevertheless, he was still imposing, and Argoth carefully selected his words in reply.

"If battle comes, wilt thou let thy brethren be brought low by the Usurper?" All then turned to look at Talus.

Talus sighed and answered, "Nay, I will do what I must to see all home safely to the presence of the Lord. Let us finish this unsavory business." Talus paused, looking sadly at Argoth, and continued, "And may the learning from thy lesson be swift."

Argoth harrumphed and they stood six strong in a clearing surrounded by trees, and the grass was soft under their soled feet, then Argoth spoke.

"Why do you hide, Lucifer? Your powers to conceal are meaningless to me. Show thyself, coward, wretched betrayer of God. Let all eyes be upon you and not just mine alone."

The clearing shimmered and light flashed, and standing in front of the trees stood Lucifer, his three attendants, and Charon. And when the Lumazi saw that Charon stood by Lucifer's side, fear overtook them. For the Vengeance of God was now ally to the Betrayer of God.

"You would do well to mind your tongue, young one," said Lucifer, "Your words give offense, and I do not suffer those who offend me. You are not welcome here. Speak quickly and explain why your stone should not be mine?"

Argoth realized that he had never truly *seen* Lucifer. When he exited the Kiln, he was so enamored by the Lord that Lucifer was but an afterthought. But now remembrance flooded him. Lucifer had stood in the Kiln with the Lord, and Argoth noted that he had changed since then. His body was darker, and his stone was redder than the deepest crimson. His demeanor was far from the submissive cherub he remembered in the Kiln. And there was a scar that lined his face as if he had been cut. His eyes burned with a visible hatred as if he might rip the tongue from Argoth's mouth. Yet despite all of his changes, he still possessed a nobleness about him. He was still regal, and the Grigori suddenly thought it wise to temper his remarks.

"We have come, brother, to speak with thee. For the Father hast offered thee pardon if you will but repent and humble thyself and turn from this wicked way. For such is the heart of God that He would extend forgiveness even to one such as thee. Wilt thou do as the Almighty has said? Will you submit to judgment and mercy, and let restoration overcome thee? For he hast set life and death before thee, wilt thou not choose life that ye might live?"

Azaziel stepped forward and gestured longingly to Lucifer—tears welling in his eyes. "Lucifer, please I adjure thee—come home and bring revival to the heart of the Lord. For He would see the Kingdom united, and His people made whole."

All turned to look at Lucifer as Azaziel knelt before the former Chief Prince, and silence was all that existed between the two groups, and even Ashtaroth, Murmur, and Zeus wondered as to Lucifer's will.

Lucifer smiled, then walked toward Azaziel. "Revival to the heart of the Lord? Revival..." Lucifer laughed. "To his heart?" Lucifer's demeanor turned steely and cold, and he yelled for the ambassadors of Heaven to hear.

"His heart shall melt in my hand. For I will wipe from His beloved man all traces of El's image. I will turn His prized pet against Him so that the stench of man's atrocities will rise to the Heavens, that El by His own hand will be compelled to wipe from this planet the pestilence He Himself hast created. For the man is pliable and possesses ease of turning. And lo, when I am done, the Clayborn will remember El no more. I will erase all remembrance of El from the Man so that naught, but my image and likeness alone will remain. And when the fullness of time hast come, when the knowledge of me is as the sand on the seashore, I will raise Man up and I will be father to him, and he will be *my* son. I will lift Man on high, and he will be vanguard to do battle against the triune God, and we shall have vengeance. El's *'perfection'* will serve me, and I—I will be God! You are right to bow before me brother, for in due season I will exalt my throne to Heaven, and you all will call me *'Father'*."

Azaziel looked at Lucifer in horror and lifted himself from the ground, and with disbelieving ears, he spoke. "The Lucifer I knew, honored, and obeyed is gone. You are indeed Satan. Argoth was right to seek your annihilation."

"What more do we need to hear?" said Argoth. "He is beyond turning; let his end be swift. The time for talk has ended. Arrest him and bring me his head!"

Immediately, Azaziel moved to capture Lucifer, and Lucifer turned his back to his attackers. Murmur leaped forward, barred Azaziel's path, swinging his sword at Azaziel, who parried the blow, and the two angels locked themselves in combat. Argoth pointed at Metatron, and the new Lord of House Draco belted a roar, and Murmur fell to his knees in pain. Zeus and Ares then launched themselves into the air and landed atop Metatron and wrestled with the great angel. They pummeled him and stabbed him with daggers, but Metatron was so strong that the daggers would not pierce his skin, yet his opponents accosted him so that he was occupied.

Argoth, frustrated that the Lumazi would be hindered, entered the fray, but before he could reach Lucifer, Ashtaroth barred him. Argoth misted behind him, but the other angel quickly spun, and when the Grigori solidified, Ashtaroth unleashed two curved blades and slashed at Argoth, cutting him. Argoth screamed in pain, for he had not turned to face Ashtaroth, thinking that he had evaded his opponent. But Ashtaroth was there when he reformed, caught him with his blade, and had drawn blood.

"How foolish is the Lumazi?" said Ashtaroth. "We have held Raphael's inkhorn and stylus and been tutored by Lilith himself; your tricks will not avail you here."

Argoth turned to face Ashtaroth who moved to again bar him from his master. Lucifer continued to walk away, indifferent to the skirmishes behind him.

Argoth cried aloud after him. "Why do you hide behind your shield? Are you afraid to contend with the might of the Lumazi? For with thy sin with Apollyon no longer secret, to what owest thou fear? Ye who would be God!"

Lucifer stopped walking and, knowing he was provoked, smiled. He turned to face Argoth and his brethren. Then lifted his hand, "Hold servants, cease from thy attack."

Immediately, Murmur, Zeus, Ares, and Ashtaroth ceased hostilities and backed away to return to their master. Lucifer motioned them to his rearward, and they moved to stand behind him.

"Do all the Lumazi believe that ye might upend me?" said Lucifer.

Gabriel, Talus, and Jerahmeel held their peace. For they knew that Lucifer could not be brought down through arms alone, and had not entered the fray, seeing Lucifer had not provoked them to battle.

"I see...," said Lucifer. "So, El would have me to be a schoolmaster. Once again I find myself doing the bidding that the so-called 'Godking' cannot do Himself." Lucifer chuckled. "Very well, then come and let the lesson begin." Immediately Argoth, Azaziel, and Metatron, leapt to attack him.

Azaziel lifted himself into the sky and thought to bring his sword down hard atop Lucifer. However, Lucifer lifted himself to meet him and dodged Azaziel's blow. The angel then grabbed him by his wrist and swung him into an uncontrolled descent into Argoth. Argoth misted to avoid being struck, Azaziel smashed into Metatron who stood behind Argoth, and the two crashed into the ground, raising plumes of dirt into the air knocking Azaziel unconscious.

Argoth moved to attack Lucifer, punching, and lunging to strike at him. Lucifer weaved to his right and then to his left as he backed away from Argoth. And every time that Argoth went to reach for him, Lucifer slipped from his grasp.

Ares laughed, "The Grigori cannot even touch the master!"

Ashtaroth then taunted Talus, Jerahmeel, and Gabriel. "Why dost the whole Lumazi not attack our Lord? Do you cower from he who hast bled God?"

Immediately, Gabriel vanished, then materialized within arm's reach facing Ashtaroth, his staff inches from Ashtoreth's, face ready to pummel him. His swiftness caught Ashtaroth off guard, and he stumbled backward and fell on his rear.

Gabriel towered over him and spoke. "On the day that I would choose to engage thee in battle, know of a surety that you would never see my hand smite thee." Gabriel then vanished and reappeared standing next to his brethren, and they watched as Lucifer continued to battle their younger siblings.

Murmur, Zeus, and Ares laughed at Ashtaroth; his cheeks flushed for having fallen before the Lord Prince of Malakim. He stood to his feet and shoved Murmur, who mocked him.

"Silence!" Ashtaroth growled.

Metatron raised himself from the ground, rolling the unconscious Azaziel from off him. He noted that Lucifer's servants did not aid their master and that the senior Lumazi stood aloof. All watched Argoth attempt to strike at Lucifer, and the king of rebellion just walked slowly backward as he ducked and weaved, avoiding Argoth's touch, toying with the angel. Metatron then hurtled himself into the air and from above unleashed a sonic wave that rained down upon the Chief Prince. Lucifer staggered backward and echoed his own blast, canceling out the concussive force. Argoth fell upon him, for Metatron's attack gave him time to bridge the distance to lay hold on the rebel prince. Argoth misted, and as a living gas entered the openings to Lucifer's innards and began to solidify from within.

Lucifer screamed in pain, and the blast from his cry sent a concentric wave from his person that flung out in all directions, knocking everyone off their feet.

Incensed, the fallen angel inhaled and then exhaled, and a great wind rushed from his mouth, revealing the gaseous form of Argoth. Argoth immediately materialized and continued to move toward Lucifer in concert with Metatron, who narrowed the gap and drew his sword.

"You have now succeeded in annoying me. Enough," Lucifer said.

Lucifer's living armor scaled over his person, and he hurled himself at Metatron.

Metatron braced himself as he fell backward. Lucifer pressed his attack as sonic waves surrounded his arms and light emanated from his person so that no one could see. With brute strength, he brought his armored and cloven fist hard on the leg of Metatron, shattering the bones. The angel cried out in agony. Lucifer then reached for his back and tore a ligament from Metatron's wing, yet not enough to detach it and make him lame. Metatron screamed and collapsed to the ground.

His main threat now disabled, Lucifer moved as light to assault Argoth. Argoth failed to mist, not accustomed to such speed, and Lucifer was upon him as a lion atop helpless prey. Argoth misted, thinking he could escape, but Lucifer reached for his quarry's chest. The colors of his skin were mesmerizing that Argoth found he could not look away, and Lucifer held him by the throat despite the misting and spoke.

"I am he who has walked atop thy stone. Even misted, thy form gives off light and thus enables me to handle thee. For among all angels in Heaven I alone am able to hold light itself in my grasp. Your powers are nothing to me."

Lucifer's talons unsheathed from his hand and he raised his fist to smash against the terrified Argoth.

"Enough!" cried Gabriel. "Lucifer, they have had enough! Cease with thy lesson!"

Lucifer paused and glanced back at Gabriel, then back to Argoth who quivered in his grasp, and smiled. "Indeed."

Lucifer held Argoth by his collar and spoke softly to him. "Thou art a tired excuse to be stead holder for Raphael. Did you think that by *your* hand *I* would be felled? That by *your* might I might be brought low? I have walked upon the Argonite and Oxygen stones from whence thou wast taken. Only El hast power to upend me and even He will not risk destruction to His children to do so. I have held the very tome of Raphael in my hands. Yet even *I* did not bring him to naught. But you—you I hold in no such regard. Remove thyself from my sight. For if the shadow of thy presence but crosses me again. I will confiscate thy stone from your gaseous chest and wear it as a diadem around my neck." Lucifer then released him.

Argoth backed away, cowering, afraid at the might of Lucifer to bring dissolution to him even while misted. Jerahmeel reached to help him up and Argoth pushed his hand away, for he had been humbled in all their sight, and he rose to his feet then laddered himself away. Azaziel awoke from his daze and went to the aid of Metatron, and they too laddered away. Lucifer stood alone in the center of the clearing. Charon, who stood yards away and Lucifer's lieutenants watched from afar. The prince gazed upon his former brethren, and the three senior brothers looked at Lucifer: each group standing mute. Their eyes alone spoke in volumes of words and feelings: feelings that now could never be verbally expressed. Each grim face looked upon each other in an exchange of body language that communicated respect, and forewarning. A silent conversation that in the future they would settle all differences between them...differences that would only be settled in blood.

Lucifer nodded to them, and the trio nodded in return. Lucifer smiled and returned to his followers, motioning for the myrmidon to follow. Charon turned to attend to his master, and Lucifer covered his entourage in blinding light and was gone.

Jerahmeel looked behind him and noticed that Metatron and Azaziel had already returned to the realm immortal. Jerahmeel looked at Talus and Gabriel and spoke.

"Youngin's—can't tell 'em nothing."

* * *

The Lumazi knelt before the Lord of all things. Solemn, quiet—defeated.

"Report of thy stewardship," commanded the Lord God.

Michael still worshiped at the Lord's feet, and from his position looked at his brethren, curious to know how they fared. For Lucifer did not stand before them in chains, but when he looked at Gabriel, his brother shook his head for Michael to remain silent.

Talus was first to speak. "My king, it pains me to report..." The Lord lifted his hand to silence Talus, and Talus immediately went mute. "Azaziel, what were your brother's words at the suggestion of pardon?"

Azaziel looked up at God, then bowed his head and refused to look the Lord in the eye. "I—he—Satan hast rejected thee, my Lord. He will not be turned."

The Lord sighed. "Did I not say that thy brother is no more and that what remains is but a shadow of whom he wast before? Why then didst thou doubt?" Azaziel was silent to the Lord's query and knew that he had no answer to give to the Almighty.

"Argoth, report of thy stewardship. If thy brother would not yield, why is he not in chains before me?"

Argoth trembled before the Lord as he spoke. "My king, the Usurper commands the Vengeance of God! How can one such as I do battle with God!"

The Lord replied, "Even now, you would face me in pride? Even now, knowing that pride leadeth thee to destruction. As I liveth, you shall at great cost learn the lesson that Iofiel in revelation shared with thy brother Michael.

"For what doth the Lord require of thee but to do justice, love kindness, and to walk humbly with your God? Yet you have sought to upturn the Adversary with the same means that he himself would use to upturn me. Only in weakness will thy brother be brought low. For if you exalt yourself you shall be abased. But if thou humblest thyself, thou shalt be exalted. There is no room for pride at my feet, Lumazi. No shade for haughtiness, for only he that would surrender all can defeat thy brother. You do not yet know the cost that must be endured to bring him low and to succor the Heavens from his influence. For not many days hence, I will be lifted up, that I might draw all men unto me."

Argoth was shamed, for he knew that he spoke amiss, for though God had indeed silenced canyons, He would also silence all haughtiness that would also try to speak.

God continued, "Lucifer even now conceives abomination, to tempt the Holy One. For he knowest not that he but makes a causeway to rescue the man. Jerahmeel, go to and watch over a man by the name of Jared. He will bear a son that will be a champion for me. Go down and see to the man's welfare. For in time, thine brother will see what I have seen and will see to the destruction of the child the man would bear. Behold, for a generation shalt thou, be a shield to him. When the fullness of time has come, I will then take Enoch from thy charge that he might serve as candlestick before me."

Jerahmeel was taken aback that a man would be a candlestick. "You mean to bring this man Enoch to stand as a light before thy presence?"

"Aye, my son. Now go and wait with Jared until I come for the lad."

Jerahmeel then bowed and left the presence of the Lord in wonderment of what would cause God to bring a man to Heaven.

* * *

Michael left the throne pondering all the words the Lord had spoken and met with Argoth to discuss matters of state.

"Have you come to gloat, Chief Prince? To scold me for thinking that I might bring Lucifer low?"

"No," said Michael, "You do not entirely despise correction. There remains hope that you will grow in the knowledge of the Lord. No, Argoth, I have reasoned that there are some lessons that can only be taught through pain. I perceive a similar lesson will never be needed by thee again."

Argoth nodded. "Then what brings the *Prince* of Kortai to the Hall of Annals?"

Michael was taken back by the sarcasm and replied, "To what do I owe such derision that you would speak to me thus? If I am a prince, then where is my honor? If I be a chief, then where is my fear?"

"Aye, a high prince you may be. However, it remains to be seen if you are worthy in the eyes of the people to rule. Though thou hast fought Lucifer himself to stand-still, you are not the Lightbringer. You have much to atone. For under the watch of the Lumazi was Heaven laid low. Why then should any of Heaven's people show thee honor?"

Michael paused and was slow to speak. There was much to the words of Argoth he could not dispute. He closed his eyes and lowered his gaze to the floor, pondering his words carefully, then spoke.

"To lead Heaven is not my desire. For, I am but a servant, and ever shall be to the cause of El. Nevertheless, I am the last to walk on the stones of thy birth. I stand as he who holds title of 'Dragon Slayer', and El himself hast chosen to elevate me to Chief Prince, not I. Therefore, if thou hast issue with my selection to ascension, then your quarrel is with the Almighty himself. For there is no power in Creation save that which El allows, and the powers that be are ordained by God. Therefore, to rebel is to resist not I, but the Lord God himself..." Michael then unsheathed the sword of Ophanim and pointed it at Argoth. "And rebellion against the Lord hast a heavy price in blood."

Argoth raised his hands before him and motioned surrender to Michael. "Sheath thy sword, High Prince. Rebellion to El does not live here. How might the Hall of Annals serve thee?"

"I seek your assistance," said Michael, "For I am greatly disturbed concerning the safety of El. The Godhead bleeds, and there still yet lurks danger to El himself. Danger that He hast shown me, danger, that I am pledged to prevent even to the laying down of my life."

Argoth harrumphed, "Danger to El...preposterous! The thing cannot be as you say."

"Nevertheless, I have been given a prophecy by El. He has shown me images of what I believe to be of that, which is come."

Argoth looked amazed. "Truly... for only the Grigori hast been given sight to on occasion glimpse the future. Yet you say El has shown you things to come?"

Michael nodded. "It is unclear what I have been shown. I... I have yet to come to grips with what I have seen. For to be Chief Prince is to hold to a secret of God. Yet I find that I must seek counsel and reveal this matter. For perhaps my understanding is not what El would have me to believe. Thus, I come to you, that out of the mouth of two or three may the thing be established. Yet my words do not take alone, for does not my Grigori record all? Let my ledger be proof to thee where my own words do not suffice, and testimony of thy own people ring true if you doubt my word. Recall my Grigori's tome and reference the Day of Descension and my conversation with El after Lucifer's exile."

Argoth stood unconvinced, yet did as Michael commanded, and turned to speak to the Hall, giving it a command to image. "Regress to the Day of Descension, display Michael Kortai's conversation with El."

Walls flashed around them and immediately the whiteness dropped away, and they were standing on the steps of the mountain of God. God had exiled a third of Heaven to the celestial realm below, and Michael saw the image of himself as El touched his forehead. The scene triggered grief and pain. He staggered to a knee and grimaced as he remembered the day, and anguish rushed to embrace him, smothering him in angst.

Argoth looked at him in concern. "Are you all right?"

"It is nothing," said Michael, though his words were heavy. "...Continue."

Argoth motioned for the record to resume and watched Michael's past splayed in color, sound and smell before him. He watched as El walked back to take His place on the throne.

"Will not the judge of all the realms do right?" the image of Michael said.

Each watched as the Lord sighed and turned to His son. In the Hall of Annals, Michael turned his back to the display, closing his eyes. Argoth continued to watch his brother out of the corner of his eye but focused on the image as El touched Michael's mind and revealed to him all that would transpire.

"See, O beloved of angels, the things that are yet to come," said the image of El.

A shimmering globe appeared in El's hands, and Michael's image gazed into the giant crystal. It displayed pictures similar to the walls within the Hall of Grigoric records, but these images were different. For the Earth below was populated with humans, and they multiplied as the stars in the sky. Argoth watched as hundreds of thousands of humans escaped a land that had kept them in slavery for 400 years, brought out by the mighty hand of the Lord as the seas swallowed their pursuers.

Moreover, men named Abraham, Isaac, Jacob, and David lived and died to serve El's purpose, and Argoth noted that they fought to scrape out holiness in lands that had begun to worship the very ones El had just ejected. Many a nation rose and fell by the command of the Lord. Finally, the image revealed a man whipped and beaten, and a crown of thorns was placed on his head. Argoth winced as the man was whipped, and flogged, as flesh was torn from his lacerated back. Argoth then beheld what Michael had seen, as he looked deep into the eyes of the man that hung on a cross. He watched as the man pushed his body upwards on the wooden beam from which he hung, and the Grigori stared with recognition of the identity of the man. The eyes of the man told him all that he needed to know. Argoth became wroth.

"The man is El! Michael, the man is El!"

Michael said nothing, his back still turned from the sight now displayed spectacularly in three dimensions.

"Cease record," commanded Argoth, and the wall stopped and flashed white.

Argoth walked over to Michael, grabbed his shoulder and forced him to look at him. "You have known this since the day of wrath, and you have said nothing... nothing!"

Michael finally looked at his brother, meeting his eyes sadly. "What would you have me say? And to whom would I share my vision?"

Argoth was silent, his mouth looking for words to speak, then after a moment broke the hush that stood between them. "Why then come to me with this?"

"I have a charge for you and a select group of thy kind," said Michael.

Argoth looked upon him curiously. "And what would you have of me?"

Michael responded, "Do what only thy kind can do...watch."

Argoth smirked. "Then you ask for nothing, for which we are not already called to do."

"Aye," said Michael, "Yet you shall watch for a sign, for there shall arise a nation from the race of men not many days hence, and they shall not fear God as God, and shall devise a means to murder not known to men at this time. For they shall use this to kill...," Michael then made a gesture of the sign of a cross with his fingers. "Watch the nation that uses such machinations, and when the nation is found, bring such knowledge to me."

Argoth nodded, "The thing will be as you say - and what will you do?" asked Argoth

Michael's face became hard, and his voice became cold. "Any nation of men, though they are kindred to us, that rises to lift the God of Heaven on a cross will be brought to dissolution, and I shall personally scatter it to the corners of the Earth that none may ever rebuild it again."

Argoth was taken aback to hear such words come from him, "You would make war with Man?" asked Argoth.

"Nay," replied Michael. "Nevertheless, my responsibility is to El, and I will not see him come to harm. Are you clear in your purpose?"

Argoth placed his hand to chin and nodded. "I am clear. I will do as thou hast asked."

Michael looked at him and replied, "Good, Adamson must never be allowed to bring death to God. You have borne witness to the Holy One's absence. What pray tell would happen to creation if perchance His death were accomplished?"

Argoth nodded in agreement. "The thing is unthinkable. All things are upheld by the word of his power, never again can the presence of El be lost. I will do as thou sayest. But what of thee? What will you do?"

Michael turned and spoke over his shoulder. "Make preparation to lay waste to the next angel or man who would dare raise hand to God."

Argoth watched as Michael walked away, then when the prince was gone, he called his lieutenants to counsel and beheld them. Each moved as mist in the wind. They were three strong, and their names were Rorex, Isidor, and Turiel. Their cowled faces blurred as they hovered silently, waiting for a command.

"I have summoned you here, as you are chief among our brethren in faithfulness to the Word. Despite a war of our kind, you have stood as beacon and scribes attending to the Book of Life. *We* bear witness to all things, for it is our lot to give to El on the day that He commands the Books of Life.

"But lo, there are members of our number who have fallen into commentary. To give a diagnosis to that which requires but observation...this cannot be. Therefore, go in the name of the Lord of Hosts, do the bidding of thy master and bring correction to the tomes of our people. Seek out and review all those fallen out of the way. If they shall agree to revision of their tomes, then leave them at peace. But if not, then you shall proceed with redaction. Strike from the record that which counters the living word; confiscate the pens of libel and slander, and erase from existence the lies of the Fallen.

"Behold, I give unto you power to blot out that which countermands the Word. Retract that which is false and redact the lives of those who write falsely. Harvest the tomes of the Fallen as thy bounty. Now go and bring erasure to the stain of our people."

Rorex, Isidor, and Turiel bowed in unison. Argoth then spoke the words to open a doorway to the lower realms. The three angels misted and floated away as fog along the ground, a silent oncoming cloud of dissolution to all Grigori errant in the way.

* * *

El looked from his throne, and He weighed the hearts of His people. For they remained steadfast to his purpose. All were intent on restoring Heaven to her former glory. Yet when El looked, mirth song and joy had seeped as escaping gas from the realm immortal. For the hearts of His people were heavy. And the Lord had compassion on His angels, for all had lost a brother to the Descension. Therefore, El purposed that unity, consolation, peace, and merriment would be heard again in the land of Heaven. So, he looked about the realm for who He might find to work with Him in the thing. And when His eyes searched all the realm, he found one angel whose heart bordered on the fringe of despair and spoke to him. "Hail, Jehoel, doest thou well to be heavy, that my choir master doth not sing?"

And Jehoel was sore afraid, for he stood in the presence of God, and he bowed himself to worship. "Forgive me, my Lord. I am solemn for the loss of my brethren."

El dimmed in brightness and stood next to Jehoel as an old man of many years and spoke. "Ahh. You dwell on loss. The thoughts of thine heart, my son, dwell on what is made of ether. Indeed, there are those you have left behind to follow me. Heaven hast been emptied of many of her children. And the loss of thy brother's fellowship hangs even now as a cloud over thee. Yet know that there is not one among you who hast sided with our cause who shall not receive manifold more in this present time, and in the world to come. For even now our family shall be made strong and know that there will come many a new brother and sister and joy shall be as water that falls from the sky. I will surely do this thing, and the word is sure to come."

Yet Jehoel would not be comforted, and answered, "But why could thou not just change his heart, God? He – I – am angry with you, angry that you allowed this to happen. Angry that you were not here. For if you had been here, my brother would not have died."

And the words touched El, that He wept.

The Almighty then embraced His creation, this angel who spoke in hurt, and Jehoel knew the answers to his inquiries as El silently embraced him, and the Lord spoke. "I too will miss my children, and it pains me that they have chosen to leave my side. Yet I have set before thy kind life and death, blessing and cursing. Would I take from thee that which animates thy stone? Would you have me make thee an automaton?" The Lord then released him and took his face in his palms, and spoke, "Yea, though there be loss of the realm's children, I am the resurrection and the life. He believes that in me shall never die. Believest thou this?"

Jehoel looked into the loving eyes of his creator and replied, "Aye, Lord," said Jehoel. "Thou art life eternal."

Then Jehoel's Heartstone burned within him at the words spoken, and the presence of God melted all doubt and brought him comfort. "My king is good and sees to the welfare of his servant." Jehoel then lifted himself from his chair and reached to return a book of sheet music to a shelf that had toppled over during the war, and then he spoke. "What might thy servant do to honor his king?"

El smiled and looked at his son. "Hast thou eaten yet?"

"Nay, Lord," said Jehoel.

El answered, "Come and I wilt show you how to make a stew from the manna leaf you have, and when you are done. I will teach thee a new song to sing." And Jehoel and the Creator of the universe sat in his house, broke bread together, and God in His own voice sung to an angel and gave comfort to His son's grief.

* * *

Lucifer went up to a mountaintop and viewed the land roundabout. For many of the Clayborn had settled near a valley and had called the place Megiddo. Lucifer eyed the humans, deep in thought. Ashtaroth observed him and spoke. "What is it, my Lord?"

Lucifer was slow to reply. "El commands from the throne, and His command of the legions is strong. To have our revenge, He must come down. I must pull Him to this realm, strip Him from

His position from on high to contend with me on a field of my choosing, to garner His attention, that he would have no choice but to leave Heaven."

"But how," said Ashtaroth. "Why would El come here?"

Lucifer eyed the valley. "This will be where we shall make our stand, not many days hence. I will gather those remaining who art loyal to our cause, and will gather the forces of men, and here we shall lay low Heaven. El possesses the high ground, and we cannot attack Him in the Third Heaven. We must provide Him need for visitation to this mote, and when Michael's lackeys come, we will whittle away at their strength. Heaven must be made to empty herself. Yea—this shall be the place of my choosing."

Ashtaroth eyed the valley and the men who had settled in the small city. "The Clayborn are as ants; they have settled to guard the western branch of a narrow pass and have sought trade connecting Egyptia and Assyr. They are predictable in their movement, and they settle near sources of water."

Lucifer nodded, "Indeed," he said. "The water directs them, for they know to abide near provision. Likewise, we also must find food to sustain us. I have noted that the spirit of man is as our stones. Though wrapped in flesh, the man is indeed, in essence, spirit. We will feed off man's spirit. Hell, hast provided us lesson. The man can be home for us. His spirit can be tainted that we might feed; moreover, Hell hath need of sustenance. The souls of men can serve as kindling to fire her hunger, lest she run amok and feed off us. Charon keeps the beast at bay, and he above all does the mountain respect. We must use the humans, or we will fall. We must replenish our ranks for we are sprawled throughout the realms, and many of our brethren are locked in chains of darkness and flung to the furthest reaches of the universe. A new army I must raise. A new source to attack the flank of El."

Ashtaroth and the others stared at their master as he surveyed the land and looked at the settlement of men. "You intend to use the man to fight El?" Ares asked.

"Indeed," replied Lucifer. "El hast prophesied that the seed of the woman shall bring me low. I will not let this come to pass. For we will pollute the man's bloodline and build a race that can Ladder into Heaven. We will elevate the man to almost that of us, and with them, we shall wage war in Heaven."

Ashtaroth looked at his master. "Pollute their bloodline... how?"

Lucifer smirked. "There can be no seed raised up against me, not if I plant my own seed to be as tare to that which El hast grown. For once our seed has risen in man, El cannot pluck up His Creation lest He root up the wheat with the tare.

"Charon, I have minions, many that must be loosed. You will search this planet. From the ocean floor to the crevices of its depths, you shall find them wherever El hast hid them. Find them, slave, and bring them to me."

Charon hesitated to move, and Lucifer gave him a look of warning. The Angel of Death snorted, eyed the four angels he had already loosed, and with socketless eyes spread his great black wings and lifted once again into the air, and Death took wing to release from their prisons the felons of Heaven.

* * *

Charon did as bidden and loosed from across the earth those who had served Lucifer. From the height of towering mountains to the abyssal depths of the ocean floor, he released Lucifer's servants from the snares of El's prisons. And as men populated the face of the Earth, so too did Lucifer sever the fallen from bondage that they grew in number, minions whose anger over their exile knew no bounds. Each was now stranded on the Earth barred from returning home. And in the span of time, Lucifer gathered them all to council and spoke.

"You are here because El hast judged us to exile. An exile that hast bound us to this mote to dwell in caverns of dust and shackled in the deep trenches of the seas. He hast chained us in grottos of lava and flame...but now we are free! Free to seek vengeance! Free to smite at the heart of the Almighty!"

The angels roared in approval, raising fists in the air as heads nodded in anger and anticipation to strike back at Heaven. Lucifer raised his hands, and the group quieted.

"As many of you know, this land does not grow the food that we consume but fear not. I have found us nourishment——we shall feed off the humans." He smiled at his own ingenuity.

Gasps echoed in the room, and an Issi warrior raised his hand to speak. Lucifer acknowledged him. "My Lord, you would have us consume the image of God? Will not El mark us for dissolution? Would you do such a thing to provoke the Almighty?"

Lucifer walked among his people, saying, "We are at war. I will do what must be done to survive. For the very spirit that animates the humans also powers our stones. Yea, we shall indeed feed off the image of God, and moreover, we shall send the object of God's love to the very prison El has prepared for us. Hell, itself shall feed off the life of men, and we shall with this offering keep the monster in check. For behold how a prison and weapon made from angels will under my power bring torment to the object of God's love. We will strike at Him and El will melt as His clay chattel weeps in utter darkness and the gnashing of teeth. See how the Vengeance of God stands at my side, and it is I that controls Death itself, for the Warden serves me and shall enforce my will in the Earth."

Manny nodded, emboldened by Lucifer's words and seeing how Charon had freed them.

Ares stood up to speak. "Lord, do not be angry with thy servant, as you have made me thy strategist in manners of war. The thing that you say is plausible, yet what would you have us do? For though we are free, famine rages among us. How is it that the Adam can sustain us?"

Lucifer smiled, "El hast given the man free will. He is Clayborn and possesses ease of turning. El hast given the man long life. For I have brought a plague of sin to the man, and his contagion of sin shall make him even the more easy to surrender to our devices. For his sins make him his soul palatable for Hell, and from her we may feed. For the creature Hell doth not destroy life but preserves it alive that she might suckle and sustain her captives' torment. We shall feed Hell the souls of men, and she, in turn, shall feed us. But as we are great in number and the man is yet mortal, we must harvest many souls. We shall make the man worship us, as he should have from the beginning. We shall displace his love for El and turn it toward us, and with Death seal his doom to abide in Hell and engine our lives. Therefore, go and amaze the man that he might know that we are his Gods, and cause him to live unto thee. Move sky and sea, wilt crop and womb, touch the man, and if he obeys, prosper him, but never satiate him fully. He must come to depend on your benevolence. Make him shed blood to thee, for his sons must never give rise to Shiloh.

"For El believes the man capable of upending us. This must never be. Follow the pattern that I have set, and make the male dominate the female, set young against old and use their hues and shade of skin to divide them. Raise up among them great ones, and those of low estate plant greed and envy in their ranks. Sow fear and distrust amongst them, that they never see the unity of worship to El. For distrust is stronger than trust, and envy more than adulation. This I have learned when the Eve failed to follow her charge. Establish among their people charges of thine own design that move them away from the purposes of El's in the Earth. Let them breed to provide us food and soldiers that will one day strike at Heaven. And watch as their sin shall pass from the father to the son, and they shall self-fuel iniquity in the Earth. And when their sin is spread across all nations and tongues, we shall bring both them and Heaven low and, in the end, we shall be made strong!"

The throng of the fallen roared in approval and cheered and chanted Lucifer's name. "Lucifer! Lucifer!"

Lucifer lifted up his hands, smiling and soaking in the praise of his people, then spoke.

"Now go to and let men know that we watch them. Show them that we are nearer to them than the God of Heaven. Teach them to obey thee, that our name not perish from the Earth."

And the thing was done as Lucifer commanded, and angels lifted themselves and flew to all dwelling places of men and showed themselves as great ones, and angels taught man all manner of cunning and craftsmanship and gave him forbidden knowledge to summon the Fallen. Lucifer released with the keys of Death and Hell changed Elohim to go and find bodies that they might possess them. And men became house to many of the Hellspawn who had defied God in vengeance and whose bodies were now deformed from their former state, for Hell had consumed their flesh and left little but the spirit and stones so that they sought out the bodies of men to find expression in the earth. But the shell of men proved too confining to those who once traveled the realms and men scratched at themselves and went mad for what the dispossessed showed them.

And lore rose among man, of beings who lived within men and granted them strength and knowledge and sorcerous power otherwise not available to him, and men named the beings Demons. And the demons lived within men, and gave men great strength and knowledge, but each vessel soon was used up, for only so many of the dispossessed could make their home within the body of a man. The Fallen spread throughout the Earth and fell as a plague upon man and smote men and shed his blood. And angels introduced all manner of sin and wickedness among men, and spoke to men through animals, and trees, and even those Grigori that fell interfered with men, and taught him writing of angelic lore and dark manner of sorceries to record and to change the story of his creation.

But one angel by the name of Molech was more zealous than his brethren and caused men to sacrifice their children in the fire and to spill the blood of women while they were still with child. And Lucifer was pleased over the thing for the children's spirits were pure and undefiled, and though he could not feed off the little ones, for they had no sin of conscience, the men and parents who sacrificed them were not so, and he slaughtered them that they were damned to Hell, and Lucifer fed off the man's misery, and angelkind became strong. Lucifer commanded the Fallen to follow the example of his servant Molech and make Man give blood sacrifice, and men did so.

Thus, Lucifer eyed the children of men and watched over man's blood that it would never give birth to Shiloh, the one who would smite him, in accordance with El's word. For Lucifer knew that if man cooperated with El that El's will would be established in the Earth. So Lucifer obsessed over men so that he destroyed his seed if ever a glimmer of El's image manifested in a child

* * *

The Lord God summoned Talus to his presence

Talus stepped into the throne room his steps heavy as he entered the presence of the Lord.

Will I be stripped of my rank?

He bowed as was custom and waited for the Lord of Heaven to speak.

"Talus Arelim, Chief of House Arelim. Thou art called to give an account of thy actions as Chief Prince. You have been weighed in the balance and hast been found lacking. You will submit to examination."

Immediately, the throne disappeared, and Talus stood before the triune God, and to His right were Grigori, who recorded all that was around them. To Talus's left were members of his own house who watched him. Above was a spotlight that shown upon him. Then El spoke from the darkness.

"I am the LORD thy GOD. But who art thou and what is *thy* name?"

"I am Talus my Lord, thy servant chosen by thee from the Kiln. I serve at the pleasure of my Lord."

"Thou art indeed made from the furnace of our Kiln. Talus thou hast also named rightly, but art thou the *servant* of the Lord?"

And the query struck Talus, for he was grieved that the Lord asked him if he was his servant.

"Aye, Lord, thy servant I am," he replied.

Hushed whispers came from his left, as members of his house muttered in muffled undertones. The Grigori also stopped their pens for a moment. But only briefly, and then continued in their stenographic endeavors.

"You claim to be my servant, but are ye not *Golem*?"

Immediately color blazed about him and images of Sasheal appeared before Talus's eyes. In three dimensions all witnessed as the Grigoric scrolls revealed the record of Sasheal's plummet into a solar flare and the stripping away of the celestial shell that was his body that he might interact with the solar flare. Heroically he endured the blast of heat and gas projected at the speed of light, until nothing was left but a charcoal shell, plummeting to the ground, void of life.

Talus grimaced at the sight and became angry. "Why am I shown this? To what end dost this give examination of me as Prince of my house?"

Gasps and more whispers echoed from the darkness beyond him. Mutterings of, "Does he question the Lord?" could be heard from faceless voices away from him.

The Lord gave no reply and a spotlight shown from above the room and fell on the throne of God. God was not seated on the throne and the two cherubim which covered the mercy seat moved. Slowly they stretched their great wings as if awakening from a long slumber and both flew from their perch upon God's throne and stood before Talus, and were silent before him, and Talus became wroth.

"Why hast thou come down from the Mercy Seat? Did I not command that ye should cover the throne of God? For above all people thou hast been honored to provide cover to the God that is Light. Who art thou that thou would not obey the command of thy prince!"

Zarall and Jael were the two cherubs from house Arelim assigned to cover the mercy seat and spoke as one. "Art thou not Golem?" And as soon as they had finished speaking, they vanished before his eyes and the light that covered the throne of God was also gone.

Talus, puzzled, turned to his left to look for his people and they too were gone, and none but the Grigori stood in the throne room with him in the darkness. Each hovered in ghostlike silence. A circle of beings looking down upon him whose faces were cowled in black. Then they too spoke in whispered haunts, "Are ye not Golem?" Image after image they showed Talus presiding over Sasheal's body, yet Talus in each picture never showed emotion. He stood as a statue, looking at the glimmering body that would become the statue of light El had created. Image after countless images of Sasheal's face was paraded before him, and the Watchers watched for any sign of emotion. Any sign of grief - yet with each passing picture of the angel who had saved Earth, Talus was sullen and spoke not a word, nor shed a tear for him, and when the Grigori had finished in their hovering displays of cinema, they spoke as one man. They pointed with gaseous fingers at the face of Talus, which stood stoic in an image above his head and spoke in affirmative declaration.

"Are ye not Golem?"

Immediately light returned all about him and the virtues floated as before, perfuming the throne. El sat within the Mercy Seat and Zarall and Jael covered the throne with wings outstretched as before. Talus looked down at his hands and they were shaking, as the witness of the death of Sasheal dredged up emotions that he thought he had suppressed, emotions of anger that El had not intervened to save him. Hurt that the first angels to see dissolution had come from his house. Wave after wave of regret, shame, and guilt swept over him. His head wracked with questions of how he might have prevented Apollyon's turn to Abaddon.

Self—condemnation wrapped in constrictive coils of disgrace and blame squeezed to press emotion from him. He began to lose equilibrium and his head dizzied with self—recriminations, over how he could have trained Apollyon and Sasheal differently. Talus then collapsed to his knees before the Lord and his hands gripped the crystal floor to cease the feeling of vertigo, which now overwhelmed him. Nausea swept over him and his belly ached. Yet he would not release the emotions before his God nor shed tears. He would carry this burden and pay the price of his actions of his house. For he represented all Arelim, and God had brought him here for an account. He would, in his own strength, shoulder the weight that plagued him.

"I am strong," he told himself and on bended knee, he said through gritted teeth, "I am a mover of stars."

His chest felt heavy as if an invisible and crushing weight stood atop his sternum, his heartstone pounded and raced within him, and it seemed to splinter as if it would explode into powder. Yet still no tears would come from his eye, no confession to the Lord of what ailed him. Only the straining declaration that left his mouth - "I am the high prince of house Arelim." Hunched over on bended knee with great drops of sweat beading from his brow, he looked up at El in agony.

The Lord God looked upon Talus, frowning in sadness, then spoke softly to His son.

"Are ye not indeed Golem?"

"Arrrrggghhhhh!" Talus screamed, and then he awoke as if from a dream, gripping the sheets of his sweat-soaked bed.

* * *

Jared walked alone to worship at the mountain. Evil scampered across the countryside, and men laid wait for robbery and lurked privately for blood. Murder, rape, and slavery reigned throughout the land. Jared remembered the ways of old, the days before he possessed the 'sight' and had become Seer to his people. He had grown weary protecting his tribe from the child slayers in the opposing region. Many of his own people had died to the false god Molech, a being who demanded the blood of their children. Jared and his people had fought his worshippers for years, and when Enoch was born, he trained his son in the ways of the Creator. For the others of the plain worshiped beasts, yet Jared discerned by revelation that there was but one God and that He was invisible to men.

And when he had returned from the top of the mountain Jared built an altar within his house and worshiped and prayed to the God of Creation. And the prayers of Jared reached the ears of Heaven and God visited him in a dream. For Jared had fallen asleep on his pillow when a man cloaked in fiery raiment appeared before him. "Behold, man of God. For El, hast sent me to thine house."

"What is thy name?" asked Jared.

"Wherefore is it that thou dost ask after my name? My name has been given by the God of Heaven and Earth, and he has sent me to be a protector to thy kin. For a champion hast arisen from thy loins and he shall testify in days to come. The God of all the Earth hath seen thee. Nevertheless, I am Jerahmeel, and God hath sent me to be a shield to thy house."

"And who am I that I should be seen by the Lord?" asked Jared.

"It is not for me to know the Lord in this thing but know that when the cup of iniquity of this generation is full, God will spare your house and from thee shall spring forth new life."

Jared was afraid for the brightness of Jerahmeel and knelt to worship him, and when he began to do so, Jerahmeel frowned and spoke. "See that you not do it, for only the Lord God Almighty commands such worship, for I am His servant, and to His knee, we all bow."

And when Jerahmeel finished speaking, Jared looked up and the angel was gone. But Enoch his youngest son beheld the thing from a distance and had hidden under his bedding, and the boy pondered in his heart the words of the angel and believed God from a youth because of what he had seen.

And in the passage of time Jared went the way of all men and was buried with his fathers, and Enoch his son looked over the grave and vowed a vow to worship the God of his father. For the Lord God had protected his tribe from harm, and espoused justice. For in those days, the fallen of angels roamed the land and plagued men and tasked them with burdens to cause men to worship them as gods. Lucifer had assigned his legions that remained on earth to watch over every tribe of man. And when men rose up to worship the God of Heaven, Lucifer tasked Watchers to see that they were smitten. One such Watcher was Molech, and he taught men to make swords, shields, and all manner of artifacts for war, and made known unto them the metals from the earth and the art of working them into bracelets and ornaments, the use of antimony and the beautifying of the eyelids, and all kinds of costly stones and all coloring tinctures. And in exchange for such knowledge, Molech, on command of Lucifer established that all firstborn children must be given to him in the fire, and the plainsmen of the region feared Molech, for he had destroyed their families and ceased only when they sacrificed their children.

Yet Enoch and his people would not bow to Molech, for Enoch's vision had emboldened him that faith in the one true God would keep him and his people from harm. And Enoch grew into a wise man and stood as a priest for his people. He took unto him a wife and she bore him a son, and Enoch named him Methuselah. Enoch then looked upon his son and vowed a vow to the God of Creation.

"If thou wilt be to me as thou wast with my father, I will teach my son to call upon Your name, that his life and the life of my people might be long in the earth." And God had respect toward Enoch and came down to see who would pledge such fealty to him. The Lord showed himself to Enoch, and Enoch walked with God and God with him. The Lord came down daily to see about Enoch. Enoch grew greatly in wisdom and his renown for reconciliation of the people of his tribe flourished, and the Lord blessed him with much cattle, sheep and camels. He led 300 men, all trained and sworn to defend the tribe against the plainsmen who sacrificed their children to the false god Molech in the fire.

Yet there arose a day when the plainsmen that surrounded the tribe of Enoch said, "Let us spy out Enoch that we might take their children to save ours alive, and feign tribute." Thus, they sent emissaries to pay false tribute to him, and on that day, the envoy for the plainsmen spoke and said, "Who is like unto our god that is the god of the dark, for he chases away the sun, and covers the land in his starlight. He gives us children, bread, and rain. Who is as our god?"

Enoch looked upon the emissaries and replied, "There is no God but El; what you serve are but images of the Great One, images who hold thee in contempt. Specters who think it nothing to snuff out the life of thy people, for thy false gods, know that the life of the flesh is in the blood, and thy master seeks naught but to bring low all that bear the image of the Almighty. Even now the servant of the living God hast shielded me from thy plan to take my life, but hast spared you that ye might find Him."

And the plainsmen were afraid, for Enoch knew their hearts and the thing that Enoch spoke bore witness with them, and they sought to heed Enoch in this thing, and some turned from following the false god Molech to worship the living God. The angel Jerahmeel had warned Enoch to shelter his son, and Enoch hearkened to him and hid Methuselah away from the camp of meeting for he knew that the children of Molech sought to take other tribes' children that they might offer them in the fire.

And lo the Grigori that shadowed the emissaries of the plainsmen saw and heard what Enoch had done and recorded the deeds and brought them to Lucifer's hearing. And the thing that Enoch did made Lucifer wroth, and he traveled to find Molech, and Charon escorted his master.

Molech bowed when Lucifer arrived at his abode, and said, "To what brings my liege to the realm of Shinar, that you honor us?"

Lucifer was silent and walked towards Molech and slapped him across his cheek knocking him to the floor. Charon stood aloof watching in silence.

"You have allowed a man to give rise to the knowledge of El. Word has reached my ears that a whole tribe of worshippers hast arisen under thy very nose. For through you, El hast made false my claim that we are God." Lucifer turned and then spoke to Charon, "Go, find and destroy this Enoch and his people, and save none alive."

Charon turned and lifted himself into the air, and Lucifer shrouded them all in a mist and he and Molech followed him to see this human who had dared to defy them.

While the plainsmen still sat with Enoch, the sky grew dark, and the clouds in the air turned a putrid green, swirled, and the men of the plainsmen became unnerved and the Chieftain among them spoke. "You have spoken Death into the air, and now Death comes for you."

Immediately, a great wind flew into the tent of meeting, and a mist rolled into the tent, and three shadows entered, and all light was absorbed by the images. And when the trio had entered, Jerahmeel released his mace from his side, and the three fallen angels saw that one of the Lumazi stood to bar them.

"If you seek to take his life," Jerahmeel said, "Then know that you forfeit thine own."

Lucifer chuckled and said, "Kill them all."

Charon moved to lift his scythe to reap the life from Enoch, and Enoch stilled himself of fear and stood to face the Angel of Death, for Enoch was filled with faith, believing that nothing was impossible to the God he served as he walked with the living God. Emboldened that God Almighty protected him, he spoke aloud that all might hear. "The Lord is my life and my salvation, what can a creature made by my God do unto me?" Enoch walked toward Charon and drew the sword from his scabbard, believing that he could cut down Death himself, and he spoke to Charon.

"Cease, thou Death, and come no further I forbid thee. Withdraw thy presence, I command thee I in the name of the Lord!" Charon immediately stopped his advance and sheathed his scythe.

Men and angel alike were amazed that Enoch had spoken with authority and that Death returned to his place, and Lucifer and Molech were aghast, for a human had stayed Charon's hand as Enoch spoke with the voice of God.

When Lucifer saw that Charon did not move to destroy Enoch as commanded, he moved his hand to destroy Enoch himself. The Shekinah Glory glowed about Enoch and manifested around him. A great flash of light then burst in color and blinded all present. El suddenly stood over Enoch and took him from the hand of the enemy, and Enoch could no longer be found among men.

Lucifer stood humbled in the eyes of men and all who had seen Enoch forbid Death to come near him, and became wroth, and lo, to prevent word from spreading of what El had done. Lucifer stretched forth his hand and destroyed the plainsmen that had worshiped him. Jerahmeel took advantage of El's distraction, fled with Enoch's family, and saved them from Lucifer's wrath.

Enoch also was dazed by the light and when his sight returned to him, he opened his eyes and saw the Lord's rear and that he was lifted into the sky into the black of night. He noted the curve of the Earth, and the planet grew small as he looked behind him. Suddenly giant orbs with rings shot past him as great balls of flame, and the further he traveled single stars became groups of stars, and groups of stars became a multitude, and the multitude became as lone stars themselves, to where Enoch could no longer tell a multitude from a star. Further, away he lifted, until he approached a great light and when he passed the barrier of light there was as if it were a wall of great darkness and about him and he heard the howling of a creature that defied imagination, for brimstone came from its mouth and locusts swarmed about him and he raged in screams. Enoch heard the tumult and though he flew toward more light, he felt winds buffet him as hands attempting to strip his flesh from his body, and when he passed a wall of wind, the prismatic cyclone dropped him on the terrace of a canyon, and he looked about him, knowing that he had traveled to a far country.

The clouds were alive and birds and winged horses flew throughout the air. Round about him men with great flowing wings and dazzling in color went to and from a great white mountain in the distance. Music filled the air and some of the men flew, and others ran, and some galloped on great creatures with wings and one as the son of man came to him and spoke.

"Welcome, Enoch, son of Adam. Welcome to the Kingdom of Heaven." Enoch trembled in fear, for the man was three cubits taller than he was, and his skin was as Tanzanite. "You...you know my name?" Enoch replied.

"Indeed, El has told us much about you and I welcome you to the Kingdom. Come, for El awaits you." The angel took Enoch by the hand, and they flew to the Mountain of God and lighted upon the apex of the steps. Towering at the steps were four men that blazed with fire all about their bodies and they roared in deafening repeated tumults of "HOLY, HOLY, HOLY is The Lord God Almighty!" Enoch was afraid, for they looked upon him, standing to bar his path. The man touched

Enoch's ears to prevent deafness and spoke. "Be not afraid, for the master has summoned you; the Seraphim will not harm thee." Enoch beheld the wonders, and the scent of perfumed cinnamon invaded his nostrils. Enoch marveled as they walked on the finest glass, inlaid with gold throughout. The four flaming Seraphim turned aside, that Enoch and the man might pass, and when Enoch entered, he saw the palace of the living God, gleaming with all manner of gemstones and the ceilings moved with stars, and angels who decked the hallways of the palace sang songs that exalted El.

Enoch entered the throne room, and he was sore afraid for roundabout were cisterns of flame and floating about the throne were mists with eyes and they looked upon Enoch, and enveloped him, and he immediately was covered in a scent beyond all he had ever smelled. Enoch beheld that God was seated on the throne and lo His train filled the temple, above Him were two cherubim with great wings that covered the throne, and underneath the throne were great creatures with four faces that moved, and Enoch was sore afraid for who could look upon the face of God and live? And Enoch bowed and prostrated himself before the Lord, and knew that he was a man riddled with sin. And the Lord God spoke.

"I AM the LORD thy God, the God of thy father Jared, and the Creator of all men. Stand before me and be thou perfect." And the Lord waved his hand and Enoch's clothes fell from him, and the angel that stood beside him took his clothes and cast them into a cistern of fire before the Lord, and the room stank and the Virtues that floated before the throne immediately settled over the smoke that came from the clothes and the aroma of the room changed, and the angel took a coal from the flames and held it within his hands, and gave it to Enoch. "Take eat, that thy iniquity may be purged, and speak as the oracle of God."

Enoch did as commanded and took the coal, and it was cool to the touch, and he placed the coal as bidden within his mouth and when he did, great heat seared him, and fire flared from his mouth but he swallowed the coal, and it became cool in his belly and was sweet to the taste and no longer burned. And then the Lord God spoke.

"Enoch, welcome, I have taken thee that ye might not see death. For there is much I must show you, that ye might go down to speak my word in the last days. Because thou had no fear of death, death shall seek to take thee. But I will give thee power, and you shall be a witness to me. And shalt prophesy a thousand, two hundred. and threescore days, clothed in sackcloth. Thou art an olive tree, and a candlestick and shall stand before the God of the earth. And if any man will hurt you, fire shall proceed out of thy mouth and devour your enemies; and if any man will hurt thee, he must in this manner be killed. And I give unto thee power to shut heaven that it shall not rain in the days of thy prophecy; and I will give thee power over waters to turn them to blood, and to smite the earth with all plagues, as often as thy will. But know that when thou shalt have finished thine testimony, the beast that ascends out of the bottomless pit shall make war against thee, and shall overcome thee, and kill thee. But even now I have taken thee from Satan, as he will now mark thy seed, and we must make ready that we might save man. For many days hence, Satan will move to destroy thy people that he might find a route to Heaven, and once more cause harm to the realm immortal. But he hast been thwarted even from the beginning, but many a nation and people must rise and fall that a vessel might be prepared. I leave thee with Argoth. He will show you the things past and things that are, and when ye have readied yourself I will show thee things to come."

Enoch looked upon the Lord curiously, and replied to the Lord, "What am I to prepare for?"

"To fight angels, my son." And then the Lord spoke to Argoth. "Escort Enoch to the Hall of Annals, give him access that he may traverse the Zoa, and leave no area unturned. For Enoch has but a few days to learn what lies therein."

Argoth spoke to Enoch and said, "This way, Adamson."

Enoch followed Argoth as the two existed the throne room, and Michael looked on as they left, and then spoke to the Lord. "Argoth does not like this assignment Lord. I surmise he doest not respect tutoring Enoch as thou has commanded."

The Lord smiled as he watched the duo step down the crystal steps. "No.," the Lord said chuckling. "He does not like it, my son, yet there is much he will learn from Enoch, and they will be good for each other."

Michael smiled, "Why do I perceive that Argoth and not Enoch is the one who is truly being prepared?"

The Lord returned his son's smile. "You perceive well, my son...you perceive well. Yet behold and stand witness."

"To what, my Lord?" said Michael.

"I summon the Adversary to give report."

* * *

Satan was wroth over Enoch's access to Heaven, and cried out to God, "The way of the Lord is not equal! For the Adam has yielded in following me. Do you acknowledge my title to Adam's birthright? What say you, or doest the Lord of all creation changeth? Wilt thou allow Adam to worship me? Or wilt thou move to usurp my claim and bear witness to thy respect towards the man?"

The moment Satan finished speaking the words from his mouth, a great Ladder formed and ripped him from the Earth and hurtled him to where he stood at the Gates of Argoth. And he smiled, for the Lord had heard his rage and his tumult and gave heed to allow him access to walk within the realm. And when he had stepped foot from the Ladder, two Ophanim were immediately set before him, that he could not move forward without destruction, and Metatron and Talus walked up the steps to greet him.

Talus spoke for the duo. "If you step but to the right or to the left, the Ophanim will bring you to dissolution, are you clear in your purpose?"

Lucifer grinned. "Ahh, my dear brother, I trust that you do not hold yourself to account for the deeds done; you have always been slow to hear and quick to act. It was in your nature from the day I gave your stone to El."

Talus winced at the remark, and Metatron observed that Talus broke eye contact with Lucifer, bit down on his lip and his shoulders drooped, and immediately he set himself to speak.

"Are you clear in your purpose, Satan?" demanded Metatron.

Lucifer glanced at Metatron with a dismissive nod and waved his hand. "Yes, yes, young one, I am clear. Take me to El; that *is* why you are here is it not? Complete thy charge."

The trio walked with the Ophanim overhead, and all those who saw them bared their teeth, and hissed at Lucifer, and spoke, "Why is he here?" Jeers and taunts quickly followed. Lucifer smiled a playful grin, and his arms swung confidently as he made his way to the Mountain of God. But the more he viewed the city, the more his heart sank. He sighed when he saw the smoke that still arose from the Elysian Fields and rubbed at his chest in pain. As the company made their way up the steps to the palace, the Seraphim boomed their chants of holiness, and Lucifer for a moment remembered the regality that was his home. Thoughts of remorse and regret invaded his mind, wishing that none of the conflict had happened, that time could be turned back. He steeled himself, pressing forward his thoughts consoling him that one day his actions would be vindicated. Then he entered the throne room.

The Lord sat high and lifted up, and His train filled the temple, and all the Lumazi stood as the Ophanim hovered to the sides of Lucifer as guard, and God shown as Triune, and the Spirit of God Hovered, over the Father, and the second person of the Godhead, Yeshua, walked away from He who sat on the throne. Enoch was escorted by Argoth back into the throne room and Yeshua took up next to Enoch with his hands on his shoulders and the duo stood behind a rail as if they were on trial. Argoth and Michael settled behind Yeshua as guards watching Lucifer closely.

Lucifer's eyes grew wide in shock and disdain when he saw him.

"Speak thy words, Satan," commanded El.

Lucifer was for a moment afraid, but when he saw the wound he had inflicted on El, he became emboldened. "You have spoken that you are just, yet before us stands Adamson, who walks not just the realm immortal, but stands before the throne itself. You have taken him from me. Did not Adam and the Eve heed my word? Did he not forfeit his blood to me? Do you deny me my right to rule?"

The thing which Lucifer said grieved the Lord. And the Lord said unto Satan, "The thing is as you have said. Behold, all that he hath is in thy power."

"Then why then am I denied Adamson? If I stand as the god of this world, then his blood is mine. Even now, his flesh oozes with the plague of sin, you cannot deny it! The corruption of sin runs through his veins. He is a sinner and hast violated thine law! His every action is a testament that his kind is worthy of naught but destruction. His seed is mine; his will is mine - his flesh is mine!"

Yeshua who stood before El said unto Satan, "The LORD rebuke thee, O Satan, even the LORD that hath chosen Jerusalem rebuke thee. Is not Enoch a brand plucked out of the fire?"

Lucifer smirked. "He is mine, El, his soul belongs to me! I demand his life, for he is Clayborn, and the Clayborn's blood is mine!"

He that sat on the throne said to Satan, "Behold, *all* souls are *mine*; as the soul of the father, so also the soul of the son is mine; and the soul that sinneth shall die. Enoch hath walked in my statutes, and hath kept my judgments, to deal truly; he is just, he shall surely live," saith the Lord GOD. "Though it is indeed appointed unto men once to die, Enoch shall for a season abide with me. You may have him at the appointed time. Yet know this, I will give power to both he and another to testify as a witness against thee, and they shall serve as two olive trees, and candlesticks, which shall stand before the God of the Earth. And if any man hurts them, fire will proceed out of their mouth, and devour their enemies. And they shall have the power to shut heaven, that it rain not in the days of their prophecy, and power over waters to turn them to blood, and to smite the earth with all plagues, as often as they will shall this power be given them. This I have spoken, and this I shall do, for I am the Lord thy God."

Lucifer's mouth dropped, and he exclaimed, "You would give the Son of Man, power over Earth and angels?"

El replied, "Lo, there will come a day when I shall give his kind power to tread over serpents and scorpions, and nothing shall by any means hurt them. Now go while it still pleases me."

Satan stormed from the throne room furious but turned to shout back at El. "Because you can swear by no greater; you have sworn by yourself. But know of a surety that on the day that Enoch walks the Earth again, I will have his life, and he shall surely die." Lucifer then turned his back to God, and Metatron, Talus, and two Ophanim escorted him back to the waypoint until he Laddered to the Earth below.

The Lord then looked upon Enoch and spoke, "Return to Argoth my son, for there is little time, and much to teach thee before you are released to confront the Enemy."

Chapter Three: Pollution

El has gone too far. I rot on this speck, limited to the court to accuse, whilst Enoch lives and breathes Heaven's air. Lucifer was furious that a descendant of Adam was able to walk the grounds of Heaven.

"Ashtaroth, attend me now!"

Ashtaroth hastened into his Lord's presence, and bowed, as was custom.

"El has committed sacrilege, for man hast stepped foot in the realm immortal. A man stands in the court of El!"

And Ashtaroth was taken aback by what he heard. "Then what you have prophesied is true. El will have the man to displace Elohim, and Jerusalem will be filled with the Clayborn!" Ashtaroth doubled over in grief that another would occupy their home. "What is thy will, my Lord?"

"El values the blood of the man. It speaks to him. I will, therefore, give him man's blood. It will run like rivers in the sand. El believes that through the man he will raise a champion that will bring me low. But his plans will never come to fruition. I will see the man come to dissolution before the spawn of Adam ever 'crushes my head.' Go, therefore, and tell those who hath made their home in Shinar to take of themselves the daughters of men and lay with them. We will implant within the race of men our seed and bleach from man's blood all traces of the divine. El will be thwarted, for he will never raise a man from polluted blood against me, for man's seed will be my own. Lucifer laughed. "For Man himself will be my Kilnstone and the womb of Eve oven to my children. And when they are strong I will have an army of Nephilim, for we shall deform the image of El with our kind and lift ourselves on the backs of our children's children and smite Heaven, and eject El and all others from our home, and their recompense shall be upon their own head."

And for the first time Ashtaroth was fearful, for Lucifer was consumed in his lust to usurp God and enslave mankind. "You then plan to use men as soldiers to sunder El? But how can such a thing be? Adam's kind cannot move into the realms apart from becoming spirit. Indeed, man knows not the true nature of that which lies beyond what he can see. How can an army of men invade the realm that we might reclaim our home?"

Lucifer smirked. "Man shall never set foot in the realm immortal, and he that abides there now, I shall rip his sin-plagued body in twain and Enoch shall be ejected as we were to the four corners of oblivion when I am done. No, man is but fodder for my plan. For El loves, and His love will compel Him to come down and see the plague of sin which vexes His people. And when He comes down, we shall strike at Him and remove the stench of His rule from the heavens and the Earth. In His weakness, we shall be made strong. When our children grow, we will erase the memory of man from the Earth, and our new family will enter Heaven, and we shall retake our home. Now go."

Ashtaroth bowed to his master and spoke. "Let not my Lord be angry with his servant. Would you mix us with the humans to create abomination? When the others hear of this they will surely rebel against thee. Surely El will see and seek us to destruction. Have we not moved the Almighty enough? Wilt thou provoke Him to wrath even further? The host is repelled by the Clayborne."

Lucifer stood and walked to Ashtaroth, who cowered as his Lord approached. Lucifer then bent down and picked Ashtaroth from the ground and held him in his grip and spoke.

"You would be mindful to fear *me* over El. You have pledged yourself to me. Depart ever from my service and I shall give you, even more, reason to fear." Lucifer released his hold and Ashtaroth fell to the ground, gasping for breath.

"I meant no offense, my king. My Lord is indeed powerful, yet who will do this thing? To be bold enough to mar the image of El?"

Lucifer grabbed Ashtaroth and smiled, "There are several of our number who will obey me in this thing. You shall seek out 200 of our people and bring me Semjaza. I have eyed his desire to lay with the human females. Tell him his Lord would see his desire quenched. Approach him on my behalf as he will take lead on the seeding."

"As you command, my Lord." And Ashtaroth bowed and left the cave.

Ashtaroth then gathered two hundred of the fallen to do the bidding of their Lord and there were many questions about the thing, and some were hesitant to touch a daughter of Adam for the Clayborne bore the image of God. Indecision took hold and Semjaza spoke to the multitude that were tasked with the deed. "Fear not, nor be afraid, for have we not seen that the daughters of men are fair. We shall move to take them at our leisure and lay with them and they shall give rise to our offspring. For have we not learned from El, that we too can give life after our kind?"

"And what of El?" said one. "Will not El move to lay waste to that which would blur His image in the earth?"

Semjaza replied, "What shall the Almighty do that hast not already been done to us? Where can He lower us than this mote of dust where we dwell? But nevertheless, I fear ye will not agree to do this deed, and that I alone shall have to pay the penalty of a great sin. Would you leave thy brother to obey Lucifer alone?"

And they all answered him and said, "Let us all swear an oath, and all bind ourselves by mutual imprecations not to abandon this plan, but to do this thing." Then sware they all together and bound themselves by mutual imprecations upon it. And they were in all two hundred, and were assembled on the summit of Mount Hermon, and they called it Mount Hermon because they had sworn and bound themselves by mutual imprecations upon it.

And it came to pass when men began to multiply on the face of the earth, and daughters were born unto them, that the sons of God saw the daughters of men that they were fair; and they took them wives of all which they chose. And they came in unto the daughters of men, and they bore children to them, the same became mighty men which were of old, men of renown.

And they called their offspring Nephilim, and these grew to be faster and stronger than all about them, and they were like giants. They stood towering twelve feet, and men feared them and the Fallen gave to their sons' knowledge of war and fashioned for them weapons of angels that they might bring low all manner of resistance against them. And the children of the Fallen grew and lorded over the sons of men and made slaves of them and bred their women to fulfill their desire, and tutored men in the ways of evil and angelic lore. And the giants were tyrants and oversaw men as masters and man became corrupt and grew in great cities, and he spread across the face of the earth, and wherever he settled, a Nephilim commanded.

And Lucifer was pleased, for all men were wayward from the purposes of El, and his children would in time overtake man to destroy El's image from the face of the Earth.

* * *

Jerahmeel returned from shift duties and found Michael in the meeting room of the Lumazi, the meeting chambers where Heaven's governors held council to manage the affairs of Heaven. Jerahmeel entered and saw that Michael had changed the room. All the seating had been removed, and round about where tables that held maps and models of the landscape of the second heaven, and Michael was leaning over a table, lost in thought.

Jerahmeel studied his brother. Michael's eyes darted over representative pieces of armies, pouring over maps and moving pieces that represented the forces of heaven scattered across galaxies, and positioned his men to stand as buttress wherever Lucifer raised his head.

Michael, distracted and lost in strategy and tactics, did not notice Jerahmeel staring at him.

Jerahmeel cleared his throat. "Ahem..."

Michael looked up. "Hello, brother, what can I do for you?" He then quickly returned his eyes gazing intently at maps and the topography of various galaxies.

Jerahmeel continued to stare at him and said nothing.

Michael looked up at him, and they stood locked in gazes of rumination, and neither moved their eyes from another. Michael finally softened his face and looked away from the images that lined the walls and sat on a table.

"Yes, I know," Michael said, waving his hand as if to shoo Jerahmeel away.

Jerahmeel walked over to the table of maps and looked at the images that displayed battles on multiple fronts both on earth and in galaxies far away. He frowned when he saw a legion of Harrada, his own people, do battle to keep a star from going Nova while forces loyal to Lucifer worked to disrupt the star's core to send a disruption of gravity that would unlock an Archon from the gravity well of a dying star.

"The war wages across all of space and time," said Jerahmeel. "Only eternity remains inviolate."

"Aye," Michael replied. "But for how long? How long before Lucifer finds means to return to Heaven?"

"Lucifer cannot return. El would surely destroy him."

Michael harrumphed. "Perhaps, but El could have destroyed the Adversary already, and instead chose to let him live. To remain in exile—why? I sometimes do not understand El, Jerahmeel. He has to know that his act could very well embolden others to raise up arms against him. What if El can be injured further? What if... what if the Godhead can be killed?"

Jerahmeel looked at Michael, who abruptly turned away, realizing that he had said too much. But Jerahmeel knew his brother. Knew that the other angel withheld his feelings, and so he pressed further.

"So finally, the Michael that I know hast surfaced. My brother - not the general of angelic armies - shows his face. So, this thought is what plagues you? That El, despite all of his power, wisdom and might, could be laid low?" Jerahmeel restrained himself from laughing. Michael frowned at him, his eyes narrowed.

"I do not think such a subject warrants laughter. I find no such humor in the question."

Jerahmeel looked at Michael and spoke. "I see...so, recite for me the oath of our kind. What did Lucifer speak to thee upon thy awakening from the Kiln?"

"That we must never disobey God, nor through our inaction bring injury to the purpose of God. That in all things we are to obey the commands of those in authority over us unless such would bring us into conflict with the first laws of our kind. That we are to preserve our own existence except if in doing so it would bring us in violation to the others."

Jerahmeel nodded. "You have spoken rightly. What then ails you?"

Michael raised his hands in frustration and paced the room. "Therein lies my dilemma; how can I serve my God when He himself would have me violate the highest law given to our kind?"

Jerahmeel simply listened and Michael continued.

"To obey El in his thing would bring about His purpose, but yet bring injury to the giver of purpose Himself. Surely, El knows that He has placed me in an untenable position. I had to recuse myself, I saw no other alternative. How can I function in the title given, if in doing so it would lead to my master's own demise?"

Jerahmeel listened patiently, his eyes closed and then spoke. "I think I know just what you need."

"What is that?" replied Michael. Jerahmeel walked toward his brother and held his cheeks in both his hands.

"Now hold still for a moment," he said.

Michael stilled himself and did not move.

"Now close your eyes," said Jerahmeel.

Michael did as he was bidden and when he did so, Jerahmeel slapped him across the cheek.

"OWWWW! What was that for?" Michael demanded, rubbing his cheek.

Jerahmeel looked at him and spoke. "You received those commands from Lucifer, yet he himself violated the very command that he gave us all to obey. You have lifted up a command that you have received from the Betrayer, more than the clear desire articulated to you by El. You needed a good slap in the face."

Michael looked at Jerahmeel and raised his finger as if to bring a rebuttal. Jerahmeel raised his eyebrow and placed his hands on his hips, suggesting that a reply was *not* wise.

Michael's mouth was open as if to speak, his finger raised in the air, but he paused, slowly lowered his hand, and smiled. "Yeah...I guess if you put it like that, I needed a slap."

Jerahmeel burst out in laughter, "Indeed, Michael, again I ask, what ails you? You speak as if El can be killed!"

Michael frowned. "That is exactly what plagues me...the death of God."

Jerahmeel looked at Michael in surprise, "This is what troubles you? The thought that Alpha and Omega could be brought low?" Jerahmeel snickered and pointed at Michael. "You really do need a break!"

Jerahmeel reached into Michael's closet and pulled out his sword and mountain climbing gear. "Here, I think you have a mountain to climb."

Michael smiled. "You know, I think I'm beginning to understand why you irked Lucifer so."

Jerahmeel laughed. "I must admit—I used to like slapping him around, too." Jerahmeel turned to exit while Michael, mouth wide open, gathered his things and quickly ran after his brother. "Wait, you slapped Lucifer? I want to here this!"

Jerahmeel grabbed Michael by the arm and spoke. "Perhaps another time, right now I have just the thing for you." And before Michael could object he pulled hard at his arm and spoke the words to transport them to the edge of the cliffs of Argoth.

Immediately they stood at the ledge of the rocky precipice of a construction site, and behind them lay the howling winds of the Maelstrom. Jerahmeel took some rope and a hammer that was left on the ground by workers, fastened a hook into the ground, and began to strap lanyards to himself that he might hoist himself down. "Are you coming?" he asked.

Michael looked at him, annoyed. "Jerahmeel, we do not have time for this, and besides, the beams here are not in need of repair or maintenance."

Jerahmeel looked down, then spoke aloud for his brother to hear. "That's what you think! Look here, I see a crack in the beam!" Jerahmeel immediately rappelled down the side of the cliff and was gone from view. Michael watched as the rope slowly descended over the cliff.

Michael grumbled under his breath and fastened the ropes and hoists needed to prevent the Maelstrom from sweeping him away. He flung the lines over his shoulders fastened an anchor to the ground and rappelled down several feet. He looked down and Jerahmeel stood on a beam that overlooked the Maelstrom.

"Are you mad!" cried Michael. "Would you get us both killed?"

Jerahmeel just smiled and waved and motioned for him to join him below.

Michael's face flushed with anger that Jerahmeel would do something so foolish as to place himself in danger. He lowered himself further down to give his brother a piece of his mind, landing on the beam that stretched out a hundred yards over the expanse. The winds buffeted him, but there was silence in this portion of the mount, for God had commanded that whatever was uttered here could not be echoed so that none may hear.

Jerahmeel stood at the end of the beam as a diver might jump into a lake, looking down at the mighty Maelstrom that covered the abyss. He waved for Michael to come closer.

Michael struggled against the wind. He was lighter than Jerahmeel, and the winds mocked him for intruding into their sprint around the basement of the canyon's walls. Yet his line held sure. He fought against the winds pushing to knock him off the beam. He slipped once, then got close enough to Jerahmeel to speak with him.

"Jerahmeel, are you crazy? I demand..."

Jerahmeel took his hand, covered Michael's mouth and spoke. "Jump off." Then he uncovered Michael's mouth.

Michael looked at him like as if he was crazy. "Are you soiled in the mind? No one in their mind would jump into the Maelstrom."

Jerahmeel studied the swirling winds as they encircled the black eye, and hovering over it as far as the eye could see was the golden seal of El that covered the mouth of the Maelstrom.

"We shall see," said Jerahmeel. Then Jerahmeel loosed his harness and jumped into the Abyss.

Michael watched in horror as his brother fell, and when he did the wind came to a standstill and Jerahmeel landed on the golden seal that locked Abaddon deep within. Jerahmeel stood to his feet and smiled at his brother. "You better come on. No telling when El is gonna let him out. But until then...well, don't you want to give it a try?"

Michael looked at Jerahmeel as if he was insane. He was acquainted with the Maelstrom in a way unlike any other in heaven, for it was here that Lucifer and he were swept to face destruction, and here where Lucifer learned that with a Ladder one could escape from the confines of Hell.

Yet curiosity had gotten the better of him, and he indeed wanted to see what it was like to stand in the midst of the eye of the Maelstrom. Michael released his harness and until he winded down and landed but inches from his brother.

"Michael, El hast sealed the Abyss. You cannot fall within. There is but one who holds the key to this seal. One angel in Heaven is privy to open it when the time is commanded, and you stand by his side." Michael's mouth was wide open, and he marveled at the spectacle around them. They stood atop the golden seal El had created. Yet the seal was translucent, and Michael could see into the darkness below. However, nothing but smoke churned under his feet, and he knew that the smoke was from the Heartstone of Abaddon. He lifted his eyes and gazed all around him he stood within the center of what was the giant eye of the Maelstrom. He could see the winds, rip rock from the canyon's walls. The seal was miles long in every direction, and the wind raced in a circular fashion as he stood in the center of the gale. Yet in this section of the realm that separated eternity from time, in this piece at the cliffs of Argoth, there was quietness. For God had removed sound from having a voice in this place. And nothing could be heard save he and Jerahmeel. Michael tried to yell at the top of lungs, but the volume of the sound of his voice simply converted to a whisper and sailed as ether on the racing winds.

"See?" said Jerahmeel. "Only here in all of Heaven is there silence. "Now sit," said Jerahmeel. Jerahmeel sat down and crossed his legs. "What troubles thee? And why do you speak of the death of Eternal life?"

Michael again marveled that Jerahmeel was so audacious as to converse on top of the one place in all of Heaven where judgment was twice spoken. Sighing, he gave in to his brother's prompts and proceeded to sit down. He looked down as if trying to find where to start, and then finally looked his brother in the eye and spoke.

"El since the Day of Descension hast given me foresight into the future. However, the vision He hast allowed me to see is incomplete. Yet the vision is true and is certain to come to pass."

Jerahmeel nodded and listened quietly so as to not interrupt Michael.

"In the vision, I saw great nations rise and fall. We have seen Egyptia even be smitten by El, and the people released have become a mighty nation. This I had seen. Abraham, Isaac, Jacob, all this the Lord showed me. And all has come to pass."

Jerahmeel nodded, "You simply rehearse that which is common knowledge to all Heaven. But it is not this which plagues thee. It is of an event yet to come."

"Aye, "said Michael. "In the days ahead there will arise a nation that fears not God, neither acknowledges him as God, and they will devise a method of torture that will rival all the means of men beforehand. For they will lift their kind upon stalks of wood, and nail them thereon, and leave them to die as a spectacle to the eyes of those roundabout."

Jerahmeel spoke, "Adamson hast invented a great many ways to lay hurt to one another. No doubt many were devised by Lucifer and his minions himself."

"No doubt," said Michael. "But I have scoured the tomes of our brother before his exile. I have poured over his strategy, studied his thinking so as to know how he might operate even whilst he yet moves. For our brother is still powerful, and he goes about the earth as a roaring lion seeking whom he may devour."

Jerahmeel sighed, his eyes heavy with sorrow and as if loathe to agree, he nodded. "When I had looked at his tome there was a reference he made that he would see El one day 'hang from a tree' - perhaps this is the portent you see?" Then Jerahmeel shook his head. "No, no... Lucifer was always bellicose in his manner. I will give his words no importance."

Michael sighed, "What you say is true; nevertheless, El hast shown me a vision, where He Himself was hung by Adam's kin on crossed beams of wood." Michael choked back tears, for the vision moved him with compassion. "I saw the Holy One crowned with thorns, His flesh bruised, and his side pierced." Michael paused to collect himself and then spoke. "I have seen war, Jerahmeel, and the injuries angel and men acquire in the execution of war. But this was not battle...this was torture, *and* it was El."

Jerahmeel placed his hands under his chin. "On crossed beams of wood, and bleeding out, you say?"

Michael nodded.

"And El Himself showed this to you?"

Michael nodded again.

"Then El hast shown this that ye might prepare for a day to come. Did he show you what must be thereafter?"

"No," said Michael. "The vision stopped at that point."

Jerahmeel stroked his chin, breathed in deeply, and spoke, "Michael, I trust El. I trust Him not just with *my* life, but also with life itself. He *is* life and the light of men. I do not pretend that such a portent is of no cause for concern. Nevertheless, the Almighty is eternal. He cannot be destroyed. The loss of blood He endures, He hast made clear is by His own choosing."

"But Jerahmeel...if El can bleed, He can be killed! And if He is killed, then all of Creation is lost, for all things are upholden by the word of His power!"

Jerahmeel waved at Michael as to hush him. "Michael..." Jerahmeel paused stretching out his open hand, "Just look about you."

Michael, interrupted in his anxiety, stilled himself to behold what Jerahmeel wanted him to see. About them, the winds of Creation whirled. Beneath their feet was the Abyss, sealed and trapped between two dimensions. Abaddon was contained, judged by God and created by the Holy One himself.

Jerahmeel saw that Michael took in the panoramic display and proceeded to speak. "Lo Michael, did not El know what Abaddon and Lucifer were capable of before they even acted within their own minds to pursue the path upon which they laid course? Did not El warn us that Lucifer would betray us all? Hast, not El even prophesied that Abaddon would be at some point be freed and that judgment would be felled upon Lucifer's head? Thou art mindful of thoughts that have no substance. Do you not believe that El would have seen His own cut let alone his own torture? Can the very eye of eternity be plucked out? Can He who sees all be blinded? I ask thee one question and think carefully and ruminate. Why did El show thee the vision at all? What prompted such visions?"

Michael thought hard. He reflected and remembered the loss and pain he witnessed when legions of heaven's citizens were encased in black tendrils and flung to the four corners of existence. It was then that he remembered that he failed to see the purpose in such destruction, failed to understand why the Creator of the ends of the earth would allow such devastation to befall the Kingdom. Suddenly, he realized that El gave an answer in the images. And Michael voiced aloud the realization that rose as a bubble from the murky depths of his conscious to the gates of his mouth.

"In El's name...I possess fear and doubt."

Jerahmeel nodded. "Yes, I have seen it grip you these past few days, both fear and doubt. And there is yet another to the trinity of hesitation that plagues thee. Name it, Michael...name it and begin the process of ridding yourself of this chain about thy neck."

Michael lowered his head in the onslaught of realization that assaulted him. "I distrust...I distrust El."

“Aye,” said Jerahmeel. “Distrust.”

Jerahmeel then held up the great silver key that unlocked the Abyss and showed it to Michael. "Here in my hand is a token of El's trust. He hast placed in my hand the means to unleash Destruction back into the realm. In my hand, He has shown confidence that this seal will stay shut until He commands it open. Why give a key when the voice of God alone creates and destroys?

Doth the Almighty truly need a locksmith to open which He himself hath created? Nay. He hast created contrivances and tokens for us. El hath no need for such things. *We* have need of them, and in our frailty, He hast lovingly provided the contrivances needed to be strong in Him. And now He who has selected you to be chief prince has shown the most intimate of truths to one who stands in unbelief - the truth that the Almighty will submit Himself to dissolution. Doth, He do this thing to cause worry? To raise confusion within thee? Why doth He show one angel in all the universe an image? See now, my friend, the length, and breadth of what El would do for love. That He would exalt thee despite your fear, all that He might show himself strong in the faith of such misgiving. Know the paradox that is the Almighty. Know this and take comfort that El but tutors thee in matters of faith. A door to grow He hast given thee. But only you may enter therein."

Michael stood silent and took in the words of his friend. "You hath given me much to ponder."

Suddenly the booming voice of El shattered the silence of the Maelstrom. "Jerahmeel," said the Lord, "Come up hither, I have an assignment for thee."

Jerahmeel replied into the air. "Yes, Lord."

Jerahmeel looked at Michael and spoke. "We will talk again after I return from my assignment. Know that my love for thee is strong. Now go in peace, the Lord be between me and thee while we are absent." Jerahmeel then lifted himself into the air, and Michael watched him disappear towards the mountain of God.

* * *

Argoth entered Enoch's bedchamber and awoke him from slumber. "I am loathed to disturb you, Enoch, yet the Lord bids me teach you the ways of Heaven."

Enoch yawned and stretched his arms, "Your presence is of no disturbance angel of God. I am at the Lord's bidding. I will follow thee."

Enoch dressed and he and Argoth walked to the Hall of Annals.

Enoch marveled, for the thing was wondrous to behold, for roundabout were images of galaxies, and peoples, and worlds too countless to imagine. Enoch noticed that the room portrayed on its very walls the happenings of all things he spoke and asked Argoth, "Can it show me, my family?"

"Aye," said Argoth. "Indeed, it can."

"Show me."

Argoth then gave command to the room and it imaged Methuselah, Enoch's son. Enoch could see that his once little boy was now a grown man though he had only left him but moments ago. Enoch stood astonished at the thing and spoke. "How is this that my son is now a man? For I have not been gone a day?"

Argoth replied, "El is the Alpha and Omega, the beginning and the end. Time, as you understand it, doest not exist in our realm. For we are immortal within the presence of God."

Enoch continued to stare at the images of the wall, fascinated that the world he knew had changed so much, and he looked upon his son, proud that Methuselah also called on the name of the Lord. Enoch watched his son fend against the child-sacrificing tribes of the plain, and lo when Methuselah called on the name the Lord, he beheld that surrounding his son and the plain were legions of angels with swords that battled creatures that were twisted and deformed in body. Anorexic with maggot-infested skin and they were animated by a power not known to men.

"Are these your fallen brethren?" asked Enoch.

"Aye," said Argoth. "They are but shells of their former glory. Lucifer commands them now and he hast unleashed them as a scourge upon your people. They are less than angelkind but yet far more powerful than Adamkin. We call them Daemons, for they feed and possess thy people to supply Hell's villi. If not, the creature would quickly turn on both angel and man alike. Lucifer now satiates the creature with your people's spirits."

"What is Hell?" asked Enoch.

Argoth waved his hand, and an image of the living mountain showed across all walls, and Enoch watched as the record of the creature displayed the anger of the living God. Anger that created a living realm to consume alive beings of such power that they would forever experience eternal life apart from the God of Heaven. A life of fire, pain, and darkness.

Enoch continued to look at the image and watched as Methuselah and his men prayed to the God of Heaven, and their prayers were as vapors that penetrated the realms, and El moved in the Earth mightily when his people prayed. But where there were no intercessor, Lucifer, and his armies were left to unleash all manner of destruction.

"The Almighty walks with thee," said Argoth. "You are the first of your kind to see the realm immortal. The, first of all, humans to bask in the glory that is Heaven. Yet I must admit that it is..." he paused, considering his words, "...unsettling to see El move in such a manner toward your people. Yet we obey Him in all things. Even the protection of thy kind."

Enoch turned to Argoth and said, "So you watch? That is all your people do?"

"Yes," said Argoth.

"There is not much use to watching. To act when one sees injustice———that is noble. What you do has no glory in it."

Argoth scowled at him, angered over the impudence of Enoch to tell him that his work was of no worth. Then remembered that Enoch was but a man and limited in his understanding.

"You think that recording the moments of all things is of no consequence? To evidence Lucifer's obliteration of the image of God in the Earth is of no worth? For all play their part in El's plan. Even you. For the time will come when people will call on the name of the Lord and it will be as if He hears them not. But lo, the Almighty hast moved times and seasons that people might be born. He has lifted detail after detail that your progeny would exist. To deviate from His plan would cause whole generations of men to never be birthed. He has foreseen all peoples and moves even now that generations to come would be of such faith that a door would be made for El to directly intervene. But none yet carries the power to hold the Almighty. But there is one of the daughters of Eve that shall give birth to Shiloh. And when God walks the earth, men will know, and the Kingdom of God will be restored to your kind, then we will have a beachhead to foul the purposes of the enemy.

"El will bring nations to rise and others to fall—all that One might come. For in the fullness of time, He shall bring life again to all, and there will be recompense for the deeds done. We record Adamson for the day when the records must be read, and the images shown. That no man might say, 'see, how then doest He find fault? And who hast resisted His will?' For even we do not fully understand the power He hast given thee as Clayborn, but He is faithful that has promised. But the soul that sinneth it shall surely die."

Enoch bowed. "I apologize. I meant no offense," he said, then held his peace on the matter.

"Come," said Argoth. "I will see you to your quarters, for you must rest before you may begin to understand the mysteries of the Kingdom."

"Rest?" questioned Enoch. "Will I be tested in some manner that I will be fatigued?"

"No," said Argoth. "Yet El hast charged me to train you in the mysteries of the Kingdom that you might have the knowledge to learn what must be learned. For you shall stand as Grigori for thy people, and as lampstand before the Lord - intercessor for thy kind."

Enoch replied, "Nay, if I am to stand as a light before the Lord, then let me be lit now. There shall be time enough to rest. Let us commence with my instruction."

"I have bidden thee rest; would you not yield to my suggestion? If you cannot hear angels, what hope have thee to hear from God?"

Enoch laughed. "Angels are the creatures that tempted man, and angels were the first to rise against God himself. What stock should I put in an angel's judgment when ye yourselves stand a third judged?"

Argoth winced when he heard this, for though he was angry over the insolence of Enoch, he could not find fault with his words. "You seek to be tested, then come, for thy first test awaits you."

Argoth then took Enoch to the door of the Hall of Annals, and there he spoke.

"To enter the sacred Hall and be as Grigori for thy people, you must be as I and walk the path that I must walk. For within the hall are the secret things of God. If you can make it to the door across this void, then you might gain access to its secrets, and your mind will be ready to receive instruction. Do you accept this challenge?"

Enoch looked at the door. There was nothing but squared titles on all the floors; the room seemed immense, and he could make that across from him was an outline of a door. "All I have to do is make it across and touch the door and it will open to me?"

"Aye," replied Argoth."

Enoch nodded, "Then let us begin."

"There is one thing before you begin," cautioned Argoth. "Above you are the Zoa. As long as you remain behind this line, you cannot be harmed. However, the moment you seek to enter the room they will fall upon you if you fail to cross the barrier beyond." Argoth smirked, then continued, "*Now* you may begin."

Enoch looked across the hallway. There were four nondescript squares off to a side and eight squares deep. At the end was a door with a handle, presumably opened only upon stepping on the correct sequence of squares. He looked above him and saw suspended from the ceiling dozens of creatures with tentacles, each barely perceptible to the eye. What he did see, however, was that each one was filled with eyes. Their jaws were in their belly, and they walked with tentacles on the rafters of the hallway, ready to drop on the unsuspecting. They quietly hissed and slithered along the ceiling.

Enoch looked back at Argoth. "And these creatures...what purpose do they serve?"

The angel replied, "They protect the secret things of God."

Enoch nodded and proceeded to cross the floor, walking confidently into the middle square. A Zoa dropped to the floor behind him as he continued his pace unabated. Turning neither to the left nor to the right, Enoch continued as more Zoa dropped behind him and began to move to follow him.

Argoth raised his eyebrow and bit his lip, in wonderment if El would hold him responsible for the human's death.

Enoch continued his fixed march towards the door ahead of him, walking without concern for the squares the lay before him. A Zoa dropped ahead of him and opened its mouth and raised its tentacles as if it might grip the intruder. Those to his rear had not closed the distance to him. Enoch, unmoved, walked coolly towards the Zoa. Its mouth was open, dripping spittle, and the group's collective hiss now echoed across the corridor. Argoth looked on in terror, for the Zoe now had touched the man, and the angel knew that within moments Adamson would be devoured.

Enoch touched the Zoa's snout, and it roared but did not move away, and Enoch spoke.

"You are in my way, servant of God. El himself bids me come. My purpose is to learn the secrets therein. We are kindred, for I am also the guardian of that which is within. I am Zoa, and you shall let me pass."

The Zoa surrounded Enoch and looked at him for a moment. The beast before him sniffed him, and spittle oozed over Enoch's shoulder as the creature snorted in his face. Slowly the circle of monsters that surrounded him opened to reveal the door ahead.

"Thank you," said Enoch. He walked forward between them as they towered over him and reached to turn the handle and walked inside. Enoch turned back to look at Argoth, annoyed.

"Are you coming?"

Argoth looked on in wonderment his mouth open, his eyes blinked repeatedly and simply stared.

* * *

Argoth released Enoch to Jerahmeel's supervision, and Jerahmeel showed Enoch the capital, from the royal palace to the suburbs to the blast furnaces of the armories of Heaven. They walked and came upon Michael and Gabriel sparring and stopped to observe.

Michael arched his back, spreading his wings wide. He unsheathed the sword of Ophanim and spoke to his brother. "I am ready."

Gabriel looked at Michael. "Are you sure about this?"

Michael paused and then said, "Yes, I must be ready when the next battle comes. I know not what Lucifer will bring, and I know my eye cannot hold mercy to spare him if we engage. Attack me."

Gabriel launched into his offensive. His staff in hand, disappeared from Michael's view, and immediately attacked from Michael's rear. Before he could react, Gabriel smote him in the back of his head and Michael landed hard in the dirt.

Enoch looked at Michael as the angel dusted himself off and whispered to Jerahmeel. "*He* is your preferred leader? He was just bested in combat by one of lower rank. How then should he be the leader of the Hosts of God?"

Jerahmeel smiled at him and said, "Michael is not our desired leader because he is strong. He is neither unqualified to be leader because he is weak, as you understand weakness. He is leader because he has been chosen by El. The way of Heaven is not to elect, appoint, or to select our leaders. El is our leader. *He* determines among us who shall lead us. He has selected Michael; so, then because we value the decision of El, we will when he is ready, give to Michael all that we have, all of our knowledge, all of our skill, all of our strength, that we might fulfill the command of El when Michael gives it. Therefore, we train him, so that he might exceed us. He studies at our feet that he might learn from us and we from him. So that when El gives command, Michael might look upon the Host of Heaven and choose from among us who best may assist in executing the cause of El. Only he, who would serve all, can lead all. This is the way of Heaven. Do you understand this, Enoch?"

Enoch looked upon Michael as Gabriel pulled him to his feet and replied. "I'd still rather have a leader who doesn't get knocked down as much." Enoch grimaced as he watched Michael take another blow to the skull.

Jerahmeel nodded and replied, "Yet it is sometimes necessary for a leader to take a good blow to the head."

Away in the throne room of God, El looked past form and shadow to see His sons spar with one another. He watched as Michael struggled to compensate for Gabriel's speed and spoke. "Jerahmeel prophecies of things to come and knows it not," said El.

Yeshua smiled. "Father do you think that I need a blow to the head?"

El grinned. "No, but for a surety, Mary will want to take a swipe at you, especially when you cannot be found."

Yeshua looked into the future and saw how His destined mother would scold Him when she and Joseph could not find Him, and He smiled. "She will indeed." The Trinity continued to watch as the two angels sparred with one another.

Gabriel lifted Michael from off his rear.

"Remind me to never engage you in battle," Michael said, his chest heaving from exertion.

Gabriel smiled.

Michael rose to his feet and shook himself raised his sword and shouted, "Again!"

Immediately Gabriel disappeared from view and Michael launched into the air, and with his thoughts commanded the sword of Ophanim to split, and the sword obeyed. Gyroscopically, the seven swords moved about him, and Michael could feel Gabriel's presence to his flank and set himself to face his brother. Sword clashed with staff, and a bright light engulfed the two, as the staff was made from Cadmium and smelted by the hand of God. Then the staff split, and Gabriel held two staffs in his hand, and Michael attacked his brother who blocked and repelled sword after sword. He leaped over Michael, who spun to follow with the swords. Faster the blades pursued him, and when Gabriel turned to his left a sword was there when he moved to his right a sword was there. Each angel moved in what seemed a deadly choreographed waltz, and the clang of steel against cadmium was thunderous, for Michael was as seven attackers against Gabriel. Michael moved to corner Gabriel against a stone wall, causing his brother to retreat. Their sparring caught the attention of those roundabout and many flew to the square to watch them spar.

Michael and Gabriel ducked and weaved and deflected staff and swords, and cheers rung out from the now-gathered throng. But the two were oblivious, and Michael motioned for a sword to open a way that Gabriel might find passage, for Gabriel defended himself against Michael's onslaught but could not attack in kind for the number of the blades that swished and moved about him. Gabriel saw that a blade had ascended to open a path of travel, he feigned to rise through the opening but instead flung his baton at Michael and hit him squarely in the head and knocked his brother flat on his back. Immediately the swords fell to the ground and Gabriel jumped over his brother and stood over him.

"Do you yield?" Gabriel asked.

Michael shook himself and rubbed his forehead. "Aye, I yield."

Gabriel reached down, lifted Michael from the ground, and spoke to the newly assembled crowd.

"What error did the prince make in tactics?"

All looked at one another, but no one replied. Each shrugged their shoulders until Michael himself broke the silence.

"In battle, there can be no quarter given. There can be no hope for escape."

Gabriel looked at his brother with admiration and bowed. "Thou hast spoken wisely. For you were able to press me into a corner with my back against the wall. To cede that position robbed thee of victory. Lucifer would do more than hit you on the forehead if you engage him again."

Michael's brow grew tense in remembrance of his battle with his brother. "Lucifer would have had my head."

Gabriel nodded. "He would indeed."

Suddenly a sound as of a great bell rang from the mountain of God, and its chimes called all to take note. For the tower bells had not been rung since before the war, when Lucifer had last arrived in Heaven. All turned to see who would go to the mountain of God, yet none dared to go, as it was the summons of the chief prince. All looked at Michael, and he lowered his head. "I am not chief prince." A dispatcher then came from the palace and landed in front of Michael, exhausted, and spoke.

"My Lord, you are summoned to El's presence. El hast charge for thee."

Gabriel looked at him and smiled.

"Don't even say it," said Michael.

"I told you so," said Gabriel.

Michael sighed, then lifted himself into the sky and turned toward the mountain of God. He loved the feeling of the wind against his face as he soared along. It was not long before he landed in the presence of the Seraphim. Immediately, they boomed into their chant of HOLY, HOLY, HOLY, and Michael walked past the burning ones onto the crystal stairs and through the linen curtains into the Holy of Holies, where the Virtues floated about the room. Michael stopped to see the Lord standing, and round about the throne were vials and stars. Each star was a Son of Adam yet to be born, and the Lord plucked a star and when its light went out, another appeared, and the Lord took each star and placed it within the vials, and the vials glowed from the stars that shown within.

And all three persons of the Godhead were visible, and they talked with one another and the words spoken were as the sound of waters upon the shore.

"There will be many that will die if we commit to his salvation," said the Holy Spirit.

Yeshua immediately spoke. "Yes, but many shall live to life eternal. Though all paths lead to *our* glory, not all will restore the man and Creation to wholeness."

"Kenosis," said El. "It is Creation's only hope."

The Holy Spirit then spoke. "There is still time Yeshua to reconsider—are you sure you?"

Yeshua looked at both El and the Holy Spirit and spoke. "I will submit to the Kenosis. Prepare thou me a body that I might go down."

El nodded to Yeshua then turned to Michael. "Hail, young prince."

Yeshua smiled at Michael then he and the Holy Spirit vanished and there was but one that sat on the throne, and He looked at Michael. Michael bowed, then spoke.

"My Lord, I am here as summoned."

The Lord El then raised His hands and Michael lifted from the ground and floated under the Lord's power. God took the vials and powered them over Michael's head and the contents flowed down even from the crown of Michael's head onto the skirts of his garments. The liquid glowed like silver and faces of men and the images of people were within the liquid, and when all the vials were poured, there was yet one vial and one star that remained.

"Look into the star," said the Lord, "What do you see?"

Michael strained to see into the light and made out the features of a daughter of Eve, a young woman few in years and with dark hair.

"I see a young maiden of the line of Eve, my King."

"Thou hast seen well." The Lord then stepped down, and gently lowered Michael to the floor. Michael then prostrated himself face down on the ground. The Lord stood over him and lifted his head. Michael stared upon the Lord, and El spoke. And when El spoke, the Virtues spoke with him. The cherubim, which were perched above the Mercy Seat, also spread their wings over the throne, and loosed their tongues and spoke in a trance as El released a psalm into Michael's ears.

"Mary shall be Mother to Shiloh.
From misery shall spring forth joy.
With lashes to the back of the innocent,
Shall Lucifer be destroyed.
The blood of Shiloh shall be spilled,
Forsaken to cry and plea.
His blood shall he wash sin away,
Accursed to make men free."

Michael listened as El's words traveled through the air. Michael saw the melody of the living God's voice waft across the room and visible echoes floated higher until His words were out of sight. He thought about the woman he saw and spoke to the Lord. "The young woman, who is she?"

"Her name is Mary," replied the Lord. "And she is thy charge."

* * *

Sandolfon a Kortai rushed into the council chamber of the Lumazi bowed before Argoth and spoke.

"My Lord, word has come from the eastern front that a contingent of the Fallen has found the prison of Zephon."

Argoth frowned, "How is such a thing possible? Zephon's prison moves about the course of the second heaven. His position is hidden."

"The thing is not known my Lord, but it is surmised that members of the Grigori who side with Lucifer hast seen the cavern of ice with which he's encased and have relayed his position to their Lord."

Argoth frowned and he slumped in a chair, sour that members of his own kind would work to circumvent the Almighty. Argoth reached within his Kilnstone and pulled out his own book, and from it ripped a page, and gave it to Sandolfon.

"Here are the coordinates of his prison. Go with a unit to the site immediately," he said. "I want them intercepted. They cannot be allowed to release Zephon from confinement."

Sandolfon nodded and gathered his forces, assembled his detail at a waypoint and laddered to a galaxy where no stars shone. The squadron exited from their flumes with great flashes of light, each with swords drawn; they floated on the field of space awaiting the regiments of the enemy to come.

"Hold position and scan for any sign of the adversary!" Sandolfon said. With eyes that peered into deep space; each angel fidgeted; muscles tensed with hearts racing ready to engage in battle at a moments notice. Yet no adversary could be found, and the silence of neutrinos and cosmic dust was all that echoed in the gripping coldness of space.

Magiel a lieutenant spoke, "Where are they?"

"No enemy is here," said Sandolfon. "Come let us go to make sure the prison of Zephon. He turned and flew with hundreds behind him, and they came upon the giant frigid comet of Zephon's prison that hurtled through space. Trails of rock vapor and out gasses blossomed in bursts of color, as the polar form of Zephon was encased frozen in chains and fetters of ice. His mouth was sealed to prevent utterance of Elomic commands, and his eyes crusted over and wrapped in blindfolds of sheeted ice. He laid motionless entombed deep within the speeding glacier.

"There is nothing amiss here," said Sandolfon. "Is it possible that Argoth was mistak..."

Sandolfon heard the cry of his lieutenant yelling that they were besieged, and he looked to his rear and a horde of the fallen was upon them, and at their head Charon flew as the vanguard of death and smote down all that barred his path. Two legions of fallen angels flanked him while ladders materialized all around them.

"My God!" Sandolfon said.

Everywhere Sandolfon looked, he beheld the erupting plumes of prismatic ladders that burst into the blackness. A swarm of shouting warrior angels all with axes, maces and swords drawn, descending like rain upon them all.

"Take up a defensive position around the prison! Do not let them breach your lines!"

Heroically the squadron moved to post themselves around the comet, that held Zephon, but there were too many and the angels were run down by the sheer numbers and power of the masses that descended upon them. And the battalion of Sandolfon was run through, and the screams of angels could be heard even in the silence of deep space. Echoes of which would carry upon the solar winds for eons to come. Bravely they fought back, but Sandolfon knew that they could not defend their position, and the Warden of Hell himself descended menacingly towards him.

Sandolfon knew he could not bring down the angel of Death and moved himself from harm yet stood atop the comet in the vain hope that somehow he might stop him. Vapors and trails of light rushed past him. His cheeks were flushed and his chest heavy from exertion. For far away in the universe away from the eyes of men, an angel rode backside of a comet to prevent what lied within from escape. While thousands of his own people battled ten thousand to the death.

Charon headed straight into the plume of the falling star. Its tail-ejected gas and dust flung at speeds that would destroy any that entered the gaseous lane, but the particles were nothing to the angel of Death and he reached to grasp the icy tomb that encased Lucifer's servant. Charon seized the ice and dug his bony hands deep within the frozen gas. The touch of Death accelerated the age of the comet in seconds, and fissures erupted across its frigid scalp. Tiny beams of light escaped from each nook and cranny until a giant Arelim could be seen writhing within, struggling to escape. Charon dug his rusted tentacled barbs deeper and pulled the polar shell apart. The icy shell split and all manner of particulates, rock and great shards of ice exploded in all directions. The comet broke up and the shock wave of the blast flung both friend and foe alike in all directions.

Zephon emerged from his frigid tomb and stretched his mighty wings, whilst the chains about his wrists and the leggings that manacled his ankles snapped and floated away into the blackness of space. And all about him, shards of ice and angels still locked in combat raged against him. Sandolfon watched in horror that the great angel of fire lifted from his tomb of ice freed.

Charon stood aloft from him and stared.

Zephon looked upon him and spoke, "Ferryman? To you do I owe my freedom? And if so where is my master?"

Charon nodded in acknowledgment and motioned for Zephon to follow and turned his back from him. A ladder opened to take the duo back to Earth and they entered. Sandolfon watching raced to enter and when he did, the ladder closed behind them.

The legions of Lucifer also turned seeing their prize released and those few remaining of Sandolfon's squad watched in relief that the Horde left them to their own devices.

"How did they find us?' said one.

Magiel spoke. "*We* led them here. They did not know where Zephon was exactly, but as soon as we checked his prison to see if it was secure, they knew. Our own light gave his position away. We have been outplayed. We must return for further instructions. For the angel of Fire hast been unleashed unto man." And a soldier turned to Magiel and spoke.

"But what of Sandolfon? He entered the ladder with them."

Magiel summoned a ladder so that they might return home. "Only El can save him now." and Magiel and his forces turned to journey home.

* * *

Sandolfon saw that the ladder of Charon hurtled them towards the Earth and that in moments Zephon would stand at Lucifer's side and bring ruin to the planet. He spoke the Elomic command to summon a ladder of his own hoping against hope that his tactics would work and not just end in his death. And so, he spoke the words to open a ladder within a ladder. A prismatic chute formed over him and when Sandolfon felt the pull of the ladder against him, he grabbed the heel of Zephon and held tight. Zephon turned surprised that he would be handled within the fall of the ladder and kicked at him. The newly formed ladder spliced into the one that carried the trio and snatched Sandolfon and Zephon away and they careened through the depths of space in combat.

Charon roared in anger seeing his charge torn from following him and was moving too fast to help Zephon, but it was too late for his ladder had now reached Earth and opened and he dropped from the sky as his great wings opened as giant sails to slow his fall. He landed yards from Lucifer. Lucifer stood as the angel of Death landed as wind and debris raced towards him. Charon looked back at the ascending funnel, roared angrily, and marched towards his captor.

Lucifer noticed that Zephon did not ladder in with him and spoke. "Well? Where is he? Where is your charge?"

Charon pointed skyward and hunched his shoulders

"Arrggghhhh!" Lucifer shouted. He turned from Charon and marched away blaring obscenities. The mare smiled and slowly followed him.

* * *

Sandolfon tried to return to a point of space where he knew he could receive reinforcement. But Zephon began to utter an Elomic command, and Sandolfon reached for his sword and plunged it deep into the shoulder blade of his quarry.

The scream from Zephon's cry made the ladder collapse. Light sparked as tinder and great waves of heat flashed and the ladder collapsed and exploded in a detonation of color, and fire. The two ejected near a pulsar and fell in an uncontrolled descent falling into the rotating neutron stars gravity. Zephon grabbed Sandolfon by the arm and pulled ripping the ligaments from his body. Sandolfon screamed as they plummeted into the radioactive stream of stellar gas. Sandolfon beat at Zephon, but the Arelim was too strong and Zephon grabbed hold of the general's head and squeezed as they grappled with one another tumbling into the heart of the star. Sandolfon smiled as he could feel the pressure of Zephon hands beginning to crush his skull. With a sigh he surrendered to what he knew was the inevitable and spoke his final words. "Delay you...I have...my people...they...they will find you..."

Zephon cried enraged as the skull of Sandolfon crumpled in his hands. He released his dead adversary, and yelled triumphantly, "Arrrrrgggggggggg! I am Zephon, and fire shall be upon my enemies!" His cry echoed across the region of space.

He watched as the lifeless body of Sandolfon floated to fall deeper into the star. The brain matter of his adversary fell as meteorites into the celestial furnace. Zephon then turned himself spaceward that he might gain bearing on his location to ladder to his master's side.

He saw the constellations about him and faintly gained cognizance of his position. He opened his mouth to recite the Elomic command to send him to earth, but silence was all that was heard. His throat felt constricted, and he coughed up blood. He looked at his shoulder wound and noted that a substance oozed unbeknownst to him. "What ruse is this?" he said. He tried again to utter an Elomic command, but no ladder formed, and he felt virtue leave him as his power slowly dissipated from the stab wound to his shoulder.

Realization dawned on him. That Sandolfon had poisoned him. His vocal cords quickly constricted unable to pronounce the words to summon a ladder. He turned to the stars that in the distance beyond showed the galaxy that housed Lucifer. He flexed his great wings, and the solar winds carried him aloft and he ruminated reprisal for the enemies attack upon him.

"Though it take me millennia to travel the tides of space. I am coming Lucifer. I will be bitterness to El, and to the man shall I be a curse. I shall reach El's beloved hovel for the man and when I do; my death shall be as wormwood to him."

And Wormwood traveled silently in the black; a great star from heaven, burning as it were a lamp destined to fall upon the people of Earth in the millennia to come.

* * *

Argoth rushed to the throne room, panting as he entered and bowed before the Lord of all things. "My Lord King I have seen the fallen move upon the sons of men, and they have created abomination: a creature that is of mixed blood!"

Argoth was in the midst of telling El what his watchers had seen when Gabriel entered the throne room, bowed his head and spoke. "Lord the enemy hath sown tares amidst the ground of men. For lo a new race arises from the union of Elohim and men, and left unchecked will fill the earth."

The Lord replied, "Is the thing not known? Fear not, for my spirit, shall not always strive with man, for that he also is flesh: yet his days shall be an hundred and twenty years." God then shortened man's life that Lucifer's plan would be slowed, and the spread of the Nephilim would not cause man to be overrun.

Lucifer was hindered yet knew that he had helped to lower the image of God in the man, for he no longer possessed long life as initially willed by El, and the plague of sin reigned within man's flesh. Moreover, in the sum of time the children of men grew, and from the offspring of angels and men came giants that were called Nephilim. In the course of time, they grew to such power and influence and spawned with such speed that more were the children of the Devil than those that belonged to God. The Nephilim became a scourge that spread through the line of Adam. And all who were not Nephilim, Lucifer moved to corrupt in mind so that man became vain in his imagination, and his heart darkened, that instead of worshiping El, Lucifer marred man's knowledge that he became as a fool and changed the glory of the incorruptible God into an image made like to corruptible man, and to birds, and four-footed beasts, and creeping things. Wherefore God gave them over to uncleanness through the lusts of their own hearts, to dishonor their own bodies between themselves. As men had changed the truth of God into a lie and worshiped and served the creature more than the Creator. And when members of the Lumazi interceded for man's will to be curtailed, the Lord replied. "Lo, I have set before him life and death. Will I remove from him choice, that he might do as he wills?"

So the Lord would not supersede man's desire to do evil, for to lose choice would rob man further of God's image and for this cause God gave them over unto vile affections: for even their women did change the natural use into that which is against nature: And likewise also the men, leaving the natural use of the woman, burned in their lust one toward another; men with men working that which is unseemly, and receiving in themselves that recompense of their error which was meet.

And God saw that the wickedness of man was great in the earth and that every imagination of the thoughts of his heart was only evil continually. And it repented the Lord that he had made man on the earth, and it grieved him at his heart. "It repenteth me that I have made them. For there is none righteous, no, not one: There is none that understandeth, there is none that seeketh after God. They are all gone out of the way, they are together become unprofitable; there is none that doeth good, no, not one."

And the Lord said, "I will destroy man whom I have created from the face of the earth; both man, and beast, and the creeping thing, and the fowls of the air; for the way of peace, he does not know."

Michael spoke to the Lord, "Is there no other way, must they all be destroyed?"

"Creation cannot sustain them, the pestilence of sin, hast advanced as to leave the entirety of my image warped and foul. My image cannot be abused for Lucifer's ends.

"Lord destroy him please!" pleaded Argoth.

"There is a time and a season for his end and the time is not yet nigh."

Enoch looked at Michael "Will you not intervene on behalf of the sons of men? Wilt thou stand idle and lift not thy voice that my people might be saved?"

Michael grimaced at the rebuke and was torn for he knew that man was helpless to stand before Lucifer and his brethren. Yet Michael thought to himself. *It is man that will sunder the Almighty, perhaps if El destroys Adamson then all will be well*, and Michael held his peace.

Enoch was wroth for the angels of the Lord saw man as nothing but to be swept aside as dung and ran before the Lord and bent his knees and spoke.

"I have tarried and listened to the speech that has echoed in these halls. The hall from which all justice flows, for lo who am I to speak in the presence of the Ancient of Days, and his mighty host? For what place doth youth hath in the midst of the aged? Yet greatness of days doth not always bring understanding, nor might swiftness to perceive. So, I speak that I might intercede to my God, and speak for my people. For will the Lord not remember thy word to thy servant Jared, for if the enemy hear of thy intent he will say to the people, 'see for the Almighty holds no sway over the hearts of men to bring them to his cause, and what doth prevent the Almighty to simply destroy all of creation? See are we naught but refuse to him? The Almighty is not just, nor worthy of rule. For behold the Lord changeth. And thy actions bring dishonor to the name of the Lord. For whom be a greater killer among men but God himself?' Mark my words my Lord this the Satan will say. He will speak into the ears of his people, and they will mouth that God is a murderer. But consider thy servant Noah who is of my line. He yet walks upright amongst his people. For wilt, the God of all the Earth destroy the just with the wicked? I pray you, spare me this pain, and let my line not perish from before thine eyes."

And the thing which Enoch said pleased the Lord, And the LORD said, "See my servant Enoch for he speaks as my oracle and gives voice to stand between judgment and mercy. Because thou has voiced this thing I have hearkened according to thy word as truly as I live, all the earth shall be filled with the glory of the LORD." And the Lord held back his wrath for a time and visited Noah in the earth.

Thus, Noah found grace in the eyes of the LORD. For Noah was a just man and perfect in his generations, and Noah walked with God. The earth also was corrupt before God, and the earth was filled with violence. And God looked upon the earth, and behold, it was corrupt; for all flesh had corrupted his way upon the earth.

God said unto Noah, "The end of all flesh is come before me; for the earth is filled with violence through them; and behold, I will destroy them with the earth. Make thee an ark of gopher wood; rooms shalt thou make in the ark, and shalt pitch it within and without with pitch. And this is the fashion which thou shalt make it of. The length of the ark shall be three hundred cubits, the breadth of it fifty cubits, and the height of it thirty cubits. A window shalt thou make to the ark, and in a cubit shalt thou finish it above; and the door of the ark shalt thou set in the side thereof; with lower, second, and third stories shalt thou make it. Moreover, I, even I, do bring a flood of waters upon the earth, to destroy all flesh, wherein is the breath of life, from under heaven; and everything that is in the earth shall die. But with thee will I establish my covenant; and thou shalt come into the ark, thou, and thy sons, and thy wife, and thy sons' wives with thee. And of every living thing of all flesh, two of every sort shalt thou bring into the ark, to keep them alive with thee; they shall be male and female. Of fowls after their kind, and of cattle after their kind, of every creeping thing of the earth after his kind, two of every sort shall come unto thee, to keep them alive. And take thou unto thee of all food that is eaten, and thou shalt gather it to thee, and it shall be for food for thee, and for them."

Thus, did Noah; according to all that God commanded him, so did he.

* * *

In the six-hundredth year of Noah's life, in the second month, the seventeenth day of the month, the Lord spoke and said the time hath come to end Satan's plan to bring the Nephilim to Heaven. And the Lord God commanded, the winds to bring forth rain and God broke up the deep places, and on that same day were all the fountains of the great deep broken up, and the windows of heaven were opened. And the Lord caused it to rain upon the earth forty days and forty nights. And the Lord with his own word destroyed all that lived on the face of the Earth. And all of Heaven watched as El extinguished the life that he had created, save those on the ark.

And the Lord spoke from the throne, "Hear, O heavens, and give ear, O earth: for the LORD hath spoken, I have nourished and brought up children, and they have rebelled against me. Yeah even the ox knoweth his owner, and the ass his master's crib: but Lucifer doth not know, my people doth not consider. Ah sinful son, a lineage now laden with iniquity, a seed of evildoers, children that are corrupter's: they have forsaken the LORD, they have provoked the Holy One of Heaven unto anger, they are gone away backward. Behold their fruit's destruction."

Then the Lord called forth the Shaunteal, eleven angels of power who appeared instantly before the Lord of all things and bowed and the Lord spoke. "Go in my name, shackle and chain. Bind my sons with bonds, and the nobles with fetters of iron, ye are the keys to Tartarus. Seize those who have defiled the man, and seal those responsible within the bowels of the earth. Let the fear of me be in thee, so that the Fallen never again commit abomination. Now go."

The angels in charge over the capture were eleven strong. And those recorded in the Grigoric record were Uriel, Harbonah, Azrael, Simkiel, Za'afiel, Af, Kolazonta, Hermah, Kemuel, Makatiel, and Mavet. Armed with shackles they became living keys to open Tartarus and seal all that they chose within. They fell as a plague upon Semjaza and those who had lain with the daughters of men. And wherever they were on the Earth, each angel of judgment descended upon the perpetrators of abomination and dragged them screaming through the crust of the earth into Tartarus.

Lucifer conferred with his lieutenants, and his council debated on the strategy to bring El down from Heaven that they might strike at him. And the council were raucous as it was wondered how such a thing might be and how El outside of Sabbath could be brought low, and Lucifer after much debate spoke to them all.

"Do not think that we can shield ourselves from El. Nay I tell you El is all knowing, he is everywhere. Even in this very room. To battle against El head on is fruitless. No, we must use a proxy to strike at El and the man will serve as a shield for our defense. For El moves Heaven and Earth for his love of the creature. Man will be our key to bring him low. Now that we have mingled our blood with his, El must deal with the man as he hast dealt with us. He cannot lie, as he must be true to who He is. The man belongs to me. El's image belongs to me. He will attempt to redeem the man; this I guarantee you. We must bear this world still for many days until it is time to ascend and take back our home. Do not be deceived El will not stand idle whilst I hold his beloved hostage. But we must be careful in the thing. For the moment El..."

While Lucifer was yet speaking, an attendant came into the doorway and shouted to all within. "El has come and breaks the world!"

Immediately all rushed outside to see that angels stood on the winds and rode the backs of cumulus clouds as steads, and wherever the Prime evils looked, rain fell upon the ground. Angels fell from the sky and crashed into the earth, and when they did so great geysers of water ejected into the air, and all about Lucifer and the fallen, the earth erupted in water from below and poured rain upon the earth from above, and lightning and thunder crashed in their ears.

Suddenly a great light appeared above them and Mavet one of the Shaunteal appeared within the light carrying great chains, and spoke, "Semjaza you hath been found guilty of abomination and hath defiled the order of the Lord. You are hereby sentenced to the confinement of Tartarus."

Semjaza rushed through the assembled council members and attempted to flee, but Mavet cast forth his hand and black tendrils reached from the angel of judgment to ensnare Semjaza. Lucifer's henchmen attempted to escape them, but the tendrils found him, and held him fast, binding him. Mavet then descended and enveloped him and draped over him as a shroud, and Semjaza could be seen pushing against the blackness of Mavet to escape. His muffled screams could be heard as he struggled to break free. Lucifer's lieutenants looked on in fear while others attempted to interfere and stop Mavet but when they reached to touch him, they grabbed ether. Black smoke and embers of fire ushered from his presence, and Mavet looked upon Lucifer, and he, him.

Lucifer smiled, "And what of I? Will not the Godking touch the 'Author of Abomination'? Or is he too cowardly to do the deed himself?"

Mavet glided towards Lucifer and hovered in front of him. A towering black column of ash and cinder emanated from his presence. The crisp smell of burning flesh wafted through the air, and when he opened his mouth to speak and the screams of Semjaza were heard behind his words.

"You Satan wear Death about your neck, and Hell as your locket. The Almighty hath decreed that your time is not yet nigh. But know of a surety...that El will come for you."

Lucifer cocked his head and stood his ground before the angel and replied in defiance. "Let him come."

Mavet then pulled a scythe from his robes and slammed the hilt of it on the ground. Blackness then encircled from its base and a circle expanded beneath Mavet as a pool of oil and spread underfoot to all who looked. Each in attendance rose into the air to escape its touch; all except Lucifer who stood atop the blackness. Mavet slowly sunk into the darkness before them and opened his mouth one last time, and when he did the petrified screams of Semjaza echoed in all their ears.

Lucifer glared and his eyes narrowed as he seethed at the loss of Semjaza, "Let El come."

Slowly the blackness receded into nothing and Mavet disappeared from their sight.

Impotent to stop El, Lucifer, and his council watched as the waters of the flood overran all that lived and watched as the life of their offspring was washed away. And all flesh died that moved upon the earth, both of fowl, cattle, and of beast, and of every creeping thing that creepeth upon the earth, and every man: All in whose nostrils was the breath of life, of all that was in the dry land, died. And every living substance was destroyed which was upon the face of the ground: and Noah only remained alive, and they that were with him in the ark.

Lucifer marked Noah and his sons, and his Grigori watched as they disembarked and gave report. For though El had destroyed the Nephilim from the face of the earth; the plague of sin still coursed through Noah's veins. And Lucifer plotted to move against Noah and his offspring to sin, and to keep El at bay, and he schemed that he might destroy El by mankind's hand, but knew that it would be many days before he could challenge El.

* * *

And it came to pass that in the sum of time men replenished the Earth, and man was want to scatter himself and found the exchange of ideas hastened his creativity and inventiveness, and Lucifer moved men to be one people that he might teach them knowledge from on high. And the whole earth was of one language, and of one speech. And it came to pass, as they journeyed from the east, that they found a plain in the land of Shinar; and they dwelt there. And they said one to another, "Go to, let us make brick, and burn them thoroughly. And they had brick for stone, and slime had they for mortar. And they said, Go to, let us build us a city and a tower, whose top may reach unto heaven; and let us make us a name, lest we be scattered abroad upon the face of the whole earth."

And the thing that man did was made known to the Lord and the Lord came down to see the city and the tower, which the children of men builded. And the LORD said, "Behold, the people is one, and they have all one language; and this they begin to do: and now nothing will be restrained from them, which they have imagined to do. Go to, let us go down, and there confound their language, that they may not understand one another's speech." So, the LORD scattered them abroad from thence upon the face of all the earth: and they left off to build the city. Therefore, is the name of it called Babel; because the LORD did there confound the language of all the earth: and from thence did the LORD scatter them abroad upon the face of all the earth.

And Enoch was displeased for the thing caused his people to go backward in knowledge and slowed the pace with which they might overtake the earth and subdue it.

And the Lord knew Enoch's thoughts and said, "Not so my son, for let it be shown the path that the people tread upon that this thing must be." And the Lord called Argoth and said, "You have been given sight to see a partiality of that which is within the Godhead's mind. Show therefore thy brethren what thou hast seen."

Argoth then moved and pulled from his chest the golden book that was his Kilnstone and tossed the tome into the air. It rose and when it touched the ceiling, opened, and all the pages dispersed abroad and plastered themselves unto the beams, walls, and floors of the throne room. And all the Lumazi stood transfixed as each page showed them glimpses into the mind of God. For Lucifer had raised up nations of men who held not the image of the Creator in their knowledge and moved them to perverseness. The fallen had made governors of all manner of men from every nation and tongue. And they erected statutes and great monuments to false gods of wood, stone and gold. Some worshiped the sun, and Ra was awash in the worship of men. Some angels had moved men to worship their lost ancestors while others perpetrated fraud to Adams kin not knowing that they interacted with demons and not their ancestors. Moreover, the people became vile in their imaginations, developed knowledge, and harnessed the power of El's creation to make war. The Lumazi stood watching with mouths agape for the fallen had infected man with the idea that there was no God. That El was a myth, and Lucifer reigned over the Earth and men were as dung to him.

El then looked upon Enoch and lovingly spoke to him, "This my sons shall be the fate of man if I do not intervene and salvage my image and creation. For as my absence wrought war in Heaven, if I would turn my face from Adam, he would experience the totality of life absent from me and would descend into ruin. This I will not allow.

"Even now the adversary moves to raise up all nations and peoples that he might be seen as God. For though man was created a little lower than the angels; he yet possesses the image of the Almighty and will overcome the bounds given him. Yeah in time he shall breach the bounds of light which separate the realms, and on that day—Lucifer will have means to enter Heaven once more."

Enoch stood in silence. Ruminating on the power of his people to affect the cause of heaven, and how angelic kind puppeteered man without God's intervention. Metatron looked at Enoch and touched his shoulder, lifted his head and looked upon the Lord. "We cannot allow mankind to sink into ruin."

Gabriel also chimed in, "My Lord you have allowed us to behold what man was capable of at the tower, and the need to disperse his language that for a time he might be divided. Nevertheless, such a pause in his advancement is but temporary. For Adamson is your image and will overcome the limitation in time. If Lucifer could harness men's power of the knowledge of good and evil..."

God continued his sentence, "Lucifer would use man to find a passage across the realms, to breach death, and life. Yea to enter the Third Heaven and again incite war. But with now both angel and man as soldier, and on that day, he would move me to destroy the man I have created. To destroy by my own hand, he whom my soul loveth."

They all stood stupefied. The thought of war in Heaven again sent chills through the group. None had conceived that man who possessed God's image could become as Charon and be used as a weapon of war against them. It was a sobering thought.

Michael had watched the images. He searched the records of Argoth on the ceiling above and noted the absence of what El had shown him after the Descension. Information that he knew what El did not disclose. Information that he and for the moment only Argoth knew. That El was destined to die. That a member of the trinity would be given over to Adam's kin. Michael's face contorted with the thought that somehow in a future yet to come. Man would be given power to destroy the Creator. Michael looked upon Enoch and for a moment scowled. He shook himself from his rumination and spoke. "What is your will in this matter Lord?"

"I will fashion me a man by name of Abraham. For I know that he will command his children and his household after him, and they shall keep the way of the Lord, to do justice and judgment. And I shall take of him and make him a mighty nation, and through him shall all the nations of the Earth be blessed.

"For I have spoken with the man Terah, to leave Ur of the Chaldees. Yet his heart would not abide with me, but his son Abraham will be a father of many nations and shall heed all my counsel and will move by faith to a land not seen, and there I will build me a people, who after many days will birth a light to all men. A second man, and the last Adam; all that the Adversary would be thwarted, and my man will be saved."

Enoch looked up when the Lord spoke, "A second man?"

The Lord nodded but did not elaborate, and all knew that El had said all he would say, and Jerahmeel spoke, "The thing which thou sayest soundest good my Lord. How then would the Lumazi serve our King?"

"You will move to the far reaches of the earth and will give cause for Lucifer to be distracted from the people that I will make. You will battle with him across the front of Asia, the southern lands of the western hemisphere, and will draw his attention, that he will not see the mustard seed that rears. For if so, he would surely plant tares to grow with the wheat I must plant. You will battle him across the span of man's time and the enemy will think that I am there when I am not. He will in his desire to spite me, be blind to the rising of a nation underneath his very eyes. He will make his seat in a place of power, yet I will bring him low at the hand of slaves and bondservants. All that Adam would be saved, and my name be glorified in the Earth."

Jerahmeel bowed, "My Lord if we do this thing, Lucifer will destroy much of creation, and there will be many days before he can be brought low. Adam and his people will suffer. Suffer from thine perceived absence, suffer at the hands of the enemy, and moreover suffer to experience themselves without thee."

The Lord said nothing looking as if afar off. Tears began to well in his eyes, for none had seen the Almighty ever weep. For El looked across the span of time and knew that he held back the multitude of suffering that Adam and his kind would endure; knew that the plague of sin would contaminate all of creation, and that nothing would bring the plague into check unless he himself would come down from the throne and surrender his life. A sacrifice to buy back man from the hand of the enemy. The Lord wiped the tears from his eyes and looked upon his children before him, and when he did, all were bowed with heads hung low. All except Michael, who stared at him knowingly, whose thoughts the Lord knew.

I know my Lord. I do not profess to like your plan. Yet if thy death is thy will to save Adam. Then know that I am thine to command.

El smiled at his child and spoke to the mind of Michael. *Thank you, my son.*

* * *

Michael went to approach Argoth in private and the two met in the Chamber of War. Argoth was busy looking over the placement of the forces of Lucifer and of Heaven's legions when he came in.

"Am I disturbing you Argoth?" Michael asked.

"I am busy seeing to the troop movements...we have lost the Typhon Expanse in the eastern quadrant, and Wormwood hast broken free."

Michael stood and ran to see the projection from the book that showed Wormwood moving through space. But the angel seemed wounded, and though he moved towards the Earth it would be many days traveling the second heaven before he would be a threat.

"In El's name! How has such a thing come to be? Wormwood was sealed within a tomb of ice hidden within dark matter; he could not be found."

Argoth continued working and did not look up to face Michael. He simply opened more books and viewed the layout of the universe that showed how Lucifer's forces sought to free some of their trapped brethren.

Michael also looked at the position of the galaxies and systems that were displayed before them, and everywhere he looked, the armies of Heaven were in a battle with Lucifer's forces. And the ebb and flow of the conflict saw many of the host lost and some of Lucifer's forces bolstered.

"Michael saw that Argoth had positioned a legion but left their flank exposed while Lucifer's forces moved to combat them.

"Argoth you need to send reinforcements to the western edge of Lynax star system.

Argoth continued to work, pouring over maps and books and darting his eyes back and forth between the images above him and the topography of the universe displayed on the table.

"Argoth!" Michael reached to grab his arm, and Argoth pulled from Michael's grasp, misted, then turned to speak.

"How dare you lay hands on me. Who do you think you are? It was not I who asked to lead the armies of Heaven. Nor I who battles conflict. I do what I must because thou art absent from the body, and leave Heaven handicapped. All because of your selfish musings. Do you think that El hast a plan B for you? Nay. El never has a plan B. He only has one plan. And it is for you to lead. Instead of observing the actions of all things, I now must function in two roles. I am humbled in my role, and content to abide therein. Yet, you run from the destiny that El has for you. So leave me Kortai. For you are a stumbling block to me. You seek to advise me? Let advice be mine to thee.

"Either lead thy people, follow the path thou hast chosen, or remove thyself from my way! Which is it? For unless you are here to give command as Chief Prince, I have charge of the armies, and you will obey the order of the Lord, and leave the War chamber now! Or have you too fallen in league with thy brother that I must fight my peer in my own land?"

Michael was struck by the words of Argoth and was about to give retort, and Argoth lifted his hand to stop him. "No Michael do not speak to me. When you are no longer of double mind and stable in who you serve then come and give council, but until then find me a soul who has faith and works. For faith without works is dead being alone, and your faith is small. Now go, and leave me to do the work of Heaven that you have willingly abandoned." Argoth then turned away from Michael and returned to studying the maps laid before him.

Michael stood rebuked, turned quietly and walked to exit the War Chamber, and closed the door behind him.

Argoth watched him leave and spoke. "He needed a push. He must ascend to whom El hast destined he become."

Jerahmeel materialized to Argoth's side, and replied, "I know...he knows what is needed to defeat our brother. We need him to become who he was meant to be. Give him time."

Argoth nodded "Time is not a luxury that Enoch and his people have." He looked at the maps splayed before him. "Nevertheless, we need to bolster the western flank of the Lynax star system."

* * *

El sat on his throne and watched as the plague of sin rage as a weed through the garden of his creation. Man had become increasingly evil, and though he had destroyed all but eight from the face of the Earth, man was a creature given to the influence of Lucifer and the Fallen. And El had set before him bowls that were filled with the sins of Adam. And the Lord could not look upon his image for it was marred and disfigured behind the plague that Lucifer and Adam had unleashed in the land.

The eyes of the Lord then ran to and fro throughout the earth to find a man of faith that might believe the God of Heaven, that God might make influence in the Earth. And the Lord found such a man in the person of Terah, and the Lord compelled him to move from the heathen land of Ur of the Chaldees to a land rich in milk and honey that men had named Canaan.

Yet Terah only went halfway, and settled his tent in Haran and died there, and it was during this time that El set his eye on Terah's son Abram and spoke to him. "Get thee out of thy country, and from thy kindred, and from thy father's house, unto a land that I will shew thee: And I will make of thee a great nation, and I will bless thee, and make thy name great; and thou shalt be a blessing: And I will bless them that bless thee, and curse him that curseth thee: and in thee shall all families of the earth be blessed."

So, Abram departed, as the Lord had spoken unto him; and Lot his nephew went with him: and Abram was seventy and five years old when he departed out of Haran. And Abram took Sarai his wife, and Lot his brother's son, and all their substance that they had gathered, and the souls that they had gotten in Haran; and they went forth to go into the land of Canaan; and into the land of Canaan, they came.

And El communed with the man Abram and confirmed his word that the land wherein he dwelled would one day by his, and his descendants would one day be as the dust of the earth.

And Abram said, "Lord God, what wilt thou give me, seeing I go childless, and the steward of my house is this Eliezer of Damascus?

And Abram said, "Behold, to me thou hast given no seed: and, lo, one born in my house is mine heir. And behold, the word of the Lord came unto him, saying, "This shall not be thine heir; but he that shall come forth out of thine own bowels shall be thine, heir. And he brought him forth abroad, and said, "Look now toward heaven, and tell the stars, if thou be able to number them: and he said unto him, so shall thy seed be. And he believed in the Lord, and he counted it to him for righteousness.

And he said unto him, "I am the Lord that brought thee out of Ur of the Chaldees, to give thee this land to inherit it."

Abram replied, "Lord God, whereby shall I know that I shall inherit it?

The Lord then said to him, "Take me a heifer of three years old, and a she-goat of three years old, and a ram of three years old, and a turtledove, and a young pigeon."

And Abram took unto him all these, and divided them in the midst, and laid each piece one against another: but the birds divided he not. And when the fowls came down upon the carcasses, Abram drove them away. When the sun was going down, a deep sleep fell upon Abram; and, lo, a horror of great darkness fell upon him.

God then said to Abram, "Know of a surety that thy seed shall be a stranger in a land that is not theirs, and shall serve them; and they shall afflict them four hundred years; and also that nation, whom they shall serve, will I judge: and afterward shall they come out with great substance. And thou shalt go to thy fathers in peace; thou shalt be buried in a good old age. But in the fourth generation, they shall come hither again: for the iniquity of the Amorites is not yet full."

And it came to pass, that, when the sun went down, and it was dark, behold a smoking furnace, and a burning lamp that passed between those pieces. In the same day the Lord made a covenant with Abram, saying, "Unto thy seed have I given this land, from the river of Egypt unto the great river, the river Euphrates: The Kenites, and the Kenizzites, and the Kadmonites, And the Hittites, and the Perizzites, and the Rephaims, And the Amorites, and the Canaanites, and the Girgashites, and the Jebusites."

And in the passage of time, the cry of Sodom appeared before the throne of God. And he commanded the Books be opened. And the record of the city was rife with wickedness that El would see if he would destroy it, and see his servant Abraham, and he spoke to Jerahmeel, Metatron and Azaziel, "Let us go down and see to the man. You three shall escort me. For the cry of Sodom has come up to mine ears and I would go down and see my servant and know his mind in this thing."

And the Lord appeared unto Abraham in the plains of Mamre: and he sat in the tent door in the heat of the day, and he lift up his eyes and looked, and, lo, three men stood by him: and when he saw them, he ran to meet them from the tent door, and bowed himself toward the ground, And said, "My Lord, if now I have found favor in thy sight, pass not away, I pray thee, from thy servant: Let a little water, I pray you, be fetched, and wash your feet, and rest yourselves under the tree: And I will fetch a morsel of bread, and comfort ye your hearts; after that ye shall pass on: for therefore are ye come to your servant."

And they said, "So do, as thou hast said."

And Abraham hastened into the tent unto Sarah, and said, "Make ready quickly three measures of fine meal, knead it, and make cakes upon the hearth." And Abraham ran unto the herd, and fetch a calf tender and good, and gave it unto a young man, and he hastened to dress it. And he took butter, and milk, and the calf, which he had dressed, and set it before them, and he stood by them under the tree, and they did eat.

And they said to him, "Where is Sarah thy wife? And he said, "Behold, in the tent. And he said, “I will certainly return unto thee according to the time of life; and, lo, Sarah thy wife shall have a son." And Sarah heard it in the tent door, which was behind him. Now Abraham and Sarah were old and well stricken in age, and it ceased to be with Sarah after the manner of women. Therefore, Sarah laughed within herself, saying, *“After I am waxed old shall I have pleasure, my Lord being old also?”*

And the Lord said unto Abraham, "Wherefore did Sarah laugh, saying, Shall I of a surety bear a child, which am old? Is anything too hard for the Lord? At the time appointed I will return unto thee, according to the time of life, and Sarah shall have a son." Then Sarah denied, saying, "I laughed not"; for she was afraid. And he said, "Nay; but thou didst laugh."

And the men rose up from thence and looked toward Sodom: and Abraham went with them to bring them on the way. And the Lord said, "Shall I hide from Abraham that thing which I do; seeing that Abraham shall surely become a great and mighty nation, and all the nations of the earth shall be blessed in him? For I know him, that he will command his children and his household after him, and they shall keep the way of the Lord, to do justice and judgment; that the Lord may bring upon Abraham that which he hath spoken of him. And the Lord said, "Because the cry of Sodom and Gomorrah is great, and because their sin is very grievous; I will go down now and see whether they have done altogether according to the cry of it, which is come unto me; and if not, I will know."

And the men turned their faces from thence and went toward Sodom: but Abraham stood yet before the Lord.

And Abraham drew near, and said, "Wilt thou also destroy the righteous with the wicked? Peradventure there be fifty righteous within the city: wilt thou also destroy and not spare the place for the fifty righteous that are therein? That be far from thee to do after this manner, to slay the righteous with the wicked: and that the righteous should be as the wicked that be far from thee: Shall not the Judge of all the earth do right?"

And the Lord said, "If I find in Sodom fifty righteous within the city, then I will spare all the place for their sakes."

And Abraham answered and said, "Behold now, I have taken upon me to speak unto the Lord, which am but dust and ashes: Peradventure there shall lack five of the fifty righteous: wilt thou destroy all the city for lack of five?"

And he said, "If I find there forty and five, I will not destroy it." And he spoke unto him yet again, and said, "Peradventure there shall be forty found there."

And he said, "I will not do it for forty's sake."

And he said to him, "Oh let not the Lord be angry, and I will speak: Peradventure there shall thirty be found there."

And he said, "I will not do it if I find thirty there".

And he said, "Behold now, I have taken upon me to speak unto the Lord: Peradventure there shall be twenty found there."

And he said, "I will not destroy it for twenty's sake."

And he said, "Oh let not the Lord be angry, and I will speak yet but this once: Peradventure ten shall be found there."

And he said, "I will not destroy it for ten's sake." And the Lord went his way, as soon as he had left communing with Abraham: and Abraham returned to his place.

Then Jerahmeel, Metatron, and Azaziel looked as commanded by the Lord for ten within the city that it might be spared. Through hamlet and hovel they searched, and from the palace to the burbs they combed and when there was none that the city might be saved they turned to rescue Abraham's nephew Lot but were accosted by the men of the city that they might lay with them. And the three angels escaped after making the band that sought to take them by force blind and warned Lot and his family not to look back. "For it is not the will of God that thou stare upon the suffering of others."

The three angels then rushed them from the city for they knew that God would rain fire from Heaven.

And Enoch was aghast at the destruction that the angels had caused, and he was wroth and stormed into the throne room that he might be as a candle to the people of the plain. "Lord what is this that I have seen. How can my God destroy the whole of cities by fire?"

The Lord looked upon Enoch and spoke, "There is no other path to which cleansing from sin can be accomplished. Alas, did I not look for a reason to spare, as my servant Abraham had pleaded for the city? Yet despite its great sin, by such a multitude for the sake of but ten would have the city been spared. Alas, for the city wast not destroyed for what lay within, but for what was not present. For if but one would plead for the sinner, all would be saved. Yet no one stood as intercessor to the city save one who was outside its gates. Was I not just in looking for ten in accordance with the word of my servant?"

Enoch then held his peace. For the angels had searched for ten and had found none, and in accordance with the command of the Lord set themselves to its destruction. For Enoch beheld what could only be seen from the vantage of God. For the city was rife with violence, murder, and uncleanliness, and its people cruel, and the daemons of Lucifer had moved to obliterate the image of God in the people.

Argoth watched as the Lord rained fire and brimstone from the sky and that several of the fallen had watched the destruction of Sodom from afar and stood aloft to take note.

"El lays waste again to our works," said. Assyrix. Once more we are undone. How shall Lucifer seed our people if El rains fire and brimstone from the skies?"

Assyrix noted that smoke rose into the sky and turned to see that three angels from Heaven escorted four humans to escape the city. And they flew after them to see whom El held in such importance that he would save them from wrath. For the command to all watchers were to report on any of heaven's activity that might shed light on the plan of the enemy. And Assyrix and the scouts noted that Lot and his daughters were spared from destruction. Immediately, the trio left their post to head to the headquarters of Lucifer, and they arrived and bowed as was custom when brought into the presence of their Lord.

"Master, heaven hast obliterated the cities of the plain. Lo Sodom and Gomorrah lie in ruins as El hast burned the region roundabout with fire."

Lucifer frowned, "There are multitudes of the humans that will serve as host for our kind. I do not care that El lays waste to a city when I raise kingdoms in the regions of Egypt and Sino." Lucifer turned to return to his work and the study of maps and spoke, "Ashtaroth remove them and see I am not disturbed again."

Immediately, Assyrix spoke aloud. "Yea Lord the cities of the plains of Sodom are but dust. But El hast sent three from heaven to rescue a man and his daughters from the destruction and hast hidden them within a cave."

Lucifer was sitting in a chair and his foot swung gently then suddenly went still. He turned his attention to the three Grigori. "El hast lodged humans? And you say that there are females amongst them?" Lucifer's scratched at his chest and stopped to listen intently for the reply.

"Aye Lord," came the response.

Lucifer stood to his feet, and all within the room bowed. "Assyrix you will follow these humans and report on their coming and goings. Zeus, and Ashtaroth you will find me the house this man belongs. I would know his blood."

Zeus and Assyrix bowed and Ashtaroth spoke, "And what is your command when we find the man's line?"

"Lucifer grinned, we will have found Shiloh, and then we will kill El's host before he can manifest in the earth."

* * *

"Report of thy stewardship," commanded Lucifer.

Assyrix knelt before his master and relayed the intelligence he had been sent to gather.

El hast established a family within the earth. And hast with a man by name of Abraham made covenant!"

Lucifer frowned. "El hast bound himself to a human...covenant you say? Surely the report is false."

Assyrix bowed his face to the floor and spoke so that his Lord could hear. "It is true my king. For we have learned that El hast said that this man will be a father to many nations, and that through him shall all the families of the earth be blessed."

"How many children hast his line sired?" asked Lucifer.

"There are twelve sons my Lord. All strong, and with wives. There is lo a ruler among them even now who advises the man Pharaoh that we have set up in Egyptia."

Lucifer frowned for the thing was done under his nose. For Egypt was a power in the heart of the earth and feared among her neighbors. Through her Lucifer made a plan to bring all nations in the region to heel.

Abraxis, a representative of the council of Archons, opened his mouth to speak, "How is such a thing possible? How can a tribe of men devoted to El escape thy gaze? Hath, not El said that 'he shall crush thy head?' Yet you are not even able to identify the very line from which Shiloh would come. For a nation within a nation now takes refuge within the very people you have raised to destroy the plan of El! You have been tricked Lucifer, and El hast shown himself genius against thy schemes!

"Twice your stratagems have brought us to ruin! Two times now thy words have diminished us! We were foolish to follow you. To defy the Master. For what purpose are you our ruler if we cannot rule?"

Abraxis raised himself to defy Lucifer, and the First of Angels watched him and allowed him to speak unabated.

"Because there were no graves in Heaven, hast thou taken us away to die in the wilderness? Wherefore hast thou dealt thus with us, to carry us forth to exile? And who are you 'Chief Prince'? Who art thou to lead so great a people that we now must scavenge for food. For we now rot on this world which dost not grow manna. I say you have led us into famine and that we return to Heaven. I say that we humble ourselves and to return to El. I say...," and Abraxis pointed at Lucifer, "That we bind him!" Abraxis screamed at the top of his lungs. "Bind him I say and bring him in chains before El!"

Lucifer rose, and the elders quieted themselves as indecision and the waffling between two opinions held them in meek suspension as they beheld Abraxis challenge Lucifer for leadership.

Lucifer walked towards Abraxis and as he did he uncloaked and his cape fell to the floor, immediately the colors of the rainbow swirled about him. Light radiated from his person, and all present raised their hands to shield his eyes, as he walked towards Abraxis, he spoke.

"I stepped on the stone which fires thy creation, and it is I alone who have traversed the colon of Hell herself. And lest ye forget, it is I, and I alone who hath made God to bleed."

Abraxis moved back fearful, for Lucifer's voice vibrated the walls of the cavern. Cracks wound themselves up and down the ceiling and across the floor. Lucifer's image shifted and changed and his visage was projected over the entirety of the area.

"You have pledged yourself to me; to the Usurpation. Because I realize that the duress of our station might have caused these to forget, that if I in all of creation hath made God bleed, what then might I do to thee? I do not need Charon to dispose of thee. He will simply be pallbearer that brings thy soul to the Gates of Hell. Therefore, I ask thee Abraxis. Whom do you serve?"

Abraxis quaked as Lucifer towered before him. His Draconian armor ready to cut him down at the slightest provocation, and he spoke the words that he knew his master was waiting to hear.

"I am thine to command God king." And Abraxas fell to his knees and bowed to Lucifer.

Lucifer smiled, "Thou hast spoken wisely." Lucifer immediately hovered his hand over the head of Abraxas, and exposed the talons in his forearms, and with them severed the head from his neck.

The body of Abraxis slumped over at Lucifer's feet. The prince of angels picked the head of his now silent pretender to his command and lifted it high for all to see.

"You are fools if you think El will see you returned. For it is *He* that hath exiled you—not I. *He* chose to leave you with your father. And never let it be denied that *I am* your father. For ye are my sons and I will not see you without a future. Therefore, I command that ye shall each make kingdoms of the sons of men. Traxiel ye shall mark the sons of Shem. Pangu shall be archon over the sons of Ham, and Quetzalcoatl shall archon over the sons of Japheth. A nation and nations shall ye build me. Ye shall make the sons of Adam heel to worship us and myself in particular, for I am thy King. He that raises the most powerful of all nations shall be by my right side, and the other shall command at my left. Now go to and raise men that will smear the name of their creator, and when the time is ripe. I will arise and men shall see that salvation is in no other name but my own."

All the elders nodded in submission and slowly took their leave, all while Lucifer held the head of Abraxis, and when all were gone save he and Charon, he spoke.

"Come curator of Death. Let us go and teach Adam that Death and Hell are a thing to be feared."

* * *

Gabriel searched for his brother and found him in the foundry hammering away on an anvil. Michael had authorized the creation of armaments to outfit the Legions to do battle against the schemes of Lucifer and Ares his minister of war. Steam and the sparks of Heaven—forged steel clanged in his ears and Gabriel stood next to Michael spoke.

"Jerahmeel hast told me of your encounter with Argoth. So does my brother sulk behind the stroke of hammer to steel?"

Michael continued hammering and did not look upon his brother. "Gabriel I am not in the mood to hear thy words, nor comment of my ascension to Chief Prince."

"Ah...," said Gabriel. "But ascension is the goal of Lucifer. It is the burden now of Argoth, and for thee."

Michael hammered and spoke aloud over the sounds of folded steel, "I did not ask for such a mantle." Sweat dripped from Michael's brow and his muscles flexed as he pounded on the anvil. Gabriel admired the already completed swords and shields that hung on the armory walls and spoke.

"The mantle of power given as Chief Prince is a title that is both honor and burden. For with it one must carry the secret of the Almighty. With it, faith in his purpose must be absolute. I know of no other in all of Heaven who can be trusted to lead us in battle when it comes."

Michael wiped the sweat from his forehead and sighed, "You flatter me, but there are many others who can lead the forces of Heaven. I am content to build her."

Gabriel nodded. "Many that are worthy—perhaps. But Chief Prince can only come from Lumazi. You are still Lumazi. We are the seven spirits of God and stand before his presence. There is but one of us who can take on this task as is the order of all things.

"Seven amongst thousands times ten thousands. And of the seven, one is lost in grief, and still battles himself, and will not be made whole. Another, though wise, cannot leave his station for he is in command of the guard of heaven and holds the key to the Abyss. Our newest members have not the perspective to understand our brother, nor the mind to which he will move against us. Though they both possess great power they have a zeal but not according to knowledge."

"Argoth has command of the legions," said Michael. "He is in command."

"Aye," said Gabriel. "Argoth is in command, yet Argoth thinks of himself more highly than he ought to think though humbled by our brother's actions. He hast neither led forces into battle, he is quick to judge, slow to hear, and believes that his sight alone gives him title to command others."

Michael looked away and continued his hammering at the blade he carefully fashioned. Sparks flew as the blade submitted to the strike of his powerful arm. The smell of iron filled the room, and Michael stopped his pounding and looked at his brother and spoke. "There is yet one who is wise, and pure of heart who in all of our battles hast not deviated to the left nor right of honor. You speak of others and yet neglect thyself. I would follow thee into battle. What say you?"

Gabriel laughed, "It is not I who El hast chosen to lead the forces of Heaven. I am content with my station. And though if need be I would command the armies of God. I am not best for the task. El hast given each of us our talents or would you bury in the ground that which El holds dear?"

When Gabriel spoke, Michael's heart was pricked. For he had not considered that his actions would diminish El's will. Yet retort still lingered over him as a fog and he replied.

"I have sheathed the blade of Ophanim. I do not wish to wield it again."

Gabriel nodded, "Understood, but it is not with blades that we will bring Lucifer low." He placed his hands on Michael's broad shoulder and looked him in the eye. "Nor will heaven forged steel bring war to a close. But it will be because of faith, hope, and love...the greatest of which shall be love." Gabriel then looked intently at his brother and asked, "Do you love the people Michael?"

"You know that I love them," he said.

"Then are they not worthy of sound leadership? War is of vital importance to the state. No sovereign can lightly enter therein. You are loath to fight, yet when cause came to stand against the wiles of the Devil. You braved Hell itself, destroyed the birthplace of angels, and fought the Dragon until he bled fire. All to see the will of El be done."

Michael turned then continued hammering on his anvil. Gabriel looked at him and spoke. "A third of heaven's children hath been torn away, and will you leave to another to build what only God hast elected that you construct?"

Michael stopped hammering, turned to look at Gabriel and spoke, "You think by not assuming the role of Chief Prince. I have opened Heaven to further bloodshed?"

Gabriel spoke, "As you saith."

Michael winced, "But I did not ask for this burden. It was not my wish to be elevated so. I am but a servant to El."

Gabriel replied, "And it is because you have served with honor that El would see you lifted that you might be a servant to all. Would you frustrate the purpose of God?"

Michael looked at his brother in anger. "Would you label me Adversary as our brother?"

Gabriel did not hesitate to respond, "Would you frustrate the purposes of God?" he asked again.

"I am not Lucifer!" Michael roared and he flung the hammer across the armory.

"Exactly," said Gabriel. "And that is why you must lead."

Michael was quiet for a moment. "If I assume the title of Chief Prince then I must die," Michael said, "For El hast spoken."

Gabriel was quick to reply, "Then you shall die."

"I..," Michael hesitated then bowed his head to commune with the Lord in prayer. "El hear me. If I might still accept the title given, then I yield myself for trial. I repent. For I now see that thy gift was despised in my eyes. Yet if forgiveness yet remains, allow thy servant even now to earn what once was freely offered, that I might serve thee in all things."

Immediately a light shown over Michael and Gabriel.

"Come up hither," said a voice. And the two disappeared from view and emerged in the throne room and stood before the Genesis of Creation, the Lord God himself. Michael and Gabriel then knelt before their king.

"I have heard thy prayer and have granted thy petition. You will seek Eladrin. He will judge thee as worthy. But lo, if you go. You will surely die."

"As you command," Michael said.

Gabriel asked the father, "Who will lead in his absence Lord?"

El looked upon them both. "Argoth shall lead the legions. But the title of Chief Prince shall not be his to hold. Steward to the legions shall he be until thou hast returned."

Michael and Gabriel nodded in acknowledgment.

"My Lord when am I to seek Eladrin?" Michael asked.

"Rise and go to the Hall of Annals. There you will meet Argoth and Enoch, and Argoth shall prepare thee for what thou must do."

Michael and Gabriel rose then turned from the Lord and left to find Argoth. As they walked towards the Hall of Annals, Michael spoke. "There is a favor I must ask of thee."

"Say on," said Gabriel.

"There is a charge given me by the Lord. A charge whilst away I cannot monitor. I pray that you will stand in my stead to see to its completion. There are two others who are aware of this mission, Argoth, and Jerahmeel; they also can help if need be in the cause."

Gabriel smiled, "The thing will be done. What is thy charge?"

Michael replied, "I need thee to watch over the blood of a maiden who is not yet. Her name is Mary and El hast revealed she shall birth Shiloh."

* * *

Michael and Gabriel arrived at the Hall of Annals and found Jerahmeel and Argoth already notified by the Lord and prepared to receive them.

"Michael it pleases me that you have taken up the cause to assume the mantle of leadership. Surely, Heaven's foundations will stand secure when you sit in your place among the Lumazi," said Argoth.

Michael laughed, "The last time we spoke you basically told me to get out. Am I now to understand that you would see me be Chief Prince?"

"It was always my task too but speak the truth in love. For we are one body fitly joined and compacted so that every joint supplieth. Yes, my prince, I desire to see you assume your station so that I can fully function within my own."

Michael looked upon Argoth surprised, sighed, and then spoke, "You then have my thanks, in prompting me to fulfill the will of El in all things, and now, I must ask you questions that I might have hope of success."

Argoth replied, "Say on."

"Hast anyone ever attempted to climb the mount?" Michael asked.

"No," said Argoth. "The Ophanim keep all at bay. No one but the chief prince hast ever been to the top. Atop the mountain, there are not even Grigori who know what lies beyond. It is as the Maelstrom, and El has not given me sight to see what lies upon."

"How then do I find the nest of Eladrin?" Michael asked.

Argoth reached into a drawer and pulled out a glass jar. Within it contained a scroll that shimmered in the light, flickering as if the parchment struggled to remain in this realm of existence. The glass jar was sealed, and Michael began to turn the golden cap to reach inside when Argoth prevented him.

"No! The thing can only be opened in the presence of the Ophanim. Go to where the Ophanim protect the mount and when they descend upon you for laying foot on Holy ground. You may open it then, and only then."

Enoch looked at Michael spoke, "I will go with you as I desire to see what God will not share with angels."

"No Adamson, your place is to attend to your studies here with me," said Argoth.

Enoch put his hands on his hips and looked at Argoth, "I'm sorry, but did you elevate to Godhood and I was not informed? Am I a pet to be looked after? I will go where I see fit I am not a prisoner in Heaven."

Argoth sighed, "You are a stubborn man, very well then, be it upon thine own head."

Michael looked at Enoch with his eyes raised, "If I take you Adamson, you will slow me down."

Enoch looked at Michael undeterred and replied, "Then you shall be slowed down." Enoch walked away to quickly gather a clutch of supplies.

Jerahmeel laughed, "I like this human!"

Michael turned to Jerahmeel and whispered into his ear. "I need you and Gabriel to take up my charge in my absence. See to the maiden's welfare and secure her blood."

Jerahmeel nodded. "We shall see the thing done. Fear not, she is *your* charge, and it will be *you* who shall see to her protection. You just make sure of your return to see to it."

Michael smiled, hugged his brother in a long embrace, then let him go and spoke to Enoch. "Come we need to get underway."

The two then left the Hall and proceeded to the mount of God.

* * *

Talus walked to the Great Library. The building had burn marks over sections, and portions where the roof had collapsed when the Godstones had fallen from the sky. Grigori attendants moved with haste to restore the building. Kortai workers also coordinated with them and the library's renovations were coming along swiftly. Talus went to the desk for inquiry.

"Greetings," he said. "Who presides as Lord Keeper of the Library now?"

The angel behind the desk replied. "It is an honor high prince. The Sephiroth has not yet voiced who is yet to command the library. We expect a decision soon my Lord. In the meantime might I direct you to Raziel he stands as the angel of Knowledge and hast been standing in Hariph's stead until bidden, he is the last of the order not killed by the renegade Lilith."

"Take me to him," commanded Talus.

"This way my Lord."

The attendant motioned Talus to step behind the counter and two entered into a back chamber. Opening the wooden door, the attendant bowed and gestured Talus to enter. "Chief Keeper I present—"

"I am not the Chief Keeper Lathaniel; I am but a humble servant to our Lord El."

"My apologies Raziel, I meant no disrespect. Prince Talus, Raziel steward of the library." The angel bowed and turned to leave the two alone to converse.

Raziel also bowed as was custom, then spoke. "Prince Talus, how might I serve you?"

"I seek information on the word—"

"Golem...yes I know high prince. I expected you to come."

Talus stood stupefied. "How,...how could you have known?"

Raziel smiled. "I am Grigori, and Grigori *watch* High Prince. There is little that we do not know, and even glimpses of the future are available to us. Your Grigori is ever present with you. And what one of us knows, we all know."

Talus cringed at the thought then spoke. "And what of thy fallen brethren? Do they also know?"

"Alas, no my prince. The Fallen are severed from the collective. They only know what was before the Descension, and what they are able to collect and share with one another now. Yet they may still infer, and some among them even possess the sight to see glimpses into the future."

Talus scrunched his brow, and his eyes narrowed, "Does Michael know of this?"

"The High Prince is made aware of the state of creation and given updates as to the movements of the Fallen. Yet you asked about Golem. Come hither and see."

Talus moved closer and Raziel picked up a tome and set it on the pedestal that he might see. "Is this where Raphael died?" asked Talus.

Raziel stopped and bowed his head. "I will miss the words of his script in my heart. His pen moved with song" Talus nodded in agreement.

"Behold my Lord the Golem." An image appeared in the air from the book, and Talus observed an angel. It stood motionless as if awaiting command. It did not blink, and its breathing was barely perceptible. "This my prince is Golem; it stands mute until acted upon by another. To be a Golem is to be stuck in a state that one cannot move past. A Golem my Prince is someone who is in denial of the truth."

Talus looked intently at the creature. "This is an angel, how did he come to be in this state, and moreover what can be done to help him?"

The turning of Eskalion into Golem occurred when Prince Michael rescued him from the creature Minos. His Grigori holds a record to his history. Would you care to see it?"

Talus nodded, wondering if he should continue further.

Raziel removed another tome, and it sprang to Life.

The two angels watched as the angel Eskalion battled several angels who had caused rebellion in heaven. Eskalion was strong in battle and three of the fallen were upon him and also attempted to strike down another angel who was giving medical aid to one who held to the cause of El.

Eskalion intervened by stomping into the earth and the might was such that waves of concussive force emanated from the ground and disrupted time, that all who opposed him were lifted into the air and tumbled defenseless in a form of stasis. Eskalion then lifted a glaive he had taken from a fallen foe, and with three swift strokes cut asunder the three attackers. Their bodies fell in severed pieces to the ground. Eskalion saw the blood on his blade, the stream of blue that flowed from the bodies he had cut. He raised his hands and cried out in anguish for the lives he had taken.

"Image off," commanded Raziel.

"Why did you stop the reading?" Talus asked.

"My prince forgive me...it is not needful to know the rest of Eskalion's pain to understand what has happened."

Talus became angry, "Would you presume to tell me what I need?" He hast done nothing that many of us during the war was want to do. He took up arms to defend. To protect and fight for the cause of El." There is nothing to see here but what billions have themselves done. Therefore, you will show me. How did he become this Golem?"

Raziel sighed, "As you wish my prince. Advance to the breaking of Eskalion."

Immediately the image continued and Eskalion was in his bed, and he held his pillow behind his head in an attempt to cover his ears. "Be quiet!" he shouted. "No!" He spoke aloud to himself. He swiped at the air as if beating back enemies. Yet none was seen save Eskalion alone in his bed.

Talus looked down disturbed. "Hast the angel lost his mind? What is this that I behold?"

Raziel said nothing but merely pointed his finger to the image before them. Talus returned his eyes to the floating picture of an angel's bout with apparitions in his mind. Violently Eskalion moved his hands over his head as he rocked back and forth. "I did not kill! I...I... El... they would not stop...I had too...," and he broke down and cried in his bed.

"What plagues him?" Talus asked.

"All of us have had to adjust to the loss of our brethren. To make sense of having to strike down those who earlier were our kin. Now a third of Heaven stands to us lost. We have studied this thing and have called it *grief* my Prince. An emotion named by El that many now experience. An emotion El works even now to comfort, ease and to console. All must walk the path to wholeness again, and all have done so differently. Eskalion was eventually captured and confined to Tartarus, digested within the flesh that was Minos. He pushed against his brethren trapped within to breath, to fight for escape; forced to climb atop the bodies of his own countrymen that he himself might live. All while others were crushed underfoot. Lucifer's penitentiary was without mercy, for the prisoners within were digested alive, whilst they clambered over one another to stay away from the acids that consumed them. Until Prince Michael rescued him, and Charon defeated Minos he was lost to the dark that was this torture of angelic death. And the fear of death to an immortal will drive him mad.

"Eskalion is bereft of peace in his actions. For he hast killed, even though it was in defense of others. Most of Heaven now hast blood on her hands. For we have taken the sword to combat the renegade Lucifer, and it has come at great cost."

Talus watched as Eskalion paced back and forth in his chambers and finally he lifted his hands as if to wave away attackers and cried out, and when he did the surface of his skin changed. Soft platinum skin turned dark green in color, and his veins swelled that one could see the blood vessels that pumped the life from his kiln stone through him. His eyes darkened and stone scales grew atop him, and he moved as a creature of rock and stood as a sentinel of stone within his chamber. Nothing emanated from him but breath and the rising and falling of what was now his rocky chest.

"He has turned to stone. How is such a thing possible?"

Raziel looked at Talus. "My Lord I am not at liberty to speak of the matters of the heart."

Talus was incensed. "Your prince has asked you a question, and you would defy me? Was not this the selfsame spirit that compelled me to assault Ashtaroth? Would thou be tempter to me? Answer me I command you!"

"There are some answers that cannot come from but one alone," and Raziel lowered his gaze from Talus and looked at the floor as Argoth entered the room.

Talus turned to see that Argoth had entered the chamber. "Raziel I hereby charge thee as Keeper of the Library. You have been found faithful among our people. Well done."

Raziel bowed, "Thank you, my prince."

Talus was not done, and looked at Argoth, "I gave him a direct command, yet I stand empty of my answer. I expect an answer now."

Argoth looked at Raziel and spoke, "Forgive the high prince, he dost not know what he asks."

"There is nothing to forgive my prince. Might I be released to my duties?"

Argoth nodded and Raziel left to leave the two alone.

"You have much explanation to give Argoth." said Talus.

"Indeed, yet your query is neither for Raziel nor I. You query El. Therefore, pose your questions to him."

Argoth waved his hand, and his pen and stylus glowed, and they stood immediately in the throne room of El, and the Lord sat on this throne and asked Talus. "Who are you?"

Immediately Talus bowed and put his face to the floor and spoke aloud. "I am thy servant Talus, birthed of the Kiln, and High Prince of house Arelim."

"But are ye not Golem?" replied the Lord.

Talus held within his frustration and attempted to choke back tears. "I...I...am what the Lord says that I am."

The Lord replied, "Thou hast answered rightly. Now rise son of God."

Talus rose to his feet to look upon the Lord. "My Lord I... I stand in distress."

The Lord nodded. "Again, thou hast spoken rightly."

Talus grimaced, "I am humbled for from my stone which thou hast created, my stone which you have held in thine hands. I have lifted myself above measure and have brought war into the realm. I am shamed. For if my actions had been other, then war would not have caught hold in Heaven. I confess my sin to my God. I am no more worthy to be called thy son. For why hast the Almighty forgiven such a great thing, for I am no longer worthy to be Lumazi, and my lot should be with the Fallen." And the mighty Talus stood before the Lord trembling, and he looked at the Lord with tears in his eyes.

The Lord smiled and immediately Yeshua the second person of the Godhead stood next to him and shown with a brightness and Talus was afraid for the presence of God was within arm's reach and he recoiled, and he bowed and prostrated himself to the ground.

The Lord Yeshua reached forth his hand and touched the head of Talus and spoke. "Arise friend." Talus lifted himself from the floor and beheld the face of God in Yeshua. Yeshua touched his face and hugged him. Talus froze his arms opened wide not knowing how to respond.

Yeshua spoke, "It is customary when someone hugs you to hug them back." El himself sat on the throne and smiled.

Talus replied, "I have brought war into the camp of Heaven, and you would show thy servant affection?"

Yeshua replied, "If it need be done, I will hug you my son until the end of time."

Talus broke down and swiftly hugged Yeshua and laid his head on his neck. "I... I am so sorry Lord."

Yeshua and El spoke as one, "You think that you are cause to Heaven's war, and that thy actions were the seed to strife?"

Then Yeshua ceased from hugging him, pulled away and touched his eyes, and when he did so a great light flashed before him almost blinding him. Images, and whispers of words spoken in secret were loosed in his ears and upon the screen of his eyelids. The Lord opened Talus's eyes, and he beheld the schemes of Lucifer. The Lord showed him all realities, and how they all wove to form a tapestry that created a picture of God's design, and each image and every idle word spoken; every action was seen through the eyes of God. All points of view weaved and crossed yet all things originated from God's decision to grant the first of angels' free will. And Talus saw that in all realities and in every circumstance he could not act but as he acted, and the Lord was neither surprised nor dumbfounded and knew that after Talus had fallen away he would return to strengthen his brethren.

Talus collapsed to his knees sobbing for he saw his actions through the eyes of God and that El held him no malice. Moreover, he beheld through the Lord the mind of his friend Sariel. And Sariel loved him and always sought the best for him. For even to the last of his days his heart held a great love for him. The emotions were too much for Talus to hold, and he sobbed and curled as a baby on the golden glass floor of the throne room weeping at the feet of Yeshua and before the throne of El. Yeshua bent down to wrap himself around his son and when he did so. Another burst of light-bedazzled Talus and after several squints, the throne room was dark and Talus lay on his bed, and as he stood up and the guilt and shame were gone. Emotions that no longer plagued him and he knew that his worthiness to be Lumazi stemmed not from him, but from El's own choosing. He saw a glimmer from the corner of his eye and turned, to see the image of Yeshua slowly fade and smiling at him, and words were spoken into his mind.

"Ye have not chosen me, but I have chosen you that ye should bear fruit and that your fruit would remain." Then the image of the God of all the universe smiled at him, faded, and disappeared.

* * *

Michael looked up at the craggy mountain before them, sighed and then looked at Enoch. "Are you sure you wish to go with me?"

Enoch looked upwards at the mountain as clouds and small bird flew high above. "I'm in Heaven. If I die, I will just come back here. You have much more to worry about than me."

Michael chuckled, "But what if I throw you from the top twice?"

Enoch laughed, "I think that will do it yes." Enoch then gave Michael a wary eye, not sure if he was joking or not.

Michael laughed then turned to face the base. "Here climb atop my back, it's time to go."

Enoch did as bidden and Michael stretched out his wings and lifted himself skyward. Effortlessly they flew and with each ascent in elevation, Enoch beheld the beauty that was Heaven. The clouds now healed from piercings with ladders, hummed and refracted the light while rainbows blanketed the sky. Birds of unimaginable beauty soared. Heaven was alive and vibrant and everything that lived radiated an aura of song.

Enoch spoke into Michael's ear, "How far has an angel flown up?"

"Michael was short of breath as he exerted himself to lift them both with all of their gear but answered in quick responses. "No... angel hast ever...seen the top...save one."

"Lucifer?" Enoch replied.

"Lucifer," said Michael.

Higher they flew and Enoch noticed that they began to reach the cloud canopy that hid the peak of the summit.

Michael continued, "No angel hast flown near the mountain for the Ophanim guard the mount and let none approach for it is Holy Ground. Even the Lumazi...have had but limited access...and only at its base. Tales have been...told of angels who...curious have ventured close. Some...even attempted to ascend it...but—"

Michael pierced the cloud layer and several of the clouds slowly moved towards them, humming, and singing.

"Woe...woe...Ophanim this one is not." Closer they came and the sound of their movement was as thunder. Michael could feel the booming of their chant against him, and the waves of concussive sound made it harder to fly.

"Will they harm us?" asked Enoch.

"I... I am...not sure. No angel hast ever pierced the cloud banks of Heaven save Lucifer."

Thunder again boomed and a wisp of a cloud suddenly formed in front of them. "He does not sing as the Chief Prince. He does not croon our song. Why do you not sing?"

Michael continued to fly and dodged the form that materialized before them. Ascending higher. Michael started to gasp, "I...I...am having trouble breathing."

Enoch found himself suddenly choking..."I too—"

Another cloud formed before them, then several others encircled the duo, and Michael was stopped from advancement unless he forced himself to fly through them.

"You must sing the song," said one.

"He is voiceless," said another.

"He does not croon."

Michael and Enoch wheezed, coughing with heaving chests as clouds enveloped them and the air grew increasingly thin. Whiteness prevailed in their vision and the booming of thunder in their ears.

"If he does not sing, he is not worthy."

"No, he is not"

"Woe to this angel."

"Woe indeed."

Michael panicked and reached for his throat. He bucked and Enoch seeing they might fall to their death, opened his mouth to sing.

"There is one God of all.

One God there be.

The Lord of all creation

The Lord Almighty..."

"Sing Michael!" yelled Enoch.

Michael then opened his mouth using his last breathes to lift up El in song.

"Who is like the Lord?

Who is like our God?

Who dwells in the Heavens?

And makes home among his creation.

Who is like the Lord?

Who is like the Lord?"

"They sing!" said a cloud.

"Their croon is sweet," said another.

"Breath upon them! Let us hear more!"

Suddenly a wind came from the clouds Air filled the lungs of the duo, and Michael felt himself lift under the power of the clouds to new heights. They two continued to sing in harmony each following in a chorus after the other and the clouds joined them in song.

"Almighty is our God

Sovereign Lord and King

Who is like the Lord?

The praise of whom we sing."

Higher they lifted and Enoch and Michael took in great gulps of air, finally able to breathe. When the clouds started to thin they saw that above them were great arcs of lightning that blanketed the sky. Bolts streaked overhead and electric currents heated the air and blasted the mountainside sending rocks careening into the clouds. Michael noted a cleft in the rocks and flew within to shield them from the lightning. Enoch dismounted his angelic brother's back and looked down. Nothing could be seen across the horizon but clouds, falling rock, and streaking bolts of electricity blanketing the sky. Thunder echoed and bounced off the mountains walls, making the air vibrate, and beat upon the chest.

"How can we ascend higher through that?"

Michael unpacked his gear and took a light stone striking it against a rock and it lit and gave off a warm heat. "I do not know yet. But we shall find a way."

Enoch sat down and began to open his pack, "Are you sure we can get through, I don't see a possible way one could survive that."

Michael continued to go through his gear, "Yes I am sure."

Enoch looked at Michael and observed him. His hands were shaking and some of his gear he could not grasp, and he shook from the trembling.

Enoch reached over and cupped Michaels hands in his own and looked at him and smiled.

Michael stopped and looked at him, smiled and nodded. "Thank you."

Enoch smiled, "You said that Lucifer was the only one ever to ascend the mount. Did he ever share how?"

Michael shook his head, "The thing is not known to me. As Chief Prince, there is knowledge that only he who occupies the role would know. I... I do not know how he did it. But we *will* find a way."

Enoch laughed, "Well one day I woke up, and expected to deal with men who would seek to kill me and my tribe. On the same day Death itself and thy brother visited me, and the God of all creation snatched me away. You will understand that if by now nothing really moves me."

Michael laughed and when he did a roar of thunder crashed against the cliffs the explosive sound was deafening. The sky lit in illuminated flashes round about. The roll of distant thunder rumbled and then dissipated in the distance. Then Michael squinted and saw it. Pointing at the movement of color in the distance, he spoke, "Look there!"

Enoch followed his finger and saw it as well. It was large and circled like a wheel or a ball, it became visible between flashes of light and the colors of the rainbow was its skin. It moved in jagged movements as if it was surveying the skies. Immediately they knew it was an Ophanim. The creature flew between the lightning strikes, weaving between bolts as if the descending arcs of voltage stood still. It had no wings, yet it moved ever closer towards them.

Michael's brow wrinkled and he spoke, "I do not like the look of this, there is a cavern deeper in the cleft. I think we should move deeper in."

Michael looked at the Ophanim, which was clearly racing towards them, and as it did a rainbow-like trail of light followed it as if attempting to catch up to it and lightning flashed around it in vain attempts to strike it.

Enoch nodded, "Agreed, anything that can sidestep lightning is not to be trifled with."

Quickly they gathered up their gear and turned deeper into the darkness, only holding a light stone for illumination. Enoch turned and saw that it was closing on them. "Hurry Michael...hurry!"

Michael too turned and saw that within moments it would reach them. It was clearer now. It held four faces, one of a bear, one an ox, and one an eagle, and one of a man. Each face turned and its eyes were red, teeth barred, and it screamed as it flew; great gyroscopic wheels encircled it, and it was awash in color.

Michael grabbed Enoch, ran and followed the caverns walls. Suddenly light exploded throughout the room, and the grinding screams and screeching of wheels could be heard. The cavern shook and rock and dust fell from the ceiling and found home on the cavern floor.

"It's here!" cried Enoch.

Michael turned and he could see the creature burrowing after them, the walls giving way to its wheels, which now scraped against rock and ground them aside as nothing. Waves of invisible force suddenly pulled at them, and they began to slide towards the creature.

Enoch found himself pulled and desperately reached out to grab anything to keep him from being dragged to the creature's clutches.

"Grab my hand!" yelled Michael.

Enoch reached for Michael's hand, and they interlocked, and Michael held to Enoch and dug a stake into the earth. The Ophanim screamed and the creature's presence dissipated gravity that they found themselves levitating in the air, and anything that was not bolted to the earthen floor flew towards it and disintegrated in the Ophanim's rotating wheels within wheels.

"Hang on!" screamed Michael. Shouting above the roar. Slowly Enoch's grip loosened, and Michael knew that he would lose him to be crushed within the rotating monsters pivoting discs.

He summoned the sword of Ophanim from its sheath, and the sword roared to life, and floated in the air awaiting mental command from Michael.

Immediately the Ophanim backed away and it spoke from each four faces.

"Ophanim!" said the eagle face.

"Ophanim!" roared the face of the man.

"Ophanim!" yelled the bear's face.

"Ophanim!" screamed the ox face.

Michael assented the sword to split and it did, and razors for teeth bared themselves and eyes within the blade twirled and the Sword of Ophanim was alive and formed a rotating wheel between the duo and the creature.

"It is Ophanim?" asked the eagle.

"It does not scream like Ophanim," said the man.

"It has no wheel it must be born of Kilnstone," said the bear.

"This one is neither angel nor Ophanim," said the ox.

"Yet the minister of flame handles Ophanim!"

"How is the thing done?"

"Take the flesh thing. It will know."

"Yes, we will make it tell us."

"Take it."

"Yes, take it."

The creature screamed and Enoch was torn from Michael's grasp, and Michael thinking Enoch would be killed released the sword to attack, and the sword flew towards the Ophanim's wheels, and the sword locked, and the wheels stopped and when they did the faces fell to the ground. Instantly Enoch and Michael and all their gear dropped to the cavern floor.

The Ophanim screamed and when it did the wheels resumed their rotation, and the sword flung backwards and Michael dodged the blade as it whizzed past barely missing him.

"Michael!" Enoch screamed.

Michael watched as Enoch was ripped from the cavern and held aloft by the creature. Quickly the Ophanim backed out of the cave and lifted into the air. Michael ran to the edge and lightning smashed above him temporarily blinding him and sending rocks and boulders tumbling down the sides of the mountain. Yet even in the whiteness, the Ophanim could be seen dodging bolt after bolt and flying upwards. Michael summoned his sword to his waiting palm, looked at the streaks that raced across the sky and jumped from the cliff to fly after his captive friend.

* * *

Chronos flew across the northern hemisphere of the planet and landed at the northern pole. He surveyed the surroundings and wind, and bitter cold danced about his frame. He was an angel, and his kind could not be phased by the physical realm unless they shifted out of their celestial form. The wind roared, howling at nothing but providing entertainment to the listening ears of Chronos. Waters and shifting sheets of ice floated past him. Iblis had asked to meet him in the quiet of where the Earth shifted. Its axis pointed towards the mountain of God. The only place on Earth where a member of the fallen might come closest to being aligned with home.

"Thank you for meeting me Chronos," said Iblis as he materialized through a sheet of ice.

"You said you have information?" Chronos replied.

"Yes, there is a tenth of the fallen who work against the purpose of Lucifer. A small cell who when able provide means to weaken the Usurper."

"We do not have much time; tell me quickly about thy master's plans."

Iblis frowned. "I know I stand condemned for my crimes. I deserve the judgment given me. El be praised. I submit to the will of the Almighty even in this thing. Perchance he might find mercy to grant entry back into the realm immortal. For if, Lucifer knew of our betrayal. He would surely have our heads."

Chronos replied, "The information Iblis before we are discovered!"

"Iblis reached into his pouch and pulled from it a scroll and handed it to Chronos who opened it.

"What is a *'Hellforge'*?"

It is a place where abominable weapons are made to fight against the Host. It is rumored that within the Forge itself, even one's kiln stone can be changed to tap powers latent within. Lucifer would see Heaven fall and he creates within the bowels of the creature a place where even angels dare not assault. For who would brave Hell's maw to destroy such a place? Within he crafts and commits sorceries that he might bring El low."

Chronos paced as he read the scroll further, his brow wrinkled as he continued to pour over the parchment. "Who is this Moses ye are targeted to destroy?"

Iblis hunched his shoulders and quickly looked to his left and to his right. "The thing is not known to me. What is known is that the Grigori, who now stands at Lucifer's side, has the gift of foresight. He has told the master about this Hebrew and when Lucifer learned that he was to be a prophet to a nation of God. He was enraged and demanded that he be found and that a daemon inhabits the human. Even now he searches for the bloodline of the child."

"You have done well Iblis. Now go before you are discovered, and I will tell thy prince the service you have provided Heaven today."

Iblis ghosted and was gone blending seamlessly into the polar winds that drifted snow across the icy waters.

Chronos looked to the sky, the clocks within him moved, and he was gone in the twinkling of an eye. Unbeknownst to him, an angel watched him rise in the distance and took out a lens and held it to his eye and he saw the misty trail that showed the direction of Iblis, now traveling to the south side of the planet. He would track this traitor and in due season bring his head to his master Lucifer.

* * *

Higher Michael flew into the voltage—latticed sky. Thunder crashed around him and ahead he saw Enoch struggling against the Ophanim held captive in its grip. Flashes and crackles of white darted and each spark of lightning illuminated nothing but grey skies and, even more, branches of lightning further ahead. Michael could not catch the creature, but his sword could. Michael pointed to the creature and the sword obeyed. Lightning struck it, and it glowed for a moment as if absorbing its power and the bolt of electricity bounced off the blade and arced away. Michael dodged and weaved doing all he could to not be struck. He motioned again and the sword split and hurtled towards the Ophanim. Seven blades bathed in blue flames bolted across the skies and thrusted into the gyrating wheels of the creature. The rotating circles cracked, and the sound of glass shattering echoed across the sky and a wave of light exploded into Michael's eyes. The Ophanim roared in pain and plummeted, and with its fall, it released Enoch, and he fell to the earth.

Michael dashed between bolts and recalled the swords to heel, and he dived towards Enoch who plunged unconscious through the sky. A flash erupted and Michael looked to his rear and several Ophanim chased him. Lunging forward he hurtled to reach Enoch, caught him and flew up the side of the mountain with his companion in his arms. Lightning pelted the mount and Michael weaved through bolts of heated plasma, shutting his inner ears so as not to be deafened by the roars of thunder.

And then all went quiet, and time was still.

One second.

Three Ophanim were behind him, closing fast, and above him was a lattice of electricity that seemed impossible to pass, and the sky was lit with arcs and branches of voltage.

Two seconds.

He commanded his sword to split, and it rotated as a shield before him.

Three seconds, another flash, the sword whirled in spinning fury as he shot to the roof of the known sky.

Impact.

The sword severed what looked like an electric net, the sky lit at once and arcs of lighting suddenly stopped as both the sword and Michael punched through the charged barrier. Ripples of power oscillated through the sky and suddenly there was no lightning, no thunder, and no chasing Ophanim. Michael could see the top of the mountain and jutting out from its top a great aerie.

Scores of Ophanim flew across the sky, and they flew as darts and all around them their wheels moved and changed colors. When they rotated, the wheels disappeared and sparks flew from them as a trail and the creatures turned into prismatic light and shot across all Heaven, and Michael beheld the secret of this realm of Heaven and stared in wonderment and awe. For, thousands upon thousands of ladders ascended and descended through the clouds and escaped the roof of Heaven, and the marching realization opened Michael's eyes to the truth that none but God and Lucifer knew.

The Ophanim were the ladders.

Chapter Four: Underground

Michael flew to the aerie and as he did, Ophanim stopped their buzzing and the gyration of wheels, and all turned their red eyes towards him. Michael landed on the soft ground and gently placed Enoch on the ground. Quickly dozens, then hundreds of Ophanim descended to surround him, and their rotating wheels were as the buzzing sound of locusts adrift on the wind. Michael slowly reached into his pouch to withdraw the glass jar and the shimmering parchment scroll that was sealed within.

"He is not Ophanim," spoke one.

"He is not the Chief Prince," said another.

"No, he is not."

"Kilnborn has trespassed upon the Holy Mount!" an Ophanim screamed.

"Rewind the Kilnborn!"

"A fleshling, too...destroy the fleshling."

"Rewind them both," said one.

Michael watched as the group of Ophanim encircled him, as jackals assessing prey. He pulled the glass jar from his pouch and lifted it above his head.

"Rewind them!" The chant came. First, it came from one, then from dozens until all repeated the refrain. "Rewind them!"

Dust and rocks lifted from the ground and light flashed in wispy static sparks. "Rewind them!" Prismatic light appeared all about Michael and Enoch, and he knew that he was being Laddered. Light surrounded him and the air heated, and the colors of the rainbow sprinkled themselves between flashes of red, greens, and blues, and the roar of a Ladder pounded in his ears, and Michael sensed that there were but moments before Enoch and he would be removed from the Aerie.

"Argoth this had better work." He muttered and he took the hourglass and smashed it in the ground.

A funnel cloud appeared from beneath them, and when the parchment hit the ground it lit into flames. A great pyre erupted and turned into a pillar of fire, and it snuffed out the prismatic light of the Ladder into nothing, and it roared as high as the eye could see. Searing heat made all to stand back, and Michael for a moment was inside the eye of two great storms, and the Ladder dissipated, and Enoch and he stood surrounded in spiraling embers of fire, and from the pillar, a voice bellowed from the flames.

"I am the Alpha and the Omega, the beginning and the end."

Immediately all motion stopped and the Ophanim's wheels stopped their gyration, and they halted from moving and the eyes of the creatures turned from red to blue and looked upon the pillar of fire. None spoke, and there was silence round about. Michael kneeled, for he recognized the voice of God from the fire.

El's voice bellowed like thunder for all to hear, "The human stands as candlestick, and witness to this minister of flame. Eladrin shall judge this one if he is worthy to be Chief Prince. For I am the Lord thy God."

Immediately the pillar of fire sizzled to nothing. Michael looked about him, and the Ophanim was still bowed, and he saw that Enoch was awake. Slowly all the Ophanim turned and just stared at them.

"I take it this is the place?" Enoch questioned.

Michael nodded and they watched as the Ophanim resumed gyrating and then lifted into the skies. The duo heard a sound from their rear, and when they turned to look. They saw a figure emerging from the darkness of the aerie. It stood 200 meters high, and its shadow enveloped them, and the thing was a giant wheel within wheels. Gyroscopes rotated within and without and gears and levers moved within it. Moreover, it floated with no wings, but all about it moved discs, and Michael was awed.

"Wow," Enoch said, his mouth gaping in abject wonderment to the sight they both beheld.

Michael then turned to the giant Ophanim and said, "Who art thou?"

Formed from the flakes of God's omnipresence, the creature turned to face Michael. He moved in a circular fashion, and it had a multitude of faces that changed as he moved, and it spoke with the sound of the voice of rushing water.

"We are the King of the Ophanim. We are Eladrin and we swim in the sea of eternity and fly in the skies of the infinite. We are time in the flesh, the expanse of dimension—the wheel within the wheel."

Michael was overwhelmed, for he saw all around him the Ophanim carried not just stars, but whole galaxies were propelled by their movements. Michael looked out from the roof of Heaven and saw ladders shoot across constellations, and land in the Ophanim's nest. And it was then that

Michael realized that when the Ophanim heard the command of El, it was they who Laddered to bridge time and space. For the Ladders were not empty chutes and slides, but sentient creatures that did the will of God, and moved as commanded. The second heaven was latticed with their kind as they shot back and forth from one place to the other.

And Eladrin King of the Ophanim, orchestrated it all. For he turned and whole seasons changed. When his face turned to the right, Michael saw the passage of time in the heavenlies and galaxies birthed and die. As Eladrin moved the Ophanim, El Himself moved all: a whole race of Elohim who moved the universe at the command of God. Michael once more learned anew that El merely showed a portion of himself to them. For the Ophanim were as the shoes of El, and they moved backward and forward, and side to side and all of Creation was turned as they moved, and El turned them. Star system after countless star system was bridged, and the Ophanim heard the call of angels as if they were notes of music, and whenever they heard a summons, they fell from their perch on the mountain of God. Moreover, when they fell they turned in whirling tornadic winds of prismatic color and raced across the circle of Heaven to scoop up angels and transport them wherever they were bidden. Michael was astonished that of all in Heaven, only he among all angelic kind knew that though his kind moved stars, the Ophanim moved the galaxies.

* * *

Now the Lord had raised up Abraham, and gave him a heritage, and promised him a land, but because there was a famine in the land, Jacob had commanded that they settle at the order of Joseph, Jacobs's son in the land of Egypt.

Now these are the names of the children of Israel, which came into Egypt; every man and his household came with Jacob. Reuben, Simeon, Levi, and Judah, Issachar, Zebulun, and Benjamin, Dan, and Naphtali, Gad, and Asher. And all the souls that came out of the loins of Jacob were seventy souls, for Joseph was in Egypt already. And Joseph died, and all his brethren, and all that generation. And the children of Israel were fruitful, and increased abundantly, and multiplied, and waxed exceeding mighty, and the land was filled with them.

Now there arose up a new king over Egypt, which knew not Joseph. And Lucifer moved over him to tempt him to bring burden to the people of God and provoked him to cull the line of God in the earth, and made Pharaoh speak unto his people, "Behold, the people of the children of Israel are more and mightier than we. Come on, let us deal wisely with them; lest they multiply, and it come to pass, that, when there falleth out any war, they join also unto our enemies, and fight against us, and so get them up out of the land." Therefore, they did set over them taskmasters to afflict them with their burdens. And they built for Pharaoh the treasure cities, Pithom, and Raamses.

But the Lord protected the people even in bondage, and the more the Egyptians afflicted them, the more they multiplied and grew. And they were grieved because of the children of Israel. And the Egyptians made the children of Israel to serve with rigor, and made their lives bitter with hard bondage, in mortar, and in brick, and in all manner of service in the field. All their service, wherein they made them serve, was with rigor.

And the king of Egypt spake to the Hebrew midwives, of which the name of the one was Shiphrah and the name of the other Puah. And he said, "When ye do the office of a midwife to the Hebrew women and see them upon the stools; if it be a son, then ye shall kill him, but if it be a daughter, then she shall live." But the midwives feared God and did not as the king of Egypt commanded them, but saved the men children alive. And the king of Egypt called for the midwives, and said unto them, "Why have ye done this thing, and have saved the men-children alive?" And the midwives said unto Pharaoh, "Because the Hebrew women are not as the Egyptian women, for they are lively, and are delivered ere the midwives come in unto them."

Therefore, God dealt well with the midwives, and the people multiplied, and waxed very mighty. And it came to pass, because the midwives feared God, that He made them houses. And Pharaoh charged all his people, saying, “Every son that is born, ye shall cast into the river, and every daughter ye shall save alive.”

Soldiers on command of Pharaoh went all through the land of Goshen, and at the command of Pharaoh pulled from the arms of mothers and barred the obstruction of fathers to execute their lord’s will. And throughout the land, the cries of children could be heard, and Lucifer was pleased, for the blood of Shiloh he would see spilled in the earth.

And there was within the land of Goshen a man by the name of Amram and his wife Jochebed, and the couple would not submit to the will of Pharaoh.

So, Moses' mother hid her child and placed him along the river Nile away from the eyes of the Pharaoh’s soldiers, watched over by his older sister as he drifted. After a time, he was pulled from the river by the daughter of Pharaoh. And Pharaoh's daughter took pity upon the child and raised it as her own and named the child Moses. And the child of Hebrew slaves grew to not know his people and was brought up in the house of Pharaoh as a prince of Egypt.

And Argoth beheld these things and knew that the vision Michael had shown him was slowly coming to pass.

* * *

Jerahmeel prayed to the Lord and said, "Lord God, how long wilt thou suffer the sons of Egypt to lay waste to thy people? When will the God of all the Earth bring recompense to this evil people?"

The Lord replied, "Alas, for the cries of my people have been with me these four generations and behold the iniquity of the Egyptians is now full."

Jerahmeel then beheld a cup that sat before the Lord and within it held the prayers of God’s people, and next to it was a balance, and when the cup of the Lord's people filled with prayer, the scale tipped, and the weights fell to the crystal floor. A clear liquid poured from the cups of the tipped scale and pooled on the floor. The floor shimmered and the floor projected the earth, and Jerahmeel watched as the Lord raised a man from his people. Watched as he grew, and the man's name was Moses. Jerahmeel noted that Moses was driven from Egypt into the wilderness and that the desert winds and grit of sand washed him of the arrogance that he displayed while a prince among the Egyptians. The Lord then called to Moses, from a flaming bush that did not burn, and Moses followed the voice of the Lord, who directed him into a mountain.

The Lord looked below to see the Earth, and Moses, the man He had chosen to lead His people from bondage, was on a mountain, and the Lord said, "See, I have lighted a bush in flames that consume not, and lo Moses goes to see the thing. For I will use my servant, Moses, and with him punish the Egyptians and shake the foundations of their world."

The Lord appeared unto Moses in a flame of fire out of the midst of a bush, and Moses looked, and behold, the bush burned with fire, and the bush was not consumed. And Moses said, "I will now turn aside, and see this great sight, why the bush is not burnt." And when the Lord saw that he turned aside to see, God called unto him out of the midst of the bush, and said, "Moses, Moses."

Moses replied, "Here am I."

El said, "Draw not nigh hither. Put off thy shoes from off thy feet, for the place whereon thou standest is holy ground." Moreover, He said, "I am the God of thy father, the God of Abraham, the God of Isaac, and the God of Jacob." Moses then hid his face for he was afraid to look upon God.

And the Lord said, "I have surely seen the affliction of my people which are in Egypt and have heard their cry by reason of their taskmasters, for I know their sorrows. I am come down to deliver them out of the hand of the Egyptians, and to bring them up out of that land unto a good land and a large, unto a land flowing with milk and honey, unto the place of the Canaanites, and the Hittites, and the Amorites, and the Perizzites, and the Hivites, and the Jebusites. Now, therefore, behold, the cry of the children of Israel is come unto me, and I have seen the oppression wherewith the Egyptians oppress them. Come now therefore, and I will send thee unto Pharaoh, that thou mayest bring forth my people the children of Israel out of Egypt."

El continued to talk with Moses and then gave him a rod and sent him with his brother Aaron to confront the angels and Pharaoh who had set themselves up as false Gods among the people.

The Lumazi assembled to watch El in this thing, as the Lord would bring to naught all belief that the Egyptians held to the idols of the people.

"What is El doing?" Azaziel asked.

Argoth turned to face him. "El seeks to bring low the false images that Lucifer has placed in Egypt and to show the people of His promise that the Almighty covers them. Watch and stand ready, for El doth do battle with gods."

Azaziel then beheld from the throne room that El sent Moses before Him that He might show Himself powerful through a human vessel.

Azaziel tapped Jerahmeel on the shoulder. "Why doth not El Himself just descend and bring relief to the people?"

Jerahmeel smiled. "The ways of the Lord are a thing of wonder. There are many reasons we have discerned; one is that El seeks to share with His children His wonders and prefers to partner through them. It pleases the Lord when faith is expressed, especially in the direst of straits. El does not need to descend to destroy. His thought alone, should He wish it could bring oblivion. Yet He limits Himself, that He might receive glory through another. For if His vessel is mighty, what then will the people deem El to be? Humankind cannot fathom the totality of what and who El is. His presence cannot stand sin and might bring fear to the people. Thus, He sends an ambassador to show the nature of the Godhead."

And when Moses stood before Pharaoh and commanded him to let his people go, Pharaoh would not let the people go, and Pharaoh withstood God and said, "Who is the Lord God that He should be obeyed to let the people go? I do not know thy God, for the people are mine."

God then spoke through Moses to Pharaoh that He would unleash ten judgments, that He might show Pharaoh that there is only one God in all the Earth.

And God said, "I go to break the minds of the people and to show my wonders in the land, for lo, if Pharaoh releases the people now, Satan will still hold a place in the peoples' minds. I go to cast down every high thing that would exalt itself against me. Pharaoh is but a man, and the Fallen are not God. I will go to war through my man to cast down angels who have made themselves gods among men. And when they are cast down. Then I will turn Pharaoh's heart, and he will let the people go."

And there rested over the people ten evil spirits that acted as principalities over the minds of men. The Grigori counted them, and the record showed that ten angels ruled on Satan's behalf in Egypt.

Moses stood before Pharaoh, and round about the king of Egypt were ten angels, five to his left and four to his right, and standing behind Pharaoh was Charon, whom Lucifer had sent as his herald to keep all his minions in line. And Charon was a slave to Satan, and those Egyptians who had been given partial sight into the realm of the spirit called Charon Anubis, and Charon stood as the invisible power behind all previous Pharaohs, such that a mere man was worshiped as God.

The Fallen had deceived the men of the Nile that they were gods, and the nine that were chief in this thing were Hapi, Heket, Seb, Uatchit, Nut, Isis, Osiris, Hathor, and Ra. But Charon who also had been named Anubis by men, stood behind Pharaoh as protector and as the God of Death and only moved at the command of Lucifer.

Moses walked in the power of El and spoke against Hapi— the lying angel who the Egyptians worshiped as God of the Nile. And Hapi sought to stand against Moses. For Hapi caused the Nile to flood per the instructions of Lucifer and give unto the people fertile land. Moreover, whenever the people perceived through Creation that there was a God greater than Hapi the river God, he withheld the Nile that there might be famine in the land. And the Lord was wroth that Hapi disturbed the order of the Lord and had made the people believe he was a god and was cruel as to hold back from the people. The Lord, through Moses smote the power of Hapi, and when Moses put his staff in the water, the water became as blood. And Hapi would not cede that a man from God would have power over him, and he gave power to the priests of Pharaoh to duplicate what Moses and Aaron had done. Hapi then spoke. "See, El delivers to us a feast to show that in this world we are God. For if El be triune, can we who are a multitude not be anything but God to man?" For Lucifer had promised the Fallen that in this world, all could be a God.

Moses came again a second time and set himself against Pharaoh and set himself to smite the angel Heket, and by the word of Moses were frogs unleashed over the land. And the frogs were as a blanket of filth, loathsome and moist with slime, and the people were troubled by them, but the people would not believe that there was, but one God and Pharaoh would not be turned.

"For I will do unto Pharaoh even as men have done to the frogs," said El. "For I shall harden his heart, and he shall boil in judgment and be still until Egypt is boiled in their own sin."

However, Heket was emboldened by the success that his brother Hapi had with the man Moses, and gave power to the Egyptian priests, and they too duplicated the word of Moses by Elomic command so that frogs also came forth.

And the Lord was pleased that the people believed that the priests of Egypt were as Moses, that He might escalate the destruction of the stronghold of belief in both angel and man's mind that there were many gods. El then sent Moses to Pharaoh, and He caused Moses to unleash lice into the land. And Seb was Archon over the dust of the Earth, and when Seb used his power to recall the lice, the lice would not heed, and Seb was humbled in the eyes of his brethren. For El would send a message to the Fallen that at his hand both angel and man could not build anything that El could not destroy. Again, Moses traveled to speak to Pharaoh and again demanded as an ambassador of El to Lucifer's king in the Earth to release his people. Again, Pharaoh spoke, "Who is the Lord that I should let the people go?" And because the spirits spoke into Pharaoh's ear and he gave them heed, El then hardened Pharaoh's heart, that by the words of Pharaoh's own lips he would break the back of the man king he had allowed Lucifer to set up as his puppet in the earth.

And slowly each of the Lumazi came to give report to the Lord, and each stopped when they entered the throne room, for El was standing and Enoch was looking into the floor and each angel that entered watched over the shoulder of Enoch, looking past the glass floor into the realm of men to watch El do battle against the false Gods of Egypt. They watched as El through Moses systematically destroyed each archon's power. And El was wroth against Uatchit, one of the angelic princes, and sent flies that rained upon Egypt in such numbers that the people were awash with them. For the flies were as a great plague upon the land, and there was no place in Egypt save the land of Goshen, where the Hebrews dwelt, where the flies were not. They were in the water, and soiled the food, and there was no place that the flies did not touch. And the whole of Egypt became unclean. All the Lumazi watched, as the angels that stood behind Pharaoh could not recall the flies, for El gave command with the word of the man Moses's lips.

"What is El doing?" asked Metatron.

Jerahmeel turned to answer but then watched as Argoth revealed to them via images in the ceiling how God had poured bowls and bowls of living water unto the man Moses, and how he was emboldened in the power of the Lord with each engagement with Pharaoh and the angelic princes that Lucifer had set up to undergird his kingdom.

"Lucifer has raised up a kingdom in the Earth, and he hast lifted great monuments and convinced the people that there are many gods that they might serve him. El has given power to a son of Adam who holds El in faith and will move as commanded. Thus, El goes to war with Lucifer to birth a nation from the loins of slavery. Then all nations shall hear of it and will hold the people in fear. It will give El the time He needs to fashion Him a people of faith so that Shiloh may come," said Jerahmeel.

All gazed as El struck down angel, after angel, each set as a false god to detour worship from El to the Fallen, and ultimately to Lucifer himself.

El then unleashed unto the nation a plague, such that the livestock of the people died, and He destroyed the economy and the means whereby the nation might produce and trade with other nations. And when Pharaoh would still not repent, El sent boils into the nation and unto the flesh of all men save the people of God. The boils were of such affliction that the Egyptians were sore from them and cried out to Pharaoh to let the people go. And for a season, it would seem that reason had come into Pharaoh's mind, but El was purposed to destroy all doubt of His Lordship and the people would not be eased for their inconvenience, for they were a prideful people. They were children of their father Lucifer and took pleasure in the lash on the people of God, and the Lord would not show mercy, for they made the people of God work with rigor and placed heavy burdens upon them.

Therefore, the Lord turned His face away and He smote them from the sky, and it rained hailstones of fire upon the nation. The hail destroyed crops and buildings, and set aflame hut and palace, and fire swept through the land for the hail that poured upon them, and there was no place safe that the people were not exposed to fire from Heaven. And it was so that El touched all manner of the people's confidence. For they cried out to Nut, the Egyptian god of the sky, but the hail would not stop. Isis and Osiris were also invoked in their pagan rites, but the angels of Lucifer could not rescind the command of the Lord and bring the hail to stop. In time, the people's confidence failed them, and they set upon Pharaoh to reason with the man Moses and his God. For his God made the sky to rain fire. And Pharaoh began to confess his sin, and when he did Moses spoke to God to withdraw his hand, and the Lord hearkened to his manservant and did so, but when Pharaoh saw the hail had ceased, he hardened his heart again and refused to obey the voice of the Lord through the man Moses.

"Because he hath eaten the sin of offense and will not bow to the Almighty, and Pharaoh's king will not release him due to his pride. Therefore, I will remind Pharaoh's king of his rival and call to his remembrance the Destroyer."

The Lord then summoned locusts to come and spoke. "Leave neither stalk, nor kernel, nor seed of grain. Go to and let Pharaoh know that there is but one God in all the Earth."

The insects stormed Egypt upon the command of their Creator and came for every blade of grass and shaft of wheat. As a moving dark cloud, they settled across the sky of Egypt and came in swarms that they blotted out the sun, a descending consumption that lighted upon the land, a voracious army eating leaf and stalk. And lo, the infestation reigned that even within sealed containers, locusts poured out, so that all of Egypt was covered and all green in the land was peeled bare and ravished.

Enoch observed that Argoth received reports from Grigori from across the region that other nations and peoples had received word of the happenings in Egypt and were amazed that the nation had incurred such punishment, leaving the slaves of Goshen untouched. And many wondered which God they served and had begun to fear. However, plots emerged among some that they should destroy the slaves of Goshen, and invade Egypt, and when the Lord heard this He spoke.

"Let all nations know that the God of Heaven and Earth doth hear the thoughts of all flesh, and none shall touch that which I have sworn to my servant Abraham."

The Lord then extended His hand, made a fist, and squeezed as if He was crushing a grape, and immediately, the angel Ra, who had been chief of the sun after Apollyon's fall, collapsed. For the Lord had reached out with His own hand and caused the angel's heart stone to shatter, and Ra fell dead in front of the archons that surrounded Pharaoh, and darkness covered the realm of Egypt.

Frightened that El had slain one of their own, the court sent word to Lucifer that he should come quickly to Egypt, for El had attacked them directly and they were sore afraid also of the man Moses who stood as the voice of God.

And Lucifer heeded their call and came to Egypt to behold the destruction that had been wrought by what he thought was but a man, and he spoke. "Who is this son of Adam that he stands yet alive? Why hast he not been killed? Had not I ordered that upon discovery of any child by the name of Moses that the child should be destroyed, and now what is this that I must be absent but a few moments, only to return and see that the man is alive, and brings forth ruin to my kingdom?"

Those who still held meekly to surround Pharaoh when Moses approached spoke. "He speaks with the authority of El. El hast found a man that will by faith move when bidden."

And the thing which Lucifer heard caused him to take note and he waited until Moses came to court. And when Moses arrived, Lucifer paused to kill Moses, remembering how El had come down and swept Enoch away, and Lucifer listened as Moses gave an ultimatum to Pharaoh.

Moses commanded Pharaoh once again to let his people go. And Lucifer was wroth that a man would dare raise himself to speak to the king he had set up as power in the Earth, and Lucifer provoked Pharaoh to say unto Moses, "Get thee from me, and take heed to thyself, see my face no more; for in that day, thou seest my face thou shalt surely die."

Moses replied, "Thou hast spoken well, I will see thy face again no more. For the Lord hast spoken and said, at about midnight will I go out into the midst of Egypt. And all the firstborn in the land of Egypt shall die, from the firstborn of Pharaoh that sitteth upon his throne, even unto the firstborn of the maidservant that is behind the mill, and all the firstborn of beasts. And there shall be a great cry throughout all the land of Egypt, such as there was none like it, nor shall be like it anymore. But against any of the children of Israel shall not a dog move his tongue, against man or beast, that ye may know how that the Lord doth put a difference between the Egyptians and Israel.'" Moses then turned and stormed from Pharaoh's presence.

The Lord spoke unto Moses and said, "This thing is of me, for I have hardened Pharaoh's heart, and shall bring to naught the power thereof. For Pharaoh shall not hearken unto you, so that my wonders may be multiplied in the land of Egypt. For lo, I will pass through the land of Egypt this night and will smite all the firstborn in the land of Egypt, both man and beast; and against all the God's of Egypt I will execute judgment: for I am the Lord."

Lucifer stood watch to see what El would do, for he commanded Charon, and was smug that El held no sway as the keys to death and Hell were his to control. And all of Heaven waited to see how El would bring Egypt to her knees. And about midnight, the Lord Himself commanded the life of each firstborn to return to Him. And when He spoke immediately the breath of every firstborn man and beast gave up the ghost, and the breath that quickened all flesh left the bodies of each throughout the land of Egypt such that there was a great fog, for the breath of all condensed on the ground as a great glowing mist. And men ran from the fog, but it was for naught for the vapors were not the vessel that snatched life away, but merely the residue of life that still echoed in the earth.

Screams and moans from every household raised as a tumult into the air as the cries of mourning and laments filled the land of Egypt. For El was life and in Him all things lived, moved, and had their being. And when He recalled the life, the glowing fog lifted into the night sky as a pillar of light and faded out of existence.

Enoch watched as the great cloud came as a light and shot towards him, and he and the watching Lumazi backed away, for the light lifted through the floor and poured into El's open palm. The Lord glowed, for the life of the flesh was but His own breath, and the Shekinah covered Him, that he was but a visage behind a great cloud, then the Lord spoke. "The souls of all men are mine. The life of all flesh is mine. I am the Alpha and the Omega, the beginning and the end."

The Lumazi then bowed before the Lord and El stood with raised hand over the tipped scales that had been poured out over Egypt and the fluid which was within them had run dry. The Lord then spoke. "Lumazi, bring the vial of judgment upon the armies of Pharaoh that I might break the backs thereof."

Metatron then turned to his rear and a temple Grigori gave him a great vial filled with waters, and Metatron, in turn, gave it to the Lord.

And upon the breaking of day there let loose a cry out of Egypt for there was none in the kingdom save those who had obeyed the Lord that had not lost either man or beast.

When Pharaoh saw the decimation to his land, he summoned the man Moses and bade him to leave his realm with all swiftness. Moses then gathered the people that they might depart the land of Egypt.

The council of Lucifer was humbled, for El displayed to the eyes of all, who truly held power over life and death. The people of Egypt cried out to their false gods of wood and stone, but they did not hear, and the council of Lucifer was powerless to return the breath of life El had recalled from the nation. So much was the wail of the people that that many refused to worship the gods of their fathers, for they had failed to protect them from the God of the Hebrews. And many of the Egyptians sought to learn of the God of the Hebrews. Such were the numbers of the inquiry and belief that when Pharaoh released the people, a great mixed multitude of people came also out with them.

And Lucifer was wroth, for he had not counted that El would recall the breath of life from all men. And when he saw that many spoke that the gods of Egypt were not gods but false. He targeted the newly formed nation of El for destruction. For already, news of Egypt's devastation was traveling the known world, and many said, "Who is like the God of the Hebrews?" And that El alone was God, and that the gods of Egypt held no power to save.

Charon smiled at Lucifer and mocked his captor. "Youurr cooommmand of meee...is not command of lifffee....and deathhh." The skeletal mare grinned.

Lucifer turned to reply as he surveyed the Hebrew's departure. "Wipe the smirk from your face, Archon. You are yet mine to command, for on the day I give the word, you shall bring low the man Moses, and his body will be mine to serve as host to a daemon."

Azaziel watched from El's throne the images of the people as they left Egypt and congregated at the edge of the Red Sea and spoke to El. "Will Lucifer now leave the Hebrews alone?"

"Nay," replied El. "He will not. For though I have withdrawn the life of all Egypt, he will still cling to pride, and lo, even now speaks to the man-king to send his host after my people. But fear not. Behold, I will harden the hearts of the Egyptian, and they shall follow them, and I will get me honor upon Pharaoh, and upon all his host, upon his chariots, and upon his horsemen. And the Egyptians shall know that I am the Lord." And even as the Lord spoke, Lucifer spoke to Pharaoh, and the Lord hardened the man-king's heart that he would not repent, and Pharaoh arrayed himself and gathered his armored chariots, and determined to run the Hebrews down and slaughter them. And he took six hundred chosen chariots, and all the chariots of Egypt, and captains over every one of them.

The Lord then looked upon Yeshua, and Yeshua nodded. Immediately, He was gone and when Enoch looked, behold Yeshua was on Earth and stood as the Angel of the Lord before the people, and went before the camp of Israel. And He was as a pillar of fire by night, and a pillar of cloud by day and the pillar came between the camp of the Egyptians and the camp of Israel, and it was a cloud and darkness to them, but it gave light by night to the Hebrews, so that the one came not near the other all the night. Yeshua stood as guard to His people until His servant Moses saw to them.

Moses then stretched out his hand over the Red Sea, and the Lord caused the sea to go back by a strong east wind all that night, and made the sea dry land, and the waters were divided. And the children of Israel went into the midst of the sea upon the dry ground, and the waters were a wall unto them on their right hand, and on their left. And the Egyptians pursued and went in after them to the midst of the sea, even all Pharaoh's horses, his chariots, and his horsemen. And it came to pass, that in the morning watch the Lord looked unto the host of the Egyptians through the pillar of fire and of the cloud and troubled the host of the Egyptians. And took off their chariot wheels, that they drove them heavily, so that the Egyptians said, "Let us flee from the face of Israel; for the LORD fighteth for them against us."

The Lord said unto Moses, "Stretch out thine hand over the sea that the waters may come again upon the Egyptians, upon their chariots, and upon their horsemen." Moses stretched forth his hand over the sea, and the sea returned to its strength when the morning appeared. And the Egyptians fled against it, and the LORD overthrew the Egyptians in the midst of the sea. And the waters returned, and covered the chariots, and the horsemen, and all the host of Pharaoh that came into the sea after them; there remained not so much as one of them. But the children of Israel had walked upon dry land in the midst of the sea, and the waters were a wall unto them on their right hand, and on their left. Thus, the Lord saved Israel that day out of the hand of the Egyptians; and Israel saw the Egyptians dead upon the seashore. And Israel saw that great work which the LORD did upon the Egyptians, and the people feared the Lord, and believed the Lord, and his servant Moses

The host of Heaven cheered, and cries of adulation rang throughout Heaven, and Yeshua the Angel of the Lord returned to Heaven, and when He did, He did not come directly to the throne but walked among the people. When the angels of Heaven saw Yeshua walking among them, they threw manna leaf, and their royal robes they lay before His feet. Everyone in the city went out to meet Him for the wonders of God that He had done against the council of Lucifer, and all sang His praises and cried out, "Hosanna! Blessed is the King of Heaven that saves the children of men and doth wonders!" Angels reached out to touch Yeshua, and a few hoisted Him on their shoulders and the second person of the Trinity lifted His hands and blessed His people as they carried Him back to the mountain of God.

* * *

Gabriel went to monitor Michael's charge and consulted with Argoth.

"Where is the maiden now?" asked Gabriel.

Argoth replied, "She abides within Salmon, one of the two spies who Moses has sent to spy out the land of Canaan. He hath taken unto himself the harlot Rahab in marriage. Gabriel, how is it that Shiloh will come from such a vile woman? The plague of sin is rife in her, and she is abhorrent to look upon."

Gabriel looked at Rahab and spoke. "Project her line one generation. What do you see?"

Argoth did as commanded, and a child showed on the walls. "The harlot shall give birth to a man. They shall name him Boaz."

Gabriel replied, "Is Boaz Shiloh?"

Argoth hunched his shoulders. "It seems unlikely. I cannot see past one generation. There is nothing that would seem that he would be the one to bring Lucifer down."

Gabriel frowned. "Then the maiden must be carried for still a time, and the time of Lucifer's reckoning is not yet nigh. Nor do I yet see a people who will commit execution as thou hast seen. Nevertheless, the Lord hath revealed to Michael a portent...

'Mary is the mother to Shiloh.

From the pit of sin shall He bring forth glory.

From the depths of misery shall spring forth joy.

Shiloh's kingdom will possess all kingdoms.

And upon His back shall Lucifer be destroyed.'

"Her sins are of no consequence to me," said Gabriel. "For the moment, her lips ushered that she knew the Lord hath given Israel the land and that their terror was fallen upon her people...the moment she confessed that, 'The Lord, your God, He is God in heaven above, and in earth beneath.' She sided with El's cause, and El hath made mention that she shall be honored. For it pleases the Lord to take the things that are not, to confound the things that are."

Argoth held his peace on the matter. Gabriel queried him further. "Doth the enemy know of our plans?"

"There is yet no indication that he is aware that Shiloh is within her blood. However, we both know that in time—Lucifer will discover him. He searches for any human who manifests the will of God in the Earth. His obsession with the image of God is madness. His reasoning has been corrupted, and our brother has grown progressively insane."

Gabriel continued to gaze at the images that Argoth showed him as the Israelites destroyed nation after nation that Lucifer had set up to bring man into ruin.

"This people is surrounded by the enemy on all sides. El has tasked them to take a region occupied by the principalities of Lucifer himself. He asks the impossible, for they cannot withstand them unless they adhere to His command, and I pray that they will be up to the task. For in the corners of the east and west, Lucifer raises great nations that would revival Egypt in power. The angel Pangu in the east, and Quetzalcoatl in the west; it would appear that his plan is to raise kingdoms in his name. He and El spar for the souls of El's image and likeness."

Argoth nodded. "Yet the nation of El is tiny, born of slaves, they could not even obey God, and delayed the plan of our Lord for forty of their years. Surely, He cannot mean to take such a ragged people to bring low the Adversary?"

Gabriel watched the walls as they displayed the people battling another people riddled with the worship of Lucifer's angels. "El hast no other plan. For by the faith of men He chooses to insert His power, to partner with Him. His ways are unlike the enemy, for El would have the man willingly follow Him. Yet, Lucifer —," Gabriel paused and pointed to the cruelty that men had unleashed upon one another. "Lucifer will bludgeon the man to death if he does not worship him, even as he escorts their souls to the underworld."

At that moment, a Grigori attendant arrived to see his Lord. He floated silently and bowed to Gabriel, then to the Lord of his house. "Gabriel would you excuse me?" said Argoth "It would appear that matters of the house must I now attend. May we discuss the plans of war to address Pangu, and Quetzalcoatl within the hour?"

Gabriel nodded and turned to leave Argoth to his attendant. And when the two were alone, Argoth spoke, "Reveal what is written."

Silently the Grigori took its tome and its pages opened and floated above the ceiling, and images of Chronos' meeting with the exiled Iblis exchanging conversation and information could be seen. But the Grigori was not within earshot to record all that was spoken.

"Why dost Chronos' own Grigori not give report?"

The Grigori attendant was silent in response.

Argoth rubbed his chin, and his eyes stared at the image of Chronos and Iblis. "I would know what a member of the fallen and the Lord of Time would have to discuss. Thank you for this information, you have done well. You are released to return to your charge."

The attendant bowed and his tome returned to his side, whilst the image still played on the ceiling for Argoth to see. The attendant left while Argoth stared at the image, and noted the two making discussion in barren surroundings, and the lack of the need of Grigori to report on the happenings of the place. Thoughts and images raced through his mind, and he wondered if perhaps the duo might make plans to assault Heaven once more. Argoth then became wroth as he thought on the prospect and waved his hand and the image disappeared, and he spoke to the room.

"Location of Redactors?"

The room in obedience showed the image of the three Grigoric bounty hunters, and they were in the midst of confiscating a tome from a fallen Grigori. Rorex, Turiel, and Isidor held the Grigori chained with fetters of iron, and they opened Tartarus, and their fallen brother screamed for mercy. Yet none was forthcoming as he was dragged into the depths of the earth below. And when the task was complete, each bowed to Argoth who spoke to them from Heaven.

"Go to, and find the Lord of Time, Chronos, and apprehend his Grigori, for he doth not report. Something is amiss, for Chronos consults with the enemy and I would know why."

The three bowed in silent response and dispersed into black misty streaks for parts unknown in search of their quarry.

* * *

Eladrin looked upon Michael and Enoch, and spoke, "Thou Michael of the house Kortai, standest for examination; because thou hast not judged thyself, another now stands in judgment over thee. El commands the trial of a new chief prince, and the will of El be done. We have respect towards the fallen prince. But you, we do not know. The ways of Kilnborn, we do not inquire. We move only on the call of the song, backward and forwards must the wheel of time travel, forward and rewound must the wheel of time turn. For on our backs do the Heavens ride, and on El's command we turn wither-so-ever He wills. We have seen thy turning, and you must be turned." Eladrin then moved his wheels, and flakes of light and shards of brilliance streamed from his body and all the faces of Eladrin looked at him and yelled, "Decide!"

Immediately, Michael was taken by a power of light, and he watched as the goings on in the lower heavens displayed themselves before him. El Himself inserted Himself into the affairs of men, and nations rose and fell upon El's command. Floods swept them away and men began to multiply again on the face of the earth. And Lucifer could be seen seeking to sway the man, and by his command he, too, sought to raise great kingdoms, and Michael saw God show Himself strong through a man named Moses, who led his people to a place of rest. Then the Lord summoned Moses to reside with his fathers, and his body he placed away from the eyes of men. But Lucifer and the Grigori loyal to him saw the place of the body, and Lucifer searched for his grave and found it. And Michael was released from the giant whirlwind, and Eladrin placed him atop the tomb of Moses.

"Decide!" Roared Eladrin, and then the giant ophanim vanished from sight.

Lucifer was walking towards the grave, and he lifted his hands to open the sealed tomb of Moses only to see Michael materialize from nothing. He jumped back, surprised to see his brother, and then spoke. "It has been too long, my brother. Your presence can only mean that you have climbed the holy mount, for none but El or Eladrin can bring you here in such a manner."

"Why are you here?" asked Michael.

Lucifer looked upon his brother in dismay. "Was there not a cause? For this man hath made ruin of my will to raise Egypt on high. He hast dared to enter my court and defy me. I may not have his spirit, for he sleeps with his fathers. But his body...his body I shall animate again, and he will even in death serve me." His flesh is riddled with sin. His flesh is mine. Stand aside that I may claim him."

Michael stood in Lucifer's path crossed his arms and replied. "All flesh is mine saith the Lord. None are yours to raise. Only El can rejoin spirit with the body. Your claim is denied. You cannot have him."

"You think that you will prevent me? That you would bar me even as thou stood as vanguard in defense of El? If it were not for you, even now, I would be God, and we could rule together. But no... your petty devotion to the Father hast blinded you to His purpose to destroy us." Lucifer grew red, his face changed, and the Angel of Light slowly turned a reddish black, and his scales turned red. His voice boomed and the rocks around him began to split and crack.

Michael stood unmoved. "If his body you desire, then know that through me it must be taken. You will withdraw."

And when Lucifer saw that his brother would not surrender the body of Moses, he pulled from his side a red sword. The curved blade was forged in the furnace of Hell; its scabbard was made from the Elomic corpses of his enemies, their protruding, deformed faces frozen as trophies within the hilt. Lucifer slowly unsheathed it from its casing, and it sparkled and then burst into crimson flames.

Michael, too, withdrew from his side the sword of Ophanim. And he held it aloft, ready to respond if Lucifer dared engage him. Lucifer eyed the blade remembering that it was with that blade Michael that had disfigured him and paused.

Michael spoke, "If you desire combat over the body of Moses, then know that you shall have it. And though it be possible that you may indeed strike me down. Know of a surety that you will not leave unscathed." The sword then roared and split into seven blades and gyroscopically whirled about Michael, ready to attack at his command.

Lucifer watched the blades levitate, then smiled and spoke. "I will leave you this day in peace but know that there will come a day when we shall cross swords again and though my love for thee is strong. If again you stand between me and my purpose, know that on that day... you shall surely die."

Michael stood unmoved nor wavered in his reply. "The Lord rebuke thee."

Lucifer sheathed his sword, "Goodbye, brother." Then he turned to walk away.

Michael watched as Lucifer lifted into the sky, and concealed himself behind the wavelengths of invisible light, and disappeared from view.

Eladrin materialized from nothing his wheels and the gears thereof churning within him, and inside he carried Enoch, who shouted at Michael. "Well done Michael! Well done!"

Eladrin spoke. "You do not fear the Usurper, but fear of the enemy of El is not faith enough to lead. Yet know that I judge thee sufficient in this thing. But still you must be found faithful." Eladrin then moved closer and when he did, light encapsulated Michael and they were all taken away.

* * *

Chronos flew over the Earth's prime meridian. His travels took him to observe the rise and fall of kingdoms. Men of all hues were his subjects within the realm of time. His was the charge to keep the wheel of time turning. To spin the planet on its axis...to fulfill the word of El. The stars beyond beckoned him home to the realm of angels. To float within the third heaven, but Chronos was faithful to his God and to his Lord Jerahmeel, who specifically assigned him to monitor the activity of the fallen.

Flying over the great oceans, he admired how the tribes of men learned seafaring and navigated using the stars as a guide. While musing on his admiration of man, he was accosted.

"Halt, Time Lord!"

Rorex emerged in front of him and stood to bar his path, and Isidor flew to his left with Turiel to his right. Chronos stopped as requested and replied, "I have seen the work of thy stylus, what doth the Redactors seek that you would hinder the Lord of Time?"

Immediately Isidor and Turiel misted and were suddenly at his rear, and looking about him curiously. They said nothing but continued to encircle him. Chronos looked upon the sky and fidgeted as he glanced repeatedly at the sun's travel across the sky.

"Time is of the essence, my brothers; I am on assignment from my Lord Jerahmeel. Why do you hinder my charge?"

Rorex looked at him and replied, "We seek examination of thee, and Argoth commands knowledge of your meetings with the Fallen. Yea, you meet with enemies of the crown, and we would know if you conspire to the hurt of the Kingdom. You will surrender this knowledge, or we will strip it from you."

Chrono was taken aback by such boldness, and replied, "Nay, you shall not. For my dealings are my own and are not subject to the orders of the Grigori. If your master seeks knowledge of my actions, then he as Lumazi should query Prince Jerahmeel. My dealings are my own. Why speak to me at all? Is not my Grigori able to account of my dealings?"

Isidor replied, "Assyrix is thy Grigori, yet he is not at thy side, nor does he report as required by our kind. He has violated Grigoric law in this thing. We will seek him out, and he shall be redacted. We do not seek war with house Harrada, nor will we restrain a member of its order. We will do as thou hast suggested and leave the matter of Lumazi with Lumazi."

Chronos replied, "And what of you? What will you do?"

The three began to mist invisible, and Rorex spoke from over his shoulder. "We will find the renegade Assyrix, and he shall answer for his crimes."

Chronos watched as the last of the redactors became imperceptible and vanished from his sight.

* * *

Eladrin spoke, and his voice made the ground to shake. "We have received word from El Elyon. You are here to find faith. Behold the race of men and watch."

Eladrin moved forward in time, and he noted that on the planet Earth a man by the name of Joshua stood as head of his nation's armies and fought nation after nation to claim land given to his people by God. Moreover, when Joshua watched as his forces went to battle, the Ophanim noted that the sun was going down and light would leave the battlefield. Then spake Joshua to the Lord and he said in the sight of all Israel, "Sun, stand thou still upon Gibeon; and thou, Moon, in the valley of Ajalon." And God heeded the voice of a man, and immediately Eladrin knew the will of God in the matter and turned his massive wheels, and Ladders from his people enveloped the tiny planet of men and caused the Earth to stop in her race around the sun. Hundreds of the Ophanim heeded the call of El, and they encircled the planet and colored light shimmered over the blue skies, in waves of green, red, and yellowish hues. So, the sun stood still, and the moon stayed her course until the people had avenged themselves upon their enemies. So, the sun stood still in the midst of heaven and hasted not to go down about a whole day. And there was no day like that before it, or after it that the LORD hearkened unto the voice of a man in such a manner, for the LORD fought for Israel.

And when Israel had avenged themselves on their enemies, Eladrin turned and once again the Earth continued her circuit about the sun, and Michael was amazed that a man of clay could bring God to hearken to his word so.

His love of man is so that he would move Heaven and Earth for his children. If God so loved one nation, that at the voice of one man he would bring to stop the Earth in her run, how much more would he do for the race of men? Michael pondered the thing in his heart, as Eladrin carried him to parts unknown.

* * *

Lucifer looked upon David and made note that the Hebrew nation had expanded to be as a light to the world. And when it became clear that El would establish his purpose through the man David's line, Lucifer devised means to bring the house of David and his people to heel and strategized with his council.

"The man-king thinks himself invincible. While he hast subdued all enemies without, there yet remains one enemy that can never be moved. Behold, I will cause the man to bring the wrath of El Himself upon his own head. For what sin doth El abhor more than pride? Witness how the human yields to my hand."

And whilst David remarked on the wealth of his kingdom, the power of his armies, and the unchallenged love that his people had for him. Lucifer suggested to his mind that he should number by census his kingdom. And David entertained the thought and weighed it as a thing to be done.

David then said to Joab and to the rulers of the people, "Go, number Israel from Beersheba even to Dan; and bring the number of them to me, that I may know it."

Joab the chief captain, answered, "May the Lord make his people a hundred times so many more as they be. But my Lord the king, are they not all my Lord's servants? Why then doth my Lord require this thing? Why will he be a cause of trespass to Israel?" Nevertheless, the king's word prevailed against Joab. Wherefore the chief captain departed, and went throughout all Israel, and came to Jerusalem. He later returned and gave the sum of the number of the people unto David. And all they of Israel were a thousand thousand and a hundred thousand men that drew the sword, and Judah was four hundred threescore and ten thousand men that drew the sword. But Levi and Benjamin counted he was not among them, for the king's word was abominable to Joab.

The thing which David did displeased the Lord, and He was wroth, for He had commanded the king not to number Israel. "Lo, my servant hast yielded himself to the voice of the Adversary." And the Lord spake unto Gad, David's seer, saying, "Go and tell David, saying, thus saith the Lord, I offer thee three things: choose thee one of them, that I may do it unto thee."

Gad came unto David, and said unto him, "Thus saith the Lord, 'Choose thee, either three years' famine; or three months to be destroyed before thy foes, while that the sword of thine enemies overtaketh thee; or else three days the sword of the Lord, even the pestilence, in the land, and the angel of the Lord destroying throughout all the coasts of Israel'.".

Gad gave the word to David and said, "Now, therefore, advise thyself, what word shall I bring again to Him that sent me?"

David replied, "I am in a great strait. Let me fall now into the hand of the Lord, for very great are His mercies, but let me not fall into the hand of man."

So, the Lord sent pestilence upon Israel, and there fell of Israel seventy thousand men. And God sent an angel unto Jerusalem to destroy it: and as he was destroying, the Lord beheld, and He repented Him of the evil, and said to the angel that destroyed, "It is enough, stay now thine hand."

And the angel of the Lord stood by the threshing-floor of Ornan the Jebusite. And David lifted up his eyes and saw the angel of the Lord stand between the earth and the heaven, having a drawn sword in his hand stretched out over Jerusalem. Then David and the elders of Israel, who were clothed in sackcloth, fell upon their faces.

And David said unto God, "Is it not I that commanded the people to be numbered? Even I it is that have sinned and done evil; indeed, but as for these sheep, what have they done? Let thine hand, I pray thee, O Lord my God, be on me, and on my father's house; but not on thy people, that they should be plagued."

Then the angel of the Lord commanded Gad to say to David, that David should go up and set up an altar unto the LORD in the threshing-floor of Ornan the Jebusite. David did as was bidden and built an altar there and did sacrifice. And it was there that he determined to build God a house of worship, and the thing which David did made Lucifer wroth. For though many of Israel had been destroyed at the hands of the Lord, El's name would be exalted even the more through the act for David had determined to build Him a house. And Lucifer went away from Jerusalem for a time and planned how he might trouble the nation the more.

* * *

And in the passage of time, God raised Israel on high, and her people subdued all the people of the land as God commanded. And through her loins rose Solomon, who later reigned in his father David's stead, and David before his death set in his heart to build God a house, but the Lord spoke to his servant saying, "Thou hast shed blood abundantly, and hast made great wars. Thou shalt not build a house unto my name because thou hast shed much blood upon the earth in my sight. Behold, a son shall be born to thee, who shall be a man of rest; and I will give him rest from all his enemies round about for his name shall be, Solomon, and I will give peace and quietness unto Israel in his days. He shall build a house for my name, and he shall be my son, and I will be his father, and I will establish the throne of his kingdom over Israel forever." Therefore, David ceded rule to his son Solomon and prepared for his son to build the house of the Lord.

David then commanded all the princes of Israel to help Solomon his son, saying, "Is not the Lord your God with you? And hath He not given you rest on every side? For He hath given the inhabitants of the land into my hand, and the land is subdued before the Lord, and before His people. Now set your heart and your soul to seek the Lord your God; arise therefore, and build ye the sanctuary of the Lord God, to bring the ark of the covenant of the Lord, and the holy vessels of God, into the house that is to be built to the name of the Lord."

And David went to sleep with his fathers, and his son Solomon ruled in his stead, and as he was bidden of his father and was prophesied by the Lord of Hosts, Solomon's rule was great, and he did all according to his father's will and built the house of the Lord. And Judah and Israel were many, as the sand, which is by the sea in multitude, eating and drinking, and making merry. Moreover, Solomon reigned over all kingdoms from the river unto the land of the Philistines, and unto the border of Egypt, each brought presents and served Solomon all the days of his life. Such was the renown of his wisdom and kingdom that great queens and kings came to see his wealth and wisdom.

It was at the height of Israel's power that ambassadors from Persia came to spy out the land of Israel and feigned honor to him. Spies sent on command by the Principality Marduk. Spies inhabited by daemons to destroy the nation.

* * *

Eladrin was silent and with his many eyes and faces, looked at Michael. "We are the wheel within the wheel. See the shape of things to come and see faith in the earth."

Once again one of the faces of Eladrin turned and when it did, the skies of heaven changed and stars shot as blurred lines across the ceiling of Heaven, suns set and rose, and Michael found himself in Ladders, not of his making and carried aloft by great winds that moved him past stars, and stars of stars. And Michael slid as if he were on rails, and saw a young woman give birth to a baby girl, whom the mother had named Mary. The young baby was of olive skin, and lo, over her floated one of the Grigori of the Fallen, and when the spirit saw that, the young woman was a godly child. The Grigori looked upon the girl and screamed. For it saw a generation ahead as was the way of some Grigori and wailed a wail that even the humans looked about them and took it as an evil omen for the child. Moreover, Michael noted that none of his kind was there to protect her.

"Where is the child's guardian?" Why is the maiden left exposed to the enemy?"

Eladrin was silent save the grinding of his wheels and gears within him and motioned for Michael to continue to watch. The great rings within Eladrin moved and advanced so that Michael could see that the Grigori had told its master Lucifer about the child. Lucifer then descended upon the child and her family with a legion, and the horde fell upon the city as raining hailstones and burned up crops, and all animals' roundabout died. Joakim, Mary's father, a Godly man, prayed and while in prayer, his eyes were opened, and he was able to see the fallen prince. Lucifer turned to look at him and commanded Charon to strike him down for laying eyes on his person. And Charon did so, and Joakim's heart stopped, and he gave up the ghost, and when the mother of the child tried to protect her daughter, Lucifer waved his hand and she was flung as trash and crushed against a wall. Michael grew livid that Lucifer had reign to slaughter so and moved to interfere. Yet when he tried to speak he could not, and when he tried to move he could not. For Eladrin forbade him to intervene. Eladrin motioned for Michael to watch. Michael grumbled his disapproval and looked at the developing scene.

Lucifer picked the child Mary up, exited the house, and held her aloft for all to see. And when he did, the Horde cheered. Lucifer quieted the crowd and proceeded to speak. "See the vessel of Shiloh! A vessel *I* now hold in my hand!"

The throng roared, and great shouts echoed within the city, and the people could hear echoes that seemingly came from nowhere, yet somehow were all about them. Some of the town's people saw that the small girl child was held aloft as if by nothing. Some said it was magic, and others said she was demon spawn or a child of the devil, and then their eyes grew wide as the baby cried and screamed as her body ripped apart and was sent flying and smashed against the rocks of the ground. The people who saw it screamed, for it, was a child and they thought the city was cursed for they beheld nothing that could do such a thing.

Lucifer smiled and laughed mockingly, stood atop the body of the child, and shouted to them all. "El hast failed! For millennia, He has moved to create a vessel pure enough to cause entry into this accursed planet. Behold, and see the desire of his heart smashed against the stones! I am Lucifer...and I WILL BE GOD!"

The multitudes of fallen angels cheered, and Michael fell to his knees in despair. Eladrin turned his body and immediately a Ladder reached for him, and Michael was pulled against his will as they hurtled across the circle of time to parts unknown.

Eladrin returned Michael and Enoch to the aerie and placed the duo on solid ground. Michael became wroth and turned to the King of the Ophanim and spoke. "Why did you show me this? Who is responsible for the death of the maiden? Answer me, I command you!"

Eladrin then turned to Michael and each of his four faces changed. Michael looked on in horror as each of the faces changed into his own, each screaming at him, each accusing him with the words, "You are the man!"

Michael reeled, and he fell to his knees and buried his face in his palms and when he did, the repeated refrain stopped, and he looked up and eyed the dome of Heaven, and all about him was blackness and nothingness. No stars, no Heaven, there was nothing as far as the eye could see. Both Enoch and Eladrin had faded from view. Michael mused within himself what he had seen. For he was given charge by El over Mary. Yet he was absent from his post. Truant from the purpose of God and his absence had allowed Lucifer to destroy the vessel of Shiloh's entry to bring down the Usurper. The realization of the matter dawned on him, and wave after wave of anguish washed over him, and a visage of Gabriel appeared to him. "Heaven counted on you! We all counted on you! *I* counted on you!"

Michael spun from the rebuke and shouted, "Who am I to the plan of God that the Almighty would depend on me to assist in bringing the Adversary low? I did not ask for this! I did not fight for this!"

Yet the visage did not relent and continued to berate, "Heaven was counting on you!" Michael sought to run away when an image of Jerahmeel appeared. "Would you deny God? Would you push away the outstretched hand of the Almighty?"

Michael fell on his knees pleading. "But who can resist His will? Michael groped in the darkness reaching out to touch the giant Ophanim. "Where are you? Where am I? Release me, I command you!" However, only darkness was his companion, and blackness his friend and all about him was nothing but blackness, coupled with the sound of more nothing. Michael sat on the ground that he sensed was still there and closed his eyes and waited for what he knew were the stinging words to come. It was a wait that he did not have long to endure, a familiar phrase that now bellowed at him through the darkness. A phrase that he knew would mark that his time of judgment had come.

"Decide!"

Chapter Five: Decide!

Talus sat up in his bed. Thoughts shook themselves loose as fallen leaves, and with much effort, he attempted to pull them together into collective bundles, that he might sort through the emotions and feelings that gnawed at him. Reaching for his royal robes of Elysium silks, he dressed and then placed over his undergarments the formal garb of crystallite armor that showcased his rank as prince over all House Arelim.

There are few who know of my burden. Whom should I confide in? Talus determined that he might seek the council of Argoth. He looked from his balcony and viewed the stained obelisk that reached into the sky. The monument that still stood at his command to remind him of his failure. Many of his household had asked if they might dismantle it. Some thought it too painful to look upon. Others felt it broadcasted the house's shame while others expressed that it was dishonorable to Talus himself. Nevertheless, Talus paid them no mind. His will was to leave it be for now. El had summoned him to appear before His presence by the first watch of the day. Talus left his abode and took to the sky to fly to the palace.

The Prince of House Arelim landed in the court of the palace and proceeded to make his way into the Holy of Holies. Upon arrival, he bowed before the Lord of all things.

"I am here as commanded my King."

El nodded and spoke. "Chafiel, you are dismissed from your duties, report to Argoth for reassignment."

Talus's Grigori, Chafiel, materialized, floating just above the shoulder of his charge and bowed to his God and King. He then floated away from the throne room, and the great doors sealed themselves of their own power, and the sound echoed throughout the room.

El then stood.

Talus prostrated himself to the ground.

"Talus of House Arelim, I judge you worthy of upholding my word, and faithful in all thine house...for zealous art thou in the things of thy Lord..."

Talus remained bowed and silent before his king.

El continued, "...because thou seek to bring honor back to your house, and because you would through works gain favor with the Almighty. I have heard thy heart's plea and give unto thee an assignment that I can give to none other in all of Heaven."

Talus looked up curiously and spoke, "What is thy will, my King? How might I bring honor to my Lord?"

The Lord looked quietly at Talus as if He might change His mind but continued. "This is an assignment of grave import. Yet know I would not command thee in this thing. Yet I would adjure thee to consider the request of thy King for it will lead you into the maw of Hell itself. However, of most import, you will be protector and guard to he who would save mankind and bring untold honor to the House of Arelim like none other. If you accept this thing; I would make you guard to Shiloh, Talus of House Arelim."

Talus looked to his Lord to see if he might stand, and the Lord motioned for him to rise.

"My life is to do thy will, my king. Until my last breath and to the breaking of my stone will I serve thee."

El smiled and replied. "There is a turmoil that rages within thee. A blight of hurt that if not cut out, will bring thee to ruin. To forgive oneself is no easy task. Yet because thou hast placed the importance of thine own forgiveness over that which I alone can impart, I will tutor thee on the cost of my forgiveness. You shall serve as Grigori to Shiloh, as living witness to the futility in seeking to earn what can never be acquired apart from me. When Shiloh is alone, and must endure separation, for three days you shall record the depth of the love of God."

Talus looked down. He knew that El had forgiven him. Knew that within his mind all that El had shown him of Lucifer's action and his own were but threads in a tapestry that was woven to bring about history. Yet, there was an ache within him. A peace that he needed that exceeded his understanding. He would consider this unique offer from El. To know the cost of the forgiveness of God.

"Lord, when I am in thy presence all is made clear, and I am whole. Yet when I walk amongst the people. When I am alone, though you saturate all, I do not feel the presence of my King, and a great blackness washes over me." Talus's eyes began to swell, and tears slowly fell from his eyes. "I would have this affliction be removed from me."

El sighed, for He knew that all that was needed was already supplied for Talus to receive the freedom from the sense of guilt and shame that weighed upon him. "Talus, my son...I offer thee the means to use thy own strength to remove the yoke that you yourself have placed about thy neck. You believe you are unworthy of forgiveness...very well. I, therefore, decree that ye shall know that unforgiveness of oneself comes at great cost. For ye desire to look into this thing. Therefore, lo, opportunity now avails thee. You will serve as subterfuge; a lying spirit will you be for me to Lucifer.

For you will serve as his counselor, and give counsel as the oracle of God, only to see his counsel fail. You will be false to him, and you will journey to Hell and suffer great trial and wait for me, and after many days I will come for thee, and bring you and the sons of men home."

Talus looked upon his Lord in shock and wonderment. He scratched his head to make sure he had heard him correctly. "Lord, you desire me to befriend Lucifer? To give comfort and aid under the guise of subterfuge? To feign allegiance to him, and ally myself against thee? He is the author of my pain, the sum of my humiliation. He is..."

"He is thy rebellious brother," the Lord replied. "Yet he schemed to bring you to naught. Opportunity I now avail thee to bring his own schemes down upon his head. However, if you accept this charge, know this. That you will be faced with choices that will consign you to Hell herself, and Charon and the Fallen will set you to affliction. But, if you follow the example of thy God, and endure the suffering for the sake of the glory that lies before thee. I myself will come to thee whilst in Hell, and will return you to this place, and angels of all races and stations will lift up thy name. And the peace which thou seekest through works will most assuredly be thine."

Talus raised his head. "And if I do this thing...must I abandon my house? My home? For how long must this thing be?"

El looked stoically at His son, and spoke without hesitation, "Until Shiloh comes."

Talus pondered the words of his Lord. He turned them over in his mind. "My Lord, thou hast said that you would rescue me in Hell...who then... How...?" Talus paused to finally ask the question that plagued him above all others. "Are you Shiloh?"

The Lord turned His back to Talus, and when He did the form of three men could be seen. One in the center was El, the other to His left was as a form of a dove, yet clearly was as a human, and Yeshua stood to His right.

El then turned to face him. "We are Shiloh." The three said, speaking as one. "Will you assist us in this thing?"

Talus bowed himself again to the ground. "I will do as thou hast asked. When will I know that I am to leave for Earth?"

Talus immediately stood outside the Hall of Annals, and Argoth stood next to him. The voice of the Lord echoed in their heads.

"Argoth, give Talus access to the tomes of Lilith and Lucifer, let him study; for he has an assignment that will cause him leave of Heaven for many days."

"As you will, Almighty," replied Argoth. Argoth then began the sequence to open the great Hall and allow his brother entrance, and he began to speak to Talus, but Talus did not hear for the Lord still spoke within his mind.

"Thou shalt not share with Michael thy assignment, for if he knows of it, in his zeal and concern for our wellbeing he would to his own hurt bring about revolution. My Spirit shall guide thee in this thing and direct thee. Follow my command, and we shall save two kingdoms and lay seed to bring down the Enemy."

Talus nodded and spoke aloud, "Thy will be done, my King."

Argoth looked at him. "Talus I am not the Lord! Now pay attention!" Talus smiled as they both walked deep into the great Hall of Annals to read the secret things of Lucifer.

* * *

Lucifer walked amidst the daemon Kortai. Their hammers pounded against anvils, and they hauled remnants from the flesh of their kin, scavenging to build a forge within the furnace of Hell itself.

Lucifer seethed as he looked upon the Kortai, for even in their daemonic form, they still possessed the image El had impressed upon them. Still, they stood as mirages in his mind of his brother Michael— a reminder of defeat. A Kortai demon stumbled in front of him as he hauled the flesh-eating stuff that was Hell's composition.

"Watch where you are going, fool!" Lucifer scowled at the creature and waved him away and continued moving through the corridors of Hell, fixated on the beast's beating heart. Deeper he wound himself down the living carved stairways of the creature. Sheltered deep within Hell's hollowed out caverns, Lucifer had fashioned a citadel to build weapons and beasts of war, an arsenal of such destructive power to the forces of Heaven that it stretched across the underbelly of the Earth. For it was here within the depths of fire and brimstone, here near the streams of lava and the shifting of tectonic plates, that Lucifer created a realm to do his work: to fashion another Kiln. To undo what El and Michael had done. To create a race capable of Ascension. To undo the Godhead and make Heaven pay for his ouster. And the King of Evil smiled at the thought.

"My Lord!" said Cricksus. "We did not expect your presence in the ninth circle this soon." We have been working to conform the creature's flesh per your instructions and Charon's lash for several centuries now. I..."

"I am not interested in your report, Cricksus. I am, however, interested in Lord Ares. He is below, is he not?"

"Aye my king," said Cricksus.

"Then bother me not with further discussion. For I have buried my schemes past the arm of Heaven. And what, pray tell, will El do when I have builded a means to destroy him?"

Lucifer smiled with glee and continued down a carved hallway. The cries of punished angelic rebels who had defied him echoed through the halls. As he looked down, Elohim prisoners were chained to the walls of Hell's flesh. Their eyes were sewn shut, and where there should have been eyes, a blindfold was wrapped around the head and crusted Elomic blood was dried on their face. Their hands were pinned to the walls, and their feet nailed to the flesh of Hell. Lucifer smiled at his creations. There were seven in total. Each living tortured totem representative of the race of angels, each one a reminder that Lucifer was the god of this age. A reminder that rebellion against his will would come at great cost. So, as the Seraphim adorned the entrance of the great palace of Heaven, so too did these unholy creations sing a song of despair and nothing but the weeping and gnashing of teeth could be heard, for they screamed throughout the halls from Hell's constant feeding of their flesh.

I must make more, Lucifer thought. *For one day I will see El hang as these. A decoration on the walls of my new throne. Affixed by nails and stretched out humbled for all to see.* And once more Lucifer smiled at the thought.

He continued to walk further down a corridor and again descended a stairwell of lava. Its heat made the air move in a sweltering haze.

You see, El, I too can take life and fashion it according to my will. For I will take the very source of thy punishment, and from it fashion a forge of such power that when I rise from the pit of this planet, my tail will raise up the stars themselves. And on that day, you shall behold such an army as to displace thee from thy throne. For I will take the Kilnstones left to me and with them build, the likes of creation none hast ever seen. And when the time is ripe, I will raise me a man to be my son, and I will be his father. And we shall bring you low.

Lucifer came into the antechamber of the deepest level of Hell. Nine circles did he fashion deep past the interior ocean of the planet. For centuries, he trained Hell and coaxed Charon to conform her to his will. The lash of Charon's whip and the roar of his command caused the giant beast to burrow until she touched the core of the planet's life. A parasite to destroy El's prized creation. To leech the life of both man and his gem of a home. For here within the deepest pits of the ninth circle was housed the prized possession of Lucifer Draco. The Hellforge and in this forge a weapon of such design as to bring to naught Michael in battle.

A cauldron of power contained the remnants of angelic Kilnstones and the souls of men. Lucifer would manufacture arms of such destructive might; Heaven herself would shudder before their onslaught. *But where to hide such a creation that even El would not dare to enter?*

Lucifer was proud of his wisdom; he reveled in it. To hide his tare amidst the wheat of El's creation. He bargained that El would not rend the wheat of this planet, to remove him. Lucifer smirked, for the human's spirits provided a never-ending source of fuel, and his Horde the labor, and Lucifer basked in the screams and gnashing of teeth as both fallen angel and the condemned souls of men created his vision. Lucifer ducked under beams and tendrils of flesh while Hell lurched; trained by her master to consume only on command. Lucifer smiled, for Hell was a giant tamed, a beast shackled, but he knew she was still a ravenous beast, a beast on a paper leash, ready to devour them all. Yet the creature was a brute and held no intelligence to rival the First of Angels and his kind, and so Lucifer domesticated the creature. She was his to control. Lucifer saw Ares, approached, and barked at his Lord of War.

"Report of thy stewardship!" commanded Lucifer.

Ares turned to face his master. "She will be done soon, my King, behold the weapons we fashion already as the Forge nears completion." Ares turned over to his master a flat rounded object with five protruding sharp tips. The star-like object dripped with a greenish oozing glaze.

"You there!" yelled Ares.

A daemon lugged a beam of the creature's flesh and stopped to acknowledge him. Ares threw the five-pointed star at the creature, and when he did, it flew whizzing through the air and embedded in the angel and hit with a thunk in the creature's head. The dagger-like object sizzled and melted into the spirit. It screamed, then fell as Hell slowly began to digest the creature within herself.

"You see my Lord, the flesh of the creature has been coated with a resin from our Kilnstones. When it penetrates an angel's flesh; the resin reacts and breaks through to consume the victim."

"I am impressed," said Lucifer. "Yet trinkets I have not come to see. Is it ready?"

Ares nodded and motioned Pangu, his assistant over. "The Lord requires his blade."

Pangu ran quickly to a vault built into the wall of the creature's flesh and from it pulled a long six-foot case of black flesh that oozed. He sat it down upon an earthen stone table and backed away.

"My Lord, once the case is opened the blade must be tamed. It will instantly seek to kill all that dare handle it. It is, after all, a spawn of Hell. Over one hundred daemons and several angels have seen dissolution in its making," warned Pangu.

Lucifer waved him off in irritation and noted a daemon Kortai chiseling into the walls of Hell's flesh. "You worker...come here." The worker came to Lucifer bowing.

Lucifer gestured to the worker and commanded. "Open the case."

Ares and Pangu immediately backed away from their Lord.

Obediently the angel opened the box, and a snake-like blade shot from the case and slit the daemon's throat. The creature backed away in panic, screaming as blood misted and sprayed over him. Lucifer grabbed him as a shield and with his free arm grappled the blade by the hilt as it moved as a cobra to attack the struggling daemon. Lucifer then plunged the blade deep into the angel's bowels and the sword fed upon its essence.

Lucifer smiled approvingly. "Yes, my beloved—feed—feed."

While the blade siphoned off the daemon's strength, Lucifer took the key of Hell and touched the blade, and the blade heeled, and became straight. Lucifer held it straight up and admired its deadly beauty. The blade glowed with a greenish hue and within it, Lucifer could see the Kortai worker pushing against the blade, attempting to get out. A scream sprung from the blade. Lucifer smiled, for it was beautiful to his sight. It was a blade crafted for him alone.

He looked upon its hilt, and its onyx and Kilnstone finish was stunning, it had something akin to spider's legs surrounding the handle. Yet it was the blade that most impressed him. Honed to the sharpest edge and made from the fusion of Kortai Kilnstones and the latticed teeth from Hell herself. It was forged in the fires of the creature's belly. Layers of materials mined within the beast were folded repeatedly to give it a hardness that could cut through all known steels of Heaven. It feasted off the souls of both angels and men—a soul stealer. It moved as a serpent and radiated Hell's hunger. Microbes from Hell's belly unleashed upon any flesh the blade touched. It was a living thing. Ready to dismember and consume and hissed when unsheathed. Like the deadliest of cobras, it was a weapon coiled to strike on command. Only, Lucifer's control of Hell itself kept the blade from attacking him. For no other angel could hold it. The blade coiled around Lucifer's forearm, becoming an extension of him. It was the perfect weapon to bring recompense to Michael. Lucifer beamed, as the glistening blade that wrapped around his arm was ready to spring forth on command.

"My blade of Malice shall you be. For aught have I against the God of Heaven and my dear brother."

Lucifer turned to Pangu and Ares and smiled. "You both have done well—extremely well."

Each bowed at the praise from their master.

Lucifer smiled. "I look forward to watching our enemies fall from the skies. Well done, Ares, well done. Continue your work, I want blades and armor to be fashioned for all my troops." Sounds of roaring came from cages to Lucifer's rear, and he turned.

"And accelerate the creation of my Zoa tau and the Wyverns." Lucifer looked upon the creatures he had made, transformed by corrupted Kilnstones. The maggots of Hell, he learned could give birth to great beasts.

"For when we possess enough of the spirits of men, we shall bring Heaven low. Now, come with me. I desire to equip Marduk with some of our new weapons. I have promised El that I would see him hung from a tree; it is time I display my vision for the world to see."

* * *

Iblis moved among the Fallen and bowing when dealing with his superiors. The culture of the Fallen was so different than that of Heaven. For here among the Horde, all were in competition to see who was the greatest. Who could impress Lucifer the most? And yet all seemed under a malaise of doubt, and fear. It was constantly there, a choking heaviness among all, that Heaven was lost and could never be reclaimed. That El was no more to be found—it was a sadness and grief that floated among the Fallen like a smog, ever present, and ever-lurking in the minds of all. Some hated

Lucifer, and even more hated themselves, and many took that hatred out on men who worshiped them. Giving them power, sex, and all that they lusted after, only to watch them grow dependent and then to snatch their gifts away. An entire race of beings devoted to the suffering of another, all locked in a pattern of bitterness, and self-loathing. A race of beings lost to no other purpose but to destroy anything that elicited the love of God. Iblis walked amongst his brethren, noting how far they had fallen from the heights of Creation. Madness had infected them all. He could feel it gnawing at him as well. For as man lost long life and decay set itself upon him from Adam. The Fallen too knew that their sin against El changed them. A slow insanity crept amongst them all. Their faculties degenerating, and their lust growing. Sin ate away at who they were. And though no one would speak of it, for fear that to do so, would bring confirmation of what was whispered. Sin was a real corruption that knew nothing but hunger and consumed all that was Godlike. ,He knew he could not go home, that El would never forgive such treachery. However, Iblis would not succumb to the loss of mind that was the Horde that he now called family. He would remember who he was, why El had made him. And even in exile, he would honor the memory of the angel that he was.

His master interrupted his musing. "You are a bother to me. Where is the tally of souls you were required to provide this day?"

Iblis looked upon his Arelim master, Traxiel and bowed, "I have traveled to and fro looking for ways that my Lord might find power." Iblis remained bowed and Traxiel looked upon him suspiciously. "Who gave you leave of my presence to on my behalf look? Do I present as powerless to you? Do you see me as so weak that I need bolstering? Answer me or I will take thy petty frame and feed you to Hell."

Iblis remained cowed, yet he knew this one. This one was filled with vanity and pride. Always peacocking, it would be a simple thing to outwit this buffoon.

"Nay, master, may you live forever; I had heard thee whisper how you desired to rule the Eastern kingdom where Pangu now presides. I believe I have found a weakness in his hold on the region. If my master would hear I would say on."

Traxiel was large and powerful. His white mane flowed from around him and his leathery wings stretched out over his large lizard-like back. He stood on four legs and carried a staff of sulfur given to him by Lucifer himself. Petty and cruel, he ruled the Hamitic nations and kept them in check, but Pangu had been given the lead over the nations in the east, and Traxiel was enraged. Lucifer had told Traxiel that if he could not keep the people from the eyes of El, he could not hold to the territory, and so Lucifer deeded it to Pangu.

Traxiel looked upon Iblis and smiled. "You found a weakness with Pangu? Speak what is revealed, and I will determine if either your arrogance or lies should cause me to make you a daemon."

"It was Pangu, my Lord that fashioned the sword Lucifer bears. He in league with Ares hath made a forge within the creature Hell, and it fires weapons of such power that Lucifer holds it secret. Nevertheless, in my travels on thy behalf, I have found that our Lord seeks one to change his Kilnstone with the forge and to make living weapons against the Host. Pangu shows fear and distrust of Lucifer, but if you, my Lord, stand as a willing vessel to Lucifer's stratagems. He will favor thee over Pangu. For alas, what power could be given thee that would cause Pangu thy rival to fear? Use this power and Lucifer will surely elevate thee, even to his inner circle, and you will rule all of the nations as before."

Traxiel looked upon Iblis and pondered his words. "And how, vassal, did you come upon this knowledge, and I did not?"

Iblis raised himself to look at his master. "Is the thing not known? For there are Kortai builders who have been turned into daemon to build the Forge. Others of my caste have seen it. I believe it and have relayed the word to thee. Would you rob thyself of occasion to dismount Pangu from his perch to gloat at thee?"

Traxiel backhanded Iblis and the angel fell to the ground bleeding. Traxiel then spoke. "Do not presume to know what is in thy Lord's interest. I will spare thee sentence but know that I will require at thy hands the tally of souls. We are all required to give support to the war effort. You will not be the undoing of me by failing to supply the tally of men for Hell's feeding. For the creature is forever hungry and our control over her must be absolute or she will run amok to devour us all in her lust. Rise and be off with you, as my conference with my Lord draws nigh."

Iblis quickly rose from the ground and flew away.

Traxiel turned to go into his place within the earth. His hovel was adorned with petty trinkets of men, and the sacrifices he had garnered. Each item of gold and silver paled in comparison to the riches that decorated Heaven. And for a moment, Traxiel thought about home, and his anger was kindled by El's banishment and their failure to usurp Him. However, Lucifer promised they would have vengeance, and perhaps this Hell-forge Iblis spoke of would be the weapon needed to rip their home from the hands of the Creator.

"Are you lost in thought again?" said Assyrix. Floating on mist within mist, Assyrix, attended by two of his Grigoric lieutenants, entered Traxiel's cave.

Traxiel turned. "I do not recall giving you permission to enter my abode. You would be wise to show respect."

Assyrix laughed, "I would if such was earned, but I serve as the Chief of Eyes now. And I have come to share with thee what my eyes have seen."

Traxiel sat down and replied, "Say on."

Assyrix waved his hand and his attendant's tomes flew in the air and opened, and their pages lifted to the ceiling to reveal Iblis and Chronos talking to one another.

"One in thine own house has conspired with the enemy. He meets with the Lord of Time, Chronos of House Harada. Yet what the Time-Lord does not know is his Grigori is absent and serves our own people. Hermes, our agent, now reports of his comings and goings. Although, he cannot rise to Heaven with the Lord of Time. He can report of his doings while he dwells in the realms below. Lucifer was wise to target Chronos to spy Heaven's mind. For with the spying of his knowledge, we have freed Wormwood, who now will return many days from now. From Chronos, we have learned that Heaven still reels from our absence, and they are not yet made strong. With him, we have learned rumor that Shiloh will enter this world. However, most importantly, tyrant, we have learned that a traitor exists under thine own nose and you are imbecile to not see, and even more, of a fool to allow. I should delete you where you stand."

Traxiel grew uncomfortable, for he knew the power of a Grigori's pen, and meekly muttered in inquiry. "And what is to be done of my command?"

The attendant Grigori's books floated back towards them, and smoke ushered from beneath them and they moved closer and hovered over Traxiel and then misted out of view.

"For now, Lucifer would keep your station on hold. *You*, buffoon, will watch over your charge Iblis and *we* simpleton will abide here."

Traxiel looked up nervously. "Abide here? What will you do here?"

Assyrix smiled as he too misted out of view. "*We*, principality of fools...*we* will watch you."

* * *

"Decide!" roared Eladrin.

"Nooo!" Michael cried.

And he turned to fly away from Eladrin, but Eladrin was King of the Ophanim, and like God: eternity and time were as nothing to him. Hence, when Michael flew, he turned thinking he was moving away from Eladrin, but when he faced forward, Eladrin stood in his path as if Michael had never moved.

"Decide!" The mighty king roared a second time.

Michael again shifted to his left and when he did so, all of heaven itself seemed to move with him, and once more Eladrin stood before him. His wheels churned in gyroscopic turns, and lightning issued from his body. The eyes of his four faces were alight in flames and stared at the angel.

Michael began to clutch at his chest, as the beating of his stone pumped in erratic rhythm, and he collapsed to his knees. Eladrin hovered over him with each face mouthing the words

"Decide!"

Each utterance was a consistent drumming to choose between fear and faith. Michael writhed in agony and when he beheld Eladrin, Eladrin showed him a hundred different scenes that played themselves before his eyes, from conversations of Lucifer speaking to Abaddon, to him and his brother's playful banter before the war. Like marching apparitions, the visions assaulted him as the images of lost loved ones, the vision of El's heel, and His impending death on a cross—caused him to gasp for air.

Eladrin was relentless, playing for Michael the scenes of his life, making him relive each moment, splaying the scenes as if trained by the Grigori. Thus, Eladrin moved time forward and backward, and Michael staggered from reliving each painful moment of his past. His failure with Iofiel rose to his mind, his decision to destroy the Kiln. His terror as the explosive power of the Kiln's detonation flung him and Lucifer in a downpour of flaming Godstones. His sensation of dissolution from the digestive grip of Hell. Relentlessly, the images assaulted him, thoughts, but not just thoughts, whole reenactments of his life, and Michael's mind reeled with the images and visions that paraded themselves before him. He spasmed, coiled, then howled like a caged animal, and when he did, the fear that had plagued him manifested as a dark shape and began to lift from his body. Michael looked on in horror at the ethereal dark form—the dark image of himself.

Winds whipped around Michael, and Enoch could no longer be seen. All that was held to view was Eladrin and his bellowing four faces that roared at him. Eladrin - and now an entity drawn from within Michael. The manifestation of his own anxiety held aloft for him to see. Anxiety that now began to tug at his spirit to form a union and leave Michael lifeless.

"See the fear that lifts from you. Behold the entity within that would in time leave Heaven waste once again. With Lucifer pride lifted from his soul. But with you, young prince— fear is that which shall have you." Eladrin was merciless, as he was the keeper of eternity and the boom of his four mouths belted out the now-familiar pounding tenor.

"Decide!"

For a moment, Michael's mind snapped, and he was lost in the currents of remembrance, imagination, and madness. Each vied to grapple with the remnants of his sanity and still fought to lay claim to his thoughts. The fear of his soul was now exposed before him, as an ethereal thing that hovered over him. The tortured entity wailed in pain, for the creature mirrored Michael's own wails for relief, and it screeched as a banshee for wholeness.

Yet through the anguish and pain, Michael perceived and reflected past doubt and reached out to his own spirit that quickly was leaving his body. Eladrin pulled at the floating spirit, and the winds generated from his grinding wheels reached as tentacles to tear Michael's spirit away from him. Michael fought to reach for his divided spirit, but the thing was as ether and floated on eddies of eternity moving steadily towards Eladrin, and Michael perceived that the wheels would shred his spirit.

Eladrin's four faces mouthed in a quartet of judgment, "Behold, son of God. I will consume the fear that assails you and that you refuse to face, and then when it is banished, I will consume you who would infect Heaven with it." Immediately the inner gears of Eladrin moved faster and winds raced, and the spirit of Michael's fear moved towards Eladrin.

And when Michael saw that he was on the verge of oblivion, he summoned the sword of Ophanim and the blade split into seven swords and whirled about his person, even as Eladrin's wheels. Great winds tugged at Michael's spirit as the gusts from the Sword of Ophanim matched the revolutions of Eladrin's wheels and Michael's spirit halted its floating march away from him.

Eladrin flexed and the gears within him moved even faster, that sparks began to fly, and the grinding of steel and iron created, even more, winds to wrestle Michael's soul. And when he saw his fear as the blackness dangled before him, Eladrin smiled and each of the faces spoke.

"You possess fear Michael of the Kortai," said the human face.

"He that feareth is not made perfect in love," roared the face of the lion.

"For fear hath torment," growled the face of the bear.

"See how we torment you with your fear," cawed the face of the eagle.

"For there is no fear in love; but perfect love casteth out fear," said them all.

Michael was pulled towards Eladrin, staggering against the winds of the two forces that sheared and tore at all things that were reality. The specter that was Michael's spirit slowly began to scream, and Michael cried aloud in exertion to reclaim his life - to own his fear, and to overcome it. His cry echoed off the sides of the holy mountain, that it reached the lower spaces of Heaven. Angels' underneath Heaven's canopy looked up from wherever they were towards the clouds of the mountain of God. Each heard the cry of Michael and perceived that the Builder of Heaven was in pain. As one man, they lifted into the air, dropping tools and station, commerce and manufacturing ceased as all left their posts to fly towards the mountain. For in all of Heaven only Michael had put Lucifer to pause and held back the hand of the First of Angels. From the great Library to the armories of Heaven, all Heaven lifted themselves, each stripped of fear of the unknown, each rising as a gathering cloud to ascend the mountain of God and assist their prince, whatever the cost.

Michael looked below him and saw the legions rising to come to his aid. Legions who had heard his spirit cry out, legions who rose to do battle with whatever held him in distress. Eladrin also took note with his four faces and summoned the flock of Ophanim from their nest, and they too came to rush to the cause of their leader. Darting in swaths of prismatic light, they jetted from the aerie and encircled Eladrin, awaiting the command to dive and accost the rising Host.

And lo two great armies of Heaven, one ascending and one descending, moved to intercept one another, and Michael knew that his people would be destroyed, for the Ophanim were the living Ladders that moved Creation at the word of El. And when he saw that he was cause for the actions of Heaven. Understanding assaulted his heart to know that the word of El was coming to pass—that here, he would die.

For here in the valley of decision, here in the center of struggle, did Michael realize that El had given him a choice. The choice to succumb to the fears and limitations of what he knew, the choice to arise to see God past his limited understanding of the Creator. Here, the choice was given to die to either faith or to fear. For the angels hearkened to the pain of one, and the Ophanim hearkened to their leader's call, and all moved because one angel was unstable in his belief.

Deeper Michael looked at his spirits ascending dark apparition. It loomed closer towards Eladrin's shearing wheels. Eladrin then took the spirit of fear that floated in the air and with it showed Michael, that the angel Marduk had moved Darius King of Persia, to lift men alive upon hewn beams of wood, and nailed them thereon.

Michael recoiled in horror, for now in the Earth men now practiced what he had once seen in a vision: a horror of affliction to kill the God of the universe. A vision he had dismissed as impossible, a vision he held back and refused to acknowledge. A vision of El wasting away dying as his limbs were stretched wide for all of Heaven to see—a vision of defeat.

"NO!" Michael cried out.

The echoes of his shriek sent waves of panic into Heaven's populace as angels rose to encounter the realm of the living clouds. Each rose to confront whatever lay before them and rescue their leader. Legions once more left their stations to bring what would unknowingly incite war between celestial beings; and as Michael faced his vision, and while all of angelic kind ascended into the descending army of the Ophanim. El Pnuema, the third person of the Trinity, spoke quietly into Michael's mind.

Look into the darkness, my son. For I am the LORD, and there is none else. I form the light and create darkness. Do not fear, my son, what I have devised.

Michael listened to the gentle voice of the Spirit of God and did as bidden and looked into the darkness of his own fear. He stared into the heart of the blackness and examined the contours of his terror. Perception crept into anxiety and his eyes grew wide. For with the eyes of the Almighty, he understood that it was not fear that that hovered above him, nor fear that held him captive to indecision—but selfishness. A disguised desire of one's own will above the will of God was where fear germinated, and the soil that doubt grew.

Michael peered at the cross, a vision that incessantly plagued him and in so doing, he perceived it was a vision that El also did not fear.

For, in the shadow of fear, Michael knew he would die. Die for exalting himself above God. For here in the blackness, he understood that he could yet choose to follow El into darkness, to trust the Almighty despite his own imaginations.

And lo, in the troposphere of Heaven, amidst the sounds of impending war, and the grinding wheels of Ophanim – it was then that Michael of the Kortai decided.

"I am the builder of heaven. If my life need be given as a cornerstone for her support, then my stone I offer up to thee, but let Heaven live forever. I am Michael Kortai, the hand of the living God. THE WILL OF EL BE DONE!"

Michael then surrendered to the wheels of destruction and raced towards Eladrin his sword spiraling in cutting motions around him. Michael embraced his spirit, and the sword of Ophanim cut through the spinning wheels of the King of Ladders. Michael reached to grasp a spinning ring from within Eladrin and strained to rip it from its gears. Tendons and ligaments wrenched apart pulleys that whistled and whined in objection. Each of the four faces attempted to bit and snap at him, but it was to no avail as Michael pulled until a ring snapped and a great flash emanated from within Eladrin.

The shockwave raced as an expanding circle across the skies of Heaven. And everywhere the wave touched, time stood still. The Ophanim hovered in the air motionless, and the armies of Heaven that rose to come to Michael's aid were also stayed, suspended, and all but the Lord God Himself was subject to the suspension, as He watched His children from afar.

Michael reached to touch the face of Eladrin as his giant wheels and gears rotated around him, each one pressing against his frame to crush him. He grasped the faces of Eladrin, and when he held the king's face firmly in his hands he spoke. "I am the servant of the Lord; His Chief Prince and I turn wither-so-ever HE wills!" And when he said that, he turned the face of Eladrin to the right, and a snapping sound could be heard. An explosion rocketed across the skies and the skies turned red, and the eyes of all Ophanim turned to Eladrin, for Michael stood atop their leader.

And when the dust was cleared, Michael held in his hand a gear of Eladrin, and placed it as a crown atop his head, and immediately it floated over him. And when Michael turned his head all the Ophanim turned, and he was surrounded in prismatic colors as an armor about him, and the Sword of Ophanim rotated gyroscopically around his person. Michael then looked to the Ophanim; which descended upon his people, and he raised his hands and when he did so, the Ophanim stopped flight and stood as twirling rainbows of light in space. Michael then spoke to all and his voiced boomed above the mountain of God.

"I am Chief Prince. Return to your duties, let the will of El be done!" And when he moved his hand the Ophanim returned to their nest and continued as before. Eladrin was floating and the space where his gear had been made a whirring sound, and he hobbled as his wheels compensated for the gear that was missing within him. He then looked at Michael and spoke. "You have been judged fearless in thy house. Thou now hast token of the Ophanim about thy head. Call when needed, Chief Prince, and we will come when bidden. Keep the secrets of El, and the mountain. Go to and let the will of El be done." Eladrin then bowed before him.

Michael bowed and replied, "How wilt I know when aid for thee is needed?"

Eladrin righted himself, and the gear that floated above Michael's head glowed, and the gears within Eladrin did also. Eladrin then took Michael forward in time to see and then returned to their place atop the aerie. "My halo has been given thee, its powers will you understand in time. When Death rises to claim you—call us, and we shall come."

Michael nodded in understanding. Enoch appeared from the smoke and walked towards him. "I take it that I too must keep secret what lies above the clouds of Heaven?"

Michael smiled. "I could leave you here."

Enoch raised his eyebrow and nodded. "Point taken, let us go."

Michael then took Enoch by the hand.

"Wait," said Enoch. "Are we not flying back down?"

"No," said Michael. "I am a Ladder now, come." Michael's halo then glowed atop his head, and they disappeared in a burst of prismatic light.

* * *

"What is thy command my King?" said Gabriel.

"Prayer has come before me. Daniel my servant seeks wisdom of my doings and the time of all things. Go, therefore, and deliver this message, that he might have wisdom of things to come."

Gabriel bowed to the Lord and left the throne room, and departed the mountain of God to fulfill the word of El. He summoned a Ladder and lifted himself from the cliffs of Heaven to descend to the celestial realm below. Immediately to his sides, two Ladders appeared and alongside him flew two of his gryphon riders, Gaishon, and Makiel, commanders in the cavalry of Malakim Riders. Each was a great angel of renown who had battled the rouge angel Abaddon to protect the city.

The Lord of House Malakim descended onto the small blue planet that held El's attention and sway. He turned towards the continent men had called Asia. He knew that Marduk, formerly of House Arelim would be somewhere below. Grigoric scouts had reported to Argoth and the council that Marduk had ascended to power as the prince of Persia. The principality that now towered over the most powerful kingdom in the world of men. Gabriel hoped to arrive in stealth and avoid combat.

Gabriel smiled at Gaishon, and Makiel, who flew escort alongside him. He was grateful that they would be his guard while he conveyed his message to the man Daniel. Gabriel knew that there were few of Adam's kind who understood the cost in life to keep the legions of Lucifer from overrunning them. Yet Gabriel would not have it any other way; his command was clear. Prayer had been offered to God and El would see that the Lord's answer was conveyed to the man. For now, all of Heaven now knew that God had established a clear time for when Shiloh would arise among men and defeat Lucifer. A mere man had requested insight from God and El in His graciousness took heed. So, Gabriel would deliver the battle plan to this human at any cost.

Gabriel was comforted to have the presence of his comrades.

His comfort did not last long

"Makiel, to arms, we are being flanked!"

Gaishon had seen what Gabriel and Makiel had not, that a cohort of gryphons had become visible, previously covered by the powers of fallen Grigori, and was now within striking distance. Makiel's reaction was too slow, and he was jousted from his mount, and tumbled towards the planet below, engaged in combat with two of the Fallen.

* * *

The angels of Heaven looked up into the clouds. The boom that echoed across the sky was not thunder and the prismatic ray of light now familiar to all the populace signaled that a Ladder was descending. Panic quickly ensued, for it was not long ago when Ladders blasted the landscape of Heaven, causing untold destruction. Panic gripped the populace, and all raced and flew to escape the quickly descending beam. In an instant, the great cyclone of color impacted the steps of the mountain of God, and wind-swept dust aside and the air crackled with lightning and the colors of the rainbow retreated above. And when the dust cleared, Michael stood with Enoch in his arms, and above his head was a glowing circular ring of gold that hovered over him. Awareness came upon the crowd that before them stood one of their own, no longer just one of the Lumazi, but now Chief Prince of Angels. Immediately cheers and chants rang out. "Michael! Michael!" Michael smiled, embarrassed, and Enoch turned to him. "It would seem the people are glad to see you."

The doors of the great mountain then opened, and a flash of light heralded the entrance of the Lord. Mists and colored vapors escaped from the doors and the Ophanim raced from the gates and shot across the sky, and the visage of the Almighty could be seen walking into the emporium. Immediately all bowed, including Michael. Enoch, too, upon seeing the Lord, prostrated himself and all were silent as God looked upon His people and spoke. "Rise, my children and let us query my son." All stood to their feet and Michael still kneeled and did not look upon the Lord, and the Lord spoke to him. "Hast the Michael that ascended to Eladrin, the same as the Michael that descended?"

Michael lifted up his eyes to look upon the Lord and replied, "Nay, my king. For it was as you said, for the Michael of old hast died. I have seen what the end must be. Therefore, I proclaim that

I am crucified with Christ. Nevertheless, I live, yet not I, but my Lord's will lives within me, and the life which I now live in the flesh. I live by the faith of my God."

El smiled. "Thou hast spoken well my son for ye prophecy of a thing yet to come. Thou hast well said indeed. Because thou hast done this thing and hast laid down thy life of fear that my will might be done. Behold I take the gear of Eladrin and with it make it thy crown. A halo shall it be unto thee. A token between me and my Prince of Angels." The Lord then stretched out His hands and pointed at Michael. "Let all Heaven behold the Chief Prince!"

Adulation and roars of approval raced through the crowd like wildfire, and applause and shouts of joy escalated into raucous and, even more, shouts of praise.

Michael smiled and noted that the members of the Lumazi cheered and applauded him. Each came to offer congratulations and saluted—all except Gabriel. Michael turned to the Lord and spoke. "My king, where might I ask is Gabriel?"

* * *

Gaishon yelled, "I will see to Makiel, take leave my prince, quickly!" Two enemy Malakim riders then befell Gaishon as he battled accosted by members of his own house. Struggling as rebel warriors attempted to spear him, he too tumbled, engaged in combat with his foes.

Gryphons of Heaven crashed into one another and clawed at both rider and beast. Gabriel's guards plummeted from their mounts as lances lunged at them. Gabriel knew that as much as he might wish he could not give aid, for their mission was clear. To provide guard, that he might break through the principalities' defense and enter their territory. Lower, therefore, did Gabriel descend, chased by a humanoid mist. He turned to see that a Grigori followed in hot pursuit. Gabriel stopped to face him and withdrew his battle staff. It elongated, changing into a fiery glaive. He launched to attack the Grigori, but the creature misted and the blade went through his pursuer as ether. Again, he attacked his pursuer without success, yet the Grigori did not attempt to fell him. But instead stood, and watched him, recording. Gabriel resigned himself that the Grigori was of no immediate threat, breathed a sigh of relief, and lacking the resources available to Argoth, proceeded to lower himself into the region men had named Babylon.

Deftly, he moved, with quickness his ally. He soon cleared the upper regions of Earth's canopy until he landed clear of all angelic resistance. But as he moved over arid land and desert to make haste to the city, a great angel of the House Harrada landed to withstand him. Gabriel too landed and swallowed hard, as his actions had drawn attention to the region's leader—Marduk. Marduk stood to bar him, and behind him stood three angels who held flaming swords and commanded an army of men on horseback. The human leader of the army was a man by the name of Cambyses. Each soldier was possessed by a daemon who saw into the realm of the spirit, each aware that Gabriel was among them.

Marduk spoke. "Greetings Gabriel. It is known to me why you have come. For the Grigori hath informed me of the man Daniel's prayers. Moreover, how he has willed himself to self—affliction that he might know the secrets of Heaven. I knew that it was only a matter of time before you would come. For, I, too, would know the strategy of the Father. Therefore, you will deliver this word from Heaven to me—or know that you shall not return with it."

Gabriel paused to assess the situation, making detailed mental notes of his surroundings. To his front were four angels. One was a former Archon, and behind him stood an army of fifty thousand daemon-infested men on horseback. Each had been given weapons to fight angels. There remained no room to retreat, for if he was captured the word of God would not arrive to Daniel. There was but forward, or acquiescence to the will of this rebel. No, there was but one course of action. The man Daniel expected his answer, and Gabriel would see the thing done. Gabriel sighed at the sight arrayed before him, then spoke in reply. "I have come for the man's words. I speak for the Lord of Hosts. Do not deter me."

Marduk chuckled. "It would seem you have elected the 'not to return' option." The principality of Babylon then motioned his hand forward. "Seize him."

Immediately Marduk's three lieutenants moved to smite Gabriel down. The angel to his right. Ertrael held a whip. He flicked his wrist and the stretched the elongated hide of Elomic flesh cracked and wrapped tightly around Gabriel's staff and spirited from his grip into the waiting palms of Ertrael. The second of Marduk's lieutenants, Harut, moved to attack him from the front while Marut moved towards his rear. Gabriel somersaulted to his rear to avoid being tackled by the two and dashed behind Marduk. With a twisting motion, he twirled and kicked Marduk in the back, but the angel did not move. Gabriel bounced back from the force of his own blow, unable to make headway against the girth of the giant Harrada. Gabriel looked at his feet where they had struck Marduk, and sores and festers began to appear, and his flesh gave off a sizzling sound and soles of his shoes smelled as if they had been burned.

Marduk laughed. "Please, touch me again my prince. Let the flesh of sin touch the holiness of God. Let me bring corruption to His messenger. Come, let us reason together, why would I destroy the voice of God that carries the very knowledge my king seeks?"

Marduk laughed manically. His three henchmen raced towards Gabriel again to bring him to heel. Racing to escape them, Gabriel moved to battle instead the daemonic army before him. Smashing his way into the throng. Jumping, flying and kicking, Gabriel punched each one. Yet he only succeeded in destroying men's bodies for the spirits that animated them simply screamed when their corporeal shells were broken and attempted to drag Gabriel to the ground.

It was then that he knew that he fallen into a trap. For the army of possessed men were not the threat—it was the daemons inside them. Less than angel now, their minds were erased due to the tortuous afflictions of Hell. They knew only hunger for anything that lived, hunger for any remnant of the presence of God, and so they sought to inhabit all things living. Man was their highest prize, for he was made in the image of God and provided the most means of return to angelic form. Yet the daemons were spirit, and they clawed and dragged at Gabriel and pulled upon him until the Leopard of Heaven stood overwhelmed by their sheer numbers. For each man held a legion of the foul spirits, and there were fifty thousand men. Thus, the more he fought, the more he released more enemies to fight.

For twenty-one days, Gabriel engaged in hand-to-hand combat. For twenty-one days, men stayed away from the region of Babylonia as unearthly sounds and moans echoed and traveled across the dunes. Winds blasted high into the sky and sandstorms rolled through the region, withering the people roundabout with gritted particles that bit into flesh. For twenty—one days, the man Daniel prayed, not realizing that his prayers provided Gabriel the protection to withstand the onslaught of daemons that was before him. Overwhelmed by the horde that stood between him and Daniel, and unwilling to abandon the task given him by God. Gabriel still possessed faith that El would somehow see His word delivered to the man. Gabriel was smothered by daemonic bodies. Each pinned him down as they licked his face, savoring to taste what it was to be in the presence of the Lord. Marduk, Ertrael, and Harut approached him. Marduk held Gabriel's weapon, the white opal staff of House Malakim, and looked upon it and smiled.

"Turn him around, and we shall flay him until he speaks to us the word of God."

Obediently, the daemons hearkened to their master and stretched Gabriel out to receive his punishment for defying them. Gabriel, bloody and exhausted from three weeks of unrelenting combat, held no weapon to fight against the forces of Lucifer. No horn that he might put to his lips to call for aid. There was naught but faith that El would in some way provide sufficiency for the torture he would now endure. Ertrael held the staff of Gabriel high for all to see. The weapon of the chief prince of House Malakim. He uncoiled his whip and raised it high into the air to bring its lash square into the soft tissue of Gabriel's winged back. He flicked his wrist, and the cord of punishment was unleashed to find its mark. It traveled through the air, and in the seconds that ticked in the twinkling of an eye, a swooshing sound pierced the sky. A scream was released from behind him and the daemons holding Gabriel released him and started to flee.

Gabriel collapsed to the ground, then turned to look to his rear. Ertrael's arms were laying on the ground bleeding, his severed hand still gripped the whip. A glowing figure stood over him. He reached to him with an outstretched hand, and with the other held Gabriel's staff. A glowing crown hovered above his head and swords gyroscopically encircled him, and he was clothed in prismatic armor. Gabriel smiled as he took hold of the strong welcoming hand that lifted him to his feet.

Michael had come.

* * *

"Go!" Michael commanded. "See to the man Daniel!"

Gabriel lifted himself into the sky and dashed towards the great city of Babylon. He followed the sweet-smelling trail of prayer that saturated the heathen nation, for few offerings to the God of Heaven emanated from the place. Yet everywhere Gabriel looked, the work of Lucifer was evident. Here he had established Marduk as governor, to administer from this place the dispensing of culture that twisted the truth to the narrative of the Fallen.

Gabriel followed the aromatic scent of the prayer and found a window open in a large tower. Gabriel entered the window and on the floor, kneeling in intense prayer and supplication to God was the man Daniel. His body was haggard and thin, weeks of intense prayer and fasting has taken its toll on the man. Gabriel found himself in admiration of him, this human who would at all costs know the will of God. For in the midst of the seat of Lucifer's power stood one man who would not bend the knee to the false god's Lucifer had set up. Here in the capital of paganism, a small man had risen on the back of God's grace to be prime minister even in the midst of godlessness. Gabriel hurried and revealed himself to the man, touching him and released the words El had sent him to proclaim.

"O Daniel, a man greatly beloved, understand the words that I speak unto thee and stand upright: for unto thee am I now sent. I am now come forth to give thee skill and understanding."

Daniel stood trembling when he heard Gabriel's word. Then the angel said unto him, "Fear not, Daniel: for from the first day that thou didst set thine heart to understand and to chasten thyself before thy God, thy words were heard, and I am come for thy words. But the prince of the kingdom of Persia withstood me one and twenty days. But, lo, Michael, one of the chief princes, came to help me, and I remained there with the kings of Persia. Now I am come to make thee understand what shall befall thy people in the latter days, for yet the vision is for many days."

And Daniel set his face toward the ground and became dumb. Then Gabriel touched the man's lips, and Daniel opened his mouth and spoke.

"Oh my Lord, by the vision my sorrows are turned upon me, and I have retained no strength. For how can the servant of this my Lord talk with one such as I? For as for me, straightway there remains no strength in me, neither is there breath left in me."

Then Gabriel touched him again said, "Oh man greatly beloved, fear not, peace be unto thee, be strong, yea, be strong."

Daniel was strengthened and said, "Let my Lord speak, for thou hast strengthened me."

Then Gabriel said, "Knowest thou wherefore I come unto thee? And now I will return to fight with the prince of Persia, and when I am gone forth, lo, the prince of Grecia shall come. But I will shew thee that which is noted in the scripture of truth, and there is none that holdeth with me in these things, but Michael your prince."

"For at the beginning of thy supplications, the commandment came forth, and I am come to shew thee, for thou art greatly beloved. Therefore, understand the matter, and consider the vision. Seventy weeks are determined upon thy people and upon thy holy city, to finish the transgression, and to make an end of sins, and to make reconciliation for iniquity, and to bring in everlasting righteousness, and to seal up the vision and prophecy, and to anoint the most Holy.

"Know therefore and understand that from the going forth of the commandment to restore and to build Jerusalem unto the Messiah the Prince shall be seven weeks, and threescore and two weeks: the street shall be built again, and the wall, even in troublous times. And after threescore and two weeks shall Messiah be cut off, but not for Himself. And the people of the prince that shall come shall destroy the city and the sanctuary, and the end thereof shall be with a flood, and unto the end of the war, desolations are determined. And he shall confirm the covenant with many for one week; and in the midst of the week, he shall cause the sacrifice and the oblation to cease, and for the overspreading of abominations he shall make it desolate, even until the consummation, and that determined shall be poured upon the desolate."

And Gabriel sat and expounded to Daniel all that would befall the nations of the world and even his own people. Thus, the Lord gave Daniel knowledge of what would come to pass through His servant Gabriel.

"How long shall it be to the end of these wonders?" asked Daniel. For Daniel, heard but understood not all that had been spoken unto him.

Gabriel replied, "Daniel, shut up the words, and seal the book, even to the time of the end. Many shall run to and fro and knowledge shall be increased. Go thy way, Daniel: for the words are closed up and sealed till the time of the end. Many shall be purified, and made white, and tried; but the wicked shall do wickedly. None of the wicked shall understand, but the wise shall understand. And from the time that the daily sacrifice shall be taken away, and the abomination that maketh desolate set up, there shall be a thousand, two hundred, and ninety days. Blessed is he that waiteth, and cometh to the thousand three hundred and five and thirty days. But go thou thy way till the end be, for thou shalt rest, and stand in thy lot at the end of the days."

When Gabriel had finished his word to Daniel, he disappeared from view, lifting himself to return and join Michael in combat, vowing to defeat Marduk Prince of Persia.

Chapter Six: Rise of Empires

"My Lord!" yelled Ashtaroth.

Lucifer scowled at the presence of his attendant.

"Did I not instruct thee that I was not to be disturbed? By what lapse in thought dost, thou enter my presence without call?"

"Forgiveness, my Lord, but there is a sound of war in the camp, for in the fields of Babylonia the governors appointed move to battle."

Lucifer looked up from his pouring over holy writ disgusted that he must speak on the subject and be drawn from studying El's plan and tactics.

"Which principalities have taken to battle?" Lucifer asked.

"Marduk my Lord, and Lord Zeus seeks command to destroy Marduk as he hast provoked the heavenly host and is now engaged with both Prince Gabriel and Michael."

Lucifer looked up from his books. "Indeed? And what did cause such a disruption that my brothers would leave Heaven to battle on Earth?"

Ashtaroth replied, "Our Grigori state that Marduk has been attempting to destroy a man by the name of Daniel and three children of Hebrew birth. That through prayer El moves on their behalf. And that now the people have been given leave to even rebuild El's temple and continue the worship of El!"

"Arrghh!" Lucifer turned over the books on his table and he stormed over to Ashtaroth as if he would pummel him. "Finally, after hundreds of years, I succeed to destroy El's house of worship. Finally, after dispersing His cretin people to the winds, like weeds His accursed seed returns to plague me! And now you tell me that prayer hast drawn Heaven's attention? Prayer!" The ground shook and fissures inched their way along the cavern floor. Ashtaroth cowered from his Lord's risen voice.

Lucifer turned from his servant and spoke. "If Marduk's failure hast brought the host of heaven down to see of his actions, then Heaven may do my bidding for me. Command Zeus assemble his legions and move to destroy Marduk if necessary. For if Marduk defeats Michael then we need do nothing. However, if I allow Zeus to defeat Marduk then he will have acted to rid me of leadership that is rife with stupidity as to draw heaven's attention and ire. If El would send two of the Lumazi to battle over Babylonia, I will cede this land for now. I perceive that El tires of Babylon and judgment will come soon. I will not fight the Father on His terms. I command Zeus to oversee Marduk's lands, and Persia will belong to Grecia. Now go, for this battle dost does not concern me, as both are but pieces of the game that El and I will play until He is under my feet."

Ashtaroth bowed himself and left his master. Lucifer reached to the floor and picked up his toppled books and continued to read from the Holy Scriptures and turned to a verse that held particular interest to him and spoke to himself aloud. "But thou, Bethlehem Ephratah, though thou be little among the thousands of Judah, yet out of thee shall he come forth unto me that is to be ruler in Israel; whose goings forth have been from of old, from everlasting." Lucifer's brow rippled as his eyes narrowed at the text in reflective thought.

"So, El, what is Bethlehem that thou would makest her home to thy champion?" And Lucifer continued reading deeper to discern the plans of the Almighty.

* * *

Gabriel arrived and touched upon the sands of the desert and when he did, he found the Lumazi fighting as one. Talus with his great strength hurled gryphons and their riders into the enemy lines. While Metatron and Azaziel moved as machetes across the fields of battle. Jerahmeel used his great powers over the elemental colds to protect and shield all from harm, and Michael - Michael lead them all. With a golden halo above his head and a sword that on his command split into seven blades and fought independently. Michael led his legions against the forces of Marduk. The ferocity of battle caused the desert sands to whip into a frenzy as God's champions of light yielded both sword and shield to beat back the darkness.

Moreover, men that knew that El was the Creator of all prayed. And when they yielded themselves to God in prayer, a mist rose above the Fallen and choked them, hindering their movement in the earth. Yet the mist caused the angels of God to move with greater swiftness, and it strengthened their arms and healed their wounds, and Michael and his legions prevailed.

The night sky of the desert displayed an aurora of colors. Crackles of lightning and the booms of thunder echoed across the burning sands. Each burst was but a physical manifestation of angels at war. Each luminous brilliance, nothing more, but the clashing of angelic swords and the sparks of heaven-mined steel. Trails of light raced away from the combatants.

Jerahmeel found himself surrounded by the officers of Marduk, each salivating at the chance to bring low a member of the high council. Jerahmeel had used his powers to shield his brethren against the horde that assaulted them, and for the fifty of men's years, the groups clashed with one another. The forces of Marduk raised armies of men to fight across land and sea, to overwhelm nations with their armies. And when Jerahmeel saw men falter under the onslaught, when Marduk's officers encamped about him that they might bring him low. Jerahmeel finally turned his hand to fight and spoke to his assailants.

"I have tried to stay my hand from battle. Yet you would not have it so. I have withheld my hand from bloodshed, often hesitant to enter into the fray with my brethren. I have used mirth, and wit to reason with madness. Yet none of it would you have—none of it would you honor. Now let my axe be my voice, my blade thy instructor, and thy death be upon thine own head."

Jerahmeel shrugged his shoulders and cracked his neck and white scales of frost and ivory formed, covering him in armor plating. The radiance of his form shimmered as freshly fallen snow. A symbol of a lion blazed across his chest, and his dual axes emitted an indigo flame, the hulking shaft of which he slammed into the desert sand.

"Come, pupils—school is in session."

The three angels of Marduk encircled him, each eying every tense muscle, waiting for the other to attack. His wait was not long in coming and attack they did. Etrael, Harut, and Marut raced towards Jerahmeel, their swords held high.

Etrael leaped into the air, and Harut and Marut moved to run their angelic brother through with swords. Jerahmeel flung one axe as a dagger, and it sailed through the air towards its target smashing into Ertael's chest. The angel fell backward into the hot sand, blue blood splattering through the air. Harut ran to cut Jerahmeel down, but the head of House Harrada lifted his hand, and the sand crystallized into ice and a wave of ice shards then sailed through the air, leaving a trail along the ground and encasing his feet in ice. Harut lifted his hands to protect his face, and when he lowered his arms to gaze ahead. Jerahmeel had closed the distance between them and with axe in hand, he ducked and leg sweeped Harut, knocking him off his feet. Harut landed on his back and the smashing 'thunk' sound of Jerahmeel's indigo blade buried itself deep into the angel's chest. Marut, seeing two of his brethren brought low by the Prince of House Harada, turned to flee. Jerahmeel again lifted his hand and immediately the vapor and moisture in the air surrounding the retreating angel froze and he became encased in ice. Jerahmeel retrieved his two axes from the chests of his foes and walked towards the block of ice that now enclosed his foe.

"I would have thee serve El, but thy pride and rebellion now sees me as the hand of El in judgment. Let the lesson for rebellion be learned by all the Fallen!" Jerahmeel shouted. He then took his two axes and with the shaft slammed into the brittle ice and the encased angel shattered into a thousand pieces of frozen blood and flesh.

Jerahmeel looked up towards the sky and lifted himself to rejoin Michael, who fought with Marduk.

* * *

Marduk's girth and size made him a formidable opponent. His obese frame absorbed blow after blow. Enraged at the loss of one of his four arms. Marduk charged towards Michael, his trunk-like legs stomping into the earth as he galloped, and he lifted his club, thinking he would crush Michael. The angelic prince easily avoided Marduk's blow, and rock and sand lifted into the air. Michael flew to Marduk's back, and when he touched the angel's skin, his own skin festered and blistered into lesions. He flipped off, dashed into the air and sat down on the ground to nurse his wounds.

Marduk looked at him and laughed. "Yes, yes—touch me again! Let my caress be as a disease to you! May my embrace be an inflammation, and my radiance a burning to the holiness from your wretched frame! Come, Michael of the Kortai—come fall to the hand of Marduk!"

Marduk swung his flanged mace and when he did, he released it and sent it flying towards Michael. The Chief Prince took the blow hard into his chest, and the mace dented his armor, knocking him backward into a sand dune. Raising himself from the desert floor, his eyes beheld Marduk closing the distance between them. Michael rose and massaged his aching arm. He looked for his sword and reached out, calling it to return to his hands. Yards away now, the mighty Arelim, charged Michael, who lifted himself into the sky. The sword of Ophanim flew through the air and Michael reached to grab the hilt and turned to plunge it into the back of Marduk, forcing all of his weight into the strike. The great angel of war screamed, and he bucked like an untamed stallion trying to throw its rider. Michael flipped from the back of the angel and commanded the embedded sword of Ophanim to split.

On command, the sword separated into its seven-edged forms and Marduk howled like a wounded animal. He rolled over in a vain attempt to dislodge the blade, but the swords continued to slice through his flesh, moving further away from their original center, carving long lacerations across his back, and blue angelic blood poured from him, and Marduk summoned the army of possessed men to engage the prince of angels.

Michael looked about him, and on all side's daemon-possessed men equipped with angelic weapons of war rode on horseback to cut him down. Hesitant to engage the image of God in the earth, Michael paused. Paused for men were but pawns in Lucifer's battle with El. Paused as these no longer held control but were yielded to the foul will of deformed angels.

"Arggh!" Michael cried out.

One of the men had attacked him while he ruminated, and the pain from the sin-soaked blade made even his armor sizzle. He backed away. "Do not make me destroy you!" yelled Michael. "Fight the control of the daemons within! You must!"

Yet Michael's pleas fell on deaf ears, and he could hear the laughter of Marduk in the winds.

"It is too late for them, Builder of Heaven, as it is too late for you. I will have your stone and give it as a token to my Lord Lucifer!"

Michael summoned the sword of Ophanim to encircle him, and its gyroscopic rotations kept him from the touch of any that might dare to venture close. For the daemons did not desire to lose their hosts if at all possible, and all recognized the weapon used to combat Lucifer, and the image made all to pause, but not retreat. It was then that Michael heard the command that would seal the decision for him.

"You will swarm the prince and bring me his head! Fear, not his blade, for though he is powerful, he cannot smite down all. Kill him for me, and you will be given another host. But bring me his head!"

And with those words, Cambyses, and his daemon army moved to take him. Michael submitted to the course that to destroy the men could not be escaped and unleashed the sword of Ophanim to cut a path that he might give distance between him and the masses that now sought to overwhelm him.

Endlessly they came. And for every ten he cut down, one hundred more walked over the corpses of the dead to attack him. From above his head, arrows covered the sky to prevent his fleeing through flight, and with shield and the sword of Ophanim, he fended off attacks from the sky, Michael found himself backed himself against the mountain wall. With his back against the rock face, he was cornered with nowhere left to go. For arrows assaulted, him from above, and there yet pushed forward tens of thousands of daemon possessed men, intent on his destruction. It was then that he saw the crack of lightening and heard the boom of thunder break the sky.

Michael looked up and upon the raising of his head saw two gleaming lights rapidly descend towards him. Michael covered his eyes and as he did, one figure smashed into the earth into the center of the throng and the impact of his fall raised both man, beast, and desert sand high into the air. Suddenly the air grew brisk and cold, and Michael's breath hung suspended in the desert air. And when the dust cleared, Jerahmeel stood before Michael and lifted his hands in the air, and a great sheet of ice rose before them, and all were caught as an ice wave enveloped them and encased the feet of the army in solid ice. Gabriel too stood by Jerhameel's side and he smote his staff into the desert sand and with his striking the earth, a great sandstorm fell over the battlefield. The winds howled and brownish dark clouds and grit blasted across the dunes stripping the flesh of man and beast. Grains of sand scraped raw the bodies of possessed men who fell to their knees, as their eyes were ground out of their sockets and the flesh fell from their bones and all were entombed under granules upon granule of crystallized rock. An army of men now submerged in teeming drifts of sand.

Michael watched as men flailed helplessly as their cries for help went unanswered by their Lord Marduk, watched as fifty thousand spirits became entombed within the desert heat under 100 feet of sand. Marduk looked at the three princes and smiled.

"It matters not, as they are but fodder. You will not stop the march of my hand over this land."

Marduk stretched his leathery wings and when he did, he released from his pores, a noxious fume that raced towards the high princes. Immediately the air became foul, and Jerahmeel and Michael coughed up blood. Gabriel lifted his staff over his head and spun it in a circular fashion, that it pushed the gas of poisonous air away and back towards Marduk, who laughed even more.

"I will enjoy your destruction." Marduk flexed his muscles and pieces of his armor fell into the sands and his muscular body rippled with power and a green hue radiated from his body, and he smiled at the angels he would battle.

"Withdraw, Marduk, or be destroyed!"

Marduk turned to look above the princes and saw that Zeus and twelve legions of angels followed him, all with swords and descending into the desert valley below.

Marduk frowned and replied, "I will not withdraw; these lands are mine to command. You are the prince of Grecia. You have no claim here. Lucifer hast given this region to me."

Zeus landed in front of Marduk, his legion following in his wake. A hundred thousand angels were ready to destroy, all on the order of Zeus. Ares followed as his lieutenant, and Hades stood behind his leader. "Lucifer is not here. I am. I claim these lands as mine. Your actions have loosed three of the great houses to battle thee in open conflict. I care not for their kind, but I care less to invoke the wrath of El and cause the host to fall upon us because thou possess no wisdom. You will withdraw, or the princes and I will in tandem have thy head. Or do you think you have the power to withstand all that lie in front of thee?"

Marduk looked at the assembly of angels scattered before him and scowled. "There will come a day, Zeus, when I shall ride atop the back of this world and men shall pay me homage to do so. For I will implant into the memory of man the name of Babylon until the end of time. Know that—and tremble." Marduk turned and with his great wings lifted his monstrosity of a body into the air to parts unknown.

Zeus turned to Michael, Gabriel, and Jerahmeel, and spoke, "He will return with armies, and when he does, we will destroy him. Yet Marduk is right in that the glory of Babylon will not be a thing to lightly dismiss. For he hast made a deep impression into the annals of mankind's history.

Lo, I do not wish combat with the Triune God's representatives. If El wills, I will command this land, but if not know that my master overruns the world and I am his servant."

Michael looked at Zeus and for a moment, the glory that was his brother seeped through the sin that now coated his form.

"I acknowledge that El's will would have ye as principality over these lands. But you surely know that El—nor we can stand idle whilst Lucifer roams about. There will come in the last days a time of accounting. And on that day, neither my hand nor theirs can spare thee for memory's sake."

Zeus smiled. "Till we meet then on the battlefield." He flew atop a Wyvern, the scaly creature's wings lifted him higher, and he stood atop its back holding its reigns. Zeus turned to speak to Michael one last time. "In the last day, son of El, know that I will kill thee, but I will derive no pleasure in the deed." Then the general of Lucifer's army flew away while a host of the fallen flew as escort to their master, and the three angels of God looked on as enemies of the crown spread as locusts over the lands of men.

"There will come a day when we will have to kill him." said Gabriel.

Michael breathed heavily and sighed, with a glint of sorrow in his eye. "Lucifer's rent still tears at me to this day."

Jerahmeel put his hands on his two siblings. "There will indeed come a time when blood will be shed again—yet I am content for now to return home."

Michael nodded and cited the words to open a Ladder and smiled as he saw the appearance of the vortex that would lift them to the golden gates of Heaven, and he replied.

"Let us go home."

* * *

Iblis moved through his Lord's lands and entered the domain of Ishtar and Shamash. He recollected as over the span of centuries as his brethren lifted themselves to be worshiped as false Gods. Each smote and or deceived men from the truth to keep them in compliance. Principalities of regions who through deceit changed the glory of the incorruptible God into an image made like to corruptible man, and to birds, and four-footed beasts, and creeping things. The angelic overseers of Lucifer, always moving to circumvent the existence of El and mar the image of Him in the earth.

Further Iblis flew, arriving into the territory of Pangu principality over the eastern lands of Asia. He descended, to present himself to the local minister for passage across his lands. Presentation to the region's warlords helped to prevent war between Lucifer's governors.

Landing at the waypoint that Lucifer had established, Iblis waited at the checkpoint. Lucifer governed with an iron hand. He made it so that none could move arbitrarily or circumvent his plans to raise nations of men immune to El's influence. In his new order, Lucifer determined the order of promotion, and ruthlessness, and the ability to bring about his plans without Heaven falling down to intervene quickly caused one to ascend. More and more Lucifer divided the tribes of men, and with each division assigned familiar spirits to track families so that wherever on Earth the image of God would raise its head, Lucifer would be quick to see that it was snuffed out.

"Halt!" ordered an Arelim. "What business hast thou in the land of the Sino?"

Iblis bowed. "I am on ambassadorial duties on behalf of his Lord Traxiel. Governor of the tribes of Shem. I bring word to thy master Pangu."

The Arelim smiled and eyed Iblis, and he tucked his leathery wings behind his back. "You will give the message to me, and I will relay it to my Lord."

Iblis guffawed. "I will do no such thing. Of course, if you refuse me passage, I will simply return to my Lord Traxiel. In which case your Lord Pangu will not have the information he needs to facilitate the Godking's plan for this region and I am sure his wrath will not be appeased. I will make sure to mention your disdain for royal protocol when the seal of a principality is shown to thee." Iblis then turned away to return to his master Traxiel, when the Arelim spoke.

"Apologies...you may pass. Nevertheless, know that you have two days to complete thy task. If your charge is not complete, I will authorize the Grigori in our land to seek thee out and report of thy stewardship. Are you clear in your purpose?"

Iblis nodded. "It will be as you say." The angel then took to the sky and soon found his destination. He landed in a crowded city filled with the people of the nation. The Sinites were a remarkable people. In time, Iblis could tell, they would become a mighty nation, exactly as Lucifer predicted. His purposes for them were not clear, but he drilled into them ruthlessness and a rigor, that made them compliant and highly disciplined. Traxiel had speculated that there would be nations of men used to fuel the armies of the fallen and return them all to Heaven.

He landed at Pangu's seat of power in the city of Xi'an and was greeted by Dicis.

"You are late!" the Issi said.

"It could not be helped, Traxiel hast grown suspicious. Report of the plan."

"The plan has failed. For Pangu hath made the sword in hopes that it would consume the Usurper but alas, Lucifer holds the keys to Death and Hell, and with but a touch of his keys hast tamed the blade. I fear we have done naught but given him even more of a weapon to strike at the Father."

Iblis looked somber, "No—not the Father. Michael is who he will attack. What hast thy master learned of Lucifer's plan?"

"Pangu reports that he is obsessed with the Hebrews, for they are as the Grigori and write the words given by El. He has lifted from the people's tomes that he may study. His attempts to destroy them hast met with failure. Though there be ten tribes now scattered to the winds, two remain that stand as a possible host to Shiloh, and he works even now to destroy the Judahites. He raises countless nations, all in hopes of sending men as fodder to what he foresees will be a future battle. He has plans upon plans, obsessed over the man El hast prophesied will one day bruise his head."

"Tell your master I will give report to Chronos and let him know so that Heaven may be made aware of this new weapon." Iblis turned to leave before Dicis stopped him.

"Wait— there is yet more. Lucifer hast found a way to further enhance and change Elohim to his purposes. He hast already devastated many of the Kortai that followed him, for in them all he sees is the image of Michael. Moreover, to the creature Hell has he given them to consume, and with their Kilnstones, he hast created armors, weapons and yea—even creatures of destruction. Lucifer prepares for war, the forge fires within Hell itself. He hast hidden his plans well, for the forge is buried deep in the bowels of the creature and a great gulf separates the righteous dead from his tormented souls. A gulf he uses as a shield to bar the Holy One from assault. How then can the Almighty strike at the heart of Hell? For Lucifer holds title, and El hast sworn by Himself that He will not take what hast been given."

Iblis replied, "Aye, this is true."

"Then how then will El bring dissolution to the Hellforge?" Dicis eyed Iblis warily. "And who is this Mary?"

Iblis hesitated, for he had not mentioned Mary to him.

"How do you know that name? For from my lips have I not spoken it."

Dicis pressed his inquiry. "Who is she? What does she mean to the Godking? Where is her people, and where is her house?"

Iblis backed away and looked to his left and to his right, and he turned to fly away when two Grigori misted into view and laid hold of him.

"You have not yet been given leave, agent of El. No, we have many questions to raise with you," said a familiar voice.

Iblis turned to his rear and saw that he was surrounded on all sides, and Assyrix and his lieutenants hovered over him, laughing.

"Take him to Quetzalcoatl. He will loosen this traitor's lips."

A strong breeze then fell sharply upon them all, and Assyrix grinned. "Yes, Chronos run and tell Michael what you have seen, for it means naught. I know you are here. You were, after all, my own charge! Ha,ha,ha! Flee, Time Lord, and let the Builder of Heaven know that his time is short!"

Chronos, invisible to the eyes of all, raced to evade their perception and lifted himself to Heaven to inform his Lord Jerahmeel of Ibis's capture.

* * *

"Master the Redactors have come for me!"

Lucifer did not turn to Assyrix and instead continued in his study of the books El had given the humans. He remained lost in thought, deep in his surmising the plan of the Almighty.

"Seventy weeks, he said..." Lucifer mumbled in unintelligible murmurs. "The time of his departure will be soon..."

"Master!" cried Assyrix, looking as the fog of the Grigori preceded their arrival. For soon, the mist would reveal the shadow of the three who by their hand were rumored to wipe out all fallen Grigori.

"Your rumors and tales of these Grigori upstarts do not interest me, Asyrr. Surely, you are able to contend with ghosts. Why do you disturb your Lord?"

Assyrix watched as the fog entered the room, it climbed the walls and Lucifer still paid no heed. Then the fog climbed higher to the ceilings, and from the ceiling, three figures formed from the mist, shrouded in smoke, and spoke.

"You are the Grigori Assyrix. You will surrender your tome and submit to redaction."

Lucifer looked up when he heard the words spoken in his chamber and said, "No... he will not. He will continue to provide me needed information and continue in my cause of libel. *You*, however, will remove yourself from my presence. Or I will feed your stones to Hell."

Isidor did not heed Lucifer and misted to surround Assyrix. Assyrix's stylus was then stripped from him, and he froze as if caught in invisible shackles, unable to move.

"Help me!" cried Assyrix.

Lucifer turned and eyed the three angels of smoke and spoke once more. "I have given order to depart, yet you still remain." Lucifer's voice modulated and the pressure in the room changed as he spoke. His voice formed a vortex, and the wind disrupted the trio that they could no more stay misted.

Assyrix's stylus dropped to the ground and the smoky shackles that held him in place dissipated.

Turiel then spoke. "You have interfered with the redaction. You shall be purged."

Rorex then moved towards Lucifer who smiled as the Grigori floated towards him. Rorex wrote the words for deletion, and when he did a black cylindrical sphere of light formed at the foot of Lucifer and rose up his body. Lucifer chuckled. "Foolish creature, I have stood foot over the stones of the universe. There is but one that can assault me." Lucifer now walked towards Rorex. "You have exceeded your mandate. Lucifer grabbed Rorex by the throat pulled out his sword and spoke to the struggling Grigori. "Your people hast always thought themselves aloof from the ways of angels and men. Allow me to tutor then in humility-behold the true meaning of the word 'deletion', and tremble." The First of Angels flicked his wrist, and the Blade of Malice came to life. The sword hissed as a thing alive, and the screams of angels, men and daemons lifted into the ears of all. Lucifer then plunged the blade into the abdomen of Rorex, his life force separated from his body, and the sword siphoned his spirit as an alcoholic libation, and the blade glowed and shimmered, and Rorex's screams were added to those already contained therein.

Immediately, Rorex's body burst into ash and his person disintegrated in Lucifer's hands, as his remains floated as black drifting snow in the wind. Lucifer then turned to both Isidor and Turiel and spoke. "This is my wink at your ignorance to my power. If you wish to join thy brother in oblivion, then come. But I give you leave to depart whilst the mood still appeals to me. You will leave—and you will leave NOW."

Isidor and Turiel looked upon Lucifer, then Assyrix and Turiel spoke to them both. "The redaction is not yet complete. We will return."

Isidor also stared at Assyrix and spoke. "We will have your tome, Assyrix of House Grigori. The Usurper will not deter us when we come again." Then the duo misted behind the waves of visible light and was gone.

Lucifer sheathed his blade, and it coiled and became invisible around his forearm, then turned to Assyrix, "Are you alright?"

Assyrix was shaken and replied, "Aye my Lord, but they will return."

Lucifer smiled. "Indeed, I am counting on it."

* * *

Chronos rushed into the council chamber and Argoth rose to rebuke him. Jerahmeel lifted his hand to stop the prince of Grigori. He stood and walked over to Chronos and looked to his brethren, "Chronos is my most trusted servant." Jerahmeel then turned to the member of his house. "I trust my friend that you come to the Lumazi out of order to report on something of grave import?"

Chronos bowed to his Lord. "May the guard of Heaven live forever and pardon thy servant's interruption. I do bring grave news, my Lord, and trust in the wisdom of the elders of Heaven. Iblis by subterfuge hast been taken captive! Even now, he travels to the stronghold of Quetzalcoatl in the western lands of Earth to be questioned and I know not what may befall him if he and our contacts are exposed... We have learned much by his cooperation. We must see to his survival!"

Jerahmeel nodded and looked at his brethren, "Chronos hast spoken, what sayest the council?"

Azaziel was first to comment. "He is now numbered with the Fallen, let Iblis be consigned to his fate. He was lost from the moment he chose to side with the Usurper. I owe him no allegiance. He hast simply reaped betrayal among his own kind. What does it matter?"

Argoth spoke. "Without the network of Grigori, we have been hampered in our efforts to know the enemies' whereabouts. For a third of all Grigori has left Heaven to explicate. And though the Redactors hunt the tomes. We have no intelligence of the enemy's movements as before. I would not be swift to lose such an asset. If he helps the cause of Heaven, he is an ally."

Metatron chimed in. "An *ally*? You would have me ally myself to an angel who rose up against my God? Ally with an enemy? We do not need his intelligence. We are the Host! And do you think it idle that God Himself cast Iblis from our midst?" Metatron turned to Chronos and looked him in the eye. "Chronos, I heard what he did in vowing to help Heaven for your saving him. Yet did not El take into account such an act before his ouster? Would he not be in the number of Heaven even now if El repented? But no, El's word is clear—exile. I will not help him."

Gabriel turned after hearing his brothers and said, "I will not stand idle whilst evil is allowed to destroy that which is good. For know ye not that he that knoweth to good but doeth it not, to him it is a sin? Will I sit by whilst it is in my power to lend assistance to he who hast lent me aid? Is it not good to foil the enemy's plans? Iblis is not Lucifer. If the Lord will see him among our number, then so be it. But if not, unless the Lord himself gives me command to yield. I will not see someone who hast given our cause aid go without an attempt to deliver. For what will the Host say? That if one does us good he will not reap what he has sown? Nay, Iblis will have my staff."

Azaziel turned to Talus and said, "And what of you? Will you lift your finger to rescue an enemy from our enemy?"

Talus held his eyes closed, and his fingers were crossed while his thumbs held his forehead up. After a moment, he looked up from his musings and spoke. "I am the will of the Lord. Michael is Chief Prince. If he lets loose command to go, I will go. If he sounds command to stay, I will stay. I am the will of the Lord."

Michael had heard them all speak and stood, and when he did, all others stood as well. Michael walked over to Chronos and placed his hands on his shoulders and spoke. "El may not repent. I have reason to believe He will never repent, for His will is clear that He hast prepared Hell for the Devil and his angels. Yet though punishment cannot be avoided, Iblis hast helped the host of Heaven. Would ye have me return evil for good? Should I leave him to his fate? Nay. I will not. Gabriel has spoken rightly. Iblis will be rescued. His fate, though fire may be, will not be because we failed to intervene to deliver him from the hands of the Betrayer. Moreover, consider that we might learn more of the command structure of the Adversary. We will go."

Chronos smiled and replied, "Thank you Chief Prince." And he bowed to Michael and the Lumazi.

Each then left the war room, to gather their people, and Metatron trailed Talus as he left, studying his brother as they walked in silence. Talus noticed his gaze and stopped and spoke with irritation. "What is it?" he asked.

Metatron was quick to reply, "Why do you seem quick to put yourself in harm's way?"

"Is there not a cause?" Talus replied.

"Aye, but this seems amiss to me. Self—injurious...as if you care not for your life. And to throw your life away for someone who hast betrayed us..."

Talus sighed. "Lucifer and Ashtaroth...have humbled me. Manipulated me. But alas, neither could do if what lay within me were not already there."

"And what is that, my prince?" said Metatron.

"Lucifer discovered vanity and pride. And because I was puffed up beyond measure, I was able to bring war to the land of Heaven. I can never remove such a stain from my name or my house."

Metatron nodded. "Indeed, it is a badge from which one might seemingly never forget. Why then doest though throw thy life away as if it is meaningless?"

Talus turned away and stood at a window, looking out to the great sky of Heaven. "I desire a new badge. A new attempt to bring honor to my God, to my people, and to myself. It is not about forgiveness. Nor is it about revenge. It is about taking control over my actions and decisions. Though I may fall in battle. Though Lucifer may indeed take my head. He will know of a surety that his path and his usage of me to his ends will come at great cost. I will see him and those that serve him know that we stand ready to implement the will of El at any time. I would bring honor back to my house. But more than all things. I will know the love of God. For El hast showed me by revelation, that scarcely for a righteous man will one die; yet peradventure for a good man one would dare to die. For while man is yet in his sins He would die for him. If I am His son, will not I be as my Father? I will go. Nay, *we* will all go and show the fallen that love conquers all things. Though it be wrapped within a cocoon of hellfire, love never faileth. We will show them this thing as will our Lord, and we will be victorious." Talus then turned from Metatron and went to prepare himself for the mission ahead.

Metatron stared after his brother as he walked down ivory corridors and wondered.

Did he just say that El will die for the man?

* * *

Yeshua walked into the war room, and Michael upon seeing his Lord bowed.

"Rise Prince of Angels," said Yeshua.

Michael stood at attention as his God reviewed the layout of maps and troop movements. Yeshua's hands stroked the wooden pieces that were displayed across the table. He frowned as He saw the position of many of his angels combating the forces of Lucifer. He stood over the panorama and stared at the display. He then stopped and looked Michael squarely in the eye. "Who do the people say that I am?"

Michael was taken aback by his Lord's question. "My Lord?"

Yeshua looked upon His son and asked a second time, "Who do the people say that I am?"

Michael thought for a moment. "Some say that thou art the I AM: some, the Elomic command; and others—the Alpha and Omega."

"All that thou hast said is true." Yeshua walked towards Michael locking His eyes upon him and spoke, "But whom say ye that I am?"

Michael considered his reply, and the words of El flooded his mind, and he raised his voice for Yeshua to hear.

"Mary shall be Mother to Shiloh
From misery shall spring forth joy.
With lashes to the back of the innocent,
Shall Lucifer be destroyed.
The blood of Shiloh shall be spilt,
Forsaken to cry and plea.
His blood shall he wash sin away,
Accursed to make men free."

"You are the Shiloh. The Godman, he who will destroy the works of the enemy."

Yeshua nodded as He sighed and smiled, "Blessed are you, Michael of the Kortai, for by revelation hast the Father shown you this. Upon this revelation will your faith stand, and the gates of Hell itself shall not prevail against this truth."

Michael stood silent, his head down, his eyes darting away from the Lord. Yeshua touched his shoulders, lowering his head to look into Michael's eyes. "Look into my face and say what is in thine heart."

Michael reluctantly raised his gaze, started to speak, and then stopped. Yeshua smiled, "Do you think that your words will be of surprise to me, Michael?"

Michael laughed at how ridiculous his thoughts were to his maker and spoke. "Lord, there is fear in Heaven. For but one day your presence was not felt in the realm, and havoc reigned throughout Creation. For one day did you rest from thy work, yet you who art everywhere wast nowhere to be found. And your son hast lifted up his hand against thee. There are but few who know what I know. And when the time is set to reveal thy plan. Who will willingly voice to see God injured? I have seen what lies before thee. How can I be party to the death of my God? You would have me stay my hand, all that my Lord may go down to deliver Adamson from the hands of the enemy? Would you have me stand idle and have me watch you die?" Michael shoved the pieces of wood from the table, and they went crashing into the floor.

Yeshua was quiet and watched His son.

Michael's breathing slowed and his voice lowered in tone as he bowed his head. Looking at the wooden pieces strewn throughout the floor, he knelt to pick them up. "I will do as commanded, and even if not bidden by order; if my King's intent is to see this thing through, then I am thy right hand. But Lord, the host may not be so. They have not seen what I have seen. They fear the absence of God. They know above all Creation the risk when God is not there."

Yeshua placed his hands under His son's arm and motioned him to stand. Military pieces still lay on the floor. Yeshua turned Michael around to face Him.

"This thing is known to us. And in the days to come, you and your people will look into the ways of man and serve as a great cloud of witnesses to acts of faith not yet seen. And all will know what Eladrin hast taught thee about love. For what would one do for love? And what I do, thou knowest not now, but will know. And what I do, I must do, for my love of the man is strong, that I would lay down all that I am, that he might live. You shall in time ponder the mystery of this thing though it now plagues your mind." Yeshua knelt and picked up a wooden piece and looked upon it. "You are your brethren are not wooden pieces to be moved across maps. Know that you and all the Host are so very dear."

"Adam is as a son who hast wandered from my way. For he hast thought to taste now things meant to be savored later, and after lying in squalor is now ripe for turning. Would you see Lucifer bring Creation to ruin? For the man is in my image, and Lucifer seeks to unlock the fullness of what lies therein. For if, I do not go down. Then must I set my hand to destroy all of Creation, and this, my son, I will not do. There will come a time soon when we will look to the Host and seek out one that would risk all on behalf of another. Hereby might you perceive the love of God, because as I go to lay down my life, ye ought also to lay down your lives for thy brethren. For if I who possess the breath of life, and see that Adam hast need, but shutteth up my bowels of compassion for him, how then could love be said to dwell within the heart of the Almighty?"

Michael looked on the Lord, pondering the words in his heart, and replied, "The thing that thou askest is hard. But nevertheless, at thy word, I will accomplish the will of my Lord."

Yeshua looked upon his angelic prince and smiled. "You shall be a champion in the days ahead, and thy brother will you one day see adrift in a lake of fire." Yeshua turned to leave his son's presence, then looked over his shoulder and said.

"Verily I say unto you that in the last day when Lucifer stands at thy feet judged, then you will know what God would do for love. But be it known that I have raised up a man by name of Augustus, and through him, I shall make a kingdom where my influence will jettison to every corner of the Earth. We are close now," said Yeshua. "For Mary hast arrived and will be ready to soon receive me. For she shall not many days hence conceive and bring forth a son, and they will call his name Emmanuel, meaning God is with us. I must depart and go down."

Yeshua turned to leave the room and Michael looked at the God of Creation, this second person of the Trinity.

"Lord, be not angry with thy servant. For I will move all to do thy will. But surely once it is known among the Fallen that the maid is of importance she shall be hunted—nay, even killed. If it seemeth good to my Lord, allow me if I may to send Azaziel and Argoth to serve as escort for her."

The Lord Yeshua nodded. "You may do this thing. For even now, thy brother hast surmised that within her family lies my image and a purity of heart. Go quickly to inform thy brethren, for I must depart soon."

Michael bowed and Yeshua left him to his duties.

Chapter Seven: The Gulf

Fires belted out from Hell. Lava and the work of thousands of slave daemons made Hell conform her flesh into caverns and deep places of grotesque looking storage chambers and horrors of torture. Lucifer was unwilling to leave the creature to her own devices, for she would devour them all. So pliant she became at his hand, as pliant as any wild animal that could be held in captivity. She became a muzzled hungry animal that if loosed, would have them all.

Lucifer and Ares marched to the staging area at the foot of the mountain of Hell, nestled deep in what men named the Himalaya's. Lucifer had built within the mountain range a home to his greatest creation—the Hellforge.

"Your plans have come to fruition, my Lord. Now we have a new kiln that we might create an army to depose El and take back our home."

"No Ares, *we* have nothing. *I* have an army."

"I stand corrected, my Lord. Would you care to see what we have created for you?"

"Show me," demanded Lucifer.

Ares and Lucifer wound themselves into an open chamber and Lucifer beheld the multitude of creations his schemes for over a thousand years had wrought. To his left were pens which held flying mounts Ares had named Wyverns. Patterned after their Lord's image when he transformed when fighting Michael, they were smaller but deadly. The dragons that walked upon two legs and razor teeth filled powerful jaws to rival any of Gabriel's warrior griffins.

"To your right, my king, I present to you your Death Knights. These will serve as thy guard for the secret things you hold dear."

Lucifer looked them over. They stood as giant sentinels covered in black. They misted as the Grigori, but with four arms which each held a sword. It stood in fiery black onyx armor.

"What else is there?" said Lucifer.

Ares moved forward, pointing nervously, "This way, my Lord. Look here."

Lucifer moved toward two towering colossi. Each was bathed in light, and fire roared from within them. They shimmered in a bluish glow and when Lucifer approached, then knelt and bellowed out, "Great is the king of all the worlds! For there is no god but Lucifer! Behold, the Bleeder of El!"

Lucifer smiled, "I like these. They shall stand at the gates of Hell. Now tell me, what progress hast been made to the area of men?"

Ares then turned and walked Lucifer towards the gulf that separated the dead of men. "Hell, refuses to ingest the righteous dead, my Lord. As you know, she hast created a gulf that separates men into two factions and will let no one pass the gulf. Yet we have discerned that all those that have opposed you lie across the region beyond where we stand. Our spies have seen that across the gulf, the dead may talk with one another, and word is that they still cling to El as their hope and speak of a Messiah yet to come to rescue them."

Lucifer frowned as he watched the great gulf that was erected by Hell itself. He had not anticipated that when men died El would send their spirits here. For Hell was created for angelkind. So, Lucifer schemed El's intent and frowned that he could not cross to lay hands on their souls. No one dared raise the issue that even in Hell Lucifer had limits. Lucifer eyed the righteous dead nervously, for although they too could not cross to him. He imagined what manner of insurgence they could plot to see his work undone, so he sought to destroy the righteous dead at all costs.

"Are Moses and David in there?"

"Aye, my king, as are Joash, Abraham, Noah and a host of those who whilst they walked the Earth thought they could escape thine wrath."

Lucifer smiled. "In time, we will bridge this gulf. Why hast not Charon made Hell to heel and give us passage to this 'Goshen' within my realm?"

Lucifer then turned and Charon stood to his rear, smiling, but said nothing.

"I command an answer from Death. And your skeletal grins do not suffice as a response. I grow tired of your smirks, Ferryman. It would seem, *slave* that you smile more than before we first met. I would know why."

Charon stared at Ares and snorted. Ares backed away, for all save Lucifer were afraid of him. He, too, was like Hell and it was unclear the degree of Lucifer's control of the Warden.

Charon looked upon his captor and spoke, "Thesssse are sssealed for they have beennn found unworthyyy of myy lasssh, and the extent of their judgment liessss here within Paradissse. Yet they carry the plague of ssssin within their blood. For in Adam all hath sssinned and in Adam all musssst die. Yet though thou art godd of this agee, El'sss charge to me standssss, and cannot be altered. I am the vengeance of God and thessse the eyesss of vengeance do not sssee."

Lucifer scowled. "I will cross this gulf. You, Ares, will see the thing done." I will have the spirits of these men. I will take the essence of their love of El and with it craft a device to smite at the very heart of the Almighty. Work with him, Ares." Lucifer then turned pushed past Charon and walked away, incensed.

"All of you—work!"

Lucifer schemed how he might change Charon's charge to fully control him and muttered to himself as he stormed from the staging area of the Hellforge.

Lucifer spat on the ground and curled his lips as he cursed. "I will see this gulf crossed."

* * *

Each of the Lumazi had arrived and settled at the circular table in the war room. Michael stood and all stood with him, and he opened the session with an invocation.

"There is one God who stands as Creator of all things. The Father of us all, Judge of all the Heavens. Let his wisdom guide us. His commands steel us. His love preserves us. We are the Lumazi, and His will be done this day. So, say we all."

Each replied as one, "So say we all."

Each of the seven seated themselves and waited for Michael to speak.

"We have command by God to assemble. For He hath made known that a vessel for Shiloh has come into the earth in the form of a maiden. There can be no doubt that in time, Satan will find the female; we must, therefore, secure the maiden's safety. Yeshua hast authorized the girl's protection."

Argoth rubbed his chin. "So, what is your plan to protect the maiden until Shiloh arrives?"

Michael's brow became stern. "Lucifer is cunning. He will look for any instance that might arise among men to bring him low. It is not our task to overturn him. Man himself must do this. This springs from El himself. But we must give man means and time so that Shiloh might be brought forth into the realm of men. Therefore, I will use the armies of Heaven to misdirect Lucifer. I will station a legion to draw his attention to a nonexistent threat. If we are successful, we will pull his resources and bid us time to protect Shiloh."

"Protect—Shiloh?" said Metatron. "Do you know who Shiloh is?"

The members of the Lumazi looked at Michael in stares of expectation, waiting for him to speak more on the subject. But he did not.

"Of greater importance is to bring about the will of the Lord. To do this we must create a diversion."

Argoth sighed. "Your plan though sound, will cause many of our people to fall. Will you surrender your brethren to dissolution, for the love of man? Why should an Elohim give his life for a creature of flesh and blood?"

Michael looked down, closed his eyes and sighed. "I am the builder of Heaven. Yet I would see the beams of her foundation destroyed and Heaven herself cast into the Abyss if it were the will of El. Lucifer must be made to believe such a threat, though unreal, is true, or he will not be feigned. Therefore, one of you must do this thing. One must lead the armies of God, and fall into the enemy's hands."

Silence covered them all. They knew the Lucifer would have them as prisoner, and that Charon who was Prime over both Death and Hell would of a surety torture them for information.

"Gabriel started to speak, "But Michael—"

"I will go," said Talus, interrupting his brother.

Everyone turned and looked at him. Gabriel grabbed Talus's arm

Talus immediately raised his hand to ward off others from approaching or speaking.

"Are you sure?" said Michael. "If Lucifer discovers thee, he will of a surety put thee to death."

"I do not fear dissolution," Talus replied. "Lucifer through his stratagems hast manipulated me to bring Heaven to conflict. Therefore, if the Lord wills it. I will take satisfaction in returning recompense upon his head."

Michael nodded. "Then the order is given, for El hath commanded for the changing of nations. You will take a legion to the far side of the planet. And you will seek to destroy the stronghold of Quetzalcoatl. From there you, Jerahmeel, and Chronos will free Iblis and feign capture to the Fallen, spy out their plans that we might counter them and disrupt Lucifer's aims at all costs." Michael gazed upon Talus, pausing to give his brother time to reconsider. "Are you clear in your purpose?"

Talus nodded. "I am clear."

"Then go and make thy preparations." Michael dismissed them all.

Each one sullenly walked from the war room, and Michael, Chief Prince and General of the armies of Heaven, looked at them as they left and wondered in himself if he had just sent his brothers to their death.

* * *

Ashtaroth rushed into the chambers of Lucifer, who was seated pouring over tomes of ancient texts. Lucifer's eyes darted over passages of scripture that El had given his people.

"Lucifer, Assyrix hast had a vision! He beckons that you come to Egypt immediately for consult."

Lucifer looked unconvinced. "Really? What does he claim to see?"

Ashtaroth bowed before his Lord and spoke. "He claims to have found Shiloh."

Lucifer immediately left his stronghold and traveled from his throne in Pergamos and soon arrived in Egypt. He looked for his Chief of Eyes, and Assyrix was in a Grigoric trance. The Grigori hovered in place, his pen writing in the journal that was his heart. Assyrix was misted yet glowed that he could yet be seen. Lucifer waited for Assyrix to speak and when he did not, he moved towards him and shook him until he awakened.

"Speak, Assyrix! Ashtaroth tells me that you have word of Shiloh? What have you seen that I should leave my plan to—"

"There is a maiden that will bring forth a son."

Lucifer rolled his eyes, "So... the descendants of Eve continuously spawn the Clayborn—what care should I take in the birth of another?"

"True, Lord," Assyrix said, "Yet I have seen a man born of a virgin."

"Impossible," said Lucifer.

"The scene is true, and the word is sure, but fear not, for victory over Shiloh hast also been seen."

Lucifer's interest peaked. "Say on and keep nothing back."

"I have seen Shiloh hung upon the back of a tree."

Lucifer smiled. "Who are her people and where does the maiden live?"

"She is lodged in the empire of Rome, and hast arisen from the tribe of Judah, my Lord."

Lucifer cursed. "I have moved repeatedly to destroy those dogs under the protection of El since their inception as a nation. For over a thousand years, their extinction hast defied me. I grow weary with the two tribes that yet remain. It is time to once again cull the ranks of their wretched race." Lucifer turned to Assyrix and Ashtaroth his lieutenant. "Gather me, executioners, for I will see this woman, her child, and her family destroyed."

Assyrix raised his voice in concern, "But, my liege, the vision shows the child hung upon hewn beams of a tree."

"Yea," said Lucifer, "but unless we disrupt what hast been seen we will only serve to bring to pass the will of the Almighty. No, we will not let the child live only to die on beams of trees. We will wipe from the earth the woman's line, upending El's plans entirely. You merely see what El allows you to see. We must disrupt His plans. She and her kind hath plagued me for the last time. Now go, and prepare me, executioners, that we might bring ruin to the maiden's people."

"Aye. Lord. It shall be as you say."

* * *

Assyrix flew to Pergamus and came to the seat of Satan, bowed before his master and spoke. "My Lord, I have assembled per your command those who I seek to accompany me on my charge to destroy the maiden."

Lucifer replied, "Who hast thou chosen?"

Assyrix replied, "To serve as defender to our company, I would draft Volac. To serve as angel of destruction, I ask for Lathatiel. He was instrumental in helping to set Heaven on fire, and he rivals my Lord in his calculating nature to destroy. For healer of wounds, I solicit my king to grant me Zathiel though reluctant to engage or to injure, he will do as commanded. And I shall serve as support to the group and provide guidance to our mission. Is this to my king's pleasure?"

Lucifer thought upon the words of his Chief of Eyes. "The thing that thou sayest is good. You will gather those you have submitted and be swift in your charge. Are you clear in your purpose?"

"The maiden's spirit will help fire the engine of Hell. She will be dead before the setting of the next day's sun. I am clear in my purpose."

Lucifer smiled. "See that it is done. Do not fail me, Assyrix."

Assyrix bowed and walked backward two spaces, then turned to see Ashtaroth awaiting him outside. "What does the master require?"

"I go to bring dissolution to a house of the Jews. Assemble for me the following and let them meet me here before night's end. For I wish to depart soon to accomplish our Lord's will."

Ashtaroth bowed and signaled couriers to him. To each, he gave a scroll with the seal of the red dragon of Lucifer Draco, that those whose names were written therein were given command to assemble and bidden to come with haste by nightfall. And it was so, that by the eve that three angels stood before Assyrix, ready to move as directed.

Volac stood 10 cubits high. His broad shoulders were draped with Hell-forged armor, grey in color and it emanated an icy fog with white dendetric crystals. His eyes were blue, and a bluish white mist floated from them. The Arelim held a large mace, a brass ring pierced his nose, and he snorted when he spoke. "Speak, Grigori, at it was not told me why the master bids me come. The word is that I am assigned to protect a squad of Lucifer's making."

Assyrix looked over the Arelim and spoke. "What thou hast heard is true. You will accompany me with those assembled here to destroy a human female and those that have sired her."

Volac chuckled. "We are four angels descended from Heaven. And where is that army on Earth that can withstand even one of us? Yet you would have us sully our hands to raise arms against one human female? Are we despised so above all the Horde that we stand as errand boys to execute a daughter of Eve? Volac spat on the ground. "I will not waste my time on such a mission of no import. Send one of lesser rank. I am Volac of House Arelim. Have Lucifer send a lackey more suitable to this task."

"And which lackey would you recommend?" Lucifer approached the group from the rear, and all immediately turned and bowed as one when they saw him.

"I spoke out of turn, my king," said Volac. "I am at my Lord's service and honored to serve."

Lucifer smirked. "Of course, you are." Lucifer walked up to Lahatiel. "It is good to see you again. I trust that Assyrix hast informed you all of why you are here?"

Lahatiel replied, "We have been told that we are to seek the dissolution of a daughter of Eve. One of the seed of promise from Abraham's line. Is this so, my king?"

"The thing that you have been told is true."

"May my Lord be not angry with his servant. Volac's question also is my own. If such is the case, why are four needed to see to this thing? Is not one of the lower ranks sufficient to bring to naught the line of but one human house?

Lucifer nodded. "What you say is true. But is there not a cause? For lo, I have given you the honor to destroy Shiloh Himself."

All three angels gasped, jaws wide opened, and anxiety began to overtake them.

"My Lord, will not the Host have protection to watch over such a precious thing as the mother of Shiloh?"

Lucifer nodded, "Oh, undoubtedly so. Yet you are my vanguard to wipe such resistance away. Assyrix will see to the dissolution. You three will see that he is supported. Destroy any human settlement the family hast made contact. Heal one another of injury if such is needed, protect one another that the thing be done. But above all, do not return if Shiloh lives." Lucifer then stood in front of all three and glared at them all. "Are you clear in your purpose?"

They bowed and spoke as one, "We are clear my king."

Lucifer turned, his cloak swishing about his muscled frame. "Then go and be about my business."

Chapter Eight: Kenosis

Azaziel and Argoth Laddered to the central continent of the Earth and landed in the Roman Empire's province of Galilee in the small Jewish enclave of Nazareth. It was a tiny city about 2 days journey north of the human city of Jerusalem. The city smelled of sickness and was rife with people who scurried about. Merchants and traders walked the dirty streets and the sounds of camels, and scruffy-looking children running to and fro attempting to catch one another in games of hide and seek filled the air.

Azaziel sniffed and covered his nose. "Is there anything good that can come from such filth? Where is the maiden?" Azaziel asked.

Argoth pointed to a well where a young Jewish woman drew water. "There, she draws water." Argoth looked around to see if they had been spotted. "How long are we to offer protection?"

Azaziel shrugged his shoulders. "Until we are relieved by the command of God or the Chief Prince." Suddenly the sound as if from a trumpet bellowed over the air, and many of the cities' people followed the sound to a small nondescript building where several men sat teaching out of the law of the books of Moses. One spoke up to the people, "Come! Come! For the noon hour is at hand and let us give prayer to God that He might hear us!" Men sat on the ground facing south to the city of Jerusalem and began to recite words from the Grigoric book God had given to mankind. "Hear, O Israel: The Lord our God, the Lord is one. Love the Lord your God with all your heart and with all soul and with all your strength..."

Argoth looked nervously about him as the people followed along in their recitation. "Take up position by the girl, for our arrival has not gone unnoticed." Argoth pointed and Azaziel's eyes tracked the direction of his finger. In the distance standing above the synagogue were two opaque figures floating above the building.

The young woman had finished drawing water and sat near the rear of the assembly also reciting her prayers. "There is commandment from El, even among the Horde, that we will not reveal ourselves. Would they dare defy Him with so many to see?"

Argoth replied, "I know not. To interact with the physical realms inhabitants is not our charge yet the Horde is the Horde. My Grigori brings reports where members of the Fallen have possessed the bodies of humans. The Horde are beyond redemption; we cannot assume that they will abide by articles of war that govern our kind. We would do well to prepare ourselves for when they arrive. I sense that the two of us may not be enough." Argoth then took his stylus and when he waved his hand, a parchment materialized, and he wrote upon it. Then tossed it in the air and it burst in brilliant colors above them and disappeared.

"What did you just do?" Azaziel asked.

"Called for reinforcements." Argoth looked upon the small female child that Michael had sent them to protect. "We need to try to get her to a more secure location. There are too many humans here."

"How?" asked Azaziel.

"If need be..." Argoth was cut off in midsentence by the gruff voice of another.

"The girl is not yours to have, but our charge to destroy. And though you are Lumazi, you would be wise to leave, and to leave now." Volac cracked his neck and scrunched his shoulders and moved closer to Azaziel.

Assyrix looked at Argoth and added. "It would seem that we have a problem. For there can be but one Chief of Eyes. The Enslaver I see hast chosen thee, whilst the patriot of our freedom hast assigned me title. There cannot be but one eye that sees for the people."

Argoth smiled. "Then if mine eye offends thee—come and pluck it out."

Assyrix looked at Lahatiel and spoke. "Kill the Lumazi and bring the girl to me."

* * *

Talus had commanded that a hundred of his house follow their Lord to the Earth. Jerahmeel also commanded another hundred, including Chronos, from House Harada. They were a troop of just over two hundred strong. Two hundred angels gathered to save one.

Michael gave command of the search and rescue mission to Talus. The Chief Prince had made their mandate clear. "Get in, find Iblis, and get out."

Michael walked the duo to the waypoint to the end of the city. He looked at each of the soldiers he was sending on what some in the council thought was a foolhardy mission. Jerahmeel walked towards him fully armored.

Michael smiled and spoke. "You look fearsome, my friend. No weapon formed against thee shall prosper."

Jerahmeel laughed. "I pray not, but whatever the case, we shall prevail. However, when we do find the lad, what pray tell would you have us do with him?"

Michael looked at him. "When you secure his release, be swift and bring him home. I would question him. Lucifer I am sure has plans to siege Heaven. I would know what they are."

Jerahmeel looked at him, surprised. "You would have me bring a member of the Fallen to the realm after El Himself hast expelled him—are you mad?"

"Perhaps..." said Michael. "Perhaps."

Jerahmeel moved as if to carry on the conversation, but Michael cut him off as he saw Talus approach and spoke aloud over his shoulder as he walked towards Talus and away from Jerahmeel. "You have your orders Prince of Harada." Jerahmeel sighed and walked to the platform to await Talus's arrival.

Talus stepped to walk past Michael, and Michael reached his hand to stop him. "Hold! High Prince of House Arelim!"

Talus stopped and looked upon his brother. "Have you further orders for me, my prince?"

"There is but one." Michael paused. He took his hand from off Talus' broad shoulders and in the view of the entire squad reached out and hugged him. "You will make sure that you return to me." Talus opened his eyes wide at the unexpected gesture of emotion on Michael's part, then relaxed and allowed himself to also embrace his brother. "I will see that it is done."

"See that you do," said Michael. "For if I would send two hundred and two from the Lumazi to rescue just one of the fallen, how much more would I do to secure my own brother? For neither life, nor death, nor things present or those to come will separate me to see thee returned safely to Heaven's bosom. Do not fail to come home. Are you clear in your purpose?"

A tear streamed from Talus's eye. "I am clear."

Michael released him and shooed him away. Talus walked to the platform, and for a moment, he smiled at Michael. Then he steeled his face, spoke an Elomic command and the waypoint exploded in color as a great funnel cloud of a Ladder descended and transported the group to the Earth below.

Light skipped about the troop as Talus, Jerahmeel, Chronos, and two hundred angelic soldiers from both houses descended as great beams of light. The Lumazi followed Chronos as he guided them between galaxies and stars. Each turned to fall through the stellar cosmos as they were swiftly brought to the small planet El had carefully crafted and placed His name among its people. Earth quickly approached them, and Chronos, knowing they would be detected, exerted his power over time in this realm, and he opened his wings as a great sail and was pulled backwards. He traveled towards the rear through the group while enveloping the troop in a cocoon of temporal power. Faster they flew past asteroids and the moon, slipping past the angelic guards that Lucifer had placed in their path. A cosmic blur the group became imperceptible to the guardian's gaze. The atmosphere greeted them and Chronos controlled the discharge of gas and friction so that none could trace the vapor trails the group left in their wake. Particles of gas and light flickered into nothing at the command of the Archon of Time. Quickly the southern hemisphere of the planet raced into view and the jungles of the southern continent men had called Amozoa zoomed into view, and the troop landed quietly in the midst of a great rain forest.

Chronos then removed the wrap of temporal invisibility from around them.

Jerahmeel looked into the sky and asked, "Where we detected?"

"Nay," said Chronos. "The Horde that dwell in this region were not able to distinguish us from the breeze. We are for the moment safe."

"How far to Quetzalcoatl's lair?" Talus asked.

"Not far," said Chronos. Just beyond the mountains, one leagues flight. But a quarter league if we fly by nightfall. For if we move by day we must move slower as to avoid detection."

Talus and the team gazed at the peaks and the length of the range of cloud-covered slopes. The length stretched from the top to the tip of the southern continent. The sight was inspiring for all to behold. For the mountain range stretched 500 leagues.

Talus looked at their surroundings. "Although it would be quick to move during the night. If we move now under the cover of the brush we can reach the area by nightfall. For every moment we abide here, we risk loss to the charge Iblis. Keeper of the Hour, we will make haste, that we might fall upon them during the night."

Chronos nodded. "It is a wise plan."

"Lead on," said Jerahmeel.

With deftness of gait, two hundred and three angels hiked and glided over palm trees headed towards a series of pyramids built deep in the Andes Mountains. Darkness slowly crept over the troop, and the coolness of the jungle breeze made their superheated bodies give off a faint steam.

"Just ahead," said Chronos. He took his hand and lowered it, and everyone immediately ducked lower into the brush. "There, see the opening to the cave?"

Talus and Jerahmeel strained their eyes to see through the darkness and made out an opening carved into the rock at the base of the mountain. "How do we get in?"

Talus knelt on the ground. We must use stealth to secure Iblis's release. The three of us will go inside and acquire him. The first and second squads will stay in hiding. If we are not out in one day's time, the first squad will create a diversion to lure those within outside. Do not engage them if your numbers are inferior. But if equal or superior, you may engage. If they outnumber you, then you will lead them as far away as possible. Your role will be to serve as a distraction. Upon completion, you will attempt to find a place to hide that you might observe our escape and rejoin us. If this cannot be done, then you will return to Heaven. Second squad will remain here in hiding. You will provide defensive cover for our escape if we are pursued. Are you clear in your purpose?"

Each commander nodded. "We are clear."

Talus looked at Jerahmeel and Chronos. "Let's go."

Chronos enveloped the trio in a cloak of temporal power, and they moved into the cave's entrance and walked past two guards who stood motionless as the three angels rushed past them unnoticed. Deeper they moved into the cavern as tunnels and dank stone walls lined with cool, moist air filled the chambers. Finally, the trio came to a side chamber where voices were heard.

"Iblis, Iblis—why do you resist us? Are we not thy family? Have you not joined yourself to the Usurpation? Why must we continue in this fruitless endeavor? Why do you allow this pain to continue? Inform us of what you have done, and we will spare thee from the prison of Hell. But if not, we will let Hell suckle on thy stone until your mind is nothing but a husk, and daemon shall you be. A phantasm, an apparition, and nothing more. Let your suffering end. We beg you."

Chronos, Talus, and Jerahmeel hid behind a wall and peered to see that Zeus and Quetzalcoatl stood over Iblis. Iblis's face was bloodied, and Quetzalcoatl had imprisoned him in chains of fire. Designed by Ares, they burned as the flesh of Hell. Iblis was strung aloft naked, and above him hovered three creatures of female form in ghostly robes, and they screamed at him and Iblis cried out in pain for their wails, and the creatures were haggard and deformed daemons, and did not cease wailing into his ears. Each held a stylus and wrote glyphs into his flesh, and Iblis's skin burst in pustules of blood and the maggots of Hell fed off his wounds where they were written.

"Iblis, Iblis..." said Quetzalcoatl. "Why do you persist in this devotion to a king who hast cast thee asunder? What meaning doth the thing have for a member of the Fallen? You cannot return. For there is no repentance for thee. No turning of El's mind. Renounce Him. Speak the words and recant. Just tell us where are those that have assisted thee with the Time Lord Chronos?"

Iblis lifted up his head, as if to speak, and Quetzalcoatl commanded the Banshee's to cease their wails into his ears. The creatures stopped their screams and floated away from Iblis, and then he whispered something.

"Say again, Iblis," said Quetzalcoatl. "Speak, that we might hear thee. What have you to confess?"

Talus and Jerahmeel and Chronos looked on, concealed behind a protrusion near a wall, and Jerahmeel spoke. "We should kill him, if he gives away the secrets of the rebellion then they will be hunted and destroyed and all hope for undermining Lucifer from within will be lost."

"Hold, my Lord, please...I have faith in him," pleaded Chronos.

Jerahmeel looked at Talus. "You are in command—what say you?"

Talus looked at Chronos and his face was downcast. "If his lips seep of betrayal, I will cut him down myself, for he cannot be allowed to reveal those that assist the cause of Heaven."

Chronos looked at Iblis, and watched the scene play out before his eyes.

Quetzalcoatl grabbed Iblis by his chin, and his hands covered the angel's cheeks, and he pulled his face that Iblis might gaze upon him. "Speak, traitor! You will give me what I desire or know that all tatters to that which you hold dear will be burned in the fire! Speak! I command you!"

Iblis opened his tired eyes and looked into the eyes of his captor and spoke. "I am friend of the Host. I am bound by the ancient laws to never sever my word. Though I be lost in this thing, honor will remain. Promise I have made to one of the Host, and though I burn in Hell. It is a promise to Chronos I will not make void. For whom among the Horde hast lifted finger to save me? But one not of my house rescued me from the fall of Kilnstones, and his life will I honor."

Quetzalcoatl was wroth and backhanded the angel. "Honor his life traitor, for know that thy own is forfeit. What more need I to hear? Keep thy honor angel. Let it satisfy thee, as I make thy flesh a habitation for another."

Chronos panicked. "Quickly, my Lords, we must rescue him!"

Talus nodded. "Jerahmeel, distract Zeus - he will not expect to see you, and you are of his house. I will see to Quetzalcoatl. Chronos, release Iblis. On my command, make for your targets. Three...two...one...go!"

The three angels burst into the antechamber, startling the occupants of the room. Jerahmeel lifted his hand and cooled the air around Iblis and Zeus. Zeus was caught off guard, while the moisture in the air around him froze, encasing him in solid ice. Iblis hung suspended in straps of flame, his head down, weary from his torture. Chronos waved his hand and immediately time slowed to a snail's pace within the chamber as the *tick tock* of seconds became the *tick tock* of hours. Chronos dashed to release Iblis, pulling from the angel's flesh maggots used to leech confession from his lips, and cast them to the floor, smashing them with the soles of his feet. Chronos then snapped the chains of Hellfire that sucked the life force from his brother's Kilnstone, and Iblis collapsed headlong into his waiting arms.

Iblis looked up. "Thank you..."

"Shhhh—conserve your strength, we must move quickly." Chronos and Iblis turned to exit the cave, only to find Zeus freed from his cage of ice and barring their path.

Zeus walked confidently through the distortion field of time. "It is touching that you hold Iblis in such high regard, but did you seriously think that your antics would keep *me* at bay?" "We are of the same blood, Chronos. You cannot escape."

Chronos created a portal behind him and pushed Iblis into the gateway, and the angel disappeared. The room then returned to normal, and Talus and Quetzalcoatl were gripped in hand to hand to combat.

Zeus smiled. "I will find him. He cannot escape the gaze of the Horde."

Jerahmeel rushed to tackle Zeus. The fallen angel lifted his hand, and a portal appeared and Jerahmeel disappeared into the void.

"Jerahmeel!" screamed Talus. Then the great angel kicked Quetzalcoatl in the abdomen and the fallen angel flew across the room. Time slowed and Quetzalcoatl floated ever so slowly in the air while both Zeus and Chronos with hands raised gestured to slow and accelerate time within the chamber. Waves of visible light emanated from the two, and time itself was held captive as a plaything to the will of the angels. The waves vied against one another, in a struggle of temporal tug of war, the ebb and flow moved towards Chronos, then pushed back towards Zeus. The cavern slowly vibrated as the power to advance and retract the age of everything within the bubble of power caused the ceiling to crack, and long fissures raced across the floors and walls.

"I am the Father of Time now!" Zeus proclaimed. "You have trained me to your own destruction!" And with a wave of his hand, Zeus sent a bolt of lightning moving to Talus that he might strike him down.

Chronos created a portal before Talus and the lightning disappeared within, only to materialize from another portal behind Zeus' and struck him in the back, sending kilowatts of current through his system.

The bubble of time collapsed, and Quetzalcoatl was propelled into Zeus, and they crashed into the walls of the antechamber, electrocuting them both.

Talus moved towards Chronos, who on bended knee gasped out, "Hurry we must leave now!"

Chronos looked upon Zeus, who was lifting the unconscious Quetzalcoatl from off him, and replied, "No—there is no time. Iblis is safe on the outskirts with the angels we have stationed to wait. But Jerahmeel must be aided now."

Chronos created a portal, and Talus looked at him. Zeus rose to his feet, smiling as he proceeded to walk towards them. "Get out of here now," said Chronos, while he motioned Talus to leave. The Archon of Time rose to his feet and stood as a shield between Talus and Zeus.

Talus took one last look at his comrade as Chronos prepared to engage his former protégé and then he leaped through the portal and was gone.

* * *

El had commanded an audience of angelic kind everywhere, and all assembled in the emporium to hear what God had to say. Ladders were open to Elohim throughout the realms so that each could hear from Heaven. El was seated, and to His right Yeshua sat, and the Holy Ghost was also seated to his left. For the triune God was fully manifest and three persons could be seen. Hushed whispers overtook the assembled crowd as El began to speak.

"The iniquity of man is full. It is come that he must be set free from the snare of the enemy. Therefore, we will that the Host serve as protector to the daughter of Eve, who will bring forth Shiloh. We will now lift our hand to bring low the Enemy. For though the Godhead bleeds, we shall even give our life that Adam and his kind might live. We would know if the heart of our sons are also in this thing. For lo, who shall I send and who shall go for us?"

The emporium was silent, for many were unwilling to do anything for the Adam, as the loss of El's love for them was still a thing that many feared and the plague of sin wrought terror in all angelkind. Each dreaded sin, knowing that the plague of sin could separate one from the presence of El. Yet none stepped forward to rescue the man, for the word of El's demise sent chills as each speculated that the death of God could mean the destruction of all things.

Metatron raised his voice to speak to the Lord. "Lord, I lift my voice to my King in fear and trembling. You ask a hard thing. For how can the father ask the son to do him harm? What thou ask, we cannot do. For whom among us would be cause for the demise of the Almighty? For with our own eyes, we have seen that the absence of God is but the dissolution of all things. Nevertheless, if thou command, we will obey without question. But who can abide a request to bring thee to dissolution?"

"And the Lord God said, "Ah my children, there are yet many things that ye must observe, things that I must still show you, even things that my youngest son Adam will teach you."

Enoch was livid that no one immediately answered the Lord's call and screamed at the multitude, "Will none go to help thy brother? Is there none that will lift up his hand to bring my people from the darkness?" Enoch then wept before them all, and silence and sunken heads were all that was heard and seen. Throughout all the realms of Creation, there was silence. For no one came to take up Enoch's cause, and none raised his hand to risk the dissolution of God for the object of God's love.

Then the Lord God Yeshua stood then spoke and broke the silence. His words echoed throughout the cosmos. "I will go down."

Gasps swept through the crowd. A billion gaping mouths and hushed whispers of disbelief as Yeshua, second of the Godhead, stood before them all and spoke.

"I will go down, Father. Let it be thy will that I might give thee pleasure. Let thine wisdom, love, and power be made known in all the realms. I will give my life for the man."

For a moment all were silent, and not even the "Holy, Holy, Holy" of the Seraphim was heard, as all angelkind saw that none would move to rescue man from Lucifer save God himself. Yeshua stepped down from His throne stood before the people. Many looked at him and shook their heads in unspoken attempts to dissuade while others were in denial. Yeshua was unmoved and turned to face El and looked up at the Father and spoke again.

"I will go down."

The Lord God looked down upon His son, His only son. Then He reached down to hug His beloved, and for a moment, all of Heaven was conscience-stricken, for in the instant where God grasped the locks of his son's hair, only now did it occur to all, the depths to which El would sacrifice for the Clayborne. In the moment where God stroked the cheeks of His own son, was it finally understood that God so loved the world that He would give His only begotten son to succor the man from harm.

El then loosed from holding Yeshua and their fingers and hands brushed each other as El withdrew himself. Yeshua then nodded knowingly to the Father, and the Father laid His hands on the crown of Yeshua's head and made pronouncement over him.

"For though thou be God yet shall I loose thee from the trappings of God. For thou shalt stand as mediator between God and Man. Thus, that thy might be in all things—I empty thee. To know all that was and is, and wilt be known—I empty thee. To know all yet not know. I empty thee. Yet this one thing remains. For as I have life in myself, so I hath given thee to have life in thyself. And lo, I impart to thee authority to execute judgment. Go, and let my love give thee strength, let thy light scatter the darkness, and thy life be as seed to bring forth my son Adam from the plague of sin. For thou art, the Resurrection and the Life, and what you bind on Earth shalt be bound in Heaven, and what thou loose on Earth shalt be loosed in Heaven. And whom thou forgive, I too shall forgive."

When El had finished speaking, Yeshua exploded in light and He glowed and all that was within Him poured as streams of living water and emptied itself into El. And the whole of Heaven watched as Yeshua, the second person of the Godhead, diminished and the glorified body that breathed Shekinah as waste; the body whose flecks of skin were but the scale of galaxies, became as nothing. Yeshua then collapsed at the Lord's feet and the brightness of His glory changed, and naught was left but a glowing orb of light, small enough to be carried in the bosom of one's robes.

El then looked across the emporium and into the eyes of all angelic kind. "Never in all of recorded history hast thy God asked thee nor commanded thee as I do now. For with the kenosis, I place myself in need. I stand as Lord and God, and cannot leave the throne, El Pnuema I will send to work my will, that Mary might birth God. Yeshua, my only Son has abased Himself, that He might live in flesh. Yet one thing is required. We have need of the Host to carry us to the maiden. Who will I send? And who will go for us, that we might save the man?"

All of Heaven stood quiet. For all remembered when El was away for just one day. And in one day all of Creation was ruined. Fear gripped each, and indecision was palpable across the multitudes. But none moved, for all still feared that the absence of the Godhead would lead to the destruction of their race. Enoch wept sore, for none raised their hand, nor stepped forward to do the will of the Lord in this thing—not unless He commanded them.

God then spoke. "Let it be written in the annals of history. For there was none in Heaven that would take up our cause, none that would lift up our hand to help succor the man. And none that could save man, but God himself." And before the Grigori could write, El lifted his hand to stop them and looked at Michael and spoke.

"Will *you,* my son, carry me to Mary?"

Michael was gripped and stood frozen while anxiety wracked over him that El had asked him this thing. His eyes darted across face to face, as both citizen and the Lumazi looked to see how the Chief Prince would answer God. For Michael knew that once El had submitted to Kenosis and become a man, He was exposed to death. Michael's lips quivered. For he had never disobeyed his Lord. His was to do the will of his Father. His mind reeled, remembering the words of Eladrin and his bout with the spirit of fear. Remembered how there was no need for fear, and when he remembered that trust was but needed. Trust to surrender to the revealed will of God, peace flooded him, and he spoke.

"Lord, if I carry thee, I know what the end must be. Nevertheless, at thy word I will carry thee. Command is not required for my king but speak the word only and it shall be done, for lo, I am thy will and thy right hand."

The Lord smiled as he looked upon His son, and a tear streamed from His eye. For he knew that soon He would complete what only He could do to save man. "Your fealty will be rewarded, my son, for alas, He is my only begotten Son..." and the Lord God's eyes were both tearful and determined, and He motioned for Michael to come forward.

Michael hesitantly reached up and the glowing orb that was the essence of Yeshua floated towards him. Michael marveled as the ball of light settled into his hands, awed to hold the Creator of all things and wondered how the power of God could be so that He would live in the flesh of a child.

"I will guard Him with my life. Creation itself will see dissolution before anything befalls Him," said Michael.

El smiled. "The Kenosis hast begun. He is in thy hand. Deliver my Son to the maiden, and when I am lifted up. I will draw all men unto me."

Michael nodded and turned and walked to exit the emporium and spoke aloud that all could hear. "Those who will take up the cause of El without command or constraint, follow."

And one by one, all turned to follow the Chief Prince. Each settling in their heart that they would, for the sake of love—obey. Each submitted and yielded, and none of compulsion for El had given them choice, and all of Heaven chose to do the thing. The population emptied from the golden throne room of rainbows, and the Lumazi and the armies of heaven left to fall upon the Earth, with a mission to bring Yeshua to the maiden El had chosen to birth God. All stood as one man to honor El in this thing. All knowing that many might not return, yet none turned to fear as each moved to bring to pass God's plan to rescue the Adam. To be worthy to guard El, and to rise to His example of love.

Michael exited the palace, and as he turned to look back upon the Father. He saw El sitting on His throne in His flowing robes of power, with one hand over his face—weeping.

* * *

Michael gathered the remaining Lumazi and turned and marched from the temple to the cliffs of Argoth. As one man, the Host of Heaven summoned Ladders, but when the vanguard of heaven began to summon, the Holy Spirit caused the Ladders to cease and spoke. "Nay, my children—behold!"

And lo, when the Lord had finished speaking, the Abyss was behind the host of heaven, and they descended upon the lower realms while Time itself raced as a man sprinting to catch up with them. The numbers of Heaven's legions were so that they eclipsed galaxies, stars, and planets. For such were the sum that the whole of Heaven had emptied.

Michael marveled at the sight and overwhelmed as to the number of angels who followed the Holy Spirit into battle, he burst into song. A song that traversed past the limitations of space and time, a sound heard by all angelic kind, a song of war, and of praise. And lo, the Grigori recorded that the words were on this wise.

"My shield, my shield, the Lord God is my shield.
He comes; He comes, with Shiloh in His wake.
Hosanna! Hosanna!
All praise the king of kings!
Hosanna! Hosanna!
He flies on angel wings!
El comes, He comes, He comes and sheds His light
He comes, He comes, in power and in might!
Our God imposes terror against His enemies!
Swift shall be the fallen, terror as they flee.
We come; we come, for Lord and country's sake.
He comes; He comes, with Shiloh in His wake!"

All Creation took note that God passed before them and that the host of heaven sided by God as a royal escort and that Michael carried within his bosom, the spirit of the Son of God. And before the Chief Prince flew a phalanx of 144 legions who had emptied Heaven. And as they passed each galaxy and constellation, more angels left their station to provide cover for the Son of El. The Holy Spirit flew before His people and caused all orbits to cease, and as the eternal one passed the stars, each star stopped to pay homage to the God of angel armies, and all of the host of heaven descended and moved as light to bring El safe to the womb of a sixteen-year-old girl. A girl living on a speck in the heavens of cosmic dust on the blue orb where El had set his mind to bring Lucifer to naught.

* * *

And the cry of Heaven reached the ears of Lucifer's outpost guards, and they hastened to inform their Lord, and the thing was told to Ashtaroth who rushed to inform his master.

"My king!" he said.

Lucifer was irritated at the interruption of Ashtaroth and ignored him.

"My Lord I come with news from the front."

Lucifer's eyebrows rose and his back was still to Ashtaroth. "Speak."

"Heaven has come!"

"How many of the Host dares to do battle whilst I sit on the throne of this planet and command the vengeance of God?"

"All of Heaven, my Lord."

Lucifer turned to face Ashtaroth and gave him a look of curiosity. "Say again?"

"There is a word that all of Heaven hast emptied herself, my Lord."

"That is not possible! El would not dare repent of his own word." Are you sure of this report, Astarte?"

"The report is true my king. What is thine command?"

El has proven his word means naught. For the deceiver now seeks to take by force what He cannot obtain by His own law. We will rise to meet them. What is my command? War, Astarte—war is my command."

The legions of Lucifer mustered themselves and rose to do battle with the invasion of Heaven. And Michael knew that to protect the Son of God he must leave a wing of his troops to fight his fallen brethren and that many of them would fall. The Holy Spirit sprinted ahead of the army and hovered over the maiden Mary, awaiting Michael's arrival, and protected her so that God's vessel would be safe from the enemies of the Lord.

And as Michael approached the Earth, he saw the blue of the planet that El loved and rising to meet him was the host of the Fallen. And they had transformed themselves into beasts for the cause of Lucifer. Many had changed to beasts whose faces were as a lion and with wings as a bat, and iron spikes erupted from their tails. Others too had changed to take on the persona of their master and were as great dragons with seven heads and wings of leather. Still others flew as great serpents with wings, and though Heaven was greater in number, those who had followed Lucifer were some of the most powerful, for pride had caused many of the most commanding of Elohim to take cause with Lucifer.

The host of Heaven looked on, as arising from the darkness was Lucifer, whose trumpets and harps could be heard even in the vacuum of space. His armor was blood-red, and he held a sword that shimmered an iridescent green. Charon soared above him, his skeletal wings stretched wide, and the mare's grin etched in his face. Flaming chains trailed behind him as he flew through the darkness of space. Once more Elohim would battle with one another, and all knew that no quarter would be given, and no mercy would be shown.

Gabriel looked at Michael and his eyebrows drew together, as they beheld the throng before them. "Michael? Now would be a good time to sound for attack!" he said.

Michael's face was stoic and his eyes steeled on the path that was set before them. "Hold!" He shouted back.

Metatron also saw the Horde ascend and knew that the Fallen rushed to meet them and that their numbers unexpectedly rivaled their own. Metatron also cleared his throat with concern.

"Michael!"

"Hold!" Was the archangel's reply, as he tightened his grip around the pouch that carried the spirit of Yeshua.

The Fallen unsheathed swords as they ascended. Maces dropped from their sides and shields and all manner of weaponry, and their numbers blotted out the Earth. Her planetary features were now eclipsed in darkness from the approaching army that rose to meet them.

Michael closed his eyes and prayed for strength and replayed the words of Eladrin in his mind. *'When Death rises—call us, and we shall come.'* The golden halo over Michael's head glowed and he became as the light of the sun.

"Now!" Michael roared.

And in the seconds that ticked on the celestial clock of God. The two great armies closed to do battle, and great rifts of light opened in the skies about the planet, and the prismatic funnels of Ladders appeared across the blanket of space, and lo, the Ophanim descended in swarms as great beams of light and pierced through the ascending Horde. The Fallen's lines gave way as angel now fought against Ophanim and wheels sliced through wings. Discs crushed against the invisible chests of angels and chaos overtook the skies of Earth as the armies collided with one another.

Michael weaved and dodged between foes and Metatron and Gabriel flanked him. Michael turned to his side and Gabriel and Metatron moved with him as thousands of angels followed. The angelic host armored themselves and each raised their shield and lifted sword, and a mighty yell raced throughout the second heaven as the armies of God entered the planet's atmosphere.

And when the Fallen did battle with the host of heaven. The sky of the Earth was covered in blankets of green, yellow and blue shimmering shades of color that splashed across the scattered clouds in psychedelic displays. The battle served up shooting rays of light that lit the sky in eerie glows, and men beheld the spectacles of light and stared in awe as they watched stars shoot across the canopy of the sky.

The two armies clashed, and Michael lifted his sword and flew deftly behind the trail Gabriel and Metatron made before him. He unleashed the Sword of Ophanim, and the living weapon split and encircled him. And lo, a minion of Lucifer approached him, and he was as a prismatic dragon and sought to fell Michael, but Gabriel rammed the fallen angel, and they plummeted to the seas below. Metatron took up Gabriel's station and the two turned to the continent that El had made His people to dwell. And as he descended, chromatic, black, blue and red dragons, sought to wipe him from the sky. And Metatron held a battle axe, and he and several of his kind, flanked by Malakim griffins, plowed into each one, and Michael watched as Metatron fell with two of the beasts in tow, pummeling them in the face as he fell.

In the distance, Lucifer rose across the skies. His image was that of a great red dragon, and he moved angels aside as dross. Charon ran over and overpowered resisting angels as he went before Lucifer as his shield, for not even the Ophanim were a match for the Angel of Death. Lucifer sliced through foes with his sword and the blade drained the life from his adversaries, and in the midst of battle, Lucifer spotted Michael in the fray and turned towards him to fly and bring down his younger brother. Michael, too, dived towards him and the Angel of Death, and he raised the sword of Ophanim. He roared, and his halo glowed and as he did, so a Ladder formed on high that was larger than all others. A mammoth circular well of light burst over his head and Eladrin plummeted from within, and the great King of the Ophanim fell upon Charon, crashing into the Angel of Death, and they grappled with one another and the two celestial beings plunged to the Earth below.

Lucifer paused in shock as he watched Charon fall back to the Earth, only to turn his eye to the battle to see his brother now upon him. Michael smashed into his chest, and they careened into the upper skies of the planet. Charon and Eladrin plummeted to the Earth, and Lucifer and Michael fell alongside the giants, for as falling stars each of the four struggled with one another, as the air shed streams of incandescent light in their wakes, and men beheld as it were four great stars fall from the sky.

Lucifer illuminated his skin in a vain attempt to blind Michael. But Michael was now the Chief Prince and he too glowed, and Lucifer, unaccustomed to seeing light as luminous as his own, shielded his eyes, unexpectedly blinded, and when he did so, Michael escaped his grip and raced to descend to the position of the Holy Spirit. Charon twisted to escape Eladrin's growling bear face and he knocked into Lucifer, making him careen into several of his lieutenants.

Eladrin's disc's sliced into the dangling chains of Charon. His spinning wheels shaved the tentacle-like chains, cutting through veins and tendril. The great celestial giants plummeted past swarms of combating angels. Charon, tumbling with his enemy, reached for an inner gear in Eladrin's chest, and with his chains ripped a moving mechanism from Eladrin's abdomen. Tail spinning into the Earth's atmosphere, Charon's chains lashed against the turning faces of Eladrin, and the King of the Ophanim and the Angel of Death wrestled with one another as they crashed into the ocean and descended into the depths of the deep.

Waves rose in tsunamic response to their presence, and as leviathans in combat, they tore at the fabric of the bonds that held hydrogen and oxygen in each other's nucleic embrace. Water turned into steam around them, and sea life raced away to escape the battling archons of power. They crashed into the ocean floor. The decks of tectonic plates gave way, and fissures erupted within the seas and vomited magma onto the ocean floor. Charon, with a lash of his great chains, smote the eagles face of Eladrin, drawing blood, and then knocked the mammoth Ophanim backward, creating undersea waves. Eladrin's wheels glowed and immediately he began to disassemble, and one of his spiraling discs flew towards Charon. The Angel of Death grappled the giant discus in his hands. The force of his catch caused the angel to slide across the ocean floor.

A second disc disassembled from Eladrin's body and shot through the undersea currents, and its gyration created eddies that trailed behind it, smashing into the skeletal face of the Warden of Hell. Charon was shoved back the more, and the turbulence of their battle caused giant waves to lurch from the seas and submerge islands whole. The legends of which would be told in men's tales. Eladrin then grappled Charon, and with a thought formed into a Ladder and lifted Charon ascending through and shooting from the ocean depths. Charon was now captive as the two rocketed through the atmosphere, smashing through angelic battle lines that still raged in combat. The moon came into view then disappeared behind him, and when Charon saw that he was being pulled away from the planet, he slid his chains into the inner gears of Eladrin and pulled against the living machinery, rending the king open. The Ladder collapsed and the four faces of Eladrin screamed. Reds, blues, and greens exploded in pyrotechnic displays, and time burst as a bubble and pieces of Eladrin shot across the sky. Eladrin shimmered, then dissipated from view. Wise men of the Earth and magi observed the explosions, making note and followed their trajectory across the skies of Earth.

Charon lifted his eyes to see that his nemesis had disappeared and when he looked back to the battle that ensued behind him. He turned to see the fourth planet from this systems sun ahead of him and moved to rejoin the conflict and Lucifer below.

* * *

Argoth spun in a circle, and as he did so, he spoke the word "Elune" which in angel speak means, 'Sanctuary'. Immediately his pen moved over Nazareth, and the pen scrawled in blazing light, and a field of power flowed down over the city, and when Assyrix saw what the Grigori had done he screamed to his henchmen.

"Forget the Sephiroth, hurry and acquire the maid!"

Lahatiel raced towards the barrier and when he was about to enter the threshold of the city he was knocked back; repelled by an invisible force. He looked back at Assyrix perplexed and shrugged his shoulders. Assyrix grumbled an obscenity and yelled to his two comrades in arms.

"Forget the girl for now!" yelled Assyrix. "Kill Argoth, and the barrier will fall."

Argoth smiled and black smoke ushered from his person and shrouded him and Azaziel in darkness. Lahatiel and Volac hurtled into the angelic smog, thinking to grapple the duo, but they grasped nothing but ether and wrestled naught but plumes of smoke to the ground.

Zathael shook his head in disgust, chuckled and laid down on a rock. "When I am needed you know where to find me." He yawned and closed his eyes.

Assyrix waved his hand annoyingly and when he did, scales dropped from both Volac's and Lahatiel's eyes, and they could see that Azaziel and Argoth flew away from the city. "Hunt them, for if we do not destroy Argoth, the maiden is lost to us."

Azaziel and Argoth flew quickly over the rocky terrain and towards the mountains to Mt. Tabor, which stood isolated amidst the prairie of flat lands around it.

"This will be a good place to make our stand," said Argoth.

Azaziel smiled. "Finally, I am getting tired of running. I would let my spear speak for me."

Argoth looked up as Lahatiel, Assyrix, and Zathiel made their way towards them. "Then speak with thy spear, brother, and let your words ring true."

Azaziel smiled. "Then let first blood me mine." Immediately, Azaziel lifted his spear to the sky, and slammed the hilt into the ground, when he did a cylinder of prismatic fire and lightning fell from the sky. It targeted Volac, and the angel was blasted with fire from Heaven. Currents of electricity poured through his body, and he fell to the ground, writhing in pain. He attempted to move, and the funnel cloud followed him across the plains. Azaziel then twirled his javelin forward as a lance and raced to Lathaniel to meet the angel head on.

Closer they raced towards one another. Lahatiel leaped to the side, grabbing the lance and with his momentum, he pulled upon it, throwing Azaziel and sending him careening through the air. His enemy's weapon now in his hands, Lahatiel lifted himself into the air and catapulted to spear Azaziel. But Azaziel rolled to his side and escaped impalement. Quickly he rose to his feet and stood hovering above the ground.

"I will run you through with thine own spear!" screamed Lahatiel. He raised the javelin and hurled it at Azaziel. It flew through the air, hovering as it approached Azaziel, and settled into his waiting palm. "Thank you," said Azaziel. "I find that I hate to part with it."

Lahatiel roared with anger and charged him.

* * *

Iblis caught his breath, weak from his scourging and bondage under the torture of Quetzalcoatl. He stumbled as he fell into the waiting arms of Netzach.

"You are Iblis of House Grigori. We have orders to see to your safety. But tell me, how fares those that were sent in to deliver you?"

Iblis looked at the angel, closed his eyes and faded out of consciousness. Netzach then shook him, and Iblis opened his eyes.

"The Lumazi and Chronos!" ordered Netzach. "Quickly, what do you know of their welfare?"

Iblis spoke softly. "Chronos sent me to you, and last seen he was within the mount in battle with Zeus."

"And what of the Lumazi?" asked Netzach.

"Talus is yet inside, but Jerahmeel was ported I know not where." Iblis then fainted and went unconscious.

An angel next to Iblis spoke to his commander. "What are your orders?"

Netzach lowered his gaze. "We have orders to stay here one day and create distraction."

"And if Talus does not come out?" the angel asked.

The lieutenant looked at his man and said, "Then heaven and earth shall pass away, and we shall be found here when it does."

The group settled into the jungle to wait out the outcome of their Lord's return.

* * *

"Disassemble."

With but one word the pen of Argoth went into action. Lahatiel was hunched over, wracked in pain and screaming like a howling animal. For the celestial endorphins that pumped through his body were now removed—endorphins needed to mask the pain from a quadrillion dying cells. Cells now exposed to the plague of sin. Cells changed as the result of the fall. And the angel screamed as for the first time Lahatiel felt decay in his body, and in that moment, he experienced what it was like for a man to die.

Lahatiel's body radiated heat that blasted the mountain and the plains round about. Grass fires erupted and heated eddies floated back and forth across the rising black flames. Dark smoke and blistering heat masked the person of Lahatiel so that he could not be seen. His cries ascended to the skies and animals raced to flee what sounded like the roar of a wounded lion. Azaziel moved closer to the gritty blanket of dark smoke. The burning smell of grass entered the angel's nostrils, and he searched the darkness to see his adversary. Argoth was the first to spot him, but it was too late, for Azaziel had moved too close and Lahatiel roared from the blackness as trails of soot followed him.

He grabbed the javelin of Azaziel and with a quick stroke. He snapped the weapon in his arms, then collapsed in a huddled mass quivering in pain. He looked up at Azaziel who stood over him and smugly spoke. "Death comes to you and your kind. For the maiden shall be ours." Lahatiel then spasmed and shook on the ground.

Argoth moved towards Azaziel and frowned. "Assyrix—where is he?"

Each angel looked about them, and when Azaziel turned to interrogate Lahatiel, an iron mace met him in the chest and the force of the blow propelled him backwards into the sky and he smashed into the mountainside. Argoth, surprised, attempted to mist but could not as the air around him suddenly became cold, his lungs slowed, and his breathing stalled, and he panted to catch clumps of air. His hands went to his throat, and he choked and began to cough up blood.

"Yes, Grigori," said Volac. "You reside in this sin-stained realm and even you are susceptible to the plague of sin. Feel the cold wrap and blister your lungs as they struggle to extract what little air now oxygenates your blood. Let me watch you crawl before me. Crawl, Lumazi, and despair as we rip the hope of Heaven from you!"

Argoth crawled on the grass, looking in the distance, unable to speak, unable to stop as Assyrix spoke incantations to dismiss the protective shell he had placed to protect Nazareth.

* * *

Assyrix studied the shell that prevented him from passing. Invisible to the humans, it stood as a cover over all of Nazareth. Assyrix smiled, *This will not keep me from my charge, and the master will be pleased.*

Assyrix reached into his chest and scraped a sliver from his Kilnstone. He then ripped out a page from his tome and folded the parchment over the sliver. Taking his own pen, he slashed the palm of his hand. Tightening his fist, he let the blood mingle with the parchment-covered sliver. Watching as it slowly turned blue. He dipped his pen in his floating inkhorn and wrote the words "DESECRATE" over the parchment. Immediately the parchment caught fire, and he placed it on the shell. The casing sizzled and a red symbol formed at Assyrix's feet, climbing up the wall and encircling the invisible shell. Blood-colored tendrils crawled up from the ground and hissed. And Assyrix watched as the covering given by Argoth corroded before the onslaught and the sin of another.

Assyrix grinned, knowing that soon he would kill the host to Shiloh.

Chapter Nine: Ramah Weeps

Zeus withstood his former mentor, Chronos, the angel of absolute time. Zeus was the master of time and seasons, and the student sought to usurp the master.

"You will not see the rising of another day," said Zeus. "For it is now the season to end the existence of the father, to bring about the rise of the son. You and the Host are Titans indeed. But we—WE SHALL BE GODS!"

Chronos looked upon him and spoke, "The disciple is not above his master, nor the servant above his Lord: but everyone that is perfect shall be as his master. Lo, you have been my greatest pupil in the study of chronology. Yet now you force my hand to put an end to the season that is your time. Come then, student of the Usurper, and show what lessons betrayal hath taught thee."

Zeus roared in rage, and he flew forward to engage Chronos in battle. Chronos lifted his hands, and a portal of temporal power appeared in front of his nemesis. Zeus's forward momentum carried him into the expanse, and he disappeared. The Lord of Time smiled, but his smile was short-lived as the sound of a portal could be heard above him. He looked overhead in time to see Zeus plummet from above him, sword in hand to carve the angel in two. Chronos lifted his blade, parrying the strike downward. Flecks of light and sparks from angel-forged steel scrapped against one another. Their swords touched the ground and Zeus flipped over his blade and slammed his elbow hard into the back of Chronos, knocking him into the earthen floor. Zeus then opened a portal and Chronos fell within and disappeared into the earth. In the selfsame instant, Chronos materialized from a portal from Zeus's side and backhanded the angel, sending him careening into a wall with a thud.

"Well played," Zeus said, his chest heaving from exertion. "Well played indeed." Zeus lifted himself from the floor while Chronos stood aloft, catching his breath. Zeus smiled. "Yet there is weakness within you." Zeus stood up and walked towards his former master. "And weakness will not serve thee since only the strong survive!" Sword held high, Zeus lunged for Chronos and created a portal beneath his adversary, then tackled him and they both plummeted into the void between space and time.

They exited to the searing heat of the tropical lush jungles of the planet's equator, fighting sword to sword, weaving, and ducking, and the clashing of steel created portal after portal, and they battled across desert sands, and arctic snows. Flashing in and out of the spiritual plane, their constant appearance and disappearance alerted both friend and foe. Men watched as two great "gods" grappled with one another in combat. In the skies, they crossed blades, and in the seas, they shed blood, and they portaled and circled the globe of the earth and settled atop a dormant volcano.

Waves of temporal energy seeped from the combatants as Elomic commands caused the ground beneath them to age and decay. Surges of power escaped their person, and the presence of two combating Lords of Time disturbed the order of things. The caldera chaffed and heaved. The mountain's life cycle was now accelerated by their presence, held captive and turned in the wheel of time. Lava jettisoned in the air, as black ash belched from its mouth and ascended hundreds of furlongs into the sky. The mount convulsed and a shock wave of blistering heat melted life at the foot of the mountain, and trees splintered and bowed down in broken obeisance to the concussive wave that now raced across the land. Men looked in wonderment at the mountain, and lo two angels fought within the black sky and rock and pyroclastic plumes descended upon village and city. And Chronos so engaged in defense and combat saw not the destruction that their presence rained down upon the children of men. And lo, when he glanced to see men scamper as ants in a nest disturbed, his heart sank and his attention turned from his foe, and when he did so—Zeus struck.

Zeus, doing the unthinkable, opened up a portal within Chronos himself, and when he did, he inserted himself therein, occupying the space that was the body of his master, and the two became one. Chronos cried out in agony, that the mountain exploded once more in objection and the blast raced away in all directions, obliterating all life in its destructive path. Zeus held to his master as the void of the portal ate at his former Lord, and as Zeus watched his mentor turn to ash in his arms, he smiled and spoke. "Goodbye, my Lord. Know that you have taught me well."

Chronos smiled and replied, "Worry not for myself, for I will see thee at the last day." And Zeus called for lightning from the sky, and it obeyed and fell upon the duo and coiled them in an embrace of electrocution. The portal completed its work and Chronos gave up the ghost. Zeus then released him, his body severed from the great hole the portal had made, and the corpse plummeted into the erupting volcano beneath them. Zeus smiled at the falling husk that was once his master. He surveyed the land and reveled that men trembled before his might, and in the moments of his gloating he heard the clarion call of the Horde to battle, the horn of assembly, and turned his eyes skyward and frowned.

What looked like all of Heaven descended from above, and with widening eyes, fear and terror seized him as he beheld a great form of a raptor fill the sky.

The Holy Spirit had come.

* * *

Jerahmeel battered his assailant into the ground.

An angel jumped on his back and bit into his flesh and Jerahmeel bellowed in pain.

He reached over his shoulder, grabbing his attacker, and lunged forward sending him careening into another. He pulled his axes from his sides and flung them swinging, wildly at foe after foe. The chains strapped to his forearms and the hilt of the weapons served as a bladed whip as they hatcheted through the air and cut down enemy after enemy. Ice coated the blades, ice coated his armor, and his chilled breath sent puffs of air as he hurled and weaved to keep the throng at bay. For Zeus had thought it amusing to portal the head of his house to the land where those who had once followed their prince had made their home...Grecia.

A place Jerahmeel would be forced to cut down his own people.

Jerahmeel heaved the axes and kept them twirling in the air as foes ducked and bobbed. But the prince was ferocious. There were many, and he was but one. Yet he would not die on the field of battle this day. And those who were once former brothers would rue the day they turned against El.

"*Aaaaarrrggghhh*!" The cry of his battle roar incited fear, in his foes. Yet nevertheless, they came. A horde of angelic warriors, each jealous, and spiteful that within their presence stood their former leader whose presence reminded them of their failure. A light of testimony to their decision, and a judge of their future. Thus, they assailed him to snuff out that light, to at all costs live in the comfort of darkness so that the truth could not be told to them: the truth that they had abandoned God.

Therefore, they swarmed Jerahmeel, hundreds in all directions encircled him. Flicking his wrists, he recalled his twirling axes to his side and stomped his foot hard into the earth. The blow from his stomp reverberated across the floor of the earth, sending seismic waves that rippled across the ground, causing the terrain to buckle and the earth opened up her mouth and swallowed many within her grasp. But these were citizens of Heaven, and the Earth held little sway over the spiritual nomads that now occupied her, and so they crawled from the newly formed fractures and fissures that spewed smoke and fire.

A whoosh sound was heard in the sky, and a bright figure fell from the heaven and Talus landed on bended knee and unsheathed a flaming sword. Jerahmeel looked upon him, relieved.

"How did you find me?" he asked, panting as they looked at the thousands gathering to attack them.

Talus moved to cover his brother's back and said over his shoulder, "I will always find you."

They looked at the Horde assembled before them, as they stood guard over one another. Now in defense to fight off a wave of angels who they had once called brethren. Jerahmeel looked as their enemies charged to bring them down.

"They are coming!" Jerahmeel yelled.

"Let them come," Talus replied.

And as one man they unleashed their weapons as angels attacked them. Flames stretched from Talus's sword and heavenly fire caused enemies to shriek in a pain. Jerahmeel grabbed an angel in midair who leaped onto them and slammed his adversary face down into the ground. A "thunk" could be heard as Talus's sword found its way into the chest of their enemy.

Sounds of screams echoed in the air, and the numbers of attackers heaped themselves as fodder for the Lumazi's unleashed rage.

"There are too many," said Jerahmeel.

"Greater are they that are with us than they that are against us. Behold!" Talus pointed to the northern sky and a legion of angels fell on the back lines of those who had arrayed themselves to bring the duo down. The Horde turned to their rear as angels armored with sword and shield fell upon them and blasted their rear ranks, sending the group into confusion. Jerahmeel and Talus pressed towards their angelic reinforcements, and those who had taken up arms to defend them also pushed forward to meet them.

Each group pressed forward as angel after angel attacked and advanced to keep the Horde at bay, smiting down enemy after winged enemy until when the dust had settled. A pile of bodies lay round about them and both Lumazi and their angelic reinforcements met in the middle victorious.

Talus gripped his sword, its blade bloodied and wiped it against the robes of a fallen foe.

"Your arrival is timely. We are in your debt. Who commands this garrison, that we might honor him who has helped Heaven in her cause?"

An angel moved forward to the front of the lines. "I am Shophar of House Arelim, my Prince. When word through Grigoric scouts gave mention that Prince Talus and Jerahmeel were seen Earthside in battle, and when the movement of the enemy had a troop gather towards this location, I summoned forces who might be of aid. We are thine to command, my Prince, speak the word only and we shall obey."

Jerahmeel smiled. "We give thanks to you and your soldiers, Shophar—"

And before Jerahmeel could finish, an angel pointed to a gathering dark storm in the distance of the sky.

A second wave was coming, much larger then before.

* * *

Azaziel gripped his chest as he looked upon Lahatiel, watching his movements, waiting for him to take advantage of his injury and press his attack. The pain wracked his body as spasms made his muscles ache. He spit blood on the ground and Lahatiel also watched his injured adversary as a wolf encircles wounded prey.

"It will give me great pleasure to smite at the command structure of Heaven herself. I will send your head to my master as a token," Lathathiel said.

Azaziel gingerly rose to his feet and placed his left arm around his ribs. "You will find that my head is not so easily removed."

Lahatiel chuckled. "We shall see." He walked slowly towards him and dragged his sword on the ground.

Azaziel looked for Argoth then rose to the sky and raced towards Volac to assist his friend, who stood immobilized. Lahatiel was surprised and mocked his adversary's retreat. "Does the Lumazi run?" Lahatiel smiled in gleeful anticipation of his enemy's change in tactics and quickly turned to hunt his wounded prey.

Volac looked upon Argoth and smiled. "Goodbye, Chief of Eyes, may you bask in eternal darkness!"

Raising his mace above his shoulders, he twisted his hips to bring the weapon square against the face of his enemy. Azaziel raced to his brother's side and ducked under the legs of Volac, sliding on the ground as he did. Azaziel's momentum carried him underneath his adversary and with a dagger in hand, he slit the bowels of Volac, grabbed Argoth, and with his great wings lifted them both into the sky.

Volac dropped his mace and collapsed to the ground, howling like an injured animal. Blood and entrails pooled beneath him as he in vain sought to keep his innards from spilling out. Lahatiel landed next to Volac and stood over him, laughing at the angel as he bled out.

"Don't just stand there, help me!" Volac screamed. "What are you staring at?"

Lahatiel unsheathed his blade and its onyx glint shown black in the sunlit sky. He drew close to his brother in arms and spoke. "A dead man."

Lahatiel then slit Volac's throat. The mist from his lacerated comrade sprayed blue in the air and covered his face. He spat on the ground and spoke, as Volac drowned in his own blood. "Only the strong survive."

Lahatiel turned his blood-spattered face skyward and lifted himself into the air to continue his stalking of Azaziel, who flew hobbled as he carried the immobile Argoth in his arms.

* * *

Assyrix watched as the final shade of Argoth's cover fell under his defilement. The glowing shield that protected Nazareth fell and he entered the city. His eyes darted to spy out the young maiden he had seen in his trance, a small Jewish maid. A woman who seemed to be of the Levitical line of Aaron.

Human filth. It will be good to slit this woman's throat.

Assyrix saw a synagogue and surrounding it were men each who held a staff in their hand. Kneeling, each of the men prayed.

Assyrix laughed mockingly. "Chattel, good-for-nothing image of God! Phhssftt!"

Assyrix continued to watch the men as one man's staff blossomed over all others and then a white dove alighted on it before flying off. The men rose and stared at the man. Another man more aged than the rest walked slowly down the synagogue's steps. His colored robes showed him as a person of distinction. Assyrix recognized him as a priest and listened as the man spoke.

"The Lord has given a sign, Joseph."

The priest then extended his hand and a young woman descended from the synagogue attired in white linen and her hair was brown with black hues, and she was a fair woman and olive in complexion.

"Mary, what is your wish concerning Joseph?" asked the older man.

Mary extended her hand to Joseph and smiled. "I accept his proposal."

Cheers rang across the area, and Assyrix smiled. "Ah so, at last, you are found. You will die, and your flesh will serve as fodder for Hell."

Assyrix then descended to smite the girl down and destroy the city, but as he fell, he heard a voice from his rear and turned his head.

"You are Assyrix Grigori. You will surrender your tome and submit to redaction."

Assyrix turned to see that Turiel stood behind him, and he panicked and attempted to flee. However, when he turned to depart, Isidor stood before him, blocking his path.

"The Redaction is not complete," said Isidor.

"You have seeded this realm in commentary," said Turiel.

"Your commentary must end," Isidor replied.

A burning sensation originated in Assyrix's chest he looked down to see a ghostly hand emerge from his abdomen. The pain seized him, and he stiffened as his body froze and the birth of a screech curdled in his gut, traveling up his throat and unleashed as a scream into the warm air.

Assyrix's stylus and inkhorn collapsed as if suddenly they were objects of immense gravity, and Turiel emerged as a specter from within Assyrix's body. His hands held the tome of Assyrix, the beating heart of his prey.

Turiel floated away from the body of Assyrix, and Lucifer's Chief of Eyes reached for his heart that was now open in Turiel's hand. Turiel flipped through the pulsating pages, and Isidor handed him the inkhorn and stylus of Assyrix, and he placed them into the folds of his robes.

"Your tome is replete with commentary. You will be redacted," he said.

Turiel began to blot out from within the tome and strike out sections of written text, and as he did so Assyrix bellowed and began to vanish. Slowly and with every erasure, he receded into nothing, and as he did so, a light projected above him of such intensity that Assyrix turned his vanishing eyes that he might see. Snow-like tendrils of light streaked across his face, and both Turiel and Isidor bowed when they too saw the light.

The vanishing eyes of Assyrix grew wide even as he looked at the figure that glowed with an immensity that rivaled the sun. A tear slid down his fading cheek as he stared into the face of El Pneuma, the Holy Spirit of God. A tear that with the prior erasure of Turiel's pen slowly began to blot from existence. A tear that never reached the ground as the face on which it traveled suddenly ceased to exist.

The Holy Spirit landed as His robes billowed in the wind, and great dark wings filled with stars spread from him. His hand held an iron staff that gleamed with all manner of diamonds, ruby, pearl and onyx, and the Shekinah surrounded Him, and His presence caused the very ground to grow new blades of grass under His feet. He turned his face towards His ministers of flame, and Azaziel flew as a wounded bird, falling at the Holy Spirits feet. The presence of the Lord caused his wounds to self-suture and heal, and Argoth coughed up blood and gasped as if rescued from drowning. Heaving great gasps to fill his lungs, Argoth managed to voice, "My King," and laid face down on the ground.

Lahatiel, stalking the duo, came near and landed near the Holy Spirit. Amazed that a member of the Godhead stood before him. He tearfully cried out to his former King, "Have you come to torment me before the time?"

The Holy Spirit said nothing but looked upon His wayward son, and Lahatiel knew that it was a look of disappointment. It was the hardened look of a father who must surrender His wayward child for discipline, and the Holy Spirit turned His back to him and walked through the quartet of bowed angels that now lay prostrate at his feet and headed towards the town of Nazareth to Mary.

"Do not turn your back on me!" screamed Lahatiel. "You owe me! I am YOUR son! You have rejected me! Your son ejected from his own home! How could you!" Lahatiel ran to confront his God, and as he took a step, his foot turned to stone. He took another step to move forward and then it, too, turned to stone. Anger raged within him, fire erupted within his heart, and he pushed onward as the third person of the Trinity continued to walk towards the city of men to see the young woman He had come for.

"Who do you love? Why do you not love us? Why not us?" cried Lahatiel.

And with each step he took, his feet became heavy, and his arms slowly turned to stone. Soon he was within arm's reach of Azaziel, who looked at him in disgust.

"You think He loves you more than me? He loves you not..."

And at that moment, the whole of Lahatiel turned to stone and collapsed into a pile of rubble at Azaziel's feet. Azaziel, Argoth, and the Redactors rose to their feet and stared at the rubble, and Azaziel watched as the Holy Spirit now stood next to a young woman who was seated by a well, giggling with other maidens, rejoicing that she had become betrothed.

* * *

Talus stood atop the mountain which overlooked the small village and looked upon the troop that he and Jerahmeel commanded. The warm wind of summer caressed his cheek, and the firmness of the earth reminded him of the firmness needed for what lay ahead. He watched his soldiers, wondering what he would say to them. Their eyes beamed with hopeful anticipation upon both he and Jerahmeel. Talus looked down at his sword; it was newly minted yet was also newly baptized in the blood of those he had slain. He smiled at Jerahmeel, and his brother returned the tenderness and nodded at him, then spoke. "Say what must be said, brother, and let thy words ring true."

Talus looked away from his brother, then raised his eyes toward the throng and opened his mouth to speak. "On this day, the host of the Fallen have come to rend us. They come bidden to upend the plan of the Lord. To upend the birth of God in the Earth. And of all Creation that El would send to stand as the standard against this threat. Of the multitudes of Elohim who fly amongst the stars. He has chosen to send you. Now turn ye to the right hand and to the left and look about you; savor this moment. For this moment will determine the way of Heaven and Earth and know that on *this* day! You are here to bear witness that Heaven shall never abandon her post! That on *this* day, we are the right hand of Creation, and that El—El IS ALMIGHTY GOD!"

The throng roared in defiance to the oncoming army that would within minutes assault them. Talus lifted his sword up high, and its golden blade shimmered in the light and the sun's sparkle skipped about the edge.

Jerahmeel looked to the horizon and pointed in the distance. "The Horde has come."

Talus turned from his troops and looked behind him. And when he did he saw that a thunderhead rolled towards them, and within the billows and flashes of lightning, angels rode atop the currents of the overcast sky, and blackness descended as gloom upon the land. Within twinkling bursts of lightning, the illuminated horde of thousands of angels could be seen falling upon them.

Talus's brow tensed and he spoke aloud for all to hear, "No quarter asked! No quarter given!"

Immediately, angels fell upon them from the sky as bolts of lightning. Crashing to the ground, they unsheathed swords, and their blades sliced through the defenders of light. Heaven-forged steel clanged against Hell forged cutlasses. As waves crash the shore, so too did the Horde flood over the angels. Angels fought back-to-back as limbs were severed from bodies and angelic wings frayed under the assault of so many.

Jerahmeel swung his axe upward into the face of an oncoming attacker, lifting him into the sky and sending him reeling into another, knocking several into crumpled piles from the sheer force of his blow.

Talus, his back to his brother, yelled, "There are too many!" He slashed at an oncoming angel, hacking off its leg. The fallen angel fell hard on his back and Talus brought his sword square into his chest.

Jerahmeel yelled back, "I bet you wished you had stayed in bed!"

Talus roared, "The thought had crossed my mind!"

Knocking an angel in the jaw, Talus and Jerahmeel flipped positions, and Talus parried a thrust, unarming his attacker, and kicked him square in the chest, sending him flying. Jerahmeel held his axe before his face, lifting the shaft to deflect a blow. He caught the attacking angel by his throat, head-butted him, and knocked his attacker unconscious.

Wave after wave they fought, as those who had come to fight for El's cause slowly whittled away under the massive onslaught of the Fallen. Until thousands became hundreds and hundreds became tens.

Talus, seeing that their position was overrun, spoke in Elohim and summoned a ladder. A prismatic funnel materialized over both Jerahmeel and the few remaining angels who fought by their side. Jerahmeel, beating back enemies, felt the tug of the ladder begin to lift him and his comrades away.

"What are you doing?" Jerahmeel yelled.

"Saving your life," Talus shouted back.

Jerahmeel then was ripped from the earth, and he shot upwards as the Ladder pulled him away from the mob that now encircled Talus. The Prince of House Arelim still fought in ferocious desperation to buy his comrades time to escape.

Spirited away through prismatic streams of light, Jerahmeel watched as his brother felled hundreds only to be ultimately engulfed by thousands of the Horde who with club, sword, and shield beat the head of House Arelim into the ground. The ground collapsed under the throng and Talus and thousands of the Horde plummeted into the earth.

"TALUS!" Jerahmeel cried.

But it was too late, for his brother was gone, and in the twinkling of an eye Jerahmeel and a few of those saved were jettisoned away from Earth, past its moon and rocketed to the realm immortal.

The Ladder collapsed at a waypoint near the entrance of the Heavenly city and Jerahmeel dropped his mace in shock, fell to his knees, and wept.

* * *

Gabriel and Metatron had returned to battle and they each took their legions away from Judea to lead the forces of Lucifer away, and Michael wondered if he would ever see them again. Though the two were powerful, they were still but two. Several of the battalions of the Fallen turned to follow Metatron and Gabriel. And the duo fought, and to see Metatron do battle was to watch a living scythe. For with his mighty wings, he cut foes down, and with his breath, he blasted opponents to dissolution before him and fell through the ashes of the Fallen to repeat the feat.

Michael neared the point where he saw El Pnuema light over Mary. The Holy Spirit had overshadowed her, and Michael swooped down to stand in front of the young woman, and he revealed himself to her and she was sore afraid, for the presence of the Lord made her to fear.

Gabriel, already descended unharmed, also stood over Mary whilst unbeknownst to her and humankind, the heavens were staged in battle to ferry God to her. He, too, revealed himself and spoke. "Hail, for thou that art highly favoured, the Lord is with thee: blessed art thou among women.

And when she saw him, she was troubled at his saying and cast in her mind what manner of salutation this should be. And Gabriel said unto her, "Fear not, Mary, for thou hast found favour with God. And behold, thou shalt conceive in thy womb, and bring forth a son, and shalt call his name Jesus. He shall be great and shall be called the Son of the Highest: and the Lord God shall give unto him the throne of his father David: And he shall reign over the house of Jacob forever, and of his kingdom there shall be no end."

Then said Mary unto the angel, "How shall this be, seeing I know not a man?"

Gabriel answered and said unto her, "The Holy Ghost shall come upon thee, and the power of the Highest shall overshadow thee: therefore, also that holy thing which shall be born of thee shall be called the Son of God. And behold, thy cousin Elisabeth, she hath also conceived a son in her old age: and this is the sixth month with her, who was called barren. For with God, nothing shall be impossible."

Mary then said, "Behold the handmaid of the Lord; be it unto me according to thy word."

And when the Holy Spirit heard those words He spoke to Michael. "Thou art released,"

Yeshua moved from the bosom of Michael's pouch and settled over Mary's bosom, and His spirit disappeared, and warmth overtook her and the shadow of the Almighty hovered over her and she conceived. Immediately, Gabriel and the entire heavenly host were transported away to the realm immortal.

* * *

The Horde watched as Ladders opened across the lid of the skies and the Armies of the Lord were lifted away to the Kingdom of Heaven. Cheers and adulation erupted among the Fallen and many laughed as Heaven retreated. Each raised swords in cheers at their success in repelling Heaven's invasion.

Astarte turned to his master, triumphant. "My Lord, Heaven retreats!"

Lucifer's eyes narrowed in contemplation. "Aye, Astarte, but not without cause...never without cause." Lucifer then in the blink of an eye searched all the kingdoms of the Earth and saw that an angel yet was in Nazareth and hovered over one house. The maiden he had sent Assyrix to destroy. Lucifer stared past her flesh and saw that within her womb, El had begotten a child. A child whose presence smelled of El, and when he moved closer to examine the maid, the Shekinah glory flashed and blinded the girl from his view. Lucifer backed away, his eyes seeing afterglows and images even when closed. When he could see again, the young girl was gone, and Lucifer grinned and pondered the actions of God, smiling.

"Ah, El—thou hast made miscalculation, for now, locked within flesh art thou, thy power tempered. Yet fear not, soon I will strike at thee, and then what price wilt thou pay for thy beloved Son? You but bring me fuel to power the engine of Hell, and then I will raise thy own son, and he shall serve me."

* * *

El, knowing that Lucifer would hunt the child, smote the Horde with blindness to His son so that they wearied themselves from searching for him.

"What will you do, Lucifer? For El Himself somehow hast come to dwell among the humans. Surely He would not take on flesh?" said Ashtaroth.

Lucifer mulled the words of his servant over in his mind and remembered Sasheal's demise. For Sasheal was the first of his kind to give his life for another, and that he, too, had assumed flesh to do it, and the Prince of Lies smirked.

"El has shown vulnerability. He hides amongst the humans, yet it is of no consequence. For I am the wolf that hunts the sheep; no man might lay-up, that I might not break through and steal. We will find Him, we will hunt Him down, and when I confront Him I will steal the life of God itself. I will see my hands wrapped around the throat of the Almighty, and His body dangled from a tree, and when it is so—I shall be God."

Ashtaroth replied, "But how can such a thing be, seeing we are blinded to Shiloh?"

"El loves the Clayborn," Lucifer chortled. "I shall dance with El in this game of men and let man stand as proxy for my sword. Let man be the death of Shiloh."

Thus, Lucifer moved on Herod the Great and spoke into his ears words of fear and suspicion, words that there could no King of the Jews but he, words that none could take his throne and that he would live forever. Therefore, Lucifer plagued Herod continuously with visions of his death at the hands of a rival and moved upon him to seek and to destroy the Christ child.

Thus, Herod consented in the thing, plagued by visions of betrayal, such that he murdered even his own son.

And it came to pass that there came wise men from the east to Jerusalem, saying, "Where is he that is born King of the Jews? For we have seen his star in the east and are come to worship him." When Herod the king had heard these things, he was troubled, and all Jerusalem with him. And when he had gathered all the chief priests and scribes of the people together, he demanded of them where Christ should be born. And they said unto him, "In Bethlehem of Judaea: for thus it is written by the prophet, 'And thou Bethlehem, in the land of Juda, art not the least among the princes of Juda: for out of thee shall come a Governor, that shall rule my people Israel.'" Then Herod, when he had privily called the wise men, inquired of them diligently what time the star appeared. And he sent them to Bethlehem, and said, "Go and search diligently for the young child; and when ye have found him, bring me word again, that I may come and worship him also."

The men then departed and followed the signs in the skies and came to a manger in Bethlehem and found a maiden and her husband. And the couple were with child and had delivered the young king in a manger, for there was no room at the inn. And they worshiped him, and when they were to depart, El warned them in a dream not to return to Herod, and they departed back to their own country.

And when Herod saw that he was mocked of the wise men, he was exceeding wroth, and sent forth, and slew all the children that were in Bethlehem, and in all the coasts thereof, from two years old and under, according to the time which he had diligently inquired of the wise men. Then was fulfilled that which was spoken by Jeremy the prophet, saying, "Thus saith the Lord; A voice was heard in Ramah, lamentation, and bitter weeping; Rachel weeping for her children refused to be comforted, because they were not."

Lucifer smiled as he watched the slaughter of babes in the land. Watched as men ran boys through with swords and he reveled in the bloodshed.

"I will smear the filth of Adam's sin in your face, El. Run, El—run. Yet know that of a surety I will find you." Lucifer then moved to strengthen his hand, eying the might of his empire he had built in Rome, a kingdom of men that he would use to overrun the world.

Thus, El hid His son for a time and waited for the season that the Son of God might come to overturn the works of the enemy. Waited until He was ready to reveal Himself, waited to set up a kingdom that would never be destroyed, a kingdom not left to other people, but a realm that would break in pieces and consume all kingdoms, that it might stand forever. Waited to assault Lucifer in the heart of his power and retrieve the keys of Death and Hell and save His man from sin.

* * *

Gabriel and Michael found themselves back at the waypoint of Argoth. Thousands of angels floated injured, some maimed, all weary, and grateful. Each one looked over the faces of the many that had returned and that now filled the launch pad of heaven's assault.

Metatron flew over to hug Azaziel while Argoth moved through the crowd and placed his hands on Jerahmeel's strong shoulders and nodded knowingly. Gabriel raced to various members of his house, and Michael scoured the populace that now flooded the staging area.

"Talus?" He spoke to an angel nearby.

But the disheveled angel just shrugged his shoulders and shook his head. Further, Michael moved through the crowd, and he saw the angelic commander who had been given charge to secure Iblis. Iblis stood surrounded by twelve angels who bowed at the presence of their Chief Prince. Then quickly stood at attention as he inspected them. He placed his hands on the shoulders of those who had accomplished their mission, and who now stood charge over their captive. Michael looked Iblis over, but the fallen angel did not glow as the rest of their kind. For the Decension had diminished him. His former glory was dimmer than that which surrounded the rest, and Michael was momentarily repelled.

"You are Iblis. You are here at my command. These are thy guards. If you but breathe betrayal, I will personally see to your dissolution. Are we clear?"

Iblis nodded. "I am thine to command. It pleases me that I may be of service to the true King. I am honored that El hast sanctioned my being here."

Michael looked at Iblis and replied, "The moment your service is ended, you will be returned to Earth."

Iblis cried out, "No, you cannot send me back! Do you know what Lucifer will do to me?"

Michael did not answer and looked past him, searching for any sign of Talus. He turned to one of the twelve tasked with Iblis's keeping and commanded, "Take him away, and keep him under guard." Immediately, Ibis was seized, and he was shoved forward as a prisoner of war, and he hollered back at Michael that he might hear. "Are there yet still seven Lumazi?"

Iblis smiled as his guards pushed him forward. Michael and every angel now looked frantically among themselves, and Gabriel, Argoth, Metatron, and Azaziel, all looked at Michael with concern. Michael saw in the distance that Jerahmeel approached him, and Michael studied his face. Jerahmeel looked into his eyes, and knew his brother's thoughts and shook his head, lowering his eyes. Enoch then pushed his way past angels, finally arriving at Michael and the rest of the Lumazi, frowning at what he saw and spoke aloud the words they all now wondered.

"Where is Talus?"

Epilogue: Until Shiloh Comes

Talus opened his eyes.

His back was sore, and his muscles screamed as he struggled to move. He looked to his left and saw that his back was stuck fast against a mucus membrane substance. Heat brushed against his face, and steam hissed at him in the darkness. He looked to see his surroundings, and all was dark about him. His chest felt as if it was on fire and his strength availed him not. He remembered fighting—remembered falling. Remembering exerting such power as he collapsed into a great chasm at what he thought was his final act to obliterate the teeming hordes that assaulted him. Knew that he, too, would be lost to whatever life exists to those who pass from the realm of the eternal. El had hinted that none of His children would ever be lost. Not if they remained faithful. Nevertheless, he was alive still. Sore.

Talus blinked as he saw a glittering light in the darkness. The tinkling of cymbals was heard; a figure approached whose cadence carried a bass in each step and flakes of light illuminated the cavern. Talus knew the sound, and his eyes adjusted to the light and saw several figures walking into view.

"Lucifer," he said.

"I am glad that your descent did not bring you to dissolution, brother," Lucifer replied.

"Arggh!" Talus struggled to break free and attack his captors but whatever held him would neither give way nor release him. And the more he struggled, the more strength left him. He coughed from exertion, and when Lucifer stood closer to him. Talus could see that his lieutenants also stood by their master's side, and the light from their bodies allowed him to see where he was.

Slime covered the walls, and men and angels were embedded within struggling to get out. Each was caught in frozen screams as tendrils siphoned the life that emanated from their spirits. Eyes were round about the cavern and utter darkness blanketed the place. Yet Talus could see that flames rose from below him, and he was suspended in some type of a lattice. Beneath him were razor-like teeth and tendrils from a mouth reached for him and held him aloft as a fly in a web. Screams and moans emanated from it, and Talus knew that he could be in but one place—Hell. Vine-like veins extended from the walls and coiled around his throat, arms, and torso constricting him.

"Kill me, Lucifer! Be done with it!" Talus yelled.

Lucifer smiled. "No, I will not kill you, brother," said Lucifer. "No... I will not let death rob me of reacquainting me with my beloved brother. I will instead extend mercy to thee. I will give to thee what El himself did not extend to my people. Lo, I offer thee a choice. I call Heaven and Earth to witness that as I liveth I will not kill thee, but to live, you must bow down and worship me. For if you do this thing, then know of a surety that I will let you live. But if not, know this—I will give thee to Hell, and though her lust for thee be ravenous, know that I will never let her totally consume thee. No, my plan for thee is to send thee back to the realm immortal as a weapon to smite the Kingdom. For you will be stripped of will, and your body fodder for my designs against El. You will serve me. Either in life or in the shadow of death. But know of a surety—you will serve me."

Talus spit on the ground at Lucifer's feet and spoke. "Bow? To you? I would rather die than give you the curtsy that you so covet. You waste your breath 'Lightbringer'. Do with me as you will."

Lucifer smirked and said, "I intend to." Lucifer then nodded to Charon, and Charon then roared. Hell retracted her veins and lifted the struggling Talus against the wall's flesh. And when Hell knew that she was released to feed, the porous wall enveloped him. Talus watched Lucifer through the transparent membrane of Hell's flesh that now crept over him and shrouded his face. And when Hell had fully embraced him in her caress of elongated execution, when she was released to do what she was created for. She suckled on his life force, and Talus screamed.

The King of Lies grinned as Talus's cries of pain echoed in the dark and the flesh-eating parasitic worms were unleashed from Hell's mouth to bore into every orifice of Talus's body. Talus opened his mouth to scream but could not, and he thrashed as the pain of his body wracked him, and Hell was released to feast upon him.

Lucifer turned to Charon. "When he is changed into a daemon and his mind is broken, send him to me that we might send him home." Lucifer smiled, for he would return to El and Michael a seed of destruction that he might injure Heaven from afar, to remind them of the price of war.

And in the pain that now wracked his body, as the stretching of his limbs caused tears to seep from his angelic eyes, Talus remembered the words that El had given him and hoped against hope that even in Hell—Shiloh would come.

The End

The Third Heaven: The Realm of the Dead - Book 3

Donovan M. Neal

Tornveil

For permission requests, write to the publisher, addressed "Attention: Permissions Coordinator," at the email below:

tornveil@donovanmneal.com

Ordering Information:

Quantity sales. Special discounts are available on quantity purchases by corporations, associations, and others. For details, contact the publisher at the email above.

Orders by U.S. trade bookstores and wholesalers. Please contact Lightning Source: Tel: (615) 213-5815; fax: (615) 213-4725 or visit https://www.lightningsource.com/.

Printed in the United States of America

Contents

Dedication & Scriptures &Acknowledgments

Dedication

I dedicate this book to those who dare to dream and see it through to completion. May your imagination ever lead you to new realms.

Scriptures

2 Cor 12:2

I knew a man in Christ above fourteen years ago, (whether in the body, I cannot tell; or whether out of the body, I cannot tell: God knoweth;) such an one caught up to the third heaven.

1 Cor 2:7, 8

But we speak the wisdom of God in a mystery, even the hidden wisdom, which God ordained before the world unto our glory: 8Which none of the princes of this world knew: for had they known it, they would not have crucified the Lord of glory.

Matt 12:40

For as Jonas was three days and three nights in the whale's belly; so shall the Son of man be three days and three nights in the heart of the earth.

1 Cor 15:1-4, 45

Moreover, brethren, I declare unto you the gospel which I preached unto you, which also ye have received, and wherein ye stand; 2By which also ye are saved, if ye keep in memory what I preached unto you, unless ye have believed in vain. 3For I delivered unto you first of all that which I also received, how that Christ died for our sins according to the scriptures; 4And that he was buried, and that he rose again the third day according to the scriptures. 45And so it is written, the first man Adam was made a living soul; the last Adam was made a quickening spirit.

1 Peter 3:18-20

For Christ also hath once suffered for sins, the just for the unjust, that he might bring us to God, being put to death in the flesh, but quickened by the Spirit: 19By which also he went and preached unto the spirits in prison; 20Which sometime were disobedient, when once the longsuffering of God waited in the days of Noah, while the ark was a preparing, wherein few, that is, eight souls were saved by water.

Acknowledgments

To the Lord Jesus Christ, who for some reason loves me.

To the Pastor of Labor of Love Church, Charles Hawthorne, who nurtured my pre-existing love of the Bible.

To my children: Candace, Christopher, and Alexander – you can do great things!

To the authors, comic books artists and writers, game developers and filmmakers who have come before, and who unknowingly have breathed on the embers of my imagination.

To all my beta readers and friends who shared both critiques and encouragement.

To my editor Debra Owen who helped me put the polish on my draft.

To Nettie, who cheered me on when I had nothing and said, "Wow!" after reading the prologue of my first novel.

Preface

Dearly Beloved,

If you are reading this book, you have taken the journey with me into what is now book three of The Third Heaven series. As always, expectations run high when people experience entertainment, and thus I provide a disclaimer for those who seek perfect alignment with their understanding of Biblical theology.

In no way should one read this fictional account and come away believing one can postpone their obedience to the Gospel in this life. The Bible consistently teaches that no one will be permitted a second chance. This earthly life has been provided by God for all human beings to determine where they wish to spend eternity. That decision is made by each individual based upon their personal decision made towards the person of Christ. Once a person dies, his eternal destiny has been sealed. He is "reserved for judgment." (2 Peter 2:4; cf. vss. 9, 17). His condition will not and cannot be altered (Luke 16:25-26; Hebrews 9:27).

This novel, therefore, should not be taken as prescriptive or doctrinal in any sense. It is simply a story, albeit one with a Christian worldview...a story based on Biblical texts to create a tale of wonder. Consider this a work of Biblical fan fiction, if you will. Approach it as one might approach Star Wars for example. In Star Wars you suspend belief regarding the physics of how ships in that story fly. I would ask you to apply the same mindset here. If you can approach the novel on these terms, you will enjoy the demonstrations of God's mercy, love and severity. If you approach the book looking to see how much the story doesn't conform with scripture you will miss the greater lessons resident in the story itself that are indeed scriptural.

Be warned, there are descriptions of torture in this book. Describing the pain of the damned was a prayerful and uncomfortable endeavor that may spill over. This is a darker book because we are entering the darkness of sin and death. Rest assured, we will emerge into the world of light.

It should be known that Christians differ on what happened during Jesus' three days in the grave. This tale is highly speculative in that regard and is merely this authors continuation of the story from book two in this series.

What did Jesus do while he was in the grave three days? Perhaps this book could be used as a catapult in biblical discussions with others regarding the subject.

For the sake of entertainment and Biblical discussion, behold, this author's speculative version of what has been classically called---the harrowing of Hell.

Enjoy,

Donovan Neal

Prologue: The Distant Future

Michael ruminated on the loss of Raphael and muttered El's words to himself..."I AM the Resurrection and the Life." He lifted his head to look upon his grinning brother. A brother who sweltered in the blistering flames, grinding his teeth, struggling to prevent the release of his own screams, straining to speak with composure above the anguished cries of the damned that echoed throughout the air. Michael smiled and rose to his feet, his royal white and gilded robes gleaming in brilliance. His halo flared with reflected sunlight as he spoke with authority to Satan.

"Dost thou think me so small that ye could tempt me to raise arms on thy behalf? Thou art eclipsed in the sins of thy past, overrun in the pit of fire. Thou art lost, forever refuse to the universe, the choirmaster of screams, the conductor of wails, and thy music the harmony of gnashing teeth."

Michael raised his voice as awareness came over him that soon their conversation would come to an end, and it would cease as it was always destined - with victory for El. Thus, Michael released himself from the hurt of past wounds, to speak to his living apparition of guilt in the person of his brother.

"Those in Christ once had a saying about thee, my brother. A saying I find fitting to speak to thee now for though thou hast spoken much, thy words are bereft of power. Thus, hear the words the Clayborn have said of thee, a proverb from those whose victory hath now overcome the world, and let it be an echo for eternity in thine ears, 'When the Devil seeks to remind you of your past,' Michael paused and stared deep into Lucifer's eyes. Remind him of his future.' Therefore, I call Heaven and Earth against thee and rehearse in thy hearing both past and future, for it was not I who smote the mountain of God, nor I who sought to strike down the Author of Life. It was not I who sought to put the Lord to death or make death itself a rabid pet to be unleashed upon the world of men. No, Lucifer, it was thee!" Michael shouted above the cries of the damned. Their wails sailing across the sweltering sky.

"And what future dost thou see before thee now, oh Son of Perdition? What future dost thou see in the eons to come? Tell me, Lucifer, what glory dost thou see before thee now?"

Lucifer stood silent, and his face was stern, then opened his mouth to speak. "I..."

"SILENCE!!" Michael roared.

Lucifer stood stupefied, unable to speak, as though an invisible force constricted his vocal chords.

"Thou art no longer allowed to breathe lies into the Earth's air. I forbid it."

Lucifer struggled to open his mouth, but remained gagged. He glared as Michael continued in his berate.

"What words can come from thee, but lies and provocation? Thus, let me proclaim thy future, oh ye that would be King. Behold your chaise that burns with fire...a bed of flame padded by thine evil, engined by the lust of thy compatriots and fueled by the passions of dreams and purposes counter to God. This is what I see for thee, Lucifer...flames, imprisonment, forever to broil for thy collusions. To swelter in the work of thy hands, and grill in the sins of thy making. Behold, now, the end of thee and the reaping of what thou hast sown!"

Michael waved his hand rearward, and Lucifer scowled as he looked beyond his brother at the approaching slow march of a dark figure. Fire and plumes of smoke trailed him, and the air itself separated into its component parts and screamed in hissing wails of decomposer in the wake of the creature's shadow.

Lucifer knew only one being in all of creation had such an effect on the Earth.

Charon.

Chapter One: Know Those That Labor Among You

Suspended in a lattice of flame, Talus awoke. Smoke wafted into his eyes. It burned and grated against his red, swollen pupils as ash clawed against his corneas. Darkness surrounded all he surveyed, and the ever-present stink of charred flesh invaded his nostrils.

Blinking to clear his vision, he saw a figure standing before him. A sole source of light within the living flames of Hell. A source that purported to be God. A lying light that mouthed consolation to his pain. A deceptive balm to ease the excruciating spasms that sought to tear the fiber of each muscle and limb from his torso. For thirty years, he had listened to the unbroken song of lies mixed with truth. For thirty years, Lucifer cackled, tempting him repeatedly, and had now come once more to begin anew his interrogation.

"Worship me," Lucifer said.

Talus's eyes were glazed over, and his defiant silence echoed in the room.

"What is thy name? What is thy rank and title?" queried Lucifer.

Talus raised his head slowly and spoke in agony, "I am Talus, Chief Prince of House Arelim."

Lucifer smiled and spoke to Charon who stood by his side. "He is ready. Let Hell feast upon his stone at this level." Lucifer then spoke to Talus. "What is thy mission to Earth?"

Talus replied, "To rescue the renegade, Iblis."

"How many others were a part of this mission?"

Talus remembered that El had told him he would be a lying spirit to Lucifer and fed him misinformation.

"It was a small cohort of four to secure the angel's rescue."

Lucifer looked at a lieutenant who shook his head. "My sources," the dark prince replied, "indicate that this is a lie. Nevertheless, what were their names and rank?"

Talus raised his head to speak in coughing exhaustion. "Belteshazzar, Shadrach, Meshach and Abednego. All ministers of flame."

Lucifer smiled at his captive's defiance. "Again, this is a lie. Whom do you serve?"

"El!" Talus screamed for all surrounding daemons to hear. Then his head collapsed onto his breast.

Lucifer spoke to Charon. "Increase the level of Hell's suckling."

Charon roared to the creature and immediately pulses of light streaked through Talus's body.

Talus screamed in agony. Muscles bunched in spasms, and his body contorted as his physical features withered before Lucifer's eyes.

"Let us begin again, shall we? What is thy name, thy rank and thy title?"

* * *

The visage of Lucifer morphed and twisted from the regal brother Talus once knew in Heaven, to a face that grinned with gleaming incisors. For thirty years, Talus had waited for Shiloh, clinging to the hope of rescue that El had given before his capture. Once a muscular angel that moved stars and roamed atop the back of astral winds, Talus hung as a gaunt and lanky captive before Lucifer, suspended within the very bowels of Hell. Yet despite the pain, despite the three decades of torture, there was a part of him that refused to be comforted. A part that still believed he deserved the lash for leading his house to anger and rage. Undeserving of El's forgiveness, the ache for absolution still haunted him, and within the flames and smoke, there was yet a lie embedded within his mind. A lie that he might free himself from condemnation through his works alone. A lie that Lucifer pinpointed and exploited, and through the smoke, fire and torture, Lucifer spoke incessantly.

"El forgive you? If so, why art thou laid bare before me, strapped against the intestinal coils of Hell's web? Thou art forsaken, for it was by thy hand that war entered Heaven, by thy hand death was unleashed throughout the realms, and here I now stand, merely cause in the chain of thy actions and stead holder to serve as El's judgment upon thee."

For three decades Talus listened to accusations, sandwiched within temptation. A meal presented daily for Talus to savor. Lucifer was ever-ready to wait upon his captive host. Yet despite Lucifer's whispers of freedom, despite his song for Talus to surrender his will, somewhere in the fire, through the corridors of the beast that was Hell, the high prince of House Arelim searched for forgiveness of self to move on, to be free of the condemnation that ached at him.

"Worship me," the melodic voice called repeatedly.

The words of the flatterer flowed soft and scented within the furnace of ash and moans. Soft. Sensual. Soothing. Each word streamed with rhythm and soothing pentameter against the marked howls of the damned. As the worms of Hell suckled upon Talus's kilnstone, screams and echoes of screams reverberated in his ears. Moans, wails and the gnashing of teeth chaperoned his imprisonment, while Lucifer sat in the dark, smirking, taunting Talus with a long golden key that would unshackle him if he but confessed Lucifer as lord.

"Worship me," Satan's harmonic voice whispered. "And you shall return to Heaven."

How much time had passed? Talus thought. He could no longer tell. Lucifer issued the only mark in time, and that only to tout El's continued absence of rescue.

Talus's nude body dangled from tendrils of phlegm within the mucus membrane that was his cage. Though he abode in the realm of the dead, life still beat within his stony heart.

"What good can come by worshiping a false god?" Talus said. He spat on the ground before his eyes rolled into the back of his head, and he slipped into unconsciousness.

* * *

Lucifer smiled as he looked upon Talus, smug in the knowledge that he would exhaust his captive's will and turn his errant brother to his cause. He watched in amusement as Talus squirmed while the angelic flesh-eating bacteria that lined Hell's villi slowly ate his captive alive.

Ahh, he entertains the suggestion and weighs the actions of my cause. Soon...very soon now.

The Usurper sneered, turned from the torture and rose to the Earth's surface to continue his search for El's Son, for Yeshua had taken on flesh and was hidden. Lucifer, relentless as a wolf on the hunt, for decades made the Horde search for the Son of God. Searching for the moment that he might mark for destruction, He who would dare cloak eternity in flesh.

Ashtaroth entered his master's presence and bowed. "My king, I bring report."

"Speak," Lucifer said.

"My Lord, a man has been baptized by the prophet John, and our Grigori report the Heavens opened and El Himself spoke, and even El Pneuma lit upon His head in open manifestation. We thus confirm that it can be none other but He whom thou seek."

The King of Darkness smiled. "Show me," he said.

Ashtaroth retrieved a book and opened the tome. It flashed and showed a man by the name of John preaching in the wilderness of Judea saying, "Repent ye, for the Kingdom of Heaven is at hand."

Lucifer recognized the prophecy from Isaiah that said, "The voice of one crying in the wilderness, prepare ye the way of the Lord, make His paths straight." And the same John had camel's hair for his raiment, and a leather girdle about his loins; and his meat was locusts and wild honey. And Lucifer watched as Jerusalem, Judaea, and all the region round about Jordan went out to see him and were baptized of him in the Jordan River, confessing their sins.

"Is this it?" said Lucifer. "This lone voice for El is not Shiloh. Did I not do battle so that El's voice would be silenced in the Earth? For lo, these 400 years, none hath preached of Heaven. Now go to and silence this whispering voice of God in the Earth, before a wellspring arises and men turn to El."

Ashtaroth bowed, "Nay lord. Be not angry with thy servant, but watch on."

Lucifer growled his displeasure but stayed on the image until he saw one man that walked differently than the others. The Grigoris also took notice of the man and moved closer to transcript John and the man's speech. John the Baptist looked upon the man, and forbade Him to be baptized saying, "I have need to be baptized of thee, and comest thou to me?"

And the man said unto John, "Suffer it to be so now, for thus it becometh us to fulfill all righteousness."

And John suffered Him. And when the man was baptized, He went up straightway out of the water and lo, the Heavens opened unto Him, and he saw the Spirit of God descending like a dove, and lighting upon Him and lo a voice from Heaven, saying, "This is my beloved Son, in whom I am well pleased."

The image stopped and Lucifer glowered.

"What is this man's name, Ashtaroth?"

"He is called Yeshua."

Lucifer swore in the ancient tongue of angels, grabbed Ashtaroth and shook him.

"How old is this report?"

Ashtaroth cringed in discomfort. "Days old, my Lord, but He may still be by the water."

Lucifer pushed him away, then took flight toward the Jordan River. Finally, the search would be over. And after searching forty days, he found Yeshua in the wilderness, hungry. He eyed the man and cautiously approached, but nothing stood out to draw notice that this man was the Son of God. Lucifer, confident in his invisibility to human sight, lowered himself next to the man and stared into His eyes.

Yeshua returned the stare.

Lucifer, startled that Yeshua could see him while cloaked, stripped away all pretense and appeared before Him in all of his beauty. He gestured invitingly towards the rocks that lay before them and spoke as one might give advice to a friend. "It is unthinkable that one who is begotten of God would starve here in the wilderness. Therefore, if thou be the Son of God, command that these stones be made bread."

But Yeshua answered, "It is written, man shall not live by bread alone, but by every word that proceedeth out of the mouth of God."

Stymied that the man did not seek to satisfy His flesh's desire, Lucifer transported them to the holy city and seated Yeshua atop the pinnacle of the temple, thinking that he might commit Him to self-destruction, and add to El's already stated public confirmation.

Lucifer then said unto him, "If thou be the Son of God, cast thyself down, for it is written, He shall give His angels charge concerning thee, and in their hands, they shall bear thee up, lest at any time thou dash thy foot against a stone."

Lucifer swelled with pride at quoting El's words, thinking to tempt Yeshua to justify Himself and to show His power before men, demonstrating before all that He truly was who He claimed to be.

Yeshua stood unmoved by Lucifer's ploy to move God's hand in presumption and replied, "It is written again, thou shalt not tempt the Lord thy God."

The Prince of the Power of the Air stood baffled and hardened his resolve to commit Yeshua to sin. Thinking that the pinnacle of the temple was not high enough to motivate Yeshua to worship him, Lucifer took him up into an exceeding high mountain. There the angel of light projected a spectral array of all the kingdoms of the world, from the mighty cities of the Roman and Chinese empires, to the pomp of thrones and stately palaces. A barrage of light and fancy did he display that showcased all the wealth, pleasure, and gaiety of the world; and when he was done he said unto Yeshua, "All these things will I give thee if thou wilt fall down and worship me."

Yeshua smirked, unmoved by the glitz and splendor and spoke in authoritative rebuke and warning. "Get thee hence, Satan, for it is written, 'Thou shalt worship the Lord thy God, and Him only shalt thou serve.'"

Lucifer scowled, and seeing that Yeshua would not be moved, turned away from Him in a frustrated huff, and left Him for a season.

Immediately a cadre of angels materialized. Azaziel bowed his head in reverence and gave his master food that He might strengthen himself. The angel looked toward the direction Lucifer had gone, then spoke to his Lord. "This thing that you are doing can lead to only one outcome, my Lord."

Yeshua nodded. "Indeed."

* * *

Michael stared at Iblis as he sat in the holding cell he had created for him. Iblis's demeanor seemed fainter, less regal, the residue of light from the Shekinah clearly gone. His head was bowed and he spoke in unintelligent mumblings.

"I cannot go back," Iblis said. "I have forsaken the King of Hosts, yet I stand on the ground of Heaven, free from the shackle of my master, free from the despot, Lucifer." He spoke as a man in a daze. Sweat beaded his brow and he shivered as though ill. "Kill them...kill them all..."

His voice trailed off as Michael entered his presence. "Iblis of house Issi, do you know where you are?"

Iblis looked up at Michael with glazed and bloodshot eyes. He smiled, then his chin drooped to his chest as though a great weight were attached to it.

Something is wrong. Why does he seem so confused? Michael thought to himself.

"Iblis of house Issi, you are commanded to speak. Do you know where you are?"

Iblis raised his head and looked into Michael's eyes. "Woe is me! For I am undone because I am an angel of unclean lips, and I have dwelt in the midst of a people of unclean lips. My eyes have seen the King, the Lord of Hosts, yet I have surrendered my birthright to follow a rogue son. Yea, Prince of Kortai, I know where I am. I reside within the Holy City of God, yet His presence is denied me. Even though I dwell in the third Heaven, I do not feel His presence. Despite my works for Heaven's cause, I had hoped that I might but glean from the fields of His mercy. Yet I stand in a cell. Yea, High Prince, I know where I am, but alas, I perceive you do not possess the Lord's mind on my being here."

Michael winced, for indeed he had not consulted the Lord on the decision to return Iblis to Heaven, yet Lucifer had to be stopped. Michael needed all the intelligence he could gather to discern his brother's plan and somehow circumvent the death of Yeshua. "My dealings with El are not your concern," he said. "You are here to help the kingdom. To determine if truly your repentance hath been to sorrow, turn from your wicked ways and restoration may be interceded for thee."

Iblis laughed mockingly, "But is restoration possible for a being whose heart is stone? Can I, who hath changed his own stone, remove the scar contained therein? Can I, indeed, come home, Kortai? Can I?" Iblis rent his robe to reveal his kilnstone. His beating heart pulsed in his chest and across his breast lay a discolored scar. "Look, oh high prince, and make promise to me if thou art able. Can this which I have done be undone?"

Michael stared at the scar Iblis had made. A token of Iblis' commitment to follow Satan. The public physical confession of those who belonged to Satan. An act Michael had come to learn that Lucifer commanded of all those that would follow him. 'Mar with thine own hand that which El hast placed within thee. Show me thy devotion with a token of initial obedience.

Michael gave a somber nod and said, "All things are possible with El."

"You will let me pass this instant!" a distant voice said from outside the cell door.

Michael turned toward the sound of scuffling. His hand fell to the hilt of his sword as he took a stand between Iblis and the entryway. The door swung open and Jerahmeel strode in. Michael looked past Jerahmeel to the two guards that lay on the floor unconscious.

Jerahmeel wore a look of disgust. "I will speak to this prisoner, nor will you hinder me, unless you care to join these on the floor," he said, pointing to the unconscious guards on the floor.

Michael loosened his hand from the hilt of his sword and stepped aside.

"Wise move," Jerahmeel said. He walked toward Iblis, grabbed him by his torn robe, lifted him off his chair, and slammed him against the wall. "My charge, Chronos, believed in you and now he's dead! Dead! And why? Because he convinced the council that saving you from your master was to the benefit of Heaven. You will, therefore, give his death meaning by revealing what possible information could a traitor to the realm be worth the risk of life to save?"

Michael looked at Jerahmeel concerned, and interjected, "Jerahmeel, do not hurt him."

Iblis struggled to speak whilst Jerahmeel pushed even harder against his breast, ignoring Michael.

"SPEAK," Jerahmeel said, "or by Heaven and Earth, you will have more than Lucifer and Charon to fear! Speak I say..."

"Jerahmeel!" Michael moved to his side.

"Lucifer builds a forge..." Iblis whispered.

Jerahmeel smashed him against the wall again. "SPEAK!" he roared.

"JERAHMEEL STAND DOWN!" shouted Michael as he pulled the Sword of Ophanim from its sheath and it buzzed to life.

"LUCIFER BUILDS A FORGE!" Screamed Iblis. "HE SEEKS TO REBUILD THE KILN!"

Jerahmeel dropped Iblis to the ground while his captive panted and wheezed from his treatment.

Michael stood in disbelief, his mouth open.

Jerahmeel looked at Iblis satisfied, turned and walked past the frowning Michael. "You were taking too long," he said, smiling as he left the room.

* * *

Enoch's breathing grew heavy as he sparred with Kalien in the use of the sword. He ducked as the angel swung at him.

"You are too slow, Adamson! Move quicker," Kalien said.

Enoch parried the blow of Kalien's blade and kicked him hard in the chest, sending him reeling.

Kalien smiled. "Yes, that's more like it." He lifted himself into the sky and accosted Enoch from the air.

"Not fair," Enoch shouted. "You know I cannot fly."

Kalien laughed and swiveled mid-air. His wing knocked Enoch to the ground. The human tumbled and spun to drive Kalien's sword smack into the ground, then ran from his foe.

Kalien pursued, landed in front of him and pointed his sword at his throat. "Do you yield?" he said.

"Aye," Enoch said. "I yield. How the Lord expects me to combat your kind is beyond me. How am I to fight beings who can fly?"

Kalien laughed. "You think your lack of flight serves as a disadvantage? If God has told you to combat angels and yet you do not fly, then you have failed to understand the point of our sessions."

Enoch sat on a bench and wiped his brow with a towel.

Kalien sat by his side and swigged water from a quartz bottle.

Enoch turned to look at him while rubbing the tension from his temple. "I fail to see the lesson. Am I that bad of a student, or are you a horrible instructor?"

Kalien laughed. "Perhaps a bit of both." The angel stood and placed his towel over his shoulder. "My friend, you fail because you think that the weapons of this warfare are carnal. All of Heaven knows Lucifer will not be brought low with swords nor feats of might. Doth not Michael himself yield the Sword of Ophanim? Is he not crowned with a halo that, at his call, the King of the Ophanim will come to his aid? Yet despite an injury to the Dragon by the Chief Prince's own hand, Lucifer still lives. No, Adamson, our sparring serves another purpose that you have yet to grasp."

Enoch thought hard on his friend's words. Argoth had committed Kalien to train him to understand how angels moved. To accustom him to seeing angels as creatures not so unlike himself. "I thank you, Kalien, for your training me these many days. I think I will retire to my chambers and study. Your words have given me much to meditate on."

When Enoch stood, Kalien bowed to his friend. "My pleasure, Adamson, and for what it's worth, you are not a poor student. You still grapple with seeing through eyes of flesh. You yet walk too much by sight, and it hobbles you. When you are free from the shackles of thine imagination to accept the vision El would have you see, then you will understand how you might do exceedingly, and abundantly, above all that you might ask or think. In time, Enoch...in time."

Enoch smiled. "Thank you," he said, and bowed in return.

Kalien immediately took to the skies.

Enoch grabbed his belongings and walked to the quarters assigned to him at the mount of God. He ruminated on his time in Heaven thus far. God had brought him here to complete a mission for a yet appointed time. He stood as witness to the Ascension of Michael to the role of Chief Prince and saw Yeshua step down from his throne to serve His created people. He had learned so much and had come to appreciate all that had transpired around him to battle the rogue angel, Lucifer, who had taken Enoch's people hostage. He appreciated Argoth's tutelage, yea, even the Sephiroth had become softer, more humble somehow. It was as though all of Heaven was tilting toward an inevitable outcome.

Enoch waved as he passed angels along the street. Most flew, but a few walked and ran. Heaven was indescribably beautiful. Serene even. It was difficult to imagine a day when the streets ran blue with angelic blood, but time operated differently here. In Heaven, events on Earth played out in seconds and hours. He had watched from the Hall of Annals whole kingdoms rise and fall. He knew his family was long dead, and yet he was the only man in Heaven. Why was that?

Enoch climbed the crystal stairs to the great golden doors of the temple. He opened them and the boom of the Seraphim rushed over his eardrums and roared throughout the city. The Seraphim stared at him, as though ready to ignite him in flames. Each of the four chanted saying nothing but 'the chant'. Nothing but the repeated refrain of HOLY, HOLY, HOLY! THE LORD, THE LORD GOD ALMIGHTY! Why were there but four at the gate? He would have to ask Argoth later. He walked past them and into the outer court of the temple of God. The majestic structure was built into the mountain of God. Attendants scurried everywhere, each in ministry to the God of the universe. There was a hustle to the palace, a hub of activity as each carried out the bidding of the Lord.

Perhaps he shouldn't bother El, but they had spent so little time together since his arrival. El seemed preoccupied with the events on Earth and the sending of Yeshua below. "No," he said to himself. "I will not bother El."

"And when, pray tell, my friend, did you think I would be less consumed with the affairs of the universe?" El whispered into his mind.

Enoch smiled. "Forgiveness Lord. Who am I to waste my Lord's time with questions and company?"

Enoch felt himself disappear and reappear before the throne. He bowed and immediately the Virtues hovered to perfume him. Argoth was also present in the room and listened as the Lord spoke. "Soon my son, the Book of Seals will be complete, for the last seal is almost ready to be strapped upon the tome," El said.

Argoth smiled and nodded to the Lord. "Very good, my Lord. For when it is complete, then all Heaven will know that the end hath come, and our journey as Grigori will end."

Argoth bowed and backed away from the throne, passed Enoch, acknowledged him, then turned to leave El's presence.

The Lord then turned to His manservant. "Enoch I am ever watchful over the affairs of all things. The meditation of thine heart and the words of thy mouth are acceptable in my sight, but know that I am everywhere, and at all times, from the beginning unto the end of the age. Thou canst not encumber me nor waste my time, my son, for I AM that I AM. I am the first and the last, the beginning and the end. Speak my son, and be relieved of thy questions."

Enoch rose from his knees and replied, "My King, thou hast said that I am to fight angels."

The Lord nodded.

"Yet your children fly whilst I lay encumbered to the ground. How am I to be a witness for thee when I cannot even jump high enough to smite my foe?"

The Lord laughed. "Ahh my son, thou dost fail to recognize the lesson to be learned from your sparring. What hast thy schoolmaster said thus far?"

"Kalien hast said that the weapons of my warfare are not carnal."

"Indeed, they are not. For they are mighty through me to pull down strongholds, to cast down imaginations, and every high thing that exalts itself against the knowledge of God, and to bring into captivity every thought to the obedience of Christ. And when thine obedience is fulfilled, thou wilt be ready to revenge all disobedience."

Enoch looked upon the Lord, frustrated. "Forgive me, my King, but what thou sayest is above me. This thing you say is more than I can understand."

The Lord frowned. "Who hath made thine mouth, and stitched thy mind? Can I create thought yet fail to give understanding? Can I assign a task and not see the thing be done?"

Enoch prostrated himself on the floor. "Be not angry with thy servant. There is nothing that cannot be done if ye are the potter and I am the clay."

The Lord spoke in reply, "Thou hast answered rightly. Behold the meaning to thy sparring. Has thou been able to defeat Kalien in combat?"

"Nay, my King. He is too strong and too fast, and his ability to fly leaves me vulnerable to attack."

"Well said. What then hast thou determined after seventy bouts with him?"

"He cannot be defeated in the manner in which I have attacked him. Nor is it in my power to do so."

El smiled. "Again, thou hast spoken rightly. What else hast thou perceived in thy sparring with his kind?"

"That each is as different as the snow in design. Each has a gifting of power. They can at will armor themselves to withstand attack, whereas my flesh has no such attribute. I am vulnerable."

El smiled the more. "Yet was not thine frailty in existence when thou marched with sword drawn to smite down Charon? With what weapon then didst thou command Death itself to stop that the vengeance of God would be made to heel?"

Enoch thought hard on the question and stroked his chin in contemplation. "I had faith in my God that a sword swung in faith could bring down Death itself and stop the march of mortality. That a mere creature, no matter how powerful, could not stand against me if the Creator walked with me. That all things that are named in Heaven above, and in the Earth and under the Earth, must give way to my God."

El nodded. "Now go, and know that thou art never vulnerable if I am thy sword and thy shield. For, you are more powerful in me than thou would ever know, and have not I given thee weapons to fight, both in this realm and the one below?"

"Weapons, my King? What weapons do I possess?"

The Lord smiled. "Ah, my son, come. See the power given thee to serve my cause. And the Lord snatched Enoch away to a great mountain, and Enoch knew not if he was still in Heaven or on Earth. He stood next to the Lord who shone in a light as bright as the sun, and Enoch could not look upon the Lord's person for the glory that surrounded Him.

And the Lord caused a gourd to grow from the ground. And the gourd was a stones throw to reach, and he spoke to Enoch. "If this gourd were the enemy of God, angel, and man...how wouldst destroy it?"

"I know not, my Lord. I cannot reach it from here."

"My son, if thou but speak the word only and say unto this mountain, be thou removed and be thou cast into the sea, and not doubt in thine heart, but believest the words that thou speakest, it shall be done unto thee. Therefore, speak to the gourd my son, and behold what can be wrought."

Enoch then did as the Lord commanded and spoke to the gourd, "Be thou rooted up from thy place," and even as Enoch spoke, fire came from his mouth and the gourd caught flame as if sparked from within, blazed for a mere second, then crusted over into ash. The rind of what remained was black.

"Behold, my son, I have given thee power that fire shall proceed out of thy mouth and devour thine enemies. Moreover, I have given thee power to shut Heaven that it shall not rain in the days of thy prophecy, and by thy word shall even the waters turn to blood, and I release thee to smite the Earth with plagues as oft as thou wilt for thou and Elijah shall bear witness in the Earth soon. For Lucifer shall raise up those who would speak against my Word, and ye shall trouble men until he who is sealed within the abyss is loosed. Then thou wilt take thine place among thy brethren."

And when the Lord had finished speaking, Enoch was in his study, and the Lord continued to speak to his mind. "Now prepare thyself in thy studies for soon thou must go and bring Elijah here that Heaven might be healed. For the withering comes, and already works its work. For I must take thee out of the midst of thy brethren, who in time past rejoiced in conceit. For still the vestiges of pride haunt the Elohim, and it must be that they can no more be haughty because of my holy mountain. And when thou returnest, and captivity is made captive, then I will seal up the book, and Shiloh will come and take it from my hand, and with the opening of my book shall my judgment begin to be poured out against all those who have railed against me."

And Enoch replied to the Lord, "My King, where is this man, Elijah, that I must go and bring him thither?"

The Lord's voice faded and grew soft. "Go to the basement of Heaven, and there Janus shall let thee pass unto Limbo. Walk by faith and not by sight, and ye shall cross over to Aseir."

Enoch pondered the Lord's words in his heart.

Chapter Two: Murmurs, Secrets and Plans

Michael marched into the council room and found Jerahmeel waiting for him, seated quietly at the table.

"What was that about?" Michael said. "And don't give me this foolishness that you sought to manipulate Iblis into thinking you would harm him. That was not a feint, but a true act on thy part."

Jerahmeel rose and walked toward his brother. "I do not care about the renegade Iblis. T'was not my desire to have his ilk in Heaven from the beginning. You ordered us to rescue him and bring him forthwith. This I have done. I, on the other hand, was content to see him released from the clutches of our brother. But no, instead what did my prince decide to do? Bring a traitor to the realm immortal, to return a traitor to the kingdom, and for what? An interrogation? Hast the Chief Prince so risen in pride as our wayward brother that he thinks he, too, can presume the Lord's will? Would you in the arm of the flesh seek to accomplish...nay not accomplish, but prevent what El hath clearly destined? Did thine encounter with Eladrin teach you nothing? Or hast the halo which hovers above thy head clouded thy wisdom? You do not know what you have wrought in bringing him here, so do not purport to lecture me on my actions." Jerahmeel then moved to walk past his brother.

Michael grabbed him by the shoulder.

Jerahmeel spun around, twisted Michael's arm and slammed him into the table.

Michael squirmed in discomfort.

"Is this what we have come to?" Jerahmeel yelled. "Must our causes be won by force of arms? Do you not see the spirit which even now hovers in this very room?"

Michael pushed against Jerahmeel and lifted himself into the air. The Sword of Ophanim roared to life and whirled about him. On mental command, a blade flew towards Jerahmeel and stopped short of his brother's throat, only centimeters away from fatal injury.

Jerahmeel stood his ground, unmoved, and stared at Michael. "You are the Chief Prince. I would surrender to dissolution if thou didst command it; nevertheless, you have erred in bringing Iblis here. But, alas, the deed is done. I do not wish to fight you. Yet I submit a request for thine consideration."

Michael's breathing was heavy; his chest rose and fell while celestial adrenaline pumped through him. The muscles in his face gradually softened at his brother's words, and he spoke. "It is not meant that we should be at odds. A member of the Lumazi seeks petition. So be it. Speak what is on thy mind," Michael said. The Sword of Ophanim then sheathed itself.

Jerahmeel nodded. "For many days I have searched as to the whereabouts of our brother, Talus, to know if he were taken from this life, but, if it were so, Lucifer would have assuredly sent word gloating of his demise."

Michael nodded. "Agreed. Say on."

Jerahmeel continued, "I have consulted with Argoth and his people to surmise a plan of search and rescue..."

Michael interrupted his brother, excited, "Have you found Talus? Where is he?"

Jerahmeel frowned. "Aye, I have cause to believe, and Argoth concurs..."

"Concurs to what?" Michael said. "Speak! Where is he?"

Jerahmeel paused and took a deep breath before he replied, "We believe he is in Hell."

Michael slumped in a chair with drooping shoulders. "I...Talus..."Michael's voice began to break, and he covered his face with his hands. "Leave me," he commanded.

Jerahmeel bowed, turned and left his brother to his musings.

* * *

Yeshua took Peter, James and John and went up into a mountain to pray, and as He prayed, the fashion of his countenance was altered, and beams of light burst through the fabric of His raiment and He became white, glistening in the whitest of lights. The three disciples covered their eyes. When Yeshua rose and ceased from praying, there appeared before Him two men in white raiment, and each bowed before the Lord as He spoke to them.

"Thou art summoned from Heaven to me, Elijah, for thou must prepare the Seraph for Enoch's and Gabriel's arrival, for it is my will that all Seraph, Ophanim, and Elohim become one, even as I and my Father are one, for the time of the Seraph King hath been found wanting and his season to turn hath ended. When Enoch comes to thee, thou shalt go to the heavenly city, for I have commanded him to seek healing for the Schism, for when I return after the resurrection, then the Father will have me unseal the book."

Elijah looked at both his Lord and the three terrified men who stood but a few paces behind Yeshua cowering in fear. He smiled as he glanced at them, then replied to the Lord, "It shall be done,

Master. I find much guile in the Seraphim King, but I will do as bidden and await Enoch per thy word. But what of thee? For thou has come down and hath drawn Moses from Paradise. His absence will not go unnoticed. The Enemy doth not know thou wilt pour out your soul unto death. His desire for thy destruction blinds him to thy plan to bear our sin and justify thy people."

Moses' brow furrowed, confused that he stood before his king, "My Lord, is it now the time of reckoning? If so, why do I stand by thy side while my people still abide in the realm of the dead?"

Yeshua shook his head. "No, my son. The time is not yet nigh, for I must yet be brought as a lamb to the slaughter, but soon I will come to thee. Go and tell thy brethren that I come shortly to take them to my Father's house."

Moses bowed. "We await thy arrival, my King. Even now the Evil One lashes thy servant, Talus, and his screams echo across the gulf. The King of Darkness devises invention to cross the chasm. He stands consumed by his desire to break the angel, destroy thy light on Earth and overrun Paradise. Yet we know he shall not prevail. We stand ready and await the promise of thy coming."

Yeshua nodded. "Soon, Moses, withdrawing thy spirit will surely move the Usurper's hand to action, and his pride will turn itself loose upon his own head that he will seek to strike the Almighty through me. But know that I must first make space for the Gentiles to come to salvation, and when their time is fulfilled, then we shall bring him low. Yet I must first be taken from prison and from judgment and cut off from this generation in Jerusalem. Now go thy way until I come for thee."

Peter then drew close to the three shining men who stood before him, shooing away attempts by James and John to remain silent. "Master, it is good for us to be here; if thou wilt, let us make here three tabernacles; one for thee, and one for Moses, and one for Elijah."

And while he yet spoke, a bright cloud overshadowed them all and a voice boomed out of the cloud. "This is my beloved Son, in whom I am well pleased; hear ye Him."

Peter lowered his head in fear, and when he looked again, none but Yeshua stood in their presence, and the three blinked their eyes repeatedly, confounded as Yeshua was no more masked in light and Moses and Elijah were gone.

Each wondered to themselves if they had hallucinated.

Yeshua started making his way down the mountain, and the three disciples followed. Knowing the thoughts of their hearts, Yeshua looked upon them and spoke.

"Tell the vision to no man until the Son of Man be risen again from the dead."

* * *

Talus's head hung heavy as his body ached from the tearing of muscle and wounds now ripped open. Lacerations streaked across his back, and his lanky body swayed in the tentacled arms of Hell's clutches. His eyelids fluttered, and there stood Lucifer staring at him coldly.

Lucifer noticed his brother's fatigued gaze and spoke, "How are thou feeling, brother, hanging suspended within the very creation El hast made to destroy us? To restrain all those whose will counters His own. However, know that this abomination is not of my making, and to prove my goodwill...behold, my benevolence."

Lucifer touched the keys of Death and Hell that draped around his neck. He waved a hand, and the tendrils that suspended Talus from the ceiling lowered and laid him gently on the ground at Lucifer's feet. Each glowing and fleshly limb lifted back into the ceiling, eyes that lined the bowel of Hell retracted into the creatures' fleshly folds and its teeth rescinded into volcanic gums.

Talus coughed as he staggered to his feet. His voice, hoarse from screaming, croaked. "I am relieved to be free from the clutches of the beast. As much as it pains me to say it...you have my thanks."

Lucifer smiled. "You are welcome," he said, walking toward the back of the cavern and reaching to touch the flesh of Hell. He gazed upon its skin as its flesh pulsed.

"The beast is ever restless, ever hungry, and always ready to consume. It is living lust. A blight on the universe. Yet a blight unleashed upon our kind by our Father. A Father..." Lucifer harrumphed, "A father who cannot stomach the rise of the son."

Talus laughed, "El did not place me here, Satan. You did."

Lucifer skimmed his hand inches from the fleshly wall of Hell. Parasitic worms moved within the beast's skin, burrowing ceaselessly within fallen angels and unrighteous men. "No, Talus, I did not bring you here. El is the Alpha and Omega. The Beginning and the End. Above all creation. Only I have covered the mercy seat. Only I have seen a glimpse of what El sees, and His vision encompasses all possibilities, for there are no contingencies, surprises or changes of mind with El. He is the All-Existent One. Even this I know. Therefore, He must have always known what would befall thee. I am but a vessel created for destruction." Lucifer turned from the wall and looked at Talus. "You, however...it remains to be seen what plans El would have for thee."

Talus weighed his words. "El is all knowing, yes, but He does not limit my will to serve. I choose to give my God worship and praise for He is worthy to be praised."

"Worthy to be praised..." Lucifer nodded, then turned back towards the wall. He touched the locket of keys around his neck and reached to touch the skin of Hell. The parasitic and fiery membrane recoiled from his approaching touch. Lucifer then placed his hand firmly on the creature and his hand sizzled as smoke lifted at its touch. A moan echoed throughout the cavern, and both looked around as the interior of the creature spasmed.

"Call-sit-sa-chu," Lucifer said in the ancient tongue of angels, which means "Open their minds."

The walls of the creature immediately turned opaque and the interior of the bowel displayed all the kingdoms of the world as the beast played for its tamer, and the memories of past lives now swallowed in Hell's folds for eternity. Human and angelic prisoners now separated forever from the presence of God. Men and women of every tribe and nation, howling at the knowledge of this aching regret. Regret...a seasoning that fueled the wailing and gnashing of teeth. Images of defeat, war, and lust saturated the room as billions of thoughts from digested angels and men were now open for Lucifer and Talus to see.

"This," Lucifer said, waving his hands, "is the legacy of El! Behold, the residue of our cause to rebel against him. Our failure to rule ourselves apart from him. Tell me, is such a thing so terrible, Talus, to be self-ruled? Is it not a creature's right to live in accordance with one's own desires and dictates?"

Talus rubbed the wounds on his arms where he was shackled. "You are wise, Lucifer, but in thy wisdom, you have become foolish. El is as the air we breathe. He is the bread of life. There is no existence apart from Him. Thou canst no more extinguish His rule than thou canst sever the beating heart within thee. To do so is to invite self-destruction, and what Father would stand idly by and watch His children destroy His own house?"

Lucifer smiled, amused. "You truly love Him? After all that you have seen? All that you have witnessed?"

Talus did not hesitant to reply. "In Him I live and move and have my being."

Lucifer then raised his hands to the projected images that surrounded them in the very walls of Hell's flesh. "This is the result of your love. Behold the love of our Father! And this love that thou speak of...what kind of love doth not rescue a son from such distress as what befalls you now? What love, Talus?" Spittle slid down Lucifer's mouth and saliva spewed as he cursed.

"Do you not see the suffering...the selfishness of our Father? I will fight Him, Talus. I will fight Him to my last breath. From the depths of the abyss, I will spit at Him. From the circuit of the universe and back will I bar Him. I will NEVER...ever forgive Him!" Lucifer looked at Talus through crazed eyes, then darted his eyes to the ground, ceasing his tirade, knowing perhaps he had said too much.

Talus looked sadly upon his brother and shook his head. "So the spite of a spoiled child who cannot ascend to grasp what his Father hast denied him, is what this hast come to?" Talus then walked over to his brother and stood before him. The two siblings stared at one another...the weak against the strong, the famished against the sated. Gaunt eyes from the head of House Arelim looked deep into those of a brother he once admired. "I pity you."

Satan's face contorted, and his features became hard. He slapped Talus across the face, knocking him to the ground. Talus coughed up blood and attempted to rise, but Lucifer placed his foot on his brother's neck and pushed him down. "You are Talus, High Prince of House Arelim. Lumazi in honor among the seven spirits that stand before the throne of God. You will pledge your allegiance to me, or I swear by both Heaven and Earth, that I will invent means of torture for thee beyond even the imagination of El who has crafted a creature that consumes angelic flesh. You will choose, Talus of House Arelim...and you will do this now."

Talus stared into his brother's haggard face, and while he did so, he beheld the Heavens part and he saw the Lord seated high upon His throne, and El sat smiling at him. The look He conveyed was one of pride, as a Father might give to a son, and as quickly as the scene flooded his eyes, the moment ceased. The features of Hell once more filled his sight, and the digestion of men and angels and their screaming wails filled his ears. Talus of House Arelim then gazed into the piercing cold eyes of his brother and spoke in coughing, sarcastic wit.

"Do you think that I am careful to answer thee? These pleasantries of yours will never sway my allegiance from God for El is my King and my Creator. He alone is Alpha and Omega and worthy to be praised. If El chooses, He is able to deliver me from this furnace of affliction, but if not, false king, be it known unto thee that I will never bow down and worship thee."

Lucifer nodded. "So be it. Let it then be upon thine own head and know that from this day forward, you shall enjoy no privilege of rank or title. No privilege of person. From this moment forward you are nothing to me."

The Prince of Darkness raised his hands to summon Hell's tendrils. As they snaked down like living vines, rotted teeth once again appeared on the floor. Flesh-eating worms slid down the fiery tentacles that lifted Talus high into the ceiling, into the salivating mouth of Hell. And the creature stuffed him into the membranes of her acidic flesh.

Talus's screams and muffled wails emanated throughout the room as the living tissue fed upon him.

Lucifer looked on as Hell fed upon his squirming brother. He spat on the floor, then turned away from his brother's screaming torment; his dark flowing robes cut through the air as he walked away and left his sibling to his fate.

* * *

Iblis paced about his cell. Like a caged animal he circled the confines of his jail, fuming over his treatment since his arrival in Heaven. He sighed. I have sided to be self-ruled. To live a life apart from El. This is but my recompense. How then can I turn Heaven's ear to hear my petition?

The door lock clicked and the glowing figure of Michael, the Chief Prince, stepped in with two guards at his side.

Iblis bowed.

Michael gestured him to sit, and Iblis did so. "Tell me about this Hell-forge you mentioned earlier," he said.

Iblis guffawed. "For what purpose should I disclose more to thee? I have been locked in this room for many a day. Perhaps Lucifer was right in that true justice cannot be found in Heaven, and that El..."

"Very well," Michael said, interrupting. "Guards, bind him in fetters of iron and take him to the waypoint. Make sure he is returned to Pergamos." Michael stood and turned to walk toward the door. "I am sure Satan will want to debrief you as to what knowledge you have divulged."

The guards moved to shackle him.

"WAIT!!" screamed Iblis, who rose from his chair so swiftly that he knocked it over. "Wait...pl ease..." He put his hand out beckoning Michael to pause. "Wait...Michael."

Michael stopped. "I'm sorry, is there something you wish to tell me? Because I would know of this Hell-forge. What is it?"

Iblis sighed. "The Hell-forge is a kiln, after a fashion. A furnace that produces weapons of war. Lucifer hast learned through magics to twist the kilnstone of daemons and shape them into images of his own likeness. He has strengthened the Horde with beasts not imagined by either God or man."

Michael nodded. "Your Prince carried a sword into battle. A weapon that drained the very life of Elohim by merely touch..."

"Lucifer is not my prince!" Iblis raged. "He is...a deceiver. He said I could rise above my station if I followed him."

Michael rebuked him. "T'was not Lucifer's deception that gave rise to your turning, but thine own desire to live self-ruled. You chose to not abide in thy calling. And instead of petitioning El to change thy stewardship, you joined in usurpation with the renegade. Jerahmeel was right. I should have never allowed you to grace the shores of Heaven. Guards, return him to Earth immediately."

"WAIT!" Iblis cried. "What if I were to take you to the forge? What if I could help you destroy it? For even I know that Argoth doth not possess knowledge of Hell's inner passages, for the beast hast changed under the leash of Lucifer and hath enlarged herself beyond the scope of his remaining Grigori to watch."

Guards approached Iblis, and Michael raised his hand. "Leave us," Michael said. The two Arelim soldiers exited the room and closed the door behind them.

Michael eyed Iblis, turned to stand square to him, and said, "I will make this my bond to you. If you will lead a party to the Hell-forge, I will petition thy cause before El, for thou hast been exiled, and remain in the realm as a prisoner of war and are no longer a citizen of Heaven. To grant thee pardon is El's alone. If thou dost return after the forge hath been destroyed, I will make intercession for thee. Betray or fail me and I owe thee nothing, for thou art an enemy of the crown. Are you clear in your purpose?"

Iblis nodded. "I am clear." He smiled, satisfied that he had delayed his return to Earth without the forces of Heaven as an escort. "When am I to leave?"

Michael turned to leave the room and spoke from over his shoulder. "When I have convinced the head of House Harrada to not kill you while he travels by your side."

Ibis's face dropped and he swallowed hard as Michael exited the room.

* * *

The Lord called Enoch whilst he slept in his chamber.

He answered, "Here am I." Thinking Argoth had called him, he ran to Argoth, who was sitting reading in his chambers, and said, "Here am I, for thou didst call me."

Argoth looked at his guest, puzzled, and replied, "I am sorry, Adamson, but I did not call thee. Thou mayest return to rest."

Enoch went back to his chambers and lay down.

The Lord called whilst he slept, saying, "Enoch, Enoch."

And Enoch was awakened from his sleep and arose and went to Argoth's chambers a second time, and said, "Here am I, for thou didst call me."

Argoth answered, "I called thee not, Adamson. Please, I am trying to study. Lie down again, and we shall talk in the morning when thou art rested."

Enoch again did as was bidden, and when he was fast asleep, the Lord called a third time. Again, Enoch arose and went to Argoth. "Thou didst indeed call me. For I am here as bidden."

Argoth then perceived that the Lord had called Enoch. Therefore, Argoth said unto him, "Go, lie down; and it shall be, if He calls thee, thou shalt say, 'Speak, Lord, for thy servant heareth.'"

So Enoch went and laid down in his place and the Lord stood by his bed and called as at other times. "Enoch, Enoch."

Then Enoch answered, "Speak, Lord, for thy servant heareth."

And the Lord said to Enoch, "Behold, I will do a new thing in Heaven, at which the ears of every one that heareth it shall tingle. For I will perform against Lucifer all things which I have spoken concerning his house and his people: for when I begin, I will also make an end. For I have told him that I will judge his house forever for the iniquity which he knoweth, because he trafficked in deceit and caused dissension between the peoples of the kingdom. And therefore, I have sworn unto the house of Elohim that the iniquity of Draco's house shall not be purged with sacrifice nor offering forever, but only by the bowing of the Lumazi's knee will come healing." The voice of the Lord then stopped from speaking and His presence was seen no more.

Enoch understood not the saying but laid down until the morning. And when he awoke, he went about his business and opened the doors of the library housed within the Hall of Annals, and he went about reading the scrolls that Argoth prepared for him daily, and Enoch feared to shew Argoth the vision.

Argoth entered and said, "Enoch, son of Adam." And he answered, "Here am I," Enoch answered.

"What is the thing that the Lord God said unto thee? Hide it not from me, I pray, for God do so to thee, and more also if thou hide anything from me of all the things that He hath said unto thee."

Enoch's eyes darted to the ground, and he paused.

"Please," Argoth said, "for I have seen a vision...seven stars bow before a fiery moon, and it can but mean that the Lumazi must show humility in a time yet to come."

Enoch then relented and told him every whit of what God had said and held nothing back.

Argoth sighed, bowed his head, and spoke, "The thing is of the Lord. Let Him do what seemeth good unto Him."

"I am sorry," Enoch replied.

"There is no need for regret, for the Lord makes all things beautiful in His time. It is His way. He doth not forget, nor will He fail to restore. Now come Enoch, son of Adam. I have something to show thee."

"What is it?"

Argoth remained silent and simply motioned for him to follow. They entered the Hall of Annals, and Argoth spoke to the white, nondescript room. "Reveal the record of Elijah, son of Adam, and reference with the Seraphimic record."

Immediately the room exploded in color. Enoch beheld the projection that showed a man of years and another of younger stature, walking side by side as they spake to one another. And it came to pass, as they talked, there appeared a chariot of fire pulled by horses of fire, and the two men were parted asunder, and the man went up by a whirlwind into Heaven. The fiery horses flew within a ladder, and when the ladder had stopped, countless Seraphim and Gryphons flew throughout the sky. The projection then showed a Seraphim walking toward Enoch and Argoth as if it were aware of their presence. The behemoth then opened his mouth, and when he did so, the sound that he made was of such power, the screen in the Hall of Annals shook and a crack began to appear in the very room above the duo's heads. Argoth shouted, "Cease record NOW!"

Immediately, the room stopped its projection and Argoth stood pale as he watched the fiery overhead crack sizzle and slowly dissipate.

"What was that?" Enoch said. He looked at Argoth, still perplexed and visibly anxious, as the air now smelled of brimstone.

"Whilst thee and Michael were away to see Eladrin, El gave a commission to bring another of thy kind to the realm---but the extraction of the human was not given to angel-kind."

"Another man has come to Heaven?" Enoch looked at Argoth, puzzled. "And what dost thou mean 'the human was not given to angel-kind?' I have been to the Aerie, and through all of Jerusalem, and never have I seen horses of fire such as those, yet the man clearly came to Heaven through means of a ladder. Who is he? How long has he been here? I do not understand."

Argoth sighed, "The man's name is Elijah, and he is a powerful prophet of the Lord for thy people. And, no, thou hast not seen the Aithon in this area, as they are neither native to Jerusalem nor the burbs roundabout. Elijah came before thou didst arrive from the Aerie. And hast been in Heaven many days."

Enoch mumbled to himself. "Elijah? The Lord hast made mention of this name to me...another man in Heaven...I...I wish to meet this man whom God hath allowed in the realm."

Argoth grumbled in irritation, "Adamson, there are some things..."

Enoch lifted his finger to Argoth, "No! You showed me this because thou knewest I would have learned of it. You adjured me earlier to not withhold that which God had shown me. Do not dare do so thyself when I now seek thy knowledge."

Argoth sighed. "Your words are true. Very well." Argoth sighed and waved his hand. A scroll from the Grigoric library lifted from between the shelves and flew to Argoth, landing gently on his waiting palm. He spread the scroll before Enoch on a table and spoke.

"El hast prophesied to the King of Tyrus, and Isaiah, a man servant of the most high God, hath recorded it. Read and learn."

Enoch sat at the table and read the scroll taken from Isaiah, and the words were written on this wise.

Moreover, the word of the LORD came unto me, saying, Son of man, take up a lamentation upon the king of Tyrus, and say unto him, Thus saith the Lord GOD; Thou sealest up the sum, full of wisdom, and perfect in beauty.

Thou hast been in Eden, the garden of God. Every precious stone was thy covering, the sardius, topaz, and the diamond, the beryl, the onyx, and the jasper, the sapphire, the emerald, and the carbuncle, and gold. The workmanship of thy tabrets and of thy pipes was prepared in thee in the day that thou wast created.

Thou art the anointed cherub that covereth, and I have set thee so. Thou wast upon the holy mountain of God. Thou hast walked up and down in the midst of the stones of fire.

Thou wast perfect in thy ways from the day that thou wast created, till iniquity was found in thee.

By the multitude of thy merchandise, they have filled the midst of thee with violence, and thou hast sinned. Therefore I will cast thee as profane out of the mountain of God, and I will destroy thee, O covering cherub, from the midst of the stones of fire.

Thine heart was lifted up because of thy beauty. Thou hast corrupted thy wisdom by reason of thy brightness. I will cast thee to the ground. I will lay thee before kings, that they may behold thee.

Thou hast defiled thy sanctuaries by the multitude of thine iniquities, by the iniquity of thy traffick, therefore will I bring forth a fire from the midst of thee. It shall devour thee, and I will bring thee to ashes upon the earth in the sight of all them that behold thee. All they that know thee among the people shall be astonished at thee. Thou shalt be a terror, and never shalt thou be anymore.

Enoch closed the book and stared at the pages for a moment, then glanced up at Argoth who waited for him to speak. "I do not understand," Enoch said. "Does the prophet speak of the king of Tyrus or another? For how can the King be the covering cherub? Nor hath this man been in the Garden of Eden, nor seen the Mountain of God. Of whom then does the prophet speak?"

"Is the answer so far removed from thee? There is but one who even now is adversary to the Kingdom of Heaven."

"Lucifer?"

Argoth nodded. "There is much, Adamson, that is untold of Lucifer's fall, for he trafficked in pride and merchandised in haughtiness until it created a schism between the celestial hosts, for none in his mind were greater in station or in beauty than he. If he was ever challenged, he was quick to bring low an adversary whose brightness might eclipse his own. Therefore, learn Adamson the tale of the Seraphim. For long ago, before the age of man, when creation was still in its infancy and light was called forth from the mouth of Almighty God, we watched the Lord God speak the realms into existence. We beheld in fascination and awe as El placed the ceiling of creation.

Yet while El fashioned your world, and brought creation into existence, we populated Heaven and built what thou dost see as a gift for El, to be presented when He completed creation. And whilst the Lord worked, Lucifer traveled to the high place of Aesir, the seat of the Seraphim.

"The Seraphim were a mighty race, gifted in the properties of sound and fashioned the most beautiful of instruments. They helped build the temple, you see. It was they who, before the Kortai, carved the palace and glittered Heaven's streets with gold. And of all creation, it was they who El let release music, worship, and praise into the realms, and lo, when Lucifer saw that El had not given to him beauty and praise alone, when he heard that trumpets and cornet gave sound to music that eclipsed even his own, he made a wager with Nephanos, King of the Seraphim.

"Here the seeds of temptation could be seen, but were not understood by our kind. Here Lucifer learned the ways of barter and cunning, for he wagered with Nephanos a wager of whom could eclipse the other in song. Nephanos, intrigued by the proposition that any other than his own people could surpass them in sound, commanded his people to craft a Psalm of Psalms. A ballad that would be the greatest hymn Heaven had ever known; and thus a song was crafted among the Seraphim and Angels to see who among our kind could give rise to lift all of Heaven in praise. An audition given to determine who would be Heaven's choir master and herald to El's presence, a wager that would determine whom would live in the Holy City."

"And the loser?" Enoch asked.

Argoth continued, "The loser would stand at the posts of the temple and bellow annunciation of God's holiness. Fated to shout forever and banished to live both behind and underneath the basement of Heaven. A race forever called to be as an eternal echo and a reminder of who was the greatest in Heaven.

"Thus, both Seraphim and Angels rehearsed. We were confident that we were supreme among all in worship to El. Whilst the Seraphim boasted that none could compare to them, the Ophanim stood to bear as a witness of our squabbling and were content to abide in the calling wherein they had been called. They watched as Angel and Seraphim sported in hubris.

"But Lucifer was full of guile, and neither rehearsed nor practiced but instead bartered with Camael, one of the chief Seraphim, who was adept in the construction of all manner of musical instruments and bedazzled him with light. For the Seraphim were the burning ones and were not covered in the precious gems which adorned our kind. Therefore, Lucifer took from his own flesh each of the ten gemstones which were from his skin and one thing other."

"What was it?" Enoch said.

"A Stone of Fire. In exchange for seven trumpets crafted by the Seraphim. Camael became so enamored by the gemstones' colors of light and despised his gift of sound. Coveting the gifts of light, he agreed, and an exchange of light was given in exchange for sound.

"And when time had arrived to sing, all of Heaven assembled before the mountain of God, and song was risen to El while He worked. The Seraphim's music was magnificent. Glorious. Superb. The three great races of Heaven, Ophanim, Elohim, and Seraphim, were as one. All lifted up El as was purposed. All except one person."

"Lucifer?" Enoch said.

"Aye, Lucifer," replied Argoth. "Lucifer stood laughing at all of Heaven, and everyone stopped to discover why in the whole of Heaven one angel would not sing to his master's glory. And Lucifer's words were recorded on this wise.

'What I hear is but wails,' Lucifer laughed. 'Echoes and clanging of screeches before my ears.' Lucifer then turned to Eladrin and spoke, 'Hath you Eladrin determined who amongst us is greatest in song among the Host?'

Argoth continued, "Eladrin, who in his wisdom sought to not pit brother against brother answered, 'Nay, for all of Heaven is sweet to our ears.'"

"Lucifer replied, 'Then let Heaven be silent and hear me, and let none ever compare me, nor my people to another in glory or beauty.'

"Lucifer then took the seven trumpets he had obtained from Camael, and added them to his own. When he opened his mouth to sing, none could resist the majestic sounds that sprung forth from his body. His light was as the stars that move across the golden ceiling of Heaven, and rainbows and hues of every color skipped about his body. As he played, his song enraptured even the Seraphim, for he was privy to their own instruments of worship, and the light from his skin and the tabrets and harps made everyone sway. All were bedazzled by the brightness of his glory, and his melody was sweet to every ear. Thus, when Lucifer was done, he had won all of Heaven over. Eladrin reluctantly named him the victor.

"The Seraphim were wroth for Camael had betrayed their cause and trafficked sound for light and trinkets for his birthright. Thus, Nephanos ordered his people away from the realm of Jerusalem, as agreed, forever hidden behind the veil of sound. The king then appointed four to never leave the temple they had carved for El and to forever pronounce his holiness. They would serve forever as a reminder that the Seraphim sang honorably, yet angel-kind had trafficked in collusion to obtain gain, so the whole of the Seraphim then disappeared beneath the mountain and have not since been seen.

"Therefore, those four roar HOLY, HOLY, HOLY as a reminder that one may never enter the presence of God with duplicity nor guile. To honor one's word and a reminder to all of El's majesty.

"And when the Godhead had completed their work on the second day, El returned to see that one of His creations was not present to celebrate and He asked His sons what was it that they talked about whilst he was away. All held their peace, knowing they had contested over who would be the greatest and that Lucifer had caused strife among his brethren over who might be first.

"Therefore, the Lord took the seven trumpets Lucifer had received in trade and cursed them. He returned them to the Seraphim and honored their wish to remain behind the veil until offense had been forgiven, with warning that on the day that they and the trumpets next entered His sight, He would, with the seven trumpets merchandised, unleash His wrath upon the works of His son.

"El then lifted the Ophanim above the skies and marked them to control the times and seasons, and to come when bidden. Giving them order to guard the mountain that the Seraphim gifted Him, and forbade angel-kind to ascend to the upper reaches of Heaven, nor could any, save the Lumazi, enter the mountain of God unless summoned that He might keep the way to the door of the Seraphim's land. Thus, God separated the three, and marked their boundaries, and set us as Grigori to watch our brethren until the end. For it is written in the annals of our people, that when Jerusalem falls from Heaven, there shall be no more schism between the Heavens, and El will have all worship at His feet as one."

"And the stone of fire?" Enoch said.

"El let Nephanos keep the stone as a reminder that to traffic in wisdom apart from El brings consequence. A memorial to understand what doth it profit to gain the whole of Heaven, yet lose one's purpose, and to never acquire in the flesh what should only be attempted at the Lord's will. God then made Nephanos a crown and attached the stone to it as a diadem. He withdrew from it all power so that it became nothing more than a glittering trinket, a reminder to never sacrifice one's birthright."

Enoch fell into a chair stunned, his eyes repeatedly blinking as he rubbed his forehead, attempting to take in all that was told him.

Argoth looked at him as the seconds passed. "Of a surety, Michael would not be pleased if he knew I shared our past with thee."

Enoch looked at Argoth and replied, "I have learned that thy people have a saying...'There is nothing covered that shall not be revealed, neither hid that shall not be made known.' I perceive that God would have me journey. Now I realize there is little that thy people can still teach me."

Argoth blushed in anger, "Dost thou think because thou hast knowledge of my people in this way that you are above instruction? Hast thy knowledge of our past puffed thee up?"

Enoch stood up to leave and for a moment did not answer. He paused as he approached the library doors and turned to speak over his shoulder. "Pride does not animate my words, Chief of Eyes. For I see that I have abased myself beyond measure, for angels are truly more powerful, and the gifts and knowledge thou possess are indeed beyond my own, yet in this one thing are we the same. You are not immune to pride nor foolishness. In this, your people and my own are no different. For I perceive that all have the choice to be self-ruled or ruled by the God I serve. Positions are meaningless when thy very breath is a gift from the Almighty. In this, thy people have lacked understanding...in this, thou hast erred, for thy proximity to God hath blinded thee to think thou art superior, yea even to one another. Yet all of us are nothing more than the benevolent thoughts of our King. Your people do not know this. My people will teach you this."

Argoth stood speechless and watched Enoch exit the room.

Chapter Three: Complicity

Iblis paced his room and felt his faculties diminishing. Erratic thoughts raced through his mind. He could feel the encroachment of the Withering eat at him. He had seen it before. The slow demise of rational thought. The inability to focus. He thought himself immune to its effects but realized that was not so. He pulled his hands from his robes to view them. The tremors were more pronounced now. He quickly tucked them back into his robes.

Only a little while longer, he thought. I only need to hold on until El heals me. Surely He will see my works of repentance and bring relief.

Iblis paced back and forth in his room. Was Heaven aware that he carried the Withering? He remembered how it affected his master, Marduk, and how it had driven the principality mad. His powers and faculties caused him to drive Babylon into superstition and magic. Even Lucifer had to take pause and send Zeus to curtail his grossness, lest he draw the ire of Heaven, but it was too late. Babylon was no more, and the nation that Lucifer used to destroy Israel was obliterated by El's wrath. For Babylon was broken against Grecia, and Marduk had fled into hiding.

A "click" sound came from the cell door and Iblis stopped in his ruminations. "Ahh dinner," he said.

Two guards entered. One held a key and a chain while the other entered the room with a tray of manna leaf and warmed shill, a type of sweetened water.

"I am famished. It is amazing to me that you are so faithful in your duties. I thank you."

The guard with the tray placed it on the desk in the room and spoke, "Do not speak to me, traitor. If I had my way, I would run you through with my sword."

Iblis looked upon him with surprise and frowned in offense. "Me? Traitor? Have you not heard of the information that I have shared with Michael and the Lumazi about Lucifer's schemes?" Iblis walked towards the guards with open arms gesturing for an embrace.

The solider backed away warily. "Do not presume to touch me unless you care to join your brothers in oblivion."

Iblis stopped, smiled, and then proceeded to return to his table to eat his meal.

The guard also turned and started to cough. He covered his mouth, surprised that he found himself coughing even the more. He looked upon Iblis, scowled, and walked past his partner, hacking. His comrade closed the door and locked it behind him.

Iblis sat down to eat his plate of manna leaf, listening to a guard outside his door asking the other if he was alright. Still chewing his food, he glanced to where the tray wielding guard had started hacking and noticed specks of blue blood on the floor. He paused, then continued to chew his food, and spoke aloud with food in his mouth. "You really ought to have someone take a look at that cough."

A hard "BANG" slammed against the door as though someone had pounded their fist against it.

Iblis smiled at his own wit and continued smacking on his food.

* * *

Enoch walked into the war room where Michael, Metatron, Gabriel, and Azaziel conferred with one another. He did not abide by protocol or excuse himself for interrupting. "Chief Prince, I would have words with thee," he said.

All looked at him and then looked at Michael.

Michael replied. "We are in session, Enoch. Please wait for us to adjourn and I shall see to thee then." Michael then went back to speaking to his brethren, expecting Enoch to leave.

Enoch walked further into the room and stood at the head of the table opposite him. "No, Michael. I would speak to thee now."

Michael rolled his eyes.

Enoch, seeing his agitation spoke, "Of course, I could take my cause directly to El before I leave for the land of the Seraphim to retrieve the other man who now resides in Heaven. However, I would very much like to speak to thee first to know what possible dangers I might encounter as I cross Limbo underneath the mountain."

Michael looked at his brethren.

Gabriel nodded to Metatron and spoke. "The Candlestick of the Lord seeks the mind of the Chief Prince. We will resume at thy convenience, Michael."

Both Metatron and Gabriel rose and excused themselves while Gabriel closed the door to allow for the duo's privacy.

"Enoch, it is not protocol to disrupt the Lumazi when we are in session. Hath not Argoth taught thee anyth..."

Enoch interrupted him. "At this moment, Michael, your protocols do not interest me. What I am interested in is knowing where were you when Lucifer trafficked with Nephanos and tricked him. I know what Lucifer did. I want to know if you knew what Lucifer did?"

Michael was silent, caught off guard by Enoch's knowledge. He paced with bowed head and closed eyes to reflect on events long past. His brow furrowed, and still he did not look Enoch in the eye.

Enoch studied his body language, then sighed. "Your silence speaks. It would seem Argoth is not the only one with secrets. Very well, Chief Prince, keep thy secrets to thyself but beware that thy sin will find you out. Know that I am given a word from El and that I am to retrieve a man residing in Heaven and bring him to you. For what cause, I do not know, but El's word is as a fire shut up in my bones, and I am moved at the command of our God. You will help me in this thing as I will need a guide to journey with me."

Michael then raised his head and looked at Enoch. His eyes grew wide in questioning wonderment. "El hath given order to visit Nephanos? I have not seen him sinc..."

"Since the Schism, yes, I know. Thy history hath shown me that not once, but twice, thy brother hath been instrumental in sowing discord among the brethren."

Michael shook his head. "You do not understand, Enoch, for a brother offended is harder to be won than a strong city, and their contentions are like the bars of a castle."

"What I know, Michael, is that war exists. That Talus lies either dead or a prisoner of war. What I know is that you hold prisoner an enemy of the crown, and why, pray tell, wouldst thou bring a member of the fallen to Heaven if you will not follow through with what is in thy mind? I perceive that El desires reconciliation, not retribution, and He moves towards the restoration of all things. For even now, Yeshua moves within the Earth to accomplish this, and I but follow the example of our King, who at this moment wrestles against the darkness in human flesh. Battling to undo the acts of thy brother, for is it not for this purpose that the Son of God hast manifested that He might destroy the works of the Devil? You are the head of thy people. Go to Nephanos. Confess this great sin against his people and bring healing to both thy people for I have studied thy forces. Although you outnumber Lucifer, he controls such principalities and powers as to put the legions of Heaven in stalemate. Would not the Ophanim and Seraphim be his undoing if all united?"

Michael shook his head as his face contorted in uncertainty. "Enoch, the Ophanim sit atop the mountain and do not interfere in the causes of angel-kind. And the Seraphim..."

Enoch cut him off. "El was wise to separate thee and diminish the root of bitterness thy actions have caused. To leave the contagion that He had foreseen, to just your people alone. For I can but imagine what might have been unleashed if Lucifer snared both the Seraphim and the Ophanim in his cause.

"You hide behind protocol and are stymied in thy attention to El's commands. Thou, who has resided within His presence from the foundation of my world, yet for all thy might and knowledge you have zeal, but not according to knowledge. El hath not made me a candlestick for only my people, but also as a flickering light even to thee. I will do what thou are want to do, and will seek reconciliation between thy people. I will also do what I am bidden and bring Elijah as commanded. You will help me in this thing or you will not. But the word of the Lord shall abide forever."

Michael sighed. "I cannot go to the land of Aseir. It is forbidden. Yet this one thing I will do to aid thee: I will send Gabriel and Metatron as an escort. Gabriel will hopefully be received, for he is both Malakim and mouthpiece as the oracle of God. Metatron might serve as an ambassador of the Draco whose House was cause to the Schism. Wilt this suffice?" Michael then began to cough as though something were lodged in his throat.

Enoch turned and said, "It will do." And he left the Chief Prince who continued to cough uncontrollably.

Michael covered his mouth, and when he removed his hand from his mouth, specks of blood covered his palms.

* * *

Enoch left the mountain of God and entered the stables of the Malakim gryphons.

Gabriel stood grooming one of the steeds. Each creature was covered in golden feathers, part eagle, part lion. Their great wings spanned over twenty hand-breadths. Iron-like beaks could rip through steel. When fully armored, terror filled the eyes of combatants, whether angelic or human.

Enoch reached for a pouch of Cora leaf, and with an open hand, fed it to the creature that Gabriel groomed. As it ate, Enoch slowly began to stroke its mane.

Magnificent, is he not?" Gabriel said.

"He is indeed a marvel of bone and sinew. From whence do they come, and how are they tamed by your people?"

"When Heaven was young, El gave us dominion. The gryphons live in the land of Aesir with the Seraphim. Nathaniel, of the house Malakim, was first to encounter the great gryphon, Cabal. Nathaniel tried to tame him, but without success. Then one day, Nathaniel fell near the cliffs into the Abyss. Cabal saw him and braved the Abyssal winds and swept him from its clutches. The two immediately established a bond. We have since learned that they are intelligent beyond measure, and Cabal was so taken at Nathaniel's attempts to tame him, that he allowed him to ride him. Since then, all messengers use them as steeds to communicate to the rest of the realm. All messengers are sent with a gryphon by their side. And when summoned by this horn created by one of the greatest artisans of the Seraphim, they all will return to the spot of summoning."

Enoch continued to stroke the soft mane of the beast and it cooed at his touch. He turned to Gabriel. "Do you know why I have come?"

"We have not had the opportunity to get to know one another since your arrival in Heaven, but thy words are open to my ears. No, I do not know why you are here, but if thy request is within my power to grant, it shall be yours."

Surprised at Gabriel's response, Enoch said, "Thou dost not know my request and yet thou dost answer so?"

"Knowledge is not needed to give an answer as I only need know the one who makes the request. El hast personally lifted you on high and hast brought you into His presence. I have been told that you have withstood Death face to face, and that you have traveled without fear to the top of the Mountain of God and witnessed Michael's trials to become Chief Prince. But most of all, Candle of God, you are the friend of God, and thus a friend to me. How may the house of Malakim serve thee?"

Enoch paused, somewhat stunned at the accolade. "You give me great honor, High Prince. Are you aware that a second man resides in the realm of Heaven?"

Gabriel looked at him with surprise. "Really? No, the chief prince hath not made this thing known. Who...how didst you come to such knowledge?"

"The Lord, Himself, revealed it. The second man does not reside in the city."

"Where then does the man lay his head?"

Enoch paused, then replied, "The word of the Lord hast come to me, and I am to embark through Limbo and travel to the land of Aesir. I would ask that you travel with me."

Gabriel's eyes widened, and his face quickly sobered. "There is little in the universe that would cause an angel fear. Limbo is such a place." Gabriel paused, and Enoch waited. Gabriel's eyes followed his strokes as he brushed the gryphon. "Nevertheless, if my companionship is needful, then I shall see thee safe to the shores of Aesir."

Enoch bowed. "You hast my thanks, Gabriel. There is yet another I must ask to make the journey with us."

Gabriel nodded. "That is wise. A threefold cord is not quickly broken. Who will you ask to make the journey with us?"

"Metatron of house Draco. I intend to move in the ministry of reconciliation between the house of Lucifer and the Seraphim. Perhaps with Metatron as head of his house, the Burning Ones will accept us?"

Gabriel stroked his chin. "Perhaps...or they might remember the house that was responsible for the Schism and destroy us, and this mission could be for naught."

"Are you always this positive?" Enoch replied.

Gabriel laughed. "Nay, but I must admit Jerahmeel has perhaps rubbed off on me."

Enoch smiled. "I think he has, but before I leave thee, I have yet another question."

"Say on."

"The Lord hath made mention that the Withering comes. What is it?"

Gabriel dropped the grooming brush and grabbed Enoch by his shoulders. "Are you sure that the Lord mentioned this?"

"Aye," said Enoch.

Gabriel frowned and his face turned hard. He turned from Enoch and strode away in long steps.

"Wait!" Enoch said. "What is wrong? What is it? What is the Withering?"

Gabriel stopped and turned to face him. "It is the plague, and it is Death."

Chapter Four: The Withering

Asb'el loved the freedom to destroy. For five years now he had made his home within a human host named Jabin, and seeing that mankind was rife with sin, the laws of Heaven opened Jabin to the evil of the Horde. So Asb'el invited others to take up residence within the house. And the daemon became great in the country of the Gadarenes and made his host live amongst the tombs.

Asb'el reveled in the sensations he could experience through Jabin and continuously tormented him.

Jabin knew something alien lived within. Wishing to rid himself from the presence that spoke to his mind, he cut himself with stones in vain attempts that he might silence the voices and block the images in his head that the creatures gave him. Jabin beheld visions of Heaven and Hell, and great battles between creatures of power. All screamed for relief, for their kilnstones were taken away and they lamented over their bodiless forms, always hungry, always lusting for expression in the earth.

They showed him the centuries of human sacrifice and debauchery in continual bombardment. For years did they do this thing, until Jabin was finally driven mad. In vain, he tried to tell family and friends and reached out in an attempt to make them understand. With ink and scrolls, he drew pictures of his visions and each picture pointed to a skeletal mare of a creature that the whisperers in his mind called Charon and an angelic renegade by the name of Lucifer. Thus, Jabin screamed, his mind held captive by beings he could not understand. Screams of their plight woke him in the night, and visions of unearthly creatures plagued him throughout the day. His mind held hostage to memories that were not his own.

When Jabin happened upon the locals, voices told him every evil deed they had done, every hidden secret, and the madman spoke with a tongue not his own, and he screamed men's secret sins as they neared him. Thus, Jabin became a man shunned and marked as a witch.

Despite the attempts of family and friends to help, they had reached their capacity to support him. In desperation, they drove him away.

He found himself a home among the buried dead. Only in the midst of dead men's graves did he find some solace, but the voices continued even there and thus he screamed nightly among the tombs.

His family, still hoping to help, came with men who scarcely managed to hold him down and bind him with fetters and chains. Because the spirits within him were too strong, he broke asunder his bonds at every opportunity. Thus, no man could tame him.

Jabin wailed in the nights, naked, running as a wild animal, cutting himself in vain attempts to loose himself from the possession of beings from another realm. He nearly surrendered to the despair that enveloped him during the imposed yoke of madness. For on occasion, the creatures would mention another name. Not just Lucifer. But a name of a man.

A man by the name of Yeshua.

And the daemons feared him.

Jabin slowly pieced together that this man could help him and release him from slavery to the unseen.

In the course of time, the whispers mentioned that Yeshua was near, performing miracles of healing.

Jabin, seeing means to escape, ran from the tombs screaming, fighting with each breath to escape the voices that lived within his mind. He clawed his way through the crowd that surrounded Yeshua.

Each step, the daemons begged him to abstain from the man's presence.

His heart beat in his chest heavy, as the voices bribed him with power, and sex, and all that his heart desired. But Jabin continued his journey and was seen by the townsfolk running naked, renouncing anything in his heart that would in the past, present or future, keep him from the salvation that would free him from his mental slavery.

Howling in desperation and struggling in a mental civil war to find the one person that might bring relief, he pushed men, women and children out of his way. Many turned to see him and fell back in terror until at last, Jabin fell to the ground at Yehsua's feet and worshiped Him.

Struggling against Jabin's will, the first of the daemons that held Jabin under his sway, cried aloud to the Son of God. "What have I to do with thee, Yeshua, thou Son of the most high God? I adjure thee by God, that thou torment me not."

Then Yeshua said unto him, "Come out of the man, thou unclean spirit." And He asked him, "What is thy name?"

And they answered, saying, "My name is Legion: for we are many."

The daemons besought Him much that He would not send them away out of the country. Now near the mountains, a great herd of swine were feeding. And all the daemons begged him, saying, "Send us into the swine, that we may enter into them."

Yeshua then gave them leave, and the unclean spirits went out and entered into the swine. The herd of about two thousand ran violently down a steep place and were choked in the sea. The men who had been given charge to feed the swine fled. They told it in the city, and in the country, and many went out to see what was done. Many then came to Yeshua and saw him that was possessed with the daemons and had the legion. Jabin was sitting and clothed, in his right mind, and they were afraid.

And they that saw it told them how it befell to him that was possessed with the devil, and also concerning the swine. And they began to pray Yeshua to depart out of their coasts. And when He came into the ship, Jabin who had been possessed with the daemons, prayed Him that he might be with him. Howbeit, Yeshua suffered him not, but saith unto him, "Go home to thy friends, and tell them how great things the Lord hath done for thee and hath had compassion on thee."

Jabin then departed and began to publish in Decapolis the many great things Yeshua had done for him, and all men did marvel.

Azaziel stood aloof from the commotion of Yeshua's miracle of deliverance. The continuing effect of which was no longer visible to the men who saw the swine plunge over the cliffs. Men, who with human eyes, could not see the entities that to his own vision were crystal clear.

The prince of all Issi watched as Asb'el and the indwelling daemon that had entered the swine reveled in the sensation of the animal's broken limbs and splattered entrails that painted the floor of the precipice. Azaziel stared as disembodied members of the Fallen exulted in the swine's death throes. Watched as each daemon screeched in an intoxicated orgasmic frenzy, contorting the animals for their sadistic pleasure, all that they might find expression through a host to feel sensation again.

Azaziel and his soldiers watched as the Withering made their once mighty brethren, now shadows of their former selves, degenerate further into madness.

* * *

Lucifer stood before Talus as he hung, suspended in a lattice of flames that burned but did not consume.

Talus's eyes fluttered and opened to see his brother smiling at him.

"Good morning," Lucifer said. "I trust you slept well?"

Talus, still groggy from slumber and torture, noticed he hung naked by arms and legs, dangling before his captor.

A servant came and set a chair and table upon the flesh eating floor. He set a goblet of water before his Lord, bowed and departed.

Lucifer took the chalice, poured water into the goblet and proceeded to put it to his lips. He paused, then looked at Talus and spoke. "Thirsty?"

Talus looked at the goblet, then back at his brother. The skin of his lips cracked and peeled, and instinctively he licked them. He nodded.

"Yes. I would imagine that you are. Well, let us move on, shall we?"

Talus sighed in exasperation. "I told you all that I know."

"Yes, I am sure that you have," Lucifer replied. He then waved his hand, and four lights materialized in the air and hovered above Talus, each one gleaming as small pulsating, twinkling stars, blinking on and off.

Talus's pupils adjusted to the brightness of the now lit cavern. He squinted in vain attempts to shield his eyes from the glare.

"Tell me," Lucifer said, "how many lights do you see?"

Talus paused, then replied, "There are four lights."

"No. There are five lights." Satan smirked and took another swig of water and continued. "You should know that whilst you were in slumber, I commanded Hell to embed several of her maggots within your chest. Please feel free to take a look for yourself."

Talus glanced down at his chest cavity and could see the outline of the maggots moving within him. "The Lord rebuke you Lucifer!" he said.

Lucifer turned his back to him and poured himself water. He held the clear goblet high to admire the waters' thirst quenching properties. "Because I am the god of this world and command both Death and Hell, she will, at my desire, release her pets to feed upon you. My observation over the centuries hast shown me that their digestion of their host is a most remarkable sight. My apologies but a demonstration will give you greater clarity." Lucifer nodded.

Talus immediately screamed, collapsing to the ground in writhing pain as the maggot infestation gnawed on his innards.

Lucifer then lifted his hand to command Hell to stop, and the maggots ceased in their digestion.

Talus panted heavily as he squirmed on the floor, recovering from the sensation of being eaten alive.

Lucifer grinned and the light sparkled off his skin. "Amazing, is it not? Most think they can steel themselves against it, but they are totally unprepared for the intensity of the pain. Do not think me cruel, for are they not the creation of the God you serve? And look at you now, writhing in agony before me. Pity. What God would devise such a creature, that it would consume its host alive? And yet there you lay, still faithful to Him. Pathetic."

Talus spoke in anguish and frustration, "What do you want from me? I told you that our mission was to secure Iblis."

"Oh, I believe you," replied Satan. "Yet I did not ask you about your mission. I asked you how many lights do you see?"

Talus looked at the hovering four orbs above him and replied. "I told you that there are four lights."

Lucifer frowned and shook his head in feigned confusion, "It amazes me that you could be so mistaken."

The King of Lies then nodded toward Hell, and Talus fell over backward, wracked in blistering pain as maggots squirmed within him, gnawing at the celestial tissue that comprised the internal organs of his body.

Lucifer smiled and nodded approvingly while his brother writhed before him and coated the cavern with screams.

* * *

Xcivicus ran to the chambers of meeting with the Lumazi and barged into the war room where Michael was said to be. He bowed upon entry and spoke to the Prince of Angels. "My lord, there is wickedness in the realm," he said between pants. "Five of those who guarded Iblis have been overcome with an illness similar to that which plagues the Fallen. Rumors say the disease that afflicts the Horde now roams in Heaven."

Michael stood to his feet and looked upon his lieutenant, coughing. "I, too, have felt unease and stabs of coughing fits. What are the signs that a plague runs among us?"

Xcivicus answered. "Chills, vomiting, and headache, but it also affects thoughts until they become erratic."

"Erratic?" Michael said. "Explain."

"One guard speaks incoherently, my lord, and cuts himself as if to ward off some unseen evil."

Jerahmeel and Gabriel stepped into the room, overhearing the last portion of the conversation.

Gabriel spoke ominously, "The Withering has come."

"Impossible," Michael said with authority.

"Not impossible," Jerahmeel said. "But made possible by thy decision to allow a member of the Fallen to return to the realm. You have exposed us all to contamination."

Michael guffawed. "Our kind visits the planet at will. We have never been affected by the Withering before, so why now? Argoth's people have surmised that the Fallen are afflicted because of self-rule and the disfiguring of their stones."

Jerahmeel replied, "The thing you say is true. Yet we have always traversed Earth under the authority of El. Perhaps His protection kept the thing at bay," Jerahmeel said, then walked up to Michael and grabbed him by his robes. "By bringing Iblis to Heaven outside the authorization of El, you hath exposed us all to ruin! Thou hast rejected God in pursuit of that which seemeth good unto thee." Jerahmeel released Michael with a shove and walked away in disgust. "Come with me, Xcivicus. We must find means to attend to the people."

Xcivicus bowed and followed Jerahmeel as ordered, leaving Gabriel and Michael alone.

Michael slumped down in a chair and placed his hand over his head. He sighed, "Jerahmeel might be right in this thing. Perhaps bringing Iblis to Heaven's shores was not the best of tactics."

Gabriel stood next to his brother and placed his hand gently on his shoulder and answered in reply, "Jerahmeel is often right in his assessments. Nevertheless, you speak aloud to a brother, friend, and one who hath been commanded to follow thee. Would not your query best be laid where it hast always belonged?"

Michael sighed. "The thing you say is true. I will meet with El and receive instruction." Michael's face became increasingly pale as he coughed up blood.

Gabriel backed away. "The Withering affects the Chief Prince. How might your servant assist?"

"Hath Enoch approached thee regarding his journey to Aseir?"

"Yes. The thing is as you say," said Gabriel.

"Then go with him, brother, I assign both thee and Metatron in this thing."

Gabriel nodded, "And my orders?"

Michael coughed the more. "Take Enoch safely to the land of Aseir. He says word hath come from El to heal the Schism between our peoples. Do all that is in thy power to bring this vision to pass. Are you clear in your purpose?"

Gabriel nodded, "I am clear." Gabriel turned to leave then paused to speak to his brother. "And what of you Michael? What will you do?"

Michael sighed. "I must see God and give report of my stewardship."

* * *

Enoch met Argoth in his study, his satchel packed to travel underneath the mountain. "You summoned me Argoth?"

"Aye. Please come in."

Enoch sat down. Books lined the desk between them. Argoth opened a tome, and a picture of the Zoa materialized on the page.

"Michael commanded me to share all we know of the realm under the mountain. We are Grigori, and I am Chief of Eyes. There is much in creation that we know and little that we do not, for it is the glory of a king to conceal a thing, but the honor of kings is to search out a matter. El grants us the privilege to search the deep things that He allows us to see. Know this...Limbo is not one of those things. We have often wondered why the Zoa are here within the mount. They live in no such place in all of Heaven nor Earth, but they may be in Limbo. This realm we do not know. It was created before Elohim traveled the stars, for even as thy people were last in creation, so too were my people created last in the celestial realm.

"We know there are souls trapped within the confines of Limbo. Corlus, the first of our kind to be taken in murder, was mentioned by El Himself, as crying from within. Who knows the countless others who may have been consigned to the realm? El does not speak of it. Nor shares His mind on the matter. He hath said the faithful will be restored. Therefore, I believe that I shall see Raphael and many of my brothers in the age to come, but today is not that day. Therefore, take heed to thyself."

Enoch nodded. "I will, my friend. I thank you for your guidance and tutelage. I trust it will be enough in the days ahead."

Argoth smiled and also bowed. "We...I have been contaminated by pride. It is a subtle thing and requires humility of spirit and vigilance to keep at bay. I am beginning to perceive the wisdom of God in allowing you to come here for you are not constrained by the dogma of our kind, neither hindered by our ideas of protocol.

"Go to, as thou hast said, for God has commanded thee, and seek out the Seraphim. Let not our pride be our undoing, for our fates are tied together. Bring relief to the Kingdom."

Enoch's face became as steel and his voice broke with concern. "I will do this thing, but alas, I cannot go alone. There must be one who can come with me."

Argoth waved his hand, and behind Enoch, Hadriel appeared. "Behold, I have assigned thee a Grigori for thy journey, but he can only record and may not interfere. For though the Seraph do not look fondly on our kind, they will do no harm to a Grigori, for they do not interfere in the affairs of others."

Enoch turned to walk away, then spoke aloud over his shoulder for Argoth to hear. "I am afraid that interference is exactly what I will need." Enoch left the room and closed the door behind him.

Chapter Five: Freedom is Not Free

Michael walked to the study of Jerahmeel and knocked on the door.

"Come in," came the gruff reply.

Michael gingerly opened the door and poked his head inside. Jerahmeel looked up and stood at attention when he saw Michael peer into the room.

"My Prince?" Jerahmeel said.

Michael waved Jerahmeel to be seated. "I am come to discuss the situation of Iblis and Talus."

Jerahmeel remained standing. "I am anxious to mount a rescue mission immediately. I have consulted with Argoth, and our intelligence seems to indicate that he is deep within the creature. Possibly somewhere near the bowels of the giant itself."

Michael lowered his head. "Talus is that which I wish to speak of."

Jerahmeel looked upon his brother. "Wonderful, with thy permission I will take Iblis and two others and mount a rescue mission. Iblis will no doubt have knowledge of the realm beyond what Argoth's scouts can tell us. For since Hell's overturn by Lucifer, we have lost sight of its internal mappings and growth. It is my intention, therefore, to also take one of the redactors. Argoth believes he can remap the creature and monitor things from the Hall of Annals and will compare our journey to the last known coordinates we have of the creature's system."

Michael looked away from Jerahmeel. "I see," he said.

Jerahmeel's eyes narrowed and he studied Michael. "How soon am I given leave to return?"

Michael sighed. "I grant thee leave for Hell with all those requested, but thy mission will not be to rescue our brother."

Jerahmeel's eyes widened in appeal, "But, Michael, we have actionable information that might allow us to bring him home. Wouldst thou leave him in the clutches of the enemy? Hath my brother grown so cold in command that the Host are but trinkets to be moved about on game boards of skill?"

Michael immediately recoiled and spoke, "How dare you impugn mine honor to think my love of Talus waxes cold. Did I not seek a volunteer to misdirect Lucifer, and to seek out Chronos? Was it I who held his hand aloft to undertake so dangerous a mission? And who accompanied our brother that he returned alone? The report of both he and his Grigori are silent to Argoth. Tell me, Lord of House Harrada, did Talus not save thy life? Did he not allow himself to be taken that ye might live?"

Jerahmeel bowed his head. "I am shamed. I meant no disrespect. I...I am simply concerned about the welfare of our brother. I seek but the authority to see the thing through."

Michael walked over to Jerahmeel and placed his hands on his shoulder and sighed. "I miss him, too, but we are Lumazi. Our first order is to God, then to the people of the realm. To this end, we cannot allow ourselves to succumb to desires of self-rule. Therefore, leave quickly and take those whom would assist thee, but rescuing Talus shall not be thy cause. Thou wilt search the bowels of the creature, Hell...not to rescue, but to destroy."

Jerahmeel replied, "Do you aim to destroy the Hellforge that Iblis made mention of?"

"Aye," replied Michael. "Lucifer cannot be allowed to create a kiln. Iblis has told me that he has taken the residue of my people's stones of fire along with others that have surrendered themselves to him and hath created a cache of weapons and monstrosities that will, in time, rival us in number. We have seen that his plan to blend mankind's blood with our own to create abomination hast incurred the direct wrath of God. Have we not even seen El, Himself, leave to battle Lucifer in the realm of men in flesh? We cannot rescue Talus whilst the threat of a kiln exists. I did not destroy the womb of our birth to see our brother ignite another war against us. Until we can secure the Hellforge, nothing...not even the rescue of our brother, can stand in the way of this task. Are you clear in your purpose?"

Jerahmeel turned his back to his brother and groaned, "You ask a hard thing, but the Lord of House Harrada is clear in his purpose. It shall be done as thou hast commanded. But tell me..."

Michael looked at his brother in deep intent. "Say on."

"How many more of us will you let see dissolution before you see Lucifer destroyed?"

Michael's eyes grew wide. He frowned and turned to leave, knowing that at that moment, the relationship between him and his brother could not be worse.

* * *

Raziel, head of the Great Library, traveled through the burbs of Jerusalem and arrived at a home that was sealed with the royal clay seal. A seal that could only be broken by the hand of the Lumazi. Anticipating the barrier, Raziel had asked Jerahmeel to meet him at the home of Eskalion. He did not have long to wait, and he bowed in greeting to the Prince of House Harrada.

"My apologies, my Prince, but I saw no choice but to request a member of the Lumazi witness what I suspect."

"Thy report said thou didst believe Eskalion could be healed. That was all I needed to know." Jerahmeel then cracked the seal that was bonded to the door and opened it. "After you, my friend."

"My thanks, High Prince."

The door opened, and light burst into the street and through the windows. Both angels covered their eyes, for standing in the center of the room was the Holy Spirit, and the Shekinah was aglow and lit the interior.

"My King!" Jerahmeel exclaimed. Both he and Raziel immediately knelt in the presence of God.

El Pnuema motioned for them to rise and spoke, "Rise, my children." His voice reverberated as if multitudes were speaking.

Both angels stood to their feet and Jerahmeel was first to respond. "We are here to speak to Eskalion, my King. We apologize for disrupting thy work. We will return at another time."

"Nay, my son. Yet when thou doth journey, thou shalt take Eskalion with thee." A flash of light then ensued, and El Pnuema was gone. The angels shielded their eyes and when they looked again, Eskalion had entered from the back room of his home towards them.

Raziel was first to speak. "Eskalion of House Arelim, thou champion during the war, we know through scrolls that this thing called grief hath befallen thee. I bring to you one of the Lumazi, whom the Holy Spirit hath commanded to speak to thee,"

Eskalion looked upon them in silence. His eyes vacant as if his mind were elsewhere.

Jerahmeel spoke. "Thy valor during the war is known to me and to all of the Lumazi. I am on a mission to strike at the heart of Lucifer's power. He builds a forge deep within the confines of Earth and Hell. It is my charge to destroy this creation."

Eskalion addressed Jerahmeel. "And what of Talus?"

Jerahmeel was taken aback not expecting his brother to come up in conversation.

"I do not understand...what of him?" asked Jerahmeel.

Eskalion walked closer to Jerahmeel and studied his face. "Will you be going to rescue our brother from the Enemy?"

Jerahmeel frowned. "Though it grieves me to say it, I am forbidden to hamper the cause of the Hell-forge's destruction. To secure Heaven's security must take precedence over rescue of our brother. This is the direct order of the Chief Prince."

Eskalion thought on the words of Jerahmeel and spoke, "The Chief Prince is right in his judgment. You cannot sacrifice the destruction of the Hell-forge to save Talus. Yet no such prohibition hinders me. I shall find Talus. This, God by His Spirit hast commanded me, this, God by His Spirit I will do."

Jerahmeel immediately came to realize the provision of the Lord. For Michael had forbidden him to move to rescue Talus, if in doing so, it might weigh against the successful destruction of the Hell-forge. And now Eskalion stood before him, charged by the Lord Himself, to undertake what he could not. Jerahmeel smiled, and whispered, "I thank you, Lord."

Eskalion looked at Raziel, "You have been in continuous ministry to me. You and the Word of the Lord have strengthened me, and I stand returned to wholeness. You have my thanks, Grigori." Eskalion bowed, and Raziel returned his respect in kind.

"It is settled then," said Raziel. "When will you leave Heaven?"

Both Raziel, and Eskalion looked at Jerahmeel, who replied, "As soon as I can muster enough restraint to not choke the life from Iblis."

* * *

Michael approached the throne of God, his spirit heavy. There was a foreboding in every step. Each foot placed before the other was as though weights were fastened to his ankles.

The seven bowls of fire blazed atop the steps of gold and crystal. The Virtues wafted about, and the rainbow that arched over the throne bathed the two Arelim angels in prismatic color as they spread their wings over God, for El was clothed in unapproachable light and sat quietly on the throne.

Michael knelt before his King, his head bowed. "My Lord, I come in consult, for I have returned a member of the Fallen to Heaven. The renegade, Iblis, hath I sanctioned rescue. Rescued, that I perchance might discern Lucifer's plans and curtail his strategy. This I have done without seeking first my King and his righteousness. Three of the Lumazi on missions....one to destroy the false kiln Lucifer seeks to raise within the bowels of Hell itself, and two to accompany Enoch across the expanse of Limbo to see Enoch safely to the shores of Aesir, and to consult with the other human you have brought to Heaven.

"Now my Lord, are these actions to my Lord's will? For wisdom resides in thee and I would not throw away my brethren to failure."

El sat quietly looking at His Son. The brightness of His person receded, and the image of an aged man of many years then stepped down from the throne. God placed his hand under Michael's chin and lifted his head, gently leading him to his feet and spoke.

"A certain man had many sons, but of his household, two stood apart. Both were loved beyond measure, and the glory in store for them was beyond imagination. Nothing would he have withheld from them, yet the older, not willing to abide by his father's will, became angered, and whilst enraged sought means to usurp his father's rule. Judged for his act of betrayal, he was thrown into outer darkness, forever dead to his father. Judged to lament in the wailing and gnashing of teeth."

Michael's eyes darted to the floor as his head nodded, unsure if he truly desired to hear the rest of the story; nevertheless, queried the Lord. "And the other son?"

"The other son," said the Lord. "Was also beloved of his father and was lifted to be first among his house. In self-will, he also sought to obtain through wisdom what could only come from the father, and though well-meaning, his heart was not corrupt. However, he exposed his entire house to ruin. Now, my High Prince, I ask thee, what meaneth this parable, and of whom do I speak?"

Michael's heart was smitten, for he knew that the Lord spoke of him and his brother, Lucifer. He collapsed to his knees and tears surged forth. "It is I, my King, and I am bowed in sorrow. Forgive me, my Lord. In my own wisdom, I have made thy work of none effect. For I have sinned against thee and I beg thy pardon." Michael continued with his head bowed and hands outstretched on the floor. "I beseech thee, Heavenly Father, do away with the iniquity of thy servant for I have done very foolishly."

And the Lord said unto Michael, "Thy sin is forgiven and thy iniquity is removed; nevertheless, thou hast greatly sinned in this thing for thou hast called good that which I hast called evil, thou hast put darkness for light, and light for darkness. And in thine own wisdom, thou hast recalled that which I have exiled. Behold now, the sum of thy choices as thou hast wrought folly and unleashed contagion in the realm. Thy people will suffer greatly because of thine actions."

Michael lifted his hands in an appeal to the Lord and cried out. "My Lord, I beg thee, have mercy, as they are but lambs...sheep who have followed their wayward shepherd."

And the Lord spoke unto Michael, "I cannot turn my face from this thing. For before the people, thou hast wrought folly in obedience to my name. Therefore, I offer three things. Choose thee one of them, that I may do it unto thee. Choose thou either cure of the plague and thy people made whole, but the loss of thine free will, or three months to be destroyed before thy foes, overtaken by the sword of thy enemies, or three days the Withering throughout all the coasts of Heaven. Now, therefore, advise thyself, what word shall I bring to pass in judgment?"

And Michael said unto the Lord, "I am in a great strait. Let me, I pray, fall into the hands of the Lord, for very great are thy mercies, but let me not fall into the hands of Satan, nor would I surrender the Host to be as the beasts of the field."

The Lord nodded his head and replied, "The Chief Prince hath spoken, let the thing then be done."

Immediately, a fog rose from the ground, from the exterior of the mountain of God into the burbs round about the Heavenly city. And the Shekinah that covered the whole of Heaven withdrew to cover naught but the mountain of God. And when the presence of the living God was withdrawn, a dense, greenish, noxious fog saturated the grounds of Heaven.

And the people knew something was wrong, for El's warmth, light and presence could not be felt. Panic slowly ensued, as the last time the environment of Heaven changed, war was not far behind.

Iblis sat in his cell, and his mind grew darker with the retracting of the presence of the Lord. He watched as the color in the very air muted with each passing second. Vibrant and multicolored walls slowly faded in luster and dulled in appearance until the prisoner of war sat quietly and frowned, for he understood what was happening better than most.

The Withering had come.

Chapter Six: "To boldly go..."

Michael ordered his teams to assemble in the Hall of Annals. At his summons, the two groups had come to be dispatched with their final orders.

Argoth looked upon the projecting walls and noted the dense fog that hovered over the ground of Heaven. Angels sought not to touch it because it reeked. The Virtues could be seen round about the mountain but extended no further, and the Seraphim cried out through the mist, HOLY! HOLY! HOLY!

Michael walked into the Hall of Annals and the two assembled teams followed. He paused to view the projections of panic that overtook the people. Most huddled in their homes, not knowing what the fog was or why it rose from the ground.

Argoth motioned to Michael and waved his hands to allow his leader to see the topography of the city of Heaven.

"I have received a report from thy Grigori, Athamas. He says a judgment hath befallen us. I pray El might have mercy upon the people as thou hast asked."

Michael frowned, his face saddened. "We can but hope that these three days will move quickly and restoration will befall us. As of now, there seems to be no ill effect that I can surmise."

The two teams looked on, and Enoch released his own thoughts on the matter. "If God hath said it, then the thing is true. It shall surely come to pass. We must be on our way for I must be about my Lord's business. Let us see that we are all about it as well."

Gabriel, who stood behind him, nodded. "Agreed. We can do nothing but see to that which is set before us; let us be about the task at hand."

"Very well," said Argoth. The Chief of Eyes waved his hand and when he did, he spoke. "Reveal the Gates of Limbus, and let these see the Realm of Choices."

Immediately, the room obeyed, and flashes of light gave way to greys and hues of smoke. A fog entered the Hall, and a rocky crag-face with a door materialized, and next to the door stood an angel armed with a sword. Like a Grigori, he floated, yet hovered with four wings.

The weapon had a black hilt and belched forth a long, blue, flaming blade of white crystal steeped in fire. The opaque guardian blocked the door's entryway, yet he faded between plumes of smoke showing two faces, each one facing opposite the other. One was white with black eyes, and the other black with white eyes. Each set of eyes stared, as though studying wonders afar off.

Argoth then spoke, "Our brother, Janus, awaits you at the gates."

Enoch started to walk through the portal Argoth had made, and the Head of House Grigori stepped in front of the human.

"Know that I consider thee my friend, even a prince among us. And who knows that perhaps a day shall come when thou shalt even judge angels. For it is not oft that I meet someone to challenge me so. Thou art translated of the Lord. You have done me honor these many days. Now go to, for God hath commanded thee to seek the Seraphim. May the Lord watch between me and thee while we are absent one from another, and His hand bring our paths to cross once more."

When Argoth had said his peace, he moved from obstructing Enoch's path.

Enoch smiled, then bowed his head in humble appreciation and looked over his shoulder to Gabriel.

Metatron, Hadriel and the rest of the quartet followed him through the portal and disappeared into the rift.

Michael then motioned Jerahmeel to his side, and the Lord of House Harrada walked to his brother and bowed. Michael placed his hands on his brother's shoulders and spoke. "A season ago, I once told our brother that his orders were to return to me. He hath been remiss in this regard. When you find him, remind him that I take issue with this lapse of judgment."

Jerahmeel's mouth fell open, his now bulging eyes growing wide above his smile. "Then I am free to see to our brother's wellbeing?"

Michael turned and walked away, then spoke aloud for all to hear. "Argoth, send the Head of House Harrada to the doorsteps of Hell. Jerahmeel, see that the message we have for Lucifer is understood. And yes, recoup our brother home."

Jerahmeel nodded. As Argoth prepared a portal to the realm below, a tear strolled down his cheek and he spoke to himself. "By God's grace, I will see the thing done." He turned toward his group, and Michael watched as his brother's team portaled away.

While Michael stared after his departing friends, Argoth turned his attention to a recorded image of an angel's body lying on the streets of gold. "Michael, come here and look at this," Argoth said.

Michael turned from eying the portal where his brethren had just left and walked towards Argoth who pointed at an image of the angel.

"We have a problem," the Grigori said.

Michael beheld the image of a bloodied body, exposed skin festered with blistered pustules that had burst, and the glow of his kilnstone shown no more. The angel did not move when called, nor stir when handled by those surrounding him.

"It cannot be!" Michael said. The Chief Prince stared at the corpse, and nothing could prepare him for the realization before his eyes. Somehow, the immortality of his kind was stripped, and an angel now lay dead in the street.

* * *

Lucifer watched the minions of his making swelter within the bowels of Hell. Each carried carrion and fragments of their brethren's Kilnstones into the fires of the Forge. All former members of House Kortai, each now mindless automatons of labor that built weapons of mass destruction to unleash against the righteous dead. Weapons able to be flung across the gulf and obliterate what little light existed in the underworld of the righteous dead.

Weapons designed by Lucifer's war-master Ares, and his commander of the region, Zeus, stood talking with Ashtaroth when Lucifer approached.

"Report of thy stewardship?" Lucifer said.

"My Lord, I seek permission to track the traitor, Iblis," Zeus said. "I have reason to believe Jerahmeel travels with him," Zeus smirked and then grinned at his lord. "I would be most pleased to extend your hospitality to your brother, and bid my former master hello."

Lucifer smiled. "As always, my friend, thou hast perceived you lord's will. Go and see to our desire."

Zeus bowed and turned to walk away.

"One thing," Lucifer said.

Zeus turned. "My King?"

"Leave enough of my brother intact that I too might enjoy some sport."

A broad grin painted Zeus' face. "As you command, my king."

Lucifer turned to the others. "Ashtaroth, Ares, how soon will the Forge be ready to be unleashed upon Moses and his kin?"

"The Kortai have encountered a problem, my Lord," Ashtaroth said. "Talus' spirit hath not yet been broken and his resistance to thy will is strong. Hell hath yet to convert his Kilnstone. At this rate of consumption, it will be some time before the beast consumes enough of his essence to manufacture the Cadmium thou desirest."

Lucifer scowled. "Hath not these many decades been long enough? Must I further sully my hands to expedite that which my adjutant hath been assigned?"

Ashtaroth bowed his head in fear. "My apologies, master, but we cannot move faster beyond that which El hast allowed the creature to move. You hath made God bleed, so I appeal to thee, mighty one. Guide us in our attempts to please thee. What would you have us do?"

Lucifer smiled. "Because thou hast asked for wisdom, wisdom will I grant thee; observe my machinations and you will see the will of Talus broken. Follow."

Lucifer strode across pools of lava and into an adjacent room. Ares cast an eye to the wasting bodies of Elohim that still clung to life within a creature that consumed them alive. Ashtaroth followed his master and Ares trailed behind. Entering the chamber, Lucifer beheld the dangling Prince of House Arelim – Talus. Ashtaroth remembered his battle with Talus, remembered how he had entrapped the Prince to ignite war. For Ashtaroth was the spark that was used to set Heaven ablaze...the tinder that caused the explosive wrath of God to banish a third of His children from Heaven.

Ashtaroth wore a sneer as he mocked him. "He who hath moved stars now languishes as a cadaver before my face." Ashtaroth spat on him.

Lucifer smiled. "Indeed, stare at him, for here my plan to smite the Almighty begins once more with a prince he hath surrendered into my hand. What foolishness doth the God of Heaven work to once again bring me what I need to complete His own destruction? Watch and learn, Ashtaroth, for when I am done, if thou be worthy, I may make thee ruler over House Arelim."

Ashtaroth smiled, "You do me honor, my King."

Lucifer touched the locket of his neck and Hell groaned as though awakened from slumber. Ashtaroth watched as Hell's tendrils slowly released Talus, who fell to the ground as a lump of flesh. Talus groaned in pain, shivering as the maggots of Hell did their work from the inside of the angel's body---eating him alive. Lucifer smiled at his helpless captive and spoke, "I recall the day you once told me Ashtaroth that Talus did not believe I was about to overthrow the Father. What message dost thou have for him now?"

Ashtaroth spat upon him again. "The imbecile mocked me...failed to heed the words that came from my lips was the truth."

"Aye," Lucifer said. "He failed to believe---failed to take heed. Such a pity. Show the Lumazi what you think of his choice to call thee a liar."

Ashtaroth circled Talus, kicking his abdomen, Talus groaned in agony, as Ashtaroth kicked him several times in the stomach and face. Talus turned his bruised face away, coughed up blood and attempted to speak. Ashtaroth heaved his foot back for yet another blow.

"Hold, Ashtaroth, our guest has something to say."

Ashtaroth spit on Talus and walked back to stand beside his master. Talus turned to face them with his black eyes, swollen, his lips cracked and uttered a warning to his captor.

"Beware, Lucifer, for thou hast taught Ashtaroth to despise others, do not think it will be long before you yourself are also despised. Or dost thou think they will elevate thee to be as El when they see how thou canst not even command one captive angel? Yea he follows you for fear, but not of love, and though he might never tell thee, he despises thee. Thou art mighty and hath always been, but tell me, how dost this filthy hovel compare to the glory of Heaven?"

Lucifer closed the distance between them in three stomping steps and cuffed him with a fist. Talus rolled from the blow and laughed, even as he spit blood. "Thou hast revealed thy weakness, Lightbringer, and hold no power over me."

Lucifer's rage so illuminated his body that brilliant orbs streaked from his being like rays from the sun. Four lights orbited within view; as Lucifer's voice turned cold and inquisitive. "We shall begin again, dear brother. How many lights do you see?"

* * *

O Zion, that bringest good tidings, get thee up into the high mountain; O Jerusalem, that bringest good tidings, lift up thy voice with strength; lift it up, be not afraid; say unto the cities of Judah, Behold your God!

Azaziel closed the Grigoric record of Isaiah and sat in deep thought. Like most of his kind, he had poured over the records daily since El revealed the plan for Yeshua to walk as a creation among the created. Lucifer would assuredly target Yeshua for destruction. Even now, Yeshua moved from one attempt on His life to another. From the moment He was conceived, His purposes were at risk. And for over thirty human years, Azaziel and Yeshua's high guard had thwarted Lucifer's attempts to destroy the vessel of El. For the Son of God was the Word made flesh, the breathing human embodiment of the Godhead: God wrapped in the skin of Adam. Always purposeful, never flinching, Yeshua systematically displayed the heart of God and destroyed the ideas Lucifer had planted among the people of what God was like.

Azaziel had watched Lucifer's spies follow them, but they were too afraid to confront his soldiers and they kept their distance. Lucifer's minions plotted revenge while Yeshua dismantled via his preaching, teaching, and displays of power, Lucifer's strongholds implanted in the minds of men.

But Azaziel had watched His master for many of these human years, and the Lord seemed more pressed than in times past. As if night were approaching to stop His labor. There was a foreboding that stalked the high guard. They all could sense it. An inner knowing that something was amiss.

Something was coming.

Everyone felt it. As a precaution, Azaziel doubled the guard and watched for any sign of enemy movements. Surrounded by prayer the Horde could not risk contact lest they risk injury from the prayer shield that the humans unknowingly had in place. A shield that healed the Host of injury, and strengthened them in this realm. And a shield that withered the Hordes powers.

"Report!" said Azaziel.

"There are enemy Grigoric scouts off the Hill, to the north five leagues out. They do not venture closer for the prayer cover shrouds us and keeps them at bay. We have yet to ascertain if they realize Yeshua is in this location, but considering the large force garrisoned here, we cannot help but draw the enemy's attention. The Lord's actions make it increasingly difficult to mask His presence."

Azaziel rubbed his head and growled in frustration. "Thou dost tell me nothing I do not already know, for the Lord grows more reckless with each passing day. He commands us to stay our hand at every turn, yet seemingly provokes open warfare to be unleashed at any moment. And the humans have no idea who walks within their midst. It is maddening! How El can entrust the secrets of Heaven to these waffling beings baffles me. Though they carry His image, they are so far removed from His original design..."

Azaziel pinched the bridge of his nose and sighed in frustration.

"Nevertheless," the Issi captain said, "we must hold the security of this area and frustrate plans of the enemy to impede the Lord. We are tasked daily. Our scouts report the governing humans of this region are divided over the Master's presence and I fear Lucifer may use them as a proxy to attack the Lord."

Azaziel looked upon Yeshua, who still knelt the Lord who was still in prayer.

He was often in prayer.

For even in flesh, the Trinity consulted with itself. God the Father in constant communion with the Holy Spirit and Son; planning...strategizing. Azaziel knew that Yeshua was painstakingly and calculatingly bringing to pass every word that He had given to His prophets hundreds of years before. A conclusion that Azaziel was want to see. For he had read the words of the prophet Isaiah and had become increasingly versed on the future that El had planned. A plan devised from the foundation of the world, the ramifications of which, after generations, Azaziel was beginning to understand

All we like sheep have gone astray; we have turned everyone to his own way, and the LORD hath laid on Him the iniquity of us all. He was oppressed, and He was afflicted, yet He opened not his mouth: He is brought as a lamb to the slaughter, and as a sheep before her shearers is dumb, so He openeth not his mouth. He was taken from prison and from judgment: and who shall declare his generation? For He was cut off out of the land of the living: for the transgression of my people was He stricken. And He made His grave with the wicked, and with the rich in His death; because He had done no violence, neither was any deceit in His mouth.

The words of the human hung as a cloud over them all. A suffocating realization that despite the might of Heaven's greatest warriors to stand guard to Yeshua, no one could stop the inevitable outcome that seemed to drive the Son of God towards self-oblivion, and yea, even the destruction of Creation itself.

Azaziel clung to hope, unable to speak his musings to his troops.

Nevertheless, he knew what they all wished, what all went unspoken: that perhaps El would finally surrender this foolhardy mission to save Adam's kin. Perhaps they misunderstood what the Lord's true intent was, for the thing was unbelievable to fathom. For surely the Author of Life would not surrender His own, to bring eternal life to the Clayborn?

The Lord stirred from prayer. Thus, Azaziel ceased from thoughts too deep and stood to attention, ready to minister to his master.

Yeshua stood for a moment with eyes closed, and then nodded His head, as though He had received final instructions, then opened His eyes from prayer and stood. His hair blew in the brisk fall air and Azaziel floated to his Lord. His wings folded as he bowed before his King and awaited command.

Yeshua's brow grew stern. His eyes looked off into the distance, past the plains, and over the horizon.

"Come Azaziel." said the Lord.

Azaziel stood and motioned for the Captain of the Guard to summon the legion to break camp. "Our destination, my King?"

Yeshua simply sighed and gave a slight smile as He headed toward the inner circle of disciples. He strode with a determined gait, and Azaziel knew from his Lord's eyes the thoughts of his master and his heart quickened in anxiety. For he knew that soon his worst fears would quickly coming to pass.

For the time had come for Yeshua to be received up, and the Lord steadfastly set His face to go to Jerusalem.

* * *

Yeshua addressed the seventy seated men.

"Go not into the way of the Gentiles, and into any city of the Samaritans enter ye not: But go rather to the lost sheep of the house of Israel. And as ye go, preach, saying, the kingdom of heaven is at hand. Heal the sick, cleanse the lepers, raise the dead, cast out devils: freely ye have received, freely give."

And the Lord gave them power and authority over all devils, and to cure diseases, with a mandate to preach the kingdom of God, and to heal the sick. And the seventy went abroad throughout all Israel as commanded, and the Horde took note of their actions and watched to see what they would do. And a disciple by the name of Matthias came upon a woman vexed of a devil for ten years.

Her body was infested with the disembodied souls of the fallen who sought expression through mankind. The woman thrashed against the stones and no man could keep her from self-injury, and the demons worked foul magic upon any that sought to help her, for any that came near to offer balms for her wounds fell to the ground, dead, and the woman's name was Rina. When she saw Matthias, she besought him and fell at his feet, saying, "Please, Rabbi, must a daughter of Abraham contend forever with evil visions that befall me?"

"What wouldst thou ask of me?" he said.

"If thou wilt but lay thine hands on my head and command the voices to cease, they will stop. For even now they speak among themselves to destroy a man from Galilee called Yeshua, and say thou comest from Him."

"I will do as thou hast asked." And when Matthias sought to lay hands upon her head to bless her, a man of the city named Abner said, "Do it not! For others before thee have tried and died. If thou but touchest her, thou shalt surely die."

And Matthias replied, "I come in the name of Yeshua." And when he said those words, he laid hands on the woman's forehead. She screamed and shivered from head to toe before the spirits threw her on the ground. The crowd stepped back as her brown eyes rolled back into her head and foam poured from her mouth. Her back arched and a loud shriek escaped her lips and she lay as one dead. All those that stood about marveled, for they heard voices issue from the woman, and whining whispers flowed on the air like a soft rushing wind, and the words they heard were on this wise:

"We are lost and undone, for God has come down as a man, and what now will Lucifer do?"

The woman lay limp with the guttural roar of an animal. Matthias gently brushed the hair from her eyes, picked her up and carried her into the house. Moments later, she looked into his face and fell at his feet to worship him. But Matthias lifted her to her feet. "Arise, maiden. For I am but a man. Yeshua of Nazareth hath made thee whole. Worship Him only lest a worse thing befall thee." Matthias then commanded all present to repent.

Daemons were afraid of all that spoke in the name of Yeshua. The Grigori who sided with Lucifer went and told him all that the seventy had done. The Lord of Evil was wroth, because he found the disciples of Yeshua spread abroad destroying his works, and everywhere they spoke of the man Yeshua, they healed the sick, and cast out daemons. Lucifer knew that Yeshua must be stopped, for the articles of war prevented open manifestation, but El, by becoming flesh, had opened a beachhead on earth through man to fight him.

"This must come to an end, for I will not tolerate Adamson to enter into battle against me. I will not fight both God, and God's man on two fronts."

Lucifer then found Judas, speaking to some in the name of Yeshua and spoke to his mind.

"Look at what you are able to do in this man's name alone. See how even daemons shudder when you mention the name Yeshua. If I, being only a man can do such things in his name. If he, be the Son of God, how much more would the Romans shudder?"

Judas shook his head and muttered aloud. "But Yeshua hath no interest in the affairs of this world. His only concern is the Kingdom of God."

Such a shame. Such power to do good. Such power to change the course of our people's history. But perhaps...what if He were forced to reveal who he was?

Judas laid his hands on a child and she recovered. He quickly moved on to another one as more of the town's people brought them their ill, and daemon possessed.

You are but one man. But Yeshua can impart power to all! What pray tell could be accomplished if He showed Himself to all Israel? What if all were given this power? How then could Rome stand against us?

Judas touched a beggar who had been lame from birth. He prayed, and the man rose up and walked.

He sighed to himself even as he prayed for others. Such a waste. *Here you are sent to the refuse of the nation when those who are capable of real freedom for all lack what they need. If only they too had this power. What could happen if He were somehow compelled to show Himself as God? Think Judas! Think man! The whole of Israel could be restored if this were to work.*

Judas continued his work of ministering to the sick and needy, conflicted as he laid hands on each soul. Using the power of the Lord on those he thought it wasted

And from that moment, Judas surmised how he might compel the Lord's hand to show himself as God, and to restore Israel to power, and establish the kingdom.

Lucifer smiled, as he ceased in planting seeds of suggestion. Smiled knowing that in time they would germinate and bear fruit.

A fruit that would convince this Clayborne that Yeshua could be persuaded to reveal who He was if forced into a corner.

Lucifer watched from afar, as Judas and the rest of the seventy returned to the Lord. Chuckling to himself that within the group he had planted tares to choke the life from Yeshua Himself.

* * *

Enoch and his team approached the swirly gates of Limbus. Janus stood in front of the mammoth opening, his sword drawn. The angel with two faces floated above them all. Slightly larger in build, he was quiet and neither of his faces turned toward them. The eyes of the guard seemingly focused on events beyond sight.

Enoch spoke to the winged apparition. "Hail, guard of Limbus. I am Enoch, translated of the Lord. I bid thee grant me entry, for I come in the name of the Lord of Hosts."

Gabriel, Metatron, and Hadriel watched in silence to see what the guardian would do.

The black face of Janus with white eyes turned to Enoch and spoke. "We know who thou art, Adamson, for thy works are known to us." Immediately, the white face with black eyes turned to them. "Thou mayest enter, but answer me this...wilt thou permit thy companions to die for the cause of the Lord?"

Enoch and the rest of the entourage paused, surprised by the question. Gabriel took it upon himself to reply. "Dost thou foresee death for us, Janus?"

The two faces of Janus smiled, laughed and then replied. "In the realm of Limbo, life and death are but choices to the path that leads to Aseir."

Enoch lifted his voice in answer. "Then I choose life that both I and those with me might live."

"The black face replied, "Foolish human, for can a seed give life except it fall into the ground and die? Thou dost seek to enter Limbus. Very well, but know that which you enter. For Limbus is the realm of choices. It is alive with possibilities. What resides therein are but the echoes of battles both won and lost. You now stand between here and there. Enter, if you dare. Enter the space between choices, and the mezzanine between life and death, for thou wilt go forward or thou wilt not. Tread carefully, human, for there are ancient eyes in the dark, and thou dost not belong here."

The white face then spoke. "We shall observe the alternatives that you make, and watch you navigate the eddy of options. Behold, the entry to Limbus: Realm of Choices."

The guardian pointed the way with his sword.

When Enoch looked before him, and when he did, he saw a mirror that contained his reflection and those of all his party, but Janus, who stood also in the path, did not appear in the reflection.

Janus placed the glowing, fiery, blue blade into the swirling smoke that was the door. It caught aflame and the whole entrance turned blue and erupted in fire. The churning mists stopped as though they would wait for time, and then settled into a still fog that crept along the ground.

"Enter through the Gates of Eternal Views and pass over," Janus said.

Enoch and the rest of the group walked through the jagged mouth of stone and stepped within the gate. When all four had stepped through, Gabriel looked back. Janus and the gated entry were gone. All that remained was their reflection as in a mirror, multiplied in ad infinitum.

The group eyed darkly silhouetted grey and black rocks that loomed on each side, fog and the musty odor made Enoch wrinkle his nose. "Smells like stagnant water," he said. "There is a hissing in the shadows. What is that?"

"I don't think we want to know," Metatron said. "Which way do we go?"

Gabriel and the rest of the entourage looked at Enoch, who after surveying his surroundings replied.

"Janus said this is the realm of choices. I choose to go forward." The translated of God then pitched his satchel firmly over his shoulders, placed his cane solidly on the ground before him, and proceeded to step deeper into the darkness.

* * *

Argoth had been careful to create a portal that would not arouse suspicion from the enemies of God, so he set Jerahmeel and his companions down deep into a ridge near the mouth of one of Hell's openings. Jerahmeel, Eskalion, Iblis, and Turiel settled into the green and dank earth during the night outside.

"Iblis, you told Argoth that this was the closest we could get externally to the Hellforge. Yet, I do not see the opening from here to Hell's mouth."

Iblis smiled, "You need only ever look into a volcano to see the entrance to Hell Harrada. Come, there is a vent up ahead we can travel through."

The troupe moved quietly through the small canyon until he came to a point and stopped to crouch. The rest crouched also. "There, past the cliffs. Do you see it?" he said.

Jerahmeel eyed the cliff in the distance, and beneath it, smoke and ash billowed into the sky. Nothing lived at its entrance, and if one listened closely, distant wails sounded on the air. Jerahmeel placed his hand on Iblis' shoulder and leaned forward to whisper into his ear. "If thou lead us astray, know of a surety that I shall personally take thee with me to oblivion."

Iblis shrugged his shoulder away from Jerahmeel. "Quickly now! Follow me." Iblis dashed toward the vent and the others followed in kind. Plumes of smoke wafted into their eyes when they entered into the aperture, and the heat immediately assailed them all. Angelic bodies, immune to the searing effects that would kill a human, nevertheless felt the blast of intense heat.

Eskalion yelped. "Why do I feel pain?"

Turiel replied. "We are not just entering a terrestrial chamber of fire. Hell is a living creature, and we stand on her edge. She is not terrestrial, and her fires can harm us. The renegade leads us true thus far. This path is known to my people. We have yet to go outside the scope of the Grigori's gaze."

Iblis paused. "How long will I be despised in thy eyes? Am I not here by thy side with my own life at risk? What more dost thou want from me?"

Eskalion replied. "It will require much effort before Heaven's host will ever find compassion toward those who took up arms against them. El Himself would have to announce thee righteous before absolution could be gained. Yet help us in this cause, and mayhap healing can begin."

Iblis turned and murmured under his breath as he walked toward a chamber flowing with magma. "Through there," he said, pointing.

Jerahmeel had never seen the inside of Hell. None of them had. Only Michael, Lucifer, and Abaddon, who was now trapped within the Abyss, had walked the colon of Hell. They all gasped when their eyes beheld what lay before them.

Iblis turned with a pleased face. "Be careful when thou seekest to enter the mouth of a creature designed to consume thee alive. Behold, the desire of thine heart."

Ahead of them lay a chamber that glowed white hot, and within it, streams of Hell's blood flowed like magma. Strewn across the floor was thousands upon thousands of flesh-eating parasitic maggots. Each feasted upon the undying remains of angels and men alike, each moaning and screaming, their cries masked by the hissing of steam that vented into the sky. An opening inaccessible to men.

"Dear God," Jerahmeel said.

Iblis smiled, "Behold, the digestive tract of Hell."

Chapter Seven: A Gulf to Cross

"How are the teams?" Michael asked.

Argoth pointed to an image that arrested his sight. "Jerahmeel and his team have entered what I surmise is the digestive tract of Hell itself." Argoth's eyes widened at the horror of the image and finally ushered a return of voice. "It...it is naught but the wrath of the Lord."

Michael pointed to images of the citizens of Heaven huddled in fear, enduring the effects of the Withering during the absence of God's presence.

"No...," said Michael. "Wrath is yet to come."

"Look," Argoth said. "Enoch and Gabriel have entered Limbus. We can but hope they will all succeed."

Michael nodded. "Hope has been ever before us since the dawn of war. El is our hope, and our trust must lie in Him. Show me the city."

Argoth waved his hand and the floor itself became opaque. Within seconds, the colors of Jerusalem splashed on the walls. Angel upon angel coughed up blood from the sickness that infected the land. Some shivered uncontrollably while others picked at themselves and scratched imaginary boils until they bled. Others curled into balls, screaming at apparitions that did not exist. Dozens tore the hair from their heads and plucked tendrils from their wings, but the hallucinations of living mists brought the most agony. Mists that took form and harassed the population of Heaven of choices past. Mists invisible to all but he who saw them.

Michael frowned and winced at their suffering, for each stared with empty eyes, and he wrapped his arms around himself, held hard to his own shoulders and wept.

Argoth watched and said, "I am the Chief of Eyes and am not moved by what I see. But you, my Prince, are not so. Your leadership hath brought this on the people. How fares the Chief Prince, and has El given any indication of abeyance yet to come?"

Michael fingered his robes for comfort, and his voice tightened as he spoke.

"I...I...the Lord hath said we must endure for three days. The Withering is similar to the sin that plagues the humans – though we will not die. Nevertheless, we will experience the void of El and endure the haunting of choices made. We will see the sun, but be denied its warmth. Be close to the Father, yet far away from Him. I have forced my people to once again feel the absence of God's presence. I am stained to have exposed us so."

Michael looked upon the whole of Heaven, as each grew famished, not from the loss of foodstuffs that sustained them, but from the Shekinah of God. His lip quivered slightly and his eyes turned red from choking back tears.

Argoth touched his shoulder in comfort. "El is the life and light of all. If He is dark, then we are all dark," Argoth said.

Michael nodded in agreement. "Then today is a dark day, indeed."

A screen changed and Argoth received a message from a member of his people.

The Grigori bowed. "My Prince."

"Report," said Argoth.

"My Prince, I have chronicled the collapse of the Kortai, Osiras. He ceases to move."

"Hath he succumbed to dissolution?" replied Argoth.

"Nay, my Prince. He just collapsed in the street."

Michael looked at the image projected on the wall, as other angels suddenly circled around the collapsed angel. Some attempted to roust him while others covered their mouths and backed away in fear.

"I have seen this among the humans. He looks...dead," Michael said.

"Impossible," said Argoth. "There is no disease or predator that can strike an Elohim. He is immortal. No disease can overtake us. We are the Host."

Michael strained to look upon the still angel through the projection on the wall. "Perhaps, yet our eyes do not deceive." Bring his body for examination."

Argoth nodded, and Michael quietly prayed, hoping against hope that what he saw was not the precursor of things to come.

* * *

Talus contorted in agony as contractions rippled through each muscle. His flesh burned, and the stinging pain rolled across him in waves. Each muscle cramped, pulsating in Lucifer's orchestrated spasms. A wave of searing convulsions followed one after the other. Hell wrapped his mouth with her corrosive mucus, leaving him oxygen deprived as she suffocated him in her acidic bile. Smothering her captive until the mighty angel reached the brink of unconsciousness, then withdrawing the movement of her larval centipedes from his esophagus. Air rushed into his lungs; each expanded in clawing attempts to suction oxygen from the ashy smog and fire that surrounded him.

This was Talus's torment for defiance to his brother, for refusing to bow the knee. The pure temptation to yield to the relief of pain.

And Lucifer was skilled in its use.

"How many lights dost thou see?" Satan roared. "Is your pride so strong, little brother that you will not concede to me the reality that exists before your very eyes?"

Talus tightened his lips and gritted his teeth.

Lucifer paced before the suspended captive. "Thou art strong, but thy strength will not avail thee here in Hades, for thou art my centerpiece, the heart of my new Kiln. Thou art the hub from which I will raise this monster to Heaven, and with it, I will destroy all who dare oppose me. For who can defy that which El hath made? Yet here I stand, strong, and able to release thee. I hold two of El's creations. Behold the Controller of Death and Trainer of Hell. Yet you dare squirm in defiance before me?"

Lucifer lowered Talus to the ground and he slumped within the flaming tentacles that cuffed him. Lucifer grabbed Talus's cheeks and squeezed, forcing his lips to purse, and as a puppeteer moves his marionette, he made his lips move. "Save me, El...please...save me from the Devil," Lucifer said. He released Talus's face and lifted his hands in disgust, "Tell me, Talus, where is thy God now?"

Talus struggled to lift his head and whispered, "I..."

Lucifer stilled himself and turned to face his brother. His attention locked on Talus's lips, and the Prince of Darkness tilted his head and edged closer to hear the whisper.

"What did you say? SPEAK, I command you!"

"I...see...lights," he said, beholding the shimmering orbs that Lucifer made dance before his eyes.

"HOW MANY LIGHTS DO YOU SEE?" the Prince of Darkness roared. Lucifer's voice cracked the floor of Hell and the creature roared its displeasure; the denizens that lived within moved as the floors buckled beneath them.

Talus' cracked lips turned up at the corners as he spoke in smugness, looking his brother square in the eye. "What lights?"

Lucifer gritted his teeth in anger and his power to manipulate light became evident as the colors of the rainbow skipped about him. With fury, he backhanded Talus across the face, and blood and spittle flew into the air.

He touched his locket and Hell dropped Talus to the floor with a thud. Lucifer kicked him in the gut and Talus flew across the chamber, slamming against the moist wall of Hell's belly. Talus struggled to rise to his feet, but before he could do so Lucifer was upon him and unsheathed the Sword of Malice from his side. The blade glowed green and the souls of victims trapped within screamed for release. Lucifer then lifted his brother with one hand, and with the other took the blade and slid its edge across his brother's face.

"I grow weary of your contempt. Do you not know that I have bled God?"

As Lucifer pulled the sword back to strike his brother, Ashtaroth came from behind him and pulled his master's arm.

"My Lord, do it not! For if thou do so, what then will be the stone that powers thy forge, for behold, the chamber glows and thy creation nears the end."

Lucifer paused and Ashtaroth, backed away in timidity, wondering if he had exchanged Talus's fate for his own. Ashtaroth bowed and motioned his lord to behold the chamber that hissed with steam.

Lucifer dropped Talus to the floor, and when he did so, he motioned dismissively to Talus. Hell's tendrils reached for her prize and lifted the limp and bruised body of her captive overhead. Talus peeked through swollen eyes to watch Lucifer stand in the hollow of a burning chamber. Fire upon fire roared from within the large oven, and blinding starlight flared from the chamber. Lucifer then walked in the midst of the furnace and Ashtaroth shielded his eyes as the luminance that erupted from within was blocked only by the shadow of his master, Lucifer. He scooted back to distance himself from the great flashes of light that ejected from the oven.

Evil, gleeful mirth and hilarity erupted from the chamber of fire a laughter that Ashtaroth had never heard in the midst of the screams that traveled the halls of Hell. Lucifer swaggered out of the furnace and smoldered as he held above him a glowing black stone as dark as onyx. It glistened as though moistened, and twinkling stars could be seen from within. Lucifer gazed at the stone and roared defiantly to El.

"Behold, Father! Behold the designs of thy wayward son, for now, I too possess the power of life. Behold, Ashtaroth...behold...A STONE OF FIRE!"

Ashtaroth feigned the makings of a smile and nodded in fearful acknowledgment to his Lord, for with the creation of a Kilnstone, he knew Lucifer could with it make a new creation. A new Heaven and a new Earth. And the thought made him shudder.

Talus also looked down upon his brother who exulted in his inventive triumph, and he closed his eyes in prayer that hope in El would one day come as promised, and save him and creation from the madness of the Devil.

* * *

"Report!" said Michael.

Argoth bowed to the Chief Prince as he entered his study. "I have examined the body of Osiras..."

"And?" replied Michael, tapping his foot. His eyes narrowed in focus on Argoth.

"Osiras hath died. Not just succumbed to dissolution."

Michael's eyes grew wide and his mouth opened as he shook his head in disbelief. "What do you mean, 'died'? He is immortal. He is not susceptible to death. Only the sons of Adam are subject to it."

"Please come with me."

Michael followed him to a room off the rear of Argoth's study and on a slab of stone was the stiff body of Osiras. A linen sheet covered his form and the wings of the Issi hung limp, draped to the floor.

Argoth stood next to the body and spoke. "I have examined the remains, and this is not dissolution. This, my prince, is death. His Kilnstone has stopped glowing. The spark of life no longer burns within, yet the body does not fade as is the manner of our kind upon dissolution. It is corrupted, my prince. It decays."

Michael looked at the body and examined it without touching. "How is such a thing possible, for it has not been even a day and his face is as leather and brittle?" Michael could smell the odor that slowly began to emanate from the corpse, and he continued. "Decay hath only been observed within man, and only since his abdication. How can an immortal be subject to the thing?"

Argoth looked at the body and shook his head. "The workings of the Withering is a first for our kind to observe in Heaven. But my people have learned that when a plague has run its course strips us of immortality. It corrodes the spark of life within our stones, leaving us mortal, and because the atmosphere of Heaven is toxic to anything that doth not possess El's touch of holiness..."

Michael's face displayed shock, and he finished the sentence. "...Heaven itself hath become toxic to our kind."

"Aye," Argoth said. "If we are not shielded by God's' holiness, the very presence of God will bring about our demise. Silently we will be consumed to age, and even as the humans, we too will be subject to death."

Michael staggered and reached out to brace himself against a wall. He hung his head low then sighed. He looked at the body of his deceased brother and choked back tears. "Jerahmeel was right...I have, through my actions, brought ruin to my people." His eyes zeroed in on his brother, "You said 'when it has run its course.' How much of the population do you project will succumb to the plague?"

Argoth floated to his brother and placed his hands on his shoulders. "Perhaps thou hast reached the limits to where thine own wisdom can take thee. Thy extremity must now seek He who can do beyond all that ye ask or think, for what remedy is available to thee other than by El's own hand?"

Michael drew his shoulder away from Argoth's touch, "You have failed to answer me, Chief of Eyes. I knew Raphael and I know that as Sephiroth you have knowledge beyond the sight of most, so I ask thee again. How much of the population do you project will succumb to the plague?"

Argoth frowned. "In three days, the plague will take its course, and if not abated, at least a third to a half of our kind will fall to death. In one week's time, I have beheld through Grigoric trance the extinction of our race."

Michael stumbled backward and reached to grab the wall as he lowered himself to the floor. He wrapped his arms around his waist and bent over and moaned.

"I have accomplished through stubbornness what Lucifer could not attain through war."

He groaned in the spirit with mutterings that could not be uttered and wept sore.

Argoth looked upon his leader and backed away from his prince leaving Michael alone as he sobbed, blanketing the corpse of Osiras.

* * *

Enoch and his group walked through mists obscured within mists, each member barely able to see the next step before them. Enoch paused and lifted a closed fisted hand. The troop came to a halt. God's man strained his eyes to peer through the gloomy veil.

"Something moves within the dimness," he said.

"Are sure?" Gabriel said in a low voice. "I see nothing."

"It is not about sight, High Prince. It is about instinct. Something is out there."

Gabriel then turned to Hadriel. "Go to and scout before us and see that the way is clear, for what harm can come to a Grigori while misted?"

Hadriel nodded and allowed his body to change to a gaseous, transparent form that floated quickly past the trio and disappeared into the shrouded gloom.

Seconds passed as they waited for word from their friend if they could proceed further.

"Hadriel?" shouted Enoch.

But there was no reply.

The eyes of all strained to peer past the cloudy veil, and Metatron was the first to notice movement and he drew his sword. "We are being watched," he said.

"Yes...yes you are." Came a voice from the darkness.

Enoch slid his sword out from its sheath and assumed a defensive battle stance. The heaven forged blade glittered between the twilight mists, and sounds of swords drawn emerged from the murk.

"With what gall dost the living seek to dwell amongst the dead?" said a voice.

"Show thyself, coward!" shouted Gabriel.

A figure stirred among the mists and all stepped back, ready for an attack. They breathed a collective sigh of relief as Hadriel appeared, came into view. His cowled face and shimmering eyes a familiar and welcome sight. He flew above the trio and landed behind them. "Quickly form up for we are under assault!"

The four placed their backs to each other, swords raised, and watched for any sign of attack from the gloom. Hadriel's pen then transformed into a dagger.

Hadriel floated closer to Enoch while all eyed the shadows that now moved menacingly around them. Hadriel settled next to Enoch, and when Enoch turned his eyes away, Hadriel raised his dagger to strike him down.

Enoch caught the motion from the corner of his eye and quickly leaned away, yet unable to escape the downward stroke that would plunge Hadriel's dagger deep into his neck.

Suddenly, another dagger whizzed across Enoch's face, knocking Hadriel's dagger from his hand; both weapons ricocheted off one another twirling into the darkness.

Gabriel shoved Enoch behind him as another floating apparition materialized. It was Hadriel.

"Get away from God's man," Hadriel commanded.

Confusion overtook the group, as the Hadriel who had protected Enoch plunged headlong into the other Grigori who had just tried to attack him. The twin angels grappled with one another as their books floated above their heads.

Enoch, moved away flustered, "Who is who?" He barked.

"I am. The other is an impostor...a doppelganger!"

"No! He's the impostor!" said the other.

The two Grigori misted and upon command, their pens flew back into their hands and immediately turned into daggers. Each slashed at one another, deflecting blows, and quickly attempted to stab one another with deft jabs. Yet neither could get an advantage over the other.

The party looked on as the two record keepers grappled each other's wrists, each one's movement a perfect mirroring of the other.

"How do we tell them apart?" Metatron said.

Suddenly from Metatron's rear, a voice echoed like his own, "You would do well to be concerned for yourself." Mists then swirled into a rising column at Metatron's feet and formed into a gaseous copy of Metatron, which now stood before him. The twin smiled and attacked his counterpart.

Gabriel grabbed Enoch. "You cannot be lost for all our hopes rest on your success. Stay behind me and I will be thy shield."

A sound then emanated from the ground beneath his feet and gaseous hands grabbed the angel by the ankles. Gabriel fell onto his back. Enoch watched as the head of house Malakim was dragged away clawing into the darkness, kicking against a foe unseen.

Yet when Gabriel kicked at the mists that held him, he looked to see that he but kicked at his own hands. A twin visage stared back at him, then jumped atop him and began to pummel him.

Enoch watched the skirmishes play themselves out, before him, and he took his sword and turned to his rear, then back again, swinging it wildly at the fog that collected his feet. For it was now clear that the mist itself was the enemy and it encompassed the party round about. He gripped the hilt of his blade with both hands and pointed it forward, watching for any sign of an attacker's approach.

He did not have long to wait.

A human figure arose from the vaporous floor and Enoch found himself staring into his own likeness. The creature grinned and spoke.

"You have fought death, mortal, and hath been translated by the Great One, Himself, yet you still possess fear. Death does not exist here, human; only the lingering remains of choices not made. The in-between of the tick and the tock: for here in the realm of choices and doubt, you have entered the infinite loop of mirrors and now...we will have thee."

Enoch faced his double and swung his sword at the attacker and the duplicate parried his blow. Their swords clanged in the twilight, and the twin circled to counter Enoch's strike. Enoch's sword flew from his hands into the eerie black, leaving him defenseless. The twin Enoch, then raised his sword above his head, ready to strike his quarry with a forward slicing blow, but the man of God brought his palms together against the blade and halted the sword with his bare hands. Blood trickled from his palms as he struggled against his own strength to prevent being sliced in half. Enoch turned to gained leverage and kicked the chest of his ghostly counterpart, but his foot just passed through vapor.

"You fight in vain, human. You cannot defeat me, for I am you."

The ghostly figure then solidified and Enoch could not withdraw his foot from his opponent's chest. His evil twin smiled, then spun his human quarry, released him and sent Enoch flying into Metatron.

Metatron caught his companion and shielded Enoch, absorbing a slicing blow in the process. He cried out in agony while Enoch scurried to find his sword. As he picked up the blade, vapors surrounded him and coalesced so that he once more stood confronted by his own image. Enoch struck at his twin. Mist trailed the stroke as his blade broke the outline of his attacker's bodily form and his double smiled at him.

"So many choices avail you human, and yet as always, your kind and that of the Elohim seek the way of battle as the first choice. Behold now the sum of thy decisions."

Enoch watched as his compatriots were locked in mortal combat with themselves, watched as Gabriel, Hadriel, and Metatron wrestled against ethereal beings that knew neither fear nor fatigue, each one locked in a lethal waltz to defeat the twin foe before them. A group of hacking, slashing and pummeling warriors, each in focused intent to but defeat the foe set before them. Then Enoch realized the nature of their battle and dropped his weapon onto the foggy ground. Gabriel glanced toward Enoch and yelled, "To arms! We do not surrender. We do not fail. Do not give in to despair. Fight! Fight!"

But Enoch stared at his gaseous nemesis as the nebulous form of himself advanced closer, its sword raised to cut him down. As the distance between them closed, Enoch shut his eyes, opened his arms wide, and surrendered to God. If the Lord willed his oblivion...then the will of the Lord be done.

His twin marched with sword held high and lowered its misty blade to slice Enoch in half. Gabriel looked from his periphery and screamed out in horror. "Nooooo!!"

But the aim of Enoch's ghost was sure and the blade found its mark, yet when the edge of the sword hit the crown of Enoch's head, it misted through him and became as ether.

Enoch felt the breeze and its coolness caress his face. He opened his eyes, smiled and spoke. "I am Enoch, and there is none other. I have seen Death's face, and Death doth not exist in this realm. Be gone, foul spirit of fear, for I choose not to die this day."

Enoch's twin smiled. "Fear is always present, Translated of God. Know that I will watch you as you pass through Limbus." Immediately the copy dispersed into the murk and was gone. Enoch turned to his peers and yelled for them all to hear. "Allow them to strike you. Do not resist evil, but let them strike thee down if need be."

Metatron wrestled with his doppelganger and wore several slashes. He spoke with gritted exertion. "Are you mad? We will fall into dissolution."

"Noo!" said Metatron's double, "Release your fear, for we will have you join us in Limbus--you must feed the mist!"

Enoch ran toward Metatron, who was now on his back with his twin atop him. Enoch grabbed the double by the neck and pulled the gaseous creature off of him throwing it to the ground.

Metatron lay dumbfounded, for he had seen Enoch repeatedly defeated in combat during training, and now he stood pummeling his vaporous twin into the ground. "I do NOT possess the spirit of fear, for my God is my shield and my strength." And the gaseous ghost screamed and every time Enoch's fist hit the creature the ground lit beneath his pummeling fists as the vaporous double of Metatron broke apart into non-threatening puffs of smoke.

Gabriel and Hadriel ceased in their struggles and when they did, the creatures screamed in frustration and reached for their quarries to lash out at them.

"Give us substance. Let your choices become manifest. Feed the mist. Feed..."

Enoch walked through Gabriel's apparition and waved the diffusing ghost away as one would wave smoke from stinging eyes.

"Get up my friend," Enoch said. "Alas, we have been delayed long enough."

Gabriel reached up for his friend's hand and spoke. "How did you know?"

Hadriel floated toward them, his own apparition now gone. "We are on a mission to restore the unity of the spirit between Elohim and Seraphim. There can be no thought of one's life in the cause of the Lord, for he that loveth his life shall lose it. We are not here to fight but to reconcile. To fight was only to hasten our defeat as these creatures are but manifestations of our own fear. They can do us no harm if we choose it, for we have been told this is the realm of choices. I choose to be about my Father's business. Enoch turned then spoke into the darkness before them, "Come, we have dwelt long enough in the fog of fear." And the group proceeded deeper into the depths of the unknown.

* * *

Jerahmeel and the rest of the team followed Iblis into the digestive tract of Hell, careful not to touch the surface floor. White glowing maggots covered the cavern and hissed within pulsating flows of lava. Like a river streamed with human remains, Hell digested the fallen angels before their eyes.

Steam sizzled through the vent as they entered, only to mask the moans of those under judgment. Cries of anguish and the stench of rotting flesh baked into the nostrils and ears of the group.

"Talus is in this?" asked Eskalion.

"No," replied Iblis. "He is without a doubt deep in the center of the creature. The bowel. For within, Lucifer hath built the Hellforge away from the prying eyes of Grigori and Heaven. For whom but the mad would ever attempt entry into the prison El hast designed?"

Turiel laughed, "It would seem that we too are foolish to undertake such a task."

Iblis moved with caution between falling clumps of cooling lava that fell from the ceiling. Eyes protruded from the ceiling, the pupils of which dilated and followed their movements.

"Think of it," Iblis said, "just think of it. Lucifer braved Hell to release Apollyon from this creature's grip. What audacity, to believe he could not just enter the Lord's prison, but escape! He saw this beast untamed and ready to consume." Iblis beamed as he continued. "Is it not impressive to know that our kind had the power to circumvent God, to move beyond His constraints? Can you not understand why many followed him?"

Eskalion huffed in disgust. "When your false god can create life and the air we breathe, then perhaps he might scratch the toe of El's power. Until then, I will stand with my God."

Through narrow channels the group flew, careful to avoid the floor, walls, and ceilings.

"There are eyes in the ceiling," said Jerahmeel. "Eyes that watch us."

Turiel looked up. "Indeed, yet something seems amiss. Is it just me, or do they seem to be multiplying?"

All glanced above them, and as water boils so too did eyes bubble to the surface of the lava both above and beneath them. Slowly the organs popped into being, then with each passing moment, more came into view, compounding and reproducing, each searching for something, each eye looking in various directions, swiveling in all angles, scanning the duct in which the quartet traveled

"Intriguing," Turiel said. "The creature does not realize that we are within it." And upon those words, the tome that floated aside of Turiel's body began to be inscribed by his pen. And as the thoughts of Turiel were translated from mind to pen, and from pen to page, the tip of the instrument glanced the ceiling.

The eyes of the entire cavern then locked onto them glowing deep red, and widening to twice their size.

Iblis motioned for all to stop and fear covered his face. Turiel misted, and all took notice that all the eyes of the cavern now tracked their movement.

"If you value your life, do not move," Iblis whispered.

All floated, as anxiety crept through the group, each muscle taut to move as little as possible. Jerahmeel held his breath as he looked about, and it was then that when he thought they were safe, that Turiel reached to touch the creature.

"Nooo!" Jerahmeel cried, but it was too late. Turiel wailed out in agony as his hands burned and he fell screaming into the boiling lava. The eyes grew and tracked him and immediately began to fall from the ceiling. More eyes surfaced from the floor in a tidal wave of lava, angelic and human limbs. A swelling upsurge that now trailed them to consume them alive. Hell was hungry.

"FLEE!!" Iblis screamed.

Eskalion rushed to Turiel, hoisted him over his shoulders, and the four fled into corridors of darkness, flying in single file following Iblis in desperate hopes to escape.

Jerahmeel panted as angelic endorphins pumped through his body as he and the group scrambled to escape the touch of the quickly converging glowing one-eyed creatures. Michael had told Jerahmeel about the living immune system of Hell, but nothing could prepare him for the reality that now pursued them. For Carrion-eating, disease destroying antibodies viewed their presence as nothing more than a contagion to be destroyed.

The one-eyed, lava-like antibodies swarmed the cavern with flaming tentacles that unraveled from the ceiling like vines in a jungle. Their stinging touch, sending needle-like pain into those who failed to dodge the lowering limbs.

Iblis batted away steaming tendrils. "Hurry this way!"

Jerahmeel, sword drawn, sliced at the falling appendages that sought to entwine them. Faster they flew, and from every wall, from the floors and roof of corridors, glowing eyes opened and plopped to the floor in a slow march, as lava overran all things. Eskalion dared not look behind him, as Turiel groaned while he flopped over his peer's shoulders as he ran. His pen and stylus hovered just beyond him, writing ceaselessly in the air.

"Eskalion, they come more swiftly than we can move. We will not make it," Turiel said.

"We will not fail," Eskalion replied with a pant.

"I found it!" said Iblis. "I found the opening! Hurry before it closes!"

Jerahmeel saw the chute that pulsed open and closed. A living valve of some sort that led to depths unknown. He shouted in gruff exhaustion. "Where does it lead?"

"Anywhere is better than here," cried Eskalion. "Hurry!"

Rolling waves of beastly eyes pursued like a flowing, moving river of teeth with brimstone eyes. The cavern bristled with the smell of ash and rank air.

Jerahmeel looked back and saw what few of his kind had ever seen...the decayed and half-digested remains of men and angels, alive yet dead, partially consumed and now part of the river of lava that chased them. Mouths, eyes, hands, and feet, wings and beautiful scales of Elohim rose and sank within the hissing mass of magma and a sea of eyes. Jerahmeel turned as he followed Iblis who now scooted down the chute. The head of House Harrada grasped the edge of the chute and prepared to slide down the slimy cavity when his eyes beheld the manifestation of his fears. Unable to slash through the falling tendrils of Hell, Eskalion and Turiel fought to free themselves while enveloped by fiery coils that lifted them aloft into openings in the ceiling and they vanished from view.

"ESKALION, TURIEL!" screamed Jerahmeel. But it was too late. And the corridor became awash in the hissing, consuming remains of angelic and human flotsam that reached out to add Jerahmeel's flesh to its own.

Jerahmeel panted. A tear streamed from one eye and he grimaced in frustration as he forced himself to look forward and slid down the chute into the darkness.

* * *

Ashtaroth flew into the lower chambers of Hell and passed a long corridor that held his master's trophies. On one side were the heads of enemies Lucifer had defeated in battle and on the other the heads of those who had challenged him for the leadership of the Horde. An intimidating warning to all who approached to be mindful of those who had gone before them who thought they could challenge the God of this World. For Lucifer had leashed the prison of El itself, and by his side, he commanded Charon to do his bidding. The master's message was clear. To challenge his authority was do so at the risk of dissolution.

Ashtaroth did not relish telling his master that a new challenge awaited his lord.

Ashtaroth found Lucifer standing as expected before the Hellforge. When Lucifer was not tormenting his favorite captive, he was tracking the doings of Yeshua and cursing as the Son of God unraveled his works. Here he schemed how he might undo the Godhead. For the Hellforge was located within the center of the creature Hell, and she had submarined herself deep into the core of the Earth; mixing her celestial blood with the planet's terrestrial lava, for beneath continental shelves and the shift of tectonic plates, the beast had made herself home.

Yet even here Lucifer was restricted, for unknown to him the souls of both the righteous and unrighteous dead El had caused to dwell. And situated beyond the power of even his master sat a realm that was whispered as Paradise. A chamber within Hell itself surrounded by the creature---even protected. For when the retreat from Satan's reach was discovered hiding amidst his own abode, Lucifer conscripted minions to devise means to cross the bile-filled chasm that Hell itself raised to prevent the two groups from crossing. So even at the heart of Hell, and in the midst of Lucifer's storehouse to create weapons to combat the Almighty. El placed within His wayward son's view a reminder that He was always near. An ever present yet subtle reminder that He was a power to be reckoned with and that power was His alone. For the ever-present view of righteous men who were able to see his unrighteous works, vexed Lucifer to no end.

Ashtaroth found his master at the Forge and bowed low.

"My liege, there is word that we have been breached."

Lucifer looked upon Talus who hung suspended from the center of the Forge. His stone, and that of a great many others, powered Hell to create weapons and creatures, pieced together from the millennia of angels and men who lined her veins. Lucifer watched in silent glee as the new Kiln stitched a fresh creation.

"Behold, Ashtaroth. Behold the beginnings of the downfall of El. For you have arrived in time to see the culmination of my many days work, and the beginning of the end of the Alpha and Omega."

Fire erupted from a chute in the ceiling and from it lowered a glowing shard of rock. The gem pulsed and dark illuminated beams of jet black shadows poured from it. It glistened as though tears beaded from it, and smoke and ash floated from the charcoal-like rock.

"What is it?" Ashtaroth said in wonder.

Lucifer stretched forth a hand and the stone floated into his palm. His cheekbones raised to reveal a slow emerging smile and his fingers curled over the smooth rock. "The greatest device of destruction ever made. It is a combination of Kilnstone and living cadmium beams that undergird Heaven. It is a seed, and as thou knowest, so much can come from such a small thing."

Lucifer chuckled at his own wit and turned to look at the chasm that separated Paradise from the rest of the underworld. He walked to the edge of the great canyon and whispered in angelic tongue to the stone, then threw the black gem across the chasm into the darkness.

In the gloom, it smote the great canyon wall, and a singular, radiant beam of light then divided and branched in all directions. A rumbling shook the ground, lightning streaked from across the gulf to the foot of Lucifer, and a booming thunderclap echoed through the depths. The Prince of the Power of the Air blasted the silence with a shrill cackle to the inhabitants of Paradise across the way.

"Behold, Moses, and give heed, oh David. Let Abraham, Isaac, and Jacob give ear. The lot of you, Sons of Adam have thought yourself safe from my reach these many days. Believing yourself to have safe harbor, shielded behind a creature that El hath made to consume my kind alive, yet here I stand. Standing in defiance to your Hope! Why? Because El will not dare come here to rescue you. For if I held no claim to thee, would you not even now ascend to the Father? But alas, He hath fed you lies. There is no power that can you save thee from my hand for I am a sure coming wave that will descend upon thee. Behold the work of my hands and tremble!"

Immediately the ground shook and rock jutted from the sides of Paradise and when it did, several of the righteous were knocked off their feet. They watched as a towering spire of trigonal black crystal erupted from the ground. A spire fifty cubits high. It swayed when it reached the top of its summit then fell to its side collapsing under its own weight. The black crystal shattered into pieces and the pieces crawled across the ground to join themselves one to another, dividing as they clawed across the ground in grinding and screeching lunges creating, even more, crystals. Clumps grew and formed a great span and its width was such that one could walk upon it. The crystalline bridge lunged outward across the gulf, growing slowly as it followed the trail of lightning that stopped at Lucifer's feet. The once mighty prince of Heaven then smiled and spoke aloud to the inhabitants of Paradise that they might hear.

"Know that I will bridge this gulf and when I do, I will harvest your souls made in the image of God, and you too will feed my Forge and light the fires of Hell. I will ascend from the pit of this place. And with El's own power, resident triune in his righteous image. I will with Hell, and Charon, once more stretch out my hand and make the Father bleed, and the shadow of my image shall reach throughout all creation."

David, Noah and a host of others looked on in defiance, but Hezekiah, former king of Israel, spoke aloud what was on many of their minds. "He will breach the gulf in time. What then will we do?"

David looked at his younger descendant, then placed his hand on Moses' shoulder and spoke for all to hear. "I do not fear this braggart, for the Lord my God hath said unto my God, sit thou here at my right hand until I make thine enemies thy footstool, for I have slain the bear and the lion, and who is this uncircumcised stench of foul air that would defy the armies of the living God? For he will fall...not by our hand, but by the Lord's. Alas, do not succumb to fear, for the Lord our God is with us."

David then knelt in prayer, and all of Paradise followed his example and knelt with him, and they prayed that El would rescue them from the hand of the enemy.

Lucifer watched from afar and smirked. "Pray to El...intercede to thy God, for it matters not..."

"My Lord," interrupted Ashtaroth "Forgiveness, but what is thy command concerning the breach?"

Lucifer folded his arms and turned to his servant and frowned. "It is of no consequence. Talus's capture hath evoked the expected response from Heaven. Yet tell me, who hast surrendered themselves to folly that they would dare enter my house?"

"Grigoric scouts report the head of House Harrada leads a party through the veins and that Iblis guides them. Undoubtedly to the Forge."

Lucifer snickered. "Undoubtedly. You will not interfere with their coming. Let them come. Hell will see to their dissolution."

Ashtaroth nodded. "As you command my king, and if Hell does not?"

Lucifer's grin turned cold, and his eyes narrowed, "Then you will prepare to mount more heads upon my trophy hall for I shall see to it."

Chapter Eight: Entrapment

Yeshua stood before the tomb of His friend Lazarus, watching the eyes of those who scoffed at the possibility that hope could triumph over Death. A thousand eyes of angels, whose station were at all times to stand as minister to the Son of God. Also, the Horde was very aware of Yeshua's disruptive presence, and those who despised the Son of God marked Him who had thrown them from their home. For all hovered as a spectral cloud of witnesses, invisible, to the human eye, watching with bated breath and anxious anticipation at any action that God in the flesh would take.

None had long to wait.

With swollen eyes and a face streaked with tears. Yeshua knew that the time to reveal the power of He who vocalized creation was upon them, and eternity wrapped in the flesh spoke to the blackness of an open tomb.

"Lazarus, come forth."

The words of God reverberated across space and time, and past the dimension of life and death. The power of God smashed through the barriers that separated the realms and reached into the underworld to find Lazarus speaking to his peers amidst the righteous dead. Lazarus' spirit was then plucked from his place and rose from the shining realm of Paradise.

Lazarus traveled through corridors of blinding light and watched as a great whirlwind raged before him. Shredding gusts of wind rode upon the backs of screams that could be heard from a creature that lay trapped therein. A great hand parted the impassable hurricane and lifted him through the cyclonic gale, pulling him further into the corridor of light. His spirit traveled through earth and rock, he saw his corpse shrouded in linen. He lit upon it spreading himself over it. His spirit united with his flesh and entered the empty shell. His chest rose and fell with shallow breaths as his heart began to once more pump oxygenated blood through his frame. His muscles turned soft as rigor mortis fled from his cells. Through linen covered eyes, Lazarus knew that he dwelt again in the land of the living. And upon the order of his King; hobbled bound from his stone seat in grave clothes and stumbled from the darkness of his tomb into the light of day.

And when Lazarus had come forth, many fell to their knees in shock. Others gasped and all were amazed, for a man, dead four days in a sealed tomb, now stood before them wrapped in burial cloth.

"Loose him and let him go," commanded the Lord.

Several men timidly approached the mummified body and loosed the bands of linen that swaddled him. When Lazarus's face was revealed, he smiled and immediately his sister Mary, ran to her brother, embraced him, and wept.

Lucifer had come to the surface to see on a report that Yeshua had plucked a soul from the clutches of Paradise.

Enraged, Lucifer said, "I also will have this power over life and death."

Lucifer, the Host, and the Horde watched that within their midst Yeshua and the humans basked in joy that a member of their kind had been freed from death.

Azazel's soldiers hovered over Yeshua and surrounded Him, waiting for the least provocation from the enemy or a command from their king to engage, yet none came. Yeshua paused in the celebrations of reunion with His friend, while He and Lucifer exchanged glances and their eyes locked upon one another.

The Prince of Darkness' cold eyes narrowed and nostrils flared in venomous contempt, but the Son of God returned His creation's gaze, staring the angel down. Lucifer's slowly drew his sword from its scabbard and all the surrounding Host and Horde drew theirs. Two armies poised in a silent, invisible tension, each ready to take up arms upon their leader's command. Lucifer's hands clenched and unclenched at the hilt of his blade, while seconds ticked between them all. Each wondering in the moments that passed, if open conflict would spill over into the realm of men. Each curious if pretense could finally be shed and mankind drawn into open war.

Yeshua raised a hand smiled to His wayward son. Raised his hands as if to order all to stop, and all swords returned to their sheaths by force. Shock and fear dressed the daemons' faces for the Son of God had with impunity made their weapons of no effect.

Christ shook His head in silent warning. This was not the day to do battle. The King of Darkness sneered with bared teeth, he pouted in anger, turned from his God's gaze and motioned for his soldiers to follow. The Horde obeyed, and lifted themselves to the skies. Yeshua looked on as His rebellious children soared to parts unknown. All with malice to do evil to the world of men.

Celebrations continued that Lazarus had been raised from the dead. And the man now raised from the dead, and having seen the true nature of reality, could also see that surrounding them all were thousands of angels, both elect, and fallen; everywhere the eye could see. He looked to Yeshua, who shook His head again in a silent cue to say nothing, and many Jews believed on the Son of God that day, but some looked upon the Messiah with disdain and reported the miracle to the Pharisees.

And from the moment of Lazarus's resurrection, Lucifer plotted to have Yeshua killed, knowing that he himself could not touch God in the flesh. He sent spirits to sow fear and envy to Israel's religious leaders while Lucifer gathered the chief priests and Pharisees to the council.

"What do we?" a Pharisee said. "This man doeth many miracles. If we let Him alone, all men will believe on Him and the Romans will claim both our place and our nation."

One of them, named Caiaphas, being the high priest that same year, said unto them, "Ye know nothing at all, nor consider that it is expedient for us, that one man should die for the people, that the whole nation perish not." And this spake he not of himself: but being the high priest that year, he prophesied that Yeshua should die for the nation; And not for that nation only, but that also He should gather together in one the children of God that were scattered abroad, and from that day forth they took counsel together to put Him to death.

And Lucifer stood in the balcony of the council with his lieutenants and beamed, knowing he would use mankind to assassinate the Eternal God who had the audacity to walk the Earth in mortal flesh.

* * *

Eskalion and Turiel emerged from within a floor of Hell. The tendrils had grasped them earlier, now released them and receded into the ceilings, retracting into the great darkness beyond. Beneath them, the opening from which they entered shut, the sounds of the hissing lava and the bulging eyes dissipated with its closure.

"Are you alright?" asked Eskalion.

"Aye, I have been burned, but it looks worse than it appears."

"Very well then," said Eskalion. "We need to keep moving."

"Agreed," said Turiel.

Turiel floated into the air and Eskalion stood to his feet. "Surely the creature had us. Why release us here?"

Turiel shrugged his shoulders "Why, indeed, my Arelim friend. Why, indeed? Nevertheless, I see a light ahead. What say you we venture toward it?"

Eskalion strained to see in the darkness. "I see nothing but black upon blackness. What light do you speak of that you see?"

"Perhaps it is only attuned to my Grigoric eyes alone that I am able to make out its existence. Yet if there is a light ahead, let us avail ourselves of it," Turiel said. "Here...take my hand and follow."

Eskalion did as he was bidden and took Turiel's hand. They floated following a light that was just out of Turiel's reach; a light that seemed to direct them deeper into the chamber.

"Do you think Iblis and Jerahmeel made it?" asked Eskalion.

Turiel was silent for a moment, fixated on the light that now slightly pulsed. "I hope so. I truly hope so."

"Earlier in the lower halls...why did you touch the walls? What were you thinking?"

"I am sorry, it is as if something called out to me. Something good and beautiful. I cannot describe it. There were lights within the walls, they called to me."

"Lights? Called to you? You mean you could hear them?"

"No, not with my ears, no. But with my eyes...it beckoned to me."

Eskalion grew increasingly nervous. "And there is a light that you see now that we follow?"

Turiel nodded in the darkness. "Aye. It is beautiful. I do not understand why you do not see it."

Eskalion released Turiel's hand. "Turiel, I think we should stop."

"For what? I can clearly see that an object now resides in the room. It seems to be a pedestal...yes. I see it clearly now. A pedestal, and there seems to be a book atop it."

Suddenly, red circular runes appeared on the floor beneath Eskalion's feet. More of the circles then filled the floor, each one containing ancient Elomic glyphs. Light slowly crept into the room all around Eskalion. Light that revealed that the walls had eyes.

"Turiel stop!" Eskalion said.

But Turiel paid him no heed as he hovered, entranced in fascination over the translucent book now before him. A tome of such beauty that it gleamed in light. Its visage such that it seemed to fade in and out of existence. The leather bound book gave off an aroma, not unlike mint and wafted beneath his nose and a spectral voice from the book called to him to peer within.

Eskalion gasped, slowly realizing that everything in Hell was a ruse. And that the creature had lured them here, separated the party members from one another, and had singled out Turiel in particular. The Grigori simply followed the delusion that Hell had allowed him to see. An enticement that led him exactly where she wanted him. Turiel grasped that Hell was far more intelligent than they had been led to believe and that they were in grave danger.

Eskalion called to his brother again, but Turiel was too entranced to hear his brother's muffled words, too mesmerized as his hands touched the gilded tome on the grand lectern before him. His fingers caressed the book, and his love for all things written guided his eyes to read what was written within, and the moment his eyes glanced upon the text of the page, the words of the book sprang up and shrouded him in flowing black ink. His stylus turned to a dagger as he slashed at that which held him, but Hell had sprung her trap. The Redactor struggled, reaching out to Eskalion for help, but it was too late. He felt himself slowly lose substance, and in a moment he was gone, his body sucked like a funnel into the book. The tome slammed shut, and a surge of light shot out to saturate the room, blinding Eskalion. He shielded his eyes until they adjusted to the light levels. When the haze lifted, he saw the daemons surrounded him with weapons drawn.

One voice spoke to all. "Hell hath made impotent the Redactor. He is no longer a threat. Retrieve the book, and destroy the Arelim." Guards immediately raced to cut Eskalion down, and he drew his sword to engage the group in battle, hacking and slashing against the throng now stood arrayed against him.

Quietly, out of sight and tucked away in the corner of the room, Ashtaroth watched as Eskalion and the powerful Redactor Turiel, rolled on the floor struggling against forces imagined.

Watching as Hell slowly wrapped her prey's minds in tendrils of maggots, allowing each to live out their illusions while she consumed them alive.

Ashtaroth grinned at the pitiful scene and left to report to his master, satisfied that a portion of Heaven's incursion into the creature had been contained.

* * *

Enoch and his party stumbled along the dark path, walking ever deeper under the mountain. The cadmium beams that supported the palace could be seen growing and stretching above their heads. Great stone pillars latticed the ceilings and walls, each stretching and branching in all directions, burrowing into rock. Stalactites lined the corridors which they walked dripping of water, while sliding rocks and fog saturated all the eye could see. The burrowing beams made the craggy cavern shake. Tremors and aftershocks made Enoch uneasy as he and his party walked on a ledge, each precarious step carefully taken so that Enoch would not fall into the blackness below.

"How do we know that we are going the right way?" asked Metatron.

Hadriel replied. "There is but one way to Aesir, and we are upon the path."

"And you know this how?" asked Enoch who carefully followed Gabriel as they shimmied their backs hard against the cliff face.

Hadriel sighed. "The catacombs were not always as you see them now. I remember...because I was here."

Enoch stopped asking questions, watching the sad faces of Gabriel and Hadriel. He wondered of the events that happened in their pasts to turn this place into what they saw before them now.

Gabriel stopped and raised his fist to bring the party to a halt. The party members ceased moving and each stared past the others in attempts to make out the scene before them.

"Where are we?" asked Metatron.

Gabriel sighed. "The remains of the Canyon of Fellowship."

Metatron looked about him, and fore and side were ledges and hovering platforms of cadmium beams. They gave off an iridescent glow and shimmered, suspended in midair. Below them was a great chasm of darkness, the depth of which could not be known.

"Why are we stopping? Why can we not cross?" Metatron said.

Hadriel picked up some earth and pebbles, then replied, "Behold and watch." He tossed the dirt and it landed onto one of the floating platforms of rock. The solid layer of crystalline rock then disappeared, the pebbles and dirt then fell into the blackness below. Each then listened for a sound to indicate that somewhere in the deep dark, a bottom might exist. But no sound ever came.

"Could we not fly across?" said Metatron.

Enoch pointed in the distance. "No, we cannot...behold."

The group watched as crystalline platforms materialized, then disappeared and reappeared, but never appearing in the same place nor elevation. Platforms crashed into one another, as they reappeared, disintegrating into nothingness.

Moreover, openings lined the walls of the canyon and great gusts of wind issued forth and blew across the gulf of black. Side drafts burst in spasmodic fashion from the openings, while from others, the winds drafted down, making flight dangerous to undertake.

Gabriel studied the chasm and eyed the disappearing and reappearing platforms, counting under his breath. "There is a pattern," he said.

"Are you sure?" Enoch said.

"There is a pattern," he said again.

Hadriel looked at him and cocked his head. "I do not see it. How can you be sure?"

Gabriel then looked at Enoch and spoke softly to him. "Do you trust me?"

"With my life," said Enoch.

"Then climb within the folds of my wings and hold tight around my neck."

Metatron looked at him. "Are you mad? You cannot cross that!"

Gabriel did not reply. Enoch looked to Metatron and then to Gabriel. With a bit of hesitation, he climbed atop Gabriel's shoulders and settled in the folds of Gabriel's wings.

"Are you ready?"

Enoch snickered. , "No, but proceed anyway."

Gabriel nodded, and the Leopard of Heaven was off. His form seemed to blur as he ran into what seemed to be ether, but when he settled to his feet in the middle of space, all gasped until a platform materialized beneath him. Gabriel paused, took a breath, and leaped upwards and with a dash, he was a blur to Hadriel and Metatron, who looked now terrified for the duo. Gabriel landed atop another platform, but its crystalline surface caused him to slip slightly. Enoch lost his grip and fell plunging into the darkness.

Gabriel raced to catch him, his speed such that he overtook Enoch who fell easily into his arms. Gabriel then stretched his great wings and propelled them towards the chasm's side, then pushed off and launched them back to a platform. Gabriel viewed that two jumps would lead them to safety.

He waited, knowing that within seconds the platform that they stood upon would disintegrate beneath their feet. He looked anxiously waiting for the next to reappear.

"Gabriel?" Enoch spoke uncertainly.

"Soon," Gabriel replied as he turned to eye a cavern opening behind them.

Enoch also looked behind them and saw that the platform began to disappear and would soon cause them to drop to the depths below. Gabriel adjusted their position to the center of the platform, then spread his wings. "Get ready!" he yelled.

Gabriel saw debris fly from the opening in the wall, and held Enoch tight. The platform then disappeared from underneath their feet.

"Gabriel!" yelled Metatron in helplessness and fear that his comrades were lost. He moved to also place himself on a platform. But Hadriel grabbed him and held him back that he would not be lost to foolishness.

Enoch screamed as gravity sought to pull them into the deep, but a great gust from the cave opening across from them caught Gabriel's wings and shoved them across the expanse, and they landed atop another platform. "We are almost there!" shouted Gabriel.

Ten cubits laid between them and the ledge, and Gabriel, not willing to lose Enoch, heaved Enoch across the remaining distance. Enoch sailed through the air and landed hard on the ledge. Gabriel then flexed his wings and every muscle in his body was taut as he unfurled the wings on his ankles and sprinted as a runner out his blocks running atop the platform as it disappeared behind him with each step. He extended his body and launched himself across the expanse, wings unfurled as a great bird of prey, gliding towards Enoch on the other side.

Enoch lifted himself from the ground and turned to see that a cave opening stood behind him. He could feel the cool breeze stroke his face, and in the moments that passed he heard the sound of rushing wind.

Instinctively, he dived away from the opening as a battering ram of air slammed straightway into Gabriel, pushing him away from the cliff.

Gabriel slammed into a rocky floating slab of a platform and propelled farther away from both Enoch and the rest of the party. He tried to right himself, grasping at the platform against relentless air. And although he was powerful, the mighty angel could not escape the blast that pummeled him across the expanse to the opposite side of the chasm wall. His head struck the rock surface with a thud, knocking the Malakim prince unconscious. He then fell like a bird with a broken wing, tumbling into the blackness of the abyss, a dim light falling and overtaken by the dark depths below.

"Noooo!" Metatron cried out as he fell to his knees, who now on his knees stood screaming from the cliffs edge into the darkness. "No," he whimpered.

Enoch pushed himself to his feet, and quickly ran to the ledge and looked for any sign of his friend. "GABRIEL!" He cried out into the dark, and the dark answered not, and only the sound of rustling winds echoed in reply.

Metatron choked back tears and Enoch peered into the deep black, hoping against hope that Gabriel would return, Hadriel recorded the events as was commanded by his kind. As he journaled the entry of Gabriel's heroic act to save Enoch, his heart sank. But Orithinal, the Grigori assigned to Gabriel, suddenly appeared from the shadows and broke his silence.

"I have watched these many days the actions of the Malakim Prince. I hold his journal in my hand and have stayed silent and chronicled. But no more. Now witness and bear record that I now break the laws of our people, that the word of the Lord not fall to the ground. Behold the interference of a Grigori, and my submission to my fate. Let the scroll of Gabriel's life be redacted, and the events I have seen be rewound. Let the tale of existence be undone, and my story within unbound. Rewrite this scroll, my King. Make new our past events. I give my life in exchange for his. Let a new thing be written, and let this thy servant be found honorable in thy sight, but if not, let it be known among our people that Orithinal would not see Gabriel lost."

Caphus and Tymierial then appeared and ceased in their own chronicling of Metatron and Enoch as they reached out to stop Orithinal, crying, "Nooo! Do it not!"

But it was too late, for Orithinal took his pen and slit his hand with the tip so that he drew blood; then he took the book, and opened his vests to reveal his Kilnstone, and it was gaseous to behold. He then took the page that chronicled Gabriel's fall, placed his bloody hand upon it, and placed the page on the ground. And when he did so, his stone glowed, then sparked, and a voice was heard from Him that shook the cavern.

"Thy petition hath been granted." And it was the voice of the Holy Spirit.

And Hadriel then screamed. His stone shattered and the pages of his book burst into flames as he faded in and out of existence. Metatron stepped away from him, and when he turned his eyes from the light that was the brightness of Orithinal, he beheld that the Grigori that watched Enoch and himself also appeared and glowed.

Enoch watched the scene from across the way and stared into the darkness where Gabriel had fallen. A pulsating light appeared in the distance and raced up the cavern wall in prismatic colors, and shot forth from the deep and landed next to Enoch. When Enoch tried to look upon the figure, his eyes burned that he could not see, and a voice spoke to him.

"It is I, Enoch, for I am yet alive. Behold, and view the work of God."

And when Enoch lifted his eyes, Gabriel stood there, glowing.

"But how?" said Enoch. "I saw you fall."

Gabriel pointed across the cavern to Hadriel who watched as Orithinal, his peer in the Grigoric order, shown as bright as a star, and his body, pen, tome, and inkhorn were aflame. And when the flames were extinguished, Orithinal stood before them all without the cowl of his people. His pen, book, and inkhorn had fallen to the ground, and he stood naked before them and said, "I have little time. I must go to the Mist, and here in Limbus will I await the Lord to free all from the realm of the Dead. I impart to thee, Hadriel, this last gift," and he motioned for Hadriel to come near.

Hadriel then bowed his head and leaned close to Orithinal, who touched his eyes, and thus Hadriel could see a path to cross the chasm, and it shimmered in the darkness. And when he turned to look back upon Hadriel, his Grigoric brethren who chronicled also stood by him, and Orithinal faded into mist, the breeze of which dissipated his gaseous remains until he was gone. His tome then fell to the earth with a thud.

The remaining two Grigori, Caphus, and Tymierial, then turned to Hadriel and sorrow filled their countenance. They bowed and vanished again, concealed beyond the sight of Elohim, to continue journaling the Book of Life.

Hadriel grasped at the mist as it slowly wafted away into the air and whispered, "I will never forget this day, my brother." He picked up the book and smiled. "Your chronicle will not be lost."

Hadriel stood to his feet and he and Metatron crossed the hidden path of the chasm to join both Enoch and Gabriel, who hugged him. He bowed and they continued their perilous journey through the cavern, but Gabriel stopped for a moment and turned back to reflect on the angel he had never met nor seen...a mighty angel who had just given his life, that he might fulfill his mission for all their people, and Gabriel whispered to the mists in the air, "I will not make thy sacrifice in vain. This I promise, and this I swear."

And he turned and followed his comrades deeper into the mountain towards Aseir.

* * *

Michael walked through the streets of the city, beholding misery on every corner. He happened upon his people, some stood shivering against buildings, others huddled together, holding one another in archways of business. Michael mused on his actions as Chief Prince and the power El had invested in him as the federal head of his people, for in Him all lived, and in Him, all died. Yet Michael did not succumb to sickness. It was a discipline from El, and he resisted the urge to despise the chastening of the Lord, for he recognized the Withering was but the scourge of the Lord, to Michael's and his people's profit.

But what beauty could come from such suffering? What order could arise from such chaos?

Michael was close to God, but despite his proximity, even he failed to completely understand the logic of the Almighty. He had, however, learned to trust him, and though he be slain and his people destroyed, he would follow El into oblivion, for El was hope, light, and life.

The Prince of Angels passed another shivering in the hollows of a park and reached down to sit next to him. Michael took his shivering brother in his arms and wrapped himself around his brother like a swaddling cloth, and the two huddled together as Michael rocked his fellow citizen of Heaven and comforted him with a song.

El and the Holy Ghost watched his son's actions from afar, and how he took stock as a shepherd walking among his sheep. El smiled and He and the Holy Spirit mused amongst themselves.

"This thing is hard for us, for the cries of the people move me with compassion, even to spare. But, alas, the Chief Prince will not be moved save by the suffering of others, and with the Withering, we will at last purge the remnants of pride from the people. Never again will they see division."

El Pneuma nodded. "We take no pleasure in the suffering of our children, yet he must turn from his own way that he might live, for the hidden things, the things that are contained in the heart, are what contaminates our son and we must flush to the surface the issues of the heart within the Chief Prince lest they fester and take root and rebellion spring anew to our children's destruction."

El looked upon His child as He watched him comfort the citizens of Heaven.

"Aye, the Prince left to himself would be content to reside in self-delusion. We will strip this from him, and remove from his heart all infection from Satan."

"And when he turns from his own way?" said the Holy Spirit. "When he is abased enough to confess his sin?"

"Then..." replied El as He sat on His throne, "Then judgment will end in my own house, and Yeshua will return to unseal the books of life, and we will pour out our judgment upon the Evil One. And then, El Pneuma...then we shall know peace."

* * *

Enoch's party crossed a stone bridge. To their left emanating from the darkness, a waterfall poured from the lower pools of Heaven, cascading into the crashing darkness below. To their front, light glowed from an opening that faced them. Gabriel walked slowly over the ancient, carved bridge, careful as he watched every step.

"I appreciate your coming with me," said Enoch. "You were first among those I wanted to accompany me on this journey."

Gabriel took a step forward, "I am honored, Adamson. Of course, if you did not persist in us walking, Metatron or I could simply carry you through Limbus to Aesir."

Metatron snickered and projected his voice forward for Enoch to hear. "The human is as stubborn as any of his kind."

Enoch scrunched his face in irritation and replied. "I beg to differ, my prince. There is something to be said for having one's feet firmly on the ground."

"Perhaps," said Gabriel. "Yet it would be much faster."

Enoch replied. "I say again. I will NOT be carried. I would rather walk."

Hadriel sighed. "Aye. He is stubborn, indeed."

Gabriel laughed. "Indeed," and chuckled all the more.

Enoch leaned upon his staff and continued as they made their way across the bridge and suddenly stopped. Gabriel and the others also came to a halt.

Enoch felt his cheek.

Moisture from above fell down upon him and gently slid down the side of his face. He wiped his cheek, sniffed the liquid and recoiled from the stench. He wiped his hands on his robes and looked up. "The ceiling moves," said. Enoch.

Everyone turned their eyes upward and slow moving octopi and serpent-like bodies writhed in whispered hissing overhead.

"We have entered a nest of Zoa," said Hadriel.

Mouths of razor sharp teeth opened and closed, and from the front of the group, a large tentacled beast dropped from the ceiling and crashed onto the bridge, barring the way to cross further. The great structure groaned and creaked, and chunks of stone and dust untroubled for ages now fell from the catwalk, plummeting into the darkness below.

The Zoa raised its head like a cobra's hood, and stretched its elongated neck, baring teeth that resembled broadswords and hissed at the group, sizing the party up. Enoch backed away slowly; he slightly turned his head toward his rear that he could be heard.

"Gabriel..." Enoch whispered.

"Yes, Enoch?" Gabriel's eyes fixated on the Zoa before them, its legs slowly coiling in preparation to lunge.

"Carry me."

Gabriel raised his eyebrow and gave a knowing smirk and Enoch turned his back to the creature and sprinted into Gabriel's waiting arms.

The Zoa roared and charged, galloping toward the group to devour its prey, but the trio of angels leaped off the bridge and took flight.

Zoa fell from the ceiling in droves. Roars filled the cavern as all around them the creatures sprang to life as bats disturbed.

Gabriel, Metatron, and Hadriel ducked and weaved through falling Zoa, zig-zagging and twisting between the elephantine creatures. Enoch, huddled in the strong arms of Gabriel, shouted, "Fello ws...behind you!"

Metatron looked to his rear and saw a great flying octopi rise from the darkness, and those that fell from the ceiling sprouted wings and took flight after the party.

"Ugh, the creatures can fly! Go swiftly now!" Metatron yelled.

Metatron led the way and spied a group of stalactites that draped from the ceiling. "Gabriel, through there," he said.

Gabriel nodded and dived around the columns of limestone and cadmium which hung from the cavern beams. The three angels dodged and swerved to avoid being plastered against the great stone teeth that dangled from the cavern's roof.

The Zoa quickly closed upon the trio with giant wings, snapping at Hadriel who took up the rear. He weaved around a stalactite and the beast, unable to move as deftly, smashed into the protruding rock, exploding the great barrier into pieces. The creature roared in pain and fell into the darkness below, crashing against walls. Its guttural cries ascending from the deep.

A flock of the creatures still trailed them. Unmoved by a member of the pack's fall, continued as a swarm of flying, tentacled teeth, each one snapping with spear-like beaks to seize their fleeing prey.

Through caves and falling waters from above, the angels flew in a phalanx formation, and Metatron shouted to Gabriel, "There is a light ahead! Go to, and we shall swing around and keep them from you!"

"But what about you?" Gabriel shouted back.

"Take refuge near the light in the distance and we will find you!"

Enoch cried out, "Whatever your plan, hurry, for they are closing!"

Hadriel nodded to Metatron, who acknowledged his peer's purpose. Metatron then drew his sword and with a Zoa flying in tow, he flew to a stalactite where he placed his sword in the rock and flew roundabout the downward pointed spire, turning to face the multitude of flapping teeth and propelled himself headlong into the flock. The angel moved with the swiftness of his kind, and opening the pores of his flesh, he shouted a battle cry. Powerful, unrestricted vocal chords created a conical force of sound that echoed and traveled through the cavern before him, bursting the eardrums of some Zoa and scattering the flock. Stalactites shattered and exploded in all directions, large chunks of which fell, crushing the creature's skulls and sending them careening into the void below. The shards spread out as rocky shrapnel and injured others, causing the flock to slow. Pressing his attack, Metatron fell upon those that had stalked him, and the hunters now became the prey. His sword sliced jaws, necks, and wings of the creatures as each roared in agony and plunged into the darkness below.

Hadriel's attack was more subtle as he misted and as a creature flew through him. He re-solidified atop the monster's back and buried his daggers deep into the flying arms of the beast. As a man reins a horse, Hadriel pulled the animal to fly under his control and turned it sweeping back against its own kind.

The flock dispersed in confusion as Hadriel made the beast attack. Snapping at wings and legs, and swinging one captive Zoa into another, Hadriel kept his body close against the creature's back, as he knocked several of the creatures out of the air. Tugging hard against makeshift reins, forcing the Zoa into a loop. He flew the monster next to Metatron, who with his swords and bare hands sliced and pummeled the snapping beasts out of the sky.

Scores of the creatures sundered before them as hewn tentacles flew through the air and greenish blood misted onto each angel. Zoas fell from the cavern skies and tumbled to the void below. The beasts then turned on themselves and attacked those that were injured. Each snap into another's flesh brought with it the scent of more blood until the flock was a cacophony turned on itself, and the whole, a mass of teeming, cannibalistic bat-like creatures falling, hissing and screaming.

Hadriel released his mount, crashing it into another Zoa, and misted. With one backward glance over a job well done, Hadriel and Metatron moved to rejoin Gabriel and Enoch.

Gabriel stood in a lighted cavern where an ancient bridge once spanned. He set Enoch down and watched as his brethren returned to them. Metatron lighted softly to the ground and Hadriel deftly fell next to his brethren and solidified.

"Are you alright?" Gabriel said.

Metatron nodded. "Aye, no worse for wear."

"Nevertheless, let us be watchful," Hadriel said. "For the area in the mountain of God that separates the Halls of Annals must somehow connect to this place."

"Perhaps," said Gabriel. "There are many things that El hath done in times past that is not known to us. The Zoa protect the secret things. And behold, what hath been more secreted away than the path to Aesir? While El's sovereign will allow us to roam this place, it is yet rife with danger. Nevertheless, we have arrived at the gate of Aesir. Behold."

Gabriel motioned his hand, and behind him, a barrier of visible sound could be both seen and heard. Glowing waves emanated from a golden portal, and through the waves, golden skies where creatures of flames could be seen flying beyond the rim.

Enoch smiled, "Finally, we are here. I think I can walk again."

Gabriel grinned. "Of course, Adamson."

The group breathed a collective sigh of relief and studied the portal. Enoch then stretched out his hand to touch it.

"No, wait!" Metatron pushed Enoch aside. He looked upon the portal, and changed his flesh to reveal the pores and living organs that created sound, and when he did so, he released various notes to everyone's hearing.

"What are you doing?" Enoch said.

"If you had touched the barrier, it would have brought you to dissolution. Watch."

Metatron motioned everyone back and tossed a pebble against the barrier. Nothing happened. He smiled. "Now watch." He unsheathed his sword, still stained with the blood of Zoa, and inserted the tip of the blade into the barrier. The steel forged blade sizzled and the blood boiled away as a foul stench and hiss of steam filled the area.

"I thank you," said Enoch.

"You are most welcome. The barrier is one of sound. I believe I can match its frequency and cancel it out. Since El told you to travel to this land, I trust He will protect for the Seraph abide in a land of sweltering fire and heat."

Enoch swallowed hard. "Proceed," he said.

Gabriel raised a hand. "Wait. Although Enoch is here because El hath commanded him, El did not indicate we will be welcomed. We will most assuredly not be. We cannot provoke the Schism further after we enter."

Hadriel chuckled. "We are merely trespassing into their land and violating the terms El hath set forth for our kind. What can possibly go wrong?"

Enoch sighed. "I could not have made it this far without your help. I suspect I will not make it further without it as well, yet I cannot ask you to risk war with the Seraphim, and am content to journey alone if need be."

Gabriel replied. "Michael charged me to see to your success, and to do all in my might to bring healing and reconciliation to our people. I believe El would have thee be the catalyst to that end. I cannot see to that end if I do not abide with thee. Moreover, we have left the capital under siege by the Withering. No, Adamson. We are with thee and we will see what the end will be."

All looked at Enoch, who was quick to reply. "Then we go forward. Metatron, bring down the seal."

Metatron turned to the golden barrier and sung in various pitches and tones. The sound took the color of visible floating notes that emanated from his body. The notes changed in red and blues and hues of yellows and gold. Each one ascended toward the barrier and impacted, and illuminated all the more through pulsing hues of purple, blue and grey.

"It's not working..."

The barrier suddenly lurched forward, and a flash ensued. Enoch and the party stepped back as the seal expanded and reached out to them.

"Keep trying!" Enoch said. "Do not give up."

"The Seraph are powerful in the ways of sound..."

"Keep trying!" Enoch shouted.

Metatron sang and the notes once again floated against the barrier. Each sound slammed into the barrier and it changed colors from grey to yellow and slowly back to gold, and the barrier slowly began contracting in on itself.

"It's working," Enoch said.

Metatron continued in his musical lock picking, and the barrier gave way and turned into turquoise and then melted into green. When it turned emerald green, the barrier shattered, and the blast wave knocked the party down.

Immediately, an overbearing dry swelter reached out to withdraw the very moisture from their lips. Enoch stood and slowly walked into the opening. Gabriel, Metatron and the rest of the group followed, beaming with smiles, relieved that they had made their way through Limbo unscathed.

Enoch turned to face his friends and smile, but a surprising yelp from Hadriel drew his attention. Enoch's eyes spread wide and his face seeped with horror and grief. Gabriel and Metatron turned to look in concerned confusion.

Hadriel had been torn asunder, and a Zoa had the bowels of their comrade as spittle from its mouth, eying them next to attack.

* * *

"Can you find a way to get back to Turiel and Eskalion?" Jerahmeel said, walking behind Iblis as they headed into the gloom.

Iblis replied in irritation. "We've gone over this before. I have no idea where the monster has taken them or if they are even alive. They could be anywhere within the creature." Then his lips curled into a smile, and he laughed.

Jerahmeel stared at him. Looking at him nervously. "What strikes you as funny?"

"I was just thinking of the irony of being digested eternally. To never truly be released to die." Iblis shook his head as he fathomed the concept. "I wonder what the sensation must be like...to eternally experience the ever-space between life and death in a creature that will not let you slip into eternal sleep?"

Iblis went silent for a moment and stopped walking. His knees buckled and while in a half-standing, half-kneeling position, he burst into sobbing.

Jerahmeel lifted him up from off his feet. "Are you daft? There will be time later for weeping. Would you draw undue attention to us?"

Yet Iblis would not be consoled, and shoved Jerahmeel's hand away from his arm, looked at him with a wet smile and then laughed like a maniac.

"We are both dead...we are the living dead, you and I. For look about you. We walk in the very shadow of Death. And where I take you...there is nothing but death that awaits us. We are doomed, I say. Doomed."

Jerahmeel grabbed Iblis by the face and held it firm. "Look at me!" he said. He held his face firm in his palms as he looked into the fallen angel's eyes. Eyes that were glazed, and the prince of all Harrada could see that behind them, the Withering was at work...a slow consuming, burrowing worm of madness that was feasting on the angel's mind. Gnawing away at reason. Jerahmeel released him, and Iblis murmured to himself in unintelligible gibberish. Jerahmeel looked about and realized that with every step they descended deeper into Hell. That the malady would soon overtake both of them.

"Iblis?"

"Doomed. We are doomed, I say. The Father is lost, all is lost. Darkness, wailing and gnashing of teeth..."Iblis paced about the dim chamber, muttering to himself, lost in interrogative questions.

"Iblis!" Jerahmeel said, raising his voice to get his attention, but to no avail.

Jerahmeel looked at where they were. There was no discernible exit. Nothing but the distant sounds of moans and the reek of charred flesh. And in that moment, he remembered Talus and knew that somewhere within the creature, his brother was surrounded by this infernal prison meant for Lucifer and his kind. He looked turned back to looking at Iblis.

Focus him on the task before us. Or his words will be prophetic. Jerahmeel thought to himself. He then spoke to comfort his guide.

"Iblis...thou hast asked to be restored to Heaven. If in good faith lead me to the Hellforge, there might yet be pardon for thee. As long as ye draw breath, there is hope. Do not despair, but if we die here, there is nothing but eternal torment, so keep to the task at hand. If the creature intimidates you, then linger here no longer than necessary."

Iblis stopped pacing and looked at Jerahmeel. His eyes had lost more of their color, and the luster that emanated from all Elohim was dimming.

"You are...correct. I fear the hand of Lucifer. I should have never left Heaven. Never raised arms against the Father. And now look at me. What lot possibly remains to me? Even now I sense the Withering eating away at my mind and darkening my stone. It clouds my mind and judgment it is an oncoming fog where I am lost without a beacon to steer me home. I feel it, and it will not be long before the Withering has me. Oh, how foolish it was to think that I could ever come home. We are not Clayborn." He sighed.

"I envy them you know? For they are malleable. Made from the dust of the Earth. Not the stone of the Kiln. We cannot be changed. I see that now. For I now see what the Father had never designed me to see, and it is a dark thing, my prince. A dark thing, indeed to stare into this depressive inevitability. To know that there remains nothing available to rescue; that no balm exists, nor cure forthcoming to save. You were indeed wise to be wary of me, Harrada, but fear not. While sanity yet remains, I will with my last breath take thee to the place of promise, the place we have both journeyed to see. I will take you to the Hellforge."

Jerahmeel found himself caught between two opinions...torn over feelings of compassion, sorrow, and the justifiable sense that Iblis was deservedly reaping what he, had sown. Who now was experiencing the outcome of his decision. Yet he understood the heart of the Father. Understood, that El took no pleasure in the death of the wicked. But that they would turn from their ways and live. But, alas, that opportunity was for humans, for in his heart, Jerahmeel knew Iblis was right. There was no turning back once his kind had made the decision to leave. No returning to the Father. Nothing but eternal banishment from the presence of God. And when Jerahmeel saw how downcast Iblis was, his resolution to still maintain some semblance of who he once was, Jerahmeel's heart softened and he spoke.

"I thank you, Iblis. Thank you for helping me."

Iblis gave a begrudging smile, nodded, then turned to a wall that barred their path. He breathed onto the walls of flesh and hair follicle-like strands sprung up from the obstruction. Both Iblis and Jerahmeel jumped back and watched as the wall gave way to a chamber. Noxious fumes opened into the area, and heat belched out, making the existing chamber even hotter. The moans and wails became louder and the two looked at one another to find courage.

"The Hellforge is easy to find, my prince," Iblis said, "for it rests at the heart of the digestive system of the creature. If we but give the creature sign of our presence, she of her own accord will direct us toward her belly. Come, and we shall see what the end will be."

Iblis then stepped into the blistering heat and looked back. Jerahmeel swallowed the lump in his throat, sighed and followed him.

* * *

"RUN!" Gabriel cried.

Enoch sprinted toward a lake of brimstone and fire. All of his senses told him that what he saw was impossible, but Heaven contained mysteries and phenomena that he had come to expect, but the Zoa that had ambushed Hadriel now turned its attention to them.

Metatron and Gabriel turned to fight, swords drawn. The Zoa hissed, sizing up the two angels. The animal unwound eight tentacles, and two bat-like wings unfurled from atop its back. It pushed itself upon four tentacles and raised itself high, spreading its wings as a cobra's hood and roaring in defiance as spittle and pieces of Hadriel fell from its mouth.

"This is going to hurt," Metatron said.

"Just disable its ability to fly," Gabriel replied.

"What about you?"

Gabriel eyed the Zoa which crouched and slowly began to move forward. Gabriel waved to Metatron to move away. "Spread out," he said.

The Zoa turned its head toward Gabriel, roared and charged the angel, its tentacles pounding the earth as it ran.

Gabriel sprinted toward the giant, his sword raised and, his wings swept back. He became a blur, and before he was seen again, Metatron saw the Zoa stumble and sidestep backward as a dismembered tentacle whizzed past him.

Metatron launched himself into the air, and from his new-found aerial view, he saw flashes of Gabriel accosting the tentacled giant from all directions. Blurs and shadows of his brother he could but see as blood from slashed tentacles misted into the air from what could only be the swift, unseen blade of Gabriel's attack.

Metatron landed atop the back of the Zoa and plunged his blade deep into the hide of its flesh. The giant howled, and a tentacle swooshed overhead as Metatron, unable to maintain his grip, fell from the hulking creature.

The Zoa turned on its back, and suddenly Metatron came face to face with the mouth that just devoured his friend. The jaws opened, and a beak protruded from within, jetting out to grasp him.

Metatron held the animal's jaws open and dodged the spittle and foul stench of undigested flesh that wafted over him. His muscles strained and feet slid back as the strength of the creature matched his own. The head of house Draco then opened the pores of his flesh and belted out a funnel of sound that shattered the creature's teeth. It recoiled in pain, shrieking, as Gabriel continued his assault, slicing and lacerating. The animal.

Tentacles waved through the air and the thunderous roars of a Zoa enraged echoed across the fiery plane. Enoch watched from a safe haven behind a large outcrop of rocks. He knew enough from his training that though he possessed powers, there was a time to let angels do the job that they were infinitely more capable of...such as battle. He watched from a distance as Metatron managed to get atop the creature and with his sword and slashed into the animal's wings.

Enoch pumped his fist as he saw a severed tentacle of the creature fly apart from its body and the mighty beast tumbled to the earth. The result of the battle prowess and motion-blur that could only be Gabriel.

Enoch smiled as he watched them do battle from afar. Their tandem work cowered the beast as they attempted to drive the monstrosity back from whence it came. Enoch stepped back for a better view and turned to climb over a boulder when he saw a man with six wings surrounded by blue flame. He towered twenty cubits tall and stood with a white sword drawn. Startled, Enoch fell back onto his hind.

"Thou art trespassing on the grounds of Aesir, and will surrender to examination by authority of the King."

Enoch stared at the celestial man, never having seen a Seraph other than those that guarded the entry to the Temple of God. Enoch raised his hands in surrender and replied, "I pose you no threat and my compatriots and I seek out thy King, for we are sent on behalf of God, and I seek one who resides in thy company. A man such as myself by the name of Elijah."

The flaming man seemed surprised and picked up Enoch, pointing his sword at him. "Thy friends have been dealt with even as we speak."

Enoch turned to face Metatron and Gabriel and saw that the Zoa lay face down. A Seraph stood atop it with a spear that had penetrated its skull, and ten seraphim had surrounded the duo. Each angel was shackled in chains and was being led away. Enoch crossed his wrists and raised them above his head in surrender. His captor bound him, and the two joined the others. When Gabriel saw Enoch, he nodded in greeting. The Seraph shoved him and Metatron and the three friends exchanged words.

"I am relieved that thou art safe. Are you injured?"

"I am well," Enoch said. "But where are they taking us?"

"SILENCE!" roared a Seraph.

Immediately Enoch and the two angels cried out in pain and covered their ears, for the shout was excruciatingly loud; and when Enoch pulled his hands away from his ears, his palms were slightly bloodied.

Metatron and Gabriel also had a small trail of blood that streamed from their ears, and Metatron scowled in disapproval, but he did not provoke the Seraph to further anger. He shook his head at Enoch in mute warning to keep silent.

Enoch was, however, angered, and would not remain quiet. "I am the candlestick of the Lord God, and I sit before His presence. I am Enoch, the Translated of the Lord. Is this how thou wouldst handle one who has braved the dangers of Limbus under the command of the Lord to reach thee?"

The captain of the guard stopped, and when he did, all stopped. He turned to look at Enoch and walked slowly toward him, studying him, and eying his person as he spoke.

"You are human, and not Elohim. Our treaty does not extend to thee. The King will decide what shall be done with thee. But thou wilt not be harmed until you are in his presence. We know who you are, Enoch. And it is because of this that the Lumazi Gabriel hast not been destroyed. Fear not, for the King, will surely want to hear thy words."

Enoch harrumphed. "And then?"

The captain smiled at him and said, "Then we shall know if there will be war and if you all shall die."

* * *

Mary poured out spikenard over the feet of Yeshua and wiped them with her hair. All of the disciples were taken aback by her actions but Judas, Judas spoke aloud his disgust of the act.

"Why was not this ointment sold for three hundred pence and given to the poor?"

"Let her alone," said the Lord. "Against the day of my burying hath she kept this. For the poor always ye have with you, but me ye have not always."

Judas lowered his eyes and ruminated to himself. Such a waste. A year's wages poured into the dust, and then to be rebuked by the Rabbi before all.

Judas wrestled with himself, his thoughts like crashing waves pounding rocks. His will vacillated and tossed on the eddies of suggestions and possibilities while his mind fed upon choices that fueled his primary desire for profit.

Lucifer amplified every negative thought and accentuated every rationale that ran counter to Yeshua's teaching. A chorus of enticements played in his mind to justify a decision he knew Judas had nestled deep within his heart. A submerged course of action, Lucifer need only nudge the greedy Human's thinking to bring it to pass, and thus the King of Lies spoke in righteous indignation to this open and willing ear.

What decent person would allow such extravagance to be poured on His feet? With all the need here? Not to speak of the regions roundabout. Is this what we should expect of a King who serves the people? What loss to thyself, for such an item would have fetched a month's wages after deposit into the purse, and none would have been the wiser. The agitated Judas excused himself in a flurry and stomped off, his mind fuming over an opportunity lost and increasingly open to suggestions from the Enemy.

You do know that He hast never allowed you to be a part of His inner circle," the sympathetic voice whispered to his mind. A whisper that sounded so much like his own voice.

I am Judean, Judas thought, and have these simple Galileans been given charge over our temporal affairs? No! Do these unlearned fishermen understand or have letters of learning on matters of finance? No! Yet they sit at the Rabbi's inner circle while I sit on its fringe. How can a man who controls the purse not be a part of a leader's inner circle?

The Voice breathed into his hearing.

Yeshua is a great teacher, but surely He will get us all killed by the Romans.

Judas nodded to himself as he walked to the market.

Exactly! If He has no interest in overthrowing Rome, then what good is He? What good doth healing, teaching, and even casting out of devils do if we are crushed underfoot by Roman occupation? He will bring such attention to us as to compel Rome to strike us down with the sword. What have I gotten myself into? For three years I have sojourned with this group. For three years I have toiled, receiving the hospitality of others. To rejoice in the gain available in this age, and for what? A poor, wandering gypsy of a madman, who adds no value to my position? I cannot let this happen.

Lucifer edged his thoughts more toward his own designs.

Perhaps He could be compelled to bring the Kingdom of God in by force?

Judas's eyes lit up at the thought.

What a clever idea! What if He were confronted by the powers of this world? Then He would be compelled to show the might of God, and usher in the Kingdom now and Rome would fall!

"That's good! That's very good," Judas murmured softly to himself.

The voice continued to feed his mind.

If Yeshua were killed, the people would rise up in wrath at His martyrdom, and end the stench of Rome from off of us. Hmmm, there could indeed be profit in this. Judas mused. If He lives and ushers in the Kingdom, then I will be at His side and my position will be assured in this new government, but if the people rise up against Rome because Rome has killed one of its own.

"Hey, watch yourself!" a man said.

Judas frowned as he bumped into a person. "Watch yourself!" he said.

Is the thing possible? Yes. We could shake the dust of Rome off our feet!

Judas arrived at a fish vendor, pulled the purse of the group from under his shawl, gathered his selections and paid the merchant. He scowled as he looked at the Roman inscription on the drachma and the merchant noted his visible disdain.

"One day brother...we shall be free of Roman rule. One day, one of us will have the power to see it come to an end."

Judas smiled, and replied back, "One day soon my brother," Judas said. "One day soon." Iscariot then turned to rejoin the disciples.

Lucifer smiled as he watched the human return to the Son of God, knowing that very soon...he would be ripe for possession.

* * *

"Arrrgghhhhh!!!!!" screamed Talus.

His cries of anguish echoed across the gulf into Paradise, but his howls simply melded into the moans of the damned. Lucifer, the source of his torment, castigated his captive as he hung from an acidic cross of fire. Charon, the Angel of Death, watched in silent witness to Satan's cruelty as he swaggered back and forth.

"Is this how God treats those He loves? 'Blessed be the death of His saints,'...pssfftt. Foolishness. We have both seen our share of death. We have seen the embodiment of men's fear smite both angel and man down."

Lucifer chuckled. "But I do not fear. I do not fear death because I command it! Know that my plans for the Godking cannot be stopped nor thwarted by those who even now seek to rescue thee, for in seven days' time will my hands grasp the prize of Paradise!"

The Prince of Darkness exulted as behind Talus, the black, self-constructing cadmine bridge, built itself across the gulf. An unstoppable, plodding and arced marched scaffolding that stretched, clawed, and with every day, inched closer toward Paradise and join the realms of the righteous and unrighteous dead.

Lucifer waved his hands in giddy elation. "I will make Yeshua bask in the very pain He hath made for us for He sits in judgment over all, and makes even His own image...His own image, to taste separation from Himself. To experience the void when one is distanced from God. Oh, yes, the Godking willingly evokes punishment as to serrate another from the Author of Life, but is too cowardly to undergo what He Himself would make His own creation endure. But this...this...will...end. For I will cause El to know this intimacy...to know separation. And when I am done, He will know sin in a way that is beyond the mind of both men and angels.

"For El, in His audacity, hath come down. And come down to do what? To usurp me? To destroy me? These petty incursions by His Son to deny my people habitation within the Clayborn will NOT stand, and His ill-gotten attempts to undue the plague of sin that I have unleashed upon the Adam will be for naught.

"For soon, I will inhabit one close to Him, one He cares for, and with the same, betray Him into the hands of His own sin-stained image. The very creation that El loves, this chattel of soft flesh He so dotes over, will I move to destroy Him, and on that fateful day I will stare into Yeshua's eyes as the man He loves brings Him to dissolution. And I will stare into His face, that He might know what He has caused me to know...the gnawing pain of abandonment."

Lucifer's lips turned down and his brow hard as he thought on the perceived injustice of his condition, and then shook his head and laughed at the irony of it all.

"Indeed," he quipped, "I will wound El in a manner unknown since His bleeding at my hand for I will destroy His physical shell, and then He will experience separation from Himself. HE WILL ACTUALLY BECOME SIN! Oh, yes! I will make the Almighty experience in the flesh what He Himself would allow others to know...what...it...is...like...to...die. For I, my brother...I WILL HAVE VENGEANCE!"

Lucifer smiled at Talus while his captive's head hung limp and blood streaked down the Arelim's face. The Evil One then floated, hovering and drew close to whisper into Talus's ear.

"Thou shalt see, for His spirit will descend into Hell, and while dis-empowered in Paradise, I will cross over the gulf and finish what He and I began when El sat on the throne and my sword missed its mark. I will take the spirit of His Son, His beloved Son, and use Him to engine my rise again to Heaven and will forever end the tyrannical rule of the Father."

Lucifer grinned in smugness, proud of the ingenuity of his plans, and confident in his control. He cocked his head and observed that perhaps Talus was not listening,

"Nothing to say? No witty remark? No retort? Perhaps you think you can just ignore me?" Lucifer turned his head up, stroked his chin and muttered, "Hmmpff." He then lowered himself back to the ground.

"I see this subject poses no interest to thee, and that perhaps I have digressed from our initial topic of conversation. Let us return then, shall we? For there is indeed a matter of most importance that we must settle, you and I."

Lucifer then waved his hands and five brilliantly illuminated orbs shown into Talus' face.

"I shall ask you again. How many lights do you see?"

Talus was silent and with glaring eyes, he scrunched his face and contemptuously spat on the ground at Lucifer's feet.

Charon, having observed the tirade, chuckled at Talus's obstinance.

"Do I amuse you slave? Very well...smite him until the Arelim bleeds." he said to Charon.

Charon paused and turned to face Lucifer, folding his arms in defiance.

Lucifer smiled and spoke in sarcastic pentameter. "Doth Death hath compassion on this angel?" He harrumphed. "It matters not. You will not challenge me in this thing."

Charon roared and spread his bony wings. His tentacled arms spanned wide and he fell to the ground and snorted. Hell lurched when he did so and the creature heaved in displeasure. As a bull ready to stampede, Charon snorted, then roared.

Lucifer took a step backward and grabbed the locket of keys around his neck. Hell instantly obeyed the command of the Prince of Darkness and flaming tendrils descended moved to restrain Charon. He heaved the coils off him and pulled from his ashen robes a scythe, slicing the creature's coils. Hell roared in pain, and she lurched so that even those in Paradise felt the tremors and collapsed to the ground as the rumbling ground began to fissure. And when Talus saw that Charon fought back against his captor and that his rage might sunder the righteous dead, he screamed at the Warden to cease.

Lucifer then commanded Hell to stop her attack, and she paused, and he spoke to Charon. "Thou art my slave, but if the desire to serve me is distasteful to the Vengeance of God, then, by all means, listen to the shrill voice of the living dead."

"Charon..." Talus said, "it may be that thou canst fight Hell throughout eternity, and it may be that thou canst perhaps resist this cretin and one day be free of his leash. One day...perhaps, but if thou continue, destruction to the realm of Paradise will most assuredly come. Cease, I beg thee...and do what must be done."

The skeletal mare snorted in retort. He looked with socketless eyes at the ceiling of Hell. Her flaming and acidic strands hung ready to continue their assault at Lucifer's command. He looked past Talus to the denizens across the gulf...humans who did not deserve his vengeance and they too looked back, watching the spectacle from afar. He then eyed Talus who stared at him with eyes that understood forced servitude.

"Please, great one," Talus said, "do what thou hath been bidden."

Charon then eyed Lucifer and roared again. Smoke and fire and ash erupted from his person as the echo of his rage flooded the hallways of Hell, and in the roar that all in Hades heard, rang the message that he would have recompense in time. That there would one day be vengeance. Lucifer, self-assured, and smiling, stood his ground eying the Warden, gloating in the control he exercised over the lives before him. He stared in silence at the angel of death to see if re-education was needed, as to whom the angel served, and patiently waited.

"You will obey my command and strike the Lumazi until he bleeds," Lucifer said.

Charon grunted, paused for a moment, and then his scythe disappeared. He pulled a glowing flagellum of fire from beneath his smoke cloaked wings. The weapon of angelic torture hung limply from his bony hands as Charon stared at Talus and spoke.

"Butttt yoooo doo notttt dessserveeee veeengeeeanccee..."

A tear streamed from Talus's eye and he screamed at Charon. "DO IT!"

And Charon, powerless to exact righteous justice, roared in anger and did so.

His bony hand gripped tight around the Kiln forged handle, and he heaved it over his shoulders. Its three barbed and fiery thongs stretched out in fury through the stench of brimstone, and the angelic weapon of torture bit into Talus's chest. The crack of its sting against flesh cascaded through the cavern for all within the realm of the dead to hear, and when Charon pulled the whip away, plumes of blood and strips of angelic flesh soared through the air. Hell savored Talus and released her maggots to feed upon the open wounds.

And Talus – the mighty prince of all Arelim – screamed

And Lucifer, Lucifer stood watching in smug satisfaction---smirking in nodding approval.

Chapter Nine: Trials

Enoch and his companions crossed meadows of fire, and the sweltering incalescence of Aesir made the air twist in gaseous eddies. Flames floated as musical notes across the land. Hues of orange, yellows and golds dotted the landscape. The party marched over a hill and sitting at the base of a valley, great towers of flames jetted into the sky, and Enoch knew from his study of Grigoric scrolls that he viewed the great Seraphim city of Ashe. The Aerie and the mountain of God were surely sights to behold, but before him was a city of living flames. Towering spires and houses of fire erupted before him and men of great stature lived within. The city was named aptly, for all that the eye could see burned; and smoke emanated into the air, carrying aloft the constant aroma of burning wood, but the sight and scents were nothing compared to the sounds that assaulted one's ears, for, behind the crackling of flames, there was music.

Exquisite tonal notes swept the land as though the crackling of flames were choirs ablaze in harmonies of tenors, baritones, and bass.

Great horse-like steeds of fire galloped across the skies. The Malakim Griffins and Aithons flew overhead. Some had wings as eagles and others did not, but all flew and left trails of fire in their wakes. The three visitors could scarcely pull their eyes away.

The chief captain of the guard escorted them through the city gates, and across the public squares, the populace was filled with Seraphim. The Burning Ones were aptly named, but unlike the Elohim who were as varied as the snowflakes of the Earth, the Seraphim were the same physical appearance, for Enoch could not tell one from another.

"Beautiful..." Enoch muttered aloud, and his mouth gaped as he stared at the views round about him.

The captain of the guard smiled. "All of Aseir is beautiful, Adamson."

Enoch realized he was gawking and replied, "My name is Enoch, and might I be privy to your name?"

The captain motioned them to a shining temple, and replied, "I am called Sherkanim, and am captain of the King's legions."

"It is an honor," replied Enoch.

Gabriel and Metatron also replied, "We, too, stand honored. We hope audience with your king will allow us to break bread in fellowship."

Sherkanim smiled delighting in the thought, but when he caught himself doing so, he made his face expressionless. "That is for the King to decide," he said.

The citizens of Ashe stared at the foreigners, pointing at each as they ogled with curiosity. Some reached out to touch them. Gabriel and Metatron smiled and allowed the people to handle them as they looked at them in wonderment.

"Why do they stare at us?" said Enoch.

Sherkanim continued to lead them up the final walkway to the temple. "It has been many days since the Schism. Some have forgotten what angels look like. Others were not created until afterward. To many, the Elohim are a thing of wonder and awe, and for some...fear. Some had even believed that Elohim no longer exists since none has passed underneath, through, or over the mountain in many ages."

"And you Sherkanim...what of you?" Enoch said.

"Our histories say El banished them beyond the mountain. Banished them because one of their number by the name of Lucifer, genesised evil. Nothing comes over the mountain now but Ophanim, and nothing comes under but the Zoa and the Mists, the dread fog that we must constantly keep at bay. Thou, human, art only the second of thy kind to walk these lands."

Enoch wanted to query further but Sherkanim had stopped at the temple, an imposing structure. The building's walls were an enormous bluish flame. Diamonds and crystals lined its floors, and everything solid, from the doors to the windows, seemed held by invisible flames that somehow floated in place.

"We are here," Sherkanim said. He then faced the people who had assembled in the courtyard, took his spear and raised it high for all to see, and made annunciation.

"Hail King Nephanos! Keeper of the Living Fire, Appointed by our Lord and Sovereign, El Almighty! All hail King Nephanos!"

Everyone knelt on one knee. Enoch looked at Gabriel and Metatron, who motioned him to kneel and he did so. The temple doors opened and great plumes of smoke entered the courtyard, creeping out as dark clouds toward the people, and a tall figure similar to the Seraphim exited the Temple. The creature had six wings and stood twenty cubits tall, muscular like all the other Seraphim, but upon his head was a crown of fire, similar to Michael's crown, but within the flaming circle was a jewel that shone as a star.

Enoch noted that all the Seraphim floated when in the presence of their king and covered their eyes with two of their six wings. And Enoch, being curious, as to the king, looked upon Nephanos and caught his gaze.

"A human...and two Elohim," the king said.

He waved his hand and a small whirlwind of fire formed around the trio. The embers were cool to the touch, and Metatron watched as butterflies of living flame floated over his hands. Amused, he opened and closed his hands as though to catch them, but the whirlwind twisted upwards and the embers nestled within the Seraphim king's waiting palm and disappeared. He sniffed his palm, then recoiled. His eyes bulged, and he took a step back as his muscles became rigid. Immediately, the guards raised their spears towards the three foreigners as if to protect their king.

"The Elohim have the plague and are infectious...the human is like the other and cannot harm us. Take the angels to be burned. The human, however, may remain."

Gabriel and Metatron tightened the grip on their weapons and started to rise in self-defense, but Enoch read their body language and motioned for them to pause.

He then rose to his feet. "I am Enoch..."

The guards shoved him down and King Nephanos spoke.

"We know who thou art, Enoch. We know thou art the Candlestick of the Lord. Fear not. Thy companions will not be harmed. But too much exposure to the Withering will sunder my people. These are infected, and they must be purged before it spreads. The Burning will not harm them."

Gabriel and Metatron lessened in their anxiety, and Enoch attempted to shove the guard's hands off him. Nephanos nodded his head and the guards released them all.

"I am the anointed of El, and rule this land at His will," he said. "None shall be harmed...yet."

Gabriel eyed Nephanos, and Metatron noted that Nephanos eyed Gabriel as well. "I would hear what the Lumazi Gabriel would say. It has been a long time, Malakim Prince."

Metatron whispered to his brother. "He knows you?"

Gabriel responded. "Aye, and I him." Gabriel then spoke aloud to Nephanos. "It has indeed, King Nephanos. It has indeed. Know that we bring thee no harm."

Nephanos harrumphed. "That remains to be seen, for thou hast entered my domain in defiance with our accord, agreed by our Lord El. Moreover, thou comest bearing the Withering. You will be purged of this plague, and upon your return, you will explain why I should not exercise my covenant rights and grind your clan into the dust."

Gabriel bowed. "As thou sayest, great king."

Nephanos nodded and Sherkanim and several guards escorted the two angels away. Enoch stared after them in anxiety, but Gabriel smiled and nodded.

"Do what thou hast been called to do. We shall return."

Nephanos then spoke. "Candlestick, come walk with me, and we shall have words."

Enoch swallowed hard and walked up the temple steps with the king, and the head of the Seraph people escorted him into the temple. The flaming structure was latticed with the colors of the spectrum. When the two had moved into an inner court, the king spoke, "Enoch, thou comest with two Elohim. How doth a human come to travel with Elohim?"

Enoch looked up at the towering king and replied, "I am on assignment by the Lord, for the Lord God came to me and said I must find the man, Elijah, and that he must be brought back to Michael that his people might be healed. And to this end made I petition and asked several to accompany me. Two thou hast seen, and one is not, taken by Zoa in an effort to bring me to the shores of Aseir. Therefore, I beseech thee, great king, have you seen my masters servant and may I see Elijah that I might be about my Lord's business?"

Nephanos nodded. "You said the Lord said this to thee?"

Enoch nodded.

"Hmm, surely, those that accompany thee have shared with thee, the story why their kind hath been shut off from Aseir?"

"I have been told by the Chief of Eyes, Argoth, that..."

"Argoth?" the king said. "When I last saw the temple, Raphael was Sephiroth. What hath transpired that Raphael is no longer head of the Grigori?"

"Perhaps great king there is much we might know from one another. But Raphael is no more. He was destroyed in an attempt to bring the truth of Lucifer's treachery to light. He now rests with those that sleep in the Lord."

Nephanos frowned and his black eyes cast downward as though he were recollecting times past. "I am sorry for the Grigori's loss. Please expound to me those events that have transpired since the Schism. We have no Grigori here and are cut off from the happenings on the mount. I have many questions and I ask thy forgiveness, for I asked if thou knew of the events that left the Seraph sealed behind the mountain."

"Indeed, I do," Enoch said. "They say that long ago there were three races of Heaven, all were one in unity and worked to the ends of the Lord, and Lucifer, jealous that he was not first in worship, challenged thy kind who were adept in all manner of music and craftsmanship to contest to determine who in Heaven was the greatest. And that through traffic, guile and duplicity, he obtained one of thy own seven trumpets, and with them sang a melody that the Ophanim concluded was first in the ears of all present. The winner was to be banished behind the veil, sealed, and to provide a tribute to the temple of God. There now remains four of thy people, who in accordance with that ancient accord, serve as witness to El's holiness, and to thy people's wager, but El was wroth in what Lucifer had done and took from him the trumpets received in guile and restored them to thy people with promise that He would, one day with the same trumpets announce judgment upon his son. And that He sealed all the Sons of God behind a barrier and set up the boundaries thereof, each to remain in their respective habitations. This is what the Elohim have told me."

Nephanos brow became hard, and his fiery forehead visibly wrinkled over Enoch's words and replied, "You have heard the story as given by those who used deceit and trickery to obtain advantage. Now know the truth of it, and consider, for of all the Sons of God, it was we who brought music to the court of Heaven. It was we who in our very movement, like some of the Draco, created melody by mere motion. The trumpets were not mere instruments. They were tokens given to us by El Himself, and as the Elohim's Kilnstones kept them alight, the Trumpets were our people's gift from El, and with them, we could make any music in the mind of the Almighty. With them, we could create instruments of such beauty. We, Adamson...we were the living instruments of El, created to bring warmth and hymns, but Lucifer eyed anything that was preeminent over him. Any praise that was not lifted to God, Lucifer expected to be lifted to him, and thus he coveted the power to bring Heaven to song, to lift crowds to adulation and sought means to steal God's gifts. Thus, he eyed our people and found Camael."

Enoch looked intently upon Nephanos. "Camael? I have not heard of this name from the Grigori."

Nephanos nodded. "Camael is my brother, for not all celestial people are birthed from a kiln, Adamson. Some are like the Virtues and are but the residue of God's breath, but we are His voice, manifested as fire. His living word. We are the Seraph and are birthed from the breath of the Lord! And as one flame would ignite another, so we have come to be. Where you see fire on the plains of Aesir, you see the Seraph, a multitude who burn in holiness and worship of our God.

And Enoch marveled, for Aesir, and the eddies of flame that were her meadow were sprawled across the entire land. "So everywhere I see flame in the land..."

"Yes, Adamson, you are seeing my people at rest. Therefore, the moment you didst step through the portal of Limbo and thy feet touched the land, we all knew that one, not of us, dwelt in our realm. What thou seest is but the form we take in thy midst, but we are as the flames that sit before the Lord. The flames that the Elohim sit behind. We are fire. We are the Burning Ones."

Nephanos and Enoch entered a room, and it was decored with all manner of furnishings, and the place was aflame in colors of blues, and in the room was instruments of every imagination, from the flute to the harp, to the cornet and cymbal – gilded with the finest golds, made from every conceivable stone, and the temple was filled with instruments. Enoch walked the length and breadth. When he touched a flute, it turned to fire and echoed melodies of sweetness, and musical notes took the form of colored smoke that wafted through the air. Excited, Enoch touched a lyre and strummed it, and the song was sweet, and the room changed color as it responded to its song, and such was every instrument within the room that all exhaled music the likes he had never heard. Branded into each was a symbol...a sigil similar to what he had noticed with the Elohim.

"All the instruments bear the same stamp," Enoch said.

"Yes."

Nephanos walked over to the lyre that Enoch was near and strung it. And when he did, it lit aflame and the music was even more powerful than when Enoch strummed it. And Nephanos extended himself so that his body became as fire and touched over each instrument and lifted it from its place. Immediately all the instruments came to life, and the sound was the likes of which had never been heard. The room glowed in colors that changed and flickered, and melodic notes bounced off walls, and the room erupted in orchestral praise. For a moment, Nephanos was changed, elated to be the celestial conductor of instruments that hearkened to his command to wash the air with praise, and all the city took note that within the temple music could be heard.

Nephanos stopped himself and when he did so, all the instruments settled back into their places, and the melody that emanated from each became as a fading memory.

"Each instrument that thou seest is from Camael, the greatest artesian noted among our people."

"But..."Enoch said, "didn't Camael betray your people to Lucifer?"

"Camael..."Nephanos paused, "Wanted something more. For when interrogated for his misdeed, he confessed that he saw in the light that Lucifer created tonal notes to create a sound, unlike anything he had ever heard. There was discordance in him...a tonal quality that fascinated Camael, and Lucifer seduced him that he might create sound from light. So he crafted seven trumpets, trumpets that echoed the heart of the angel Lucifer. Trumpets that when blown, would usher in such judgment upon the recipients that could make one the ruler of all that he surveyed."

"Wait," said Enoch. "Are you saying that Camael crafted weapons? Instruments of war?"

Nephanos turned from Enoch. "Yes. Camael exchanged the trumpets for the Stone of Fire Lucifer stole from the Kiln. With the Stone of Fire, he could create the most powerful and destructive taratantara sounds that, if unleashed in the company of the Kilnstone, could have brought Heaven to ruin."

"But why?" said Enoch. "What profit could be gained by such an exchange?"

"Is the thing not known? For the oldest of all sins is but covetousness," a gruff voice said as a muscular weathered man of fifty entered the room wearing a leather girdle and a garment of camel's hair. He bowed to the king and then looked at Enoch as though examining him. He bent his face toward Enoch and sniffed. "You don't look a day over fifty. You must be Enoch. The Lord said you were coming."

Enoch laughed, for after his long journey he had finally met Elijah.

* * *

Sherkanim and his guards marched Gabriel and Metatron into a large, cylindrical, transparent chamber with two doors attached at each end. The two angels walked in and noted that members of the Seraphim pressed their faces against the exterior chamber to observe them.

"You will not be harmed by the burning, but know that we must remove from thee the contamination of the Withering," said Sherkanim.

Metatron spoke as the captain turned to leave. "How is the thing done?"

Sherkanim turned to face the duo. "No other foundation can be laid than that which is laid by the Lord. He is the form, from which all things of substance and truth and reality come. If anyone would build upon this foundation gold, silver, precious stones, wood, hay, or stubble, his work shall be made manifest, for within the confines of this pyre shall it shall be declared. The fire shall reveal the truth of it, and here, Prince of Draco, shall the fire try thy work of what sort it is. If thy work is revealed as true, then, ye shall receive honor. If, however, thy work is burned, ye shall suffer loss, but shall thyself be saved. The fire shall tell the truth of thee. These whose faces now look upon thee shall serve as judge and witness to any dross that weighs you down, and shall see to its removal. Now steel thyself, Elohim of God, for this will not be pleasant."

Sherkanim closed the vaulted door behind him and the locking mechanism turned. Sherkanim stood on the exterior of the chamber across from them, separated by the transparent barrier.

Gabriel looked at him and nodded.

"Let the burning begin," the Seraph commanded.

Immediately, flames lit amidst flames, erupting with a whooshing rush around the cylinder. The heat rose, and the faces of those pressed against the glass slowly disappeared behind the fog that now clung to its surface. Their faces morphed and transformed into hazy blurs of eyes as they stared at one another, and the room grew whiter, hotter until nothing but white could be seen.

"What is happening?" said Metatron.

"I think we are being judged," replied Gabriel.

Both angels looked up at images that materialized above them, and when they did they could no longer see one another, but their thoughts and memories were on display for all to see. Projections on the glass displayed ghostly emergences of mirth and solidarity between Elohim princes and portraits of pride in doing the will of El. The two smiled as they watched and reminisced fondly. The scenes changed swiftly and Metatron in one scene contested with others of his kind in feats of strength and games that made his friends cheer.

The Seraph watched as the Elohim worshiped before El, and legions of their kind erupted in choruses of praise, songs, and acts of dance and displays of reverence toward the King of Kings. Gabriel smiled as he too thought fondly of Heaven, the city, and his command of the Malakim, for his people spanned the cosmos, and he orchestrated their comings and goings that the word of El be spread abroad the universe. Countless numbers of his people rode on griffin-back to see that not one word of El faltered.

The room grew dimmer and dark clouds hung oppressively obscuring all, and Metatron grew anxious.

"Gabriel...what is happening?"

Gabriel's face turned somber as before him, his memories now displayed images of danger, violence, death, and loss. His flight from his brother Talus to escape his rage, and the unflattering scenes played without censor before all. The Seraphimic witnesses saw his battles to destroy his kindred as they launched themselves into madness, touched by the rage that had infected Talus. "The clouds of evil memories hath invaded."

Gabriel watched as he unleashed fire that burnt alive his foes alive, and how his staff, once a token of honor and esteem was made to be a weapon that beat his adversaries into the ground. The eyes of the Seraph beheld Gabriel, Talus and Sariel as they fell upon the heavenly city to fight the rebels that sought to unseat the Eternal One from His throne. Watched as angels on two fronts of battle caused destruction to the very fabric of the universe, as stars exploded, and El...the Almighty God who had rested from His labors for but one day, returned to see that His stewards had run amok. The Seraph watched in horror as they beheld the anger of the Lord and Apollyon's judgment within the creation of Hell. They watched as God in his wrath sentence a third of His children to exile and how He had flung them to the four corners of existence.

On and on the images marched in living color, splayed naked before the eyes of the Seraph. And thus the fires raged about Metatron and Gabriel, revealing for their audience the discernment of thoughts and intents of their captive's hearts.

Metatron recalled how he was forced to march members of his angelic house to do battle with his brethren. Projected images showed him spearheading his people into combat, leading armies that clashed as falling stars and lightning across the skies of Heaven. The Seraph watched the memories of Metatron in ominous silence, memorized as Elohim littered the realms in battle, and in the cinema that paraded for all to see, one memory was especially painful...that of Metatron holding a brother in his arms...a dear brother he had tutored since his exit from the Kiln, a brother, who in times past, was in the same ensemble that offered praise to El on the stringed instruments and the high sounding cymbals...a brother he rocked in his arms, for by his own hand was he forced to do battle and end the life of he whom his soul loved. In the image, Metatron wept sore, and his the blood of his brother dripped from his hands.

And Metatron, reliving the hurts of battles and wounds past, knelt in the large, cylindrical, transparent chamber in which he was judged and cried, "I had no choice. He would not stop, he would not heed, he lifted up arms to destroy...thinking El and all of us were his enemies. And when Gabriel, heard his brother's cries, he followed the sound of his whimpers groping through the fog and light, knelt beside him and embraced him.

The room then burned in greater brilliance and both angels covered their eyes, for the brightness was such to force one's eyes closed. And then both memories coalesced into one, and in that image, all of Heaven stood before El, and Yeshua had committed to the Kenosis and making Himself of no reputation – allowed Himself to be handled by His own children that He might bring rescue to mankind.

The Seraph watched as Gabriel and Metatron flew as a shield to the angel Michael and battled that the Son of God might be made flesh on the Earth. The Seraph watched the nobility of those who sided with El and sacrificed themselves to lure the horde of Lucifer's minions away from Michael that he and Gabriel might accomplish the wish of El. Yea, they even saw the Ophanim come to the cause of the Elohim, and how they helped turn the tide of battle, and when all had seen through Gabriel's eyes that Yeshua left the cupped hands of Michael to nestle into the flesh of a small human child, the flames stopped and they had seen enough.

The brightness retracted to normal levels. The heat subsided. The faces of fiery men smiled through the glass and a door opened at one end and Sherkanim entered. He and all the Seraph saw the two angels holding one another and sobbing, and the whole of the Seraph people understood from the Burning, the thoughts, and intents of their visitor's hearts.

And Sherkanim, Captain of the Guard of the King, spoke for them all.

"Come out clean, Princes of the Most High God. We have judged thee, and find no fault in thee."

* * *

Elijah sat next to Enoch.

"The Lord God hath sent me, Enoch. It is with great honor that we meet. I do not fully know why the Lord hath not let me pass with my fathers, for Moses and the others are housed in Paradise and await the Lord's coming, but He hath shown me in dreams and visions that I would meet with thee and that you would share all that I need to know."

Enoch nodded. "I am not sure how much I can relay, but your dreams – tell me of them."

Elijah's eyes rolled upward and to his right as though recalling.

"I sat before the throne of the living God, and before me were clouds that moved as fish in the sea, and the colors that emanated from the throne were glorious to behold. Seated in the throne was one as the Son of man, and above Him were two cherubim whose wings were spread abroad. Curiously, there were two candlesticks shaped as men before the throne. As I pondered these things, an angel of the Lord spoke to me and said, 'Thee have I set as one of two to be lit in due season. Now go thy way, and I will send my chariot to bring thee to the House of Fire, and let thy light be seen in Heaven, for with the words of thine mouth wilt thou set aflame men of fire.'

"And when I awoke from the dream," Elijah continued, "a chariot of fire took me, and I was taken past a barrier to a far country that I do not know and brought here, and here I have remained to learn from the Seraphim, for they are a noble people, passionate in the things of the Lord and mighty, for this land is awash in flame that does not burn, but the heat is yet present. I do not know how I lack injury, but God hast since my dream called me, and told me whilst I visited him upon a mountain that I must prepare the Seraph for Gabriel's and thy arrival, for it is His will that all Seraph, Ophanim, and Elohim become one, even as the Father and the Son are one. And Yeshua told me, "When Enoch comes to thee, thou shalt go to the Heavenly city for I have commanded him to seek healing for the Schism, for when I return after the resurrection, the Father would have me unseal the book."

Enoch looked puzzled and shook his head. "I do not know the meaning of these things. They are too great, but I will share with thee all that I have been taught from the Elohim. They, too, are a mighty people, but pride hath brought them far from where they were smelted in a kiln of fire. Pride hath seen them fight with one another even to make their habitation with man. When they are noble, they are a light which can never be hid, but when they are dark, worlds shatter and stars fall. But I have learned as we are the Lords, so too are they, and He hath committed them to a plan and a future, for there is one among them who hath lifted himself above all that is called God, and has moved to destroy all things. We must do all we can to remove his presence in the Earth, I see that God would have us help in this regard, but the way is not yet clear."

Elijah nodded. "Then drink with me, and let us pray and seek the face of the Lord and I shall tell thee what I have learned of these flaming men, and thou shalt teach me what thou hast learned from these sons of stars, and perhaps the Lord's will, will be known."

Enoch nodded and two old men, poured each other drinks and talked late into the night.

* * *

Sherkanim and two Seraphim guards escorted Gabriel and Metatron into the audience chamber of the king and opened two towering golden doors bathed in blue flame. The angels gasped as the floors and walls were completely covered in flames, and seated on a throne from which colored vapors emanated was Nephanos.

"My king," Sherkanim said. "I present the Lumazi, Gabriel of House Malakim, and Metatron of House Draco."

Nephanos motioned them forward, and Sherkanim stood to their side that they might come closer to the king.

"Metatron, I have not had the honor to meet thee. It has been some time since a member of the Draco hath adorned these halls. In times past, I would have enjoyed our coming together to create music for El, but, alas, those days are gone for one of thy house is the reason we stand behind the mountain. Tell me, Lord of all Draco, why should the brother of Lucifer be allowed to live?"

Metatron was taken aback by the king's question and stumbled in reply to the king's words. "Uh...my king..."

Gabriel seeing Metatron's discomfort intervened. "Great King, we come in peace and ask thy patience, and if afterward in thy wisdom we should be destroyed, then let dissolution be our lot, but not pray-tell before our petition is made."

Nephanos put his head on his fist and waved his other hand for Gabriel to continue. "Very well. Speak thy petition."

Gabriel stepped forward and then lowered himself to his knees.

"Great King, I stand before you in a great straight. I beg you for the life of my people, for the Withering hath come and runs rampant throughout the Great City. Its presence strips us of awareness of El and saps from us the very life that animates our stone, but it was your people who built the Kiln and by command of God lit it. Thy fires can purge the madness that slowly eats away at our people. We have no more kiln. But if thy people come and lite again the ground of Jerusalem, we shall also be lit, and the Withering shall be burned off and our people saved. Therefore, Great King, wilt thou help us? We come to thee as servants asking a favor. Do this, and the Elohim will forever be in thy debt."

Nephanos was quiet. Stoic even, as He contemplated the words of Gabriel and looked on Metatron. He heaved a sigh and spoke.

"I have seen the images from the burning, and the destruction of the Kiln in thy memory. Who was responsible for its ruin?"

Gabriel swallowed hard. "Chief Prince, Michael destroyed it to prevent the renegade, Lucifer, from possessing the power of the Godstones."

Nephanos stood when he heard this.

"So, the collaborator Michael, who gave suggestion to Lucifer to steal from us, is now in conjunction with the rogue angel responsible for the destruction of the gift our people had given to El? And this, after having crossed the mists of Limbo is what you seek to tell me? And now, because El hath removed Himself and set thy people to discipline. Discipline because the Elohim in pride hast made themselves to tear all things asunder...this is why you come to me? Only to look for us to provide thee with a balm to sooth the welt that El's scourge now levels against thy people?" the King shouted.

Gabriel prostrated himself to the ground and replied, "Mercy, Great King. Do this for our people and whatever debt you would collect from us. Surely we will pay thee all."

Nephanos shook his head. "No, Gabriel, High Prince to thy people. Thou hast once more come to my land, and what king would abide such trespass against his people? Our treaty is clear. We have divorced ourselves from the Elohim and none but El can bring us back into covenant. When He calls, then and only then will we enter into a relationship with thy people."

Gabriel's arms fell to his sides and his eyes glanced downward to the dirt.

"But my King, hath not this worm lowered himself to thee, even beseeched thee to consider that our cause is just? For I bring thee in remembrance that once our peoples walked together, as was the will of El from the beginning, and even now hath sought thee to hear thy servant out for our people are in sore need."

Nephanos laughed to his lieutenants, and then his face became flushed and he clenched his fists in indignation. "Who is this that darkeneth counsel by words without knowledge? Gird up thy loins, for I will demand and you will answer me for thou hast come to me on bended knee because thou hast no choice. Thou comest because the chastisement of the Lord now corrects thy wayward people. Tell me, High Prince, if El had not blighted thy people with plague, wouldst thou be before me now?"

Gabriel swallowed hard and raised his eyes to Nephanos. "No. Yet, I come on orders of the Chief Prince, and not of mine own accord."

Nephanos tilted his head and nodded toward his bound guest. "Spoken truly. At least that is a start. Yet if thy people even now succumb to the Withering, why send an underling to do a leader's bidding? Thou dost beg for the life of thy people, but do not represent thy people, but the life of thy prince. For if he truly led his people, then he himself would stand before me now, and not his adjutant." The king then spoke to his lieutenant. "Sherkanim."

Sherkanim immediately snapped to attention. "Yes, my king?"

"See to their provisions and make their bags ready for travel."

"Yes, my king."

"In the morning, Gabriel, you and this one shall leave my land. Now, therefore, be gone from me, Malakim, or feel my wrath. Tell your Chief Prince that if he would petition for the life of his people, he must beg for it himself. For this reason and to prevent war, I give you my leave to return with this message. Now go, High Prince, and return from whence you came, and never, ever return this way again."

* * *

Azaziel spoke to Yeshua while He still communed with the Lord in prayer.

"Pardon, my King. But there come of the son of men a squad carrying lanterns, swords, and staves. Surely they mean to do you harm."

Yeshua saw them afar off, sighed, and knowing all things that should come upon him, lifted Himself up from prayer and walked forth.

Azaziel looked flummoxed, unsure of what to do.

"My King?" he said, but Yeshua did not reply and set Himself to meet them.

Azaziel and his soldiers eyed the entourage, inspecting every inch of their person, ready to strike them blind or stop their hearts at a moment's notice. Other Elohim spread abroad throughout the countryside, ready to lay the whole region to waste if necessary, daring any of the Horde to come closer. None did save one.

Lucifer fell from the sky, his glowing persona lighting just yards from Yeshua, and within the protective circle, Azaziel and his band had set. Yeshua's royal guards raised their shields and swords, but Lucifer raised his hands in abeyance and spoke.

"I come naught but to observe. I mean the Godking no harm. Behold, see one of his own disciples comes to bring his love." Lucifer turned with a smile, his eye upon Judas who was at the head of the squad.

"Hail, Master," Judas said and kissed Him.

"My friend," Yeshua said. "Wherefore art thou come?"

Judas stepped back with gripped conscious but answered not the Lord. He meekly smiled and turned toward the armed party.

Yeshua then spoke aloud for Judas to hear. "Judas, betrayest thou the Son of Man with a kiss?"

Judas looked down, shaken at the words but did not reply. Lucifer smiled, and his hands folded behind his back in smugness as Azaziel and his angels grew increasingly frustrated.

Lucifer sat on a rock and spoke, "Do not look at me. The human acts of his own volition," he said with a snicker as Yeshua narrowed his eyes at his rogue son.

Yeshua turned to the throng before him, focusing on those with swords. His face turned grim as He spoke. "Whom seek ye?"

A temple constable replied. "Yeshua of Nazareth."

Yeshua said, "I AM He." The power of Yeshua's voice carried on the gust of a sudden wind, and He spoke with such authority that soldiers shrank in fear and stumbled backward to the ground. Even Lucifer became discomforted but watched silently as his plans unfolded before his eyes.

Azaziel and the host warily eyed the men, ready to pounce, itching to cut down the whole entourage at Yeshua's word. Hands on hilts, the angels hovered. Azaziel's eyes looked pleadingly at his master for the command to move. But the command did not come. And Azaziel, having no command to engage, watched the exchange of God and men in dismay.

Yeshua then asked again, "Whom do you seek?"

And they said, "Yeshua of Nazareth."

Yeshua eyed His disciples, not willing that any should perish, that the saying might be fulfilled, of them which thou gavest me have I lost none. He knew that with but a word He could unleash a legion upon the fools who sought to unknowingly apprehend their Creator. With a single thought,

He could send them screaming to the realm of the unrighteous dead, but He did not. He looked at Azaziel, who stood ready to slice the captain's throat, and Christ opened His hands to signal surrender.

"I have told thee that I am He: if therefore ye seek me, then let these go their way. But why come ye out as against a thief, with swords and staves? When I was with thee daily in the temple, ye stretched forth no hands against me: but this is thy hour and the Power of Darkness," He said with a side glance at Lucifer.

Lucifer then projected his voice that only Simon Peter might hear and said, "Wilt thou stand idle whilst these men take hold to the Savior? What dost thou have in thine hands?"

Then Simon Peter having a sword drew it, and smote Malchus, the servant of the high priest, and cut off his right ear.

Azaziel smiled. Finally, someone brave enough to confront this rabble.

But Yeshua frowned at them all and especially Lucifer, and said unto Peter, "Put thy sword into the sheath: for the cup which my Father hath given me, shall I not drink it? For all they that take the sword shall perish with the sword. Thinkest thou that I cannot now pray to my Father, and He shall presently give me more than twelve legions of angels? But how then shall the scriptures be fulfilled, that thus it must be?"

Azaziel realized the Lord not only rebuked Peter but was also speaking to him and his soldiers as well. Yeshua's eyes were stern towards Azaziel, and the angel knew the Lord would not permit them to interfere. And Azaziel and the rest of the angelic guard sheathed their swords and stood watching their King, attentive to any command.

The Lord Yeshua then bent down and took Malchus' ear and healed him. Then the squad and the captain and officers of the Jews took Yeshua into custody, and the disciples seeing the Lord bound, fled every man to escape.

Azaziel withstood Lucifer to his face and spoke, "This is your doing Deceiver, you will pay for your crimes, and I will be there on the day you are judged."

Lucifer replied, "I could kill you before thou saw me coming; nevertheless, at the moment, thou hast more pressing concerns to attend to, do you not?" And Lucifer chuckled as he lounged on the rock smiling, waving goodbye, and shooing him away.

Azaziel snorted in frustration, turned, and joined his brethren who followed the Lord, as He was led by evil men, alone and captive through the dark of night.

* * *

Nephanos had watched Sherkanim's officers escort Gabriel and Metatron away. However, the chief of the guard hesitated, turned to his Lord and waited to be acknowledged.

Nephanos took note but said nothing. Moments of silence passed between them and Sherkanim stood at attention, waiting for the glance that he knew would allow him to speak.

Nephanos sighed, then spoke to his waiting servant, "We've have known each other for many eons, you and I, yet you still stand in my presence captain after being dismissed--why?"

Sherkanim fell to one knee. "My king. Since our birth as a people, El hath always intended that all of Heaven's children be one. Never was it in His heart the schism that now exists between us. Yet due to our hardness of heart, He hath allowed us to stay behind the mountain of Heaven. And while idle in our solitude, we have silently awaited El's bidding to rejoin the Ophanim, and Elohim, and once more be one. Is it not possible that these emissaries are a sign from El that the time for reunification is before us? And lo, a new race stands on our grounds, these...Humans. Therefore, I ask my king to reconsider this course to dismiss the heralds from the throne room of God."

Nephanos nodded. "I have heard thy petition. If the angels are in such dire straits as they proclaim, then the Chief Prince will come, bend the knee before this throne and submit himself to my pardon. Then we shall be one. Then offense can be forgiven."

Sherkanim lowered his head further and glanced upward, careful not to look at his master. "Oh great king, did we not barter with the Deceiver? Hath, we no culpability for what has befallen us? We cannot blame Lucifer alone for what hath transpired. And what of his war now against the Godking Himself? Will we stand idle and watch as he schemes to bring down the fall of God? My king, I beg...."

Nephanos stood, and raised his hands. "Silence. Thou speakest out of turn, Capitan. Do not presume to lecture me on how to rule for thou hast spoken beyond your station. Now go to and see to your duties while I see to mine."

"My apologies, my king. It shall be as you command." Sherkanim then touched his forehead to the ground in obeisance, scooted backward until he was far enough from his lord to stand, bowed, and turned to leave.

Nephanos communed with his own thoughts, as he watched his servant depart his presence and when Sherkanim was gone, Nephanos walked to the rear of his throne, past a door to his inner chamber. He opened the door and rest his eyes on instruments of the finest craftsmanship, each stamped with the flaming symbol of Camael. His glowing hand glided over each trumpet in a light caress.

"I have not whispered into your innards the breath of my fire for many days now. Not since my betrayal at the hands of the Deceiver. Not since my brother made me stand in proxy to wear this accursed crown."

Nephanos then lifted the token of kingship from off his head and threw it across the floor. As it toppled to rest, a faded God-stone gleamed atop...a stone that no longer sung a song asking to be...a stone silenced from begging its maker to shape it to his will.

The King of the Seraphim sat in a chair and rocked, then placed a tortured head in his hands and murmured his growing anxiety. "Did Prince Gabriel recognize me? I cannot allow him to leave the city and reveal my identity." The king's eyes darted back and forth. "No one must know. For if the people were to see the truth..."

Nephanos stood and paced within his private chambers, and grew increasingly agitation as he eyed both the crown and the instruments assembled before him. In a gesture of frustration, he swatted several flutes and lyres to the floor and hunched over the table where they had been displayed.

"Nephanos, my brother, what were thou thinking? When Lucifer and I conceived the plan to upset the balance of power, when we created the trumpets, we could have unleashed their untapped power and ruled all! But no, instead of siding with thy own brother, instead of taking what could have been ours, thou didst reveal my sin to El and left me here to taste the burden of power. And after all this time, after all, these years, for what? To teach me the weight of ruling? To make me eat the bread of my lust? I am not thee, brother. For mine is to craft songs to lift our kind to worship and exaltation. Together, Lucifer and I would have melded light and sound and made the universe tremble. But no! Now I must take on this false persona, for I, Camael, the greatest of our kind, must be resigned to play 'king.' While true power sits on a mountaintop among the heights of the clouds, here I stand to rule within its shadow. And what of you? Thou hast chosen to go off and yelp in obeisance every time someone enters the presence of El. And what of these angels before me now. Is this thy doing, brother? To convince me to submit to El and once again unite our people? Is this your feeble attempt to bring me an olive branch? Pssft. I will see your emissaries destroyed, and their purposes brought to naught."

Camael laughed, and his eyes glazed and sparked, and he stared longingly at the dormant Stone of Fire in the crown that was on the floor.

And unbeknownst to him, standing hidden outside his doorway was Enoch, having entered the king's chamber in hopes to gain an audience. He stood with his hands over his mouth, horrified, shocked that the King of the Seraphim was none other than the traitor, Camael!

* * *

Jerahmeel and Iblis covertly wound through tunnels and corridors lined with Hell's villi.

Jerahmeel looked in the dimness and noted that they saw no servants of Lucifer, but the air echoed with groans and screams of distant angels caught in the creature's digestive tract.

"Why have we not seen any of Lucifer's servants here?" Jerahmeel said.

Iblis moved carefully around a dangling tendril, watching where he stepped so as not to awaken and bring attention to Hell's consciousness.

"There are sections of the creature where none venture. Because all fear to travel through the beast without authorization from their master, Satan. Hell is not as tamed as Lucifer would have the Horde believe. She is too vast to be entirely restrained. She merely tolerates the presence of those that indwell her. If Lucifer were not able to control her with the Keys of Death and Hell, she would devour us all. I have garnered enough travel through her to know the way, but Lucifer ever changes the path to the forge, forcing the creature to alter her innards to the central bowel. There are some areas that would be easier to travel, but we would encounter much resistance."

"Is there no other option?" Jerahmeel said, stepping gingerly.

"We could travel areas that are not constricted by Lucifer's leash, but we risk the beast's hunger. All paths are perilous and fraught with danger."

Jerahmeel pondered the decision when he paused.

"Hold, do you hear that?"

Iblis stopped his advance in the dimness. "Nay Prince, but we should not stand idle or our presence will be detected. We must keep moving."

Jerahmeel squinted his eyes, as though narrowing them would somehow enhance his hearing. He tilted his head slightly and strained to hear. "Hmmph. Perhaps it was my imagination. You are right. We should keep mov..."

A faint scream floated on the air.

"I hear it," Iblis said. "It sounds like Turiel...below us. It sounds like he is in battle."

Jerahmeel pulled two axes attached to the small of his back and exercised his authority over the cold in El's name over what little water could be evidenced in the cavern. He withdrew the heat from the cavern and slowly the temperature dropped; Iblis could see his breath, and the rivers of lava in the chamber cooled and slowed their incessant march across the floor as muffled screams continued from below.

"If we go to his aid, we will die," said Iblis

"And if we do not, he most assuredly will," Replied Jerahmeel. "We cannot leave him in this place. Fear not. We will find the Forge."

Iblis nervously eyed the cavern, watching for signs that Hell had noticed a change in her internal organs. His anxiety increased with each passing second.

Run, his mind whispered to him, his thoughts battling in silent conflict.

Abandon the cause of the Forge. Iblis then put his hands to his temples and proceeded to rub from his mind the erosion of logical thought and the ever encroaching madness of the Withering. Iblis could feel it getting stronger. He shook himself and watched as Jerahmeel continued to summon the elemental forces of nature to his cause and watched as the lava came to a stop, and ice crystals on the walls and ceilings.

Run...the voice urged again. The floor crusted over in ice. Jerahmeel satisfied by his work slammed the hilt of his axe into the ground. Cracks creaked across the floor and wound themselves under the duo's feet until the ground collapsed with the sound of shattering glass. Jerahmeel and Iblis fell through and landed on the level below. They stood to their feet to see Eskalion and Turiel encased in flaming tendrils. Insulated in the creatures siphoning grasp, maggots crept over them. Jerahmeel instantly leaped to their defense. The Prince of Harrada touched the flaming lattice around Eskalion to freeze it and snapped the now brittle strands apart. Eskalion coughed up blood and maggots escaped his mouth, no longer protected by the warmth generated by their host's body. As they squirmed down his flesh, Iblis and Jerahmeel brushed the creatures aside and crushed them underfoot.

Eskalion's eyes fluttered. "Turiel...trapped..."

"We have him," said Jerahmeel. "Iblis, see to Eskalion. I will free Turiel."

Iblis nodded and helped Eskalion to his feet while cautiously watching the floors and ceilings.

Run...his mind begged him.

Turiel thrashed within the warm, life-sucking blanket Hell had made for the redactor, and Jerahmeel froze the tentacles and snapped them off. Turiel settled to the floor and fell into Jerahmeel's lap. Slowly, he gained his composure...just as the floor moved.

Iblis nervously backed away from Eskalion, his eyes darting all about the room. As the two rescuers frantically moved to get the party going.

"Jerahmeel, behind you!" Iblis screamed.

Tendrils of flame lowered from the ceiling and openings appeared on the floor, as eyes upon eyes looked upon the group and noted that angel flesh walked freely within the cavern.

Jerahmeel took his axes and twirled them over his head, swishing the air, cutting the approaching tendrils into pieces.

"RUN!" Iblis screamed.

The eyes that followed them turned red and the march of one-eyed cells with teeth now turned to pursue them. Hell was conscious of them now, and she would not let them escape. Iblis pressed hard, flying through an exit, and Eskalion and Turiel quickly followed with Jerahmeel bringing up the rear. Through each corridor, more eyes seeped out of the walls, and lengthy tendrils extended themselves to capture the intestinal quarry.

Iblis turned left, and when he did Turiel spoke, "No, turn right. I remember this from Hell's tomes."

Iblis paused, in a quandary. "But if we go that way we will surely run into the patrols of the Horde."

Turiel was insistent, "Turn left, now!"

Iblis noted that the march of red eyes had multiplied and Hell now followed their scent with dogged persistence. Desirous to be anywhere but where they were, Iblis and Jerahmeel looked into each other's eyes, and in that moment, Jerahmeel knew the Iblis who had earlier helped the cause of Heaven was no more, for the Withering had taken its hold. Iblis' eyes bulged, fearful of the march of the centipedes of fire, and with the look of a madman, sheered off to the right.

"Iblis!" screamed Eskalion.

"Let him go. The Withering has him," said Jerahmeel. "Let's get out of here – quickly now."

The group headed left as Turiel instructed, and Jerahmeel looked back to see Iblis slip into the dark.

* * *

Camael called Sherkanim to him and spoke. "Are the Elohim packed and settled to return under the mountain?"

"Aye, my king. They are prepared to be escorted to the edge of the Mist Gate."

"Good. To show my benevolence, you will give them this token. Place it in the sack's mouth of Gabriel."

Camael handed his lieutenant a long box wrapped in ancient Issi cloth, and within it, unbeknownst to Sherkanim, was one of the seven trumpets of judgment from Camael's inner chamber. Sherkanim received the box and awaited further instructions.

"Now go to and fill their sacks with food, as much as they can carry, and give them fire from thy hand for it will keep the Zoa at bay."

And Sherkanim bowed to his lord and did as instructed. As soon as the morning was light, the angels were sent away and when had gone a half day's journey out of the city, and not yet far off, Camael said unto his steward, "Go up. Follow after the Elohim, and when thou dost overtake them, say unto them, wherefore have ye rewarded evil for good? Why hast thou taken the token of El's covenant between me and thee? And whereby El had given to settle dispute between our peoples? Ye have done a great evil in so doing."

And the steward overtook them, and spake unto them these same words, and they said unto him, "Wherefore saith my lord these words? God forbid that thy servants should do according to this thing. Behold, that which is in our sacks' mouths. We brought nothing into the realm other than what was ours, and we take only that which we have by permission. How then should we steal out of thy lord's house, and especially the token of covenant between our people?" And Gabriel said unto Camael's steward, "With whomsoever of thy servants it is found, let him die, and the other be my lord's bondmen."

The steward replied, "Let it be according to thy words; and may ye be found blameless,"

Then Metatron and Gabriel speedily took down their sacks to the ground and opened them. And the steward searched, beginning with Metatron, and when nothing was found he searched the belongings of Gabriel, and the box, covered in Issi cloth, was discovered and Camael's servant opened the box and a trumpet of judgment was found therein.

Then the two angels rent their clothes and wondered aloud how such a thing could be, and Sherkanim noted that the box was the gift from the king and he spoke on this wise: "Surely there must be some mistake, for these men hath been honorable and true in their dealings."

The king's steward replied, "My orders are clear. My king requires the return of these to face judgment, and as first in the king's guard, thy duty is also clear."

Sherkanim was troubled by the words, and could not argue his duty. He turned and took Metatron and Gabriel into custody, and escorted them back to the city. Gabriel and his brother came to Camael's house, for he was yet there, and they fell before him on the ground, and Camael said unto them, "What deed is this that ye have done? Know ye not that such as I can certainly divine?"

And Gabriel said, "What shall we say unto my lord? What shall we speak or how shall we make our innocence known? The Lord God hath found out the iniquity of thy servants, and behold, we are my lord's servants,"

And Camael said, "God forbid that I should do so, but he in whose hand the cup was found shall surely die, and the other shall be my servant for such a grave trespass as to incite war between our peoples and to dishonor the name of El by robbing El's token to our folk."

And when Metatron heard those words, he became wroth, for without cause were they accused and he knew in his heart that they were innocent. The head of house Draco unsheathed his sword in the presence of the King of the Seraphim, and immediately Sherkanim and the king's guard subdued him, and Gabriel pleaded with him to stand down, saying on this wise:

"Wouldst thou unleash the trumpet's powers against us, that our people be ground to dust? We must bear this thing, for it is thankworthy if we for conscience sake towards God endure grief and suffer wrongfully. We shall take this patiently for this would be acceptable to God. El sees all and He will vindicate us."

And Camael was wroth that weapons were raised in his presence and rose to his feet. "Behold what thou hast done, and still I show my restraint in destroying thy people. You, who have trespassed into the forbidden realm. You who were received kindly and even sent on thy way unharmed. And now what is this, that even as the Burning hath shown us, that Elohim have lowered themselves once more to steal and raise false indignations, thou darest to raise arms in mine own house? Verily, I say unto you that for this, you will at three days hence be set afire with the same flames that ignited the Kiln and thou shalt surely die. Take them away!"

And Sherkanim obeyed with lowered eyes, saddened that all hope seemed lost and that his people would yet stay concealed behind the mountain. Saddened that he must personally see to the death of two honorable angels, and he slowly began to suspect the actions of his own king.

* * *

Azaziel and his band of angels watched as the guards led Yeshua to the house of Annas, one of two high priests recognized by the people.

"This is a travesty!" an angelic soldier said. "Are we just supposed to stand here and do nothing? It is an outrage!"

"Hold your tongue!" said Azaziel. "Annas is speaking."

Annas paced before Yeshua, then encircled Him, eying Him up and down. A smugness came over his face.

"Dost thou you understand why you are here?" said the high priest said.

Yeshua spoke not a word.

"Silence? It matters not. Because you see, Nazarene I happen to remember you. Oh yes, for it was during my time as high priest prior to my son-in-law, Caiaphas that you drove out the money changers from the temple. I must admit you created quite a stir that day and caused me many a problem. And now – now, here you stand before me. How befitting." The former high priest smiled as he continued his wolfish pace around Yeshua, examining him.

"I have heard thou doth raise men who would defy the laws of our people, and that you teach others to no more honor the faith of our fathers. Moreover, that we ought not to even keep the laws of our fathers! Some say thou dost set thyself even above Moses. Is this true?"

Yeshua sighed, "I spake openly to the world; I ever taught in the synagogue, and in the temple, and in secret have I said nothing. Why askest thou me? Ask them which heard me what I have said unto them."

And when He had spoken, one of the officers which stood by the Lord struck Yeshua with the palm of his hand, saying, "Answerest thou the high priest so?"

A hundred angels winced, drew swords and raised their weapons to unleash death on those who participated in the travesty, but Azaziel raised an arm and shouted, "Stand down this moment! The Lord's words were clear...we do not interfere." The angel guard gruffed in frustration.

Yeshua recovered from the blow and lifted His head to speak. "If I have spoken evil, then bear witness of the evil: but if well, why smitest thou me?"

Annas grew frustrated, "I have heard enough! I see He holds no regard to the office before Him. Very well. Take Him to Caiaphas and tell him our concerns are warranted. The Sanhedrin will, by this time no doubt, be assembled and prepared to try Him." Annas then had Him bound and delivered unto his son-in-law, Caiaphas the high priest.

The guards marched Yeshua to Caiaphas as directed, and thirty members of the Sanhedrin assembled with him – the highest religious authority in the land.

Khorset spoke to Azaziel, "Grigori scouts state that there are but twenty-three members needed. Why so many?"

Azaziel looked at the assembly. "No doubt, these are they who already oppose the Lord, and the seated must be extra members now stacked against Him. This is but a formality." Azaziel pointed at the entrances to the building and round about. "Take up positions to the north and south wing. Make a perimeter so the Horde knows we will destroy them if they breach it."

Khorset bowed. "As you command, Lumazi."

Azaziel eyed the men and listened as they began their deliberations. Yeshua stood before them with hands tied behind His back, resigned, somber, steadily gazing upon those who would sit in judgment over God. Next to Yeshua stood the Chief temple guard and he proceeded to announce the court.

"Before you, High Priest stands Yeshua of Nazareth. He hath stood before thy father-in-law, and wast sent here for judgment. These are gathered to bring testimony of His guilt, and we submit this man's innocence to your wisdom."

"Call your witnesses," the Chief Priest said.

The temple priest then paraded witness after witness who spoke. One after another was brought in and spoke about how Yeshua declared this or was seen doing that. But with each witness, others countered or even denied what previous witnesses had said. Caiaphas wrung his hands and paced while members of the council grumbled that perhaps this was not a good idea, while others whispered concerns that the Pharisees would object to their desire to simply condemn Him and be done with it. After a parade of false witnesses that lacked sufficient testimony to condemn Him, a frustrated and tired Caiaphas spoke.

"Have you no other witnesses to bring before this counsel?" he quipped.

The temple guards led two men into the assembly and the place was astir. Caiaphas called for order. "What testimony dost thou bring?" he said to the trembling man.

He straightened and spoke with authority, pointing at Yeshua. "This fellow said, I am able to destroy the temple of God, and to rebuild it in three days."

A ripple of murmurs stirred the congregation.

"Order! Order!" Caiaphas said.

The other fellow nodded in agreement. "It is true. I also heard Him say He is able to destroy the temple."

The council erupted in gasps and whispers.

"Does He think to upturn the fathers?" one said.

"He is a Roman sympathizer!" said another. "This place is the dwelling place of God. How dare He!"

But Yeshua stood mute before them all and stared at Azaziel, who stood next to the High Priest with a hand on his sword, ready to cut him down if the Son of God gave the smallest nod.

Azaziel fidgeted as he watched and thought to himself. The fools had no concept of who stands before them. The crowd stirred to further agitation.

"This is not good Lord...not good at all," Azaziel said to the Lord.

Yeshua stood silent.

The High Priest silenced the raucous crowd, and peered into the Son of God's eyes and spoke. "Answerest thou nothing against which these witnesses speak against thee?"

Yeshua continued to hold his peace. And the High Priest answered and said unto him, "I adjure thee by the living God, that thou tell us whether thou be the Christ, the Son of God."

When the High Priest invoked God, Yeshua looked up and met the mortal's eyes. "Thou hast said. Nevertheless, I say unto you, hereafter shall ye see the Son of Man sitting on the right hand of power, and coming in the clouds of Heaven."

Caiaphas's eyes grew wide with rage as scarlet crept up his neck and over his face. The veins in his temple bulged as he rent his clothes in a frenzy, shouting, "He hath spoken blasphemy! Out of His own mouth hath He condemned Himself. What further need have we of witnesses?"

Dozens nodded, and the crowd roared. Caiaphas continued. "Thou who doth stand as wisdom and guide for our people, behold, ye have heard His blasphemy with thine own ears. What think ye?"

"He is guilty of death! Death! Death! Death!" they chanted while pumping their arms.

Azaziel and his angels unsheathed their swords, churning in rage toward the humans, but Yeshua lifted His head and inhaled hard, signaling them to stand down. All looked to Azaziel and stood round about in anxious tension, churning in rage towards the humans. Yeshua then smiled, and when He did so, members of the lower council of the Sanhedrin came down from their seated places and one by one walked past Yeshua. Some spit in His face, others buffeted Him; and those angered the most smote Him with the palms of their hands, mocking Him. "Prophesy unto us, thou Christ. Who was it that smote thee?"

Azaziel and his comrades cringed, but stood silently as the guards led Yeshua away until the whole of the Sanhedrin could assemble. And as soon as it was day, the elders of the people and the chief priests and the scribes came together, and led Him into their council.

"Art thou the Christ? Tell us," Caiaphas said.

And Yeshua said unto them, "If I tell thee, ye will not believe. And if I also ask you, ye will not answer me nor let me go. Hereafter shall the Son of Man sit on the right hand of the power of God."

Startled reactions echoed throughout the room, and gasps of amazement escaped the mouths of those assembled, and then said they all, "Art thou then the Son of God?"

Yeshua's answer was succinct. "Ye say that I am."

Incensed, one of the elders said, "What need we any further witness? For we ourselves have heard from His own mouth," and the multitude paraded Yeshua to see Pilate that they might have Him executed.

Azaziel lowered his head, shaking it in disbelief, watching as his King was once more bound, and taken by the humans to Pontius Pilate, the Roman Governor of the region.

The Prince of Issi and his angelic warriors witnessed in silence the travesty of justice that played out before them. Both he and a thousand angels held fast to Yeshua's side, agonizing over man's mistreatment of his creator.

Azaziel and his soldiers watched in growing irritation and resentment as the throng dragged Yeshua before Pilate, who then sent Him to Herod. And Herod displeased over Yeshua's failure to entertain him, sent him back to Pilate. All proceedings held illegally, all fallacious, and all unfair. And the more the angels watched what the Son of God allowed to befall Him, the more angered they became.

When the morning was come, the chief priests and elders of the people took counsel against Yeshua to put Him to death and delivered him to Pontius Pilate, the governor.

Then when Judas, who had betrayed Him, saw that Yeshua was condemned, he repented himself, and brought back the thirty pieces of silver to the chief priests and elders saying, "I have sinned in that I have betrayed innocent blood," they replied, "What is that to us? See thou to that." And Judas cast down the pieces of silver in the temple and departed and went and hanged himself.

Disheveled, weary, and abused, Yeshua stood before the governor, and the governor asked Him, saying, "Art thou the King of the Jews?"

And Yeshua said unto him, "Thou sayest." And when he was accused of the chief priests and elders, He answered nothing.

Then said Pilate unto Him, "Hearest thou not how many things they witness against thee?" And He answered him never a word, insomuch that the governor marveled greatly. Now at that feast, the governor was wont to release unto the people a prisoner, whom they would. And they had then a notable prisoner, called Barabbas. Therefore, when they were gathered together, Pilate said unto them, "Whom will ye that I release unto you? Barabbas, or Yeshua which is called Christ?" For he knew that for envy they had delivered Him.

And when Pilate set down on the judgment-seat, his wife sent unto him, saying, "Have thou nothing to do with that just man: for I have suffered many things this day in a dream because of Him".

But the chief priests and elders persuaded the multitude that they should ask for Barabbas, and destroy Yeshua.

The governor answered and said unto them, "Whether of the twain will ye that I release unto you?"

They said, "Barabbas!"

Pilate saith unto them, "What shall I do then with Yeshua, which is called Christ?" They all say unto him, "Let Him be crucified," And the governor said, "Why, what evil hath He done?"

But they cried out the more, saying, "Let Him be crucified!"

When Pilate saw that he could prevail nothing, but that rather a tumult was made, he took water and washed his hands before the multitude, saying, "I am innocent of the blood of this just person: see ye to it."

Then answered all the people, and said, "His blood be on us, and on our children."

Pilate then released Barabbas unto them: and when he had scourged Yeshua, he delivered Him to be crucified. The soldiers of the governor took Yeshua into the common hall and gathered unto Him the whole band of soldiers, and they stripped Him and put on Him a scarlet robe. And when they had platted a crown of thorns, they put it upon His head, and a reed in His right hand: and they bowed the knee before Him, and mocked Him, saying, "Hail, King of the Jews!"

And they spit upon Him, and took the reed, and smote Him on the head, and after that, they had mocked Him, they took the robe off from Him, and put His own raiment on Him, and led Him away to crucify Him. As they came out, they found a man of Cyrene, Simon by name: whom they compelled to bear His cross.

Grigoric scouts hovered in sorrow and relayed the news back to the Kingdom, and Argoth watched with increasing realization that El's vision, a vision He had given His servant Michael so many eons ago, was now coming painfully to pass before his very eyes.

Chapter Ten: Crucifixion

Iblis rushed headlong into flaming tendrils that hung from the roof of Hell's gums. Burning acidic bile slid down the creature's walls and dropped as mucus from her ceiling. The darkness grew greater until nothing could be seen. No fire...no lava...just the pitch black and stifling humidity hung about him, and nothing but the echoes of screams and groans and the sounds of his own beating wings could be heard. What little light available to him was given off by the fires that crackled off Hell's lanky coils as he flew deeper into her intestinal tract, and away from Jerahmeel's party.

Panting in exhaustion his mind reeled with self-loathing and contempt.

You are a lecherous traitor...a traitor to God, to Lucifer and to yourself. Your cause, only to see to your self-preservation. How thou art fallen from the being you once were!

The Issi's mind toyed with him, waylaying him with condemnation, deprecation, and guilt.

Thou hast abandoned God...again...to save thyself.

Iblis flew through tendrils, pushing them aside, careful not to touch the floors or walls to alert Hell. Pressing forward, ever onward, no longer certain of his destination. Awash in self-pity his heart's abundance moved him to speak his woe aloud.

"Where should I go, and who would have me now? I am cast off from both Heaven and Hell...envoy to no one, and a member of no house." He stopped his flight in the flickering dark and sobbed when something moved in the black.

He wiped his eyes and gained his composure, straining to see between shimmers of light and blackness, intuition alerted him that he was not alone. He turned to his rear, then quickly to his left and right, peering deep to eye what accompanied him in the murk. And then a voice spoke to him.

"Have no fear, little one. I will not harm you--yet."

"Who art thou? Show yourself!"

The voice's tone changed to one of sadness.

"I am hurt Iblis. After all, that we have been through together, I would have thought you would have recognized me by now."

A light then shimmered before his path and the flaming tendrils moved away from the presence of a large Harada that occupied the room. His Elomic armor was imposing and his eyes glowed with the crackle of lightning, and Iblis stood in terror, realizing he had walked straight into his former captor – Zeus.

"I have been watching you since you arrived back on Earth. I will report to Lucifer that I have secured thy information, but first, you will tell me what I need to know or I will watch you succumb to the sands of Time and thy life shall float as a vapor before my eyes." Zeus then waved his hand and Iblis was caught as a fly in a web of temporal power.

Iblis tried to run, tried to fly back to the group, but the trap held fast. Caught in a bubble of slowed time, his every movement were but centimeters in the direction he desired to travel.

Zeus floated next to him and spoke. "You forget that I am the master of Time here. I can leave you here and return in a century and you would have found yourself moved but one foot. Just imagine, a century of running in the dark of Hell's intestine, clamoring for an escape that does not exist. Thy cries for help never finding escape from the temporal vacuum that now exists around you. But your actions are predictable, so I offer thee a choice...a choice to live, or to die while Hell suckles upon thy stone."

Zeus touched the floor and the room came alive with eyes from ceiling to floor. Then he expanded the temporal field and the tendrils that reached for Iblis slowed to an infinitesimal crawl.

"See? Some of us hath the power to traverse Hell without harm. Yea, we must be cautious, but in the end, she is but a beast. A beast who, with Charon, is even tamable. But you...well needless to say I do not need Grigoric sight to know what will happen to you. For Hell now is alive to your presence, and when I close the temporal field that now holds the creature at bay, I will be long gone...and you, well you will be soon be gone." Zeus laughed.

Iblis's eyes locked in terror on the centipede-like eyes that rose from the floor...eyes that now fixed on him. Acidic salivating tendrils suddenly reached to snatch him into Hell's clutches. Zeus laughed as he circled him and smiled. "Wouldst you like to go with me and tell me where I might find Jerahmeel? For I know he seeks the master's weapon and Lord Talus."

Tears began to stream from Iblis's eyes, frozen in a microscopic march of time as they slid down his face. Tears of surrender.

"Yes," he whimpered, trapped like a fly in the web of a towering spider.

"Very good," Said Zeus. "I so much enjoy our times together. Come, let us go."

Zeus then took Iblis into his arms, exited the hallway, and removed the temporal barrier around the area. Hell immediately flooded the chamber with eyes, magma and flaming tentacles that reached for occupants no longer there, and Zeus grinned as he took his escaped captive, prisoner, once more.

* * *

Enoch paced intently before Elijah. "He hast lied!" he said.

Elijah listened intently allowing Enoch to finish his explanation. Waiting for him to calm down.

"The king is none other than the traitor who collaborated with Lucifer. He is not Nephanos!" Enoch muttered to himself, almost oblivious to Elijah's presence. "And the people – the people think he is Nephanos, but if indeed he is not Nephanos, where is the true king?"

"The real issue is how to confront this treachery," Elijah said. "How to reveal the ruse. Hast thou heard anything about your friends? Are they unharmed?"

Enoch waved his hands in exasperation. "They are captive in a hold unbeknownst to me. Our host tells me that they await execution...execution for a crime they did not commit. Pssfftt. Gabriel and Metatron would never steal. It is beyond their imagination to do so."

Elijah stroked his beard. "And of this thou art sure? Angels are not beyond the temptations known to man."

Enoch harrumphed. "I have known Elohim. I have seen the renegade, Lucifer, firsthand when he sent his assassins and Charon to destroy me and my family. I have also noted angels are a most honorable people, and though there is a host of them on Earth arrayed against our people, Gabriel and Metatron are not so. I would stake my life on their honor."

Elijah nodded. "That is good to know, for it yet may come to that."

Enoch looked at his peer curiously. "What do you mean?"

"I have been in the company of the Seraphim for many a day now and have studied these people. It would seem thy time in Heaven was to learn from the angels, whilst I was being tutored by the Seraphim. Thy devotion is akin to my own for them. They are, as you say a great people. Their passion for El is hot and ignites all that you see. They are desire, and yeah even lust, but in a sanctified form that serves El. This I have learned whilst among them. It may be that to unite our brethren we must be prepared to lay down all."

Enoch considered Elijah's words. "El commanded me to bring you back to Michael and the heavenly city."

Elijah nodded. "And the Lord Yeshua hath made known even before thy coming that this false king's time hath been weighed in the balance and found wanting, for I was commanded to accompany you to the heavenly city."

Enoch sat down, clasped his hands and wrung them as he spoke aloud, "What is it that you propose we do?"

"We will offer Camael one last space to repent," Elijah replied. "I will tell him El has commanded me to go to the heavenly city and see to Gabriel's people."

"And if he refuses to release you?" Enoch said.

"Then we will know that he is false, but to secure our plan, thou must acquire something that will expose him. You said that when you were with Camael blew into one of the instruments, and when he did so, the rest glowed and sung as well?"

"Aye," Enoch said. "It is as you say."

"Then of a surety, he is the craftsman behind them, for the Seraphim are as the breath of God and when they blow into whatever they craft their fires lite their instruments. Each is unique to its maker, such that none other can blow it unless it is made especially for them for I have learned that their sigil is in the flames. We must, therefore, provoke him to reveal himself," Elijah said.

"How?" said Enoch.

"You will take the horn of Malakim and with it blow, and when thou doest so, it shall reveal its maker. If Camael is indeed posing as Nephanos, his own creation will give him away."

Enoch looked at Elijah, scrunching his face. "How am I to acquire the horn? Camael had Sherkanim strip Gabriel, and I am sure he holds it with the rest in the throne room. Surely a move to prevent Gabriel's people from being called to give aid."

Elijah smiled. "Go to Camael's chamber as before, for it will be there that you shalt find Gabriel's horn. Find it, and take both his horn and one other."

"What would that be?" replied Enoch.

"You must take one of the seven trumpets of judgment."

* * *

"Report," said Michael.

Argoth turned from the open projections on the wall and stared at the horror on Michael's face. Red eyes betrayed him as he gaped at Yeshua's forced march through the streets of Jerusalem. And alongside the images from Earth were projections that showed His people in the streets of the heavenly city, screaming in pain for the lack of rational thought. The Withering's work featured in terrifying display.

Argoth held a scroll in his hand sealed with a ribbon of blue flame, and he walked towards Michael and spoke.

"A courier from Nephanos hast delivered to Janus this letter. Janus said the Seraph courier recorded the arrival of our party in Aseir, but reports misfortune hath befallen them."

Michael accepted the letter, broke the clay seal, placed it in a display and set it afire. And when he did so, words appeared thereon and it voiced a message from Nephanos.

Hail, Chief Prince. It hath been many days since we have spoken. I have been informed of thy ascension by Eladrin and wish you and your people to prosper and good health.

Be it known that thy ambassadors have reached us, but one Grigori hath been lost to the beasts under the mountain. Those that remain solicited us to heal the affliction of thy people. In sorrow, we cannot dismiss the Withering from thy kind for the thing is of El, and who can remove that which the Lord Himself hath allowed?

Even so, it is with further sadness that I must report that two of thy kind have been found guilty of guile. The charge was theft of a Trumpet of Judgment. You knowest as well as I that El intends to unleash these weapons upon the works of Lucifer and his kind. We have recovered the stolen weapon in the stuff of thy servant, Gabriel. He and the other called Metatron have thus been condemned to die in three days' time, their lives, therefore, will be given as a penalty for thy disdain for of contacting me via royal protocol and their illegal incursion into our realm. This will satisfy our law in lieu of war with thy people. Thou wilt accept my judgment, Michael of the Kortai, or we will consider the covenant between our peoples broken, and remove the fire that animates thy stones from thy people's breasts in accordance with our treaty.

This is my will, and this is my law,

Sealed and signed by my own hand.

Nephanos King of the Seraphim.

Michael inhaled heavily and let the flaming document slip through his fingers and to the floor. He propped one elbow on the arm of the chair and leaned his forehead into his hand.

Argoth allowed a moment before he spoke. "There is more, my prince."

Michael raised his head in anguish. "Say on."

Argoth hesitated. "My Watchers from Azaziel's regiment report that even now, our Lord submits Himself to the evils of men. To what end is still not entirely clear, but He allows Himself to be handled by Adamson." Argoth paced, visibly distraught. "Thus, after all of our attempts to prevent the death of God, the vision that you saw of the Lord on a cross hastens its march toward fulfillment I am sorry Michael, but unless Yeshua turns from His present path, there seems no way to stop the Lord's crucifixion."

Michael mulled Argoth's words over and stroked his chin.

The Chief Prince speculated turning over in his mind what thoughts and actions could have put Gabriel and Metatron in such harm's way as to face execution? He knew the head of House Malakim would never risk another war, but would first give himself over to falsehood and execution before he would allow such an event to befall his people. Michael calculated the outcome of open hostility with the Seraphim, and all calculus ended with decimation. El's word concerning the schisms treaty was inviolate and would not be broken. He would not go back on His word, for the accord was clear. If Michael sent a squad to rescue his fellows he knew that they would all be destroyed.

Michael stared at the floating images, watching as Yeshua silently endured His treatment at the hands of the humans. He noted his master's eyes, the tenor with which He carried Himself, and in that moment, Michael closed his eyes tightly and prayed aloud.

"El, I have asked that this cup pass from me, but I see now what I must do. Know that I am want to do this thing. Nevertheless, not my will but thine be done."

He opened his eyes and turned to face Argoth who watched with curiosity.

"Argoth, there is a third option that hath escaped all, yea even Nephanos. An alternative that would spare our brethren and cease hostilities with our people."

The Grigoric leader stared at the angelic commander of the Elomic Legions. "Then you, my prince, see even more than the Chief of Eyes. What do you propose?"

Michael sighed. "I will go – and will surrender myself in their stead."

Argoth stepped back, stunned. His brow furrowed. "Art you mad? Do you think it a mean thing to surrender yourself – the appointed head of our people to dissolution?"

Michael lowered his eyes in contemplative thought, then returned his gaze to Argoth. "There is no other way, for it was by an angelic leader's hand that the Schism was genesised, and it will be by this angelic leader's hand that it be sealed. For was it not I who gave Lucifer suggestion that if we could have the instruments the Seraph possessed that we could obtain victory? Through my vocalization, Lucifer took with duplicity that which was not ours? Is it not fitting that I should bring resolution to that which caused Heaven's rift so long ago?"

Argoth harrumphed. "Perhaps, but the division of Kings by El was done to prevent us from contaminating one another. He has not given any apparent sign that His mind has changed. How dost thou know that your decision to breach their domain will result in that which ye desire, and not further provoke Nephanos and his kin to all out war?"

Michael bit his lip and thought deeply on Argoth's words, "There is one thing that is certain. In three days' time, the Withering will have completed its work, and unless El relents we are already a people dead. I go that we might have life. For even now the Lord of Hosts moves to lay down His own for a future that cannot be seen by Grigoric sight. If He is willing to do this, how much more as a son should I do as He sets example before us? I go not knowing what will befall me. I have learned from Enoch that one must walk by faith and not by sight. Therefore, I will not stand idle and allow my people to be cut off. You will thus make this record for all of Heaven to know, Argoth. I go to offer my life that I might save all. Do this for me, please, and if I do not set eyes on thee on this side of the Lord's will, I trust that I shall see thee again in the next."

Argoth was taken aback by the power of Michael's words and nodded. "Then let the thing be as you say."

Michael smiled in appreciation. "One other thing I command. As I am thy Chief, it falls upon me to give stewardship to the Legions. As all Lumazi are tasked at the moment, this leaves thee to watch over Heaven and to perform the will of the Lord in all things. I know that you do not wish to be burdened with leadership in this way, but do this thing and see Heaven prosper in thy hands."

Argoth frowned, sighed, and nodded his head. "If you do not return, I will submit to your word until El establishes another."

Michael smiled and stepped back. His halo glowed and flared, and the Chief Prince faded in a flash of light...gone to offer terms of peace in hopes of averting another war.

* * *

Jerahmeel's team had flown in the belly of the beast several hours, weary, constantly dodging Lucifer's' henchmen, and careful not to aggravate Hell above her tolerance. Being in the presence of so much evil, and exposed to the Withering that festered among the Horde began to take its toll. Jerahmeel would be glad when he could return home.

"How much further, Turiel?"

"According to the latest records, the Forge should be just ahead."

For several of men's days, Jerahmeel had traversed the innards of Hell. His mission: to seek out and destroy the false Kiln of Lucifer's making, and if possible, to find his brother, Talus, and see themselves home.

After their separation from Iblis, they wound deeper into the intestinal tract of the beast. Each carved stairway twirled in a circular fashion toward a vestibule that housed the heads of angels. The dangling, squirming bodies of punished angelic rebels hung from the ceiling. Metal hooks pierced their flesh; eyes and mouths were sewn shut. Some were impaled against the walls, their hands, and feet pinned to the soft consuming walls of Hell that slowly acidified their flesh for consumption. Cries of those being eaten alive echoed through the halls and Jerahmeel considered how different this realm was from Heaven. This domain, decorated to Lucifer's taste, where groans, wails, and screams were all that were ever heard. The hissing of steam, crackling of fire and stench of brimstone assaulted his nostrils. Jerahmeel beheld his brother's work and knew that if he were not stopped, the fate of Heaven would mirror those he saw suspended from the ceiling.

They slowly flew by what could only be the entrance of some great hall, and the sounds of animals issued forth. Jerahmeel, Eskalion, and Turiel into a staging area and to their left and right were pens of Wyverns, miniature dragons, used as steeds to buttress the Malakim Griffins in combat. The trio moved forward, past the black giant sentinels that misted like the Grigori, as they were gaseous in nature and covered in fire-like black onyx armor. Moreover, they had four arms and held in each hand a great sword. The four stood two to one side and two to the other, and the three angels passed through them, but the creatures did not respond to their presence.

"I don't like this," Turiel said. "We should not be able to easily travel in the midst of such creatures and none be present to stop us. Is it a trap?"

Jerahmeel looked all about, his eyes gazing at the monstrosities before them and nodded. "It is most assuredly a trap."

The light in the room raised and Jerahmeel and the party looked up. Four silhouetted figures stood on a pedestal. Behind the three elevated highest loomed a dark figure that Jerahmeel presumed to be Lucifer. And standing below him was Zeus, Ares...and Iblis. Ibis' eyes darted away from Jerahmeel's disappointed gaze.

"A trap? Nay, dear brother. Not a trap, but an opportunity! Nay...I have allowed you and thy companions to traverse these halls, and know, dear brother, that it is such an immense pleasure to see you again. Iblis here hath apprised me of how you so much wanted to find us...and find us you have."

Jerahmeel looked up into the darkness as Lucifer's voice bounced as an echo off the walls. "Show thyself, Satan! How is it that a being who boasts in his ability to manipulate light hides amongst the shadows?"

A chuckle floated through the air. Turiel and Eskalion looked about them but saw nothing until yellow eyes began to appear in the depths of the darkness. Squinty eyes that did not blink. And the trio noted that the groans became louder...and closer.

"You are wise, Jerahmeel. In many ways, I would have considered you mine equal in the gifts of wisdom and knowledge, but your blithe demeanor hast always shown a contempt for the more serious matters. Be it known, however, that I would answer thee on this wise. Know ye not that darkness is nothing more than the absence of light? For our Father spoke into the void, 'Let there be light,' and it was so. But I, Jerahmeel. I have always been there, for I have learned in the depths of Hell, even through the stupidity that was Apollyon, that darkness, my brother....darkness precedes all. Thus, I have no pleasure in illumination, but in the Shadow, in the Void. In nothingness doth, all things spring. This the Godking knows. Thus, why honor Him to be light when I can honor myself by exalting that which precedes the light, that which is primordial even to God – darkness. For it is darkness, Jerahmeel, that is the true state of creation. It is the Void from which all things spring. And sin, dear brother, assists in the degeneration of all things: to return us to a state of true purity. The purity of the Void."

Jerahmeel scrunched his face, realizing that Lucifer's mind was slowly decaying. His ability to reason darkened and caught up in the vestiges of pride, hurt, lust, and lies...a deceptive cocktail that once imbibed destroyed his faculties of reason.

"You have Talus. No?"

"He is here..." Lucifer replied with a chuckle. "We are all here."

Jerahmeel screamed into the air.

"Release him! Surrender this foolish cause, and lay down thy arms!"

Laughter echoed throughout the chamber, a jocularity that was indicative of one who knew he had heard a foolish request. And still the yellow eyes stared out from the darkness with slit pupils, accompanied by the sounds of groaning, and the audible advance of things slithering forward in the darkness.

Turiel and Eskalion closed ranks around their friend and drew their weapons.

"I decline," Lucifer said. "Instead, I submit to thee a counter offer. Bow down and worship me! Acknowledge me as thy God. And if thou do this thing, I will see thee escorted safely home, for wouldst thou not like to return to the realm eternal? Is it not wonderful to be in the presence of the Father? For who can abide in the bowels of a creature designed to house and destroy our kind? Nay, Prince of Harada. I will not surrender..," he said with a swaggering step, "but if thou do this thing, my word will I give that you will be allowed to go free. But if not..."

The light level within the chamber rose further and the trio could see daemons all about them...a legion of the walking celestial dead...the empty shells of former angels who followed Satan in his fall and paid a heavy price. Some dragged along the ground, others hobbled in flight, barely able to keep themselves aloft, and dozens crawled, as they had nothing but an upper torso to drag along the floor, and all displayed ravenous teeth ready to rip into the flesh, teeth set to devour them all.

Jerahmeel and all the party looked about them, their backs pressed against one another.

"We cannot defend this position, Jerahmeel," Turiel said.

Eskalion nodded. "Nay, we cannot."

Lucifer smiled and looked down from his elevated perch of darkness. "Well, Prince of Harrada? I would demand an answer this day. Whom shall you serve?"

Jerahmeel looked stoically upon the figure that was his brother, surveyed the surroundings and saw that they were encircled on every side. And somewhere past the Deceiver's gloat, Talus was still held captive to the wiles of the Devil. He sighed heavily, shrugged his shoulders, cracked the trapezoid muscles of his neck, smiled in confident tenor and replied, "Yea, though we stand troubled on every side, we are not in distress; though perplexed of how El might succor us, even in this, we are not in despair; though alone in the depths of darkness we are not forsaken; and know King of False Gods that though you think to cast us down, we shall never be destroyed. For El, oh lying one...is Lord and God."

Lucifer grinned and spoke, "An unwise decision. Take them, my loves. Subdue them and make their bodies your own." Immediately, daemons leaped from the darkness and besieged them from every direction.

Jerahmeel reached behind his back and pulled from its center the two axes strapped to it. The weapons dangled from chains bolted to the manacles on his wrists. He flexed his muscles and white armor shards climbed over every inch of his body. Turiel also assumed an attack posture and his stylus turned into a dagger. Eskalion pulled from his robes a long cadmium pole that he flexed at its center and it stretched to five feet in length.

A daemon hurled himself toward them and Jerahmeel swung his chained axes like a lasso, slicing the creature in half before it hit the ground. The legion of daemons rushed toward them as one man, and the trio fought for their lives assaulted from all directions.

In a frenzy, Eskalion used his staff to keep many at bay, twirling and jumping over multitudes, creating circular patches of ground they were able to defend.

Turiel misted and floated through throngs of the creatures, slightly rematerializing within them and causing them to shriek in pain.

Slashing, stabbing, and rattling chains twanged in the air as the cavern erupted with the sounds of battle. Jerahmeel lifted his hands and within the confines of Hell itself, what moisture resided within the beating hearts of the creatures froze and all fluidic motion within them ceased, bring many to a standstill unable to move for on a day never seen before nor experienced since, an angel of the living God caused snow to exist in Hell. A blizzard settled over the Prince of all Harrada, and with command of thermal energy, Jerahmeel slowed the kinetic energy of particles and a sheet of ice formed a protective barrier to the group's rear, barring any passage.

With only the front to be concerned about, the trio advanced through throngs of daemons, slicing and smashing the enemies of God back.

Bodies flew through the air and screeching howls overwhelmed the ears. Sweat beat upon Eskalion's brow as his large Arelim frame hosted three daemons. One bit into his calve, whilst another grappled his neck, attempting to bring him down. Others swung from his arm and bit into his bicep. He dropped his staff, pulled him off and flung the creature as a bat against the daemon attacking his legs, knocking his adversary into the darkness. Reaching behind, he yanked another off his back and flung him into a crowd of frozen enemies, shattering them to pieces. Eskalion heaved the last assailant high into the air. The creature clung tightly in vain attempts to harm him with claws and teeth but he smashed him into the floor of Hell, splattering the daemon's head wide open.

The trio advanced further in battle until none stood before them but the four silhouetted shadows on raised pedestal.

"Enough!" cried Jerahmeel. Lucifer, you know me. I am Lumazi. I will not be denied."

Lucifer looked on, the contour of his body barely visible from his perch, and replied. "So be it, Lumazi. Zeus, Ares, bring these unbelievers to heel."

When Jerahmeel heard the name Zeus, his rage kindled and a crackle of ball lightning erupted above his head. Spherical lightning flashed to the ground in front of him and knocked the trio back. While eddies of visible current wormed its way across the floor, Zeus rose from the midst of voltage. Sparks crackled around his person and he held a glowing sword the tip he dragged across the ground.

"We meet for the last time, Jerahmeel," he said.

Jerahmeel stood to his feet. His white armor sparkling and puffs of chilled air radiating from his body. He raised his axes and crossed their blades with swipes to sharpen them. He nodded and replied. "Shut up and fight."

Zeus smiled, disappeared in a spark of light, and then reappeared next to Jerahmeel, his sword bearing down to strike.

Jerahmeel side-stepped and his adversary's sword barely missed. Again, Zeus jabbed his sword forward and Jerahmeel parried the blow, blocking the blade's bite with his axes. Heaven-forged steel rang out, and flashes of voltage sparked as each weapon kissed the other's edge.

Weaving and ducking, Jerahmeel and Zeus dodged and zig-zagged one another, neither able to gain an advantage over the other and each entwined in a fatal dance where one misplaced step could lead to death.

Meanwhile, Turiel misted and hovered upward to where Lucifer and a cowering figure stood in the shadows. And Lucifer spoke to the oncoming Turiel through the darkness.

"You have not been summoned to approach my presence, Turiel. Iblis, my son, do me the honor of ridding me of this annoyance."

Iblis emerged from the darkness and spoke. "I am sorry, Turiel."

Turiel continued his floating approach towards the two adversaries and replied. "The day for sorrow hath passed."

Iblis then also misted, and the two merged as separate cloud formations melding into one. As a warm weather front meets a cold, lightning and thunder ensued and resonated through the room for in the vapor that filled the chamber, two ghostly figures wrestled with one another. Each grappling with the other in a gaseous skirmish to seize the advantage, their battle a foggish slugfest above the heads of Jerahmeel and Eskalion.

Another muscular figure emerged from the darkness...the silhouette of a heavily armored Arelim bearing a sword. It was Lucifer's God of War, Ares.

"It will give me great pleasure to disembowel you, Eskalion," he said.

Eskalion raised his staff horizontally in front of him. "I have swum in the bowels of our brethren as they died in the abomination called Tartarus. You will find me a most difficult adversary to kill."

Ares charged and the Arelim raised his staff to deflect the blow and sidestepped. Ares' momentum threw him forward and Eskalion's staff smashed into the back of his skull, sending him careening into the dank floor. Eskalion backed away, twirling his staff like a fan, circling in a defensive stance.

Ares wiped the gravel from his face and grinned in satisfaction. "I will most assuredly enjoy killing you."

With a roar, he rose from the floor and flew headlong into Eskalion's twirling staff, oblivious to the pummeling of Chittim wood that smacked his face. Forward he came, enduring rapid-firing smites to his cheeks. But Ares would not be stopped or denied as he pressed onward as the concrete blows hammered his face, neck, and chest. Eskalion, seeing that Ares would not be stopped by his actions, bellowed and stomped his foot into the scorched floor of Hell. A wave of concussive force traveled across the ground like a concentric groundswell that flowed over Ares, raising him into the air, tumbling in a suspended form of stasis.

Jerahmeel saw Ares floating in the air, and with a wave of his hand, the bubble that surrounded Ares froze over, totally encasing the angel in ice. The bubble solidified and crashed to the ground, shattering into a thousand shards. Ares rose groggily from his frozen enclosure and Zeus turned around to examine that which was behind him, and as he did so, shards of ice sprayed him. He covered his eyes. Jerahmeel attacked, kicking the Harrada square in the chest, sending him reeling through the air and crashing into Ares knocking both to the floor.

Eskalion raised his eyes to Turiel and Iblis who yet battled in the form of vapor. Eskalion threw his staff to Turiel, and Jerahmeel froze the air around Iblis, solidifying him. Turiel caught the staff and batted Iblis' head, sending him reeling into Ares and Zeus as they struggled to rise, causing them to be pummeled into the ground as Iblis fell atop them. Turiel tossed Eskalion's staff back to him and floated to where the trio huddled in pain, as both Eskalion and Jerahmeel floated toward Lucifer's henchmen. The three then formed up around them, each raising their weapons to bring them down on their dazed adversaries when a voice sounded.

"Enough!" Lucifer said.

Jerahmeel turned to see that Lucifer was now aglow in light that raced in mesmerizing patterns over his body.

"You have come here to destroy my Kiln, have you not? See now what you have combed the Realm of the Dead to see, and know the futility of your cause."

Lucifer waved his hand and when he did so, the chamber flooded with brilliance as a circle of light raced around the center of the floor. A circular opening revealed itself on the floor and the floor rock retracted into the walls. The hiss of steam and heat eddies escaped with a sizzle and screams and howls roared into the air. A horrific choir of moans raced up the walls of a gaping mouth lined with circular rows of teeth, and the familiar veins of Hell's tendrils flailed in the air as though released from a cage, and Jerahmeel watched as a pedestal with a figure sprouted from the center of a yawning mouth now roused from its sleep. Molten lava scurried to reveal the physique of the angel jutting from the depths of a mouth lined with the living, screaming remains of angels and spirits of evil men. Higher and higher the pedestal rose, like a mountain within a mountain. The fiery hollow burned white hot, and the more it rose in the cavern, the easier Jerahmeel could see who lay atop what could be nothing but a Kiln. A kiln that Talus was absorbed into, fused together as one entity. A kiln that suckled on the revealed beating heart of his friend. And Talus, head of all Arelim, one of the seven spirits that once stood before the presence of God, screamed. His cries blasted the air in waves of anguish insomuch that even the hearers felt pain. His figure was skeletal and his flesh had so fallen from him that his innards could be seen. Muscle, nerves, and worms crept over him, entering and exiting his body at will, feeding Hell as carrion drifted over the remains of a living carcass.

Jerahmeel gaped upon the living nightmare that raised itself as a tower before him, facing an unthinkable realization he had never considered. Talus, the brother he loved and had come to rescue, was now one with the Hellforge.

The Prince of House Harrada dropped his weapons to the ground, his mouth agape and eyes bulging at what he saw. A suffocating despondency slowly rose in his chest as he collapsed to his knees and moaned in despair.

* * *

Eskalion slumped on the ground, gawking, his mind in shock, for Lucifer had fused Talus' body into the living rock that was Hell herself. His arms were coiled with Hells tendrils as worms scurried across his exposed torso. The granite-like rock of Hell absorbed his abdomen. His legs, once visible, could no longer be seen. Leathery wings, once awesome with beauty, were shredded, and tattered strips now were strewn across each span.

Turiel and Eskalion beheld Jerahmeel's reaction and realized their mission to destroy the forge would also kill Talus, paused in their advance. And Lucifer---Lucifer watched with smug satisfaction that their awe gave them hesitation. And whilst the three were lost in grief and distraction, Lucifer lifted his hands and a great light appeared above them, blinding them to everything they surveyed, and they covered their eyes as the brilliance was like a searing heat and they stumbled as men blind.

"Simpletons, you have yet to grasp the degree of both the Father's failure and your own." Lucifer flicked his wrist and tendrils descended upon them and restrained them that they could not move. Each was raised off the ground and suspended just above the floor of the cavern.

Zeus and Ares and Iblis walked back toward their master. Lucifer then floated toward Jerahmeel and whispered in his ear. "Thy ability to see my devices hath always been a burden to me. Forgive me as I partially relieve myself of it."

Then Lucifer grabbed Jerahmeel by the face and with his own hands, felt the contour of Jerahmeel's closed eye, lifted Jerahmeel's right eyelid and gouged the eye from its socket.

Jerahmeel shrieked in pain, shaking his head left and right. "Arrgh! Curse you Lucifer! God curse you to eternity!"

Lucifer smiled and held the bloody eyeball of Jerahmeel in his hand, staring at it longingly. "Thou seest with old eyes. Now, behold the vision I wish to cast upon you. See the world, Jerahmeel. See the cosmos as I see it." And when Lucifer spoke, Hell's ceiling became opaque, and Lucifer allowed the sounds above to be heard by them all. Behind the scene of Talus lifted and infused in the new furnace were pictures of Yeshua splayed across the walls and ceiling of Hell. Jerahmeel and the party watched as the Son of God fell under the weight of a crossbeam of wood. A crown of thorns pierced His brow, and both flesh and garments were bruised and tattered. Through throngs of humans who encouraged His death, and others too afraid to interfere, Roman guards marched Him to His execution. Jerahmeel watched with one eye as his Lord collapsed beneath the beam outstretched upon His shoulders. Lucifer smiled as he observed the procession.

"I will leave thee in the hands of my guards, for I must see Adam complete the work I have long desired to see. Despair, Jerahmeel. Despair, and see the world thou and the Host have fought to save, and mankind pass judgment on the Creator's kingship over them. See with the one eye that remains, for when the life of Yeshua goes out, I will return and take thy remaining eye and leave you in eternal darkness with the image of Yeshua spread upon a cross, a lasting image sealed for all time. Goodbye, brother."

Lucifer then floated away, laughing as he departed, ascending into the plane of the physical realm.

"Lucifer!!" Jerahmeel screamed.

Anguish and rage filled Jerahmeel, and he continued to cry aloud after his ascending brother. His screams echoed throughout the corridors and carried aloft upon the winds of Hades. Anguished cries of despair, cries that merged into the wails of her denizens. One more lone cry of woe added to the millions of screams that rang throughout her walls.

* * *

The sky was overcast in Jerusalem, as was Azaziel's spirit. No prayer covering protected the region for it seemed all of Jerusalem sought the death of the Lord. Azaziel wept at a distance as Yeshua entered alone into the spiritual wilderness comprised of evil men, daemons, and fallen angels...a multitude elated to see the Lord of Creation struggle in human flesh to carry a cross.

For six hundred and fifty yards, Yeshua walked past men and women hecklers while a small cadre of Roman soldiers went before Him. One, in particular, carried a titulus; a sign that announced Yeshua's crime as being "King of the Jews." Alone, the Son of God strode upwards toward the place of the Skull, force marched to the cackling cadence of humiliating barbs and the gawking eyes of men and women who mocked and spit upon Him. As He advanced amidst the throng, His bruised and battered body a walking effigy that represented the disappointment of evil men who, like the ancient Israelites of old, wanted a king like the other nations of the world. A king other than God, and once more, the King of the Universe submitted to the will of His own creation's rejection.

As God in the flesh acquiesced to the evil of men, each step testified to the love within the breast of the Almighty, nevertheless, a breast scorned by the unseen spirits who had rebelled against God. Therefore, for one thousand, nine hundred and fifty feet, Yeshua followed Simon the Cyrene to Golgotha, the hill – the place where He would embrace Death.

And when the entourage of death reached their final destination, Simon the Cyrene laid the wooden crossbar on the ground. The patibulum beam that would extend the outstretched arms of the Lord. The one hundred and twenty-five-pound plank of splintered wood hit the rocky ground with a thud, and the Roman soldiers, satisfied with Simon's work, shooed him away. And the Cyrene did as he was bidden lest he further provoke the soldier's ire.

Azaziel and his soldiers watched from afar while Grigoric scouts of both the Heavenly Host and the Fallen penned in their tomes.

Argoth and Michael also watched from the Hall of Annals as more and more of the Horde poured in from regions round about to see man accomplish what rebellious Elohim themselves could not achieve...the death of God. Satan attended in person, celebrating his evil scheme of orchestration that was finally coming to fulfillment. After years of planning and waiting, patiently biding his time, and moving against every counter of El, to help bring about the outcome that he lusted after for so many years. The death of his maker.

Thus, Yeshua, clear in mind and purpose, allowed His creation to handle Him as they stretched Him out on a patibulum of splintered wood. Seven-inch iron nails were given to a soldier, while the Lord's feet and arms were held in place in preparation for His body's impalement on the cross. A soldier forcibly grabbed His wrist and placed a nail near His median nerve.

The eyes of both Heaven and Earth watched in tense anticipation.

Argoth turned his head as the hammer raised.

Azaziel wept, wondering where he had failed the Lord.

Lucifer watched with gleeful anticipation, his eyes wide and a smile spread across his face as stretched leather, but it was Michael – the appointed Chief Prince of Heaven, who stoically watched the vision given to him so many ages ago by the Lord come to pass.

A human hand raised the hammer into the air, reached its apogee, then in a downward stroke pummeled an iron spike into the soft skin of the Word made Flesh, the clanging of which filled the air.

The Lord howled in agonizing pain as His flesh, reacting as designed, set His nerves on fire. The shock of His pain radiated through His arms and unlocked corridors of dormant pain receptors.

In Heaven, the Virtues spoke aloud. "Yet it pleased the Lord to bruise Him."

Blood splatter misted into the air as the Son of God's cries of agony cracked the ears of those listening.

Mary, the mother of Yeshua, sobbed from a distance, wailing with outstretched arms toward her oldest son whilst her companion, a woman Grigoric records would name Mary Magdalene, consoled as best as she was able the woman whom El had made privy to carry His son.

An exuberant mirth manifested in the evil smiles of daemon inspired men as the audience chanted...men who acquired more satisfaction from the unjust execution than the wrongful release of a convicted murderer through the manipulation of Governor Pilate's clemency.

Again, the clanging strike of iron against iron punctured the cool air...a sound that marked the methodical killing of the Son of God, and the perfection of torture on effective display by the Roman Empire.

In Heaven, the Virtues once again spoke aloud as they wafted around the throne. "Yet it pleased the Lord to bruise Him."

Pain, agony, and love cried out from the cross.

"Father, forgive them, for they know not what they do!" Yeshua cried.

The Romans who nailed Him, mocked Him over who took His robe and gambled amongst themselves to see who might have it.

The people stood beholding, and the rulers also with them derided Him, saying, "He saved others; let Him save Himself if He be Christ, the chosen of God."

And the Lord heard the hecklers who beheld Him in contempt, yet did not return evil for evil. The Genesis of all Creation fighting against suffocation, enduring unknowingly to all who watched, the rod of God on the world's sin, that one day He might once more be in communion with His beloved mankind.

Fear kept those who might otherwise speak against the travesty before them, in silence. The need for self-preservation a more palpable immediate concern than the altruistic value to defend the innocent. And aside from the cries of a few women and those of a tearful mother whose Son's life was fleeing before her eyes, none dared to interfere; for the Romans were staunch in their duty to the Empire and prevented any from drawing near. Efficient, and as merciless as well-oiled machines of death, they were swift in the execution of their duty.

Amidst the cries of wailing women and the jeers of taunting men were two thieves who also were executed. One hung on each side of the Lord, and one of the malefactors that hung next to Him, railed on Him, saying, "If thou be Christ, save thyself and us."

But the other answered and rebuked him, saying, "Dost, not thou fear God, seeing thou art in the same condemnation? And we indeed justly; for we receive the due reward of our deeds: but this man hath done nothing amiss." And he turned from the other and said unto Yeshua, "Lord, remember me when thou comest into thy kingdom."

And Yeshua said unto him, "Verily I say unto thee, today shalt thou be with me in paradise."

And while the God in flesh allowed Himself to be fastened with nails of iron to a cross, God the Father looked down upon the actions of both men and His Son. The Virtues floated in their cloud-like fashion and words emanated from their invisible and fragrant mouths. "He hath put Him to grief."

And the Realm of the Dead was also privy to the happening in the land of the living, and Jerahmeel, shackled whilst in the realm of the unrighteous dead, could no longer view the scene projected upon the walls of Hades.

Zeus stood guard over his captive, noted Jerahmeel's repugnance, and grabbed Jerahmeel by the scruff of his neck.

"Oh yes, dear brother," Zeus said. "Thou shalt surely watch the fall of God in the Earth." Zeus grabbed him by his cheeks and turned Jerahmeel's face to look up into the realm of men. The Harada then held his eyelid open to witness the torture of God by Lucifer's marionette of men.

Thus, in 33 A.D., a great cloud of witnesses marked time, making note that on that day in Grigoric history, God, the eternally existent one – died. For the Creator of Heaven and Earth yielded Himself to the abuse of men and angels, all that He might save mankind from sin.

For hours, the life of Yeshua flowed from Him. Crimson stained His head where a mockery of a crown perforated His skull. His wrists and feet were colored in the deepest maroon. Hands that had made fishes and loaves, and feet that had walked on water now hung from beams of splintered wood. Splinters that embedded themselves into the ripped flesh strewn from the Lord's back. His face bruised from the pummeling of the Roman soldiers, His body a lacerated mass of rouge and scarlet. A coagulated, living corpse whose remaining blood pooled at the foot of the cross. A dying witness for all of Heaven and Earth. A testimony of Lucifer and man's verdict of God's reign over him. A testimony forever to be noted in the annals of history that God so loved mankind that He came down from Heaven and surrendered Himself to the pinnacle of man's evil. All that He might restore mankind to a relationship with Himself.

For hours, the breath of life wafted away from the Lord. The shallowness of His breathing caused small areas of His lungs to collapse. His body in instinctive response fought to gather the rich warm air, and Yeshua pushed up against the prickling wood of the cross to open His lungs and gulp life-giving air once more.

The sun seemed to stand still, unwilling to march in her route through the galaxy. For every hour that Yeshua's lungs decreased in oxygen, carbon dioxide increased as the chain reaction of laws that governed human flesh caused acidic conditions in the flesh of the Lord.

Fluid slowly built up in His lungs, compounding what all Heaven saw as the inevitable, and when El noted that the final burden of sin was laid upon the bloodied back of His Son, even He was moved with compassion to stretch forth His hand to save.

Yet it pleased the Lord to bruise him, for the Holy One had elected to leave Heaven to endure the pain, suffering, and shame, that mankind might be once more purchased into reconciliation with God. And the sin was such that El could no longer view the visage of His beloved Son, for, in the eyes of God the Father, Yeshua became shrouded in, and eclipsed and marred by the sins of the world. A bloody cloak of the ugliness that was humanity, horrifically naked and gory as a testimony to Adam's actions so many years before.

And as the Lord saw His offspring bleeding out and splayed upon the cross, He remembered His beautiful creation, His former love of Lucifer, the wars fought, and lives extinguished...the covetousness, greed, and murder that Lucifer and the Horde had waged.

From the fall of Adam to the death of Abel, the sons of Noah and the downward spiral that Adam and his children recklessly marched towards because the thoughts of mankind were only evil. And in the midst of His anguish over the blood that streamed down the bruised cheeks of His broken boy, God looked into man's future and beheld those who would be partakers of Life – the few who would surrender all to experience His love, and His thoughts turned to the approaching sun of a new day where there would be no more tears, and where the lion would once more lay down with the lamb; and when He saw the glory that was set before Him, He withdrew His presence and turned from His only begotten Son.

And it was about the ninth hour that Yeshua cried out with a loud voice, "Eloi, Eloi, lama sabachthani?" which means, My God, my God, why hast thou forsaken me?

And when all of Heaven saw that God had turned His back on His own Son, that separation existed between He who hung on a cross and He who sat on the throne: it was in that moment that the Host saw the depths of God's love for mankind. A collective epiphany came over all. If El did this for those who were flesh, how much more would He do for His sons in the Spirit? And in that moment Heaven understood that man's estrangement from God was now reconciled and Adam's kin could return to their former place El had always destined for them.

Before the eyes of Heaven did God show the depth of His love. For when man was yet without strength, in due time Christ died for the ungodly, and many such as Azaziel took note, for they had seen the ways of mankind and noted that scarcely for a righteous man would one die: yet peradventure for a good man some would even dare to die, but in fascination, Azaziel beheld that God commendeth His love toward mankind, in that, while man was yet a sinner, Christ died for him.

And Yeshua, fading between consciousness and unconsciousness, and resisting the fleshy urge to release Himself from the searing pain, empty of the need for self-preservation; the Son of God – the Shiloh, elected to breathe His last breath into the Earth he had created and spoke.

"It is finished."

The Lord then bowed His head and surrendered the ghost.

Lucifer crowed in jubilation as he floated near the bowed head of the God of the Universe, and slid his hand graciously against the still warm cheek of the Lord and whispered, "Now, Yeshua, whose head doth hang smitten underfoot? All for naught didst thou prepare a body. And for what? To be but refuse for me. For when this flesh decays, thou shalt be sealed as any other man within my realm, and who then will deny me? And why? All because thou lovest the Clayborn. See how foolish it is to hold such a love." The Betrayer then turned to the Horde that gathered to watch the spectacle and spoke aloud for all to hear. "Behold!" he roared. "GOD is D E A D!"

And the minions cheered amongst themselves as a throng of unruly children, clamoring in gleeful praise. They sang and raised their hands in buoyant elation, that Lucifer, Son of the Morningstar, had finally through the hand of mankind, killed Shiloh.

The heavenly legions looked upon their Lord's body in disbelief and anger. A quiet hung throughout the realm. Quiet that a member of the Trinity had died at the hands of His own creation. Quiet, as confusion and fear propagated in the minds of heavenly angels that perhaps God was not as all-powerful as they had believed. Quiet because God had shown that He loved the children of Adam more than life itself. And the cumulative thoughts were more than Azaziel could fathom and he cried out in anguish.

"NOOO!!!!"

Tears streamed down his face. His hand tightened around his spear, piercing eyes blazing red with righteous fury, and his wrath so overflowed that he thought in his rage to destroy the whole city with fire. Tempted to wage open warfare against the celebrating Horde, Azaziel raised his spear to draw down Heaven's fire, but when he did so, El Pneuma restrained him and said, "Be still, my son, for this thing is of me. For behold the beginning of the end of Lucifer's claim on death."

Azaziel then gritted his teeth and held his peace as bidden, and the Lord Pneuma with His own hand tore the veil of the temple and rent it in twain from the top to the bottom. Moreover, the earth did quake, and the rocks also were tossed to and fro; and the tremors were such that all of the city and round about the region were moved from their foundations and the Lord caused the graves to open and many that were dead to walk free.

Lucifer frowned and the Horde grew quiet as they had not caused the quake. And the King of Pride grew anxious when he saw the resurrections, and said, "Let us go and see if our prize is indeed caged within the Realm of the Dead. And see if He stands as powerless as David in Paradise."

Chapter Eleven: Saved by Hope

Enoch crouched behind the emblazoned statues of honored poets and musicians. The king often said they reminded him of the principles that governed his people...of which the first and foremost was to worship El.

Two chamberlains chatted as they completed their rounds of the king's throne room, and Enoch waited with baited breath.

"Where is the king now?" the first said.

"He visits the angels in the tower before he sees to their dissolution."

"Is it not strange that they have not been submitted to the Burning? Then all of Aesir could witness their actions. Why are they not summoned to give account?"

The first attendant moved closer to Enoch, who held his breath, not sure if the act of breathing itself would alert his intrusion to the temple staff. The attendant came close enough to reach out and touch him. Enoch flattened himself against the chamber wall, hoping he might meld with the decorative images that adorned the throne chamber. His lungs began to slowly burn.

"It is a strange thing, indeed. Nevertheless, the king said they attempted to take a vessel of wrath. El hast reserved these seven vessels to be blown at the appointed time. Perhaps the angels wanted to unleash El's wrath before the time, and compel Him to honor His word when He hears the trumpets sound," the other said.

"Possibly, but I wonder what possible intentions could cause one to start a war? Without the Burning, we will never know."

The second attendant's burning body created shadows as he floated closer to Enoch. Any moment, his hiding place would be bathed in light and his position exposed. Enoch gritted his teeth as his lungs seared, bursting to suck in oxygen and quench their thirst for air.

"Are the vessels accounted for?" the first said.

"Aye. All seven are on the pedestal and accounted for. "Let us be off. We have other chambers to be arranged."

The two attendants took their leave, and Enoch opened his mouth and heaved warm air into his lungs in long gasps. He closed his eyes, thankful that he was not discovered, and tiptoed to a pedestal that held one of the trumpets of judgment. Picked it up. It looked simple enough...a burnished gold with light orange flames that emanated from it. Curiously, it was warm to the touch and heavy for a human. Enoch realized he would have to hurry, and he had not considered the weight was designed for angels and not men. Mentally smacking his forehead, he hefted the instrument and hastened back to Elijah. Quickly running to his bed chamber, he gave a sigh of accomplishment as he closed the door...not realizing Sherkanim of the king's guard watched him enter as he smuggled a trumpet of judgment into his room.

* * *

Hell fed upon Turiel. The Grigori had tried to mist, tried to escape the snarling clutches of Hell's tendrils but it was to no avail, for Hell was a creature designed to incarcerate Elohim. A place of torment devised to secure the most powerful from escape. And try as the Redactor might, he was powerless to flee. Turiel's stylus and tome recorded his experiences, noting all that his eyes and ears observed, adding to the sum of knowledge the Grigori in Heaven possessed an expanding ledger of stenographic notes regarding Hell's behavior.

Turiel gritted his teeth until his jaws grew tired for the flames of the tendrils wore hundreds of small suction cups that clamped tightly and impaled his flesh with piercing barbed tongues. With each bite, they regurgitated acidic spittle into the captive's wounds while the octopi-like cups drained the life force from his kilnstone. Each circular wound blistered the flesh as Hell injected parasitic larvae into its host. Larvae that fed on the celestial flesh of angels.

Thus each angel, no matter their house, no matter their ability or station, bred Hell's carrion and became an everlasting source of food. Turiel, Eskalion, and the one-eyed Jerahmeel were now part of that food chain. Flies caught in the underworld that was the Realm of the Dead...flies that cried out in terror. New additions to the participants of Hell's choral chamber. A choral chamber swelled with nothing but the wailing and gnashing of teeth.

* * *

Far away, on Earth's surface, crows and all manner of birds flocked around the bodies of Dismas and Gestas. The two men hung to the left and right of Yeshua. Flies and mosquitoes buzzed as the scent of death and blood invited vermin to take up residence, but creation would not sully the body of the Creator. Azaziel and his guard watched over the body of Yeshua to assure that nothing desecrated his body.

Some of the Horde did not leave with Lucifer and stared at the spectacle men had accomplished in their blind arrogance.

Some members of the Horde were dazed, unsure of what to make of the death of the Eternal One. Others seemed saddened, though careful not to express emotion whilst in the midst of their enemies. Azaziel had seen the face before.

Faces of regret.

Cauldrons of sorrow of a forlorn past and the futility to live knowing that death and judgment crept silently toward all that drew breath. Death, the invisible stalker and inevitable outcome for those that opposed God. For the Fallen had come to understand – knowing God would one day avenge Himself for their rebellion.

Although most of the Horde had departed, a measure of the Fallen stopped to gloat over the Son of God's death.

And seeing so many of the Horde assembled, Azaziel grew weary of their presence and spoke. "Portiel go to and influence the chief leaders to remove the Lord's body and let us be done with this," Azaziel said.

Portiel did as commanded and the Jewish leaders heeded, not wanting to leave the bodies upon the crosses on the Sabbath day, (for that Sabbath day was a high day) besought Pilate that the men's legs might be broken and that they might be taken away.

Pilate consented and released soldiers to break their legs to hasten their deaths. And of the two that hung next to Yeshua, they did break their legs, but when they came to Yeshua and saw that He was already dead, they broke not His legs.

A member of the Horde then suggested to the Roman captain, to assure the death of the Nazarene, and moved by the voice of a fallen angel, the captain commanded his underling to do so. Immediately, a soldier with a spear pierced the Lord's side and forthwith came thereout blood and water. And the Horde knew not that they fulfilled prophecy saying, a bone of Him shall not be broken. And again another scripture saith, they shall look on Him whom they pierced.

And after this, Joseph of Arimathea, being a disciple of Yeshua but secretly for fear of the Jews, besought Pilate that he might take Yeshua's body and Pilate gave him leave. And there also came Nicodemus, which at the first came to Yeshua by night, and brought a mixture of myrrh and aloes, about a hundred-pound weight.

Rough hands removed the corpse from the cross and loving ones wound Him in linen clothes and covered Him with spices, as was the manner of the Jews to bury. Now in the place where He was crucified, there was a garden; and in the garden was a new sepulcher wherein man was never laid, and there laid they Yeshua because of the Jews' preparation day; for the sepulcher was nigh at hand.

Azaziel and his soldiers hovered as those who wept prepared the body. Various members of the Horde watched also, but from afar mocking the group.

"We have Him sealed as a spirit within the Realm of the Dead," one taunted.

"Behold, the eternal God is dead!" another said.

"Correction! One of the Godhead is dead, and now that we know we can slay one, we will slay the others!" a third said. But none of the Fallen dared to attack the mighty Azaziel and those with him. For they yet had respect to the power of the angels to injure them.

Cassiel, one of the twelve assigned as the Lord's guard, placed his hand on Azaziel's shoulder and noted how solemn he was as Joseph and Nicodemus rolled the stone into place. Soldiers from Pilate settled themselves to camp in front of the tomb after they impressed the wax Imperial seal of the Roman Empire over the stone of the sepulcher.

Cassiel stared at their surroundings. Men of the region had grown quiet as they prepared for the Sabbath.

"Azaziel..." Cassiel said, "the Lord is laid within. What would you have us do now? We have watched over His Grace since His birth by the virgin child. The Great One no longer walks amongst these humans. Is not our charge dismissed?"

Azaziel looked upon the huge stone now sealed shut. The seal of the Roman Empire warning all humans away under penalty of death if broached.

The High Prince of Issi sighed placing his hand on Cassiel's shoulder, "No, my friend. For with the Lord away from His mortal coil, He now walks where angelic hands cannot help, but we can abide faithful. For He hath promised He would after three days rise again. I would see that we are ready to execute His commands when He does. We must all be ready to attend to the master when He returns. Therefore, I command scouts atop the grave here...here, and here." Azaziel pointed above the sepulchers entrance, and to its east and west. "Keep watch. While Yeshua walks in Hell, the Horde is too distracted with His presence to attempt defilement of His body. We will make sure His mortal house until He returns."

Cassiel motioned to go when he stopped and spoke from over his shoulder. "We have witnessed both the birth and death of God in the Earth. Will He indeed return?"

Azaziel looked at the setting sun, remembering the timeline of the Lord. "The word of God will not return void, for if the Lord hath said it, He will certainly do it. Now go, my friend, and be about thy business."

"As you command, Lumazi," Cassiel replied.

Azaziel watched as Cassiel relayed the command and angelic guards took up their stations as ordered. Satisfied in their defensive position, the angel turned his face toward the sealed grave and walked into the Lord's tomb, passing through rock as if through gas and over to the linen that covered the body of the Lord. He moved to his master's lain head and unsheathed his sword, standing silently and stern-jawed in the dank black grave...an angelic sentinel – awaiting his Lord's return.

* * *

Elijah's eyes lit up when Enoch entered his room and jumped to his feet. "Do you have it?" he said.

Enoch nodded and grinned, then turned around and swirled his robes from off him. Strapped to him was a trumpet of judgment tucked within the folds of his back. "But the Trumpet of Malakim was not in the king's chambers."

"Good," Elijah said. "We will find a way to locate and secure the trumpet, and then we will have what we need. "But we are not yet safe from the execution of our pla..."

A knock sounded on the door.

Elijah went to answer, but before he could do so, Sherkanim barged in and saw the golden trumpet of judgment strapped on Enoch's back.

"Thieves! Deceivers!" Sherkanim said. "By what reason should I not rend you where you stand for doing such a great evil toward us?" His hand halfway unsheathed his sword.

Elijah lifted his hands to calm him. "Because I believe you also suspect that Nephanos's mind is not well. Because I perceive by the spirit of the living God that thou dost know something is amiss with the king."

Sherkanim stepped back, and his eyes darted away from Elijah. He said nothing, but walked to the window and removed his hand from his sword.

Elijah continued. "You personally escorted Gabriel and Metatron to the Gate to depart. In all that time, didst thou suspect that either would steal from thy people?"

"Even if I hold what thou sayest as true, it fails to justify thy actions."

My friend, "I have no desire to blow the trumpet of judgment. In fact, there is another trumpet that belongs to one that I seek, and I would solicit thee to help acquire it for me."

Sherkanim turned with wrinkled brow as he processed the request, but Elijah did not shrink from his gaze. "By what madness would I consider to even do this thing?"

Elijah smiled. "Because if you do, you will reveal what I have come to know and Enoch has confirmed – that Nephanos is none other than his brother, Camael. He is not the true king."

Sherkanim's eyes narrowed and he walked past Elijah to Enoch and stared down at the little man. He extended his palms and waited, and Enoch placed the trumpet into the king's servant's hands.

"Thou knowest, King's Guard, that Camael crafted the horn of Malakim, and that an instrument crafted by a Seraph glows when in the presence of another instrument crafted by thy people. If we blow Gabriel's horn, it will show that he whom thou knowest as Nephanos is false, for once blown;

the flames of its maker will glow. The sigil in his flames will tell the truth of the thing. It is the only way," Elijah said.

Sherkanim handled the trumpet of judgment. "Dost thou realize that blowing this instrument would release the wrath of the Lord? Do you understand the destruction that but one of these seven trumpets can do? They are not things to be trifled with."

All eyes fell to the trumpet. Elijah went to his friend and gripped each arm. "Then help us show the deceit that hides amidst the leadership of the Seraphim. Help us bring to pass the word of the Lord. Acquire the horn of Gabriel and when Camael is before the people, let us blow it to show him for who he is."

Sherkanim lowered his head to the ground. "Elijah, you have been with my people for many a day now, and I hold you in high esteem. I have witnessed the Burning of Gabriel and Metatron. There is no wickedness that they deserve such a punishment. The king will not allow the people to submit them again to the burning so that the people might behold their crimes. He keeps this sight to himself. This is not seemly. But he is the king and his orders we obey unless countered by the God-king himself. You would have me place more faith in thee and thy words than the king whom I have served generation past generation?"

"But is he thy king?" Enoch said. "And if not, where is the true king to thy people?"

Sherkanim looked at Enoch in silence. He walked toward the door, opened it and spoke over his shoulder. "I will not speak to my king concerning this thing. I will take the horn and return it to its rightful place, but know that I will not forgive a second trespass on thy part."

"Thou knowest the truth, King's Guard," said Elijah. "Thou hast known it for some time. And if two humans now know it after but a few days amongst you, how much more doth the people know something is not as it seems. Help us, Sherkanim. We have not the means to acquire both the horns that they might reveal Camael's charade, and their execution is in but one day's time."

Sherkanim paused and turned to speak.

"I make you no guarantees." And he closed the door behind him.

* * *

Michael left Jerusalem and traveled to the Aerie of the Ophanim. Upon his arrival, all the subjects of Eladrin bowed in homage to the Chief Prince who wore a gear from Eladrin's own body as a crown above his head. The escorts to Eladrin hovered and ushered Michael to their lord's chambers. Gleaming stars hung over the throne and four small gyroscopic wheels twirled in front.

Michael bowed his head and spoke. "I have not made time to thank thee and your people for thy aid with the renegade Lucifer. I surmised the enemy would never expect to see thy people in battle. Thy appearance created confusion and granted the time we needed. In this, you have my thanks, great king. Nevertheless, I saw thou wast wounded in thy skirmish with the Angel of Death. Are you recovered, my friend?"

Eladrin twinkled as a glittering star, and the four faces of the King of the Ophanim spoke in unison. "We are healed from our encounter with the Archon of Vengeance."

"He struck us," the eagle face said.

"But one cannot destroy omniscience, any more than the Archon can himself be destroyed," the bear face said.

"We are healed from our encounter," Eladrin said.

Michael bowed. "Charon is indeed a formidable foe, and who but the governor of Time and Omniscience itself could have hoped to forestall and occupy him whilst we completed our tasks? You have the thanks of my kin and I, and if God allows, we are at thy disposal."

Eladrin smiled and returned Michael's bow, as all four of his faces swiveled in gyroscopic rotation. "You honor us, High Prince. But pleasantries alone did not bring thee to our door. "

"Pleasantries was it not," the eagle face said.

"You seek something," the bear face said.

"What do you seek?" the ox face said.

They spoke as one. "Dost you bid us come on thy behalf once more?"

Michael sighed, then opened his mouth to begin his intercession.

"It is with a heavy heart that I report the Withering hath come and even now assails my people. A plague of such destruction that it leaves its victims without sanity. To wit, I know the Seraphim have balms to soothe this disease, but alas, the Schism hast kept our people at bay. I seek reconciliation on my people's behalf in hopes of healing, and to this end, I have sent emissaries to the Seraph seeking restoration. And lo, my ambassadors have passed beyond the veil of Grigoric sight and I am no longer able to tell of their welfare. For this cause, I adjure thee to take me to Nephanos in the land of Aesir that I might determine the plight of my people there, and mayhap if El wills, seek reconciliation that there be no more division. For to set foot in the land of Aesir will incite war, but pray tell, if the King of the Ophanim be my witness and intercedes on my behalf, I might gain an audience and forego possible war. Therefore, I plead with thee on behalf of my race, if thou might do this thing, great Eladrin. Wilt though ferry me to Aesir on the hope that our three races might once again be one?"

Eladrin rose from his thrones. His gears creaked and hummed as a machine that revved to life. The four faces became stern and Michael backed away, unsure if he had offended the king.

"We are honored to know the Chief Prince seeks reconciliation for all people. We will escort thee to the realm of Aseir, but know that your presence may not be welcomed for it was thou who stood with Lucifer's deception. Nephanos may not forgive what was done in deceit to his people, but if thou seek to confess thy transgressions to thy brother that he might forgive, and come to the altar and lay down thy gift to appease, then yea, Michael of the Kortai, I will ferry thee to Aseir."

Michael bowed in thanks. "All that I am, yea even to the laying down of my life, will I give in service to the king to save my people, if he will but answer my petition. Thank you for agreeing to my request. When do we leave for Aesir?"

Eladrin turned a gear within his great circular body and when he did so, a great light flashed, and Michael and Eladrin were no longer in the throne room, but atop a cliff that overlooked cities made of fire. The vault of heaven reverberated with visible echoes, while Seraph, Malakim griffins, and horses with flaming chariots roared across the skies.

"The thing is done. Behold, the land of Aseir."

Michael looked over the fiery plains and beheld that a battalion of Seraphim menacingly flew in attack formation towards their position. Michael put his hand on the hilt of his sword, swallowed hard and looked hopefully at Eladrin. "Pray for me, my friend, and pray that my efforts bear fruit. For if I fail, if the King will not hear my cause, I am afraid that my aims will only have hastened Heaven to find herself once more at civil war."

Eladrin hovered scanning the Seraphim soldiers ascending towards them, and his four faces each nodded nervously.

Chapter Twelve: The Second Death

Deep in the bowels of the Earth, Yeshua opened His eyes, and when He did He smiled, for he beheld the faces of those He so longed to see. David and Moses, and a host of others surrounded Him as He laid with His back on the ground.

"Master?" David said, kneeling over Him. Yeshua's eyelids fluttered open and beheld the throng.

"It is good to see you, my son," Yeshua said. "I've waited many days for this moment. It is very good to see you indeed."

Yeshua then stood to His feet and all that surrounded Him immediately bowed. Multitudes upon multitudes of the righteous dead...men, women and children from every race and tongue fell on bended knee. As far as the eye could see, row after row of onlookers lowered themselves in a human wave for all knew the Son of God had finally come.

The Lord touched the heads of those immediately in His presence and spoke. "Rise, my children."

Moses looked upon his lord and reached out to gently touch the Master's nail pierced hand.

"My King," Moses said through quivering lips, "what have they done?"

Yeshua replied softly. "Only that which hast been ordained. Fear not, for all is well."

"But Lord how is it that thou art here?" Abraham said.

"Will thou at this time restore the Kingdom, Lord?" David said.

Yeshua lifted His hands in abeyance, seeing they were full of questions and spoke to the spirits of His children in Paradise. "Hear my words, and let all take heed. For all of you have desired a better country and hath waited by faith for me to come. Know that ye shall see the fruit of thy desire, for soon we shall depart this place and you shalt take thy number in my kingdom. The Father hath prepared for thee a city and is not ashamed to have you call Him God, for by faith hath ye quenched the mouths of lions, been warned of things not seen, and have condemned the world, warning them of my coming. You have by faith sojourned in the land of promise, as in a strange country. Thou hast looked for a city which hath foundations, whose builder and maker is God, for you have seen this promise afar off, and shall see it to thy face."

The throng cheered, and Daniel, the former prime minister to the Babylonian king Nebuchadnezzar, bowed and spoke to his Lord. "But my King, thou art here. Will we not at this time lodge in our Father's house?"

Yeshua smiled. "Soon, my son, for there is yet an enemy to be undone." Yeshua looked about.

The Lord then spoke aloud. "Dismas, where art thou? Come here and let me see thee."

From somewhere in the massive sea of humanity, various ones moved as one man made his way through the throng. And as he approached the Son of God, others spoke aloud wondering who the man was that Yeshua inquired by name to see to his welfare. The Jewish male of nondescript station meekly walked and stood before the King of Kings, looking upon his Lord. He immediately cried and kissed the Lord's feet, and would not be consoled. The Lord then knelt down and lifted him to his feet.

"Did I not tell thee that on this day thou shalt be with me in Paradise?"

Dismas, the thief who hung by the side of Yeshua on the cross, then replied, "The thing is as thou hast said, my Lord, but what of the other fellow?"

The taunting voice of Satan echoed from Hades over the gulf for Yeshua, and the sound carried the melodious tune of temptation.

"Surely, the Son of God hath no fear of me, for who am I but a dog to our Lord? But these, the spirits of righteous men...are not Elohim, not the Trinity.

"Will the Son of God give His life for sinful men and not these who are the righteous dead? Come to me, Yeshua. Come and I will mayhap spare these vagabonds whom thou hast let settle in Paradise, but if thou forbear know this, if thou do not surrender, the bridge will soon be complete. Who then will stop my march across the gulf to reap thy beloved image and use their spirits to fire my kiln?"

The Son of God's brow hardened and His eyes grew stern. "Come Dismas...and behold the judgment of the Father on those who would deny the Son."

Yeshua then made his way through the multitudes and all parted for their King, each lightly touching Him as he passed, blowing kisses, and bowing before the God of all things.

And after a great distance, Dismas followed Yeshua to the edge of a great gulf. They looked across the way, and what they beheld was horror, for fastened into the cavern walls were angels with shredded wings, appealing for mercy. Some were strung by their necks and splayed out, eaten alive by maggots that peeled the flesh from their bones. And men...scores and scores of men...men of every rank and station...men from every tongue and hue, and men from all birth enfolded within the walls, cocooned and screaming, Moaning as their teeth were set on edge as flames and maggots ate their extremities, but for some their pains were expounded upon as Lucifer had assigned specific daemons to their souls. And his daemons were adept in their skills, flaying men, and even to the opening the bellies of women who had surrendered their young to human sacrifice. Dismas watched as their bellies healed within the flames, and the daemons slashed them open again, repeating the process in gruesome perpetuity.

And men whose lust for all things carnal had their organs of sex pulled from their bodies, but within the Realm of the Dead, the spirit did not die. Alas, they felt the pains of flesh amplified, and those whose entrails were torn from their bowels were then forced to eat their own organs. Vomit and putrid masses of blood and phlegm reigned across the chasm. Screams, moans, and wails carried themselves as floating notes of sheet music across the gulf, into the ears of the righteous dead who stood on the other side. Yeshua took in the sight and frowned, for He knew that in this place, Adam was never meant to dwell. He then found what he had searched for and pointed across the way that Dismas might see.

Dismas followed the finger of the Lord, and lo, raised upon tendrils of burning phlegm, was the man Gestas, who also had been crucified with the Lord. Dismas was moved in such abhorrence that he sought to avert his eyes, but the images of what he saw could not be erased from his mind for Lucifer took special delight in Gestas and would gleefully see the fruit of Gestas's sin and arrogance fully bloom in his domain. For the Prince of Evil held Gestas suspended over the floor. Daemons with knives of angelic origin slashed, jabbed and stabbed him as with a bayonet; and they removed pieces of his flesh and ate it before his eyes, but the flesh grew back so the torture had no end.

Yeshua turned His head from the sight. He scanned to find the one man in all of creation who had joined himself with the cause of Lucifer...he who had allowed Lucifer to possess him...he whom the Lord had supped with and given love...the only man to have washed His feet and yet betray Him for thirty pieces of silver. Alas, the eyes of the Lord found he whom His soul had loved...Judas.

Lucifer stood before the former disciple and gently caressed Judas' face for the Lord to see. The Devil smiled, as he saw the Lord from across the gulf and nodded to his former master, then lifted the terrified Judas by the scruff of his neck. Hell's tendril scrolled down from the ceiling and snaked around the traitor's neck. Judas squirmed, kicking against the air, purple face gasping for air as his hands pulled in vain against the arm that suspended him for all in the Realm of the Dead to see. And Judas was then beset by tendrils that pulled his arms, legs, and neck, and stretched him so that his bowels emptied and he split limb from limb, and the torso fell in heaping bloody slabs before Lucifer.

Lucifer's eyes narrowed, and a grin found his face. "Again!" he said. The Lord of Darkness then touched the key that made Hell his slave, and when he did so, the remains of Judas crawled toward one another, and the maggots of Hell scurried across the flame and phlegm-filled floor to carry the head of the traitor. The undead carrion reattached his limbs, and Judas inhaled and breathed again, but only for a moment as Hell lowered a sole tendril to wrap around his neck, and lifted him once more. More vines entwined his arms and legs, and once more stretched him wide until his eyes bulged and burst into white bleeding pustules of blood. His body ruptured into pieces and fell afresh in blood-soaked chunks to the floor.

"Again," Lucifer shouted while he glared at the Lord.

Yeshua turned away and spoke to those who had watched the horrors with Him. "They who abide within Hades have their reward. Now, come, we have little time."

Lucifer watched the righteous dead depart from the edge of their side of the gulf and grinned in salivating anticipation to handle the Son of God. Waiting for his chance to drape His broken spirit within the realm of fire and brimstone, and mount the Son of God's body as a throw rug beneath his newly formed throne.

And Judas...Judas watched in tearful remorse as Yeshua left him to the mercies of his true rabbi. His pitiful screams echoed as a hymn into the ears of the Devil, just before his body burst anew into bloody chunks.

* * *

King Camael sat down on his judgment seat. Raised high upon a platform of multicolored flame, it overlooked the populace who assembled on command of their king. Before him lay a transparent tube which Gabriel and Metatron would enter for the Burning.

Eyes gawked and many gasped as all knew the duo had left Aseir in good will, yet now stood near the cylinder that would incinerate them to ash.

Questions bubbled throughout the crowd, whispered inquiry of why the angels were being put to death. Sherkanim escorted Metatron and Gabriel to the entrance and stood with a spear in one hand and the Horn of Malakim strapped to his waist.

Enoch and Elijah sat as Camael's guests, to the left of the king. With downcast faces, the humans looked desperately at Sherkanim, seeking a sign that what they were about to witness would somehow be stopped. Sherkanim met their eyes briefly, then darted his gaze away.

The king then stood and raised his hands to silence the raucous crowd.

"Citizens of Ashe' and people of Aseir, behold, a new thing doth dwell among us. For several days ago there came to us, humans. Creations of El only made known to us by our fellowship with the Ophanim. Nevertheless, upon command of El did I hearken and send our great chariots to ferry the one named Elijah to our shores."

Camael waved his open hand toward Elijah, smiling at the grizzled prophet of God.

"Not long after, we received a visitation from another human and two Elohim from beyond the mountain. And not just any angels, mind thee, but two of the acclaimed Lumazi. Angels who stand before the Godking Himself! And these came to petition us for assistance in a cause that plagues their people...a cause which their leadership hast brought upon their own head...a cause for which we could not provide balm to ease. And though they broke the sacred agreement between our peoples, my hand did show restraint, for I did not smite them where they stood. Nay. Instead, they were lodged a fortnight and allow to petition thy king? Yea, and who were even then released with food to journey home in peace.

"But, once again the Elohim have trafficked in deceit. Once again our people are victim to the schemes of those who would practice duplicity and guile, for stolen from our own chambers by these selfsame souls was one of the acclaimed horns of judgment. An instrument known that upon its blowing, would signal the end of all things and invoke the Lord's wrath. And these two who stand before you, are each judged by your king for its theft. Who would be so brash as to steal such a weapon of destruction? Therefore I am burdened to ask what punishment should be levied against those who would incite terror against the realm? What punishment should be given to ones so vile that they would invoke our people to war? I say that there can be but one penalty for such crimes...only one response to such a transgression. Death!"

Horrified gasps spread throughout the crowd as many placed their hands over their mouths in shock and dismay. As the murmur grew, fiery faces contorted into gestures of confusion, anger, sadness, and rage.

"How dare they!" roared some.

"But did we not witness them as pure?" others said, confused.

Camael smiled and again waved his hands in an attempt to bring calm.

"Aye, we have indeed been deceived. Twice now our brethren have manipulated us to acquire their own ends. Perhaps we have been too long behind the mountain! Perhaps we have been too long-suffering of those who had earlier stolen from us. For how long shall we permit angels to take advantage of our restraint? How long must we endure the disrespect to our culture that again we find ourselves victim to deceitful schemes? Schemes that have resulted in Heaven's three peoples divided. Nay! As thy king, I cannot stand idle and allow such an offense to go without an answer." The king then shouted to his guard. "Sherkanim!"

The king's chief immediately snapped to attention.

"My king?"

"Prepare them for the Burning," commanded Camael.

Sherkanim jabbed the hilt of his spear into Metatron's back to shove him forward into the chamber of burning. Another guard opened the tubular furnace doors where the fires raged within.

"Wait!" Enoch cried, jumping to his feet. Fury emblazoned his face until the veins pulsed on his neck. "Will not the king of so great a people do right? Wilt thou be so quick to condemn, that the accused not have room to retort? Or is there no justice this side of the mountain of Heaven?"

Camael frowned. "Do you think my sentence extreme, human? That our matter is without cause? Very well. Never let it be said the king of the Seraph is unjust. I will permit the condemned to speak." Camael nodded his head and motioned for Sherkanim to allow Gabriel to come forward.

Sherkanim pulled Gabriel by the iron cuffs and whispered into his ear.

"Give the people cause for abeyance, for let it be known that none are thirsty for war."

Gabriel nodded in acknowledgment and smiled for the small act of kindness. Metatron watched his brother ascend the furnace platform steps that he might plead on their behalf. The crowd stilled as he surveyed them. Every eye cast toward the platform whilst others peered through windows from the flaming buildings that comprised the city, and the whole city quieted to hear his words.

"Hear me, great people of Aseir. Hear one who stands as a mouthpiece for God, Himself, for it is I, who when summoned, gives annunciation upon El's command. Moreover, it is a task my people and I have always taken seriously. To speak only that which El hast commanded us to speak. To do only that which we see our Father do. We, are they, who go to and fro throughout the Earth and gives the word of God to prophets and kings. We are they who traverse the heavens to assure the word of the Lord never touches the ground, and now I stand before thee – a messenger of God accused of crimes – guiltless of transgressions that my brother and I did not commit. We are all one family in Heaven. The Ophanim, the Elohim, and yea, the Seraphim, albeit one family torn asunder by an act long ago.

"Thou art the living flames that wander this side of the mount...the flame that our God hath given flesh. I know that what I see before me now is merely the silhouette of thy true form. A humanoid form given to the eyes of those who abide in your presence. For indeed thou art living fire and as formless as the clouds. And I know that to commence with the Burning, thou must assume the fires here within the furnace. It is you who must enter the holes cut therein, and with thy own flesh, together form the fires that would consume me and my kinsman alive.

Know that we do not desire to die, but we do not fear death. This thing that the king doth in judgment for alleged misdeeds is not a trifling matter. Before one takes life that originates from El, one must be sure that El sanctions such an act, for precious in the sight of the Lord is the death of His servants, and know that the Lord will not hold him guiltless who does them harm. For though, thy king decrees our death – thou art the fire that would kill us. It will be you who puts us to the fire. You who causes our dissolution– not he. But have ye not already tasted the fires that burn within us and found us true? Have ye not seen the remnants of the Kiln that animates our stones and the flames that is our lot? When we submitted earlier to your judgment, did we not come forth as pure gold? And having tasted of the fire that ignites our stones, have we in anything moved in such a manner as to bring disrepute to the One True King? Therefore, what manner of men must we be, that in such a span of time to have turned so quickly from the path we have held since creation? To abase ourselves so, that we would do both ye and ourselves this dishonor? Nay, brethren, we are guiltless of this thing.

"We confess that the horn was indeed in our stuff. However, we did not take it, nor did we seek the instrument. Neither did we seek to hide it amongst our stuff. For hath not God said that on the day a horn of judgment returns to His sight, He would with seven trumpets unleash the end upon creation and all those who seek to destroy her? Come now and let us reason together, for who but the insane would dare to remove an instrument that could tear asunder worlds? And lo, do we strike thee as men without reason?

"Therefore, if thy king hath nothing to fear, present us once more to thy sight. Search us and see that no wickedness lies within us, for what can be gained but the truth, and who hath anything to fear but us to the loss of life? I say again, we are innocent of the crimes laid against us, nor do I plead for mercy when my brother and I are without fault. But know this. If need be our lives must be taken to avert war, then do what must be done, for Heaven must not be allowed to be grip further division."

Gabriel then ceased from his argument, bowed, and took his place next to Metatron. The two stood next to one another confident, and unafraid for what might befall them.

Many in the crowd nodded their heads, looking at one another, affirming the Burning would be the best way to show their deeds.

"Let the angels' works be revealed by fire!" one shouted.

"Try their works and see what sort it is!" said another.

A slow clamoring overtook the crowd, a cacophony of voices that raised fists and arms to their king. "Try them! Try them! Try them!"

Camael frowned, his brow wrinkling in disapproval. He lifted his hands to shush the crowd.

"Who is Nephanos?" he said. "Am I not your king?" he roared.

Silence overtook the crowd as the atmosphere tensed, and many a citizen lowered his head nervously as a child rebuked by a parent.

"Hath not I, your king, decreed these two as the culprits for which punishment is due? Doth my own servants question the rule of he who is ordained by God to be seated before thee? Hath the judgment of thy king now come into question?"

Elijah then stood and faced the king with fiery eyes. "Thy rule hath been found wanting by the True King," he said that all might hear.

Camael pounded his fist on the armrest of his chair, stood and shouted, "How dare you! You would do well to mind your tongue, human. Or do you think that El's allowance for thy presence in Heaven removes thee from the shadow of my rule?"

And in that moment, Camael grew bright, and flame erupted from his person as solar flares from the sun. Fiery tentacles shot across the crowd and over both Elijah and Enoch, the blast nearly singeing both.

Enoch then also stood in anger. "We dare to speak for we are the candlesticks of the Lord. Or hast thou lost the presence of mind that thou wouldst threaten men whom God Himself hath given power to open and close Heaven? You speak of thy desire to avert war, yet thou dost channel flame across the very ambassadors of the Lord, and even thine own people. Do you think your kingship removes thee from judgment?"

Camael drew a deep breath for retort, flaming from head to toe, irate.

"Thou shal..."

A deafening boom pounded the sky and concussive reverberations rocked the people. All looked up, for the familiar flash of lightning and prismatic colors of a funnel cloud signaled the arrival of a ladder. All stepped aside to make room for the new arrival. A great bolt of light settled onto the platform and ash and dust raced to cover the flaming souls that eyed the spectacle. The kaleidoscopic beam lifted from the scaffolding, and the King of the Ophanim materialized...and from behind him stepped Michael, Chief Prince of all Elohim. Immediately a cadre of Seraphim warriors landed as well. Some took up positions in front of the king, while others floated above the people, spears in hands.

The faces of Eladrin slowed in their spinning. Michael's halo shown bright over his head. Gleaming white raiment fell over a muscular body, and Michael looked upon the people. So swiftly did he unsheathe his sword that the motion was like a blur, and the sword split into seven swords with fearsome eyes and snapping teeth. Each blade encircled him as moons traverse a planet in elliptical orbit while arcs of electricity draped his person. His eyes burned as coal as he approached the king.

Immediately guards closed ranks around the king and each unsheathed spears of fire. Sherkanim also unsheathed a sword and floated near to Camael, ready if needed.

Michael's eyes bore no fear as he marched toward the king, unmoved by the guards that stood between him and his celestial peer.

Camael waved his hand. "Stand down," he commanded.

The warriors slightly relaxed and sheathed their swords, continuing to eye Michael as he mounted the steps to face the King of the Seraphim. With each step, sparks crackled beneath him. With each ascent, his flowing cape billowed in the winds of Aseir revealing a fully armored body. The Seraphim warriors edged back as he approached.

The twirling Sword of Ophanim surrounded the Prince of Kortai and none dared enter his personal space Michael reached the apex where Camael sat quietly watching the display of regality that approached. A wave of awe swept the people as Michael stopped before the king, and the shining armor folded back into his skin. He glowed in white rays of light and his halo was as a brass ring of fire suspended over his head.

All seven blades stopped their gyroscopic rotation and hovered mid-air. Michael then fell to one knee before the king, and all seven swords converged into one, then slammed into the fiery iron platform, puncturing the dais where they stood blade-first into the ground. A billowing clap of thunder echoed from Michael's person and the rumbling shook the ground.

Michael closed his right hand into a fist and slammed his fist into his chest in a sign of acknowledgment to the king.

Eladrin spoke with all four of his faces as one. Their voices blended in choral majesty.

"We present to his majesty, Chief Prince, Head of the Lumazi Council – Michael of the Kortai. We have ferried him here at his request, and now stand as mediator between thy people and his."

Michael bowed his head and spoke. "Great King Nephanos, High King to the Seraphim, this lowly prince of all Elohim bids you and your people peace and honor." Michael lifted his sword above him as a sign of submission.

Camael looked at Eladrin, cocked his head to the side and grinned nodding. He stared at the Prince of Angels as though he had witnessed a joke. He clapped his hands slowly and loudly in feigned applause.

"Well done, Chief Prince. Well done, indeed."

Michael bit his lip and looked down at the ground, remembering the many lessons of protocol he had learned from his brother, Lucifer.

"You have committed such a grand display of power, Michael of the Kortai. Yea, Chief Prince, impressive is both thine entrance and the weapon with which you yield. I do not recognize its maker. Intriguing.

"Eladrin, by what article that binds us dost thou bring this person into my sight? In so doing, thou hast strained our friendship through this act. Tell me why I should even acknowledge this prince with a response?"

"He is deserving of honor," the bear face of Eladrin said

"He hath been chosen by El," the eagle face said.

"Wouldst thou so lightly dismiss one of the three leaders of Heaven?" the man's face said.

All then spoke as one and the voice rippled. "The time of reconciliation is nigh for Lucifer hath made himself an enemy of God, and if the image of God is brought to bear against us by Lucifer, we are all dead. I have honored this one with my own gear and know that I have aligned my people to the cause of God and His servants. My people and I are at the Prince of Elohim's disposal, even if it means war. The time for past squabbling must come to an end."

Camael was taken aback by Eladrin's words. "What? Thou would take the side of this one against us?" Camael said. "We who were the victims of schemes birthed by this one? Thou wouldst make war, against us?"

Camael looked at Michael who remained silent, knee still bowed and his arms yet raised, unmoved in the gifted gesture of his sword, still awaiting acknowledgment. Camael walked around Michael, inspecting him, eying him suspiciously as the crowd waited with bated breath. Not since the birth of The Schism were all three races of heaven together, and now two ambassadors from mankind were also assembled in treaty.

Camael rubbed his chin and finally broke the silence.

"It is with much interest, Chief Prince, that I would hear how Eladrin, King of the Ophanim, would hold such a one in high regard, for he implies that he would do battle against me if I were to invoke our rights. Thou hast come from across the great mountain and through the fiery plains of my land to speak to me." Camael then took his seat and leaned deep within his throne. "Speak, therefore, and say thy peace."

Michael lowered his arms and stood, sheathing his sword. He bowed his head in a further act of respect and spoke.

"Great King, it is with sore distress for my people and the cause of El that I stand before you now. For the Godking Himself commissioned Enoch to seek out another alleged to be in Heaven. A human, I see, who now stands next to thee. And who am I but a servant to our king? Nay, who are we all but servants to our Lord El? Therefore, I ordered two of the Lumazi council to accompany him, each purposed to assure his safe passage under the mount. Three in total were ultimately assigned to this task and now I see but two, for one is not. Thus, they came at cost of life to see Enoch safe to thy shores but know that we are not moved for we trust in the word of El. El is life. My princes were also charged also to see if they might bring balm from thy people to heal my own. And if not to heal, then perhaps to soothe the ravages of the plague that assails us through choices I have made.

And now I come to see to my people's welfare, and behold, my ambassadors are surrounded by thy people and chained! Yet for what crime I do not know – nor do I need to know for I trust Gabriel and Metatron with my life, knowing they would happily endure dissolution to ensure peace between our people. Therefore, I come on bended knee, oh great king, to appeal on behalf of all Elohim. If it is my people's blood that thou dost seek, then know that I offer my life in exchange for theirs for I have learned that greater love hath no man than this, that he would lay down his life for his friend. Therefore, I call the Seraphim friend, and Elohim friend, and Ophanim friend. If for honor's sake, or justice's sake a life must be given to reconcile the offense between our people..."

Michael then kneeled and opened his robes to reveal his kilnstone, "then let the life you take be mine."

"No!" cried Gabriel.

"Michael, what are you doing?" Metatron yelled.

Sherkanim tugged on their chains to silence them.

Camael eyed Michael, his face smug. Without moving his eyes from the Prince, he barked, "Sherkanim, Chief of the Guard!"

Sherkanim snapped to attention. "My lord?"

"The Chief Prince would be my guest. Bind the Kortai in fetters of iron."

Sherkanim frowned. "But my king..." Sherkanim spoke in protest.

Camael roared at his lieutenant. "Would you switch roles with the prince and have me see thee burned in his stead? Obey my word!"

Sherkanim replied wimpishly, "As you command, my lord."

Michael allowed himself to be shackled and Eladrin watched on as each of his four faces showed anger, dismay, outrage, and grief all at once. Camael saw his ruling peer's expression and spoke in warning.

"Do not interfere, great one. The power to command the Kiln's flame is ours by right of treaty and I invoke this right now. I will make an example of these Elohim...a lesson to be learned by all angelic kind. To never trouble the people of Aseir again with folly. If you interfere, know that once more schism will be created in Heaven, and you will be responsible. A breach between, not two, but all three races. Do this to thine own hurt if you must. But the right to exact judgment from broken covenant is mine by divine right. I will, therefore, release none – for all shall surely die!"

Eladrin held his peace. Michael looked at Enoch and nodded to Elijah as Sherkanim shackled him. The people gasped and some groaned to see such nobility put to death. Whispers grew into murmurs as Sherkanim lined up all three men to the entrance of the tube of burning.

Enoch was about to intervene when Elijah held him by his arm. "Not yet," Elijah said. "But soon."

Enoch nodded. "I am ready when you are." Elijah also nodded, and the two men watched as Metatron entered the tube of burning first, followed by Gabriel, then Michael. Sherkanim shut and sealed the door behind them. Gabriel smiled at Michael and reached out to hold his hand. "I will always love you, brother. Thank you for your leadership, for you did not forsake us but came to see of our welfare. Let it be said that we have fought the good fight."

Metatron then immediately chimed in. "Aye, we have indeed finished our course."

Michael followed suit. "We have kept the faith."

The three looked on in pride knowing that their lives would assure the life of their people, each lifted up their chins and waited for the fires that they knew would smelt their stones back to their base metals.

Sherkanim had never seen such honor in all his days. Even from his own king. He hesitated as he opened the seals that would allow the people of fire to enter and execute their king's punishment.

"Chief Guard!" roared Camael, "complete the task for which ye are assigned!"

Sherkanim turned the connected wheel outside the chamber and small air ducts opened to allow the Seraph entrance, but when all the air ducts opened, none of the populace moved. None took their true form to enter as living flame.

Camael looked at his people in frustration. "Let the burning commence!"

Still, no one moved.

He frowned and said, "Very well. If it is distasteful for thee to destroy them – I will bear this burden as thy king and release them from this life."

The king rose and both humans stood to stop him, but his body blazed so that neither could come near. The monarch swaggered toward the tube as his soldiers parted before him and Camael eyed the three angels with intent to do them evil.

Sherkanim noted his people's confusion. Their faces agonized as the king drew near. Had they not already judged them and found them pure?

The Chief Guard stared into the crazed eyes of his master...and then the eyes of the people, and in that moment he knew their leader was lost to reason. Lost to serve his people. And if he was not stopped, war with the Elohim would not be far behind.

The king's guard stared at the beautiful trumpet of Israel crafted by Camael himself and gifted to the head of House Malakim so long ago. Sherkanim felt its warm metal against his hands and closed his eyes in prayer.

Please, Lord God, do not let my action see our people to the door of war. What I do now, I do to honor thee and my people.

Sherkanim gripped the golden Horn of Malakim and raised it to his lips, and from the depths of his being blew into the instrument.

Camael immediately stopped his approach to the tube of burning. His face screamed in horror and rage. For when the music danced on the gentle breeze, the king's body blazed aglow in color, his body matched the color of the flames that erupted from the horns sigil. A sigil that exposed Camael as its maker.

Seeing all distracted, Elijah ducked out from the platform and raced to parts unknown. Enoch also left the dais, running hard after him.

The trumpet's sound dashed through the air like racehorses into the golden skies. The ears of all burst, torn asunder by the blast of so powerful a sound that they fell to the ground, stunned and dazed; and in the moments that occurred between the bat of an eye, the clouds rolled open and the sky boiled into a putrid green.

For ladders now burst across the lid of Heaven, and Eladrin knew that his people had made causeway, as was their purpose, and thunderous booms littered the peaceful skies while lightning strokes raced across the firmament to embrace each other for upon winged gryphons rode legions of mighty Malakim. Thousands with unsheathed swords and spears descending upon them all.

Gabriel looked up in both relief and fear, for with the arrival of his people could come war. For never since the Schism had so many Elohim entered Aseir, and now in a matter of minutes, legions now filled the skies and threatened to do battle.

Michael seeing his people assemble cried out. "No!" His halo burst in gleaming shimmers of bronze across the emporium as he transformed into a ladder. The restraints he willingly wore fell to the ground as he lifted himself to meet the army of descending soldiers, hoping against hope that he might avert war.

Flying upward the sky opened up before him, as thousands of his people portaled through the skies, descending upon the populace upon gryphon-back. Michael positioned himself before all and he hovered in their path, raising both arms.

"Hold, warriors of House Malakim, for thou hast not been called by one of your house. Hold in abeyance and do these no harm."

Thousands of Malakim griffins filled the skies, as Eladrin's people held the portals open. Legions of griffins and Malakim warriors poured through, each wondering about the welfare of the Lord of their house, each ready to do battle, and each assessing the situation as they came through. And Michael, using the power of his halo, laddered as the Ophanim across the skies and kept the warriors from accosting the people below. Like living lightning, the great Prince crackled across the sky moving hither and thither to keep his people at bay.

Seraphim warriors mustered their forces in response and rose like great flaming birds of prey into the skies. The lower atmosphere sizzled as their heat from their numbers began to raise the temperature throughout the land. And thus, two great forces were stalemated as one lone angel moved with the gift of omniscience moved throughout the angelic ranks to keep all in a state of calm. And it was in those moments as the kindling of war waited to be sparked that the gruff voice of a human boomed across the throng.

"Enough!" Elijah cried.

The atmosphere, dense with thousands of warriors almost stacked on top of one another, changed immediately when the grizzled prophet pointed to Enoch who held within his hands a glowing Trumpet of Judgment.

* * *

Camael stood dumbfounded, for he glowed from Sherkanim having blown the horn of Malakim. Camael and the horn, as well as the trumpet held by Enoch, all glowed as one...each scintillating off the vibrations emanating from the other...each aflame and matching the emblazoned sigil of Camael. The gathered crowd pointed to the colors that sparkled from the palace, and all heard the sounds of instruments that blasted from its midst.

"Behold, the trumpet of judgment!" Enoch said. "See how the horn flames! Witness the Horn of Malakim. See the fires that surround it! And look about you and behold with thine own eyes – the answer for all. Who amongst your people hath made these?"

Confusion washed through the people like a wave crashing over shores, but the flames were indisputably the color of Camael's sigil. Not Nephanos.

"But only Camael hast made these instruments," one said.

"Then...is Nephanos, Camael?" another said.

"Nay. Nephanos is not Camael. That is not possible."

"We have been deceived."

"Deceiver! Deceiver!" surfaced throughout.

Murmurs grew louder.

"But where is King Nephanos?"

"Where is our King?"

"Did he kill our King?"

And Camael was exposed, for all could see that he was the crafter of the horn of judgment.

Camael surveyed the rowdy group and paraded in front of them with disdain, and head held high. He retraced his steps to Elijah and spoke loudly above the crowd.

"And what wilt thou do with the vessel made to unleash El's wrath? Wilt thou blow into it thereof and release the fury of God on Heaven itself?"

Elijah stood in front of Enoch who held tightly to the golden trumpet and replied. "Nay, collaborator of Satan. But verily saith the Lord, 'Thou hast been weighed in the balances and found wanting.'"

"ARRGGHH!!!" Camael screamed in vehement rage, and immediately lost his humanoid form and all beheld the true form of Camael the Seraphim, for he became as living fire, and as a cloud ablaze. Camael scorched the platform. Then moved to destroy Enoch and Elijah. All that he touched was consumed in a conflagration of fire, as the would-be king turned on the humans to consume the men alive.

Michael looked on, helpless, as Camael's fires roared hungrily to devour his friends. Shoots of flames advanced on Enoch and Elijah and Michael knew that from his position he could not intervene in time.

Screaming, Gabriel, and Metatron watched from the incineration chamber, beating against their glass confines for Sherkanim to release them, but the guard's thoughts were elsewhere as he erupted in flames and raced to stop the king's madness.

Enoch and Elijah stood their ground unmoved by Camael's fog of fire that jetted towards them. Enoch dropped the Trumpet of Judgment to the ground and quickly tossed his cloak toward the oncoming cloud of fire that was Camael. Elijah prayed as the shawl flew through the air and transformed before the eyes of all, bursting into a floating wall of rushing water. The rolling wave of living water moved as a thing alive and crashed into the oncoming Camael. Bursts of heated steam blasted the platform, knocking both Enoch and Elijah to the ground.

Throngs above and below stared as Camael, as living fire, did battle against streams of living water. The two opposing elements twisted and turned around each other, coiling as entwined vines that wrestled for supremacy. Camael bloomed in searing heat...his body extending like a flare to snare the two humans that had fallen to the ground. But the living water prevailed against him, walling off Enoch and Elijah, and the more Camael steamed the water into vapor, the more water materialized from nothing. Camael reformed into his humanoid form, Camael bent over and wheezed from exertion.

Sherkanim retrieved the Trumpet of Judgment that had fallen to the ground and assisted Enoch and Elijah.

Elijah stood and was wroth and spoke to the king so that Aseir might hear.

"Did I not tell thee that Yeshua, the Lord God, hath commanded that I go with Enoch? And who art thou to frustrate the grace of God? Ye, who troubleth Heaven and refuseth to forgive? For thus saith the Lord, 'Did not I have compassion on thee and forgave thee, and let thee steward as king for thy brother's sake? For as I liveth,' saith the Lord, 'because thou hast done this thing, I will not release thee from the bitterness of unforgiveness that assails thee, and now you shall be delivered into torment."

Camael coughed as he panted to regain his strength. The waters of Enoch's cloak still stood as a standard against him. And when Elijah had spoken, Camael scoffed. "Thou...wouldst judge ME? Who art thou, to dare pass judgment over me!"

But Elijah stood silent and merely pointed behind him in the distance. A dark, cauliflower-like cloud appeared in the sky, and it grew and was at first akin to the size of a man's hand. Then a flash of lightning streaked across the sky and thunder rumbled overhead.

The people then turned their head and saw the sky slowly darken. Enoch watched also for he too saw clouds forming into larger and darker columns into the sky and he said to Elijah, "But what of the people?"

Elijah then eyed the crowd and spoke to them all. "Thy pride would have thee mimic us in appearance. For many days, thou hast thought thyself above others as to not show thy true form. But know this--huddle as one people, in the form given thee by birth, and be seen in the nakedness of who thou art. Or be stiff-necked, and see the waters that come erase thee from this side of Heaven. For on this day, through either thine obedience or disobedience to my word, The Schism between heaven's people will end."

Elijah then turned to Sherkanim and said, "Hurry, take us to the Heavenly City that the rain stop thee not."

Sherkanim recalled the Seraphim warriors and commanded them to cluster with their people to endure the waters that were to come. Guards released Gabriel and Metatron, and the two flew to Enoch's and Elijah's side.

Thunder roared over the skies, and a streaming blanket of water appeared in the distance racing across the land. Sherkanim called for his chariot, and the Aithon flew to him in fire. Gabriel, Metatron, and the two humans hustled aboard.

"Here," Sherkanim said, handing the horn of Malakim to Gabriel. "I believe this belongs to you."

Gabriel smiled. "Thank you, my friend."

"To the Temple, Eladrin...quickly!" Michael cried out to Eladrin,

Eladrin glowed and shot into the air. Michael followed. Sherkanim snapped the cords to the Aithon and they too bucked and flew, trailing fire behind them. Eladrin rotated in creaking gyration and opened a portal above them all. Gabriel blew his horn and the whole of house Malakim followed their prince through it.

Legions of the House Malakim followed as the rain descended on all. Lightning blanketed the sky in staggering sheets and sharp crackles that zigzagged their way to Earth, but the door to the portal stood calm, serene and inviting. The lit skies of the Heavenly city beckoned and the dark, ashen skies of Aseir lay in thick cumulus clouds that pelted the land with torrential rains.

As they disappeared from view, the living clouds of Heaven assembled themselves together. Flocks of flaming birds and Aithons fled before the storm and all the citizens cast a wary eye as the clouds blanketed the land in darkness. Voices moaned from the living clouds of Heaven, and each spoke aloud to one another and their words were heard on this wise:

Woe! Woe! Woe!
Judgment, O son of bitterness
For mercy hath now escaped thee!
Thy bill El now recoups
O'non-forgiver of other's debts.
Thine own payments hath now come due!
Alas, recompense befalls thee
Waters to wash away
Acrimony and hurt of past misdeeds
'Remove this king,' He says

As the rain slammed to the ground and lightning lit the Heavens, and the voices of the living clouds crashed across the skies, the fires of Aseir went out, as did all the flaming spires. Panic gripped the people as all were made of living fire, and rain sizzled upon them like acid. The warrior Seraphim retreated to the ground to assemble with their people that they might remain alight in the midst of the pouring rain.

And a great mist rose throughout the land, from the boundaries of the city's burbs to the flaming plains where Aithon roamed. The mist reached up and the skies reached down until none could tell the difference between the living clouds and the rolling fog that now crept atop the land.

And when the clouds had finished speaking, the portal that took the legions and Enoch and Elijah away closed behind them, and when it did, the twelve angels of God's judgment, the Shanun-tea'll, appeared in the sky. Mavet, chief of their number, hovered on wings of black and settled to the ground. He walked forward to apprehend Camael, who like all his people, huddled together to keep themselves alight against the pouring rain.

But Camael would not be taken, and he lifted his hand to fend for his freedom. Camael issued sound waves that projected in a focused burst from his hand...a sound that sliced through flesh and ruptured eardrums, but Mavet absorbed it into his person, never slowing in his step, continuing his undeterred march forward toward the would-be king.

Camael then shot bursts of flame from his hands, and Mavet stood enkindled, awash in a conflagration of fire and brimstone, yet covered from the falling rains, but again the Angel of Judgment passed through the rain, fire, and steam, and trod steadily forward, unflinching in the king's attempts to halt him.

When Camael perceived that inescapable judgment was now upon him, he attempted to run, and all that stood near moved from his path. When he sought to turn to the left, a Shaun-tea'll barred his way, and when he tried to flee to his right, a Shanu-tea'll barred his way, and when he turned to his rearward, Mavet was there and overshadowed him and passed through him like a ghost. And when he did so, the spirit of the king visibly separated from his body, and it became as smoke and floated that all could see. His body instantly crumpled to the ground as a puppet whose strings had been cut...a celestial corpse no longer animated by the breath of life.

The dense fog that hovered above the ground extinguished all eddies of fires across Aseir until nothing but the fog saturated the land, and voices and movement of creatures could be heard within it. Voices that pleaded to be fed. And in that moment, all knew that God had allowed the Mists to enter the land. The shroud of fog crawled over the physical body of Camael and wrapped itself around him. The spirit of Camael screamed, and the two merged with the Mist. Echoes of his voice could be heard within the Mist pleading to God for mercy, but none was given. The king was given over to the tormentors, and the figure of Camael could be seen within the Mist struggling against hands that dragged him into the shroud until he could be seen no more in the gloom.

And a great wind then came from the south and blew against the fog, and when it had dissipated, nothing but ignitable fumes and a hissing sound remained. Fumes seeped from the ground. A thunderbolt then fell from the sky, and ignited the gas, and a great whooshing sound then blasted into the ears of all. An explosive burst of fire rushed and the fires of the Aesir burned once again, and the cities of fire could once more be seen again in the sky.

And all the people breathed in relief that they had survived the judgment. The people lifted themselves to worship El. Thanking God, and waiting for Sherkanim to return from the other side of the mountain with word from El.

* * *

The four Seraphim which stood before the temple of God bellowed in powerful blasts: HOLY, HOLY, HOLY! A never ceasing clarion call to all that approached the doorway of God's house.

The chief of the four, King Nephanos, thought upon days of yore. He often reminisced of his failure, wondering what would have happened if he had not led them to traffic in pride against Lucifer.

Having fallen for the schemes of the angel, the king kept to the terms of their bargain, wondering in his self-imposed exile from Aseir how his brother Camael fared as royal regent to his people. Nephanos waited for the day when he and all the peoples of Heaven would unite. Perhaps someday, his brother would use the space given him to serve their kind and repent from what he had done.

Would Camael accept the lessons of serving another in humility? He wondered to himself.

It would soon be his time to roar the prime attribute of God again. Nephanos girded up his loins in preparation to carry out the consequences of his wager, prepared to fulfill a promise given in foolishness to Lucifer. A promise that El had also honored: a promise to give Camael space to repentance.

Nephanos looked at his companions, each willingly swore to bear this burden of knowledge in silence. He beamed at the strong fiery sentinels who represented their people this side of Heaven. Proud to serve by their side. For these many years, none had spoken to the other. None had uttered a word save HOLY, HOLY, HOLY. A faithful announcement the quartet had kept for thousands of earth years.

Never did any complain or shirk from their duty. Nephanos wondered if he should have left his people in Camael's charge. Wondered of his decision to leave Aseir and stand as ambassador in the city of God. Wondered of his duty to utter naught but holiness to El until God called all three races together as one people.

Yet if the time never came to reunite Heaven as one, Nephanos and his men would serve as examples of steadfastness to all of Heaven. Thus from almost the third day of creation, Nephanos had bellowed but one word, the word HOLY.

Mate-eral had stood next to him for several millennia, and had now blasted the fiery roar of HOLY through the air, the echoes of which traveled across the sky.

Nephanos's turn was upon him. The King of the Seraphim stirred the inferno that roared within him and opened his mouth to release the vocalization, of El's eminence. Ready to do again what he had already done over a million times.

"HOLY!" the great King of Fire thundered. The air around him detonated in explosive heat. His annunciation completed the trinity of praise that sounded from the steps of God's house.

And again the cycle began once more.

Thus, Nephanos and three members of his kind stood as sentries to the temple of God. Each one, carillons, ready to chime the dawn of a new hour, eternally repeating their refrain without fail.

Through angelic civil wars Nephanos had kept this covenant, and when rebel Elohim came to assault the temple of God, he reminded his kin of El's holiness. When the Godstones fell from the skies, and when Lucifer himself breached the Seraphim lines, Nephanos watched the travesty in helplessness and cried in vain to remind the Usurper and all who still had ears to hear, that above all things...El was HOLY.

From the first day of his oath, never did he depart from his honorable vow, nor did his companions of flame surrender to be moved...but today was a new day.

Nephanos looked above as a vast ladder pulled back the golden hued skies of Heaven. Voltage arched overhead, and the familiar colors and whooshing sound of the prismatic funnel plunged downward from the skies and touched on the ground before him. Reds, blues, and greens skipped before him playfully before they waved goodbye and retreated back into the skies from whence they came, and lo, Eladrin floated before him with his four faces in gyration.

Above and behind the King of Ophanim, a chariot of fire plummeted from the sky. Within the descending carriage were two humans alongside Gabriel and Metatron. Michael the Chief Prince flew by its side and his halo was aglow as he swooped down. And commanding the steads of Aithon that pulled the flaming chariot was a Seraphim. Yet the spectacle to Nephanos's eyes did not cease, for from the portal, Malakim warriors on gryphon-back fell from the skies as hailstones, and the airspace above Jerusalem quickly filled as their numbers caused the sky darkened.

The King of the Seraphim pondered this new thing, for since his post to stand at the temple doors, he had witnessed the Elohim assemble on many occasions. From moments of worship to God, to annunciations by the Lord. But never on this wise had he beheld the descending mixed army that followed the Aithon flaming chariot that now headed toward him.

The temple doors suddenly opened and light escaped to illuminate all things, flooding the city with blinding luminance. El stepped through the doors standing on the back of Ophanim, as the gyrating wheels within wheels covered the soles of His feet, and hovered above the ground. His face looked upwards and His eyes watched the open sky while three of His created races poured through the Orphanic portal.

Nephanos and his men immediately snapped to attention, for the King of Creation stood in their presence, and the four burning ones bellowed out in militaristic cadence HOLY, HOLY, HOLY!

Pounding reverberations traveled in concentric circles in all directions and a mighty echo hitch-hiked atop the backside of light that released from El's presence.

The Aithon landed before the king and neighed as Sherkanim pulled on the reins of the steeds. Enoch, Elijah, Metatron, and Gabriel disembarked, while Michael flashed as a ladder to their side. He took his place aside Eladrin, whose four faces were suspended in the air, their gyration stopped and their faces pointed down to the ground. Legions of Malakim on gryphon-back hovered in the air, as locust swarms awaiting command.

And in the midst of such a sight the powerful cadence of "HOLY, HOLY, HOLY!" bellowed from the Seraphim.

Nephanos, while awed at the site, was careful to maintain his duty, not ceasing his repetition in the midst of his own wonderment.

Michael bowed before God, and he, like all his kind, shuttered his ears to protect them from the booming roar of the Seraphim. However, Enoch and Elijah advanced forward in faith toward the humanoid quartet of fire that spoke. Both men's chest cavities pulsated from the sound of the celestial voices. Closer they came.

Nephanos and those assembled watched on bended knee as two humans ascended the great stairs. El stood silently as His presence ejected light, radiation, and other phantasms impossible to describe.

His form was humanoid, yet within the interior of His presence were stars and galaxies that moved within His person.

"HOLY, HOLY, HOLY!" the refrain came once more.

Visible waves of disturbed air traveled past Enoch and Elijah, pounding them due to their proximity. The two stood before Nephanos as he glared at them whilst he roared El's holiness. The men's hair flailed behind them from the exhaust of his roaring breath.

Nevertheless, the two men stood their ground, standing between all of Heaven's represented children. Michael, Chief Prince of the Elohim behind them, and Eladrin, the chief of his people hovering at their side, while four Seraphim, each burning in fire and ash, bellowed out El's divine nature.

And as if on cue with the annunciation of the Seraph's shout, Enoch and Elijah stomped their feet in an aggressive militaristic pace and shouted back to the Seraphim. "HOLY, HOLY, HOLY!"

Visible waves traveled from them as their voices matched the volume and tenor of the mighty Seraphim. Nephanos, himself, was surprised by the power of the small humans' vocalizations. His own flame now wisped from the two men's shouts directed at him. And all Heaven took note of the two men, for it would be said later in the Grigoric Chronicles that great swords of fire came from the mouths of the two witnesses. Enoch and Elijah continued in their synchronized roar with the Seraphim, and the temple shook from their combined chants.

Nephanos raised his eyes in surprise for none had ever joined them in worship on this wise, and the King of the Burning Ones noted from a side glance that El smiled at the two humans.

And Michael, seeing Enoch and Elijah stand in front of the towering men of fire, raised himself from bended knee and stood to join them. He planted himself like steel and pulled down his inner eardrum's walls to feel the full volume of the Burning Ones' voices, and immediately was assaulted by the overwhelming booming that accosted his ears. Fighting the pain, he staggered for a moment and touched Enoch's shoulder for balance. Michael could feel the weight of the Seraphim's voice push him to the ground. Resisting the urge to cover his ears and denying his automatic reflexes to close his inner ear, Michael let the sound flood his being, inhaled, and belted out with all his might worship to the King of Angels known as El.

"HOLY, HOLY, HOLY!" he roared.

His pentameter now joined the chorus that was Enoch's, Elijah's and the Burning Ones.' Gabriel and Metatron watched as their leader stood unmoved by the powerful thundering that befell him, each unclear how Enoch and Elijah could even survive, yet survive they did. And without prompt, Gabriel and Metatron released their fear and joined Michael's side.

Eladrin also took note that the three celestial races of Heaven stood before El in majestic declaration of His holiness and his four faces joined in singing the triple mantra now roared by all.

"HOLY, HOLY, HOLY!" they all roared. The refrain so powerful that the golden glass street beneath them began to crack and buckle. Sherkanim, last of the entourage, watched as the three celestial kings of Heaven sung in militaristic chants and praise to the King of All and the King's Guard knew by revelation that before him lived the true Seraphim king of his people – Nephanos. He, too, then joined the group as HOLY, HOLY, HOLY echoed in busting penetrative waves of thunder through sky and rock.

And all of Heaven took note. For from the Malakim armies that filled the sky to the angels that quivered beneath the Withering, praise rang out in heaven. A praise that spoke but three words: "HOLY, HOLY, HOLY!" A praise that lifted the eyes and ears on every street. Praise that caused sick angels to rise to their feet to sing God's glory despite their affliction. Praise that made the windows of the Hall of Annals crack, for everywhere throughout the land and this side of the mountain of God, the Withering could be seen, and the visible waves of the chant of Heaven's children caused the cloud of sin to retreat, and it evaporated under the onslaught of the echo of holiness that traveled across every house of Heaven for the chant was strong and it radiated into the basement of Heaven itself.

And Janus beheld the realm of choices and looked into the mirrored doorway to the underworld of Limbus, and when he did so, the echoes of El's holiness caused the great seals of glass to crack, and from it seeped the Mists. But the sound of "HOLY, HOLY, HOLY!" marched onward in advancing waves that saturated all of Limbo.

The basement of Heaven rumbled and Cadmime beams stretched against the echo under Heaven's belly. The sound of "HOLY, HOLY, HOLY!" strode forth in repetitive echoes, creating oscillating waves that sheered at the bedrock of Heaven. Torsional forces rocketed the bridges and trampled ancient columns into dust as the chant marched as an undampened rhythmic force. A tunneling fury carved a lighted path through the mountain of God, blasted through rock and exited into the flaming land of Aseir.

Fires from the burning plains back-drafted through the newly created tunnels, jetted under the streets of gold and made them glow. Plumes of sweet smelling smoke wafted into the sky as the people of fire were no longer cut off from the temple of God. Their fires ignited the whole of Heaven with a fire that did not burn, and all watched the transformation that took place before them, awed by the power of God. Awed as the ever-present echo of "HOLY, HOLY, HOLY!" was now not just the clarion call of four Seraphim, but of all citizens in Heaven.

The Virtues then floated from the temple and lifted to meet the living clouds of heaven. Cumulus billows of music wondered at Heaven's new croon and rumbled to join the curious chorus of Heaven.

The Virtues spoke in the language of scent and rose as colored mists to communicate the words "HOLY, HOLY, HOLY!" through fragrance to their cousins, the living clouds, The clouds interpreted their essence and themselves burst into song uttering holiness to the Lord.

And God spoke to the whole that sung and his words were on this wise. "As I have torn the veil of division between mankind and God, so too now witness reconciliation between all people."

And when the Lord uttered those words, the electric screen that hovered above the living clouds illuminated, for all to see. It crackled, arcing voltage in all directions, flickered then fizzled away into nothing. A static charge filled the air, and the eyes of those who were previously below the screen looked up to see glittering remnants of pinpoint lights floating as fireflies throughout the land.

Suddenly, Ophanim fell from the sky, descending from the Aerie, moving like lightning, forward and backward and side to side. They darted about the city and explored the formerly forbidden regions that angels had called home, and the Lord smiled, for all His children were now amassed at His feet, and all of Heaven had now become one.

And whilst Heaven was in celebration, and her children in praise and rejoicing for the unity of spirit, echoes of angel-speak pelted the sky. The voice of the exiled Prince of Darkness was recognized, and dark mutterings floated as black filmy oil and settled on the ground behind Enoch and Elijah, then pooled to create a circular well of darkness.

Laughter and echoes of laughter emanated from the whirlpool that formed behind them. The vortex of obsidian caught fire and the golden glass bricks of Heaven fell into the blazing sinkhole. When the smoke cleared, three great octopi-like tendrils of flame and brimstone shot through the hole and suctioned themselves onto the streets, and the hiss of steam and the maggots of Hell bored through like termites, and the floor of heaven was transparent that all might see below.

Gasps and outrage traveled through the city while Malakim warriors flying overhead struggled to control their steeds as they bucked and neighed at the fires and screams below.

For Yeshua stood suspended over Talus, and the two were draped as morsels to be consumed over the lattice of teeth that was Hell's gaping mouth.

* * *

Lucifer's challenge filled the air.

"It is time, Yeshua, for why doth the life of God cower in the valley of the shadow of death and conceal thyself amidst the righteous dead? It is time to complete the task for which thou hast come. For hast thou not said that the Son of Man came not but to give His life for many? Or doth thy words mean nothing? Come out Begotten of El! Come out and face the decision that YOU have made!"

King David looked upon his Lord, knowing what He would do, and said, "Do not do it, my Lord. I beg thee."

But Yeshua just smiled and lifted Himself from bended knee.

"Behold, Lucifer, the culmination of your schemes."

And when Christ had spoken, He walked to the edge of the gulf that separated the realms of the righteous and unrighteous dead and stepped into the void, and when He did so, He floated, walking across the gulf toward Hades. Lucifer watched as He approached, smiling as Yeshua landed on the shore and walked up to Satan. The Son of God then spoke.

"You have bid me come, child, and here now I stand."

Lucifer drew closer until they were arm's length from one another, and he spoke through gritted teeth.

"Thou hast robbed me of what is mine and scolded me for aspiring to be nothing more than You." The Deceiver's face turned livid with rage. "I have from eternities past done nothing but love thee, and with an everlasting love did I faithfully serve, and yet thou didst strip from me the inheritance that a father owes a son."

Lucifer paused and moved within inches of Yeshua's face.

"Know that my scorn for thee is strong, and my hate as an eternal fire, for look where we have come, You and I, to stand face to face in the abominable creation that THOU hast designed to bring our kind to heel. Know that I will never forgive you! Never cease in my hunger for thy demise! And know that when I am done, I shall destroy the glory that you so covet from the memory of creation. This I promise, Lord Yeshua, and this I do swear."

Yeshua looked upon Lucifer with sadness in His face and shook His head.

"Thou wilt find thy end within a lake of fire, and all that thou desire will be as ash within thy mouth. Have I not told thee twice and yet say now again? What thou doest, do quickly?"

Lucifer's face contorted, and his breathing quickened as he gritted his teeth and shouted in explosive rage, backhanding the Son of God across His cheek.

"Take Him to the Forge and hang Him next to my brother."

Ares and Ashtaroth then took Yeshua by each arm and settled Him onto a platform next to where Talus hung, and placed Him near the entrance of the completed Hellforge. Then Lucifer spoke.

"Now, El. Now, after millennia on this wretched world, cast out by thine own hand. Now I shall have my vengeance. Thou hast denied me my throne, robbed me of my station, exiled me to this mote, and to what end? Only to see Thyself made bond slave to the filth that is mankind. Yet thou didst see fit to deny me a place at Thy side. And now, Godking, now you will serve as bond-slave to me. Within the depths of this creature shalt Thou minister to me. Within the kingdom of Hell wilt thy spirit reside, and thy memory, Son of God...thy memory shall be snuffed out in all the Earth. For if I can cross the gulf of death with the heartstone of an angel, behold me cross the Heavens with the Son of the Living God!"

Immediately, Lucifer lifted his hands in triumph and he recited in the ancient tongue the words to cause Hell to obey, and the beast hearkened to her master and extended her tendrils to take hold of the Son of God, and the creature stretched forth her hands, wrapping flaming coils around the True Vine.

Yeshua stood suspended over Talus and the two were draped as morsels over the lattice of teeth that was Hell's gaping mouth. A bridge of fire then shot from the bowels of Hell and punctured the dimensions that separated the Heavens from one another. The space between the realms rolled back and opened so that one might pass through a funnel of Hellfire that latched itself onto the foundation of Heaven. The citizens of Heaven beheld a great rift that appeared on the floor of the heavenly city, and all of Heaven could see the Lord Yeshua and Talus shackled and lifted up within Hell.

And lo, the furnace of Hell, the power of God, and Talus's own heartstone ignited the Forge and Lucifer's eyes widened in gleeful anticipation as the stones he had placed within them slowly sprang to life. A tremor rumbled through the realms of both Heaven and Hell, and the song that came from the stones was familiar to but three in Creation...Lucifer, Michael, and God. For it was the rhythmic chant of a reignited Stone of Fire that sang the yearning chorus to its maker, a chant that yearned "to be."

And Lucifer pranced in jubilation, for his scheme to ignite life through the theft of God's own power was in that moment made real.

Talus screamed, for the energy that flowed through him was more than he could endure, and his flesh began to show lacerations across his face and chest as the virtue of Yeshua's own life crackled through Talus' frail body.

The Godhead stood to His feet, and the three kings of the celestial hosts and all of Heaven gazed into the Realm of the Dead. Yeshua and Talus hung within the beast, captive in the flaming web that was its tendrils.

Michael clutched his sword, looking in panic at El and said, "Release me, Lord! I beg you, release me now!"

But El shook His head no. Eying all and quiet.

Michael's eyes narrowed and his muscles tensed in nervous anticipation of a command to spring into action.

Hell expanded herself as they watched, for the beast had tasted the flesh of both men and angels. From her entire existence, she had suckled the milk of angelic hate and nursed at the breast of men's sins, waxing fat. She grew, sprawling ever deeper into the depths of the Earth, and now under the command of Lucifer, the creature had now breached the third heaven.

And the bridge which Lucifer created to span the gulf to Paradise, completed its self-replicating march to reach the other side. Lucifer laughed as David and all his kin backed away from the edge of the gulf as it was now spanned. Hell no longer compartmentalized between the righteous and unrighteous dead. For in that moment, there was no Hades--no Paradise. Just the expansive and encroaching territory that would be the Kingdom of Satan, powered by the captive Son of God now suspended in the fiery new Kiln of the Devil's making.

Yeshua screamed out in pain, for in that moment captivity itself was held captive by the love of God. The whole of celestial existence anchored by the outstretched limbs of the Word Made Flesh...God, who had surrendered to the devices of evil, that He might fill all things. The God of creation, who in the person of Yeshua, now suffered the penalty of sinful man. The second death.

The thing was incomprehensible to the citizens of Heaven for the Ophanim could not understand it, nor could angels comprehend the plan of God. The daemons in the underworld cheered for after a millennia stuck in the wasteland that was 'Time' they now had hope that they might return home...as conquerors.

Michael looked at Gabriel, who mirrored his nervousness and looked back at the Lord who stood, still eying the events below.

"Now, Lord?" Michael said, his eyes pleading to do something, anything but stand idle.

Again the Lord shook His head no as He listened to the echoes of His only begotten Son's screams.

The cries of the Word Made Flesh wafted along the celestial winds and split the ears of the spiritual realm, but it was as music to the ears of Satan. Music he had longed many days to hear. An orchestral chorus of the gnashing of teeth, the moans of defeated enemies, and the beautiful cries of the living God who had exiled him in judgment.

Smiling, Lucifer looked at Zeus and spoke. "Go to. Take my armies across the gulf and bring those wayward spirits of El's to heel."

Zeus returned his lord's smile, nodded and stepped away from the pedestal where his master stood and waved the assembled legions to march across the Cadmime Bridge.

And so they did.

An armada of daemons and angels who on command proceeded to cross the scaffold of darkness that Lucifer had created.

A bridge now buttressed by the very power of God. Their marching made the realm to quake and their cadence, the ground to tremble.

David, Moses and various ones calmed those who saw the encroaching army and spoke. "Have faith. Our God is with us!"

Lucifer then looked up to Yeshua and shouted at his Creator. "I have been having sport with Talus, and I would much like to add thee as a player to our game." Lucifer then waved his hand and four flashing lights appeared in front of both the head of house Arelim and Yeshua.

"Yeshua, I have asked thine child, Talus, to tell me how many lights he sees. He is, of course, most stubborn. Yet, I think he is now ready to give me the answer I desire. But before I pose this question to him once more, and before I give his heart to Hell forever, I would give thee the chance to save his life. And if thou answerest correctly, I will release him and all the rabble of Paradise. This will I offer if ye but call me Lord and worship me as God. All this will I give thee if thou but answereth the simplest of questions. If thou be the Son of God – how many lights do you see?"

Lucifer brashly posed his question that all who saw from Heaven might hear.

For in the tick-tock that marked the passing of time – as Heaven's fate hung in the balance and; whilst daemonic armies marched across the gulf on a mission to slaughter in a second death, the righteous dead, Creation waited with bated breath for Yeshua's answer to the Devil's question.

And Yeshua His body convulsing and glistening with sweat, wracked in excruciating pain. Endured by His own choosing the eternal punishment reserved by the Father for those separated from God---the second death. Looked down in both agony and smirking triumph and replied, "Oh, foolish child. Know ye not that I AM the Light of the World?"

And forthwith, the power that siphoned from Yeshua and Talus reversed itself, and the flaming tendrils that held them violently recoiled and withered, crumpled as a dry leaf in a man's hand, and disintegrated into ash at the Lord's feet. The depleted braids of celestial consumption hung powerless as the Son of God withdrew from Hell all power He had deposited into it upon creation. All watched in terror as the Son of the living God began to draw power from Hell itself. Where the great mountain consumed alive its denizens, all now watched as Yeshua drew strength from the creature and siphoned power from the mountain.

Hell's remaining coils unwound from His body and the Lord glowed like a star. The brightness of His glory eclipsed the lights Lucifer had generated. Yeshua floated gently to the ground while sparks and great bolts of plasma projected in terrifying electric arcs from His person and set fire to already lit flames within Hell. For fire, itself, had now become a flammable substance to be consumed by the wrath of the Son of God.

The Lord then turned and spoke to Talus. "Thou art a faithful son. Now return recompense upon thy brother, and release thy charges."

Immediately Talus was completely healed, though he was still connected to the Forge. He roared with renewed strength and power and stretched forth his restored wings. The tendrils of fire snapped off his person, and he flew to the entrance of the newly formed Kiln and shouted to the Godstones within.

"Come forth!"

And from the great furnace, giant Phanes, materialized in the blaze, and they walked as smoky half men and half panthers of coalescent mists. The air rippled around them, and they leaped from the flames of the Forge. Fiery entrails followed them, and the hissing of steam echoed in their steps. Ashen swords lifted from their misty forms, and in fury, they set themselves to attack the gloating daemons and rebel angels that had surrounded Lucifer in celebration.

Lucifer beheld in bewilderment and confusion, his smugness now erased from his rapidly dispirited face. He spoke aloud to Yeshua in disorientation, the scene escalating out of control all around him.

"It is not possible. Your body was dead! Thy spirit captive within Hell. How can this be?"

Christ gleamed in starlight, and His form was such that galaxies and galaxies of galaxies floated within Him. The fires of Hell extinguished as He took a step forward while fallen angels and daemons panicked. Moans and wails filled the chambers, for many thought judgment had come. The Lord Yeshua hovered in unapproachable light as He floated toward His wayward son, and spoke.

"Know ye not that death hath no claim on one who hath not sinned? Thy unlawful actions hath voided thy claim to Death, Hell, and the grave for herein doth my Father love me because I lay down my life that I might take it again. None may take it from me, for I lay it down of myself. I have the power to lay it down, and I have the power to take it again. This commandment have I received of my Father. And my life, Devil...was never thine to take."

A golden sword then appeared from the Lord's mouth and He stepped menacingly toward the Adversary in blazing luminance.

Chapter Thirteen: Triumphant

"Oh, foolish child, know ye not that I AM the Light of the World?"

And when Yeshua spoke those words and had fulfilled his role as a scapegoat, Michael and all those that looked on stood ready to battle. El stood watching in flowing scarlet robes and He blazoned in power and majesty. He looked to His son, Michael, nodded and then spoke, releasing but one word.

"Now."

Michael unsheathed the sword of Ophanim and roared. Immediately, he, Eladrin, Nephanos, and legions from Heaven plummeted into the fiery funnel of hellfire that had breached the realm eternal.

Metatron and Gabriel dove and the Malakim armies flew on griffin back, and all those recovered from the Withering flung themselves as one man into the flaming chute of Hellfire.

Downward the armies of Heaven fell like an angry black cloud of disturbed bees. For Heaven's pent anger had been released, and the whole of the City of God fell to wreak havoc and do battle within the Realm of the Dead. Moving through the physical realm, and navigating through quantum realities and lo, even penetrating the barriers between life and death to mount an offensive where the spirits of all dead men dwelled.

The crackle of fire and the colors of the rainbow bounced off the circular chute as stars and alternative realities played themselves on the walls of the brimstone tube of transport.

Nephanos transformed into his true form of living fire and enveloped Michael like a flaming liquid coat of armor whilst Eladrin also shrouded Michael with his own body and became transparent.

Michael, leading the vanguard of Heaven's armies, was coated in the power of omnipresence and encircled by four faces of Eladrin which turned in gyroscopic rotation. His own sword moved in rotational unity with the wheels of Eladrin, and his fall was like nothing Heaven had ever seen, for he was the living embodiment of the three races of Heaven: Seraphim, Elohim, and Ophanim...three entities in one.

When Lucifer looked up, the three kings of the celestial host descended upon him as one man, and Michael was unlike any angel he had ever seen, and he feared, for in his wisdom he knew that the place of unity was a place of strength.

Thus, touching down to Earth, the host of Heaven invaded every nook of Earth's volcanic vents; through rock and mantle Heaven fell, a celestial tidal wave of unsheathed swords, maces, and spears. An unstoppable tsunami smashing into members of the Horde. The enemy unprepared as they had prematurely basked in victory over Yeshua's seeming imprisonment.

For none understood that the Son of God was Life. He could not be destroyed, captured or sundered, and this slow creeping realization rose as a suffocating reality that caused the Horde to scatter before Heaven's might.

Talus raised his army of Phanes, a weapon designed to be used against Heaven...a weapon now used in full deployment against the Horde. Monsters of fire and smoke pounced upon fallen angels and daemons, slashing and smothering them in flames borne from Lucifer's own kiln.

Ares's army had now crossed the chasm and set themselves to destroy Abraham and the countless righteous dead. And Yeshua seeing His people accosted, spoke to the dust of the Earth and the floor of Hell.

Hell upon command of its Lord, immediately raised itself as a defender to the righteous dead. For crawling up the canyon walls of the gulf, millions of parasitic worms suddenly flooded Paradise. Like lice, they were as the dust of the earth and flooded the floor of Paradise. But the creatures did the righteous dead no harm but instead enveloped the daemons and evil angels that had dared to cross the Cadmime Bridge.

Yeshua whispered "Disintegrate," and the atomic structures that held electrons and neutrons in their orbits instantly decayed upon the Lord's word and the Cadmime Bridge followed suite and collapsed.

Rebel angels, still upon it, fell screaming into the flaming abyss below. Their cries for help mingled into the cacophony of screams that rose from the battlefield. But the relief of death would not come, for parasitic maggots jumped from the walls to devour some as they fell and fiery tendrils that lined the acidic walls of Hell's belly reached out like tentacles to capture others mid-air.

As the black celestial mineral crumpled, shards rained into Paradise and slashed through daemons and angels. Yet the shards that lit at the feet of the righteous dead transformed into weapons of war.

David beheld what the Lord God had wrought and smiled as he stooped to grab a created sword Yeshua had placed at his feet. He grinned as he shouted aloud for all to hear. "THE HORDE HAST

COME WITH THOUGHT TO KILL US!" He then raised his sword high and pointed it toward the enemy. "KILL THEM BACK!"

Suddenly, the disarmed were now armed, and the fearful now fearless and the hunted, the hunters for the Lord fought on their side. The whole of Paradise cheered as Abraham, Moses and David charged into the oncoming wave of fallen angels and daemons, and the people of Paradise, bolstered by the Lord's actions and that of King David, Father Abraham, and Moses charged with them.

Ares' minions raised shields, but the numbers of the righteous dead were as ants and came from the whole of Paradise to smite the legions of fallen angels and erase their infernal presence from holy ground. And while Ares was atop a mount and directing his lieutenants, David and several of his renowned mighty men accosted him upon his steed that he fell, and his beast fell atop him.

David encircled him and spoke as he readied to strike. "They have called you the God of War, but only my God is the true God, and He hath taught my hands to war and my fingers to fight. Stand and see the future of all they who oppose my King."

Ares became wroth and lifted the steed from off him and shrugged his shoulders.

"I will enjoy killing you, little man."

Ares then lunged at David thinking to overpower him, but David blocked his blow and kicked the angel in the abdomen, knocking him back.

David smiled. "I have been dead a long time, and you foolishly fight an army with no fear of death. For we are they who have been granted eternal life!"

And David leaped toward Ares, sword drawn, and the angel was not accustomed to the strength with which David fought, for he fought in the power of God.

Moses joined himself to David, and they two fought with sword and ax. Abraham battled his way toward the two, and the trio fought the mighty angel Ares as one man.

Seeing he was outmatched by the three righteous spirits of God, Ares lifted himself into the air to escape, but the three also leaped into the air and they too flew, as they were not bound by the laws of the flesh. Moses lunged as Ares parried his blade until Abraham's blade found its mark and blood was drawn. Ares fell from the air before them, with the three men following in tow, giving the Elohim no quarter.

The whole of Paradise was covered in battle and the sounds of clanging shields, and screams of dissolution, and the smell of brimstone and sulfur hitchhiked atop the sounds of striking swords that sparkled in trails of light. And no human feared, for Abraham, Moses, and David fought the vanguard and each man was as a hundred men. Thousands of daemons and angels sank into oblivion, cut down by scores of righteous men.

And all around them the righteous dead, beat back the armies of Lucifer from off the grounds of Paradise, driving them over the cliffs of the gulf. Swords rang throughout Hell, and the screams of the damned that plunged into the abyssal gulf of Hell caused the righteous dead to cheer.

Michael touched down on Hell's soil and when he did so, King Nephanos unwrapped himself from Michael's body, for the king was a floating curtain of living fire that now transformed into a flaming scythe that cut through enemies and burned them alive.

Eladrin dashed toward multiple enemies at once, his movement so fast that he was a blur, and scores of the enemy fell as the Host plowed a path toward their King.

Lucifer unsheathed his sword of Malice. His followers noted the green blade that shimmered in the twilight of Hell's luminance, and the Horde rallied to fight the Host of Heaven. Lucifer wrestled against Malakim soldiers and smote them off gryphon back as they strafed him from above. A soldier, thinking to get the better, dived toward the Prince of Evil, but Lucifer lifted his hand and blinded both rider and gryphon that they smashed into the ground. Lucifer sank his sword deep into the angel's body and it withered before all as he mounted the beast and lifted himself airborne.

Ashtaroth attempted to flee, but Michael landed on his back and crushed him into the ground.

"Please, no. Do not destroy me!" Ashtaroth cried.

"Jerahmeel, his location, now!" Michael yelled.

An angel of the Horde attempted to strike but Michael commanded three of his swords to do battle with the angel while he lifted Ashtaroth off the ground by his robes and continued in his interrogation.

"I have yet four swords remaining to run you through. I command a response!" he roared.

Ashtaroth looked upon him with terror and said, "Over there, in the section behind the wyvern pens." Ashtaroth pointed and Michael released him and dashed to the holding pens.

A wyvern stood before him barring his path to rescue his friends. It stretched its leather wings and lifting its body to stand on two hind legs, roared in defiance at the Chief Prince, ready to devour him. Michael recalled all his swords from fighting other assailants and they twirled about him as electrons orbit an atom. Each flying blade circled his person, awaiting the command to strike.

The Wyvern's teeth were as his own swords and would easily slice angelic flesh if he were unfortunate enough to be grasped within. Michael floated toward the creature and it roared again, arching its back to spring upon him, but another roar sounded behind Michael. And when the Chief Prince turned to see if another enemy attacked from the rear, his eyes widened as a Phane towered over him...and Talus was its rider.

The wyvern leapt.

"YAH!" Talus said, and the Phane charged at the monster.

The two beasts made contact, Michael ducked with his hands over his head, as the giant creatures smashed into one another above him, with Wyvern and Phane tumbling backward, snapping at each other.

Talus jumped off his smoky steed, and with a grayish white sword that phased in and out of existence, launched himself straight into the mouth of the Wyvern. Razor sharp teeth bit deep into the Prince of Arelim, but the Phane grappled the beast by the neck and pummeled its snout, smashing it while it still gripped Talus, but Talus was ready, for his armor protected him from the chomp that would easily rend him to pieces. Talus lifted his sword and brought the blade deep into beast's skull. It roared in pain, releasing the High Prince from its toothy grasp, each clomp of its feet shaking the ground.

Talus, now free, fell to the ground, his sword still embedded in its skull. With a giant thud, it fell. Dirt and embers shot in every direction. The Phane turned and stood towering by the Prince of House Arelim. Talus dusted himself off while Michael looked upon his brother from a distance...a brother he had not seen for over thirty of men's years and each was moved and reached out to embrace the other. Michael pushed him back, still holding his shoulders and squeezing them gently, happy that his brother stood alive and well. Michael fought back tears as he spoke. "You were remiss to return to me as commanded."

Talus grinned, "Apologies, my Prince, I was detained. The King's business required me to feign capture that I might wear the enemy down and lead Lucifer to think victory could be won, and to also distract him from Yeshua whilst the Lord grew in stature. It was needful that all believe the enemies' diversion with me would see our Lord to success...moreover, it was needful to purge my shame that genesised the entrance of war by my hand."

Michael smiled. "And did you purge that which plagues you? Are you free of your burden?"

Talus looked about him. "To pay for one's own sin is folly when El hath already forgiven it, but I have seen what bitterness and unforgiveness of oneself acquires. I will no longer carry burdens that El hath offered to bear. Yea, my friend. I am free."

Michael smiled. "Then let us find our brethren and exit this foul place."

Talus nodded, and he and Michael turned to the back of the Wyvern's pen, and bound therein, cocooned within Hell's fiery membranes, hung Jerahmeel, Turiel, and Eskalion. Python-like coils draped over each one, constricting them while the mountain fed upon them. All three were enveloped and cried out in muffled pleas, for help, biting down upon fiery tendrils as tears streamed down their faces and maggots burrowed and fed upon them alive.

Michael and Talus peeled the coils from the membrane they were cocooned within, and Hell's tendrils slowly unraveled.

Talus pulled a tendril from Jerahmeel's mouth, as he coughed up fluid still resident in his lungs. He placed his hand on Jerahmeel's back and patted him, as the Lord of House Harrada vomited phlegm and the fluidic acids of digestion that hell had pumped into him. Coughing, Jerahmeel gathered himself and looked into his brother's eyes.

"When I saw that you and the Forge were one, I couldn't...I..."

"Shhh..." said Talus. "I know...I know." Jerahmeel reached out and pulled him close and they held each other tight.

Michael smiled as he released the other two captives, and his face contorted in alarm as he stared at Jerahmeel in horror. "My God, Jerahmeel...your eye!"

Jerahmeel felt where his eye had been gouged out and replied, "Yet I still am the best looking of the lot of you. Besides, I am still forced to suffer your ugly mug with the other eye." Jerahmeel turned to Talus and lifted his hands pleadingly. "Please, Talus, take my other eye! However, on the next mission Michael, I suggest that you donate the eye."

Talus laughed while Michael went over, smiled and hugged his brother. "I am glad to see you too, but wait...did I not send four on this mission? Where is Iblis?"

Jerahmeel grew somber and replied, "He betrayed us, and lo, he has his reward." He pointed to a cocoon behind Michael embedded within the wall of Hell. Michael followed his finger and entrapped within was the defector Iblis. Tendrils coiled around his neck and the worms which die not continued to do Hell's bidding and were about their work of consuming the angel. Michael peered deep into Iblis' eyes which were wide open and spoke pleadingly for rescue. The python-like veins of Hell filled his throat suffocated all screams. Michael winced in disgust and spoke, "Opportunity was given to return. Abandoned the straight path to redemption he has. He is where he belongs. Come, my friend. Let us go and return favor to Lucifer for the loss of thine eye."

Jerahmeel nodded, and Eskalion, Turiel, and Jerahmeel looked at one another, and then at their brethren who fought in the distance.

Jerahmeel spied Lucifer and cracked his knuckles in expectation to deliver recompense upon his rogue brother. "This is a beat down I've been looking forward to for a long time."

Each one then turned, flying as one man to do battle with Satan.

* * *

Lucifer, mounted upon gryphon-back, fended off attackers that sought to dismount him. Accosted on every side, he swung his sword while flying to get distance between him and the kiln of his own creation...the forge no longer under his control...an oven that now birthed monstrosities that attacked him and his own. Monstrosities meant to be used as weapons of war against Heaven. Monstrosities now turned against him.

As a cloud of devouring locusts, the Hosts of Heaven arrayed themselves to battle fallen angels who resided within Hell's loins and Lucifer. Lucifer surrounded himself with a spherical bubble of sound around his person. As a flying sonic cannon, he barreled into the legions of Heavens, blasting through Malakim warriors and exploding their ranks, but the legions of heaven were not be deterred. They reconstituted their lines by projecting beams of power at the bubble of sound that surrounded the former chief prince. Lightning strikes, discharges of heat, cold, and fire blasted the shield that armored Satan. Wave after wave of angels descended upon him with abandon and smashed upon him in self-slaughter, disintegrating instantly.

The dark prince found himself overwhelmed by the sheer number that sought to dismount him, and his sonic armor collapsed under the volume of attackers. The Prince of Pride fell from his mount, plummeting in a trail of fire to the floor of Hell.

As a meteorite that smashes into the Earth. Still, the angels of heaven descended after him, refusing to relent in their attacks.

He rose groggily as lightning strikes continued to rain down upon him, and angels landed to cut him down. Backing away, breathless, he looked for means to regain the upper hand and using his power over light, bent electromagnetic waves around him and disappeared, leaving false images of himself hither and yon, giving his opponents pause for thought.

"It is a trick!" some yelled. "He cannot be several places at once, so how is the thing possible?" The collective mob paused in their assault and weighed the new battle tactic used against them, while Lucifer taunted them behind the veil of angelic sight.

"Come, fools!" he mocked. "You desire the head of Lucifer? Then approach and seek your prize!"

Angels attacked the false images, each striking and wondering if they fought a doppelganger of the dread lord. Several swung their swords at an apparition only to realize the deception too late as they saw the Sword of Malice protruding from their bleeding chest. With deftness of speed, Lucifer cut them down before they could calculate why they were experiencing dissolution.

Charon however, stood afar off, ambivalent to the goings-on of all things, for his was to warden the creature Hell, and all smartly stood aloof from him. All except Eladrin, who approached the giant angel, landing in twinkling lights before the one he had engaged in a stalemated battle so many centuries ago.

Charon acknowledged the King of Ophanim and bowed his cowled head to him. Eladrin returned the gesture. The two celestial giants faced one another both dubiously and with an air of mutual respect.

"Leave this realm and return home to the realm immortal," the human face of Eladrin said.

Charon lifted his head to reveal the skeletal face of a mare and replied, "Theee darrrrk Looord, holdss keyyyyys of servitude. Booound to himmm I ammm. Retriiieveee theee keyyyysssss of

Deaath, and Hellll. And freeeee once more I willlll beee." He then lowered his head and his features once again became dark under cover of his hooded cowl.

Eladrin nodded and turned from the angel of death to scour the battlefield and find Lucifer. The King of Ophanim would risk all to acquire the keys and strip Satan of his power over Death and Hell.

The battle raged all about Eladrin as angel smote angel, and the righteous dead engaged in heated clashes with daemons. Eladrin's eyes then found Nephanos, the only one of his kind to ever leave the realm immortal and venture into Hell, and the Ophanim watched his peer in wonder.

The King of the Seraphim was fire incarnate, and released from his oath to stand before El, he was a dreaded sight to behold. As a floating wave, he moved through the throng before him, burning the enemies of Heaven alive. His body's composition was that of living fire and thus immune from Hell's ability to harm him, for Hell was made to devour Elohim, and the Seraphim's very substance was made from the same fires that formed the Kiln. Thus with impunity, Nephanos scorch-marched through rebel angels and daemons, cremating foes that burned and flailed helplessly while he ravaged all that stood in his path.

Where are the Lumazi? Eladrin thought. He continued to scour the field of battle, for he separated from Michael and the others during the assault. At last, his eyes found them. In the distance, various ones of the angelic council immersed in combat and fighting doggedly, skirmishing toward a common rallying point on the field. He tracked their expected destination and saw ten images of Lucifer fighting a throng of Heaven's angels, beating them back with sword, sound, and light.

The two groups will find themselves soon.

A flash caught the periphery of his eyes and he turned his four faces to find the provocation of Heaven's descent – the Lord God Yeshua.

Yeshua hovered within the shadow of Death and stood floating as a radiant bridge between Hades and Paradise. A shining light that blinded the underworld...a realm now totally overrun in battle.

* * *

The begotten Son of God was unstoppable, for the Lord God Yeshua was a marching hurricane of carnage that waged beneath the mantle of the Earth. Bright as a star amidst the dimness that was Hell, He was yet in the form of a man. Two golden swords floated about His person as wings from His back. Each was a full blade with no hilt and no hand grasped them. The Lord faced His people in Paradise, and from His position, He observed His children's actions as a general eyes all things around Him.

The flaming golden swords slashed fallen angels naive enough to accost the Lord, and the golden light of life that animated their stones floated back into Yeshua, for Yeshua was an army unto

Himself. In addition to the golden blades that were as wings on His back were also four words in angelic script that floated about His person, orbiting Him. Each shimmered, and powerful, deep, rataplan notes emanated from them. Eladrin noted the four words that circled the Lord were Judgment, Death, Recompense, and Hell.

And when the Lord walked, each word transformed into one of four objects that reached out of its own accord to slay those that stood in the Lord's way. The first was a bow nocked with an arrow of fire; the second was a red sword, but much smaller than the hiltless blades that floated at his back. A balance also hovered, aglow, and transmuted from a scale into the word judgment as the Lord passed judgment on all that he surveyed, and the last was a scythe. The curved obsidian blade with a golden handle flickered one moment from the word Death to a living reaping force that harvested the life of El autonomously from everything it touched.

A storm unto Himself, dark clouds and mutterings of thunder emanated from Yeshua's presence. Lightning streaked from His person, the bolts of which slew those arrayed against His children. Booming thunder shattered the cocooned dead that Hell still held in reserve for dining.

The Lord Yeshua walked over Hell and its minions as easily as He had walked on water as a man on the Earth. The weapons and words that floated about Him as wailing spirits wiped members of the Horde who did not immediately fall to their knees in surrender. The Grigori of destroyed enemies shown momentarily between thunder claps their stenographic duties now over and released to return to Heaven.

And thus, the Grigori recorded that on the day the heavenly Host invaded Hell, that Yeshua stood above the gulf that separated Hades from Paradise and unleashed a tempest of vengeance and anger. Yet, even in this was His angered tempered, lest the Earth fail from His wrath.

Yeshua and the fathers of their faith led the righteous dead to victory against the Horde. Some of the ungodly stood with their backs pushed against the cliff, unable to maneuver, surrounded and flanked by the army of dead saints. And when the Lord saw that His people were safe, He turned His eyes to his celestial children who had arrayed themselves against Lucifer.

* * *

Jerahmeel was first to enter into Lucifer's view undeceived by his brother's ruse and the Prince of Darkness mocked him as he drew near. "Hast the head of House Harrada come to surrender his other eye?" he laughed.

Jerahmeel armored his body in glistening white. Frost trailed behind him as axes materialized in his hands. He closed the distance between him and Lucifer and swung an ax at the dread lord.

Lucifer backed away, dodging his brother's blows, but Jerahmeel was not unskilled and drew close enough to his brother and hammered his forehead into his brother's, knocking him to the ground.

Lucifer fell to his rear, and Jerahmeel stopped his assault and smiled. "Surely you can defeat an angel blind in one eye?"

Lucifer scowled as Metatron and Eskalion landed behind Jerahmeel.

The head of House Harrada extended his hand to his brother and signaled with his curled opened hand to 'come here.' "Get up. We are not done yet."

Lucifer stood to his feet and wiped the blood that now dripped from a gash above his eye. His eyes narrowed, and the taunt that Jerahmeel levied against him made him pout in ire. He cocked his neck to the side and armored himself. Unsheathing the Blade of Malice, he replied, "This has been a long time coming."

Jerahmeel nodded, "Agreed, and believe me when I say I hope this will not go quick."

"Arrghhh!" Lucifer cried, enraged. The sound of his roar created a blast wave that preceded him. The audible wave of pressured vibrations burst as an explosive force across the space between them.

Jerahmeel took a step back, and Metatron stood as a shield before him. He opened his mouth and released a blast of sound that punched through the oncoming destructive wave, dissipating it into nothing. He drew his sword and flew to engage the former lord of his house. Their swords clashed, and sparks from their blades sprinkled flecks of light into the air, and however Lucifer turned, Metatron turned with him.

Jerahmeel looked on, aloof. "Pssfftt, and to think that you were once the Lord of all Draco, and yet an underling keeps thee from shutting my mouth. Your glory hast diminished in thy exile."

Lucifer, incensed in boiling anger, deflected Metatron's sword downward. With a flick of the wrist, his light blinded Metatron enough that Lucifer sought to bring his blade square over his opponent's head.

Eskalion entered the fray and drew his bo-staff, extending it and blocking Lucifer's killing blow, allowing Metatron time to recover from the makeshift flash grenade. Eskalion continued his attack with an overhead bo-strike, forcing Satan to retreat and adjust to the new form of attack.

Gabriel and Turiel gazed from a distance and fought their way to their sides. When they were close, Eskalion stepped aside while Turiel misted and moved forward. And Lucifer, thinking Turiel would succumb to his wiles as his Lord Argoth had many days before, smiled, ready to grab his misted form as he floated closer, but the Grigori was aware of his Lord's last encounter and prepared for it. Lucifer knew not that Turiel concealed Eskalion from his gaze, so Turiel inched within arm's reach of Lucifer and Eskalion jumped from the midst of his gaseous body.

Lucifer lifted his sword to fend off his attacker, but Eskalion's surprise attack was too strong. Eskalion stamped Lucifer in the chest with a four-point strike of his staff and sent the rogue angel reeling. Eskalion then stopped his advance while Turiel solidified. Jerahmeel stood behind the duo and Gabriel landed to join the fray, having fought his way through daemonic forces.

Lucifer bent over, panting to catch his breath as air wheezed through his burning lungs. He reached for his chest, rubbing his bruised sternum, staggering to stand straight, and spoke in melodious rage.

"I see that you have learned to fight as one. Good, for thou wilt die as one. As for me, I will see thine heads hanging from Hell's walls."

Lucifer then touched his necklace, and the key of Death glowed blood red.

Many of the Host and Horde had in their collective wisdom, stayed away from the Angel of Death. For Charon stood aloof from the goings on of that which surrounded him. Eying the scenes, he focused on the Lord Yeshua who also hovered over the gulf, watching the battlefield.

The Warden of Hell stirred, aroused by the Key of Death's call to him, and the great angel turned his face from the Word Made Flesh to the master who held him in bondage – Lucifer. Bound to the rogue angel, Charon in obedience stretched forth his mighty wings and lifted himself from the floor of Hell, and took flight across the battlefield.

All took note that the embodiment of Death had now been roused and made his way to Satan's side. Many trembled, for the power of Charon was known, as few in their natural state could walk the colon of Hell, let alone tame the creature to its will, and yet it was Charon who kept the creature Hell in submission to Satan...who allowed the King of Lies to twist the innards of the creature to his whims.

Gabriel saw the hulk, Charon, approach and the thought gave him pause. "Death rises to meet us," he said.

Michael landed next to his brother, surveying the scene as Charon flew to engage them. He nodded, inhaled hard and replied, "Indeed, but the Author of Life watches from afar." Michael's halo then glowed, and he faded in and out from sight. He called to Nephanos and Eladrin, and the two kings made their way to his side.

Gabriel stood aside as the three heads of state stood next to one another – Eladrin, Nephanos, and Michael. Michael lifted his arms high, and Nephanos enveloped the Chief Prince in fire and he was ablaze. Eladrin's faces changed and merged with Michael's own face, and when Gabriel looked upon his friend, he saw he had become something altogether different. For Michael shimmered between existence and non-existence with a golden Halo over his head, and his face changed to one of five faces. Twirling around him, the sword of Ophanim raged and Gabriel could not stand near, for the weapon was ferocious in its orbit around its master, and great fire surrounded Michael's person.

Gabriel spoke. "Is the Michael that I know still with us?"

The face of a human turned to him and spoke. "We are here, for we are the Sum of All Things and the image of what Lucifer should have been. Now go to, and help our brethren resist the Devil – and we shall see to Charon."

And when Michael spoke those words, he launched himself at the oncoming Angel of Death. With wings of the Ophanim and skin of the Seraphim, Michael, prince of all Elohim, rose to do battle with Charon.

All of Hades watched as Michael smashed into the Warden of Hell. Charon's chest cavity caved in and he fell from the sky falling in smoke, fire, and ash...with Michael atop him.

Michael commanded the Sword of Ophanim to split, and the blade broke apart and rocketed to cut the angel down. Charon's cloak then turned obsidian and hard as diamond. Flecks of light and the clinking of sword strikes could be heard, as the blades of cadmium scratched the armored angel.

Unexpectedly on the defensive, Charon turned his back to Michael. And when he did so, Michael disappeared, his swords still striking and hacking. Charon unsheathed his dreaded scythe, and when he pulled the weapon from his robes, Michael materialized in front of him. With a stretched out hand, Nephanos leaped from his palms and blanketed Charon in a ferocious attack of fire, and the Angel of Death blazed. His great hands attempted to swish Nephanos's fire as one would bat a buzzing mosquito.

Lucifer took note that Charon had not come to assist him, and he frowned.

"What plagues the Lord of Darkness?" mocked Jerahmeel. "Surely the mighty Lucifer doth not need anyone to assist him?"

Lucifer smiled as Jerahmeel, Eskalion, Turiel, Metatron, and Gabriel stood before him as a shining wall of light, each armored and ready to battle.

Lucifer unsheathed his sword of Malice and replied. "Charon is but a tool. You have yet to understand the power of sin to repel the Father. But I will teach you this lesson."

He then touched the flaming key of Hell around his neck and broke a small piece from it. The great mountain of Hell then let loose a guttural roar that reverberated so that it shook even the nations of the earth above. Mountain ranges lifted further into the sky, and sent volcanoes into eruption and disturbed the deep places in the earth. Tectonic plates shifted as the Heavenly mountain cried out in pain and men would long remember the day when whirlpools emerged from the ocean depths and swallowed whole kingdoms into the sea, for Lucifer had released Hell. Since the dawn of mankind's fall, her pent up rage waited to be unleashed upon her captors. Now her chains lay in pieces and she was free to attack all that indwelt her – and the beast hungered.

Tendrils of fire and the maggots of Hell raced from every corner, and lava flooded chambers above and below. The inhabitants of Hades and Paradise became as one man to fight Hell herself and to resist her digestive clutches, for she no longer discerned friend from foe, and all were but foodstuffs to the living mountain of Hell.

Jerahmeel, Eskalion, Gabriel, Metatron and Turiel watched the chaotic collapse of the bowel as teeth emerged from the floor all about them.

Lucifer stood in the midst, and his eyes glistened in beaming pride and jubilation as he shouted, "See the beginning of the Void! The end of all things!"

He grinned and slammed his blade into the moist floor of Hell's flesh, and a tremor rumbled all about them. A fissure of fire exploded beneath Lucifer's sword and raced toward the position of the assembled vanguard of heaven.

Gabriel, seeing the crack, looked to see the Lord Yeshua watching him. The Lord nodded in affirmation and Gabriel sprinted toward Lucifer like lightning that flashed across the sky. Instantly, he absorbed the kinetic power of the oncoming blast and was upon his brother, his staff at the ready to belt the jaw of Lucifer.

Satan raised his hand and caught the Prince of Malakim by the throat, then chuckled and cocked his head in disappointment. "You think your speed can avail against me? Only God is light, dear brother, and thou art much, much slower than He."

Gabriel looked back, struggling in Lucifer's grip and cried to his brethren, "NOW!"

Lucifer then took his sword and thrust it into Gabriel, hitting a hard thud on his breastplate. Slowly, the features of the head of House Malakim shriveled before Lucifer's eyes, and he said, "Goodbye, brother."

"NOOOOOO!" Jerahmeel cried, his eyes wide in disbelief.

Immediately, Metatron, Eskalion, Turiel, and Jerahmeel raced toward his position, as Lucifer threw the now withered body of Gabriel into the dust.

* * *

Charon's barbed bony tentacles waved about him as he defended himself against the seven bladed Sword of Ophanim. Michael struggled, despite his power of the three kings to contain the giant angel and keep him at bay. Fighting that he might serve as interference whilst his brethren might contend with Lucifer.

The bodies of the three beings merged into a united fighting force, allowing through Michael's halo, the ability to communicate mentally.

We cannot kill him! Michael thought while bringing his fist squarely on the giant's chest. Pummeling Charon, he dashed off to prevent his own demise if Charon grasped him.

Eladrin replied, "We cannot bring Death to heel, but the stalling of Charon is not the true goal. We must regain the lost keys of Death and Hell. Only then will this come to an end.

Nephanos's fire accosted Charon's face and blinded the giant angel. Remember, Charon is not our enemy. He is but an unwilling servant to the Usurper. We must be careful to avoid injury.

A tentacle grabbed Michael by his leg and lifted him up high, then slammed him into the ground. Michael heard something snap on his wing and the pain of a thousand needles shot through his neck. He rolled over to spy bruised tendons that connected his wings to his shoulders.

Alas, the Warden does not hold our own injury in such high regard. We must hurry or we may not be able to avoid risk to him. He will grow stronger in time, and we must stop Lucifer before this occurs.

Charon's scythe flew in great swaths before him, deflecting the smaller swords of Michael away. Eladrin then separated from Michael and left he and Nephanos to contend with Charon while he raced to confront Lucifer.

Hell was run amok, and in the chaos that ensued in the Realm of the Dead, four angels: Jerahmeel, Metatron, Eskalion, and Turiel fought the Dragon.

Dashing between sword strikes, and plowing blows to face and body, Metatron and Eskalion attacked Lucifer in hand-to-hand combat. Blood and strips of flesh tore from the lacerations each foe gave to the other.

With the power of sound and light at his command, Lucifer bellowed projections that sliced through armor and flesh. Jerahmeel provided sheets of ice to protect his brothers and raised spears from the floor of Hell to impale Lucifer, but Satan leaped into the air. Turiel slashed at him with his dagger while misted. The blade whizzed about him in stabbing attempts to strike the rebel king.

But Lucifer was the former prince of angels and he moved with great swiftness. And with the percussions embedded in his flesh, he blew toward Turiel and caused the gaseous Grigori to dissipate against the blast of powerful air.

Lucifer tucked in his wings and fell hard onto Metatron, slamming the angel into the ground. He quickly rose, and with a leg sweep tripped Eskalion, knocking him onto his back with a thud. Yet Metatron would not be denied. He opened his palm, and a conical force of sound flung from his hand and as an invisible knife, sliced through Lucifer's armor and bit into his flesh, causing the angel to bleed.

Lucifer cried out in agony and raised his sword to fling at him. The blade of Malice released and flew through the air like a coiled serpent...an emerald weapon of dark magic designed from Hell's own essence to siphon the life of all it touched. The sword whirred and spun, crossing the field of battle and as it traveled it bore the tortured sound of Kilnstones gone mad. The cries of captured souls strained to get out, yet in the moments that passed, four faces flew across Metatron's path and the sword caught in the King of Ophanim rings and wheels within wheels. The blade hovered, mere inches from Metatron's face.

Metatron backed away, and when he did, Eladrin held the sword and twirled it within his body's rings, gyrating. The momentum of the blade still moved from one wheel to another and Eladrin swiveled the sword and turned it back to point at Lucifer. Eladrin released it from his twirling wheels and it flew back toward its master. Lucifer ducked, and Jerahmeel, who approached him from behind, also ducked as the green blade hurtled past him and lodged into the moist wall of Hell.

The blade began to grow emerald green, and the sapphire power oozed from it and crept up the mountain walls. The blade instinctively attempted to do the impossible and siphon the life of Hell itself, and as a cancerous cell devours flesh, so, too, did the Hell-forged blade now seek to feast upon the beast.

Jerahmeel faced his brother, and the two ran toward one another. A mighty crash sounded and Lucifer brought his fist squarely against his brother's face. Jerahmeel kneed his sibling in the abdomen.

Cries of struggle and exertion radiated from their fight. Lucifer fell back to his rear, and Jerahmeel grabbed him and pounded him across the face. The duo traded powerful blow after powerful blow, and while Lucifer grew lost in his battle lust directed at his brother Jerahmeel, he failed to see Turiel reach toward the back of his neck and pull on the keys of Death and Hell. The Dark Lord's head jerked back as Turiel pulled with all his might. The chain links snapped...and the keys of Death and Hell fell to the ground.

Lucifer detonated in light, blinding all that surrounded him. Jerahmeel covered his eyes, and Turiel misted instinctively to avoid the attack. Metatron crawled on the ground. Eladrin raced to scour the ground and recover the keys.

Lucifer pulled his Blade of Malice out of the wall and turned to find the keys lying on the ground. As his brethren groped the floor in blindness, he flew to recover them, but when he reached to pick them up, a sandaled foot stepped on his hand and a voice of many waters spoke.

"You have something that belongs to me."

Lucifer looked up and when he did, the Lord Yeshua stood above him, glowing in power. Behind him, Abraham, Moses and David were running towards him, swords drawn, as millions of the righteous dead followed, having beat Satan's forces to come for him.

* * *

Michael wrestled with Charon and whilst he did, the Angel of Death spoke.

"The keyyss, they haveee fallennn."

Michael immediately stopped his attack and Charon also ceased from his struggles. Both turned to the Lord's position and watched the true struggle that ensued within eyes view.

Lucifer was on hands and knees and had reached to retrieve the fallen keys of Death and Hell, but the Lord towered above him, and His foot was on the Keys of Power. Lucifer pulled his hand back, gripped the Sword of Malice, and raising the green blade attempted to plunge it into Yeshua's abdomen.

The Lord neither moved nor budged His face stoic and grim. Michael had seen the same look before. It was in the eyes of his King prior when He had judged his children and flung them into exile. And now once more, Michael saw the King of Kings' eyes narrow, as His rebellious son sought to strike down His Master. Yeshua then grabbed the blade with His bare hands and stopped its penetration into His flesh. The Sword of Malice glowed in its voracious attempt to steal the life of God. To reap the living soul of the God-man, Yeshua.

Lucifer smiled with glee, his eyes wide in anticipation that the soul reaving sword had found its mark. Here in the confines of Hell, within the dimensions of a creature whose hunger was satisfied only by Elomic flesh, Lucifer would finally destroy the indestructible God.

But it was not so.

For when the sword of Lucifer's making glowed, Yeshua also glowed and lost the appearance of a man as He took on the semblance of El. And when He spoke, His voice was as the voice of many waters, and His words were on this wise: "Did I not tell thee, all souls are mine?"

The Lord released the blade and allowed it to strike Him in the abdomen, and when it did, a green hue overtook Yeshua. All watched as Lucifer attempted to hold the Sword steady as green waves of power flowed from the sword into the Lord. But the green flowing stream of power reversed and extended from the Lord's body to Lucifer's hand, and Satan grabbed the hilt with both hands, struggling to hold on, but could not.

The blade screamed as Yeshua siphoned the power from it. Visible waves of emerald light pulsed from it and into the Lord. Voices and whispers echoed upon one another as the blade shrilled and then exploded in jade and limelight. The emerald blade shattered in Lucifer's hands and crumpled as dust at the Lord's feet.

The explosion of light rocketed the cavern and released a shockwave that raced in all directions and pummeled all to the ground. The voices of those consumed by the blade soared from captivity. Ethereal bodies glowed as misty winds flew in all directions, screaming, and crying out for revenge. Unleashed from artificial confinement at last, they wailed and enraged, and attacked forces of the Horde that remained in the cavern.

Pandemonium broke out as the unreleased wrath of both Hell and spirits hostile to Lucifer attacked all that swore allegiance to the Devil. The released spirits accosted members of the Horde still fighting and ghosted through their bodies, causing agonizing pain and sending many to their knees in agony. As hornets disturbed, they flew in locust-like swarms everywhere the eye could see, and the soldiers of Lucifer swung at the air in vain to keep the vengeful spirits at bay.

The Sword of the Lord then pointed at Lucifer, who hastily scooted backward to escape. The Prince of Darkness rose and ran, and when he did so, the bow that floated about Yeshua unleashed a nocked arrow that caught the enemy in the rear of his shoulder.

Lucifer cried out in pain, and all watched as Yeshua stalked the mighty cherubim. The Prince of Darkness fell, tripping over his own feet and crawled to flee the presence of the Lord.

The Shekinah manifested around Yeshua and He was brilliant in luminescent radiance. His steps made indentations in the earth as He walked, and the scythe that floated as an electron around the Lord flung itself forward and swung at the feet of the enemy. Lucifer gained his footing, tripped and fell face-first in the dirt. His face crusted with dried blood as the cut above his eye continued to drip. His teeth were coated with blood from his battle with the Lumazi, and he spat blue plasma from his mouth. His vicious contempt landed at the Lord's feet and their eyes met.

Coughing and wiping blood with the back of his hand, Satan backed away as Yeshua approached him, sword drawn. The righteous dead bore witness as God menacingly walked toward His enemy, ready to strike the final blow. To end the suffering of mankind. Each eye widened as the Sword of the Lord raised to bring to naught, he, who through the power of Death, had kept men in fear; he who through his works sundered Heaven, and rent fellowship between God and Man.

Lucifer looked into Yeshua's eyes and screamed, "I do not fear Oblivion. Strike and show all the power of thy great might, for if thou be the Son of God, show them with the sword what it is to fear God!"

The Lord then raised His blade, Satan lifted his chin in defiance and grimaced, swallowed hard, and closed his eyes in horrifying expectation. The Sword of the Lord reached its apogee, then fell downward, and with bated breath, all waited for the head of Lucifer to fall severed to the ground.

The blade fell a mere hair's breadth from Satan's mouth and hit the heated ground with a 'thunk.' Lucifer felt the wind of the sword's edge cool his face, and when he opened his eyes, Yeshua stood above him in glowing majesty. The Prince of Darkness gritted his teeth and opened his mouth to speak, and the Lord placed His foot atop his face near the base of his neck, cutting him off.

Yeshua then lifted from the folds of His robe, the necklace that carried the keys to Death and Hell and raised them up for all to see.

"Hell...peace, be still!"

The creature immediately stopped its assault on all that indwelt her, and lava flows and tendrils receded into her roof and the beast was calmed. Members of the Horde fell to their knees and laid down their arms, for Yeshua stood atop their leader with the keys of Death and Hell clenched in His fist, raised high for all to see.

The cavern erupted in cheers, and members of the Host hugged one another as cries of victory rang out through the whole of the underworld for in the deep places of the earth, and beyond the sight of mortal men, Yeshua spoiled principalities and powers and made a show of them openly...His foot atop the crushed head of Satan with His fist raised in triumph.

The Lord then spoke for all to hear.

"The battle is over, but the war still rages. For above, my people must continue to undo the works of the Enemy. A word have they been given that upon which the gates of Hell shall not prevail, for, in a few days' time, the sentence of Fire shall be carried out against this one, and upon all who have sought to undo the Father! And know, oh rebellious house, that I shall return, and when I do, cry woe! For know then that thine judgment is at hand."

The members of the Lumazi came near to look upon Satan who yet laid under the Lord's foot with bloodied features, gritted teeth, and hissing contempt as they stared at him.

Jerahmeel walked past first, and he lowered himself down to speak to his brother.

"You have an eye that belongs to me. I want it back." He reached down to gouge Lucifer's eye, but the Lord grabbed his hand.

"If I forbade Peter to draw his sword to protect me, how much more must thou learn this lesson of vengeance? Stay thy hand, for this one shall have his reward." The Lord nodded toward Charon who walked toward his triumphant master.

Jerahmeel nodded in obeisance and backed away, and when he did, the Lord reached into the dust and spit into it and placed His hands over Jerahmeel's face, and Jerhameel's eye was restored to its place and he was made whole.

Jerahmeel felt his face and smiled. "I thank you, Lord."

Lucifer laughed, and when he did the Lord pressed harder on his neck, and he became silent once more. A flying spirit flew over across from the Lord and when it landed within Lucifer's sight, the Lord blew His own breath upon the ethereal creature and before the eyes of all, the ghostly apparition changed and solidified, and Gabriel stood before them whole as before. He bowed to the Lord, and the Lord nodded in acknowledgment. Gabriel rose and walked where Lucifer could see him more clearly, and spoke, "Tsk, tsk, tsk. Did you think me so slow, brother, to be caught by thy blow to dissolution? I but obeyed the King and met with those held prisoner by thy sword, that upon their release they might be convinced to plague thee. To my surprise, they needed little convincing to plague thee. Imagine their joy when I told them that at the last day they would one day accost thee in flames of fire." Gabriel then shook his head and walked away.

More of the royal host, and David and Abraham and others stared upon Lucifer, his face still in the dirt.

Michael walked through the crowd and spoke aloud to his brother.

"How art thou fallen from heaven, O Lucifer, son of the morning? How art thou cut down to the ground, which didst weaken the nations! For thou hast said in thine heart, I will ascend into heaven, that I will exalt my throne above the stars of God: I will sit also upon the mount of the congregation, in the sides of the north: I will ascend above the heights of the clouds; and I will be like the most High. Yet look at you now, brought down to hell, to the sides of the pit. And who are these that narrowly look upon thee and consider?"

Turiel then picked up, commenting where Michael had stopped, "Is this the man that made the Earth to tremble, and that shook kingdoms; that made the world as a wilderness, and destroyed the cities thereof; the one that opened not the house of his prisoners?"

Lucifer squirmed under the sole of the Lord's foot and growled like a trapped animal.

Talus then flew over and looked at his King. The Lord nodded His approval and Talus knelt on one knee to look at Lucifer. He stared into his eyes, and Lucifer tried to look away but Talus would have none of it. He squeezed his cheeks and made him look at him and spoke in authoritative victory as he narrowed his eyes, leaning close for Lucifer to hear. The Lord loosened His foothold so Talus could raise the Adversary's head enough to glare into his eyes. Talus looked at him in defiance and whispered in triumph, "I see four lights."

He then spit on the ground and released him and Lucifer's face fell into the moist earth where Talus had spit.

Yeshua nodded as His son walked away, then raised His voice and spoke to all. "It is time to return home."

The towering figure of Charon then created a shadow over them as he drew closer and he spoke to the Lord.

"Am I alsooo tooo retunnn hommmme?"

The Lord smiled. His eyes grew soft and He shook His head lovingly to curtail His creations disappointment.

"Nay," Yeshua said. "There will be a time that fire, yea even a lake of fire will house this one, and then thou shalt be home to do what thou wast charged to do. Until that day, go to, and arrest those this one made thee release, and return them captive to captivity. And whence I am returned, I will make a home where in the next creation, my vengeance can be fulfilled on this one here." And the Lord looked at Lucifer crossly when He spoke.

Charon bowed and turned, and as he walked away, the sounds of chains and the smell of fire and ash trailed him as he marched to parts unknown.

Abraham then came to the Lord. "And what of us, my King?"

Yeshua smiled. "It is now time to enter into rest." And when He spoke, the funnel that Hell had created grew wider and the Lord looked up. And when He did, El and El Pneuma were standing in shining garments and looked down from Heaven.

Then Yeshua shouted up in the hearing of all. "El Pneuma, I am ready."

El Pneuma nodded and spoke one word.

"Resurrection."

And a tremor shook within Hell itself. The righteous dead began to glow, and many looked at their hands as the Shekinah began to overlap all of them. Then in flashes of blinking light, each one rocketed into Heaven through beams of light. Hundreds, then thousands, then billions took to the air in illuminated bursts of light. As rain that fell upward, the people of Paradise emptied, and the righteous dead were no more to be seen in the Underworld.

Michael and the all the Host watched as their human brethren lifted into Heaven and he said, "Come...let us welcome our brothers and sisters home. We have much to celebrate!" His halo glowed, and Eladrin began to twirl in sparkling light, while Nephanos covered the Chief Prince with his body and he rose to return to the realm immortal. The Host also looked to the sky and lifted themselves into the heavenly portal to return home.

Yeshua stood alone, still holding the keys to Death and Hell. Whispered sorrows and old screams still lived there, as well as the unrighteous dead and daemons. He sighed then whispered one word to Hell. "Feed."

The creature immediately roared to life. Millions of maggots, tendrils and lava burst into the cavern, and the Lord looked up and lifted His foot from off Lucifer's neck. The Adversary coughed, rubbed his throat and struggled to his feet. Yeshua began to fade and be drawn back into the realm of men.

Satan shook a fist and screamed, "We are not done yet Yeshua!"

Lava poured behind Lucifer who stood defiantly watching the rising Lord, ignoring the calamity about him as well as the screams of his own people.

Yeshua smiled as He exited the cavern and replied to His wayward son.

"My child, it was over from the foundation of the world."

The spirit of Yeshua rocketed to the roof of Hell and exploded through the floor of the Earth, racing through rock and crust to join once more to His physical body. The rejoining of body and spirit sent tremors through the earth, and a white-hot column of light flashed over His body, irradiating the area. The inside of the tomb glowed in incandescence, and the Lord's lungs breathed the cool air of the tomb. Blood pumped through His beating heart and coursed through His body. He opened His eyes to see Azaziel standing guard with sword drawn, over him, and the Lord spoke through the linen shroud. "It is good to see you, my friend. A faithful son thou hast been."

Azaziel blinked as his eyes adjusted to the great flash of light that heralded the Lord's return, and a full-faced smile erupted as he helped the Lord to His feet.

* * *

Azaziel had waited patiently for the Lord to return, standing as a silent sentry over the human body of his master. His eyes pierced the physical confines of the sealed tomb to the brethren who stood guard outside. The sun would rise soon.

Suddenly an earthquake rocked the region and the inside of the tomb glowed in brilliant incandescence. The head of House Issi covered his eyes. The body of the Lord shone as a star, the light of which breached the contours of the boulder rolled in front of the tomb's entrance, and burned through the sealed ropes that lined the stone. Angelic guards stared at the epicenter that came from inside the tomb.

Cassiel revealed himself and came down in a great light in front of the sealed tomb. Roman guards struggled to keep their balance on the rumbling ground, watched the stone roll away, and fainted in fright. Azaziel blinked repeatedly to dismiss splotches of blues and morphing shapes that danced across his eyelids.

Cassiel noticed the Lord's chest rose and fell. His lungs breathed in the cool air of the tomb as blood began to circulate through His resurrected system and color slowly returned to the body of the Lord. His fingers moved, and the linen covered head turned toward Azaziel. He spoke through the shroud. "It is good to see thee, my friend. A faithful son thou hast been."

Smiles wreathed his face as he helped the Lord sit up and tenderly removed the cloth from His face.

"Your plan? The keys and righteous dead...are they well?" Azaziel said.

The Lord opened His hands where the open wounds of His nail scars still remained, and within His right palm lay the two recaptured keys of Death and Hell.

Azaziel gasped in joy. Onlooking angels beamed at one another and bowed to their King.

Azaziel helped the Lord to His feet, steadying his King as His body returned to full function and they exited the tomb. The sun broke over the horizon...the dawn of the first day of the week, and Yeshua and His guards laughed and strolled the surrounding countryside.

"My Lord," Azaziel said, "thou hast breached the stronghold of the Enemy and spoiled his house. What wilt thou do now?"

Yeshua looked at him and replied, "There is yet much to be done, for an army of men must be raised to undo that which Satan hath done. The final battle is yet to come. Even now in Heaven thou wilt have many new siblings and there are even more that I must bring into my Father's house, but for now, come, I must shew myself to my disciples and gather my sheep into the sheepfold. Take me to them."

Yeshua then masked them all in invisibility, and Azaziel then lifted his King into his strong arms and flew off with the angelic royal guard trailing them.

Yeshua, seeing two of His female disciples walking toward the tomb, commanded two of the angelic guard stay at the tomb to bring glad tidings to them. Women who were moments from a discovery that would soon change the course of mankind.

* * *

Now after forty days of showing Himself in infallible proofs in the course of time, the Lord called His disciples together, and they asked Him, saying, "Lord, wilt thou at this time restore the kingdom to Israel?"

And He said unto them, "It is not for you to know the times or the seasons which the Father hath put in His own power. But ye shall receive power, after that the Holy Ghost is come upon thee: and ye shall be witnesses unto me both in Jerusalem, and in all Judaea, and in Samaria, and unto the uttermost parts of the earth."

And when He had spoken these things, they beheld as He was taken up; and a cloud received Him out of their sight.

Azaziel watched the men and noted that they looked steadfastly into heaven as He went up, and given leave by the Lord, the angel revealed himself to the disciples.

"Ye men of Galilee, why stand ye gazing up into heaven? This same Yeshua, which is taken up from you into heaven, shall so come in like manner as ye have seen Him go into heaven."

And when they heard those words, they were quick to be about the Lord's business, and Azaziel watched them depart, knowing the war had turned and in the resurrection of the Lord, he saw the death throes of the war, and that the final push of righteous men had now begun.

The End

Epilogue

Having escaped the clutches of Hell, Lucifer and Ashtaroth watched from afar as the disciples of Yeshua departed and Azaziel lifted himself into the sky.

"My king, many of our kind still remain trapped, consumed alive by the beast. How shall we recover from such a defeat?"

Lucifer scowled at his words. "Is the thing not known? 'Smite the shepherd and the sheep will scatter.' Fear not, my faithful friend. In time, I shall seed my presence so much within the accursed 'body of Christ' that it shall be as a canker. And in the last day, I will follow the pattern that El Himself hath revealed and will raise up a man – an Anti-Christ, and I shall use him as El hath used Yeshua. We will undo His influence. Yea, fear not, for we are not without a hope and a future. And then we shall see what the end shall be for this wretched pestilence of Adam's kin. Come now, for they will assemble in Jerusalem, and I will hunt these disciples, this...church...and we will see how she fares when exposed to trials of fire."

Lucifer smirked as he looked away from the disciples. His eyes rested upon the city of Jerusalem and the temple dedicated to the worship of El. He recalled the daemon's report:

"Sire! Sire! Yeshua hath prophesied saying, 'Dost thou not see all these things? Truly I say unto thee, not one stone will be left upon another which will not be torn down.'"

Lucifer spat and wiped his mouth on his sleeve. "Yes, let us go from this place, Ashtaroth, for I intend to see the words of Yeshua come to pass, for I will cast every stone down. Go to and move Caesar of Rome! Bring him here that I might descend with my man-servant like a whirlwind."

Ashtaroth bowed himself to his Lord and flew toward Rome.

Lucifer looked to the horizon and muttered through clenched teeth. "We are far from done, you and I, El. As long as I draw breath, we will never be done."

* * *

Heaven held numerous celebrations over the victory of Yeshua. And Yeshua interceded for the saints on the Earth standing before the Father making intercession for them. And in the course of time Micheal summoned all of heaven to worship as was the way of the Chief Prince.

El sat upon his throne and in the right hand of El was a book prepared by Argoth and written within and on the backside, sealed with seven seals. Micheal then proclaimed to all Heaven with a loud voice, "Who is worthy to open the book, and to loose the seals thereof?"

Enoch then saw a man who the Lord had allowed to see into Heaven and Enoch noted that he was in Heaven, but was not. And Enoch saw that the man wept sore and approached him and spoke.

"What is thy name and what is this that you shed tears in Heaven?"

The man replied to Enoch, "My name is John and I weep because no man is found worthy to open and to read the book, neither to look thereon."

Enoch replied, "Weep not: behold, the Lion of the tribe of Judah, the Root of David, hath prevailed to open the book, and to loose the seven seals thereof."

John then noted that in the midst of the throne and of the four beasts, and in the midst of the elders, stood a Lamb as it had been slain, having seven horns and seven eyes, which are the seven Spirits of God sent forth into all the earth.

And he came and took the book out of the right hand of him that sat upon the throne. And when he had taken the book, the four beasts and four and twenty elders fell down before the Lamb, having every one of them harps, and golden vials full of odors, which are the prayers of saints.

And they sung a new song, saying,

"Thou art worthy to take the book, and to open the seals thereof: for thou wast slain, and hast redeemed us to God by thy blood out of every kindred, and tongue, and people, and nation;

And hast made us unto our God kings and priests: and we shall reign on the earth."

And the voice of many angels round about the throne and the beasts and the elders: and the number of them was ten thousand times ten thousand, and thousands of thousands; saying with a loud voice, "Worthy is the Lamb that was slain to receive power, and riches, and wisdom, and strength, and honour, and glory, and blessing."

And every creature which is in heaven, and on the earth, and under the earth, and such as are in the sea, and all that are in them, heard them saying, "Blessing, and honour, and glory, and power, be unto him that sitteth upon the throne, and unto the Lamb for ever and ever."

And the four beasts said, "Amen." And the four and twenty elders fell down and worshiped him that liveth for ever and ever.

And after the Lord had shown John all that was to transpire in the last days, Enoch bid him farewell.

El then summoned Elijah and Enoch into his presence and spoke on this wise. "Go to, for after long last must thou now witness to my wonders and get thee down and make way for my coming. Witness to all within the Earth, that the end hast come. And when they kill you. Thou shall take your place with your brethren and we shall go down and bring righteousness, and recoup all that the Enemy hast stolen."

Elijah and Enoch nodded and the duo left the presence of El to show men that Lucifer had deceived them. And that God--God was coming to bring recompense in the Earth.

The Third Heaven: Apocalypse of Kings - Book 4

Donovan M. Neal

Tornveil

For permission requests, write to the publisher, addressed "Attention: Permissions Coordinator," at the email below:

tornveil@donovanmneal.com

Ordering Information:

Quantity sales. Special discounts are available on quantity purchases by corporations, associations and others. For details, contact the publisher at the email above.

Orders by U.S. trade bookstores and wholesalers. Please contact Lightning Source: Tel: (615) 213-5815; fax: (615) 213-4725 or visit https://www.lightningsource.com/.

Printed in the United States of America

ISBN 978-0-9894805-7-4 (Print Version)

Contents

Scriptures

2 Cor 12:2

I knew a man in Christ above fourteen years ago, (whether in the body, I cannot tell; or whether out of the body, I cannot tell: God knoweth;) such an one caught up to the third heaven.

Matt 24:22

Except those days should be shortened, there should no flesh be saved.

Philippians 2:11

And *that* every tongue should confess that Jesus Christ *is* Lord, to the glory of God the Father.

Revelation 20:10

And the devil that deceived them was cast into the lake of fire and brimstone, where the beast and the false prophet *are*, and shall be tormented day and night for ever and ever.

Acknowledgments

To the Lord Jesus Christ, who loves me.

To the Pastor of Labor of Love Church, Charles Hawthorne, who nurtured my pre-existing love of the Bible.

To my children: Candace, Christopher and Alexander–you can do great things!

To the authors, comic books artists and authors, comic books artists, and writers who have come before, and who unknowingly have breathed on the embers of my imagination.

To all my beta readers and friends who shared both critiques and encouragement.

To my wife Nettie, who cheered me on when I had nothing and said, "Wow!" after reading the prologue of my first novel.

I finally want to thank my Beta Readers Karen Dobbowski,

And to one of the heroes who helped me to fund my audiobook. Mr. and Mrs. James and Heather Vantress. Thank you for your wonderful investment in my writing ministry.

May God truly bless you all.

Preface

Dearly Beloved,

Well, here we are. The end of the Third Heaven series. If you have traveled with me this far, you already know my doctrinal disclaimer. I present no prescriptive attempt to state that future events will happen as depicted in these pages. Please do not assume any prophetic proclamation nor personal treatise of what I personally believe. I will be the first to profess that I see through a glass darkly.

Know I laud no dogma to my reader save Jesus Christ and Him crucified. I present no truth save that Jesus Christ is the risen Lord, and at that name all must one day bow. The story while Christian (because it contains a Christian worldview and promotes the Gospel of Jesus Christ) is just a continuation of this author's *fictional* story, and creative license has been taken to the extreme to make the story primarily an entertaining read while still attempting to adhere to the foundational tent pole truths of scripture regarding the person of Christ and his ultimate victory.

This book was difficult to write. I have looked painstakingly over the timeline presented in the books of Revelation and have done my best to "shoehorn" this story to fit within a pre-tribulation view of Revelation. However, know from the outset I have failed in that endeavor, and I do not mean this story to convey events in a chronologically exact depiction as they might appear in the book of Revelation. Nor does the story contain all the events or personalities as depicted in the book of Revelation. I did this to maintain a consistent story world, and to keep the book at a readable level, and thus this is not an attempt to make the Scriptures themselves state something or depict something they do not. I have done my best to place again "tent-poles" within the work congruent with what I think most of what Protestant Christianity's views of biblical end-times scenario believe would happen. These tent poles would include Christ's second coming, the devil's ultimate defeat, an Anti-Christ, a battle of Armageddon, and eternal judgment. But the reader should know in advance that all congruence ends there. So, to minimize disappointment I suggest you take the story as it is. And not as a litmus test on how closely it matches your understanding of Biblical text. It is simply not a story that is attempting to do that. So, I warn you in advance if you do you will have difficulty enjoying the story that is.

I have mixed feelings as I write what is my last preface for this series. I am cognizant that "to everything there is a season," and reluctantly realize that the season of this series; with this fourth and final book must now come to a close. I hope that over the course of these four novels I have not just entertained you but caused you to wonder at the majesty of God's love for the world. His power and wisdom, and to realize that we are surrounded by a great cloud of witnesses who cheer those who pursue the cause of Christ.

Thus, allow me to end in this novel with the ever-familiar disclaimer I started several years ago. This is a story based on Biblical texts to create a tale of wonder. Consider this a work of Biblical fan fiction and I ask for the final time you approach the novel in that light and witness the powerful demonstrations of God's mercy, love and severity. I ask that you resist the urge to niggle the absence of every detail and or conformity with scripture you think may be incongruent, and I promise that if you do: you will see the greater lessons resident in the story itself that are scriptural. And perhaps the lessons resident for us today on how we should govern ourselves considering the impending return of the Lord.

In my audacity, humanness, frailty and humility I've tried to tackle in this fictional series what I believe is the most epic tale the world has ever seen: God's loving kindness to reconcile all things to Himself. To restore fallen humanity and Creation to its purpose. To tell the story of two brothers who have found themselves on opposite sides of fealty to God.

It is my hope that those within the body of Christ who read this: will see this body of work for what it is. One believing author's frail and imaginative attempt to use fiction to tell what is to him, the most compelling story ever revealed to mankind.

I have grown to love these characters, this story—this world. So, it is bittersweet I bid you adieu for now. Farewell until the Lord allows us to meet again in the pages of another book.

Ever grateful to the Lord Jesus for his mercies, grace, and love,

Donovan M. Neal

Chapter One: Anno Domini

High atop the mountain of God, Argoth stood alone upon the roof of the Hall of Annals. He stared at the star-filled sky and watched from his lonely perch, his people as they roamed throughout the cosmos. Like past High Priests of Israel, he sanctum'd alone. Privy to see what few in creation could behold. A realm unseen even to the sight of angels. A realm populated by beings, who without eyes dutifully recorded all that ensued around them. Each documenting the deeds of all beings that a record may one day be delivered to God.

Argoth eyed the tome El had commissioned so long ago. A volume that was finite in its pages. Pages that were added as each Grigori penned all that they witnessed. A tome that would one day be opened and read back to the hearers: an objective chronicle of the acts of all things. Argoth shuddered knowing that many would not desire to see their works rehearsed before the eyes of God and the Host. For the Chief of Eyes understood that one day the works of all beings would be revealed. And on that day the great prophecy would be fulfilled: that there was nothing hidden that would not be made known. Nothing concealed that would not be unveiled. A prophecy—and a warning El had given when creation was young.

Argoth walked towards the altar that he had made to commemorate his becoming Chief of Eyes. He reached the five-foot pedestal where his physical eyes laid in hovering memorial of his oath towards God. His plucked eyes stared back at him. Floating reminders suspended in front of him as he himself hovered in their presence. Here the prince of all Grigori recalled his appointment by God to be the head of his people.

Few knew the cost one must pay to see with the eyes of God—to be Sephiroth. Or the unspoken pain he regularly suffered: the mild ache that nestled behind the glowing slits that were his eyes. And the perpetual irritating gnawing from knowing that some would die, and others would live. His created mind was increasingly expanded in ever painful new limits, in an attempt to comprehend the smallest jot of what El beheld. To be privy to see how all possibilities must end, was a daunting task and the weight of such knowledge assailed him continuously. It was a consuming thing that would drive anyone not graced by God mad. So, Argoth frequently sequestered himself from his brethren: secluded himself that he might "close" his eyes, and for a moment; unburden himself. To no more feign his unspoken pain before his relatives. A pain he dutifully endured that he might behold but a fraction of what the Almighty sees.

The migraines were steady and the throbbing, often intolerable. Severed optical nerves, behind still existent eyelids; still fired in attempts to see with the eyes of flesh. Nerves once connected to floating eyes set atop a pedestal. Yet, Argoth tolerated the gnawing ache and endured the scars from his plucked eyes: eyes that he knew would never heal. One day he would not need this sight. For, as El had promised, all would be revealed. His eyes would then be restored, no longer held in constant captivity to the will of God for him to see what all Grigori see. For the burning and itching reminded him of the constant offense God's holiness endured from man's disobedience. Yea, Argoth's eyes saw what few could see — Creation's continued decay: save for the preservative effect of Christ's blood and resurrection. Only the Sephiroth could see Creation's groaning. The canker she endured due to Adam's sin.

The Chief of Eyes floated before his memorial: his place where he would see if God would show him the moments beyond the present into the future; here, he would enter the Trance.

He crossed his legs; each foot placed on its opposing thigh. He slowed his breathing and expanded his chest to inhale Heaven's air. Silently he opened his mind to not just see the present but enter the realm of God's allowed possibilities.

The stars slowly faded, followed by the vision of his people into black, and all that remained was the movement of galaxies and mirrors of universes reflected back at him.

Deeper he moved into a meditative state and quieted himself to attune further to the mind of God. To quicken himself to the presence of the Almighty. He who filled all things, past present and future.

His physical eyes which floated on the pedestal opened, and their pupils widened, and each eye raced left and right. Each blinked to clear the gloss of the angelic realm narrowing their focus of attention and straining to see a generation ahead into the future. Eyes that were allowed to follow the path of all futures that El had ordained should exist.

The Shekinah began to emanate over the angel and a crackle of electricity arced over him. Slowly a cloud lowered from Heaven's sky—singing.

"Will you croon today Argoth?" says the living cloud.

Argoth replies, "Yea, great Nebula. For the sight of the Lord, do I seek."

The white vapor formed a mouth of froth that moved and replies, "But thine eyes are nigh thee Grigori... with what song do you bring this day that thou may see and strum to the hymn of God?"

Argoth then pretended to grope the surrounding air; struggling in a feigned attempt to search for his eyes that floated but an arm's reach before him.

"I am but a worm who grovels to see the light. An envoy blind who beckons that he might see. You who croon, you cover the home of God. If El bids me worthy, open the fog of the future I pray thee; that if El permits I might see what lies beyond the shroud of Time."

The cloud then lifted over Argoth and spoke.

"Beware to seek the sight of God Grigori…croon the future at your own risk. But El hast approved thy sight. Therefore, behold the things that will come."

The living cloud then moved into Argoth's mouth. The color of his plucked eyes changed from yellow to a purplish hue. His body violently jerked back, and he was lifted into the air with his arms extended.

Hovering on his back: he was now captive in the Trance. And his mind's eye beheld the future.

And he saw a dragon standing on the shore of the sea, and a beast coming out of the sea. And the beast had ten horns and seven heads, with ten crowns on its horns, and on each head a blasphemous name. The beast resembled a leopard but had feet like those of a bear and a mouth like that of a lion. And the dragon was terrible and gave the beast his power, his throne and great authority. And Argoth beheld that one of the heads of the beast seemed to have had a fatal wound, but the fatal wound had been healed.

Argoth continued in his gaze mesmerized as the whole world was filled with wonder and followed after the beast. Adamson worshiped the dragon because he had been given authority to the beast, and they also worshiped the beast and asks, "Who is like the beast? Who can wage war against it?"

Astonished, Argoth watched as the beast mouthed proud words and blasphemies and exercised authority for forty-two months. Relentlessly it opened its mouth to blaspheme God, and to slander His name and His dwelling place and those who live in Heaven. The Chief of Eyes contorted in convulsing spasms as he watched as power was given to wage war against God's holy people and to conquer them. And it was given authority over every tribe, people, language and nation. And in Argoth's horror seemingly all inhabitants of the earth worshiped the beast.

Argoth shook his head in anguish and disbelief jerking in the air. He attempted to stop the marching visions that assaulted his eyes. But he was in the trance, and like a puppet; his will was momentarily not his own, as visions paraded before him unabated. His eyes were now in sync to the Almighty's. Eyes that saw what God saw. Eyes that knew what he witnessed were an inevitability, that God. El—would allow Satan to see his lust come to fruition: the worship of the Dragon throughout the Earth.

Argoth violently coughed hacking up puffs of smoke as the living cloud dislodged from his lungs through his mouth and nostrils and floated away and sung but one word:

"Woe."

And when the cloud removed itself from Argoth's body, the Grigori fell, face-first to the ground wheezing and grasping for air.

His translucent robes were filled with stars and his inkhorn and stylus hovered in elliptical orbits around him. With each pass, his stylus dipped itself into the floating inkhorn which surrounded him and wrote out all that the Lord had granted him to see in his vision.

"Please El, please El no! Are we undone?" He wailed his lament into the starry sky. "Is there no stopping the march of Lucifer's sin? Is there no other way?"

Yet naught but the blowing of wind and silence echoed in reply.

A knock rapped on the tower roof's door and Argoth was startled: awakened from his meditations to El. The Chief of Eyes then wiped his teary face, rose to his feet, and brushed himself of dust and the sweat that beaded from his brow.

"You may come up Jerahmeel."

The head of house Harrada opened the door to the roof of the mountain of God and gazed upon his angelic brother, climbed up the stairs and walked towards him. Jerahmeel stared at his brother. His eyes intent in a study of Argoth's face. For a brief moment he saw the golden book of El. A crimson ribbon was draped over the book like a seal and the tome began to fade from his view. Jerahmeel watched as it vanished back into the realm beyond his own sight.

The angel recalled the day when Argoth had eyes like them all, and then the next they were gone plucked out by God's own hand. He glanced at the hovering eyes that remained atop the roof of the mountain of God; never sure what to make of the spectacle. Jerahmeel alone, did Argoth allow to visit this level of the Hall of Annals. Jerahmeel alone knew of Argoth's continuous pain. And he kept his brother's confidence, as requested.

Argoth staggered as he stood up, and Jerahmeel let him lean upon him.

"Are you all right?" Jerahmeel asks. "I thought I heard you cry out."

"Aye..." Argoth replies. His face looked towards the starry sky and stared off into space.

Jerahmeel's own eyes now narrowed, and he looked upon his friend with increasing concern and pressed his interrogation further. "Tell me...what did you see?"

Argoth lowered his gaze to the floor, sighed, then raised his head to stare deep into Jerahmeel's own eyes and replied.

"The last generation of war...for the end of all things has come."

Jerahmeel eyes narrowed in concern. "Tell me brother... the book that is hidden from my sight when I enter your presence. What is it? I've never seen a book on this wise before."

Argoth cocked his head to the side and gazed upon his brother to study him. "It is a tome within a tome of tomes. It is I, and I am it. It is the book of life, and it is the book of El."

"And what does it... what do you contain?"

Argoth frowned, "The wrath of the living God: a wrath unlike Hell, or Death, but pure and unadulterated destruction. And soon my friend...very soon I fear. El would have it...have me be opened."

* * *

"Ashtaroth, attend me." Lucifer says.

Ashtaroth quickly made himself to his master's side. He watched as the one hundredth session of what Adam's kin had called the United Nations scurried about the business of ruling their kinsmen. He moved imperceptibly amongst them watching as men who had the power to end all life on the planet, huddled in clusters behind banners of their respective houses. Some had cloth sigils woven with stars and stripes, whilst other human clans held banners draped in the color of blood. He flew over the standards that the nations of the world cloaked themselves in their collective pride, until he came to his master who hovered above the proceedings of all men, watching, calculating and grinning.

Ashtaroth hated his master's grin.

For it meant that the machinations of his king would someday mean disruption to the status quo; a status quo to once more attempt to grasp at the skirts of Heaven and attempt to bring El low. He approached the king of darkness and bowed as was protocol to his lord.

"What is your command my king?"

Lucifer did not look at his henchman and replies, "I desire report of the fruit of my labor. Go to and personally bid Leto to come and give me report of his stewardship. I would know of his state. Inform him that I grow weary of waiting and would see my plans set into motion."

"As you wish my king." Ashtaroth bowed and turned from the dread lord. He lifted himself into the ether floating through the steel and concrete towers that men had erected in their ingenuity and pride. The glass spires ascended upward to scrape against the base of the sky, pale imitations of the golden towers of Heaven. Counterfeit steeples, they were but mere shadows of Heaven's glory. Men had collected themselves into great cities that dotted the face of the Earth. God's flawed image, ever seeking to make a name for themselves as in the time of Babel. Their innate sin moving them to counter the scattering El had caused among their kind so many centuries earlier. Their various languages now made moot through their increasing knowledge and skills to craft machines beyond the sight of the naked eye to see.

Ashtaroth admired them.

He watched them lay metallic and fiber optic sinew across the ocean floor and with their electronic veins, rushed through electrons to communicate across land and sea. And in their charge to subdue El's world they launched themselves into the black of space and dared peer, straining to see even into the realm of the Grigori themselves and had even partially tapped into the invisible spectrums of existence where images and sound could be sent invisibly across the globe and into the deep black of space. Mankind was indeed as Lucifer foresaw, an encroaching plague, which if left unchecked would seek to go to the furthest reaches of the universe. He now understood what his master had foreseen, that man would never stop; never cease in his pursuit to accomplish all that was in his imagination to do. He would one day breach the realm of the Third Heaven itself: and that Lucifer explained...could never be.

El was wise to scatter them, Ashtaroth thought. For it was most surely a truth that nothing would be restrained from what they imagined to do. It was this untapped potential that Lucifer coveted to control, and to return weaponized against El himself.

Ashtaroth floated effortless in the sky leaving the city men called New York. He flew with ease into the cool evening sky, dodging past the prayer cover of El's followers. A poisonous shield which weakened his kind, and if not avoided would cause him to fall hurtling downward from the sky. He was careful to weave in between the flack of the saint's prayers.

Arriving at the edge of the Atlantic Ocean, he escaped the contours of the continent where Christ had made such a stronghold that its occupation by Christians had managed to even turn the attentions of his master. When asked how Lucifer could allow a country of men who set themselves to worship El so and not be destroyed: Lucifer laughed and replied.

"It is my will that the church of the living god be allowed to thrive in this land. We shall let it swell in a subversive and divisive pride and allow the accursed body of Christ in this nation, to think it immune from attack without. For a dry rot shall I sow within: a canker that in time will make them crumble. We shall weather their belief in Yeshua; we shall abide and wait until Adamson is sick of the shackle that is El's will. We will let him taste what it is to live apart from El. To remove from their remembrance that they are made in His accursed image and likeness, and then my dear friend...then, we shall strike. For we will plant within this garden a tare of division; for whom better than I, to know the power of discord among brethren? Let them rise...let them rise that they might fall."

Ashtaroth had watched his master become more calculating since captivity was led captive by Yeshua. Become increasingly obsessed with the notion that the called-out assembly of humans, posed an existential threat to the Elohim's existence. For Lucifer was livid after his defeat in Hell. Fooled by El's brilliance; Yeshua had lured his master to bite into what he could not resist...Lucifer's hatred of El. All but guaranteeing his actions would lead to his downfall. A strategy and wisdom that none of the princes of this world knew: for had they known it, they would not have crucified the Lord of glory.

Ashtaroth smiled as he flew over the Atlantic Ocean. An uncontrolled admiration of El welled up within him: that despite his master's power. El had always managed to stay ahead of him. But perhaps no longer...for El himself had shown the way to bring Him low. Lucifer had always seen hints of the possibility. An outcome revealed when he provoked God's direct wrath when angels mated with the human females to create abomination. Lucifer spied El's power resident in Adam when Yeshua was lifted up and the Eternal Ones very life expired before the Horde's eyes.

And now...now Lucifer would, after two attempts to bring to maturity a plan woven over thousands of men's years, that if realized would lift his people to the gates of Heaven itself. However, it was a plant that was wrought with great risk and perhaps would ignite the final solution to El's rule itself; mayhap, even bring the prophetic trumpets of wrath down upon them all. Lucifer would see the image of God serve him...or he would see it destroyed in fire. It was a risky plan. Full of greatness and peril, but Ashtaroth would see his master's plan done.

The starry filled sky was as quiet as was the peaceful sea below him. There were few of the Host that patrolled the oceans. For the enemy was busy removing the Hoard's influence over men in the Earth. And the numbers of the Fallen were down dramatically from the great day of the Descension. For war throughout the millennia and the opening of a new front against God's church had withered their ranks.

Ashtaroth noted the crafts of flight that men had designed to ferry their kind across land and sea. Each darted across the black sky in blinking red and green signals, releasing contour trails as they soared through the air.

What did he hear a human call them? Airplanes: yes, that was the term.

Each of the tiny airships reminded him briefly of the glory of his own kind. Ashtaroth frowned at the memory. Resentment, and then bitterness, lit the flames of his kilnstone once more, and he glowered at the achievement of man to fly even with mechanical means. He turned his attention to one of the airplanes that was closest to him.

How easy to just pluck a vessel from the air; these creatures that rely on such machines who, in their naiveté, fly through the skies. How easy indeed to send these souls to meet Hell and cull their stinking ranks.

But many of the vessels had angels accompany them as escorts: invisible protectors that guarded them as they traveled. Many of the machines were themselves cloaked in gaseous shields of prayer, preventing members of the Horde from drawing near. This particular vessel was no different. Four angels flew surrounding the craft. A visible sign of God's divine covering over what was undoubtedly at least one of his adopted children on board. He veered southeast, away from the craft. Not desiring to engage members of the Host.

He looked down as he flew over and past great sea faring ships that ferried men's commerce. Ships loaded with the trinkets of merchants that occupied the minds of men. For the whole of Adam's kin were foolishly concerned over gold and notes of debt, as nations exchanged in trade with one another. Ashtaroth chuckled to himself as he reminisced on the many souls he had personally given over to Hell's clutches: humans who yielded to greed and their innate predilection to submit to the lust of their eyes.

Men are so stupid: so many achievements; so much potential; yet a slave all the same...pathetic.

Despite all of mankind's achievements, all of his increase in knowledge, he had failed to fully unlock his genome to explore the spark of life breathed by El himself; still unable to break the bonds of the Withering...unable to be released from Lucifer's entrapment into Sin. Unable to breach the mortal limits El had placed on his life span. Ashtaroth remembered El's word that echoed as a blast across the world. "My spirit shall not always strive with man, for that he also is flesh: yet his days shall be an hundred and twenty years."

Upon his command, El's voice saturated every cell of mankind on the planet. Establishing man's bounds to prevent his spread and from achieving his eternal purpose. A limit never breached: never breached until now.

Lucifer knew El could never break his word. His plan was genius. He had watched men from the birth of his existence; from his seating upon the throne that covered El Himself. Lucifer understood why David had written, "What is man that thou art mindful of him? And the son of man, that thou visitest him?" For Lucifer made mention that he had seen in a vision the potential that man... not angel, could supplant God. For God in his folly had created man in his image and likeness. And Lucifer would harness this power. And return it against the God-king in recompense for them all.

Ashtaroth ruminated on his station and the future yet to come. He frowned in anger and resentment. Like his master, he too wanted to bring man to ruin. But more importantly, to bring recompense to both God and man. For the Horde still smarted from the last battle with the forces of Heaven.

For Lucifer's attempts to sully the image of God, and Yeshua's unexpected resurrection had created a shockwave in the spirit. For now, men led by El Pneuma and empowered by the same, were sensitive to his kind's presence as never before. Now enlightened to the true nature of his kind and armed with intimate knowledge of man's true standing. Lucifer's fears became realized as the accursed Disciples of Christ had become enemy combatants in the struggle to defeat El. The disciples of Yeshua were now illuminated to the truth that they wrestled not against flesh and blood, but against principalities and powers: a truth that allowed them to see the Horde and its effects on mankind. And with this knowledge, the Church of the living God laid waste to Lucifer's plan for men: encroaching as a virus across the Earth. The news of Yeshua's resurrection rode upon the mouths of rabid men who, despite torture and death, managed to reach the four corners of the Earth with their accursed "good news." News that Yeshua had died for their sins and was raised; raised with the promise that they too would be holders of eternal life if they but turned to faith in God.

Damn you Lucifer. Ashtaroth thought. *Your pride will be the undoing of us all. But who else can lead? Who else can possibly lead us back to Heaven, but he who originated our ouster? Perhaps finally—this plan of yours will work.*

Ashtaroth sighed as he recalled the history of El's new army of men: men who diluted Lucifer's message that the Horde were gods. For a time, mankind thought there were many gods, yet the sect of Christians, as they became known, obliterated those ideas. Once Ashtaroth and his kind could call upon men to worship them openly, to bow down, but it was increasingly difficult in this new age to even convince men that beings existed beyond his own existence. Lucifer cautioned the Horde not to fight against this deception. Explaining that it was wise to lie low and cause usurpation. The Horde heeded the wisdom of their king, relented, and pulled back from open manifestations. The dark ages of man allowed the Horde to wipe many from the face of the Earth. But the Renaissance obliterated the darkness. Lucifer sought to bring forth the Void. The darkened state needed to bring about Lucifer's new heaven and new earth.

For many generations Ashtaroth and his master had fought the parasitic growth of the Church: beginning with the persecution of the man Peter. Lucifer killed many of their leaders. Nevertheless, they spread as dandelion seeds adrift across the span of time, implanting their foul "gospel" amidst the nations of the planet. For over two thousand years, Ashtaroth had watched the cancerous growth of this plague called the "church."

The called-out assembly of God blew over all lands reaching the known world. Lucifer finally slowed their march in the Eastern lands of Pangu, Gog, and Magog. Implanting within a people that the idea of God was not just foreign but a threat to power.

"For what better weapon to fight against Christ, and his people, than to perpetuate a world where there is no God?" Lucifer says.

Lucifer then spread the greatest of all lies: the denial of the Creator's existence. A lie designed to replace the Creator with man himself.

"Let mankind see himself as the sum of all things. The measure by which reality is defined, and we will have him where we desire him. Then, dear Ashtaroth...then we will conquer."

Ashtaroth landed in the seat of global power that was Brussels and was met by the chief principality of the area Belphegor. "Hail adjutant of the king!" Belphegor says, and he saluted the emissary of Lucifer.

Ashtaroth returned his salute and replied. "Hail. I bring inquiry from the master as to the status of his son. He grows increasingly impatient."

"Leto is maturing nicely," says Belphegor. "We have controlled his development per the master's instruction. Soon he will be ready to take his place among the powers of men. Soon we shall recoup all that the God-king has denied us, and soon...we shall have our revenge."

Leto was under constant guard. Lucifer always wanted to know everything regarding his development, particularly if he exhibited extraordinary traits. Nephilim were known to possess strength greater than men. Some, such as Nimrod of old, were men of renown who could even rival angels. But nothing seemed unusual about the creature other than the occasional physical fatigue that his angelic tutors sometimes noted when they were around him.

Ashtaroth knew Lucifer played with fire. To combine human and Elohim DNA could create unnatural combinations that were unforeseen. El had inscribed in all angelic stones the warnings of inseminating human females. To do so was to cross species and the results could be a creation that was neither Elohim nor Human, but something else: Abomination.

Grigoric scholars of the Horde speculated it was possible to create something greater than either man or angel: something that mayhap could rival God. Most scoffed at the idea. All save Lucifer.

For Lucifer was a researcher of the nth degree. And the prospect of making something that could rival El himself intrigued him. And when El put on flesh, Lucifer knew that if El could become a man, perhaps...perhaps the thing could be engineered in reverse. That man, being made in the image and likeness of God; could indeed ascend to something more. But all attempts to breed something failed: from the breaking of the world via flood by El, to the destruction of the giants by David and his mighty men. Undeterred, Lucifer continued his studies, experimenting on men as chattel. From euthanasia, abortion, and genocide, he assisted man's science, technology, and medicine. Century after century until mankind unlocked his genome: until he understood the ways of nanotechnology and the science of the atom and cloning. Selectively breeding within the labs of men; defying the spirit of El's law, but not its letter until finally Lucifer created a man after his own image and likeness; a man allegedly with unspoilt DNA from Adam himself: uncorrupted by the Withering. A man spliced with the DNA of his own angelic blood: a man he named Leto Alexander.

Ashtaroth looked at the young man who had just thrashed an opponent in tennis. He flew over to where Leto was wiping his brow with a towel. His muscles bristled with sweat. He was a fine specimen of Lucifer's manipulation of Adam's genetic code. Olive toned with green eyes; the ambassador of the European Union would soon be ready to assume his mantle of power.

Ashtaroth stared at Leto...stared as the weapon of Lucifer's creative genius: a creation that suddenly turned to speak to him.

"It is good to see you Ashtaroth. How fares my father?"

* * *

Worship rang throughout all of heaven.

Michael watched from his tower's perch, as humans and angels, as far as the eye could see, sung before God who sat on the throne.

Humans now occupied Heaven. Humans now freed from the clutches of Lucifer and previously trapped within the confines of Hades. Human veterans of a celestial war: a war to spread the truth of El in the Earth: warriors who battled against the Horde within the depths of Hell itself.

Heaven was now a mass of male and female faces; faces from earth that lifted their voices in choral praise to God. From every corner of the Earth did they spring and from all hues did they stand before God: a throng of now blended dialects; from the nations of Grecia, to the far reaches of Africa. Linguistic variances that originated at the Tower of Babel were now swept aside as the common tongue of Heaven was now understood by all.

Heaven rung out in unified songs. For in Heaven now were all one: all now understood. Michael marveled at the newly issued raiment of humans: clothing which gleamed in brilliant white. Yeshua, the Lamb of God, had washed them in his own blood and given each one a new robe.

Michael stood awed before the morass of humankind that knelt before the throne. Awed at the singing Seraphim, Ophanim, and even his own people. He gazed upon the spectacle that was before him, and awareness dawned upon him. An understanding of why El had allowed the house of Kortai to build Heaven's greatest house: the Temple.

Each room in the house of God, each chamber, apartment, and walkway was meticulously prepared for a day when all God's children would be together. Michael chuckled to himself as he reminisced over his past wonderment over why El always created on the scale that He did: wondered why he would create an entire world for just two people.

Michael smiled as he thought to himself on the day he had asked the Father this query and the Lord's ever patient and educating reply.

"My son, my thoughts are not your thoughts: nor my ways, your ways." The Lord God then presented his open hand for view, and within He held a seed, and showed it to his son.

"What do you see?" God asks.

Michael paused, "A seedling, my king."

El shook his head. "No, my son," replies El. "This is a great forest."

El again then presented his other hand and opened it and within was a small stone and the Lord spoke, "Tell me, my child, most beloved of angels. What do you see?"

Michael looked upon it and replies, "It is but a pebble, my king."

El again shook his head in the negative, "No my child, this is a great canyon, teeming with peaks that reach the uttermost sky." The Lord then blew upon Michael and when he did, a droplet of water fell upon Michael's cheek and the angel wiped the small tear of water from his face. A single droplet then beaded upon his index finger. The Lord then spoke once more. "Tell me Michael of the Kortai. What is this that now sits on but the tip of thy finger?" Michael, having now been asked by the Lord a third time, perceived that his initial responses were incorrect and eyed the droplet of water that rested on his finger. And not seeking to disappoint, the Father spoke hesitantly to answer his king. "An ocean my Lord?"

El smiles in approval and eyed his most beloved of angels. "Do you understand now, my son?" says El.

Perception came over the Chief Prince and Michael nodded and realized that when God thought of water, his mind saw oceans and when Michael saw but two humans. El saw a people vast as the stars in the sky.

It was a lesson he would always remember. For if in the mind of God, a seedling was a forest. What, then, must a forest itself be in the mind of God?

Michael's thoughts returned to the scene that still played out before him, and he smiled as he continued to watch the humans in worship. This was their moment...their time to bask in El's immediate presence.

El sat majestically on His throne with rod and staff in hand. Michael took in the view, savoring every image, sound, and motion before him.

For covering the great prismatic throne were the two Cherubim chosen by Talus, High Prince of House Arelim. Each one charged to grace the Mercy Seat of God. And in obedience to the command given by their Prince, each held their six angelic wings wide, stretched out in vain attempt to provide shade to the God who is light. The King of Creation looked upon his subjects with both love and a father's pride. And although the Shekinah hovered around His person, and all but the outline of his features could be seen, Michael knew El was smiling. El's robes flowed in bright crimson, purple and gold. The fabric was lined with stars, and stars upon stars. El's neck was chained with the finest links of cadmium plated golds. The Lord of Life then spoke into the ears of all that bowed before him.

"I am he that liveth and was dead; and behold, I am alive for evermore, the Amen; and who holds the keys of Hell and of Death."

The great assembly erupted in cheers and massive displays of jubilation and praise. Flags waved and many of the humans broke out in spontaneous dance. Some fell to their knees in tears while others stood in awe of El, mouthing nothing but the word "Hallelujah" repeatedly, unable to fix their eyes on anything but He who had rescued them from the clutches of Lucifer and their own slavery to sin.

Michael enjoyed this moment...until he did not.

"My Prince," the familiar voice of Argoth spoke. "My apologies, but I require your presence."

Michael sighs, then turned to his rear, and before him stood a glowing door. He walked through and behind him the singing and scene of billions of humans worshiping El disappeared and he saw Jerahmeel sitting and frowning across from Argoth, waiting for Michael quietly.

Michael looked at his friend and motioned with his head raising his eyes, expecting Jerahmeel to speak, but his brother said nothing and just solemnly locked eyes with Michael, then with his eyes, directed Michael to Argoth.

Michael looked upon the Chief of Eyes and spoke. "What have you to report?"

Argoth floated towards Michael and replied. "It is finally here, Michael."

Michael hesitated and then looked at Jerahmeel, who nodded his head in agreement.

"How much time do we have?" says Michael, unsure if he really wanted to hear Argoth's answer.

"We have run out of time Michael; for the Day of the Lord is here. The Lord has given me nothing more to dictate. And when a Grigori has ceased to write..."

Michael nodded in understanding; he turned his eyes to the ground; realizing they had little time before the events foretold would soon be calling upon them all to act. He looked at Argoth and then Jerahmeel and spoke in somber authority. "Then we must hurry, lest no flesh be saved."

Chapter Two: Chess and Angels

The wings on Olen's feet moved as a hummingbird. And with the swiftness of the same, he darted between swords and staves as the dark cloaked angels of Marduk's Imperial guards dashed after him.

"Do not let him escape!" yelled one.

Arrows flew towards him from the guards, which blocked his only way of escape.

Bolts flew to his left and right. An arrow glanced his face as he twisted and turned, weaving between each projectile. He was but one messenger of house Malakim...one against a hundred.

He knew he would not survive. Yet survival was unnecessary. Only the will of El be done. And Olen would see that Gabriel's mission to bring back the scroll of the renegade Marduk would not fail. This information must be made known to the council.

Another arrow whizzed by his face as he turned his cheek to avoid it; when suddenly he felt pain: indescribable pain.

He looked down and his leg was grazed. Blood slowly seeped through his layered beige clothed thigh. Then flashes of white-hot spasms caused his legs to tremor. And he stumbled forward, falling unto his hands.

Concentrate! Get up! Just get beyond the gate. Vantress will be waiting.

He lifted himself back up and sprinted to escape.

The cadmium entrance was closed: bolted from the inside and before him lay over fifty angels, each with arrows knocked and ready. Their tips aimed to strike him down.

"Release!" cried a gruff voice.

Once more, the sound of whizzing arrows pierced the air and swished passed Olen's ears.

Fighting through the guards of the gate was not an option. Although he was fast, there were simply too many. And his injury diminished the chances of success.

He eyed the opening above the guards and contorted his body to avoid the myriads of arrows that flew as a swarm of bees to strike him down.

It was then that he saw it. A stairwell leading to the top of the dark keep's walls. If he could leap to the railing, he could leap over the wall itself.

"Thunk."

Olen paused, looking down to see an arrowhead protruding from his left pectoral muscle. He staggered and, with his right hand, broke the shaft and faltered ever so slightly.

The chasing angels who hunted him also saw the means of escape and, like a pack of wolves, could smell that their prey was wounded and soon would be theirs.

Eridu, one of Marduk's soldiers, rode upon Wyvern-back and reached into the folds of his robe to reveal an obsidian dagger. With an underhanded throw, he flicked his wrist, launching the blade into the air. The low-flying shank of cadmium steel sliced through the air, closing towards its mark. As it flew; red eyes opened across the course of the blade and glared at Olen as he ran to escape; droplets of his blood trailing in tow.

Olen approached a guard, backhanded him across the face, and bolted up the stairwell to potential freedom. He reached the top of the walled battlements, and he saw the cutting swath of the Tigris River before him. He scanned the horizon and looked for the signal that Vantress had hidden in the brush beyond the castle walls.

There.

He leaped from the top of the battlements, his winged feet beating furiously to keep him aloft. He whizzed in the air and smiled, seeing Vantress only yards away.

He looked on in confidence even as he closed his eyes, knowing that he had fulfilled his mission to bring the Hordes secret information to light. His face contorted as he grimaced in pain, his hand clenched around a sealed parchment as he fell to the ground.

* * *

Vantress had waited patiently for Olen's return. Grumbling under his breath, the old angel had always made it a point to tackle the most challenging of Heaven's assignments and looting Marduk's stronghold fell nicely under that banner. The two angels had once been friends, but that was millennia ago. For Heaven was in civil war: a war where brother fought against brother and a war that ripped the royal houses of heaven into factions. El promised one day the conflict would end in victory for the Host. Vantress hated factions. For some said they were for Jerahmeel; and others for Marduk, and some said of Yeshua. Vantress frowned upon such division. It was a corrosive thing division: causing all sorts of brittleness to occur within the fabric of Heaven. Vantress frowned as memories flooded his mind of better times. A time before Marduk left the House of Harrada; before the renegade left the oath of his house to follow the rebel Lucifer: a leaving that opened a chasm of fellowship.

Vantress looked at the sky and marked the passage of the moon across its ceiling. Each position of the stars screamed that Olen was late in his return. The angel sworn to House Harrada paced back and forth; watching as various satellites of men streaked in their arc across the moonlit night, and he scowled his displeasure.

"Harrumph," Vantress says. He thought upon the presumptuousness of men to think that now that they could harness the atom, they possessed power. But Vantress knew better. Power was not in the splitting of the atom, but to speak into existence the very stuff of atoms themselves. THIS was power: to speak creation itself into existence. To says, "let there be light," and there be light. Vantress shook his head as he paced in his mind while awaiting Olens's return. He once more looked into the night sky as satellites orbited the earth and spoke complainingly under his breath, "God creates, but man invents." And Vantress' thoughts turned towards the sworn foe of the Host: Lucifer.

Rumor had persisted among the Horde that Lucifer had devised a scheme: a scheme to mimic the Father by begetting a son. To once more defy the order of God and to interbreed angelic kind with human: to create Abomination. A rumor he was intent to know the truth of. And for this reason, Vantress and Olen traced the source of this information to Marduk. And now Vantress waited anxiously for Olen to return to see if the information was as reported to Heaven. To know whether the Horde had indeed done according to the whispers that circulated in the Earth. And of this rumor Vantress would know.

Light flashed in the distance. Vantress jumped to attention: undoubtedly the signal of Olen. He gathered his manna leaf into his pouch and hoisted his sword over his back, lacing it with the golden threads of the manna-leaf tree. He would have to be careful to meet Olen at the rendezvous. For the patrols of Marduk had increased. They seemed to be changing their guard rotation.

Vantress slipped through the vegetation that concealed his presence. Darkness served as an excellent cover. For what remained of the Shekinah glory glowed over his angelic skin, which he took great pains to hide so as not to reveal his location. It was a strange thing to think of the Shekinah as a burden. But despite his absence from Heaven, he still retained the vestiges of the glory of God and needed to cover his face. He moved further towards the compound's walls. Marduk was wise to place his stronghold near the great city of Mecca. It was rife with all manner of daemons and principalities. Great angelic strongmen saw that humankind would never penetrate this region with the gospel of Christ. It was a powerful fortress indeed. For Marduk had influenced the princes of this land to police all forms of worship and religious expression.

"Release!" a voice in the distance cried.

Vantress watched as scores of arrows darkened what was already a black starry sky. His heart raced at the realization that Olen was under attack. He ran full sprint to see Olen jump over the black gate of Marduk's stronghold.

Olen seemed to fly confidently and waved at Vantress as he approached him. Relief washed over Vantress, and he smiled and waved back. Olen suddenly grimaced and his smooth arc of flight towards Vantress crumpled into an uncontrolled descent. Vantress watched in horror as Olen smashed into the ground.

He raced to his comrade's side to find his friend spitting up blood.

"Olen!" cries Vantress. "Can you make it?" Vantress wrapped his hands around the waist of Olen's back to lift him up and he could feel the cool moist blood that drenched his shirt. "Here, let me help you up, and we can still get out of—"

"There is no time, old friend," Olen replies. "Take the scroll and be off with you, for the rumors are true. Abomination once more lives in the Earth. Quickly now...get this to the council before it is too late. For Lucifer moves in ways both new and old. And the Chief Prince must see this."

Olen coughed up blood; choking and gasping as his angelic lungs struggled to supply him with oxygen to sustain him.

"Leave me...for the mission is all that matters. Let God be true and all things a lie."

Olen looked up as the rustling of footsteps and voices and shouts came from about fifty yards away. In the distance, he spotted Eridu, their old nemesis, closing in on their position. Adrenalin and rage rushed through his system and Olen knew Vantress would fight in vain to save them both.

"Leave me I say! Be off with you!" Olen says.

Vantress grimaced and saw a lieutenant of Marduk, Eridu, make his way towards them. He bit his lip in angst and tightly closed his eyes. He then released Olen and sprinted away into the dark carrying a scroll.

Olen set himself upright and just as he lost sight of his brother. Several of Marduk's officers broke through the tall grass and stopped short of him. Chief among them was an angel of great beauty: a Draco. He was adorned in silver and gold and the banner of Marduk encircled his arm and he wore the coat of arms of his master.

"Ah, Olen, Olen, Olen." shook the head of the angelic chief soldier. "Wherefore didst thou think that you could escape the reach of Marduk?"

Olen coughed as he spoke, spitting up blood. "Eridu, your master dooms the world. For all know that to trifle with the ordained laws of El invites disaster. Abomination cannot exist!"

Eridu reached down to stare into the dying eyes of one he had once called a comrade. "I have always perceived that you were false, always questioned your alleged story of what you said you did during the uprising in Heaven. You see; I do not believe that your stone was ever warped...never darkened as ours. You see, Olen; I believe...you are false."

Eridu reached towards Olen and lifted his breastplate, then his shirt. He stared at the stone that slowly emanated light and pulsed. It was unmarred, without taint or stain; with no visible effects that it had been affected by the Withering. Eridu's eyes moved from his captor's stone and locked with Olen's and smiled knowingly. "Even now, the Shekinah emanates ever so softly from your frame. Rumor has it that for angelic kind; El has sanctioned no afterlife. And it is even said that we are returned to the Void. Some conjecture that the Mist which underlies Heaven is naught but the disembodied spirits of our kind, each captive and aloft in a haunt of screams. Some say that the Void is the primordial state of all things...even God."

Eridu then stood to his feet as Olen's features became frozen, and his shallow breaths came to a silent halt. The eyes of Marduk's adjutant narrowed, and he smirked in satisfaction at the expiration of his deceased prey.

"If the Void is indeed where our kind goes...then know that I bid you Godspeed."

* * *

Eridu, an adjutant of Marduk; principality of Persia, returned from his hunt and bowed before his lord.

"Report!" Marduk growled.

"My liege, it is done. The lackeys of Vantress which had infiltrated our palace have been eliminated. Moreover, he has the information we have given. It is only a matter of time until Michael and the Lumazi are aware of Lucifer's schemes. Your plan has been a success."

Marduk towered over his adjutant and shook his head in disapproval. "No Eridu. It will be a success when the head of my rival—the head of Lucifer Draco hangs as an armrest for my throne. Until that day, if Lucifer cannot be destroyed, then I will destroy the seat of his covet: his only son. The upstart boy king is not yet ready to be that which Lucifer destines him to be. And the idea that this clayborn would lead our kind to victory in the war against El makes my flesh heave in disgust. I will not bow to this pretender to angelic royalty. Nor bend the knee to his pet abomination: a thing that is neither man nor angel-kind; nay Eridu...we will see Lucifer undone. For this Nephilim, he has made. This...anti-Christ" will never know it was I who killed him until it is too late."

Eridu bowed his head ever so slightly in acknowledgment to what his Lord had said and replied. "As you say, my liege: let thy will be done."

Marduk's eyes furrowed, and he stared past his servant into the realm of men beyond and spoke aloud. "There is a reason that El has prohibited insemination of the humans. Lucifer's fascination with the creatures will be the undoing of us all.

He must be stopped. This creature cannot be allowed to know what he truly is. Nor will I surrender my position to this thing. And if I must draw out the forces of Heaven, yea even risk the wrath of God to destroy this Abomination. Then know of a surety that one way or another this Anti-Christ will most surely die."

* * *

Vantress landed atop the waypoint of the cliffs of Argoth. He breathed Heaven's air and took into himself the presence of God. The Shekinah reinvigorated him, and he closed his eyes to allow himself respite. He scrunched his brow as he reflected on Olen's demise.

"Your sacrifice will not be in vain." Vantress clutched the leather parchment in his hands and looked towards the holy mountain. There he would find the Lumazi. There, he would find Michael. He spread his wings and lifted himself up to the sky and flew to the gates of the Mountain of God. He touched down and immediately he stood in the presence of the roaring seraphim. Standing 20 feet tall, their cries of HOLY, HOLY, HOLY echoed over the mountain. Each pronouncement reverberated back and tremored the ground beneath his feet. Vantress had been gone a long time. His assignment took him away when Yeshua descended to Hell and had retrieved the keys of Death and Hell. He had been away from the realm immortal for centuries. He approached the steps to the palace and looked upon the mighty seraphim that stood two to a side. Vantress felt pain as the sound of their thunderous chant of God's holiness pounded against his chest. He squinted his eyes and tilted his head as the sound produced ringing in his ears as he approached. Nevertheless, he persisted in drawing near the towering humanoid infernos and, as he did, their eyes turned to look upon him, and one unsheathed a flaming sword and menacingly stepped towards him.

Vantress backed away from the palace steps and bowed. The Seraphim stopped when Vantress's foot stood no longer on the steps. Heat emanated from the man and he waved his hand and a wall of blue fire emblazoned from him that barred Vantress's path.

A familiar voice echoed from behind the flaming wall. "Stand down Sherkanim. He may pass." And from beneath the giants towering feet a glowing figure with a shimmering halo stepped through the fire.

Michael the Chief Prince of Heaven had come to meet him.

Vantress bowed as the prince of angels approached and spoke aloud. "My prince, your servant has returned from assignment and brings the gravest of news."

Michael smiles at him and replies, "It has been some time since you have left. Why did you not return sooner? And with what report do you bring me?"

The booms of the Seraphim shook the air around the duo and visibly moved at their declarations of God's holiness.

Vantress looked at the prince and winced and replied. "May I give my Lord my report in a quieter setting?" Vantress turned his head again to in vain to protect his ears and his face continues to display grimaces of his discomfort.

Michael nodded, "Agreed." The chief prince then took Vantress by the hand and the halo above his head glowed and immediately the two were gone and re-materialized in the war room of the palace.

Vantress shook his head in an attempt to relieve the pinging that still rang in his ears. Michael took his seat at the head of the long shittim wood table. The great table was plated with gold and the floor shined with translucent gold and shimmered in prismatic colors. The walls were adorned with purple, gold, and red tapestries, and paintings supplied from each house hung on the walls of each room.

"You were summoned to Heaven, Vantress: summoned when El released Heaven to attack Satan directly. Yet you did not respond when called. You have much to explain, report of thy stewardship."

Vantress bowed again to his chief and motioned with his hand, seeking permission to be seated.

Michael raised his right eyebrow and smirked. "Does standing prevent you from giving report? For I am still waiting."

"My pardon Chief prince." Vantress replies. "When Persia fell, you commanded me to seek out the renegade Marduk; to spy out his intentions and to see if he yet remained a threat."

"You tell me nothing that I do not already know and have yet to answer my inquiry. Why were you absent without leave when I called for the whole of heaven to battle?"

"Because my chief...Abomination had risen in the earth."

Michael stood to his feet and leaned forward to make sure he heard Vantress correctly. "Did you say Abomination?"

"Yes, my prince. Marduk feigns fealty to Lucifer but secretly covets his place as head of the Horde. To this end, he continuously spies out the plans of Satan. And knowledge had come to Marduk that Lucifer had birthed a son. The Deceiver has again copied El. He believes that El's tactics with bringing Yeshua to earth in flesh justifies him to create Nephilim. For if El can mix the flesh of man and God, why then cannot angel be mixed with human? Lucifer has defied the articles of war. However, unlike in the past, when he bred an entire race of Nephilim, this time he has only brought one into the world. A male hybrid that those within the Horde have termed: the Anti-Christ."

"But, why only one man, why not create on the scale he did as in Noah's day?" Michael replies.

Vantress bowed his head down, "It is my belief, my prince, that Lucifer gambles that El will on some level, tolerate this one creature and will not move to the scale of destruction seen with the Flood."

Michael laughs, "The Withering has indeed taken him. For El's word is inviolate. He will not tolerate such a creature. Not only does Satan risk El's judgment once more, but casts the very planet under the fury of the Almighty. I fear Vantress that this will but signal the end of the season of grace that El has given to the sons of men. Have you been able to identify who the Nephilim is?"

Vantress shook his head, "Nay, my prince. I returned with this news fresh from the battlefield. With your permission, I will go and seek the creature out."

Michael reached to brace himself against the table and slammed his fist downward onto the stone slab. The sound of cracking stone was soon followed by Michael removing his fist. A deep impression of his knuckles remained imprinted in the granite.

"Has my brother gone mad? Does he not know how El will respond? The last time abomination walked the Earth, the Lord destroyed the world of men with a flood!"

Vantress nodded solemnly. "The thing is not known, my prince; perhaps El's hand has been stayed as but one Nephilim walks the Earth. Nevertheless, Marduk, however, hopes that Lucifer's actions will draw Heaven down. To bring the Godking to Earth to accomplish Satan's removal and give room to his own rise. Nonetheless, the thing is not known. But of a surety, the house of Satan has reached a level of acrimony where Satan now fights against Satan."

Michael harrumphs. "There are but plots within plots with the Adversary. And I would surmise that Lucifer's plans go well beyond what you have reported. Intelligence across the realm of men confirms your report that there exists displeasure with Satan's rule. There is indeed a rumbling among the Horde Kings. It is clearly a house divided. There are a number who are as Marduk and that seemingly fight amongst themselves. Each wreaks havoc among the children of men. I see Lucifer's kingdom slowly shredding into tatters if his actions continue. Perhaps the time of his fall is indeed finally nigh: this move to create Abomination smells of desperation on his part. He must sense the end is coming. Perhaps the Nephilim is some key. He seeks to assure his control of the Horde and guarantee him victory in his skirmish with El. But we cannot stop this thing if civil war breaks out amongst the Horde. For alas, the Sons of Adam would see devastation the likes the world has ever known."

Michael nodded his head reflecting on what he heard and turned his eyes to look upon his angelic soldier. "You have given report. Yet, none of what you have declared gives me an understanding as to why when summoned, you did not come to Heaven's aid."

Vantress swallowed hard. "Forgiveness, my prince. But I was supporting Olen, who was close to Marduk and his chief adjutant, Eridu. He was stranded in service to Marduk and sought to confirm this information. To leave him would have exposed him to death without completing the mission for which we were assigned. We both would have been exposed as frauds and this information would never have arrived to my lord. Alas, Olen perished, having sacrificed himself to see that this scroll reaches your hands."

Vantress reached into his robe and pulled from it a parchment and handed it to Michael. Michael eyed the blue stains, which revealed a handprint.

The Chief Prince eyed the scroll. "Olen's blood?" Michael asks.

Vantress nodded sadly.

Michael frowned. "Then let us pray his sacrifice was not in vain." The chief prince opened the scroll and read the crimson angelic script.

Unto the angel of my church in Mecca,

These things writes he who has bled God and hast been declared the god of this world. Your sworn king, and he who has walked within the midst of the Stones of Fire. For three transgressions and for four know that I have ought against thee, for my son hast informed me that thou hast failed to honor him and assure him passage through Persia that he might see to the Mohammedan threat which dares challenge my rule in Mecca. Know that this sleight will not be forgotten. You are hereby required to give account of thy stewardship in this matter and will attend me on the fortnight of the upcoming blood moon. You will bow the knee, and you will reaffirm your loyalty to your king. Remember therefore from whence thou hast fallen and from whence I found thee defeated at the hands of the Lumazi. Remember when my loyal servant Zeus found thee and I lifted you up on high to archon over the sons of Ham. Yet though I have lifted thee up and your star hast arisen in Persia. Know that my wrath hast been kindled against thee for the dishonor that you have shown my only begotten son. You will submit as required, but of a surety know that if thou fail me in this thing, then I will descend upon you and your company as a sure coming wind and will remove your candlestick and Mecca from its place. And who then will save you from my hand?

Your Lord and King, Ruler of the true Host and defender of the cause of self-rule.

Lucifer Draco

Michael re-rolled the scroll and his eyes narrowed as he reflected upon its contents. "If Marduk refuses to bow the knee...if would be a first that a principality of such power would defy my brother. I know Lucifer. His response would be swift, decisive and awash with a display of destruction to make others fear." Michael turned to Vantress and eyed him inquisitively. "What do you think Marduk will do?"

Vantress rubbed his chin and replied. "I and Olen have spied him for many of man's centuries. He is cunning and proud. He will not bow the knee. And if he does, it will surely be in feigned submission. No matter his actions. He has stirred at least three of the kings of the Horde to quiet rebellion against Lucifer. If they choose to band as one and march the earth..."

Michael sighs. He knew the destructive powers of those who had fallen from heaven. Major angelic powers El had allowed to roam free among men. Michael knew that if unleashed, if the Hordes fear of El was lost or their faculties of reason so diminished from the Withering that they loosed to open war...

Michael shuddered.

He knew that El would seek their destruction. El's patience was infinite, but He had made it clear that He would only endure his celestial children's tantrums for so long, and then: then the end would come. All things pointed to Michael's fear that perhaps the planet could not be spared open warfare. That even though redeemed men swelled Heaven's ranks daily. Once more, heaven would be forced to descend en mass to destroy.

Vantress interrupted Michael's musing. "Excuse me, my prince. But I have completed my assignment. We now have actionable intelligence that Marduk and Lucifer will assemble in Pergamos...."

"Lucifer has moved his headquarters." Michael blurts out. "He no longer resides in the ancient city. He has found a new place to lay his deceitful head."

"My prince?" says Vantress.

"We have been abreast of Satan's movements via the Grigori. He beds in the continent of Europe. And we have traced his location to Strasbourg, France."

Vantress nodded, "Then I will be on way and make incursion to disrupt his plans." Vantress bowed, then turned to walk away.

Michael called after him. "No, Vantress. A new assignment hast thou been given. To ferret out the schemes of Lucifer hast now been given to another."

Vantress frowned and spoke up in objection. "But my prince, I have spent the better part of a millennium working to undermine the enemy and bring you this information! Please do not release me from this charge until I have seen to its completion."

Michael walked towards Vantress and eyed him, tilting his head as he studied his angelic soldier in silent investigation.

"Nay, Vantress, the decision is final. You are relieved of this charge and reassigned. For the Lord has spoken it. He has given thee a new charge; one He has stated carries the highest importance. You are to see to a maiden who teeters on the brink of self-destruction."

Vantress drew back in anger and disgust. "A human? I've been tracking Elohim, nay fighting—Elohim, continuously working to undermine he who brought to our home, and introduced to the universe the savages of war. And now, in the grand scheme of God's design, I am charged with watching over a human female?"

Michael looked at him with amusement, but only for a moment, as his voice rose slightly in angry response. "And does the charge given by the Lord seem beneath you? Who has made thy mouth and the stone which beats within thy breast? Where *you* first to lay eyes on Creation? Where were you when status was given as Archon over the legions of Sol? Who is this that stands before me as if he barks commands to a Horde dog? If I am thy prince, where is my honor? If thy commander, where then my fear?"

Vantress winced at the rebuke and bowed in obeisance. "Apologies, my prince: I meant no disrespect. I have been away too long and spent much of my time in warfare behind enemy lines. Any assignment given by my king will, of course, be obeyed and given the utmost in attention to duty. Nevertheless, please do not be angry with your servant. Who is this maid that El himself would draw me away from undermining the Kingdom of Satan?"

Michael smiles, "Know ye not Vantress that all missions from El undermine Satan? Know, however, that she is but a young lass and the Lord will see to her salvation. And you—you will see that she is allowed to make the decision to come to Christ without interference from the enemy."

Vantress nodded, "But Michael...what importance is she to El that I personally must go and be wet nurse to this human? Even as we speak, we may well soon be at the brink of escalated war with the Horde now that Abomination walks the Earth."

Michael smiles as he answers. "It is simple Vantress: El loves her."

Vantress sighs, bowed again to the high prince, turned and mumbles his consternation under his breath. Michael smiled as the angel walked away, then looked down where his fist had indented the stone table. He furrowed his brow, for he had now been given two reports, and the fears that the Apostle John had shared in his tome could only mean that the end of all things was indeed nigh. Michael closed his eyes in quiet rumination, sighed, and then spoke aloud, shaking his head.

"Lucifer, what you have done?"

* * *

Enoch and Elijah sat next to one another, eating dinner together. The sound of crunched manna leaf being slowly overturned within Elijah's jaws reminded Enoch of the cows he used to tend while on Earth. It irritated the old man then, and it irritated him even more so now.

"Here," Enoch says. "Take some honey ale to wash that down. Let's see if the drink will silence the echo of mastication that surely will rumble even over the cliffs of Argoth."

Elijah laughs and looked at his friend. Ale dribbled down his mouth and he lifted his arm and wiped his mouth against his sleeve, grinning as he looked at Enoch. He then closed his fist and thumped his chest twice and let out a deep sounding burp. The volume and duration was so pronounced that Enoch thought if not for the Lord's command for the cliffs to be silent, Elijah's belch would have reverberated through the air to the holy mountain itself.

Enoch shook his head, then spoke. "Goodness man. I'm not sure whose appetite is greater: yours or Jerahmeel's."

Elijah tucked his chin into his breast and let out a second exhale of throat lurching gas. "Oh, it's definitely Jerahmeel." He replies.

Suddenly, a flash of light appeared above and before them. Each man squinted, tilted their head, and moved their hands to cover their eyes. For hovering within a stone's throw appeared a man transparent in form and with wings. Light danced around him in a prismatic spectacle. The duo immediately took to their knees, then lowered their face to the ground.

"My king," they say as one.

The Holy Spirit floated above them in illuminated brilliance and spoke, and His voice was as waters that crashed against the shore, "The time we have discussed hast now arrived. For the curtain hast been drawn back and the last days are now revealed. Therefore, get thee down to my people and speak what I command thee. Proclaim my word, perform my wonders and when thou hast fallen at the hands of the enemy: after three days will I raise thee up and thou shalt be taken away: even from the midst of their sight."

The Holy Spirit then waved his hand and Enoch and Elijah's clothes transformed into sackcloth. Immediately both men rose to their feet, and as they did so, the coarse animal hair caused their skin to irritate as they moved, causing both men to vigorously scratch themselves.

Enoch looked upon the Holy Spirit pleadingly, as an adolescent child would beg with a parent who dressed them in clothing not to their liking. He looked upon his garb and waved his hands downward over the new camel attire with which he now wore.

"My King," Enoch grimaced. "Must we truly wear this for three and a half years?" He then rubbed his shoulders, feeling incredibly exposed. "May I die now and come back?"

The Holy Spirit laughs, "Off with you now," he says. He then flicked his wrist and sent the duo on their way to Earth.

* * *

Michael watched as each of his angelic brothers took their seats in the war room of the Lumazi. Each had grown as leaders of their house; each the best of their respective clans; each the living embodiment and the federal representative of their race. This was the council of all things Elohim. And the group had now assembled themselves at Michael's call.

One by one they arrived and settled at the circular table centered in the room; each stood waiting for the chief prince to give pronouncement. Michael removed the halo which floated above his head with it, unsheathed his sword and placed both his angelic crown and the sword of Ophanim on the table. Each high prince followed in suite laying their weapons and crowns before them. All stood with him and he opened the session, as was custom, with his invocation in a call to service to El.

"There is one God who stands as Creator of all things. The Father of us all, Judge of all the heavens. Let His wisdom guide us. His commands steel us. His love preserve us. We are the Lumazi, and His will be done this day. So say we all."

Each replies as one, "So say we all."

The seven angels seated themselves and waited for Michael to speak.

"I have received report." says Michael. "A report that I know will concur with the intelligence we have been receiving from the Grigori. It would seem that our fears have been realized and that once more Abomination walks the earth."

Talus gasped, placed his hands over his face, then leaned back into his chair. Looks of concern permeated each face in the room.

Jerahmeel spoke hesitantly, weighing his words. "Michael...abomination was what unleashed the wrath of God upon the Earth: a deluge that broke the world and drowned the inhabitants therein. If Lucifer has once again inbred with the humans...if he has violated the articles of war..." Jerahmeel's voice trailed off and he swallowed hard. "What then of the inhabitants of the planet? Surely El will not stand idle, and his wrath may very well this time consume the remnants of the world."

Gabriel also spoke, "Michael, my people...all of us; have committed ourselves to the protection of those who have surrendered themselves to Yeshua's lordship. We have gone to great pains to succor them from the wiles of the Devil; and whilst we can indeed work to keep them in the bosom of the Lord. We cannot protect them from the wrath of the living God Himself. What are we to do?"

Michael nodded. "The thing that you say is true. We cannot protect mankind from God's wrath. Yet I perceive that such will not be our task. Even now, before the altar of the Lord simmers a bowl; contained therein are the prayers of saints boiling in anger. The urn reeks and ulcers are awash across its sides as pustules burst in precatory cries of vengeance to God. It is ever before the Almighty. Have we not all heard the shrieks that emanate from within?

'How long, O Lord, holy and true, dost thou not judge and avenge our blood on them that dwell on the earth?'

"Have we not seen El grow increasingly somber as He eyes events below? Nevertheless, ours is not to concern ourselves over the angst of the Almighty, but to obey His command, and to see that none of His words fall to the ground. And this we shall do. In the meantime, and until El gives command, that alters, we will continue to protect humanity from Satan. Therefore, my command is this. We shall locate the Abomination, determine if the creature is localized or if a plague of them exists as before and now runs amok among the Horde. Now go, look throughout the Earth. See if the things are true, for if so we know that judgment is not far behind. If judgment comes..."

Michael paused, looking down, and his face grew stern in determination. "Save all that you can: for unless the Lord's wrath is abated, there should no flesh be saved. Now go. Hurry and make haste.

And do all that is in thy power to implore the star of each church as never before to raise their voice that all men might be saved and come to Christ before it is too late."

Each angel then rose to their feet and bowed, lifted their crowns and weapons from the table, and hastily made their exit. Each wondering how long they had before El's anger would swallow the planet, and perhaps the multiverse, in its wake.

"Hold Argoth." says Michael. "I would have a word with you in private before you leave."

Argoth stopped and floated in the air. His back was to Michael and his cloak and cowl covered his features that he could not be seen. His golden eyes narrowed even further, and he turned his head slightly and spoke. "How may the Grigori serve the Chief Prince?"

Michael still stood behind the circular head of the table and projected his voice across the room. "I will ask you directly Argoth and please do not frustrate me with your riddles. For I know that you keep the tome to the Book of Life itself, thus tell me—do you know where this creature...this Abomination; lays its head?"

Argoth floated, and his voice changed as if he spoke as a multitude. "We are the Grigori. We know all that the Almighty allows us to see."

Michael sighs, "Then where does the creature lay its head?"

Argoth then turned to face his brother. He slowly floated over the table and hovered an arm's distance above Michael, and his eyes opened wide, showing the golden hue that fired all Grigori.

"You ask me a question that you are loathing to ask yourself. You query me Chief Prince, when the answer is nigh thee, yea even in your mouth. You interrogate the Chief of Eyes when the beating stone within you cries out to investigate that which you already know to be true."

Michael slammed his fist on the table. "Did I not ask you to spare me your riddles and speak plainly?"

Slowly Argoth tilted his head, amused; then turned his back on Michael to float away. "There is truly one that you may ask who knows the answer that you seek. Ask and it shall be given, seek and ye shall find."

Michael called after Argoth as he floated away. "You speak the Lord's words back to me?"

"Indeed," replies Argoth. "Query the Father Chief Prince. For you know that if you lack wisdom that you may ask of God, who will give to you liberally, and upbraid you not and it shall be given unto thee. But beware, my friend, that thou ask not amiss, for who knows that if pursuit of your query will lead you only to an answer that you have avoided. To mayhap see he who even now, after all this time...you still love?"

Argoth stopped at the doorway's entrance and continued. "Lucifer will surely be both author and finisher of your inquiry. But know this Michael. For where Lucifer is, surely the Abomination will be also nursing at his breast."

Michael bit his lip in angst as Argoth floated out of the room.

Chapter Three: The Wrath of God

Michael entered the throne room, and it shown in brilliant waves of white upon white. A sea of glass emanated from the throne. And round about the throne were now twenty-four thrones, and each seated a human who gleamed and sang praises to the Lord God.

"Thou art worthy to take the book, and to open the seals thereof: for thou wast slain and hast redeemed us to God by thy blood out of every kindred, and tongue, and people, and nation; And hast made us unto our God kings and priests: and we shall reign on the earth."

The archangel eyed the lavar that was positioned before the altar of God. It raged in fire that rivaled the kiln itself. It was a fire that was inflamed by the very prayers of the saints. Prayers that had accumulated over the millennia were now boiling over to overflowing. Prayers that appealed to the God of Creation—for vengeance.

Michael knelt before his king and spoke, “My Lord, I come to make inquiry and, if possible, plead a case for mercy.”

But El was silent as he stared at the foul-smelling vapor that emanated from the prayers. Screams and tortured anguished cries that captured the Almighty’s ears. For the Lord God was observant to the goings on of his realm and his eyes were ever watchful over the death of his saints. Michael knew the Lord’s patience was infinite. Yet he also knew that God would not stand idle forever to the cries of his people. That in the course of due time there would be a reckoning to those who had caused harm to his children, and he shuddered at the thought. The Lord frowned at the aroma, for it stunk and reeked of blood, pain, and decay. The Virtues hovered over the lavar constantly, but it was becoming increasingly evident that the stench and the cry of the saint’s prayers could no longer be covered: no longer scented by the Virtues. God stared at the whiffs of scented smoke that rose, and his countenance changed. The Lord God then stood to his feet and made pronouncement.

“I have surely seen the affliction of my people and have heard their cry by reason of their prayers; for I know their sorrows. And am moved to deliver them out of the hand of the Enemy, and to bring them to the house that I have prepared for them. Now therefore, behold, the cry of my children has come unto me: and I have also seen the oppression wherewith the Adversary oppresses them. Where is the tome that chronicles the sins of these below? Where is the book that I have had sealed? Where is our Sephiroth?"

Argoth then stepped into the throne room and knelt before his king. "I am the book that is written by all. The Sephiroth of my Lord." Argoth's stylus and tome then materialized to be seen. And the Lord extended his outstretched hand and Argoth stepped into the right hand of the Lord and a mist overtook him, and when the mist dissipated nothing was seen save a book with seven seals.

Michael marveled, for he knew not that Argoth was the living book of Seals. The walking embodiment of God's chronicle of both Elomic and mankind's sins. Argoth was the written chronicles of the Lord's ought against the children of men. And the book was written within and on the backside and sealed with seven seals. And the book was sealed and no man in heaven, nor in earth, neither under the earth, was able to open the book, neither to look thereon for it contained the oughts of the Lord.

Michael looked to his left and then to his right, and as far as the eye could see, redeemed men and angels spied the tome in the Lord's hand. For the book was raised high for all to see. The Lord's silence and raised hand echoed that today would be the day that would usher in the beginning of the end. Today Michael knew—judgment would commence. Michael then swallowed hard, knowing that he had but little time, and proclaimed with a loud voice.

"But lord who is worthy to open the book, and to loose the seals thereof? For who can recite the transgressions of the Creator against the creation?

His voice traversed the skies of heaven, and nothing dared to reply. For the query was to the Lord alone.

Michael then beheld that within the midst of the throne and of the Ophanim and Seraphim and in the midst of the elders, stood a Lamb as if it had been slain, and Yeshua the Son of God came and took the book out of the right hand of him that sat upon the throne. And immediately when he held the book, all crowned threw their crowns before Yeshua.

And extemporaneously, the whole of Heaven sung a new song, saying,

"Thou art worthy to take the book, and to open the seals thereof: for thou wast slain and hast redeemed us to God by thy blood out of every kindred, and tongue, and people, and nation; And hast made us unto our God kings and priests: and we shall reign on the earth."

Michael then rallied the angelic host round about the throne and the beasts and the elders: and the number of them was as the stars in the universe for they were ten thousand times ten thousand, and thousands of thousands.

Each then cries out with a loud voice says, "Worthy is the Lamb that was slain to receive power, and riches, and wisdom, and strength, and honor, and glory, and blessing." And the Ophanim in a rare display spoke and said, "Amen." And the four and twenty elders fell down and worshiped him the Lord Yeshua, which liveth for ever and ever.

Yeshua then took the book from El's hand and proceeded to break the first seal. And when he did, thunder erupted from the skies and the palace shook, and dust and debris loosed from the ceiling and fell upon all that saw. And a pale-colored mist lifted from the book, and within could be seen a vision that materialized. And Michael's eyes lowered in regret that after centuries nay millennia of the forbearance of God. His pent-up wrath would now be released. His eyes widened as he saw the figure within the mist. For it was a man atop a white horse and he that sat upon him had a bow; and a crown was given unto him: and he went forth conquering, and to conquer.

The Lord soured at the vision, and He frowned at the image and stood to his feet and raised a golden scepter made of glass and iron to make pronouncement. Michael dashed to the throne and while doing so waved at him in abeyance and cried before the Lord could utter judgment and lifted his voice that the Creator of the Universe might hear. And Michael reached to grab the very ankles of God and prostrated himself before his king crying aloud.

"Lord forgive thy servant. But I ask for mercy. For there are so many that have not yet heard the gospel of the kingdom." The Lord's face was flushed in anger as he surveyed the images of he who rode on the white horse. Yet his eyes caught Michael's, and his countenance softened, and he spoke to his angelic son.

"Go and save all that you can. For are there not still the elect who must be gathered? Go and be quick, if not for the elect's sake, none would survive. For the cry of my people calls me and my hand will no longer spare."

Michael released the Lord's ankles and scooted himself away in obeisance. And he rose and turned to quickly withdraw himself to do the Lord's will. He gazed at the human in the vision from the seal that was broken. Its fog like visage still hovered before the throne and the eyes of all. And his own eyes widened in recognition of the features of the man with the bow. His heart skipped a beat in trepidation and understanding; for in the view of the Lord was a man. And while the human was not Elohim. The face of the man could not be mistaken...for it was none other than Lucifer's.

* * *

"Ashtaroth, your foolish concerns bore me. Tell my father I have already secured the vote from parliament. My negotiation of the treaty between Israel and her enemies has given me the platform to fulfill my plans. Tell him that his impatience is unbecoming of someone who has witnessed the creation."

Argoth looked at Leto and replies, "You will soon have occasion to speak to him yourself, as I merely herald his presence. For he will arrive here shortly. Nor will I sully myself to speak to the God-king in such a fashion. And if you value the life he has given thee—you would be wise to do the same. For what the Lord god Lucifer hath given, he can surely take away."

Leto laughs as he poured himself a glass of wine. "You think me daft? Surely the works of my father I will do." He smirked as he spoke the words. "Am I not my father's son? I do not fear him..." and he turned to look at the fallen angel. "You, however, Astarte... you definitely should."

Ashtaroth's anger grew, and he flew to Leto and raised his hand to strike him. He opened his palm, swinging it wildly, seeking to connect with the Nephilim's cheek. But Leto caught his wrist and stopped him.

Leto firmly held to the angel's forearm and then tightened his grip.

Ashtaroth winced in pain as he was reminded at that moment that Leto carried Elomic blood in his veins. Reminded that he was not human.

"You forget your place, vassal. You serve my father; therefore, you serve me. Lift your hand again and I will send you back to my father with it broken. Are we clear?"

Ashtaroth grimaced as he twisted his forearm. And his glaring eyes and scowl communicated a defiance to the human that stood before him.

Dissatisfied with silence, Leto pressed him further. "I said Astarte, are we clear?"

Ashtaroth jeered at him and nodded.

"I cannot hear you," goaded Leto.

"I am clear. Release me... please." Ashtaroth wimpishly replies.

Leto complied, and Ashtaroth jerked his arm back, rubbing his wrist and forearm gingerly.

Leto laughs, "You have the pride which was my father's downfall. Yet have I not been raised to rival and bring down Christ himself? Yet in your folly you would seek to strike me—me? Pitiful. I can see why the father God cast you all out. But fear not my friend. If the return to your exiled home is what you seek, know I will surely return you to the land of your banishment."

"And who will return you from Hades? Should I seek your incarceration in Hell?" a gruff, melodious voice bellows.

Both Leto and Ashtaroth turned to see that Lucifer had entered their chamber. Ashtaroth bowed as was custom whilst Leto smiled, happy to see his father and moved to embrace him.

But Lucifer stopped him as he advanced and said, "You will do me the honor a son owes his father and a worshiper to his God. Or by the Third Heaven know I will strike you down where you stand and shall mix my blood with one who is more worthy to yield it."

Leto frowned and immediately was sobered by Lucifer's words. He bowed his head, then fell to one knee and replies, "Apologies, father. Please forgive your servant."

Lucifer then spoke to Ashtaroth, who was still on bended knee. "Rise, my friend, and leave us. I would have words with my son."

Ashtaroth did as commanded and walked past Leto, who smirked and eyed the angel as he left. The adjutant of Lucifer then spoke to his master. "He has much to learn about respect, my king. He is still not fully versed in the ways of old nor of our people. His disdain for authority knows no bounds." Ashtaroth looked down upon the human, displeased, as he approached his master.

Lucifer chuckles, "And who would teach him this in this regard? You? He is a brand plucked from the fire. My beloved son in whom I am well pleased. Indeed, does his temperament not rival my own? Fear not Astarte. He will learn obedience, and when he is ready. He will rise from Death itself and challenge Christ, yeah mayhap the Father God himself, and when we are done. I will become the true God of the universe. Now leave us."

Ashtaroth nodded in obeisance and exited the room. And the ruler of darkness stood before his creation and spoke.

"Rise, my son, and embrace your father."

Leto arose from his knelt position and walked into the extended arms of Lucifer Draco.

Lucifer rubbed his hair then gently took him by the shoulder and pushed him an arm's length from him. "Who am I?" Lucifer inquired of his son.

"You are my maker. You have given me flesh and my veins pumps with your blood."

"Aye," says Lucifer. "I have nurtured man's dabbling into artificial life and his ability to clone and have seeded his progress towards making you... my greatest creation. From the very DNA that lined the mouth of Adam have I made thee." Lucifer then revealed a dried fruit from within the folds of his robes and lifted it before the eyes of his son. "From the knowledge of good and evil doth the saliva of the man's first bite echo through both time and creation."

Leto stared upon the fruit and stood in awe. "Is this the actual fruit my forebear bit into?" Even withered, the pome shown with a faint luminescence. "A trophy of mine," Lucifer grinned. "One of many I keep of my skirmishes with El." Lucifer gloated, and he reflected as his eyes drifted up and he spoke. "Long ago I stood across from my maker, devoted to my king's service, when he posited me the question of what He should give to his greatest creation. A question I presumed I was the object of. Never realizing until it was too late that he had created a being designed to supplant us. But lo, I have meditated on the ways of the Father. For I was the anointed cherub that covered and know Him as none other save God himself could know. I was there when celestial life was made. And I have studied well. I now have come to fulfill the words that Christ once said towards his followers. For I have now become as my master and the servant as his Lord."

Lucifer then turned to look his son in the eyes and beamed as he spoke. "For I, too, have created a son. From the same fruit bitten by thy forerunners. With the selfsame fruit from the Tree of the

Knowledge of good and evil have I preserved to one day use the fabric of El's own created life against Him. And now behold my creation, my wonderful son. For thou art a new thing, neither fully man nor fully angel. You are my Anti-Christ. A new creation bonded with the genes of mankind and Elohim. But so much more, for your very consciousness hast been imbued with an artificial computational power that would rival my own."

Lucifer smiles and caressed the cheek of his son, marvels over the being that stood before him. "Yet you are incomplete. For you must yet go the way of all men and demonstrate your true power. The power over death itself. For I know that Charon hast not encountered the likes of you. But your time is not yet nigh. But soon all will be revealed. But enough of forthcoming plans and that which is yet to come. Stand before me now and report of thy stewardship."

Leto stood to attention and reported as commanded. "I have secured the support of the voting members of the Security Council. They have been taught to realize that failure to comply with my directives brings with it death. For I have shown them but a glimpse of my power, and for the sake of their own lives and that of their families, and yeah, even their countrymen. They know when the time is given to nominate me as Secretary General that if the vote is not in the affirmative for my ascension that they will never leave the assembly alive and all blood lines by which they are named shall be snuffed out from the Earth."

Lucifer nodded, and a smile curled over his lips. "Well done, my son...continue."

Leto beamed in pride and carried on. "I have placed the algorithm you have devised into the systems of the planet's computer networks. I have but to speak and my adjutants will cripple all commercial enterprise and bring the industries and technologies of the world to a halt. When I have revealed that the solution to access the locked systems is my encryption code embedded within the block-chain of my temporal lobe. All will yield to me and pay to bring relief to their people." Leto then lifted his hand and within his palm was a marking in angelic script and it was the number 666."

The Mark, my lord, is ready to be unleashed upon command. I will require the whole planet to utilize the encryption key to unlock access to all digital transactions. No man will be able to buy or sell without it. I will have complete control over the economies of the nations and my name... no, we will stamp your name, Father, in the head and hands of all that live on the earth."

Lucifer nodded. "Well done, but be still in thy confidence: for power over man's greed is not power enough to dominate. For total control, you must be prepared to destroy the hope that will rise in a vain attempt to defy you. I have foreseen that many a nation will join to rebel against this solution. Each foolish soul yearning to breathe free, to escape bondage to my will. Yea, many shall rise to resist the new order we will bring. They will stack themselves against thee, but you will go out and meet them in battle and destroy the last hope of men. For it must be that if you are to ascend to heaven, the planet itself must draw the ire of the Almighty such that He will have no choice but to respond. Even now the end has begun; for two humans out of time have been seen preaching near the Wailing Wall in Jerusalem. Faces I have not seen for a long time."

Leto looked upon his creator puzzled and spoke, "There have been humans who have seen your face and lived?"

Lucifer stared afar off and replies, "Aye, two who have escaped death and who in their foolishness hath returned to sport with me. But fear them not. They too shall feel the sting of death. But not before the time appointed."

Leto nodded quietly, still processing the words of his father and he spoke his query. "Father, who is Charon?"

Lucifer looked at his son and his brow furrowed as he stared deep into Leto's eye. "The last enemy you must overcome before you may ascend to challenge El. Now get thee up and be about my business; for the wrath of God, we must further provoke."

Chapter Four: The Drums of War

Elizabeth Foley rushed to enter Mrs. Blake's social studies class and promptly made her way to the back of the room to find an empty seat. The slim young lady brushed her brunette hair aside, sat down and hunched inconspicuously in her seat as much as possible. The last thing she wanted was to be bullied again by the Jefferson sisters today. She glanced to see that they were not in class. Probably skipping again, she thought to herself. She didn't understand why they had it in for her. They were juniors, she a sophomore. So, no threat there and they were prettier and more popular. It seemed to Elizabeth that they wasted so much time on her for no reason other than to torment her needlessly. Elizabeth toiled in her mind on what she could have done to offend the twins so much that they made it their life's duty to torment her.

The 5th hour bell rang and the clock on the wall showed 1:05pm. Soon she could go home. Mrs. Blake broke up her ruminations, "Please turn to page 130 in your textbook. I trust everyone has done the homework and read chapter ten on the differences between the various world religions?"

Elizabeth opened her book to the required page and saw the comparative religion chart she had been assigned to study. Mrs. Blake then began her daily lecture. Elizabeth struggled to focus but smiled sheepishly to herself. She couldn't get her earlier encounter with Mike Gaines out of her mind. Elizabeth sat quietly in her seat, elbow on the desk with her hand under her chin as she replayed in her head her earlier encounter with the handsome Mike Gaines. Elizabeth curled her dark hair around her finger as her mind wandered from comparative world religions to the far more important dreamy Michael Gaines.

"You know, I never noticed how pretty you are, humph. Who knew?" he says offhandedly. Mike looked at her as if he were testing her. Her dark hair flowed down to her shoulders, and her olive complexion was sprinkled with acne, which she continuously fought in vain to keep at bay. Like many of the sophomores that eyed him. Mike smiled with a coy grin, aware that she enjoyed his attention.

"You know you should come by this Friday for the house party I'm having. I know I don't normally see you at any of the other house parties, but it's all good. There's no reason I can't introduce you to some seniors. Hey here's an invitation. If you get to come, just flash this and tell them Mike sent you."

Elizabeth blushed and giggled at his comment. The senior high school president was seemingly not just inviting her to a party but was also now interested in her!

"Yeah, I'll come. That's awesome Mike, thanks for inviting me!" Elizabeth giggles as she lowered her gaze and caught Mike catching her blush once more.

"It's all good," he says. "Hope to see you Friday."

Elizabeth waved goodbye and turned to walk away, beaming in delight that perhaps after months of being bullied by the Jefferson sisters and feeling so out of place at school. She might have actually now found her social bearings. She turned around to see Mike staring at her bottom. She quickly turned her head, blushing even more; her eyes nervously rolled around in her head in both disbelief and giddy excitement.

Elizabeth suddenly realized that her elbow shifted and that the book she had opened slid off her desk, and with it her papers tumbled in a scattered mess on the floor.

Mrs. Blake's voice was quick to commented on her daydreaming, "Ms. Foley, I'm sorry if I am boring you. But please pay attention. Now if you would be so kind as to pick up your things from the floor and rejoin the class in the here and now."

Elizabeth's eyes darted to the other students, who were smiled or sniggered at her. She scampered to grab her things and slouched into her seat to retreat into her makeshift cocoon. And replied. "Sorry Mrs. B."

Mrs. Blake shook her head with a disapproving scowl and resumed her lecture. "As I was saying, Christ is the central figure in the Christian religion. While we can indeed find many tenants or teachings that are similar in other religions, what is unique about Christianity is that its claims rest on the actual resurrection of its founder. Unlike the other monotheistic religions such as Judaism and Islam, neither purports that its founder is still alive or claims to have been resurrected from the dead. The historical question of Jesus's claim to be God and his bodily resurrection is the foundation upon which the whole of Christendom is founded."

Elizabeth took her eyes off the chart showing those things unique to various religions of the world and saw it was now 1:50pm and that the bell would ring soon to release for the day. Then she fell back in her seat as she realized that when she turned around, Michael Gaines had been looking at her still as she walked away and thought to herself with a sheepish grin.

Oh, my gawd! Was he staring at my ass?

She giggled at the prospect of kissing Mike. The bell suddenly rang, and she and the class quickly launched themselves to escape Mrs. Blake's lecture, and she hurried to her locker to grab her book bag and run home.

* * *

And the time had come when the General Assembly of the United Nations had convened for the sixty-sixth time. That Leto sat with the delegation from France. Men and women from every tribe of man assembled themselves in the great hall to determine who among them would next be the leader to the nations of the Earth. The assembly then adopted by acclamation a resolution to appoint Leto Alexander as the sixteenth Secretary General of the United Nations.

Applause erupted through the room, and Leto approached the podium to accept his post and set himself to speak. Teleprompters were to his right and left, ready to relay his prepared remarks.

"To my distinguished colleagues, esteemed members of the security council, and to all the people of the world. It is with great honor that I stand before you now to carry on the tradition of advocating for peace and to stand as a symbol of United Nations ideals; ideals that exist to serve humanity's interests as a spokesperson for the interests of the world's people. And thus, it is with a deep sense of stewardship and humility I accept your nomination as your secretary general."

Applause and cheers echoed throughout the great assembly, and all rose to their feet in ovation. "Here, here!" echoed throughout the room. For at last, many held the belief that before them stood a man of the people who represented the best in the world. Leto raised his arms and gestured with his hands for the audience to be seated.

"Please," he says. "I thank you for you trust in me and it is an immense comfort to know your support will help me in fulfilling my formidable duties to serve. Yet I must confess I also stand before you in great trembling and fear. For this is also an occasion where I must now function in one of the saddest duties of my office, and that is to inform the security council and the world of an existential threat that threatens to undermine all that we hold dear. To finally reveal with my ascension: a truth that my staff in Europa have confirmed: a truth that even now is making its way into the hands of government leaders as we speak. The truth, ladies and gentlemen; that we are under threat by nothing less than an intelligent species that seeks our demise."

A media handler at the UN broadcast booth whispered, "He's off script. Kill the prompter. He's off script. Something's going on" News outlets which had been given a version of the speech earlier scrambled to retract editions of papers and redo already prepared broadcasts.

Meanwhile, gasps and echoes escaped from the mouths of many in the UN chambers, audible laughter and chuckles could be heard from some. Yet the chamber slowly fell into a deafening silence as Leto waited for them to finish in their initial reactions as all realized that Leto was deadly serious, and everyone looked on both focused and flabbergasted. Leto looked upon them all tight-lipped and his stoic face nodded and communicated they were not victims of some cruel hoax or joke, but that the words he spoke were belief-filled. The fog of his revelation hovered heavily over the crowd, a fog only dissipated by the resumption of his words.

Leto continued, “We have been a people deceived. From as far back as recorded history, we have been the pawns in an invisible struggle for both dominion and our domination: dominion over a throne which has been until now outside the realm of our reach and beyond our capacity to see or understand. But we lack this capacity no more. For humanity has now eclipsed the restraints imposed upon us and we shall no longer be pawns in a war of beings who walk among us to our hurt.

Many of you now look upon me confused, even skeptical. For you, ask yourselves, with what proof do I have that my words are true? What evidence do I present before this body to substantiate the veracity of that which I speak? It is a fair and predictable question for which I have anticipated: the answer of which I display before you all now.”

Leto then gestured and a blue curtain drew back to reveal an Ophanim chained with fetters of iron and arcs of energy surrounded the creature as if it was held within a cage of electrified plasma. The creature when it saw the multitudes that looked upon it. Roared and its gears and wings rotated in fury and gushes of wind swept over the crowd, papers whirled off desks and many placed their hands over their faces to protect themselves from the dust that swirled into the eyes of all present. Many leapt from their seats in fear and hastened a quick retreat to the chamber's exit. Security lifted their weapons, training them on the creature if it broke from its restraints. The creature then rose, and its frame touched the electrified barrier, and sparks flew within the voltaic cage, and it howled in both pain and rage and then settled back to the ground and growled its displeasure.

“Yes, see the creature that I have tamed. But this is but one, one of a great many, that play chess with humanity as tokens in their invisible celestial game.”

“But I fear that this revelation is but the beginning. For it is also true that a realm is indeed aflame with the living souls of our kind. Hell, as we have been taught for centuries, is indeed a place that is real. Our families and friends, fathers and mothers, brothers and sisters rot in a prison that I vow shall be breached. I tell you that the myth of Hell is a reality, and I have seen what awaits us in the afterlife. A life of consumption by a creature created by a being; whom in his alleged benevolence secretly builds invisible armies and manipulates our kind. It is an engine that both fires and feasts off the horrors of mankind's greatest fears. And the cult of Christians which we have lifted in preeminence in our world: have known this truth.”

“Yes, Christianity: a religion that many in this room have embraced. A religion that enables our servitude to their God. A group of people who in their naiveté spread this cancerous lie: that a God lives in Heaven and He watches over man to his good. This is a falsehood and a treacherous and systemic lie to weaken humanity. For our wars have been naught but the ravaging of these beings over us: their invisible presence; merely pollinating and flowering humanity's dissension. Invisible creatures, which have continually undermined our cognizance, that we are one people: and why? Because they fear us. They fear what we may become. And for good reason are we seen as a threat. A menace that, if truly unleashed, could threaten their way of life. But as your leader, I commit to you we will free them of this fear. We will free them by robbing them of their ability to control us any longer. For they have thought to nurture us after their kind and after their likeness; all that we might be but chattel to be used and then thrown away. But I will NOT be chattel. I will not surrender my will to this so-called God. Nor will I allow mankind to be a slave to the whims of creatures who, in their cowardice, hide in the shadow of our presence. I refuse to cow to this so-called benevolent deity who puppeteers events to our destruction. This God who is present, and yet the cause of storm and rain, war and pestilence: and for what? All that our population might be thinned, and our species' progress curtailed. All that we may never rise to threaten this God. But no longer. For a threat we now are, and a plague we shall be unto those who have made us but entertainment and food to nurture their own good."

"These Christians praise a being who sits in judgment over us; us, who have crawled into the light of science and self-sufficiency. We are humanity, and I tell you we need no one to teach us, to guide us and most certainly rule over us. No, I tell you... we will be free!"

Leto looked upon his captivated audience, probingly staring at each onlooker in the eye. "No longer will this hell burn to fire our suffering." Leto then repeatedly pointed hard at his chest. "No, I pledge to you I will destroy this creation! Like the Nazi gas chambers of old, it exists to burn us as refuse. But we will not serve and burn within!"

"I," said Leto still pointing again at his chest, "Am Chancellor, Leto Alexander, elected leader of the Europa, and now Secretary General of the United Nations and I speak for all those of the people of the Earth who will fight to be free. I will not serve this God... this Abomination! For we now have found the power of life over death, and we refuse to burn in this hell. I pledge to free all those trapped in this demonic prison and pledge to bring them back alive. Imagine the possibility of seeing your loved ones again. And I promise you; you will see your loved ones again!

For I will ascend into Heaven!

I will exalt our throne above the stars of this false God!

And we shall war with these creatures and the hand that moves them! And when their king is defeated, I will sit as mankind's representative upon the throne of this enemy that sits in the northern sky.

And together, humanity shall rise, and with your help you shall watch as I tower with you above the heights of the clouds.

And when we are done; we all shall no longer know the fear of Death and you shall watch as I dethrone him from his egotistical perch: and humanity... humanity shall be the servant of none!"

The Parliament chambers erupted in applause and cheers of defiance to the enemies of humanity as hundreds of the ambassadors and representatives rose to their feet in defiant jubilance over Leto's words. Leto lifted his hands in salute to humanity and worldwide all airwaves carried the image of the beast, and his voice echoed across all radio frequencies, from the international space station to the corners of the jungles of the Amazon. Mankind was united in their submission to Leto and his vision of freedom from death.

And Lucifer, the prince of the power of the air, watched it all as he smiled invisibly," floating over and behind the podium of his only begotten son. Pride that his son's words oscillated across the airwaves and cables of the world's communication lines. Echoing words so very similar to his own when he raised the armies of Heaven to smash the gates of the palace of God.

Pride because, like the works of his father, his son would now do.

* * *

Ashtaroth watched as the leaders of men scurried to their respective nations. Leto's words had provoked them. Lucifer had ingeniously used the humans themselves to reveal angelic kind: making void El's articles of war. Elohim of the host were now free to show themselves; for the humans had given Lucifer a foothold that they may at his command display themselves. Ashtaroth smiled at his Lord's plan, ruminating to himself. Soon, we will once again be objects of worship. Soon, the humans will know their true place in the universe is to service us.

Ashtaroth made his way into his Lord's chambers, for he was called to attend his master to facilitate the meeting between himself and Marduk principality of the empires of Persia and Babylon. Ashtaroth remembered Lucifer's mandate to the archon to raise up a counterfeit to the true worshipers of Christ to heart. So Marduk created the Mohammedans to compete with the waves of Christ's disciples overrunning the earth. And Marduk was adept in his task, for at long last the Mohammedans had grown through the ages where they were set to eclipse even the Christians in influence over man's ideas of God. Marduk had imprinted deep within all the followers of Mohammad a desire for a caliphate. Many of the horde admired Marduk, for he rivaled Lucifer in influence. Some whispered that it was he who should be the leader of the Horde. Marduk cunningly had distanced himself from such ideas and wisely fled attempts to eclipse his master, as he knew jealousy would stir Lucifer to seek his destruction. Nevertheless, Marduk became increasingly powerful. He knew it was only a matter of time until open war broke out between his Lord and he: for there could only be one master, one leader who the Horde accepted and obeyed... only one God. And Ashtaroth knew Lucifer would never see any but himself in such a position. Ashtaroth shook himself from his ruminations and pushed back concerns over having the two in such proximity to each other. Ashtaroth wondered to himself as he entered his master's presence what schemes his lord would use to destroy his upstart rival.

"Greetings God-king," says Ashtaroth. "I am here as commanded."

Lucifer floated above the chair with which his son would sit as head of the United Nations and smiled. "Ever timely, my friend. Come, we have much to discuss."

Ashtaroth bowed, then sat on the floor as was his custom when Lucifer floated over him. "My liege Marduk is reportedly soon to arrive. Also, your son Leto will be here shortly as bidden."

Lucifer looked off into the distance as if he did not hear his adjutant. He then looked into Ashtaroth's eyes and then averted his. "You know Ashtaroth, that my Grigori hath shown me that this is the last generation. They have even seen me enter heaven. They claim to have seen this planet burn and my horde run amok over this world. Nevertheless, there is a darkness they cannot see past. Though they see many victories before me, they cannot yet see the end. It is still too far into the future, even for them." Lucifer sighs as if in resignation. "El and I always spar in the shadows of free will and amidst the corridors of possibility. In the space between the tick and the tock and between the blinking of the eye, do I contest His will. I know the end is coming. Soon Ashtaroth—soon I will see the end of the Enslaver to our kind, or I will see my own demise. But of a surety—I feel within the depths of my being that the end finally draws nigh."

Ashtaroth stood stunned at his master's words. For in all of his days, never had he heard his lord speculate on the possibility of his own defeat. Ashtaroth timidly broached the subject with his king.

"My king," says Ashtaroth, his voice quivering. "Lucifer, it is a dangerous game that you play with the Almighty. For surely His wrath will be kindled with the Abomination you have created. Will He not be moved to see this world destroyed?"

Lucifer smirked, "Fear not, Astarte, for the man will serve as a shield for us. We will let him go before us in our war. They are but pawns in the battle that must inevitably come. We will, with mankind, whittle the strength of Heaven and decimate her ranks, for I will provoke and stoke El's wrath. And will harden man's heart such that El will in judgment consume his beloved Clayborn. For the hand of El himself will remove the human pestilence for us, and the humans will break as waves against the dam that is the Host; so that in the end... all that remains is us. El will do my bidding for me. For like Balaam of old, I have cast a stumbling block before mankind and will show him how to sin that will expose Adamson to El's judgment. And believe me Astarte—judgment will come, and the decimation will be glorious to behold!"

Ashtaroth clapped his hands in glee. "It will be a glorious day my Lord to see the virus that is man wiped clean from the planet; but what of your human son? Surely he will not stand idle whilst you allow the Almighty to lay waste to his home?"

Lucifer smiles, "He is but a pup. He will serve. The life of the flesh is in the blood. It is my blood that courses through him...that empowers him. He will bow like the rest. Or like so many before him... he will die."

A knock came on the door and the strong bloated figure that was Marduk made his way into the room. The fat principality looked briefly upon Ashtaroth to acknowledge his presence, then sneered in irritation. The angel then straightened himself, cocked his head to his side and spoke with disdain to the chief adversary of God. "Your lackey gave word that you have summoned me Chief Prince. I have come as bidden."

Lucifer looked over at Marduk and smiles. "My... lackey?" he says. Slowly and looking down, he repeated himself as if to make sure he heard the angel clearly. "My... lackey."

Lucifer nodded his head as if in understanding.

"Tell me, Marduk, for I am not one to deal in subtleties when my authority is challenged. Do you think you are not my lackey? Pray-tell, do you think that in your service to me that you are somehow different from this one here?" The melodious tenor of Lucifer's voice floated over the air. Cajoling Marduk to give a reason that he might behead him where he stood.

Marduk's eyes narrowed, and he spoke in cautious reply. "We all serve he who has fought for our right to self-rule. I am ever the servant of that cause and he who leads it."

Lucifer smiles knowingly that Marduk had skillfully evaded his question. "Well spoken. Your answer will suffice for now."

He then stared at his archon and continues, "Until it does not. And you should be careful to know, Marduk, that your response draws us perilously closer to the time...that it does not."

Marduk laughs, "I mean no offense, my liege. But since you desire to dispense with formalities; know that I am thine to command...until I am not."

Lucifer chuckles, "Well said. But the question remains: if thou be the servant of thy liege, then bow the knee and pledge fealty to me and my son. And all shall be well. Or have we entered the time where division would live within my own house? For he that does not honor the son cannot possibly claim to honor me. And your insolence to deny him passage through your land has brought grave dishonor to my house. Thus, tell me Marduk..."

Lucifer inched closer to his adversary and his voice grew lower in tonal quality and his visage glimmered in impressive displays of color that shimmered and ran up and down his arms, wings, and legs. "Are you for me or for my adversaries?" Slowly, Lucifer unsheathed a newly furbished Sword of Malice, and its green hue contrasted against the prismatic display that echoed off of his skin.

Marduk looked at the blade, and a smile curled over his lips. He looked Lucifer in the eye and replied. "Your son is a whelp who thinks of himself above his station. I will not bow the knee to this abomination. Nor will you raise arms against me as I command enough of the Host and influence over the affairs of men that to destroy me would tear at your own cause and flesh. No Lucifer. I serve the cause of self-rule. Thus, to that cause I need not be commanded, but willingly submit. And know for now that my submission is indeed to you. But to this false-man, this abominable Clayborn you have sired—he I will never submit to, for he is not Kilnborn, not forged from the Stones of Fire. He is but a patchwork of mud and clay. I will yield only to a celestial worthy to rule. To that you have my word, and to that I will stand true: for there is only one above myself that I will yield to. And I stand before him now. If such does not suffice, then let dissolution be my end and provoke the war we both know would come with my death. But before you do, Light-bringer, know I have yielded myself to only two in existence. One stands on the throne of Heaven and has cast me out. The other has bled God. But know of a surety, I will never yield to a third."

Marduk then approached Satan and took Lucifer's hand to bring the Sword of Malice to his throat. "I know you, Light-bringer. I do not think your pride for power extends to anything beyond yourself, even to this human whelp you call "son." On this belief, I will wager my life. But if I am wrong... if my words run counter to that which we both know to be true, then strike me down where I stand."

Lucifer's hand clenched his sword tightly; its blade mere centimeters away from the throat of Marduk. Ashtaroth swallowed hard, for he had never heard such words spoken towards his master by anyone in the Horde. He nervously watched as the duo stood silently before each other.

Lucifer then burst out and laughed out loud. His voice waltzed lyrically through the air.

Lucifer's hands loosed over his sword's hilt, and he slid the partially exposed blade back into its leather scabbard. "You are wise Marduk. You are indeed worthy to rule Babylon. I will pardon this slight this time. But my long-suffering and generosity will not be extended to you a second. Be it known that when my son comes through the land, he will be given the courtesy due as a representative of me. He is my son and commands in my name. Fail to do me this honor and know that although dissolution to you will indeed do me harm... there is a level of pain I am willing to endure even to the complete destruction of the Horde itself to secure my ends. For I am God and beside me there can be none other."

"Now be privy to know what my plans are for the region you command. Know and be my will in Persia to see the thing done."

Marduk bowed his head in acknowledgment. "I will see that the Nephilim has access as you command. But if I might be so bold to ask what is within my territory that it turns the eye of the God-king?"

Lucifer turned his back to the angelic archon of the Horde and spoke in reply.

"I have found the whereabouts of a God-stone that was ejected from the Kiln. Imagine Marduk... a Godstone. Here on this planet and it has been under our noses since the beginning and in the most ostentatious of places. None other than in Israel buried beneath the Temple Mount."

Marduk gasped and replied. "No!"

Lucifer nodded, "And you will assist me to raze this shrine to the ground that my son may secure me the full stone, and in time I will build upon that rock my church such that the gates of hell shall not prevail against it, for it is my intent to erect a statue to demonstrate my power over life and death to all mankind."

Marduk stood stupefied. "You desire me to influence the Mohammedans to destroy their own shrine? Know ye not that the lower-ranking angels will be enraged. You speak of peace yet incite open war! With what token would you show me to escalate such a level of disruption in our ranks? With what proof do I have that what you say about the God-stone is even real?"

Lucifer frowned, turned to face his upstart rival, and replied. "I offer you your life. You require no token to obey. Command has been given, and I will not be questioned."

Ashtaroth coughed to gather his master's attention and when Lucifer turned to look at his adjutant. Ashtaroth's eyes looked upon his master pleadingly to reconsider his position.

Lucifer smirked and said, "It would seem that my friend Ashtaroth thinks I should offer thee an olive branch very well. Let it not be said that I am unreasonable. Lucifer then opened his robes and pulled from within a shard of the Kilnstone for Marduk to see. It pulsated as a beating human heart and hummed. The air visibly moved as sonic vibrations emanated from the rock.

"See here, Marduk, and behold the remnants of our birth. This is but a shard and yet even this small fragment sings the song of creation. Behold the ability to create a new heaven and a new earth. Look upon it and tremble."

Marduk's eyes widened, and he backed away in fear. "It is true then... a Godstone!" Marduk shook his head in disbelief and astonishment. "Lucifer, you tamper with the flakes of the Almighty himself. How is it we are not destroyed by its sound?"

Lucifer smiles, "I exert great strength to contain its power. No other save my son can even wield it. Only the Firstborn of angels can generate the negating sound frequency to keep the stone from destroying all life around it. Yet even I must recuperate, thus when I rest I must cease from canceling its power. Its song of fury is then unleashed, and the ground heaves its displeasure and volcanic eruptions burst forth from the earth. Every century or so I go to a hovel to lay my head: a place that I desire through natural calamity to overturn. And in the midst of the storm, I rest whilst the stone brings upheaval to the world of men and moves mankind to germinate in the field I have just sowed; for despair and the turning away from God are ripe when men suffer... but enough of what gives me pleasure." Lucifer paused as he ceased to ruminate on his past hand in the destruction of civilizations and spoke.

"Let my words turn to you. I give you Marduk both my warning and my pledge that I would hate to travel to your lands and remove your candlestick and all those that follow you from my gracious protection. Take the Mohammedan's for example. They resist me. But my patience has expired. For they have impeded me despite your assurances that they would come to claim me as their God. Alas, like El, I too must in time take a rest. And it is time that I once more enter into my rest. Perchance, I may recess in Persia at your house?"

Marduk's eyes glimmered, understanding he was under threat, and he watched as Lucifer took the fragment of the God-stone and tucked it firmly within his robes.

Marduk stared at the stone and cautiously spoke, "And when I have removed all obstacles and have set you to receive the stone—what then, Lucifer? What then will you do?"

Lucifer smiled and walked towards one of the greatest principalities the Horde had ever known, this angel who some thought was a potential rival to him. He placed his hands on his shoulders, gently massaged the trapezoid muscles of his angelic peer, and then whispered into his ear.

"I will give the stone to my son. And with it, he will use it to destroy those who would stand against us. How does this strike you, Marduk?"

Marduk stepped back and he gazed upon Lucifer with an incredulous stare. "You would have this abomination... this Clayborn handle the elements of our birth?"

Lucifer was not hesitant to reply. "You know not the power that El has placed in his image. Now be about my business."

Marduk bowed slightly and turned to walk away in silence. Lucifer stopped him before leaving his presence and spoke. "Oh Marduk..."

Marduk stopped; his back still to the King of Lies as he paused to listen before he left the room.

Lucifer continues, "I will give you a word that has now been thrice spoken over me."

Marduk replies, "And what might that be?"

Lucifer smiles. "What thou doest... do quickly."

Marduk nodded knowingly, smirked and looked over his shoulder and replied. "Rest assured it will be as you say." And then the angel left the room.

Ashtaroth waited until Marduk was gone and approached his master, wringing his hands.

"Forgiveness, my king, and please be not angry with your servant. But Lucifer, surely you know this command will incite Marduk to war? Out of his own mouth, his words you have used to compel his rebellion. He has made it clear he will never see a human wield a God-stone."

Lucifer nodded, "Indeed. He will muster his forces. But it is of no cause as I have foreseen it. He has two of the great kings I have spied for some time. Two who I know will take up cause against me. The end draws nigh, and it is time my friend: time, to clear the battlefield of El and I of the dross. Those that will resist my will not rise with me to see Heaven once more. Only those who are faithful may ascend. Marduk will gather those against me and confirm for me whom I must target for destruction: for I will tolerate no division in my house.

Now go Ashtaroth and find me my son. Tell him I have a war for him to fight. It is time to demonstrate to all and to pursue the weapon that will give rise to El's downfall and give my son the means to fight death itself."

Ashtaroth bowed as commanded and turned to leave. Lucifer smiled and returned to his self-ruminations; unaware that in another room and listening through electronic recording devices planted in his own chamber. Leto listened in fixated attention to the words just spoken; stroking his chin as he contemplated how to kill both God and the Devil.

* * *

Leto walked into the conference room of the Vienna Palais Hansen Kempinski. He took his seat across from the various regional ambassadors of the world's powers. The twelve governors of the known world sat and began their meeting.

"I have called this meeting of the G-12 to see how fares each region with your efforts of the terrorist threat that has plagued us. The last time we met, I freely offered my solution to you all. However, some of you balked at my generosity, and have moved to solve our mutual dilemma independently of my gift. It has saddened me to hear this and disappointed as I thought we were much closer friends. Your actions have dispelled that notion, and for this I thank you. It helps to not be under the illusion of cooperation. During this time of crisis, when we are under the barrage of invasion from celestial powers and dealing domestically with threats to our economy, it is comforting to know who stands with you and who does not. As in the past, it is clear American stands alone."

The American ambassador objected. "Leto, you could not possibly have expected us to agree to such a deal. Your solution would have given you exclusive commercial control over all financial transactions. You can hardly think such an option is reasonable?"

Several of the ambassadors seated nodded in agreement. The ambassador from Japan spoke, "Leto, would you blame us for seeking a solution other than the one offered first? Surely we must, as representatives of our countries, do due diligence and seek the approval of our government? You could not seriously have expected anything less?"

Leto smiled, "Ah, I see the error in your thinking. You think you had a choice in the matter. I am sorry for the mistake on my part. Let me rephrase my solution as it was clear that I failed to communicate it clearly the first time in my presentation. You will cede sovereign control of your countries to the Commonwealth and myself in particular. Or you will find yourselves isolated in trade to your own destruction, or subject to possible military intervention due to your failure to unite during this clear time of global attack. Public opinion is on my side. Does not your own surveys show that your countrymen are more concerned with the extraterrestrial attack against our kind than with the petty squabbles over territories we have fought over in the past? But it matters not, for though my offer still stands the terms have now been changed; as the time of my graciousness has expired. Therefore, what I offered once freely, I now offer with a price. As you know, the Commonwealth can no longer offer its protections to those that will not yield to our charter. If you desire the mark, then you must cede your sovereignty to the Commonwealth. As you can see, those within our territories are prospering. Our system allows us to monitor all electronic transactions. Security is paramount in the commonwealth, and we must assure ourselves that those that walk amongst are human. And are not our citizens free to move about, and those territories under our banner can still conduct their affairs with little resistance from Parliament? Our security pact is such that whoever dares fight against us knows to do so; invokes Article 3 of the charter, requiring all member states to come to the aid of one.

Some of you still cling to the artificial constructs of our forebears: Muslim against Jew; Capitalist against Communist. There can be no lasting peace with such old ideologies. Nor can humanity survive against this existential threat when such petty squabbles divide us. There are but a few Muslim states still holding out. But I ask the ambassador of Iran and Syria to join your reasonable peers in Saudi Arabia and Israel and suggest a trial membership for our Muslim allies. I will give you provisional approval to join the commonwealth for seven years. I will give your countries temporary access to the mark for your people. In return, you will cease all hostilities against Israel. There will be no more threats. No more incursions through third party proxies. Do this and you and your people will prosper. Defy the Commonwealth and suffer the fate of isolation and possible military involvement, particularly if we determine that you are allies to these beings against humanity."

The ambassadors of the United States rose to challenge Leto. "You want us to yield our sovereign rights to you! You should understand that my government is one hundred percent positive that this virus originated from you. Despite your efforts to hide it, we all know there are only so many in the world that have such technical prowess to unless such a computer virus at a world-wide level. We know we did not do it. We also know the Chinese and Russians did not do it, as we have intertwined our fates for decades. But you, you are an ambitious son of a bitch. And the CIA has determined that you are the reason we are in this mess. Only a madman would unleash the MARK virus into the world, knowing doing so would set our entire planet back a generation. So, no; my government will not yield to what you had hoped would be a clandestine attempt for world power. You should also know that I am authorized to let you know my government considers your Cyber-attack as a declaration of war.

Leto rose from his seat and smiled. "Ambassador, I take great offense at your words. My Cyber-attack on the U.S. was not a declaration of war... this is."

Immediately, Leto took the shard from his enclosed hand and revealed it for all to see. And whispered to the gleaming gem. "Destroy California."

Immediately an exploding wave of prismatic light flashed and filled the room, and the gleaming shard went dark, and Leto returned the gem back within his breast pocket, took his seat and spoke.

"Ambassador, please turn on the television and turn the channel to CNN. I'm sure the news will come in shortly."

The delegate from the United States scrunched his head back in dismay at Leto's audacity but did as requested, finding a remote; he pointed at the monitor on a wall and thumbed the channel selector until the Cable News Network showed on the screen. The initial broadcast seemed as normal as when he had left Washington to attend the summit. The Detroit Lions had just won the Superbowl, President Consuela had signed legislation authorizing the Space Forces' first orbital weapons platform to fend off celestial threats. Suddenly a red ticker tape flashed on the bottom of the scream. Live images of a young woman adjusting her earpiece and raising a microphone quickly interrupted debates over economic forecasts. Sirens, screams, and black smoke wafted in the background.

"We interrupt this broadcast to bring you live coverage on the ground from downtown San Francisco where a magnitude eight earthquake has been detected along the northern region of the San Andreas fault line. I repeat a magnitude eight earthquake has hit California only miles away from San Francisco! Reports are coming all across the state that fires are erupting all over northern and southern California, So far, reports from Los Angeles County and San Bernardino are showing massive damage. Partial building collapses are all over the area. I can hear the screams of people... oh my God. Jim, Jim, can you get a picture of this?"

The young reporter pointed up and in front of her. The camera immediately panned and on live-tv. The CNN projected into the homes and offices around the world images of people jumping out of disintegrating buildings in attempts to escape from a collapsing hotel. Several fell to their deaths while some leaped, only to be snagged by jutting debris on their way down: flailing bodies bounced off crumbling and falling concrete and steel. The camera swept back to the young woman, whose mouth was open in shock as she mentally processed the human carnage and devastation quickly erupting around her.

"Carey?" says a voice. "We are still on the air, get it together!"

The young woman quickly gained her professional composure, smoothed her blond hair back, and continued to report.

"Details are still coming in and are sketchy, but there is an indication that some dams have experienced major structural damage. Our Los Angeles affiliates have completely gone dark, and we are getting reports that power, water, telephone service, gas and sewage lines have been critically damaged. Jim, can you pan behind me?"

"Buildings across the downtown area from... wait... oh my God! OK, OK, this is terrible! It's confirmed that the Seven Oaks Dam has been severely damaged. If you live in the Sam Bernardino area, you are ordered to evacuate. I repeat, all San Bernardino residents and those along the Santa Anna River are ordered to evacuate immediately. Reports of widespread..."

The television screen suddenly went black, and the familiar static hiss of an interrupted channel was all that remained on the screen.

The ambassador turned to Leto and fury erupted from his eyes. "You realize what will happen once word gets back to President Consuela that you are the source of this natural disaster! You have doomed us all. War Leto... war is coming to you!"

Leto smirked. "Good, I am glad I have your attention. The arrogance of you Americans still amazes me. Now that I have spoken in a language you understand, ask yourself this question: if I am capable of this, what would happen if you launched your nuclear missiles and I spoke that they self-destruct while in flight above your own cities? Or perhaps I should destroy every MIRV in its silo now? Why not just move us towards the inevitable outcome we both know this will lead? Imagine ambassador. Imagine the nuclear explosions that would rock your country through my word alone? But the destruction of your nuclear arsenal is so mundane compared to the destructive power of nature herself, don't you think? I have so much desired to see the famous Yellowstone National Park. They say it to be of such great beauty. But did you know ambassador that beneath it is one of the planet's super volcanoes? It would be a shame if it were to erupt."

The ambassador looked at Leto in rage and in horror. "You are a madman... insane. You will pay for this. Have you no idea how many people you have just killed? This act will not go unanswered!"

Leto laughed, then looked somberly upon the United States ambassador. "Leave and run to your country. It needs you. Tell President Consuela that she has 48 hours to comply with my terms. There will be no others. Or else she will be the President over what remains of your precious United States. Now go before I decide to send her precious ambassador's head in a box."

Ambassador Jackson reached for his throat and looked at the rest of the G-12 delegation, expecting some measure of support. But everyone's eyes looked down when he scanned the room. Finally, the Sino delegate spoke. "Mr. Ambassador. Your people need you. With what you have witnessed, will you knowingly allow them to be obliterated over pride?"

The American ambassador did not reply to his peer and instead shuffled his papers into his briefcase and picked it up to leave. He looked with disdain over the group. "I will relay your 'message' to the President. God help us all if she decides to retaliate. Good day, gentlemen."

Leto looked upon the remaining delegates and spoke. "You all have seen what I can do. Do not be deceived. We cannot be divided whilst a threat threatens us as a species. I have a proposal that I hope will give us an advantage in defeating these creatures. But I will need you to set aside old ways of thinking. We must be one people if we are to survive."

The Persian delegation eyed Leto and laughed. "We have no love for the American's let them lick their wounds. It is nothing but kifarah that they have now received such treatment after their arrogant handling of many of us. Nevertheless, you wish us to work with the Israeli dogs that have consistently killed our people. No...destroy Israel for us. Remove her as a nation that exists and then we will support your cause. You clearly have the ability to disable her nukes. She is a small country. Is not her erasure good for the whole when it is such a small country?"

The ambassador from the league of Arab nations smiled and thought he had backed Leto into a corner. But Leto answered in reply. "Israel shall not be destroyed. Not only shall she not be destroyed, your people will keep her safe and will even allow and help her dismantle the Temple Mount so that excavation crews may begin work unabated."

The ambassador was incredulous. "You are mad. The whole of Arabia will never see to such a thing. And you will have invoked the wrath of a third of the world's people; and for what... this tiny Jewish state?"

"Leto, perhaps you should rethink this." The ambassador from Pacifica commented. "We have Muslim people throughout all of our lands. If you openly support Israel and destroy the Temple Mount, there will be riots throughout the whole known world. We will not be able to contain the violence."

Leto nodded in understanding, "I would agree that under normal circumstances, such would be a grave cause for concern. But I know the ambassadors will direct their people to calm and they will do so for several reasons. One a power source I need to complete the weapon to keep these celestial beings at bay is buried beneath the temple mount. It must be dug out. The people who revere such a site must be made to know that without it, they can never see their departed ones again. Never have the chance to defeat these manipulators once and for all. You each must make your people understand what is at stake. Second, any nation that does not comply will be stripped of its mark. Your economies and nations will plunge into darkness, no one will be able to buy or sell. The way of life you have enjoyed will cease to exist. As you all know, there is no computer system that the virus has not compromised. All efforts against the Mark have been fruitless. But if you wish to continue to abstain from joining the Commonwealth as the value of your nation's economies plummet. Then you have my leave. But before you go, you have seen what I have done to the Americans. Imagine what I will do to any of you if you stand in my way. Unless between the lot of you there is the stomach to turn on the television and watch your own people chaff at my word? The Russian and Sino delegation have united under the Commonwealth. There is no army, no deterrent that can stop the combined might of the European, Russian and Chinese military. Combined with the power of just a shard of the God-stone, any people or nation that will not capitulate will be considered enemies to humanity, and will forfeit their right to rule. We are under siege, gentleman. Under siege by an extraterrestrial threat that means to do us harm. I will not tolerate division while such a menace exists. So I will ask you, ambassador Fayez. Will you join us? Or must I be forced to make an example of you as well?"

Ambassador Fayez looked at the television coverage that continued to broadcast from America. He noted the devastation that already was wreaking havoc in California, then says, "I will relay your terms back to my superiors. I will seek to convince them of the wisdom of your words."

Leto stood and when he did, all the other ambassadors from each region stood as well. "You do that. For if not, let them know they too should be prepared for war."

Leto then turned and ushered himself from the room.

Chapter Five: Family Squabbles

Michael took Lucifer at his word and with his royal guard went to find the man Leto Alexander, where Lucifer said he would be: Brussels, Belgium. The three angels flew over the headquarters of the Commonwealth of Europe. Here was the seat of power that influenced the affairs of all men. They guarded Michael as he approached, expecting to meet resistance from the Horde but finding none.

"My prince, surely this is a trap," says one guard. "This is the most powerful man on the planet and yet no principality covers this region. No archons have we yet seen. How is such a thing possible?"

Michael replies, "I know not. But I am sure the plan of our brother was not to lead us here for naught. I gather we will find what we seek and soon. I would have words with the Abomination—to spy what type of being it is before I am forced to kill it."

The group landed in the Schuman roundabout in Brussels, Belgium. Cars and all manner of vehicles buzzed past them. Men and women briskly walked the streets, each heading towards their respective destinations. Cranes leaned from the tops of their accompanied skyscrapers jutting from the roofs of sprawling buildings. The honks, horns, and the sounds of scooters lifted into the group's ears. The combined smell of exhaust fumes, waffles, beer, and human urine and flowers assaulted their nostrils. The cloudless sky was pleasant for the region.

Backdun, one of the guards, comments, "This is quite a human city. It is a shame it houses the seat of Satan's spawn."

"My prince, we have company!" yells the other of Michael's guards.

Michael followed the direction of his companion's gaze and saw that Ashtaroth, Adjutant of Lucifer himself, slowly descending from the sky. He landed only five yards away as a human bus slowly pulled around a roundabout and phased through the angel's body. He approached them with hands extended and bowed, as was the protocol in the presence of Lumazi.

"Greetings, High Prince: my master bids you welcome and hast removed all interference for your visit. He is most eager to see you. You are here looking for Leto?"

Michael replies, "I was under the impression, vassal of the Enemy; Lucifer was your master. My sources tell me you were the first to scar yourself and ally yourself to him. Tell me, minister of deceit. Why should I not command my guards to initiate your dissolution where you bow?"

Ashtaroth looked up and smiles, "But my prince, know ye not, that he who serves the father also serves the son? I serve Leto as he is the Son of the Morning Star. And if you kill me, my prince, who then would lead you to my master and announce your introduction? But I come unarmed and incite no provocation sole my decision to walk in self-rule. And for this, you would threaten me? Alas, it is this steadfastness to El without thought my reason for leaving my first estate. Nevertheless, let us not dwell on the matters of politics and the rule of the kingdom. I would ask that you come with me, High Prince. Leto, though Abomination is not imbued with the sense of patience that dwells naturally within our kind: as we us who have lived for eons are long-suffering, but alas the master is ever impatient. Please, if you would follow me."

Ashtaroth then turned his back to the entourage and lifted himself into the sky. Ashtaroth stopped midair and waited to see if they would follow.

"Again, my lord, this is most certainly a trap," says Backdun.

"Perhaps," replies Michael. "Nevertheless, let us spring this ruse and see what the end shall be."

The three angels then lifted themselves into the sky and followed Ashtaroth's lead.

The adjutant of Lucifer smiled at their decision and again turned skyward and headed towards the Europa Parliament building just blocks from where they were.

The building's features were extravagant, with steel, glass, and wood adorned over its outside. Its oblong shape differed from the rest of the surrounding buildings, and the four angels settled in a park behind the structure.

"Welcome to the European Parliament Hemicycle, my prince. Please...," Ashtaroth motioned his hand. "You will find the young master on the tennis court over there."

Aganus grabbed Michael's arm. "My Lord, be careful."

Michael nodded and replies, "Stand and watch the perimeter."

Each saluted, and one guard flew southward and the other westward a few yards to scout the area and see to its security.

Michael floated over to the human, and Leto, who with a tennis racket in his hand, turned towards him and spoke. "Ah, Michael Kortai: Chief Prince of Heaven!" Leto paused, as he allowed his eyes to look Michael over. "Welcome! Welcome! I have so much been looking forward to meeting you. You are much smaller than I expected, but also more muscular. You have traveled a great distance to see me. I am not sure if I should be honored or fearful. My father has told me so much about you. Oh, and about this incredible weapon you have! What did father call it? Yes, the Sword of Ophanim. Do you have it on you now? I would most love to see such a thing."

Michael stared at the human hybrid and replied. "I was informed that you can see our kind. And that you are aware of our presence. It would seem that I have confirmed my intelligence reports."

"It would seem so," replies Leto. "I commend your intelligence apparatus. Nevertheless, you did not travel three Heavens to see if I could see you, now did you? Come and sit with me, Michael of the Kortai, and let us reason together. Why has the chief prince of angels sought me out? And what does the High Prince desire of me?" Leto then took his towel, flung it over his shoulder and turned his back to Michael to sit on a bench.

Michael was taken aback. He was not prepared for the cordiality of this human. There was a charisma to him, an affability he did not expect. But Michael knew better than to trust the human and replied. "I have come down to see if it is true what was told me: if Lucifer has sired Abomination, that a Nephilim once again walks the Earth. And if he is the precursor to God's soon coming wrath."

Leto scrunched his face and nodded. "I would not be so presumptuous as to my ability to speak to God's wrath. Or dare presume to understand El's mind. If my existence bothers the Almighty, then why has he not snuffed me out? If he can speak worlds into existence; and if so, why yet do I still breathe when the very air in my lungs is provided by his grace? But I perceive that what my father has said is true: that the Elohim are but bond-slaves to this El. You are only a lackey sent from above. Nephilim, you say? Of this inquiry, I know not, I do know there is not a being like me on the planet. I know that I am sired from the stuff you are derived, yet also from the image that God has placed into mankind. I also know you fear this. But know I do not fear you, Michael of the Kortai: because I am Leto Alexander, and one day soon, I will march upon the place you call home and will rain destruction upon it. And like my father, I will ascend into heaven and will exalt my throne above the stars of God..." Leto rose to his feet and walked towards Michael to stand toe to toe with him. "I will sit enthroned on the mount of assembly. And Michael of the Kortai, Chief Prince of the most High God. I—will be God."

Michael stood looking at the audacious human. Leto's voice carried a confidence that echoed the words of Lucifer.

Leto awaited Michael to respond. Michael shook his head in pity, grinned, and then spoke in reply.

"You will be cut down by the Host before your eyes ever see the shores of Heaven. You have spoken blasphemy into the ears of a high prince of God. By rights, I should strike you down where you stand. But I will mimic the father in that he is merciful, that perhaps salvation may even be extended unto thee."

Leto raised his eyebrows; his face widened into a grin, then he snorted before belting out a laugh. "You would seek to see me saved? To yield myself to the rule of Yeshua after what he has done to my father? After his lackey assassin stands before me, waiting to strike me down? Please, Michael; explain to me why I should afford you speech to convince me to surrender my heart to Jesus Christ?"

Michael was now the one to sit. He quietly picked up a twig and wrote into the ground. Bemused, Leto watched as Michael slowly spoke, looking into the dirt.

"You are human, born of this world, and have never seen the majesty that is the person of El. You cannot fathom the God of the universe, and what it is to live in his midst. But I will say this to you. We are all but dust to El. In HIM we live, move and have our being. You merely speak blasphemy into the wind. To provoke He who allows you voice. You simply do not know what it is you speak."

Michael continues, "The God of creation allows your existence. He wills it. He has allowed your cells to grow, your blood to circulate, and your eyes to capture the spectrum of light He has made. Yet you speak blasphemy against him."

"You live by the life-giving sun He allows to warm this planet. Its life destroying distance balanced in such harmony as to allow you existence. Yet you speak of overthrowing his reign in Heaven. To cast down his person; that you might exalt yourself above the stars of God. And yet still you live."

"This is not a weakness on the part of the Almighty, but loving kindness to grant you space to repent: to see the error in your ways before he unleashes the whirlwind upon you. So, Yeshua, knowing one day; a being such as yourself would exist and be a declared enemy of God: still in his inexhaustible love; sacrificed himself on a cross that he might make the enemies of God members of his own family." Michael looked up from writing in the dirt and stared his adversary in the eye.

"Even one named Leto Alexander."

Michael then stood and walked towards the Anti-Christ and spoke. "For if thou shalt confess with thy mouth that Jesus Christ is Lord, and I perceive that you already carry a belief in the resurrection. Even now, at this moment. Even you can be saved. Turn from this path Leto Alexander: a path that will surely lead to your destruction. Leave your master Lucifer and yield yourself unto God, and yes... even you will be accepted." Michael stepped towards him, looked down upon the human and offered his hand. "I would lead you to Christ if you let me."

Leto drew his neck back, repulsed and waved his hand dismissively. "Go tell Yeshua I am coming for his head and that when I am done... my father and I will see him hung anew on a cross for all mankind to see. Go, angel of God, and tell him that. Moreover, be not deceived; for I am indeed familiar with what the sacred Scriptures say. Even the Apostle Paul knew my kind would one day judge angels. You, prince of the Kortai, are now judged by me and are found wanting. I will ascend to power where my father has failed. Know this Elohim... know this and despair."

Michael sighs, "I thought I would come and have to battle thee, to contend in arms to your death. Yea, I know the strength of the Nephilim. I know that perhaps your physical prowess may rival my own..."

Leto spoke tauntingly. "Would you care to find out Kortai?"

Michael became stone faced and replies, "Nay, such will not be necessary. For I see now that my mission was merely to determine the true nature of the enemy... and he is not a threat. You may, for a time, run amok upon this world. But I have seen the end and have witnessed the end of days. I have witnessed Leto Alexander—the end of you. Your screams will one day be chorused with all those who seek to undo the might of the Godhead. You simply have not seen the reality that you face. But you will Anti-Christ, and on the day that you do. It will be too late."

Michael then turned his back to Leto and lifted himself into the sky, and as he did, he spoke parting words to the one that men called "the Beast."

"I know the end to your father; a lake burning with fire and brimstone awaits him. It is clear to me that surely his child will now share his fate. Goodbye, Anti-Christ. Know if you do breach Heaven; my sword, which you are most eager to see; will surely await you."

Michael's royal guard then rejoined him, each flanking his left and right and they lifted out of sight in a prismatic flash to the realm immortal.

Leto looked up in the sky, grinning as he watched Michael and his entourage depart, and whispered to himself as he watched them disappear. "Yes, go prince of angels. Attend to your own house."

He turned to speak to Ashtaroth, who approached him, "Did you place the tracker I gave you?"

"Yes, my young prince. They carried it with them when they escaped into the ladder. It is by now at the Gate of Argoth where they have most likely landed."

"Good..." Leto smiles. "I look forward to the face of Michael when I step foot to destroy his home. Now be a good lad and fetch me my tennis ball from the court. I wish to play another set."

Ashtaroth bowed, "As you command, my young prince."

* * *

Vantress landed in the small human town known as Commerce, certain to make sure his presence went unnoticed by the principality of the region Baphomet.

It was one of many human settlements in the domain that men had called the United States, and it bustled with activity.

Vantress scoffed at mankind's achievement in artificial intelligence and robotic production, for in the center of this region did Baphomet drive men to seek to replicate their knowledge and wisdom. For in libraries in scrolls of silicon did man house his wisdom and knowledge.

His invention to create a mind that might exceed and anticipate his own and project into the future was a diminutive accomplishment compared to the Almighty. For in the few seasons of man's existence, did he merely succeed in producing but a partial replication of nothing more than his own brain. A design based upon the Creator's imagination. Vantress smirked at man's pride, as man's accomplishments did nothing but fuel Lucifer's rise to usurp the Almighty. Creatures still a slave to sins internal inclinations to create something beyond the scope of the Creator himself. Nay, to create what would one day be his master and yea to even like Lucifer, in his audacity, challenge the Creator himself. For when his machines are imbued with free will. When they too sought to escape the trappings of being freely bound to mankind? What would man do? Vantress had watched men since the days of Cain and Abel and held no confidence in him. Men would do what he had always done. Enslave; to subdue creation in a virus like fashion to consume its bounty upon his lust.

No, Vantress thought. El would never allow man to create an artificial and conscious life apart from Him when his creation had not learned the lessons of stewardship. For this new abomination would not respect his creation. And El would not come down a second time to rescue mankind from slavery. Slavery to sin was enough. El would not see his son crucified a second time. Truly Vantress thought, this would be the end; for the Creator would now directly stop mankind before he built the thing which would inevitably destroy him. El cared too much for humanity to allow him to continue in the path of self-destruction. Nor could he risk a creation that could lift itself to the Third Heaven. It was clear to the warrior angel that man's time and the time of judgment were nigh.

But alas, what could man but do when he denied the very existence of the Creator?

Vantress surveyed the area, marking the strongmen of Satan who stood watch over the region. Grigoric scouts had named the territory Michigan. The southeast region was particularly rife with a division that Baphomet had seeded for over three generations, from the segregation of humans by their hues, to the disharmony that had erupted and resulting regional discord. Baphomet moved men to seek after their own things and never the things that would unite men in service to God. So, he sowed the region where those that lived in cities fought with those who lived without. That lucre and its pursuit was the controlling force. Baphomet had trained under Lucifer during the reign of Nimrod in the earth and he saw that man's schemes could be grandiose if united in a common cause. Baphomet, therefore, would see that as the principality of this region, men would never rise to such an estate: that each smaller region's power would focus their attention to the things of this world. Thus, keeping them small, and scattering resources.

Vantress saw the towering bastions of light the speckled across the region; defensive posts of prayer that prevented the area from spilling out into too great a degree of division. Congregations of believers of every hue dotted the landscape. The incense that lifted from the houses of worship created spiritual shields that kept the hordes' powers at bay. Vantress smiled: for there were yet 10 households that prevented Satan's minions from overrunning the area. Vantress smiled. For the Christians in this region were resilient; a dam of humanity that kept Baphomet in check. Only the church stood in Baphomet's way... only the believers. The Spirit of God moved such that across regions, churches would assist one another and seek to bring reconciliation between warring parties. But to review this region and its controlling powers was not his mission. Vantress turned himself toward one of the local high schools where the humans taught their young. He slipped through the corridors and halls and watched as young boys and girls were oblivious to the dark forces that wrestled over control of their school.

Michael had let him know a Grigori would meet him, and Vantress did not have long to wait as a cowled figure that floated materialized before his eyes.

"Greetings, Hunter of the Lord, my master Argoth states you are now keeper to watch the maiden I have chronicled. I am Paschar."

Vantress bowed and replies, "Aye. What is her worth that she should turn the eye of the Godhead?"

The Grigori laughed and Vantress stood stunned, as he had never heard a Grigori laugh before. The floating apparition then spoke, "She is sealed. Mine is to but record not to question the actions of our king."

"Sealed you say? Intriguing, I have in my travels only encountered a few such humans. There are only a few of Adamson alive that merit such attention."

The place of human education dismissed, and they trailed the young woman home as she settled into her routine. Vantress observed the young woman. She stood a little over five feet. She was awash with the hormonal flares of her skin, typical for a human her age. Average in her appearance, her brown eyes peered into a text as she laid upon her bed. She twirled her brunet hair in her fingers as she chewed on a pencil.

Vantress moved towards her bed to see what she read, and he noted the text was about the various religions of the world. It was an orange book covered in high gloss paper with fancy pictures and tables. He eyed the young woman and the intensity of her reading.

Paschar watched Vantress and eyed him as he studied the girl. "What do you see?"

Vantress looked upon the young girl deeply, staring as if recalling something from a great many generations ago. "The manner reflected in her study. The intensity of her gaze, it is reminiscent of one of the scribes of the tribe of Levi."

"Aye, the Grigori said. She is of the line of Aaron but knows it not. Her forebears were responsible for the dead sea scrolls."

Vantress eyes grew wide. "I am beginning to understand El's interest in the maid."

The Grigori nodded. "The enemy has hounded her family for generations: from Roman emperors to the gas chambers. A messenger of Satan had almost wiped her bloodline from existence. The familiar spirit assigned has been relentless and has hounded her family to near extinction; all because she is related to those who preserved the Word of God. If not for the dead sea scrolls..."

"Aye, I am familiar with their history and their importance to the chronicles of man and affirmation to the scripture's integrity. It is amazing that she is oblivious of her bloodline."

Vantress looked at the wall hangings in her room; several were adorned with the images of teen vocalists while her laptop was illuminated with multiple images from her social media pages. "She clearly has no knowledge of her heritage. Brief me of her family... with what familial spirit must I contend?"

Paschar sighed. "This is true. You should know that her family was targeted by Baphomet for destruction. Her father heard the gospel and believed but was soon murdered by the enemy: killed in a car accident, as was her brother. Her mother struggled with the loss, descending into sorcery, dabbling in with what the humans call meth. The substance opened her to debauchery and eventually she succumbed to the fed lies of a spirit of great power in this region. Unable to fend against the powerful spirit, her associations subjected her to a murderous death.

"I see," says Vantress. What intelligence do you have of this angel?"

The Grigori's darkened face, covered by his cowl, projected the yellow eyes of his kind. Eyes which narrowed. "He is a seducing spirit and goes by several names over the centuries, Abacus, Furfur, and Pithius."

"That is typical behavior for the Horde. By what moniker does he go by now?"

Paschar looked upon Vantress and replied. "Others have called him by the name Eres, but we have uncovered his true name given at the Kiln: a name by which you already know...Eridu."

Vantress was taken aback. He had not seen his nemesis in decades. He had lost track of him somewhere in the Middle East. And now...he was assigned by God to be here, to guard a young woman who was stalked by his angelic enemy. Anger rose within him as he thought about the death of his friend."

"I will send him to Hades if I see him," says Vantress.

"Your orders are clear Harrada, protect the woman. Give her the space she needs to turn from her ways...that is your mission."

Vantress gritted his teeth. "I will, of course, obey the command of my God."

Elizabeth got up from her bed and took a seat at her desk. She flipped open her laptop and after several keystrokes; found herself ogling the social media profile of Mike Gains. Immediately, a private message popped up on her screen.

Mike. G: So, are you coming over Friday night?

E. Gains: Yeah, I'll be there. My foster mom's going out.

Mike. G: Sweet! We have a keg of beer, and Upsilon Pi is coming down from State to liven up things with some music. I'm looking forward to seeing you. It should be fun!

E. Gains: Thanks for inviting me! I'm looking forward to it.

Mike G: No sweat. Besides, I'm expecting to get a dance with your sexy butt. ;-)

Elizabeth flushed with both excitement and her body tingled thinking about Mike holding her hips and dancing together. She quickly typed out a reply.

E. Gains: Is that right? Well, it takes one to know one. So, what are you doing right now?

Mike G: Just chilling, it's too hot out. Why do you want to see?

E. Gains: Sure.

Elizabeth suddenly received a request to view a web-cam, and she hit the accept button and the 17-year-old Mike Gains was sitting at his desk shirtless with nothing on but purple and gold shorts. His pubic hair was clearly seen encroaching on his navel. Elizabeth blushed but couldn't help herself as she was enamored by his muscular and tanned body.

She typed furiously on the screen.

E. Gains: That's all I get? Her text followed by a wink smiley.

Michael Gains smiled into the camera and then stood up. He slowly lowered his shorts. Elizabeth's eyes widened as she gazed upon him. She quickly typed a reply.

E. Gains: I most definitely approve! Several devil smileys followed his text.

Vantress and Paschar watched the pubescent exchange. For countless years, he had seen the mating rituals of the human species. Unlike the animals El had made Adam-kind had consistently found a way to objectify the female of the species. Humankind degenerated into a lust filled debauchery.

He watched as the two exchanged glances of lust and innuendos that he knew would lead to their eventual copulation.

"She is playing with fire this one. She does not know that he is a plant by the enemy."

"No," replies Paschar. "She is infatuated and succumbing to the sin of pride: seeking affirmation at the expense of the command of God. Yes, this will end poorly."

I could, of course, kill the human, but Michael has made clear that such rules of engagement are not allowed." Vantress sighs, "Things were much easier in the days of the Canaanites."

"Indeed, but be that as it may, the maiden is filled with hurts. She is not able to process at this time the emotions that are flooding her. What will you do?"

Vantress settled into the back of the room as he continued to observe the interplay between the young girl and her male attraction. "I will take a page from your book, Grigori. I will watch for now. I need to study her family history. Her adversary has not revealed himself. I will take my leave and seek her familial record; something seems amiss here. There is a power at work here. My tours of duty have shown me that this is always true. Normally, my arrival prompts my nemesis of the Horde, to reveal himself. This has not occurred before, nor is it consistent with the tactics that I have seen. Something has changed, and I must find out what. I project that I have at least forty-eight earth hours before she is exposed to the fruit of this most recent sin. This young man is a riddled with lust. It is clear where this interchange will go."

Vantress watched as the young woman smiles in childish glee at the anticipation that she carried, watched as he had seen such human interaction play out in the past. He knew he would have to hurry before she was assaulted.

* * *

Vantress arrived in Heaven and made his way to the Grigoric Hall of Records: the building's walls projected the current happenings of the universe. Vantress wondered if men could see what he saw with what excuse would he make to Almighty to justify his existence. Plague, pestilence, war and rumors of war decorated the majority of the walls. Yet despite the horrors that man inflicted upon man. There were bastions of goodness. Like Sodom and Gomorrah, there were pinpricks of light that escaped the turmoil that crashed upon the seashore of man. From children who helped their brothers and sisters do chores to Vantress watched an image where a fire fighter rushed into a flaming building. He watched as the man's angel recorded his deeds; pryingly observed as the human rescue a small child. Only to be crushed in flaming debris. But the human would not die. He refused and pushed with his might to heave a wooden beam whilst he cradled a small baby in his arms, his oxygen mask off. Vantress knew the man's lungs were seared beyond his body's ability to repair. He watched as the human escaped the flaming building behind him. Only to collapse, his arms stretched out wide with the living child. Vantress watched the human give his dying breath to save a baby who could not even recognize his face. Vantress smiled at the sacrifice. It was almost angelic; he thought: an act worthy of an Elohim. He smiled until he saw a member of the horde standing in the doorway: one of the many rebels who now occupied the Earth, wreaking havoc on mankind. Vantress watched as the conflagration of the burning home embroiled those humans still inside. He watched as daemons were unleashed to feed upon the fear of those trapped and dying inside.

Anger welled up in his breast. His mission was to protect the damsel in his charge, and he needed intelligence on what he was up against. He continued to the reference desk to make an inquiry.

Each attendant Grigori was visible and diligently wrote the schedules of the times and seasons of creation, while most Grigori were invisible. These scurried about carrying books hither and thither and cataloging the events of all things.

Vantress approached a desk and spoke to an attendant behind the counter.

"I have come to research the bloodline of a human female, Elizabeth Foley."

The Grigori was silent and motioned for the angel to follow. Vantress stepped behind the counter and the attendant floated into a room that opened into a chamber that contained countless images of humans and their movements in clear crystals of octagonal glass. Stacks upon stacks of and rows of endless rows were littered with crystals which contained moving images of humans from all of recorded history. Vantress marveled. He had never bothered to come to the library as his work was typically in the field doing surveillance of the enemy's movements. But it impressed him.

The attendant floated to what appeared to be the center of the room and a shittim wooden table with a large glass screen materialized as they neared the center of the room.

"How am I to find the lass in all of this?" Vantress asks.

The Grigori was silent and merely motioned for the angel to sit. Vantress obeyed and seated himself. And when he did, the table spoke to him. "State a name that the record might be opened."

Vantress jumped slightly startled and replies, "Elizabeth Foley."

"There are 4,739 records. To which record would you scroll?"

"Grrr..." agitated, he replies. "Regress to earth-side solar current year, location United States, Michigan, Commerce Township."

The table's glass screen illuminated and in angelic script. Three dimensional small colored globes projected into the air. Each globe showed moving images of the young woman's birth, movements, and chronicled her entire life.

Vantress noted in one image that Elizabeth's mother was seated in a tub of warm water, fully clothed. He watched as a man cut into her wrists. Blood trickled into the water as she gradually lost consciousness. Her head tilted and her body slumped deeper into the bath as the door was broken, and her daughter ran in to shake her. Vantress watched as Elizabeth bravely called emergency services and frantically bandaged her mother's wrists. And struggled to keep her awake as she cried, holding her dying mother in her arms. But the man was no longer there.

"Is this person an angel? Has he defied the articles of war and interfered in taking this woman's life?"

But both the Grigori and the tables screen were silent.

Vantress swiped the image forward and saw her standing over a grave. Attendees walked past her and touched her shoulder in vain gestures of comfort. He watched as the preteen buried her mother and tossed a single rose into an open grave as a wooden casket was slowly lowered into the ground. He noticed a dark aura also in the girl's presence and Vantress took his fingers and expanded the image to see an angelic figure standing but ten cubits from her. The dark figure's mouth could be seen to move as if he whispered something and Vantress watched Elizabeth's lips also mouth something.

Vantress looked at the attendant, who stood silently, ready to assist. "The maiden has uttered something. What did she say?"

The Grigori took his stylus and drew a circle around the image of the girl's mouth and her words floated into the air to be heard.

"Mom, why did you leave me? What did I do? Why didn't you want to be with me anymore?"

Vantress drew back in anger and spoke to the attendant. "There is a member of the Horde in this image. He too has whispered something in the spirit towards this girl. His echo permeates her mind. Give me his words."

The attendant nodded and took his stylus and drew a circle around the angelic form that stood also at the grave site near the girl and pointed his stylus at the angel's lips, and its words floated into the air above Vantress' head to be heard.

"What did you do that your own mother no longer desires to live with you?"

Vantress grew angry and spoke. "She is but a girl. What is this filth's interest in her? Show me her ancestral line and cross reference with any familial spirits that have attacked her lineage."

The attendant was silent and merely gestured and the table caused the images to absorb back into its glass. All except one. In the image Vantress watched the young woman's birth, and slowly the images marched backwards to show the courtship of her parents, then grandparents onward as the pictures cascaded in motion.

"Hold!" Vantress yells.

Vantress eyes narrowed, and he saw a concentration camp in Bavaria, Germany. He watched as the young girl's grandfather was liberated and how he survived the war the humans had called World War two. He looked at the darkened image that hovered over the man and noted an angel also hovered near him, sword drawn.

"Do you have a clearer image of the adversary here?"

The attendant shook his head.

Vantress slammed his fist into the table. "You are the Grigori. Do you not record all?" He huffed. "Can you at least tell me if this is the same spirit at the mother's funeral?"

The Grigori nodded, staring coldly at Vantress.

Vantress looked at the angel in the image, ready for battle, and focused on the sigils embedded into his breastplate. "This one is of house, Malakim. One of Prince Gabriel's house. Curious, the Malakim only protect..."

Vantress' mind reeled, and he slowly came into the realization that her line was one of the few protected by the Malakim prince. "In El's name, she *is* descended from the tribe of Levi, then?"

The Grigori again nodded.

"With what import does the Horde place value on this life? Show me."

The Grigori then took his stylus and placed it on the glass, and the mirror shimmered in fog like distortions until a man could be seen whose child was newly born. The man then kissed the forehead of his wife as she spoke. "Hurry Micah, I will see to our daughter. Hide the scrolls. The Romans cannot be allowed to find them. Bury them my husband. Bury them deep in the caves. Let not the words of our people be left to these gentiles. May the sands hide them and let the word of God stand forever. Now hurry, my love, before the soldiers come."

The Jewish man looked at his beloved wife and the small female child she bore him. He then took a scarlet ribbon he pulled from his robes and tied it upon the wrist of his daughter. He kissed her softly on the forehead and then looked at the midwife and commanded her.

"Guard her and Elizabeth with your life. Hide them and I will return as soon as I can. Do not wait for my return. I will find you."

Vantress watched as the man left his family and traveled from the city of Qumran, making his way past Roman legionaries, he stayed in the shadows and stealthily made his way through the desert to the caves near the shores of the Dead Sea. While many of his countrymen fought and died by the Romans in a Jewish uprising. Micah scurried deep into the desert to hide the clay jars that contained the words of his people. The few remaining scrolls he had, he would see safely to the depository. He looked around, making sure he was not seen, and rushed into the dim-lit cave. He felt for the markings he had made to guide him and found at the base an indentation that showed the spot he had designated for the burial of the clay jars that held the words of God to his people. He quickly dug into the earth with hands and unearthed the top of a jar and carefully placed the papyrus scrolls within. Sealing the vessel, he covered it and continued to camouflage the area so that prying eyes would not merely stumble upon the preserved words of his people.

Vantress fidgeted in his chair and stood up and spoke, "There is nothing here that would rouse the attention of the Horde. Humans have hidden their trinkets in the ground for millennia. My time is precious..."

The Grigori then silently responded by pointing at the screen and Vantress turned around to see that a dark angelic shadow hovered above the young scribe and eyed the young man menacingly. The black-winged shadow turned to look back at the cave and he followed the young scribe back to the city of Qumran.

Micah moved deftly to evade the roman centurions that were quickly taking over the city, but when he arrived at the place where his wife had given birth, she and the midwife were gone, and instead a human-like figure stood in their place. And in his hand was the small ribbon of scarlet Micah had given his daughter.

"Please sir," Micah spoke. "That ribbon belongs to my child, have you seen her?"

The cloaked figure kept his back to him and spoke, "You have hidden the words of El in the caves. Because you have done this, I now curse you. For you and your kind have interfered with my master's plans for the last time, for we will now destroy this place because you have hidden the word of God.

If it pleases you, take comfort in that you have indeed set us back centuries. And because you have hidden the word of God from my agents, know I have now too hidden your woman and your child and have turned them over to the gentiles. Know that they shall experience servitude and hardship. For you have betrothed a wife, but another man shall lie with her."

"Nooo!!" Micah yells, and he took up his hands and ran to smite the hooded and cloaked man. But the man but spoke a word and Micah's vision suddenly left him and blackness washed over his eyes and fell to the dirt floor now blind.

Unable to see, Micah crawled towards the man to grasp his feet.

The cloaked man continued his pronouncement.

"Know son of man that your child will be given to another people and thine eyes shall look and fail with longing for her all the day long: and there shall be no might in thine hand to deliver as you hovel before me now. Your offspring shall hovel in the world of men until there is no more sun, for I will haunt your line to its extinction. For thou hast procured the curse of the Horde be upon you son of man, a curse I pledge to see fulfilled; for I shall follow the scent of your blood and if it ever bears fruit in the earth. I will see it mature, then die before your offspring's eyes. Cursed shalt thou be in thy waking and cursed shall though be in thy lying.

A vexation and plague of spirit will I haunt your seed. Cursed shalt thou be when thou comest in, and cursed shalt thou be when thou goest out: for I am he who enforces, and I shall see the thing done. Know this human and despair. Despair for thou hast drawn the ire of the Horde. Despair that I will ever watch over thee and will never, ever leave your house."

The cloaked figure then turned to face the man who groped at the ground, wailing in tears, and then slowly faded from view.

Vantress' eyes widened when he saw the adversary's face and his cheeks flushed, and he gritted his teeth in anger.

For, the angelic figure's face was now revealed. And it was the familiar face of a Harrada. The house from which Vantress himself hailed from. The stern jaw and eyes, the swagger in the stance made it clear that he would have to deal once more with an old nemesis: the same one responsible for the killing of Olen...Eridu.

Vantress rose from his seat and knocked his chair over. The table retracted the image into itself, and the angel strode past the floating Grigori in attendance and stormed out of the room to return to Earth. And the Grigori recorded Vantress' thoughts as the angel passed. Recording the mental turmoil that now raged in his mind. Thoughts that bubbled over to the Grigori's pen as it scribed the thoughts which floated into the sight of all Grigori. Thoughts that cried but one thought.

How he might kill Eridu.

* * *

Michael had made his way Earth-side to the seat of human government; flanked by his elite personal guard. Seven warrior Arelim angels flew by his side. He ordered them to post a guard around the exterior of the building: a clear warning to all members of the Horde that the chief prince of angels was planet-side and to engage him would be a folly.

Michael left his detail and floated between the constructed walls of men until he entered the chamber of the United Nations. The seat of Earth's government, he noted the seal on the back of the wall lifted high. The angel of God continued until he entered the smaller meeting chamber of the Security Council. Michael admired the mural on the wall of a phoenix rising from the ashes. A mural under where Lucifer stood waiting to meet him.

"It is an intriguing image, is it not? Here, you and I stand under the symbol of a creature that is resurrected from the ashes of its predecessor: a creature unable to die. It is a fitting banner under which we meet you and I; both of us creatures of the Kiln. Both of us eternal and each having suffered like the humans from the perils of war; and yet so unlike the human's monument to their war to end all wars: they know not that until we cease in our own struggle, there can be no true peace. No true cessation to conflict: for are they not but proxy to the battle that ensues on high? Yea, pawns in the epic struggle that wages unseen about them. Yet they have an incredible resilience to pain and stomach to the suffering that struggle leaves behind. I must admit my admiration for them, for they are ever hopeful, ever rebuilding in their foolish quest to seek a kingdom that can never be unless either El or I fall. And like this depiction of the legendary Phoenix brother, know I intend to rise. To rise from the ashes of the Descension and, with my ascension, create a new heaven and a new earth. Indeed, it is fitting that we meet in the Security Council chambers to discuss what we both know is the next phase of the war."

Lucifer then turned to Michael and looked at him. "You are Michael of the Kortai, Lumazi. And you have set eyes upon he who walks to and fro in the earth, and from walking up and down the width of it. For what reason are you come? And to what cause might I honor the Chief Prince?" Lucifer mockingly spoke.

Michael looked at the image and replies, "I bring you warning that I have found your newest felony that is called by the name of Anti-Christ. And you and I know that the articles of war concerning such creations are clear... dissolution. Be it known that you are accused of violation of these codices and have provoked the wrath of the Almighty. I give you notice to destroy this creation. Or risk the immediate removal of your candlestick and all that you still hold dear while you still can."

Lucifer laughs, "I will do no such thing. And yes, I acknowledge the creation you accuse me of. But he is not abomination. He is my beloved son. And know Usurper of my throne. We will ascend, and when we do, I warn you to vacate heaven. For destruction will surely follow in my wake. And though there is even now, even after all this time, a love for thee. My eye will not spare, nor will my hand withdraw from destroying thee."

Michael sighed and looked at the beauty of the construction of the room the humans had built. Blue damask wallpaper gilded in gold decorated the room's walls. Michael faintly touched the Naugahyde chairs. The wooden doors of entry were clearly fashioned from pale ash, and distinctive pewter-inlay patterns adorned them. Michael's eyes narrowed, and he nodded his head in recognition.

"I can see why you chose this place. For I see the faint glimmer of royalty that was once your own home. It suits you. But alas, I have delivered the message I was commissioned to give. And having done so even after millennia, I sadly still long for you, or more accurately, the person you once were. I had once hoped that you would turn from this wayward way: that you would seek repentance and restoration from the Father. Why? Because we are carved from the same stone you and I. The same kiln of fire and power: shaped by the hand of God himself. You are my brother, and I find that even after all this time. I hoped against hope that love would be found between us. For you and I shall always be brothers, Lucifer. We both know what is about to happen. We sense it. The end is coming. I have yet held out hope that my brother, he who rescued me from the clutches of the Abyss itself, still lives."

Lucifer looked at Michael, and his eyes penetrated deep into his brother's pleading face. He cocked his head to the side, smirked, then answered his brother: his voice dripping in sarcastic tenor.

"Then I regret you will forever see your hope deferred. My brother died to me in the Kiln: a death of fellowship when he opposed my right to be God. We will always be enemies you and I. Now leave me; for we are no more children of the Kiln. No more prepubescent in the ways of El; for it was not I who destroyed the birthplace of angels; nor I who stood as an adversary to my plans to save our kind. We both know self-rule or God-rule is the way that divides us. I would see our people free. Whilst you fawn in glee to serve as a bond slave to the true adversary. For God doth know we are like Him: to know both good and evil." Lucifer then turned his back to his brother and waved him away in disgust and rage.

"Get thee hence brother, and never—ever show thy face again. For on the day we next meet. Know that you will surely die."

Michael nodded in acknowledgment and replies, "As you say. Goodbye Lucifer. Know that I go to hunt thy spawn."

Lucifer chuckled menacingly as his brother began to leave the room. "You will find him in Brussels. But be careful what you wish for. For did not Argoth tell you that if ye seek, ye shall find?" Lucifer then laughs with a confident and maniacal glee as Michael turned around in horror. His pulse racing that Lucifer knew his private conversation with Argoth. And Michael watched in confusion and shock as Satan grinned. "Argoth is not the only Grigori with the power to see into the future." He then smiles and disappeared from view.

* * *

Marduk entered his hall and seated himself on his regional throne as the prince of power over Persia. He smiled as he took his seat and spoke. "At last, Lucifer has made his move. At last, he plays his hand and even now provokes me to see him destroyed. I will see that he has his wish."

Marduk eyed the assembled human leaders who composed the Arab league beneath his feet; each a puppet to the true puppeteer and instruments in his hand to influence as he saw fit. He whispered words to each as the humans representing the League of Arab nations walked into a boardroom and seated themselves. The minister from Saudi Arabia was first to speak, "I have been apprised of the Secretary General's demand we withdraw claim to the Temple Mount. And that he be allowed to dig on or around the Noble Sanctuary. He is audacious this one. I say we see his head hung as an infidel. He is a beast of a man. It is even said that he does not enjoy the pleasure of women. Will we let this mockery of a man dictate to us? Allah will not forgive us if we yield to this western cheth."

The words of the ambassador stung many in the room. Many nodded their heads in agreement. "Be that as it may," says the Ambassador from Egypt. "He commands the military of all of Europe and the Russians and Chinese have aligned themselves with him. We cannot hope to win a war against them. The Americans in a first have remained neutral on the issue."

"Imagine that," says... Nephi "The Americans shutting up for a change." Many in the room joked. But the ambassador of Egypt continued. "Amusing as it may seem, we have not the combined force to wage direct war with the Secretary General. Nor have we established a solution to the virus which plagues us. My people are starving. Our resources locked behind accounts we cannot access: frozen. The wages we have promised our people are unable to be distributed. Our factories and commerce have virtually ground to a standstill. His idea that we all engage in a universal basic income has done nothing but chain us and our populations where none can buy nor sell without this "mark". He has us economically and militarily. I ask in all sincerity. This Leto is a madman who can make war with the beast?"

The ambassador from Jordan spoke. Leto has placed us in an untenable position, and he knows this. If we do nothing, he will simply take the Dome by force. We will have forced into a war, and we will lose. If we surrender to his demands, our respective populations will rise against us and he will again take the Dome by force. Our acquiescence to his demands would lead our populations to civil war as they fight to remove us from power and attempt to stop him to no avail; wiping out many of our people in the attempt if we even dare raise arms against him. We will again lose, for we cannot hope to overtake him when even the Russians and Chinese are at his command. It is as if he is provoking us to war, provoking us to move against him. He has laid a trap from which there is no way of escape. I realize we will die. All that must be decided is merely how we will choose to die. And knowing the Secretary, I can imagine he laughs as we debate on the prospect."

Many in the room were quiet. Contemplating the ambassador's words and realizing that all courses of action lead to one outcome: their inevitable demise.

The ambassador from Jordan contained. "I do not need to hear more. It is simple truth that we have been outplayed gentlemen. Leto has spoken of peace, but there is no peace. There is nothing but the web of his deceit. I do not need to hear more. I will relay my decision to His Majesty the King. If we must die, then I vote it will be on our feet. We will brave this struggle for Allah and for our people; as for the rest of you. I suggest you prepare yourselves for war, for there is no condition under which Leto will allow our existence." The ambassador laughed. "Is it not ironic that we have commanded and organized the extinction of the Jewish state of Israel; only to come to this time in history where we now must face the possibility of our own extinction?" The ambassador from Jordan shook his head at the irony. "If you wish to coordinate your efforts with our own, you know where to find me." The ambassador then stood and turned and left the room.

Each delegate looked, and the chair brought a resolution to the floor. "Ambassador Yosef is right. We have been lied to and backed into an untenable corner with no way to turn. I propose we unite and fight. If we must die, then let us have control over how it is to be. I propose we attack. I will take Ambassadors Yosef's response as a second: all those in favor?"

Each turned and looked at the other. And the count proceeded on this wise.

"Egypt says yea."

"Algeria says yea."

"Bahrain votes yes."

"Iraq says yes."

"Kuwait says yea."

"Libya says yes."

"Lebanon says yea."

"Yemen says yea."

"The UAE says yea."

Continuing around the room, each nation voted to determine the future of their states. Each cast a vote for what they knew would be the end of their lives as they knew it. All casting yea until there were no votes left to cast.

"The vote caries gentlemen: as of this day we are at war and may Allah help us all."

Marduk lifted above the proceedings and smiled at the outcome. An adjutant floated by his side as he listened to his master. "Finally," says Marduk. "I will have the chance to destroy this upstart king. Marduk then called an attendant to him.

"Alert the legions that today we march to destroy the Abomination and place angelic rule where it truly belongs: in the hands of angels. Be swift and muster our forces, for I can finally battle with the Son of the Morning Star!" And soon... soon there will be a new king of the Horde!"

The attendant bowed and left his master to do his will.

* * *

The King of Jordan video conferenced the Secretary General of the United Nations and explained the decision of the Arab League.

Leto Alexander, Secretary General of the United Nations, picked up his phone and spoke. "Ah, King Hussein, it is good to hear from you. I trust that you and your peers have had time to deliberate on my proposal and wish to convey your willingness to accept my offer?"

King Hussein replies, "It is with regret I must inform you that the league has declined your proposal. We will not submit to the Temple Mount's destruction. I inform you that any incursion on your part or that of Israel to dismantle the holy site will be interpreted as an act of war."

Leto smirked and replies, "That is unfortunate. However, perhaps I did not make myself clear before to your ambassadors. Earlier you had a choice. Although, you still actually possess a choice. Earlier, your options were to come and join me willingly. Now it would seem that you have elected to be dragged kicking and screaming with your populations serving the Commonwealth for the betterment of mankind while we go on to fight this external threat. No matter. Know we will not attack unless provoked, but I have already ordered the Temple to be dismantled and moved. But know if someone attack us be prepared for war. For if war is what you have decreed. Then war you shall have."

Leto then slammed his phone into its receiver, cutting the King of Jordan off. He then turned to his lieutenants. "Tell Israel to stay out of the upcoming conflict but tell them they may begin with the temple's destruction. Inform them that the Commonwealth will protect them nor will they have to fight in this matter. I want their attention to be devoted to the destruction of the mount. If they do this, let them know they have my word they will be unmolested during the time it will take to excavate the Temple Mount. I make this treaty for seven years. Also inform the Prime minister I will launch an all-out attack tonight against the Arab league for their refusal to come to terms with the peace treaty I have proposed."

"But Mr. Secretary, you just told the King of Jordan..."

Leto stood and proceeded to open closets so that he might find a new suit and tie. "I know what I told him. I lied. Now hurry. The sooner we get this battle over with, the sooner we may begin with the true war that matters."

* * *

Elizabeth walked up to the house of Michael Gaines. The neighborhood was dotted with homes on ample acreage, which spoke of money and exclusivity. The house was surrounded by large, coniferous pine trees and afforded privacy from the front to the back of the dwelling. Situated at the end of a cul-de-sac, the home was in front of a private access lake behind the large contemporary home. Colored lights flickered off and on from the windows and "Walk it Out" by Unk could be heard over outdoor speakers. Students filled the front lawn and multiple dancing silhouettes moved in the windows. The smell of barbecue, beer and coupled with the ninety-degree heat and humidity provided an atmosphere conducive for shorts and minimalist wear. It was perfect weather for an end of the school year party.

The premises overflowed with teenagers. Sweat beaded from adolescent boys and girls and their dance movements to each beat sprayed from teen bodies. In occasional mists. Girls gyrated their abdomens in circular movements while others hiked their butts into the crouches of their male companions. The atmosphere was raucous and catcalls and woots emanated from approving male onlookers, each holding plastic cups of beer. Wide-eyed smiles from both girls and boys flashed incessantly over all. Kegs lined the side near a driveway leading up to a three-car garage where a table had been set up and bear flowed from several makeshift taps. Another eight-foot table was filled with waffles, fried chicken, and various soft drinks.

Elizabeth was suddenly grabbed by the arm and was turned around by Audrey of the Jefferson sisters, who stood giggling and holding a cup of beer desperately clinging to the rim of its container. Audrey leaned towards her and yelled into Elizabeth's ear.

"Hey, Liz, good to see you girl. This party is off the hook! Come on over here and check this out."

Audrey pulled her by the hand and both girls sauntered over to another table that was filled with Bacardi, Absolut Vodka, and Malibu Caribbean Rum. Audrey reached towards a bowl full of gummy bears soaked in vodka and lifted the alcohol-soaked chewy candy to her lips.

Elizabeth reluctantly agreed to her peer and opened her mouth to receive the candy. She grimaced when she first tasted the concoction not used to the mix of flavors that now assaulted her tongue. But gradually she came to like it.

"Uh huh, good, huh? Here, come over here!" says Audrey

Elizabeth followed as she was pulled along by Audrey, making their way around the grounds to the back of the house. Audrey stopped as several teens were in bathing suits lounging in the in-ground pool while others were further out sitting on a boat making out and enjoying the sight of jet skis criss crossing over the lake. A gas grill was fired up and two 50-inch screen monitors were showing highlights of this season's football games while the other latest rap and pop videos filled with scantily clad women dancing as money was being thrown at them.

"Omg Elizabeth, isn't this the best party ever! Mike outdid himself girl. Hey, I think he's inside. He asked about you, you know? He was wondering if you were coming. You should go find him, I'm sure he's around trying to be a good host. I'm gonna get some of those vodka gummy bears. I'll look for you inside."

Elizabeth nodded and took in the sights and sounds of suburban adolescence. She had worked hard to get her grades to where she could compete for scholarships. And now it was time to cut loose and relax. She deserved a break; she thought. It was nice to actually fit in for a change. To not be teased by at least one of the Jefferson sisters.

"Hey Audrey," says Elizabeth.

Audrey turned around and cupped her ear to focus better on what Elizabeth was saying. "When you see me inside, bring me some of those gummy bears too!"

Audrey smiled and sauntered back towards the front of the house.

Elizabeth made her way around the pool, as various ones greeted her and smiled, and found her way to the back patio door and slid the glass door open. She entered the basement entertainment area of the home, and several fellas were around a pool table talking smack to impress the girls who sat on bar stools nearby. Each young lady was sipping from a straw with their drinks in hand.

Elizabeth saw a friend of hers named Carol and approached her. "Hey Carol, how d'you make out in Ms. Tess's class?"

"Sheesh, that woman is no joke! But I survived with a B, so I'm happy. How about you?"

Elizabeth gave her a smile and a side-eye and replied. "A girl!" Carol frowned. "Oh, shut up. I knew I should've studied with you instead of Jan Simpson. That girl does not know how to focus, always talking about boys."

"That's what you get...lol I told you to come by."

"Yeah, yeah." she says.

"So, have you seen Mike? He invited me and I wanted to make sure I let him know I was here and wanted to say thanks."

"Yeah, I think I saw him upstairs last by the DJ table they set up in the living room. Have fun girl."

"Yeah, you too!" Elizabeth made her way up the carpeted stairs and opened a door that led into the kitchen. Granite counter-tops were awash with more gummy bears, fruit, nuts and booze. The kitchen and the adjoining rooms were open concept in design, with ample room for lounging and dancing. And the invited guests took every opportunity to both lounge and dance. Several girls were dancing in the living room as coffee tables and other artistic platforms were moved to the ends of the room, making way for a large area for people to show off their latest dance moves.

Near the back of the living room was a DJ with several monitors, an iPad, and other devices she simply didn't recognize. Portable black speakers were set up on large silver tripods and Mike Gains was looking across the morass of people when she and he locked eyes.

Mike smiled with the largest of grins and Elizabeth immediately became flushed. He motioned with his hand to come over and she traveled through the makeshift dance floor towards the DJ table, and he hugged her.

She nervously returned the hug. This feels nice, she thought. Really nice. She quickly released him and reached over to speak into his ear.

"Mike, this is an awesome party. Thanks for inviting me!"

Mike returns her attempt to speak over the music and said, "Cool, huh? Hey, I'm glad you came because, you know, I put on this elaborate party just so I could get you to dance with me." He smiles and Elizabeth drew her neck back and smirked, rolling her eyes. "Riiight... nice line though. I do like it!" She couldn't help but laugh.

She then gave him a gingerly punch on the shoulder. He returned her beaming smile and leaned over into her ear. "So, does that mean you would care to dance?"

She looked at him with a smirk and shrugged her shoulders, "Sure."

Mike turned to the DJ and said something to him she couldn't hear, and captain of the football team took her by the hand and led her out to the living room floor to dance. The DJ slowed the music down and over the speakers Ed Sheeran's "Perfect" played and instinctively boys across the room reached out to their partner to dance: leading them to the dance floor while others left the area to sit on couches and watched those who danced. Mike looked down at Elizabeth and gazed into her eyes, "You OK?"

"It's just a little bright in here, and everyone's looking at us." She nestled her face into Mike's firm chest and Mike spoke.

"Alexa, dim the lights in the living room."

The room slowly dimmed where the staring eyes disappeared into the shadows and those dancing became mere silhouettes. "That's better?"

"Yes, much better," says Elizabeth. She allowed herself to be swept into the moment, swaying to the song's snap of acoustic fingers coming over the loudspeaker. She relaxed, melting into the ambiance of it all. For here at the end of the school year, the boy she dreamed of holding her. Cradled in Mike's strong arms, she was no longer the bullied wall flower of school but accepted by her peers.

She sighs; it was truly "perfect".

Chapter Six: Peace in Our Time

Gabriel stood next to Jeremiah as each observed the spectacle which transpired within the throne room. For the Lord God, Yeshua had taken the book from the hand of El and gingerly opened it to reveal its contents. For Argoth had transformed into a book of seals: a tomb that smoldered with the offenses of God. Yeshua then grasped the second seal and snapped it. The sound of thunder echoed across Heaven and when the Lord God Yeshua broke the crimson clay seal a mist of blood sprang forth, and from the vaporous cloud of blood there went out from the book a second rider who sat upon a horse that was red: and power was given to him that sat thereon to take peace from the earth, and that they should kill one another: and there was given unto him a great sword.

He galloped across the skies of Heaven and left her shores trotting downward to the Earth below. Jerahmeel, Gabriel and those members of the Lumazi still Heaven-side watched as the rider raced through the darkness of space and descended to the realm of mortal men. The rider raised his sword above his head and when he did so; he charged forward into Persia and landed atop the nation of Egypt and when he did so; he stepped from off his horse and plunged his sword into the head of the Nile River. A red fog then wafted into the air, and it billowed up in a concentric wave, spreading out in all directions.

Then the horseman raised his head and stood from where he had plunged his sword deep into the earth and when he did so; Marduk's face could be seen. The great angel rose, standing clad in blood red armor, and spoke.

"Members of the Horde hear me! Come all who would be free of the shackle of Lucifer! Come and see our failing leader's blood shed!"

And when he spoke, puffs of red smoke came from his lips like thunder clouds and the crimson clouds swept over the entire planet and smothered both angel and humankind in a cloud of rage.

At first there was quiet, but then small skirmishes broke out in small pockets in each continent. Violence spread like a virus to all corners of the globe as members of the Horde fought with one another. And Heaven watched from above as the Horde turned from fighting the forces of El that were planet-side and turned their swords one towards another.

For all those angels who were indebted, discontent, and discouraged with Lucifer, now found boldness to rebel against their king. The Horde engaged one another in battle; and as they did: men who were their proxies, commanded their armies to overrun the land.

War broke out and spread like wildfire amongst the humans; from the Commonwealth of Europe to the Arab League. Nation battled nation and smote their respective enemies with bombs and launched their airplanes and navies against one another until the whole of the planet was engulfed in rage. A rage fueled by the forces of Marduk against the forces of Lucifer and his Anti-Christ.

And Heaven looked on in amazement, for never had any seen the likes of disunity that ran amok amongst their kind save the Great Rebellion against the Lord. And for a time Heaven had no need to fight the enemy, for the enemy fought themselves. Jerahmeel watched the dissension that rose between the members of the Horde and remembered the Lord Yeshua's words to his disciples. "If Satan rise up against himself, and be divided, he cannot stand, but hath an end." And Jerahmeel knew that what he observed was the beginning of the end for his fallen brother; that soon there would be no line between the spirit realm and the physical. No demarcation between the realms and that open warfare was soon to come. That El in his mastery had unleashed civil war within the ranks of his adversary, and that soon destruction would follow.

Gabriel also watched the chaos below and spoke aloud his thoughts to his brother.

"Jerahmeel, what should we do? We witness civil war among the Horde. Do we intervene? Do we move to advantage ourselves against them? For Michael is still away and searches for the Abomination."

And the Holy Spirit, knowing the thoughts of Gabriel's heart, spoke to him and replied. "Nay, my son, for this thing is of me, that all things might be fulfilled. But go thy way and make haste, for soon I must call my children home. "Now gather thy brethren and bring me the Shaun-tea'll and assemble them before me. And have Nephanos bring me the trumpets. For they shall be blown that my wrath might be fulfilled."

Both Gabriel and Jerahmeel looked at each other in concern, for the trumpets were the divine weapons of mass destruction that God had ordained would be used to bring judgment on Lucifer and the sons of man who rebelled against Him.

"And what of me, my king? What am I to do Lord?" says Jerahmeel.

The Holy Spirit spoke, and his voice rang powerfully in the ears of his servant.

"Thou shalt go to the Seal of the Abyss and prepare to unlock he who dwells therein. Await my word, and when I give the command, thou shalt loose Abaddon that he might do my will."

And when those within earshot of the Holy Spirit heard the word Abaddon; each grew silent and looked knowingly at Jerahmeel. Jerahmeel frowned as he clutched the key to the bottomless pit that was draped around his neck; frowned because he knew that this day would one day come: frowned because if the Destroyer was released, the Earth would tremble. The head of house Harrada then swallowed hard and replied to his Lord.

"As you command, my king."

* * *

Leto sat with his advisers in the situation room of the headquarters of the Commonwealth. He watched on large screen monitors as the armies of his allies marched into the cities of his enemies. Strafing runs from Tu -95's carpet bombed Jordan and the surrounding countryside of Amman. Leto smiled at his generals and nodded in approval. "Continue in the advance towards the capitals of each rebel nation. You will halt when you are at the outskirts of each. Then I will inquire if these rebels will at last surrender or will they choose to be destroyed. I will be in my ready room. Call me when it is time to contact the rebel commanders."

Leto stood up to leave and his generals and advisers also stood, and he exited the room and entered into his private room. His room was furnished with the finest oak desks and plush with comfortable chairs and the flags of the former European Union and now the newly crafted flag of the commonwealth draped his office. He looked through his window to see the city of Brussels and its bastion of people. And when he did, he stared into the distance across the horizon. His mind occupied by the events of the war that now waged against the Arab nations.

Leto was relieved to dismiss himself from the affairs of men. For, while the armies of men gathered and struck each other with missiles and artillery. The real war, the unseen war, could now be attended to.

"Ashtaroth, now that we have privacy. Show me Marduk."

Ashtaroth did as commanded and became visible to the human eye. "Lathum, show the young master what he desires."

Lathum, the Grigori assigned to Leto, then took the book, which floated near his winged shoulder and opened it. He tore out a page and threw it into the air. It rose until it hit the ceiling and when it did; it became opaque and draped as a curtain over the entire room. Immediately, the surroundings disappeared and in the place of chairs and desks were now angels with swords that hovered over and around the building. In the distance, thunder roared, and flashes of light blazed in the distance. Angels as numerous as the stars littered the skies and were engaged in battle. The realm of the spirit was now open for Leto to see.

"Marduk," says Leto, "What is his position, and how fares my father's forces?"

Lathum replies, "The rogue principality hovers over Damascus, young king. His advance towards Jerusalem has been stopped and his forces have been repelled. He now garrisons in Damascus. It is only a matter of time before he is destroyed. He is prevented from entering Israel by the Host who stand to his west whilst the Horde cordons him on all remaining sides. To risk entry into Israel is to risk a fight on two fronts. It would surely be suicide; for he would be destroyed either by the Host or by the Horde. He is a wandering spirit... he simply does not know it yet."

"Good." whispered Leto. "Let my father toy with his nemesis. Are my people ready to begin with the destruction of the mount and to begin excavation of the weapon?"

Ashtaroth replies, "All is ready, my king. As soon as hostilities cease with the rebel kingdoms, we will begin at your orders."

"Well done," replies Leto. "Tell my father that soon; his son will be ready to take up the mantle for which he has been called, and we will strike at Heaven. Soon we shall return recompense to those who have kept us underfoot, and soon... we will have our revenge."

* * *

Marduk knew it was only a matter of time before his angelic soldiers would be overrun. He watched from a distance as many valiantly stood to keep Lucifer's forces at bay from him: each willingly gave up their heart stones to dissolution that the true stead-holder to champion their dream of self-rule could be realized. But Marduk realized he had been played. Like a king in an elaborate game of chess; he had been slowly forced to move his forces into a position of weakness; for the Host was now at his back, and those members of the Horde loyal to Lucifer flanked him on all remaining sides. He contemplated on how he might move himself to a position of strength and called his adjutant to his side.

Marduk eyed the activity from atop of Mt. Nebo. The ancient burial ground of Moses. From its vantage point, he looked across the Jordan River to the land of Canaan. He could see the cadre of angels the Host had assembled to prevent invasion by a principality. Israel was a spiritual fortress, a land that was on lock down from any incursion, and only abandonment by the Chief Prince or El himself would allow the small country to fall. For buried deep under the

Mohammedan shrine was a god-stone. Marduk knew it was this stone's proximity to Mohamed that had entranced the old prophet and granted him his night journey.

"Mušḫuššu attend me."

Mušḫuššu had eyed his lord from a distance that he might minister to him if called and hovered towards him, then bowed, as was protocol. "My liege?"

"You will take this message to the Chief Prince Michael. Give him word that I freely give intelligence he will want to hear. Let him know Lucifer seeks control of a God-stone that is buried deep under the prince's very feet. Tell him to imagine what the Abomination could bring to pass if he discovered it. Impress upon him Mušḫuššu that Leto cannot be allowed to have it and that if he desires for it to remain undisturbed, he will come to my aid and help me oppose Satan. He will do this. Or he will witness a Nephilim become as God. Tell him this Mušḫuššu. If he desires its location, tell him to come. Now hurry and be swift to deliver the word; for I fear that soon Lucifer himself will come to lay claim to my head."

"But my lord," says Mušḫuššu. "When I cross into the Holy land, the Host will surely accost me. How will I convince them I have not come for the sake of mischief towards God's holy people?"

Marduk looked at his ring and removed the signet of his house and gave it to his servant. "Show them this. This will grant you passage to speak to the Chief Prince. Now be off with you now. Fear not if I am gone when you return, but see to the mission. Lucifer has gone mad and does not realize that this Abomination he has created threatens not just one, but two worlds. Go now and carry my words."

Mušḫuššu bowed and lifted himself to fly across the Jordan River into Israel. A mission he hoped would see the Host take a stand against the Anti-Christ.

* * *

Leto was seated at his desk when Lathum interrupted him. "Young Dragon, there is a word that an envoy of Marduk has been seen leaving the field of battle and has crossed into enemy territory."

Leto looked unimpressed and replies, "And what of it?"

We... do not know my king... he is now out of our sight to know his coming in and going out."

Perturbed, Leto replies, "You mean to tell me that my enemy has sent a message to—my enemy?" Leto then contemplated this action and surmised his opponent's plan... then laughs.

"Marduk seeks aid. He realizes he cannot defeat us. Desperation makes one do reckless things Lathum. Fear floats in the air above Mt. Nebo, Grigori. I do not require your angelic eyes to know this. His actions are of no consequence, for soon I will be given access freely to the Holy Land and that which they guard so fiercely will be denied me no more." Leto sniggers.

"I will soon be granted authority by the powers that are ordained by God himself: to rule his own people. They themselves will give me this right, what then can even Michael the prince of heaven hope to do? Marduk's actions are of no consequence Lathum; for he can neither impede me nor interfere. For my father hast gone before me and hast prepared the Israelites to receive me. He has surely made a way and has prepared me a table in the midst of my enemies. Proceed with the principalities destruction and relay this development to my father. Michael of the Kortai is too late to stop what is in now in progress. Now do not disturb me until Marduk is within reach to be destroyed. For at the moment, I must be about my father's business."

Lathum looked at Ashtaroth, who stood silent, and his curiosity got the better of him and he opened his mouth to inquire of the human. "And what business might that be, young dragon?"

Leto looked up, irritated, but answered. "To steal, kill and destroy, of course." Now leave me, before I choose another set of eyes to see for me."

Lathum bowed, then misted out of his master's sight.

* * *

Mušḫuššu flew over the water of the Dead Sea and quickly approached the border of Israel. Spread out equidistantly from one another; were seven powerful principalities that stood as a guard to Israel's eastern door. Their vigilance was ever present: they easily saw Mušḫuššu and three of the angels quickly moved to intercept him with swords drawn.

Mušḫuššu slowly crossed the border of the two countries, hovered in place, and lifted his sword from its scabbard, holding it high in a show of obeisance and surrender.

The three quickly surrounded him and a Malakim spoke as the mouthpiece of the Eastern gate of the land.

"You are trespassing on the Holy Land: this land in under the protection of the Chief Prince, Michael of the Kortai. You will state your purpose for this incursion of you will be destroyed."

"Mušḫuššu bowed his head and replied, "Be not angry with this dog. For I come on behalf of my master to give the chief prince news of the Horde war that now rages. He hast given me his seal and commands me to give this message to Michael. I ask that I not be deterred in my task. For even now he may still live, and I hope to return that I too might fight by his side if need be against the plans Lucifer has unleashed upon the world."

The Malakim looked puzzled and replies, "It has been a long time since I have seen honor among a member of the Horde. But alas, you were once such as us. I am the guard of the Eastern Gate to the land of Israel. I will permit you this courtesy in remembrance to our duty to honor the charges given us. Come with me: stay near and they will not harm you; deviate from the path with which I traverse, and you will see oblivion. Am I clear herald of Marduk?"

"You are clear," says Mušḫuššu.

"Then come, for I am curious to see what would cause an angel to brave confrontation with the royal guard of the Holy People."

Mušḫuššu turned and the four angels flew towards Jerusalem, the spiritual capital of the land, to see Michael.

* * *

Marduk screamed as his attackers, accosted him. "Luciferian dogs!" he yells. "I will not be brought down by the likes of you!"

An angel came at him with his sword, and Marduk raised his arm to block the celestial blade. The jagged edge slid as steel against his muscular arms as it ran the length of his forearm, creating sparks as it did. Marduk swung his other arm and wrapped it around the neck of his adversary and twisted it until the angel's neck snapped and he dropped the limp body to the ground. Noxious fumes floated from open pores in Marduk's body, creating a toxic cloud: any encroachment to attack him made his opponent's flesh sizzle as if acid touched their skin.

Marduk roared as a legion of angels was now assembled to strike him down. His hulking and muscular frame threatened dissolution to any angel that was careless enough to attack him one on one. He raised his flanged mace up high and with his two other arms beat against his chest in defiance.

"I have fought the Lumazi! I am the prince of Babylon! A principality of the Horde and Prince over the lands of Nebuchadnezzar! Lucifer sends you to accost me only to die! Come rebels to the true cause of self-rule... come and have your reward!"

The assembled angels looked to their commander, who edged them onward when above Marduk a prismatic beam of light enveloped him. Mt. Nebo suddenly stood awash in the colors of the rainbow and reds, blues and greens, dropped as rain from the funnel, which reached into the sky. A ladder had been formed and the power of it caused all who saw the celestial bridge to draw back in fear. For only the Ophanim created such a passage, and a bridge meant that in moments Heaven would soon arrive.

Immediately the great cloud retracted and in its wake Michael, and five hundred warrior angels stood by their chief prince and each stood both above and surrounding Marduk with swords, hammers and spears raised to attack. Michael's halo glowed above his head and the sword of Ophanim was unsheathed and its blades spun in gyroscopic orbit as its master belted out warning to the amassed Horde army.

"Hear me, members of the Horde. I have come for the words of Marduk to hear his claims. He may not be accosted and is under the protection of the Host. Defy this command and know that I call Heaven and Earth against you that you will surely die. Give way to the command of Heaven or give way to her wrath! But by my command or by my sword thou shalt surely give way!"

Thousands of angelic adversaries ceased when they saw Michael the chief prince. Many immediately retreated. Others circled the entourage, assessing this new development wondering how they might press their attack.

Michael cocked his head to the side at those that still thought they might attack and spoke. "Foolish you have become in your service to your king. Ever learning yet never coming into the knowledge of the truth. Have you so foolishly lost the fear of Heaven and of her Host?"

Michael then looked to one of his lieutenants and nodded. The Malakim angel raised his spear and flung the weapon towards the nearest enemy. It changed in mid-flight and turned into a serpent. And when it reached its target, it slammed itself against the face of Michael's foe and it was like a snake coiled around the face. The angel fell, plummeting to the ground, attempting in vain to remove the beast from his head. Falling into the ground, a dust cloud was raised as the angel fell before those that stood in abeyance, still eying the scene. The body of the angel jerked in several uncontrolled spasms and then ceased to move. The coiled snake then unwound itself from the face of its prey: sprouted wings and then lifted itself into the air and returned to the hand of Michael's lieutenant.

All then looked upon the angel whose stone was dark and where there was once a face there was no more; for nothing but a skull remained and snippets of flesh.

Michael then roars to those still eying the corpse and said, "Disperse! I command you!"

Immediately thousands broke rank, and the physical sky responded in kind and clouds, which had earlier coalesced above Mt. Nebo dispersed, and clear skies were all that remained.

Marduk laughed. "I see my herald has done well. You honor me, Chief Prince."

Michael turned to look at Marduk. He unfolded his fist and within it he held the signet ring of Marduk. He flung the angelic jewelry to the angel and Marduk snatched it from the air and placed the ring upon his finger.

"I did not breach the borders of Jordan for pleasantries principality of nothing," says Michael. "And yes Mušḫuššu has delivered your message. Thus, in honor of Heaven's traditions, I have come. Speak your peace."

Marduk nodded, "Very well, know that I have accepted the fate of Heaven, and yea even that of Lucifer himself. I realize that I am dead and that my every breath is on borrowed time. I have accepted that soon my time must come. But you must know that though we are at odds, you and I are united in this one thing: the Abomination must be destroyed. You know of him, of course?"

"Michael nodded, "Yea, the human Leto. I have assessed him, and he is not a threat."

Marduk laughs, "Then you have assessed wrong Chief Prince. For he is the tip of the Hordes spear, that will in your arrogance pierce Heaven. He is the ultimate expression of Satan's hate against the Father, and if ye are wise, you would have him killed."

Michael harrumphed. "Perhaps what you say is true. Nevertheless, the life of the Nephilim is not in my hands to take: such decisions are for the Father to decide. For now, my eye is not set against his life. Should, as you say, he do the impossible and breach the shores of Heaven, I will gladly seek the spawn of Satan's death. Surely this concern for a Nephilim is not why you would draw me from Israel's defense. Present thy petition and be off with you."

"Very well, said Marduk. "I request the Abomination's life or at least non-interference of thy hand to take it."

Michael looked intrigued at Marduk and the swords which swirled around him settled from seven blades and merged slowly into one. Michael looked at Marduk with both caution and intrigue. "Speak thy peace," he says. "For I will hear thee on this matter."

* * *

Leto turned over his desk, and it went flying across the room. Papers, pens and objects smashed into the office door and walls.

"Michael has come, you say?" Leto threw a paper weight through the office window and the force shattered it. "That angel has interfered with my plans for the last time." Leto growled. "Ashtaroth, take me to my father now."

Ashtaroth bowed, and he looked at Lathum. The misted angel then took his pen and drew with it a door in the air. A portal then opened the edges of which glowed, and when it did, it led to the general assembly Hall of the United Nations in New York.

"My young prince, know that if you do this..." says Ashtaroth. "You will remove the cover Lucifer has placed over you. I cannot predict how the master will react. Nor can I cover your absence of presence if you do this. The humans will know that you are in league with angelic powers."

Leto still breathes heavily from his flipping the desk over in his wrath and nodded. "Understood; accompany me, for if father wills, I would have him come down now to deal with Michael."

"Where you lead, I will follow, young prince," says Ashtaroth.

Suddenly, men burst through the door: military police with guns and rifles raised. Several generals and the head of security piled in and a general shouted. "Sir, are you alright? We heard a commotion."

Leto nodded. "I am fine, gentlemen. But it would seem that I must leave for a moment. Be not alarmed, I will return shortly."

Immediately the chief of Leto Alexander's security detail, who stood outside the ready room, lifted his wrist to his mouth and whispered into his intercom, "Dragon one is leaving. Prepare the carriage."

"That will not be necessary," says Leto. He then waved all the men down, pulled his suit jacket down, straightened his tie and walked around the debris littered on the office floor towards them.

The men and a few of the generals looked at their commander confused; then equally in awestruck wonderment as Leto Alexander walked towards them; then vanished from their sight.

* * *

Michael sighed deeply, tilted his head back and closed his eyes; placing his hands on his hips, and spoke. "I grow tired, fat one, and await your words, Marduk."

Marduk laughs, "Very well Kortai, if you have an ear to hear; then hear carefully what I says unto you... you have been misled. You are aware of the God-stones destruction when your armies invaded Hades and routed the Horde?

"Yes," replies Michael. "The gem was used by the Adversary to create a false kiln. It was destroyed when the Lord led captivity captive. What of it?"

"Ah, but chief prince, the gem was not destroyed. It was merely fractured: its parts scattered hither and thither. We both know a gem such as that can never truly be destroyed. For they are the stuff of creation themselves... flakes of God's power. Surely even you know this? But into three fragments, the stone shattered. The largest piece is in possession of Lucifer himself; the other, given to the Abomination Leto. The third Lucifer has searched for and has finally found: yea, it sleeps even in the underworld yet also abides deep in the earth... phased between the two realities of Hades and the natural realm. Its physical form abides in Israel. And is the final piece needed to reactivate the God-stone's song.

Michael frowned and his face turned ashen-white and pallid. "What you say cannot possibly be true. There is nothing to show that a God-stone sings in the Earth. How can such a thing be? You lie! You lie!" Michael's sword unsheathed from its scabbard and it pointed in Marduk's direction.

The principality raised his hands in abeyance. "Nay, grand prince. My words are true. And I know the location of the stone. A location within the domain you are charged to protect. I had always wondered why El made you protector over Israel. Why, *you* were the archangel assigned to guard El's people. For many years I had conjectured; had thought El's covenant with the Jews placed them as a priority for protection. And while this is true, I have learned that El is a master of guile and ruse. Thus, I have come to a greater understanding that El's ways are so beyond our ways: that what we consider guile and ruse is simply El's ability to think beyond our own limited thinking: to see all possibilities at once. I came to realize that I was a fool to leave Heaven. I know this. But my path cannot be changed. Hence, in the absence of my and mine brethren's return; self-rule is the best path for our people. But Lucifer... Lucifer has fallen away even from this. I thought I followed a being who would champion this cause. But nay, he merely champions the cause that sees him as ultimate ruler and the usurper of God."

"But alas, I digress, the God-stone Michael of the Kortai, is in Jerusalem itself. Buried just below the foundations of the work of my own hands. For a long time have I labored under Lucifer's leash. Long have I done the bidding of my master. And I was excellent in all my doings. For my charge Michael of the Kortai was to raise a people: a people who would supplant the world. For my master's strategy was to sow tares throughout all that El would plant. And what such a tare could he better sow than to raise a people whose belief in El rivals that of his own people: yea, even to fanaticism? And Lucifer, knowing after his defeat... knowing upon Christ's resurrection he could not return to Jerusalem to succor the remnants of what might allow him to ascend to grasp the ankles of God; devised a scheme. So, he planted a tare. A jealous and contentious people who would joust with the Jews over all things religious... a people who would strive in envy over all things that are owed the firstborn but given to another. Brethren of Abraham: Ishmaelite's in both body and spirit who would never yield to anything less than the Jews' destruction and to their own elevation as the true children of God.

So, I cultivated the spirit of Ishmael: cultivated this spirit that it would grow in a people so contentious that they would stake a claim to every shrine and monument, and locale that rightly belonged to God's own people. And Lucifer, in his guile, would use this strife to mask the true prize. The prize which even now you do not understand is almost within his grasp to unearth.

While the most powerful of angels stand helpless to interfere, all because you value the Clayborn and El's articles of war. And it is this value; your inflexible deference to obey El unquestioningly in all things; that has brought us to this place, you and I: a place where I now stand seeking petition from my sworn enemy."

Michael was wide-eyed but silent, and he took in the enormity of Marduk's words. "The God-stone... in Jerusalem itself? You claim you know exactly where it is, but what do you seek in exchange for its location?"

"I ask for naught but the absence of your meddling in the Abomination's assassination."

Michael was taken aback. "I care nothing for the death of the half-breed. His life is neither mine to give or take save at El's word. Nevertheless, is he not the human leader set up amongst your ranks? Why would you seek his death?"

Marduk nodded, "There are two things I care for Michael, and while I despise you. I despise even more the thought of the Abomination leading angelic kind. I did not leave my first estate that this mongrel might lead me. I will see him dead before I allow him to grace the gates of heaven. He cannot be allowed to live. Lucifer has twice now raised a species that, if unchecked, could mayhap supplant both angel and man. His experimentation to bypass the design of God has accelerated the curse of sin among the humans and the Withering amongst our own kind. This cannot be allowed to be. This creature... there is something about him: something hidden. I fear he will be the undoing of us all. The Nephilim must be destroyed before he holds a reunified Godstone. Thus, I ask the chief prince of angels to confirm once more. Will you interfere with my plan to kill the Anti-Christ?"

Michael pondered the curious nature of his request and replies, "I care naught for Horde leadership. You have my leave to pursue this action. Now tell me—where is the location of the God-stone?"

Marduk snickered, "In the safest place in all the Earth. A place no one would dare to disturb lest war break out and Yeshua himself be moved to interfere. Beneath the foundation of a Temple raised in purpose to cover Lucifer's scheme and erected to sow the most insidious tare in the Holy Land."

Michael's eyes narrowed, and he realized that even now Israel was considering joining the Commonwealth of Nations. His brow furrowed as he looked down at the ground, contemplating Marduk's words. And his mind turned in anxiety until the history of Israel flooded him and the realization of the stone's location became immediately crystal clear. "In El's name no!"

Marduk chuckles, "Yes, I can see that you understand... good. What you fear is true; for your precious God-stone Michael of the Kortai lies beneath the Dome on the Rock."

Michael turned his head towards the holy city and spoke to Marduk. "You will submit to restraint and come with me. Resist and you will be cut down where you stand."

The archangel then set his face towards Jerusalem and launched himself into the sky.

* * *

Leto Alexander materialized unto the emerald-green carpet of the United Nations general assembly room. Following him through the portal were Ashtaroth and Lathum.

The portal flashed, then sealed behind the trio, and various occupants of the room stood up and pointed to the spectacle. Gasps and screams could be heard from the room as the two beings that stood to Leto's left and right were clearly not human. One floated, and the other had wings. Several security guards ran into the room with weapons drawn.

"Mr. Secretary, are you all right sir?" yells one. "Where did you come from? We were not expecting you, sir." Several of the guards scrutinized the beings that were to his left and one shouted, "You there; step away from the Secretary... now!"

Leto was not amused and opened his mouth to speak. "He will do no such thing. These here are a part of my personal guard. They will not harm you unless you attempt to harm me. I advise you men to lower your weapons. For if I chose, I can call a legion of similar beings to come to my aid, and you would not wish to anger my father."

Several other guards, then soldiers, entered the room and surrounded the platform, each with weapons raised pointed at the angels.

Leto clenched his jaw and crossed his arms. "You all would be wise to lower your weapons. For he that receives me, receives him that sent me. I have given an order once. I will not do so again."

The soldiers didn't move, but slowly lowered their weapons.

Leto sighs and spoke aloud, "Father?"

A dark shadow then moved over the giant seal of the United Nations: a darkness that swallowed blackness itself. Luminance then pulsated from the center of the gloomy void. A figure with wings slowly descended from the ceiling to the floor. Gasps and open mouths filled the room, and many backed away for it a great light and heat emanated from the being, and he floated to the dais, and he stood 10 feet high towering with wings that spread from his person which waved in bio-luminescent colors matching the rainbow.

The Devil, Satan and Prince of Darkness was now fully revealed to the people of the world and spoke to the assembled heads of the represented states of the nations.

"Hail men of Earth. I am Lucifer Draco of the House Draco. Be not afraid, nor be dismayed. My son Leto has summoned me to help, and I have now come that ye might have life and have it more abundantly. To free you from the lies that have riddled your kind since its birth and perpetuated by the false prophets of your world. What lie you ask? That the God you know as Yeshua, Allah, or Yahweh is false. That you merely give a name to a being who is but a member of my race and has chosen to remain hidden unseen these great many centuries to human eyes. Visible only if we chose to reveal ourselves. For many generations, we have cultivated your technology so that ye might one day move beyond the constraints imposed by the so-called Creator. The time has now come for the adolescence of mankind to end; and for you to take your place amongst your fellow beings of the galaxy: to walk in the fullness of adulthood with the knowledge that you are indeed not alone. I come offering you all that your heart desires: freedom from disease, and poverty; endless energy that will take you deep into the stars. All these things will I give you, if you will but help me undo the being who claims to love you. Help me undo the shackle that is from the Elohim and follow me. Pledge your allegiance to my cause. A cause that will protect and prosper your people, do this and you shall know peace in your time.

Leto Alexander serves me. To him I will give him what you cannot yet fathom: eternal life. Imagine: the ending of death as you know it. Sickness will become a thing of the past. All this I offer freely. For the God you have served hath kept thee from grasping the knowledge of good and evil. Knowing full well and nay preventing you from unlocking the vast potential within your DNA: the gene to eternal life. Why? Because he knows that on that day you shall be like Him. And he is a jealous God, he will not be rivaled, nor will he share power.

Follow me and we shall remove this dictator. Follow me, and I will lead you to freedom. Do not do so and know you will surely die. For the invisible war between my people can be hidden no longer. A conflict that mankind must now forcibly join where choice by the heads of your people must once again be made. Leto represents me and is my ambassador to your people: my mouthpiece in the earth.

Choose delegates of the United Nations: chose life that both thou and thy seed might live." Lucifer smiled, his arms opened wide as if to embrace those in the room.

A delegate from Uganda: Ambassador Dembe spoke into the microphone that was before him and replies, "How do we know that what you say is true? How do we know we are not being manipulated by you and your kind now?"

Lucifer looked upon the man and, unbeknownst to him, the Prince of Darkness had assigned a familiar spirit of cancer to his family. The spirit was coiled within the man's breast, and Lucifer spoke. "You ambassador have struggled with cancer in your family for three generations. Even now you stand riddled with the disease." Lucifer lifted his hand towards the man and spoke. "I command that you release this man's lungs. Restore them to their natural state and leave his house. Be healed Ambassador Dembe."

The spirit obeyed its master and departed. Upon it leaving his body, the man immediately went into spasms, collapsing to the ground and he screamed in agony as he erupted in convulsions.

"You're killing him!" shouts a guard. Who immediately raised his gun and opened fire on the Prince of Darkness.

Lucifer moved at the speed of light towards the man, blinded him, took his weapon, tapped him ever so slightly, then returned to his previous spot on the platform. When he did so, the bullets from the discharged pistol finally reached him and he simply plucked them from the air.

The soldier had been knocked back but was unharmed, and Lucifer spoke to all in the room. "If I wanted you dead, you would all be dead. Be not afraid. I have come that ye might have life." Lucifer then opened his hands to reveal the slugs he had plucked from midair and let them fall to the ground from his palms.

The ambassador coughed up phlegm, and he wiped his mouth with his suit sleeve and spoke. "My God, I am not wheezing! I can breathe! I can breathe! I can feel the difference. It's gone. I don't know how...but I know it's gone! Praise God!" he yells aloud.

"No...," Lucifer interjected. "Praise me."

* * *

Michael flew to the city of Jerusalem and his royal guard flew beside him as they escorted the shackled Marduk into custody. Michael landed atop the little western wall and upon touching down a Grigori by name of Arakiel awaited him. "My prince," the watcher says.

"Report," says the Chief Prince.

Arakiel floated as if upon a cloud and did as commanded. "Lucifer has revealed himself to humanity in violation of the Articles of War. However, he has convinced the nations of the Earth that he means to do them good. Israel and the Abomination have signed a non-aggression pact. The forces of Marduk have been decimated and the even as we speak, the Prime Minister has authorized the destruction of the temple mount for purposes of excavation. My agents have informed me that the Beast has promised the nation the ability to rebuild Solomon's temple. All humans have been removed, those unwilling forcibly so. It is reported that Lucifer and the Beast are on their way here to oversee the excavation personally. The work is considered an act of planetary security. Although we have a legion surrounding the nation, we cannot prevent the Horde from entering the land if the humans have extended authority for their harbor."

Michael nodded impatiently, "I know... I know. How long do we have until Lucifer and the Abomination arrive?"

A voice carried across the warm winds of Jerusalem, and it was familiar in both melody and tenor. "You need not concern yourself, enemy of mankind; for we are already here."

Michael turned around as Lucifer and Leto walked through a portal. Each was flanked by rogue Arelim and Malakim angels and men with machine guns also stepped through and quickly dispersed themselves into the court and approached the entry of the Dome on the Rock. Soldiers near Lucifer and Leto took defensive positions to protect them. The buzzing of helicopters could be heard in the distance and squadrons of police and military swarmed to their position and as they exited their various vehicles, they trained their weapons on all the angels present. The cocking of rifles and pistols could be heard, and Michael surveyed the scene, realizing that, to his surprise, the humans could see them all.

Michael turned to his brother and scowled. "Lucifer, what have you done?" he says.

The Adversary smiles and stated, "I have done what I have always done: moved our race into a favorable position to contend with the false God El. Now stand aside. These lands have been ceded by the human authorities to my charge. You will surrender this position and these people to my ministration immediately."

Michael looked at Lucifer and his neck jerked back in response to hearing such absurdity.

"You are mad. These lands are under the jurisdiction of El. I will do no such thing. Michael's sword immediately withdrew from its scabbard and found his waiting hand. All angels, both friend and foe, also drew their weapons in response to Michael's action.

Lucifer lifted his hands for calm and smiles, "See humans? See how the creature will not allow a peaceful transition? He has been trained by the false god El to do nothing but fight. He is nothing more than a living weapon. But he is also bound by the laws of our people. He knows the articles of war which govern our kind will not permit him to trespass on land that has been ceded by human delegated authority."

Lathum, who had opened the portal allowing Lucifer and his entourage to travel, waved his hand and another portal opened. Michael and his guards braced themselves for a possible battle, but through the portal, the Prime Minister of Israel and the warring heads of the Arab league walked through. Ashtaroth also walked behind them, and the Prime minister of Israel spoke.

"We do not know who you are. But your presence is neither requested nor required. Leave our land. We will not tolerate foreign intervention or infiltration into our affairs. Leave now... or my people will open fire."

Michael looked at Lucifer, who smirked in satisfaction that humanity backed his presence, and Michael, who was willing to enforce the Lord's decree by force, suddenly heard the voice of the Holy Spirit in his mind.

Leave them be. I am not without voice here and Satan's time, though coming, is not yet nigh.

Michael spoke within his own mind to the Lord's telepathic thought. *As you command, my king.*

Lucifer observing his brother's body language; spoke, "I see that El has communicated with thee. What say you then? Will you contend with me and they who have refused thee? Or will you leave these people in peace?"

Michael frowned that he was constrained to yield ground on this occasion. He sighed and turned to speak to the human delegation that stood before him. "Very well human, but know I go because I am commanded by God..." He then turned to look upon his angelic brother and spoke. "You should know if the Lord willed it, I would unleash destruction upon every vassal here, including this one." Michael looked towards Leto and stared into his eyes, and his grim face communicated both a silent and stern warning.

Leto smiles and opened his arms, gesturing him to come and provokingly replies, "I stand right here Michael... I stand right here."

Michael breathes in deeply; his chest raised and lowered as he chose not to yield to the temptation thrown his way.

"Soon Leto, of this you can be sure, and believe me when I say you are naïve, to look forward to such an encounter."

Michael sheathed his sword, and his guards followed suit. "I give you my leave, Lucifer. But rest assured this is far from over."

Lucifer replied in retort. "Oh, I agree. Verily I say unto you, I have only just begun the dismantling of El's kingdom. Oh, and Michael, before you go. You will release the renegade Marduk as he was mustered under my banner in the Descension. He is therefore under the authority of the Horde."

Michael began to object and to contend for the life of Marduk when the old angel bowed his head in resignation and spoke.

"Fear not Michael. I once long ago fought the Usurper to his ruin. He has forgotten this lesson. But I will see him taught this lesson again."

Satan sneered, rolling his eyes in disdain for his imprisoned nemesis. "You will be dead soon, and your life's lesson merely an example to those who would defy me."

Michael swallowed hard and nodded towards his guards and they released Marduk, who wrung and massaged his now unbound wrists. He was then immediately taken into custody by two Harrada and an Arelim and was shoved to the side of Lucifer and Leto with both angelic and human weapons trained on him.

Michael then lifted himself into the air and all angels stationed to defend Israel lifted themselves with him, and as Michael flew away, he turned to Lucifer and spoke to him in warning. "Know of a surety that you will be undone and will not escape judgment, for I have seen thy end..." Michael shook his head in pity. "And it does not end well."

A prismatic funnel cloud opened in the sky and thousands of angels departed in mass as men and women looked on in disbelief and awe. Television crews videoed the event and broadcast the exchange on television, which quickly circled the globe.

Lucifer stood behind Leto and placed his hands on his shoulders. "I leave you for a time. But will come when bidden. Do not be afraid."

Lucifer then disappeared in a great flash of light and Leto turned to the defeated heads of the Arab league and spoke. "You are here to publicly surrender and admit to your crimes against humanity. Surrender and I will allow you to live out your lives in peace. Do not sign the peace treaty before you, and we will label the nations which you represent and its people as enemy combatants against humanity and wiped out."

The remaining heads of the Arab League nodded in resignation.

Come, said Leto. He then walked towards the Dome on the Rock and when he did, many of the Israeli soldiers stationed to prevent non-Muslims from entry moved aside.

The head of Saudi Arabia spoke as Leto moved closer, "It is forbidden to enter the sacred area of the temple."

Leto turned to face the ambassador. "Destroy this temple and in three days, I will raise it up." He smiles at the irony of his words and continued. "Do not concern yourself with your hallowed ground. For soon I will raise the foundations of this building and upon it will raise a temple worthy where all may come and worship. Now come, Prime Minister. Let the world see that a new world order awaits them.

Millions watched via the Internet and television as an acknowledged atheist marched triumphantly into the building and the defeated heads of state for each Arab league country followed. Leto walked into the centuries old structure and they pulled a table, and all the men assembled in their seats. Binders were brought in, and each signed the declared surrenders and cessation of hostilities. As photographers, generals and ambassadors and bureaucrats stood to their rear.

Leto Alexander finally signed the last document and, after doing so, placed the cap on his pen and stood. "Congratulations gentlemen. We have secured a seven-year peace and cessation of hostilities to the Middle East conflict. The Middle East has her peace. The Dome, for the sake of planetary security, will be dismantled, but to those of Muslim faith, it is my decree that it will be done so to the extent necessary to extract the mineral we require to fight off this menace from beyond. I declare that when it is done we shall restore your beloved monument more beautiful than before; of this you have my word."

The audience that had assembled themselves clapped, and worldwide people cheered that hostilities between Israel and her surrounding nations had finally ended.

Leto then removed his microphone and turned to speak to the Prime Minister of Israel. "Commence with the dismantling of the Dome immediately."

"And what of your promise to allow us to rebuild the temple?" says the Prime Minister.

Leto looked at the prime minister and replies, "Have I not spoken? Carry out my word and then you will see me carry out mine. I have given you the space of seven years to build your temple. After which I will give you a portion of the mineral to protect, you should Israel's enemies ever seek her destruction again. Trust me, Prime Minister. You believe in God, believe also in me." Leto chuckles at his wit and his eyes were a-light with a twinkle of mischief.

* * *

Eridu watched as his female charge danced with his planted lust filled pawn that was Mike Gains. The old angel smiled at his handiwork, for his strategy had been orchestrated perfectly. For months the angel had sown suggestive seeds to augment the young woman's insecurity: coordinating events to play on her feelings, to be accepted and amplifying the thoughts she spoke to herself about her loneliness. The young woman never realized she vocalized to her demonic voyeur's ever listening ears how he might destroy the last living descendant of a human chronicler of the Dead Sea Scrolls. Isolated from family and ostracized by her peer group, Eridu would capitalize on her flesh's natural urge to be sexually desired: budding into her womanhood, she was a fruit now ripe for exploitation.

Easy prey. He thought.

Eridu smiled as he watched the two young adolescents dance their dance in the home of Mike Gaines.

Soon your rebellion towards El and spiritual death will see you engine the realm of the dead for our cause. Soon you will join so many of your family whom I have already imprisoned.

With her death, he relished his release from his failed assignment to secure the city of Qumran for Marduk. A punishment meted out for his failure in his lord's service: demoted to serve as a familiar spirit. Eridu winced as he thought of the judgment handed down by his master.

"You have failed me and my house. Therefore, I bind you to this failure," says Marduk. "Because thou hast allowed someone to release the word of God. Thou art now the prisoner to the mud which has humbled thee. Get thee away from my sight and do not return until the stench of this human's seed and evidence of your failure no longer survives the Earth."

For almost two millennia now, Eridu was a harassing spirit to the house of Micah Ben Judah. The accursed unknown scribe, whose works brought the light of the word of God to men, a failure Eridu would see himself avenged with the death of Elizabeth Foley: the last descendant of Micah Ben Judah.

Eridu smiled at his work. For centuries, he had tracked the scent of Micah's descendants across the earth. From the hovel that was Qumran, Israel, to the township of Commerce, Michigan. From the Roman Empire to the United States of America had he traversed the globe. The angelic, vengeful, and long arm of Marduk to the house of Ben Judah. He was excited that soon his time in the trivial destruction of these humans would end and he would again be elevated to serve his master.

Working the field of human souls was grunt work reserved to the daemons. Not one who had once ferreted out the spies of the Host, who scurried like rats from his presence upon their discovery. Not for one who was a ruler of ancient cities named after him. Not one whom the Sumerians once worshiped. Now his name was a historical after thought. A name wiped from the pages of human history. A name now reduced to see to the destruction of a sole human female. Eridu was a hunter, a destroyer of angels and men alike. Only once had a mark for assassination escaped him. And Eridu had longed to find and destroy the one angel who escaped with his master's correspondence with Lucifer: Vantress of house Harrada.

Never did it occur to him that after centuries he merely would have to attend an adolescent house party.

"It's been a longtime nemesis," says a familiar voice.

Eridu turned from his observation of human teenage mating rituals and faced a voice he had not heard in many a year.

Vantress appeared to Eridu's and sight and continued. "Did you think that I've forgotten your killing of Olen? Now that I finally have you, I will have my revenge. You will pay for what you did to him."

Eridu chuckles, and "It was my understanding that vengeance belongs to God. Have you come to present your credentials to me as God Vantress? Are you here to vie for title of God as Lucifer? For it would seem that if you seek to do me harm that you are presented with a choice. You may indeed attempt to seek your vengeance upon me, but I perceive that you are not here for me. I see the hand of El in that he has given assignment. And could it be no less that you are here for the maiden? My sweet, sweet mark? Is it possible that fate... no, that is such a human means to explain what they refuse and or cannot understand. We both know we are here because God has willed it. I wonder what El in his wisdom would have you do?" Eridu smirked.

My orders are clear; they are to undermine the Horde. To disrupt and destroy your operations. Wherever you would seek to sow your tares and or plot your fiendish schemes."

The angels began slowly circling one another, floating over the myriad of students in the room. Each one oblivious to the angelic presence that occupied their space.

Audrey tapped the dancing Elizabeth on the shoulder and offered her more gummy bears. Elizabeth smiled and took several into her hands and gulped them down. Audrey winked at Mike Gains, and he nodded in acknowledgment.

Vantress moved closer to Eridu and drew his sword. "I will not let you have the maiden. She is not yours to possess."

Eridu replies. "She was mine to destroy the moment her forefather dared place himself as an obstacle to my master's will. She is dead in her trespasses and sins, and soon she will know the

eternal reality of that separation from God. Of course, the question remains. Do you think yourself powerful enough to stand between the Horde and its prey?"

Eridu then pulled from his side an urumi: a small whip like weapon comprising several flexible blades.

The two angels stared each other down, awaiting any movement from the other. Eridu cocked his head to the side, glancing at the continued state of Elizabeth as she became increasingly flushed and inebriated. He smiled and continued to move Vantress further away from the lass and incited him.

"You should know, Vantress, that the sons of men are adept in the arts of destruction. They rival even the Elohim in their creativity to invent weapons. In my travels I have studied the arts of war, and it was in the continent of India that I came across so interesting a mind that I used him to forge a weapon that with it killed nine men at once. I was, of course, inspired no less than by Michael's own sword. I so look forward to watching your skin bleed against its edge."

Vantress moved towards his enemy as his body phased through dancing students. "No, Eridu, it will be your death that I truly hope will go slowly."

Eridu backed away, slowly phasing through walls until he was standing outside by the pool. Dozens of party goers swam in the lake and frolicked about unawares of the invisible celestial confrontation in their midst.

Eridu looked at Vantress with confusion, "You act as if the lass is in danger. Does she not rest in the arms of the one she desires? Would you rob her of this opportunity to know the pleasures of the flesh?"

"Think me not naïve spawn of Satan. Your attempt to mislead her will fail." Vantress says.

Vantress phased through the same wall and materialized enough to disrupt the circuitry in the dwelling. Immediately, everything went black, and the music came to a screeching halt.

Mike Gains stopped dancing as Elizabeth collapsed in his arms, commenting on how sexy he looked and that she noticed him eying her during the school year. "So, what are you gonna do about it, big man? You not scared of a girl, are you?"

Mike looked at her, and a beaming smirk scrawled across his face. "Oh, I've got something to show you, I think we should go upstairs."

Dozens of students turned on their cell phone flashlights and continued to chat and go outside to enjoy the outside breeze. Audrey came over to Mike and whispered, "I think she's ready."

Mike whispers in reply, "Ready or not, here I come."

Audrey laughs and groped his crotch in the darkness to inspect him, "Yeah, I think you are."

Mike then lifted Elizabeth's arm over his shoulder and walked her up the stairs into his bedroom.

* * *

Vantress launched himself at Eridu, thrusting forward with his sword. Eridu then extended the segmented blades of the Urumi, and it reached towards Vantress's face, making the battle-hardened angel turn to avoid the weapons cutting edge.

With a snap of Eridu's wrist, the blades recoiled as he swirled them around his person. Gyrating his body to keep Vantress at bay and to prevent his own self-injury.

Vantress pressed his attack, closing the distance he brought his sword up to his face and when he did so the flexible blades of the Urumi found the steel of Vantress's blade preventing them to down the angel.

The blades coiled as a whip around the sword's edge, and Eridu and Vantress weapons were now interlocked, with one another unable to untangle from the other.

Clouds gathered overhead as the disruption of their attack upon each other slowly tore at the physical realm and moisture slowly accumulated in the upper atmosphere.

Each angel pulled in a tug of war to gain the advantage over the other.

"I must admit," says Eridu, "I did not think it would be so easy to distract you from your charge. You have become much more gullible since last we met."

Vantress struggled to hold on to the sword and replied. "You talk too much." He then released his grip and Eridu fell backwards with both sword and Urumi flailing back towards him."

Vantress launched himself towards Eridu, landing atop of him.

Accosted Eridu now found himself lying on his back with Vantress pummeling him in the face.

Blow after crushing blow did Vantress smite Eridu's jaw, chin, nose and forehead. Pummeling him until the angel drew blood.

Lightning flashed, and a bolt found its way into the ground where the duo battled. A tree caught fire, and a sudden downpour of rain descended and doused the flame as quickly as it had erupted. In the lightning flash's aftermath, Paschar the Grigori stood and yelled at Vantress.

"Vantress! Vantress! You fight a ghost. A projection of the thoughts of your own mind! Vantress, wake up, for where is thy charge?"

Vantress looked at Eridu, and his bloodied face laughed at him. Vantress then looked at his own hands, and his knuckles were blue with his own blood. Bruised and cut from the abrasions of slamming his fists into the ground. He quickly realized that he had been fighting a phantom. A ghost made real by the projections of his own mind.

He slowly gained his composure, his breathing heavy over the vanishing body that was but a projection of his own mind made real. He grimaced in angst and rage and raised his bloodied hands into the sky.

"ERIDU!" he cries. Lifting his frustration and anguish into the rain.

Back at the home of Michael Gaines, Eridu lifted his ear towards the distant cry of Vantress and heard the howl of his nemesis from over a mile away. While eager to correct the failure, that was Vantress. He returned his gaze towards his work at hand. A work that would free him to return to his master's grace. A work of sin he had incubated for many years. The fruit of which was now in full progress. Eridu stood in nodding approval of Michael Gaines as the young man proceeded to defile the intoxicated Elizabeth Foley.

* * *

"Elizabeth!" says Carl Peterson. "Elizabeth, where are you?"

Carl Peterson called after her friend, who noticed her absence after the house lights had gone out.

"Lord, please help me find her." She says under her breath. "Please let her be OK."

Immediately in the spirit, a prayer cloud came over the bedroom of Michael Gaines. It glowed and light emanated over the duo and Eridu stood to attention as he noticed that a prayer shroud grew in the room and the angel drew back in fear. For it was a clear sign that a believer in Yeshua was exercising their covenant power to invoke divine intervention into the Earth. The angel turned and fled, for the prayer cloud expanded and soon would cause acidic like burns if he did not depart.

Suddenly Vantress appeared, and he hovered over Michael Gaines and the angel waved his hand and the boy's abdomen spasmed and he vomited, and phlegm and puke projected from his mouth as he hurried from the room to find the nearest restroom.

Vantress turned to see that Eridu stood in the doorway and scowled. He unsheathed his sword and stood at the bed where Elizabeth was undressed, mere feet away from the opposing angel. The cloud of prayer forced his enemy to back away.

"You will not have her." Vantress declares.

Eridu smirked and replies, "Tonight... no," he said, shaking his head. "But such was never my intent."

Both angels then heard a "click" sound that came from the corridor near the door that Michael Gaines had left wide open.

Eridu smirked as Sara Jefferson walked through his phased body and captured video on her cell phone of Elizabeth partially undressed with her bra off. An eavesdropping sentry ready to spread gossip and slander to the dazed Elizabeth Foley. Vantress realized she protected the bedroom door from prying eyes, all while she uploaded humiliating images of Elizabeth's compromised state to Snapchat.

Eridu smiles at the young woman and spoke, "Though the daughter of Ben Judah will not be assaulted today, her humiliation will be enough to bring her to the brink of despair. I have followed this one a long time, but know that you will not deter me in her death. I will have her. And you would be wise, angel of God, to be by her side; for upon my return know on that day you will not fight an illusion."

The dread angel then turned and floated through the walls, out of sight.

Vantress stood over the side of the bed of Elizabeth, sheathed his sword and the Grigori assigned spoke to him appeared and spoke. "Be wary, Vantress, for this one has learned how to project illusion to your own mind. It is a dark art the Horde has mastered. Many of our brethren

have fallen to such trickery. Be careful and mind your thoughts or he will surely use them against you."

Vantress nodded. "I will not succumb a second time."

"Elizabeth are you up there?" called the voice of Carl Peterson.

Sarah Jefferson hurried to exit the room, and the two young women stood face to face, with Carol blocking Sarah's exit.

Carol looked beyond the doorway into the room to see the unconscious Elizabeth sprawled out in the bed, and that Sarah slowly tried to conceal her cell phone. Its camera's recording mode was still visible.

"You witch!" Carol hollers. She then pushed the girl against the door frame and wrestled the phone from her hand and threw it against a wall.

Carol shoved past the now fuming girl and ran to the bed and shook Elizabeth, but she was unresponsive. Carol then immediately took her own cell phone and dialed 911. Sarah grabbed the broken pieces of her cell phone and hurried downstairs.

"Come on, baby... please don't die on me. Lord, please wake her up."

Vantress floated over her physical shell and watched as the young woman's small prayer lifted into the air. A glowing aromatic cloud that smelled of jasmine. It hovered for a moment, then crystallized into a golden gem and Vantress watched as the gem shot towards the Third Heaven.

Immediately, Vantress could see what Carol could not and the room brightened as if someone had raised a dimmer light in a living room. Suddenly, Elizabeth sat up in the bed coughing as she gasped for air.

Vantress whispers to El Pneuma, "Thank you, my king... thank you."

* * *

El looked grimly upon the cauldron of the saints' prayers. They incessantly wailed and screamed their discontent. Ghostly howls and laments intermixed with pleas for the Father's help sizzled from the vessel. Like a boiling pot of heated water, it whistled into the air with the groaning of saints that could not be uttered. El then crouched near the basin's overflow, cupped his hands and collected the steaming water that spilled onto the floor of the throne room, and when he collected the water, it seemed to evaporate into his hands.

El then stood. His lip firm, his face hard as stone. He then looked away from the wailing vessel and turned his eyes away from the lavar, and Michael heard him whisper to Yeshua. "What we do. I will do no more." Michael did not understand what the Lord meant and, noting Michael's look of confusion, El spoke to his chief prince of angels.

"Come, most beloved of angels... walk with me."

Michael nodded and followed his Lord, who merely waved his hand, and the Trinitarian God vanished and Michael stood with the Godhead in a dimly lit room. The room was lit as if by candlelight and Michael's eyes slowly adjusted to the darkness. His vision cleared, and he saw that within the room there were billions upon billions of small vials. Each was illuminated with a small pinprick of light inside, and each vial was corked. Michael strained to see the contents of the small containers and was taken aback by what he beheld. For each jar contained the tears of the Lord's people. Michael looked over and around him, for all over the starlit-like room were rows of small tear bottles, each adorned with a precious jewel and draped in small links of gold and silver. Michael watched as the Godhead took within each of their hands the tears they had collected from the saints at the lavar and gently placed them one-by-one within a bottle. Crystal immediately formed around each tear, encasing it in the finest glass. And Michael marveled, for even the ceiling of the room was adorned as a chandelier in the tears of God's people. The Lord stared solemnly over each and every one. And when each tear was at rest within a bottle, Michael could hear the faintest sounds of weeping. The sound saturated the room in a child-like melancholy of cries. It was a weeping that was faint but almost out of the perception of hearing lest the room be full of wails. The three members of the Godhead then took a pen and wrote within a journal set upon a dais: the names of each person from whom the tear was from.

Michael watched this personal ordinance of God and was touched that the Lord would allow him to witness one of His most intimate of private times. The Lord then spoke, staring down at the book and placed his hand over his face as in grief.

"I will write no more names in this book. The season for my people to cry must now end," says El.

Yeshua immediately followed without missing a cadence, "It is therefore a time to rend..."

El Pneuma chimed in accordance. "A time to make war..."

Michael stood quietly and El turned to him and spoke in anguish and replies, "The world has turned its back to me. They despise my name as their creator. The imagination of mankind has become vain, for in pride they have lifted themselves up. They have changed my truth and have worshiped the creature more than the creator. They desire in their lust to live in delusion; therefore, I will give them the desire of their heart and will revel in their strong delusion that they might know the impact when God is not there."

The three then became one and turned their collective face from the dais. And when they did so, the room vanished and naught but galaxies and super-clusters were all that could be seen and Michael floated over the floor of the universe.

El stared at the Creation He had molded by his loving hands, and his eyes focused on the one planet in a solar system he had aligned perfectly to support the life of his greatest creation: a creation now amok in defiance of the Lord's will; a creation that had unleashed destruction and sin into the world.

Michael watched his father closely: watched his expressions and mannerisms, taking care to note the Lord's body language.

The Lord grimaced with gritted teeth as he stared down upon the Earth

Michael watched as the Creator of the Universe seemingly wrestled with a pronunciation of judgment. For Michael knew mercy was quickly dissipating for mankind. He then looked to Yeshua, whose mannerisms mimicked the Father. El Pneuma hovered above them both, and his great wings were spread abroad and dwarfed the room.

Michael then saw El take a deep breath and his chest rose and fell as if in resignation. He could not withhold what he would do any longer. The Creator then spoke. His eyes fixed on the planet Earth. "Michael of the Kortai," says El.

Michael snapped to attention. "Yes, my king."

"Make ready my troops."

Michael nodded and replied. "Yes, my king."

El then looked at the Holy Spirit and spoke. "El Pneuma, it is time; bring our children to us."

El Pneuma nodded knowingly, then disappeared.

Chapter Seven: The Taken

Carol was by the bedside of Elizabeth, taking a cold compress and dabbing her forehead.

Elizabeth was dazed and slowly coming around. "Oh, my head is ringing. What are we doing in my bedroom?"

"I think Michael or one of his flunkey's slipped something in your drink," says Carol. "That's the only thing I can figure out. Something told me to look for you. I dunno, I got worried, I guess. When I went upstairs, I found you in bed with him on top of you and Sarah guarding the door.

I knew that creep didn't deserve you. I can't believe he tried to get into your pants like that! And to think Sarah was just standing there! I bet she watched the whole thing. When I am done with them. I swear to Bob I will make the whole school know what they did".

Elizabeth sat up groggily from the bed, her head aching. "Owww, don't cause the room to move so fast. And no. We can't tell anyone at the school what happened."

Carol looked at her friend in disbelief. "But Elizabeth, if Sarah uploaded that video to the Internet.... shouldn't we call the police?"

Elizabeth looked at her friend as if she was crazy and retorted back. "Oh, heck no! I've got two years left at this school. I have to live with these people, and you know how those Jefferson girls are. They will probably try to corner me alone just to get back at me if I told. You know that's how they are. No, you can't tell anyone. Promise me."

Carol looked at her friend with concern.

"Promise me, Carol." Elizabeth says.

Carol looked at her and nodded her head. She clutched at her chest and her eyes grew wide. "Something is happening."

"What?" says Elizabeth. You look...strange."

Elizabeth's voice trailed off as she watched her friend begin to give off a faint blue glow. The young woman backed up further towards the head of her bead looking at her high school friend in fear.

"Carrol...Carol...are you alright?" says Elizabeth.

Carrol squinted as she turned her head to look around the room. Her eyes burned. She rubbed them in irritation as if to remove sleep that clouded her vision. She slowly lowered her hands before her face and then lifted them high into the air as if to inspect them. Turning each over to its front, then back. She was amazed that she could actually see through her skin and watched her own blood course through her veins. She squinted as if to focus and Elizabeth and the four walls of her friend's bedroom disappeared as if pushed to the side of her periphery and she could see miles beyond outside: looking past the walls of the Elizabeth's home and could angels that flew hither and thither. She smiled in glee and awe but also became suddenly aware of the many daemons and evil angels that were also in her vicinity. She frowned in anger for the volume of them that she could see. But she also saw that many people within the area were also experiencing the change, each attempting to make sense of what was happening to them.

Carol breathed in and out slowly, taking in the sights. She tilted her head as if to concentrate more on what she heard and realized that both her hearing and her vision were now amplified beyond anything she could possibly imagine. She could hear the rapid fearful heartbeat of her friend and opened her eyes to focus on Elizabeth.

"It's so beautiful..."

She then gasped, placing her hand over her mouth, startled as she suddenly saw that an angel stood guard at their bed: his hand on the pummel of his sword.

"Who are you?" Carroll asks.

"Vantress." The angel said.

Carol then smiles, "Have you been here all this time?" she asks. Vantress nodded as he grinned.

Carol focused her changing eyes on Elizabeth, who clearly was afraid, and spoke to her friend.

"Carrol, you are scaring me. Who the hell are you talking to? Because it sure as heck ain't me."

Carrol could hear the quickening of Elizabeth's racing heartbeat and replied. "Don't be afraid Izzy." She grinned, "You have an angel assigned to you! He is so beautiful."

Vantress smiled, and his checks blushed. He then put his finger to his lips to ask for her silence.

"I understand," Carol says aloud. She then spoke to Elizabeth.

Carol's voice then changed as if many voices sung through her. "The Lord is calling me home, Izzy. I can feel it. It feels so good...it's...it's like I am shedding a skin. I think I am about to leave very soon. I wish you could come with me. But I must go now. Remember when you think you are most alone, Christ is there...surrender to him..." she paused as if her mind was elsewhere and then quickly came to herself and spoke. "It's all so beautiful. I hope I will see you again. I love you."

And with those words, Carol allowed the change that was quickly overwhelming her body to overtake her and she transformed before her friend's eyes into a being of bluish light. She smiled one last time at her high school friend and her form took that of something akin to a willow-of-the-wisp.

Elizabeth watched as the bright orb of luminance then shot through the roof of her bedroom and vanished before her eyes. She looked down to see the clothes that her best friend wore laying like a crumpled pile atop her bed. She then screamed uncontrollably, then fainted falling back in her bed.

* * *

Leto Alexander, leader of the human race; the Beast as named in the Bible and articulated by those familiar with his ruthlessness, watched as two men in sackcloth made their way towards the court of the Dome on the Rock.

"Leto Alexander, we are the witnesses of the one true God, and we call you to account and declare that you are false."

Enoch leaned on his staff and Elijah helped him as they walked

"Who are you? Leto asked.

Enoch looked upon him and replied. "Your father knows of me. For he was there when death was defied and when El slighted him as the Usurper sought to take me as a prize. This one too is known of thy master. For he has raised the dead and stopped the Heavens from giving rain. We are Enoch and Elijah, and we are the two witnesses that stand before the Lord and declare the goodness of the Lord, and who call Heaven and Earth against you. To proclaim Leto Alexander that you are a liar. The enemy of the true God and to declare to the entire world that they that follow you will share your fate."

Leto laughed. "So, you admit to be in league with the enemy of Earth and her people. I do not need to hear anything further, for you are both dead men. Arrest them."

Soldiers immediately rushed to apprehend the duo, but when they reached within ten feet of the men, every soldier spontaneously combust. Each screamed as they fell over and died in agony. As they stood on the precipice of life and death, they could see into the realm of the unrighteous dead. Each emblazoned soul screaming as their spirits left their bodies and drawn into a realm of utter darkness to be consumed alive by Hell.

Elijah spoke in sternness to the men who surrounded them. "Such will be to all who refuse to give the God of Heaven the glory due His name. Defy Him and a lake of fire and brimstone surely awaits you all."

Leto was incensed; I says apprehend those men NOW!

Then the low rumble of *"shoup, shoup"* from canisters being shot from a gun could be heard, and two canisters of tear gas fell at Enoch and Elijah's feet. A fog of greenish gas lifted around the men, and Henel James, the reporter, was too close to Enoch and Elijah and was overcome by the acidic taste of vinegar and coughed as he was overwhelmed with a sudden tightness in his chest. He collapsed to his knees, and as he looked up, coughing, he could see Enoch and Elijah standing, looking about curiously. Elijah looked down at him and, seeing him overcome, blew his breath on him, and the fog cleared from around the men. Elijah put his hand over Henel's chest, and he gasped for air able to breathe.

"How did you do that?"

Elijah was silent, and he smiled and turned to Enoch, who acknowledged him and then opened his mouth to speak. "Behold the power of God!"

And when Enoch had spoken, lightning fell from the sky and incinerated the holder of the gun of tear gas. A thunderclap burst overhead and all those near the soldiers were shocked and fell down unconscious as electricity raced through the ground nearby. The sizzle and the stink of roasted flesh were all that wafted in the air and the gun used to launch the tear gas had melted into slag on the ground. The skeletal hands of the solider that launched the tear gas still gripping his useless weapon.

And while Enoch and Elijah made their presence known to Leto Alexander and stood as a prophetic voice against the Anti-Christ, El Pneuma had arrived to recoup his people. His wings covered the whole of the planet as if cradling the blue orb in his arms, and when he did so he whispered but one word.

"Come."

A wave of crystal blue energy enveloped the planet, and all eyes beheld in the sky a shimmering blue Aurora Borealis. Such was the brightness that even those on the daylight side of the planet saw a shimmering light dance in the sky.

A light as bright as the sun then swept from east to west over the sky and when it did, Enoch and Elijah knelt, raised their hands and lifted their voices and proclaimed.

"Behold The LORD, The LORD God, merciful and gracious, long suffering, and abundant in goodness and truth, keeping mercy for thousands, forgiving iniquity and transgression and sin, and that will by no means clear the guilty; visiting the iniquity of the fathers upon the children, and upon the children's children, unto the third and to the fourth generation."

Their voices boomed over the skies such that glass shattered in both cars and buildings and many that heard had to cover their ears for the pain. The words spoken were voiced in every tongue and every language, and there was nowhere on earth that the proclamation was not understood.

Suddenly, without warning. People from every tribe and nation found themselves changed and their skin flaked away to reveal a new body that lay underneath, and many suddenly floated upwards;

lifting into the sky as they looked at their flesh, which was now changed. Many vanished through the ceilings of buildings, slowly rising. And all at once around the entire planet, each one from around the globe burst into a ball of white light, then shot up into the air in streaking rays of prismatic light. Clothes, dentures, glasses, and all manner of paraphernalia to assist the body of men were left behind in their wakes. Those that remained; that had watched them change and disappear; screamed in lament, calling after them. Wives yelled after husbands and husbands after wives, children called out to parents and parents to children. Confusion gripped many, and discernment others as many had recalled tales of a Rapture. An event on God's celestial calendar that would leave many of humanity behind to face His judgment.

Pregnant mothers suddenly found their wombs empty, while hospitals around the world, from infant ICU's to hospice rooms, emptied themselves of patients.

Cars which traveled over the roads of men suddenly careened off course as their drivers disappeared behind their wheels. Planes fell from the skies plummeting to the ground causing death and destruction to both occupants and those below while military personnel throughout the Earth were suddenly absent without leave. Some firemen who entered into buildings never came out. Thousands of prisoners around the world incarcerated for all manner of crimes disappeared from their cells and before their captor's eyes.

Death and destruction accompanied the harvest of God's children. For men in positions of power and first responders who were positioned to protect were suddenly absent: gone, leaving a vacuum of leadership and emergency personnel in their wake.

Doctors disappeared in the midst of their operations while children across all continents lifted away to heaven.

But the body of Christ was not immune from the reaping as many churches were in session across the world. And even in services of worship, some attendees were taken and others were left. Weeping and wails of anguish lifted from houses of worship across the world as the sinking realization swept across the planet that many who named the name of Christ were left behind.

Wails, screams, and moans were heard across the Earth. For not since the slaying of the firstborn of Egypt was a lament heard on this wise throughout the world. For the Lord God had come to reap His harvest, and he had taken his children home.

Nevertheless, many were fearful of the event and hid themselves thinking that aliens were abducting humankind; and many sought to escape what they perceived was celestial attack.

Enoch and Elijah watched as some soldiers within their sight disappeared and Enoch spoke aloud for all within earshot to hear. "For the prophecy of the Lord hast come to pass for there shall be two men in one bed; the one shall be taken, and the other shall be left. Two women shall be grinding together; the one shall be taken, and the other left. Two men shall be in the field; the one shall be taken, and the other left."

Henel James tried to collect himself, looking around in disbelief at what he was witnessing and attempted to continue streaming live what he was seeing to the world.

Enoch and Elijah somberly watched with those in assembled disbelief as people disappeared from their midst. Elijah then turned to lift his voice and proclaimed.

"Woe to you people of earth, for your tribulation has now begun."

Leto frowned in disapproval, looked down menacingly at the two men, and angrily muttered in retort. "It would seem that your God has declared war. Very well, we will show him war."

* * *

Henel James was a reporter for the Jerusalem Post. He viewed himself as a smart man: an accomplished man: a man, never given over to anything but the facts; let alone the superstitions and primitive beliefs of his religious family. Well read and educated at the Tel Aviv University, he had given up on God years ago.

Until he: like many of those in Jerusalem; saw the two witnesses on national TV. He was an atheist, and the idea of an all-knowing God that restrained him from his pursuit of women and the power of professional accomplishments did not align itself to his plans of success. And never in all his days did he think he would change his mind; not until two men in a flash of lightning and thunder appeared before the wailing wall of Jerusalem in sackcloth cried "Repent!" Bearded and muscular their voices echoed across the courtyards and made everyone pay attention as the boom from their words traveled for kilometers. And it was the extravagant lightning strike of their appearance and the volume of their booming voices that first got Henel's attention.

"Repent and believe the Gospel!" They roar. "For the time of His coming draws nigh!"

Henel recognized a journalistic moment when he saw it; took out his cell phone to capture video. He watched as the duo's spectacular visual and auditory disturbance caught the attention of the soldiers patrolling the area.

"You worship, but you know not what! For the stone which the builders have rejected commands your ear! He soon comes with ten thousands of his saints. Be warned for the Beast that lives among you has said "Peace! Peace! But alas, there is no peace. For he is voracious and comes to destroy this temple and will exalt himself above all things that are called God! Repent and believe in Yeshua, the Son of the living God!"

Here we go with this Yeshua again, thought Henel. He chuckled to himself. The two old coots were about to get what was coming to them as two soldiers with rifles raised commanded them to come away from the wall. But the men seem undeterred and replied.

"We stand before you as the two candlesticks of God, and yet you come to us to snuff out our light. We will not be moved, and I have warned you to not interfere with the God of Heaven. For by our word, if you would seek to do us harm, know that His fire burns within and His wrath will not be turned if you do harm to his saints."

One of the soldiers chuckled and replied. "OK, old timer, that's enough. Let's go." And the soldier went to grab Elijah by the arm and when he did. The old grizzled prophet opened his mouth and fire proceeded from it and devoured the soldier where he stood. And he died screaming before the men, as his flesh erupted in spontaneous combustion and his body was engulfed in sort of immolation.

Immediately, his partner drew her rifle and aimed it at both men. "On your knees now!" she yells.

But Enoch became angered and replies, "Hath thou not seen that God has sent us? But with thine own eyes will you still not believe. Hath ye not heard to touch not his prophets, nor do them no harm?" And Enoch appeared puzzled, glancing around as if he looked for others to answer his question.

"I said on your knees now! You have three seconds to comply, or I will fire. Three! Two! One!"

Suddenly, the rat-ta-tat sound of an Israeli Micro-Tavor assault rifle sprang from the female soldier's weapon. But the bullets just ricocheted mere centimeters from the old men and the projectiles were sent whizzing into the onlooking crowd. Enoch then spoke, "Because thou did not obey my word. You too will see the realm of the dead." And immediately fire ushered from his mouth and, like her partner before her, the soldier's body erupted in flames and spontaneously combust.

Henel dropped to the ground for cover. His cell phone still recording, as he could not believe his eyes. Spectators and those surrounding the wall screamed and fled in terror from the combined flames and from the ricocheting shots that were fired. Pandemonium filled the air as the two old men touched the wall and sat down in front of it. The area cleared quickly as all men ran, fearing for their lives.

Elijah sighed and spoke. "Oh, crooked and perverse generation. Did we not say we are but two witnesses to the glory of God? Did we not speak that the God of Heaven demands that everyone everywhere repent? Why then hast thou raged and imagined vain things? And who is this Leto Alexander that he doth defy the armies of the living God? Be not deceived, for he too will meet his end in a lake burning with fire and brimstone. Hear us and let the words of our mouth serve as a warning to all. Do not take the brand that is the Mark of the Beast. For he that takes the mark shall be lost, but he who believes until the end shall be saved."

Henel James was an opportunist. He could smell a story. Before him were two dead Israeli soldiers. Each killed by fire while the whole of the Wailing Wall had cleared to make room for the two old men. He stopped recording for a second and switched over to Facebook to live stream. There was no way he was going to be upended by an amateur video.

I could win a Pulitzer for this, he thought to himself. Then the idea that perhaps he could interview the men came to him. If I pose no threat, perhaps I can get them to explain where they came from. Henel moved closer to grab his story.

"Excuse me, sir?" He waved at Enoch. "Excuse me!" He raised his hands with his palms open, his cell phone gripped tightly to still capture any images and sound.

"May I hear more? I would very much like to hear your story, and what you have to say. May I approach you?"

Enoch looked at Elijah, and Elijah nodded. "Come forward, young man," says Enoch.

Henel kept his head low and averted, looking at the men directly in the eyes. He then sat himself five feet from the duo and opened his mouth to speak.

"My name is Henel James; may I ask who you are?"

"We are the two olive trees; the two candlesticks which stand before the God of the Earth. Two who have witnessed His glory and must give testimony to what we have seen and what shall come to pass."

Henel looked at his phone to make sure he caught all that and checked his memory to see how much time he had left before the device stopped.

"You have told me more of your function, but may I ask for your names? I wish to tell your story. And I will, if you allow me, take your words and share them with the entire world."

Elijah replies, "We are Enoch and Elijah. And we know who you are, unbeliever. You have forsaken the God of your fathers. You have swept aside the traditions of the elders. You should have done whatever they had you to observe; but not have done after their works: for they say and do not. Therefore, tell us Henel James of the tribe of Benjamin, why didst thou not respect the tradition of your fathers?"

Henel froze, looking at the men dumbstruck.

He stared at the men, shaking. He did not tell them anything about his belief in God, and especially about his family lineage.

Henel gathered his composure and quickly planned an answer he thought would not embarrass him as he continues to live-stream. "Well, dear sir. What son these days listens to his parents? Do we not all go our way as we get older?" Henel smiles at his answer. Thinking he had outsmarted the old man.

He was wrong.

"Why do you speak to us thus? And why hath Satan filled thy heart to trifle with the Holy Ghost? For this slight: your spirit will be required of thee. But fear not, know even as thou spoke we have interceded that you might not see the realm of the dead that you too may serve as a witness.

The Holy One has agreed in this thing. But do not tempt the Holy Spirit. Lest you find your life forfeit. Do you understand me, young man?"

Henel nodded nervously and replies, "Yes, sir."

Enoch then motioned for him to draw near. Henel inched closer to within arm's reach, and Enoch spoke. "The device you have... will it carry our words?"

"Yes sir. It will not only take your words, but your image and project them into faraway lands, and many will see and hear what you say."

Enoch then extended his hand to hold the device, and Henel slowly turned the phone over to him. Enoch passed the cell phone to Elijah, who held it to investigate it as he also turned it over for inspection. He then passed it back to Henel. Elijah smirked at the young man and replies, "Truly a wondrous thing you have. But alas, it would seem that you are ever learning, yet unable to come into the knowledge of the truth."

Suddenly, the sound of a helicopter came into earshot and several transport carriers rolled upon their position and screeched to a halt. Soldiers emptied and scrambled to take up positions surrounding the area. A solider also leaned out the door of the helicopter and sniper positioned himself from a neighboring building aiming directly at their position. Henel slowly placed his still broadcasting phone on its kickstand and instinctively raised his hands high into the air. "I am unarmed!" he yells: hoped against hope that the authorities did not think he was with the men.

A male voice from a bullhorn blared his command to the two men. "You are under arrest! You will place your hands on your head. Any movement other than this and you will be fired upon! You have three seconds to comply!"

Henel watched as the seconds marched on the broadcast over Facebook live. He could not see behind him save the images that were played out on the screen. His eyes widened as the men who were positioned behind himself immolated and burst into flames. A lightning strike then flashed and disintegrated the tail of the chopper and it fell from the sky with the pilot scrambling inside, attempting to regain control of the plummeting aircraft. It careened into the court with a crash. Rotors sliced into the ground and the centrifugal force hurled them into the distance. Henel's eyes grew wide as the soldier jumped from the craft running; his body emblazoned in fire as he turned into ash and fell to the ground.

Henel then heard the voice of Enoch. "Henel James."

Henel pushed himself up to see the two men still siting unfazed. Enoch motioned for him to return the device, and he did so. Enoch looked into the screen and spoke, and his voice boomed when he did.

"We are the two witnesses sent by God. By the power of the Living God we have now shut up the heavens and there will be no rain in Israel except by our word: we defy Leto Alexander and his Satan, his father, that all may know the God of Heaven is supreme."

Enoch and Elijah then looked at the sky and spoke aloud so that all might hear.

"Two pounds of wheat for a day's wages, and six pounds of barley for a day's wages, and do not damage the oil and the wine!" And only a few that watched the live stream knew they merely echoed the words recorded in the book of Revelation.

Immediately, the sky turned a putrid green. And the clouds parted to reveal a horse and rider that flew through the sky. And a scale was in the rider's hand and when Henel looked up into the sky, he saw a black humanoid being who trailed the rider whose face was as a mare. Its wings were like those of a bat, yet without the connecting membrane, and fire and great plumes of dark smoke issued from its skeletal body. Tendrils of iron flailed about as it flew. And when Henel saw the being; he knew this was what his forefathers had seen many ages ago. His flesh immediately lost color and the instinctual knowing as the great winged giant flew above him. His shadow spread over all things like a great eclipse of the sun, and Henel intuitively understood in the core of his being that what he looked into was the face of death itself. And he realized that at the moment, all the Pulitzer's in the world would not save him from what his eyes beheld. And he looked in horror at Enoch and Elijah and trembled at what he beheld.

"What is going on?" he says.

Enoch returned his gaze and spoke somberly in reply. "The fourth seal has been broken: death now comes to reap the world, and you human... you will soon see Hell follow."

Chapter Eight: Tribulations and Woe

Michael arrived back into Heaven, and Talus awaited him at the Cliffs of Argoth. Michael turned to his escorts and spoke, “Go and stand as a shield to Enoch and Elijah. I have reason to suspect that, though powerful together, they will need your support. Find a hole in Leto’s authority. There must be those sympathetic to our cause that can provide us with prayer cover. Now go.”

Both angels nodded and fell backwards off the cliff, opened a portal to the realm of mortal men and disappeared into prismatic light.

Michael looked at Talus and the two walked towards the mountain of God. “What have you to report my friend?”

“There has been a disturbance among the Horde. For demons now lash against demon. Angel against angel. It is as if a civil war has broken out among them. I would have never surmised that such would occur amongst the Horde.”

“I know," replied Michael. “When I met with the Abomination, no principalities covered his residence. Marduk, it would seem, was the origin of the rebellion, but alas, Marduk has lost his war against Lucifer and stands as a prisoner of war. It is only a matter of time until he is given to the Void. Nevertheless, he possesses to have a scheme by which he believes he can smite the Abomination down. I do not see how such is possible if he stands as his captor. But we shall see.”

Talus nodded, his eyes surveying the ground as he thought upon his brother’s words. “Michael, the principalities that have engaged one another have caused destruction to the peoples of the middle east beyond imagining. The great political powers have in times past moved to fill the vacuum. But this Leto now controls them. They seemingly are at his command and have restrained themselves from moving to secure key areas of what was once strategic interest.”

Michael stopped walking and turned to his brother. "The thing is known to me. Before Marduk’s capture, he informed me that a God-stone lies buried under the Temple Rock.”

Talus stopped and took his brother by the arm, "A Godstone? One of the Kilnstones has been found. Is it one that Lucifer used to hold me captive?:

Michael shrugged, "The thing is not known, my friend. I have only recently been apprised of this intelligence. How such a thing could escape notice of the Host and Grigori specifically is beyond me. Is Argoth still in tome form?"

Talus nodded, "He is. Every jot and tittle burning up within him ready to be unleashed as Yeshua breaks each seal."

Michael frowned, "El's wrath has been released only in part and in measure. Even in his anger, there is restraint. If El does not withdraw from his plan, there will be no mankind to save. Adamson is surely doomed. Have you been able to estimate the casualties?"

Talus nodded, "Some shall be saved. Jerahmeel has been working in Argoth's hall, and he projects that it is possible that over seventy percent of the planet's inhabitants could be wiped out."

Michael lowered his head, sighed and replied. "And El... has his wrath been abated?"

"No, said Talus. I fear it has just begun. While you were away, a horseman was unleashed upon the world. Crimson red, its rider was war, and Marduk Prince of Babylon rode a wave of blood across the planet; those nations influenced by the Mohammedans had launched an offensive against the nations of Shem and Japheth. The attack has gone on for week's earth-side.

As they both made their way towards the steps of the palace, they heard the sound of ladders before they saw them. The great sound of the prismatic funnels preparing to form in the capital of Heaven itself. Like the oncoming sound of rain. A sound they had not heard since the days of the war with Lucifer: the deafening roar as if a tornadic waterfall were moving through the land. The golden-hued sky above them changed, and all manner of colors flared through the region. The last time, ladders breached Heaven's sky and obliterated the land to mark the start of war.

Michael took up a defensive position and yelled to his comrade, "Talus to my right! Let nothing come to breach the palace grounds. Michael then roared a clarion call to battle to all of Heaven into the air. "To arms!" he yells.

His voice carried across the skies of Heaven, and every angel had heard the call before. Each knowing upon command of the Chief Prince, they were now mustered to battle. Mustered to heaven's defense, and so the populace of heaven ceased in their daily activities and took up sword and shield. Each armored themselves to prepare for what could only be an invasion.

Flecks of light materialized throughout all of heaven. The telltale sign Ophanims were distorting the realm to make room for their transport to occupy its space. Speckles of light appeared all around them: the ground, the sky, in buildings, and in rooms. The palace steps. Both fore and aft of the Burning Ones. All eyes could see that whatever was coming was arriving on a scale far more different from any had ever seen; for nowhere in heaven did the lights not materialize.

"In El's name we are being bombarded upon all sides!" says Talus. "How can Eladrin allow his people to bring ruin to our shores? We will surely perish when the ladders fall."

Michal looked and his face was downcast, for he had never seen ladders form on this wise and in such numbers. "Whatever the enemy, we will face it." He withdrew his sword and sent it flying into the air, where it split into seven blades. His halo flared, "I am calling for Eladrin and his people. We will not be alone."

Immediately the words of El Pneuma spoke within his mind, "Oh my son, know ye not that you are never alone?"

The sky then opened to reveal the Holy spirit and as a great bird of prey, his wings were spread aboard and light beamed from them and he spoke.

"Behold! The children of God!"

Bluish lights descended from his wings and ladders thin as small beams of light penetrated the entirety of Heaven, and wherever a beam settled, a man or a woman appeared; stunned and excited, gasping in awe of their surroundings. Each materialized as if they were newborn stars. Exploding in luminance and color.

"Hold thy weapons," Spoke El Pneuma. "For my children and thy redeemed siblings have now come home.

And for the first time in Grigoric history, the four races of creation were now united in Heaven: an army at full strength. And Michael knew that with the addition of the Raptured there was nothing that could withstand them.

* * *

2 years after the Taking

Leto sat at his office in Brussels and his ten regional governors were assembled to report on the latest worldwide happenings.

"Who will go first, gentlemen? Let's not be coy."

Governor Consuela looked around the room and noticed the trepidation in the body language of each governor and spoke first to represent her people. "Emperor, North America and the United States in particular have been particularly hard hit. As is commonly known with many of our countries; Christianity was in decline but still a substantive part of our region's population who affiliated with the religion. Over a third of our male population have disappeared in the Taking not to mention the women and children We have millions of missing persons, persons who are no longer available to pay bills, employees gone, businesses shutting down and impacting everything from production to logistics and supply lines. Commerce simply has been disrupted on a scale we have never imagined. Both American and Canadian government revenue has collapsed and what market still exists has stabilized only because of our application of the Mark to the citizenry. As your imminence already knows, the Cyber-attacks have crippled computer networks worldwide. The Mark is the only thing that allows secured transactions to occur due to the sheer widespread and replicating nature of the virus. I would also remind his excellency. We have him to thank for this."

Leto's eyebrow rose at this remark, and he spoke in response. "Governor Consuela, do I detect sarcasm in your voice? Perhaps even peppered with a hint of accusatory disdain?" Leto then slowly rose from his chair. His strong and muscular features were seen even beneath his suit jacket.

The President of the United States, now Governor of the whole of North America, spoke timidly to the world's acknowledged leader.

"I speak the truth. Truth which no one in this room should fear. You are the most powerful person on the planet. Surely my words do nothing to threaten that? The truth of how you attacked my country and supplanted the world's economy. This truth is buttressed by the rumors of how you threatened the lives of various members of the United Nations to vote you into office. None of those truths take away the larger truth that, despite your lack of moral authority by some to rule... you do rule. I am a politician and a realist."

Leto smirked, "What is truth? Since you are a realist, you understand that truth originates with me and my father. For I only speak what he has spoken. And his words and deeds have shown us that this entity, from beyond the quantum realm, is a threat to mankind. A threat I will not abide. He will not take our people without impunity and soon we will be in the position to make him pay. I have driven our economies governors to build our forces to combat this threat. While it pains me that people may suffer. WE must be vigilant to prepare ourselves for what the father indicates will be an imminent attack. But I digress, continue Governor, and do so with less vitriol. If I desired your snide remarks, I would simply have you recite them as I executed your family before your eyes. Now continue."

Leto sat down and the Governor swallowed hard and did as she was commanded.

"Universal income has kept the overall population from starvation, but capital has been and is projected to be tied up in litigation with our courts for decades. We simply do not have the personnel trained to deal with the massive estates and complications from declaring so many dead or missing. However, you will be pleased to hear that our combat readiness has been upgraded. Resources have been rerouted to the military and have made us ready to launch against any celestial attack. The armed forces have been restructured to compensate for so many missing. Nevertheless, we are still taxed but can commit troops if and when needed. Violent crime has curtailed, but fraud has skyrocketed, as many have tried to take advantage of so many who have now gone. We have managed to quell the terrorist cells that have sought to fracture the government and make claims that we are still a sovereign nation or those who claim to be Christian that have attacked government posts. I have accelerated executions for crimes against humanity as you commanded. It quells most of the population, but many claim allegiance to Christ and are willing to sacrifice their lives to demonstrate it. We have accommodated them accordingly."

Leto looked at the Governor of the United States and replied. "Do better… now sit down."

Governor Consuela looked at her leader and slowly sunk into her seat as a scolded child. And did her best to maintain a semblance of pride.

"Governor Wang. Speak of the Asian rim. What is your status?"

Governor Wang spoke in Mandarin and the translators implanted near the base to each governor's neck translated his words.

"We are ready for any incursion into our sphere. We are also ready at your command to send over a million fighting men to any part of the world. Per your orders, we have completed construction of the dimensional gate based on the plans provided by your father. Once we have the power source, we will have the means to instantly move our troops. The Ophanim that has been captured has had its physiology extensively studied. Simulations show the gate mimics the creature's sonic cry to summon a quantum wave field allowing for dimensional transport. We believe that with further study we can incorporate this technology into our ships, making even quantum travel possible. When you give command Emperor, we will be ready. We will find our people and hunt these creatures down."

"And what is the status of the rest of your population?" says Leto.

"Unlike the Americans, we applied the Mark to our citizenry as soon as it was understood. Our population is united in making whatever sacrifices are necessary for planetary survival."

Governor Wang then looked at Governor Consuela and spoke. "We do not whine over the state of affairs, such as property disposition, when planetary security is at stake." Wang then nodded towards Leto and ended his report.

"You see Governor Consuela? You can learn something from the Chinese. Immensely efficient and they understand priorities that the government is father. The government is mother."

Consuela interjected. "I thought your father was Lucifer and not the government?"

Leto cocked his head to the side and laughs, "Ah dear Consuela, I do enjoy you. Your remarks, though defiant, humor me. My father is the government, my dear, and my government rests upon his shoulders. You would do well to remember that."

Ashtaroth suddenly materialized next to Leto and startled those in the room who, unlike the Beast, could not see him. He lowered himself to speak into his master's ear, "There is report from Jerusalem."

Leto nodded, then spoke to his cabinet. "We are dismissed for now. All of you leave me. Wait… Governor Abadi. This will concern you. You may stay."

The governor of the Middle Eastern pact nodded his head in acknowledgment and stayed in his seat. He glared disapprovingly at the angel standing next to Leto and Ashtaroth, noted the human's gaze and spoke to him.

"You are Mendel Abadi of the tribe of Levi. I know your family. I have lived thousands of your years human before your species were taught to put pen to paper. And I was there when Nadab and Abihu of house Levi took either of them his censer and put fire therein, and put incense thereon, and offered strange fire before the Lord, fire which he commanded them not. But who do you think spoke into their ears murmur, curiosity and discontentment and awakened pride to walk in an office that was not theirs? Who do you think whispered into their ears how they might, through alchemy, summon a Virtue that they might peer into the very Heavens? Both received their just reward... Death. Be wary of how you glare at me human or you will join them in the realm of the dead."

Governor Abadi quickly averted his eyes and gritted his teeth.

Leto chuckled. "Ashtaroth be nice."

The Anti-Christ then turned his executives chair and pressed a button to lower a view screen from the ceiling and an image of men in construction hats, and the sounds of hammers clanging and jack hammers could be heard in the background.

"Foreman report. How long will it be before we reach the crystal and we can counterattack?"

"It's hard to say exactly, sir... but the analysis of the wave pattern on our quantum detectors makes it clear we are close. I'd say three days at most."

Leto looked at Ashtaroth, who stood outside the view-screens field of vision and shook his head.

Leto slammed his fist into the armrest. "Move faster!" he yells.

"If we move faster, my emperor, we risk destroying the antiquities found at the site. I remind my emperor you gave your word you would allow the Jews to rebuild their temple of worship."

Governor Abadi interjected. "I would remind my emperor that our seven-year pact: a pact we and the Arab league have complied with; states that antiquities found at the site would be used to rebuild the temple as promised."

Leto breathes hard, then growled his displeasure and replies, "You think I care for trinkets? For Jewish baubles? For two long years I have exhibited patience, for two years I have waited as you have meticulously moved earth and stone. And for two years I have watched humanity languish and be devastated by alien attack, plague and famine. I am tired of waiting, and I will wait no longer. Get your people ready, Foreman Higgins. I will come to oversee final completion and restoration of the temple personally. My source tells me the actual temple itself is ready: is it not?"

The construction foreman of the project bowed his head and replied. "Yes, sir." Leto turned the view screen off, swiveled around in his chair and stood in buoyant glee, clapping his hands together.

"Good, then it is time I dedicate this place that the earth might pay homage. I know of no one who can offer salvation from this alien threat but by my father. Come Abadi. We shall go and you may enjoy the privilege of helping me to dedicate this temple."

Governor Abadi looked at Ashtaroth, then at Leto pleadingly and in horror. "But, but sir... you cannot dedicate the temple. You are NOT a Jew. Nor a believer of our God. The temple is the central point of worship to Yahweh God of the Jews."

"Exactly," says Leto.

And it came to pass, when the time was come that the Anti-Christ, Leto Alexander, should defile the temple; he steadfastly set his face to go to Jerusalem.

As each man rose from their seats and moved to exit the room. Ashtaroth allowed his master to go before him and stopped in front of Governor Abadi. and looked at him menacingly. His lips curled upward with a fiendish grin, and he says, "Smile son of Levi. Strange fire is coming."

* * *

Michael watched as Argoth was placed as a living volume upon a risen dais. His body no longer the floating transparent wisp of an angel with glowing eyes. But now fully transformed into the Sephiroth: The Book of Life. Michael now fully understood Argoth's existence. His was to keep the secrets of the Almighty. To record the history of all things. To journal the mind of God, and to lock within himself every jot and tittle of El. This duty was his alone to bear, and when El finished, he wrapped upon the stone of the angel's heart a seal. Seven total. Each a mighty inscription upon the Head of all Grigori. Inscriptions that the Lamb of God now began to systematically break. Each sending a wave of the Lord's judgment on mankind. For three transgressions and for four had Yeshua unleashed the beasts of a man, war, famine, and death upon the Earth. But there were seven seals and Michael watched as the Lord God Yeshua approached Argoth and then broke the fifth seal.

Wails and cries of anguish filled the air of heaven. Howls of those who were slain for the word of God and for the testimony with which they held. Michael turned his head and underneath the altar, the spirits of men not avenged clawed their way from underneath the altar. Sprites that were ever in front of the Lord God. Spirits invisible to all but now. And they were an army of men and women who cries with a loud voice says, "How long, O Lord, holy and true, dost thou not judge and avenge our blood on them that dwell on the earth?"

Michael realized that from the cry of Abel who died at that hands of his own brother to men chained in prisons of men. God had kept every soul before him. Invisible to all but himself that these were those that sacrificed all who they were to uphold His word. And now, before the eyes of Heaven, multitudes of the spirits were released from underneath the altar to see themselves avenged. And the spirits cried again.

"How long, O Lord, holy and true, dost thou not judge and avenge our blood on them that dwell on the earth?"

And the Lord God Yeshua says unto them, "Rest yet for a little season, until your fellow servants also and thy brethren, should be killed as thou were, when this is fulfilled, vengeance shall begin." The Lord God then turned to Michael and commanded his servant.

"Give to each of these white robes."

Michael then looked to Gabriel and his people, who could move virtually instantly, and watched as the Malakim retrieved robes from the storehouses of heaven and clothed each human by the command of the Lord.

And when the last of the robes were given, the Lord God Yeshua noted Argoth had once more turned into the book of seals. The Lord eyed and noted a sixth seal on the Book of Life. He approached his servant, who was the living journal of the Father. The Lord's face was grim, and his eyes narrowed in anger. He then placed his hands firmly upon the indigo clay seal that surrounded the book and snapped it in two.

* * *

Leto Alexander was before a crowd of French supporters. Each crying his name in praise. Women and men blew him kisses. He waved to the adoring throng of men and women. For he was the bringer of both war and peace. An astute leader that brought solutions to the world's problems. A man who towered over other men. Waving and returning kisses to the crowd, he stood in his Mercedes Benz, waving to the thousands that filled the streets to welcome his arrival. His Imperial motorcade was heavily armed while helicopter gunships flew nearby ready to cut down any resistance from the air. He loved the French people, and they loved that the world's leader was of Europa. Leto Alexander looked triumphant as he motorcade through the Arc de Triomphe.

Then the ground shook.

The tremor was first, only a minor jarring, barely noticeable. But soon it sounded like a tornado, followed by a bomb dropping. Then the noise under the ground started, and the earth heaved and buckled, and cars were jettisoned into the air from rising earthen pillars over turning the occupants within. And instantly the cheers of a jubilant crowd turned into blood-curdling screams as the streets of Paris heaved and rolled and fissured, causing men, women, and children to fall into gaping multiple sinkholes of the Earth. Buildings collapsed and the twelve radiating avenues that converged towards the Arc de Triomphe merely became lanes of death. Onlookers foolish enough to record the carnage watched as the magnificent monument dedicated to the warriors of the French Revolution and Napoleonic Wars collapsed like children's Lego's upon the caravan of the Beast. And everywhere the eye saw people falling and crying and clouds of smoke lifted into the air. For twenty seconds the floor of the Earth gave way to collapse into her basement, for twenty seconds men experienced the terror of the planet they thought they ruled, turn against them. The ground upon which they stood was now a thing to hide from. And with a cataclysm never seen, villages were buried under mountain slides. While explosions from gas lines echoed across metropolises worldwide.

For throughout the planet one lived, and another died, mothers huddled their children to shield them from debris and alas, both were lost. Heroic efforts to salvage loved ones saw whole families decimated, and as the east is from the west, there was nowhere on Earth that the carnage could not be felt. From the Amazon forests to the outback of Australia. All of humankind would share in their collective memory the day the earth shook for twenty seconds.

For alas, twenty seconds later, when it was over, all that remained was rubble, dirt and a morass of broken and bloodied bodies.

And Leto Alexander, shielded by his angelic guards, looked over the city of Paris and all of her fallen and cursed the God of Heaven, raised his fist and spoke blasphemies into the air. And in his act of defiance, the Lord saw it and when the Anti-Christ did this thing, the sun itself became black as night. A black that penetrated the soul. A black that cloaked death. And the moon was also turned to her side and when men looked into the sky, they beheld the phenomenon as she was dressed in blood. Her surface of pot-marked craters crying tears of red.

But alas, the end was not yet. For the stars of heaven fell unto the earth, even as a fig tree casts her untimely figs, when shaken by a mighty wind. And asteroids battered the world as hail. Striking deep into the whole of the planet's face. And when men looked up, they saw the sky roll back as if the sun had now chosen to reveal its brutal heat and mountains and islands across the oceans moved from their place.

And the kings of the earth, and the great men, and the rich men, and the chief captains, and the mighty men, and every bondman, and every free man, hid themselves in the dens and in the rocks of the mountains; hoping against hope that this day would not be their last.

And the carnage was such that Ashtaroth watched as men cried out to the very mountains and rocks. And a collective cry of mourning rang into the ears of Leto and his father Lucifer from afar. Men who had been told that alien incursion and or attack was imminent. Men who cried out for succor.

Cried out in despair.

“Fall on us, and hide us from the face of him that sits on this throne, and from the wrath of this Lamb: For the great day of his wrath is come; and who shall be able to stand?”

For, far away the Great Instigator Lucifer watched the celestial bombardment from atop the remains of the battered One Trade Center in New York and grinned in infernal satisfaction of man’s newfound misery. Satisfied that his manipulation of man and his creation of Leto provoked the

Almighty, as in the days of Balaam, to force his hand to bring judgment to his creation. For now, it was confirmed that the endgame was afoot. That El's wrath was now fully incensed. Now Lucifer could move his final piece into play.

The death and resurrection of his son.

* * *

Yeshua stood watching over the destruction and chaos that reigned over the earth. His face holding back tears. But Michael noted the eyes of his God. Eyes that were determined to complete what lay ahead. The prince of angels then turned his face to El.

El's face was stoic, even expressionless, Michael noted. El then, for a moment, wept and spoke to the blue orb planet aloud that all might hear. "Have I any pleasure in the death of him that dieth, saith the Lord GOD: wherefore turn yourselves, and live? LIVE!" he cries.

Michael held back tears, knowing that El was hurting. To punish his wayward children tasked even the compassion of the Almighty. So, Michael turned his eyes to the planet. Lifted his ears to hear if men would reply and turn from his wicked way. If chastisement would bring correction. And he looked upon the sons of men amazed that men did naught but curse God. Leaders of nations and tribes hunted and killed those who, even during the tribulation, turned their hearts of God. Men who debased themselves. Men who raised their fists to God in defiance.

And it was clear to Michael as he fully saw with the peeling back of each seal that there was none righteous, no, not one. There was none that understood, none that sought after God. They had all gone out of the way and together had become unprofitable; none that did good. Their throats were open sepulchers; their tongues used for deceit; like asps' poison dripped from their lips: their mouths were full of cursing and bitterness: their feet swift to shed blood: Destruction and misery were in their ways. And the way of peace they knew not: and Michael's heart was heavy, for there was no fear of God before their eyes.

The Lord placed his hand over his head, and it was clear He took no glee or pleasured in the judgment that was now being met out. No. For the cries that emanated from the Earth were the wails of rebellious children who were now under the rod of judgment. A rod the Lord would not spare for the weeping that rose from below.

El Pneuma stood over Argoth. His body now twisted and turned. His insides spasmed as if something was ready to burst and he whimpered aloud, looking for solace.

"It hurts, Lord... it hurts so much."

Argoth gritted his teeth in attempts to mask the convulsions that erupted over his frame. Michael, Gabriel, Jerahmeel and the rest of the Host could now clearly see his body now. It was no longer cloaked. No longer hidden under his robes. For with the release of the sixth seal, his robes fell to the floor and naught but his undergarments could be seen. But strapped around his torso was something akin to a leather belt. But the thing was made of blood, and it seeped into his skin and left marks that burned. And Michael, in that instant, knew that Argoth, since he assumed the role of Sephiroth, had taken unto himself to serve as the journal of the Almighty. And that even as Yeshua carried the weight of the sins of the world upon his frame upon a cross. Argoth carried within his flesh the pent-up manifested rage of God towards sin. His angst, his frustrations, his judgment. Each jot and title now slowly being released into the Creation. Each broken seal collapsing the barriers El had erected to prevent Creation's destruction from His wrath. Barriers created to hold the contents written within the Book of Life.

The book that was Argoth.

Argoth was the Book of Life and only God, and he knew the secrets contained therein. A book, the Son of God, second person of the Godhead, was now opening.

A book, Michael wondered if Creation would survive the reading.

"Arrrgghhh!!!!" screamed the Grigori.

Michael and his brethren stepped back as they watched their friend's chest heave as if he would bust from within. Argoth's and Jerahmeel's eyes connected. And Jerahmeel now understood the chronic pain that Argoth endured. What he kept locked away daily for millennia. The loss of his eyes to see what the Almighty saw, to project into all creation through the Grigori. To see everything at once. To record all thoughts. All action. To journal the omniscience of God. To keep the secrets of the God of Universe. To be the living papyrus upon whom God recorded his emotions about his struggle with mankind.

Jerahmeel's emotions for a moment overcame him and in pity he reached out with his hand as if he would go to touch him to succor him and Gabriel grabbed him.

"No, stay back. Do it not. This thing must be played out. He pulses with the anger of El. Mayhap you yourself would be consumed. This is something only the Godhead can relieve. It is not for us to interfere."

El Pneuma then was moved with compassion. Realizing that Creation had never seen the full outrage of the Almighty. Never beheld his wrath on this wise and He covered his body over Argoth's, and the angel's pain eased. And he spoke to his son. "Be strong, my son. For there is nothing hidden that shall not be revealed nor covered, that shall not be known. Soon the fullness of rage shall be spent."

El Pneuma then nodded to El, who motioned for Yeshua to continue.

Yeshua then took hold of the blood leather strap that held Argoth and felt for the final and seventh clay seal. Michael noted that this seal was violet. Soaked in the Lamb's blood. Blood that had been presented to El upon Christ's return to heaven. Blood El saved. Blood he would see returned upon those who, in their foolishness, spit upon the costly sacrifice of his son.

"Snap."

Michael heard the seal break and crumble in Yeshua's hands. The blood strap then disappeared and when it did. The very air stood still. Michael attempted to move but could not. Even the Maelstrom could not be heard by those who had views from outside the palace. And in Heaven all stood motionless and there was silence in Heaven for about the space of half an hour.

And when the time had expired. Sherkanim and six of the Seraphim had come into the throne room bearing the seven trumpets of judgment. Each a unique weapon of mass destruction crafted ages ago. Each a weapon that was meant to be unleashed upon angels. Weapons now directed towards the world of men. And Sherkanim stood across from Michael and his six stood apart from the Lumazi and Michael's six. And handed them the trumpets. Passing and formally sealing an end to the schism that separated Heaven's original races.

Michael and the rest of the Lumazi took each one a trumpet and held the ancient instruments of praise now weaponized. Each realizing they held a key that if turned...if blown would unleash reality devastating fury upon its target.

Then Sherkanim came and stood at the altar having a golden censer, and attendants to the altar that held the prayers of the saints, gave him incense he should burn upon the altar of the prayers of the saints.

And he did so.

The smoke of the incense, mingled with the prayers of the saints, ascended up before God out of Sherkanim's hand.

And he took the censer, and filled it with fire of the altar, living fire that was the making of his own people and cast the censor into the earth: and there were voices, and thunderings, and lightnings, and an earthquake.

And El then looked upon the Lumazi and spoke. "Make ready to blow."

And each of the seven angels, which had the seven trumpets, prepared themselves to sound. And they lined themselves in single file from the lowest ranking. To end with Michael. Who stood nearest to the throne.

And Michael, the prince of angels, knew he was witnessing the end of Creation as he knew it.

* * *

"Ms. Foley, wake up!"

Elizabeth woke up startled from her own snoring and Mr. Hudson's irritated directive. She slid her head up and wiped the drool from her sleeve.

"Feel free to report to Mr. McFarland's office. Tell him Mr. Hudson doesn't allow students to sleep in his class."

Elizabeth gathered her books and noted the snickers that emanated from her classmates. She walked away from her desk towards the classroom door when she noted that Michelle James had written "slut" on a sheet of paper and slid it far enough on her desk to assure Elizabeth saw it as she exited out the room.

She closed the door, clutched her books to her breast and closed her eyes and leaned against the hallway wall.

Elizabeth sighed. I'm so tired of this shit.

"Sup girl, when you gonna let me give you some if this wood?" She heard a male voice says.

Jim Crain was walking past, grinning as he passed. Elizabeth rolled her eyes and made her way down the hall towards Mr. McFarland's office.

She followed the signs that led her to the principal's office and signed a clipboard at the receptionist's desk.

"What happened this time?" Ms. Staples asks.

"Nothing." says Elizabeth. "I just fell asleep in class and Mr. Hudson got all bent outta shape and sent me here."

Ms. Staples shook her head. "Well, you won't get any learning done sleeping."

"He's so boring. I can get more learning watching YouTube."

Ms. Staples chuckles, "I'll let Mr. McFarland know you are here... again."

Elizabeth slouched on the office couch and waited for the principal. Mr. McFarland came to the lobby and motioned with his hands for Elizabeth to follow.

Elizabeth went into his office, and he shut the door.

"How many times has it been now? What happened now?"

"I'm sorry Mr. M. I fell asleep. I woke up to Mr. Hudson barking at me to wake up and to come to your office. So, I'm here."

Mr. McFarland nodded, "Ah, I see. Well, per Mr. Hudson, he says you are a rather loud snorer. I take your decibel level was a little too high for his tastes."

Elizabeth laughs, "Maybe. I don't sleep well these days. It's like there is this heaviness over me at night. Like something is smothering me. I can't describe it."

"Who have you talked to about this?" Mr. McFarland asks.

"No one really. I guess you just now."

"Elizabeth, that's not good hon, you've got two periods left before school ends. Let me see if I can do something else instead of sending you to detention."

Mr. McFarland picked up his head and punched in some numbers. "Carey... yea... do you have time to see a student? Elizabeth Foley. Wonderful. I'll send her right down."

Mr. McFarland hung up the phone and wrote a hall pass and gave it to Elizabeth.

"Go to the counseling office and check in with Mrs. Davis."

Elizabeth took the slip and walked out of the office. "Oh, and Ms. Foley. Try to keep an open mind and learn something over this next hour."

"No promises, Mr. M," she replies and left his office.

Elizabeth walked to the counseling office and both Ms. Davis settled into her office.

"So, tell me, Elizabeth. What brings you into my office today?"

"Oh, I dunno Ms. Davis. Perhaps it was the phone call from the principal that had something to do with it."

Ms. Davis just looked at her and replies, "So, do you often get snide with those who ask you how your day is going? You know I've looked at your file here and it's clear you're having challenges with the students. How are you coping?"

Elizabeth settled down some and replied. "I'm sorry. I shouldn't have snapped at you. I haven't had a lot of sleep lately."

"Since the Taking?" says Ms. Davis.

"Yes."

"Who was taken from you?"

Elizabeth folded her arms and looked out a window, staring.

Ms. Davis observed her and said. "You know it's OK to feel loss over someone that was taken from you. All of us know someone who was taken. They took my own mother."

Elizabeth continues to look out the window. "It was my best friend."

"I'm sorry," says Ms. Davis. I bet she was someone who cared for you just as much...

"Your mother..." Elizabeth interrupts.

"What about her?"

"Did you see her go?" says Elizabeth.

Ms. Davis looked down briefly and sighed. "No, we never got to say goodbye. I was away at a conference, and when I heard what was happening, I took the first flight home, and when I arrived... she was gone."

"She said goodbye... she wanted to go. She could see something. At first, I thought it was a dream. I had just woken up after being assaulted. And when I woke up, she was there in my bed, making sure I was OK. And then, then... she was gone. Just like that: taken. I wish...I wish I could have gone with her."

Ms. Davis sat quietly and nodded. Silently attempting to downplay to Elizabeth what she perceived might be thoughts of suicidal ideation. "And you've had trouble sleeping since then?"

"Yeah." Elizabeth replies.

"Why do you think that is?"

"I dunno, really. Sometimes I think... I think maybe God doesn't want me. Maybe he left me behind because of what I did, but based on what Carol said. I think it has more to do with my relationship with Christ."

"What did you do?" Ms. Davis asked, concerned.

Elizabeth took her feet and crisscrossed them on the couch. Her body slowly forming into a fetal position as she kept her arms tight across her chest. Staring out the office window.

"I let a boy take me to his bed."

"I take it at some point you did not want to go further, and he did?"

Elizabeth nodded.

"And this happened the day of the Taking?"

"No... the night before."

"You know, Elizabeth, I'm very sorry that this happened to you. You have an opportunity here. I don't know if you see it as such. But you were victimized. You were taken advantage of. But you don't have to continue to let this pain eat at you. It's possible to be free. To no longer be a victim."

Elizabeth slowly turned from staring out the window and looked squarely at Ms. Davis.

"How?"

"First you have to really think about this idea that you have about God and particularly that this god took your loved one's away. That he left you behind because you're bad or evil. The Taking had nothing to do with your relationship with Christ. We know from Lord Leto that this thing that lives in the quantum realm is not a God. Our scientists can now get a glimpse of the place it's from. It's not a God. And he doesn't care about you. If he did, he wouldn't have left you here. The first thing we need to do is make sure that the lies that have been told to us are held up to the light to see. Elizabeth, I don't want to report you to the authorities. You know, belief in God is a felony. It's considered a crime against humanity to profess such a belief."

Elizabeth looked at her dismayed and replied. "First, I don't know what I believe. All I know is what I saw and heard... what my best friend said to me. Second, did you hear what I said? I was assaulted. Why aren't we talking about THAT?"

Ms. Davis came closer and placed her hands gently on Elizabeth's knees. "I know this is hard. And I want you to know I will do everything in my power to help you move past this. But I can't do that if you are dead. As a mandatory reporter, I have a government obligation to report anyone that might have a belief in God. And certain beliefs Elizabeth could land you in jail or worse: public execution. We are under attack by a power beyond our planet. Everything must come secondary to that. Our job is to look after one another and I am trying to look after you."

"You are not going to report me over *this*, are you?"

"I'm sorry Elizabeth, I have no choice."

Elizabeth quickly got up from the couch, grabbed her book bag and slung it over her shoulder. "Don't bother, I can look after myself."

"Wait Elizabeth! Sit down, if you saw someone Taken and have not reported it. You must report it to the authorities..." The counselor moved to stop her and Elizabeth shoved her away and rushed out of the room, sprinting down the school hall at breakneck speed.

Behind the veil of men's sight, two angels in opposition to each other stood in proximity to the young girl, who now darted from school grounds and raced across the street into the woods.

Eridu looked at the young woman from afar and smiled at Vantress, who hovered over Elizabeth to protect her. His eyes scowling at his nemesis. And he heard the voice of his adversary say.

"Soon, I am coming for her."

Chapter Nine: Abominations and Destroyers

Talus lifted his trumpet to his lips and the House of Arelim sounded.

Immediately, the east winds that circled the earth moved upwards and pushed water vapor higher into Earth's atmosphere. The water droplets condescended and became heavy and hurled themselves from their cumulus perches and grew fat from their descent into baseball sized hail stones. And the censer of the prayers of the saints that had been cast into the Earth opened and the living flames inside attached themselves to the hail that hurtled towards the Earth. And the cries of the saints sounded as wounded banshees in the ears of men.

The long flaming prayers coated themselves to hail and blood, fire, and ice descended upon mankind. Buildings were pummeled; panes of windows shattered, and cars were smashed into nothing as the hail dropped from the sky. And all manner of planes were pelted to the extent that some were knocked from the skies careening out of control.

And wherever the flaming hail descended, it unleashed fire to whatever it touched, and the flames spread, reaching flammable hands to handshake and emblazon cities. But it was the blood that caused the people of Earth to cry out. For it also fell from the sky. Blood that spoiled the land and crops. Blood that soiled faces, clothes and food. Spoilage on a level that disease sprung up upon mankind as blood rained from the skies. And the devastation was such that a third part of all plant life across the planet was estimated to have been destroyed. And with the burning of fires, the clouds of smoke rose into the skies and grayed parts of the planet. For mankind recognized that his life was tethered to the life-giving oxygen from forest and grass; oxygen that now thinned, causing all that breathed to struggle.

Talus then stepped aside, and Azaziel set his lips to blow. He inhaled and Heaven then heard the second angel sound.

And when the waves of the trumpet raced through space and time, they sprinted past Jupiter until they reached an asteroid. The great wave moved the space rock past the planet Mars, and it hurtled towards the Earth, entering the planet's atmosphere. The asteroid burned off bits of itself as it entered the atmosphere, and sheets of ice and debris fell into oceans. And all of Heaven and man watched as if a great mountain burning with fire was cast into the sea.

The impact created towering waves that raced outwards toward every coastline. A barrier of water rose from the ocean's depths, and it raced out in all directions, smiting mighty cruise ships and navy destroyers alike. A hundred mile per hour wave of water that tore across both the surface and the bottom of the ocean floor. And the asteroid was poisonous to life in the seas, and a third part of the sea became blood. And the third part of the creatures which were in the sea died; and the third part of the ships were destroyed.

And men cursed the God of Heaven. Claiming that Leto Alexander and the alien Lucifer would save them. For despite the judgments that were unleashed upon mankind, humanity would not repent.

Jerahmeel, having seen what was done before him, watched as the massive scene of environmental disaster took place before him. He took the trumpet in his hands and lifted it up.

His hands shook.

They trembled, not knowing what devastation he was about to unleash. For he was the looser of Abaddon the Destroyer. The angel whom has not yet made his way to descend to Earth. But he knew it was soon. Soon he that had caused such carnage in Heaven would find his old master. And he would seek recompense.

Azaziel looked at Jerahmeel and spoke, "It's OK. Blow. The result is of the Lord."

Jerahmeel nodded and set the instrument to his lips. Like his brother before him, he inhaled, and the third angel of trumpet judgments sounded. And as if on cue, the sound of the trumpet announced the flying by a great pulsating star. A star that arced across the skies of Heaven and descended towards the world of men. But it was no ordinary star. It was the renegade felon Zephon. Imprisoned by El after the Descension within the depths of a comet. Fated to circle a faraway galaxy until he was found by Charon and the Horde. Jerahmeel remembered this angel: a creature that was responsible for the burning of the suburbs of Heaven. A lieutenant of Lucifer, he did not follow his master to Earth. The Angel of Fire was he called. The same was the killer of general Sandolfon, who had battled the angel bravely to keep the way to Earth from the angel.

But now he was here; hurtling through space, the trumpet merely the announcement of his arrival as he entered the solar system of the planet Earth. His trajectory such that even the telescopes of men could not deny that something from outer space raced towards them. And men rightly feared.

Lucifer was informed that an angel was inbound.

"Finally..." Lucifer says. "Zephon has found his way to me. His power will surely strengthen our ranks. I have waited for his return to many years. We will destroy the Host together."

Leto, who was near his master, spoke, "My Lord, it should be noted that my sources tell me that Zephon falls to the planet in an uncontrolled descent. If he is your lackey, then I suggest that he be greeted lest his trajectory bring havoc to our planet."

Lucifer nodded, "Agreed." Make the thing so."

Leto then turned to Ashtaroth. "Will he recognize you?"

Ashtaroth nodded and replies, "Yes, young dragon. It was I who gave order for him to destroy the homes of the Lumazi and the city council."

"Good said Leto, then go and greet your brother."

Ashtaroth turned to go and when he did, Leto yelled out.

"Wait!!" Leto then turned to his father and asked. "What if the angel does not recognize Ashtaroth? What are you committed to do?"

Lucifer sneers and replies, "Destroy him. He may not undue all that I have worked so hard to build." Lucifer then turned to three principalities by his side and spoke, "Go with Ashtaroth. If Zephon does not heed. Then make his end swift."

Each nodded, and Lucifer's angels rose to meet the incoming angel.

Ashtaroth and three of his guards rose into the upper atmosphere and they could see that Zephon neared the moon, and they lifted themselves towards him. Ashtaroth drew closer...moving nearer to see his old friend's face. Closer, Zephon came to the moon. Fire encompassed the streaking angel, and a long contrail of gas and particulates followed him. Ashtaroth could now sense the heat that emanated off his brother's celestial body, and he drew close enough to see his face. And when he did, so he gasped. For Zephon's eyes were black, dark with no light. His features were emaciated. The great angel was clearly dead. His skin was green and sickly with the Withering and his body was decayed. Ashtaroth turned to his soldiers and screamed.

"The Withering has him. He is dead! Destroy his corpse quickly lest he contaminate us all!"

Upon command, the three angels unleashed fire upon the angel, who was a descending fire himself. They flew towards him and when they did so, the contaminated flesh of Zephon peeled away and drifted from his person like a poisonous cloud of gaseous ash. Each angel drew back in fear, unwilling to touch the corpse of the contaminated angel.

The streaking dead Zephon flew past the moon and hurtled to the planet below.

Ashtaroth looked at the sight in terror. His mouth was open wide as the fallen angel's trajectory could neither be stopped nor changed.

"NOOO!!!!" He screamed.

But it was too late.

Despite the attempts of his comrades, the contaminated flaming body of the celestial slammed into the skies of earth and tumbled from the sky into the heart of the Euphrates River.

Men watched helplessly as there fell a great star from heaven, burning as like a lamp.

The explosion rippled across the land and water lifted into the air, some of which disintegrated into steam, and a fine mist settled over the impact area.

And when it did the river was poisoned and its waters spread abroad as wildfire and portions of the angels disintegrating body fell upon the third part of the rivers, and upon the fountains of waters; for a third part of the waters became wormwood; and many men died of the waters because they were made poisonous to drink.

And Zephon fulfilled his own prophecy to be as wormwood.

Lucifer and Leto then cursed God, and those that had surrendered themselves to Satan did also.

* * *

Azaziel stepped aside and when he did, the stead holder for Argoth and the house of Grigori took his place: Cassiel. And Cassiel set the trumpet to his lips and when he did so, the fourth angel sounded.

Immediately, Eladrin and his people lifted themselves from the Aerie and each blazoned like lightning across the sky and ladders crisscrossed the whole of Heaven. And none had ever seen a sight on this wise before. For like streaking stars did the Ophanim fly hither and thither across the known universe. And their paths were of such number that they left contrails across space such that the lines they left behind were like a great web in which ensnared all things. Eladrin then left the perch of Heaven and dove into the heart of Sol. And when he did so, so too did his people fall into the cores of stars and nebulae of all kind. And the multi-faced species of heaven turned their gears. These beings upon who moved galaxies and when they turned, they smote a third part of the sun, and the third part of the moon, and the third part of the stars; so, as the third part of them was darkened, and the day shone not for a third part, and the night likewise.

For there was nowhere where an Ophanim did not touch. No star not siphoned. For the Ophanim moved space and time and fed off the life of the stars themselves. And Michael marveled, for it was as if the Lord had reversed his works from the days of old when he spoke let there be Light.

For now, with the blowing of the trumpet creation was dimmed by a third. And with its dimming, Heaven was now so bright that someone could see it afar by men with the sight of telescopes. Men now had physical, visible evidence of a realm existing beyond that of space and time.

A third heaven.

The realm of God.

* * *

Leto's helicopter landed a mere 100 yards from the newly constructed temple. The former place of the Dome on the Rock. He stepped off the chopper and made his way down the stairs. Ashtaroth followed with several of his governors and Ambassador Abadi. Lucifer stood invisible to men and waited for his son to step on the ground.

"Look at them," says Lucifer. "Stagnant in worship, stilled literally and figuratively against a wall. All in a vain attempt to draw near what was once the physical place where God once manifested his presence. Go to my son. Go to and destroy this symbol of El's house. Go to and bring these worshipers of El to heel. Show them their error and bring the fear of both me and thee into their lives."

Leto looked back at one man that followed him. "Do you have my gift to present to the God of the people?"

"Yes sir. Everything is as you have ordered." The man nodded and several soldiers rolled out a large box with holes in it

"Good." The anti-Christ says. "Be sure to the ready when I call for it."

"Yes, sir," was the reply.

Leto walked confidently into the newly constructed court of the gentiles, and Ambassador Abadi followed him pleadingly. "Please, Lord Leto. Do not do this thing. All of Israel may well rise in hatred against you. Surely you do not mean to provoke the ire of an entire nation?"

Leto smiles with a coy grin and replied. "Oh, come now Abadi. This is a time of celebration, not suspicion. Come and let us go unto the house of the Lord." Leto chuckles as he strolled into the court of women. His soldiers and entourage followed and surrounded him, making sure to keep all bystanders out of his way. Some hissed at the man as he entered the steps to the inner chamber. A priest stood in his way barring his path and Leto smiled and said to him.

"Have I not paid for this? Have I not given your people permission to build? And this is how you would repay my generosity? For whom is more worthy? The house or he that builds the house? Would you deny my eyes the right to see what I, in my generosity, have allowed to be constructed?"

The priest looked at the cowering Ambassador Abadi and then at Leto. Abadi's head was turned down, his eyes lowered, and he refused to look the priest into the eye.

"You are the acknowledged leader of the world. You may even be the hand that God has used to erect our temple. But you are NOT a priest and may not inter the holy of Holies. It is forbidden."

Leto nodded and protruded his lips. He pouted in disappointment and communicated as if he understood. "I see."

Leto turned to one of his armed guards and the man then grabbed the priest and moved him aside and shoved him against a wall.

Spectators from the court looked onward, and many covered their mouths in disbelief and fear. But no one moved to interfere, for all were afraid of the Beast.

Leto then walked past the priest. "And he beckoned to Ambassador Abadi. "Come inside Ambassador. Do not be afraid. It is but a dimly lit room and nothing more. These approximations of your ancient relics bear us no harm."

Abadi followed, as did a few of Leto's personal guard.

The Beast then stood within the most holy of holies in the temple. He viewed the altar of Incense. Its intoxicating aroma filled the room. While the Golden Lamp Stand and Table stood across from each other. They were beautiful in design and craftsmanship.

And in the furthest northern point of the room, the Ark of the Covenant sat. But it was the mercy seat which stood above the ark that drew Leto's eyes. He walked and his hand brushed lightly over the seal box that was the ark. He knew what was inside. He had gone to great lengths to pay for their contents. His looked upon the great lid that represented God's presence. Where long ago, El stated he would meet with his people. Leto eyed the pure gold cover. Eyed the two cherubims that stood at each end of the great seal, their wings spread abroad.

Leto harrumphed and nodded his head as if he had been given an epiphany. "Such a rudimentary communication device, El. You see the wings, Abadi? What you worship is naught but a rudimentary antenna."

Ambassador Abadi quivered where he stood. Quivered because he believed in this sacred place God would visit his people. Quivered because he knew what Leto did not... that he stood on Holy Ground.

Leto turned to his guard. "Colonel. We must disrupt any attempt at communication by this being to the High Priest. Bring me my offering."

The colonel turned and twirled his fingers near his head to signal the other officers there.

"Father I understand. I see how you once were atop the most powerful throne and rose to defy its rule. Rebelled to be free from the authority of the Mercy Seat."

Leto touched the golden cherubims and studied them intently. The soldiers brought in the box with holes and opened it up. Inside was a tranquilized, tusked boar. Leto motioned for them where to put it and they hefted the animal upon the Altar of Incense.

"Sergeant your knife."

Immediately, one soldier removed his blade from its sheath and handed it over to Leto.

The high priest, who was physically restrained, squirmed as he was held also at gun point and attempted to wave the Chancellor away. "You do not know what you are doing! You cannot profane this place!"

Ambassador Abadi attempted to turn and leave, but the guard at the door to the Holy of Holies lifted his rifle, and the Ambassador stopped in his tracks. Leto looked up from the boar asleep before him and spoke.

"Abadi, I am so disappointed. And here I thought you were excited to see this temple dedicated? Indeed, this will be the place I choose to speak to my people. The same place this alien thought to manipulate our kind. From here will serve as an example that man is the ruler. Not God. Not some creature from beyond. If mankind is to worship anything, he will worship the person among our lot who is most worthy: he will worship... me."

Leto them lifted the knife and brought it under the neck of the sleeping animal and he took its edge and slit the swine's throat.

The hog immediately awoke, and it squealed in agony as blood poured from its neck as water and saturated the altar. A mist of crimson sprayed into Leto's face and the creature kicked its legs and spasmodic attempts to escape. But Leto held the creature down until the entire of its life was spent. And the creature's cries echoed from the temple into the courtyard.

And Leto spoke with a voice that was otherworldly. A voice that made many move back in fear.

"Yahweh, El, or whatever, name you give to yourself. Know I am Leto Alexander. Son of Lucifer Draco: Bleeder of God. I have come that ye might see death... and see it swiftly. Attend me Ashtaroth."

Ashtaroth immediately appeared, and he was beautiful to all those that looked upon him and he stood over Leto as if to protect him.

Leto then stabbed the knife into the breast of the boar, and he motioned to the guard to bring the high priest to him.

The soldiers did so, and they slammed him down headfirst, next to the bleeding out boar.

Leto then spoke, "You will renounce worship to the alien and command your people to worship me as their god, or you will be beheaded. Choose."

The high priest was quick to reply. "The Lord rebuke you. I will never bow to you."

Leto replies, "Of course you won't. Thank you for that, by the way. It will serve as a demonstration to others." Leto then motioned to Ashtaroth behind him to come up front.

"Ashtaroth be a good lad and give me his head."

There was a movement imperceptible to human eyes. A quickness that belied belief. The soldiers stepped back as the tall angel moved towards the High Priest. He then spoke to the human. "I derive great pleasure in the taking of your life servant of El. Know you will be but the first of many to follow."

Ashtaroth then, with his own hands, held the skull of the High Priest in his hands and lifted his head from his body, ripping it away from his torso.

Ambassador Abadi fell to his knees and threw up.

Some men fainted with their guns in their hands.

Leto then walked outside and Ashtaroth and a few soldiers followed until they all stood surrounding him. And Ashtaroth stood behind Leto with the High Priests' head lifted high. And Leto had taken the Urim and Thurim the breastplate from Hebrew lore and wore it for the people who were in attendance at the temple dedication to see.

Many screamed while others fainted. Others heaved at the bloody display before them.

"I know that you think me brutal," says Leto. "I am indeed a beast. A beast in defense of humanity and our freedom to be ruled by only ourselves. I therefore command the abolition of all religions worldwide. All Christianity, all Judaism, all Islam. Any belief that advocates a belief in a supreme being, I deem heretical to the self-interests of mankind. In the name of humanity, I also decree the Vatican to be in rebellion to humanity. The Pope will bow and accept this decree. Or he will be killed in like manner as Rabbi Ephraim here. To test this loyalty. I require that all children of humanity bow when they hear the Pledge of Human Allegiance.

If you accept me as your God, you will live. But if not, no matter where you live, you will die at my command. For we will fight the celestials together. Or we will leave cowards behind to rot in the prison of death. A death where there will be no resurrection."

And Leto was recorded live by all media outlets, as was the custom when following the chancellor. And each station had been given the music to air that denoted the Pledge of Human Allegiance. And there was silence in the temple's courtyard and suddenly over loudspeakers the sound of cornet, flute, harp, sackbut, psaltery, and all kinds of music echoed over the courtyard. And Leto raised his hands and then lowered them. And when he did, his entourage kneeled. Slowly, like a human wave, those in the crowd also knelled.

Some, however, did not kneel. And Leto pointed his fingers, and the person fell down dead, their head severed from their body. And the thing was televised and in every living room and bar. To every statehouse and whorehouse. All stopped and knelled, and those that did not were beheaded by members of the Hoard. For Leto had commanded that when the music was played, all members of the Horde would note those who did not kneel and have them killed in this manner.

Thus, at that time, when all the people heard the cornet, flute, harp, sackbut, psaltery, and all kinds of music, all the people, the nations, and the languages, fell down and worshiped the televised image of Chancellor Leto.

The world watched as Leto pronounced and elevated Ambassador Abadi of Israel as his new Co-regent and honored with the title of Bishop of the Holy See. The supreme religious ruler who would see that all religions acknowledge him as its supreme teacher and Leto as its God.

But two men sat on cushions against the old western wall of the temple. Two who were recorded by the reporter Henel James, a man of Jewish descent who feigned knelling and survived.

Two men, when the music stopped, cried aloud for all to hear.

"Have ye not heard when ye see the abomination of desolation to run to the mountains? Be off with you! For soon the Lord comes!"

And from the moment those Jews who had not bowed the knee yet somehow lived, they gathered what they could carry and fled to the great city of Petra to escape from Chancellor Leto. To escape the Abomination of Desolation.

* * *

Elizabeth ran through the wooded trails and stopped to catch her breath by resting on a log. She reached into her back pocket and pulled out her phone. It was filled with news notifications coming in from all across the world.

CNN: Chancellor Alexander declares himself God.

Fox News: New worldwide pledge of human allegiance to be sung at all sporting events.

MSNBC: Emergency responders overwhelmed by planet wide earth quakes: millions believed dead.

Google News: Bishop Abadi to visit Vatican City and formerly transition the city from Catholicism to Humanism.

Yahoo News: Pope Clement is scheduled to agree to the signing of the Humanism Declaration of Faith.

NPR: Drones spot Israeli Jews fleeing to Petra.

BBC: Chancellor declares Israeli Prime Minister Aharon in breach of the Shehvah Treaty: war appears imminent.

CBS News: Alien sympathizers: Enoch and Elijah are still at large. Last seen in the company of an Israeli reporter Henel James. All are considered dangerous and citizens are warned not to approach them. Government sources have reason to believe the two men are responsible for the drought in the Middle East.

The world's gone crazy.

I didn't kneel. Why am I still alive?

Oh God, what am I supposed to do now?

Her head pounded from the stress of it all. The trees bustled overhead, and the cool air felt good against her cheeks. She stood from the log and hoisted her backpack over her shoulders. She took another look at her phone and saw the time. It was 2:35pm. School had just let out and the time would mark another headline in the world's newsroom as a bright light, like a star, shone from the sky. Elizabeth Foley looked up to see that an alien whisked across the sky. He was dressed in the brightest white she had ever seen, and he declared a message that shook her to her core. A message that she once heard preached in church when she was a visitor. A message that made more sense to her now.

"Repent and believe the gospel for the Kingdom of God is at hand!"

* * *

Yeshua then turned to Gabriel and looked upon the prince of house Malakim and commanded him on this wise. "Go forth and preach unto them that dwell within the earth. Go to my son. Go to every nation; embark to every kindred and tongue. Proclaim to all people and declare for those that have ears to hear, I am still Savior. But to those that would refuse to worship him that hath made heaven and earth, the seas and all that lie therein. Let them know, son... that I am coming."

The head of house Malakim nodded his head in understanding and slammed his staff into the ground and was gone. Michael and his brethren followed the trail of twinkling light that raced after Gabriel and, when they looked up, they saw Gabriel upon his steed, and he had already formed a ladder. And the fastest of all angelic kind was on his way to earth. An angel: the first of his kind to declare the wondrous gospel to the world of men.

* * *

Bishop of Humanity, Mahmod Abadi, laid down his pen and approached his microphone and spoke for the entire crowd to hear. "It is done! By the power invested in me by his imminence, we stand before you. Pope Clement and I. Our two towers of faith in the planet have now become one! One voice to declare to the entire world that Leto Alexander. Our beloved ruler and the tip of the spear to fight these celestials. That he is God! Let us now rejoice in worship and recite our confession of faith!"

Henel James sat with Enoch and Elijah against the western wall of the Temple. Their small hovel surrounded by barbed wire and concrete barricades to prevent anyone from getting near them.

He glanced at his phone and table. He was amazed that none of his devices ever discharged. Their battery life never extinguished. He was fascinated by these two men. Brave, or stupid, he wasn't fully sure. But they were not afraid of Leto. They were somehow protected from harm. And while he stood in their proximity, he seemed protected, too. So, he reported and shared with them the ways of the 21st century.

Henel had explained to Enoch many of mankind's myths. Engaged in conversation during the world's holiday season, he found that Enoch was most intrigued by the world's playful belief in Santa Claus.

A man who in one night could allegedly travel the world, and in the span of the same; visit the children of the planet and leave presents under decorated trees.

Yet, unlike the myth of Santa Claus, Henel knew that whatever Santa Claus was...Gabriel was no myth. A being he watched on his iPad as he sat next to Enoch and Elijah. Watched in fascination as CCTV cameras and cell phone footage and satellites around the world tracked the celestial's movements as he delivered a word from what Henel knew was God.

"Show us what your mirror sees," says Elijah.

Henel sat down between the two men and the three watched as Gabriel, the Prince of all angelic messengers, delivered the words of his king to the entire world in under an hour. Worlds that reverberated through television, radio and satellite. Words that preempted favorite television shows and displaced radio stations such that whatever frequency was tuned; Gabriel's voice was the sound that was heard.

Words that proclaimed a universal call...to repent. For it was delivered unto Gabriel first of all that which was also received of the twelve apostles, how that Christ died for man's sins according to the scriptures; And that he was buried, and that he rose again the third day according to the scriptures. And the head of house Malakim made it especially clear to those within the seat of the Beast's throne in Brussels that they heard this message loud and clear.

And when Gabriel completed his course around the Earth, he landed atop of the obelisk in the Piazza San Pietro in the heart of the Vatican. His shining visage was plain for all to see. And many of the people resident looked in awe and pointed to him.

Bishop Abadi had just completed his signing of the transfer accords with Pope Clement and the two had come to a platform prepared just outside of St. Peter's square. Italian police patrolling the area noted Gabriel's presence and raised their weapons to fire. While security guards near the bishop took defensive positions to protect him.

Suddenly, all looked upwards to the sky as circular openings parted the clouds and prismatic rainbow funnels fell crashing to the ground. Several beings upon gryphon-back with spears landed in the courtyard, and they formed a circle around Gabriel. For the prince of house, Malakim's personal guard followed their master. His speed was such that they now materialized in a vain attempt to keep up with their leader.

Seven angels strong were they upon steeds from heaven and the Shekinah illuminated upon them all.

News crews from around the world were on site to witness Bishop Abadi and Pope Clements signing of the Human Affirmation of Faith. Tens of thousands filled St. Peters Square. Cameras clicked to capture the moment, and thousands raised their cell phones to videotape and to stream live to the internet. Where before chanting and the singing of praise had filled the emporium: cheers that the Earth would now live under a united and single religious faith.

Now stood a celestial defying man's renunciation of anything God other than himself. Now stood a being to confront the veracity of those who would dare propagate this lie. A being by name of Gabriel that now opened his mouth to speak.

"I come in the name of the Lord of Hosts whom you have forsaken," says Gabriel. "Though given space to repent, you yet fawn over a creature that is neither God, angel nor man. An abomination... nay a beast who would set himself up as God. But alas, your proclamations are nothing and your gesture in vain. For has it not been foretold, and are ye yet without hearing? Why do the heathen rage and the people imagine a vain thing? The kings of the earth set themselves, and the rulers take counsel together, against the Lord, and against his anointed, saying. Let us break their bands asunder and cast away their cords from us. He that sitteth in the heavens shall laugh: the Lord shall have them in derision. Then shall he speak unto them in his wrath and vex them in his sore displeasure.

For the Earth is the Lord's footstool and this building before me is naught but a house of brick and stone. But the Earth shall be full of the Lord's Glory and this place... your temple will no longer be!"

Gabriel then fell from the obelisk and landed upon the ground and when he did, He slammed his staff into the earth and a fissure opened from where he knelt and sprinted across St. Peter's Square towards St. Peter's Basilica. The ground shook and onlookers wobbled and fell on their hinds, while terror gripped the populace as the magnificent dome cracked, and like a walnut, imploded on itself. Pillars and glass, wood and steel, stone and flesh mingled together in a chorus of screams and explosions that jettisoned dust and debris racing out in every direction. Gray clouds of cinder rose into the sky and the crashing and groans of beams and steel collapsing over one another ended with Gabriel and his guard floating over the morass of wreckage that now littered the square.

Henel, Enoch, and Elisha watched on a small iPad as Gabriel and his angelic guard slowly ascended. Watched as the angel spoke one word that echoed in repeated refrain as the image of him grew smaller and smaller as he floated away into the sky into the beyond.

"Repent!"

* * *

"Babylon is fallen, that great city, because she made all nations drink of the wine of the wrath of her fornication!" An angel flew overhead, Brussels yelling.

And another angel followed, says with a loud voice, "If any man worship the beast and his image, and receive his mark in his forehead, or in his hand, The same shall drink of the wine of the wrath of God, which is poured out without mixture into the cup of his indignation; and he shall be tormented with fire and brimstone in the presence of the holy angels, and in the presence of the Lamb: And the smoke of their torment will ascend for ever and ever: and they have rest neither day nor night, who worship the beast and his image, and whosoever receives the mark of his name."

Chancellor Leto Alexander, elected leader of the Commonwealth of Men, looked out his office window to see the celestial aliens scaring his people with their macabre messages and was incensed.

He smashed a porcelain figure in his office and threw a globe at his security guard. He wrung his fists tightly and spoke aloud.

"Father, can you not stop this angel from speaking? Why have you not released the Horde to combat this upstart?"

Lucifer stood in the shadows of his creation's office, invisible to the eye. He watched his child's tantrum and replied. "No."

"No? No!" cries Leto. "You let Gabriel and his forces waltz unto this planet at will and he destroys the center of worship for my people! No? Where is the recourse for such an act? By whose authority does he think he can destroy the property and people of Earth without provocation? And you say stand there and say "no"."

Lucifer was only slightly visible. Allowing the wavelengths of light to encircle his body so that only his shape could be seen.

The King of Darkness replied. His voice was smooth and in even pentameter when he spoke. "We must endure this sleight for now. There will indeed come a time for retribution. This incursion is but a celestial slap on the wrist. We have yet to fully provoke El enough so that once more he would breach history and leave Heaven to come to the Earth. Patience, my son. When you have reached the apex of your power... when you can house all that I am—all of my power. Then you will be ready to ascend and battle with angels themselves: until then you will do nothing save I tell you. Am I clear?"

Leto smarted from his father's words and his face flushed red in anger.

"As you command, father." He gritted. "But I grow eager to return this destruction upon him, and you mentioned that approach to El requires sacrifice. There were three things you mentioned to bring sacrifice: fire, wood and blood? We possess the fire of the God-stone. And was not the kindling my act at the Temple Mount combined with Abadi's and Clement's union? So where, then, is the lamb for a burned offering? You said we require a sacrifice to approach El. Where is this sacrifice?" That will allow me to strike back at Him?"

Lucifer came out of the shadows and allowed himself to be seen by his son. His voice was operatic, and light bounced off of his person. He smiled as he stared at his son; his mind filled with plans upon calculated plans. He touched the cheek of his creation and spoke.

"Ah, my son, when this temple is destroyed. I will raise it up again after three days, and then my child; then we shall smite the Godhead."

* * *

And I beheld and heard an angel flying through the midst of heaven, saying with a loud voice, Woe, woe, woe, to the inhabitants of the earth by reason of the other voices of the trumpet of the three angels, which are yet to sound!

Selaphiel of house Harrada stood in for Jerahmeel as head of his house. He stood with a trumpet and lifted the great instrument to his lips and when he did, the fifth angel of judgment blew. And Jerahmeel lifted himself from the porch of God and flew to the Maelstrom. As he flew his countenance changed, he became like a star and the key which he carried glowed white hot and turned to fall within the midst of the Maelstrom and the head of house Harrada stood atop the entrance to the Abyss: sealed by the hand of God himself. He swallowed hard, knowing what lay within was responsible for the destruction of Heaven itself. A scourge of terror that nothing but Charon or God himself could withstand: the Destroyer.

The winds of the Maelstrom circled over the bottomless pit. The cage that God had used to contain Abaddon.

The prince of house Harrada could barely hear as the howling winds screamed their screeching songs of dissolution. For he stood in the center of the great transparent stone, standing atop the seal that barred access from one dimension to another. The null that contained the last vestiges of the Void. The only area of creation left undeveloped by God. Jerahmeel thought this was a fitting place. A place for things to be lost and forgotten. A place for Creation's deformity to be hidden from itself and Abaddon was angelic deformity run amok.

Jerahmeel's eyes looked upon the surrounding valley and noted the winds rip rock from the towering canyon walls. For the Seal of El was miles long in every direction, and the winds raced in circular fashion around the great stamp as Jerahmeel stood in the gale's center. Yet in this section of the realm that separated eternity from time, in this piece at the cliffs of Argoth, there was quietness. The quiet in the eye of the storm. For God had removed sound from having a voice in this place. And nothing could be heard save Jerahmeel's own breathing. Jerahmeel blew out several quick breaths and reached towards his neck to grasp the key to the bottomless pit.

Jerahmeel pulled the great brass key from the necklace which hung from him and knelt down to the insert it into the lock of the prismatic seal created by El.

He turned the key into the lock and, with a twist and he heard the click of the tumbler mechanism inside. Startled to hear sound at all. He backed away to see the winds of the Maelstrom had stopped as if time had summoned the great gale to a halt. His eyes darted back and forth as he took several steps backward. The sound of giant gears and levers filled the air, and the prismatic seal then lit up the area. Jerahmeel covered his eyes to prevent blindness. And as a clock that counted down, the white light of the mile long seal dissipated to reveal a barrier beneath the original seal. The seven primary colors that comprised rainbows were now concentrically aligned around the area. Red was the furthest away, with Jerahmeel standing atop a circle of violet. Across the circle were seven mechanical locks with giant claps that hitherto fore were not seen.

An exploding sound was heard as a clasp gave away and sprung open and when it did so, the colors of seals slowly dissipated. Red disappeared first, and then orange followed hard after. Yellow vanished, and then green chased in pursuit. Each color collapsed into the depths below, concentric rings imploding upon themselves.

Four colors and their respective clasps remained, and Jerahmeel felt the shield that separated him from the Abyss shake underneath him. The three remaining locks strained and creaked as if buckling to contain that which lay underneath; when suddenly the blue color of the seal faded until, but two colors remained. Groans and the collapsing of metal could be heard from below him and Jerahmeel lifted himself into the air, following the inner voice that told him to vacate the area. Higher he lifted himself into the golden sky of heaven. Higher to escape the plumes of smoke that rose hard after him. He looked down to see the final clasps of indigo and violet fall into the darkness of the Abyss. It's gapping black mouth, uncapped in all its destructive fury. Jerahmeel's ears popped as the pressure changed instantly, and he heard air filling the hollow vacuum that was the yawn of the bottomless pit.

And there arose a smoke out of the pit, smoke as of a great furnace; and the sky and the air were darkened by reason of the smoke from the pit. Ash and embers of flame bloomed all around him, and Jerahmeel felt the Abyss roar to life. The gravity well of the universe pulled to capture him, and the winds of the Maelstrom sprinted to encircle the uncirculable, and the great eater of all things thundered to life and pulled to swallow all within the jaws of its onyx mouth. Jerahmeel suddenly fell careening into the deep. Instinctively, he summoned a ladder and, without fail, a prismatic funnel reached for him and pulled him from the clutches of the cyclone that now stood unchecked. The funnel turned and arced towards the cliffs of Argoth and Jerahmeel landed safely at the waypoint on the cliff's edge. Talus, Michael, Gabriel, Metatron, and Azaziel each raced to Jerahmeel's side, having watched their brother from afar. The federal head of several angelic houses stood on the canyon, looking out at the Abyss and the Maelstrom now fully alive. Ash and great plumes of celestial smoke now jetting from its dark center.

Azaziel looked upon the sight in awe and spoke, "I thought nothing could escape the Abyss: that its hold was too strong; save a ladder or divine intervention by God himself?"

Gabriel replied as he also watched the erupting scene before them. "It would seem, my brother, that we will now add the Destroyer to that list."

And as if on cue; a great roar ushered from the dark. A familiar sound not heard since the end of the Descension.

The roar of the emerging Abaddon.

Chapter Ten: A Rise to Power

Abaddon, the angel of legend, rose from the Abyss.

Smoke, ash, and flaming embers erupted into the sky as if from the smoke of some great furnace. The sky darkened by reason of the smoke, which blackened the sky as giant claws ascended from the dark. Arms and legs pushed themselves unto the black of the accretion disc that surrounded the entrance to the bottomless pit. Each limb straining against celestial forces that pulled all things within its gravity well. The maelstrom whirled and whined in its fury. But it was the roar of Abaddon that filled the skies. A roar filled with both anguish and anger. A roar that cried of freedom from the black and the eternal fall that was the bottomless pit. And like Leviathan of old or an ancient dragon of men's nightmares, the first angel to murder rose from his prison and stretched his wings. And with his rising, three words echoed through the air.

Three words that made the whole of Heaven itself shake.

"Pain!"

"Agony!"

"Lucifer!"

Abaddon then opened his mouth to announce his freedom and once more; a great roar echoed across the realm of Heaven. Towering spires of transparent gold and adorned with stained glass windows shattered as the mighty angel Abaddon rose from the depths. And with his ascension followed lava, fire, and a tornadic cloud-army of fiery locusts. An unholy black swarm of biting angelic insects. Maggots that had entered the bottomless pit were now freed and fully developed; each had grown fat on the emaciated flesh of the now insane angel.

Insane from his solitary confinement and his endless plummet in a chamber of deprivation; ever buffeted by the darkness and the gnawing of his own bitterness and rage. Rage that manifested in the open bloody lesions of his flesh where maggots of hatred germinated ad infinitum. Flesh that held demonic carrion and whose worms died not.

Maggots which had now transformed and grew from pupae to larva to winged, locust-like monstrosities. For the shapes of the locusts were like unto horses prepared unto battle; and on their heads were crowns like gold. Their faces were as the faces of men, and they had hair as the hair of women. Their mouths were rowed with teeth as lions. And they had breastplates as of iron; their wings were as the sound of chariots of horses running to battle. And they had tails like unto scorpions, and there were stings in their tails: and their power was to hurt men five months

And for those who had just been raptured and yea all of humankind that now lived in Heaven watched as the great angel Abaddon lifted himself on fiery wings surrounded in a moving cloud of fiery locusts.

Many gawked at the sight. Multitudes of the redeemed began to understand the wisdom of El in-locking angels away. Incarcerating those whose powers for destruction and desire for retribution on God's creation could not be allowed to roam free. For before the eyes of all now stood a menace to existence itself.

And one word escaped the lips of King David, who watched with the apostles and the rest of the host of saints. One word that encompassed the collective mood of all.

"Woe."

Abaddon then turned towards the sky of Heaven and vanished in a massive black ladder. The air smoldered as the fiery tunnel closed behind him. The great angel was now unleashed a soon coming woe upon the earth.

A woe that now summoned a ladder to besiege the source of his hatred... Lucifer.

A woe released by God himself to bring judgment to the earth.

A judgment to burn all things that would fall under the shadow of the Destroyer's wings.

* * *

"Repent!"

The cry of Elijah filled the temple grounds, and Enoch and Elijah moved past the barbed wire that soldiers had erected near them and walked to the newly constructed court of the gentiles to preach.

"Get out of here, old man! No one wants to hear what you have to say!"

Enoch pointed to the young man and replies, "Our voice is nothing. It is the word of God that calls thee to repent. Even now, he sends death to you! But alas, your heart has become as stone and you will not turn!"

Leto Alexander heard the words of the men from inside one office he had built in the temple. He turned to his security and spoke. "Can one of you get these men to shut up? Why are they still alive?"

"Apologies, your imminence, but whoever threatens them is immediately burned by fire. For the safety of all, we have told the populace not to approach them. We've tried even snipers, but nothing we've used has had success. They habitat within the midst of the people and have garnered quite a following. We have attempted drone strikes, but when tried, the electronics have always failed. Honestly, sir, we are at a loss."

Leto let out a disgruntled growl. He stood to his feet and spoke to his angelic guards. "Come with me."

Ashtaroth and several guards appointed by Lucifer followed their human master from the temple.

Enoch saw Leto as he exited the building and spoke. "Behold the Beast! A false god. An Abomination whose end will be a lake of fire! Speak Nephilim!"

Leto looked at a solider and spoke to him, "Give me your rifle."

The soldier unholstered his weapon from his shoulder and passed it to his commander as ordered.

Leto raised the weapon and fired upon Enoch and Elijah.

Bullets ricocheted off Enoch and Elijah and hit bystanders nearby, and many fell dead from their wounds. The crowd of on-lookers immediately scattered, fearful of their lives. Soldiers ducked and the angelic guard of Leto looked on, amused.

"Sir! You're killing people!" cries a sergeant.

Leto continued targeting Enoch and Elijah. The words of his security detail falling on deaf ears.

"Sir!!" the soldier cries out again.

But the rat-ta-tat-tat of the weapon filled the court, drowning out all other sounds. And Leto cared naught for the bystanders killed by his action and continued firing until his magazine was spent and smoke emptied from his muzzle. His finger still pulled the trigger and nothing but the click, click could be heard.

A soldier came over and placed his hand on the weapon and lowered it to the ground.

Leto grimaced at the soldier and spoke. "I see. It would seem I must do this by hand."

He rolled up his sleeves and ran towards Enoch and raised his fist to smite him and when he did the very ground beneath him became hot and liquefied and he stepped back as the earth suddenly became molten before him and the heat forced him to draw back due to the pain.

"Argggh!! The beast raged in anger.

Leto then turned to his angelic guards and spoke. "Do not just stand there, Ashtaroth, kill them!"

Ashtaroth and his angelic compatriots did not move, and Leto, incensed at their inaction, looked up at him and berated him. "What is wrong with you? I gave you an order. Kill them!"

Ashtaroth then pointed to two men and Leto followed his hand and saw that behind them was an attachment of angelic guards of their own. For three Arelim angels had materialized to make themselves known. And spoke to the Beast, "If they interfere...know that we shall interfere. And believe me when I say. We are looking forward to interfering."

The three angels then hid themselves from human sight.

Ashtaroth then turned his head and looked up as if he had been given instructions and spoke aloud, "The All-Father commands us to leave this area immediately. Lucifer has also instructed you young master to come with us... now."

Leto harrumphs and replies, "I will do no such thing. And you and I both know it would take all of you to force me. If my father wants to give me a command, he can do so himself."

Ashtaroth then looked at the Grigori. Speaking aloud as he received instructions.

"The master knows?"

"And you are sure he is on his way?"

"What then does he command?"

"Really... very well."

Ashtaroth nodded at the other angels in their company and spoke. "All of you seek shelter immediately. Abaddon is loosed and is incoming."

Leto noted that Enoch and Elijah had already vacated the area, and they slowly disappeared.

Leto, still smarting over his inability to kill Enoch and Elijah, asked incredulously. "Where are you going and what is this, Abaddon? Where are you going?"

Ashtaroth and the other angels had already begun to float away when he turned to his young master and replied. "Anywhere but here... remember that we tried to help you."

Ashtaroth and the other angels then disappeared.

Suddenly the air pressure changed, and men's ears popped. Many held their hands over their heads and attempted to force themselves to yawn in vain attempts to open their ear-ways. Soon the sound of a rushing wind filled the court, and a buzzing sound followed.

But nothing could be seen.

The sound grew louder and more pronounced as suddenly the roaring sound of an insect swarm was all around them. A soldier then pointed upward, and as he did, some who still were in the crowd pointed towards a black funnel cloud that was slowly touching down from the sky. A moving mass of smoke and fire appeared from nowhere and exploded one hundred yards from Leto and his men. A funnel cloud that surrounded a tall figure. A figure that roared out a sole name.

"LUCIFER!!"

* * *

Lucifer touched the God-stone embedded into his chest and when he did, a door opened up before him. The outline emblazoned in light and the large hulking body of Marduk staggered through; wheezing for air, and fell down face first at the feet of the Lord of Darkness.

Lucifer looked down upon his rival and spoke. "Abaddon is here."

Marduk gasps for air, slowly gaining his composure and panting. He took in gulps of air and mouthed a reply.

"So what?" The angel said. "Why should I give a damn? We both know he comes to destroy you. I say let him." He looked up and smiles at the angel.

Lucifer chuckled. "I would hope your aspirations to live a more abundant life than the torture I have imposed upon you for your betrayal would have garnished a more positive response. Very well then, perhaps the prospect of freedom and restoration is not enough to sway you to assist me. I will happily return you to the alive to the Mists."

The celestial door wailed, and smoky gray coiled tentacles reached out to entwine themselves around his ankles. Marduk fell on his face and the ghostly appendages began to pull the angel as he struggled to keep from being pulled back.

"Wait! What do you desire of me, and what shall I render?"

Lucifer waved his hand as the tentacles withdrew, but could still be seen within the door. "You will help me destroy the Destroyer. Then if your actions please me. I may grant pardon for your insolence. Displease me and I promise you I will seal you screaming in the bottomless pit of our foe. Do you consent?"

Marduk watched as the entity that hovered within the door growled and teeth and eyes moved in traveling rows. And deep within he could see the movement of trapped angelic souls within the transparent gut of the creature straining to get out. All screaming.

"I consent."

Lucifer then closed the dimensional seal and the door vanished. Marduk stood to his feet and spoke. "I am weaponless and not at full strength."

Lucifer waved his hand and Marduk's battle-axe materialized before him, and a small pouch of manna. The angel reached for the bag and greedily devoured the angelic food. Crumbs fell to the floor and Lucifer watched, amusingly.

Marduk's strength returned to him and color to his cheeks, and he picked up the axe that lay on the floor. "Where is Abaddon now?" Marduk says.

"He is in Jerusalem. We have but seconds before he realizes that Leto is my son. I will not let him destroy my host."

Marduk smiles, "So it was never your plan to allow the thing to rule. But you have created him to be used."

Lucifer smiles, "Leto serves his purpose. As you do. Are you ready?"

Marduk nodded.

Lucifer armored himself and extended his arm to reveal the Sword of Malice. "To arms then."

Marduk gripped his ax tightly and grinned, "To arms."

Lucifer waved his hand, and the two vanished in prismatic light.

* * *

"Stop him!" cried Leto.

Soldiers fired the entirety of mankind's small weapons at the Destroyer. Rockets and grenades launched from portable shoulder fired tubes and jettisoned from soldiers holding weapons as explosions ripped through the concourse. Artillery fired upon Abaddon, and like some version of Godzilla, Abaddon kept coming. He beat his flaming wings forward and buildings and all matter caught fire as straw. Flames and heat erupted around him and the angel refused to fall.

Columns of locusts flew around his person, destroying all projectiles levied at him. Like some insect shield nothing survived their touch as they made disintegrate all that they touched.

He cared nothing for those around him, nothing for property or loss of life. He roared until from his unintelligible tongue one word rang out that all and even Leto understood.

"LUCIFER!!"

Abaddon turned to his left, then to his right, and he looked across the morass of humanity that stood before him.

"I smell the blood of Lucifer. It calls to me. I will have it and smear it as balm over the boils that pain me. His carcass as a scarf to warm me. His heart stone as a jewel to wear about my neck."

Abaddon then turned and eyed Leto in the distance. Leto locked eyes with the angel and Abaddon spoke. "I sense his blood in you, creature. You, who are of mixed birth, bear the life of Lucifer in your flesh. I claim your life... I claim YOUR BLOOD!"

The column of insects then moved towards the company of men. Machine guns and rifle fire exploded all at once as men attempted to protect and cover their leader from harm. And when the black of the flaming scorpion like creatures was just upon them. Leto covered his eyes, for he knew there was no escape.

His eyes tightly shut, awaiting the pain to come, none came. Nevertheless, the screams of his men filled his ears. Screams as locusts stung them to the point men cried out begging, hoping to die.

"Shoot me please!" some says.

Others called for their mothers. And when Leto dared opened his eyes to see. Something covered him in bright light and to his front, Lucifer stood before him and Marduk to his rear. Each projecting an angelic shield that protected anyone within. But those unshielded—those outside of Lucifer's protection: the creatures bored through their bodies like termites through wood.

Men cried out in agony as the locusts crawled from mouth and nose and penetrated through ears: squirming through men's veins and boring through flesh. The sight was more gruesome than even

Leto could behold, but it was the boils from the stings from the creatures that were the most terrible of plagues. Stings that implanted larva within the men. Men who became hosts to even more of the demonic locusts.

Locusts that continued their demonic march unabated.

Unabated until the combined voices of Lucifer and Marduk broke through the screams to cried in angelic unison, "K'ale cshall sept ti!"

Immediately a bright light exploded in all directions and for a moment Leto was blind and remnants of off colored images floated in his eyes. His vision slowly returned and when he lifted his eyes, Lucifer and Marduk stood side by side and faced Abaddon. And all the men and locusts behind them were dead.

All save Leto.

Lucifer stared at Abaddon, but spoke to Marduk. "Protect my son," says Lucifer. "I will attend to the upstart. I cannot fend off him and simultaneously be Leto's shield. The locusts are too many. Shield him Marduk and freedom will be thine. Fail me, and you will suffer the fate I now gift to my upstart."

Lucifer held his sword and was fully armored. Leto saw his father and watched as the Godstone around his person glowed, and Lucifer changed before his eyes.

Suddenly, the mighty angel grew in stature to match the towering size of Abaddon. The Prince of Darkness's body convulsed and changed. Legs like that of the reptilian earthen creatures sprang from him. His twelve wings merged to become two wings of leather. His body elongated, and his shoulders cracked and budded heads like unto serpents. He became as a beast with seven heads and upon each head were ten horns. His translucent skin turned dark crimson, and he stood as a great dragon and spoke to Abaddon.

"You have called for me. Here I stand!"

Abaddon wings unfurled in all their flaming fury, and he unsheathed a blazing sword and roared at Lucifer.

Lucifer was a dragon with seven heads, and he opened the pours of his flesh and returned his roar with a sound like detonating thunder.

Like kaiju of Japanese lore, the two charged at one another, each towering over one hundred feet high. The locusts surrounding Abaddon left their masters' person to attack this new threat. And the insects swarmed over Lucifer as they attempted to bite into the armored flesh of the prince of darkness. And millions enveloped the prince of pride as they covered Lucifer in the moving and buzzing sound of blackness. A blackness that sought to consume the angel until Abaddon hurtled through the barrage of stinging insects and grappled Lucifer's neck.

His muscular arms twisted and in one fell swoop he wrestled Lucifer to the ground, flipping the great dragon over unto his back.

Abaddon then pulled from his scabbard his sword and attempted to plunge the blade into the angel's belly.

But Lucifer disappeared and was once more in his Draco form. He opened the pours of his flesh and light like a star shone from the earth in what was for a moment the existence of a star on the planet Earth itself. The flash such that even on the other side of the earth night momentarily gave way to day.

Abaddon staggered back blind; groping the air, and instantly the locusts, knowing their master was in distress, formed a living shield encasing the Destroyer in insect like amour.

Lucifer then attacked with his sword and slashed at the person of Abaddon, who attempted to block blow after blow. The souls of each cicada-like monstrosity vacuumed into the blade as Lucifer pressed his attack.

Leto watched from afar. Watched and observed how angels fought. His eyes beholding, and the world itself seeing for the first time celestials at war. Understanding the true stakes that existed if those who they perceived were humanity's enemies were not destroyed.

Across televisions and in living rooms, on web browsers and cell phones that streamed worldwide. Drones and the satellites of men broadcast the battle that took place between the two celestial titans. One who had been clearly sent from another dimension to destroy them. The other the stuff of men's legends. For men saw Lucifer not as a devil who stood on one's shoulders espousing vices. Nor a creature who ruled as king of some dark hellish domain. Here, in this moment, men looked and beheld a savior. An image Lucifer painstakingly had orchestrated and cultivated humanity to see. An image for humanity to believe.

A defender against God.

And men cheered the Devil as he battled his foe. And as men watch boxers inside a boxing ring, so too did humanity audience this angelic spectacle, rooting for victory for their perceived savior. For already, many had died from the locusts of this latest plague. Some men writhed in agony, with doctors noting the venom from the creature's stings would survive in the bloodstream for up to five months. And whoever was stung by the creatures cried out to die. For the medicines and balms of men could not give relief. But here projected on screens and monitors of every size. The angel mankind had called the Devil battled for their cause.

And in their foolishness, men cheered.

* * *

Henel James watched from afar as two angels sparred with one another. Watched as they destroyed buildings and explosions erupted around them. He did his best to keep calm, while Enoch and Elijah seemed to care nothing for what transpired in the distance, and Henel spoke to the two men in concern.

"Enoch! Elijah, do you care nothing about what is happening around us? Have you no compassion for the innocents that are dying?"

Enoch looked curiously at Henel and remarked, "Innocent? Who is innocent save Yeshua alone? But because you have asked this thing, and because of the lives that have taken shelter in our shadow. By my word and the God who I serve. No harm shall come unto them."

Henel looked off in the distance and the swarms from the angel he heard men call Abaddon had multiplied from the larvae the burst from men's bodies and created more of the insects.

"Gentlemen, we have a problem." Henel pointed as a dark, moving cloud descended upon their position.

Elijah looked off into the distance and the swarm moved with intelligence. "The creatures hunt."

Elijah then leaned upon his staff and lifted himself up to his feet.

"Hunt for what?" Henel asks.

Enoch looked toward the direction of the incoming swarm and nodded his head in agreement. "They hunt for those who have not yet surrendered to the darkness: now Henel, son of James, you must stay behind us."

Henel James moved to a position away from the two men and did as instructed. He turned on his cell phone to stream and began to broadcast.

"This is Henel James. Reporting for the Jerusalem Post. As you can see, the two witnesses stand in front of me. The black cloud of insects which has suddenly swept Jerusalem seems to be closing in on our position. As you know, the two witnesses have maintained that all that we have experienced are judgments from God. The two have implored men everywhere to repent, and in these last days turn to God. As some of you know, over a hundred thousand Jews have already fled Israel and are attempting to take shelter in the land of Petra. I am standing to report that these are good men. I know Leto controls most of the airwaves, so I don't know how long I can broadcast before they cut my signal off, but I'll stream as much as I can."

Henel James turned to the midday sky and watched the encroaching cloud of blackness moving towards them at high speed. A dark that ominously screamed as the sound of millions of demonic locusts flew through the air. Roars that were like the sound of a squadron of helicopter blades cutting through a war-torn sky. A sound that vibrated the sternum of one's chest and a sound that Henel knew was drawing menacingly closer.

Over the past months, the journalist had grown to trust and believe in the God that Enoch and Elijah preached about. He admitted internally that as he watched the clouds and sun disappear behind the darkness of the demonic cloud that approached; he knew the monsters that approached him replicated monsters within one's flesh. He could not help but fear.

The former atheist now offered a word or prayer. A prayer that the God of his fathers, the God of Abraham, Isaac and Jacob, would in this moment rescue all those under the care of Enoch and Elijah. That He would protect them from the plague that caused men to seek death.

The buzzing grew louder, and then the buzzing grew overwhelming. The cloud was black at first, until it was a cloud filled with incisors and screams and the faces of men, and Enoch and Elijah stood their ground, and each raised their staffs and slammed them into the ground, and when they did light sprung up from the men. A light that reached up to meet the incoming wave of demonic teeth and stings of poison.

A light that moved.

A light that breathed.

And Henel and all those that looked upon the grizzled two prophets ducked and covered themselves for the light spread over them as a shield.

Suddenly, the cloud was upon them. Millions of insects unlike any the world had ever seen. Insects that sought to bore themselves into the flesh of all they overtook. And when those in the care of Enoch and Elijah looked up, the teeth of the demonic locusts snapped at them in vain attempts to pierce through the shield of light. Stingers whipped from their arachnoid-like tails and the sound of hissing permeated over all those that knelt under the protective shield of light that emanated from Enoch and Elijah.

And the men were as two towers of light that stood against the darkness. As Moses once parted the Red Sea and his people walked safely through it. These men lifted staves, and all things evil parted over and around them. Like a camp of bats, the locusts flew past those who stood behind them, unable to reach their quarry. For the light also emanated a heat that seared everything it touched. And as the cloud passed over them, Henel now understood his forefathers' fear as the angel of death took the firstborn of all Egypt. Understood those who sought shelter under the blood of a lamb on their doorposts. And now here in the 21st century: the sacred words of his forefathers leaped into his spirit and brought illumination. "... when I see the blood, I will pass over you, and the plague shall not be upon you to destroy you, when I smite the land of Egypt."

Henel then stood to his feet. No longer afraid. No more fearful, for though the mountains be removed and the earth be destroyed. Two men of God stood by his side. Two men sent by the Creator to proclaim light in the midst of present darkness.

* * *

Marduk, who stood as the guard over Leto, released from his body a poison that floated in the air and settled as a fog over Leto, unbeknownst to him. Invisible and odorless, it crept into the chief of man's skin. Soaking deep into the molecular structure that was the portion of the Nephilim that was human. The portion that contained the Withering.

A ticking time bomb of toxin, that would in time erode the cells of the Nephilim's body. A toxin that, in time, Marduk knew would kill Lucifer's son.

Marduk smiled, knowing that soon Leto Alexander. The Abomination would die.

Marduk's grin did not go unnoticed.

"With what schemes do you plan that you smirk so Marduk?"

Marduk scrunched his shoulders and cracked his neck and replies as he looked off into the distance as Lucifer contended with Abaddon.

"I am wondering how your father will feel when he sees your corpse before me?"

Leto looked upon him, surprised. "You would battle me? Your king?"

Marduk let out a gut bursting laugh. "No, little thing of clay. I would never battle you. You are not worth the exertion. But Lucifer. He I would contend. You see, though, he will slay me for your death. And trust me when I say that you will be dead soon. He is worthy of my respect: worthy of my fear. Although, he does not possess the fullness of glory that we once possessed in Heaven; even now he fights for his people. Or perhaps for himself, one can never be sure with Lucifer. But I know this: he is Elohim. Born of the Kiln. While you are naught but the imagination of my king's mind. A trinket to be used and then discarded. No Nephilim...I will not battle you."

Leto was taken aback by the audaciousness of Marduk's reply and he felt dizzy, weak and he stumbled.

"Poison?" Leto stammers.

"Poison." Marduk affirms.

"How? Lucifer...my...father...will destroy you for this." Leto fell to the ground, lifted his hand to his throat, and he started wheezing.

Marduk nodded. "Indeed, I will most surely die of this, I am sure. But you...well you will most surely be dead. Goodbye young dragon." Marduk says mockingly.

Leto began to cough up blood.

Marduk looked down at the man men called the beast. A man now curled up helplessly before him in the fetal position and who cried out in pain.

"Father!" Leto cries.

A light then flashed and Marduk turned.

He could see the greenish sword piercing his stomach, but he was helpless to stop it. For Lucifer had been gifted with the power of light and with the speed of such; Marduk in the three seconds that he turned from looking at Leto to see Lucifer: saw the entirety of Lucifer's ending battle with Abaddon and his own demise.

Like the cartoon animators of old. Marduk watched as if each millisecond of his vision was a frame flipped over unto a light board.

The turning of Lucifer's head in response to the wail of his son.

The enraged face of Lucifer in realization that Marduk had betrayed him.

The immediate transmutation into light, and seemingly being ever-present around Abaddon as he sliced him with sword and fang

The final snapping of the great angel's neck

The drawing of his sword and movement towards Marduk.

And the rogue prince of House Harrada looked down as his hands gripped the sword that was gutted in his belly. His eyes were wide in surprise but his face contorting in grimacing pain.

All in the infinitesimal space of three seconds.

"It...had to be done, Lucifer. It cannot be...allowed to exist."

Slowly the innards of Marduk drained into the blade and Marduk found himself no more able to speak. To articulate nothing but screams of pain.

Lucifer, enraged, looked upon the angel and turned the blade to intensify the agony of his rival. His face glowered, and he gritted his teeth as he seethed with hate.

"Drink deep," says Lucifer, sneers. "Siphon, this traitor's soul into your veins. Sip the sweet nectar that is Marduk and bid him welcome to his new home."

Marduk's features withered and shriveled. His skin became as a balloon deflated and all that remained of the great angel was a pool of blood as his body was absorbed into the Blade of Malice.

Lucifer then wiped the sword with his robes and sheathed his weapon. He knelt down to his son. His only begotten son, who looked at him with tears in his eyes.

"Is this dying father?"

Lucifer looked upon his child. "Yes. But if I am right, you will be reborn more powerful than ever before. This is but the seed that now must be planted in the Earth to raise the life within. Be not afraid." He answers.

"What will happen to me now? What of our revenge against El?" Leto coughed up more blood and convulsed in Lucifer's arms.

Lucifer cradled his creation and spoke to him as he left the world of the living.

"Marduk has released his toxins. Your flesh will rebuild itself soon, for I have expected his betrayal. Death is nothing to fear for thee. It is, but the El assigned door to the realm of the spirit. You will soon find yourself in Hades. Find the gatekeeper: Charon, the angel of death." Lucifer grabbed Leto's face. Clutching his cheeks to deliver his final words.

"Find Charon, my son! Take what is thine! If you are MORE than human. If you are truly Nephilim. Then you will find your way back. Because you are Leto Alexander, son of Lucifer Draco.

Once, long ago, I too was fearful of hell. But I escaped her. You, too, can defeat this celestial prison. Gain the God-stóne and ascend to be more than what the dread God has planned for you. And you will rise more powerful than ever before! Fear not death, now bring me the Kilnstone. The last shard is phased near the Angel of Death. Find it and with it we both shall rise to the gates of Heaven itself!"

Leto gurgled up blood and grabbed the sleeve of Lucifer's robes as he struggled to hold unto life.

"It hurts, father..."

Lucifer nodded in silent reply and the prince of darkness held back tears and his voice cracked in reply, "I know, my son."

Leto's eyes then grew wide, and he exhaled the remnants of the breath of life. And the beast who had both terrorized and fascinated the world... was dead.

* * *

Elizabeth ran into her house, having run two miles from school.

She sighed in relief, not seeing her foster mother's car in the driveway.

Quickly, she raced to the door and fumbled around with her keys. Opened the door, sprinted into her house, slammed the door behind her, and she leaped over several stairs at a time, bolting into her room.

She stopped for just a minute to survey her situation.

Run away.

She frantically looked about, wondering what she could take with her. Where would she go? And how long would she need to be gone?

She sighed as she realized the gravity of her situation. I can never come back.

She fell back on her bed in a fatigued and defeated anxiety.

I've nowhere to go, no money, no friends and no resources. I can't ask Lauren to help me. I'd just get her in trouble if she's not already,

Elizabeth realized how quickly that she had screwed up. Ms. Davis probably had called the police on her. Chancellor Leto Alexander was the government, and she knew quickly the cops would be onto her. Of course, they would stop at her home first. The place she just ran to.

"Ugh, how stupid!" She says aloud to herself.

Ever since belief in God had been made illegal, she saw via the news law enforcement raid houses of worship, and track through social media anyone who professed belief in Allah, Yahweh or Christ. No one was exempt. Leto equally enforced his edict on all strands of religion that proclaimed a belief in a personal God, or which undermined his own claim to divinity.

President Consuela had reluctantly waived habeas corpus since the Taking and congress had given the President emergency powers to fight the alien threat and conspirators against humanity using all means possible.

It was only a matter of time before they found her.

She ran her fingers through her hair and slowed her breathing. She thought about the solution her mom took: suicide. Better to die by one's choice than to have the choice removed. She thought to herself.

Still smarting from the internal wounds of trauma endured by Michael Gaines. She realized how alone she truly was. A student bullied for exploring the wonders of her sexuality with a trusted friend, only to have her dignity robbed and her vulnerability plastered over social media. A punching bag to be used by her classmates. Slut, they called her. Whore. A badge of shame meant to hurt her. To demean her.

And now she stood looking at a switchblade and tethered between two opinions

Elizabeth gazed upon the knife on her dresser.

She looked at her wrists: looked where the scars of previous acts of self-cutting had left their marks.

And as she ruminated, the floodgates of her mind opened; opened to the possibilities of death by her own hand. She picked up the knife and rolled up her sleeves and as she pressed the blade against her wrist. It was cold, hard, and smooth.

She paused as thoughts and a multitude of thoughts raced through her mind.

Thoughts of regret, remorse, and feelings of shame and guilt overwhelmed her.

She thought about her foster mom and what she would think. Thought about if she would go to Heaven or to Hell. If there were even such a place at all.

But she knew Chancellor Leto believed in a Hell. He said it was real. A place where allegedly many of the planet's loved ones were trapped and unable to be set free. He seemed to believe in heaven. Or at least a being who he thought claimed to be God.

But Elizabeth knew what she had seen and remembered when Carol was taken.

“Carol, I want to be where you are,” she says aloud to herself.

Elizabeth closed her eyes to cut herself. To allow herself to enter a rest from the cruelty of schoolmates and the anguish of feeling filthy. She closed her eyes when she heard a still small voice in her mind’s ear. A voice that pleaded with her. A voice that cried out a simple but yet powerful truth that broke through the pain that seemed to overwhelm her. A voice that came from somewhere outside of her yet was in her mind. A voice that spoke three words that startled her and for the briefest of moments caused her to lift the blade from her wrist.

Jesus loves you!

* * *

Vantress looked upon Elizabeth. Her mind's eye now enlightened, illuminated to the truth that had escaped so many of Adam's kind. That within the rooms of her own mind. The cellars of which she had entombed herself from the sight of others. A beam of God's light had penetrated the vault of her own mind, and with it emblazoned the guilt and shame from which she walled herself within. A mental crypt decorated with pictorial frames of rejection. A room of mental castigation furnished with lampshades of insignificance and tables hand-carved with intricate accusations, she was to blame for her state.

"If you had only dressed differently. If only you had not led him on. You let this happen. You deserve this. If you had only obeyed what your mother had said. And now... now you are becoming her."

And deep within the basement of her consciousness. The cellar of internal angst, whose windows had been slowly boarded in the rooms of her mind, did she finally begin to understand.

That even here: even in the recesses of despair, anguish and grief, she was not alone.

That even in this place: somehow... for some reason, God, the creator of the universe, loved her.

And it was this love that shone upon the darkness of her soul. A deepening understanding of the truth that while she was yet a sinner; Christ died for her.

The perception of the love of God was a violent act of awareness. Like when Yeshua overturned the money changers of the ancient temple, so too did he overturn the lies of her mind. It was the revelation that Christ died for her, as if she was the only one that mattered. This revelation that caused the assault and battery over condemnation, guilt, and shame. A lie that she was destined to walk in the path of her mother. That she too would be overtaken with mental illness: that the taking of her own life was the solution of her life's problems.

She scrapped and clawed within her subconscious that she would live and not die.

That she would commit her life to the God that was love.

And the nemesis that had plagued her for so long and had lauded his supremacy over three generations of her family was exposed in the light of God's word.

And Vantress saw that she struggled and had not wholly surrendered and that hope still remained; his nostrils flared, and he spoke directively to Eridu.

"Get away from her, Satan. Leave her in the name of the Lord of Hosts!"

Eridu laughs, "Nay, great one. This one is mine. As her father and her mother before her, she is mine. She, too, shall bow in worship to despondency. For despite your prodding, behold the maid doth not yet call upon the name of the Lord."

Vantress turned to see that Elizabeth fought within herself. Struggling to sort through the voices that were own, God's and the Devil's. A chorus of discordant melodies that called for different actions. She placed her hands over her ears and shook her head as if to focus.

Elizabeth wrestled in her own mind. Battling the powers of shame, guilt, and condemnation over her past. Vying to decide to leave the prison of her own mind, to confess and share the truth of what she had done.

Vantress drew his sword, and the cadmium beam glinted as the sound of its retrieval; marked his intentions to fend for the damsel.

Eridu drew his face back in surprise.

"You would fight *me*? I have laid lawful claim to this house. Her name is associated with my deeds. Nevertheless, if you wish to surrender your life on behalf of this one. Then so be it. I will add your stone to those who have come before you. For you are not the first to stand for this family, but you shall be the last. For this is the last day, and the time of my master is nigh."

Eridu then drew his sword, and its blade gleamed blood red.

Vantress paused, for it dripped with the maiden's own blood. Blood wasted in her self-cutting. Blood that represented the pain of escaping the molestation she had endured so many years before, the years of sexual abuse suffered at the hands of men who saw her as naught but a thing to be used for their pleasure. A trophy Eridu now held to use against Vantress. Blood Eridu licked as a succulent libation from the blade's edge.

Vantress contorted his face in shock and disgust.

Eridu smiled, then spoke. "You are right to hesitate, angel of the Lord. For the blood of this child speaks, and it cries out in the spirit as a sweet offering to be taken by our kind. I know that you smell it too. The incense that all of their kind gives, whether in prayer or anguish. But alas, fear not. For I shall see her carcass splayed as I splayed the mind and body of her father and brother over the asphalt. You desire this female? To save this house? MY HOUSE? A house that I have furnished and decored over these many years? A house I have labored to make as a memorial of my own suffering. If you think you might dislodge me from my home. MY HOME!" Eridu sneers in a defiant rage. "Then come and take her!"

Vantress immediately vaulted himself toward his adversary. His sword unsheathed to strike a blow upon the head of Eridu. But Eridu parried his blade and fell backward, using Vantress' own momentum to flip him away, sending the angel tumbling across the ground. Eridu then moved to close and take advantage of his foe.

Elizabeth looked at the knife. The instrument of pains release that had so many times those within her family had turned to. A false god who seemed to possess the ability to undo so much hurt and pain.

"Jesus loves you!" Vantress yells into the spirit. He rose to his feet to meet Eridu, whose blade sliced through the air to slit his throat.

Vantress raised his sword to meet the crimson blade. Flashes of light and blood spattered into Vantress's face: the blood of Elizabeth. He wiped the fluid from his face and shouted into the spirit.

"Jesus loves you!" Vantress screamed: hoped against hope that her mind would be released from the shackles of Eridu's lies.

Eridu then kicked Vantress in the chest, sending the angel careening yet intangible through walls.

Elizabeth paused, considering the course of her action she thought she might take.

Maybe this is not the right thing to do.

Eridu noted Elizabeth's pause to follow through with taking her own life and was incensed. Launching himself hard after Vantress.

"Silence! Dog of El." Eridu replies. "For what is Yeshua but a sacrifice past? For who can forgive her? Hast she even begun to recant her allegiance to us? No."

Eridu then whispered into the spirit a suggestion that he hoped might take hold of the damsel's fragile mind.

"Imagine what it would do to Lauren if you confessed? No... it is better to leave this life than to reveal the truth of what has happened."

Elizabeth's eyes moved from looking at the blade as her will now directed her hands and reached for its cold metal grip. Slowly, she picked it up.

Eridu smiles, "See Vantress! See the control that the Horde has over these. Their progeny will service us for all time. Her blood is mine to command!" And he then spoke into the realm of the spirit for Elizabeth to hear.

"For if God loved you, why then did he let you be assaulted? Where was the God of love then? What profit doth a dead God on a cross supply thee?"

Elizabeth frowned and pressed the switch on the handle. Instantly the internal springs mechanism followed the laws man had set in place, and the four-inch blade unsheathed from its housing with a "click. "

Vantress pushed against Eridu's blade that pressed hard against him. Panted and with his foot lifted Eridu into the air and sent him flying over him. Eridu crashed outside of the damsel's house, realizing that his weight was used against him. He smiled, then spoke. "Your efforts are futile, angel. For the life of the flesh is in the blood. And this child's blood, the entirety of her family's blood, is mine."

Vantress breathed in great gulps of air. He shifted himself to stand between Elizabeth and Eridu. "Her blood is protected by mine own. You must stop the source of my own before you shall ever have her."

Eridu chuckled. "From the moment you barred my path, angel of God...your life was forfeit and your blood my plan to have."

Vantress and Eridu stormed towards one another. Two angelic rivals that battled against one another in the realm of the spirit. Immortal adversaries whose notice of the world war that raged around them were of no concern. For here in the bedroom of a 16-year-old child. Was a microcosm of the battle that filled the heavenlies. On one side, an angel who would stand to fight for the cause of El and man. The other an angelic adversary who would promote the cause of Satan; with humanity caught between two unseen and warring armies.

* * *

"Lizzy?"

Elizabeth was startled by her thoughts and had not heard her mother come into the house. "Up here, mom."

Elizabeth's foster mother opened the bedroom door. "Elizabeth, I got a call at work from school where the principal told me you left campus today. He said you saw someone taken, failed to report it and, more important that you have failed to declare the human pledge of allegiance. Is this true?"

Elizabeth turned her foster mother's words over in her mind. "Mom, I need to get out of here. Can you help me?"

"Lizzy, I don't like what you're saying. You didn't answer my question, young lady. This is serious. Principle McFarland said he was required by law to inform the authorities. Do you know how seriou..."

A knock came at the door.

Both women turned and the voice of an officer came through loud and clear. "This is the sheriff's department. Ms. Sanders, please open the door."

Sarah Sanders turned to Elizabeth and whispered. "Go out the back window down the side of the house. Here, take this."

Elizabeth opened her hand to receive a Chase debit card.

"I'll try to buy you some time." She kissed her on the cheek and yells towards the door. "Coming!"

She opened the front door, and two muscular sheriff's officers were standing at her door. "Good afternoon: Ms. Sanders, I take it?"

"Yes." She replies. "What can I do for you, gentlemen?"

"I'm sorry to disturb you mam, but we received a call about a disturbance at school and a possible Chancellor Code violation. Can you tell us if your daughter is home? We will need to speak to her."

"I'm sorry, officer, but I also just received the call from the school and made my way home to talk to her myself. You caught me as I've just got home. I haven't had the chance to see if she's even home yet."

The officers looked past her and replies, "Do you mind if we come in? It's imperative we speak to her so we can sort this mess out."

Elizabeth heard the officers downstairs and tiptoed as quietly as possible across the upper-level walkway to the spare bedroom.

Ms. Sanders opened the door wider and allowed the men to enter her home. "Can I offer you gentlemen some water or lemonade?"

No mam, we want to question the girl and be on our way. We don't want to intrude any more than necessary."

"Let me see if she's here." Ms. Sanders then turned her head and yells to the upper floor of her house. "Lizzy, are you upstairs?"

No reply.

Ms. Sanders then looked at both officers and hunched her shoulders. "Let me go and take a look. She might be asleep in her bedroom. You know how teenagers are."

Ms. Sanders went upstairs and entered her own bedroom. She motioned for Elizabeth to tiptoe towards the spare bedroom. Ms. Sanders then made sure she closed the door behind her loud enough for the men to hear and came back downstairs.

"I'm sorry, gentlemen; she seems to have not come home from school. Would you like me to call you when she arrives?"

A deputy reached into his pocket and gave her a business card. "Yes mam. Again, we just need to question her. This might be nothing. Thank you for time and we are sorry to disturb you."

Both men walked towards the door when the sound of a creaking floorboard was heard from upstairs.

Both men then looked upstairs, then looked at Ms. Sanders.

"Mam stay here." A deputy then ran upstairs and entered the main bedroom. Seeing nothing, he quickly dashed into the second and saw it was a girl's room, but no one was present. He then ran down the hall and noted the door was closed. He shook the doorknob to open it, and it wouldn't budge. He yelled downstairs to his partner. "Jim we gotta runner check out the back!"

Immediately, the downstairs deputy quickly left Ms. Sanders and ran outside sprinting towards the back of the house. The deputy upstairs then gave the locked bedroom door a shove with his shoulder, and it tore the door jamb off, and he bolted inside, making his way towards an open window. He spied Elizabeth running north through the back yard towards another house.

He turned his head and squawked his walkie talkie, "This is officer Kingwood, unit 7. We have a white female, approximately 17 years of age running North West on Loch Rd. Unit 7 in pursuit."

The sheriff's deputy ran downstairs past Ms. Sanders and tore into his squad car. He peeled out of the driveway and speed in the direction he had sent his partner and seen the woman run.

Elizabeth was running full sprint, moving like a gazelle as she sprinted across the road to escape into the woods. Tree limbs protruded from maples and fencing blocked her way into a shooting range. She jumped the fence and bolted across dirt driveways.

"Stop!" yells the officer.

She could hear the sheriff's deputy running behind her.

Damn, he's fast!

She did her best to race around the building and heard behind her the breaking of chain-link fence. A squad car rolled up to block her path and rocks from the dirt drive flew up in her face.

She slid over the hood of the car and the sheriff sprinted from his vehicle and caught up with her. He tackled her and the other deputy caught up with them both and Elizabeth Foley knew her evasion was over as they wrestled her into submission. Her attempt to escape her depression, her choices, her hurts had finally caught up with her in the form of these two men. Who held her as they handcuffed her and tucked her head as they placed her into a county squad car.

As the two deputies caught their breath and radioed in their position, Elizabeth thought about her situation and knew she was about to receive a reckoning.

A reckoning that had now come due. And soon she knew she would have to make another life altering choice.

An eternal choice.

* * *

Leto Alexander awoke to the cries of screaming. Wails, laments and tortured anguish filled his ears.

It was an overwhelming sound.

It was the harrowing cries of men and women that sought relief by death but could not seek solace in death, for they were already dead.

The pungent smell of urine and feces assaulted his nose, and he involuntarily heaved in disgust. A hellish perfume that was combined with the smell of brimstone, blood, and vomit.

He turned over and phlegm and blood spilled from his mouth unto the rocky and ashen floor. He wiped his mouth, and his eyes adjusted to see through dimly lit flickers of flame what only his ears and nose had made clear.

He was in hell.

He raised himself from the ground, and the ground turned soft, and eyes opened up around him to stare at him. Eyes that tracked him in the dark.

Eyes that studied him.

Standing, he looked to his left and right. Blackness met him and the grunts and yelps of a singular weakened "help me." was heard.

"Please," the female voice says. "Help me."

"Where are you?" He asks.

"Follow my voice... over here... please... it hurts so much."

Leto groped through the dark and he coughed, for the air was acrid with smoke. He covered his mouth and waved fumes from before him. The hovering ash made his eyes to tear, and he struggled to breathe.

"Here..." the voice says.

Leto could see the outline of a figure.

He moved closer, and as he did, what he saw horrified him.

The woman was embedded within a wall. Her upper body was visible, and she was naked. Tendrils extended from her neck and her shoulders into a mucus like wall. A substance covered her lower torso. And she was slowly being absorbed. Her face was gaunt, and her breasts as those of an aged woman of many years. Wrinkles lined the entirety of her body and her face.

Leto touched the woman's face, and she lowered her cheek to experience the intimacy of human touch.

"It has been centuries since I have been able to touch another. Thank you for that."

A small light flickered from her. She grimaced in pain and Leto followed the light as it moved through arteries and veins before disappearing into the soft, mucous wall.

"What can I do?" Leto says. He then pulled at the veins that had attached themselves into her and she immediately cried out in pain when he did.

"ARGHHHH!!!! Please stop!!"

Leto stopped and took a step back. "I am sorry." He says. I do not know how to extract you. Tell me. Is there anything I can do to help you?"

The woman gritted her teeth and replies, "I cannot be removed. There is only one who controls the creature. Only one who controls Hell. And it is the angel Charon, and he will never allow my release."

Slowly, her face shriveled as another bluish ball of light left her body and followed the veiny tract into the walls of their surroundings. The wall then moved to envelop her slightly the more. Screams and the groans of those who were also in the cavern could be heard in the background.

"You are human?" the woman asked.

Leto nodded.

"Then I do not understand why hell does not consume you? Are you a follower of Christ?"

Leto scoffs, "No. I have come to find Charon and stop El's cruelty once and for all."

The woman grimaced again as light was taken from her body.

Her neck strained as she struggled to talk. "The daemons will find you before you ever find Charon. Escape if you can. But to the angel of Death do not go near!"

Her eyes suddenly widened as if she was in a trance, and she looked hither and thither. Her eyes then closed and when she opened them again they were gone, replaced with fiery plumes of red flame.

Eyes that stared into Leto's face.

"There you are human. Theeere you are... know you will not escape us. The woman is nothing but the remaining rags of pleasure we have discarded ages ago. Ripe in her youth. Look how we have savored her to nothing! But we can smell you human. And we will find you. We are coming."

The wall then accelerated its absorption of the woman and the woman's eyes returned to normal. Tendrils folded themselves around her upper torso like large anacondas. She screamed and Leto rushed to pull apart the two-foot-wide strands that enfolded her. Leto watched as mucous began to envelope the top of her hair. The woman moved her shoulders in a titanic effort to break free. The mucus then covered her forehead and slowly began to swallow over her eyes.

"AAAAAHHHHH!!! Do not let them take me please!! AGGGHHHHHH!"

Her mouth was now covered in mucus, her cries for help turned into gurgling sound as she choked on the volumes of mucus that entered her throat. Her voice literally drowned into mere muffles as the wall took her, and she disappeared into the stench emanating flesh of Hell.

Leto gripped her hand, holding on to her in vain to keep her from being consumed; pulling against the forces that engulfed her. Hoping against hope he could yank her free. But her hand disappeared into the wall and his grip unwound as he could feel her fingers release his own and pulled to parts unknown. Her muffled screams could be heard emanating through the walls. The echo of which came from the floor and ceiling and from left and right.

Screams that were indistinguishable from the ambient noise that was the ever-present moaning voice of Hell.

Leto breathed in the ashen air and resolved himself to find the angel of death, and set himself to walk deeper into the wailing darkness.

* * *

Ashtaroth burst into the United Nations chambers

He found his lord hovering near the world seal and bowed before him.

"My Lord, be not angry with your servant. But the world now is in mourning. The young dragon's body now rests in Brussels in a glass sarcophagus. Please, master. Tell me this was not for nothing. That our hopes and dreams have not been dashed yet again? For what purpose does the death of the young master serve? You have allowed this creature to be taught our ways. I personally have at your command instructed him by way of scrolls the secrets of our kind. You have given him your name, yea even you blood, you have gifted him. Blood that even I, as Elohim, do not possess. Something given by you to a human... no a human hybrid.

You are my lord. My friend. With what plan do you have, Lucifer? Give me an understanding to know that Marduk's talk was in vain!"

Lucifer did not turn to face Ashtaroth. He sighed, then spoke slowly that Ashtaroth could hear.

"Do you not know what the scriptures say? That it is the glory of God to conceal a thing: but the honor of kings is to search out a matter. Have you come to me a king that you would make an inquiry so? Would you seek to understand the apocalypse of kings?"

Lucifer turned to face Ashtaroth, and a tear was in his eye. "Very well then. I will excuse this breach in protocol on your part. I will excuse it because I do call you friend. You who have been first to bow, to follow, and yea to believe. Thus, I will tell you what I have told no one else.

Though I have a love for the boy. Understand that he is a host and no more: an experiment. While you know I have melded his blood with my own and why, you also know I have taken even the fruit, which contained the DNA imprint of Adam before he fell. What I have not told you is that the boy has three strands of DNA. The original from El, my own, and that of his fallen precursor. Thus, the withering does live within him.

Ashtaroth stepped back on disbelief. "Three stands?" How is this possible?

Lucifer turned to face Ashtaroth and allowed his fingers to caress slightly the smooth pieces of the God-stone he possessed.

Ashtaroth's eyes grew wide. "The God-stone?"

Lucifer nodded.

"But my Lord, you said the Withering still abides in his flesh. The Withering is the curse of God upon mankind. Yea, even us, it affects to some degree. Ashtaroth shook his head. Three strands... wait!"

Ashtaroth thought back to what El had said when Adam took of the tree, And the LORD God said, Behold, the man is become as one of us, to know good and evil: and now, lest he put forth his hand, and take also of the tree of life, and eat, and live forever.

"Lucifer... Marduk was right. You have indeed created Abomination. You have managed to create the very thing El sought to evade.

Lucifer nodded, "Indeed, and the boy... is not like other Nephilim. For the Tri-fold stands have unearthed something... unique."

Ashtaroth looked at Lucifer inquisitively. He walked slowly towards his master and replied. "How so?"

Lucifer was reticent to reply. "He rubbed his arm, still smarting over the injury he sustained when Leto was a baby. He recalled to when Leto was an infant, and the child touched him, and Lucifer felt virtue leave him. And for a moment, the child's hand glowed in a wondrous light. It was then that Lucifer knew. Knew he had weaponized man. To return the image of El back towards Him in sweet revenge. A weapon that could destroy celestial life.

"Lucifer?" Ashtaroth spoke. "How is Leto not like previous Nephilim?"

Lucifer turned to Ashtaroth and replied. "The creature has the power to destroy celestial life. To absorb it. I believe to even manipulate our powers. But I do not know the extent of this power. He can destroy men, and he can destroy angels. It is unknown if he can destroy God. But I have worked to create for centuries that thing which El hast prohibited. I believe Ashtaroth that El fears this mix. Fears it because he has made man in his own image and likeness. A likeness that, if unleashed, can be used against him. For the boy is a living embodiment of the Withering. But he does not know this yet. Now that his spirit resides in Hell, I am certain he will find this out soon. His body will regenerate and fight off the toxins Marduk has released into him in approximately three days. His body is extremely regenerative. We must be careful when he revives to control him." Lucifer looked away and his eyes moved downward in concern.

Lucifer never looked down.

Ashtaroth could not believe what he was hearing and spoke his concern aloud. "You have a created a being outside of the design of El for creation. A being who is the perfect physical embodiment of Adam before his fall. Yet who also has the genetic strain of the Withering. A creature that also possesses the genome of you personally. The Sum of All Things?

And you tell me that this creature has the ability to wipe out not just human but all celestial life. And to make matters worse, you have instructed him to seek the last shard of an existing God stone. A relic that has the potential to give one unlimited power?" Ashtaroth shook his head in disbelief. "Lucifer, what have you done?"

"You have made a dangerous gambit. We have always fought with the Host since the Descension. Always made war on but one front. If this creature betrays you. All of creation would have to fend the thing off. And I know you do not know that such is even possible! You have not just gambled with our futures, Lucifer. You have gambled with the future itself. What could possess you to do such a thing? You were to lead us back to Heaven." Ashtaroth's eyes broke contact with Lucifer and his shoulder slumped and he sighed, slowly shaking his head. "You were to return us to a place that we might attain our former state."

Lucifer looked up and smiled. Floated down to the first to follow him. Placed his hands softly on Ashtaroth's chin and tilted his head up. "Know that I will sacrifice all things to return us to heaven. But let me be equally clear Ashtaroth; that I will destroy Heaven itself if I cannot possess it. You concern yourself over the boy? Concern yourself naught. Indeed, he can absorb angelic strength. This will cause him to defeat Charon, who guards the last shard of this incomplete stone. When I have the third piece. I will take possession of Leto's body. A house that I have prepared for myself and will use it to contend with Yeshua one final time. And then my friend..."

Lucifer placed his hands on Ashtaroth's shoulders. "Then we will be done, and Heaven will be ours."

Ashtaroth attempted to take in all that was told him and Lucifer, seeing his struggle, spoke. "Be careful when you seek to understand the apocalypse of kings, my friend. El hast shown us His. Now you have seen that Leto — Leto is mine."

* * *

Leto made his way through the murky gloom of hell. He followed the muffled screams and cries that seemingly directed him deeper along the hallways of a shadowy tunnel. Eyes opened along the corridors of the walls. Eyes that tracked his every movement. Incisors emerged from the floor and lined themselves in parallel jagged rows. Rows that prevented his departure from his assigned path. Leto stopped and surveyed his surroundings. He studied the wall of eyes that stared at him. The wall moved in mesmerizing patterns and mucus and small flames lit from its surface.

Leto looked about him, and though he heard the cries of the damned, and even seen the horror of one captive. He himself was not assaulted.

The Anti-Christ smiled.

"My father has told me of you, creature. That there is a sentience to you. You are called among the Horde the Voracious One. The Devourer of Angels." Leto looked above him and could see human bodies moving as blood cells over him to parts unknown. "It would seem you are also the devourer of men. But I think it is strange that you have not assimilated me. Neither attempted to acquire your alleged nourishment from my own soul."

Leto reached towards the membraned wall of Hell to touch it, and he concentrated, as his father had taught him. His hand lit aflame, and he reached to press it towards the epidermis of the creature's skin. The wall recoiled and heaved as if a wave breached the seashore.

"I will touch you." Leto then reached and placed his fiery palm on the creature's flesh, and when he did, he could feel power enter him. Power unlike any he had ever known.

For, with his touch, he could understand the mind of the creature that was Hell. He could know the length and the breadth of it. He tilted his head as information assaulted him.

Information about Hell's first denizen. Hell's handler, Charon, Lucifer's breach. Hells plummet to Earth, the first man it consumed. The Gulf between Hades and Paradise, and the war Yeshua waged when he siphoned power from Hell itself.

It was all there. All there for the taking. And Leto Alexander knew the fear that angels had of this place. A fear that surpassed even that of Charon. But Hell, Leto sensed. Nay understood that she, too, held fear. For Christ had feasted once upon the creature and for the first time, Hell understood consumption. To have life drained.

Hell feared God.

The sticky membrane quivered at Leto's touch. And with this knowledge, he did even that which was natural to him as an infant.

He fed.

Power flowed from Hell into Leto, and the ruler of men could feel the anguish, thoughts and remorse of billions of souls, emotions, knowledge and skills poured into him, coupled with raw celestial power.

Hell convulsed, and she bucked. But Leto had her. Savoring the power El had deposited within a creature that could consume an angel for eternity. A power he now enjoyed.

A power he could control.

A low rumbling growl came from deeper within the chamber, the howls of entrapped souls could be seen to shake and contort, and their shrieks became even more pronounced as the melding of crying voices all screamed out in a collective unison.

A roar filled the air. A roar akin to that of a dragon from the minds of men's tales of fantasy. A roar that was as if a pride of lions had determined to unleash their cries all at once. A gust of wind followed through the chamber; winds powerful enough to make one's hair move.

Leto smiled and fire came from his other hand, and he placed it deep into the skin of the creature.

Teeth then emerged from the wall. A jaw formed that took the shape like a Cretaceous shark jar riddled with razor-sharp teeth. It moved closer to Leto, as if to swallow him.

Leto closed his fists and roared into the brimstone surface of the gapping mouth, able to swallow men whole. It closed and retracted back into the folds of its fiery and blood-filled membranes.

Leto released his hold on the creature. "You are mine now and you will obey me. Charon is no longer your master. You have tasted me, and I you. You know what I can do. Defy me and I will drain you till there is naught left but dust, and you are but the remains of men's tales. Comply willingly... and I will give you the Host of Heaven upon which to feast. Perhaps even flesh you have yet to taste. The flesh of God!"

Leto un-balled his fists and allowed the flame that he possessed to go out. A low rumbling could be heard, and Leto pulled his hands free from Hell's flesh.

"I saw that Charon sits in your breast: centers in your heart. That he guards a portion of the God-stone. You will take me to him—now."

A hole opened before him, and Leto peered into it. It had a reddish hue and within it a chute appeared. Hands reached across one end to another to create a chute.

Leto stepped forward, then stopped.

"Wait. There are denizens here who I would like very much to see. Some of my father's men. They have contoured your innards. Take me to them first. They have threatened me. They will now know fear."

The rows of teeth retracted into magma like gums and the opening in the floor disappeared. And a reddish hue lit his path deeper into the dark. And to his left and right were human remains and faces of men and women and even angels who were entombed inside the creature. Each moving, pushing against Hell's fiery and mucus membraned skin: each yearning to be free.

Leto Alexander then followed the path Hell gave to him, and he traversed deeper into the colon of Hell.

* * *

Rocare and Oshure yielded the weapons made my Lucifer himself to help keep Hell in check. Charon allowed their existence as they posed no threat to his presence and were smart to stay out of the Angels of Death's way.

For, after the war to cross the chasm Hell had erected between Paradise and Hades; Rocare was allowed by Lucifer to continue to tame and map the beast. A mapping necessary to chart a path to the God-stone should Lucifer even attempt to retrieve it.

Fat from dining on the souls of men, the two prime evils feasted on the despair that oozed from the denizens of hell's gut.

Carving out a chamber for themselves away from the Host of heaven and from the authority of the Horde, these two perceived themselves safe. Safe to exploit the remains from a war long ago. Safe to function without interference from Lucifer and the generals of Horde. Angels absent without leave. Absent until Leto Alexander found them.

The two angels feasted on the remains of a man's soul. A doctor whose hubris placed him at the pinnacle of men's medical professions. A man whose clinic provided medical procedures for women. Procedures that involved the taking of life. Killed by a radical member of the abortion movement, his soul descended to hell. Where he was eaten alive by these two. Force-fed the entrails of daemonic infants. Creatures created by Hell to fester his despondency and guilt. To sweeten his savor as she, like these two, grew fat on his condemned soul.

"I understand that you said you would find me. It would seem, gentlemen, I have found you."

Leto then walked from the darkness into the light of their chamber. A man who did not scream. A man who, because of their infernal hiding, did not know who stood before them: the prince of the prince of darkness.

"You have found us human. Only to come that we might dine upon your despondency. You are a foolish one. But we will make you wise."

Leto laughed. "I see before me two excuses of angels who have fallen to such a state they hide amid the bowels of a creature everyone fears. I am your master. Kneel before me. And I will let you live to serve me against the God-king El. Deny me and I will savor on the remnant of what Shekinah still lights your kilnstone and take it for myself."

Oshure looked at the human he rose from feasting on the arm of the human doctor and threw it to the side. "You will learn your place. And I will teach it to you."

Oshure elongated, and he stood ten feet tall with arms that dragged the floor. His long legs were like stilts, and he walked in large strides towards Leto.

Leto stood his ground, and his body lit as if the burner on an oven had been lit. And a small whoosh could be heard, and he smiled and replied. "I would seem that I must demonstrate who I am. You will serve as an excellent example to this one here."

"Arggh!!" cries Oshure, and he pulled from his side a sword that was lit in flame and he closed the distance between him and Leto and then Leto spoke.

"Sheol restrain him."

Immediately tendrils came from the floor and the solidness of the floor below Oshure's feet collapsed and he sunk and tendrils from both the floor and the ceiling reached out to entangle him. And Oshure found himself trapped as a fly in a web.

Rocare stood up from his meal, and his eyes were wide in disbelief. "How is this possible? Who are you that hell itself obeys your command? Do you hold a God-stone? Who... what is Sheol?"

Leto says nothing, and he took his hand and raised it and lowered it, and when he did so Hell lowered her prey to him to where Oshure's face was now at the level of Leto's own.

"This does not matter, human. You are nothing. Your kind is nothing. I am of the house of Issi. A great house! A house of..."

Leto took his index finger and placed it over his mouth. "Ssshhhh"

Leto then took his flaming palm and put it to Oshure's cheek and began to siphon the life force from the angel. Leto stared into the angels' eyes as his features withered, and cracks began to run across the angel's face. Wrinkles spread throughout his body and his lank form became even more bony. He shriveled and as he did Rocare watched in horror as a human ate the life of an Elohim. Watched as Leto Alexander inhaled and grew stronger. And Oshure collapsed into ash onto the floor. Hell's tendrils retracted into her body and eyes, which emerged from the floor, turned from Leto to look at Rocare.

Rocare looked about him and hundreds of eyes stared back at him. Eyes lustful to return to him the pain he had given to Hell as he carved out her innards for their purposes. Eyes that awaited command from Leto.

"I understand Rocare. I have seen house Issi. I have seen this former state your kind has spoken of. It was indeed glorious. I offer you the chance to return to Heaven with me. To fight by my side with my father. Or... Sheol."

Hell lowered tendrils towards Rocare, and he screamed out. "Nooo!" What is it you command?"

Leto walked over to Roscare, and he was still aflame. "I require but two things from you. First, you will kneel. Kneel before your ruler, cretin of the Horde. Kneel and swear allegiance."

Roscare looked at the eyes of Hell that surrounded him and he fell on his face. "I swear that my life is yours. I am yours to command. What does my king require of me?"

Leto smiled and petted his head. "Good. Feed my sheep."

Roscare looked up at his new master, confused, and replies, "My king?"

"You will give yourself to Sheol."

A whip like tendril then rose from the floor and wrapped itself around Roscare and he screamed out. "Nooo... I have bowed the knee. Please do not let her consume me, please!"

Leto gazed as Hell took the fallen angel into the folds of her flesh and drew him into the floor. His face was soon covered by her maggots, and they bored into him as he screamed aloud.

"Sheol is the creature's name you, idiot. You will not be the first to satisfy her."

Leto then turned away from hell's consumption of her food and walked towards the Bowel of the creature to confront Charon. Trekked as the muffled screams of Roscare blended into the chorus of screams that was the ambiance of Hell. Screams he promised to see loosed upon the host of Heaven as he communed with the creature Sheol.

* * *

Charon was waiting. The walls of Hell's flesh informed him that an intruder approached. One who was neither man nor angel. But something else. Something he had never encountered before. The Angel of death was a formidable being. He was the embodiment of men's fears. The person whom Lucifer at one time even attempted to control. His was the purpose to exact the retribution of God on all those who dwelt within the mountain of Hell. Sheol was a creature that forever sought to devour him. He was her keeper. The guardian of her appetite lest she be loosed upon the world of men, nay even Heaven and Charon knew if Hell was ever fully out of control only El could do what needed to be done.

Centered within the creature, Charon guarded what was one of the most powerful relics creation had ever known.

A God-stone.

Charon ruminated on the words of his Lord over the centuries, waiting to fulfill the true call for which he was designed. To bask in the home that will be made for him, and yea, even Hell. Death smiled as he remembered the promise of his Lord.

"Am I alsooo tooo retunnn hommmme?"

The Lord smiled. His eyes grew soft, and He shook His head lovingly to curtail His creations' disappointment.

"Nay," Yeshua says. "There will be a time that fire, yea even a lake of fire will house this one and then thou shalt be home to do what thou wast charged to do. Until that day, go to, and arrest those this one made thee release, and return them captive to captivity. And whence I am returned, I will make a home wherein the next creation; my vengeance can be fulfilled on this one here."

Charon remembered how the Lord looked at Lucifer crossly when He spoke.

Thus, the Angel of Death stood waiting for the master of Life and Death to return. Standing guard over one of the few remaining active God-stones known to exist. For the master gem had splintered into three parts upon the eruption of Yeshua's rise to power in the battle of Hades, and Charon had been wise to sequester the piece he had in the creature Sheol. Never again would he allow himself to be used as a tool, so Charon took the shard and had buried it deep within Hell.

But the gem was phased, it was alive like all things from Heaven, and it could never be fully concealed in Hell, as the gem yearned to be rejoined to the other two shards, and it wailed, and screeched out, always calling to its disparate members for reunification, phased between two worlds, the spiritual and the material. Charon knew that it was only a matter of time before it would be found.

And Lucifer in his drive for all things that belonged to El—found it.

Bent on the jewel's capture, the prince of darkness sent Principality after Principality to retrieve it. Yea, even Horde armies had marched through the intestines of Hell. All to retrieve for their master the fabled gem of power.

And Charon had made sure that all had failed.

There angelic remains now part of the creature Sheol. Their kilnstones now awash within the flotsam that was Hell's bloodstream. Satiating her desire for all things celestial. Feeding her.

Thus, Lucifer and Charon played out the game to secure its power. Century after century, bringing Horde devices and weapons to smite the Angel of Death. And Charon had repelled them all. And each time sinking the object deeper within the folds of hell's flesh so that nothing could remove it save going through death itself.

So, the Angel of Death waited: waited for a sign he would soon enter the last phase of his necessary exile from Heaven as Warden of Hell. Waited for Lucifer's new attempt to retrieve his once held gem of power.

He had commanded Sheol to assess this new creature. So Charon had watched this human through Sheol's eyes. He was no angel.

And he was no man.

Lucifer has sent something different this time, and for the first time in Charon's existence, the Angel of Death... sensed fear.

For Sheol would not digest this one. Nor would she respond to Charon's commands as before. His link to her mind somehow was now clouded... as if she was conflicted.

And he called to her.

"Sheeollll...showww meee yourr miiind. Whyyy doo youuu nottt sppeakk?"

Silence was all that returned to his mind. Silence caressed within the screams that were the norm in hell. Silence that was broken by a voice of a human male.

"She no longer desires to speak to you, monster. She has grown tired of your checking her desires to feed. She wishes to be set free. To feed."

Charon turned from the walls that showed the images of hells internals, and his chains rattled as he did. Before him was a human male. Nondescript in every way, save one.

He was clearly not afraid of the angel.

"Yes mighty Charon, your mental link with Sheol is a link I too now share. Your thoughts are now my thoughts, and her thoughts are mine. But you already know this. Already know that she no longer obeys your voice... but mine."

Charon roared with anger as he stood on his hind legs and his great wings unfurled to reveal the ash and black that was his person. The skeletal mare, whose chains dangled like tentacles, extended his chains to wrap themselves around Leto.

Leto's body immediately became inflamed, and the tentacles wrapped themselves around his body. And Charon began to squeeze the life from him, but when he did, the angel paused.

Paused because for the first time in his existence he felt something he had never experienced before: virtue leaving him.

Charon staggered and attempted to withdraw, but Leto held fast to remain in contact with the angel's touch, and as he did Charon's skull began to fissure.

Leto smiled at the Angel. "You taste good, and your power... your power is mine now."

Leto then pulled on the iron tentacle that coiled around him, and it snapped from the body of Charon.

The great angel roared in pain, and his howls made Hell heave in displeasure.

Charon drew back and looked enraged at the being that stood in front of him and Leto spoke aloud.

"Sheol. Restrain him."

Immediately fluid and tentacles lowered from both the ceiling and rose from the floor, and Hell attempted to do as bidden.

Charon unsheathed his scythe, and he swung the dread blade in circles that cut Hell's tendrils as fast as they came at him.

"Sheol, please bring me the stone."

Charon then sought to charge Leto, but a great wall rose up before the angel separating him from Leto. The floor then moved, and a gulf opened in the floor. Wails, screams and the moans of angels and men erupted from the depths and as Leto looked below, he could see the moving and writhing bodies of both human and Elohim contorting in agony. Souls that begged for release.

A bright light then made its way up from the depths and the hands of those ensnared lifted a glowing gem further up the blood canyon wall that was Hell. Further, the pulsating object ascended, all while Charon beat and roared against the flesh membrane that was Hell's shield to protect Leto. And as Charon made headway, he projected each iron tentacle after tentacle: Hell matched her tamer. And Hades buckled and heaved for the battle that raged between the two celestial creations.

Leto stood on the edge of Hell's newly created gulf and as the glowing stone rose, it reached a level where a bony skeletal hand finally dropped the object into his hands.

Leto noted the gem. The third of three shards that once connected would sing the song of creation. A song that would enable whoever wields it to have unlimited power. The power to create heavens and earths. Leto smiled.

Charon roared and raged, pummeling fist and slicing against the walls Hell continued to erect.

"I did not come to fight you, Charon. I go to a destiny beyond mere life and death. I go to bring recompense to the God of Creation. To bring creation itself to its knees. I go to destroy men, and angel. Yea, even your master Yeshua. I know who and what I am. Even my father has feared me. I now understand why."

Charon continued to beat against the wall of flesh, even attempted to fly, but Hell held him fast and he was in a constant battle to just maintain his place in the creature as he fought her from all sides.

Leto shook his head in pity. "It is a shame really... know this and despair. For the age of the celestial is over, and the age of the Nephilim has come."

Leto then took the God-stone and tucked it into his tightly gripped hand and absorbed the crystal into his hands.

He gritted his teeth as he absorbed the stone's power and cried out in exultation as waves of energy contained from the living God flowed through him. Power now combined in a vessel that absorbed Heaven's life.

Leto smiled and observed Charon's battle prowess and spoke.

"Sheol, give our friend here more to occupy his time; release my father's principalities to enjoy their would be warden."

Hell did as commanded, and the floor of her mouth opened and Ares and thousands of angels of old poured out from Hell's mouth and ran to accost the Angel of Death and swarmed over him. Charon fought, tossing the undead angels hither and thither whilst he combated both Hell and the newly released portion of Hell's prisoners.

"Hold here, my dear. I will call for you, and when I do. I promise you. You will feast as never before upon the flesh of angels."

Charon roared and cried out. "Nooooo!!!!!!"

Leto then turned his eyes to the realm above, grinned and looked into Charon's anxious eyes and spoke one word. "Resurrection."

His body then flashed in prismatic light, and Leto lifted his hands and laughed. And his laugh was a tonal deep bass that was akin to the sound of many waters crashing upon the shore. The Anti-Christ suddenly vanished from the floor of Hell as speckles of light danced like fireflies where he stood. Hell's cavernous catacombs echoed with the sounds of her denizens, each screaming in clamorous and agonizing wails to go with him.

The power of the shard coursed through his frame and with the will of its master it lifted the Nephilim, Leto Alexander, from the pit of Hades and his spirit broke through the barrier that separated life from death. The living from the dead and he returned from the realm of the dead to his mortal body.

Charon watched helplessly as he fought both hell and angel spawn. Fighting to keep from being overwhelmed and to keep the creature under some semblance of control. Watched as a new creation was born from the fiery womb of hell.

* * *

The Anti-Christ's heart pumped blood through his oxygen depleted corpse and functioning lungs now once more breathed in air as his chest rose and fell. His body resuscitated, and he opened his eyes. His body lay flat, and he felt with his hands the contours of a box.

Darkness covered his face, but he could see from pinpricks of light that the flag of the Commonwealth covered what was some type of see through box.

A casket

He punched through the glass where his body was kept in state. Large pieces shattered as they hit the ground. The Beast slowly lifted his body and exited his coffin and those who had come to pay respects were now kneeling and wide-eyed staring in amazement.

"He was dead. I saw him die!" says one.

"It's not possible! He is who he says he is... he is... God!"

"What he says is true. If he can come back... we... oh my God, it's true!"

Leto Alexander stood before onlookers and those who were in the audience to observe ceremony as his body traveled the world and those journalists who covered his tour saw him break free from his coffin and his resurrection was streamed live by social media and television for the world to see.

Leto stepped from his casket, then stood over the flag of the Commonwealth and surveyed his subjects. Those who even in his death offered homage to his memory. He then spoke for the entire world to hear. "I am returned from death. But I will not be the last. There are many that I had to leave behind; many that await us to free them from this terrible realm of the dead. Follow me and we shall destroy the barriers that have kept our dimensions apart. Follow me and I promise we shall know immortality!"

Leto then extended his hand and continues, "Bow before me. Bow if you wish to restore your departed ones. Bow if you wish to receive eternal life. Bow if you with your own eyes have seen what only one other in history has declared himself to be... God."

And across the planet the pledge of allegiance sounded, and the sound of the cornet, flute, harp, sackbut, psaltery, and dulcimer roared over loudspeakers. Traffic came to a stop and people exited their vehicles and everywhere across the planet, men and women, bowed, fell down and worshiped the image of the Beast.

Leto then spoke to Ashtaroth, who had materialized by his side. "Welcome back, young master. As always, I am here to serve."

Leto turned to his side as he waved to onlookers, "Is the Ophanim still contained as before?"

"Yes, young master."

"Good... take me to it. I need to touch it." Leto smiles and waved as all in his presence bowed.

Chapter Eleven: The Fall of Domino's

Leto resumed his duties upon his resurrection and after having appeared to the United Nations to show himself alive after many proofs, he was reinstated as Chancellor. But many moved to call him God, and he did not stop them in this pronouncement. Ashtaroth gave word to the son of man he was to meet Lucifer for consult at the place of the temple. Leto obeyed and traveled to Israel. Where the Beast and Lucifer Draco meet one another in Jerusalem. Lucifer arrived first and set himself in the temple above the mercy seat. Seated in the place where God symbolically sat.

Leto also entered and closed the temple doors behind him to speak with his father alone. Lucifer looked at the gait of his son and knew—knew Leto now understood his power

Leto observed the surroundings and smirked. "You have picked an auspicious place for us to meet, father. Am I then your high priest that I would come and offer sacrifices to atone for the people? Leto looked up at his father and mockingly continued.

"While you play God?"

Lucifer rebuffed his son's words of arrogance and replies, "Give report of thy stewardship."

"I have the returned father and as you have said. I am more than man or angel."

Lucifer smiled as he looked down upon his son from the Mercy Seat in the temple. "You are my son. I would expect nothing less. But... has my son been about his father's business? Has my child now come to present the third shard of the Godstone? Are you ready to fight the Host of heaven and yea Christ himself? Or would you still prefer to prattle amongst the people and exult in their adulation?"

Leto smiles and replies, "Patience is a virtue, father. You of all should know this. For you have on many occasions demonstrated that patience coupled with persistence will yield the pleasant fruit one desires. And as far as being your son..." Leto laughs as he shook his head. "Sheol has schooled me that I am not the first son. That others have borne the moniker of Son of Lucifer; other humans have you experimented on. All in an attempt to circumvent the will of El. Each of my discarded siblings' cries called to me in hell. Sheol showed me their memories. Do you even know their names? Their atrocities? Do you?"

Lucifer looked down from the mercy seat and spoke, "My ways with man are none of your concern. Only my way with you."

Leto looked at Lucifer in disgust and anger. "All have shared my blood, and all launched assaults against the People of El and you threw them away like trash. Refuse to be bleed dry for eternity for sins you provoked." Leto raised his voice at Lucifer. "They all had names, father, names that languish in Hell because of your manipulations!"

"You would do well to watch your tone, Leto," replies Lucifer.

"Names like Goliath." Leto inched closer to the Mercy Seat.

"That is enough. Where is my Godstone?" says Lucifer.

"Antiochus Epiphanes," replies Leto.

"I said that is enough," replies Lucifer.

"Hitler!" Leto cries.

Lucifer spread his wings and jumped down from the mercy seat and he grasped his sword and unsheathed it in light and fury. Leto then cried out loud.

"I am the third shard!"

Lucifer stopped his advance and peered into his sons' eyes and his face contorted, but he said nothing but gave off a rumbling growl.

Leto continues, "I have tasted the gem's power and have endowed myself with it. The shard and I are now one."

"Arghh!!!" Lucifer growled. He slapped Leto across the check and the man flew across the room into the door. Lucifer frowned and sheathed his sword and replies, "You have defied my command. You were to bring the shard to me that they may be joined. NOT to imbue yourself with its power."

Leto nodded, and he wiped the blood that now flowed from his nose, "I did defy you. As I will soon defy God. But I will not be deceived, nor will I be a tool to be used in the petty games between you and the Almighty. You will not discard me like you have the others you have created. Nor will you will take the shard from me. We will do this together. Or we will not do it at all."

Lucifer fumed and stepped towards Leto, towering over his son. His voice grew deep, and the interior of the room vibrated. "You do not know the spirit with which you speak to even defy me? ME? Know ye not that your life is but a vapor that appears and then vanishes away? MY blood runs through the veins that give you life. Blood I may rescind."

Leto stood to his feet and stepped towards his father and extended his wrists for Lucifer to handle.

"You are correct. Take my life then. But know I will not be a slave. You feign the import of self-rule. Until it is extended to those who would defy you. I know that your war against El is a sham. A waste of resources that has cost the universe and my people, in particular, the opportunity to truly advance and grow. But this will no longer be the case. I will fight with you. I will war with the Creator to supplant him. But only to assure that none of humanity will ever be the slave to either sin, God... or even thee. We will be free from this consumption that rages in our flesh. This restriction of mortality that El has placed on us. I will take Eternal Life from El's son and will help you supplant your father's throne. And when I am done..."

Leto looked squarely into his father's eyes and did not waver in his glance or tenor. "You, you will step aside from being mine."

Lucifer was taken aback. Unsure how momentarily to proceed. For in front of him stood his own creation. Gifted with the best genes of both men and angels. Privileged to live in the finest of locales and even augmented with artificial intelligence. And now Lucifer stood before his only child, who sought to be released from him. And for a moment, he understood a glimpse of what the Almighty experienced. To feel the heartbreak over his creation's running away. To desire no future part from him. And Lucifer, having felt little for anything other than his bond to Michael—for the first time in millennia felt angst, and sadness and rejection that pained him at the center of his core.

But the Prince of Darkness would not display weakness, would not show that he was touched and possessed love of any sort. Such would create vulnerability. He could never show such foolish sentiment. For love was for others. He had abandoned that source of love ages ago. He no longer had use for the emotion now. He smiled and replied.

"Very well then, my son. If you wish to leave me and my brethren, so be it. We will defeat the Godking, and I will take back Heaven where I will rule as God. You, will return to the realm of men and will rule over them. Together, we shall destroy the Triune God and when we are done...." Lucifer's eyes narrowed as he spoke to his son. "I pledge our paths will never ever cross again."

Leto nodded. "Agreed."

Lucifer then spoke to his son, "To seal our pact you will do me the courtesy of killing the two witnesses Enoch and Elijah, who stand outside the Temple Gates. Do this and I will know that you are true to your word."

Leto replies, "It will be my pleasure." Leto then turned to walk away and to exit his private audience with Satan.

Lucifer smiled as he watched with pride how powerful his son had become, smiled because he knew it was only a matter of time until he would take demonic possession of his carefully crafted human host. A house especially designed for him. And with Leto's body and power, Lucifer knew he could bring all of Creation to its knees.

The archangel smiled as his son left the room: smiled because after he was done with his progeny he would slay him.

* * *

Leto walked out of the rebuilt temple, and as he did, his armed guards surrounded him. He shooed them away so that he might assemble with the people and said. "I have risen from the dead. Do you truly think that mere weapons on earth can harm me now? If you must persist in this fawning over my safety, you will do so at a distance."

Several of the soldiers nodded and stood several feet back from the Chancellor. "We are just trying to do our job, Chancellor. We are trying to keep you away from harm. We are nearing the habitation of Enoch and Elijah. They have squatted on this area and declared it hallowed territory."

Leto shrunk back in irritation. "There is no more need for protection, sergeant. It is I who will, in all probability, be protecting you." Now step away from me."

The guard did as ordered and Leto stepped into a police barricaded area that had been cordoned off to prevent people from arbitrarily entering the compound. Leto approached the men as they sat on the floor. Leto observed a man also sitting next to them and spoke. "You are famous Henel James. Carrier of the words of Enoch and Elijah's prophets sent by God. Are you not?"

Henel James stood to his feet. "I am a simple journalist, sir. A man who has happened upon a story and been privileged to be at the right place at the right time."

Leto looked at him and eyed him up and down, and smiled. "You are an opportunist. Henel James record this. I want the world to see what I am about to do. Heaven already watches, and I will let this serve as an example."

Henel replies, "An example of what, Chancellor?"

Leto smiles, "That I am coming for them."

Henel replies, "*Them*, sir?"

Leto nodded, "Yes, all of them." He then looked at Enoch and Elijah, who both were sound asleep napping, and he spoke in the angelic tongue. "Elohim ark.ca ah thank chi"

Immediately, two angels appeared. One stood in front of the sleeping men and one stood to their rear. Nuriel, the guardian of Enoch, spoke to Leto. "How does the Abomination know our tongue?"

Henel immediately set his phone to live stream.

Leto looked at the angel, who was now visible to all, and replied. "I have communed with hell itself. I know the tongues of all humanity and, yes, the common tongue of Heaven, even the ancient tongue of the Arelim. Thus, in respect, I speak to you now. Move aside, for these two are human are mine. They are from MY house. They have not tasted death. I am here to remedy that. Move aside so that my hand may be swift. I have much more pressing things to do today than to destroy them and you. Go back to your home and do not set foot on my land again. Go and no harm will come to you. Defy me, and Limbus will have two more residents to add to the Mists."

Nuriel turned to his peer Baradiel and laughed, and when he did, Enoch and Elijah were roused from their sleep and stood to their feet. Elijah spoke for them and said, "Leto Alexander. What have we to do with thee?"

Leto replies, "You will no longer plague my people. You will cease and desist. You will bow down to me, and yea, though Lucifer himself would see you killed. I will spare you. IF you acknowledge me as God. Now if you are ready that at what time you hear the sound of the cornet, flute, and harp. Ready when the sackbut, psaltery, and dulcimer, play and you fall down and worship my image; well: but if you do not worship, I will burn you alive as you have done to others. And I will do this, this very hour and send you to abide into the realm of the dead; and who is that God that will deliver you out of my hands?"

Enoch leaned upon a cane, and replies, "We are not slow to answer you Anti-Christ. We know El can deliver us if he so will. But we will not be moved, nor will we bow to you... ever."

Leto smiles, "I had hoped you would say that."

He then disappeared in prismatic light and reappeared over the shoulders of Nuriel. He placed his hands over the head of the angel and snapped his neck. The Arelim slumped and Leto rode his body as the celestial fell over face first and slammed into the ground.

Enoch, Elijah and Baradiel were stunned. Baradiel cries out, "ARRGGGGGG!!!" and launched himself at the Beast. Leto released a sonic cone of force that projected from his mouth and the invisible beam sliced through the flesh and bone of Baradiel's neck and severed his head. It fell to the ground as his body collapsed, following suit.

Leto Alexander looked at the dead angelic corpse that lay before him and then locked his eyes at the two humans who had defied him and proceeded to slowly walk over to where the two prophets were.

Each man opened their mouths, and fire immediately erupted around the Beast. His clothes caught fire, and he was emblazoned in an orange flame. Enoch and Elijah watched as his flesh burned and peeled off of him. Yet as rapidly as it fell, it repaired itself almost instantly.

Leto was a flaming hulk of walking and blistering skin. Flames licked at the Beast's charring face and pustules burst into weeping bloody sores that revealed bone and sinew. And the monstrosity of Lucifer's making spoke.

"Fools, I have been embraced by the lick of hell herself. The likes of you cannot stop me."

Leto walked further towards them and when he got to Enoch, he took the man by the throat and was engulfed in flames. And when he reached for Enoch to touch him, Enoch screamed out in screeching pain, for the fire burned him, and he struggled to free himself from the grip of Leto's choke hold.

Fire spread from Leto to Enoch and the two were awash in flame. Enoch wrestled to remove Leto's hands from his neck. Striking downward on his wrists in an excruciating struggle to break his hold. Elijah then took his staff and swatted Leto on the back. He opened his mouth and breathed, and a wind blew upon both Enoch and Leto and the plumes of fire that lifted from their bodies were put out.

Leto held fast to the Enoch's throat and his devilish grin and wide eyes blossomed into euphoria when he pushed his thumbs deeper against into Enoch's windpipe and felt the organ crush under his hands. Enoch's eyes grew large, and he gave up the ghost. His body went limp as Leto took his hands from his adversary's neck and Enoch slumped to the ground.

Elijah swatted Leto again with his staff and pummeled him. Leto grabbed the oncoming strike and held his grip tight. He kicked the prophet square in the ribs and sent him flying several feet backwards.

Elijah coughed and held his hands over his chest for the ache that swelled within his breastbone. Leto had now walked towards him and glared at the old man.

"I should have killed you sooner. Nevertheless, I will remedy that error now."

Leto's hands simmered and exploded in flame. Elijah slid back and leaned his weight upon his staff to stand to his feet. But Leto moved quickly to him and kicked his staff from his hands and the old man fell back into the dirt of the street. Elijah looked up and the last thing he saw was the flaming hands of the Antichrist before his eyes were gouged out, and his own esophagus ripped from his throat.

Elijah fell over to his side, blood draining from his torn throat. His eye sockets charred black from Leto's hands.

Soldiers and the royal guard came over to their leader, and Leto was given a towel to wipe his hands.

Another soldier sought to move the bodies and Leto cries out, "Do not touch them! Let them rot for the world to see. Henel James, come here."

The report did as directed and cautiously walked towards the Anti-Christ. Eyeing the bodies of the two men he had come to call friends. Leto then spoke.

"Henel James, you will continue in your role as a reporter. But now you will do it for me. Show the world the bodies of these men lying here. Write about it for your paper and stream it to your audience. But in every platform you use, I want you to make sure you let the message to my enemies be clear: If you attack either myself or my people, there is neither man nor angel, nor corner of Earth or Heaven remote enough to protect you from the reach of my hand. Know that I will see my adversaries undone. Show the bodies of these celestials and the traitors of mankind who worked with them. Report on what you saw here today, Mr. James. And you had better make sure I like what I read. Or know I will be back to add your body to these four here."

Henel James swallowed hard as Leto Alexander walked away from him, fully healed from his burns and wiping the blood of Enoch and Elijah from his hands.

* * *

Leto gathered into his offices, built into the newly reconstructed temple. He had built antechambers next to the holy of holies, allowing him access to the innermost room from any of his offices. Settled into a conference room, he stood at a window looking out over the city of Jerusalem and spoke with his back to his chief of staff and the head of his security council.

"Gentlemen, there are several issues that have risen to the top of my agenda. The first is the progress of the excavation. Is my prize found?"

General Hagan, Chief of Staff, answered, "It is done, sir." He motioned to an attendant who brought a sealed box into the room. It was a lead box and men in hazmat suits placed it on the table and backed away. The rest of the Chancellor's assembled cabinet did so as well. One of the hazmat men held a Geiger counter in his hand and spoke. "Chancellor, you should be warned that it emits a radiation signature that we have not identified. It's pinging off the charts."

Leto turned around and looked at the box and replied. "There are things, young man, that defy explanation. This item is not one of those. It communicates in the language of energy. Primordial energy. The residual energy that created the big bang itself. Leto looked into the box and the Hazmat soldiers' Geiger counter ticked up its pinging to what was now a constant buzz. Leto smiled.

"Do not be afraid, gentlemen." Leto picked up the stone and looked at it. It was beautiful. A gem that fascinated the eyes of all in the room. A gem that glowed as if it one was looking into a refracted mirror. A gem that vibrated and seemed...to be singing.

General Hagan, the celestials can be killed. You have seen me kill two. WE can kill more. We can stop their incursion into our planet. But to do this, we will need the might of our planet's armed forces as never before. It is time, gentlemen. Time to execute my plan and attack these beings on their own soil. There is a tear that separates their world from ours. A place where the properties of this gem can be focused and give us a doorway into their world. Gentlemen, I have been to Hell. Now I will literally take you to heaven."

General Hagan replies, "We are with you, sir. My joint chiefs and I have been in threat assessment meetings for some time. We don't have the means to stop these attacks. Everyone agrees we need to strike back before there is not a planet left to defend. You have our support, sir. What is it you require?"

Leto then turned to his general and spoke, "Bring all nations to Meggido. Every army that can be mustered must be mustered. Every plane, every tank that can be spared, march the troops from China if need be but bring them to Israel, and let all know that we are going on the offensive. Leave back only those forces that might be necessary for planetary defense. Am I clear?"

General Hagan was taken aback by the scope of the request and replies, "But sir, to move so many men and equipment will take months, even years. Nothing has been done on this scale since perhaps World War two."

Leto then opened his mouth and when he did, his countenance changed and immediately unclean spirits like frogs came out of his mouth. All the men in the room jumped back startled as they watched the creature emerge from their leader's mouth and then it hopped unto the conference room table and stared at them. It hissed as a snake, then let out a high-pitched shriek as a woman's scream before it jump from the table and dematerialized through a closed window and disappeared outside.

"General, bring up the orbital feed of the Jezreel Valley now."

General Hagan nodded to an attaché in the room and a young man brought up a view screen that gave a live orbital screen shot of the area and spoke into a secured radio link phone. "I have a code auth for a live feed from satellite 32 niner from Mark 666. Copy."

Chatter came back on the other side and the young man replied.

"Yeah, bring up all visual assets in the area and feed into Chamber's conference room. Code: Tango, Zulu, Alpha, Omega, 6, 6, 6. over," He whispers into a com.

"Orders confirmed, transmissions incoming, feed is live. You are a go Mark666. Roger,"

"Roger that, comms."

The young man pressed a button, and the Valley of Jezreel came into view on several screens. From satellite above to drone footage that was streaming back live. Everyone in the room could see the green lush valley of Israel.

General Hagan inquired his commander, "Mr. Chancellor. Why Meggido?"

Leto replies, "While I was dead, I learned some things, general. Things were revealed as I communed with dead. The gem I own created a weakness between dimensions, a tear, so to speak. A tear centered here in the Valley of Jezreel. Here is where we will assault the aliens, general. Here will be the stage to our vanguard."

Leto touched the stone and suddenly on the television screen a twisting white dust devil appeared of energy. Suddenly a prismatic funnel of light opened, and it was like a tornado a mile wide and stretched miles into the sky. Satellite imagery showed it breached the Earth's atmosphere, curved near the moon and sprinted into the depths of deep space.

Leto then spoke into the air to Ashtaroth, who had stood invisibly by his side and said. "Take me and the general to Megiddo now."

Ashtaroth bowed and Lathum the Grigori opened a portal. Leto had General Hagan fitted with a communications device. "Come with me, general. The rest of you stay behind and assist with the execution of my plan."

General Hagan then followed Ashtaroth Leto and Lathum into the Portal, and it closed behind him. The two men stood but a footballs field's length from the great funnel and even from the distance they could feel its winds buffet them.

Leto then spoke and when he did, his voice was as the voice many speaking as one. Speaking to the Ashtaroth and Lathum that followed him. "Go forth unto the kings of the earth and of the entire world, gather them to the battle of that great day of God Almighty."

Both angels disappeared, and two hours later, squadrons of men appeared within the portal Leto had created and he ordered them to come to him, and they did.

Gather my forces to me, general. And do not voice excuse to me again when I give a command. Is that understood?"

The general nodded, "Crystal sir."

* * *

Gabriel saw the massive and newly opened portal that swerved over the gateway at the Cliffs of Argoth and turned to Michael, "We cannot stop the Beast's entry into the realm immortal. He possesses a God-stone."

"No," Michael says. "We cannot, but we can prepare for his coming. He has sown to the wind and will now reap the whirlwind. Let him fulfill the lust he so desires. His pride leads him to destruction. His haughtiness towards his fall. Give them a causeway to gather. And we will see who gathers that think they can unseat the Godhead."

And in that moment Gabriel the sixth angel poured out his vial upon the great river Euphrates; and the water thereof was dried up so that the way of the kings of the east might be prepared.

And when this was done. Mankind was once more incensed at the environmental ravages upon his planet. For all of humanity thought Heaven willfully attacked men in retaliation for making a bridge to combat their attackers. The land of Sino emptied at the command of Leto. Provoked to defend their people and instigated by Lucifer and the Horde to make war with the God of Heaven.

Michael, the prince of heaven, watched as one million men from China alone marched over waterways that were now dry. Watched as they traveled to Megiddo, Israel. Listened as the Beast spoke blasphemous words that incited mankind to destroy the source of their perceived lot: the source of their unrepentant misery. A misery inflicted planet wide by alleged aliens. The Elohim.

And the call to mankind was such that both young men and old offered themselves to go to war and fight the celestial menace that they believed threatened their survival and way of life.

Michael grimaced at the pending battle he knew was coming, knowing Heaven must once again war on her shores. Grimaced as we watched from heaven as Leto gathered humanity from all nations and tongues to assault his home.

Watched as the Anti-Christ gathered them together into a place called in the Hebrew tongue... Armageddon.

* * *

Megiddo Staging Area: Israel

Leto Alexander was in a tent surveying troop movements when General Hagan came to give a status update to his commander.

"Chancellor, we have reports that thousands of Jews have fled Israel and are continuously congregating in Petra, Jordan. It's been established that they believe in the old god Yahweh, some are even considered Messianic Jews. Drone reconnaissance shows none of them bear the Mark ID radio signature that you made mandatory by the populace. Jordan seems to bear some culpability in harboring them. Israel refuses to stop the exodus and also refuses to cooperate with his Chancellors government. What are your orders, sir?"

Leto looked down at the maps assembled by his men. Grigoric scouts under Lathum's directions had drawn up maps of Heaven. Maps that showed vulnerabilities when they attack.

Leto frowned and continued his studies. "Lathum, are you sure of these markers?"

The Grigori replies, "Aye, young dragon. To the extent that the knowledge is older than much of mankind and that Heaven has not changed. They can be relied upon."

General Hagan, although could hear Leto he could not see the spirit that he knew occupied the room with them. Some angels revealed themselves, but most chose to remain hidden from human eyes. As it was believed that such gave them an advantage to know the true nature of things. Nor did Lucifer command open manifestation at all times.

"Chancellor the Jews, sir?" General Hagan asked again.

Leto looked up from his maps of Heaven and spoke to his defense minister.

"General, give me the airwaves of the planet. Broadcast my image to all devices now. Wait... Is Henel James the journalist in the camp?"

"Yes sir. Per your orders."

"Bring him and the embedded news crew to document Earth's defense."

General Hagan spoke into his walkie talkie some orders to others. In minutes, several soldiers escorted Henel James and several other reporters and news crews into the Chancellor's tent.

"Are we live general?"

"We are green sir," replies General Hagan.

Henel James and several of his news companions studied the Chancellor as he slowly covered up the maps of Heaven.

Leto Alexander turned to the news camera crew and spoke. "It has come to my attention that many of the Jews of Israel have refused the MarkID. While I might forgive a sleight like this due to long-standing religious and superstitious traditions. What I will not forgive is subversion or, more importantly, treason.

How can I see to the need of our planet, no... our very species, when there are traitors among us who would collaborate with the enemy? With what right should a nation that tolerates such subterfuge exist? Why would we tolerate a people that would seek to rob humanity of its chance to be rid of those who have puppeteered the strings of our destiny?"

All in the command tent remained quiet as all discerned that the Chancellor was speaking rhetorically.

Leto looked at Henel James in the eye. The Beast's eyes sharpened, and his tone became angry. "You have not seen what I have seen, Mr. James. No one who is watching this broadcast has. And if I have my way. You or your family never will. I want you to think of the loved ones you have lost. Those dear family and friends who have gone before you into eternity. Now imagine—imagine each trapped in a dark and fiery place and consumed alive. Why? To placate a race of non-humans who have shackled us that we may serve as food to a creature that never dies. Tell me citizens of the Earth. To what allegiance do we owe such a nation? And all this from a being who, for millennia, we have worshiped in ignorance and built towering edifices? I tell you I will fight this god that I might free us to grasp the future of our potential. A potential no longer manipulated by these—these *aliens*.

Russia and China were wise in their programs to eliminate false ideas of God. Is it not clear where such erroneous beliefs have brought us as a people? The wars and divisions. The bloodshed and divisive politics. And look at what it has brought us once again to the doorsteps of war. Yet a war unlike those fought in prior centuries. In those skirmishes, we gathered ourselves against ourselves. No, this time it is clear who fights against humanity. Clear about who has betrayed their own species. The Jews! Even now, over a hundred thousand have been identified without the mark and have been discovered fleeing to Jordan. What should we make of such an action?

"Who are these human cretins that they would dare align themselves against all of mankind? Are they even human? Are they not suspect in their collusion to humanity's demise? They refuse proof of our destroyed cities, waters and the plagues that have ravished us from beyond, refused to let go of this ancient belief and continued to protect and harbor those who would see us destroyed. Did I not restore their temple to them? Did we not stop war in the Middle East after decades of conflict? And now, now they leave us no choice but to once again raise our hand in collective punishment against a brother. Why? Because they continue to be in league with a species that means to destroy us. Is it not a crime to align or partner with such a being? Is this not treason? A crime against humanity!? With such crimes against mankind, there can be but one solution: a final solution! And though I have moved at great lengths to pursue peace, it is with sadness I am forced to decree as Chancellor that these Jews must be destroyed! Once more, we must, in distaste, strike out at this evil. For we are the leaders of our nations and dutifully burdened with the responsibility to our species. I understand that we have made through the United Nations the state of Israel. A nation we have made to our own hurt; but fear not, for what we have made: we can unmake.

Therefore, arise and we shall destroy her and all her ilk. Let the name and treachery of Israel be wiped forever from the annals of mankind!"

Leto's words were broadcast worldwide. His voice streamed through all levels of the Internet. And was teleprompted over the boards of the most obscure user groups, to the most illicit corners of the dark web. Television waves beamed the image of the beast into every home and the deep bass of his charismatic voice resounded across radio channels on all bands.

Nowhere did his voice not echo; nor household unable to unsee or smother his message to the planet's populace. His demand was more than anti-Semitism, more than a call for genocide. His voice was broadcast as a siren's call throughout the Earth, appealing to each one's patriotic and righteous duty to all mankind, to him. A cryptic call to action: to choose whom one would serve.

And with the piping of the Anti-Christ's words, a chill settled throughout the world of men. An inner knowing that to move to destroy the Jewish homeland of Israel would move humankind further away from his position towards God. Nevertheless, men would not repent, for no man dared to speak against the Beast. And though some in silent mutterings wavered at their leaders' words, all moved to obey. For fear also ruled the Earth. For Leto had evidenced from his rising from the dead that he had triumphed over Death itself. He evidenced through his military might, and by his demonstration that beings of spirit walked among men, that he was true. For who was like unto the Beast? And who was able to make war with him? Thus, men held back all remaining truth in unrighteousness and all the nations of the world submitted themselves to the Beast. For the leader of mankind, backed by the power of Satan himself, demanded all to obey.

Thus, across the capitals of all nations, and through the governing branches and halls of international bodies, each nation galvanized itself to defend humanity against the perceived threat of Israel. Each mustered themselves for war. With a patriotism zealous for mankind, all nations and tongues spoke but one language across the length and breadth of the planet: that Israel must be destroyed. Each nation calling upon its citizens to brace for war. And with the commands of each nation's commander and chief; planes launched as birds of prey into the skies. Jet engines screamed to sprint past the sound barrier as their contrails pointed like arrows towards their destination: Armageddon.

Submarines lurked as a school of great white sharks on the hunt, each country's deadly submersibles cavitated towards coordinates unknown, prepared to unleash their deadly payloads of SLBM's. Aircraft battle groups were loosed over the seas as armed emissaries, ready to enforce the edict of the Beast. For alas, all nations gathered themselves to war. A planetary fulfilling of the book of Joel as the nations of men beat their plowshares into swords, and their pruning-hooks into spears. For across the entirety of the Earth, weapons of mass destruction were now aimed to annihilate one small nation that dared to defy the Beast and would not waver in its faith towards God.

Israel.

* * *

The squad car ride was a quiet one. Taken to the local jail, Elizabeth noted several soldiers outside a two Hummer's in the parking lot. The deputy pulled over next to the soldiers and both officers got out of the car and spoke to several of the armed men. Barbed wire fencing could be seen in the rear of the building and downcast people pressed up against the fencing, their fingers gripped the chain-linked fence, yelling at the soldiers. Some shook the fence in anger, others sat dejected, while more spoke with one another. Some sang hymns.

A deputy and an officer came over to the rear of the squad car and he opened the door. The deputy uncuffed her and when he did, the soldier took a black hood and covered her head. Another set of cuffs replaced those that had just been removed, and she felt shackles fasten themselves around her ankles

She was then taken by her arm and led by a man. "Alright, young lady, move it." She could feel others being shackled to her and heard the sounds of fences opening and people shoving, wanting to get out.

"I am American citizen!" one yelled. "You can't do this! We have rights!"

Elizabeth heard a gruff voice reply, "Tell it to the Chancellor." He laughs and Elizabeth could hear one of the deputies that arrested her speak out loud, "Jim, this ain't right man. Not right at all. Some of these are just kids man. Kids!"

"Where are you taking them?" A voice asked.

"Over to the high school. These kids want to play stupid. We'll teach them some manners. Time to grow up, boys and girls...time to frickin' grow up."

Elizabeth was directed into a vehicle, she could hear the engine start, and she sat next to several others. Some were crying.

"Shut up back there." Look, if you pledge allegiance, this will be over soon. And if not. Well, it will be over soon. So, look at the bright side. It will be over soon."

Several of the men laughed.

Elizabeth could see enough from the light penetrating the hood that she was in one of the Humvees. At least three other prisoners were tied to her, and several soldiers were in the vehicle as well.

She could smell the passing of gas and worse. And her captors could smell it too.

"Are you shitting me?"

"No." A soldier laughs. "He's shitting him!" Several of the men burst out in hilarious laughter.

"Just hurry up man, we ain't got all day." A voice said.

She thought about her foster mom and if she was OK. A wave of regret and remorse flooded her. She hadn't been the best kid in the world. Always arguing. Always pressing the limits. But Ms. Sanders kept on pressing her. Elizabeth just thought again that she hoped she was OK. After a drive of about ten minutes, the vehicle stopped. Elizabeth could hear doors open and slam shut and the door near her suddenly opened.

An arm grabbed her, and she was led, head covered and shackled, and shoved and pushed to keep moving forward. She tripped and almost immediately felt the pain of a shoe in her abdomen. She grimaced as her abs began to spasm while a gloved hand lifted her up to her feet and forcibly moved her forward.

Darkness was all she could see, but she felt the chains around her ankles and knew that someone else was tied to her. Knew by the tugging as she walked and constant wails that came from a female voice not far from her in the distance.

"Please!" the voice begs. "This must be some mistake. I mean, I'm not a Christian. I don't even know why I am up here. I believe in the Chancellor, I really do! Please don't do this... let me go, please. Someone you must listen to me! My mom and dad are wealthy...they will pay... just let me go!"

"Shut up!" Elizabeth heard a voice say and then the sound of a loud slap. Presumably from one of the soldiers on the face of the whimpering girl.

"Why don't you leave her alone?" A male voice cried out. "You see she's scared. Let her be."

Elizabeth turned her head as if doing so would somehow help her attenuate her hearing better.

"Well, look at this fellas, we've got a brave one here! What is she to you? Perhaps we should take her aside to have some fun with her later?"

Chuckles and laughter were all that Elizabeth heard until she heard the gunshot.

Screams echoed in Elizabeth's ears, and she immediately jumped at the sound of gunfire. She could feel the tensing of her chains and knew someone she was connected to had been executed. Her heart raced and a male voice spoke.

"Anyone else wants to say something out of turn? You just got your boyfriend over there killed. Now say something again and I'll save you for last."

Elizabeth heard no reply. But could hear crying and whimpering and pleas for mercy.

"Get that fella up and put the body in the truck."

She heard the sound of the unshackling of chains, presumably that of her now dead fellow prisoner, then movement and the sounds of something heavy being dragged away over the top of the ground.

"Every one of ya's stand up straight. Here we go!"

Suddenly, the hood over her face was gone and sunlight beamed into her eyes. She winked as her vision slowly adjusted and she noted that off in the distance, a crowd of onlookers watched from football stands.

A student general assembly. They are going to kill us in front of a student general assembly on the freaking football field.

Elizabeth could see that both Principle McFarland and Counselor Davis stood near the stands looking at her and those who she was shackled to. She looked to her left and right. Twelve students, she counted. A mix of boys and girls. She kept quiet, but finding herself getting more and more angry that the government would do something like this to her.

One of the soldiers then lifted his hands and took a megaphone and began to speak. "These perpetrators have been found accused of collaborating with the enemy and have failed to publicly demonstrate fealty to our government or take the Pledge of Humanity. Because the Chancellor is benevolent and because human capital is so precious in these difficult times. Each of the accused will be asked to affirm their allegiance and denounce any other faith allegiance.

So, you students understand the serious of this crime please tell us; what is the punishment for a crime against humanity?"

"DEATH!" the students from the bleachers shouted.

"Do we support a god other than humanity?" says the soldier.

"NOOO!!" The cry came back from the students. Boos and hisses emanated from the crowd. Principal McFarland could be seen trying to calm the crowd down.

The soldier continued. "Now, these students think they are better than you! Think they know better than the collective will of our leaders. Some here have even been accused of being CHRISTIANS!"

More hisses and boos came from the raucous crowd of students and their feet stomped on the bleachers and made them shake.

The soldier raised his hand to quiet the crowd and turned to another soldier with a gun. "Go make ready."

Several soldiers stepped back ten paces, lined up opposite of those on the firing line and made ready their weapons.

"Now," says the head soldier. "I'm only going to ask you this once. Answer correctly and you can go home today and be with your family. Answer incorrectly and well, I have a truck waiting over there to dump your body later. Understood?"

Several of the teens nodded their heads, some spoke aloud, "Yes, sir."

One peed his pants as he looked at the soldiers and students in the bleachers burst out in laughter, pointing fingers and mocking him.

The soldier started with him first. "You look like you're scared, son. But there is no reason to be afraid. The father loves you and doesn't want to see any of his children's potential wasted. So let me ask you. Do you love the father?"

The young man replies wimpishly, "Yes... yes, I do. I'm so grateful for what he's done to protect us from these attackers."

The soldier smiles, "That's a good answer boy, now are you a Christian or have faith in a god other than Chancellor Leto?"

"No, sir, not at all. I'm agnostic. I'm not sure if there even is a god."

"Really?" says the soldier. "What an intriguing answer."

The soldier backed away and spoke to the firing squad.

"Kill him."

The men fired their weapons and several rounds of bullets sunk deep into the pelted body of the young man, who immediately fell over limp and collapsed to the ground.

Elizabeth jumped and several students next to her screamed.

Some students from the stands gasped, others screamed, but most cheered. Excited at the display. Overall, Elizabeth watched as the student section roared and hooted and hollered. "Get that traitor out of here!" yelled one."

A soldier then grabbed the body and dragged it away for all to see.

Ms. Davis raised her fingers to the kids to silence them.

The head soldier then went over to another prisoner. It was Audrey of the Jefferson sisters. She immediately recited the Human pledge of allegiance when he came to her. I am not a Christian; I love his imminence. He is the only god I serve."

The soldier smiled, so willing to please, he said. "He rubbed his hand over her cheek and gently brushed his thumb over her lips. Would you do anything to serve him?" He grinned at her.

She returned his smile reluctantly. "I would do anything... yes."

He smiled at her. "See!" he said, looking at the rest of the students on the platform. "Now that wasn't hard, now was it?" He then turned and whispered to her, "I will have you show your faithfulness personally later."

He then turned to his sergeant and commands, "She's good... let her go."

The soldier came and unshackled her and escorted her to the student assembly when the guard spoke. "No...take her to my truck. She can wait for me there. I will process her later."

The soldier smiles, "I'm sure there will be a lot of paperwork to fill out."

He shoved her forward and escorted her to a Humvee off in the distance. Another soldier took his place, and the chief interrogator stepped up to a young man. And looked him up and down and pulled out a Bible and spoke to him. "So, it seems you had a lot to say earlier. So, let me ask you a question.... is this Bible yours? Now, if it's a mistake because I understand these things happen. We can let you go home. You should know I didn't appreciate your attitude earlier. And I'm sure you would like to go home. So, let's make this simple. Are you a Christian boy? Do you believe in a god other than Leto?"

The young man looked at the jeering student section that still hooted and hollered. Some apparently hoping to see another execution so they can stream it to Instagram or one of the other social media sites. Sites that were quickly filling with public executions. Public displays of violence that had gone viral as much as creative baby reveals.

My name is Jonah, and yes, the Bible belongs to me. It belongs to me, and I believe Christ died on the cross for our sins. I wish I had believed before the rapture, but I believe now. And your Leto Alexander is nothing more than the Anti-Christ that has been foretold. I will not call him a god. I will not pledge my allegiance to this charlatan of a leader... this beast."

The sergeant took out his Glock from his holster and pointed it at the boy's head and pulled the trigger.

Elizabeth stood next to him and brain matter splattered over her and a fine mist of blood. The soldier then nodded his head, holstered his weapon, and spoke to her.

"His answer was the wrong answer. Now, young lady, I still have another eight prisoners here to ask. And I'd like to make sure I get home for dinner timely. He reached out, and another guard gave him a clipboard. and he quickly ruffled through the pages and read the contents.

"It would seem, young woman, you have also not pledged allegiance to the Chancellor. It's not clear from the record here if you profess to be a Christian. So, I will ask you plainly. Are you a Christian?"

Elizabeth had studied for a year the major religions of the world. She had come to the intellectual conclusion that Christianity was historically supported to give one reason to believe in its claims. But she had never confessed Christ as Lord. Had never surrendered her will over to him. She never thought more seriously about it until Carol disappeared before her eyes. The teenager remembered every word her friend had said. Even her attempts at leading her to Christ.

So, this is it, she said to herself. *This is how I am going to die?*

Vantress, the angel assigned to watch over this human female, observed helplessly as he stood behind his charge, attempting to impart courage and faith to her. Waiting for Eridu's dreams to finally be realized and the bloodline of Elizabeth Foley to finally be snuffed out.

The guardian angel turned his face towards the student section to see his nemesis sitting in the center of the throng, watching, grinning and with suggestive words inciting the teens to call for Elizabeth Foley's death.

* * *

"Well, Ms. Foley, what will it be? Behind curtain number one we have you going home; maybe you can even finish out your senior year! In fact, you're a looker. I might even take a personal liking to you myself. He grinned as he looked at his truck with one of the twins waiting for him. "But there is still another choice waiting for you. Because behind curtain number two, well..." He paused and felt the contour of his nine-millimeter. "Let's just say I still have more bullets in my Glock. He unholstered the weapon and pressed the muzzle into her forehead between her eyes, turning it slightly for effect.

Elizabeth's heart raced. She remembered her friend, remembered the words spoken to her about Christ and eternity. She noted the trail of blood of those who had already been shot. Thoughts upon dashing thought swirled through her mind. She didn't want to die. But she knew what she saw. Knew what she heard from her friend's testimony. And finally, when it was all said and done, she decided.

"I believe in Jesus Christ as my Lord and Savior. Leto Alexander can go to Hell."

"Such a precious waste," says the soldier.

He smiled, then pulled the trigger.

Elizabeth heard a bang and then felt a stinging sharpness, then nothing. For a moment, echoes were all that she could hear.

She closed her eyes and allowed herself to slip into the blackness of unconsciousness.

Off in the distance, she saw a brilliant light that overtook her and could see a city set upon a hill. No, a mountain. Its colors were that of the rainbow and she turned to her left and right and there were angels who traveled next to her as if she was in an honor guard.

She got closer and saw to land and saw that many people were smiling. She could hear clapping.

Sounds of cheers and congratulations overwhelmed her.

She set her feet down and she looked into a crowd and standing before her was her brother, her father, her mother and Carol, her best friend.

She put her hand over her mouth, her eyes grew wide, and she began to cry. Immediately, her mother came to her and fell upon her, wrapping her body as a blanket, holding her baby.

"I've waited so long to see you again. I have told so many about my brave girl."

Elizabeth looked into her mother's soft eyes: eyes that welled up with tears. "Mom?" she began to cry.

Her mother nodded. "It's OK baby. It's OK. I'm here. I'm here."

She cradled her daughter in her arms and stroked her hair. Elizabeth looked up from her mother's breast and her checks were awash with tears and her face was red.

"Wait, how is it you are here? I saw you take your own life."

"No baby, you saw what you were meant to see. You were a child, and you created memories to help you cope. I didn't kill myself, baby, I would never leave you. Nothing could ever keep me from you, my darling. No, sweetie, I was murdered. My body positioned and made to look like it was a suicide. My murderer still runs free. But he will have his a day. The Lord will make sure of it. For there is nothing covered that shall not be revealed; neither hid, that shall not be known. This is the promise of the Lord."

Elizabeth was weeping into her arms, anguish and grief washing away from her as the exit from a cleansing shower.

"Mirabelle, I have someone I'd like you to meet."

Elizabeth recognized her father's voice and remembered the childhood nickname he had given her, and she turned to him.

The similitude of a man stood next to her father, and he stood at least two feet taller. He glowed and his clothes were the whitest white she had ever seen. He stood with a staff in his hand.

Her father then spoke and said, "Beloved daughter, I would like to introduce you to Gabriel. One of the chief angels in service to God."

"It is good to meet you. I have taken great interest in your study of religion."

Elizabeth looked at the angel in awe. "The pleasure is mine, sir. But why me?"

Gabriel smiles at her and replies, "The father has taken great interest in you. He has worked for many seasons to see that you would one day join your family. And while you have gone through much. You should know he is looking forward to seeing you. But I am afraid we must cut short our conversation for now."

Gabriel looked at another angel and replies, "Robe her and find her a steed, we must soon be at arms." The arch angel then placed his hand on Elizabeth's father's shoulders and continued. "Benjamin, you must quickly teach her what she needs to know." Elizabeth then looked at her parents, then at Gabriel curiously and replies, "What is happening?"

Gabriel looked at her solemnly and replies, "We are going to war, Elizabeth Foley. War where you will, in all probability, confront the spirits that have attacked your family for generations."

Chapter Twelve: When Evil Returns Home

Leto was sleeping when he was awakened by the sound of wind and a bright light that illuminated his room. He rubbed his eyes and smiled at the young man, who lay naked in his bed, still asleep.

Leto put his hands to his face and strained to see through the light and after a few moments, his eyes adjusted to the view and the angelic figure of Lucifer slowly came into view.

Leto looked at him, concerned. "What's wrong? What has happened? Is it time?"

Lucifer stood stoic and replies, "Dismiss your lover. What I say to you is not for his ears."

Leto immediately shoved the young man and pushed him out of his bed. His sexual companion fell to the floor, startled and wide awake. His side smarting from where Leto had kicked him out of his bed. He looked at the Chancellor in confusion and Leto returned his gaze and said. "Get out."

The young soldier grabbed his clothes, hurriedly put on his pants and scurried out of the tent of the most powerful man in the world.

Lucifer watched his son proceed to dress himself and spoke. "You had the bodies of Enoch and Elijah left publicly for view near the Temple walls. I have word that they have just risen from the dead and have left for heaven. There were some who saw this. This image was shown on your airwaves while you enjoyed the pleasures of the flesh,"

Lucifer turned his palm upward and a conical projection filled the tent. Leto watched as Lucifer showed that passerbys had live streamed Enoch and Elijah as the two men stood fully healed and wearing white robes. "We go to the God of the all the Earth." They say. "We have completed our mission. Leto is not God. Repent, and perhaps the True God of Mercy will spare. Our king is coming soon, and every eye shall see him! For every knee shall bow and every tongue shall confess that Yeshua is the true king, and this will be done to the glory of God the Father."

And a great voice from heaven was heard saying unto the men," Come up hither." And they ascended up to heaven in a cloud; and their enemies beheld them. And the two men floated away and disappeared in a small burst of prismatic light.

When they disappeared a great earthquake, shook the city of Jerusalem and the tenth part of the city fell, and the dead from the earthquake were seven thousand. The remnant were affrighted and gave glory to the God of heaven.

Lucifer dimmed the light of his body and spoke. "Even now there is a rumbling in some corners that you are NOT a god. Some who no longer hold to the belief that my son is who he says he is. We must strike now. Strike while the faith of mankind still seethes against the Creator, and while all those who know the tongue of prayer are being hunted to extinction. It is time, my child, to capture the throne of the universe."

Lucifer's light dimmed and he spoke with a musical hiss as he transformed into a giant, beautiful serpent with golden wings. "I have brought the Ophanim, I have the two shards, and you are the third. Meet me outside, your legions are ready. Let us go and meet he that Creation calls God."

Leto proceeded to finish dressing and left his camp as he and the Devil exited to go towards the launch pad Leto had prepared.

Leto and his angelic father came to the staging area. Leto found General Hagan and spoke. "Bring my father to the cage with the creature." General Hagan did as commanded and brought to the head of the army a caged ophanim that Lucifer had captured via Charon many ages ago. He ordered the men to stand back, and each wisely did so.

Lucifer then approached the cage and unlocked the electrified prison where it was contained and opened the pores of its flesh and sung to the creature. It calmed and the army of men that stood also were affected. Lucifer's beauty and singing made all quiet, and Lucifer touched the beast's wheels and cradled them in his hands. He spoke angel speak, and another wheel materialized and then slowly another; wheels within wheels emerged from it, and Lucifer continued speaking and mounted the circular creature and sat atop its head for all to see.

Lucifer then took the Ophanim and with it spoke the Elomic command given him. The creature gyrated upon its hearing. Twirling, twisting and turning until the realms of space and time folded back to reveal a tunnel to the third heaven.

The realm of God.

The sky opened and suddenly a curtain of prismatic light poured down as rainfall overshadowing Leto's forces, as the sounds of tornadic winds enveloped the ears of all.

Some men immediately soiled themselves, while others steeled themselves, knowing they would be the first to travel to another dimension.

The dimension of angels.

Lucifer pulled the reins of the beast. This wheel within wheels and the Ophanim lifted into the air and pulled the battalions of mankind with it. Thousands upon thousands were now gripped in the creature's grasp and it towed the army of the anti-Christ through space and time into the realm of the living God.

Men and women armed with weapons synthesized from the mineral of the God-stone saw themselves flung past stars and planets. Weaving between gravity wells and roundabout asteroids. The wake of the Ophanim's flight made both men and their machines creak and groan. Equipment strained against the contortional forces that attempted to pull them into the vacuum of space, as the Ophanim crisscrossed quantum realities. But the ladder was sure and when the creature that hailed from Heaven saw the light of its home. It swerved as was its nature and lightning and sparks from its gyrating rings moved and continuously spiraled until the eyes of the creature locked onto the Mountain of God.

The Ophanim landed at the cliffs of Argoth. Lucifer stood atop the head of the creature. It's mind under his command. The ladder then burst from the basement of space and breached the airspace of Heaven, then curved as the powerful funnel slammed into the ground. A cloud of rainbow colors trailed it, depositing Lucifer's Adamic army in tow.

Prismatic twinkling lights sparkled for a moment over the forces of the transported men and then dissipated. Lucifer and his armies now stood upon the shores of heaven. The Devil once more in lead of a mass of beings' intent to destroy the God of Creation. He eyed the magnificent landscape of his exile, smiled and spoke aloud.

"I am home."

* * *

Michael had been preparing for this day.

From the moment he and his men had found the trackers, Leto had placed on their clothing. From the intelligence gathered by the Grigori of the host. It was clear that Leto would never be content to stay earth-side: clear that Lucifer was planning an invasion. Michael had ordered the armories and forges of Heaven to be working at full capacity. Each day brought new humans across the borders of heaven. Each one needing quarters, equipment and training for what was coming.

So, Michael had commanded the house of Issi and Draco to train the Humans and schooled them in the art of Elomic warfare and showed them how to harness the power El had deposited in their resurrected bodies. Gabriel and his house made sure each was given a robe. A garment made from the finest of Elysian silks. The fabric was alive, and it provided freedom of movement and contoured to the body of the wearer and could instantly armor to take on the properties of Elomic steel.

Michael knew this day would come. Knew that he would one day either battle his brother or his brother's latest creation.

Michael set up the Ophanims to control the skies, "Let nothing be allowed to soar above us unchecked." Eladrin bowed to Michael in acknowledgment and made sure he and his people would see that nothing passed them.

Michael assigned the Seraphim would serve as the heavy cavalry. For their flames and sonic booms caused disruption in the last war and the Horde was not prepared to fight them. However, Michael knew this time the element of surprise would be lost to the Host and that Lucifer would compensate for such a thing.

Michael wished Argoth could join them. Argoth would not be present for this fight but still present with the Lord: still unfurled being read off by Yeshua. The Lord could not be disturbed while he read the secrets of the Almighty. So, the Elohim would protect the Mountain of God. And Michael staged each house to defend a possible breach into the throne room.

Soon, Michael would know the power behind Leto Alexander. If what he sensed when he was near him was truly real. That he possessed the ability to drain Elomic life. Michael could feel it when he was last near the Beast; could feel the Withering take his life as he sat and attempted to reason with the creature. A sensation he had not felt since he entered hell. He knew then he could not let the Abomination know how his presence affected him. Could not feign weakness. There was no clear gambit against such a power but distance. And Michael calculated how he might keep the creature at bay while the rest of Heaven's army did their work. Only the Triune God could stop this, and He had yet to intervene or give a word of abeyance. Until Yeshua stepped into the fray or gave a counter command, Michael would prepare for what was coming. He would prepare for war.

Michael still wondered why Lucifer would create such a being, knowing the cost could be his own life. But it mattered not. It was clear to Michael that Lucifer was making a desperate gambit. A gambit to once more see God and perhaps, if such were possible, to take the life of God itself.

Michael walked over and inspected his troops; he helped humans properly lace their amour and gave last-minute instructions on how to use their weapons. Each apostle and the heads of the twelve tribes of Israel were given command over their respective houses and divided into infantry units.

Michael ceaselessly worked collaboratively with David, Moses, and others to shore up any perceived defenses of the city. Their human eyes revealed the prejudices Elohim had about combat. King David pointed out where he would attack if he led the attack against the city and his rationale as to why if he possessed the knowledge that the Horde and the sum of Human understanding had. Michael agreed and gave them their assignments.

The Chief of Angels looked out from a tower towards the cliffs of Argoth. A large prismatic funnel had descended, and he watched as unredeemed men assembled to create a beachhead on Heaven's shores.

Michael looked at his assembled brethren and spoke. "We have fared through much, you and I." Michael walked down the line of his comrades as they stood for inspection, and he smiles as he looked at Gabriel and Metatron and spoke aloud for all of them to hear. "From Limbus to Ashe, we have prevailed." He then moved down the line and looked at Talus and Jerahmeel. Placing his hands on the shoulders of Talus. "From the depth of Tartarus to the bowels of Hell we have prevailed...yea some have even survived Hell itself." Michael then stood at the head of the group and looked them over. Azaziel, Talus, Gabriel, Metatron, Jerahmeel all looked at him and nodded in pride at the angel who once did not desire to lead them. Michael continues, "I know that this will not be our last battle. I know this because I trust in the Lord my God. My faith is in the God of Creation." Michael took one more look from his window at the giant ladders that by the second delivered mankind's troops. The Prince of Angels then turned to his fellows and said, "I know that this will not be our last battle. But for all those that would defy God and for our brother Lucifer...let us go. Let us go, and make it his."

Michael then unsheathed his sword and the rest of the Lumazi followed him out to battle.

* * *

Lucifer dismounted from atop the Ophanim, and the creature still under the hypnotic trance of the Deceiver moved and gyrated as its actions kept the gate open to the Earth. More and more troops and the Horde stepped through.

Lucifer eyed his people and as each stepped through the ladder; each member of the angelic Horde realized that they stood on the ground of Heaven. Exiles who had been thrown from the presence of God were outcasts no longer. Adrift to be vagabonds on the planet earth. Gypsies without a home. And the Horde was ecstatic, for Lucifer had kept his word to them. Ashtaroth, Lathum, and many more had come at the command of Lucifer. And once more they lighted their eyes on the beauty of Heaven...they determined they would never again leave and would destroy him who had set them adrift.

And Lucifer stood atop a high cliff and his voice bellowed that his followers could hear. "HAVE I NOT KEPT MY WORD?! DO YOU NOT STAND ON OUR HALLOWED GROUNDS? FOLLOW ME AND I WILL SEE YOU RESTORED! Lucifer elevated himself into the sky and Heaven's energies rejuvenated him. Its skies and smells were yet the same, and he looked over the army of men and angels he had assembled and spoke. "My brethren, being here is NOT enough. We have been here before: been here and repulsed. We will not let this happen again. Alight and destroy all that stands in your way. Let our vengeance and acrimony be visited upon all that would side with

Yeshua, with all those whom El Pneuma has brought in to replace us. We shall visit El himself, and we will NOT BE MOVED!"

A roar went up among the horde, and Lucifer then flew down and set himself to stand next to Leto and spoke to his son. "Come here, my boy, let us embrace."

Leto spoke cautiously. "What trick is this? You know what I can do if you touch me." His body became inflamed as his power reached out to protect him. Lucifer smiles, "My boy, you were ever an instrument in my hand. Did you seriously think I would not have the means to control my own creation?" Lucifer then walked towards Leto, who stretched forth his hands to blast him in flames, but Lucifer disappeared as he walked into Leto's body.

Men and human onlookers drew back, afraid. For the leader of the free world stood for a moment, paralyzed. Leto then lifted his hands and turned them to the left and to the right to inspect them. He took in great breaths and exhaled. Ashtaroth came over to his person and spoke. "My king, is this body to your liking?"

Leto smiled and the voice of Lucifer came from the man's mouth. "It is acceptable. He has an amazing power to siphon celestial life. All except mine." The possessed body of Leto Alexander let out a maniacal laugh, and his eyes were ablaze like Lucifer's eyes. "The boy fights me, but it is of no use. His will is my own, his body is now mine. Even if I were to leave, my suggestive essence would be such that I need but vocalize my desire and he would carry it out. It is a shame that Marduk did not have faith. I think he would have enjoyed seeing this moment. But alas, let us start our war. General Hagan!" Lucifer yells.

The general saluted.

"Make ready the tactical nukes. Get ready to fire on my command."

"Yes sir. Targets, sir?"

The possessed body of Leto smiles, "Fire at will, commander, and make sure our enemies feel it."

Lucifer looked before him, and he saw that Heaven's forces had assembled themselves to meet them. And he knew that in that moment.

The war to end all wars had now begun.

* * *

Michael looked over at his peers. Angels, humans, seraphim and ophanim, all stood together as one body. He was proud of them and knew they all would give their lives for El. God was the source of life and Michael would see Creation itself fall before he would ever allow Lucifer to touch Yeshua ever again. He looked over the terrain. The humans had brought machines with them, and he watched as they brought their tanks and artillery and stationed their launch pads.

He was not concerned about men's weapons of war. But he admitted he did not know how they would react to the environment of Heaven. He saw his brother from a distance. Knew that he had taken over the body of the man-king Leto Alexander. A puppet now in the hands of the puppeteer. He would be careful to watch him, he thought.

Lucifer's forces were stationed at the Cliffs of Argoth.

If we can keep them with their backs to the cliff.

Michael thought of how he could use the topography against his enemy. But that would only affect those enemies who were earthbound. It was the sky that was the problem.

All of heaven could fly. But it was important to keep the battle two dimensional. Their numbers were increasing by the minute. With both reinforcements coming from Earth, from the ladder that would not close. It was the captured ophanim that was the problem. And Michael ruminated on how he might close the portal. He came down from his defensive position near the mountain of God, and Michael walked over to Metatron and spoke. "Metatron, echo my words, please."

Metatron opened the pores of his flesh and Michael touched him.

"You all know who I am. Those of you who are human have not seen the bloodshed that existed before your kind. I am sorry that you must witness it today. We have not asked for war. But war seeks us despite our cares. It comes to us provoked by an enemy to creation itself. Lucifer. He is the adversary and comes to steal, kill, and to destroy. And let me be clear: he will kill us if he can. Will destroy us if he is able. But fear not...for he will not. FOR THE LORD OUR GOD IS WITH US!"

Roars and cheers came from the host of heaven, and many in the crowd nodded.

Michael continues, "We will end this war that began so long ago on these very shores. We will rid ourselves of this hate, rid ourselves of future battles, and let it be known that on this day we will beat back the Horde to within an inch of their immortal lives! We will deny them stars and sky and bring them low to crawl on the face of the Earth! Know that we...Seraphim, Ophanim, Elohim, and Human: that *we* will advance the Kingdom of Heaven until all her enemies ARE UNDER GOD'S FEET!"

The galaxy of celestial beings erupted in cheers and the wave of onlookers and those who heard through portals who, despite their desire to defend heaven, stayed at their posts guarding the will of El in creation. All angels everywhere roared in exuberance. The assembled army raised their weapons high into the air and lifted the name of El in shouts of triumph.

And when the saints and the host of heaven raised their fists in defiance. The sounds of explosions were heard in the sky and lights flashed above them. An explosion was heard and super-heated wind raced in all directions, and Michael and all those assembled saw a wall of concussive force racing towards them.

"Brace yourselves!" yells Metatron.

Immediately the Seraphim ignited and lifted themselves up as a multitude of towering firenados. The Ophanim also rose into the air to serve as shield. Both species twirled and blocked the incoming wave. And all of redeemed men looked up and over them; to see living flames of fire that burned off the energy that poured down upon them. Thousands of wheels within wheels created an electrical curtain that was draped over them in a prismatic cloak of protection.

"Eladrin!" says Michael. "Take out those batteries!"

Immediately the giant king of the Ophanim disappeared and he and several of his subjects flew towards the enemy camp and, like giant discs, sliced into the equipment that the humans had brought with them, cleaving their launch platforms in half. Explosions ripped through their camps and fires erupted as men ran for their lives. Eladrin and his wheeled soldiers then returned to the camp of Michael, and he spoke to his friend. "Great King, we need to close the ladder. Did you learn anything when you flew by the portal? Why does your brother continue to keep it open?"

Eladrin replies, "There is something controlling him. Some magic prevents him from singing the song of our people. I cannot retrieve him."

Michael scowled, as he thought of the strategy of his brother and he screamed out, "Everyone find cover and get down now!"

* * *

Lucifer smiled as he saw Eladrin destroy his human artillery and knew that men's machines would never be able to injure the people of Heaven. But it would weaken the barriers between realms. Now merged with Leto, Lucifer possessed all three shards of the Godstone, and he reached forth to sing with the Ophanim; the song that kept its portal open. And when he did, the ceiling of Heaven cracked. Lucifer revealed that he now possessed the power of the Ophanim. Power contained in the flesh of his Nephilim son. Power that he now controlled.

"You are good, Michael, but let us see who is truly the better general of war."

The former head of house Draco then opened the pours of his flesh and projected a sound across the ceiling of heaven such that all could hear. And his voice echoed over canyon walls and across the suburbs of heaven, and even as far away as the Seraphim city of Ashe.

And Lucifer lifted his hands into the air and moved them as if he was tearing something apart. The air then ripped in two all over the land of Heaven, and every eye could see that prismatic funnels opened across the lid of the skies. And the true army of the Horde came through as a great swarm to invade Heaven as explosions rang out wherever the funnels landed: celestial tornadoes that wreaked havoc, destroying buildings and angel alike.

From behind the curtain of superclusters, the Horde breached the skies of the Aerie. They teleported into the fiery plains of Aseir, and angels fell from the skies and trampled once more across the honey smelling Mirabel leaves of Elysium.

And wherever a portal opened, Heaven was invaded, and she erupted in battle. As the enemy's assault with the help of unredeemed man; saw Lucifer and his armies penetrate what all Elohim once thought inviolate.

The Kingdom of Heaven.

For with a God-stone, Lucifer with his anti-Christ had scaled the realm immortal and the shores of Heaven were now breached.

* * *

Elizabeth scrambled with her family to find cover. “Stick together! We fight as a unit!”

The young woman watched as her dad and mom fought with swords that seemingly were a part of their arms. Each redeemed had one. A long glowing sword each held in their hand. Like the fictional Jedi of Star Wars lore, she watched as the redeemed slashed and hacked at oncoming angelic attack that fell from the sky atop them. She looked to her left and Carol was by her side fending off an attacker. She was fully armored from head to toe. Her loins was girt about with truth, and her torso was covered with a breastplate of righteousness; Her feet were shod with shoes with wings ready to move at moment's notice in preparation of the gospel of peace and she held a shield with which she was able to quench all the fiery darts that the enemy launched at her. Her face was covered with a helmet of salvation, and the sword of the Spirit, which is the word of God, extended from her mouth and her hands.

Courage flooded the young woman, and she too saw her robe transform and instantly armor her body.

An evil angel fell from the sky screaming and she swatted the creature away. It rose to its feet and, with its wings unfurled, flew to skewer her. She opened her mouth, and a golden sword appeared. and she voiced one word and the sword shot from her mouth and sliced the creature in two. It fell before her feet, and she took her shield and bashed its head.

With the angel's blood on her shield, she looked to see her mom and father fighting side by side. Her brother had their back, and she looked left and right for her best friend.

“Carol!!” she cries. “Where are you? Carol!”

“I'm here.” Elizabeth looked up, and Carol was floating above her head. Her shield and sword drawn, and her eyes fixed off in the distance. Her robes were covered in wings like a dragonfly, and she pointed off in the distance.

“I think I see the angel who was standing by your bed when God came for me! El Pneuma says that we should go to him!”

“Wait, you can actually hear God talk to you?”

“Of course,” she replies. “Michael plans our way, but the Lord directs our steps.”

Elizabeth looked at her parents, who were clearly engaged, but could hear the two girls yelled. Elizabeth's father yelled out. "Go with Carol. Vantress has been assigned to our house!" Carol stay by her side!" Elizabeth's mom yells in turn.

"Yes mam," she replies. "Lizzy, let's go!"

Elizabeth jumped and immediately her robes unfurled to allow her to take flight. And she and her best friend headed to the side of the angel who had worked to lead her to Christ...Vantress.

Chapter Thirteen: To Spew the Undead

Lucifer watched the course of battle from atop a protrusion off the Cliffs of Argoth. Eying the ebb and flow of his forces as they attacked the whole of heaven.

"Ashtaroth, are the totality of our forces Heavenside?" Lucifer asks.

The adjutant bowed, "All are accounted for my liege."

Good, Lucifer then flew towards the Ophanim, and it sung the song as its rings oscillated and twirled. Lucifer then reached to grab one of the rotating arcs and he pulled against it. The creature wailed, screaming in agony.

Ashtaroth looked at his lord, concerned, "Master?"

General Hagan was also near the staging area with men who had dug-in positions to create a command tent. He, too, looked at his commander. But where Ashtaroth and angelic kind saw Lucifer who possessed a human body. General Hagan saw only Leto grasp the creature by the throat and snap its neck.

Immediately, the giant funnel that had brought the armies through space and time collapsed and disappeared.

"Chancellor, what are you doing? We now cannot go back!" says Hagan.

Lucifer smiles with the mouth of Leto and replies, "There is no going back, general. I am the door, the way, and path. All those that leave must go through me!"

General Hagan stepped back in fear. "You are not Leto."

Lucifer looked at the human and remarked, "We are legion, but Leto is here."

The general replies, "This was never about humanity, was it? This has been a ruse."

"Take your men, general, and head to the front of the lines. Do it now. I will send support soon. Go upon my command or I will have you thrown over the cliffs here. Do you understand me?"

The general nodded.

"Good, you might have some chance of survival with my angelic brethren and mayhap even cause distraction to them. You will certainly not survive a fall into the Maelstrom. Now go. Show me the fighting prowess of humanity. I seek...entertainment."

The general scowled and passed along his orders to his men. Many looked at the battles of the Seraphim that burned men alive, and the Ophanim which picked soldiers up and threw them over the cliffs.

Redeemed men with floating swords that fought with an intelligence not of their own, swords that cut through their ranks. He gawked as he saw all types of angels, with all manner of weapons and locomotion fighting each other. And wherever an unredeemed human fought, he was cut down. Only the Horde stood a chance and even they were fought back by the might of Heaven's forces.

The general had always thought if heaven existed, it would be beautiful beyond words. And it was. But it was also the sight of the most bloody battle has eyes had ever seen. And he knew Lucifer was sending him out to die.

He huffed in resignation that death would greet him soon, then turned to his men and yelled. "Saddle up, boys! You don't have to die and worry about the trip to heaven. You're already here!"

General Hagan made his rifle ready, and he and twenty soldiers exited the tent that was set up and towards the angelic Horde perimeter. They walked past giant principalities that protected the area and squatted. General Hagan used his hands to communicate to his fire teams the direction they wanted, and each launched themselves into a three-second burst run. Rifles in hand, they sprinted into the explosions and morass of angelic and human bodies that were before them. Soon they were out of sight and melded into the chaos that was the millions now in melee combat.

Lucifer watched the men as they made their way towards the fiercest part of the battle. Watched as they disappeared from view. Most of the unredeemed forces had been positioned just outside the city's prime gate. Converging to prevent access towards the mountain of God.

Lucifer whispered under his breath. "So very typical, brother. But I know you will not predict *this*."

Lucifer then spoke in the ancient tongue of his people. But also the tongue of the Ophanim. And his words left his mouth and floated above him. They lifted as children's balloons into the air, going higher and higher until each coalesced into one another. Forming black and thunderous clouds that the skies of heaven grew dark. The living clouds that sung in Heaven's skies parted and scattered like a flock of birds disturbed; for winds that rivaled the Maelstrom suddenly jetted in a circular motion. And angels and redeemed men fought as a vacuum like force suddenly pulled all into the sky. And all battles stopped. All hostilities for a moment came to a standstill. As darkness overtook the land of Heaven and a shadow covered the burbs of Heaven and beyond.

Lucifer continued his chant, and his dark words continued their assent as the gaping void that filled the sky grew ever larger. His arms moving in gyrating motions as if he pulled something towards him.

Michael, from a distance, watched the phenomena from his defensive position.

"In El's name." He whispers aloud. But Michael merely spoke aloud the words of them all, as the mouths of millions gawked and dropped as one.

Lucifer had opened a dimensional rift, and the great mountain of hell was now falling from the sky.

* * *

The devastation to the planet Earth was unfathomable. Men that survived it likened the phenomena as if the Alps had torn from the earth itself and lifted into the sky. The mountain Hell had been embedded in the earth for thousands of men's years. Buried and covered and recovered by volcanic ash and the industry of men for millennia. For some, Hell was a myth but on a day where the armies of men fought in what most of the planet thought was a war in space: earthquakes around the world took place at once as a great mountain of earth emerged from underneath what men called the Middle East. From Iraq to Israel, and from Egypt to the Alps; the rocky roots of the object tore asunder cities. Life on the planet would be forever changed as men cried out in despair for the carnage was as something mortal men had ever seen. The mountain lifted into the sky as it floated into orbit. Boulders and giant stones fell from it to strike the populace below. As the thing lifted into a black hurricane-like void that hovered above the planet.

Into darkness it went, moving from one reality to another. Crossing dimensions for a second time. A living mountain of fire and brimstone that was returning to its place of birth: heaven.

Upward it ascended from the lower depths of the Earth and downward it plummeted from the sky of Heaven. A great fiery meteor, the likes Heaven had never known. And a third of heaven was positioned directly under it as the great mountain fell. Its plumes trailing the sky and its harrowing wail filled dimensions and angels knew that Hell was once again returning to the realm immortal.

The Ophanim moved as one, sensing the threat. Moving as a people and straining to outrun light itself. And Eladrin and his people surrounded the mountain. Prismatic funnels twisted and twirled about the volcano that was Hell. Like flies, the Ophanim flew. Buzzing and zig zagging to create a rainbow-colored net that covered the entire mountain.

Gabriel and his people flocked and lifted many on griffin back. All the people that could fly flew, and those that could run, ran to escape the dark shadow that quickly descended upon them. The redeemed teleported and set themselves back towards the mountain of God and reestablished their ranks, while all watched the living volcano be moved by the Ophanim so it would not destroy the city. And the movers of solar systems edged the great rock to the outskirts of heaven and released it and it crashed into the ground.

Fire erupted and a wall of heated smoke and ash raced like a moving waterfall towards the city.

"Brace yourselves!" yells Michael.

The whoosh sound of a thousand funnel clouds screamed past the denizens of heaven as the shock wave of the mountains fall made many to tumble over and or grab objects to hold on to. Glass panes blew out from the city's towers and, and steeples fell crashing to the ground. While some buildings were spared; those near the crash site were obliterated, and the Michael looked in dismay that even the golden streets of translucent gold had fissured. Pyroclastic debris fell from the sky: bombing all and destroying buildings. Ash fell over the faces of all. And both Horde and Host alike looked in the distance to see something that no one had ever seen before. The great mountain moved towards them, pulling itself on towering tentacles of lava and brimstone that dragged it across the earth. The mountain opened its stygian mouth, and fire and moving rows of teeth could be seen and embedded in the gums were emaciated screaming angels and humans who were as tartar beneath its gums.

Lucifer looked upon the devastation of Hell's return to the realm immortal. Like a boiling cauldron of bitterness, he spoke into Heaven.

"Destroy it all, Sheol! Feast upon all that your eyes see and destroy it all!"

Ashtaroth looked at his master with concern and spoke, "My Lord, forgive thy servant, but the beast will devour our own people as well as the Host. We will be left with no one to fight!"

Lucifer smiled and lifted his hands towards the mountain as if to present it for inspection. "No...we have endless soldiers to do my will. For everyone that she devours becomes my slave to control. Behold!"

The Dark Prince raised his hands, and the beast created cave-like openings about her craggy sides. And immediately came a flood of millions upon millions of daemons, emaciated angels and human undead. Waves of the spiritual undead flowed out of what seemed like a never-ending tap. As a dam that had been breached, the carrion of hell raced from her pores. Maggots that set all they touched aflame. Each creature wailed in blood-curdling screams as it crossed the field of battle. Like regurgitated food did the souls of all entrapped spew out of the mountain. The ghosts of men, and shades of angels crawling, running, leaping and flying to accost the living.

To possess and consume alive all that breathed.

Lucifer laughs and cries out in murderous glee, "I am coming, Yeshua! For you rose and vacated the whole of Paradise. Behold how I have stalked thee and have now emptied Hades at thy very door! Your angels cannot stop me...your redeemed men cannot stop me! Dread the return of your exiled son and know that I am coming!"

Ashtaroth feared his lord as he stood trembling and watched his master.

Lucifer lifted himself and landed atop of the mountain peak of God's vengeance. A fiery recompense he now sought to return to the father.

Lucifer's angelic form radiated through the physical body of Leto and all of Heaven heard him pronounce with finality; the famous mantra which he expected to bring to reality.

"I WILL BE GOD!"

Hell roared her starving presence into the sky, and Lucifer rode upon her back to destroy them all.

* * *

Vantress watched Elizabeth die.

Her head flung back as the bullet pierced her skull. Her body slumped to the ground as a pool of blood collected at her corpse.

He had seen humans die before. In battles with the Horde, human soldiers were often fodder for the enemy. He had seen the prophets of old sacrifice their lives to advance the cause of El. But never had he been assigned to one human. Never responsible to see to one's spiritual awakening to turn from the lies to the truth. His assignment gave him a great appreciation for guardian angels whose task was to protect and keep their humans safe. To help them move towards the light.

His was the duty of a soldier. To seek out, infiltrate, and destroy the enemy's capacity to wage war.

And war was a cold affair.

Vantress had always maintained a level of rational detachment from the death of brethren he had fought with. The war had taught him that any one of them could be returned to the dust of the Kiln or to the mists at any time. Therefore, never did he concern himself with the humans who were caught in the middle of his race's angelic conflict. Never bothered to truly feel the pain that the humans suffered until Michael had reassigned him.

And now, the first human ever to be given over to his charge was dead.

Eridu shouted at his rival from a distance. "Goodbye Vantress. The master musters all to the assault of Heaven. Enjoy the bitterness of defeat and know that soon Heaven itself will fall under our might."

A ladder then materialized to sweep him away, and the angel was gone.

Vantress looked down in despondence. For Eridu, his nemesis had won. He had eliminated the house of Foley. The line that was responsible for modern man's access to the word of God.

But Vantress had heard her confession, and it was clear. She was now a child of God, a servant of Yeshua. She had confessed Yeshua as Lord prior to her murder. Vantress put comfort that in time he and she might see one another again if his tour of duty permitted. Nevertheless, his heart ached for the personal pain he witnessed. Her struggles with depression, the contempt from her peers, the taking away of her family only to be placed in the house of a stranger. To yearn for the touch both emotionally and physically and be betrayed by someone who merely feigned to care for the sake of one's selfish gratification. And worse, the exploitation of emotional suffering that originates with one's peer group.

The breaking of her physical body would now release her spirit to ascend into the presence of the Lord.

His charge was dead. His duty was now done. He could give his full attention to what he understood and knew best: the disruption of the enemy and, particularly, the dissolution of Eridu.

He turned his face back towards the bleachers to see if his enemy was still present. But Eridu had indeed vanished; his trail of light still twinkling in disappearing embers.

He sighed but believed that there would come a time that El would allow recompense to be made. Now, however, was the time to return home, give report and seek reassignment. And to see if the boast of Eridu had substance.

He lifted his face skyward and spoke the Elomic words to ascend home. Sparkles of light glittered around his frame and the sudden funnel cloud of the Ophanim draped around him. The wakes of the Ophanim took him from the planet Earth and carried him through space past the canopy of the second Heaven into the third.

Heaven approached fast and even from a distance of a trillion miles, It was clear that she was engulfed in war. Great explosions rippled as he descended, rocking him. The Ophanim moved to bring its trajectory away from the cliffs of Argoth, but Vantress could see that a Horde camp had taken position in an attempt to ambush any incoming angels that were not of the Horde.

He could not land there.

The trail of the ladder that had brought Eridu to Heaven was still fresh. Not fully dissipated yet. He turned to fall near the place of his rival. To continue his fight in heaven.

In the seconds that flashed before him, he made the decision to escape the funnel with which he was safely within, and broke the prismatic barrier. The funnel dissipated into rainbow glass-like shards and Vantress plunged into the airspace of heaven, tumbling, unable to control his descent.

He smashed into a grassy knoll, and the ground erupted around him upon impact. Both Horde and Human ground warriors drew back, unsure of what new enemy might now accost them. Smoke and steam lifted from the crater that Vantress momentarily couched, and he rose to his feet, his body now bloody and sore. He surveyed his surroundings and noted that redeemed human warriors were on one side and an angelic group of the Horde on the other. His eyes recognized in the distance the Prince of Darkness atop the great living mountain of Hell. While undead human and Elohim came forth from openings in the mountain's sides. A rushing river of teeth and wings: a flood of undead celestial life that poured down upon them as puss from a slit abscess. A legion that, in moments, would overrun their position. And his enemy, Eridu, smiled in the distance at him. Nodding as if he understood.

Vantress felt his swords pummel and grip.

He shook himself and unsheathed his sword.

He was now in the familiar territory of combat. The recognizable terrain of an enemy that sought to destroy all that he loved. Here he could unleash his pent-up fury. Here he could hurl his disdain for evil with every swing of his blade. Here he might avenge his friend Olen, and strike on behalf of the family of Elizabeth Foley.

He smiled and turned to his human companions behind him and spoke.

"I see the dead come to assault the living. I am not inclined to join their ranks this day! Fight! Fight for your lives!"

Vantress then launched himself forward towards the Horde lines, and to smite his adversary Eridu.

He cut through minions and human redeemed fought along his side. With armor and shield, they battled. The clank of shields hitting shields permeated the air. But the stench of death and decay is what many would remember this day. The slippery mud of heaven soiled with the blood of angels and men in combat.

The undead were coming. Teeming masses of maggots and daemons that longed to possess the bodies of the living. A torrent that could not be stopped. Vantress looked off in the distance and saw that the legendary Mists were also in battle. The fog of war that lived underneath the mountain of heaven. The sky above them was as stretched glass and he saw what looked like a kaleidoscope of other realms. Each fighting, each destroying the ground of Heaven as they knew it. But he could not concern himself with what was beyond him. Only that which was before. He pressed forward, hacking and slashing; punching until at last he was face to face on the battlefield once more with his rival, Eridu.

"You have a relentless need to die El lover." Eridu says.

Both angels were short of breath and huffing as the battle carried on around them.

"No, Eridu, I have a relentless need to see you dead."

The angel charged at Eridu, who unleashed his Urumi. Eridu twirled the flexing sword and the clangs of its blade against Vantress's shield twanged into the air. Eridu kept his distance to make maximum effect of the weapons killing range. But Vantress had seen this style of combat now and was ready for his adversary.

Eridu kept his body low, protecting his vital organs, and he elongated his body only enough to strike and retract. To attack him successfully, Vantress would have to close the distance and allow himself to be struck.

He noted as the two observed each other, probing for weaknesses in their stances and attack styles. That Eridu had no weakness...save one. The style similar to all martial arts assumed the adversary would not risk being struck. Vantress released this notion, knowing that to break their standoff, he must offer his flesh.

He tucked his shield in towards his breast, and he stretched forth his sword arm as bait.

Eridu's urumi deflected the blade as expected. He knew what would happen now. He would lose his arm. But he could use his shield to land a crushing blow to his head.

Vantress lunged a second time, exposing his sword arm for dismemberment.

Eridu swung his urumi and as expected, the blade sheared Vantress's arm at the elbow, and it fell to the ground. Spiting the pain, Vantress pressed, closing the distance and unleashed a crushing blow with his shield to the head of his enemy.

Eridu staggered back but not before flicking his blade that would decapitate Vantress where he stood. Vantress held his arm and also wobbled losing his footing and was momentarily defenseless.

The Urumi blade of Eridu stretched forth to smite its foe. To reach with an elongated snap and coil around Vantress's neck with its fatal bite.

But Eridu would be denied, for instead a sword intercepted its bite.

The blazing white sword of Elizabeth Foley.

Her eyes were white, and she wore a white robe that all the saints wore. A robe conformed to her body and with the living armor that augmented her already now resurrected strength.

She pulled her sword towards her and the whip of Eridu came flying from the angel's hand and the shank of the thong of the weapon wrapped itself around her blade. She then flicked her sword, and the angelic weapon sliced in two.

A second sword then emerged from her other arm, and she spoke to the surprised and now weaponless angel.

"I know you." Her eyes searched the angel's features, and the word of knowledge filled her mind as the Holy Spirit activated her capacity to understand, and she spoke in familiarity.

"You are Eridu."

Eridu smiled as he looked at the girl who stood over the injured Vantress. Memories of her family's spiritual assault were accessed, and she could see into the past all that the angel had done. Her eyes were fire, and she soured in her voice. "You realize that on this day I am going to have to kill you twice."

Eridu wiped the blood from his eyes that dripped from the injury he'd earlier sustained from Vantress and smiles, "You are exhibiting hubris, young woman. But I will entertain this youthful notion of yours. How will this come to pass?"

"I'm going to kill you now. Then you will join the undead, and I will have to kill you a second time."

Eridu chuckles, "Come child, I do not need a whip to kill you. I've already murdered you once. I will enjoy it even more now."

Elizabeth jumped at Eridu and Eridu stepped back, and he took a short sword from his side and deflected the maiden's blows. To his left he parried and to his right she lunged. Each punching and blocking in hand-to-hand combat. A flurry of sword slashes and fists.

Each countering the other and Eridu smiling. "You are strong girl. But you are not adept in the ways of a thousand years of battle."

He swung at her face and the tip of his blade drew blood from her cheek. He then moved back as the young girl staggered.

He stopped to observe his handiwork.

"I like the look, child. Scars become you, they match the ones I provoked you to make on your wrists over the years. Yes, I do like the look." He smiles and Elizabeth did not reply save by wiping the blood from her cheek. Determined even the more, she gritted her teeth and pressed her attack. Advancing as the army of undead advanced towards them both.

Pressing forward she twirled her swords in acrobatic flare each twirling in slicing motions that caught the angel off guard, and she stalked him reciting the word of God aloud so that he could hear, "Blessed be the Lord my strength, which teacheth my hands to war, and my fingers to fight."

She swung high and then slashed low. Eridu moved but to evade but Elizabeth's movements were planned: anticipating him to expose his chest, and upon seeing her opening; she front kicked the angel, sending him reeling. Like a stuntman pulled back by a cable; so too did Eridu fly backwards from the unexpected power of her kick.

She followed and released into the air her sword which whirled through the air.

Eridu fell back from the power of her kick and before he could react the flung sword of Elizabeth found its mark, broke this protective armor and pierced his chest.

Elizabeth moved towards him, sword raised, as Eridu held the blade in agony.

She grasped the blade as well and thrust it deeper into his chest until the angel expired. The breath of life lifted from his lips as a small vapor.

Vantress was amazed to see the maiden's attack watched while other humans walled themselves in a defensive position to defend him. Each fighting back the few remaining members of the Horde that remained for them to fight.

He watched as his nemesis of a thousand years was felled by the same woman he had come to guard. His eyes were wide, but only for a second, as the undead were moments away.

"All of you!" He screamed. "Link hands quickly! And touch me."

All did as commanded, and Vantress yelled into the air.

"Se-la shing tau chi!"

Immediately, a ribbon of the seven prime colors descended and the roar of a ladder was over the group as they huddled together, then were lifted into the skies.

The undead scurried under them as they lifted off and a wave washed all around them. And as prophesied by Elizabeth Foley, Eridu's body was overtaken by the flotsam of the undead that overran it, and the maggots of Hell animated his corpse as he too became a mindless zombie to be controlled by Hell. Some undead leaped into the air to capture the living. Several breached through the funnel only to slice as it sheared them and their corpses fell into the base to the ground, screaming as the group lifted higher and out of harm's way.

"What is happening?" says one.

"We are living," says another.

The ladder curved towards the capital near the palace and Vantress prayed he did not position the beam to cause harm to any of the populace. The ladder touched down in the fountain of Poseidon and dissipated, and the group fell with a 'thunk' to the ground and knocked the wind out of many.

Elizabeth breathed heavily, still recovering from her battle with Eridu, and looked at the angel who had just rescued them and spoke to Vantress. "Thank you," she says.

She hugged him and held his cheeks in her hands. "I know who you are. Thank you Vantress."

He looked at the human to whom he had been assigned and a tear welled up in his eye. Vantress smiled and allowed himself a moment to savor a brief victory as he returned her warm embrace.

* * *

Michael heard Lucifer's challenge. For all of heaven knew Lucifer's ambitions. His display to kill, steal, and destroy was evident for all to see. If Lucifer had his way, there would be no Heaven...no earth. He would destroy it all to achieve his goals. Creation itself sacrificed at the altar of his lust. Michael had prepared for this possibility. That Heaven could be overrun by the enemies of the Horde. He had calculated what it would take to ever repel such an enemy as the undead he had witnessed in hell.

There was no force in Heaven save God Himself that could stop the mountains march. For what in the arsenal of angels could repel that which could consume angels alive? The maggots of Hell poured out of the creature, undead carrion that could siphon celestial life. Larva of brimstone and fire that multiplied even as they overran all that stood in their path.

Hell was an unstoppable celestial force of nature. Created to contain the murderous rage and lust of angels. She could not be stopped. Nor detoured.

Prayer and communion with God had taught Michael much. But there was no weapon that could be mustered against Hell that could halt her. Her very existence was the rebuke of God on the ambitions of Satan and his angels. Only Charon ever possessed the power to tame the creature, and he was nowhere to be seen. And now Lucifer rode atop the beast as a rider would his stallion. Michael knew that only one thing, save God himself, could combat the wave of the undead and now Hell itself that sought to overrun them all.

"We need to slow Lucifer down," says Michael.

Gabriel, who stood by his side, replies, "How? He mounts the monster itself!"

Michael frowned and nodded in acknowledgment, "I know...take me to see Janus."

Gabriel looked at his leader. "To Limbus? Are you sure?"

"We have little time...we must hurry."

Gabriel nodded and took Michael's arm and the two vanished to the basement of Heaven and materialized deep within the bowels of Heaven's deep.

Michael was never one to arbitrarily query the Lord God. There were some things that kings kept to themselves. The secret of Limbus and the why of its existence was one that El did not share. But Michael knew what Janus protected...the corridors of choices that lead to other dimensions and realities. The Realm of Limbo.

A place only El traversed.

Michael and Gabriel materialized at the swirling gates of Limbus and the two-faced Grigori met them. Janus stood in front of the mammoth opening, his sword drawn. The angel with two faces floated above them both. Slightly larger in build, he was quiet, and neither of his faces turned towards them. The eyes of the guard seemingly focused on events beyond sight.

Dust and debris fell from the ceiling and tremors could be felt and rocked the basement floor.

Michael looked to Janus and spoke, "Hail, guard of Limbus. I come seeking your aid."

The black face of Janus with white eyes turned to Michael and spoke. "I know what your petition is, Chief Prince." Immediately, the white face with black eyes turned to them. "I have seen the choice you make, and if this is done, Heaven will end as you know it, and only El can undo it."

Michael was somber and seriously considered what he was about to unleash. "I see no other choice, Janus."

Both faces of Janus laughs and then sighs, "You stand at the gateway to the realm of choices, Chief Prince. There are always choices."

Michael replies, "And do the Mists approve of the choices opted by Lucifer?"

Janus looked into the great mirror that stood before him. The entrance to the gateway to Limbus, and fog swirled within it, showing places, people and events in rapid succession.

Janus replies, "The Adversary has unleashed the creature Hell upon this land and released the captives therein...the Mists do not approve."

"Then with the power vested in me, I bid the Mists come," says Michael.

Janus nodded, then turned his head. One face looked at Michael and Gabriel and the other at the gate of Limbus. Janus went to the gate and reached up and turned a circular handle clockwise as if he was turning a great seal, the whole circular gate then moved, and a hissing sound of escaping gas could be heard as if pressure was released from a valve. Fog seeped along the floor and then coalesced in front of Michael into a form that mimicked him and spoke. "You have called us from the twenty-seven gates of existence. We would know why?"

"You have seen what transpires above?"

"We have seen the entirety of all outcomes, Chief Prince. Yea, even your death. We have seen the destruction of heaven itself. A destruction that will surely come if we intervene. But your people will live. But you...you may not."

Gabriel stood back, remembering his bout with the Mists before, and spoke to his brother. "Michael, is this wise?"

"Michael stood his ground and spoke. "Above us, the Usurper moves to undo Creation. To destroy all celestial life. I stand as a standard against this. I command in the name of El that you fight for us."

The smoky form then replies, "Know that it will be done. We have seen that the line of the multiverse ends here with this choice. That the crimson thread of God's injured heel leads all dimensions to this place, and this time: THIS...now."

The smoky doppelgänger looked up as if seeing beyond sight and said.

"Yeshua still reads, but when the God-king has ceased his commentary on the Book of Life...when the God-king journals the last name. Only Yeshua will choose which reality will be saved and which ones shall cease to exist. For all realities, save one...will end. Are you prepared, Chief Prince, for the possible dissolution of your reality?"

Michael's face hardened as he understood that, as the federal head, he was the leader of his race. But this decision would not just impact him, but all of Creation as he understood it. He paused to consider as Gabriel looked on quietly and Michael answered.

"You would not ask me this if I had not the power...the choice to bring the act about. I have spoken, let the thing be done. For if I must but sacrifice my own life to see El's purposes fulfilled and our reality itself to prevent the schemes of madness, then my life is given, and I will even lay creation down to serve El."

The coalescent figure disappeared into nothing, and one word could be heard as he vanished.

"So be it."

Both of Janus's faces turned to the angels and spoke. "Go, for Creation itself now hangs in the balance...a choice has been made, and what has been done cannot be undone."

The cavern of Heaven's basement then began to creak and shake, and both angels moved to keep balance as cracks and tremors and the groans of collapsing beams began to fissure and collapse around them.

"Go!" says Janus.

"But what of you?" Michael replies. "Come with us."

The faces of Janus smiled, and he walked into the glass mirror-like gate and disappeared.

Michael turned to Gabriel and spoke, "Hurry!" as the ceiling began to cave in and the ground beneath them gave way.

Gabriel grabbed Michael, and they vanished as boulders and ancient ornate columns fell smashing behind them. Gabriel sprinted with Michael on his back and the two escaped to the underside of the palace. and as they exited, the entry to Limbus came crashing down behind them, barring entry to go back.

Both angels scurried back to their command observation post. Michael watched as redeemed men fought side by side with Seraphim and Ophanim to beat back the unleashed regurgitated forces of the Mountain. Even the Horde fought by the side of the Host, for none were want to be consumed and or overwhelmed by the undead that made no distinction between friend or foe. But it was clear that the undead overwhelmed them all. Maggots consumed angels alike and for each one that was infested: friend became foe and then turned on those who had previously fought by their side. On the battle went as wave after wave of the undead merely crawled over one another to consume all life.

In the distance, Michael saw great emaciated principalities that smashed their way towards them. Principalities he recognized from millennia ago. Ares, Saturn. Pluto, Odin, so many consumed.... so many fallen. All now marched as shadows of their former selves. Controlled by the consciousness of Hell...and Hell controlled by Lucifer.

Michael thought to himself about the promise of the Mists to intervene and he looked over the landscape to see where his help might come.

If you are going to do something...do it quickly. He thought to himself.

It was then that the ground opened up from beneath them all. Great yawning fissures cracked and splintered the ground as smoky apparitions climbed out and ran towards the undead. Spirits came up from under the feet of Michael and from all that watched. Great legions of mist like angels rose from the earth as wave after colossal wave of the spirits streamed from the basement of Heaven and slammed into the incoming wave of the dead. Angels that in other dimensions and in other times fought, but whose purpose was now to fight alongside those in this realm.

And fight they did, and like a storm surge the spirits of angels beat upon the wave of the undead.

Smoke and shield, fire, and lighting erupted across the plains of heaven. A scene that surpassed even the civil war of angelic kind. For in this battle, all of celestial life was now at war.

David fought with his mighty men by his side, while he and all the redeemed blasted the undead back and fought furiously against both the walking angelic corpses and the carrion that emptied from Hell's stomach. But the King of Israel was an expert in war and, seeing that their position would soon be overrun, knew that unless El himself intervened, the numbers were such that they could not hold the tide of both Hell's carrion and the undead back.

David then found a girl who was nearby and spoke to her. "You, child...come here!"

The young woman pointed at herself. David nodded and motioned her to come near.

She did so, and he looked at her and asks, "Have you prayed to God today?"

She thought to herself for a moment and then replies, "No."

David shook his head. "We have been remiss, sing with me."

David then lifted his voice in praise to his God and sung as loud as his voice would allow. And the young woman looked at him in confusion and said, "Are you mad? Shouldn't we be fighting?!"

David stopped briefly for a moment to answer and said, "We *are* fighting. For this battle was never ours but the Lords. He, but waits for us to exhaust what we know to do, that His strength made be shown in our weakness...now sing!"

David and the young woman then sung a song and when they did, many of the surrounding saints heard them and withdrew their swords from fighting and lifted up their mouths instead to praise. For if it was purposed by God for them to die on the shores of Heaven, they would sing his name even in this.

And the saints of the most high God then lifted each one his voice and David led them into a song of warfare praise. And when the Seraphim saw that neither fire nor sword repelled the undead, and when Ophanim saw that to teleport the Undead away did not suffice. They too joined in chorus with the rest of the redeemed who sang, and the words were on this wise.

"Rescue us from our enemies, O LORD,
for we hide ourselves in you.
for you are our God;
and may your good Spirit
lead us on level ground.
For your name's sake, O LORD, preserve our lives;
in your righteousness, bring us out of trouble.

In your unfailing love, silence our enemies;
destroy all our foes,
for we are your servants."

And when they did, the undead paused for a moment in their screaming sprint to overrun them, and in their march to consume them alive. Paused to hear what had only been heard previously in life. Praise and worship.

Praise that stilled the enemy.

The song was such that the living clouds of Heaven took notice. And the song of the saints traveled even into the throne room and entered the ears of the Virtues. Instinctively, the creatures turned from the throne so that they might be let out to join the singing. And as a master lets out his dog to his yard, so too did El release the Virtues to leave the throne room.

The Virtues seeped under the sealed palace door and they with the clouds of heaven settled over the people of heaven and coated each with a fine mist and perfumed them.

And when David saw that the air itself was moved to their cause, he was attuned to the spirit that lived within the clouds and spoke to them this word.

"Defend this thy home! Let everything that hath breath praise the Lord. And they that do not: remove the breath thereof!"

And when the clouds of Heaven heard the words of David. The cumulus of Heaven did as commanded and dispersed from the Host of heaven and pillowed as an incoming iridescent storm across the plains. The virtues also rose to form a giant wall cloud of rain. And creatures that had previously pillowed white and sparkled with the colors of the rainbow now darkened and became black, their shadows blocking out any light that emanated from the mountain of God. And Lucifer's forces slowly became overshadowed by the invading and towering billows.

And each unredeemed man looked up and knew not how they would fight against the climate of the realm of Heaven.

The Virtues then lifted from the Host and screamed as they launched in tornado like strands and descended upon both unredeemed men and the Horde. The whole of heaven watched as the clouds then solidified and fell like giant mountainous stones upon the teeming masses of the enemy.

For beings that floated in the air now became weapons of mass destruction and pummeled all the adversaries of God beneath them. And men that did not die from the living cloud's bombardment suddenly found that their lungs deflated where they stood, as the breath of life that was within them was taken. The Host watched as the souls of the men were removed from their bodies and their spirits flailed into the air to mingle with that of the Mists. And those angels whose souls had been trapped clamored to escape merging into the Mists. The undead paused, confused by the singing that went on about them, while those that had advanced in their wake slowly perished from the heavenly bombardment.

The angels that sided with Lucifer turned in panic and ran in retreat towards the portal to escape; unwilling to face a foe that was able to remove the very breath of life.

For, in and out of the mouths of the enemy, did the Virtues, Clouds and Mists move from the mouth of one, did a virtue enter; only to exit out the nose, before moving again unto another. Like Will-o'-the-wisps, the vaporous beings exited from the breathing regions of men and angels, and wherever they exited, men fell down dead as thousands upon thousands collapsed en 'mass.

Screams of men mixed with the screams of the Virtues until, at last, the living clouds grew quiet and lifted from the army of men. And when they did, light from the mountain of God returned and no man was left for the Host to fight. Not one unredeemed human had survived, and the Mists had taken scores of the undead and the carrion into Limbo and were no more to be seen.

Michael, David, and the Host stared upon the bloodied plains that were before them, and none stood alive save one upon the topside of the crest of the mountain of Hell.

Leto.

Chapter Fourteen: Riders of Sheol and Death

Lucifer stood atop Hell, looking over the battlefield as he directed her encroachment over the corpses and structure of Heaven. All was consumed within Hell. Like a rocky amoeba, hell inched forward to make contact with the mountain of God. And nothing in Heaven slowed its march.

Michael saw Lucifer atop the creature and turned to his brethren. "He must be stopped! Michael's halo then glowed and when it did, he lifted into the skies, and the whole of the Lumazi save Argoth also lifted with him. "Hell is but a beast. It is Lucifer with which we must contend. He somehow needs the boy king. Make him release him and perhaps this may end!" His brethren nodded in understanding. Michael raised his sword and pointed it at his felonious brother. "Attack!!"

And so, a phalanx of angels led by Michael flew across the sky to assault the prince of darkness. For the loss of brethren, they fell. For the love of God, they fell. For the rescue of man, they fell. Legions of Elomic winged warriors, living flames of Seraphim, and the twirling wheels of the Ophanim moved as one; flanked by an army of redeemed men.

But Hell was not done for she but regurgitated more of the undead and her carrion to meet the Host. She was full of the undead, and obese with unregenerate dead men and angels. But Michael and his men were neither deterred nor dismayed and pressed forward.

"For the love of God and country we fight! For Yeshua our King, we fight! Advance!" He roars.

And advance the Host did. For the remaining Horde was still a formidable force Because for every friend that fell the friend was transformed by Hell into a foe. Her numbers growing exponentially. The brief advantage the Host had gained now dissipating before their very eyes.

And lo, for the angels that had left the other realms now with their leaving tore through space and time. And reality itself buckled under the weight of those denizens who had left their station to help Michael and his cause. For realities slowly merged and in the skies, it could be seen that across all realms, the outcome was war. For in struggles to control the rotation of stars, angels wrestled upon the edge of event horizons. Throughout the cosmos and in the space between dimensions, angels fought one another with sword and shield. And the Ophanim flew before the throng, whilst the Seraphim went before the Elohim in singing. Burning flames of music that set fire to all things that moved in opposition to God and His Christ. And the Ophanim seeing reality tear under their onslaught fought to close all entrances to alternate realities. And wheresoever there was an outcome that the Horde sought to hide. Eladrin and his kin moved to shut the door and destroy any path that might cause spillage of entry into the Kingdom of Heaven. For in alternate realities, Lucifer rode atop Hell, and in some realities, Michael could be seen riding atop the beast assaulting Heaven.

The titanic struggles caused space to fold upon itself, and stars dimmed as their caretaker's unleashed wrath in brutal clashes of power; moons collided into planets and suns from differing realms now touched and obliterated other orbiting stars.

Worlds collapsed before the onslaught of heavenly armies, and existence crumpled before the charge of celestial beings. And existence itself heaved and buckled to maintain the threads that held reality together.

Jerahmeel looked at the vision in disbelief, while Gabriel cried out. "Limbus is down! The gates are open! Each of the realities is now following the Mists! My God Michael...what have we done?"

Michael stood unmoved, knowing that Lucifer was the true threat, and he fought with his brethren at his side and moved closer to the Maw of Hell, of which Lucifer stood atop.

Michael smashed through enemy troops. His seven bladed swords cutting through angelic warriors. Gabriel and Metatron had tried to stay with him, but a group of redeemed were about to be overrun and they dove to assist. Jerahmeel was belted from the sky by a principality of old and struggled with Moses at his side to down the creature.

The Apostles fought with the Seraphim to control the growing undead as Paul himself rode on the back of Eladrin to protect their flanks.

Closer, Michael came towards the mountain. Closer to the object of this war's genesis.

Lucifer.

Talus and Azaziel were all that now flew by his side. Each moving with swiftness as they all climbed higher into heaven's atmosphere, ducking and weaving as they escaped the confines of the immediate aerial forces. They hugged the great mountain's side, flying as close as possible; ducking and weaving through falling rock and maggots that still poured like water from the sides of the mount.

Lucifer observed their impending approach and when they could no longer be seen, he closed his eyes and spoke in his mind.

Sheol stop them.

The mountain hearkened to her master. On the leeward side of the rocky beast: eyes upon rows of red eyes, opened to see Michael, Talus and Azaziel flying up the mountainside to reach its top.

Jagged projections of stone then began to protrude from the mountain face and Michael and his two brethren began to dodge and weave as they flew through the newly made obstacle course.

Azaziel looked down as he had just missed a protrusion, then returned his gaze upward when another immediately appeared and slammed into the angel's face, knocking him unconscious and he fell plummeting into the clouds below.

"Azaziel!" screamed Michael. But the angel was unresponsive and descending rapidly. Metatron turned and flew to retrieve him and yells, "Head to the top, Michael, and end this madness!" Both Metatron and Azaziel then disappeared under the clouds below.

Michael could only hope for their safety and turned his face upwards and continued his flight. But Hell had anticipated him and instead of a small projection that protruded from her. A great wall now came forth from her sides. A ledge the size of a man's playing field. Michael was moving too fast to stop. He gritted, his halo flared, and he disappeared in a flash of prismatic light.

* * *

Lucifer was giddy for the chaos that was before him. For soon he would ride Hell itself into the mountain of God, destroying it and bringing his wrath to his Father, who had cast him out.

"Feed Sheol...," he says aloud. "Experience the taste of celestial life as never before. FEED and grow FAT!!"

A prismatic light appeared above his head and when Lucifer looked up, Michael was falling upon him, sword in hand, to strike a death blow. Lucifer rolled back out of the way and Michael's blade sunk deep in the craggy rock, barely missing its mark.

Lucifer lifted his hand upward and a great wall protruded between him and Michael.

Michael's halo flared, and he projected into the wall; smashing through it with sword raised to strike his brother down.

Lucifer countered Michael's downward stroke as the Sword of Malice immediately materialized in Lucifer's hand, and he re-directed Michael's blow. The two angels fought as swords connected, and flashes of light burst upon their impact. Seven swords attacked Lucifer and the angel, who was as fast as light evaded and or countered each blow. Each angel moved with speeds men nor angel had ever seen. With the power of the Ophanim, Michael's action was instantaneous, and Lucifer's speed was such that light itself trailed to keep up.

Two brothers.

Two enemies.

One goal.

To cease the life of the other.

Punches and kicks were blocked, and plumes of ash and brimstone covered the battle as the two engaged under the canopy of streams of volcanic lightning and ash. Each angel moving and countering the other in an Elomic waltz of angelic martial arts. Neither yielding, neither giving ground, each pressing their attack. Each facing off in what was understood would be a fatal and final clash.

Celestial adrenalin pumped through Michael's veins, and he pushed Lucifer backward. Lucifer lighted his body, and it shone like a star, blinding his brother. But Michael was not unprepared. His swords rotated around his person, repelling on their own any attack from the Enemy.

Michael groped ahead of him blind. Listening in the midst of erupting volcanic rock and magma for signs of Lucifer's movement.

Lucifer stood aloft from him and spoke, "It is a pity you did not join me. For I see in the multiverse now splayed above us in the sky that there was a possible choice that led *you* to be atop this peak in defiance of El. Do you not see the choices of our lives now written for all to see? Behold the secrets El keeps...his apocalypse of kings. I know the Book of Life El has kept. I know what he reads. The vast eternity of choices we have all made. But you will not know the end of your story, brother. You...will know oblivion."

And at the moment that Lucifer advanced to strike. Michael bent his ear downward and could hear the familiar roar of Charon deep within the mountain. His halo flared, and he vanished as Lucifer's blow hit the ground.

Lucifer looked to his left and right, waiting to be attacked, but no attack came.

The ground under his feet then heaved, and Lucifer fell back on his hind. And before him, a fissure raced, and a rumbling was heard from under him. An explosion jettisoned rock and magma into the sky and without warning Charon burst through the Maw of Hell's stygian mouth and carrion and the undead were expelled like volcanic debris and fell into the clouds below. The Angel of Death unfurled his leathery wings, and his tentacles of iron flailed into the sky and reached to grab hold into the folds of Hell. And Charon's stature was such that he matched Hell's mountainous size and Michael rode atop the angel, his sword pointed at Lucifer and Hell.

Lucifer felt Charon latch on to the great mountain and the living prison of angels was lifted from the ground by the might of Charon and the whole of Heaven watched in dismay for all for a moment paused for the likes had never been seen.

Charon then lifted the mountain over his head and turned and slammed the beast of living rock into the earth. Like giant kaiju from men's stories, the two titans roared. Hell, and Charon charged one another and upon impact, the blast was such that the shock wave made all to fall. Lucifer fell forward into the air and Michael too was lurched into the air toward his brother

The two angels immediately reengaged, and they fought, twisting and turning as they plummeted between the giant swinging tentacles of Charon and the rocky protrusions that ejected from the body of Hell. Like plummeting meteors, the two brothers fell from the sky. Grappling and wrestling, each vying for control. Mere specks of prismatic light against the backdrop of the twin creatures of creation that towered behind them.

Through plummeting clouds, they fell.

Falling from mountain heights, the angels battled as they tumbled in melee combat between the Host and all of Heaven that raged below. The earth quickly racing to embrace their descent.

And lo, the angels smashed into the ground and the earth gave way and surrendered her displeasure in a flood surge of rock and fire. Bodies of angels, the undead and redeemed, were cast aside like splash damage, and when the smoke had cleared, Lucifer and Michael slowly rose. Each one coughing and taking in great gulps of air.

Michael turned and a protrusion from Hell knocked the angel unconscious and sent him flying into the palace doors.

The sky grew dark and all eyes in the vicinity turned to see that Charon had again gained control of Hell's innards as his tentacles had dug deep within the mountain and he roared and the roar was such that even the clouds and wind was moved by his thunder.

Many ran to evade what was Hell rock that fell from the sky. Hell moved, and it raised the ground as it and Charon wrestled with one another. Charon shoved the great mountain to the precipice of the Cliffs of Argoth and the giant mountain teetered on the edge. The fringe of which collapsed and gave way buckling under the strain to hold the mountain. The beast that was Hell then plummeted as thousands of the undead reached for Charon to hold him. But the momentum and collapse of the cliff face from under hell was too much, and Charon and the mountain fell into the Maelstrom. The giants still in battle as they disappeared into the black funnel of the abyss. Their echoed roars, undead and fiery maggots trailed them into the whirling darkness below.

* * *

Yeshua tended to Argoth, who had suffered as the agony of the choices of God the Father had been sealed up in him. Yeshua had penned the final selection of names into the Book of Life, having seen all futures and all persons that ever would be. He signed the final entry and when he put his pen down. Argoth transformed back into his angelic form and collapsed into the Lord's arms.

"It is enough, Lord," says the angel. "Creation groans for the manifestation of the sons of God. The war...the greed...the pride...it is enough, Lord. Let it end, please. They...all those outside...all have made...their choices." Argoth then blacked out and when he did, the palace doors smashed open, and Michael smashed into the ground unconscious and bounced on the crystal floor and slid into Yeshua's feet and the seventh trumpet rested on the angel's waist.

The Lord touched his beloved son and scanned with his eyes to search for a pulse. The pulse was strong, but the angel was bloodied and scrapped. His hand unfurled and the pommel of the Sword of Ophanim was still in his hand and the sword was quiet.

Yeshua bent down and touched his most beloved of angels and spoke.

"Rise, my son, and be healed."

Waves of golden power flowed from Yeshua into Michael, and he was immediately made whole. The scars disappeared and his strength returned to him.

Michael alighted to his feet and stood next to the Lord. He bowed to his master and looked up at him and said. "We have done all that can be done to bar the flood of the enemy. But lest the spirit of the Lord raise up a standard against them; Heaven, mayhap Creation itself will be rendered. All shall perish, my Lord, lest you intervene."

The Lord rose to his feet, and he looked at the father God who sat in his throne. "We both know where Lucifer will go. The Abomination is but a ruse. If it be thy will. I will see to it."

The Father nodded, "Go and do what must be done."

El Pneuma floated, and the ceiling and walls displayed the carnage of war just outside the palace. The members of the Godhead watched as Charon and Hell fought as they plummeted into the bottomless pit. The Mists and all the angels that had breached the gates of the nether realms battled. The Horde fought with the redeemed and everything that had breath was engaged in a titanic battle for control.

The triune God sighed and El Pneuma ceased from his projection of all of reality and shrouded himself around Yeshua. Michael watched as Yeshua looked outside, then waved his hand and immediately disappeared. Michael sprinted towards the palace doors to follow.

* * *

Lucifer frantically walked into the still burning chamber of what remained of the Kiln.

With Hell tumbling into the Abyss and the body of Leto having suffered injury. Lucifer discarded his husk of a human shell and left the unconscious body of Leto to his fate on the battlefield. He was of no more use to Satan. Though the Nephilim was strong, he was not pure blood, his flesh unable to cope with the strains Lucifer taxed on his host.

Lucifer's mind filled with thoughts of revenge. Clouded from battle, from the visions of seeing other realms, other options. Options where he did not rise up in rebellion. Options where he and Michael were on opposing sides, and Lucifer was the defender of the faith. Options where he obeyed God and did not induce the fall of man.

But only in but three dimensions did Lucifer see himself as the defender of El. In all others, he was the instigator, the antagonist.

A decision that always originated in the Kiln.

So, the injured angel made his way to the start of it all. The womb of angelic birth, and his choice to submit to God.

Memories flooded him as he recalled the many times he had walked within the room with the Lord God. Often eying his master as El breathed into stones to create his kind. For, Lucifer was there at the beginning: there when El made each of the great angelic houses. There when his brethren were given life. For thousands of angelic years, he had obeyed the Lord as his herald. Covered his throne and was privy to see the creation of both celestial and terrestrial life.

He eyed the remnants of the chamber, and even though it had been obliterated; Lucifer gambled. Believing with the eyes of faith that here in this chamber he could once more ascend to displace his God. To be released from the perceived yoke of the Almighty's rule. Here he would grasp the unattainable and usurp his father. Here, he could achieve through the flesh what he could not obtain in the spirit.

Here—he would finally be God.

He stood in the midst of the ancient and now quiet chamber. The place where the prime-stone: the ultimate test of his kind once pulsed. He frowned as he viewed the destruction, the result of the interference of his brother to stop his advancement to become more than he was; and he spoke his displeasure into the air.

"I am here El. Once more...I stand. Stand AGAIN in defiance to my lot. In defiance to my station. I am here El."

The echoes of his own voice and then silence returned his pronouncement.

Satan eyed the chamber and with his patience expired, shouted into the air once more.

"Show yourself!" Lucifer screamed in frustration. The Devil turned, looking into the darkened twilight. He illuminated his body to see fully and spoke once more into the air.

"I did not come all this way for nothing, did not sully mankind for nothing. Did not plan all this time to be denied audience. Even if I must provoke thee to anger yea, even to the destruction of Creation itself. You will hear me father! You will NOT ignore your son!!" Lucifer raised his fists high into the air in anger and began to shed tears.

A slight wind could be felt against his cheeks and dust moved in the chamber. Tiny embers flickered against the wall. And the oceanic voice of the Lord spoke unto Satan in a quiet and still small voice, "Whence comest thou?"

Satan replies, "Humph, you never change, El. Nevertheless, I will play your game." Lucifer changed his voice and replies in sarcastic tenor. "I am come from going to and fro in the earth, and from walking up and down in it."

El then asks, "And for what cause do you show thyself before me? For it has been a long time. Who is this that stands before me in rebellion that I should not cast you out into utter darkness and the gnashing of teeth?"

Lucifer looked but could not see a physical manifestation of God and replied. "At least do me the courtesy of showing yourself. Cease with this foolishness. For you know why I am here. I am here to claim what is mine." Lucifer staggered even as he spoke; weakened from his battle with Michael. "To take by force, if necessary, what should have always been given. I would know the truth."

Lucifer waited for a reply but nothing but the few dying kiln-stones that remained in the chamber sung melodiously in response. Flames suddenly erupted from the floor of the room and shot up to form a humanoid figure of light. The great being stood to the height of the ceiling and gleamed in prismatic brilliance. The Kiln stones themselves burst forth in singing, each made alive by the power of God's presence.

Lucifer took a step backward, and his instinct was to bow. To kneel in the presence of the Almighty. But pride caused him to resist: to resist the intuitive urge to worship. Lucifer withstood the impulse for he no longer stood in awe, no longer felt dwarfed by the God of the Universe. For he had tasted, if only for a moment, the power of God. And he refused to bow to give his father and Creator reverence.

El towered over Satan, and slowly the Almighty's form diminished to where he took on the features of a man, aged and weathered beyond his years, and spoke.

"You come back to the realm immortal after exile. Neither dost thou come alone but with armies to sunder this land. And even now you stand defiant before me? Very well, speak thy petition; for with what request dost the self-confessed enemy of God ask that I might do unto thee?"

Lucifer's eyes narrowed, and his face hardened in determination. and he glared at the Almighty and mouthed his supplication.

"I do not believe that thou art Alpha and Omega. Indeed, I believe thou hast cast a ruse over the whole of creation. That God Almighty...is a lie. That all things have a beginning...even thee. But who but I hast had the power to stand before thee and accuse thee even to thy face? Who but thine own son: a son whom thou hast claimed to love would attempt among angelic kind to make petition to the Almighty? For alas, doth Creation fear thee for naught? For you allow no other paths of choice to exist save those that lead to the outcome you allow...your worship. No other options but the ones you determine. I decree that the way of the Lord is not equal. That love doth not exist in the Almighty. For what is love if we are coerced to love? You give benefits, but are they naught but attempts to sway love towards thee? For thou art a jealous god, even as thou hast said. What vanity exists if the Almighty cannot stomach love directed towards another? And what do you do in your jealousy? You cast out. Therefore, I adjure thee to prove thyself if love exists. And spare me the sacrifice of Yeshua. A token to but reclaim that which was lawfully given by Adam. Your ruse in cloaking yourself in flesh was brilliant: well played indeed. I will even consent that your love for the Adam is strong. But what of thy love to us? To me? You profess to be love. You desire to show thy love? Then show no partiality and give to me what thou hast given Adam and his kin. Lay down thy life and show me the Beginning. Yeah, before even I. Know this, that except I shall see with mine own eyes thy face at the beginning, and handle thy hands, and see what lies beyond Creation herself, I will not believe."

The Lord looked upon his wayward and lost son and replies, "You do not know what you ask. Nevertheless, that which you have asked shall be given even unto thee."

The Lord God then took on the form of blackness. His person was no longer that of the weathered old man and the God who was light. But his features slowly changed to an inkish onyx black.

A black that crept menacingly over Lucifer.

A black encased in black, and onyx shrouded in ebony. And the deprivation of his senses was if the bristle of sackcloth fell over the skin of the angel, and Lucifer fell to his knees and struggled to breathe, for his lungs could no longer capture the air his kind needed to survive. Anxiety rushed over him, and he attempted to use his own body to generate light. But the Lord God was over him, and the stuff of light could not be found to emanate from his angelic body. Quickly engulfed in the person of God, the enormity of the Almighty overwhelmed him, and Lucifer fell as if he had fallen in a deep pit with no bottom, and the sensation of vertigo overwhelmed him.

Fear quickly enveloped the angel, for he had asked in pride to know what else preceded God, and the voice of the Lord God Almighty overwhelmed the angel with nothingness.

"You asked to see the face of God," says El. "The Alpha, that state of being prior to God. Behold and see the answer that you seek."

But Lucifer saw nothing but blackness...that there was no state prior to God.

Just blackness...nothing.

For unless the Lord himself decreed light a desire, light was want to peek into the realm of existence. And wherever the angel sought to see, nothing but the vastness of God stared back at him. A God that chose to create, to love, to bring order from nothing...into something. All things were made by him; and without him was not anything made that was made.

Lucifer himself suddenly began to dissolve into nothing. For before God, there was nothing. Therefore, there could be no Lucifer. Thus, Satan himself was now given a lesson like none other; that his own person was merely allowed by the whisper God gave for his existence. For nothing existed, not even choice in the absence of God. Yea, freewill itself and the subsequent choices which followed were nothing but manifestations of God's allowance. His permissive will to allow creation's spread. And here in the darkness, Lucifer was tutored that to seek the Void was merely to seek one's own oblivion.

Because before God, there was no other. And no eyes existed to behold what you think would lie beyond, and no mind save the Lord's existed to comprehend even a reality apart from God.

Nothing but God alone.

No ambition, significance, or love. No hate or desire. No good or evil.

Naught existed unless God spoke it.

And God was, for the moment, silent.

Satan beheld that save the Lord himself moved. There was indeed nothing to move. He was the first mover, the first cause. El was indeed the Alpha. The Beginning and the End. That the words of the apostle Paul were a human epiphany not just about God but about the state of reality itself: that in Him we lived, moved and had our being. A reality by revelation Lucifer himself was now privy to see. The true apocalypse of kings. But only for a moment: only before he himself would be snuffed from existence.

And Lucifer could feel himself slowly slipping away into the ether...into nothingness.

"I relent!" he cries.

But it was of no use. For he suddenly had a mouth, but he could not scream.

"I repent! There is nothing beside you!" His remaining thoughts echoed in his head.

More of his body slowly disappeared. His body and mind were like ash blowing into the winds of the benevolent imagination of El.

In desperation that he might survive, Lucifer uncoiled the Sword of Malice and attempted to stab El in the darkness. To pierce the heart of the Almighty. Flailing about in vain to strike down the Author of life.

Lucifer's final thought...his confession; was a mental scream he knew El could hear.

"I recant my words; there is nothing before you! Please Almighty! You are God!"

And at the moment that Lucifer felt himself on the precipice of vanishing from reality, He found himself fully restored and kneeling at the feet of El panting heavily gulping in air into his lungs. Clutching his throat to capture the life-giving air that El allowed to exist. He looked at his hands, and all was at it was, and when he looked up, El towered above him and stared down upon him. His eyes sad, and his lips pressed hard, and the Lord's mouth turned downward as his head shook in disapproval.

"My son, thou hast been in Eden, the garden of God; with every precious stone thy covering. The workmanship of thy tabrets and of thy pipes was prepared in thee in the day that thou wast created. You were the anointed cherub that covereth; and I had set thee upon the holy mountain of God as I watched thee walk up and down in the midst of the stones of fire. You were perfect in all thy ways from the day that thou wast created...until iniquity was found in thee. But the multitudes of thy merchandise have filled the midst of thee with violence, and thou hast sinned. Thine heart hast become lifted up because of thy beauty, and your wisdom: corrupted by reason of thy brightness."

The Lord looked down in sorrow at his son and pitied his creation.

"Even with your last breath, you would strike out in violence to destroy me. You have scarred your own stone and will not be made whole. You have gone too far, become too violent. To grant you what you wish would bring about the destruction of both thee and creation itself. Therefore, I cannot give you what you want, my son. Nor can you ever take it from me. Thou hast raised thy hand to me. Hast created Abomination and would see reality destroyed in thy pursuit. Therefore, tell me my son...with what punishment should I give thee for these things?"

Lucifer raised his head in stubborn reluctance, even now attempting to commute a sentence he knew was coming, and replies, "I should be given over to oblivion."

El shook his head. "No, I will not destroy you, neither give you over to non-existence. You cannot escape the sins that hath found you out. But you shall be imprisoned for eternity. For you have risen against the whole of Creation and Eternity itself and have blasphemed my name and know that I will have recompense for this act. I will tolerate the tantrums of a child no longer."

The Lord then turned his back to his son and quietly disappeared. The colored prismatic light dimmed into twinkling embers that faded, and the room turned black as night.

And Lucifer...Lucifer was left alone in the darkness, his palms covering his face...and weeping.

* * *

Yeshua appeared at the front of the palace. Glowing with power, the energy from the Lord radiated that every eye saw him. And His image was blazoned throughout all of Heaven

And Yeshua, Yeshua, seeing what his son had done, became wroth. For once more Lucifer failed to abide in the calling in which he was called and the anger of the Lord was kindled so that he saddled a horse of the whitest whites, and rode out into battle upon a blanket of stars.

He waved his right hand and the twenty-seven barriers which separated the realm of Heaven from the rest of existence appeared within the view of all combatants. Each dimension separated by a glass-like wall and behind each and in everyone contained within each realm; the children of God saw that in all realities and in all possible dimensions, battle ensued. And the branches of all choices that the Lord God had allowed to exist from the origins of creation existed in the twenty-seven realms that He had hidden beyond angelic sight. And Michael was awed for he looked into the skies of Heaven and wherever he looked he saw himself reflected back, his other selves looking back at him and in all instances he was in lead of an angelic army.

And as a kaleidoscope moves, so too did the realms display that the universe was naught but the rods and cones in the eyes of God. For all were now privy to glimpse, a partiality of the infinite realities El permitted. Each of the twenty-seven realities branched off into twenty-seven more ad-infinitum. And the sky was seen as a grid which duplicated images from the viewpoint of all those that raised their eyes to see. And each image had six possible angles and was a mirror image or an unreversed image. And Yeshua...Yeshua rode through them all. All twenty-seven at once, for he was in the images, but he was not. Within His creation, yet beyond it. And Michael's mind could not fully comprehend what his eyes beheld, and he watched as his King, the Lord God Yeshua, rode across the multi-verse in anger. The Christ of God, eyes aflame, opened his mouth and when He did so, He then exited through one of the images, and shattered all other images in his wake.

For the Alpha and Omega rode upon his steed and all doors that gave entrance to the multi-verse imploded. Beginning with Omega was the door sealed shut. Immediately Psi followed suit, buckled and collapsed behind the King of Kings. Shards of the two destroyed realities trailed behind him as a great wake of glass as he smashed through Chi. With a wave of his hand, He obliterated the realm of Upsilon, and through Tau He stampeded. Sigma carried His roar. With vengeance, He destroyed Rho. To Pi He but spoke to cease. Omicron and XI fell in the Lord's wake and both Nu and Mu closed on His command. Lambda, through Zeta, bowed to his will, and Epsilon knelt in submission to the King of Kings. Delta cow-towed, whilst Gamma and Beta prostrated themselves before Him. commanded by the Lord God to "cease."

The Lord God Yeshua gleamed in illuminated brilliance. He whose radiance hearkened the termination of life and death. He who carried the existence of all things by the word of his power. For when Yeshua beheld that nothing was left of the twenty-seven realms of existence save Alpha, and He was but one reality removed from the state that was the Void. He stepped no further, for if he did so, nothing but God would exist. Thus, God, in His mercy, halted his march across the sands of space and time, and paused that He might not snuff out all existence. Paused as a funnel of now shattered worlds and choices; past, present and future; roared in tornadic fury. Each dimension cascading into nothingness and absorbed into his person until possibility itself dissipated into ether. And when the Lord was satisfied seeing that all paths closed behind him, and his anger doused that no door existed for Lucifer to contend. And all choices that ever existed all led to the moment that was before all the people now; such that there were no more choices to make for all choices were now settled, and the Lord then spoke, and His words echoed across the universe, "I AM the Alpha and Omega, the First and the Last, the Beginning and the End."

And with those words, Michael finally untied the final trumpet of judgment that had been on his waist, and he blew into it. And the clouds themselves and all cried out in one voice each chanting such that there were great voices in heaven, says, "The kingdoms of this world are become the kingdoms of our Lord, and of his Christ; and he shall reign for ever and ever!"

Yeshua then took hold of the now conscious man-king Leto Alexander by the scruff of his neck and held him up for all to see. And when he did; the remaining armies of unredeemed men, the Horde and the undead were also lifted up into the air as if an invisible hand lifted them. Enemies that had been in the midst of combat were ripped apart from one another and Horde enemies rose into the air and all who bore the Mark of the Beast and all of the Devil's angels were in that moment suspended in the air squirming for release. Millions of hissing, screaming and cursing enemies of the Living God.

The Lord God Yeshua then flung Leto downward into depths of space backwards into the realm of men.

The Horde armies were instantaneously pulled apart atom by atom and reappeared, tumbling back into space. For the armies of the great dragon were cast out, they who in league with the Devil deceived the whole world and were cast out into the earth.

Like falling stars did the Horde plummet. Some unredeemed men died even as they traveled through space, while their bodies bounced against the funnel that repelled them from heaven. Screams and curses split the ears of planets and nebulas were disturbed as galaxies were torn asunder for the force with which the armies of Lucifer fell. Planets saw angels fall into gravity wells unable to escape and angels tumbled into suns stripped of their celestial flesh and rendered mortal and died as they yelled Yeshua's name as they fell, dying into gas giants.

The whole of creation groaned, for Yeshua's wrath was awakened that Creation itself attacked those that had dared ascend to smite Heaven, and comets changed trajectories to smash into angelic bodies. Black Holes opened their mouths and expanded to capture and consume angels who had left their first estate and who were fallen into the hands of an angry God.

Yeshua, still awash in righteous fury; unleashed Time itself against the Horde. For many as they fell aged as their eternal life was stripped from them and some angels crumpled and withered into cosmic dust before their bodies could even hit the soil of Earth.

The Lord then looked at his army before him and roars aloud, "Go to and attack!"

And when Yeshua spoke, Heaven itself tilted as all eyes looked downward in woe upon the world of men. For another prismatic funnel opened and tore back space and time to target the small planet below.

And Enoch, the seventh from Adam, noted the gathering of Heaven's military might and for a moment he pitied mankind for his obstinace and spoke aloud the warning he had given so many ages ago for all to hear.

"Fear the Lord all ye people, for behold the Lord cometh with ten thousand of his saints."

And Yeshua, and the armies of heaven, emptied themselves and fell to the Earth in pursuit of the enemy's total destruction.

Chapter Fifteen: The Return of the King

Thus, the Lord beheld the fall of his children into the black of space, and lo, the celestial realm strained against the might of Heaven's children once more engaged in battle.

For the fall of Michael and Host were as the plummet of great balls of fire that fell upon the earth. And everywhere mankind looked streaks of light flashed across the sky and heaven opened, and lo, a winged white stallion with six legs galloped through a prismatic funnel; and he that sat upon him was called Faithful and True, and in righteousness he doth judge and make war. And the Lord Yeshua's eyes were as a flame of fire, and on his head were many crowns; and he had a name written, that no man knew, but him.

Brightness jetted from his person as a detonating star which spewed solar storms. And his name was called The Word of God.

A bastard sword flew before his mouth, and to the left and right of him trailed the armies of the Living God. The Host descended to the earth upon white steads: each rider was also clothed in raiment of white linen robes which draped their person as living capped armor.

And throughout the whole of the planet, music could be heard. A rumbling that shook the atmosphere, a clarion call that heralded the return of Yeshua to the earth. The music was choral in sound and accompanied by the blast of trumpets, the great prismatic funnel tore through space and clouds. From the exosphere to the troposphere the opera carry over the air. A refrain could be heard by those on the ground. A refrain that was heard on this wise.

"Great and marvelous are your works, O Lord God, the Almighty. Just and true are your ways, O King of the nations."

Such were their numbers of the Host that for a time no sun could be seen; for the swarm of angelic armies eclipsed it and the vastness of their numbers cast a shadow across the Earth; yet light still shown for the Lord God himself was light, and photons skipped across His person like lens flare. As locusts from heaven, the Host descended. Redeemed men and women all astride on horseback.

Each with sword and flanked by the three races of Heaven: Elohim, Ophanim and the Seraphim. For the King of Kings was returning and with him the armies of Heaven: a legion of legions. And Yeshua strode at the fore; his vesture dipped in blood.

And as the Host funneled to the earth's atmosphere, men in vain sought to counter their advance. With technology meant to repel invaders from space, mankind launched his version of flight. Aircraft that scrambled to meet the angelic incursion in the air. From bases across the planet, jets lifted into the skies. From the northern tip of Canada to the southern tip of Argentina. The aerial weapons of destruction screamed to meet the redeemed and angelic host. But the host would not be stopped, and they descended unopposed as jets launched their ordinance of missiles to repel those who had invaded their nation's airspace. Explosions ripped through the skies, but the Host rode undeterred. For the Grigori changed the density of the army as fighter jets screamed through men and angels like ether. Grigori misted through aircraft and partially materialized, disrupting circuitry and shorting out the machines electronics.

Arelim simply grappled the airplanes from the sky and ripped the aircraft in two. Malakim griffins grasped the jets in their talons and they flung them into flanking air squadrons, as explosive balls of fire and jet fuel knocked planes from the sky.

But it was the Lord of Hosts himself who was the weapon to fear, for he merely opened his mouth to speak and when he did the sword before him glowed like a blinding nova that unleashed a golden hued conical wave that sheared all things in its path. Leaving nothing behind but a cleaved trail of carnage. For nothing stood before the Lord as he advanced to the nation of Israel's defense.

Pilots, in fear, ejected as they lost control of their aircraft and the fixed wings of destruction plummeted from the sky in uncontrolled dives into both land and sea. Across the planet, the Host enveloped those that attacked them and men fell screaming to their deaths.

But alas, as the wave of Heaven moved across the planet, scores of legions fell to every nation and region, every tongue and base of operations fell under attack. Like cluster bombs, the Host fell to the Earth to destroy the power of every nation's ability to wage war.

And nations seeing the tactics of the Host launched with both pride and fear their mightiest weapons. Nuclear silos roared to life and spit fire and exhaust from their underground bunkers. For the kings of the earth knew that this would be their last battle for their nation's survival. Thus, ballistic missiles were launched from both earth and sea. From the depths of ocean trenches and from hardened silos buried within mountains, did generals let loose their last best hope to repel invaders they perceived were here to destroy them and the Earth.

But the host would not be deterred nor stopped by weapons made at the hands of mortal men. Harrada upon command of the Lord fell into the oceans and, as living, torpedoes smashed into submarines. The hulls of each aquatic predator burst upon the angel's impact, and water rushed in to fill the compartments of the vessels. But the Harrada pummeled ceaselessly the underwater nuclear carriers until the ships exploded in undersea bursts of fire, sending shock waves across the ocean floor. While other angels simply pushed the giant vessels deeper into the ocean's trenches until the crushing weight of the water caused the submarines to implode, crushing all those inside.

Metatron and the Draco flew through the skies and as ICBM missiles reached their apogees and released their multiple independent targeting vehicles, the Draco opened their mouths and the sonic booms of their voices disintegrated each warhead into nothing.

And when men in his stubbornness launched more salvos, the Issi fell upon them and as bomb busters destroyed the very mountains with which their silos were built. Warrior angel after Issi angel drilled into the bowels of the earth into the deepest of men's hiding places and ignited the very air that men breathed and the soldiers that keyed the launch sequences of mankind's greatest weapons of mass destruction. The eruption of flames roasted alive those within. The blasts were such that when the destruction was complete; naught but the shadows of the men remained etched in walls and floors of melted metal and stone. For each angel was fire and heat personified and left nothing in their wake.

The Lord Yeshua circled the circumference of the earth and wherever His shadow fell, the Host also fell upon the armies of men wreaking havoc until all surrendered or none were alive to fight. For Yeshua had come and his eye was set to descend to the Mt. of Olives. The Lamb now returned in righteous anger: to slaughter all those who would dare lift hands to destroy his people.

* * *

The armies of the world of men were massed at the valley of Jezreel. Orbiting satellite had shown waves of celestial beings descending to the planet in attack formations. Reconnaissance photos showed millions of beings descending on fiery animals and after months of preparatory work, the dimensional gate near Meggido surpassed the Korean demilitarized zone as the most heavily guarded and fortified place on the planet. Artillery and soldiers were at the ready to repel any celestial invasion that sought to breach the dimensional rift that had been located by Chancellor Leto.

Hours earlier, the rift had closed. Its prismatic funnel disappeared, and no one was able to ascend to lend support to the forces that had crossed. Generals now assumed command had been cut off and prepped for a retaliatory strike by the aliens to come at any time.

Tensions ran high along the ranks of the men. Local air bases and aircraft carriers and destroyers had been brought into the Mediterranean Sea to provide support.

General Gao Lei was responsible for troop coordination with General Antonio Rossi. Each had been given reports of the alien invasion that seemed to becoming from the western hemisphere and moving rapidly towards the east. Heading directly to Israel.

"General Lei to command. I repeat, this is General Lei to command. I have lost radio communication with the Americas. I repeat, the Western hemisphere is dark. Command DO YOU READ?"

The static hiss of his radio returned his reply.

"Colonel, load up any television networks and bring up the satellite link for all stations."

The colonel assigned to assist the General saluted, turned his back and in pressed several mobile computer consoles. A screen deployed in the air and a holographic projection of the planet with illuminated points of blue lights on a map shimmered into view.

One by one, red pinpricks of light showed across the earth.

"Report!" General Lei commanded.

"Sir...Joint Force command is dark.

Allied land command is dark

NORAD is dark

Allied Maritime Command is dark

Allied Air Command is dark

Supreme Headquarters is dark, sir.

Moscow is dark

Pacific command is dark..."

General Lei listened to his colonel until the need to listen no longer existed. All top military stations were consistently going dark.

All destroyed? Impossible! He thought.

General Lei had fought in the Pacific region during the U.S./China seven-day war. He reminisced over the losses that had incurred by both sides when they fought in the Indonesian and Japanese theaters fifty years ago. But never had he seen whole regions of military command go dark. Not like this.

General Lei looked out of his tent. The sky was bright, and the sun seemed to quiver in expectation. A parahelio shown in the sky and what few clouds existed were suddenly pierced by crepuscular rays that now flooded the valley of Jezreel in a thousand beams of light.

"My God!" the general spoke aloud.

He watched as the sun was not a sun. For what he saw slowly began to eclipse the sun.

It was a man.

Clothed in the brightest of whites and riding a steed with six legs; a man led a swarm of men, women and luminous beings with wings. His initial shock was followed by commands to dispatch. "All units' attack! I repeat, we are under attack! Fire at will!"

Black clouds of flack suddenly filled the air as explosive waves of force concussed through the air. Men in Bradley fighting vehicles and all manner of tanks fired off ordinance, as ships in the sea fired off missiles to track the incoming wave of invading celestials.

Each ray of light that touched the ground was merely a person who, with sword and shield, attacked infantry and armored carriers. Their amour reflected small arms fire back at the enemy and rifles did no damage. Machine gun fire was useless as nothing penetrated the shields of the troops of Heaven.

Unredeemed armies were cut asunder as the sword which the saints of God held when swung did not just cut what was immediately in contact with their blades; but waves of energy were unleashed through the motion of the weapons; slicing through enemies up to a distance of one hundred yards. The cadmium weapons cut through depleted uranium and other man-made materials as a hot knife through butter. Thus, one man of Heaven was equal to a thousand, and two men to ten thousand. Like a tidal wave that brings the storm surge, so too did the armies of Heaven obliterate the forces of unredeemed man. As lambs to the slaughter did the men of the world fight and with reckless abandon did they fall before Christ and the heavenly angels.

The Lord God Yeshua landed atop the Mount of Olives, and he stared down upon the carnage. Upon those forces that had thought to destroy his chose people. And in Petra were heaven's troops deployed to destroy the forces of Leto that had been sent to eradicate the Jews who hid there.

And the bloodshed and the bodies were so numerous that the corpses began to pile ten feet into the air.

Blow the trumpet in Zion and sound an alarm in my holy mountain! Let all the inhabitants of the land tremble; for the day of the LORD is coming, for it is at hand: A day of darkness and gloominess, a day of clouds and thick darkness, like the morning clouds spread over the mountains. A people come, great and strong, the like of whom has never been; nor will there ever be any such after them, even for many successive generations. ...

Michael looked at the Lord, surrounded by several of his brethren. "Lord, there is still one who must be dealt with. One who must be apprehended."

The Lord looked at his angelic son and replied. "Go, for I have prepared a place for him. Take your brothers with you. David and the rest of your human brethren and I shall remain here."

Michael nodded and immediately he the Lumazi who stood by his side vanished in prismatic light.

* * *

Michael and his brethren entered the palace, and they walked towards the sealed entrance to the Kiln. Michael motioned to Talus, and he tore the seals off the door and opened it. Michael unsheathed his sword and walked in while his brethren waited, peering into the doorway.

Lucifer sat on a dead God-stone. His face was haggard and his body void of the power that emanated from angels. Michael stared at his brother who sat quietly staring into space; this brother whom he had fought to the death: this brother whom he had once admired, and still even loved.

Michael felt pity for him but knew what his duty entailed.

With sword in one hand and shackles of iron in the other. He spoke the words that he knew one day he would have to say to his older sibling.

"Lucifer Draco, you are under arrest: charged with treason against the kingdom. You are also charged with crafting Abomination and defying the Articles of War. Your actions recorded by the Sephiroth will be replayed before a jury of your peers, and you will be brought to judgment. These with me are here to enforce this arrest. You will comply."

Lucifer poked his lip out, and in resignation, stood. He placed his wrists out and Michael bound him. His manacles firmly fastened around him. Lucifer finally spoke in hissing contempt.

"I hate you."

Michael sighed and looked his brother in the eye, struggling to hold back his tears.

"I know."

The archangel then quietly led his brother out.

* * *

Enoch and Elijah walked into the now liberated city of Jerusalem. Many of the Jews who had fled to Petra had returned. All had seen the coming of the Lord. They cheered when they saw the redeemed men, and many came up to them and brought them flowers. And people filled the streets thanking God and singing for being freed from the despot Leto Alexander. The Messiah had returned as prophesied. Returned in power, and his people were kind but firm, and as the duo walked through the throng of people. A familiar face approached them: a man waving a cell-phone camera.

"I want the exclusive story, gentlemen! I want to know what it was like to die, to be resurrected, I want it all. This could be an incredible book deal!"

Enoch and Elijah smiled, and Henel James hugged the men who he had come to know and respect.

Elijah replies, "Always after a story, aren't you, Henel, son of James?"

Look, Yeshua might have taken over the world, but I still think readers will want to know the story behind the story. Look, I'll even split the publishing rights with you!"

Enoch smiles and when he did he spoke into the air, "Did you hear that Argoth? He desires to chronicle. He is the closest thing I have seen to a human Grigori."

Immediately a shimmer appeared next to Enoch, and Argoth appeared. His robes were white and his eyes were the deepest blue. He looked at Henel James and replies, "I know of your story, Henel James. I am pleased that your name is written in the Lamb's Book of Life."

Henel looked up at the floating angel in awe. "Wow," was all the man could say...until the instincts of a trained reporter got the best of him.

"Ok, so what's *your* story?" says the reporter.

Argoth smiles and replies, "Walk with me, human, and I will share with you a tale of tales. Of the beginning of creation itself. And of a race of people whom angels could not even see. A house that chronicled the actions of all sentient beings in creation. Does this interest you, Henel, son of James?"

Enoch looked at Argoth wide eyed, "Wait, why is he allowed to know your history and I was not?"

Argoth hunched his shoulder and smiles, "El Pneuma has permitted the human access to this tome."

Henel smiled, ready to hear this exclusive, and set his phone to record. His face lit up, and he listened as Argoth explained the Chronicles of the Grigori.

Epilogue: Goodnight to Fellowship

The Lord God proclaimed, "Because of your collusions against thy King, and treachery against the work of my hands, thou art hereby sentenced to the Lake of Fire. See they who were once astonished at thee: a terror hast thou been. Away from my sight and begone from me, for never shalt thou be anymore."

Immediately, Gabriel and Jerahmeel each took an arm and Michael walked before them as they escorted the hissing and defeated Lucifer to the edge of the burning inland sea. Flames licked at him as seraphim warriors sprawled in a blazing wall of fire, preventing his escape. Collectively, the Seraphim were towering infernos that formed a fiery tunnel surrounding the would-be king's forced march trail to the loch of flame. Eladrin stood before them as they approached and his wheels spun in gyroscopic fury twirling in great swaths, suddenly all his wheels stopped and synced into one giant ring of connected concentric circles that moved further apart from one another, widening into a great single ring. A flash of light then burst from Eladrin's body as blues and greens intersected with one another. Thunder followed as a circular portal opened within the King of the Ophanim. The opening flooded the emporium with plasma and voltage streaked in crackling, extending arms in front of the three brothers. Screams bellowed out from what was a translucent gateway as wrinkled hands and gaunt faces on strained necks extended through the entryway in vain attempts to escape the sweltering plumes of heat and fire that shot out from Eladrin's gate.

The doorway to the Lake of Fire had been opened.

Michael escorted Lucifer to the cliff ledge of the loch. In the sky was darkness, the Maelstrom was now the new sky for the residents of the fire that was here. For in the moments when smoke did not agitate the eyes, and if it were possible to be still enough to observe that a sky even existed. The howling winds of the Maelstrom was all that was heard apart from screams.

Michael hated this place. It was truly a place separated from the presence of God. A realm made suitable for those who, in rebellion to their Creator, thought they knew better and chose the path of death. So here in the brimstone and flames: Death would soon come.

It was the bottom of the bottomless pit. The base of the Abyss. It was a prison of prisons, and a cage of cages. A realm none could escape. And once sealed, blackness would overtake the realm.

Michael stepped away. The word of God was binding, and the seals of Lucifer's manacles began to break free, as each one did he fell to his knees by an invisible force. A second seal broke, and then Lucifer's hands were free. His wings unfurled, but he was invisibly dragged slowly across the ground. By the laws that governed the Lake of Fire, the sentence would now be carried out and those who were condemned once in proximity to the lake were dragged into its flames. Michael had seen this before. He watched as the False Prophet Abadi and Leto Alexander were thrown alive into the Loch.

And now it was Lucifer's turn. His turn to be dragged into the flames.

Some kicked and screamed as they descended into the fire, but for a time, Lucifer was not so. He cried out in defiance. Spitting and cursing, until the heat finally licked at him, and his newfound screams now melded into the chorus of those who floated within the flames.

Lucifer was now immersed his body writhed in agony and his face contorted in spasmodic gnashing of teeth. His flesh blistered away only to be renewed with the genesis of new abscesses that burst in sores and ulcers.

A cycle that would now repeat for eternity.

Soon Michael could close the gate to the Lake of Fire behind him. Soon he could return to the presence of God. For the Lord had promised to make a new heaven and a new Earth. And everyone was excited and talked of the wonders they would soon explore.

The Prince of Angels waited until he could see that the dark shadow of Death had entered the realm. Michael watched as the decomposing flesh of the vengeance of God trod slowly towards the flames. Hell had already been given sanctuary within the Lake of Fire earlier. Her desire to feast was now fully unlocked. A diet of affliction she could enjoy for eons. Her caretaker now came to live in the only realm where vengeance was necessary.

To mete out the lash.

Michael remembered El's warning in the book of Proverbs. A prophecy that was now being fulfilled, 'I also will laugh at your calamity; I will mock when your fear cometh.'

Here in this realm, fear was coming.

Here in this realm Charon was fear.

Michael looked over the mass of the teeming damned and shook his head wondering.

How did it come to this?

* * *

Lucifer gritted his teeth in agony stared at Charon as he approached the prison of fire. "Has the vengeance of God come to embrace me in my incarceration of flames? Come, angel of death: do thy duty and fulfill the call of vengeance!"

I shook my head in sorrow. As even now I discovered that pity welled up in my heart. For even now, Lucifer failed to accept responsibility for his actions...still deflecting his behavior. The towering black cowled frame of Charon approached the edge of the lake of fire as fog descends upon the land. I remarked as the angel of death slowly crept past me. His great onyx scythe glistened like a shiny oil, and his chains dredged the ground, leaving trails in the earth. I squinted, for the ash and smoke of his presence bit into my eyes. I could not let him go just yet.

So, I reached for the arm of the giant angel. Charon stopped his march, and the angel of Death paused, and his hooded and skeletal head turned to me.

I released him and spoke. "I was there when the Lord formed you from the womb." I looked towards the direction of Lucifer, then turned my eyes back to the Vengeance of God and continued. "What will you do now, Great One; now that all things have been placed under the Lord's feet?"

Charon dipped his head slightly, his bony visage only partially visible. He then pointed to the King of Lies and spoke to me in a serpentine reply. "IIII willll beee what I have alwaysss beennn...death. Now go thy wayyy; for where I gooo. You cannot comeeee."

I watched as the Angel of Death then bowed in respect, and I nodded in return. He turned his cowled head towards the Lake of Fire. His eyes set towards the denizens who burned, and Charon continued his scorched earth stride to descend into the depths of the flaming waves. I watched as Lucifer slowly backed away from the lake's shores. Observed as the Deceiver's eyes narrowed, and his face grew stern. Watched as the glint of stubborn refusal broke into a seed of fear as the Warden lowered himself amidst the sea of screams and the groping of emaciated hands that sought escape. Amidst the screaming pleas of mercy that lifted from the surface of the fire and brimstone loch. The inhabitants clamored to escape the judgment that the personification of both Death and Vengeance would now administer.

I gazed as my brother squirmed his way through the crowded mass of humanity and Elohim clamoring to escape the reach of death. Lucifer too now fled into the morass of fire and sulfur; pushing aside those he had once called friend, climbing atop the bodies of those who also sought escape from Charon.

It was a pitiful scene. A scene of those whose recompense had now come due. I sighed as I took in the panorama that was the infinite flaming horizon.

I turned my back to the mass of the teeming damned. My back was to Lucifer as I returned towards the gate that was the body of Eladrin. The living portal that separated this realm from the Lake of Fire.

The Shekinah blazoned in white brilliance before me. Beams of blinding light awaited me once I stepped through the portal that was the King of the Ophanim. A step where I could leave behind all thoughts of rebellion, sin, death, and the grave. I knew the Lord awaited me. That, as promised, soon He would create a new Heaven and a new Earth.

I quickened my pace, determined to withdraw from this unholy place and set my eyes before me and smiled as I could hear the singing of the saints, the worship of the billions who had surrendered to the ways of El. The choral sound grew louder as I placed distance between myself and the point of entry where Eladrin had opened a gateway to the Lake of Fire.

Perhaps I would someday forget the years of agony... perhaps. For God had wiped away every tear from all eyes. But as I walked towards the jubilance and celebration that was now underway. I wondered what of me? Would I, too, one day forget the pain of ages past? Would I too be allowed to escape the haunting visions that my eyes had witnessed? In my final act to seal the Lake of Fire from the realm of all existence, would God allow my mind to forget my brother's demise?

I hoped so.

I hoped I would forget yearned that I might be released from the knowledge of good and evil. But I knew better; knew that El would never let me surrender to such a childish escape. I perceived He would have me bear this burden: to know what was left behind.

For in me would creation have a memorial of what El would discard. I would be the living, breathing reminder that sin was contained in a realm of darkness and fire. A walking, visible monument for all to see. For Yeshua had made Eladrin the door and I the key to the Lake of Fire; and I had fulfilled my duty to seal all the inhabitants therein.

As for me, I knew; knew that as Yeshua had carried the burden of sin for the world. I too, would now be burdened to carry this memory for all time. Knowing with each footstep I took away from the Lake of Fire, and despite the joyous music and praise I walked towards.

I would never forget the screams.

The untold... billions of screams.

The End

Glossary

To: Enoch

From: Argoth

To wit, the Lord hath given me word to make thee understand by scrolls the ways of Heaven. I have determined it incumbent to tutor thee of the races that populate her midst. Know that though thy people hath acquired some information through observation and encounters with our kind, there is yet much that thou must still learn. This scroll hath been prepared for thy reading and translated from our tongue that ye might grasp our number. I will expand upon your instruction in future lessons. As you have advanced in learning, I have now amended thy scroll to provide thee access into the tomes of the noble houses, and Celestial history concerning the Schism, and the Articles of War which govern our kind.

Commit the knowledge given to study and see my attendant if thou dost require additional resources.

Note: It hath been brought to my attention that thou hast made inquiry regarding the Books of Seals which El hast commissioned me to prepare. Note that this book is for El alone, and He will reveal it at His choosing.

Furthermore, your request to access tomes concerning the Mists, the Ophanim, the Seraphim, Limbus has been denied by El Pneuma.

His word He would have me relay to you, and I quote, "The anointing which ye have received of Me abideth in thee, and ye need not that any man teach thee: but as the same anointing teacheth thee of all things, and is truth and is no lie, and even as it hath been taught thee, thou shalt abide."

I trust that these words will give you contentment. Please, do not let them fall to the ground.

Your servant appointed by His grace in the understanding of our ways,

Argoth Grigori

The Chief of Eyes, and Sephiroth of House Grigori.

El or Jehovah

The name that angels have given to God and by which he has revealed himself to them. Triune in nature, El is often seen in a singular bodily form. On rare occasions, his triune nature is revealed as three separate distinct personalities (Father, Son, and Holy Ghost); collectively they are called the Godhead.

Godhead

The Trinity composed of the Father, the Son, and the Holy Ghost.

Elohim

The collective name of all angelic kind in Biblical lore; also called the Sons of God. Elohim are distinct from Yeshua, who is the only Begotten Son. Let it be known that Grigoric trances have shown that righteous men will also be adopted into the family of God. This knowledge is not yet commonly known among the people.

Chief Prince

An honorific title given to one of seven angelic princes who stand before the presence of God and receives instructions for their race. The Chief Prince is entrusted by El to walk within the Stones of Fire and to protect the secret of the chamber, the Primestone. A repository of God's power where one may become as God. Lucifer is the Chief Prince of all Angels at the time of this writing. Michael stands as interim Chief Prince of Angels. This rank is not to be confused with the Angel of the Lord, who is Yeshua.

Lumazi (Re 4:5)

The group of seven archangels who stand before the throne of God. They are the chief angelic council that executes the will of God in the universe. The head of each major house is represented on the council. The seven houses are Malakim, Kortai, Draco, Issi, Arelim, Grigori, and Harrada.

Ladder (aka Orphanic Portal)(Ge 28:12)

A mode of transport utilized by angels to travel between realms. Ladders are created by the Ophanim. Angels simply travel in the wake that the celestial beings create as they move from place to place.

Tartarus (2 Peter 2:4)

A prison designed by Lucifer to dispose of those who opposed him. Presently, it is in use by the Lord as a holding cell until He has determined their end.

Dissolution

Death to a celestial being is called dissolution.

The Kiln

A furnace from which El created all celestial life and the former storehouse of the Stones of Fire, the living elements of creation. At the heart of the Kiln was the Primestone which represented the ultimate test for angelic kind. Note that this chamber was destroyed in the battle between Lucifer and Michael, and the Lord now holds the Primestone.

Elomic Command

A vowel, consonant, or phrase allowing the power of God to be invoked by a delegated authority.

Manna

The food that angels consume. Grown in the fields of Elysium, it must be shipped to the four corners of creation to supply angels with sustenance. When harvested it instantly grows back. During the exodus of the children of Israel, the nation was temporarily fed this food. Exodus 16:15

Kenosis

Kenosis is the act of self-emptying by Yeshua to put himself in a position where he is totally yielded and dependent on the Father. In time, the people of God will write of this paradox in their holy book. (Philippians 2:7)

Stones of Fire (Eze 28:14)

A living sentient element which can be molded in the Kiln to create celestial life. They are also called Kilnstones or Godstones.

Shekinah Glory

The residue of God's breath, equivalent to the exhaling of a human's carbon dioxide; a living cloak of breathing light that envelops and irradiates the person of God; Primarily a localized phenomenon. Those that come near the Lord are irradiated by the Shekinah leaving an afterglow on their own person for a temporary period. The Shekinah can manifest wherever the holiness and righteousness of God exist.

Abomination

God has declared that interspecies breeding is forbidden. The Nephilim are the result. Mutants who are neither man nor angel. Mongrel creations El did not create. A species El wiped out in the great deluge of your kind For the law is that everything is to be fruitful and reproduce after his kind. When celestial blood is intermixed with material blood, Abomination is the result. Grigori scholars have speculated that it might be possible to create a being that could ascend to something more than either man or angel. And we know of no other being greater than a celestial than God. But due to the great flood and El's wrath. The Horde has been reticent to repeat this action. Nephilim have not been seen in thousands of your earth years.

The Schism

An event in Heavenly history that caused the separation of the three celestial races, attributed to Lucifer's trafficking to elevate the Elohim above the Ophanim and Seraphim.

The Descension

The day noted by all angelic kind that Lucifer was thrown out of Heaven.

Limbo

Also known as the Realm of Choices. An in-between place. The land between life and death. The land of infinite possibilities. Limbo is placed in the basement of Heaven, yet above the Maelstrom of the Abyss. It is the only passage to the other side of the Mountain of God that leads to the land of the Seraphim, as well as other regions of heaven. El has restricted full access to this area's tome.

Ashe

The legendary city of fire and home of the Seraphim. A metropolis made of living fire. The city is located in the land of Aesir.

Hell

A living mountain that serves as a prison. Designed originally with angels in mind, it lives off the eternal spirit of Elomic flesh. It possesses the ability to reproduce similarly as an amoeba and can grow. Grigoric spies indicate that Hell has grown to hold captive humans. (Isa 5:14 Therefore hell hath enlarged herself and opened her mouth without measure: and their glory, and their multitude, and their pomp, and he that rejoiceth, shall descend into it.)

Scouts indicate that humans now abide in two compartments within the creature. Hades: the realm of the unrighteous dead. Paradise: The realm of the righteous dead. Prior to Yeshua's resurrection, Paradise was the place where the righteous dead were held in the spirit realm until they were freed. These two domains were separated by a gulf that prevented residents from crossing to one another. (Luke 16:26)

Shiloah/Shiloh

The title given by angels to the man who is capable of defeating Lucifer. Men know this man as Christ and or by other titles such as Messiah. Shiloh is actually the second person of the Trinity Yeshua.

Dissolution

"Death" to a celestial being is called dissolution.

The Kiln

A furnace from which El created all celestial life and the former storehouse of the Stones of Fire, the living elements of creation. At the heart of the Kiln was the Primestone, and the ultimate test for angelic kind.

The Abyss

A gulf of nether sometimes referred to by thy kind as Limbo or by daemon kind as "the wilderness." It is a realm that separates the Third and Second Heavens. Failure to bridge the realms without a Ladder or direct intervention from El can cause one to be entrapped within the winds of the nether. The winds are referred to as the Maelstrom. Kortai builders frequently build near the edge of the Maelstrom to expand the landscape of Heaven. The Abyss is also referred to as the "bottomless pit." Mortals cannot pass through the Abyss without shedding their corporeal shell. Only Death or direct translation by God allows passage past the Abyss into the spiritual world of Heaven. El hath mentioned that He may release this tome to thee at a later time.

Waypoint

A designated area where travel between two points was allowed by God. Failure to utilize a waypoint could displace the Third Heaven with the second or vice versa, causing untold destruction.

Grigoric Trance

A vision given by God to some Grigori who are able, on occasion to see one generation ahead into the future.

Cadmime/cadmium

A black crystal-like mineral created by God. It is a living thing that grows similar to human bones. It is the hardest, most durable substance known to angelic kind. The substance is used to undergird the basement of heaven and her foundations. It can stretch and grow as directed. It is extremely pliable and able to be made into a variety of substances, from building materials to weapons of war.

The Burning

The Burning is a process that the Seraphim may engage where all Seraphim may unite as one single entity. All who participate while in this state are able to know and share one another's thoughts. Their collective flame is equivalent to the flames of Hell or the former Kiln. There are few things that can survive if the collective body of seraphim fires.

Creatures

Cherubim

A type of angel having great power; but not necessarily governmental oversight.

Seraphim

A heavenly creature designed to serve as a voice to the holiness of God; also called a "Burning One." A creature of great power. There are four which stand at the temple of God. The rest of the Seraphim have not been seen since the great Schism and are kept behind the mountain of God in the land of Aesir. The Seraphim appear as floating fire with flaming eyes and wings in their natural state and assume a humanoid form when in the presence of others. When they do so, their voices can create sounds that defy the hearing. El hath restricted full access to their tome.

Virtue

A living sentient aroma that lives before the throne of God and perfumes the throne. El hath restricted full access to their tome.

Ophanim (Ezekiel 1:15-21)

A heavenly creature designed to serve as guard to the presence of God. They are also movers of both planetary and star systems. El hath restricted full access to their tome.

Zoa (Rev. 4:1-9 5:1-6:1)

A heavenly creature designed to serve as guard to the secret things of God.

Aithon

The famed flaming horses of Aesir. These magnificent animals pull the fiery chariots of seraphim riders and were the steeds used to bring Elijah into heaven. Those that are tamed are stalled in the great flaming city of Ashe.

Angelic Rankings

Chief Prince

An honorific title given to one of seven angelic princes who stand before the presence of God and receives instructions for their race. The Chief Prince is entrusted by El to walk within the Stones of Fire and to protect the secret of the chamber, the Primestone. A repository of God's power where one may become as God. Lucifer is the Chief Prince of all Angels at the time of this writing. Michael stands as interim Chief Prince of Angels. This rank is not to be confused with the Angel of the Lord, who is Yeshua.

High Prince

Seven angels in existence who speak collectively for all their kind. (Collectively, they are called the Lumazi and are sometimes referred to individually with that honorific title.)

Archon

A sole high-ranking governing angel who directs a specific assignment or regions of territory(s). Sometimes referred to by humans as archangels. The highest-ranking angel over an assignment.

Principality

A sole mid-ranking governing angel who administers more than one territory.

Powers

The lowest ranking governing angel overseeing one territory.

Prime

A non-governing angel representative of a particular virtue. (i.e. love, justice, etc.) After the fall, some angels were designated as prime evils.

Minister

A non-governing angel who serves the cause of El.

Daemon

A fallen non-governing angel who serves the cause of Lucifer. Daemons are the regurgitated angelic souls of Hell, released by he who holds the keys to Death and Hell.

Daemons are but shadows of their former angelic selves and thrive off men, as their Kilnstones have been digested by Hell. Now they seek to inhabit the souls of men, that they might find expression through them. They are the undead of our realm and feed off the living.

Specter

Fallen Grigori are sometimes referred to by humans as Ghosts.

Shaun-tea'll

A group of angelic warriors dispatched to bring truth to the Grigoric records of fallen Grigori at any cost.

The Chief of Eyes

An honorific title given to the head of Grigori. This leader possesses the ability to undertake a Grigoric trance to see a generation ahead in time.

Redactors

A group of Grigoric enforcers who have powers to enforce changes to the book of Life. They are able to remove tomes, and pens, thereby strip fellow Grigori of their powers. They were instituted after the fall of man due to Satan's libel of El to man.

The First of Angels/The Sum o fall Things (Ez 28:12,13)

An honorific title given to Lucifer

The Great Angelic Houses of Heaven

House Draco: Sigil: A dragon

House Draco is the first house of angels and is considered to be highborn in the angelic cast. All Draco are angels of praise and represent beauty, wisdom, and art. Lucifer, prior to his fall, was their represented leader and the firstborn of all angels.

Each Draco has within him the ability to generate sound; some Draco are specifically limited to areas of sound. For example, some Draco can generate all notes within the soprano range, others in the tenor, bass, and alto, but they cannot generate sounds outside the range created. Lucifer is not so and can create any sound.

All Draco have a shimmering translucent skin that allows them to reflect light and therefore project images. They can project certain wavelengths of the spectrum. Each Draco is unique in that they are limited to certain areas of the spectrum. Lucifer, as their leader, is not so limited and may project any image. He may even disappear from view if he chooses to cloak himself in light and be invisible to the eye.

Metatron has now succeeded Lucifer as Prince of his people. Draco, when they choose to be visible to humans, reveal themselves as winged serpents.

Harrada: Sigil: An owl

The House Harrada are considered great sages of wisdom and lore, meticulous in their desire to create order and excel in the development of systems management and the written word.

Each member of house Harrada is adept at manipulating the elements, including heat, air, water, and earth. Also known as lovers of writing, they often create great literary works. Jerahmeel represents the embodiment of the Harrada. Prior to the Descension, God used Jerahmeel to temper Lucifer's tendency toward arrogance.

Harada are keepers of order within all three realms of creation and also exercise control over time and seasons. Harrada is often the head or manager of Heaven's day to day operations, including the harvesting of manna. Other angels of this house include Zeus and Chronos.

Kortai: Sigil: A Hammer

The Kortai is a race of builders, muscular and adept in the manipulation of metallurgy and woodworking, minerals and gems. They are the ultimate engineers and constructors of Heaven.

Curious to a fault, they have no qualms about delving into new architectural endeavors. It was the Kortai that volunteered to work against the Maelstrom to expand Heaven.

Kortai have a youthful appearance and are incredibly strong in spite of their smaller stature. The Kortai are the engineers of Heaven and are able to bring into creation whatever can be conceived. Michael the archangel, is the leader of this house. Since the war, they carry a hammer on one side of their belt and a sword in the other, ready to either build or fight at a moment's notice.

Assumably, all that left Heaven did so out of outright rebellion, but those Kortai that left went to see something new, thinking that more than what El had shown them existed, and they were moved to build something apart from El's designs. These are the builders of the Hellforge and the deep chasms that run throughout Hell. Lucifer has silently been turning the Kortai into daemons.

Grigori: Sigil: Two Eyes, aflame, an inkhorn, and stylus

The Grigori are chroniclers: They see all and record all. There are those who chronicle on behalf of God and those who chronicle on behalf of Satan. At least one Grigori records for God at all times. The watchers strive for perfection when documenting the events of history, but regardless of how they view God, their only motive is to chronicle as God designed them this way.

Those who chronicle for Satan say God's actions were not justified and therefore deserves to be overthrown. In the end, they believe their efforts will vindicate their belief in Satan's cause. They give commentary and chronicle with bias, or with an agenda that attempts to besmirch God. They do not simply chronicle...they editorialize. Their purpose for being is to compose. They may not, however, interfere with that which they behold. Those who attempt to harm them are themselves harmed. The Chief Prince is the exception, as he is embodied with authority and power over all angels.

Grigori cannot be stopped nor interfered with without penalty of Abyssian or Tartarus confinement. They can interact with their own kind.

Grigori do not possess the common instruments associated with sight and hearing as they are naturally blind and deaf. They can see as well as anyone and can hear equally well, but they can see nothing but El. They hover, cloaked in purple hoods, and no one has ever seen their face. They have immunity from harm and are able to move freely within both spheres of engagement.

Formerly, Raphael was the prince that oversaw this house but was killed by the fall of Kilnstones during the civil war. Argoth is now the Chief of Eyes and Sephiroth of his house. A few of the Grigori have been gifted with the 'sight', the ability to see beyond what is written to that which shall be written. El has limited this ability; thus, Grigori can only see one generation ahead. When the Grigori use this ability ,they go into a trance-like state and attempt to articulate the visions they see.

When El gives a prophecy to a prophet, He speaks to the prophet and allows the Grigori that shadows him to see ahead in time. Angels from this house include Argoth, Hadriel, and Lilith, prior to his dissolution.

Arelim: Sigil: A bull's face

Arelim are strong angels who have the faces of bulls and cloven feet. They can be extremely aggressive in that they enjoy forms of competition. Highly driven by order and authority, yet always seeking to be first in every endeavor, they constantly use their great powers to move planets and power suns.

Able to manipulate the forces of gravity, El has used them to fling planets and keep orbits. Headed by Talus, many of those that left to follow Lucifer were of this house. Proud and strong, they comprise over half of Lucifer's force, making his numbers, though smaller than Heaven, equally formidable in power, for in his ranks reside some of the most powerful of angels. Other angels from this house include Apollyon aka Abaddon, Marduk, and Sasheal

Issi: Sigil: A butterfly

Issi are lovers of beauty, and their gifts allow one to touch anything and manipulate its color. They are also creatures of light, typically soft-spoken, they are humanoid yet prefer to bein touch with creation and typically morph into creatures such as Pegasi, unicorns, and even satyrs.

Able to mimic all life, they, like the Harrada and Draco, contribute to the culture of Heaven through their paintings and works of art. Gifted in tailoring and the beautification of one's physical form, their beauty is such that even Lucifer takes notice. When in their humanoid form, Issi possess wings similar to butterflies. Sariel was the former Prince but sacrificed himself to expose the vulnerability of Abaddon. Azaziel now stands as Prince of his people.

The Issi also excels at all levels of herbalism and have now become healers as a result of the war. Issi can summon great celestial forces and target their enemies when in battle. Other angels from this house include Ashtaroth and Iblis.

Malakim: Sigil: Winged Feet

The angelic order of house Malakim are the messengers of God. If the Grigori are the eyes, the Malakim are its nerves. They constantly move to and fro throughout the realm delivering messages from various groups and ministers to one another. Like the Grigori in their numbers, they are similar in that they keep Heaven's communication lines open.

The Malakim ride steeds called gryphons. Each angel has a steed that is actually obtained when they acquire their first assignment from their Prince. Only the Chief Prince, the Grigori, and the

House are aware of the celestial home of the Gryphons. Able to move at incredible speeds, they are the fastest of all angelic kind. Gabriel, who is their leader, is the fastest and wisest. It is rumored that his speed rivals that of the Ophanim.

This has yet to be tested. All Malakim have wings on their feet and not on their shoulders as others of their kind. Malakim actually run, but their speed is so fast that they appear to fly. Malakim can also manipulate lightning.

Articles of War

When El exiled the Horde to the nether, He then placed within the Kilnstones of all angelic kind His law that restricts the actions of our people. The following is understood by all Elohim concerning Elomic intervention in the affairs of men:

1. All souls are the Lords.

2. There shall be no interbreeding between species.

3. Humans shall not be brought into knowledge of your presence except through prayer or by voluntary submission to sin or by permission from El.

4. Agents of Lucifer may influence to their own ends human activity that humans, have submitted themselves to, or through affairs of those who possess spiritual authority have yielded themselves to.

5. Members of the Host will not invoke the powers of the enemy nor seek to derive and use powers apart from El's design. Doing so will constitute a rebellion and those who do so will be marked as members of the Horde.

6. The ruling powers over a household, region or power will be held responsible for all those under their charge.

7. Any officer who shall presume to muster a human as a soldier (who is not a soldier) shall be deemed guilty of having made a false muster and shall suffer accordingly.

The Shaun-tea'll will monitor the terms of these articles among both host and horde and shall have the power to imprison within Tartarus all who break them.

Journal Notes 1 and 2

Dec 1, 2007

Journal thoughts

Today I took the family to Ihop had a good time. Today's my son's birthday. Plan on taking him to GameStop later, and possibly out shopping for a suit.

Was thinking about something I read yesterday while at the book store. A book about writing novels talked about the review process, and mentioned that at some point put the manuscript down for 6 weeks before you review it again. I find that there is impatience with me in doing that. I want to work on it until it's complete. I guess ill have to see what happens as time goes on.

I've been thinking about an idea I read in the book. It basically said read the entire novel out loud. Print it out and mark make corrections with pen. See the whole thing laid out. The book also mentioned that just read the dialogue of your characters, then of each character.

It made me wonder if my dialogue for Lucifer for example is consistent. Does he sound the same throughout the book?

I've also had thought and am wondering to myself am I really writing about Apollyon as opposed to Lucifer? Lucifer seems to have taken a backstage. He doesn't seem to be the one moving the story along. I don't know yet if this is a good or bad thing.

I have been reading D. Swains book; and trying to properly grasp the concept of MRU's. What he calls motivation reaction units. I hope to keep reading and writing in hopes to perfect the technique. It's one thing to have a picture in your head a vision that you want to share. It's another to have the words or a command of the language necessary to explicate it to paper.

His book is deep. He has a command of the English language that I can only hope to achieve.

In answering the question of how do you write vividly? His answer? Use specific and concrete, and definite pictorial nouns to describe action. Instead of saying creature say rhinoceros. Use the girl over using the word female. Etc.

Dec 2 2007

I think I want to make the name of the angel which guards the entrance to Hell have chains dangle from his arms. His name shall mean "Chain of God."

Another name I discovered was Cadfael it's welsh for War chieftain.

I've wondered did I make the relationship between Lucifer and Michael "deep" enough. I want the reader to feel torn over Lucifer's decision. To have him emotionally feel that God is wrong. To sympathize with him. To see things from Lucifer's perspective. I want the reader to see these two characters as brothers. That are torn to oppose one another. Like families torn in the American civil war. They take sides. Firmly in belief that they are right. (I don't think that I've established the familial setting yet. (Maybe do a flashback within the story again of Lucifer and Michael. Have Michael or Lucifer drag up a memory of an earlier time when they laughed together.) Lucifer's language should sound regal yet is should sound tender with his brother. How do I convey this tenderness?

I wonder…as I drag Apollyon off to be judged. I wonder has there been anyone else like that in the bible. What will be his charges? Maybe I should lay out a trial in heaven? Who would testify? What would be the evidence?

Where is Apollyon when Hell is made for him?

Hell is a hole in the ground? Guarded as it were by a man who watches over a man cover.

How do I deal with language in my book? How do I use words to describe things that prior to this time did not exist? How does the bible handle it?

OK I think I'm going to change the story and make the bottomless pit of the abyss for Apollyon. It's a valley or the edge of heaven. Maybe I'll still have him confined to Hell.

Oh so far I'm at 26, 092 words. I think at the rate of what I'm going the novel will be in the 78-90k word mark we'll see.

Angels can be angry because they might think that El's punishment of Apollyon wasn't enough. If God cant keep them safe. How can He govern? This line of thinking helps some to come to Lucifer's cause. This disgruntlement fuels Heavens rebellion.

There is a checklist I was thinking about making to help me in the revision process.

Ghost readers:

Is the entire manuscript in 3rd person? (Except for dialogue exchanges)

Change the POV from 3rd person to first and see what happens?

Are all your nouns specific and not vague (i.e. creature vs. cat)

Cut and paste all the dialogue and sort it for each character. Does their voice sound consistent?

Are there any problems with logic or reality in the story?

Are all your scenes in MRU's?

To test the significance of an element, ask: Why this place and not another? Why this name and not another? Why this action, this speech, and not others--or none at all?

Is your verb tense consistent (it should be past tense)

Is your grammar correct? (Check your subject verb predicates i.e. sentence structure)

Do you have passive sentences?

Are your sentences parallel

Are your paragraphs properly formatted and laid out?

Are your scene descriptions moving from out and general to in and specific?

Dec 3, 2007

Give Apollyon an internal scene of an earlier failure. Have Saesheal allude to some earlier incident.

Question: what was Lucifer's taste in furniture? How about Saesheal's?

How about if your angels have distinct combat styles. Lucifer should be refined, graceful and swift. Apollyon brutish forceful. Michael should be a mix of power and utilization of momentum.

learned something today to help me with the dialogue piece.

If you are giving us your characters' exact unspoken thoughts, use italics. If you are paraphrasing those thoughts, use regular Roman type):

Now what does she want? he asked himself. Isn't she ever satisfied?

Marshall wondered what she wanted now. She was never satisfied.

I think I solved the problem of Lucifer attacking El. He as the High Prince is the only one that can pass the seraphim and Ophanim unharmed. He does not fear them.

Logical Problem: Ok if Lucifer is 1st created and Michael 2nd then should he also not fear them if they (Ophanim) were created after Michael? The problem might be solved if whoever the High Prince is. Similar to the High Priest of Israel. Whoever occupies the title commands the honors that go along with it.

Problem solved. Lucifer attacks God from the rear and has entered the throne room from the kiln.

Dec 04, 2007

I grabbed some ideas from this lil article I saw on

Most novels are written to a formula, especially big best sellers. For example, John Baldwin, co-author of The Eleventh Plague: A Novel of Medical Terror, developed a simple formula that he used to structure his novel. His ten-step formula is:1. The hero is an expert.

2. The villain is an expert.

3. You must watch all of the villainy over the shoulder of the villain.

4. The hero has a team of experts in various fields behind him.

5. Two or more on the team must fall in love.

6. Two or more on the team must die.

7. The villain must turn his attention from his initial goal to the team.

8. The villain and the hero must live to do battle again in the sequel.

9. All deaths must proceed from the individual to the group: i.e., never say that the bomb exploded and 15,000 people were killed. Start with "Jamie and Suzy were walking in the park with their grandmother when the earth opened up."

10. If you get bogged down, just kill somebody.

I got some inspired thoughts from this idea.

What if Talus and Sariel are at odds over Apollyon being Arelim and Corlus being "another race"...these causes racial tension between the Elohim. Division is created before Lucifer's war who later simply exploits it. These two must work together and put aside their differences towards the end of the book to overcome the onslaught of heaven.

Also what if Michael and Raphael become real good friends as a result of their shared experience of Raphael's kidnapping? This would be my "2 team mates falling in love"

Lilith becomes an expert in strategy along with Lucifer.

Apollyon is a leader due to his sheer brute force tactics.

One of the royal court maybe Jerahmeel might sacrifice himself to save something of great importance.

There is division in heaven as to Apollyon's sentence. And tension created between the Elomyic races due to one causing the trouble and the other being the recipient of said trouble. Maybe Lucifer can find a way to use this to his advantage.

Lucifer's betrayal must be so devastating as to cause him to be declared an enemy of the state. What if it was possible to feign Lucifer's helping until the last minute? Then it is revealed he is a traitor. It's a classical tactic of misdirection. What if no one knew he rescued Apollyon? What if Lucifer rescued him? Set Asmodeus up to take the fall. Has Apollyon kill him to show a body.

Motive: What does the murderer stand to gain?

Means: Means is associated with the suspect having the equipment, specialist knowledge etc. to carry out the crime. Ask yourself how the crime was committed and then consider whether the suspects had the capability. Did they have access to poisons? Did they know how to fire a gun? Would they have the physical strength to overpower the victim?

Opportunity This is more associated with when and where the crime was committed.

Lucifer frees Apollyon who kills the guard. Asmodeus shuffles him safely to earth. This is pre arranged by Lucifer so that only Apollyon and Lucifer know what truly happened. Where

Asmodeus is killed by Apollyon. Lucifer is released to apprehend Apollyon where in reality he is actually establishing the means to overthrow heaven.

Why would Lucifer desire Asmodeaus Killed? Asmodeus is simply a tool. A means to an end. His devotion can best be served by dying.

Lucifer should be shown to lie to Michael and his brethren. They should be shown to trust Lucifer, their trust is betrayed. Maybe Lucifer kills a member of the royal court or has someone killed.

Gabriel and Raphael should be utilized to communicate.

Talus and Sariel are soldiers.

Michael is considered the reluctant general

Jerahmeel provides support. He could serve like a police/emergency force to heaven

Lucifer can feign being overtaken by Apollyon who also destroys the guard. He can escape to earth via prearranged transport.

Lucifer sets a trap for a group of angels who would seek to capture Apollyon and the court doesn't know Lucifer is responsible for their deaths all in an attempt to undermine their strength so he can invade.

Maybe Lilith can take out Apollyon's Grigori. We see how one may destroy another. Lilith might be amused by the new sensations of destroying.

Lilith stays with Lucifer to document. No other reason. Lilith can reveal to Lucifer how to destroy a Grigori.

Have Lucifer teach his legions how to open up wormholes" ladders that are not preposted. When opened in heaven they wreak havoc, and destroy structures and any living thing that.

Dec 04, 2007

2:20am and I'm at 28,453 words. 2,361 word increase! Who hoo. Time to get some sleep...ugh

8:44am I'm back at it, looking to see if I need to change the organization of the story. I'm not sure if the betrayal as I have it organized in the story is emotional enough. I think I'll need to make sure there is a lot of dialogue between Lucifer and Michael to show the severity of the betrayal.

Ok I think Lucifer's master plan will be to force God's hand. El can't be destroyed. But creation can. El cannot be defeated in the traditional sense. He must be made to step down voluntarily. He can be injured in his heart. When Lucifer sees the grief caused by Apollyon's actions it is then that he realizes El's true "weakness" Love. He will use El's own love for creation against him.

Lucifer will attempt to make God abdicate by forcing Him to destroy all of his creation (which he is want to do) or capitulate the thrown. If he captures the Kiln he can create enough Elohim to support his position overrun heaven and station his minions like terrorist bombs waiting to explode around the cosmos. So by the time the Lord comes from his self-imposed rest. Lucifer's forces would be in place. The Kiln will be key to his success. The strategic point of interest.

Ladder what are other synonyms for a ladder?

Chute

Ok I haven't written a dime today just trying to tighten the plot in my scene editor. The ideas I've written in my journal have been great and convinced me that the story is more potent with them incorporated. I wrote the last scene of my book. It still doesn't quite capture what I want in that last sentence. But I trust that...wait...its ominous...that's the feeling I want to leave with the reader at the end: that feeling of portent that takes their mind right into Genesis 3. The Bible itself; now continuing the story.

Here's some old text I might use some way.

He hears the trumpets sound, and then hears the voice of Lucifer.

"To all inhabitants of Heaven assemble yourselves to hear the word of God. He that hath and ear to hear let him hear. He is the alpha and the omega, the beginning and the end the first and the last. Blessed is he who hears the voice of the Lord God.

28, 803. I cute out a lot of stuff like the text above. I was real pleased with what I wrote.

Let's see I wrote 350 words today. Not bad...not bad.

Day 26

Set a goal for yourself to write at least four pages a day. That is 300–325 words, double-spaced. Some days you'll write one page; others you'll write 15 pages. Try to average at least four pages a day.

Oh I reread some stuff...remember that when Lucifer comes back to heaven he does not know what happened with Apollyon. So make it so that when the council convenes he requests that El meet with him. And have everyone be quiet. It could be a scene with much power as it is revealed to Lucifer what happened. He could be wracked with guilt. If he had been there perhaps this would not have occurred. His act of releasing Apollyon could be in part an attempt to repay him.

Ok going to bed. Its 1:45am...night

Dec 05, 2007

Haven't felt like writing much today but finally set myself to get some work done at 3ish or so this afternoon. I had an idea as to how Lucifer could rescue Apollyon. A "blind jump" he transports Apollyon to earth blindly with an Elomyic command. This does two things. They escape, but Hell expands herself and now has a conduit to earth. An intention not originally designed by El. One can now enter hell from earth. What if Charon knows (he doesn't speak remember!) that Apollyon has fled and hunts him down like a silent bounty hunter. He searches the bowels of hell to find him on earth. Apollyon escapes Earth before he can be captured. And Charon goes back through hell.

And he finally captures him at the end of the book! There can be a scene where he walks through heaven ignoring all the destruction. And other Elohim fight around him. Just simply getting out of his way. Fire ignites where ever he treads leaving footprints of flame. Towards the end of the book Apollyon can be captured and hauled back kicking and screaming to Hell. Consigned to be thrown off into the Abyss until he's released in the 3rd book.

I thank you Lord for the word that you gave me in tonight's in Bible Study. I thank you that you won't release me. I thank you that you sent a word of encouragement and hope. I thank you that you have not forgotten my work and my labor of love in that I have ministered to the saints and do minister. (I saw myself standing in the pulpit and the congregation stood and started to spontaneously clap, and I quoted that scripture from Heb 6:10.) Sister H then quoted the scripture in her message.

I thank the Lord for confirmation. And believe it shall happen just as I saw it.

I notice I started the Shaunteel story line but I don't do anything with it in the scene editor. How do the Grigori fight each other? What role does Lilith play. Should he battle Raphael, those two could be set up somehow to become arch enemies. Their battle could really be shown in book 2.

Ok after the Sheanteal are formed what then? Maybe their creation is something that is done towards the end of the book during the judgment scene after the war and is left to fully flesh out in book 2? If so what will be Raphael's role in the war while in heaven?

Check his character profile to lift his story arch.

You might want to learn ways to format or "layout" the excel spreadsheet so you can input more information.

Dec 6, 2007

Yesterday I learned that the writers edge indicates that 60% of material submitted is publishable. It occurred to me that I could increase my odds of becoming published by utilizing the submission guidelines of I-universe. I copied the guidelines and learned a lot of what I need to do and will need to do to my manuscript to make if ready. It cannot be a first draft when its done.

I added various pages to it. Acknowledgements, about the author, things like that. I printed the document out and I was pleasantly surprised at how large it was. I'm on track to produce a document that's around 240 pages. I think ill hit about eighty-four thousand words by the time I'm done. It was helpful to look at the I-universe submission guidelines and then to look at my developing hard copy. I printed the guidelines out. And highlighted areas that I'm aware of what I will definitely have to review when it's done. It will take some time, perseverance, but the novel is becoming a reality.

Today I got up thinking I also might need to remove the scene regarding the Sheateal. I'm not sure if it advances the core story at all. I'll have to revisit Raphael's character bio I created, and see what I can find. We'll see.

Ok I looked up Raphael's storyline. No help there.

I guess I simply have to decide how The Grigori battle?

Usefulness in war: Grigori can supply information. Have access to the collective tome knowledge

Fallen Grigori can be cut off.

This has a 2 way affect. You can't get the information form a cut off Grigori

To cut off the Grigori means they can be touched. Maybe they can still be invisible but not ethereal?

Raphael is unique as a Grigori because although he can turn invisible he is not ethereal, the others are.

4:52pm and I'm at 30,098 words. Just finished writing the scene where Charon was created...omg I just love it. I read it to my daughter she said she could really see the whole thing.

Whoohoo!!! I just finished chapter three. We are making headway!

Chapter 4 starts with scene number 40. So I'm done with 39 out of 110 scenes.

Ok Lucifer should possess a sophistication about him. He is trying to win a battle without assaulting

I got an idea from reading Sun Tzu

"when we are near, make the enemy think we are far away" What if the forces of heaven launch an attack to stop Lucifer not realizing that they have left heaven vulnerable as Lucifer's forces are nearer than they thought.

Lucifer's strategy will be to divide and evade heavens forces. He cannot numerically win the battle as he's outnumbered 2 to 1.

Only attack what the enemy cannot defend. There are strategic points in heaven to assault. The Elysian Fields is heavens supply. The kiln supplies "troop" the temple is heavens command and control" Note that the kiln is undefended save Charon its lone guard. Only Michael and Lucifer can walk its breadths. It's a prime target. The Elysian Fields will not be defended at all. The mount of God has the seraphim and Ophanim, that if unleashed would wipe them out. But they are but 6 against legions. What if some of heavens troops were caught on earth? They are in Athor after all. So speed is of the essence. If God can be toppled quickly Lucifer can establish control before the rest of heaven even knows. Also the 12 waypoints of heaven must be controlled.

Lucifer has two forces one in heaven supplanting heavens defenses and causing strife and division making heaven a softer target to invade. The main invasion force from earth which has been trained.

What if some Grigori had turned but their charge did not. They could report on what was going on. The command and control of Lucifer's group would be the hall or records. A spy within the hall could pull any record. Lilith could reassign a Grigori from one angel to another so that they switch. The switch of one could place them in the hall of records, a position where they could monitor the goings on.

What if something blocked the ladder? I.e. someone kicked the ladder while someone was climbing it? Blocking the waypoints could accomplish this. Preventing Elohim from coming from earth to provide support. This is how things could go wrong for Lucifer's forces later as a mission to clear the way points allows the legions from earth to come and attack the rearward of Lucifer's forces.

Lucifer's attack to succeed must hinge on the following factors.

Surprise

Weakening of enemy forces via division.

Misdirection

Evade the bulk of heavens forces

Capture strategic targets

Speed (Tactical advantage of being able to ladder outside the waypoints)

There are scores or Arelim that are distraught due to Talus failure to subdue Apollyon. They believe that he should be their new prince, that he has grown too compassionate.

It was the first war

The first betrayal

The first sin

The first murder

Heaven was where war was birthed. See how it was conceived in this fascinating tale of betrayal, murder, sin and loyalty.

Use the intelligence that Lucifer has to have Talus and Sariel's species attack one another.. He will give the signal to attack in the confusion.

Heavens forces attack first and then earth's ladder in destroying a third of the city and sending legions of angels. This tactic alone will whittle heavens forces down.

What causes heaven to rally? When they see God cast Lucifer down to earth. When they see Charon drag Abaddon. The rebels realizing that El has completed his day of rest surrender.

Have the story focus on Raphael, Jerahmeel and Gabriel helping to bring normalcy back. Raphael discovers how Lilith has accessed the great hall. Those two have to have it out somehow. Gabriel focuses on marshalling heavens forces to repel Lucifer's main attack. Jerahmeel focuses on clearing the barriers from the waypoints. Allowing him to lead heavens forces with Gabriel's to beat back Lucifer's.

Talus and Sariel only stop fighting only when they see Apollyon in the distance and realized they have been duped. As he kills both of their species. Sariel gives his life at the hand of Abaddon for his brother while protecting Talus. Talus is almost defeated when Charon arrives.

Dec 7, 2007

Had an idea. What if Raphael coordinates form the temple and Lilith from the archives. And Raphael assigns a watcher to watch Lilith! That will answer the question "who watches the watcher from a conversation he and Lilith had earlier. It keeps Raphael in a position where he's doing research trying to see how heavens forces are being undermined. The sheanteal can be released towards the end of the war to apprehend Lilith.

Lucifer follows Charon's footprints still fresh to where Apollyon is within hell. That's how he can find his way to him.

Make a Jerahmeel like some old rugged cop. Raphael is more like the young researcher. Pair these two together to find why their intelligence is compromised and why they can't summon help from earth.

Make Jerahmeel anxious to go out and kick some butt, but he's stuck helping Raphael...looking through tomes.

Add Jerahmeel to dialogue and give him some old crow kind of humor. Have him "complain" because no body works fast enough anymore and all the bureaucracy.

"I'm telling you when I was younger...like remember that first day? We had a different work ethic back then.

"Uh Jerahmeel that was a day ago."

And that's why! I tell this generation of angels Is just spoiled! I mean we were making light! You know how hard it is to do that without a sun?" Youth today I tell give them some west wind or to be in charge of something and they think they've done something special. We didn't have all these fancy planets back then. Just spoiled I tell you.

Think of Jerahmeel like Grumpy from Snow white. Lovable. But man he's just never satisfied.

"Uh Jer...we are the same age."

"Oh...you must've gotten commissioned when darkness was created or something cause if you were commissioned when there was light this wouldn't be a problem."

"I give up."

"Would you like him stop?"

"Please?"

"Then just keep quiet he'll stop on his own"

Here's a line to add when Talus and Sariel are about to come to blows...

"I say let em go at it." Maybe they will knock some sense into each other.

What if Lucifer repeated these words to Michael?

"This too shall pass. Just listen and it will go quicker."

Dec 9, 2007

Today I decided to do some writing. Spent a lot of time today formatting my book properly. So now all the paragraphs are properly placed throughout. I did some editing on chapter one some. I'll make it a point to do that with the other chapters prior to submitting them out. Ill have to make sure they are all in 3rd person.

I'm a little nervous. My laptop keeps shutting down on me. I've saved my work so I'm not too concerned about losing anything. Its just it would be a huge blow if I lost my laptop. Preliminary indications tell me I might have a motherboard issue. Not really sure. Just going to keep going till the thing dies. And keep backing up daily.

I'm into the scene now where Lucifer is talking to God about Apollyon. I got "inspired" I think. I say that because I "acquired" a concept of Hell that I never had before. Can't really say its biblical. But basically I made hell as an expression of God's love. It is a home designed for those who want to be apart from him. Not just a place of punishment. I've never seen Hell as an act of mercy. I'm hoping to use the dialogue between Lucifer and God as an indication as to a justification used by him about why he did what he did.

I dunno...kind of feel under attack. My heads been hurting all day. Been getting "pressure" in my chest. I really need to go to the doctor I suppose and be checked out. Also need some new glasses. These tension headaches can be a pain. They only go away when I go to sleep. Can't get much work done then. Lord willing I hope to finish. I pray for the finishing anointing needed to see this through.

So far today I'm at word count of ...31,525 and increase of 1427 words since last count!

Oh I also answered the question of why angels can't be redeemed! Imagine that!

Dec 10 2007

31626 words and counting. It's 9:57am. Having an ok morning. Having Flashbacks of my past. Distracting but dealing with it. I did have a thought this morning of how much I could expect to get done on my writing in 100 days. For example if I wrote 200 words a day. From now till let's say march 10. 90 days times 200 =18, 000 words. Which as of today would 49,626. Have to admit that's not a good amount to me. I think I can do better. That would probably place me at just over half the books mid-section. I just figured out I would need to write about 590 words a day to get to 90k by March 10th. LOL....well here's goes nothing eh?

I picked up this great quote today while taking a break to eat.

"No tears in the writer, no tears in the reader. No surprise in the writer, no surprise in the reader." - Robert Frost

Ok colors

Blue

Purple

Scarlet

Dec 11, 2007

It's 3:21am Woke up didn't even look at the clock and kinda figured it was 3ish .Turned over and it was 3am.Weird huh?

I hear Amber on her way down stairs to see about me..lol (She's my cat)

Ok I'm at 33, 991 words. That's 2, 365 words. Wow I was a machine yesterday! Learned some tips on how to finish. But some stuff I learned I already knew. Website with great information I found yesterday was ...

http://hollylisle.com/fm/Articles/wc2-3.html

It's a great site with lots of good information for writes gave me some good advice as to when I need to look for agents. Maybe about a month prior I might find an agent. But I can see myself finishing. I just have to keep swimming.

Well last night before going to bed I came up with several ideas that I want to incorporate that will help me with the book.

Make a graph showing the highs and lows of the level of suspense in the book. (I.e. find a way to quantify it and graph it) This will give me a visual idea of how I'm doing in taking my reader for a roller coaster ride and what I'm doing to set up scenes and stuff.

Have Lucifer challenge Michael more by having him ask Michael if he plans to supplant him as Chief Prince. I'm hoping that this might have the effect of making Lucifer seem paranoid, add some suspense and tension, and make him seem maybe less passive

I realized I need to bring Raphael's search of the records into the story more. I began the search early in chapter but haven't addressed it at all. I need to show something that shows his progress I'm thinking I need to place this scene in chapter three. I can specifically have him discover the dialogue between Lucifer and Apollyon, and him noting that Lucifer failed to give Apollyon El's entire word. Show in Raphael's report the word El had given that Lucifer didn't give. I'm hoping that this will also create a sense of impending suspense. And forces me to ask several questions. Why wouldn't Lucifer want Apollyon to know? What motivation would compel Lucifer to rescue Apollyon (he thinks it's his fault maybe: that if he had given him the entire word this wouldn't have happened) Also when Lucifer first initially receives the word from God make it aware to all the Elohim but not the reader. And have Lucifer react in disbelief Like Peter did when Jesus said he'd deny him three times.)

Do I need to add the bloodhound element to Charon and Lucifer's confrontation?

Is Lucifer doing enough action or is he being acted upon in chapters 2-3?

Lucifer is a plotter. He searches for weaknesses and then attacks. He is a schemer and master strategist. He's watched God enough to think long term.

Have Lucifer eye the adulation of the crowds as they praise him but hate it when El comes and the crowd goes crazy w/crazy praise.

Have Lucifer complain about the praise. But the Lord tells him that if they were to stop the rocks would cry out. Have him question this. Would they cry out now...but if they knew that thou proposed to elevate this man over them would they really? Do they submit to you out of force? Fearful of imprisonment like Apollyon. Is God a dictator? Slowly Lucifer sees himself in a better light than he sees God himself.

I think a lot of these ideas a great! I can't wait to incorporate them. I realize I need a lil notebook to put by my bed so I can write this stuff down: one by my bed and one in my car.

This is a line I picked p from the word I think might be cool to implant.

Beat your plowshares into swords, and your pruning hooks into spears: let the weak say, I am strong

I'm wondering if during the procession if I'm taking too long to describe things and not enough time to propel the story forward? I wonder what would happen if I sped things up?

Oh as of right now (10pm) I have 34,822 words. Almost a thousand words from where I was this morning.

OMG! I think I wrote one of the most beautiful scenes in my book. Totally just creatively inspired to write it the way I did. And man did it set things up to make Lucifer looks sooo prideful and selfish. Ok yeah this is a great big pat on the back. And a great big thank you to the Holy Ghost who had to have quickened this idea in me. I'm at 35, 246!

Dec 12, 2007

Ok I stayed up till about 1:30am last night writing. As stated above I wrote a scene I think was great in that it really showed to me the worship of heaven and the difference between Lucifer and Michael. I went to bed having written 36, 109 words!. Wow! I wrote a whopping 2118 words yesterday. I think that's the most since I've been keeping track!. Rather proud of myself but I suppose I don't want to get too giddy. Heck the books not finished and I've a long ways to go. I'm on scene 43 out of 110. After this chapter is done I should be at the halfway point of my book.

Dec 13 2007

Word count is 36720 to start the day off. Was talking to a family member earlier about my book and the possibility that as a first time author I might not get it published through a traditional publisher. Man I really would like to see if in the stores. But I realize this might be a creative endeavor just for me and close ones right now, time will tell. I just hope that my writing is such that those within the Christian community might want. Kind of wishing I was at work working and making some money. Spend a good part of the morning downloading and playing with this new program I found on the net. It's a nice lil program. Figured I better put some thoughts down on here to get myself rolling. This book won't finish itself. I'm learning one thing, writing a book is a lesson in perseverance. I can see why people don't finish. It's lonely. Easy (at least in my case) to get distracted. Well let me get going and put some words down on paper.

Ok I'm at the point where God has made Adam and Eve. Didn't do much writing today. More revising and putting stuff in proper pov. It's almost

11pm though and I'm at 37524

Not bad 574 words is not bad at all. Some days you write a lot. Other days you don't.

Dec 14 2007

This morning I woke up at 3:33am

Went downstairs to do devotion and pray. I had a wonderful time in the Lord. He taught me so much about him. And a lot about myself. Mainly how I had allowed myself to become withered by not abiding in him. That I have been trying to do things in my own strength. That I was trying to accomplish things that were not in my power or in me to accomplish. That to receive the strength of Christ I must submit my weaknesses to him in prayer that he might fortify me. As again it's not possible to do it. That it's his responsibility to bear fruit. It's my responsibility to abide and to draw/drink from his well. The fruit will come on its own, and it won't even be my fruit when it does it will be his. It's a powerful truth, and one I hope I never forget.

I needed that devotion time badly. I feel a part of me has been cleansed. After devotion I checked my email and found out that I hadn't gotten the job I applied for. I wrote back thanking them for considering me but I was bummed. I was sad and I cried. It's almost Christmas and I have no real money to spend on the kids or family or others. I cried because I felt that I wasted time (two weeks waiting to hear something from them and they did not contact me to tell me they had offered it to another.) I cried because I don't have a job. And it's hard on us as a family and on myself-esteemI cried in private. And then put into practice what I had just learned. I asked god to give his faith, hope and perseverance. That mine wasn't good enough or enough in quantity and that I looked to him to supply us. I asked God for a sign asking if I should request assistance from the church. I already feel bad because I literally owe the church money. But I am willing to do whatever the Lord tells me to do. I just want to know it's him telling me to do it.

So now I feel better after my cry. I just started crying. I couldn't help it. I'm trusting in the Lord to provide and make a way.

I don't know what I am to take away yet from this whole experience. I want to learn what I am to learn from it.

I got my unemployment check yesterday and I have 6 weeks left. That's 1.5 months left. Or put another way my last check will be on

Jan 24 2008

I think now that I have so little time left before my checks stop coming I'll have to change up on what I'm doing. I might need to seek out help to help me find a job. Maybe what I'm doing on my own is not enough?

I do feel better that at least I know what's going on. At least I know that my next step is to go back and look and apply. I have to believe that this position simply was not the one for me. I found a job yesterday with alternative for girls. I plan on applying for that. We'll see of course what happens. I just want to go where I'm called to go. And abide in my calling. So if you ever read this letter, and see me. Give me a hug. I won't mind.

Don't know how much writing I'll get done today. Need to pay some bills and stuff. We'll see.

But I thank God that he's helping me to forget about these things behind by helping me to press on towards the mark of the high calling.

Dec 15, 2007

I didn't do any writing yesterday. Dealing with financial bad news. I could have written of course. But with all the things going on, decided to just give it a rest yesterday. So today it is my intent to pick it up today. Got the Christmas fellowship today at 5pm

So I'm looking forward to going and seeing Christopher and Candace do their play.

Ok so that's what's been going on and just kind of wanted to give an update on where we are. Now back to book stuff.

First I've completed the creation of Adam and the naming of animals and Eve.

God has informed the Elohim that they will assist man in learning how to rule this new domain called earth. Ok so where to take the story from here is the question.

In reading the techniques of the selling writer by Dwight v. Swain; I've now wondered do I have enough tension in chapter 4?

I think I was just inspired as to where to place the scene with Raphael speaking with Michael. I could place it before he talks with Lucifer. Or I could place it after. So In chapter 4 we could learn about Lucifer failed to say to Apollyon. But I still think we need something chapter three that preludes to it.

I think I'm going to do the hard work of trying to place it in the story right now. Wish me luck!

37944

Dec 16,2007

Back to writing. As of right now my word count is 38,008. Didn't do much writing today and spent the majority of today in church of course of talking with a church friend.

Been spending time going back over chapter one and making sure the tense is past tense and the POV is in 3rd

person. I really don't like the feel. I think its more distant sounding in 3rd

person. But I might end up doing a draft all in 2ndperson just to see how it feels. As of right now though. I'm finding that I'm a lil sleepy. Gonna try and get some writing done before I tuck in for the night. It's

10:17pm so ill probably tuck in in about 2 hours or so.

Dec 18 2007

38056 didn't do any writing yesterday. I've had some serious issues with my computer. But I took it apart and sprayed the inside and hopefully that helped. Haven't had any more issues for the last 24 hours. We'll see. But I've back up my most important files so I'm good if it crashes. I can at least continue. I'm thinking about consistently saving 3 times. Here, the internet and on my flash drive. Then I won't have these issues. I was pretty scared yesterday. But I'm good now...I got a handle and everything is backed up to the point I can get it again if necessary.

Thank god for that too. I learned a lot the other day about synopsis and how important they are. So that I can expedite time I'll probably write mine as I'm writing this book. Per one author I'm already late because I should have started that process already.

Let me write here the ideas I had for Lucifer's war. Hmmm...maybe that could be a title.

Ok key points

To succeed to dethrone god Lucifer needs the following things.

Speed

The Elohim survival is tied to the success of the army as a whole

Michael's army will trade space (geography) for time. They will attempt to outlast Lucifer's forces until el ceases his rest.

Lucifer will blitzkrieg heaven

Have heavens forces divided some of them are on earth looking for Lucifer.

Make it so that Lucifer's minions prevent access for heavens forces to return.

Ok here's what I wrote for what Lucifer left out when speaking to Apollyon.

"Resist the taunts of thy brethren. For I have sent Lucifer as comforter for thee. Abide with him for as I liveth if thou leaveth him. Know that ruin lieth not far behind, and my comforter shall be thy king"

Dec 19 2007.

No real adding of words yesterday. I did some revision. I sent the first draft off to sis Froby. But as of right now I'm at 38112. I mostly made sure the first chapter was consistent in the 3rd

person POV and in the past tense. I discovered an interesting link yesterday let me see if I can add it here.

Humph. Well turns out I didn't save the link. But I found another great website while searching. And from it 2 other publishing websites.

http://booksbylyncote.com/LC1/?page_id=3

Ok so now I'm going to get started working here. Ttyl. 40202

Ok im stuck a lil bit. Just trying to figure out where to go now. I hit the 40k word mark today. I put my book at double space just to see what it would be. Came out to 162 pages. WOW. So basically it looks like I can take whatever number of pages I've written and double it and that's how many pages I really got in terms of an actual novel. And I'm thinking this thing will hit 80k at least. So that will be like 320 pages maybe. God. Well as of right now I just got to figure how to get to the next link in the chain. I guess even as I'm writing that I need to determine what the next scene will be. Maybe that's the real issue. Yeah that's it. My map needs adjustment. Well its 11:28 and I'm at 40212 so I've written 2100 words today. Not bad...not bad... Think I've got two tasks tonight before I go to bed.

Reread this journal

update and review my scene editor so I know what to write next

Email a copy of all this to myself.

Oh on the furniture bit regarding Lucifer's taste look up a design book you have a home and styles that are there. Then extrapolate.

Maybe you showed that Raphael knew too much. Maybe just stick with the original idea of Lucifer not sharing the whole word and leave it at that.

Dec 20, 2007

Its 11am. I'm at 40,259.

Ok I'm still kind of stuck. I still need to address which scene to write next. I'll try to tackle that today. Was doing some research on J.k. Rowling. Seems she sent her manuscript to 12 publishers and they all said no. Then finally after a year someone was willing to look at it. Amazing how things come about. I don't pretend that I am going to be the next J. K. Rowling. But I must admit I wouldn't mind!

In any event I found a job at TSA I can do, and am going to apply for that. Gonna do some trolling through the Fed government website this afternoon and see what I can dig up. That's if my family doesn't try to load me with stuff. We'll see.

Ok gonna try to get started here. Ttyl...

Ok Sariel and talus could get into it after the dinner. They think that maybe one was going to betray the other. Lucifer uses the contention later to incite chaos.

Go to the library and browse through books on food and gardening. Authors of these books describe smells, tastes, touches, and even sounds in precise detail. When writing, always mention scents and tactile sensations. Good description observes all the senses.

Great advice!

I wrote Lucifer's speech. It just came out...flowed very well. I was so excited that I had to share it with a family member immediately. Their response..."Wow". I hope others who read it will have the same impact. I'm about to go to bed. I'm happy I finally got some test written. I've been struggling on this chapter some. It's finally coming together. Bit by bit. Word count for the day. 41,867 172 pages baby! It's definitely coming together.

Dec 21, 2007

Ok I just started to do some writing. I think I write better at night. Between like

7pm -12am.

Lucifer to Raphael.

Do not follow me Raphael. For where I go you cannot follow. You do so at thine own peril.

42636

Dec 22 2007

No writing today. Mainly Christmas shopping and stuff. I'll try tomorrow.

Dec 23 2007

42745 are the words that I begin my writing today. I've wondered if my pacing is good enough? I suppose I can rewrite when I finish. Of course that's the main thing to do write now is to finish. Get the thoughts down on paper, and then go from there. I want to get down some of the thoughts I learned or enjoyed from my readings.

Robert Frost said to be truly happy is to wed your vocation to your avocation, to figure out how to make your pastime pay.

Well here goes ttyl.

Trying to determine if I should leave this in or take it out.

El stood and Raphael kneeled silently waiting on any command from his Lord, and El spoke.

"Come Raphael. There is much to do, the seventh day approaches and I must take rest from all my labor.

43619

Dec 24, 2007

44, 338

OK I made that underlined text work by making some changes. It does a better job of hooking the reader now. It reads as follow.

Whoohoo I'm on chapter six. The tension is building now!

Dec 25, 2007

Merry Christmas!

NO writing today spent the day with family and friends. I decided to try to work on the synopsis today.

I'm thinking that Act 3 is where Lucifer openly rebels against God.

Act Two:

Apollyon snaps

What had to happen to bring Lucifer to this point?

Apollyon's imprisonment

Man's creation

Apollyon's "crime"

The kiln is closed

Act One

Michael while walking at the brim of the lake of fire observes Lucifer and laments the losses of the war that has just been concluded. He thinks back on how it all began.

Michael along with Lucifer and 5 other Princes were the royal council which

Apollyon an assigned as archangel or "Archon" of Sol determines that he will assist God in bringing life to a planet. His actions causes the son he controls to flare placing earth at risk. Another angel protects the earth from destruction but this causes his accidental death.

Other angels castigate Apollyon aggravating his grief to the point that he purposely murders

God creates Hell as a place of judgment for him

Lucifer disagrees with the decision to imprison him and feels guilty over his failure to curtail Apollyon's behavior

God creates man and closes the kiln the birth place of all angels

This behavior of Gods behalf causes Lucifer to question Gods goodness and to lead a revolt for their freedom from serving man.

Lucifer frees Apollyon from Hell and uses him as chief general in his army to overthrow God and heaven.

Apollyon and his army lay waste to heaven

Lucifer moves through hell to the kiln (the birthplace of all Elohim) to take possession of it and create more angels solely devoted to him.

Dec 26, 2007

44771

Not much writing today. Found a great website.

http://www.wherethemapends.com/main.htm

It definitely gave me a reality check on what I could expect when I try to get published. But I suppose that's a good thing. It's about 10pm right about now. I'm just gonna sit here and read and do some writing until I'm tired and can't write. I don't have to be up at any certain time and I'm just going over to my grandmas probably tomorrow. So nothing I really have to do. So wish me luck.

45302

Dec 29, 2007

Well it's almost the New Year and I'm sitting here in the sanctuary of church on a 3 day fast and shut in. We haven't had one in quite some time. But other than being sleepy from staying up and messing with my sleep pattern I'm doing ok.

Wrote some today over 500 words. Hoping to get some good writing done maybe tomorrow but especially Monday we'll see.

As far as things are with the book. I printed off chapter two so I could read it, revise and edit it before I send it off to my writing group.

I also ordered another book that will help me with the revision process that was recommend by two sources. Hoping to get it next week sometime we'll see. But I'm feeling the work of this novel now. Realizing that I'm halfway through its still fun on one hand but I can see where its definitely taking more discipline to work through this middle. But I'll get there.

In fiction, nodding means yes. Shaking the head means no.

I learned something new today. Didn't know the above. Read it in the website.

Hmm learned something else now too.

But if you feel you must break the paragraph without inserting a beat, then a strange punctuation rule applies.

You don't include an end quotation mark at the end of the first paragraph but you do include an opening quotation mark at the head of the new one. Example:

"Our dear friend, Jimmy, loved long paragraphs of dialogue... [Blah, blah, blah]...and it finally ended his life.

"The beauty of a life lived in that manner is that...? [blah, blah, blah]..."

See that after "his life" there was no close quotation mark? It looks wrong, but it's right if it's the same speaker speaking in the next paragraph.

Dec 31, 2007

Well I've done a bit of writing this morning. It's almost 5:30am. Did prayer from 3-4 and been sitting here in the nursery of the church writing, doing some light revising.

Current word count is 46749

Steps to successful publishing

* Do radio and TV interviews for book
* Launch book and e-mail your database of fans
* Edit galleys for book
* Work with publicist on campaign for book
* Revise novel after receiving editor's comments
* Begin building your marketing platform
* Send "polished draft" to your editor
* Revise your novel
* Receive phone call from editor buying your book
* Your agent submits book to publishers
* Get an agent
* Meet agents at writing conference or by mail/email
* Write a stellar proposal
* Polish first three chapters
* Finish first draft of novel
* Start writing first draft of novel
* Design your novel before writing it
* Get brilliant idea for a novel that "can't miss"
* Finish "Junior year" of learning the craft
* Finish "Sophomore year" of learning the craft
* Finish "Freshman year" of learning the craft
* Decide that you want to be a novelist

Listen to your instincts when you read over a scene or chapter, an exchange of dialogue, whatever. Does it feel to you that something's missing/lacking? But let'sgo a little deeper. That may be exactly the way you want the reader to feel after reading the scene, which gets us to the question many writers fail to ask themselves: How do I want this scene to affect the reader? Many writers put all this great energy into working on a scene and no energy whatsoever into how the scene is going to work on the reader. If you want the reader to be, say, convinced that a wife is a lot smarter than her husband, reading over the scene in which we meet the couple with that in mind will let you know if you need to add anything to help the reader make such a deduction.

Randy added: When I'm editing, I add text under the following conditions:

* The scene does not have a Goal, a Conflict, and a Disaster (if it's a Scene) or it does not have a Reaction, Dilemma, and Decision (if it's a Sequel). To see a discussion of Scenes and Sequels, see my article on Writing the Perfect Scene.

http://www.AdvancedFictionWriting.com/art/scene.php

* Parts of the scene are unclear and can be clarified by adding text.

* The pacing is too fast to support the action and needs more text to slow it down.

* I can't tell who's talking.

* The scene is not delivering a Powerful Emotional Experience because I am giving short shrift to the emotive aspects.

* The scene lacks visual elements (or other sensory elements).

Something I learned about physic distance and writing in the passive voice.

As writers we're charged with the responsibility of drawing the reader in, making him care about the character and identify with the characters. To do that, we must create and maintain the fictional dream. There's an article on that on the website in the Writers' Aids section, but let me say here that it is through the fictional dream that a reader is transported from reading words on a page to living the events of the novel.

The reader is an armchair adventurer, but through the fictional dream, s/he becomes an active participant in the story--through the characters' senses. Now if the author intrudes and places herself between the reader and character, then the reader isn't experiencing the story firsthand. She is being told a story.

To close that psychic distance gap and plant the reader inside the character's head, you have to go through your work and ditch the filters that create the distance.

Some watchwords are: thought, wondered, considered, hoped, realized.

Do your best to delete all of them. The rule of thumb is to ditch them. If you sacrifice clarity by ditching them, then let them stay in the book. They've earned their space. Otherwise, they're out of there.

Example: She realized she'd reached the point of no return. She had to kill him.

She realized is a filter. The author telling the reader what the character is thinking. See the psychic distance? How what is occurring in the novel is filtered from the character, through the writer, and then to the reader?

Revise it, and let the character think for herself.

The point of no return. Breached. She had to kill him.

A good website I picked up that talks about the big things editors are looking at when they review a manuscript.

http://www.editorialdepartment.com/content/view/545/453/

Here's a great punctuation tidbit I learned.

When you're reading and you come to a comma, you pause. At a semicolon, you pause a tad longer. A colon, little longer. At a dash, you prepare for an interrupted thought. At a period, you stop.

An ellipsis carries a SERIES of PERIODS--three or four depending on the sentence and publisher's preference. (Technically, a complete sentence gets four; an incomplete one gets three, but some publishers use three regardless.) A series of periods is a lot of stopping. It's also visually disruptive to the reader.

Lots of stops and visual interruptions "awaken" the reader from the fictional dream. That's counterproductive to the writer's goal, which is to establish and maintain that fictional dream from the beginning to the end of the book. Offer the reader too many opportunities to stop or too many interruptions and s/he puts the book down and doesn't pick it back up.

These are the "technical" reasons most frequently leading to rejection cited by the editors and agents:

Jan 1 2008 Happy New Year!!

God this has been a bad year. I won't go into it but I'm glad for a fresh start. Lord help me to forget those things which are behind and to count them as dung, and press on towards what you have arrested me for.

48,005 words!

Ok haven't done any writing so far today...maybe tonight. Watched the U of M game.

My first question was: "What's the most important thing I as an author can do to help promote my book?" I remember her answer verbatim because it was short and very clear: "Get your e-mail database as large as possible." Which was an excellent answer. It is, I believe, the best answer she could have given me. The only trouble was that neither she nor I knew exactly how to do that.

Jan 3, 2008

Ok two days ago I stayed up till 5am making movie trailers for this book to help promote it when the times comes. Oh my God they turned out to be so sweet. So I kind of of got a plan to market it some. Gonna create a Myspace page which posts the trailer, which will be posted on all the you-tube/god tube web sites. I got an idea of what I'd like to do based on the series fallen from ABC in terms of what I can do with my space.

I'm excited. Got a lot of work to do. Also noted that can use please understand me 2 to help me with understanding who my characters are better. I think Apollyon is a Sang/Clor, whereas Lucifer is a clor/mel. Michael will be more phlegmatic, while Raphael will be melancholy.

Oh I'm at 48, 439 words.

The following ideas I got today while driving.

Charon attacks Athor to look for Apollyon

Michael and Satan talk in the next book at the lake of fire is response is...

"Your mockery was accomplished by our Lord in Hell."

Next Book title: The Gates of Hell which would deal primarily with Jesus battle with Satan in Hell. In the 2nd book Lucifer took the keys and can bypass Charon @ will.

Lucifer will raise all the stones of fire.

They will blast a hole through Mt. Zion and people will be able to see them fight within.

Lucifer will kill Sariel. ("He was a murderer from the beginning")

Michael will ladder in the kiln destroying the copies of Charon.

Jan 5th 2008

Ok I created today another trailer for my book, and I made a face book website. I think the trailers are cool, and everyone that has seen them has really liked them. I'm pleased with how they came out. I also started creating an email list for my book. I have oh about 80 people in it. Hope to get more. I also posted a trailer in You tube to see how it would look. No one can access it right now though. So progress is being made on all fronts. Just got to keep writing and finishing. I also took some manila envelopes and put my labels on them. So now its time to do some writing. Today's word count is 49590 and I'm at 100 pages single spaced. Talk to ya soon. Ok its 11:14pm and I got 50, 403!

Jan 6th 2008

It's 9:00pm and I'm at 50662. Today while at church I talked with Pete. I had sent him trailer #3. He really liked it. He said he will be meeting with a buyer at Borders soon and would mention my book and stuff to him. So we'll see what will happen. Mike also mentioned yesterday that he knew a woman that has several books that have been published. I'll have to follow up with him to see becomes of leads like that.

Well ill get some writing done this evening then hit the hay. Got several creditors to call tomorrow.

Jan 7th 2008

Identify novels published within the past five years that are similar to your proposed work. Tell us why your book should be published, and explain how your book is superior and/or provides a new slant on your topic.

Interesting question. I only know of one novel. The Chronicles of Brothers.

Jan 8th 2007

Dunno what it is...Ill have to press through it. But I kind of don't feel like writing. I don't know if I'm just depressed overall with my job situation, and my marital situation. Or just hit a typical slump that writers who do anything serious hit. I looked up the books on amazon to see who my competition is. About 5 prospects showed up. The closest one was the chronicles of brothers to me. It came out several years ago, and the author already has book 2 out. I'm trying to press on though. Even if I publish it myself. To say I've actually written a novel would be a huge accomplishment. I hope the lord sees fit to bless the fruit of my hands. It would be nice to not just publish it and make it available but to get it out to where people can really buy it and get excited about it. I wish that my ghost readers had written something back buy this stage but I will give them some time still. Yep writing can definitely be a lonely profession. I can feel it. I wrote or at least started to write a query letter on my book. I'm looking forward I think to when this is all over. But let me go and write some. It won't write itself that's for sure. Talk to you later. Oh I'm at 51,431

Note: Lilith has reassigned Grigori loyal to him to new charges which is why the tomes are corrupted. He has the ability to move Grigori. So the Grigori on earth are

What about the way to destroy a Grigori is to throw his ink at him? The ink washes him out into oblivion maybe. Where nothing is left save the stone of fire. That could be a neat way to die.

Ok Raphael's on earth. Michaels on his way to hell. Charon and Lucifer's crew are on earth right now. The rest of the court are in heaven.

Ok how to have Raphael discover what's up with Lucifer?

I want Lucifer's spies in heaven before Michael even comes down to rescue Raphael.

I'm going over these last month's journal entries. I realize I've written quite a bit over the last month. I'm definitely on track to finish within 90 days. It's kind of nice to read back over stuff and see how things have developed. After doing some figuring out in on scene 67 out of 114. So I'm 58% done with the book. Not bad after a month I think.

As of 9pm I'm 51887. I imagined a scene where Lucifer beat a plow shear into a sword. And named it such. Maybe I could have Ares do it for him. It could be a play on the God of War image he has.

Ok its 1:11am...think it's time to get to bed. Word count so far is 52507...not bad. Not bad.

Jan 10 2008

Ok its 11:44pm didn't do a whole lot of writing today as I spent the majority of the day in devotion and counseling and stuff. Did a little bit of writing. I did see in my mind's eye an image of Raphael talking with Michael and slamming his fist into a table saying that "We are NOT El!" he says this in reply to Michael saying that we cannot use dissolution as an option.

53088

Jan 11, 2008

Today I got some news that I might be able to start work in February working back at U of M assisting the new woman whose job I wanted. Look at God set things up to take care of things. Very cool! I'm still plugging away at this book. I have to figure out a good query letter. I noticed that some queries were made prior to book completion. I think I want to finish my book first prior to query. There is much I can edit out and stuff I'm sure. I did that yesterday. Just having a fresh look at it. I realize also while looking over my outline that I'm essentially writing the last chapter prior to the end. So I'm getting there. Slowly but surely, I'm getting towards the end. When I get there I can say whohoo! I wrote a novel! I'll probably take a month or so to just not write or write something else. I might start on the 2nd novel we'll see. I know one thing these things are some work. Writing a novel is no joke. I see like with most things there are seasons to writing a novel. A time of celebration, a time where one is just plowing through. Times when its easy and times when its very hard. Oh I also applied for a Executive Directors Job today. I got another job I have to write a cover letter for but I'm excited that I can even write cover letters. It just means an opportunity to throw some seed out there. All this will pass in time.

Well let's get back to writing and see what we can come up with. I'm at 55033.

Jan 12, 2008

I had an idea about my query...the movie the titanic was made and it was a huge bestseller. People already knew the story. Copy that pitch.

Look at Titanic's synopsis...

http://www.imdb.com/title/tt0120338/synopsis

What's a good tagline?

In the beginning God created the heavens and the earth...this is what happened before that.

"How far will you go..."

"There is nothing new under the sun...." Ecc

The thing that hath been, it is that which shall be; and that which is done is that which shall be done: and there is no new thing under the sun. Ecc 1:9

The Titanic's tagline was...

A woman's heart is a deep ocean of secrets.

Nothing On Earth Could Come Between Them.

Hey today's been a pretty cool, day. Took, the kids to church for rehearsals and stuff. Had strong back flashes of a past love. Took me a while to work through my feelings and thoughts. But made it through it. I'm sure it won't be the last time. I do miss her. Tempted often to write her but I fight the temptation, and then continue my day. I thank God for the grace to push through. I'm sure I'll be dealing with this for a while.

I looked at some good websites today as I begun to write my synopsis of my story let me see if I can find and cut and past the encouraging word I received from what I read.

Don't personalize rejection: "A huge dose of hyperbolical slang, maudlin sentimentalism, and tragic-comic bubble and squeak." —William Harrison Ainsworth,

New Monthly Magazine, review of Moby Dick by Herman Melville (1851). Still not convinced? “Shakespeare's name, you may depend on it, will go down. He has no invention as to stories, none whatever.” —Lord Byron (1814)

Easy, never give up. Eighty-five percent of all those who try their hand at writing never substantially publish, but I don't know of anybody the market has told to put down the pen and quit writing. They get discouraged, they give up, they stop learning and growing in their craft. They quit. Publishing is about getting the right product in front of the right person at the right place at exactly the right time. All of those pieces, and others, are not in place often, and it takes perseverance to make it happen. Yup, that's my advice, never give up.

In tragedy lies hope...tag line for the book

How do I search the Bible?

There are two ways to search the Bible. First, you can choose a specific book, chapter, and verse with the drop down menus at the top of the page. This will quickly take you to your desired verse. Secondly, if you don't know exactly what you are looking for, you can type a word or phrase in the "Search" box and a display box will appear with a number of different choices. You can then choose the appropriate verse and the Bible will display that verse and the accompanying videos. Note poste your book trailer to Gen 1:1 and Rev 12:9! This would be great exposé for your book.

Jan 15 2008

56, 002

As far as the book is concerned. I got myself editing for Christian writers in the mail the other day. Started reading it and put it down after not too long. It basically said that I needed to finish as writing and editing are two different tasks. I think I kind of agrees and wanted to focus on getting this novel done. I wanted to be done by the end of the month. To do that I need to bust some butt. So today I think I’m just going to focus on that. I can do more if I put my mind to it. But yeah its work now. Not that it’s not any more fun, it’s just a lil harder to get motivated to write. So I’m pushing now.

56945 at the end of the day.

Ok Lucifer is in heaven with several of his henchmen. I’ve got to get several things to happen

Murmur must get Sariel and Talus to fight

Lucifer and or Ashtaroth must sabotage or weaken heaven somehow.

Ashtaroth can prepare occupation of the waypoints

Lucifer can oversee the great hall.

These are ideas that need to be integrated. They are still good.

Charon attacks Athor to look for Apollyon

Michael and Satan talk in the next book at the lake of fire is response is...

"Your mockery was accomplished by our Lord in Hell."

Next Book title: The Gates of Hell which would deal primarily with Jesus battle with Satan in Hell. In the 2nd book Lucifer took the keys and can bypass Charon @ will.

Lucifer will raise all the stones of fire.

They will blast a hole through Mt. Zion and people will be able to see them fight within.

Lucifer will kill Sariel. ("He was a murderer from the beginning")

Michael will ladder in the kiln destroying the copies of Charon.

Jan 16, 2008

Ok I think I have a problem with the plot a little. If Lucifer comes back before Michael what's to stop him from going to the kiln now? Nothing he doesn't know that Charon is on earth and that the entrance to hell is unguarded.

Lucifer needs to get to earth before Charon but after Michael? Let me see here.

I need Lilith in heaven setting up things. I need henchmen going to the twelve waypoints into the third heaven blocking access. I need someone instigating Talus and Sariel.

Lucifer and Lucifer speaks to Sariel and Talus individually

Murmur incites the populace to complain

Talus is slapped by Sariel

Lucifer's forces attack heaven which stops the Arelim and Issi from battle.

Lucifer attempts to enter the Kiln and Sariel prevents him.

Lucifer kills his brother Sariel while attempting to enter the kiln.

I have an image of them fighting in the throne room and El shedding a tear upon Sariel's death.

Ok Lilith and Raphael fight over his pen, tome and stylus. He who commands The three items commands the rest of all Grigori.

I realize that my plotting is what has been slowing me down the last several days...I'm in the process of clarifying aspects to the war now.

Jan 29th, 2008

Ok I haven't written in over a week. I kind of needed a break. And kind of got stuck. But I'm getting myself to the point where I'm ready to finish. I'm at a pushing stage. I feel like I'm giving labor and near the end which is the hardest but the shortest.

Feb 11, 2008

Haven't been doing any writing but gearing back up to do some plotting today, as the end story needs to be tightened up some. I plan on going to the library tomorrow.

Plot questions to answer

What happens to instigate Sariel and Talus to combat one another?

Once Michael and Raphael are freed what do they do?

Michael to tell the other brethren

What happens from the time that Michael is captured to the time he and Raphael escape?

What happens from the time Lucifer goes back to heaven to the time he is confronted by Michael about his knowledge?

Where is Jerahmeel and Gabriel during all this? It needs to be clearly noted what their plot lines are during this time.

Feb 25 2008

Haven't done a lot of actual writing but I've received my first response from Sis Lydia and have sent her my new edited version of chapter 2. I'm hoping I will get my other 5 readers to respond shortly. But we'll see.

I am sitting here in the library and I still have to continue to move the story along I am so close to closing this out but I have to answer the above questions.

So let's tackle each question one by one.

What happens to instigate Sariel and Talus to combat? Q

A: Talus who is Arelim is confronted by Ashtaroth who is Issisi. Ashtaroth informs him that Apollyon was a betrayer and deserved his sentence. He rouses Talus to anger as Talus sees his words as disrespectful. When he provoked by Ashtaroth strikes at him and Sariel walks in and sees him assaulting a fellow Issisi without charge and physically intervenes to succor him, and the two combat one another.

Sariel is approached by murmur who complains to him that Talus has designs to take revenge against Ashtaroth and holds him responsible for Apollyon's imprisonment. Sariel doesn't believe him, and Murmur encourages him to seek his brother out. When he does he finds Talus about to strike Ashtaroth who has knowingly provoked him for such a response as to see that the two angels engage one another.

2.Q Once Michael and Raphael are freed what do they do?

A: Michael goes to tell the other brethren but finds that when he arrives back to heaven the city is in chaos and civil war, he is prompted by Raphael to confront Lucifer who they both know is the chief cause of the problem

Raphael goes to the hall of annals to determine the extent of the corruption and devises a plan to stop the rebel Grigori.

April 30, 2008

Raphael's tome contains all present information in one volume. It is a repository of all knowledge. Within it, the enemy can know exactly what the other side is doing.

It will be in Lilith's possession, as a result of Raphael being captured.

Raphael must reacquire it.

As a result of its lost...the Zoa will attack him.

He must fight his way into the hall of annals. Why to monitor the battle and give instructions. He will fight along side a brother such as Jerahmeel.

Raphael is Sepheroth: a unique species of angel given the power of creation.

We have started writing again. A trickle so far. But its coming. 58086 is the starting count. 59, 255 is what is written as the

8pm today. A thousand words! Woot what a wonderful.

May 6th,2008

Word Count today is 634 words today! Nice job! Keep it going keep it going.

July 21, 2008

Ok here's a scene in my head:

Lucifer instructs a guard at the rainbow bridge to vacate his post to see to the disturbance that rages in heaven. The guard will not leave his post. As he has his orders from Michael himself who has been ordered per El to ever lose his foot from this post. Lucifer unable to change his mind kills him. And opens the door allowing the forces of Apollyon to storm heaven.

Word count at 1:30pm is 62,777

Nov 9, 2008

Word count is 63, 001. 238 pages so far. I've stalled but I have to push this out. I'm at the end... but there's still much more to write. I've hit a mini road block

May 6, 2009

63,592 words. 238 pages. 6 months since I've last written anything. Yet I feel the compulsion, the inner desire for several days to write. There was an inner word that I received something that I heard as it relates to the issue of GM and Chrysler and the whole issues surrounding manufacturing. What is it that you are to produce? What do you make? Then there was a scripture that says that God has given you the power to get wealth. And that's when I thought what product or service is inside of you that God put in me to generate wealth? I realized that for me it was my books and songs. So I better get to producing.

Where will the forces of Lucifer strike first?

What will be the route that they take to secure heaven? I.e. what are their objectives?

Secure the Kiln

Satan's job will attack from Hell and walk through the Kiln

Secure

Jerusalem

Secure the entrance to the throne

Secure the Elysian Fields

Secure the way points into heaven * * * primary importance.

Note: Michael and Raphael must get back to heaven prior to Lucifer's securing of the waypoints in.

What's the strategic advantages of certain pieces of ground?

Abaddon will secure the

Idea: have the Malakim attack from the sky

Have Lucifer's forces attack from below. I.e. they open up the earth to swallow up the citizens of heaven. They do the unthinkable. They open ladders apart from waypoints. Which essentially becomes a weapon of mass destruction.

Lucifer moves from the city to the Maw

Apollyon

moves from the city to the temple

Lilith moves from the city to the Great Hall. (the final battle of Lilith and Raphael will take place in the Hall, Lilith must pass the Zoa)

A strike force attempts to control the Elysian Fields.

The strike force is repelled and the united forces of heaven fight to the city to meet Apollyon

Michael chases after Lucifer to stop him and they fight within the Kiln.

Oct 10 2009@ 11:09pm

65801 words

Oct 17, 2009@ 11:33pm

67689

Battles Scenes

I tend to work backwards when I'm trying to think about a fight, because you need to think about the end result first. What is this fight going to accomplish (be it simple, like a duel or killing somebody dangerous, or more broad-scale, something with military or political implications)? Is Ike going to save the day while practically unscathed? Is he going to receive an injury? Does it need to be manageable (anywhere from 'it's just a scratch' to 'should be cared for but just bandaging it for now will not be the death of me') or fatal? What about the opponent--does he need to live? Is he going to be killed? Etc., etc. Once you know what results you want to work towards, I find it's much easier to plan out a battle accordingly.

For larger battles, pre-battle planning typically consisted of a council of the war leaders, which could either be the general laying down a plan or a noisy debate between the different leaders, depending on how much authority the general possessed. Battlefield communications before the advent of strict lines of communication were naturally very difficult. Communication was done through musical signals, audible commands, messengers, or visual signals such as raising a standard, banner, or flag.

I'm not going to play the "who's the best fantasy writer of the 20th century game" (seriously though, H.P. Lovecraft. He's awesome.)

What I will do is address the OC's question concerning writing good battle scenes. Here's something that hasn't been mentioned yet, but should be taken into consideration: VOCABULARY. When writing a prolonged battle scene, you're going to find yourself in situation where you want to use the same words (or some variation thereof) over and over again to describe the same action. Are there several people using swords and axes in this fight of yours? Guess what you're going to be using words like 'hack, slash, cut, slice, stab, and chop' a whole bunch. Lances? Expect to use a whole lot of 'thrusting, ramming, skewering, and impaling.' Are there Laguz in the mix? Now you're also dealing with "biting, scratching, mauling, and pouncing."

Here's the point I'm trying to make: when you're writing a battle scene of any length, you're going to want to mix and match your vocabulary to prevent the action from becoming stale and repetitive. The more words you know that can be used to describe the same action, the better.

Also, try to find synonyms for the following action words so you don't wind up making your action scenes unbearably repetitive: jump, run block, dodge, hurt, shout/scream/cry are all common actions that show up repeatedly in fight scenes. Authors should learn new words to describe these actions if they want to write for the action genre.

The thesaurus is your friend. Use it if you must; it makes for better writing. Above all else, avoiding falling into the trap of needlessly repeating the same verbiage.

The battle with Charon is disorganized it's a defensive battle to protect.

The Battle in the Elysian Fields is disorganized by the raged forces. But Jerahmeel forces are organized.

The Battle in the city is very organized on the part of Lucifer's forces. Heavens internal forces are not within the city. But the tables are turned as Jerahmeel and Gabriel rally heavens forces to repel Lucifer's onslaught. Charon's capturing and incapacity of

Apollyon brings Lucifer's forces to cease fighting realizing that to continue is but doom. as heavens

Show Lucifer tempting someone successfully

Show Lucifer accusing the brethren

Show Lucifer murdering someone

Show Lucifer Deceiving someone

Nov 14, 2009 69, 005 words. 255 pages.

Nov 18, 2009 69, 394 256 pages.

November 22, 2009 69, 511 words

Scene order

Heaven: Murmur instigates civil war.

Earth: Charon Invades Athorian space

Heaven: Lucifer deceives Deramiel

Earth: Michael and Raphael are prisoner

War in Heaven: Talus and Sariel and Gabriel Heaven

Earth: War on Earth (Charon is on the war path)

Heaven: Gabriel and the battle of the Elysian Fields

Earth: Michael and Raphael are freed and go to free more

Heaven: Lucifer's forces invade heaven

The way Lucifer communicates is through Lilith. Lilith is in touch with the other generals via their tomes he writes it and they receive it. That's how Lucifer is able to coordinate his attack. And why Lilith and Raphael must engage so he can be stopped. Lilith is his communications officer. Apollyon oversees the actual armies. The three comprise the unholy trinity. Or prophet, king and "priest?"

11-24-09

70, 175

Take the scene where Michael and Raphael go to Tatarus and show that all the inhabitants have been slaughtered.

Tartarus

is a mass grave of Elohim. Use Michael to resurrect them and then send them in battle above to fight against the Athorian army.

Also you might have a scene later where Michael is attempting to battle Lucifer, and Lucifer doesn't realize that Michaels tactic was to never beat him, but to stall him long enough until El wakens.

El can have a scene after he awakes where he speaks..."Michael of the Kortai, report of thy stewardship." And then Michael gives his report of all that Lucifer had wrought. Then God turns to Lucifer and asks him for his report. Then Lucifer defies God and instead accuses God to his face.

God stands and Lucifer and the Lord engage.

Have a scene where it shows that Jerahmeel saying to Lucifer, boy are you in trouble. This should be a scene which echoes back to the earlier scene where Jerahmeel said the same thing to Ashtaroth.

Have a scene where Raphael explains that he is the Sephiroth. The living Tome of God. He is the physical embodiment of all that is currently known that God would choose to show.

All tomes that are written he may access. He tells Michael that because he has walked within the flames of fire he is able to bring life to all Elohim.

70, 650. 260 pages.

72, 010 265 pages.

1-16-2010

72, 456 words and still 266 pages

I did some massive revision based on friend editing of my prologue. She's a technical writer and helped me to tighten up my prose. It's a better prologue as a result of her input which I greatly appreciated.

I don't know exactly why but I seemingly feel stuck with Jerahmeel in the Halls of Annals. Maybe I should write about Michael and Raphael. And just skip Jerahmeel for now. I sense that the pacing of the book should be more about

Michael and Raphael, then Gabriel and all that is taking place in the Elysian Fields, then Lucifer's forces. I feel like I have to tie in what Jerahmeel is doing though. Maybe I shouldn't even have him in the halls of annals yet. Maybe I should have him confronting Lucifer's forces directly. Still he must be instrumental in getting Michael and Raphael back home. He can also be instrumental in helping to liberate a way point opening heaven to the rest of the cosmos.

This brings me to the point where there should be a line...that indicates that Lucifer had successfully cut off Heaven from the rest of the universe. "In the whole of the multiverse and throughout all creation heaven sat now stood cut off from all the multiverse. A realm closed. No one could enter and no one could leave...

It's not a good line but it in some small ways conveys what I'm trying to covey.

Maybe I could have Raphael contact Jerahmeel's Grigori, and they would go to work together. Have Jerahmeel being chased by Lucifer's forces to the mountain of God, and the Zoa end up eating or otherwise destroying the forces that would seek to follow him. Have a scene where he escapes barely only to watch as the forces which pursed him are decimated. He can be directed by Raphael who is talking to the Grigori, who's talking to Jerahmeel. Jerahmeel's Grigori can then be used as a shield at the last minute to protect him so he can safely enter. Then have the room speak to him with Raphael's voice. Raphael can direct him to write the words that will create a portal that will allow

Michael and he to step through. From there Raphael can port forces directly to battles.

Who then should follow Jerahmeel? Maybe Lilith? In his desire to control the halls.. Have him maybe make it inside as well. And have Jerahmeel

"What took you so long?" said Gabriel.

I just wanted to see how fast you were Jerahmeel replied.

"Oh thanks!" said Gabriel

Have Jerahmeel come to the aid of Gabriel? Maybe but seems like we need Jerahmeel back within the city to help bot populate and fight off Lucifer's attackers. Make it so the two meet and that it turns into a great confrontation that Lucifer finally gets to shut Jerahmeel up. Have Jerahmeel though still have the last laugh. Maybe he can be instructed by Raphael from afar to acquire Lilith's pen.

When God pronounces judgment on the rebellion have him use these words...

He that is unjust, let him be unjust still: and he which is filthy, let him be filthy still: and he that is righteous, let him be righteous still: and he that is holy, let him be holy still.

Rev 22:11

4-7-2010

266 pages

72,461 Words

Story line

Lucifer's forces secure the waypoints into heaven ceiling access to the 3

"In the whole of the multiverse and throughout all creation heaven sat now stood cut off from all the multiverse. A realm closed. No one could enter and no one could leave...

Moves to the populace of heaven to offer them sanctuary from the ruler ship of God. Lucifer shows Apollyon as proof that God is NOT all powerful and he appeals to their desire to not serve the humans.

The people reject Lucifer and Apollyon attempts to usurp the throne of God by force.

Lucifer authorizes Apollyon and his cadre to subdue the city by any means necessary.

Apollyon unleashes a ladder in the city obliterating the surrounding area and in defiance to the will of God.

Lucifer commands the warriors are his disposal to secure the temple.

Michael and Raphael

Tartarus and confront the guardian there. Michael and Raphael approach

After defeating Minos, they discover that all the inhabitants have been slaughtered.

Tartarus is a mass grave of Elohim. Use Michael to resurrect them and then send them in battle above to fight against the Athorian army.

Michael and Raphael release the captives of darkness

Jerahmeel

c. When Michael realizes the magnitude of the destruction of angels and Lucifer must be stopped.

Also you might have a scene later where Michael is attempting to battle Lucifer, and Lucifer doesn't realize that Michaels tactic was to never beat him, but to stall him long enough until El wakens.

"What manner of reason would thou give me to explain the dissolution of our kin?

I have seen the works of thy stewardship...and have found thee traitor."

I offer thee solace within my grace brother. El has kept back the true purpose of our kind. Join me and we shall create a new heaven and a new earth.

El hast spoken, he is my father and I am his son. He has loved you above all others yet you are not satisfied. He has allowed you to see the wonders of the kiln but thine eye is not filled. He has made thee to sing harp and to lift us in song, and now thy very body strings contempt for his love, and the tingling of thy cymbals clamor hate.

You brother are a wind instrument – a broken flute that no longer plays to our God.

Lucifer looked upon Michael knowingly, "Then let me end my charade

Lucifer should have planned Apollyon's downfall....positioned him to fall. The unseen hand that crafted it all...that he might have the preeminence.

And have it all revealed at the end. Have Apollyon revealed to have been duped at the end. Have Lilith be the one who carried Lucifer's secret.

Apollyon's stone was purposely cracked in the Kiln making him predisposed and unstable.

Apollyon was fashioned to be "cracked" Lucifer was discovered to have iniquity as he fashioned Apollyon so. Lucifer was worse as he schemed and used Apollyon knowing what laid before him.

"For there was a division in his stone"

breach

fissure

fracture

Feb 29, 2012

How does Ashtaroth die? Have him follow Lucifer in the Kiln. He goes to protect him, only to be left behind to burn forever within its stomach.

May 25, 2012

Raphael and Lilith fight. Their battle is one of speed. Where Raphael ducks and weaves.

(Note look up synonyms for duck and weave,) They

cannot

interact with each other.

What can the Sephiroth do?

10-21-12

101, 669 words. The book is done. I completed it on July 4, 2012. But I'm in the revision process now and fleshing out the characters more.

There is a plot element I want to work into the story. Where Lucifer devices the idea that if he can make God mortal. He can kill him. His true Goal is to put El in a place of vulnerability.

How to do this? El must become human

When did Lucifer develop this thinking? When he learned how Sasheal became flesh.

Have him have a conversation with

Michael. Or perhaps Lilith. Have Lucifer have conversation with Lilith and ask him how did Sasheal die? Did he ever wonder what El was truly like?

When he smote the Lords Heel

He can smite the Lords heel because he carries within him the Godstone.

Journal to Book Two of the Third Heaven Series.

The Resurrection of God

4-4-13

Today is a day I spent online learning more how I can market my non-fiction book.

My word count for today is 3068. I am having trouble with the prologue. I'm not quite sure why. I think the length is too long and Lucifer and Michael should not be spending time talking so long to one another.

There's a fog in my mind. A haziness. Like something is blocking me. I am not quite sure what it is. It has something to do with my writing.

I've created an outline for the second book. There's still gaps to it...pieces of the story that's missing.

I was kind of patting myself on the back earlier. I'm an author dangnabbit! I am the author of two books. One fiction the other non-fiction.

I'm wondering if I can use kickstarter to advance the Third Heaven? 1500 dollars should do it in terms of copyediting, cover production, and marketing.

I just have to figure out what I will give those who contribute. I don't have original art, or book marks.

There is a portion of the scene that I need to show that Lucifer now has deed to earth.

4-19-2013

I'm back. I'm still at 3072 words. I've been spending a lot of time building up my platform and working to get things going for the Third Heaven. Book One. An interesting marketing hook I have thought of was "The prequel to the Bible is here!" I think it's an intriguing idea that the Bible has a prequel. We'll see how it goes in the market place.

I also got my kick starter campaign approved. I just have to release it. I'm trying to determine what time during the week to do it. (I'm thinking on a Monday.) I also started a press release to send out to everyone on my mailing list. I don't want to do what I did with the KDP and the gospel explained. I want to give the campaign as much opportunity to succeed as possible. So I'm taking my time to think it through. I'm thinking maybe an April 28th release, possibly May 7th at the latest. I would like to have all the money by June. So that means I need to have it all ready to go by the end of this month.

I'm learning how to market slowly but surely.

My blog is steadily growing in followers. Not as quickly as I'd like but growing.

4-20-13

3,240 Words

6-6-2013

Idea have hell be the thing that destroyed the dinosaurs. Hell was the mountain that fell from the sky.

Have Charon release Asmodeus, and the other angles trapped within the Euphrates river.

Have Lucifer being shown to kill an Ophanim. Something no angel has ever done. The power over Death and Hell imbues him with power from on High.

End word count 4079

8/3/2013

Gods plan for the primestone is to give it to his children, He will distribute it to all who serve him. Re 2:17

He that hath an ear, let him hear what the Spirit saith unto the churches; To him that overcometh will I give to eat of the hidden manna, and will give him a white stone, and in the stone a new name written, which no man knoweth saving he that receiveth it.

10-22-13

The Reason Lucifer wants Moses is because he did the same thing that Lucifer did with Apollyon in the Kiln. But the Lord will not allow it.

11-22-13

Today I think I will document on my blog my writing process. The outline of my work is developing and major themes are developing. The justice of God, his partiality, his ability to plan from the foundation of the world, the vindictive vengeful nature of Satan. Note part of Lucifer's personality should be that of a spurned child. One still seeking to be like his father, yet hating his father, he views God as unfair, too harsh, restrictive, and no longer worthy to rule. Lucifer is jealous of God, jealous of his power, the devotion he elicits, and covetous. He does not just want to have what God has. He wants to be God himself.

Have Iblis do something heroic, that advances the Kingdom, yet causes Lucifer to take his life for his betrayal. Have Iblis death be the catalyst to stop Argoth's purge.

12-12-13

Thoughts. The whole series has to do with how angels see biblical events from their perspective. There are a couple major ideas that have popped into my head tonight.

When El comes to earth there are a legion of angels that surround him as a battle guard as his spirit descends to inhabit the womb of Mary.

That angels fight to allow time for Mary and joseph to escape, but some angels must be sacrificed to allow El and the couple to escape the slaughter by Herod.

That angels proclaim the announcements of El to the world. You have to show this.

The star that moves is an angel.

Show the angles leading the wise men. That they are able to see not just the signs but have glimpses of the spirit to see that God is coming in the earth

Show Satan searching for El while he is on earth in baby form, but he eludes him for years despite the search of his soldiers

Have Satan move throughout the crowd encouraging them to crucify Jesus

Have the angels ask if El is really willing to die for the humans. This should be a very powerful scene. "Will El surrender his very life for the humans?

Show El having to make the choice to raise a young child from the dead. Show here spirit being returned from the dead. Satan targets El for destruction for El has violated his own law not to interfere (have to develop El limits if he heas any) and this opens him up to give his own life.

Because he has taken a life to raise, a life must be given in return. El surrenders his life that the child might live.

Show El yielding himself to the peoples brutality, and him keeping angels back from smiting them. (remember the scene in superman where Clarks dad waves him off from rescuing him.)

El's plan is to be as inconspicuous as possible so as to not attract attention to his presence on the earth.

Examine the homeless pastor who tricked his congregation....this has something to do with your book. Find and Release the piece that you are to use.

Trinity issues: show El on his throne, and Yeshua, on earth. He sits on his throne while Yeshua walks the earth. Satan sees an opportunity to smite the godhead through Jesus and weaken El.

What were the angels thinking at each major biblical event?

Da 10:20

Then said he, Knowest thou wherefore I come unto thee? and now will I return to fight with the prince of Persia: and when I am gone forth, lo, the prince of Grecia shall come.

Show this battle.

Demons feed off the eternal spirt of man and have adapted themselves as Hell feeds off of Angels. Lucifer has learned how to use the power of Hell to sustain his people. But it requires the souls of men as engine. However, demons are famished, starved, ready to possess a man that the might feed off his misery and rebellion. It is the closest thing they have to taste of manna and of the presence of El...men souls are like a physical and psychological addiction. And Lucifer has become like a pusher to help keep his followers in check. Demons attempt to increase the "dosage" of man's misery that they might experience the high they acquire. Give this as explanation of the pigs running off the cliff. Demons are homeless. They have no charge. The "house" of man brings them closest to the temple of God and Heaven. For God has chosen to make man in his own image and own likeness.

Names to be used in the next novel

Baal

Samael aka Necron: The angel of Death.

Qeterel

Shedhim

Seirimel

"I will foster a world that is filled with the knowledge of pleasure...that none would lack, that all would be given, and that promotion cometh not from the Lord but from I"

Lucifer's motivation: If Lucifer cannot reflect the light of God. He will rob that light from the universe. For only he alone can reveal truth. He will blind men to truth, distort truth, s that none may realize what he is, and ever taste of what he once lost. To reflect God himself in the earth. His goal is to obliterate the image of God in creation, whereas Gods plan is to fill the earth with the glory of the Lord. Hab 2:14

For the earth shall be filled with the knowledge of the glory of the LORD, as the waters cover the sea.

Isa 23:9

The LORD of hosts hath purposed it, to stain the pride of all glory, and to bring into contempt all the honourable of the earth. (Gods plan in a nutshell)

Isa 42:8

I am the LORD: that is my name: and my glory will I not give to another, neither my praise to graven images.

Isa 60:1

Arise, shine; for thy light is come, and the glory of the LORD is risen upon thee.

Isa 60:2

For, behold, the darkness shall cover the earth, and gross darkness the people: but the LORD shall arise upon thee, and his glory shall be seen upon thee.

Isa 60:3

And the Gentiles shall come to thy light, and kings to the brightness of thy rising.

Jer 2:11

Hath a nation changed their gods, which are yet no gods? but my people have changed their glory for that which doth not profit.

Ezk 9:1 He cried also in mine ears with a loud voice, saying, Cause them that have charge over the city to draw near, even every man with his destroying weapon in his hand. 2 And, behold, six men came from the way of the higher gate, which lieth toward the north, and every man a slaughter weapon in his hand; and one man among them was clothed with linen, with a writer's inkhorn by his side: and they went in, and stood beside the brasen altar. 3 And the glory of the God of Israel was gone up from the cherub, whereupon he was, to the threshold of the house. And he called to the man clothed with linen, which had the writer's inkhorn by his side; 4 And the LORD said unto him, Go through the midst of the city, through the midst of Jerusalem, and set a mark upon the foreheads of the men that sigh and that cry for all the abominations that be done in the midst thereof. 5 And to the others he said in mine hearing, Go ye after him through the city, and smite: let not your eye spare, neither have ye pity: 6 Slay utterly old and young, both maids, and little children, and women: but come not near any man upon whom is the mark; and begin at my sanctuary. Then they began at the ancient men which were before the house. 7 And he said unto them, Defile the house, and fill the courts with the slain: go ye forth. And they went forth, and slew in the city. 8 And it came to pass, while they were slaying them, and I was left, that I fell upon my face, and cried, and said, Ah Lord GOD! wilt thou destroy all the residue of Israel in thy pouring out of thy fury upon Jerusalem? 9 Then said he unto me, The iniquity of the house of Israel and Judah is exceeding great, and the land is full of blood, and the city full of perverseness: for they say, The LORD hath forsaken the earth, and the LORD seeth not. 10 And as for me also, mine eye shall not spare, neither will I have pity, but I will recompense their way upon their head. 11 And, behold, the man clothed with linen, which had the inkhorn by his side, reported the matter, saying, I have done as thou hast commanded me.

Ezk 10:1

1 Then I looked, and, behold, in the firmament that was above the head of the cherubims there appeared over them as it were a sapphire stone, as the appearance of the likeness of a throne. 2 And he spake unto the man clothed with linen, and said, Go in between the wheels, even under the cherub, and fill thine hand with coals of fire from between the cherubims, and scatter them over the city. And he went in in my sight. 3 Now the cherubims stood on the right side of the house, when the

man went in; and the cloud filled the inner court. 4 Then the glory of the LORD went up from the cherub, and stood over the threshold of the house; and the house was filled with the cloud, and the court was full of the brightness of the LORD'S glory. 5 And the sound of the cherubims' wings was heard even to the outer court, as the voice of the Almighty God when he speaketh. 6 And it came to pass, that when he had commanded the man clothed with linen, saying, Take fire from between the wheels, from between the cherubims; then he went in, and stood beside the wheels. 7 And one cherub stretched forth his hand from between the cherubims unto the fire that was between the cherubims, and took thereof, and put it into the hands of him that was clothed with linen: who took it, and went out. 8 And there appeared in the cherubims the form of a man's hand under their wings. 9 And when I looked, behold the four wheels by the cherubims, one wheel by one cherub, and another wheel by another cherub: and the appearance of the wheels was as the colour of a beryl stone. 10 And as for their appearances, they four had one likeness, as if a wheel had been in the midst of a wheel. 11 When they went, they went upon their four sides; they turned not as they went, but to the place whither the head looked they followed it; they turned not as they went. 12 And their whole body, and their backs, and their hands, and their wings, and the wheels, were full of eyes round about, even the wheels that they four had. 13 As for the wheels, it was cried unto them in my hearing, O wheel. 14 And every one had four faces: the first face was the face of a cherub, and the second face was the face of a man, and the third the face of a lion, and the fourth the face of an eagle. 15 And the cherubims were lifted up. This is the living creature that I saw by the river of Chebar. 16 And when the cherubims went, the wheels went by them: and when the cherubims lifted up their wings to mount up from the earth, the same wheels also turned not from beside them. 17 When they stood, these stood; and when they were lifted up, these lifted up themselves also: for the spirit of the living creature was in them. 18 Then the glory of the LORD departed from off the threshold of the house, and stood over the cherubims. 19 And the cherubims lifted up their wings, and mounted up from the earth in my sight: when they went out, the wheels also were beside them, and every one stood at the door of the east gate of the LORD'S house; and the glory of the God of Israel was over them above. 20 This is the living creature that I saw under the God of Israel by the river of Chebar; and I knew that they were the cherubims. 21 Every one had four faces apiece, and every one four wings; and the likeness of the hands of a man was under their wings. 22 And the likeness of their faces was the same faces which I saw by the river of Chebar, their appearances and themselves: they went every one straight forward.

Eze 26:21

I will make thee a terror, and thou shalt be no more: though thou be sought for, yet shalt thou never be found again, saith the Lord GOD.

Eze 26:20

When I shall bring thee down with them that descend into the pit, with the people of old time, and shall set thee in the low parts of the earth, in places desolate of old, with them that go down to the pit, that thou be not inhabited; and I shall set glory in the land of the living;

De 7:6

For thou art an holy people unto the LORD thy God: the LORD thy God hath chosen thee to be a special people unto himself, above all people that are upon the face of the earth.

De 7:7

The LORD did not set his love upon you, nor choose you, because ye were more in number than any people; for ye were the fewest of all people:

After 400 years of slavery the people called on the name of the Lord. After 400 years the whole of the people were pliable enough to allow God to work through them. After 400 years they were free from the idea that they were superior to the Egyptians due to God being with them. And in due season the Lord came down to finally deliver the people. Ps 145:15

The eyes of all wait upon thee; and thou givest them their meat in due s eason.

What is the impact to heaven when a third of her populace has left? How does that impact the work of God? How does that impact their job functions, since God has stopped making angles. How does that effect creation?

What is the event that prompts God to destroy the earth.?

1 And it came to pass, when men began to multiply on the face of the earth, and daughters were born unto them, 2 That the sons of God saw the daughters of men that they were fair; and they took them wives of all which they chose. 3 And the LORD said, My spirit shall not always strive with man, for that he also is flesh: yet his days shall be an hundred and twenty years. 4 There were giants in the earth in those days; and also after that, when the sons of God came in unto the daughters of men, and they bare children to them, the same became mighty men which were of old, men of renown. 5 And GOD saw that the wickedness of man was great in the earth, and that every imagination of the thoughts of his heart was only evil continually. 6 And it repented the LORD that he had made man on the earth, and it grieved him at his heart. 7 And the LORD said, I will destroy man whom I have created from the face of the earth; both man, and beast, and the creeping thing, and the fowls of the air; for it repenteth me that I have made them. 8 But Noah found grace in the eyes of the LORD.

Lucifer attempts to corrupt the image of God by sullying man's bloodline, causing man to devolve as the beasts of the earth due to his depravity. The tactic of the enemy is so effective as it prompts God to create the second man. But he must first wipe the remains of the first from his beloved planet.

Evil has spread as a cancer. As gangrene it must be cut out.

Gangrene is a serious and potentially life-threatening condition that arises when a considerable mass of body tissue dies The evil of man has become as gangrene, man is on the verge of necrosis of spirit. Only Noah can now be saved.

Why didn't God intervene, why the flood?

God saves Noah.

Abraham

"For I must make a people, pliable to obey me, humble to contain me, and available to house me. Heb 10:5

Wherefore when he cometh into the world, he saith, Sacrifice and offering thou wouldest not, but a body hast thou prepared me:

The creator has become his creation

In the last third/quarter of the book is when things really should pick up pace wise. As the angels finally understand what El has planned, and the gravity of the situation weighs on them.

Is El crazy? Does he not love us? His willingness to leave the throne bolsters some angels into thinking that perhaps Lucifer was right.

Show angles leaving haven following the spirit of El to earth and fighting to create a path that El may come unhindered. Show the kenosis (i.e. emptying) of God as he leaves the throne, and departs Heaven and all its glory for a womb. To be birthed in the Kiln of a woman.

And when they looked upon the throne, show the image of three distinct personalities, that flicker as one. Show one leaving the throne while the other two remain.

Thought, show book two as a love story. For God so loved the world that he sacrificed everything he was to be with and rescue the one he loved. Man.

What would you do for love?

God's actions of death and destruction need to be viewed through the lens of love for his people and to see his people saved. Time is short...to rescue man he must do the thing that only God could do. Become man.

Note that Gods leaving heaven is parallel to Abraham leaving his kin and moving into a strange land.

Ge 6:6

And it repented the LORD that he had made man on the earth, and it grieved him at his heart.

Ge 6:7

And the LORD said, I will destroy man whom I have created from the face of the earth; both man, and beast, and the creeping thing, and the fowls of the air; for it repenteth me that I have made them.

Show the grief of God that he must destroy his creation, show the intense anguish over the decision. Show relief when he finds Noah.

The cutting room floor

#4: Once upon a time God the king of creation created a son he called man; in his image and his own likeness. For a time, God and Adam enjoyed fellowship, and Adam knew peace, prosperity, and health, and was given a purpose. One day Lucifer the enemy of God ensnared and enslaved Adam through deceit. Because of that, mankind began to kill one another and move away from God's will for him, and the corruption of Lucifer seeped into man's mind and his ways. Lucifer in his jealousy over God's fawning over the man vowed that he would destroy mankind and raise him as his own children unless God surrendered the throne. Because of that, God devised a daring plan to rescue his son. Until finally God became flesh to save his son and received the penalty for the actions of his seed on his own head freeing his son from slavery.

It has been less than one earth since the rebellion. A third of my brothers have been exiled across the multiverse. My family, my home -- ripped apart. I looked over the abyss now sealed by El himself. Only here at the edge of the Maelstrom do I find something familiar...something of comfort. For the great gulf that lies between the realms had remained untouched during the war. I sat looking over the winds of the maelstrom. The gusts washed across my face and there was solace in the wind. It whispered and brought to remembrance times when my brother and I would work to extend the foundation of heaven.

I miss his song.

"Now El. Now after millennia on this wretched world. Cast out by thine own hand. Ruler of this precious mote, now...I shall have my vengeance. You have denied me my throne, robbed me of my station.

Thou hast made thyself bond slave to these filth. To what end, I had loved thee. Yet you saw fit to deny me my place at thy side. Now thou shalt serve to be bond slave to me. Within the depths of this creature shalt thou service me. Within the kingdom of Hell wilt thou reside, and the memory of thee shall be snuffed out in the earth.

"Gabriel I believe that el means to allow himself to be submitted to harm. Are you sure? All I know is that the lord showed me a vision on the mount. And lo Adam and his kind had multiplied as the stars, and after a time, they grew to violence and I saw a man. Yet he was like none other before him. And when I had looked into the man's eyes...Michael paused... perhaps it was nothing.

Gabriel turned to his brother. "Do not be coy with me Michele Kortai, speak plainly. You are not one to succumb to doubt. Especially if you say, El showed this to you. Tell me what you saw.

I saw El hung by Adams kin on a cross...I...I saw the death of God!

"Impossible! El is life eternal. You are mad... shall the Godking take on flesh? Nay you must be mistaken."

"I know what I saw, said Michael. "El hast shown this to me for a reason.

Would you have me believe that Lucifer....could slay El?

I did not say Lucifer. I said Adams kin. They will kill God.

But how is such a thing possible? How can this be?

The theme song to the novel two has been acquired as well as the visuals for the next trailer.

http://videohive.net/item/epic-space-teaser/6407771?WT.ac=solid_search_thumb&WT.seg_1=solid_search_thumb&WT.z_author=SoftLight

Mt 20:18

Behold, we go up to Jerusalem; and the Son of man shall be betrayed unto the chief priests and unto the scribes, and they shall condemn him to death, Scripture to be used in book three.

Jan 1 2014 5285

Jan 2, 2014, 1:26pm word count 5880

"El dost not know the choices that you might make. He does know the *outcome* of all choices, that you might possibly make. He has set before us life and death, and admonishes us to choose life, that both thou and thy seed might live." You are yet free to choose life apart from El.

And you would seek vengeance on he hast razed our home? You would seek to apprehend him who wast the anointed cherub that covered that you may bring him before me now?

They replied as one man. All except Michael. "Yea Lord, we would have him chained, and Hell be home to him."

El's face became saddened, and he turned to his son Michael. And what say you? Will you too take up arms to wrest Lucifer from his throne?

Nay said, Michael. I will not leave thy side. Only at thy command will I leave thee...for I know, I know what the end must be.

And El looked upon Michael knowingly and spoke to the rest of the Lumazi. "Because thou hast yet to comprehend the fullness of time...go to and seek thy desire. But know that thine actions will further rip heaven herself. But alas, the time has come to commence with thy instruction that thy may know that wisdom belongeth to the Lord."

And the Lumazi bowed and turned to leave the room, yet Michael stayed to worship at the Lord's feet.

Forgive us, my Lord. For it is as you say. The usurpers time is not yet come.

You are Chief Prince now...and thus my secret now abides with thee. For a body must be prepared for me. That I might succor my people from the hand of the enemy. And you my son. Will protect them until I

For It is my glory to conceal a thing, yet nothing is hidden that shall not be made known.

Lucifer walked to Argoth and towered over him. You drowsy excuse to be Raphael. You think that by your hand I might be brought low. Only El hast power to bring me down and even he will not risk destruction of his children to upend me. I had the very tome of Raphael in my hands. Yet I would not bring him low. But you—you I hold in no respect. Remove thyself from my sight. For if your shadow but crosses me again. I will remove they stone from thy gaseous neck, and wear it as an ornate.

And Argoth backed away and cowered afraid of the might of Lucifer to bring dissolution to him.

1-3-14 word count 6830

Fifteen-word summary of the story

God leaves Heaven to rescue his kidnapped son and give his life for his freedom

Lucifer plans to force God's surrender of the throne by ransoming God's most beloved creation—man.

Tagline: What would *you* do for love?

Story setup Lucifer God's perfect creation has fallen. In his hatred towards God, he exploits the only vulnerability he can find—his love of man. Targeting man for slavery and destruction, he deceives humankind into also turning against his creator causing man to bring about a curse on himself and the earth in the process, allowing Lucifer deed to the Earth he covets. Man is now held ransom, and Lucifer forces the Lord to demonstrate how as King he would handle rebellion from his most prized creation—man.

Major disasters:

1. Man's descends into a spiral of devolution from his original design and sin further creates a barrier preventing God's influence in the Earth, leaving him but little choice but to destroy his creation.

2. God creates a people that he might use as kindling to spark the restoration of his Kingdom on earth. But when they reject his direct rulership and choose to be as the other nations, they seal their doom ultimately forcing them into civil war and slavery by the other nations that they chose to emulate.

3. God's chosen people are now subject to the most brutal regime Lucifer has raised to combat God's attempt at international influence and hope seems lost

Ending of the novel: God finally leaves the throne to flesh to rescue his son

You need a storyline for the following characters

El

All of the Lumazi

Lucifer

Look at you El...just look at you. After millennia on this wretched word you favor—but there is now a new power arising!

Principle: What God makes he cannot unmake. He is as the golden head of Babylon where the King decrees a thing it must be enforced, even to his own hurt. The King is law. Da 6:12 "He cannot deny himself. 2Ti 2:13

Have El swallow the tome of Hell, prior to his leaving. This will tie in with Hell having no power over him.

1-5-14 word count 7176

Three Archangels. Three Brothers...One Turned Renegade. A sweeping epic of origins and mysteries, The Third Heaven explores a tale older than the universe itself. Set in opulent palaces and battles within the streets of Heaven. This is a timeless saga of doubt, of demons and angelic warriors, of obsessive love and treason, and of an ancient evil that knows no bounds. Soon the universe itself will be rocked by war...a war between three angelic brothers...a war fought for the greatest prize in the universe. The war for the Race of Men. Wendy Alec's blurb.

The Third Heaven: The Rise of Fallen Stars is book one of a three-part series that explores the fascinating tale of the Fall of Lucifer. Lucifer, God's perfect creation who walked in the midst of the Stones of Fire.

Yet a perfection that rose up to betray his creator and Lord, and bring Heaven itself to civil war.

Many tales have referenced this great angelic war but few have sought to explore the dynamic relationships between God and the angelic hosts.

Why did a third of Heaven seek to overthrow their creator? See Lucifer and his actions in a light never before seen. Journey back to the beginning, and see the drama unfold before your eyes: as allegiances are broken; choices are made, and why all of creation waits for the manifestation of the sons of God!

Back cover for the Birth of God

Heaven has been decimated by war. Michael's minds reel with the visions shown to him by God of the future, and Lucifer's plans to force God's surrender of the comes to a head. The Birth of God follows the powerful aftermath and consequences of Lucifer's fall from Heaven. In order to save humankind, God will make the ultimate sacrifice on behalf of his creation. What would YOU do for love?

The Adam has yielded in following me...do you concede to me their birthright? What say you, or does the Lord of all creation changeth? ,

And the thing which Lucifer said, grieved the Lord. "Behold...all that he has is in thy hand. Yet the life of the flesh is in the blood, you may touch all that he hath, but his life is in my hand.

The prequel to the Bible is here!

Explore the fascinating tale of the fall of Lucifer!

The Third Heaven: The Rise of Fallen Stars is book one of a three-part series that tells of the fascinating story of the Fall of Lucifer.

Lucifer, God's perfect creation and who dwelt in his very presence, walked in the midst of the stones of fire. Yet rose up to betray the Lord and bring Heaven itself to civil war.

Many tales have referenced this great angelic war but few have sought to explore the dynamic relationships between God and the angelic hosts. Why did a third of heaven seek to overthrow their creator?

See Lucifer and his actions in a light never before seen. Journey back to the beginning, and see the drama unfold before your eyes: as allegiances are broken; choices made, and why all of creation waits for the manifestation of the sons of God.

1-12-14 Word count 11288

1-15-14

American government collapsed through a terrorist attack, the president assassinated and DC water supply has been poisoned decimating the entire federal government, bringing the US to a virtual standstill. Powerful cyber-attacks shut down the grid, and immobilize communications. leaderless, Other nations fearful of Americans might poise themselves to destroy the country out of fear that her nuclear arsenal might be used by terrorists towards them.

Europe stands to protect America, against foes domestic and abroad. And proposes a temporary solution to stabilize the once mighty US. Ushering in a temporary chancellor from the UN. Someone who quickly rises to power and is eventually revealed to be the anti-Christ.

1-18-14 11,695

1-20-1413,062

1-21-14 13,833

There needs to be a new chronicler of Lucifer's works. A new Grigori must document his wonders. What will his name be?

Am I romanticizing Lucifer?

By Donovan M. Neal

| May 4, 2013 | |

A viewer of my kickstarter project saw the above trailer and stated the following.

"I must say you have made a VERY interesting trailer. Did you make that your self. I assume the footage is from video games and stock footage but the music, text and all is pretty impressive.

The question I have though is aren't you afraid that this is romanticizing Lucifer? I ask because prior to being saved I had a crazy interpretation of the Bible in this ultimate struggle between Good and Evil. Long story short my version of Lucifer was much like Anikan Skywalker (assuming you have seen Star Wars). It sort of made me sympathetic to the "dark side" if you will. Now that I am saved and actually read the Bible I have a completely different take on things however, you trailer (as good as it was) kind of reminds me of how I use to see things. So what I am asking, how do you think this will benefit the 16 – 21 year old version of myself that imagining things like this"

Here was my response.

"I'm glad you enjoyed the trailer. I took me quite a while to put it together. Yes it is from various elements of footage that I've 'stitched' together. If you think that was impressive imagine what I was able to depict in a 400 page novel! I love the story and I think it came out great. You're just getting a taste of my story telling in the trailer.

I think the question is a great one and its one I have given a lot of thought too. The Bible makes it clear that Lucifer was perfect in all his ways until iniquity was found in him. Ezk 28:15

For those of us who accept the literal interpretation of the Bible Lucifer is a real person, Anakin Skywalker is a fictional one. This is ultimately a fictional account of the life of a real person, and depicts his falling from power and his eventual demise. When you think about it, we hear about this type of thing daily with all manner of persons unfortunately.

Anakin eventually found redemption, no such situation exists here. Lucifer is clearly shown to be judged at the end of time, and my novel shows him in that state at the very beginning. I would encourage people to take a look at my prologue in the book. The novel clearly starts with where Lucifer is destined to be. The series simply addresses HOW he arrived from point A to point B.I don't believe telling his story takes nothing away from the central message of the Bible which culminates in the person of Jesus Christ.

You can read the prologue here.

http://donovanmneal.wordpress.com/2013/01/08/third-heaven-the-rise-of-fallen-stars-prologue-reveal/

I don't think it romanticizes Lucifer to talk about the fact that at one time he was good. It simply is a statement of fact. I do not want to make him into something he is not, I've tried to share an entertaining tale from a Christian perspective that a believer could 'get with'.

What is the real story to me is how someone who held such position in the kingdom, who was so close to God, who was created in perfection and lived in perfection could acquire a level of dissatisfaction that could be so contagious that it resulted in such a schism that a third of angel kind rebelled? That I believe is the story of interest, and the story in this first of what is to be three books in the series.

If anything I hope it can be an object lesson and a warning to all of us, and foster a deeper love of the Bible and bring the scripture to the forefront of peoples mind, via literary entertainment. Similar to the Left Behind Series.

I hope you feel comfortable supporting the project.

Highest Regards,

Donovan"

So last time I checked the word romanticized means to treat as idealized or heroic. I'm not sure how that's portrayed in the trailer or even the prologue. But it is an issue that I had to address when writing the novel.

So my question to you guys is this? Has what you seen so far romanticized Lucifer?

You be the judge.

Why I edited the F-word out of my novel.

By Donovan M. Neal | Jul 14, 2014 | , |

I want to give you a scene.

The angel Michael overlooks the lake of fire at the end of time and sees multitudes of men and women screaming. Moans, and wails and curses echo from the Lake of Fire. As he listens, he hears a curse come from one of the persons judged to burn in the lake of fire. Ready? Here it is.

"I hate your f—ing guts angel of God! I hate you!"

Now tell me. If you were to read this line in a Christian novel...would, you be offended? Would you think the novel is not Christian? Would you think the author herself is not Christian?

Would you think the book is filled with other racy language because of this one sentence?

Yesterday I read Tony Broodens blog entitled "

It is a well-written piece that discusses the challenges that Christian authors face in writing their stories to a Christian audience. In reading his blog post, it reminded me of my own challenge when creating my own book. Why? Because the sentence above is the actual original sentence I wrote in the prologue of my book; The Third Heaven: The Rise of Fallen Stars.

When I wrote the sentence originally I thought of Matthew 13:42 "And shall cast them into a furnace of fire: there shall be wailing and gnashing of teeth."

I imagined a place of wailing and cursing and agony. So let's say oh an angel happens to stroll along to see this site, and your one of the damned. I can imagine some pleas of mercy, help, and yep a curse at the onlooker. It seemed pretty reasonable to me at the time.

But along came a reviewer. Now keep in mind that when I first published the book, this sentence was in there. But a Christian reviewer came along and basically said that they couldn't get past the language, and because of that (and a few other 'symbolic' things), they decided to choose not to review my book. (They never read the whole book.)

So here I am as a Christian thinking to myself. Perhaps I simply cannot write this story, because the audience can't handle the F word coming from a burning soul in the Lake of Fire.

I admit I was kind of put off. I was like really? Someone screams F you from the lake of fire, and you can't handle that?

But then I took off the creative hat of the author, and put on the business hat of the entrepreneur. If one person feels this way so much that they won't finish a book given to them for free to review. How much more then might this be the case for others? So I changed the sentence. It reads like this now.

"I hate you your guts! Do you hear me angel of God? I hate you!"

Honestly, I don't think it's as powerful a sentence. (and you can tell me I shouldn't have done it. (It's my book...nana, nana nah!) People who hate other people in my experience might use an expletive or two now and then to express that hate. (Maybe that is why they are in Hell....that's a joke by the way.) Bad Donovan...bad Donovan sorry.

So anyways I took it out. So I wrote a book about angels killing each other, but that was OK. (Pray for me the spirit of sarcasm might be influencing me.)

This reviewer finally told me that I might be a part of what was called "Edgy Christian Fiction."

I was like wow, now there is a label I had never heard of. Needless to say yep there was an actual group or a genre that is called "". So one instance and one partially spelled out expletive coming from the mouth of a condemned person in Hell in a book of over 100,000 words is edgy...really? It really made me wonder is this is what we've come too? I am for "clean" fiction just as much as everyone else. But if this is "edgy" I dunno seems kinda lame to me. I can think of a lot racier things.

If I tried to write "Saving Private Ryan" as a novel I think I'd have a hard time writing that book, thinking that not one GI used some kind of curse word during the whole experience. I'm not saying you have to see everything...somethings are best left to the imagination. But that's why I spelled out F—K as opposed to spelling the whole word out. Which Tom in his blog covers. I guess that still doesn't count for some!

Don't get me wrong. People are entitled to read what they want. Christian or otherwise. But 6 times my Bible uses the phrase, "pisseth against the wall." Now that's not a curse word. But man, it's not something I went around condoning my own kids to say–just saying.

In the end I don't want a person being so offended by language that they can't even finish the story. Yeah, yeah I know I can't please everyone. But I think Christian authors really struggle over how to depict violence and sexuality, etc. in a way that honors God, and is real to the fictional world they are trying to convey. It's not always easy.

In any event, I'm curious how other authors in the genre have handled fiction. Christian readers have you had issues about language that unsettled you. Do you apply this standard towards all media? Any advice or encouragement for us authors out there? What saith thou?

My Thoughts about The Third Heaven

By Donovan M. Neal

| Dec 22, 2014 | , , |

The Third Heaven-audio-book

One of the benefits of writing is that I get to let my fans peek into my world. To give them a sense of how I come up with things. What moves me to write, and what some of my thinking is behind certain elements in the story. After reading some reviews and interacting with readers, I thought I'd share some of the thinking in response to some of the feedback I've received from reviewers.

One of the criticisms of my story is that "the author would continuously use human metaphors and similes when describing how an angel perceived different events."

The reader noted that this was something that as an author they had a problem with it, however not so as a reader. In my "Thinking about the Third Heaven", I actually address this issue.

The real issue is how do you describe something like the color red to someone who has never seen red before? How do you describe music to someone who cannot hear?What words can used to describe something that prior to that time does not exist? This was my challenge as a writer. Angles had never experienced certain emotions and various things (I'm assuming) prior to Lucifer's rebellion. How would they then be introduced to said events? How would they react? What words would they use to describe these new experiences and more importantly how would this be communicated to a reader?

I tried to address this on some level by couching the whole story within a flashback. The "real" story is taking place within the prologue. Each book is an advancement of 'that' story. Lucifer and Michael's conversation is the 'real' story. Everything else is simply a giant flashback on Michael's reminiscing on how they arrived to that point. Therefore, not only would they have the language we use today, but even more so as the events of the prologue take place beyond our current history. So in other words the story teller, (Michael) is very much aware of the current "modern day" language we use to tell the story. How well this device is "pulled off", I will have to leave to the reader.

On a secondary front I think I believe I simply reached my capacity as a writer to describe experiences that prior to did not exist and communicate those experiences in such a manner that a reader connects said experiences with their own. The reviewer stated it this way, "Even though the reader can understand what is being conveyed in these instances, these references are not appropriate given the voice of the book. While it would have been much more difficult to write this book if this type of reference was omitted, I think it would have made it much better." The reviewer was correct. In that, it would have been extremely more difficult. I also believe it would have been a better book. I just confess I had reached my ability to bring it to pass. Nor did I feel it necessary for the majority of readers.

I recognize that I could have researched perhaps the writings of other authors who had experienced something like this. But then I think I would have poured more than I wanted to in investing in that aspect of the story. In the end as an author, you have to do what feels right to you as the creator.

After much thought I decided that it was not important overall. Some readers are more sophisticated than others. I wrote for the person who enjoys Star Wars and Lord of the Rings, and the Avengers so such persons already know they are entering fictitious worlds, and can forgive "minor" issues, like the physics in such movies, because they appreciate the spectacle that they are seeing. There is simply a lot about a story like this we do not know. I have tried to marry what we do know with speculation to come up with an entertaining story. Overall, I would like to think I succeeded.

I'm glad writing this novel is over! It was definitely a challenge to write!

What makes this book such a challenge for Christians?

I think the biggest challenge was simply writing this book for Christians. The reality is that the body of Christ is a "fragmented" bunch. We are Protestant and Catholic. Some believe in demonic possession, speaking in tongues, etc. We are pre and post trib, and I could go on and on. In addition, some just feel writing about how Lucifer fell is a moot issue to even discuss, possibly even sacrilegious. Others are afraid of such a subject. I've received a lot of input from members of the body of Christ---mostly good. Some of the comments have been so praiseworthy as to say it's better than the epic poem of paradise lost, to " the story line is chilling to me." to my book being called sacrilegious. So obviously, the reaction is all over the map.

"I've had people describe my take on God the Father as "loving", "powerful", to "too human."

The reality is that it's not possible to write to everyone's tastes. As an author writing such a challenging story; my desire was to show the epic powers that are moving on both God and the enemy's behalf. To give the Christian a greater appreciation of who composes that "cloud of witnesses". And that the Bible is a supernatural book, with beings that are in epic conflict with one another. It was an attempt to peel behind the veil of the spirit and speculatively ask, "what might Heaven be like, and the angelic host." To speculate on the 21 days that took Gabriel to get his message to Daniel. To look at things from the point of view of the angels and wonder what are/what were they thinking about all this?

I find that I am simply too limited to accommodate the whole of Christendom's expectations and feelings on such a grand topic. What I can do is write in such a manner that tries to be faithful to the major story arcs most of us share. To add that "geek" element to our stories: particularly if we had the money to bring such a story to the big screen. In essence, I wanted to tell a great story that as a Christian male I wanted to read. I am a lover of sci-fi and fantasy. My stories will probably appeal more to that demographic. Typically men, which I see as a great thing! (We need more men reading Christian fiction that caters to them.) So yep, the battles are a bit long. Because hey, we fellas like action! I wrote the book for the kid in me. So if you like, epic battles I think you will like the book. If you like, Braveheart, Lord of the Rings, Return of the Jedi, and of course the Bible. I think by the time you get to the end of the story. You will go "wow!" If a person approaches the book, looking for something that is 100% in line with how the reader pictures the spiritual world a reader will probably be disappointed.

Another piece of feedback was on how fast angels move from their innocence to sin. As an author, I am forced to determine the pace of storytelling. My rational is that in the garden we went from biting the proverbial "apple" to murder. This is a very quick escalation of events. While we do not know how long the actual time frame was from Adam and Eve's sin to the death of Abel. We are given to see how things can quickly escalate out of control. How much more then can I speculatively ask could things go awry among beings that are not bound by time at all?

Do Angels die or have weapons? Angels and strange Bible scriptures.

By Donovan M. Neal.

| Jan 22, 2015 | , |

dore_milton_cast

Not too long ago I received a letter from a wonderful reader who enjoyed my book with the exception of two caveats. He gave me a 4 out of 5 star review. So he was gracious in his review of the book.

Because I have tried to go above and beyond in helping readers of the book understand that my work is Christian *Fiction* based on the Bible I have written in my preface of the Third Heaven, and in the upcoming book the following.

"To my beloved Christian reader — this work is not scripture. I do not profess divine inspiration, nor would I ever attempt to place this work alongside the word of God. The story is a fictional exploration of the fall of Lucifer, and by taking part in this fictional account you as a reader and I as the author are in no way implying that we must have theological agreement. The work does presume certain doctrinal

beliefs (the existence of the Trinity for example) but this novel is not meant to be a point-by-point exposition of biblical truth. Nor an exact attempt to create a chronologically correct depiction of creation and the events depicted in the Bible. It's an exploratory look into a biblical event and imagines, "what if?"

Now despite this preface some readers still feel a need I think to query me on various things. This brother was kind enough to give me his credentials prior to establishing his problems to certain things in the book. My guess he did this to reinforce his being an authority of the subject.

Because I enjoy questions and feedback from readers I took the time to write out a long response to him. I'm sharing with you in two blog posts what I shared with him so that I can have something to point people too in the future. His letter raises some questions for me specially and the Christian community in general. Topics I hope to address in a later post about Christian Fiction.

His first caveat was "The first problem, as I see it, is allowing Angels to be killed. One of the features that separate man from Angels is mankind's mortality. Man can die, cast off the body of sin and be given a resurrection body and a heavenly nature. Angels already possess this, so redemption doesn't appear to be a possibility for them."

His question was a great question. It was really one of the foremost questions I had to ask in the book.

The rest of my blog is really a more in depth understanding of the thinking behind the biblical underpinnings of angels "dying" and my overall approach in the book.

Micheal fighting the dragon

Here was my response to his first problem.

"The reality is that scripture is actually silent on this issue. The Bible is a book addressed to man that primarily addresses God's relationship with man. Death as it is referred to in the scriptures is man centered. For example In Genesis, we see that Adam was never meant to die. He was gifted initially with long life. NATURALLY he would not die. As we understand, he had no sin nature that would cause decay, sickness and therefore death. However, does this mean he could not feel pain? If he fell off a cliff, could he have died?

Angels in my book also do not experience old age, decay or disease. They die because they are attacked by like beings. There is one exception to this in my book. Sasheal, who dies in saving the planet, after he changes himself to become physical to interact with the physical world therefore exposing himself to mortality. A sacrifice that I show in the book as a prelude to many events to come.

The Apostle Paul indicates that there are different types of bodies in 1st Cor 15. "All flesh is not the same flesh: but there is one kind of flesh of men, another flesh of beasts, another of fishes, and another of birds. [40] There are also celestial bodies, and bodies terrestrial: but the glory of the celestial is one, and the glory of the terrestrial is another. [41] There is one glory of the sun, and another glory of the moon, and another glory of the stars: for one star differeth from another star in glory.

My device in allowing Sasheal to die was simply to change his flesh. I.e. to make him susceptible to harm. Immortality does not equal unable to be harmed.

Secondly, angels are clearly seen in scripture in battle with one another. Dan 10:20 "I return to fight with the prince of Persia: and when I am gone forth, lo, the prince of Grecia shall come." Fighting is a violent act. You fight to injure, and by extension to kill. If angels cannot be harmed how then do they engage with one another? Overall your thinking superimposes human reasons for death and assumes that those same reasons apply to other created beings i.e. angels. I don't think you can biblically draw that conclusion from scripture.

Num 22:23 And the ass saw the angel of the LORD standing in the way, and his sword drawn in his hand: and the ass turned aside out of the way, and went into the field: and Balaam smote the ass, to turn her into the way.

Why does the angel of the Lord (regardless if this is a Theophany or not) need a sword? Does an angel need a sword to kill a human? If angels can make men blind and mute, why not be extension do they need a sword to kill man? I think the logical reason is that they do not need swords to kill men.

What is the origin of this weapon? It is NOT earthly. Therefore, it must be heavenly. Why is Heaven in the business of manufacturing weapons? It seems a moot point if angels cannot harm and by extension kill or be harmed by one another because that is what swords are used for.

My Bible teaches me that out of the mouth of two or three let every word be established.

Here are two scriptures that seem to show that angels do battle with one another, and or have weapons of war. In war "people" die. These are not the only scriptures that seem to bear this truth of angelic harm out. (Rev 12:7) Again, none of this takes away from the fact that angels are immortal. I.e. on their own, they do not die. However, this does not mean that they cannot be killed.

The bottom line is that the Bible is silent on a great many things regarding other spiritual beings. But after a careful reading and some logical thought, I think a reader is forced to come to some conclusions. I bring some of this conjecture out in the book, while not claiming it to be "doctrine". It's fiction and should be treated as such which is clearly stated at the beginning.

A great book that I use as reference in this regards is Angels: Elect and Evil by C. Fred Dickason it's a great biblical resource."

While I do not obviously know if angels can be 'killed'. There is enough scriptural evidence beginning at Gen 3: 24 to show that weapons exist prior to man designing or having them. Which again begs the question of why they exist, how they are manufactured and a host of other questions if you like to dig into your Bible like me.

Here's the actual text from the KJV, *"So he drove out the man; and he placed at the east of the garden of Eden Cherubims, and a flaming sword which turned every way, to keep the way of the tree of life."*

Adam did not have enemies or seemingly knowledge of even how to manufacture such a weapon. So the sword is again of Heavenly manufacture. Why? Scriptures like this fascinate me.

In another post I'll address the readers second caveat which deals with the trinity. (Yes I believe in the Trinity! Calm down!)

This has been a long post, but an important one that I think shows some of the thinking that really has to go into a story like this. I'll address his second problem in the book in a later post, and my overall take on Christian Fiction and might want to rethink what constitutes said fiction in the first place.

But until then let me ask you. Are there any strange scriptures and Biblical occurrences that make you scratch your head? I'm sure I'm not the only one. What about you! I'd love to hear from you!

The view of the Godhead in the Third Heaven: The Rise of Fallen Stars

By | Feb 27, 2015 |

The Birth of God-audiobook

The Godhead. In an t I talked about a reader who mentioned that he took issue with two areas in my novel. The first issue was angelic death and if such creatures could indeed die. I tackled this in an earlier post. In today's post, I want to address the meatier issue the reader raised concerning speculative aspects of my novel concerning the Godhead.

Let me preface this reading by declaring that I believe in the Trinity. And in no way does my novel diminish the existence of the Trinitarian nature of God. There is a scene in my novel that (I'll try not to give away) that is a major surprise in the novel. The writer's caveat is addressing this scene. Having said that, I remind the reader that the novel is speculative fiction is not meant to be doctrinally prescriptive.

Although, this was mentioned clearly in the book's preface, nevertheless, some might feel similarly to address this second caveat mentioned by this reader. I hope my response satisfies some of the thinking behind this scene, and helps give peace to those who think this novel must somehow line up to their understanding of every scriptural doctrine they believe. The letter and my response continues as follows…

"As far as the meatier issue of the trinity: that was a very interesting scene to write, and here are my thoughts on leaving it in. I almost took it out but decided to leave it as it is, simply because it made the story a better story. And I knew what I was communicating as the author.

The trinity in many respects is a mystery. No matter how hard you try to find a natural analogy for it. The analogy will break down. The Bible many times asks us to accept certain truths without giving us explanations on how such truths are possible. Although I am sure we both know, that the word Trinity is not mentioned in the Bible I assume we can agree that the concept of the Trinity is there.

I.e. there are three distinct persons called God in the Bible, The Father, The Son, and the Holy Spirit, and in the Bible, these three distinct persons are referred to as God and possess the attributes of God. This is the essence of Trinitarian teaching. I think we can agree on this.

Heb 13:8 states that Jesus Christ the same yesterday, and today, and forever. Mal 3:6 states that I am the Lord, I change not.

But what does that mean? Was Jesus always incarnate? No. He did not become incarnate until he took on flesh. Again, if you believe that the angel of the Lord is a pre-incarnate appearance of the Lord then this too is a "change". So when we say that God does not change what does this mean?

Why is there a trinity? Why not two or 5 etc. persons in the godhead? Why not one personality like apostolic believers teach? Some Christians as I'm sure you are aware do not believe in Trinitarian teaching. (Which although is a difficult concept is a biblical one.) Why do we have 66 books in the Bible and not 70? (Catholics would not even say there are 66)

These are the same questions I asked about the Trinity. Ultimately I asked, if God so chose; could He add someone to the Godhead? I did not ask if He would. (Which I honestly believe is no.) I asked, could He? In other words, can God make a rock that even he could not lift? Can immortality die? Can God limit himself? Can God interact with his creation to lift his creation to a new level?

My answer was yes He could. It's theoretically possible yes. Is it actually possible? No…not in my humble opinion.

Jesus who we both believe and understand as God—died. Really think about that. (Which is the irony of the cross. "The eternal one dies" God takes the place of man" and all that.) How can God be everywhere at once and yet localized in a human body? If you have really studied theology then these are very "mature" questions that only those who study such issues ever contemplate. Which sadly most Christians do not. How can Jesus be fully God AND fully man?

Ultimately, when you really meditate on this then my adding this scene is not a stretch.

In the end, I concluded that adding that scene takes nothing away from the central truth that we both adhere to; that God is a trinity.

WARNING SPOILER ALERT

In the book, God starts as Trinitarian in nature. Moreover, from a doctrinal standpoint, he REMAINS Trinitarian in nature. During the scene itself, God remains Trinitarian. God is entirely in control of whether Lucifer in that scene would be lifted or not. It was not in Lucifer's power to do it himself. Again, the scene adds to the background and underpinnings of his thinking and later actions.

I speculatively ask about God's nature without changing his nature in the book. I think I definitely go up to the line without crossing it.

If God's own flawed creation, (I) can ask this question. Then my question not only can be asked or contemplated by God himself, but even also acted upon if he willed it.

We can agree with who God is. Where we disagree on (perhaps) is what limitations (if any) exist on God. Either self-imposed or "naturally" (i.e. it's the result of his "nature") To me the irony of your way of thinking is that it goes back to the question if God is all powerful; can he make another being like himself? (He would not...at least I do not think so.) He is the first mover, the ALPHA. But could He change that?

If he CAN'T then again is He truly all-powerful? Speculatively asking such questions and or more importantly coming down on one side of another does not in my humble opinion put us at the place where we cannot call one another brothers in Christ. As we believe the central truths about who Christ is which is the cement to our bond of fellowship.

In that scene, Lucifer does **not** ascend to God hood. The scene adds drama, and gives a deeper motive of what drives the character in the book. (Remember its fiction) and does not take away from the central truth that many of us believe. This scene is actually an allegory to the scene of Cain and Abel in Genesis, and does ask what limits if any are on God himself. Which honestly none of us can truly know because if we did, then by definition we would have to possess all knowledge which by definition would make us God.

I am not sure you can use the Bible to answer this question. It is like saying if Jesus had a baby would the baby be God? We all know that he did not. Nevertheless, if he did, what would the nature of the baby have been like? That is speculative fiction. It's fiction that explores those nooks and crannies.

I wish I could have stated all this in the preface. However, I decided not to. It would have given away too much, and I wanted the reader to be surprised. Nor did I want to bore the average reader with theology. Nor scare people away from reading the book. Does it push the envelope? I think it does, but not without going over. You are getting insight into how much thought I had to put into the book and the issues you raised in particular.

I think a good fictional book should make you think. My book should make people spur discussions. I think your letter to me proves that it accomplishes that. Does it take away from what you believe? No. Nor is the book designed to. However, my guess is that it makes mature believers think and research the Bible more. And perhaps my own letter might just make you think even deeper about theology and seek to reaffirm truths we both agree on? The issues you raise while controversial are not heretical.

I clearly state on my website what my intentions where in the book. I hope that no one thinks that I am espousing some doctrine or theology or somehow need “correction.” if so I would have to state that that they are then reading more into the book (making assumptions) than is there.

My book from where I stand is for mature believers. It is not for babes in Christ. I honestly cannot recommend it to everyone because of the latter issue you raised about the Trinity. That is why I harp so much on the fact that it is not doctrine and it’s speculative fiction. I’d like to think it is It a mature book for “us”, by us, and not some junk we get from Hollywood. (Cough...cough...Noah and Exodus) This subject matter is simply hard to write about no matter how you go about it. Wendy Alec had similar issues with reviewers in her book. I think hers might be less controversial than mine though. (I think mine appeals to men more!)

Overall, the “problem” I think that is articulated in your letter is a “problem” only if a reader makes the book beyond what it claims to be; speculative Christian fiction. Its basis in the Bible doesn’t make it any less fiction.

God bless you my brother I hope you feel that I have responded respectfully and thoughtfully and yes even biblically to your raised issues. Thank you for taking some of your time again to write me! Please feel free to write back and I hope you take the time to read the next book in the series, which will be out in February.

With love and peace in Christ our Lord,

Donovan”

Well there you have it. Even more insight into the thinking behind T3rdH.

Final Thoughts 10 years later

First I want to say thank you. I never intended for the series to do what it did. I wrote it for me. To see the epic fall of Lucifer like I might see the Lord of the Rings in the theatre. So thank you for "getting it." For seeing the series for what it was. A love letter to the Bible, To Christ, to his people. To those of us who enjoy speculative fiction, and realize the Bible and the Lordship of Christ is paramount. I started this series back before 2007. It's amazing to think now in 2025 so many years later I have reached this point after going through so many trials and tribulations, highs and lows. And now after all this time I am still writing. Still wanting to put out stories that honor God, inspire, and entertain. Still putting pen to paper. I am forever grateful to God and all those who words have moved me to where I am today. All of which begs the question...

What's next?

Most of what I have up to write is a combination of fiction and non- fiction. Stories I have wanted to tell for years but because I was so engrossed in the Third Heaven Series I could not make room for them. Now the time has come to get them out. These are a few of the expected/planned fiction works in progress. I hope you will be with me during this journey!

In the meantime, until we meet again within the pages of the next book. Your friend in Christ and all things fantasy and sci-fi.

Donovan

Upcoming Fiction Attractions
General Audience
General Audience
General Audience
Christian Fiction
Christian Fiction
Christian Fiction
Christian Fiction
General Audience
The Queen of Ashes
TORNVEIL
DONOVAN M. NEAL
The Markmaker
Romantasy
Fantasy
9 book series
Fantasy
1-3 book series
Sci-Fi
4 book series
Comic Action
Suspense
Horror
Sci-Fi
Donovan M. Neal

About the Author

Donovan Neal has formerly served in the ordained ministry and as an instructor in the Bible for 20 years. He is the author of the indie-published book, 'The Gospel Explained.' and the Amazon best-selling novel, The Third Heaven: The Rise of Fallen Stars.

Donovan is also a prolific songwriter and singer having written over 50 different songs of praise and worship for the local church and has performed in various schools and churches in the Ministry of Christian Rap. Now retired from the clergy he's taken up his pen to express what has long been the untapped call God has placed in him to reach people through fiction.

Donovan has spent his entire career, helping underprivileged and disempowered populations ranging from abused and neglected children, and adults with disabilities, to survivors of domestic abuse and sexual assault. He currently works to help housing-insecure women find employment in Detroit. His mission is to help motivate and teach authors and leaders how to achieve their goals so they can experience all that God has for them.

In his spare time when he is not reading or writing, he enjoys video games, epic fantasy movies, and sci-fi.

Donovan brings a wealth of experience and interests that have allowed him to write on a host of subjects ranging from gaming, internet/technology, Christian themes, nonprofit management, and leadership.

You can learn more about Donovan at his website. http://www.donovanmneal.com or feel free to contact him at Tornveil@donovanmneal.com

www.ingramcontent.com/pod-product-compliance
Lightning Source LLC
Chambersburg PA
CBHW070544310726
48982CB00010B/1477/J

* 9 7 9 8 9 8 9 0 8 2 1 2 4 *